EVERYMAN,
I WILL GO WITH THEE,
AND BE THY GUIDE,
IN THY MOST NEED
TO GO BY THY SIDE

MURASAKI SHIKIBU

THE
TALE
OF
GENJI

TRANSLATED AND INTRODUCED BY
EDWARD G. SEIDENSTICKER

EVERYMAN'S LIBRARY
Alfred A. Knopf   New York London Toronto
108

THIS IS A BORZOI BOOK
PUBLISHED BY ALFRED A. KNOPF

First included in Everyman's Library, 1992
Translation Copyright © 1976 by Edward G. Seidensticker
First published in Great Britain by Martin Secker & Warburg Ltd., 1976
Reprinted by permission
Introduction Copyright © 1992 by Edward G. Seidensticker
Bibliography and Chronology Copyright © 1992 by Everyman's Library
Typography by Peter B. Willberg
Eighth printing (US)

US website: www.randomhouse.com/everymans

ISBN 0-679-41738-9 (US)
1-85715-108-9 (UK)

A CIP catalogue record for this book is available from the
British Library

Library of Congress Cataloging-in-Publication Data
Murasaki Shikibu, b. 978?
[Genji monogatari. English]
The tale of Genji / Murasaki Shikibu.
p.   cm.—(Everyman's library)
Translation of: Genji monogatari.
ISBN 0-679-41738-9
I. Series: Everyman's library (Alfred A. Knopf, Inc.)
PL788.4.G4E5   1992   92-52930
895.6′31—dc20   CIP

Book design by Barbara de Wilde and Carol Devine Carson

Printed and bound in Germany by GGP Media GmbH, Pössneck

INTRODUCTION

Little is known with certainty about *The Tale of Genji* except that it has existed and been held in high esteem for almost a millennium. We will probably never know exactly when the author lived, and almost certainly we will never know exactly when she wrote her book and in what form it emerged from her pen – or, more properly, brush. Most if not all of it was probably written in the early eleventh century AD by a court lady known as Murasaki Shikibu. A diary from the mid eleventh century establishes that it existed by then as a work of 'more than fifty chapters'. The accepted count today is fifty-four. There is no holograph of even the smallest fragment. All recensions must be based on texts from several centuries later.

The early eleventh century was a time when eastern Europe was doing better culturally than western Europe, and East Asia may have been doing better than either. Depending on definitions, western Europe had just emerged from or was about to emerge from the Dark Ages. Romanesque styles still prevailed. High Gothic would not come for another two centuries. The great early English literary endeavor, *Beowulf*, was two centuries in the past. Nothing more of great moment, except to specialists, would come until Chaucer, almost four centuries after the likely date of *Genji*.

It is arguable that Japan was enjoying a more golden age than China. The great T'ang period, ever since which, many a pessimistic Chinese will tell a person, China has been in decline, ended in 907. Japan was then a little over a century into the Heian period, its finest time. The Fujiwara, first of the great families (in another culture they might be called palace wardens) which through most of pre-modern Japanese history ruled in place of the titular rulers, or emperors, was consolidating its power. From the late tenth century until the death in 1027 of Fujiwara Michinaga, grandest of the Fujiwara ministers, the power of the family was at its greatest. Michinaga made brilliant use of a device hit upon by the family some time earlier, marrying its daughters to emperors, whose children could then be manipulated. Heian may be the period in Japanese history when women were most important.

Murasaki Shikibu's count of years was probably shorter than the almost three score of Michinaga. He must have been a very few years her senior. It was a good time to be alive. The T'ang had been a time of vigorous borrowing from China. Now, with the weakening of central power in China, Japan withdrew from the continent and set about putting all the importations to its own uses. In prose narrative, at any rate, and perhaps in all the arts, the *Genji* was the best thing it produced. Perhaps too it was the best thing anyone was producing the world over.

Accretions and modifications during the following centuries were probably not of such magnitude as to change the essential shape of Murasaki Shikibu's original. At least one chapter, 'Bamboo River', is widely thought to be spurious, and the two preceding chapters, both short, are also suspect. It is also possible that chapters have been lost. Japanese texts often carry a chapter title for which no chapter exists. The title suggests that the chapter described Genji's death, absent from the tale as it exists today. Whether or not it was ever written is not known.

Murasaki Shikibu's place in the genealogies is clear. She was a Fujiwara, and she and Michinaga shared a common ancestor in the paternal line six generations back. We do not, however, know her given name. Except for consorts and princesses of the blood, the names of well-born ladies are not listed in the genealogies. Of the sobriquet by which she is traditionally known, the second half, Shikibu, designates an office held by both her father and an elder brother. Murasaki may derive either from the name, or designation (Murasaki Shikibu was even more fastidious than the genealogists in avoiding personal names), of an important lady in the *Genji* itself or from the fact that it means 'purple', and the first two syllables of her family name mean 'wisteria'.

By the time of her birth her branch of the family had fallen to the second level of the court aristocracy. Her father held modest positions in the capital and twice served as a provincial governor. Provincial governors are generally treated with contempt in *The Tale of Genji*, but their layer of the aristocracy did more for the literature of the day than any other. Almost no one denies that it was a fine day, or that the *Genji* is the supreme masterpiece of classical Japanese prose narrative, and quite possibly the whole of Japanese literature, including the modern period.

Murasaki Shikibu was married in 998 or 999 to a distant kinsman. Since there are reasons for believing that she married rather late for the time, it seems likely that she was in her early twenties. Of her childhood we know little save what she herself has told us. A famous entry in the journal ('set of memoirs' might better characterize it) called *Murasaki Shikibu Diary*, which describes events at court from late 1008 to early 1010, tells how her father, observing her capacity for learning, lamented that she had not been born a boy. Her father became governor of Echizen, on the Sea of Japan almost due north of Kyoto, the capital, in 996. She probably went with him, returning shortly before her marriage. Her only daughter was born in 999, and she was widowed in 1001.

She went to court, in the service of the Empress Akiko or Shōshi, some time around the middle of the first decade of the eleventh century. The *Murasaki Shikibu Diary* has to do chiefly with the birth of two sons to the empress, events of political importance, since both princes became emperor. In her 'diary' Murasaki tells us that she came to court on the twenty-ninth day of the Twelfth Month of the Oriental lunar calendar, a date which would convert to early in the following year under the Western calendar. Unfortunately she does not tell us which year. The lunar years 1005 and 1006 seem the most likely.

Akiko was widowed in 1011. There is documentary evidence that Murasaki Shikibu remained in her service for perhaps two years thereafter, but the dates of her retirement from court and her death are not known. One can visit a spot in the northern environs of Kyoto that is described as her grave; and the marvel is that it might just possibly be. Some argue the absence of her name from documents where it might well be found as evidence that she did not long outlive Akiko's husband the Emperor Ichijō. Others argue, more subjectively but no less convincingly, that the last chapters of the *Genji* suggest a sadly wise and ageing author. If we assume that Murasaki Shikibu died in 1015, then the probability is that her life lasted barely four decades.

The *Murasaki Shikibu Diary* suggests strongly that at least a part of her great work had been written when she entered Akiko's service. Perhaps she began it in the early years of her widowhood, and perhaps, since there must have been scores of women with equally compelling political and economic claims and since the grand ladies of the day thought literature important, her book was the occasion for her being summoned to court.

Among the many *Genji* problems debated by scholars is whether or not the book is finished. The answer must be that we do not know. The last chapter is in some respects different from the others, notably in its title. All the other chapter titles derive from specific incidents in the chapters themselves. 'The Floating Bridge of Dreams' is more abstract. This deviation may mean that Murasaki Shikibu (we do not know at what date the chapters acquired the titles they now have) set it apart, announcing it to be her finale; and yet the chapter has an air of anticipation about it, as if it announced the beginning of a whole new cycle. The main point may be that such considerations are irrelevant. Murasaki was no Aristotelian, planning her beginning, middle, and end before she set brush to paper. One may imagine that if the reader of 'The Floating Bridge of Dreams' had asked her whether that was all, she might have replied: 'We will see tomorrow morning.' And by 'tomorrow morning' she had fallen into her last decline.

The action of the *Genji* covers almost three-quarters of a century. The first forty-one chapters have to do with the life and loves of the nobleman known as 'the shining Genji', Genji or Minamoto being the name given him as a commoner by his father, an emperor. Genji is born in the first chapter and is fifty-two by the Oriental count in the last chapter in which he figures. Three transitional chapters, the chapters most likely to be spurious, come after his death. The hero of the last ten chapters, Kaoru, who passes in the world as Genji's son but is really the grandson of his best friend, is five at the time of Genji's last appearance and twenty-eight in the last chapter. It has long been held by Japanese scholars that Murasaki Shikibu thought of her tale as historical, set perhaps three-quarters of a century before her time. If the historical setting were detailed and consistent, then of course she would have brought it gradually from the early or middle tenth century to her own day; but it is not. All that can be said is that a vaguely nostalgic air hangs over the narrative and that the setting is vaguely antiquarian.

Like most great works of fiction, the *Genji* 'means' numbers of things. One of them may derive from this fact, that the life of the hero seems to belong to the past. It receives its most explicit statement in the startling sentence at the beginning of Chapter 42, in which we learn that Genji has died since the conclusion to the preceding chapter. It asks that the work be read as a parable in pessimistic Buddhism. Genji's successors are of altogether lesser stature. The world is in decline and the good days will not come again.

A widely held belief in Heian Buddhism was that the religion itself, like everything else, was caught in an irreversible process of decline. The last sad stage, in which forms would remain when faith was gone, was expected to begin several centuries after the death of the historic Buddha. One chronology held that this event would occur in the eleventh century. So, with the Buddhist law itself entering an inferior age from which there could be no recovery, there could be no hope for improvement in the affairs of man, so ephemeral and insignificant by comparison.

It is not possible to say exactly what period Murasaki Shikibu thought herself to be writing about, but the reigns of the Emperor Daigo and the Emperor Murakami, covering most of the first two-thirds of the tenth century, have long been coupled together as a golden age when benevolent rulers were secure in their power. Murasaki Shikibu may well have shared the view, and selected the two reigns as a time worthy of her hero.

We may read another kind of Buddhist parable into the tale. Buddhism is a sprawling, contradictory body of doctrine. Common elements run through most of it, however. One has to do with the illusory nature of surface phenomena, including the evanescent meeting of elements that is the human being. A sense of evanescence is as much a part of Murasaki's world as the air that encompassed it. Similarly pervasive is Karma, the law of cause and effect, which holds that all actions by sentient beings, whether good or bad, work themselves out, in this life or in lives to come. The chickens must eventually come home to roost.

In the fifth chapter Genji has a brief affair with his father's best-loved lady (the Heian court was polygamous). In Chapter 36 the young princess whom he has taken for his wife bears the child whom the world takes to be Genji's. He knows the truth, that the child is the product of an affair between the princess and the son of his friend Tō no Chūjō. He is sure that he is being punished for the earlier dereliction, and his feelings are especially painful because he must wonder whether his father also knew, though he gave no indication of knowing. The reader too is left in doubt.

Although most of the significant action takes place in the women's quarters of the palace and the noble houses, and although harem politics were not as important in Japan as in China and the Mohammedan countries, the tale may also be read as political. The picture contest in Chapter 17, which has that expression for its title, may seem a trivial and extravagant endeavor on the part of some silly courtiers to please the child who is their emperor (he is Genji's son by his father's consort). In fact it is an intense political struggle. The parties are the Fujiwara, represented by Tō no Chūjō, and the royal family, represented by Genji, who has been reduced to commoner status by his father so that he may be in a more strategic position to resist the Fujiwara. The result is one which could not conceivably have occurred in Murasaki Shikibu's day, victory for the royal family. Hers was a day when no prince of the blood had the slightest chance of successfully resisting the Fujiwara. So even as the story seems to look back to a day when this might have been possible, it also seems to be a protest against the rampancy of Michinaga and the other great Fujiwara.

The *Genji* lends itself to all these readings, but what is most important about it brings us to a great contradiction. If human life and individuality are illusory, as Buddhism held them to be and the *Genji* itself does not cease telling us they are, then why was Murasaki so interested in them that she produced a narrative conspicuous for the life and individuality of its characters?

Early reviewers of the Arthur Waley translation, when it was coming out between 1925 and 1933, remarked upon the astonishing modernity of the work. It is not easy to know exactly what they meant, though yet another theme running through the *Genji*, the quest for a parent, is certainly a very modern one. Genji is drawn to his father's consort because she resembles his dead mother. In the chapter in which the child is born he finds the great love of his life, a niece of the lady, closely resembling her. In the chapters after Genji's death the quest for a mother is replaced by the quest for a father. The young man produced by the liaison that made Genji so strongly aware of the workings of Karma has doubts about his birth and senses that he has no real father.

The vigor of the characterization, however, must have been the most powerful element contributing to that sense of modernity.

The *Genji* has frequently been characterized as the first great novel in the literature of the world. 'Novel' is a complex and elusive word, but at least in English-speaking regions it designates a form of prose narrative distinguished from other forms by its concern with the tribulations, the ups and downs, of believable human beings. The *Genji* describes the highest levels of Heian society, so high that the governor who was god to the rustics out in the provinces could himself be treated like a rustic buffoon. Yet all the important characters fall within the range of ordinary human experience. Even as we are not, most of us, either saints or villains, so the characters in the *Genji* are not. Genji himself may in the first chapters seem too good to be true, but he improves as the action proceeds. The principal consort of Genji's father works much mischief, but she is not a wicked woman. She is a strong and determined mother, no more. The Rokujō lady brings on the death of rival ladies, but she does it unintentionally. She is depicted as a lady of remarkable attainments, more sad than villainous. Indeed she is one of the most compelling characters among them all. Perhaps forty or fifty characters emerge as of some importance, and they emerge with remarkable vitality, each one a believable person distinct from all the others. Here we have reason enough for calling the *Genji* a novel. It would be difficult indeed to think of an earlier piece of prose narrative that would so brilliantly qualify for the designation.

Murasaki Shikibu had a rich tradition of Chinese historical writing and Chinese and Japanese lyric poetry to draw on. As for prose fiction, she had little more than the beginnings the Japanese themselves had made in the tenth century. Prose fiction is not a genre the Chinese much admired at the time, or were very good at. Interesting beginnings these were, and, in a fragile way, beautiful beginnings; but little in them seems to anticipate the appearance of a romance which is more then a romance, in that it shows believable people in real situations. When romancers of the tenth century attempted characterization, and it is of a rudimentary sort, they write fairy stories; and when they write of such matters as court intrigues, the characterization is so flat that it can hardly be called characterization at all. The diaries of the tenth century may perhaps have been something of an inspiration for Murasaki Shikibu, but the awareness that an imagined predicament can be made more real than a real one required a great leap of the imagination, and Murasaki Shikibu made it by herself. Though numbers of romances from the tenth century are known to have been lost, the evidence is that the important ones survive.

The figure of the imaginative leap may suggest that a mature genius suddenly appeared, displaying her full array of talents from the first page. That is not quite the case. The tale begins somewhat uncertainly and gathers strength and confidence as it goes along. Since the years between the two world wars the theory has been widely discussed among Japanese scholars, some of whom accept it and some of whom do not, that the chapters were not written in the order in which they are always presented and read today. Several of the early chapters, including the second, third, and fourth, seem to stand apart from the main narrative as short stories or independent episodes. This clearly (though not necessarily) suggests that these chapters were written and added later. A further difficulty is that they are of uneven quality, some from the hand of a sure and experienced writer, some from a tyro. Read in the order in which we conventionally have them, they reveal steady growth and maturing; or it might be more appropriate to say that there are spurts in the process, so that the figure of an imaginative leap might be changed for one of a series of leaps, each bolder than the last.

The Waley translation came out in six volumes, each with a separate title, suggesting independent but related stories, like the Barchester or Palliser novels of Trollope. There is no basis in the original for such an arrangement. The novel contains no formal divisions other than the fifty-four chapters. One wishes that it did, because one could then direct the reader to the best of the independent but related novels, and suggest that, the taste having been acquired, the others be taken up in any convenient order. Though the 'short story' chapters do stand apart, no segment of the main narrative except the beginning is independent. The best that can be offered the prospective reader is assurance that Murasaki Shikibu gets better all the time.

The tale quite clearly breaks in two with Genji's death; but there is an earlier break, as Genji goes into his middle and late forties. If it may thus be thought of as falling into three parts, the first part still has a great deal of the tenth century in it. The hero is an idealized prince. Though there are setbacks, his early career is essentially a success story. It has long been argued, and rather persuasively, that Murasaki Shikibu had a historical personage in mind. If so, then certain inadequacies in the characterization of the early Genji may be accounted for by the fact that she could assume in her initial readers or listeners considerable knowledge of her model.

Then, some two-thirds of the way through the sections dominated by Genji, there comes a tidying up and packing away of things, as by someone getting ready to move on; and the matter of the last eight chapters before Genji's disappearance from the scene is different. Enough of romancing, Murasaki Shikibu seems to say, and one may imagine that she is leaving her own youth behind; the sad things are the real things. Shadows gather over Genji's life. The action is altogether less grand and more intimate, the characterization more compelling, than in the first section.

Then, suddenly, Genji is dead. We learn almost nothing of his last years, nor, though the chronology of the *Genji* is on the whole precise, do we learn how long he lived. Once more, and very boldly this time, Murasaki Shikibu has moved on. After the three transitional chapters come what are generally called the Uji chapters. The pessimism grows, the main action moves from the capital to the village of Uji, both character and action are more attenuated, and Murasaki Shikibu has a try, and many will say succeeds, at a most extraordinary thing, the creation of the first anti-hero in the literature of the world.

No sensible critic or scholar would argue that nothing at all was done to change Murasaki Shikibu's manuscript during the two centuries and more between its composition and the date of the earliest texts; and many have argued that the Uji chapters are by someone else. Tradition has assigned the authorship of these chapters to her daughter, Daini no Sammi. The scholarly argument against such ascription seems less persuasive than the intuitive one: it may be difficult to imagine a genius building so much on so slight a foundation; but it is almost impossible to imagine a second genius taking over without preparation at such a high point in the development of the first. The historical fact is that whoever wrote the *Genji* had no successors, and so the theory of mass genius has very little to support it. Later romances are by comparison rather poor stuff.

Changes and additions in detail may have come later, but the narrative points essentially to a single author working over a long period of time, herself (few would dispute the use of the feminine pronoun) living long enough to have immediate knowledge of the shadows that fall over her book, shadows that come with age and experience, and working to the end. If her own life went on into the years when sadness comes into Genji's life, then she probably died in the second or third decade of the eleventh century. Her book may seem unfinished, but to the lady herself the word 'unfinished' would probably not have meant a great deal.

One has only to riffle through the *Genji* to see that it is studded with short poems, here set off from the main prose narrative as they are not in the Waley translation. They perform social functions from trivial dalliance to earnest courtship, and serve to emphasize moments of heightened emotion. If the *Genji* is loosely constructed and inconclusive, it is also strongly lyrical, especially in its treatment of nature and fusion of man and place and season, of foreground and background. In probably no major Occidental work of fiction is one so constantly aware of the seasons and the phases of the moon.

The poems are frequently untranslatable. This need not surprise us, for the movement from the translatable to the untranslatable tends to run parallel with that from prose to poetry. There is a particular reason for the untranslatability of Murasaki Shikibu's poetry: it abounds with puns. A pun that can be translated perfectly is very rare indeed.

Only a few of the puns are explained in the footnotes to this translation. Explanation has seemed necessary when the absence of it reduces a poem to nonsense and when, as with 'Heartvine' and 'Channel Buoys', a pun is given great prominence as a chapter title. It would be difficult to say how many other puns there are, but the number is probably greater than the number of poems, which is almost eight hundred. Punning is probably the single most common rhetorical device in the poetry of early and middle Heian.

If it is common, however, it is far from daring or exuberant in *Genji* poetry. A conventional vocabulary of puns had already been put together a century or so before Murasaki Shikibu's day, and she was not an innovator in poetic matters. Some of the puns are so common that the introduction of one image into a poem will immediately introduce a second. A pine tree, for instance, usually brings with it a suggestion of unrequited love, for *matsu*, 'pine', means also 'to wait'. Mention of the long summer rains usually does double duty, having reference also to a time of sad, brooding tedium. Falling rain or snow is also the passage of the years; autumn is also surfeit or neglect; a fisherman is also a nun; the river, barrier, and gate of Osaka suggest a meeting, as also does the province or lake of Omi; an iris is also discernment or a pattern; a rat is also a root and a cry; an imperial progress, as in the title of Chapter 29, is also a deep snow; to pluck, as of plants, is also to heap up or accumulate, as of years; a letter or other specimen of calligraphy is also a trail; a wild goose also suggests evanescence or transcience. One of the most common puns in the last ten chapters is upon the name of the village in which they are principally set – Uji suggesting gloom.

Between two languages as remote from each other as Heian Japanese and modern English, there is bound to be much besides puns that is untranslatable. Conspicuous among the untranslatable elements are the elaborately agglutinative conjugations of the verbs and adjectives. Since nothing can be done to render them into English that is other than strained and impossibly mannered, they present a problem that must be lived with and need not be grappled with, and so in a sense are no problem at all. They make life more difficult for the translator from Heian Japanese into modern Japanese. Though the old language and the new are far apart, particularly in their conjugations, the one is successor to the other and of the same agglutinative nature. So the translator into modern Japanese is constrained to do something about them. The great novelist Tanizaki Junichirō published three translations of the *Genji*. The largest number of differences among them has to do with conjugation. These too make up the largest number of discrepancies among the many texts that survive from the Japanese Middle Ages, the thirteenth century through the sixteenth.

They may also, if indirectly, constitute my chief reason for thinking a new translation necessary, to supplement if not to replace the Waley translation. Waley elaborates upon the original most ingeniously, and says much that Murasaki Shikibu left unsaid. The flow of her narrative, in terms of thoughts and incidents, is rather sparse, despite the fact that, because of the conjugations, her sentences may move with the slow grandeur of the Nile. It may be that Waley elaborated in order to imitate her rhythms. If so, the endeavor is a worthy one. It risks giving a distorted impression, however, of the flow of her mind and brush. The present translation tries to follow the sequence of incident and thought without elaboration, and to say as little as Murasaki Shikibu said.

Edward G. Seidensticker

NOTE ON THE
TOPOGRAPHY

The principal east-west streets of the Heian capital were numbered from north to south, with Īchijō, or 'First Avenue', at the northern limits and Kujō, 'Ninth Avenue', at the southern. The streets most frequently mentioned in *The Tale of Genji* are Nijō, Sanjō, Gojō, and Rokujō, or 'Second Avenue', 'Third Avenue', 'Fifth Avenue', and 'Sixth Avenue'. Genji's residence for the first twenty chapters is on Nijō, which ran along the wall of the palace. In Chapter 21 he moves south to Rokujō.

NOTE ON THE TEXT

The present translation is of the complete text of *The Tale of Genji*. There exists an abridged edition in Vintage Books with later revisions by the translator.

SELECT BIBLIOGRAPHY

BOWRING, RICHARD, trans., *Murasaki Shikibu: Her Diary and Poetic Memoirs*, Princeton University Press, Princeton, 1982.

BOWRING, RICHARD, *Murasaki Shikibu, The Tale of Genji*. In *Landmarks of World Literature*, Cambridge University Press, Cambridge, 1988.

FIELD, NORMA, *The Splendor of Longing in the* Tale of Genji, Princeton University Press, Princeton, 1987.

PEKARIK, ANDREW, *Ukifune: Love in* The Tale of Genji, Columbia University Press, New York, 1982.

PUETTE, WILLIAM J., *Guide to* The Tale of Genji, Charles E. Tuttle Company, Rutland, Vermont, and Tokyo, 1983.

SHIRANE, HARUO, *The Bridge of Dreams: A Poetics of 'The Tale of Genji'*, Stanford University Press, Stanford, 1987.

WALEY, ARTHUR, trans., *The Tale of Genji*, 6 vols., George Allen and Unwin, London 1925–33. One-volume edition, George Allen and Unwin, 1935. Also Houghton Mifflin, Boston, 1935: and Modern Library, New York, 1960.

CHRONOLOGY

DATE	AUTHOR'S LIFE	LITERARY CONTEXT
Mid 8th Century		Composition of *Beowulf*. *Manyoshu*: collection of over 4000 poems in Japanese.
750		
c. 751		World's earliest surviving printed text, a Buddhist charm, in Korea.
762		Death of the Chinese lyric poet, Li Po.
764–770		Empress Shōtoku's *Million Charms*, Japanese Buddhist texts, printed.
794		
800		
842		
846		Death of the Chinese poet Po-Chü-i.
867		
868		The earliest dated printed book, the Chinese Buddhist *Diamond Sutra*.
878		
Late 9th Century		Revival of English Christian literature and culture under Alfred.
c. 890		Japanese renaissance in poetry, novels and painting.
891		*Anglo-Saxon Chronicles* begin.
906		
910		
911		
933		
947		
952		Confucian classics first printed.
955		
960		
962		
c. 963–72		Liudprand of Cremona writes *Atapodosis*, his chronicles of Otto I's visit to Italy (962–3) and his letter describing his own visit to Constantinople (968–9).

HISTORICAL EVENTS

Islam: Albarid dynasty comes to power.
Paper-making spreads from China to the Muslim world.

Japan: Heian-Kyō established as the capital.
Charlemagne crowned Holy Roman Emperor.
Collapse of the Tibetan Empire.

Emperor Basil I revives Byzantine power.

Alfred, King of Wessex, defeats the Danes.

China: fall of T'ang dynasty.
Benedictine Abbey of Cluny founded.
Rollo becomes first Viking duke of Normandy.
Foundation of Delhi.
China: establishment of Liao dynasty with its capital at Peking.

Otto I of Germany defeats the Magyars at Lechfeld.
Sung dynasty seizes power in northern China.
Otto I crowned Holy Roman Emperor.

DATE	AUTHOR'S LIFE	LITERARY CONTEXT
966	Birth of Fujiwara Michinaga.	
969		
971		
973		
c. 975	Birth of Murasaki Shikibu.	
979		
982		
986		
987		
990		
996	Murasaki's father becomes governor of Echizen, and Murasaki probably accompanies him there. Fujiwara Michinaga becomes minister of the Left.	
998/999	Murasaki marries a distant relation.	
999	Birth of her daughter.	The scholar, teacher and letter writer, Gerbert, becomes Pope Sylvester.
Late tenth century		Welsh Arthurian tales of *Culwych and Oliven*.
c.1000		Earliest surviving manuscript of *Beowulf*. Composition of Norse Eddaic poem *Voluspa* (*The Song of the Sybil*).
	Composition of *The Tale of Genji*.	
1001	Death of her husband.	
1002		
c. 1005	Murasaki goes to court in the service of the Empress Akiko, a daughter of Michinaga.	
1008-9	Birth of two sons to the empress, and consequent further rise of influence of Michinaga.	
c. 1010		*Decretum* of Bunhard, bishop of Worms.
1011		
c. 1015? during following decade?	Death of Murasaki.	

CHRONOLOGY

HISTORICAL EVENTS

Islamic Fatimid dynasty conquers Egypt.
University of Al-Azhar founded in Cairo.
British princes acknowledge Edgar as their overlord.
Revival of Anglo-Saxon art and culture.
Sung dynasty reunites China.
Vikings discover and colonize Greenland.
Japan: accession of Emperor Ichijō at the age of six.
France: accession of Hugh Capet.
Peru: expansion of Inca empire.

Incas establish their capital at Cuzco.
A great age of Chinese painting and ceramics.

St Stephen crowned King of Hungary by Otto III.
Spain: decline of Moorish power in Andalusia.
The Viking Leif Ericson discovers America.
Birth of Edward the Confessor.

Death of Emperor Ichijō.

DATE	AUTHOR'S LIFE	LITERARY CONTEXT
1016		
1018		
1020		Death of Firdusi, writer of the Persian national epic *The Shahnama*.
1027	Death of Michinaga.	
1035		
1045		
1055		
c. 1059	*The Sarashina Diary*, in which *The Tale of Genji* is said to consist of 'fifty and more chapters'.	
1066		
1071		
1096		
c. 1100		Composition of *Rubáiyát* by Omar Khayyam.
1120		*Alexiad* of Princess Anna Comnena.

CHRONOLOGY

Contents

Contents

Principal Characters

AKASHI EMPRESS. Also the Akashi girl, the Akashi princess. Genji's daughter by the Akashi lady. Consort of the emperor regnant at the end of the tale.

AKASHI LADY. Daughter of a former governor of Akashi. Installed by Genji in the northwest quarter at Rokujō. Mother of the Akashi empress.

AKIKONOMU. Daughter of a former crown prince and the Rokujō lady. Consort of the Reizei emperor. First cousin of Genji and Asagao.

AOI. Genji's first wife. Daughter of a Minister of the Left and Princess Omiya. Sister of Tō no Chūjō. Mother of Yūgiri.

ASAGAO. Genji's first cousin. Daughter of a brother of his father.

BENNOKIMI. In attendance upon Kashiwagi and later the Uji princesses.

EIGHTH PRINCE. Brother of Genji and father of the Uji princesses, Oigimi and Nakanokimi, and of Ukifune.

EMPEROR. (1) Genji's father, whose abdication is announced at the beginning of Chapter 9. (2) The Suzaku emperor, Genji's brother, who succeeds to the throne at the beginning of Chapter 9 and abdicates in Chapter 14. (3) The Reizei emperor. Thought by the world to be Genji's brother, but in fact his son by Fujitsubo. Succeeds to the throne in Chapter 14 and abdicates in Chapter 35. (4) A son of the Suzaku emperor who succeeds to the throne in Chapter 35 and is still reigning at the end of the tale.

EVENING FACES, LADY OF THE. A lady of undistinguished lineage who is loved by Tō no Chūjō and bears his daughter Tamakazura.

FUJITSUBO. Daughter of a former emperor, consort of Genji's father, and mother of Reizei emperor.

GENJI. Son of the emperor regnant at the opening of the tale.

HIGEKURO. Son of a Minister of the Right, husband of Murasaki's sister and of Tamakazura, and uncle of the emperor regnant at the end of the tale.

HOTARU, PRINCE. Genji's brother. Husband of Makibashira.

Principal Characters

HYŌBU, PRINCE. Brother of Fujitsubo and father of Murasaki.

KAORU. Thought by the world to be Genji's son, but really Kashiwagi's.

KASHIWAGI. Son of Tō no Chūjō and father of Kaoru. Married to the Second Princess, daughter of the Suzaku emperor.

KŌBAI. Younger brother of Kashiwagi.

KOJIJŪ. A woman in attendance upon the Third Princess.

KOKIDEN. Daughter of a Minister of the Right. Wife of Genji's father, sister of Oborozukiyo, and mother of Suzaku emperor.

KOREMITSU. Genji's servant and confidant.

KUMOINOKARI. Tō no Chūjō's daughter and Yūgiri's wife.

LOCUST SHELL, LADY OF THE. Wife of a governor of Iyo. Installed by Genji among his lesser ladies at Nijō.

MAKIBASHIRA. Daughter of Higekuro. Wife successively of Prince Hotaru and Kōbai.

MINISTER OF THE LEFT. Several characters. Initially, the husband of Princess Omiya and the father of Aoi and Tō no Chūjō.

MINISTER OF THE RIGHT. Several characters. Initially, the father of Kokiden and Oborozukiyo and the grandfather of the Suzaku emperor.

MURASAKI. Daughter of Prince Hyōbu, niece of Fujitsubo, and granddaughter of a former emperor.

NAKANOKIMI. Second daughter of the Eighth Prince.

NIOU, PRINCE. Son of the emperor regnant at the end of the tale and of the Akashi empress.

OBOROZUKIYO. Sister of Kokiden.

OIGIMI. Oldest daughter of the Eighth Prince.

OMI, LADY OF. Long-lost daughter of Tō no Chūjō.

OMIYA, PRINCESS. Genji's paternal aunt. Mother of Aoi and Tō no Chūjō.

ONO, NUN OF. Ukifune's protector.

ORANGE BLOSSOMS, LADY OF THE. Sister of a lesser concubine of Genji's father. Installed by Genji in the northeast quarter at Rokujō.

REIZEI EMPEROR. Thought by the world to be Genji's brother, but really his son by Fujitsubo. Reigns from Chapter 14 to Chapter 35.

ROKUJŌ LADY. Widow of a former crown prince, Genji's uncle. Mother of Akikonomu.

ROKUNOKIMI. Daughter of Yūgiri and wife of Niou.

SAFFLOWER LADY. Impoverished, but of royal origins. Installed by Genji among his lesser ladies at Nijō.

SECOND PRINCESS. (1) Daughter of the Suzaku emperor and wife of Kashiwagi. (2) Daughter of the emperor regnant at the end of the tale and wife of Kaoru.

SUZAKU EMPEROR. Genji's brother. Reigns from Chapter 9 to Chapter 14.

TAMAKAZURA. Daughter of Tō no Chūjō and the lady of the evening faces.

THIRD PRINCESS. Daughter of the Suzaku emperor, wife of Genji, and mother of Kaoru.

TŌNO CHŪJDŌ. Son of a Minister of the Left and Princess Omiya and brother of Aoi. Father of Kashiwagi, Kōbai, Kumoinokari, Tamakazura, and the Omi lady.

UKIFUNE. Unrecognized daughter of the Eighth Prince. Half sister of Oigimi and Nakanokimi.

UKON. In attendance upon Ukifune.

YOKAWA, BISHOP OF. Brother of the nun of Ono.

YŪGIRI. Son of Genji and Aoi.

CHAPTER 1

The Paulownia Court

In a certain reign there was a lady not of the first rank whom the emperor loved more than any of the others. The grand ladies with high ambitions thought her a presumptuous upstart, and lesser ladies were still more resentful. Everything she did offended someone. Probably aware of what was happening, she fell seriously ill and came to spend more time at home than at court. The emperor's pity and affection quite passed bounds. No longer caring what his ladies and courtiers might say, he behaved as if intent upon stirring gossip.

His court looked with very great misgiving upon what seemed a reckless infatuation. In China just such an unreasoning passion had been the undoing of an emperor and had spread turmoil through the land. As the resentment grew, the example of Yang Kuei-fei was the one most frequently cited against the lady.

She survived despite her troubles, with the help of an unprecedented bounty of love. Her father, a grand councillor, was no longer living. Her mother, an old-fashioned lady of good lineage, was determined that matters be no different for her than for ladies who with paternal support were making careers at court. The mother was attentive to the smallest detail of etiquette and deportment. Yet there was a limit to what she could do. The sad fact was that the girl was without strong backing, and each time a new incident arose she was next to defenseless.

It may have been because of a bond in a former life that she bore the emperor a beautiful son, a jewel beyond compare. The emperor was in a fever of impatience to see the child, still with the mother's family; and when, on the earliest day possible, he was brought to court, he did indeed prove to be a most marvelous babe. The emperor's eldest son was the grandson of the Minister of the Right. The world assumed that with this powerful support he would one day be named crown prince; but the new child was far more beautiful. On public occasions the emperor continued to favor his eldest son. The new child was a private treasure, so to speak, on which to lavish uninhibited affection.

The mother was not of such a low rank as to attend upon the emperor's personal needs. In the general view she belonged to the upper classes. He insisted on having her always beside him, however, and on nights when there was music or other entertainment he would require that she be present. Sometimes the two of them would sleep late, and even after they had risen he would not let her go. Because of his unreasonable demands she was widely held to have fallen into immoderate habits out of keeping with her rank.

With the birth of the son, it became yet clearer that she was the emperor's favorite. The mother of the eldest son began to feel uneasy. If she did not manage carefully, she might see the new son designated crown prince. She had come to court before the emperor's other ladies, she had once been favored over the others, and she had borne several of his children. However much her complaining might trouble and annoy him, she was one lady whom he could not ignore.

Though the mother of the new son had the emperor's love, her detractors were numerous and alert to the slightest inadvertency. She was in continuous torment, feeling that she had nowhere to turn. She lived in the Paulownia Court. The emperor had to pass the apartments of other ladies to reach hers, and it must be admitted that their resentment at his constant comings and goings was not unreasonable. Her visits to the royal chambers were equally frequent. The robes of her women were in a scandalous state from trash strewn along bridges and galleries. Once some women conspired to have both doors of a gallery she must pass bolted shut, and so she found herself unable to advance or retreat. Her anguish over the mounting list of insults was presently more than the emperor could bear. He moved a lady out of rooms adjacent to his own and assigned them to the lady of the Paulownia Court and so, of course, aroused new resentment.

When the young prince reached the age of three,* the resources of the treasury and the stewards' offices were exhausted to make the ceremonial bestowing of trousers as elaborate as that for the eldest son. Once more there was malicious talk; but the prince himself, as he grew up, was so superior of mien and disposition that few could find it in themselves to dislike him. Among the

---

*All ages are by the Oriental count, not of the full years but of the number of years in which one has lived. Thus it is possible to have a count of three after a full year and two days, one at the end and one at the beginning of another year. All ages are either one or two above the full count.

more discriminating, indeed, were some who marveled that such a paragon had been born into this world.

In the summer the boy's mother, feeling vaguely unwell, asked that she be allowed to go home. The emperor would not hear of it. Since they were by now used to these indispositions, he begged her to stay and see what course her health would take. It was steadily worse, and then, suddenly, everyone could see that she was failing. Her mother came pleading that he let her go home. At length he agreed.

Fearing that even now she might be the victim of a gratuitous insult, she chose to go off without ceremony, leaving the boy behind. Everything must have an end, and the emperor could no longer detain her. It saddened him inexpressibly that he was not even permitted to see her off. A lady of great charm and beauty, she was sadly emaciated. She was sunk in melancholy thoughts, but when she tried to put them into words her voice was almost inaudible. The emperor was quite beside himself, his mind a confusion of things that had been and things that were to come. He wept and vowed undying love, over and over again. The lady was unable to reply. She seemed listless and drained of strength, as if she scarcely knew what was happening. Wanting somehow to help, the emperor ordered that she be given the honor of a hand-drawn carriage. He returned to her apartments and still could not bring himself to the final parting.

'We vowed that we would go together down the road we all must go. You must not leave me behind.'

She looked sadly up at him. 'If I had suspected that it would be so –' She was gasping for breath.

'I leave you, to go the road we all must go.
The road I would choose, if only I could, is the other.'

It was evident that she would have liked to say more; but she was so weak that it had been a struggle to say even this much.

The emperor was wondering again if he might not keep her with him and have her with him to the end.

But a message came from her mother, asking that she hurry. 'We have obtained the agreement of eminent ascetics to conduct the necessary services, and I fear that they are to begin this evening.'

So, in desolation, he let her go. He passed a sleepless night.

He sent off a messenger and was beside himself with impatience and apprehension even before there had been time for the man to reach the lady's house and return. The man arrived to find the house echoing with laments. She had died at shortly past midnight. He returned sadly to the palace. The emperor closed himself up in his private apartments. He would have liked at least to keep the boy with him, but no precedent could be found for having him away from his mother's house through the mourning. The boy looked in bewilderment at the weeping courtiers, at his father too, the tears streaming over his face. The death of a parent is sad under any circumstances, and this one was indescribably sad.

But there must be an end to weeping, and orders were given for the funeral. If only she could rise to the heavens with the smoke from the pyre, said the mother between her sobs. She rode in the hearse with several attendants, and what must her feelings have been when they reached Mount Otaki?* It was there that the services were conducted with the utmost solemnity and dignity.

She looked down at the body. 'With her before me, I cannot persuade myself that she is dead. At the sight of her ashes I can perhaps accept what has happened.'

The words were rational enough, but she was so distraught that she seemed about to fall from the carriage. The women had known that it would be so and did what they could for her.

A messenger came from the palace with the news that the lady had been raised to the Third Rank, and presently a nunciary arrived to read the official order. For the emperor, the regret was scarcely bearable that he had not had the courage of his resolve to appoint her an imperial consort, and he wished to make amends by promoting her one rank. There were many who resented even this favor. Others, however, of a more sensitive nature, saw more than ever what a dear lady she had been, simple and gentle and difficult to find fault with. It was because she had been excessively favored by the emperor that she had been the victim of such malice. The grand ladies were now reminded of how sympathetic and unassuming she had been. It was for just such an occasion, they remarked to one another, that the phrase 'how well one knows'† had been invented.

---

*To the east of the city.

†A poetic allusion, probably, but the poem cited by the earliest commentators is otherwise unknown, and therefore suspect.

The days went dully by. The emperor was careful to send offerings for the weekly memorial services. His grief was unabated and he spent his nights in tears, refusing to summon his other ladies. His serving women were plunged into dew-drenched autumn.

There was one lady, however, who refused to be placated. 'How ridiculous,' said the lady of the Kokiden Pavilion, mother of his eldest son, 'that the infatuation should continue even now.'

The emperor's thoughts were on his youngest son even when he was with his eldest. He sent off intelligent nurses and serving women to the house of the boy's grandmother, where he was still in residence, and made constant inquiry after him.

The autumn tempests blew and suddenly the evenings were chilly. Lost in his grief, the emperor sent off a note to the grandmother. His messenger was a woman of middle rank called Myōbu, whose father was a guards officer. It was on a beautiful moonlit night that he dispatched her, a night that brought memories. On such nights he and the dead lady had played the koto for each other. Her koto had somehow had overtones lacking in other instruments, and when she would interrupt the music to speak, the words too carried echoes of their own. Her face, her manner – they seemed to cling to him, but with 'no more substance than the lucent dream.'*

Myōbu reached the grandmother's house. Her carriage was drawn through the gate – and what a lonely place it was! The old lady had of course lived in widowed retirement, but, not wishing to distress her only daughter, she had managed to keep the place in repair. Now all was plunged into darkness. The weeds grew ever higher and the autumn winds tore threateningly at the garden. Only the rays of the moon managed to make their way through the tangles.

The carriage was pulled up and Myōbu alighted.

The grandmother was at first unable to speak. 'It has been a trial for me to go on living, and now to have one such as you come through the dews of this wild garden – I cannot tell you how much it shames me.'

'A lady who visited your house the other day told us that she

---

*Anonymous, *Kokinshū* 647:

> Reality, within the depths of night,
> Has no more substance than the lucent dream.

had to see with her own eyes before she could really understand your loneliness and sorrow. I am not at all a sensitive person, and yet I am unable to control these tears.'

After a pause she delivered a message from the emperor. 'He has said that for a time it all seemed as if he were wandering in a nightmare, and then when his agitation subsided he came to see that the nightmare would not end. If only he had a companion in his grief, he thought – and it occurred to him that you, my lady, might be persuaded to come unobtrusively to court. He cannot bear to think of the child languishing in this house of tears, and hopes that you will come quickly and bring him with you. He was more than once interrupted by sobs as he spoke, and it was apparent to all of us that he feared having us think him inexcusably weak. I came away without hearing him to the end.'

'I cannot see for tears,' said the old lady. 'Let these sublime words bring me light.'

This was the emperor's letter: 'It seems impossibly cruel that although I had hoped for comfort with the passage of time my grief should only be worse. I am particularly grieved that I do not have the boy with me, to watch him grow and mature. Will you not bring him to me? We shall think of him as a memento.'

There could be no doubting the sincerity of the royal petition. A poem was appended to the letter, but when she had come to it the old lady was no longer able to see through her tears:

'At the sound of the wind, bringing dews to Miyagi Plain,
    I think of the tender *hagi* * upon the moor.'

'Tell His Majesty,' said the grandmother after a time, 'that it has been a great trial for me to live so long. "Ashamed before the Takasago pines† I think that it is not for me to be seen at court. Even if the august invitation is repeated, I shall not find it possible to accept. As for the boy, I do not know what his wishes are. The indications are that he is eager to go. It is sad for me, but as it should be. Please tell His Majesty of these thoughts, secret

---

*Lespedeza japonica, often called bush clover.

†Anonymous, *Kokin Rokujō, Zoku Kokka Taikan* 33903:

> Ashamed before the Takasago pines,
> I would not have it known that I still live.

until now. I fear that I bear a curse from a previous existence and that it would be wrong and even terrible to keep the child with me.'

'It would have given me great pleasure to look in upon him,' said Myōbu, getting up to leave. The child was asleep. 'I should have liked to report to his royal father. But he will be waiting up for me, and it must be very late.'

'May I not ask you to come in private from time to time? The heart of a bereaved parent may not be darkness, perhaps, but a quiet talk from time to time would do much to bring light.* You have done honor to this house on so many happy occasions, and now circumstances have required that you come with a sad message. The fates have not been kind. All of our hopes were on the girl, I must say again, from the day she was born, and until he died her father did not let me forget that she must go to court, that his own death, if it came early, should not deter me. I knew that another sort of life would be happier for a girl without strong backing, but I could not forget his wishes and sent her to court as I had promised. Blessed with favors beyond her station, she was the object of insults such as no one can be asked to endure. Yet endure them she did until finally the strain and the resentment were too much for her. And so, as I look back upon them, I know that those favors should never have been. Well, put these down, if you will, as the mad wanderings of a heart that is darkness.'† She was unable to go on.

It was late.

'His Majesty says much the same thing,' replied Myōbu. 'It was, he says, an intensity of passion such as to startle the world, and perhaps for that very reason it was fated to be brief. He cannot think of anything he has done to arouse such resentment, he says, and so he must live with resentment which seems without proper cause. Alone and utterly desolate, he finds it impossible to face the world. He fears that he must seem dreadfully eccentric. How very great – he has said it over and over again – how very great his

---

*Fujiwara Kanesuke, *Gosenshū* 1103:

> The heart of a parent is not darkness, and yet
> He wanders lost in thoughts upon his child.

†Another reference to the Kanesuke poem.

burden of guilt must be. One scarcely ever sees him that he is not weeping.' Myōbu too was in tears. 'It is very late. I must get back before the night is quite over and tell him what I have seen.'

The moon was sinking over the hills, the air was crystal clear, the wind was cool, and the songs of the insects among the autumn grasses would by themselves have brought tears. It was a scene from which Myōbu could not easily pull herself.

> 'The autumn night is too short to contain my tears
> Though songs of bell cricket weary, fall into silence.'*

This was her farewell poem. Still she hesitated, on the point of getting into her carriage.

The old lady sent a reply:

> 'Sad are the insect songs among the reeds.
> More sadly yet falls the dew from above the clouds.†

'I seem to be in a complaining mood.'

Though gifts would have been out of place, she sent as a trifling memento of her daughter a set of robes, left for just such an occasion, and with them an assortment of bodkins and combs.

The young women who had come from court with the little prince still mourned their lady, but those of them who had acquired a taste for court life yearned to be back. The memory of the emperor made them join their own to the royal petitions.

But no – a crone like herself would repel all the fine ladies and gentlemen, said the grandmother, while on the other hand she could not bear the thought of having the child out of her sight for even a moment.

Myōbu was much moved to find the emperor waiting up for her. Making it seem that his attention was on the small and beautifully planted garden before him, now in full autumn bloom, he was talking quietly with four or five women, among the most sensitive of his attendants. He had become addicted to illustrations by

---

*The bell cricket of the Heian Period seems to have been what is today called the pine cricket, *Madasumma marmorata*, and the Heian pine cricket has become the bell cricket.

†'A sad message comes from court to join the sadness already here.'

the emperor Uda for 'The Song of Everlasting Sorrow'* and to poems by Ise and Tsurayuki on that subject, and to Chinese poems as well.

He listened attentively as Myōbu described the scene she had found so affecting. He took up the letter she had brought from the grandmother.

'I am so awed by this august message that I would run away and hide; and so violent are the emotions it gives rise to that I scarcely know what to say.

'The tree that gave them shelter has withered and died.
One fears for the plight of the *hagi* shoots beneath.'

A strange way to put the matter, thought the emperor; but the lady must still be dazed with grief. He chose to overlook the suggestion that he himself could not help the child.

He sought to hide his sorrow, not wanting these women to see him in such poor control of himself. But it was no use. He reviewed his memories over and over again, from his very earliest days with the dead lady. He had scarcely been able to bear a moment away from her while she lived. How strange that he had been able to survive the days and months since on memories alone. He had hoped to reward the grandmother's sturdy devotion, and his hopes had come to nothing.

'Well,' he sighed, 'she may look forward to having her day, if she will only live to see the boy grow up.'

Looking at the keepsakes Myōbu had brought back, he thought what a comfort it would be if some wizard were to bring him, like that Chinese emperor, a comb from the world where his lost love was dwelling. He whispered:

'And will no wizard search her out for me,
That even he may tell me where she is?'

There are limits to the powers of the most gifted artist. The Chinese lady in the paintings did not have the luster of life. Yang Kuei-fei was said to have resembled the lotus of the Sublime

---

*By Po Chü-i, describing the grief of the T'ang emperor Hsüan Tsung upon the death of his concubine Yang Kuei-fei. Uda reigned in the late ninth century and died in 931. Tsurayuki and Ise were active in the early tenth century. The latter was one of Uda's concubines.

Pond, the willows of the Timeless Hall. No doubt she was very beautiful in her Chinese finery. When he tried to remember the quiet charm of his lost lady, he found that there was no color of flower, no song of bird, to summon her up. Morning and night, over and over again, they had repeated to each other the lines from 'The Song of Everlasting Sorrow':

> 'In the sky, as birds that share a wing.
> On earth, as trees that share a branch.'

It had been their vow, and the shortness of her life had made it an empty dream.

Everything, the moaning of the wind, the humming of autumn insects, added to the sadness. But in the apartments of the Kokiden lady matters were different. It had been some time since she had last waited upon the emperor. The moonlight being so beautiful, she saw no reason not to have music deep into the night. The emperor muttered something about the bad taste of such a performance at such a time, and those who saw his distress agreed that it was an unnecessary injury. Kokiden was of an arrogant and intractable nature and her behavior suggested that to her the emperor's grief was of no importance.

The moon set. The wicks in the lamps had been trimmed more than once and presently the oil was gone. Still he showed no sign of retiring. His mind on the boy and the old lady, he jotted down a verse:

> 'Tears dim the moon, even here above the clouds.*
> Dim must it be in that lodging among the reeds.'

Calls outside told him that the guard was being changed. It would be one or two in the morning. People would think his behavior strange indeed. He at length withdrew to his bedchamber. He was awake the whole night through, and in dark morning, his thoughts on the blinds that would not open,† he was unable to interest himself in business of state. He scarcely touched his break-

---

*'Even here in the palace.'

†Ise, on 'The Song of Everlasting Sorrow,' *Zoku Kokka Taikan* 18158:

> The jeweled blinds are drawn, the morning is dark.
> I had not thought I would not even dream.

fast, and lunch seemed so remote from his inclinations that his attendants exchanged looks and whispers of alarm.

Not all voices were sympathetic. Perhaps, some said, it had all been foreordained, but he had dismissed the talk and ignored the resentment and let the affair quite pass the bounds of reason; and now to neglect his duties so – it was altogether too much. Some even cited the example of the Chinese emperor who had brought ruin upon himself and his country.*

The months passed and the young prince returned to the palace. He had grown into a lad of such beauty that he hardly seemed meant for this world – and indeed one almost feared that he might only briefly be a part of it. When, the following spring, it came time to name a crown prince, the emperor wanted very much to pass over his first son in favor of the younger, who, however, had no influential maternal relatives. It did not seem likely that the designation would pass unchallenged. The boy might, like his mother, be destroyed by immoderate favors. The emperor told no one of his wishes. There did after all seem to be a limit to his affections, people said; and Kokiden regained her confidence.

The boy's grandmother was inconsolable. Finally, because her prayer to be with her daughter had been answered, perhaps, she breathed her last. Once more the emperor was desolate. The boy, now six, was old enough to know grief himself. His grandmother, who had been so good to him over the years, had more than once told him what pain it would cause her, when the time came, to leave him behind.

He now lived at court. When he was seven he went through the ceremonial reading of the Chinese classics, and never before had there been so fine a performance. Again a tremor of apprehension passed over the emperor – might it be that such a prodigy was not to be long for this world?

'No one need be angry with him now that his mother is gone.' He took the boy to visit the Kokiden Pavilion. 'And now most especially I hope you will be kind to him.'

Admitting the boy to her inner chambers, even Kokiden was pleased. Not the sternest of warriors or the most unbending of enemies could have held back a smile. Kokiden was reluctant to

---

*The Yang Kuei-fei affair was the immediate cause of, or perhaps the pretext for, the disastrous An Lu-shan rebellion.

let him go. She had two daughters, but neither could compare with him in beauty. The lesser ladies crowded about, not in the least ashamed to show their faces, all eager to amuse him, though aware that he set them off to disadvantage. I need not speak of his accomplishments in the compulsory subjects, the classics and the like. When it came to music his flute and koto made the heavens echo – but to recount all his virtues would, I fear, give rise to a suspicion that I distort the truth.

An embassy came from Korea. Hearing that among the emissaries was a skilled physiognomist, the emperor would have liked to summon him for consultation. He decided, however, that he must defer to the emperor Uda's injunction against receiving foreigners, and instead sent this favored son to the Kōro mansion,* where the party was lodged. The boy was disguised as the son of the grand moderator, his guardian at court. The wise Korean cocked his head in astonishment.

'It is the face of one who should ascend to the highest place and be father to the nation,' he said quietly, as if to himself. 'But to take it for such would no doubt be to predict trouble. Yet it is not the face of the minister, the deputy, who sets about ordering public affairs.'

The moderator was a man of considerable learning. There was much of interest in his exchanges with the Korean. There were also exchanges of Chinese poetry, and in one of his poems the Korean succeeded most skillfully in conveying his joy at having been able to observe such a countenance on this the eve of his return to his own land, and sorrow that the parting must come so soon. The boy offered a verse that was received with high praise. The most splendid of gifts were bestowed upon him. The wise man was in return showered with gifts from the palace.

Somehow news of the sage's remarks leaked out, though the emperor himself was careful to say nothing. The Minister of the Right, grandfather of the crown prince and father of the Kokiden lady, was quick to hear, and again his suspicions were aroused. In the wisdom of his heart, the emperor had already analyzed the boy's physiognomy after the Japanese fashion and had formed tentative plans. He had thus far refrained from bestowing imperial rank on his son, and was delighted that the Korean view should so

*In the southern part of the city.

accord with his own. Lacking the support of maternal relatives, the boy would be most insecure as a prince without court rank, and the emperor could not be sure how long his own reign would last. As a commoner he could be of great service. The emperor therefore encouraged the boy in his studies, at which he was so proficient that it seemed a waste to reduce him to common rank. And yet – as a prince he would arouse the hostility of those who had cause to fear his becoming emperor. Summoning an astrologer of the Indian school, the emperor was pleased to learn that the Indian view coincided with the Japanese and the Korean; and so he concluded that the boy should become a commoner with the name Minamoto or Genji.

The months and the years passed and still the emperor could not forget his lost love. He summoned various women who might console him, but apparently it was too much to ask in this world for one who even resembled her. He remained sunk in memories, unable to interest himself in anything. Then he was told of the Fourth Princess, daughter of a former emperor, a lady famous for her beauty and reared with the greatest care by her mother, the empress. A woman now in attendance upon the emperor had in the days of his predecessor been most friendly with the princess, then but a child, and even now saw her from time to time.

'I have been at court through three reigns now,' she said, 'and never had I seen anyone who genuinely resembled my lady. But now the daughter of the empress dowager is growing up, and the resemblance is most astonishing. One would be hard put to find her equal.'

Hoping that she might just possibly be right, the emperor asked most courteously to have the princess sent to court. Her mother was reluctant and even fearful, however. One must remember, she said, that the mother of the crown prince was a most willful lady who had subjected the lady of the Paulownia Court to open insults and presently sent her into a fatal decline. Before she had made up her mind she followed her husband in death, and the daughter was alone. The emperor renewed his petition. He said that he would treat the girl as one of his own daughters.

Her attendants and her maternal relatives and her older brother, Prince Hyōbu, consulted together and concluded that rather than languish at home she might seek consolation at court; and so she was sent off. She was called Fujitsubo. The resemblance to the dead lady was indeed astonishing. Because she was of such high birth (it may have been that people were imagining things) she seemed even more graceful and delicate than the other. No one could despise her for inferior rank, and the emperor need not feel shy about showing his love for her. The other lady had not particularly encouraged his attentions and had been the victim of a love too intense; and now, though it would be wrong to say that he had quite forgotten her, he found his affections shifting to the new lady, who was a source of boundless comfort. So it is with the affairs of this world.

Since Genji never left his father's side, it was not easy for this new lady, the recipient of so many visits, to hide herself from him. The other ladies were disinclined to think themselves her inferior, and indeed each of them had her own merits. They were all rather past their prime, however. Fujitsubo's beauty was of a younger and fresher sort. Though in her childlike shyness she made an especial effort not to be seen, Genji occasionally caught a glimpse of her face. He could not remember his own mother and it moved him deeply to learn, from the lady who had first told the emperor of Fujitsubo, that the resemblance was striking. He wanted to be near her always.

'Do not be unfriendly,' said the emperor to Fujitsubo. 'Sometimes it almost seems to me too that you are his mother. Do not think him forward, be kind to him. Your eyes, your expression: you are really so uncommonly like her that you could pass for his mother.'

Genji's affection for the new lady grew, and the most ordinary flower or tinted leaf became the occasion for expressing it. Kokiden was not pleased. She was not on good terms with Fujitsubo, and all her old resentment at Genji came back. He was handsomer than the crown prince, her chief treasure in the world, well thought of by the whole court. People began calling Genji 'the shining one.' Fujitsubo, ranked beside him in the emperor's affections, became 'the lady of the radiant sun.'

It seemed a pity that the boy must one day leave behind his boyish attire; but when he reached the age of twelve he went through his initiation ceremonies and received the cap of an adult. Determined that the ceremony should be in no way inferior to the crown prince's, which had been held some years earlier in the Grand Hall, the emperor himself bustled about adding new details to the established forms. As for the banquet after the ceremony, he did not wish the custodians of the storehouses and granaries to treat it as an ordinary public occasion.

The throne faced east on the east porch, and before it were Genji's seat and that of the minister who was to bestow the official cap. At the appointed hour in midafternoon Genji appeared. The freshness of his face and his boyish coiffure were again such as to make the emperor regret that the change must take place. The ritual cutting of the boy's hair was performed by the secretary of the treasury. As the beautiful locks fell the emperor was seized with a hopeless longing for his dead lady. Repeatedly he found himself struggling to keep his composure. The ceremony over, the boy withdrew to change to adult trousers and descended into the courtyard for ceremonial thanksgiving. There was not a person in the assembly who did not feel his eyes misting over. The emperor was stirred by the deepest of emotions. He had on brief occasions been able to forget the past, and now it all came back again. Vaguely apprehensive lest the initiation of so young a boy bring a sudden aging, he was astonished to see that his son delighted him even more.

The Minister of the Left, who bestowed the official cap, had only one daughter, his chief joy in life. Her mother, the minister's first wife, was a princess of the blood. The crown prince had sought the girl's hand, but the minister thought rather of giving her to Genji. He had heard that the emperor had similar thoughts. When the emperor suggested that the boy was without adequate sponsors for his initiation and that the support of relatives by marriage might be called for, the minister quite agreed.

The company withdrew to outer rooms and Genji took his place below the princes of the blood. The minister hinted at what was on his mind, but Genji, still very young, did not quite know what to say. There came a message through a chamberlain that the minister was expected in the royal chambers. A lady-in-waiting brought the customary gifts for his services, a woman's cloak, white and of grand proportions, and a set of robes as well. As he poured wine for his minister, the emperor recited a poem which was in fact a deeply felt admonition:

> 'The boyish locks are now bound up, a man's.
> And do we tie a lasting bond for his future?'

This was the minister's reply:

> 'Fast the knot which the honest heart has tied.
> May lavender, the hue of the troth, be as fast.'*

The minister descended from a long garden bridge to give formal thanks. He received a horse from the imperial stables and a falcon from the secretariat. In the courtyard below the emperor, princes and high courtiers received gifts in keeping with their stations. The moderator, Genji's guardian, had upon royal command prepared the trays and baskets now set out in the royal presence. As for Chinese chests of food and gifts, they overflowed the premises, in even larger numbers than for the crown prince's initiation. It was the most splendid and dignified of ceremonies.

Genji went home that evening with the Minister of the Left. The nuptial observances were conducted with great solemnity. The groom seemed to the minister and his family quite charming in his boyishness. The bride was older, and somewhat ill at ease with such a young husband.

The minister had the emperor's complete confidence, and his principal wife, the girl's mother, was the emperor's sister. Both parents were therefore of the highest standing. And now they had Genji for a son-in-law. The Minister of the Right, who as grandfather of the crown prince should have been without rivals, was somehow eclipsed. The Minister of the Left had numerous children by several ladies. One of the sons, a very handsome lad by his principal wife, was already a guards lieutenant. Relations between the two ministers were not good; but the Minister of the Right found it difficult to ignore such a talented youth, to whom he offered the hand of his fourth and favorite daughter. His esteem for his new son-in-law rivaled the other minister's esteem for Genji. To both houses the new arrangements seemed ideal.

Constantly at his father's side, Genji spent little time at the Sanjō mansion of his bride. Fujitsubo was for him a vision of sublime beauty. If he could have someone like her – but in fact there was no one really like her. His bride too was beautiful, and she had had the advantage of every luxury; but he was not at all sure that they were meant for each other. The yearning in his young heart for the other lady was agony. Now that he had come of age, he no

---

*Throughout the tale, lavender (*murasaki*) suggests affinity.

longer had his father's permission to go behind her curtains. On evenings when there was music, he would play the flute to her koto and so communicate something of his longing, and take some comfort from her voice, soft through the curtains. Life at court was for him much preferable to life at Sanjō. Two or three days at Sanjō would be followed by five or six days at court. For the minister, youth seemed sufficient excuse for this neglect. He continued to be delighted with his son-in-law.

The minister selected the handsomest and most accomplished of ladies to wait upon the young pair and planned the sort of diversions that were most likely to interest Genji. At the palace the emperor assigned him the apartments that had been his mother's and took care that her retinue was not dispersed. Orders were handed down to the offices of repairs and fittings to remodel the house that had belonged to the lady's family. The results were magnificent. The plantings and the artificial hills had always been remarkably tasteful, and the grounds now swarmed with workmen widening the lake. If only, thought Genji, he could have with him the lady he yearned for.

The sobriquet 'the shining Genji,' one hears, was bestowed upon him by the Korean.

CHAPTER 2

The Broom Tree

'The shining Genji': it was almost too grand a name. Yet he did not escape criticism for numerous little adventures. It seemed indeed that his indiscretions might give him a name for frivolity, and he did what he could to hide them. But his most secret affairs (such is the malicious work of the gossips) became common talk. If, on the other hand, he were to go through life concerned only for his name and avoid all these interesting and amusing little affairs, then he would be laughed to shame by the likes of the lieutenant of Katano.*

Still a guards captain, Genji spent most of his time at the palace, going infrequently to the Sanjō mansion of his father-in-law. The people there feared that he might have been stained by the lavender of Kasugano.† Though in fact he had an instinctive dislike for the promiscuity he saw all around him, he had a way of sometimes turning against his own better inclinations and causing unhappiness.

The summer rains came, the court was in retreat, and an even longer interval than usual had passed since his last visit to Sanjō. Though the minister and his family were much put out, they spared no effort to make him feel welcome. The minister's sons were more attentive than to the emperor himself. Genji was on particularly good terms with Tō no Chūjō. They enjoyed music together and more frivolous diversions as well. Tō no Chūjō was of an amorous nature and not at all comfortable in the apartments which his father-in-law, the Minister of the Right, had at great expense provided for him. At Sanjō with his own family, on the other hand, he took very good care of his rooms, and when Genji came and went the two of them were always together. They were

---

*Evidently the hero of a romance that has been lost.

†*Tales of Ise* 1:

> Kasugano lavender stains my robe,
> In deep disorder, like my secret loves.

Kasugano is on the outskirts of Nara. As already noted, lavender suggests a romantic affinity.

a good match for each other in study and at play. Reserve quite disappeared between them.

It had been raining all day. There were fewer courtiers than usual in the royal presence. Back in his own palace quarters, also unusually quiet, Genji pulled a lamp near and sought to while away the time with his books. He had Tō no Chūjō with him. Numerous pieces of colored paper, obviously letters, lay on a shelf. Tō no Chūjō made no attempt to hide his curiosity.

'Well,' said Genji, 'there are some I might let you see. But there are some I think it better not to.'

'You miss the point. The ones I want to see are precisely the ones you want to hide. The ordinary ones – I'm not much of a hand at the game, you know, but even I am up to the ordinary give and take. But the ones from ladies who think you are not doing right by them, who sit alone through an evening and wait for you to come – those are the ones I want to see.'

It was not likely that really delicate letters would be left scattered on a shelf, and it may be assumed that the papers treated so carelessly were the less important ones.

'You do have a variety of them,' said Tō no Chūjō, reading the correspondence through piece by piece. This will be from her, and this will be from *her*, he would say. Sometimes he guessed correctly and sometimes he was far afield, to Genji's great amusement. Genji was brief with his replies and let out no secrets.

'It is I who should be asking to see *your* collection. No doubt it is huge. When I have seen it I shall be happy to throw my files open to you.'

'I fear there is nothing that would interest you.' Tō no Chūjō was in a contemplative mood. 'It is with women as it is with everything else: the flawless ones are very few indeed. This is a sad fact which I have learned over the years. All manner of women seem presentable enough at first. Little notes, replies to this and that, they all suggest sensibility and cultivation. But when you begin sorting out the really superior ones you find that there are not many who have to be on your list. Each has her little tricks and she makes the most of them, getting in her slights at rivals, so broad sometimes that you almost have to blush. Hidden away by loving parents who build brilliant futures for them, they let word get out of this little talent and that little accomplishment and you are all in a stir. They are young and pretty and amiable and carefree, and in their boredom they begin to pick up a little from their elders, and in the natural course of things they begin to concentrate on one particular hobby and make something of it. A woman tells you all about it and hides the weak points and brings out the strong ones as if they were everything, and you can't very well call her a liar. So you begin keeping company, and it is always the same. The fact is not up to the advance notices.'

Tō no Chūjō sighed, a sigh clearly based on experience. Some of what he had said, though not all, accorded with Genji's own experience. 'And have you come upon any,' said Genji, smiling, 'who would seem to have nothing at all to recommend them?'

'Who would be fool enough to notice such a woman? And in any case, I should imagine that women with no merits are as rare as women with no faults. If a woman is of good family and well taken care of, then the things she is less than proud of are hidden and she gets by well enough. When you come to the middle ranks, each woman has her own little inclinations and there are thousands of ways to separate one from another. And when you come to the lowest – well, who really pays much attention?'

He appeared to know everything. Genji was by now deeply interested.

'You speak of three ranks,' he said, 'but is it so easy to make the division? There are well-born ladies who fall in the world and there are people of no background who rise to the higher ranks and build themselves fine houses as if intended for them all along. How would you fit such people into your system?'

At this point two young courtiers, a guards officer and a functionary in the ministry of rites, appeared on the scene, to attend the emperor in his retreat. Both were devotees of the way of love and both were good talkers. Tō no Chūjō, as if he had been waiting for them, invited their views on the question that had just been asked. The discussion progressed, and included a number of rather unconvincing points.

'Those who have just arrived at high position,' said one of the newcomers, 'do not attract the same sort of notice as those who were born to it. And those who were born to the highest rank but somehow do not have the right backing – in spirit they may be as proud and noble as ever, but they cannot hide their deficiencies. And so I think that they should both be put in your middle rank.

'There are those whose families are not quite of the highest rank but who go off and work hard in the provinces. They have their place in the world, though there are all sorts of little differences among them. Some of them would belong on anyone's list. So it is these days. Myself, I would take a woman from a middling family over one who has rank and nothing else. Let us say someone whose father is almost but not quite a councillor. Someone who has a decent enough reputation and comes from a decent enough family and can live in some luxury. Such people can be very pleasant. There is nothing wrong with the household arrangements, and indeed a daughter can sometimes be set out in a way that dazzles you. I can think of several such women it would be hard to find fault with. When they go into court service, they are the ones the unexpected favors have a way of falling on. I have seen cases enough of it, I can tell you.'

Genji smiled. 'And so a person should limit himself to girls with money?'

'That does not sound like you,' said Tō no Chūjō.

'When a woman has the highest rank and a spotless reputation,' continued the other, 'but something has gone wrong with her upbringing, something is wrong in the way she puts herself forward, you wonder how it can possibly have been allowed to happen. But when all the conditions are right and the girl herself is pretty enough, she is taken for granted. There is no cause for the least surprise. Such ladies are beyond the likes of me, and so I leave them where they are, the highest of the high. There are surprisingly pretty ladies wasting away behind tangles of weeds, and hardly anyone even knows of their existence. The first surprise is hard to forget. There she is, a girl with a fat, sloppy old father and boorish brothers and a house that seems common at best. Off in the women's rooms is a proud lady who has acquired bits and snatches of this and that. You get wind of them, however small the accomplishments may be, and they take hold of your imagination. She is not the equal of the one who has everything, of course, but she has her charm. She is not easy to pass by.'

He looked at his companion, the young man from the ministry of rites. The latter was silent, wondering if the reference might be to his sisters, just then coming into their own as subjects for conversation. Genji, it would seem, was thinking that on the highest levels there were sadly few ladies to bestow much thought upon.

He was wearing several soft white singlets with an informal court robe thrown loosely over them. As he sat in the lamplight leaning against an armrest, his companions almost wished that he were a woman. Even the 'highest of the high' might seem an inadequate match for him.

They talked on, of the varieties of women.

'A man sees women, all manner of them, who seem beyond reproach,' said the guards officer, 'but when it comes to picking the wife who must be everything, matters are not simple. The emperor has trouble, after all, finding the minister who has all the qualifications. A man may be very wise, but no man can govern by himself. Superior is helped by subordinate, subordinate defers to superior, and so affairs proceed by agreement and concession. But when it comes to choosing the woman who is to be in charge of your house, the qualifications are altogether too many. A merit is balanced by a defect, there is this good point and that bad point, and even women who though not perfect can be made to do are not easy to find. I would not like to have you think me a profligate who has to try them all. But it is a question of the woman who must be everything, and it seems best, other things being equal, to find someone who does not require shaping and training, someone who has most of the qualifications from the start. The man who begins his search with all this in mind must be reconciled to searching for a very long time.

'He comes upon a woman not completely and in every way to his liking but he makes certain promises and finds her hard to give up. The world praises him for his honest heart and begins to note good points in the woman too; and why not? But I have seen them all, and I doubt that there are any genuinely superior specimens among them. What about you gentlemen so far above us? How is it with you when you set out to choose your ladies?

'There are those who are young enough and pretty enough and who take care of themselves as if no particle of dust were allowed to fall upon them. When they write letters they choose the most inoffensive words, and the ink is so faint a man can scarcely read them. He goes to visit, hoping for a real answer. She keeps him waiting and finally lets him have a word or two in an almost inaudible whisper. They are clever, I can tell you, at hiding their defects.

'The soft, feminine ones are likely to assume a great deal. The man seeks to please, and the result is that the woman is presently looking elsewhere. That is the first difficulty in a woman.

'In the most important matter, the matter of running his household, a man can find that his wife has too much sensibility, an elegant word and device for every occasion. But what of the too domestic sort, the wife who bustles around the house the whole day long, her hair tucked up behind her ears, no attention to her appearance, making sure that everything is in order? There are things on his mind, things he has seen and heard in his comings and goings, the private and public demeanor of his colleagues, happy things and sad things. Is he to talk of them to an outsider? Of course not. He would much prefer someone near at hand, someone who will immediately understand. A smile passes over his face, tears well up. Or some event at court has angered him, things are too much for him. What good is it to talk to such a woman? He turns his back on her, and smiles, and sighs, and murmurs something to himself. "I beg your pardon?" she says, finally noticing. Her blank expression is hardly what he is looking for.

'When a man picks a gentle, childlike wife, he of course must see to training her and making up for her inadequacies. Even if at times she seems a bit unsteady, he may feel that his efforts have not been wasted. When she is there beside him her gentle charm makes him forget her defects. But when he is away and sends asking her to perform various services, it becomes clear, however small the service, that she has no thoughts of her own in the matter. Her uselessness can be trying.

'I wonder if a woman who is a bit chilly and unfeeling cannot at times seem preferable.'

His manner said that he had known them all; and he sighed at his inability to hand down a firm decision.

'No, let us not worry too much about rank and beauty. Let us be satisfied if a woman is not too demanding and eccentric. It is best to settle on a quiet, steady girl. If she proves to have unusual talent and discrimination – well, count them an unexpected premium. Do not, on the other hand, worry too much about remedying her defects. If she seems steady and not given to tantrums, then the charms will emerge of their own accord.

'There are those who display a womanly reticence to the world, as if they had never heard of complaining. They seem utterly calm. And then when their thoughts are too much for them they leave behind the most horrendous notes, the most flamboyant poems, the sort of keepsakes certain to call up dreadful memories, and off they go into the mountains or to some remote seashore. When I was a child I would hear the women reading romantic stories, and I would join them in their sniffling and think it all very sad, all very profound and moving. Now I am afraid that it suggests certain pretenses.

'It is very stupid, really, to run off and leave a perfectly kind and sympathetic man. He may have been guilty of some minor dereliction, but to run off with no understanding at all of his true feelings, with no purpose other than to attract attention and hope to upset him – it is an unpleasant sort of memory to have to live with. She gets drunk with admiration for herself and there she is, a nun. When she enters her convent she is sure that she has found enlightenment and has no regrets for the vulgar world.

'Her women come to see her. "How very touching," they say. "How brave of you."

'But she no longer feels quite as pleased with herself. The man, who has not lost his affection for her, hears of what has happened and weeps, and certain of her old attendants pass this intelligence on to her. "He is a man of great feeling, you see. What a pity that it should have come to this." The woman can only brush aside her newly cropped hair to reveal a face on the edge of tears. She tries to hold them back and cannot, such are her regrets for the life she has left behind; and the Buddha is not likely to think her one who has cleansed her heart of passion. Probably she is in more danger of brimstone now in this fragile vocation than if she had stayed with us in our sullied world.

'The bond between husband and wife is a strong one. Suppose the man had hunted her out and brought her back. The memory of her acts would still be there, and inevitably, sooner or later, it would be cause for rancor. When there are crises, incidents, a woman should try to overlook them, for better or for worse, and make the bond into something durable. The wounds will remain, with the woman and with the man, when there are crises such as I have described. It is very foolish for a woman to let a little dalliance upset her so much that she shows her resentment openly. He has his adventures – but if he has fond memories of their early days together, his and hers, she may be sure that she matters. A commotion means the end of everything. She should be quiet and generous, and when something comes up that quite properly arouses her resentment she should make it known by delicate hints. The man will feel guilty and with tactful guidance he will mend his ways. Too much lenience can make a woman seem charmingly docile and trusting, but it can also make her seem somewhat wanting in substance. We have had instances enough of boats abandoned to the winds and waves. Do you not agree?'

Tō no Chūjō nodded. 'It may be difficult when someone you are especially fond of, someone beautiful and charming, has been guilty of an indiscretion, but magnanimity produces wonders. They may not always work, but generosity and reasonableness and patience do on the whole seem best.'

His own sister was a case in point, he was thinking, and he was somewhat annoyed to note that Genji was silent because he had fallen asleep. Meanwhile the young guards officer talked on, a dedicated student of his subject. Tō no Chūjō was determined to hear him out.

'Let us make some comparisons,' said the guardsman. 'Let us think of the cabinetmaker. He shapes pieces as he feels like shaping them. They may be only playthings, with no real plan or pattern. They may all the same have a certain style for what they are – they may take on a certain novelty as times change and be very interesting. But when it comes to the genuine object, something of such undeniable value that a man wants to have it always with him – the perfection of the form announces that it is from the hand of a master.

'Or let us look at painting. There are any number of masters in the academy. It is not easy to separate the good from the bad among those who work on the basic sketches. But let color be added. The painter of things no one ever sees, of paradises, of fish in angry seas, raging beasts in foreign lands, devils and demons – the painter abandons himself to his fancies and paints to terrify and astonish. What does it matter if the results seem somewhat remote from real life? It is not so with the things we know, mountains, streams, houses near and like our own. The soft, unspoiled, wooded hills must be painted layer on layer, the details added gently, quietly, to give a sense of affectionate familiarity. And the foreground too, the garden inside the walls, the arrangement of the stones and grasses and waters. It is here that the master has his own power. There are details a lesser painter cannot imitate.

'Or let us look at calligraphy. A man without any great skill can stretch out this line and that in the cursive style and give an appearance of boldness and distinction. The man who has mastered the principles and writes with concentration may, on the other hand, have none of the eye-catching tricks; but when you take the trouble to compare the two the real thing is the real thing.

'So it is with trivialities like painting and calligraphy. How much more so with matters of the heart! I put no trust in the showy sort of affection that is quick to come forth when a suitable occasion presents itself. Let me tell you of something that happened to me a long time ago. You may find the story a touch wanton, but hear me through all the same.'

He drew close to Genji, who awoke from his slumber. Tō no Chūjō, chin in hand, sat opposite, listening with the greatest admiration and attention. There was in the young man's manner something slightly comical, as if he were a sage expostulating upon the deepest truths of the universe, but at such times a young man is not inclined to conceal his most intimate secrets.

'It happened when I was very young, hardly more than a page. I was attracted to a woman. She was of a sort I have mentioned before, not the most beautiful in the world. In my youthful frivolity, I did not at first think of making her my wife. She was someone to visit, not someone who deserved my full attention. Other places interested me more. She was violently jealous. If only she could be a little more understanding, I thought, wanting to be away from the interminable quarreling. And on the other hand it sometimes struck me as a little sad that she should be so worried about a man of so little account as myself. In the course of time I began to mend my ways.

'For my sake, she would try to do things for which her talent and nature did not suit her, and she was determined not to seem inferior even in matters for which she had no great aptitude. She served me diligently in everything. She did not want to be guilty of the smallest thing that might go against my wishes. I had at first thought her rather strong-willed, but she proved to be docile and pliant. She thought constantly about hiding her less favorable qualities, afraid that they might put me off, and she did what she could to avoid displaying herself and causing me embarrassment. She was a model of devotion. In a word, there was nothing wrong with her – save the one thing I found so trying.

'I told myself that she was devoted to the point of fear, and that if I led her to think I might be giving her up she might be a little less suspicious and given to nagging. I had had almost all I could stand. If she really wanted to be with me and I suggested that a break was near, then she might reform. I behaved with studied coldness, and when, as always, her resentment exploded, I said to her: "Not even the strongest bond between husband and wife can stand an unlimited amount of this sort of thing. It will eventually break, and he will not see her again. If you want to bring matters to such a pass, then go on doubting me as you have. If you would like to be with me for the years that lie ahead of us, then bear the trials as they come, difficult though they may be, and think them the way of the world. If you manage to overcome your jealousy, my affection is certain to grow. It seems likely that I will move ahead into an office of some distinction, and you will go with me and have no one you need think of as a rival." I was very pleased with myself. I had performed brilliantly as a preceptor.

'But she only smiled. "Oh, it won't be all that much trouble to put up with your want of consequence and wait till you are important. It will be much harder to pass the months and the years in the barely discernible hope that you will settle down and mend your fickle ways. Maybe you are right. Maybe this is the time to part."

'I was furious, and I said so, and she answered in kind. Then, suddenly, she took my hand and bit my finger.

'I reproved her somewhat extravagantly. "You insult me, and now you have wounded me. Do you think I can go to court like this? I am, as you say, a person of no consequence, and now, mutilated as I am, what is to help me get ahead in the world? There is nothing left for me but to become a monk." That meeting must be our last, I said, and departed, flexing my wounded finger.

> '   "I count them over, the many things between us.
>   One finger does not, alas, count the sum of your failures.

'I left the verse behind, adding that now she had nothing to complain about.

'She had a verse of her own. There were tears in her eyes.

> '   "I have counted them up myself, be assured, my failures.
>   For one bitten finger must all be bitten away?"

'I did not really mean to leave her, but my days were occupied in wanderings here and there, and I sent her no message. Then, late one evening toward the end of the year – it was an evening of rehearsals for the Kamo festival – a sleet was falling as we all started for home. Home. It came to me that I really had nowhere to go but her house. It would be no pleasure to sleep alone at the palace, and if I visited a woman of sensibility I would be kept freezing while she admired the snow. I would go look in upon *her*, and see what sort of mood she might be in. And so, brushing away the sleet, I made my way to her house. I felt just a little shy, but told myself that the sleet melting from my coat should melt her resentment. There was a dim light turned toward the wall, and a comfortable old robe of thick silk lay spread out to warm. The curtains were raised, everything suggested that she was waiting for me. I felt that I had done rather well.

'But she was nowhere in sight. She had gone that evening to stay with her parents, said the women who had been left behind. I had been feeling somewhat unhappy that she had maintained such a chilly silence, sending no amorous poems or queries. I wondered, though not very seriously, whether her shrillness and her jealousy might not have been intended for the precise purpose of disposing of me; but now I found clothes laid out with more attention to color and pattern than usual, exactly as she knew I liked them. She was seeing to my needs even now that I had apparently discarded her.

'And so, despite this strange state of affairs, I was convinced that she did not mean to do without me. I continued to send messages, and she neither protested nor gave an impression of wanting to annoy me by staying out of sight, and in her answers she was always careful not to anger or hurt me. Yet she went on saying that she could not forgive the behavior I had been guilty of in the past. If I would settle down she would be very happy to keep company with me. Sure that we would not part, I thought I would give her another lesson or two. I told her I had no intention of reforming, and made a great show of independence. She was sad, I gathered, and then without warning she died. And the game I had been playing came to seem rather inappropriate.

'She was a woman of such accomplishments that I could leave everything to her. I continue to regret what I had done. I could discuss trivial things with her and important things. For her skills

in dyeing she might have been compared to Princess Tatsuta and
the comparison would not have seemed ridiculous, and in sewing
she could have held her own with Princess Tanabata.'*

The young man sighed and sighed again.

Tō no Chūjō nodded. 'Leaving her accomplishments as a seam-
stress aside, I should imagine you were looking for someone as
faithful as Princess Tanabata. And if she could embroider like Princess Tatsuta, well, it does not seem likely that you will come on
her equal again. When the colors of a robe do not match the seasons, the flowers of spring and the autumn tints, when they are
somehow vague and muddy, then the whole effort is as futile as
the dew. So it is with women. It is not easy in this world to find a
perfect wife. We are all pursuing the ideal and failing to find it.'

The guards officer talked on. 'There was another one. I was
seeing her at about the same time. She was more amiable than the
one I have just described to you. Everything about her told of
refinement. Her poems, her handwriting when she dashed off a
letter, the koto she plucked a note on – everything seemed right.
She was clever with her hands and clever with words. And her
looks were adequate. The jealous woman's house had come to
seem the place I could really call mine, and I went in secret to the
other woman from time to time and became very fond of her. The
jealous one died, I wondered what to do next. I was sad, of course,
but a man cannot go on being sad forever. I visited the other more
often. But there was something a little too aggressive, a little too
sensuous about her. As I came to know her well and to think her a
not very dependable sort, I called less often. And I learned that I
was not her only secret visitor.

'One bright moonlit autumn night I chanced to leave court
with a friend. He got in with me as I started for my father's. He
was much concerned, he said, about a house where he was sure
someone would be waiting. It happened to be on my way.

'Through gaps in a neglected wall I could see the moon shining
on a pond. It seemed a pity not to linger a moment at a spot where
the moon seemed so much at home, and so I climbed out after
my friend. It would appear that this was not his first visit. He

*Goddesses, patronesses of autumn and therefore of dyeing and of weaving and sew-
ing. Tanabata and her lover the Herdsman (the stars Altair and Vega) met annually
on the seventh of the Seventh Month; hence Tō no Chūjō's next remark.

proceeded briskly to the veranda and took a seat near the gate and looked up at the moon for a time. The chrysanthemums were at their best, very slightly touched by the frost, and the red leaves were beautiful in the autumn wind. He took out a flute and played a tune on it, and sang "The Well of Asuka"* and several other songs. Blending nicely with the flute came the mellow tones of a Japanese koto.† It had been tuned in advance, apparently, and was waiting. The *ritsu* scale‡ had a pleasant modern sound to it, right for a soft, womanly touch from behind blinds, and right for the clear moonlight too. I can assure you that the effect was not at all unpleasant.

Delighted, my friend went up to the blinds.

' "I see that no one has yet broken a path through your fallen leaves," he said, somewhat sarcastically. He broke off a chrysanthemum and pushed it under the blinds.

' "Uncommonly fine this house, for moon, for koto.
     Does it bring to itself indifferent callers as well?

' "Excuse me for asking. You must not be parsimonious with your music. You have a by no means indifferent listener."

'He was very playful indeed. The woman's voice, when she offered a verse of her own, was suggestive and equally playful.

' "No match the leaves for the angry winter winds.
     Am I to detain the flute that joins those winds?"

'Naturally unaware of resentment so near at hand, she changed to a Chinese koto in an elegant *banjiki*.** Though I had to admit that she had talent, I was very annoyed. It is amusing enough, if you let things go no further, to exchange jokes from time to time with fickle and frivolous ladies; but as a place to take seriously, even for an occasional visit, matters here seemed to have gone too far. I made the events of that evening my excuse for leaving her.

---

*A Saibara (a sort of folk song taken up by the Heian nobility):

> It is good to rest beside the well of Asuka.
> Deep the shade, cool the water, sweet the grasses.

†*Wagon*, a six-stringed koto apparently native to Japan.

‡A pentatonic scale, resembling the Western minor without its half steps.

**Banshiki* or *banjiki* is based on B. The koto is the thirteen-stringed *sō*.

'I see, as I look back on the two affairs, that young though I was the second of the two women did not seem the kind to put my trust in. I have no doubt that the wariness will grow as the years go by. The dear, uncertain ones – the dew that will fall when the *hagi* branch is bent, the speck of frost that will melt when it is lifted from the bamboo leaf – no doubt they can be interesting for a time. You have seven years to go before you are my age,' he said to Genji. 'Just wait and you will understand. Perhaps you can take the advice of a person of no importance, and avoid the uncertain ones. They stumble sooner or later, and do a man's name no good when they do.'

Tō no Chūjō nodded, as always. Genji, though he only smiled, seemed to agree.

'Neither of the tales you have given us has been a very happy one,' he said.

'Let me tell you a story about a foolish woman I once knew,' said Tō no Chūjō. 'I was seeing her in secret, and I did not think that the affair was likely to last very long. But she was very beautiful, and as time passed I came to think that I must go on seeing her, if only infrequently. I sensed that she had come to depend on me. I expected signs of jealousy. There were none. She did not seem to feel the resentment a man expects from a woman he visits so seldom. She waited quietly, morning and night. My affection grew, and I let it be known that she did indeed have a man she could depend on. There was something very appealing about her (she was an orphan), letting me know that I was all she had.

'She seemed content. Untroubled, I stayed away for rather a long time. Then – I heard of it only later – my wife found a roundabout way to be objectionable. I did not know that I had become a cause of pain. I had not forgotten, but I let a long time pass without writing. The woman was desperately lonely and worried for the child she had borne. One day she sent me a letter attached to a wild carnation.' His voice trembled.

'And what did it say?' Genji urged him on.

'Nothing very remarkable. I do remember her poem, though:

' "The fence of the mountain rustic may fall to the ground.
    Rest gently, O dew, upon the wild carnation."

'I went to see her again. The talk was open and easy, as always, but she seemed pensive as she looked out at the dewy garden from

the neglected house. She seemed to be weeping, joining her
laments to the songs of the autumn insects. It could have been a
scene from an old romance. I whispered a verse:

'   "No bloom in this wild array would I wish to slight.
        But dearest of all to me is the wild carnation."

'Her carnation had been the child. I made it clear that my own
was the lady herself, the wild carnation no dust falls upon.*
'She answered:

'   "Dew wets the sleeve that brushes the wild carnation.
        The tempest rages. Now comes autumn too."

'She spoke quietly all the same, and she did not seem really
angry. She did shed a tear from time to time, but she seemed
ashamed of herself, and anxious to avoid difficult moments. I went
away feeling much relieved. It was clear that she did not want to
show any sign of anger at my neglect. And so once more I stayed
away for rather a long time.

'And when I looked in on her again she had disappeared.

'If she is still living, it must be in very unhappy circumstances.
She need not have suffered so if she had asserted herself a little
more in the days when we were together. She need not have put
up with my absences, and I would have seen to her needs over the
years. The child was a very pretty little girl. I was fond of her, and
I have not been able to find any trace of her.

'She must be listed among your reticent ones, I suppose? She
let me have no hint of jealousy. Unaware of what was going on, I
had no intention of giving her up. But the result was hopeless
yearning, quite as if I had given her up. I am beginning to forget;
and how is it with her? She must remember me sometimes, I
should think, with regret, because she must remember too that it
was not I who abandoned her. She was, I fear, not the sort of
woman one finds it possible to keep for very long.

*Oshikōchi Mitsune, Kokinshū 167:

            Let no dust fall upon the wild carnation,
            Upon the couch where lie my love and I.

    For the pink, or wild carnation, she has used the word nadeshiko, which com-
monly refers to a child. He has shifted to the synonymous tokonatsu, the first two
syllables of which mean 'bed.'

'Your jealous woman must be interesting enough to remember, but she must have been a bit wearying. And the other one, all her skill on the koto cannot have been much compensation for the undependability. And the one I have described to you – her very lack of jealousy might have brought a suspicion that there was another man in her life. Well, such is the way with the world – you cannot give your unqualified approval to any of them. Where are you to go for the woman who has no defects and who combines the virtues of all three? You might choose Our Lady of Felicity* – and find yourself married to unspeakable holiness.'

The others laughed.

Tō no Chūjō turned to the young man from the ministry of rites. 'You must have interesting stories too.'

'Oh, please. How could the lowest of the low hope to hold your attention?'

'You must not keep us waiting.'

'Let me think a minute.' He seemed to be sorting out memories. 'When I was still a student I knew a remarkably wise woman. She was the sort worth consulting about public affairs, and she had a good mind too for the little tangles that come into your private life. Her erudition would have put any ordinary sage to shame. In a word, I was awed into silence.

'I was studying under a learned scholar. I had heard that he had many daughters, and on some occasion or other I had made the acquaintance of this one. The father learned of the affair. Taking out wedding cups, he made reference, among other things, to a Chinese poem about the merits of an impoverished wife.† Although not exactly enamored of the woman, I had developed a certain fondness for her, and felt somewhat deferential toward the father. She was most attentive to my needs. I learned many estimable things from her, to add to my store of erudition and help me with my work. Her letters were lucidity itself, in the purest Chinese. None of this Japanese nonsense for her. I found it hard to think of giving her up, and under her tutelage I managed to turn out a few things in passable Chinese myself. And yet – though I would not wish to seem wanting in gratitude, it is undeniable that

*Kichijōten or Śrīmahādevī.
†Po Chü-i, Collected Works, II, 'On Marriage,' the first of 'Ten Poems Composed at Ch'ang-an.'

a man of no learning is somewhat daunted at the thought of being forever his wife's inferior. So it is in any case with an ignorant one like me; and what possible use could you gentlemen have for so formidable a wife? A stupid, senseless affair, a man tells himself, and yet he is dragged on against his will, as if there might have been a bond in some other life.'

'She seems a most unusual woman.' Genji and Tō no Chūjō were eager to hear more.

Quite aware that the great gentlemen were amusing themselves at his expense, he smiled somewhat impishly. 'One day when I had not seen her for rather a long time I had some reason or other for calling. She was not in the room where we had been in the habit of meeting. She insisted on talking to me through a very obtrusive screen. I thought she might be sulking, and it all seemed very silly. And then again – if she was going to be so petty, I might have my excuse for leaving her. But no. She was not a person to let her jealousy show. She knew too much of the world. Her explanation of what was happening poured forth at great length, all of it very well reasoned.

' "I have been indisposed with a malady known as coryza. Discommoded to an uncommon degree, I have been imbibing of a steeped potion made from bulbaceous herbs. Because of the noisome odor, I will not find it possible to admit of greater propinquity. If you have certain random matters for my attention, perhaps you can deposit the relevant materials where you are."

' "Is that so?" I said. I could think of nothing else to say.

'I started to leave. Perhaps feeling a little lonely, she called after me, somewhat shrilly. "When I have disencumbered myself of this aroma, we can meet once more."

'It seemed cruel to rush off, but the time was not right for a quiet visit. And it was as she said: her odor was rather high. Again I started out, pausing long enough to compose a verse:

' "The spider must have told you I would come.
        Then why am I asked to keep company with garlic?"*

'I did not take time to accuse her of deliberately putting me off.
'She was quicker than I. She chased after me with an answer.

---

*There was a belief, apparently imported very early from China, that a busy spider foretokened a visit from a lover.

‘ "Were we two who kept company every night,
    What would be wrong with garlic in the daytime?"*

‘You must admit she was quick with her answers.’ He had quietly finished his story.

The two gentlemen, Genji and his friend, would have none of it. ‘A complete fabrication, from start to finish. Where could you find such a woman? Better to have a quiet evening with a witch.’ They thought it an outrageous story, and asked if he could come up with nothing more acceptable.

‘Surely you would not wish for a more unusual sort of story?’

The guards officer took up again. ‘In women as in men, there is no one worse than the one who tries to display her scanty knowledge in full. It is among the least endearing of accomplishments for a woman to have delved into the Three Histories and the Five Classics; and who, on the other hand, can go through life without absorbing something of public affairs and private? A reasonably alert woman does not need to be a scholar to see and hear a great many things. The very worst are the ones who scribble off Chinese characters at such a rate that they fill a good half of letters where they are most out of place, letters to other women. "What a bore," you say. "If only she had mastered a few of the feminine things." She cannot of course intend it to be so, but the words read aloud seem muscular and unyielding, and in the end hopelessly mannered. I fear that even our highest of the high are too often guilty of the fault.

‘Then there is the one who fancies herself a poetess. She immerses herself in the anthologies, and brings antique references into her very first line, interesting enough in themselves but inappropriate. A man has had enough with that first line, but he is called heartless if he does not answer, and cannot claim the honors if he does not answer in a similar vein. On the Day of the Iris he is frantic to get off to court and has no eye for irises, and there she is with subtle references to iris roots. On the Day of the Chrysanthemum,† his mind has no room for anything but the Chinese poem

---

*The word for ‘daytime’ is homophonous with a word for numbers of strongly scented roots..

†The Day of the Iris fell on the fifth of the Fifth Month, and the Day of the Chrysanthemum on the ninth of the Ninth Month. The plant here called iris is more properly a calamus or sweet flag.

he must come up with in the course of the day, and there she is with something about the dew upon the chrysanthemum. A poem that might have been amusing and even moving on a less frantic day has been badly timed and must therefore be rejected. A woman who dashes off a poem at an unpoetic moment cannot be called a woman of taste.

'For someone who is not alive to the particular quality of each moment and each occasion, it is safer not to make a great show of taste and elegance; and from someone who is alive to it all, a man wants restraint. She should feign a certain ignorance, she should keep back a little of what she is prepared to say.'

Through all the talk Genji's thoughts were on a single lady. His heart was filled with her. She answered every requirement, he thought. She had none of the defects, was guilty of none of the excesses, that had emerged from the discussion.

The talk went on and came to no conclusion, and as the rainy night gave way to dawn the stories became more and more improbable.

It appeared that the weather would be fine. Fearing that his father-in-law might resent his secluding himself in the place, Genji set off for Sanjō. The mansion itself, his wife – every detail was admirable and in the best of taste. Nowhere did he find a trace of disorder. Here was a lady whom his friends must count among the truly dependable ones, the indispensable ones. And yet – she was too finished in her perfection, she was so cool and self-possessed that she made him uncomfortable. He turned to playful conversation with Chūnagon and Nakatsukasa and other pretty young women among her attendants. Because it was very warm, he loosened his dress, and they thought him even handsomer.

The minister came to pay his respects. Seeing Genji thus in dishabille, he made his greetings from behind a conveniently placed curtain. Though somewhat annoyed at having to receive such a distinguished visitor on such a warm day, Genji made it clear to the women that they were not to smile at his discomfort. He was a very calm, self-possessed young gentleman.

As evening approached, the women reminded him that his route from the palace had transgressed upon the domain of the Lord of the Center.* He must not spend the night here.

*A god who changed his abode periodically and did not permit trespassers.

'To be sure. But my own house lies in the same direction. And I am very tired.' He lay down as if he meant in spite of everything to stay the night.

'It simply will not do, my lord.'

'The governor of Kii here,' said one of Genji's men, pointing to another. 'He has dammed the Inner River* and brought it into his garden, and the waters are very cool, very pleasant.'

'An excellent idea. I really am very tired, and perhaps we can send ahead to see whether we might drive into the garden.'

There were no doubt all sorts of secret places to which he could have gone to avoid the taboo. He had come to Sanjō, and after a considerable absence. The minister might suspect that he had purposely chosen a night on which he must leave early.

The governor of Kii was cordial enough with his invitation, but when he withdrew he mentioned certain misgivings to Genji's men. Ritual purification, he said, had required all the women to be away from his father's house, and unfortunately they were all crowded into his own, a cramped enough place at best. He feared that Genji would be inconvenienced.

'Nothing of the sort,' said Genji, who had overheard. 'It is good to have people around. There is nothing worse than a night away from home with no ladies about. Just let me have a little corner behind their curtains.'

'If that is what you want,' said his men, 'then the governor's place should be perfect.'

And so they sent runners ahead. Genji set off immediately, though in secret, thinking that no great ceremony was called for. He did not tell the minister where he was going, and took only his nearest retainers. The governor grumbled that they were in rather too much of a hurry. No one listened.

The east rooms of the main hall had been cleaned and made presentable. The waters were as they had been described, a most pleasing arrangement. A fence of wattles, of a deliberately rustic appearance, enclosed the garden, and much care had gone into the plantings. The wind was cool. Insects were humming, one scarcely knew where, fireflies drew innumerable lines of light, and all in all the time and the place could not have been more to his liking. His men were already tippling, out where they could admire a brook

---

*Marking the eastern limits of the city.

flowing under a gallery. The governor seemed to have 'hurried off for viands.'* Gazing calmly about him, Genji concluded that the house would be of the young guardsman's favored in-between category. Having heard that his host's stepmother, who would be in residence, was a high-spirited lady, he listened for signs of her presence. There were signs of someone's presence immediately to the west. He heard a swishing of silk and young voices that were not at all displeasing. Young ladies seemed to be giggling self-consciously and trying to contain themselves. The shutters were raised, it seemed, but upon a word from the governor they were lowered. There was a faint light over the sliding doors. Genji went for a look, but could find no opening large enough to see through. Listening for a time, he concluded that the women had gathered in the main room, next to his.

The whispered discussion seemed to be about Genji himself.

'He is dreadfully serious, they say, and has made a fine match for himself. And still so young. Don't you imagine he might be a little lonely? But they say he finds time for a quiet little adventure now and then.'

Genji was startled. There was but one lady on his mind, day after day. So this was what the gossips were saying; and what if, in it all, there was evidence that rumors of his real love had spread abroad? But the talk seemed harmless enough, and after a time he wearied of it. Someone misquoted a poem he had sent to his cousin Asagao, attached to a morning glory.† Their standards seemed not of the most rigorous. A misquoted poem for every occasion. He feared he might be disappointed when he saw the woman.

The governor had more lights set out at the eaves, and turned up those in the room. He had refreshments brought.

---

*'The Jeweled Flask' (*Tamadare*), a 'vulgar song' (*fūzokuuta*):

> The little jeweled flask is here.
> But where is our host, what of our host?
> He has hurried off for viands,
> Off to the beach for viands,
> To Koyurugi for seaweed.

Koyurugi, in the province of Sagami, is introduced to suggest the abundance of the viands which hang shaking (*yurugi*) from the host's shoulders.

†The word *asagao* seems to have referred to several morning flowers, and only in more recent centuries specifically to the morning glory.

'And are the curtains all hung?'* asked Genji. 'You hardly qualify as a host if they are not.'

'And what will you feast upon?' rejoined the governor, somewhat stiffly. 'Nothing so very elaborate, I fear.'

Genji found a cool place out near the veranda and lay down. His men were quiet. Several young boys were present, all very sprucely dressed, sons of the host and of his father, the governor of Iyo.† There was one particularly attractive lad of perhaps twelve or thirteen. Asking who were the sons of whom, Genji learned that the boy was the younger brother of the host's stepmother, son of a guards officer no longer living. His father had had great hopes for the boy and had died while he was still very young. He had come to this house upon his sister's marriage to the governor of Iyo. He seemed to have some aptitude for the classics, said the host, and was of a quiet, pleasant disposition; but he was young and without backing, and his prospects at court were not good.

'A pity. The sister, then, is your stepmother?'

'Yes.'

'A very young stepmother. My father had thought of inviting her to court. He was asking just the other day what might have happened to her. Life,' he added with a solemnity rather beyond his years, 'is uncertain.'

'It happened almost by accident. Yes, you are right: it is a very uncertain world, and it always has been, particularly for women. They are like bits of driftwood.'

'Your father is no doubt very alert to her needs. Perhaps, indeed, one has trouble knowing who is the master?'

'He quite worships her. The rest of us are not entirely happy with the arrangements he has made.'

'But you cannot expect him to let you young gallants have

---

*A Saibara, 'My House' (*Waihen*):

> The curtains all are hung.
> Come and be my bridegroom.
> And what will you feast upon?
> Abalone, *sazae*,
> And sea urchins too.

The *sazae* is a mollusk, *Turbo cornutus*. The song is somewhat ribald.

†He is sometimes called the governor and sometimes the vice-governor.

everything. He has a name in that regard himself, you know. And where might the lady be?'

'They have all been told to spend the night in the porter's lodge, but they don't seem in a hurry to go.'

The wine was having its effect, and his men were falling asleep on the veranda.

Genji lay wide awake, not pleased at the prospect of sleeping alone. He sensed that there was someone in the room to the north. It would be the lady of whom they had spoken. Holding his breath, he went to the door and listened.

'Where are you?' The pleasantly husky voice was that of the boy who had caught his eye.

'Over here.' It would be the sister. The two voices, very sleepy, resembled each other. 'And where is our guest? I had thought he might be somewhere near, but he seems to have gone away.'

'He's in the east room.' The boy's voice was low. 'I saw him. He is every bit as handsome as everyone says.'

'If it were daylight I might have a look at him myself.' The sister yawned, and seemed to draw the bedclothes over her face.

Genji was a little annoyed. She might have questioned her brother more energetically.

'I'll sleep out toward the veranda. But we should have more light.' The boy turned up the lamp. The lady apparently lay at a diagonal remove from Genji. 'And where is Chūjō? I don't like being left alone.'

'She went to have a bath. She said she'd be right back.' He spoke from out near the veranda.

All was quiet again. Genji slipped the latch open and tried the doors. They had not been bolted. A curtain had been set up just inside, and in the dim light he could make out Chinese chests and other furniture scattered in some disorder. He made his way through to her side. She lay by herself, a slight little figure. Though vaguely annoyed at being disturbed, she evidently took him for the woman Chūjō until he pulled back the covers.

'I heard you summoning a captain,' he said, 'and I thought my prayers over the months had been answered.*

She gave a little gasp. It was muffled by the bedclothes and no one else heard.

*Chūjō means 'captain,' the rank that Genji holds.

'You are perfectly correct if you think me unable to control myself. But I wish you to know that I have been thinking of you for a very long time. And the fact that I have finally found my opportunity and am taking advantage of it should show that my feelings are by no means shallow.'

His manner was so gently persuasive that devils and demons could not have gainsaid him. The lady would have liked to announce to the world that a strange man had invaded her boudoir.

'I think you have mistaken me for someone else,' she said, outraged, though the remark was under her breath.

The little figure, pathetically fragile and as if on the point of expiring from the shock, seemed to him very beautiful.

'I am driven by thoughts so powerful that a mistake is completely out of the question. It is cruel of you to pretend otherwise. I promise you that I will do nothing unseemly. I must ask you to listen to a little of what is on my mind.'

She was so small that he lifted her easily. As he passed through the doors to his own room, he came upon the Chūjō who had been summoned earlier. He called out in surprise. Surprised in turn, Chūjō peered into the darkness. The perfume that came from his robes like a cloud of smoke told her who he was. She stood in confusion, unable to speak. Had he been a more ordinary intruder she might have ripped her mistress away by main force. But she would not have wished to raise an alarm all through the house.

She followed after, but Genji was quite unmoved by her pleas.

'Come for her in the morning,' he said, sliding the doors closed.

The lady was bathed in perspiration and quite beside herself at the thought of what Chūjō, and the others too, would be thinking. Genji had to feel sorry for her. Yet the sweet words poured forth, the whole gamut of pretty devices for making a woman surrender.

She was not to be placated. 'Can it be true? Can I be asked to believe that you are not making fun of me? Women of low estate should have husbands of low estate.'

He was sorry for her and somewhat ashamed of himself, but his answer was careful and sober. 'You take me for one of the young profligates you see around? I must protest. I am very young and know nothing of the estates which concern you so. You have heard of me, surely, and you must know that I do not go in for adventures. I must ask what unhappy entanglement imposes this upon me. You are making a fool of me, and nothing should surprise me, not even the tumultuous emotions that do in fact surprise me.'

But now his very splendor made her resist. He might think her obstinate and insensitive, but her unfriendliness must make him dismiss her from further consideration. Naturally soft and pliant, she was suddenly firm. It was as with the young bamboo: she bent but was not to be broken. She was weeping. He had his hands full but would not for the world have missed the experience.

'Why must you so dislike me?' he asked with a sigh, unable to stop the weeping. 'Don't you know that the unexpected encounters are the ones we were fated for? Really, my dear, you do seem to know altogether too little of the world.'

'If I had met you before I came to this,' she replied, and he had to admit the truth of it, 'then I might have consoled myself with the thought – it might have been no more than self-deception, of course – that you would someday come to think fondly of me. But this is hopeless, worse than I can tell you. Well, it has happened. Say no to those who ask if you have seen me.'*

One may imagine that he found many kind promises with which to comfort her.

The first cock was crowing and Genji's men were awake.

'Did you sleep well? I certainly did.'

'Let's get the carriage ready.'

Some of the women were heard asking whether people who were avoiding taboos were expected to leave again in the middle of the night.

Genji was very unhappy. He feared he could not find an excuse for another meeting. He did not see how he could visit her, and he did not see how they could write. Chūjō came out, also very unhappy. He let the lady go and then took her back again.

'How shall I write to you? Your feelings and my own – they are not shallow, and we may expect deep memories. Has anything ever been so strange?' He was in tears, which made him yet hand-

*Anonymous, Kokinshū 811:

> As one small mark of your love, if such there be,
> Say no to those who ask if you have seen me.

somer. The cocks were now crowing insistently. He was feeling somewhat harried as he composed his farewell verse:

> 'Why must they startle with their dawn alarums
> When hours are yet required to thaw the ice?'

The lady was ashamed of herself that she had caught the eye of a man so far above her. His kind words had little effect. She was thinking of her husband, whom for the most part she considered a clown and a dolt. She trembled to think that a dream might have told him of the night's happenings.

This was the verse with which she replied:

> 'Day has broken without an end to my tears.
> To my cries of sorrow are added the calls of the cocks.'

It was lighter by the moment. He saw her to her door, for the house was coming to life. A barrier had fallen between them. In casual court dress, he leaned for a time against the south railing and looked out at the garden. Shutters were being raised along the west side of the house. Women seemed to be looking out at him, beyond a low screen at the veranda. He no doubt brought shivers of delight. The moon still bright in the dawn sky added to the beauty of the morning. The sky, without heart itself, can at these times be friendly or sad, as the beholder sees it. Genji was in anguish. He knew that there would be no way even to exchange notes. He cast many a glance backward as he left.

At Sanjō once more, he was unable to sleep. If the thought that they would not meet again so pained him, what must it do to the lady? She was no beauty, but she had seemed pretty and cultivated. Of the middling rank, he said to himself. The guards officer who had seen them all knew what he was talking about.

Spending most of his time now at Sanjō, he thought sadly of the unapproachable lady. At last he summoned her stepson, the governor of Kii.

'The boy I saw the other night, your foster uncle. He seemed a promising lad. I think I might have a place for him. I might even introduce him to my father.'

'Your gracious words quite overpower me. Perhaps I should take the matter up with his sister.'

Genji's heart leaped at the mention of the lady. 'Does she have children?'

'No. She and my father have been married for two years now, but I gather that she is not happy. Her father meant to send her to court.'

'How sad for her. Rumor has it that she is a beauty. Might rumor be correct?'

'Mistaken, I fear. But of course stepsons do not see a great deal of stepmothers.'

Several days later he brought the boy to Genji. Examined in detail the boy was not perfect, but he had considerable charm and grace. Genji addressed him in a most friendly manner, which both confused and pleased him. Questioning him about his sister, Genji did not learn a great deal. The answers were ready enough while they were on safe ground, but the boy's self-possession was a little disconcerting. Genji hinted rather broadly at what had taken place. The boy was startled. He guessed the truth but was not old enough to pursue the matter.

Genji gave him a letter for his sister. Tears came to her eyes. How much had her brother been told? she wondered, spreading the letter to hide her flushed cheeks.

It was very long, and concluded with a poem:

'I yearn to dream again the dream of that night.
    The nights go by in lonely wakefulness.

'There are no nights of sleep.'*

The hand was splendid, but she could only weep at the yet stranger turn her life had taken.

The next day Genji sent for the boy.

Where was her answer? the boy asked his sister.

'Tell him you found no one to give his letter to.'

'Oh, please.' The boy smiled knowingly. 'How can I tell him that? I have learned enough to be sure there is no mistake.'

She was horrified. It was clear that Genji had told everything.

'I don't know why you must always be so clever. Perhaps it would be better if you didn't go at all.'

'But he sent for me.' And the boy departed.

The governor of Kii was beginning to take an interest in his

*Minamoto Shitagō, *Shūishū* 735:

> Where shall I find comfort in my longing?
> There are no dreams, for there are no nights of sleep.

pretty young stepmother, and paying insistent court. His attention turned to the brother, who became his frequent companion.

'I waited for you all day yesterday,' said Genji. 'Clearly I am not as much on your mind as you are on mine.'

The boy flushed.

'Where is her answer?' And when the boy told him: 'A fine messenger. I had hoped for something better.'

There were other letters.

'But didn't you know?' he said to the boy. 'I knew her before that old man she married. She thought me feeble and useless, it seems, and looked for a stouter support. Well, she may spurn me, but you needn't. You will be my son. The gentleman you are looking to for help won't be with us long.'

The boy seemed to be thinking what a nuisance his sister's husband was. Genji was amused.

He treated the boy like a son, making him a constant companion, giving him clothes from his own wardrobe, taking him to court. He continued to write to the lady. She feared that with so inexperienced a messenger the secret might leak out and add suspicions of promiscuity to her other worries. These were very grand messages, but something more in keeping with her station seemed called for. Her answers were stiff and formal when she answered at all. She could not forget his extraordinary good looks and elegance, so dimly seen that night. But she belonged to another, and nothing was to be gained by trying to interest him. His longing was undiminished. He could not forget how touchingly fragile and confused she had seemed. With so many people around, another invasion of her boudoir was not likely to go unnoticed, and the results would be sad.

One evening after he had been at court for some days he found an excuse: his mansion again lay in a forbidden direction. Pretending to set off for Sanjō, he went instead to the house of the governor of Kii. The governor was delighted, thinking that those well-designed brooks and lakes had made an impression. Genji had consulted with the boy, always in earnest attendance. The lady had been informed of the visit. She must admit that they seemed powerful, the urges that forced him to such machinations. But if she were to receive him and display herself openly, what could she expect save the anguish of the other night, a repetition of that nightmare? No, the shame would be too much.

The brother having gone off upon a summons from Genji, she called several of her women. 'I think it might be in bad taste to stay too near. I am not feeling at all well, and perhaps a massage might help, somewhere far enough away that we won't disturb him.'

The woman Chūjō had rooms on a secluded gallery. They would be her refuge.

It was as she had feared. Genji sent his men to bed early and dispatched his messenger. The boy could not find her. He looked everywhere and finally, at the end of his wits, came upon her in the gallery.

He was almost in tears. 'But he will think me completely useless.'

'And what do you propose to be doing? You are a child, and it is quite improper for you to be carrying such messages. Tell him I have not been feeling well and have kept some of my women to massage me. You should not be here. They will think it very odd.'

She spoke with great firmness, but her thoughts were far from as firm. How happy she might have been if she had not made this unfortunate marriage, and were still in the house filled with memories of her dead parents. Then she could have awaited his visits, however infrequent. And the coldness she must force herself to display – he must think her quite unaware of her place in the world. She had done what she thought best, and she was in anguish. Well, it all was hard fact, about which she had no choice. She must continue to play the cold and insensitive woman.

Genji lay wondering what blandishments the boy might be using. He was not sanguine, for the boy was very young. Presently he came back to report his mission a failure. What an uncommonly strong woman! Genji feared he must seem a bit feckless beside her. He heaved a deep sigh. This evidence of despondency had the boy on the point of tears.

Genji sent the lady a poem:

'I wander lost in the Sonohara moorlands,
  For I did not know the deceiving ways of the broom tree.*

*Sakanoe Korenori, Shinkokinshū 997:

O broom tree of Fuseya in Sonohara,
  You seem to be there, and yet I cannot find you.

The 'broom tree' of Sonohara in the province of Shinano disappeared or changed shape when one approached. Fuseya means 'hut'; hence the hut of the lady's answering poem.

'How am I to describe my sorrow?'

She too lay sleepless. This was her answer:

> 'Here and not here, I lie in my shabby hut.
> Would that I might like the broom tree vanish away.'

The boy traveled back and forth with messages, a wish to be helpful driving sleep from his thoughts. His sister beseeched him to consider what the others might think.

Genji's men were snoring away. He lay alone with his discontent. This unique stubbornness was no broom tree. It refused to vanish away. The stubbornness was what interested him. But he had had enough. Let her do as she wished. And yet – not even this simple decision was easy.

'At least take me to her.'

'She is shut up in a very dirty room and there are all sorts of women with her. I do not think it would be wise.' The boy would have liked to be more helpful.

'Well, you at least must not abandon me.' Genji pulled the boy down beside him.

The boy was delighted, such were Genji's youthful charms. Genji, for his part, or so one is informed, found the boy more attractive than his chilly sister.

CHAPTER 3

The Shell of the Locust

Genji lay sleepless.

'I am not used to such treatment. Tonight I have for the first time seen how a woman can treat a man. The shock and the shame are such that I do not know how I can go on living.'

The boy was in tears, which made him even more charming. The slight form, the not too long hair – was it Genji's imagination that he was much like his sister? The resemblance was very affecting, even if imagined. It would be undignified to make an issue of the matter and seek the woman out, and so Genji passed the night in puzzled resentment. The boy found him less friendly than usual.

Genji left before daylight. Very sad, thought the boy, lonely without him.

The lady too passed a difficult night. There was no further word from Genji. It seemed that he had had enough of her. She would not be happy if he had in fact given her up, but with half her mind she dreaded another visit. It would be as well to have an end of the affair. Yet she went on grieving.

For Genji there was gnawing dissatisfaction. He could not forget her, and he feared he was making a fool of himself.

'I am in a sad state,' he said to the boy. 'I try to forget her, and I cannot. Do you suppose you might contrive another meeting?'

It would be difficult, but the boy was delighted even at this sort of attention. With childish eagerness he watched for an opportunity. Presently the governor of Kii had to go off to his province. The lady had nothing to do through the long twilight hours. Under cover of darkness, the boy took Genji to the governor's mansion in his own carriage. Genji had certain misgivings. His guide was after all a mere child. But this was no time for hesitation. Dressed inconspicuously, he urged the boy on, lest they arrive after the gates were barred. The carriage was brought in through a back gate and Genji dismounted.

So young a boy attracted little attention and indeed little deference from the guards. He left Genji at an east door to the main hall. He pounded on the south shutters and went inside.

'Shut it, shut it!' shrieked the women. 'The whole world can see us.'

'But why do you have them closed on such a warm evening?'

'The lady from the west wing has been here since noon. They have been at Go.'

Hoping to see them at the Go board, Genji slipped from his hiding place and made his way through the door and the blinds. The shutter through which the boy had gone was still raised.* Genji could see through to the west. One panel of a screen just inside had been folded back, and the curtains, which should have shielded off the space beyond, had been thrown over their frames, perhaps because of the heat. The view was unobstructed.

There was a lamp near the women. The one in silhouette with her back against a pillar – would she be the one on whom his heart was set? He looked first at her. She seemed to have on a purple singlet with a woven pattern, and over it a cloak of which the color and material were not easy to determine. She was a small, rather ordinary lady with delicate features. She evidently wanted to conceal her face even from the girl opposite, and she kept her thin little hands tucked in her sleeves. Her opponent was facing east, and Genji had a full view of her face. Over a singlet of white gossamer she had thrown a purplish cloak, and both garments were somewhat carelessly open all the way to the band of the red trousers. She was very handsome, tall and plump and of a fair complexion, and the lines of her head and forehead were strong and pleasing. It was a sunny face, with a beguiling cheerfulness about the eyes and mouth. Though not particularly long, the hair was rich and thick, and very beautiful where it fell about the shoulders. He could detect no marked flaws, and saw why her father, the governor of Iyo, so cherished her. It might help, to be sure, if she were just a little quieter. Yet she did not seem to be merely silly. She brimmed with good spirits as she placed a stone upon a dead spot to signal the end of the game.

'Just a minute, if you please,' said the other very calmly. 'It is not quite over. You will see that we have a *kō* to get out of the way first.'†

---

*The description of the rooms hereabouts is confusing. The 'shutters' (*kōshi*) seem to be between the veranda and the rooms, an unusual arrangement.

†*Kō* (Sanskrit *kalpa*) is a Buddhist term for an enormous passage of time, the next thing to eternity. In Go it refers to a situation in which the two players could take

'I've lost, I've lost. Let's just see what I have in the corners.'
She counted up on her fingers. 'Ten, twenty, thirty, forty.' She
would have had no trouble, he thought, taking the full count of
the baths of Iyo* – though her manner might have been just a
touch inelegant.

The other woman, a model of demureness, kept her face hidden. Gazing at her, Genji was able to make out the details of the
profile. The eyelids seemed a trifle swollen, the lines of the nose
were somewhat erratic, and there was a weariness, a want of luster,
about the face. It was, one had to admit, a little on the plain side.
Yet she clearly paid attention to her appearance, and there were
details likely to draw the eye to a subtler sensibility than was evident in her lively companion. The latter, very engaging indeed,
laughed ever more happily. There was no denying the bright
gaiety, and in her way she was interesting enough. A shallow,
superficial thing, no doubt, but to his less than pure heart she
seemed a prize not to be flung away. All the ladies he knew were
so prim and proper. This was the first time he had seen one so
completely at her ease. He felt a little guilty, but not so guilty that
he would have turned away had he not heard the boy coming
back. He slipped outside.

Apologetic that his master should still be at the beginning, the
boy said that the unexpected guest had interfered with his plans.

'You mean to send me off frustrated once more? It is really too
much.'

'No, sir. But I must ask you to wait until the other lady has
gone. I'll arrange everything then, I promise you.'

Things seemed to be arranging themselves. The boy was very
young, but he was calmly self-possessed and had a good eye for the
significant things.

The game of Go was apparently over. There was a stir inside,
and a sound as of withdrawing.

'Where will that boy have gone?' Now there was a banging of
shutters. 'Let's get the place closed up.'

'No one seems to be stirring,' said Genji after a time. 'Go and
do your best.'

and retake the same stones for all eternity without affecting the larger disposition of
forces. To cut the exchange short, the player whose stone is first taken must play
elsewhere on the board before returning to the scene.

*Her father's province was noted for its hot springs.

The boy knew well enough that it was not his sister's nature to encourage frivolity. He must admit Genji when there was almost no one with her.

'Is the guest still here?' asked Genji. 'I would like a glimpse of her.'

'Quite impossible. There are curtains inside the shutters.'

Genji was amused, but thought it would be bad manners to let the boy know that he had already seen the lady. 'How slowly time does go by.'

This time the boy knocked on the corner door and was admitted.

'I'll just make myself comfortable here,' he said, spreading bed-clothes where one or two of the sliding doors had been left open. 'Come in, breezes.'

Numbers of older women seemed to be sleeping out near the veranda. The girl who had opened the door seemed to have joined them. The boy feigned sleep for a time. Then, spreading a screen to block the light, he motioned Genji inside.

Genji was suddenly shy, fearing he would be defeated once more. He followed the boy all the same. Raising a curtain, he slipped into the main room. It was very quiet, and his robes rustled alarmingly.

With one part of her mind the woman was pleased that he had not given up. But the nightmare of the earlier evening had not left her. Brooding days, sleepless nights – it was summer, and yet it was 'budless spring.'*

Her companion at Go, meanwhile, was as cheerful as could be. 'I shall stay with you tonight,' she announced. It was not likely that she would have trouble sleeping.

The lady herself sensed that something was amiss. Detecting an unusual perfume, she raised her head. It was dark where the curtain had been thrown over the frame, but she could see a form creeping toward her. In a panic, she got up. Pulling a singlet of raw silk over her shoulders, she slipped from the room.

*Fujiwara Koretada, in his collected poems:

> The nights are wakeful, sighs fill all the days.
> Never before have I known so budless a spring.

The poem is acrostic, *konome*, 'buds,' suggesting also sleep.

Genji was delighted to see that there was only one lady asleep behind the curtains. There seemed to be two people asleep out toward the veranda. As he pulled aside the bedclothes it seemed to him that the lady was somewhat larger than he would have expected. He became aware of one odd detail after another in the sleeping figure, and guessed what had happened. How very stupid! And how ridiculous he would seem if the sleeper were to awaken and see that she was the victim of a silly mistake. It would be equally silly to pursue the lady he had come for, now that she had made her feelings so clear. A new thought came to him: might this be the girl who had so interested him in the lamplight? If so, what had he to lose? It will be observed that a certain fickleness was at work.

The girl was now awake, and very surprised. Genji felt a little sorry for her. But though inexperienced in the ways of love, she was bright and modern, and she had not entirely lost her composure. He was at first reluctant to identify himself. She would presently guess, however, and what did it matter if she did? As for the unfriendly one who had fled him and who was so concerned about appearances – he did have to think of her reputation, and so he said to the girl that he had taken advantage of directional taboos to visit her. A more experienced lady would have had no trouble guessing the truth, but this one did not sense that his explanation was a little forced. He was not displeased with her, nor was he strongly drawn to her. His heart was resentfully on the other. No doubt she would be off in some hidden chamber gloating over her victory. She had shown a most extraordinary firmness of purpose. In a curious way, her hostility made her memorable. The girl beside him had a certain young charm of her own, and presently he was deep in vows of love.

'The ancients used to say that a secret love runs deeper than an open one.' He was most persuasive. 'Think well of me. I must worry about appearances, and it is not as if I could go where my desires take me. And you: there are people who would not at all approve. That is sad. But you must not forget me.'

'I'm afraid.' Clearly she was afraid. 'I won't be able to write to you.'

'You are right that we would not want people to know. But there is the little man I brought with me tonight. We can exchange notes through him. Meanwhile you must behave as if nothing had happened.' He took as a keepsake a summer robe the other lady seemed to have thrown off.

The boy was sleeping nearby. The adventure was on his mind, however, and Genji had no trouble arousing him. As he opened the door an elderly serving woman called out in surprise.

'Who's there?'

'Just me,' replied the boy in some confusion.

'Wherever are you going at this time of the night?' The woman came out, wishing to be helpful.

'Nowhere,' said the boy gruffly. 'Nowhere at all.'

He pushed Genji through the door. Dawn was approaching. The woman caught sight of another figure in the moonlight.

'And who is with you? Oh, Mimbu, of course. Only Mimbu reaches such splendid heights.' Mimbu was a lady who was the victim of much humor because of her unusual stature. So he was out walking with Mimbu, muttered the old woman. 'One of these days you'll be as tall as Mimbu yourself.' Chattering away, she followed after them. Genji was horrified, but could not very well shove her inside. He pulled back into the darkness of a gallery.

Still she followed. 'You've been with our lady, have you? I've been having a bad time with my stomach these last few days and I've kept to my room. But she called me last night and said she wanted more people around. I'm still having a terrible time. Terrible,' she muttered again, getting no answer. 'Well, goodbye, then.'

She moved on, and Genji made his escape. He saw more than ever how dangerous these adventures can be.

The boy went with him to Nijō. Genji recounted the happenings of the night. The boy had not done very well, he said, shrugging his shoulders in annoyance at the thought of the woman's coldness. The boy could find no answer.

'I am rejected, and there is nothing to be done for me. But why could she not have sent a pleasant answer? I'm no match for that husband of hers. That's where the trouble lies.' But when he went to bed he had her cloak beneath his own. He kept the boy beside him, audience for his laments.

'It's not that you aren't a nice enough boy, and it's not that I'm not fond of you. But because of your family I must have doubts about the durability of our relationship.'

A remark which plunged the boy into the darkest melancholy.

Genji was still unable to sleep. He said that he required an inkstone. On a fold of paper he jotted down a verse as if for practice:

'Beneath a tree, a locust's empty shell.
Sadly I muse upon the shell of a lady.'

He wondered what the other one, the stepdaughter, would be thinking of him; but though he felt rather sorry for her and though he turned the matter over in his mind, he sent no message. The lady's fragrance lingered in the robe he had taken. He kept it with him, gazing fondly at it.

The boy, when he went to his sister's house, was crushed by the scolding he received. 'This is the sort of thing a person cannot be expected to put up with. I may try to explain what has happened, but can you imagine that people will not come to their own conclusions? Does it not occur to you that even your good master might wish to see an end to this childishness?'

Badgered from the left and badgered from the right, the poor boy did not know where to turn. He took out Genji's letter. In spite of herself his sister opened and read it. That reference to the shell of the locust: he had taken her robe, then. How very embarrassing. A sodden rag, like the one discarded by the fisherman of Ise.*

The other lady, her stepdaughter, returned in some disorder to her own west wing. She had her sad thoughts all to herself, for no one knew what had happened. She watched the boy's comings and goings, thinking that there might be some word; but in the end there was none. She did not have the imagination to guess that she had been a victim of mistaken identity. She was a lighthearted and inattentive creature, but now she was lost in sad thoughts.

The lady in the main hall kept herself under tight control. She could see that his feelings were not to be described as shallow, and she longed for what would not return, her maiden days. Besides his poem she jotted down a poem by Lady Ise:

The dew upon the fragile locust wing
Is lost among the leaves. Lost are my tears.†

*Fujiwara Koretada, *Gosenshū* 719:

The robe I left: as sodden with the brine
As the fisherman's of Yamaga in Ise?

†From her collected poems. It is very rare for a poem not by Murasaki Shikibu herself to be given in full.

CHAPTER 4

Evening Faces

On his way from court to pay one of his calls at Rokujō, Genji
stopped to inquire after his old nurse, Koremitsu's mother, at her
house in Gojō. Gravely ill, she had become a nun. The carriage
entrance was closed. He sent for Koremitsu and while he was waiting
looked up and down the dirty, cluttered street. Beside the nurse's
house was a new fence of plaited cypress. The four or five narrow
shutters above had been raised, and new blinds, white and clean,
hung in the apertures. He caught outlines of pretty foreheads beyond.
He would have judged, as they moved about, that they belonged to
rather tall women. What sort of women might they be? His carriage
was simple and unadorned and he had no outrunners. Quite certain
that he would not be recognized, he leaned out for a closer look. The
hanging gate, of something like trelliswork, was propped on a pole,
and he could see that the house was tiny and flimsy. He felt a little
sorry for the occupants of such a place – and then asked himself who
in this world had more than a temporary shelter.* A hut, a jeweled
pavilion, they were the same. A pleasantly green vine was climbing a
board wall. The white flowers, he thought, had a rather self-satisfied
look about them.

' "I needs must ask the lady far off yonder," '† he said, as if to
himself.

An attendant came up, bowing deeply. 'The white flowers far
off yonder are known as "evening faces," '‡ he said. 'A very
human sort of name – and what a shabby place they have picked to
bloom in.'

*Anonymous, *Kokinshū* 987:

> Where in all this world shall I call home?
> A temporary shelter is my home.

†Anonymous, *Kokinshū* 1007:

> I needs must ask the lady far off yonder
> What flower it is off there that blooms so white.

‡*Yūgao, Lagenaria siceraria*, a kind of gourd.

It was as the man said. The neighborhood was a poor one, chiefly of small houses. Some were leaning precariously, and there were 'evening faces' at the sagging eaves.

'A hapless sort of flower. Pick one off for me, would you?'

The man went inside the raised gate and broke off a flower. A pretty little girl in long, unlined yellow trousers of raw silk came out through a sliding door that seemed too good for the surroundings. Beckoning to the man, she handed him a heavily scented white fan.

'Put it on this. It isn't much of a fan, but then it isn't much of a flower either.'

Koremitsu, coming out of the gate, passed it on to Genji.

'They lost the key, and I have had to keep you waiting. You aren't likely to be recognized in such a neighborhood, but it's not a very nice neighborhood to keep you waiting in.'

Genji's carriage was pulled in and he dismounted. Besides Koremitsu, a son and a daughter, the former an eminent cleric, and the daughter's husband, the governor of Mikawa, were in attendance upon the old woman. They thanked him profusely for his visit.

The old woman got up to receive him. 'I did not at all mind leaving the world, except for the thought that I would no longer be able to see you as I am seeing you now. My vows seem to have given me a new lease on life, and this visit makes me certain that I shall receive the radiance of Lord Amitābha with a serene and tranquil heart.' And she collapsed in tears.

Genji was near tears himself. 'It has worried me enormously that you should be taking so long to recover, and I was very sad to learn that you have withdrawn from the world. You must live a long life and see the career I make for myself. I am sure that if you do you will be reborn upon the highest summits of the Pure Land. I am told that it is important to rid oneself of the smallest regret for this world.'

Fond of the child she has reared, a nurse tends to look upon him as a paragon even if he is a half-wit. How much prouder was the old woman, who somehow gained stature, who thought of herself as eminent in her own right for having been permitted to serve him. The tears flowed on.

Her children were ashamed for her. They exchanged glances. It would not do to have these contortions taken as signs of a lingering affection for the world.

Genji was deeply touched. 'The people who were fond of me left me when I was very young. Others have come along, it is true, to take care of me, but you are the only one I am really attached to. In recent years there have been restrictions upon my movements, and I have not been able to look in upon you morning and evening as I would have wished, or indeed to have a good visit with you. Yet I become very depressed when the days go by and I do not see you. "Would that there were on this earth no final partings." '* He spoke with great solemnity, and the scent of his sleeve, as he brushed away a tear, quite flooded the room.

Yes, thought the children, who had been silently reproaching their mother for her want of control, the fates had been kind to her. They too were now in tears.

Genji left orders that prayers and services be resumed. As he went out he asked for a torch, and in its light examined the fan on which the 'evening face' had rested. It was permeated with a lady's perfume, elegant and alluring. On it was a poem in a disguised cursive hand that suggested breeding and taste. He was interested.

> 'I think I need not ask whose face it is,
>   So bright, this evening face, in the shining dew.'

'Who is living in the house to the west?' he asked Koremitsu. 'Have you perhaps had occasion to inquire?'

At it again, thought Koremitsu. He spoke somewhat tartly. 'I must confess that these last few days I have been too busy with my mother to think about her neighbors.'

'You are annoyed with me. But this fan has the appearance of something it might be interesting to look into. Make inquiries, if you will, please, of someone who knows the neighborhood.'

Koremitsu went in to ask his mother's steward, and emerged with the information that the house belonged to a certain honorary vice-governor.† 'The husband is away in the country, and the

---

*Ariwara Narihira, *Kokinshū* 901 and *Tales of Ise* 84:

> Would that my mother might live a thousand years.
> Would there were on this earth no final partings.

†*Yōmei no suke*. Once thought among the undecipherables in the *Genji*, it is now thought to refer to someone who has the title but not the perquisites of vice-governor.

wife seems to be a young woman of taste. Her sisters are out in service here and there. They often come visiting. I suspect the fellow is too poorly placed to know the details.'

His poetess would be one of the sisters, thought Genji. A rather practiced and forward young person, and, were he to meet her, perhaps vulgar as well – but the easy familiarity of the poem had not been at all unpleasant, not something to be pushed away in disdain. His amative propensities, it will be seen, were having their way once more.

Carefully disguising his hand, he jotted down a reply on a piece of notepaper and sent it in by the attendant who had earlier been of service.

> 'Come a bit nearer, please. Then might you know
>   Whose was the evening face so dim in the twilight.'

Thinking it a familiar profile, the lady had not lost the opportunity to surprise him with a letter, and when time passed and there was no answer she was left feeling somewhat embarrassed and disconsolate. Now came a poem by special messenger. Her women became quite giddy as they turned their minds to the problem of replying. Rather bored with it all, the messenger returned empty-handed. Genji made a quiet departure, lighted by very few torches. The shutters next door had been lowered. There was something sad about the light, dimmer than fireflies, that came through the cracks.

At the Rokujō house, the trees and the plantings had a quite dignity. The lady herself was strangely cold and withdrawn. Thoughts of the 'evening faces' quite left him. He overslept, and the sun was rising when he took his leave. He presented such a fine figure in the morning light that the women of the place understood well enough why he should be so universally admired. On his way he again passed those shutters, as he had no doubt done many times before. Because of that small incident he now looked at the house carefully, wondering who might be within.

'My mother is not doing at all well, and I have been with her,' said Koremitsu some days later. And, coming nearer: 'Because you seemed so interested, I called someone who knows about the house next door and had him questioned. His story was not completely clear. He said that in the Fifth Month or so someone came very quietly to live in the house, but that not even the domestics had been told who she might be. I have looked through the fence from time to time myself and had glimpses through blinds of several young women. Something about their dress suggests that they are in the service of someone of higher rank.* Yesterday, when the evening light was coming directly through, I saw the lady herself writing a letter. She is very beautiful. She seemed lost in thought, and the women around her were weeping.'

Genji had suspected something of the sort. He must find out more.

Koremitsu's view was that while Genji was undeniably someone the whole world took seriously, his youth and the fact that women found him attractive meant that to refrain from these little affairs would be less than human. It was not realistic to hold that certain people were beyond temptation.

'Looking for a chance to do a bit of exploring, I found a small pretext for writing to her. She answered immediately, in a good, practiced hand. Some of her women do not seem at all beneath contempt.'

'Explore very thoroughly, if you will. I will not be satisfied until you do.'

The house was what the guardsman would have described as the lowest of the low, but Genji was interested. What hidden charms might he not come upon!

He had thought the coldness of the governor's wife, the lady of 'the locust shell,' quite unique. Yet if she had proved amenable to his persuasions the affair would no doubt have been dropped as a sad mistake after that one encounter. As matters were, the resentment and the distinct possibility of final defeat never left his mind. The discussion that rainy night would seem to have made him curious about the several ranks. There had been a time when such a lady would not have been worth his notice. Yes, it had been broadening, that discussion! He had not found the willing and available one, the governor of Iyo's daughter, entirely uninteresting, but the thought that the stepmother must have been listening coolly to the interview was excruciating. He must await some sign of her real intentions.

*They wear *shibira*, apparently a sort of apron or jacket indicating a small degree of formality.

The governor of Iyo returned to the city. He came immediately to Genji's mansion. Somewhat sunburned, his travel robes rumpled from the sea voyage, he was a rather heavy and displeasing sort of person. He was of good lineage, however, and, though aging, he still had good manners. As they spoke of his province, Genji wanted to ask the full count of those hot springs,* but he was somewhat confused to find memories chasing one another through his head. How foolish that he should be so uncomfortable before the honest old man! He remembered the guardsman's warning that such affairs are unwise,† and he felt sorry for the governor. Though he resented the wife's coldness, he could see that from the husband's point of view it was admirable. He was upset to learn that the governor meant to find a suitable husband for his daughter and take his wife to the provinces. He consulted the lady's young brother upon the possibility of another meeting. It would have been difficult even with the lady's cooperation, however, and she was of the view that to receive a gentleman so far above her would be extremely unwise.

Yet she did not want him to forget her entirely. Her answers to his notes on this and that occasion were pleasant enough, and contained casual little touches that made him pause in admiration. He resented her chilliness, but she interested him. As for the stepdaughter, he was certain that she would receive him hospitably enough however formidable a husband she might acquire. Reports upon her arrangements disturbed him not at all.

Autumn came. He was kept busy and unhappy by affairs of his own making, and he visited Sanjō infrequently. There was resentment.

As for the affair at Rokujō, he had overcome the lady's resistance and had had his way, and, alas, he had cooled toward her. People thought it worthy of comment that his passions should seem so much more governable than before he had made her his. She was subject to fits of despondency, more intense on sleepless nights when she awaited him in vain. She feared that if rumors were to spread the gossips would make much of the difference in their ages.

On a morning of heavy mists, insistently roused by the lady,

See note, page 56.

†This is curious, since the guardsman's warning was not against women of the lower classes but against fickle women. There have been theories that some part of his discourse has been lost.

who was determined that he be on his way, Genji emerged yawn-
ing and sighing and looking very sleepy. Chūjō, one of her
women, raised a shutter and pulled a curtain aside as if urging her
lady to come forward and see him off. The lady lifted her head
from her pillow. He was an incomparably handsome figure as he
paused to admire the profusion of flowers below the veranda.
Chūjō followed him down a gallery. In an aster robe that matched
the season pleasantly and a gossamer train worn with clean elegance, she was a pretty, graceful woman. Glancing back, he asked
her to sit with him for a time at the corner railing. The ceremonious precision of the seated figure and the hair flowing over her
robes were very fine.

He took her hand.

'Though loath to be taxed with seeking fresher blooms,
   I feel impelled to pluck this morning glory.

'Why should it be?'

She answered with practiced alacrity, making it seem that she
was speaking not for herself but for her lady:

'In haste to plunge into the morning mists,
   You seem to have no heart for the blossoms here.'

A pretty little page boy, especially decked out for the occasion,
it would seem, walked out among the flowers. His trousers wet
with dew, he broke off a morning glory for Genji. He made a
picture that called out to be painted.

Even persons to whom Genji was nothing were drawn to him.
No doubt even rough mountain men wanted to pause for a time
in the shade of the flowering tree,* and those who had basked even
briefly in his radiance had thoughts, each in accordance with his
rank, of a daughter who might be taken into his service, a not
ill-formed sister who might perform some humble service for him.
One need not be surprised, then, that people with a measure of
sensibility among those who had on some occasion received a little
poem from him or been treated to some little kindness found him
much on their minds. No doubt it distressed them not to be always
with him.

*In the preface to the *Kokinshū* one of the 'poetic immortals' is likened to a woodcutter resting under a cherry in full bloom.

I had forgotten: Koremitsu gave a good account of the fence peeping to which he had been assigned. 'I am unable to identify her. She seems determined to hide herself from the world. In their boredom her women and girls go out to the long gallery at the street, the one with the shutters, and watch for carriages. Sometimes the lady who seems to be their mistress comes quietly out to join them. I've not had a good look at her, but she seems very pretty indeed. One day a carriage with outrunners went by. The little girls shouted to a person named Ukon that she must come in a hurry. The captain* was going by, they said. An older woman came out and motioned to them to be quiet. How did they know? she asked, coming out toward the gallery. The passage from the main house is by a sort of makeshift bridge. She was hurrying and her skirt caught on something, and she stumbled and almost fell off. 'The sort of thing the god of Katsuragi might do,'† she said, and seems to have lost interest in sightseeing. They told her that the man in the carriage was wearing casual court dress and that he had a retinue. They mentioned several names, and all of them were undeniably Lord Tō no Chūjō's guards and pages.'

'I wish you had made positive identification.' Might she be the lady of whom Tō no Chūjō had spoken so regretfully that rainy night?

Koremitsu went on, smiling at this open curiosity. 'I have as a matter of fact made the proper overtures and learned all about the place. I come and go as if I did not know that they are not all equals. They think they are hiding the truth and try to insist that there is no one there but themselves when one of the little girls makes a slip.'

'Let me have a peep for myself when I call on your mother.'

Even if she was only in temporary lodgings, the woman would seem to be of the lower class for which his friend had indicated such contempt that rainy evening. Yet something might come of it all. Determined not to go against his master's wishes in the smallest detail and himself driven by very considerable excitement, Koremitsu searched diligently for a chance to let Genji into the house. But the details are tiresome, and I shall not go into them.

*Tō no Chūjō.
†Tradition held that the god of Katsuragi, south of Nara, was very ugly, and built a bridge which he used only at night.

Genji did not know who the lady was and he did not want her to know who he was. In very shabby disguise, he set out to visit her on foot. He must be taking her very seriously, thought Koremitsu, who offered his horse and himself went on foot.

'Though I do not think that our gentleman will look very good with tramps for servants.'

To make quite certain that the expedition remained secret, Genji took with him only the man who had been his intermediary in the matter of the 'evening faces' and a page whom no one was likely to recognize. Lest he be found out even so, he did not stop to see his nurse.

The lady had his messengers followed to see how he made his way home and tried by every means to learn where he lived; but her efforts came to nothing. For all his secretiveness, Genji had grown fond of her and felt that he must go on seeing her. They were of such different ranks, he tried to tell himself, and it was altogether too frivolous. Yet his visits were frequent. In affairs of this sort, which can muddle the senses of the most serious and honest of men, he had always kept himself under tight control and avoided any occasion for censure. Now, to a most astonishing degree, he would be asking himself as he returned in the morning from a visit how he could wait through the day for the next. And then he would rebuke himself. It was madness, it was not an affair he should let disturb him. She was of an extraordinarily gentle and quiet nature. Though there was a certain vagueness about her, and indeed an almost childlike quality, it was clear that she knew something about men. She did not appear to be of very good family. What was there about her, he asked himself over and over again, that so drew him to her?

He took great pains to hide his rank and always wore travel dress, and he did not allow her to see his face. He came late at night when everyone was asleep. She was frightened, as if he were an apparition from an old story. She did not need to see his face to know that he was a fine gentleman. But who might he be? Her suspicions turned to Koremitsu. It was that young gallant, surely, who had brought the strange visitor. But Koremitsu pursued his own little affairs unremittingly, careful to feign indifference to and ignorance of this other affair. What could it all mean? The lady was lost in unfamiliar speculations.

Genji had his own worries. If, having lowered his guard with an appearance of complete unreserve, she were to slip away and hide, where would he seek her? This seemed to be but a temporary residence, and he could not be sure when she would choose to change it, and for what other. He hoped that he might reconcile himself to what must be and forget the affair as just another dalliance; but he was not confident.

On days when, to avoid attracting notice, he refrained from visiting her, his fretfulness came near anguish. Suppose he were to move her in secret to Nijō. If troublesome rumors were to arise, well, he could say that they had been fated from the start. He wondered what bond in a former life might have produced an infatuation such as he had not known before.

'Let's have a good talk,' he said to her, 'where we can be quite at our ease.'

'It's all so strange. What you say is reasonable enough, but what you do is so strange. And rather frightening.'

Yes, she might well be frightened. Something childlike in her fright brought a smile to his lips. 'Which of us is the mischievous fox spirit? I wonder. Just be quiet and give yourself up to its persuasions.'

Won over by his gentle warmth, she was indeed inclined to let him have his way. She seemed such a pliant little creature, likely to submit absolutely to the most outrageous demands. He thought again of Tō no Chūjō's 'wild carnation,' of the equable nature his friend had described that rainy night. Fearing that it would be useless, he did not try very hard to question her. She did not seem likely to indulge in dramatics and suddenly run off and hide herself, and so the fault must have been Tō no Chūjō's. Genji himself would not be guilty of such negligence – though it did occur to him that a bit of infidelity* might make her more interesting.

The bright full moon of the Eighth Month came flooding in through chinks in the roof. It was not the sort of dwelling he was used to, and he was fascinated. Toward dawn he was awakened by plebeian voices in the shabby houses down the street.

'Freezing, that's what it is, freezing. There's not much business this year, and when you can't get out into the country you feel like giving up. Do you hear me, neighbor?'

He could make out every word. It embarrassed the woman

---

*On whose part, his or the girl's? The passage is obscure.

that, so near at hand, there should be this clamor of preparation as people set forth on their sad little enterprises. Had she been one of the stylish ladies of the world, she would have wanted to shrivel up and disappear. She was a placid sort, however, and she seemed to take nothing, painful or embarrassing or unpleasant, too seriously. Her manner elegant and yet girlish, she did not seem to know what the rather awful clamor up and down the street might mean. He much preferred this easy going bewilderment to a show of consternation, a face scarlet with embarrassment. As if at his very pillow, there came the booming of a foot pestle,* more fearsome than the stamping of the thunder god, genuinely earsplitting. He did not know what device the sound came from, but he did know that it was enough to awaken the dead. From this direction and that there came the faint thump of fulling hammers against coarse cloth; and mingled with it – these were sounds to call forth the deepest emotions – were the calls of geese flying overhead. He slid a door open and they looked out. They had been lying near the veranda. There were tasteful clumps of black bamboo just outside and the dew shone as in more familiar places. Autumn insects sang busily, as if only inches from an ear used to wall crickets at considerable distances. It was all very clamorous, and also rather wonderful. Countless details could be overlooked in the singleness of his affection for the girl. She was pretty and fragile in a soft, modest cloak of lavender and a lined white robe. She had no single feature that struck him as especially beautiful, and yet, slender and fragile, she seemed so delicately beautiful that he was almost afraid to hear her voice. He might have wished her to be a little more assertive, but he wanted only to be near her, and yet nearer.

'Let's go off somewhere and enjoy the rest of the night. This is too much.'

'But how is that possible?' She spoke very quietly. 'You keep taking me by surprise.'

There was a newly confiding response to his offer of his services as guardian in this world and the next. She was a strange little thing. He found it hard to believe that she had had much experience of men. He no longer cared what people might think. He asked Ukon to summon his man, who got the carriage ready. The

---

Karausu. The mortar was sunk in the floor and the pestle raised by foot and allowed to fall.

women of the house, though uneasy, sensed the depth of his feelings and were inclined to put their trust in him.

Dawn approached. No cocks were crowing. There was only the voice of an old man making deep obeisance to a Buddha, in preparation, it would seem, for a pilgrimage to Mitake.* He seemed to be prostrating himself repeatedly and with much difficulty. All very sad. In a life itself like the morning dew, what could he desire so earnestly?

'Praise to the Messiah to come,' intoned the voice.

'Listen,' said Genji. 'He is thinking of another world.

> 'This pious one shall lead us on our way
> As we plight our troth for all the lives to come.'

The vow exchanged by the Chinese emperor and Yang Kuei-fei seemed to bode ill, and so he preferred to invoke Lord Maitreya, the Buddha of the Future; but such promises are rash.

> 'So heavy the burden I bring with me from the past,
> I doubt that I should make these vows for the future.'

It was a reply that suggested doubts about his 'lives to come.'

The moon was low over the western hills. She was reluctant to go with him. As he sought to persuade her, the moon suddenly disappeared behind clouds in a lovely dawn sky. Always in a hurry to be off before daylight exposed him, he lifted her easily into his carriage and took her to a nearby villa. Ukon was with them. Waiting for the caretaker to be summoned, Genji looked up at the rotting gate and the ferns that trailed thickly down over it. The groves beyond were still dark, and the mist and the dews were heavy. Genji's sleeve was soaking, for he had raised the blinds of the carriage.

'This is a novel adventure, and I must say that it seems like a lot of trouble.

> 'And did it confuse them too, the men of old,
> This road through the dawn, for me so new and strange?

'How does it seem to you?'

She turned shyly away.

*In the Yoshino Mountains south of Nara.

'And is the moon, unsure of the hills it approaches,
Foredoomed to lose its way in the empty skies?

'I am afraid.'

She did seem frightened, and bewildered. She was so used to all those swarms of people, he thought with a smile.

The carriage was brought in and its traces propped against the veranda while a room was made ready in the west wing. Much excited, Ukon was thinking about earlier adventures. The furious energy with which the caretaker saw to preparations made her suspect who Genji was. It was almost daylight when they alighted from the carriage. The room was clean and pleasant, for all the haste with which it had been readied.

'There are unfortunately no women here to wait upon His Lordship.' The man, who addressed him through Ukon, was a lesser steward who had served in the Sanjō mansion of Genji's father-in-law. 'Shall I send for someone?'

'The last thing I want. I came here because I wanted to be in complete solitude, away from all possible visitors. You are not to tell a soul.'

The man put together a hurried breakfast, but he was, as he had said, without serving women to help him.

Genji told the girl that he meant to show her a love as dependable as 'the patient river of the loons.'* He could do little else in these strange lodgings.

The sun was high when he arose. He opened the shutters. All through the badly neglected grounds not a person was to be seen. The groves were rank and overgrown. The flowers and grasses in the foreground were a drab monotone, an autumn moor. The pond was choked with weeds, and all in all it was a forbidding place. An outbuilding seemed to be fitted with rooms for the caretaker, but it was some distance away.

'It is a forbidding place,'† said Genji. 'But I am sure that whatever devils emerge will pass me by.'

---

*Umanofuhito Kunihito, *Manyōshū* 4458:

> The patient river of the patient loons
> Will not run dry. My love will still outlast it.

†The repetition in almost identical language suggests a miscopying.

He was still in disguise. She thought it unkind of him to be so secretive, and he had to agree that their relationship had gone beyond such furtiveness.

> 'Because of one chance meeting by the wayside
> The flower now opens in the evening dew.

'And how does it look to you?'

> 'The face seemed quite to shine in the evening dew,
> But I was dazzled by the evening light.'

Her eyes turned away. She spoke in a whisper.

To him it may have seemed an interesting poem.

As a matter of fact, she found him handsomer than her poem suggested, indeed frighteningly handsome, given the setting.

'I hid my name from you because I thought it altogether too unkind of you to be keeping your name from me. Do please tell me now. This silence makes me feel that something awful might be coming.'

'Call me the fisherman's daughter.'* Still hiding her name, she was like a little child.

'I see. I brought it all on myself? A case of *warekara*?'†

And so, sometimes affectionately, sometimes reproachfully, they talked the hours away.

Koremitsu had found them out and brought provisions. Feeling a little guilty about the way he had treated Ukon, he did not come near. He thought it amusing that Genji should thus be wandering the streets, and concluded that the girl must provide sufficient cause. And he could have had her himself, had he not been so generous.

Genji and the girl looked out at an evening sky of the utmost calm. Because she found the darkness in the recesses of the house frightening, he raised the blinds at the veranda and they lay side by

---

*Anonymous, *Shinkokinshū* 1701, and 'Courtesan's Song,' *Wakan Rōeishū* 722:

> A fisherman's daughter, I spend my life by the waves,
> The waves that tell us nothing. I have no home.

†Fujiwara Naoiko, *Kokinshū* 807:

> The grass the fishermen take, the *warekara*:
> 'I did it myself.' I shall weep but I shall not hate you.

side. As they gazed at each other in the gathering dusk, it all seemed very strange to her, unbelievably strange. Memories of past wrongs quite left her. She was more at ease with him now, and he thought her charming. Beside him all through the day, starting up in fright at each little noise, she seemed delightfully childlike. He lowered the shutters early and had lights brought.

'You seem comfortable enough with me, and yet you raise difficulties.'

At court everyone would be frantic. Where would the search be directed? He thought what a strange love it was, and he thought of the turmoil the Rokujō lady was certain to be in.* She had every right to be resentful, and yet her jealous ways were not pleasant. It was that sad lady to whom his thoughts first turned. Here was the girl beside him, so simple and undemanding; and the other was so impossibly forceful in her demands. How he wished he might in some measure have his freedom.

It was past midnight. He had been asleep for a time when an exceedingly beautiful woman appeared by his pillow.

'You do not even think of visiting me, when you are so much on my mind. Instead you go running off with someone who has nothing to recommend her, and raise a great stir over her. It is cruel, intolerable.' She seemed about to shake the girl from her sleep. He awoke, feeling as if he were in the power of some malign being. The light had gone out. In great alarm, he pulled his sword to his pillow and awakened Ukon. She too seemed frightened.

'Go out to the gallery and wake the guard. Have him bring a light.'

'It's much too dark.'

He forced a smile. 'You're behaving like a child.'

He clapped his hands and a hollow echo answered. No one seemed to hear. The girl was trembling violently. She was bathed in sweat and as if in a trance, quite bereft of her senses.

'She is such a timid little thing,' said Ukon, 'frightened when there is nothing at all to be frightened of. This must be dreadful for her.'

*We do not learn much about 'the Rokujō lady' until Chapter 9. There is a theory that 'Evening Faces' was written considerably later than the present succession of chapters has it.

Yes, poor thing, thought Genji. She did seem so fragile, and she had spent the whole day gazing up at the sky.

'I'll go get someone. What a frightful echo. You stay here with her.' He pulled Ukon to the girl's side.

The lights in the west gallery had gone out. There was a gentle wind. He had few people with him, and they were asleep. They were three in number: a young man who was one of his intimates and who was the son of the steward here, a court page, and the man who had been his intermediary in the matter of the 'evening faces.' He called out. Someone answered and came up to him.

'Bring a light. Wake the other, and shout and twang your bow-strings. What do you mean, going to sleep in a deserted house? I believe Lord Koremitsu was here.'

'He was. But he said he had no orders and would come again at dawn.'

An elite guardsman, the man was very adept at bow twanging. He went off with a shouting as of a fire watch. At court, thought Genji, the courtiers on night duty would have announced themselves, and the guard would be changing. It was not so very late.

He felt his way back inside. The girl was as before, and Ukon lay face down at her side.

'What is this? You're a fool to let yourself be so frightened. Are you worried about the fox spirits that come out and play tricks in deserted houses? But you needn't worry. They won't come near me.' He pulled her to her knees.

'I'm not feeling at all well. That's why I was lying down. My poor lady must be terrified.'

'She is indeed. And I can't think why.'

He reached for the girl. She was not breathing. He lifted her and she was limp in his arms. There was no sign of life. She had seemed as defenseless as a child, and no doubt some evil power had taken possession of her. He could think of nothing to do. A man came with a torch. Ukon was not prepared to move, and Genji himself pulled up curtain frames to hide the girl.

'Bring the light closer.'

It was most a unusual order. Not ordinarily permitted at Genji's side, the man hesitated to cross the threshold.

'Come, come, bring it here! There is a time and place for ceremony.'

In the torchlight he had a fleeting glimpse of a figure by the girl's pillow. It was the woman in his dream. It faded away like an apparition in an old romance. In all the fright and horror, his confused thoughts centered upon the girl. There was no room for thoughts of himself.

He knelt over her and called out to her, but she was cold and had stopped breathing. It was too horrible. He had no confidant to whom he could turn for advice. It was the clergy one thought of first on such occasions. He had been so brave and confident, but he was young, and this was too much for him. He clung to the lifeless body.

'Come back, my dear, my dear. Don't do this awful thing to me.' But she was cold and no longer seemed human.

The first paralyzing terror had left Ukon. Now she was writhing and wailing. Genji remembered a devil a certain minister had encountered in the Grand Hall.*

'She can't possibly be dead.' He found the strength to speak sharply. 'All this noise in the middle of the night – you must try to be a little quieter.' But it had been too sudden.

He turned again to the torchbearer. 'There is someone here who seems to have had a very strange seizure. Tell your friend to find out where Lord Koremitsu is spending the night and have him come immediately. If the holy man is still at his mother's house, give him word, very quietly, that he is to come too. His mother and the people with her are not to hear. She does not approve of this sort of adventure.'

He spoke calmly enough, but his mind was in a turmoil. Added to grief at the loss of the girl was horror, quite beyond describing, at this desolate place. It would be past midnight. The wind was higher and whistled more dolefully in the pines. There came a strange, hollow call of a bird. Might it be an owl? All was silence, terrifying solitude. He should not have chosen such a place – but it was too late now. Trembling violently, Ukon clung to him. He held her in his arms, wondering if she might be about to follow her lady. He was the only rational one present, and he could think of nothing to do. The flickering light wandered here and there. The upper parts of the screens behind them were in darkness, the

---

*The *Okagami* tells how Fujiwara Tadahira met a devil in the Shishinden. It withdrew when informed that he was on the emperor's business.

lower parts fitfully in the light. There was a persistent creaking, as of someone coming up behind them. If only Koremitsu would come. But Koremitsu was a nocturnal wanderer without a fixed abode, and the man had to search for him in numerous places. The wait for dawn was like the passage of a thousand nights. Finally he heard a distant crowing. What legacy from a former life could have brought him to this mortal peril? He was being punished for a guilty love, his fault and no one else's, and his story would be remembered in infamy through all the ages to come. There were no secrets, strive though one might to have them. Soon everyone would know, from his royal father down, and the lowest court pages would be talking; and he would gain immortality as the model of the complete fool.

Finally Lord Koremitsu came. He was the perfect servant who did not go against his master's wishes in anything at any time; and Genji was angry that on this night of all nights he should have been away, and slow in answering the summons. Calling him inside even so, he could not immediately find the strength to say what must be said. Ukon burst into tears, the full horror of it all coming back to her at the sight of Koremitsu. Genji too lost control of himself. The only sane and rational one present, he had held Ukon in his arms, but now he gave himself up to his grief.

'Something very strange has happened,' he said after a time. 'Strange – "unbelievable" would not be too strong a word. I wanted a priest – one does when these things happen – and asked your reverend brother to come.'

'He went back up the mountain yesterday. Yes, it is very strange indeed. Had there been anything wrong with her?'

'Nothing.'

He was so handsome in his grief that Koremitsu wanted to weep. An older man who has had everything happen to him and knows what to expect can be depended upon in a crisis; but they were both young, and neither had anything to suggest.

Koremitsu finally spoke. 'We must not let the caretaker know. He may be dependable enough himself, but he is sure to have relatives who will talk. We must get away from this place.'

'You aren't suggesting that we could find a place where we would be less likely to be seen?'

'No, I suppose not. And the women at her house will scream and wail when they hear about it, and they live in a crowded neighborhood, and all the mob around will hear, and that will be that. But mountain temples are used to this sort of thing. There would not be much danger of attracting attention.' He reflected on the problem for a time. 'There is a woman I used to know. She has gone into a nunnery up in the eastern hills. She is very old, my father's nurse, as a matter of fact. The district seems to be rather heavily populated, but the nunnery is off by itself.'

It was not yet full daylight. Koremitsu had the carriage brought up. Since Genji seemed incapable of the task, he wrapped the body in a covering and lifted it into the carriage. It was very tiny and very pretty, and not at all repellent. The wrapping was loose and the hair streamed forth, as if to darken the world before Genji's eyes.

He wanted to see the last rites through to the end, but Koremitsu would not hear of it. 'Take my horse and go back to Nijō, now while the streets are still quiet.'

He helped Ukon into the carriage and himself proceeded on foot, the skirts of his robe hitched up. It was a strange, bedraggled sort of funeral procession, he thought, but in the face of such anguish he was prepared to risk his life. Barely conscious, Genji made his way back to Nijō.

'Where have you been?' asked the women. 'You are not looking at all well.'

He did not answer. Alone in his room, he pressed a hand to his heart. Why had he not gone with the others? What would she think if she were to come back to life? She would think that he had abandoned her. Self-reproach filled his heart to breaking. He had a headache and feared he had a fever. Might he too be dying? The sun was high and still he did not emerge. Thinking it all very strange, the women pressed breakfast upon him. He could not eat. A messenger reported that the emperor had been troubled by his failure to appear the day before.

His brothers-in-law came calling.

'Come in, please, just for a moment.' He received only Tō no Chūjō and kept a blind between them. 'My old nurse fell seriously ill and took her vows in the Fifth Month or so. Perhaps because of them, she seemed to recover. But recently she had a relapse. Someone came to ask if I would not call on her at least once more. I thought I really must go and see an old and dear servant who was on her deathbed, and so I went. One of her servants was ailing,

and quite suddenly, before he had time to leave, he died. Out of
deference to me they waited until night to take the body away. All
this I learned later. It would be very improper of me to go to court
with all these festivities coming up,* I thought, and so I stayed
away. I have had a headache since early this morning – perhaps I
have caught cold. I must apologize.'

'I see. I shall so inform your father. He sent out a search party
during the concert last night, and really seemed very upset.' Tō no
Chūjō turned to go, and abruptly turned back. 'Come now. What
sort of brush did you really have? I don't believe a word of it.'

Genji was startled, but managed a show of nonchalance. 'You
needn't go into the details. Just say that I suffered an unexpected
defilement. Very unexpected, really.'

Despite his cool manner, he was not up to facing people. He
asked a younger brother-in-law to explain in detail his reasons for
not going to court. He got off a note to Sanjō with a similar explanation.

Koremitsu came in the evening. Having announced that he had
suffered a defilement, Genji had callers remain outside, and there
were few people in the house. He received Koremitsu immediately.

'Are you sure she is dead?' He pressed a sleeve to his eyes.

Koremitsu too was in tears. 'Yes, I fear she is most certainly
dead. I could not stay shut up in a temple indefinitely, and so I
have made arrangements with a venerable priest whom I happen
to know rather well. Tomorrow is a good day for funerals.'

'And the other woman?'

'She has seemed on the point of death herself. She does not
want to be left behind by her lady. I was afraid this morning that
she might throw herself over a cliff. She wanted to tell the people
at Gojō, but I persuaded her to let us have a little more time.'

'I am feeling rather awful myself and almost fear the worst.'

'Come, now. There is nothing to be done and no point in torturing yourself. You must tell yourself that what must be must be.
I shall let absolutely no one know, and I am personally taking care
of everything.'

'Yes, to be sure. Everything is fated. So I tell myself. But it is
terrible to think that I have sent a lady to her death. You are not to

*There were may Shinto rites during the Ninth Month.

tell your sister, and you must be very sure that your mother does not hear. I would not survive the scolding I would get from her.'

'And the priests too: I have told them a plausible story.' Koremitsu exuded confidence.

The women had caught a hint of what was going on and were more puzzled than ever. He had said that he had suffered a defilement, and he was staying away from court; but why these muffled lamentations?

Genji gave instructions for the funeral. 'You must make sure that nothing goes wrong.'

'Of course. No great ceremony seems called for.'

Koremitsu turned to leave.

'I know you won't approve,' said Genji, a fresh wave of grief sweeping over him, 'but I will regret it forever if I don't see her again. I'll go on horseback.'

'Very well, if you must.' In fact Koremitsu thought the proposal very ill advised. 'Go immediately and be back while it is still early.'

Genji set out in the travel robes he had kept ready for his recent amorous excursions. He was in the bleakest despair. He was on a strange mission and the terrors of the night before made him consider turning back. Grief urged him on. If he did not see her once more, when, in another world, might he hope to see her as she had been? He had with him only Koremitsu and the attendant of that first encounter. The road seemed a long one.

The moon came out, two nights past full. They reached the river. In the dim torchlight, the darkness off towards Mount Toribe was ominous and forbidding; but Genji was too dazed with grief to be frightened. And so they reached the temple.

It was a harsh, unfriendly region at best. The board hut and chapel where the nun pursued her austerities were lonely beyond description. The light at the altar came dimly through cracks. Inside the hut a woman was weeping. In the outer chamber two or three priests were conversing and invoking the holy name in low voices. Vespers seemed to have ended in several temples nearby. Everything was quiet. There were lights and there seemed to be clusters of people in the direction of Kiyomizu. The grand tones in which the worthy monk, the son of the nun, was reading a sutra brought on what Genji thought must be the full flood tide of his tears.

He went inside. The light was turned away from the corpse. Ukon lay behind a screen. It must be very terrible for her, thought Genji. The girl's face was unchanged and very pretty.

'Won't you let me hear your voice again?' He took her hand. 'What was it that made me give you all my love, for so short a time, and then made you leave me to this misery?' He was weeping uncontrollably.

The priests did not know who he was. They sensed something remarkable, however, and felt their eyes mist over.

'Come with me to Nijō,' he said to Ukon.

'We have been together since I was very young. I never left her side, not for a single moment. Where am I to go now? I will have to tell the others what has happened. As if this weren't enough, I will have to put up with their accusations.' She was sobbing. 'I want to go with her.'

'That is only natural. But it is the way of the world. Parting is always sad. Our lives must end, early or late. Try to put your trust in me.' He comforted her with the usual homilies, but presently his real feelings came out. 'Put your trust in me – when I fear I have not long to live myself.' He did not after all seem likely to be much help.

'It will soon be light,' said Koremitsu. 'We must be on our way.'

Looking back and looking back again, his heart near breaking, Genji went out. The way was heavy with dew and the morning mists were thick. He scarcely knew where he was. The girl was exactly as she had been that night. They had exchanged robes and she had on a red singlet of his. What might it have been in other lives that had brought them together? He managed only with great difficulty to stay in his saddle. Koremitsu was at the reins. As they came to the river Genji fell from his horse and was unable to remount.

'So I am to die by the wayside? I doubt that I can go on.'

Koremitsu was in a panic. He should not have permitted this expedition, however strong Genji's wishes. Dipping his hands in the river, he turned and made supplication to Kiyomizu. Genji somehow pulled himself together. Silently invoking the holy name, he was seen back to Nijō.

The women were much upset by these untimely wanderings. 'Very bad, very bad. He has been so restless lately. And why should he have gone out again when he was not feeling well?'

Now genuinely ill, he took to his bed. Two or three days passed and he was visibly thinner. The emperor heard of the illness and was much alarmed. Continuous prayers were ordered in this shrine and that temple. The varied rites, Shinto and Confucian and Buddhist, were beyond counting. Genji's good looks had been such as to arouse forebodings. All through the court it was feared that he would not live much longer. Despite his illness, he summoned Ukon to Nijō and assigned her rooms near his own. Koremitsu composed himself sufficiently to be of service to her, for he could see that she had no one else to turn to. Choosing times when he was feeling better, Genji would summon her for a talk, and she soon was accustomed to life at Nijō. Dressed in deep mourning, she was a somewhat stern and forbidding young woman, but not without her good points.

'It lasted such a very little while. I fear that I will be taken too. It must be dreadful for you, losing your only support. I had thought that as long as I lived I would see to all your needs, and it seems sad and ironical that I should be on the point of following her.' He spoke softly and there were tears in his eyes. For Ukon the old grief had been hard enough to bear, and now she feared that a new grief might be added to it.

All through the Nijō mansion there was a sense of helplessness. Emissaries from court were thicker than raindrops. Not wanting to worry his father, Genji fought to control himself. His father-in-law was extremely solicitous and came to Nijō every day. Perhaps because of all the prayers and rites the crisis passed – it had lasted some twenty days – and left no ill effects. Genji's full recovery coincided with the final cleansing of the defilement. With the unhappiness he had caused his father much on his mind, he set off for his apartments at court. For a time he felt out of things, as if he had come back to a strange new world.

By the end of the Ninth Month he was his old self once more. He had lost weight, but emaciation only made him handsomer. He spent a great deal of time gazing into space, and sometimes he would weep aloud. He must be in the clutches of some malign spirit, thought the women. It was all most peculiar.

He would summon Ukon on quiet evenings. 'I don't understand it at all. Why did she so insist on keeping her name from me? Even if she *was* a fisherman's daughter it was cruel of her to be so uncommunicative. It was as if she did not know how much I loved her.'

'There was no reason for keeping it secret. But why should she tell you about her insignificant self? Your attitude seemed so strange from the beginning. She used to say that she hardly knew whether she was waking or dreaming. Your refusal to identify yourself, you know, helped her guess who you were. It hurt her that you should belittle her by keeping your name from her.'

'An unfortunate contest of wills. I did not want anything to stand between us; but I must always be worrying about what people will say. I must refrain from things my father and all the rest of them might take me to task for. I am not permitted the smallest indiscretion. Everything is exaggerated so. The little incident of the "evening faces" affected me strangely and I went to very great trouble to see her. There must have been a bond between us. A love doomed from the start to be fleeting – why should it have taken such complete possession of me and made me find her so precious? You must tell me everything. What point is there in keeping secrets now? I mean to make offerings every week, and I want to know in whose name I am making them.'

'Yes, of course – why have secrets now? It is only that I do not want to slight what she made so much of. Her parents are dead. Her father was a guards captain. She was his special pet, but his career did not go well and his life came to an early and disappointing end. She somehow got to know Lord Tō no Chūjō – it was when he was still a lieutenant. He was very attentive for three years or so, and then about last autumn there was a rather awful threat from his father-in-law's house. She ran off and hid herself at her nurse's in the western part of the city. It was a wretched little hovel of a place. She wanted to go off into the hills, but the direction she had in mind has been taboo since New Year's. So she moved to the odd place where she was so upset to have you find her. She was more reserved and withdrawn than most people, and I fear that her unwillingness to show her emotions may have seemed cold.'

So it was true. Affection and pity welled up yet more strongly.

'He once told me of a lost child. Was there such a one?'

'Yes, a very pretty little girl, born two years ago last spring.'

'Where is she? Bring her to me without letting anyone know. It would be such a comfort. I should tell my friend Tō no Chūjō, I suppose, but why invite criticism? I doubt that anyone could reprove me for taking in the child. You must think up a way to get around the nurse.'

'It would make me very happy if you were to take the child. I would hate to have her left where she is. She is there because we had no competent nurses in the house where you found us.'

The evening sky was serenely beautiful. The flowers below the veranda were withered, the songs of the insects were dying too, and autumn tints were coming over the maples. Looking out upon the scene, which might have been a painting, Ukon thought what a lovely asylum she had found herself. She wanted to avert her eyes at the thought of the house of the 'evening faces.' A pigeon called, somewhat discordantly, from a bamboo thicket. Remembering how the same call had frightened the girl in that deserted villa, Genji could see the little figure as if an apparition were there before him.

'How old was she? She seemed so delicate, because she was not long for this world, I suppose.'

'Nineteen, perhaps? My mother, who was her nurse, died and left me behind. Her father took a fancy to me, and so we grew up together, and I never once left her side. I wonder how I can go on without her. I am almost sorry that we were so close.* She seemed so weak, but I can see now that she was a source of strength.'

'The weak ones do have a power over us. The clear, forceful ones I can do without. I am weak and indecisive by nature myself, and a woman who is quiet and withdrawn and follows the wishes of a man even to the point of letting herself be used has much the greater appeal. A man can shape and mold her as he wishes, and becomes fonder of her all the while.'

'She was exactly what you would have wished, sir.' Ukon was in tears. 'That thought makes the loss seem greater.'

The sky had clouded over and a chilly wind had come up. Gazing off into the distance, Genji said softly:

'One sees the clouds as smoke that rose from the pyre,
    And suddenly the evening sky seems nearer.'

Ukon was unable to answer. If only her lady were here! For Genji even the memory of those fulling blocks was sweet.

---

*This would seem to be a poetic allusion, but none has been satisfactorily identified.

'In the Eighth Month, the Ninth Month, the nights are long,'*
he whispered, and lay down.

The young page, brother of the lady of the locust shell, came to
Nijō from time to time, but Genji no longer sent messages for his
sister. She was sorry that he seemed angry with her and sorry to
hear of his illness. The prospect of accompanying her husband to
his distant province was a dreary one. She sent off a note to see
whether Genji had forgotten her.

'They tell me you have not been well.

> 'Time goes by, you ask not why I ask not.
> Think if you will how lonely a life is mine.

'I might make reference to Masuda Pond.'†

This was a surprise; and indeed he had not forgotten her. The
uncertain hand in which he set down his reply had its own beauty.

'Who, I wonder, lives the more aimless life.

> 'Hollow though it was, the shell of the locust
> Gave me strength to face a gloomy world.

'But only precariously.'

So he still remembered 'the shell of the locust.' She was sad and
at the same time amused. It was good that they could correspond
without rancor. She wished no further intimacy, and she did not
want him to despise her.

As for the other, her stepdaughter, Genji heard that she had
married a guards lieutenant. He thought it a strange marriage and
he felt a certain pity for the lieutenant. Curious to know something of her feelings, he sent a note by his young messenger.

'Did you know that thoughts of you had brought me to the
point of expiring?

> 'I bound them loosely, the reeds beneath the eaves,‡
> And reprove them now for having come undone.'

---

*Po Chü-i, Collected Works, XIX, 'The Fulling Blocks at Night.'
†Anonymous, Shūishū 894:

> Long the roots of the Masuda water shield,
> Longer still the aimless, sleepless nights.

‡The girl is traditionally called Nokiba-no-ogi, 'the reeds beneath the eaves.'

He attached it to a long reed.

The boy was to deliver it in secret, he said. But he thought that the lieutenant would be forgiving if he were to see it, for he would guess who the sender was. One may detect here a note of self-satisfaction.

Her husband was away. She was confused, but delighted that he should have remembered her. She sent off in reply a poem the only excuse for which was the alacrity with which it was composed:

> 'The wind brings words, all softly, to the reed,
>   And the under leaves are nipped again by the frost.'

It might have been cleverer and in better taste not to have disguised the clumsy handwriting. He thought of the face he had seen by lamplight. He could forget neither of them, the governor's wife, seated so primly before him, or the younger woman, chattering on so contentedly, without the smallest suggestion of reserve. The stirrings of a susceptible heart suggested that he still had important lessons to learn.

Quietly, forty-ninth-day services were held for the dead lady in the Lotus Hall on Mount Hiei. There was careful attention to all the details, the priestly robes and the scrolls and the altar decorations. Koremitsu's older brother was a priest of considerable renown, and his conduct of the services was beyond reproach. Genji summoned a doctor of letters with whom he was friendly and who was his tutor in Chinese poetry and asked him to prepare a final version of the memorial petition. Genji had prepared a draft. In moving language he committed the one he had loved and lost, though he did not mention her name, to the mercy of Amitābha.

'It is perfect, just as it is. Not a word needs to be changed.' Noting the tears that refused to be held back, the doctor wondered who might be the subject of these prayers. That Genji should not reveal the name, and that he should be in such open grief – someone, no doubt, who had brought a very large bounty of grace from earlier lives.

Genji attached a poem to a pair of lady's trousers which were among his secret offerings:

> 'I weep and weep as today I tie this cord.
>   It will be untied in an unknown world to come.'

He invoked the holy name with great feeling. Her spirit had wandered uncertainly these last weeks. Today it would set off down one of the ways of the future.

His heart raced each time he saw Tō no Chūjō. He longed to tell his friend that 'the wild carnation' was alive and well; but there was no point in calling forth reproaches.

In the house of the 'evening faces,' the women were at a loss to know what had happened to their lady. They had no way of inquiring. And Ukon too had disappeared. They whispered among themselves that they had been right about that gentleman, and they hinted at their suspicions to Koremitsu. He feigned complete ignorance, however, and continued to pursue his little affairs. For the poor women it was all like a nightmare. Perhaps the wanton son of some governor, fearing Tō no Chūjō, had spirited her off to the country? The owner of the house was her nurse's daughter. She was one of three children and related to Ukon. She could only long for her lady and lament that Ukon had not chosen to enlighten them. Ukon for her part was loath to raise a stir, and Genji did not want gossip at this late date. Ukon could not even inquire after the child. And so the days went by bringing no light on the terrible mystery.

Genji longed for a glimpse of the dead girl, if only in a dream. On the day after the services he did have a fleeting dream of the woman who had appeared that fatal night. He concluded, and the thought filled him with horror, that he had attracted the attention of an evil spirit haunting the neglected villa.

Early in the Tenth Month the governor of Iyo left for his post, taking the lady of the locust shell with him. Genji chose his farewell presents with great care. For the lady there were numerous fans,* and combs of beautiful workmanship, and pieces of cloth (she could see that he had had them dyed specially) for the wayside gods. He also returned her robe, 'the shell of the locust.'

'A keepsake till we meet again, I had hoped,
And see, my tears have rotted the sleeves away.'

There were other things too, but it would be tedious to

---

*Because the sound of the word *ōgi*, 'fan,' bodes well for a reunion, fans were often given as farewell presents.

describe them. His messenger returned empty-handed. It was through her brother that she answered his poem.

'Autumn comes, the wings of the locust are shed.
A summer robe returns, and I weep aloud.'

She had remarkable singleness of purpose, whatever else she might have. It was the first day of winter. There were chilly showers, as if to mark the occasion, and the skies were dark. He spent the day lost in thought.

'The one has gone, to the other I say farewell.
They go their unknown ways. The end of autumn.'

He knew how painful a secret love can be.

I had hoped, out of deference to him, to conceal these difficult matters; but I have been accused of romancing, of pretending that because he was the son of an emperor he had no faults. Now, perhaps, I shall be accused of having revealed too much.

CHAPTER 5

Lavender

Genji was suffering from repeated attacks of malaria. All manner of religious services were commissioned, but they did no good.

In a certain temple in the northern hills, someone reported, there lived a sage who was a most accomplished worker of cures. 'During the epidemic last summer all sorts of people went to him. He was able to cure them immediately when all other treatment had failed. You must not let it have its way. You must summon him at once.'

Genji sent off a messenger, but the sage replied that he was old and bent and unable to leave his cave.

There was no help for it, thought Genji: he must quietly visit the man. He set out before dawn, taking four or five trusted attendants with him.

The temple was fairly deep in the northern hills. Though the cherry blossoms had already fallen in the city, it being late in the Third Month, the mountain cherries were at their best. The deepening mist as the party entered the hills delighted him. He did not often go on such expeditions, for he was of such rank that freedom of movement was not permitted him.

The temple itself was a sad place. The old man's cave was surrounded by rocks, high in the hills behind. Making his way up to it, Genji did not at first reveal his identity. He was in rough disguise, but the holy man immediately saw that he was someone of importance.

'This is a very great honor. You will be the gentleman who sent for me? My mind has left the world, and I have so neglected the ritual that it has quite gone out of my head. I fear that your journey has been in vain.' Yet he got busily to work, and he smiled his pleasure at the visit.

He prepared medicines and had Genji drink them, and as he went through his spells and incantations the sun rose higher. Genji walked a few steps from the cave and surveyed the scene. The temple was on a height with other temples spread out below it. Down a winding path he saw a wattled fence of better workmanship than similar fences nearby. The halls and galleries within were nicely disposed and there were fine trees in the garden.

'Whose house might that be?'

'A certain bishop, I am told, has been living there in seclusion for the last two years or so.'

'Someone who calls for ceremony – and ceremony is hardly possible in these clothes. He must not know that I am here.'

Several pretty little girls had come out to draw water and cut flowers for the altar.

'And I have been told that a lady is in residence too. The bishop can hardly be keeping a mistress. I wonder who she might be.'

Several of his men went down to investigate, and reported upon what they had seen. 'Some very pretty young ladies and some older women too, and some little girls.'

Despite the sage's ministrations, which still continued, Genji feared a new seizure as the sun rose higher.

'It is too much on your mind,' said the sage. 'You must try to think of something else.'

Genji climbed the hill behind the temple and looked off toward the city. The forests receded into a spring haze.

'Like a painting,' he said. 'People who live in such a place can hardly want to be anywhere else.'

'Oh, these are not mountains at all,' said one of his men. 'The mountains and seas off in the far provinces, now – they would make a real picture. Fuji and those other mountains.'

Another of his men set about diverting him with a description of the mountains and shores of the West Country. 'In the nearer provinces the Akashi coast in Harima is the most beautiful. There is nothing especially grand about it, but the view out over the sea has a quiet all its own. The house of the former governor – he took his vows not long ago, and he worries a great deal about his only daughter – the house is rather splendid. He is the son or grandson of a minister and should have made his mark in the world, but he is an odd sort of man who does not get along well with people. He resigned his guards commission and asked for the Harima post. But unfortunately the people of the province do not seem to have taken him quite seriously. Not wanting to go back to the city a failure, he became a monk. You may ask why he should have chosen then to live by the sea and not in a mountain temple.

The provinces are full of quiet retreats, but the mountains are really too remote, and the isolation would have been difficult for his wife and young daughter. He seems to have concluded that life by the sea might help him to forget his frustrations.

'I was in the province not long ago and I looked in on him. He may not have done well in the city, but he could hardly have done better in Akashi. The grounds and the buildings are really very splendid. He was, after all, the governor, and he did what he could to make sure that his last years would be comfortable. He does not neglect his prayers, and they would seem to have given him a certain mellowness.'

'And the daughter?' asked Genji.

'Pretty and pleasant enough. Each successive governor has asked for her hand but the old man has turned them all away. He may have ended up an insignificant provincial governor himself, he says, but he has other plans for her. He is always giving her last instructions. If he dies with his grand ambitions unrealized she is to leap into the sea.'

Genji smiled.

'A cloistered maiden, reserved for the king of the sea,' laughed one of his men. 'A very extravagant ambition.'

The man who had told the story was the son of the present governor of Harima. He had this year been raised to the Fifth Rank for his services in the imperial secretariat.

'I know why you lurk around the premises,' said another. 'You're a lady's man, and you want to spoil the old governor's plans.'

And another: 'You haven't convinced me. She's a plain country girl, no more. She's lived in the country most of her life with an old father who knows nothing of the times and the fashions.'

'The mother is the one. She has used her connections in the city to find girls and women from the best families and bring them to Akashi. It makes your head spin to watch her.'

'If the wrong sort of governor were to take over,* the old man would have his worries.'

Genji was amused. 'Ambition wide and deep as the sea. But alas, we would not see her for the seaweed.'

Knowing his fondness for oddities, his men had hoped that the story would interest him.

---

*Or, depending on the text, 'If the girl were to become countrified.'

'It is rather late, sir, and seeing as you have not had another attack, suppose we start for home.'

But the sage objected. 'He has been possessed by a hostile power. We must continue our services quietly through the night.'

Genji's men were persuaded, and for Genji it was a novel and amusing excursion.

'We will start back at daybreak.'

The evening was long. He took advantage of a dense haze to have a look at the house behind the wattled fence. Sending back everyone except Koremitsu, he took up a position at the fence. In the west room sat a nun who had a holy image before her. The blinds were slightly raised and she seemed to be offering flowers. She was leaning against a pillar and had a text spread out on an armrest. The effort to read seemed to take all her strength. Perhaps in her forties, she had a fair, delicate skin and a pleasantly full face, though the effects of illness were apparent. The features suggested breeding and cultivation. Cut cleanly at the shoulders, her hair seemed to him far more pleasing than if it had been permitted to trail the usual length. Beside her were two attractive women, and little girls scampered in and out. Much the prettiest was a girl of perhaps ten in a soft white singlet and a russet robe. She would one day be a real beauty. Rich hair spread over her shoulders like a fan. Her face was flushed from weeping.

'What is it?' The nun looked up. 'Another fight?' He thought he saw a resemblance. Perhaps they were mother and daughter.

'Inuki let my baby sparrows loose.' The child was very angry. 'I had them in a basket.'

'That stupid child,' said a rather handsome woman with rich hair who seemed to be called Shōnagon and was apparently the girl's nurse. 'She always manages to do the wrong thing, and we are forever scolding her. Where will they have flown off to? They were getting to be such sweet little things too! How awful if the crows find them.' She went out.

'What a silly child you are, really too silly,' said the nun. 'I can't be sure I will last out the day, and here you are worrying about sparrows. I've told you so many times that it's a sin to put birds in a cage. Come here.'

The child knelt down beside her. She was charming, with rich, unplucked eyebrows and hair pushed childishly back from the forehead. How he would like to see her in a few years! And a sudden realization brought him close to tears: the resemblance to Fujitsubo, for whom he so yearned, was astonishing.

The nun stroked the girl's hair. 'You will not comb it and still it's so pretty. I worry about you, you do seem so very young. Others are much more grown up at your age. Your poor dead mother: she was only ten when her father died, and she understood everything. What will become of you when I am gone?'

She was weeping, and a vague sadness had come over Genji too. The girl gazed attentively at her and then looked down. The hair that fell over her forehead was thick and lustrous.

'Are these tender grasses to grow without the dew
Which holds itself back from the heavens that would receive it?'

There were tears in the nun's voice, and the other woman seemed also to be speaking through tears:

'It cannot be that the dew will vanish away
Ere summer comes to these early grasses of spring.'

The bishop came in. 'What is this? Your blinds up? And today of all days you are out at the veranda? I have just been told that General Genji is up at the hermitage being treated for malaria. He came in disguise and I was not told in time to pay a call.'

'And what a sight we are. You don't suppose he saw us?' She lowered the blinds.

'The shining one of whom the whole world talks. Wouldn't you like to see him? Enough to make a saint throw off the last traces of the vulgar world, they say, and feel as if new years had been added to his life. I will get off a note.'

He hurried away, and Genji too withdrew. What a discovery! It was for such unforeseen rewards that his amorous followers were so constantly on the prowl. Such a rare outing for him, and it had brought such a find! She was a perfectly beautiful child. Who might she be? He was beginning to make plans: the child must stand in the place of the one whom she so resembled.

As he lay down to sleep, an acolyte came asking for Koremitsu. The cell was a narrow one and Genji could hear everything that was said.

'Though somewhat startled to learn that your lord had passed us by, we should have come immediately. The fact is that his secrecy rather upset us. We might, you know, have been able to offer shabby accommodations.'

Genji sent back that he had been suffering from malaria since about the middle of the month and had been persuaded to seek the services of the sage, of whom he had only recently heard. 'Such is his reputation that I hated to risk marring it by failing to recover. That is the reason for my secrecy. We shall come down immediately.'

The bishop himself appeared. He was a man of the cloth, to be sure, but an unusual one, of great courtliness and considerable fame. Genji was ashamed of his own rough disguise.

The bishop spoke of his secluded life in the hills. Again and again he urged Genji to honor his house. 'It is a log hut, no better than this, but you may find the stream cool and pleasant.'

Genji went with him, though somewhat embarrassed at the extravagant terms in which he had been described to women who had not seen him. He wanted to know more about the little girl. The flowers and grasses in the bishop's garden, though of the familiar varieties, had a charm all their own. The night being dark, flares had been set out along the brook, and there were lanterns at the eaves. A delicate fragrance drifted through the air, mixing with the stronger incense from the altar and the very special scent which had been burnt into Genji's robes. The ladies within must have found the blend unsettling.

The bishop talked of this ephemeral world and of the world to come. His own burden of sin was heavy, thought Genji, that he had been lured into an illicit and profitless affair. He would regret it all his life and suffer even more terribly in the life to come. What joy to withdraw to such a place as this! But with the thought came thoughts of the young face he had seen earlier in the evening.

'Do you have someone with you here? I had a dream that suddenly begins to make sense.'

'How quick you are with your dreams, sir! I fear my answer will disappoint you. It has been a very long time since the Lord Inspector died. I don't suppose you will even have heard of him. He was my brother-in-law. His widow turned her back on the world and recently she has been ill, and since I do not go down to the city she has come to stay with me here. It was her thought that I might be able to help her.'

'I have heard that your sister had a daughter. I ask from no more than idle curiosity, you must believe me.'

'There was an only daughter. She too has been dead these ten years and more. He took very great pains with her education and hoped to send her to court; but he died before that ambition could be realized, and the nun, my sister, was left to look after her. I do not know through whose offices it was that Prince Hyōbu began visiting the daughter in secret. His wife is from a very proud family, you know, sir, and there were unpleasant incidents, which finally drove the poor thing into a fatal decline. I saw before my own eyes how worry can destroy a person.'

So the child he had seen would be the daughter of Prince Hyōbu and the unfortunate lady; and it was Fujitsubo, the prince's sister, whom she so resembled. He wanted more than ever to meet her. She was an elegant child, and she did not seem at all spoiled. What a delight if he could take her into his house and make her his ideal!

'A very sad story.' He wished to be completely sure. 'Did she leave no one behind?'

'She had a child just before she died, a girl, a great source of worry for my poor sister in her declining years.'

There could be no further doubt. 'What I am about to say will, I fear, startle you – but might I have charge of the child? I have rather good reasons, for all the suddenness of my proposal. If you are telling yourself that she is too young – well, sir, you are doing me an injustice. Other men may have improper motives, but I do not.'

'Your words quite fill me with delight. But she is indeed young, so very young that we could not possibly think even in jest of asking you to take responsibility for her. Only the man who is presently to be her husband can take that responsibility. In a matter of such import I am not competent to give an answer. I must discuss the matter with my sister.' He was suddenly remote and chilly.

Genji had spoken with youthful impulsiveness and could not think what to do next.

'It is my practice to conduct services in the chapel of Lord Amitābha.' The bishop got up to leave. 'I have not yet said vespers. I shall come again when they are over.'

Genji was not feeling well. A shower passed on a chilly mountain wind, and the sound of the waterfall was higher. Intermittently came a rather sleepy voice, solemn and somehow ominous, reading a sacred text. The most insensitive of men would have been aroused by the scene. Genji was unable to sleep. The vespers were very long and it was growing late. There was evidence that the women in the inner rooms were still up. They were being quiet, but he heard a rosary brush against an armrest and, to give him a sense of elegant companionship, a faint rustling of silk. Screens lined the inside wall, very near at hand. He pushed one of the center panels some inches aside and rustled his fan. Though they must have thought it odd, the women could not ignore it. One of them came forward, then retreated a step or two.

'This is very strange indeed. Is there some mistake?'

'The guiding hand of the Blessed One makes no mistakes on the darkest nights.' His was an aristocratic young voice.

'And in what direction does it lead?' the woman replied hesitantly. 'This is most confusing.'

'Very sudden and confusing, I am sure.

'Since first the wanderer glimpsed the fresh young grasses
  His sleeves have known no respite from the dew.

'Might I ask you to pass my words on to your lady?'

'There is no one in this house to whom such a message can possibly seem appropriate.'

'I have my reasons. You must believe me.'

The woman withdrew to the rear of the house.

The nun was of course rather startled. 'How very forward of him. He must think the child older than she is. And he must have heard our poems about the grasses. What can they have meant to him?' She hesitated for rather a long time. Persuaded that too long a delay would be rude, she finally sent back:

'The dew of a night of travel – do not compare it
  With the dew that soaks the sleeves of the mountain dweller.

It is this last that refuses to dry.'

'I am not used to communicating through messengers. I wish to speak to you directly and in all seriousness.'

Again the old nun hesitated. 'There has been a misunderstanding, surely. I can hardly be expected to converse with such a fine young gentleman.'

But the women insisted that it would be rude and unfeeling not to reply.

'I suppose you are right. Young gentlemen are easily upset. I am humbled by such earnestness.' And she came forward.

'You will think me headstrong and frivolous for having addressed you without warning, but the Blessed One knows that my intent is not frivolous at all.' He found the nun's quiet dignity somewhat daunting.

'We must have made a compact in another life, that we should be in such unexpected conversation.'

'I have heard the sad story, and wonder if I might offer myself as a substitute for your late daughter. I was very young when I lost the one who was dearest to me, and all through the years since I have had strange feelings of aimlessness and futility. We share the same fate, and I wonder if I might not ask that we be companions in it. The opportunity is not likely to come again. I have spoken, I am sure you see, quite without reserve.'

'What you say would delight me did I not fear a mistake. It is true that there is someone here who is under my inadequate protection; but she is very young, and you could not possibly be asked to accept her deficiencies. I must decline your very kind proposal.'

'I repeat that I have heard the whole story. Your admirable reticence does not permit you to understand that my feelings are of no ordinary sort.'

But to her they seemed, though she did not say so, quite outrageous.

The bishop came out.

'Very well, then. I have made a beginning, and it has given me strength.' And Genji pushed the screen back in place.

In the Lotus Hall, voices raised in an act of contrition mingled solemnly with the roar of the waterfall and the wind that came down from the mountain.

This was Genji's poem, addressed to the bishop:

'A wind strays down from the hills to end my dream,
And tears well forth at these voices upon the waters.'

And this the bishop's reply:

'These waters wet your sleeves. Our own are dry,
And tranquil our hearts, washed clean by mountain waters.'

'Such is the effect of familiarity with these scenes.'

There were heavy mists in the dawn sky, and bird songs came from Genji knew not where. Flowering trees and grasses which he could not identify spread like a tapestry before him. The deer that now paused to feed by the house and now wandered on were for him a strange and wonderful sight. He quite forgot his illness. Though it was not easy for the sage to leave his retreat, he made his way down for final services. His husky voice, emerging uncertainly from a toothless mouth, had behind it long years of discipline, and the mystic incantations suggested deep and awesome powers.

An escort arrived from the city, delighted to see Genji so improved, and a message was delivered from his father. The bishop had a breakfast of unfamiliar fruits and berries brought from far down in the valley.

'I have vowed to stay in these mountains until the end of the year, and cannot see you home.' He pressed wine upon Genji. 'And so a holy vow has the perverse effect of inspiring regrets.'

'I hate to leave your mountains and streams, but my father seems worried and I must obey his summons. I shall come again before the cherry blossoms have fallen.

'I shall say to my city friends: "Make haste to see Those mountain blossoms. The winds may see them first." '

His manner and voice were beautiful beyond description. The bishop replied:

'In thirty hundreds of years it blooms but once. My eyes have seen it, and spurn these mountain cherries.'*

'A very great rarity indeed,' Genji said, smiling, 'a blossom with so long and short a span.'

The sage offered a verse of thanks as Genji filled his cup:

'My mountain door of pine has opened briefly To see a radiant flower not seen before.'

There were tears in his eyes. His farewell present was a sacred mace† which had special protective powers. The bishop too gave farewell presents: a rosary of carved ebony‡ which Prince Shōtoku

---

*The *udumbara* was believed to bloom only once in three thousand years, and announce the appearance of the Buddha or a king of like powers.

†*Toko*, a sort of double-pointed spike used in esoteric Shingon rites.

‡Kongōji, literally 'diamond seed,' thought to be the seed of a tree of the fig family.

had obtained in Korea, still in the original Chinese box, wrapped in a netting and attached to a branch of cinquefoil pine; several medicine bottles of indigo decorated with sprays of cherry and wisteria and the like; and other gifts as well, all of them appropriate to the mountain setting. Genji's escort had brought gifts for the priests who had helped with the services, the sage himself and the rest, and for all the mountain rustics too. And so Genji started out.

The bishop went to the inner apartments to tell his sister of Genji's proposal.

'It is very premature. If in four or five years he has not changed his mind we can perhaps give it some thought.'

The bishop agreed, and passed her words on without comment. Much disappointed, Genji sent in a poem through an acolyte:

'Having come upon an evening blossom,
   The mist is loath to go with the morning sun.'

She sent back:

'Can we believe the mist to be so reluctant?
   We shall watch the morning sky for signs of truth.'

It was in a casual, cursive style, but the hand was a distinguished one.

He was about to get into his carriage when a large party arrived from the house of his father-in-law, protesting the skill with which he had eluded them. Several of his brothers-in-law, including the oldest, Tō no Chūjō, were among them.

'You know very well that this is the sort of expedition we like best. You could at least have told us. Well, here we are, and we shall stay and enjoy the cherries you have discovered.'

They took seats on the moss below the rocks and wine was brought out. It was a pleasant spot, beside cascading waters. Tō no Chūjō took out a flute, and one of his brothers, marking time with a fan, sang 'To the West of the Toyora Temple.'* They were handsome young men, all of them, but it was the ailing Genji whom

*'Katsuragi,' a Saibara:

> See, by the Temple of Katsuragi,
> To the west of the Toyora Temple,
> White jewels in the Cypress Well,
> Bring them forth and the land will prosper,
> And we will prosper too.

everyone was looking at, so handsome a figure as he leaned against a rock that he brought a shudder of apprehension. Always in such a company there is an adept at the flageolet, and a fancier of the *shō* pipes* as well.

The bishop brought out a seven-stringed Chinese koto and pressed Genji to play it. 'Just one tune, to give our mountain birds a pleasant surprise.'

Genji protested that he was altogether too unwell, but he played a passable tune all the same. And so they set forth. The nameless priests and acolytes shed tears of regret, and the aged nuns within, who had never before seen such a fine gentleman, asked whether he might not be a visitor from another world.

'How can it be,' said the bishop, brushing away a tear, 'that such a one has been born into the confusion and corruption in which we live?'

The little girl too thought him very grand. 'Even handsomer than Father,' she said.

'So why don't you be his little girl?'

She nodded, accepting the offer; and her favorite doll, the one with the finest wardrobe, and the handsomest gentleman in her pictures too were thereupon named 'Genji.'

Back in the city, Genji first reported to his father upon his excursion. The emperor had never before seen him in such coarse dress.

He asked about the qualifications of the sage, and Genji replied in great detail.

'I must see that he is promoted. Such a remarkable record and I had not even heard of him.'

Genji's father-in-law, the Minister of the Left, chanced to be in attendance. 'I thought of going for you, but you did after all go off in secret. Suppose you have a few days' rest at Sanjō. I will go with you, immediately.'

Genji was not enthusiastic, but he left with his father-in-law all the same. The minister had his own carriage brought up and insisted that Genji get in first. This solicitude rather embarrassed him.

At the minister's Sanjō mansion everything was in readiness. It had been polished and refitted until it was a jeweled pavilion,

*A kind of mouth organ.

perfect to the last detail. As always, Genji's wife secluded herself in her private apartments, and it was only at her father's urging that she came forth; and so Genji had her before him, immobile, like a princess in an illustration for a romance. It would have been a great pleasure, he was sure, to have her comment even tartly upon his account of the mountain journey. She seemed the stiffest, remotest person in the world. How odd that the aloofness seemed only to grow as time went by.

'It would be nice, I sometimes think, if you could be a little more wifely. I have been very ill, and I am hurt, but not really surprised, that you have not inquired after my health.'

'Like the pain, perhaps, of awaiting a visitor who does not come?'*

She cast a sidelong glance at him as she spoke, and her cold beauty was very intimidating indeed.

'You so rarely speak to me, and when you do you say such unpleasant things. 'A visitor who does not come' – that is hardly an appropriate way to describe a husband, and indeed it is hardly civil. I try this approach and I try that, hoping to break through, but you seem intent on defending all the approaches. Well, one of these years, perhaps, if I live long enough.'

He withdrew to the bedchamber. She did not follow. Though there were things he would have liked to say, he lay down with a sigh. He closed his eyes, but there was too much on his mind to permit sleep.

He thought of the little girl and how he would like to see her grown into a woman. Her grandmother was of course right when she said that the girl was still too young for him. He must not seem insistent. And yet – was there not some way to bring her quietly to Nijō and have her beside him, a comfort and a companion? Prince Hyōbu was a dashing and stylish man, but no one could have called him remarkably handsome. Why did the girl so take after her aunt? Perhaps because aunt and father were children of the same empress. These thoughts seemed to bring the girl closer, and he longed to have her for his own.

The next day he wrote to the nun. He would also seem to have communicated his thoughts in a casual way to the bishop. To the nun he said:

---

*A poetic allusion, apparently, not satisfactorily identified.

'I fear that, taken somewhat aback by your sternness, I did not express myself very well. I find strength in the hope that something of the resolve demanded of me to write this letter will have conveyed itself to you.'

With it was a tightly folded note for the girl:

'The mountain blossoms are here beside me still.
    All of myself I left behind with them.

'I am fearful of what the night winds might have done.'*

The writing, of course, and even the informal elegance of the folding, quite dazzled the superannuated woman who received the letter. Somewhat overpowering, thought the grandmother.

She finally sent back: 'I did not take your farewell remarks seriously; and now so soon to have a letter from you – I scarcely know how to reply. She cannot even write 'Naniwa'† properly, and how are we to expect that she give you a proper answer?

'Brief as the time till the autumn tempests come
    To scatter the flowers – so brief your thoughts of her.

'I am deeply troubled.'

The bishop's answer was in the same vein. Two or three days later Genji sent Koremitsu off to the northern hills.

'There is her nurse, the woman called Shōnagon. Have a good talk with her.'

How very farsighted, thought Koremitsu, smiling at the thought of the girl they had seen that evening.

The bishop said that he was much honored to be in correspondence with Genji. Koremitsu was received by Shōnagon, and described Genji's apparent state of mind in great detail. He was a persuasive young man and he made a convincing case, but to the nun and the others this suit for the hand of a mere child continued to seem merely capricious. Genji's letter was warm and earnest. There was a note too for the girl:

*Prince Mototoshi, *Shūishū* 29:

Fearful of what the night winds might have done,
    I rose at dawn – were my plum trees yet in bloom?

†A poem said to have been composed by the Korean Wani upon the accession of the emperor Nintoku, making congratulatory reference to the cherry blossoms of Naniwa, seems to have been used as a beginning lesson in calligraphy.

'Let me see your first exercises at the brush.

'No Shallow Spring, this heart of mine, believe me.*
And why must the mountain spring then seem so distant?'

This was the nun's reply:

'You drink at the mountain stream, your thoughts turn elsewhere.
Do you hope to see the image you thus disturb?'

Koremitsu's report was no more encouraging. Shōnagon had
said that they would be returning to the city when the nun was a
little stronger and would answer him then.

Fujitsubo was ill and had gone home to her family. Genji managed a sympathetic thought or two for his lonely father, but his
thoughts were chiefly on the possibility of seeing Fujitsubo. He
quite halted his visits to other ladies. All through the day, at home
and at court, he sat gazing off into space, and in the evening he
would press Omyōbu to be his intermediary. How she did it I do
not know; but she contrived a meeting. It is sad to have to say that
his earlier attentions, so unwelcome, no longer seemed real, and
the mere thought that they had been successful was for Fujitsubo a
torment.† Determined that there would not be another meeting,
she was shocked to find him in her presence again. She did not
seek to hide her distress, and her efforts to turn him away
delighted him even as they put him to shame. There was no one
else quite like her. In that fact was his undoing: he would be less a
prey to longing if he could find in her even a trace of the ordinary.
And the tumult of thoughts and feelings that now assailed him – he
would have liked to consign it to the Mountain of Obscurity.‡ It
might have been better, he sighed, so short was the night, if he had
not come at all.

'So few and scattered the nights, so few the dreams.
Would that the dream tonight might take me with it.'

*Anonymous, *Manyōshū* 3807:

> Image of Shallow Mount upon Shallow Spring.
> No such shallowness in this heart of mine.

†No earlier meeting has been described.
‡Kurabunoyama, thought to have been either in Yamashiro or in Omi.

He was in tears, and she did, after all, have to feel sorry for him.

'Were I to disappear in the last of dreams
Would yet my name live on in infamy?'

She had every right to be unhappy, and he was sad for her. Omyōbu gathered his clothes and brought them out to him.

Back at Nijō he spent a tearful day in bed. He had word from Omyōbu that her lady had not read his letter. So it always was, and yet he was hurt. He remained in distraught seclusion for several days. The thought that his father might be wondering about his absence filled him with terror.

Lamenting the burden of sin that seemed to be hers, Fujitsubo was more and more unwell, and could not bestir herself, despite repeated messages summoning her back to court. She was not at all her usual self – and what was to become of her? She took to her bed as the weather turned warmer. Three months had now passed and her condition was clear; and the burden of sin now seemed to have made it necessary that she submit to curious and reproving stares. Her women thought her behavior very curious indeed. Why had she let so much time pass without informing the emperor? There was of course a crucial matter of which she spoke to no one. Ben, the daughter of her old nurse, and Omyōbu, both of whom were very close to her and attended her in the bath, had ample opportunity to observe her condition. Omyōbu was aghast. Her lady had been trapped by the harshest of fates. The emperor would seem to have been informed that a malign spirit had possession of her, and to have believed the story, as did the court in general. He sent a constant stream of messengers, which terrified her and allowed no pause in her sufferings.

Genji had a strange, rather awful dream. He consulted a soothsayer, who said that it portended events so extraordinary as to be almost unthinkable.

'It contains bad omens as well. You must be careful.'

'It was not my own dream but a friend's. We will see whether it comes true, and in the meantime you must keep it to yourself.'

What could it mean? He heard of Fujitsubo's condition, thought of their night together, and wondered whether the two might be related. He exhausted his stock of pleas for another meeting. Horrified that matters were so out of hand, Omyōbu could do nothing for him. He had on rare occasions had a brief note, no more than a line or two; but now even these messages ceased coming.

Fujitsubo returned to court in the Seventh Month. The emperor's affection for her had only grown in her absence. Her condition was now apparent to everyone. A slight emaciation made her beauty seem if anything nearer perfection, and the emperor kept her always at his side. The skies as autumn approached called more insistently for music. Keeping Genji too beside him, the emperor had him try his hand at this and that instrument. Genji struggled to control himself, but now and then a sign of his scarcely bearable feelings did show through, to remind the lady of what she wanted more than anything to forget.

Somewhat improved, the nun had returned to the city. Genji had someone make inquiry about her residence and wrote from time to time. It was natural that her replies should show no lessening of her opposition, but it did not worry Genji as it once had. He had more considerable worries. His gloom was deeper as autumn came to a close. One beautiful moonlit night he collected himself for a visit to a place he had been visiting in secret. A cold, wintry shower passed. The address was in Rokujō, near the eastern limits of the city, and since he had set out from the palace the way seemed a long one. He passed a badly neglected house, the garden dark with ancient trees.

'The inspector's house,' said Koremitsu, who was always with him. 'I called there with a message not long ago. The old lady has declined so shockingly that they can't think what to do for her.'

'You should have told me. I should have looked in on her. Ask, please, if she will see me.'

Koremitsu sent a man in with the message.

The women had not been expecting a caller, least of all such a grand one. For some days the old lady had seemed beyond helping, and they feared that she would be unable to receive him. But they could hardly turn such a gentleman away – and so a cushion was put out for him in the south room.

'My lady says that she fears you will find it cluttered and dirty, but she is determined at least to thank you for coming. You must find the darkness and gloom unlike anything you have known.'

And indeed he could not have denied that he was used to something rather different.

'You have been constantly on my mind, but your reserve has made it difficult for me to call. I am sorry that I did not know sooner of your illness.'

'I have been ill for a very long time, but in this last extremity – it was good of him to come.' He caught the sad, faltering tones as she gave the message to one of her women. 'I am sorry that I cannot receive him properly. As for the matter he has raised, I hope that he will still count the child among those important to him when she is no longer a child. The thought of leaving her uncared for must, I fear, create obstacles along the road I yearn to travel. But tell him, please, how good it was of him. I wish the child were old enough to thank him too.'

'Can you believe,' he sent back, 'that I would put myself in this embarrassing position if I were less than serious? There must be a bond between us, that I should have been so drawn to her since I first heard of her. It all seems so strange. The beginnings of it must have been in a different world. I will feel that I have come in vain if I cannot hear the sound of her young voice.'

'She is asleep. She did not of course know that you were coming.'

But just then someone came scampering into the room. 'Grand-mother, they say the gentleman we saw at the temple is here. Why don't you go out and talk to him?'

The women tried to silence her.

'But why? She said the very sight of him made her feel better. I heard her.' The girl seemed very pleased with the information she brought.

Though much amused, Genji pretended not to hear. After proper statements of sympathy he made his departure. Yes, she did seem little more than an infant. He would be her teacher.

The next day he sent a letter inquiring after the old lady, and with it a tightly folded note for the girl:

> 'Seeking to follow the call of the nestling crane
> The open boat is lost among the reeds.

'And comes again and again to you?'*

*Anonymous, *Kokinshū* 732:

> Like the open boat that plies the familiar canal,
> I find that I come again and again to you.

He wrote it in a childish hand, which delighted the women. The child was to model her own hand upon it, no detail changed, they said.

Shōnagon sent a very sad answer: 'It seems doubtful that my lady, after whom you were so kind as to inquire, will last the day. We are on the point of sending her off to the mountains once more. I know that she will thank you from another world.'

In the autumn evening, his thoughts on his unattainable love, he longed more than ever, unnatural though the wish may have seemed, for the company of the little girl who sprang from the same roots. The thought of the evening when the old nun had described herself as dew holding back from the heavens made him even more impatient – and at the same time he feared that if he were to bring the girl to Nijō he would be disappointed in her.

'I long to have it, to bring it in from the moor,
    The lavender* that shares its roots with another.'

In the Tenth Month the emperor was to visit the Suzaku Palace.† From all the great families and the middle and upper courtly ranks the most accomplished musicians and dancers were selected to go with him, and grandees and princes of the blood were busy at the practice that best suited their talents. Caught up in the excitement, Genji was somewhat remiss in inquiring after the nun.

When, finally, he sent off a messenger to the northern hills, a sad reply came from the bishop: 'We lost her toward the end of last month. It is the way of the world, I know, and yet I am sad.'

If the news shocked even him into a new awareness of evanescence, thought Genji, how must it be for the little girl who had so occupied the nun's thoughts? Young though she was, she must feel utterly lost. He remembered, though dimly, how it had been when his mother died, and he sent off an earnest letter of sympathy. Shōnagon's answer seemed rather warmer. He went calling on an evening when he had nothing else to occupy him, some

---

*Murasaki, a gromwell from the roots of which a lavender dye is extracted. Lavender, in general the color of affinity or intimacy, suggests more specifically the *fuji* of Fujitsubo, 'Wisteria Court.' It is because of this poem that the girl is presently to be called Murasaki. The name Murasaki Shikibu also derives from it.

†South of the main palace.

days after he learned that the girl had come out of mourning and returned to the city. The house was badly kept and almost deserted. The poor child must be terrified, he thought. He was shown to the same room as before. Sobbing, Shōnagon told him of the old lady's last days. Genji too was in tears.

'My young lady's father would seem to have indicated a willingness to take her in, but she is at such an uncomfortable age, not quite a child and still without the discernment of an adult; and the thought of having her in the custody of the lady who was so cruel to her mother is too awful. Her sisters will persecute her dreadfully, I know. The fear of it never left my lady's mind, and we have had too much evidence that the fear was not groundless. We have been grateful for your expressions of interest, though we have hesitated to take them seriously. I must emphasize that my young lady is not at all what you must think her to be. I fear that we have done badly by her, and that our methods have left her childish even for her years.'

'Must you continue to be so reticent and apologetic? I have made my own feelings clear, over and over again. It is precisely the childlike quality that delights me most and makes me think I must have her for my own. You may think me complacent and self-satisfied for saying so, but I feel sure that we were joined in a former life. Let me speak to her, please.

> 'Rushes hide the sea grass at Wakanoura.
> Must the waves that seek it out turn back to sea?*

'That would be too much to ask of them.'

> 'The grass at Wakanoura were rash indeed
> To follow waves that go it knows not whither.

'It would be far, far too much to ask.'

The easy skill with which she turned her poem made it possible for him to forgive its less than encouraging significance. 'After so many years,' he whispered, 'the gate still holds me back.'†

*There is a pun on *mirume*, 'seeing' and 'sea grass.'

†Fujiwara Koretada, *Gosenshū* 732:

> Alone, in secret, I hurry to Meeting Hill.
> After so many years, the gate still holds me back.

The girl lay weeping for her grandmother. Her playmates came to tell her that a gentleman in court dress was with Shōnagon. Perhaps it would be her father?

She came running in. 'Where is the gentleman, Shōnagon? Is Father here?'

What a sweet voice she had!

'I'm not your father, but I'm someone just as important. Come here.'

She saw that it was the other gentleman, and child though she was, she flushed at having spoken out of turn. 'Let's go.' She tugged at Shōnagon's sleeve. 'Let's go. I'm sleepy.'

'Do you have to keep hiding yourself from me? Come here. You can sleep on my knee.'

'She is really very young, sir.' But Shōnagon urged the child forward, and she knelt obediently just inside the blinds.

He ran his hand over a soft, rumpled robe, and, a delight to the touch, hair full and rich to its farthest ends. He took her hand. She pulled away – for he was, after all, a stranger.

'I said I'm sleepy.' She went back to Shōnagon.

He slipped in after her. 'I am the one you must look to now. You must not be shy with me.'

'Please, sir. You forget yourself. You forget yourself completely. She is simply not old enough to understand what you have in mind.'

'It is you who do not understand. I see how young she is, and I have nothing of the sort in mind. I must again ask you to be witness to the depth and purity of my feelings.'

It was a stormy night. Sleet was pounding against the roof.

'How can she bear to live in such a lonely place? It must be awful for her.' Tears came to his eyes. He could not leave her. 'I will be your watchman. You need one on a night like this. Come close to me, all of you.'

Quite as if he belonged there, he slipped into the girl's bedroom. The women were astounded, Shōnagon more than the rest. He must be mad! But she was in no position to protest. Genji pulled a singlet over the girl, who was trembling like a leaf. Yes, he had to admit that his behavior must seem odd; but, trying very hard not to frighten her, he talked of things he thought would interest her.

'You must come to my house. I have all sorts of pictures, and there are dolls for you to play with.'

She was less frightened than at first, but she still could not sleep. The storm blew all through the night, and Shōnagon quite refused to budge from their side. They would surely have perished of fright, whispered the women, if they had not had him with them. What a pity their lady was not a little older!

It was still dark when the wind began to subside and he made his departure, and all the appearances were as of an amorous expedition. 'What I have seen makes me very sad and convinces me that she must not be out of my sight. She must come and live with me and share my lonely days. This place is quite impossible. You must be in constant terror.'

'Her father has said that he will come for her. I believe it is to be after the memorial services.'

'Yes, we must think of him. But they have lived apart, and he must be as much of a stranger as I am. I really do believe that in this very short time my feelings for her are stronger than his.' He patted the girl on the head and looked back smiling as he left.

There was a heavy mist and the ground was white. Had he been on his way from a visit to a woman, he would have found the scene very affecting; but as it was he was vaguely depressed. Passing the house of a woman he had been seeing in secret, he had someone knock on the gate. There was no answer, and so he had someone else from his retinue, a man of very good voice, chant this poem twice in tones that could not fail to attract attention:

'Lost though I seem to be in the mists of dawn,
    I see your gate, and cannot pass it by.'

She sent out an ordinary maid who seemed, however, to be a woman of some sensibility:

'So difficult to pass? Then do come in.
    No obstacle at all, this gate of grass.'

Something more was needed to end the night, but dawn was approaching. Back at Nijō, he lay smiling at the memory of the girl. The sun was high when he arose and set about composing a letter. A rather special sort of poem seemed called for, but he laid his brush aside and deliberated for a time, and presently sent some pictures.

Looking in on his daughter that same day, Prince Hyōbu found the house vaster and more cavernous than he had remembered it, and the decay astonishingly advanced since the grandmother's death.

'How can you bear it for even a moment? You must come and live with me. I have plenty of room. And Nurse here can have a room of her own. There are other little girls, and I am sure you will get on beautifully together.' Genji's perfume had been transferred to the child. 'What a beautiful smell. But see how rumpled and ragged you are. I did not like the idea of having you with an ailing lady and wanted you to come and live with me. But you held back so, and I have to admit that the lady who is to be your mother has not been happy at the idea herself. It seems very sad that we should have waited for this to happen.'

'Please, my lord. We may be lonely, but it will be better for us to remain as we are at least for a time. It will be better for us to wait until she is a little older and understands things better. She grieves for her grandmother and quite refuses to eat.'

She was indeed thinner, but more graceful and elegant.

'Why must she go on grieving? Her grandmother is gone, and that is that. She still has me.' It was growing dark. The girl wept to see him go, and he too was in tears. 'You mustn't be sad. Please. You mustn't be sad. I will send for you tomorrow at the very latest.'

She was inconsolable when he had gone, and beyond thinking about her own future. She was old enough to know what it meant, that the lady who had never left her was now gone. Her playmates no longer interested her. She somehow got through the daylight hours, but in the evening she gave herself up to tears, and Shōnagon and the others wept at their inability to comfort her. How, they asked one another, could they possibly go on?

Genji sent Koremitsu to make excuses. He wanted very much to call, but he had received an ill-timed summons from the palace.

'Has he quite forgotten his manners?' said Shōnagon. 'I know very well that this is not as serious an affair for him as for us, but a man is expected to call regularly at the beginning of any affair. Her father, if he hears of it, will think that we have managed very badly indeed. You are young, my lady, but you must not speak of it to anyone.' But the girl was not listening as attentively as Shōnagon would have wished.

Koremitsu was permitted a hint or two of their worries. 'Perhaps when the time comes we will be able to tell ourselves that what must be must be, but at the moment the incompatibility overshadows everything. And your lord says and does such extraordinary things. Her father came today and did not improve matters by telling us that nothing must be permitted to happen. What could be worse than your lord's way of doing things?' She was keeping her objections to a minimum, however, for she did not want Koremitsu to think that anything of real importance had occurred.

Puzzled, Koremitsu returned to Nijō and reported upon what he had seen and heard. Genji was touched, though not moved to pay a visit. He was worried about rumors and the imputation of recklessness and frivolity that was certain to go with them. He must bring the girl to Nijō.

He sent several notes, and in the evening dispatched Koremitsu, his most faithful and reliable messenger. Certain obstacles prevented Genji's calling in person, said Koremitsu, but they must not be taken to suggest a want of seriousness.

'Her royal father has said that he will come for her tomorrow. We are feeling rather pressed. It is sad, after all, to leave a familiar place, however shabby and weedy it may be. You must forgive us. We are not entirely ourselves.'

She gave him short shrift. He could see that they were busy at needle-work and other preparations.

Genji was at his father-in-law's house in Sanjō. His wife was as always slow to receive him. In his boredom and annoyance he took out a Japanese koto and pleasantly hummed 'The Field in Hitachi.'* Then came Koremitsu's house, he would be called a lecher and a child theif. He must swear the women to secrecy and bring her to Nijō immediately.

'I will go early in the morning. Have my carriage left as it is, and order a guard, no more than a man or two.'

Koremitsu went to see that these instructions were carried out. Genji knew that he was taking risks. People would say that his

---

*A Saibara:

> I plow my field in Hitachi
> You have made your way, this rainy night,
> Over mountain and over moor,
> To see if I have a lover.

appetites were altogether too varied. If the girl were a little older he would be credited with having made a conquest, and that would be that. Though Prince Hyōbu would be very upset indeed, Genji knew that he must not let the child go. It was still dark when he set out. His wife had no more than usual to say to him.

'I have just remembered some business at Nijō that absolutely has to be taken care of. I should not be long.'

Her women did not even know that he had gone. He went to his own rooms and changed to informal court dress. Koremitsu alone was on horseback.

When they reached their destination one of his men pounded on the gate. Ignorant of what was afoot, the porter allowed Genji's carriage to be pulled inside. Koremitsu went to a corner door and coughed. Shōnagon came out.

'My lord is here.'

'And my lady is asleep. You pick strange hours for your visits.' Shōnagon suspected that he was on his way home from an amorous adventure.

Genji had joined Koremitsu.

'There is something I must say to her before she goes to her father's.'

Shōnagon smiled. 'And no doubt she will have many interesting things to say in reply.'

He pushed his way inside.

'Please, sir. We were not expecting anyone. The old women are a dreadful sight.'

'I will go wake her. The morning mist is too beautiful for sleep.'

He went into her bedroom, where the women were too surprised to cry out. He took her in his arms and smoothed her hair. Her father had come for her, she thought, only half awake.

'Let's go. I have come from your father's.' She was terrified when she saw that it was not after all her father. 'You are not being nice. I have told you that you must think of me as your father.' And he carried her out.

A chorus of protests now came from Shōnagon and the others.

'I have explained things quite well enough. I have told you how difficult it is for me to visit her and how I want to have her in a more comfortable and accessible spot; and your way of making things easier is to send her off to her father. One of you may come along, if you wish.'

'Please, sir.' Shōnagon was wringing her hands. 'You could not have chosen a worse time. What are we to say when her father comes? If it is her fate to be your lady, then perhaps something can be done when the time comes. This is too sudden, and you put us in an extremely difficult position.'

'You can come later if you wish.'

His carriage had been brought up. The women were fluttering about helplessly and the child was sobbing. Seeing at last that there was nothing else to be done, Shōnagon took up several of the robes they had been at work on the night before, changed to presentable clothes of her own, and got into the carriage.

It was still dark when they reached Nijō, only a short distance away. Genji ordered the carriage brought up to the west wing and took the girl inside.

'It is like a nightmare,' said Shōnagon. 'What am I to do?'

'Whatever you like. I can have someone see you home if you wish.'

Weeping helplessly, poor Shōnagon got out of the carriage. What would her lady's father think when he came for her? And what did they now have to look forward to? The saddest thing was to be left behind by one's protectors. But tears did not augur well for the new life. With an effort she pulled herself together.

Since no one was living in this west wing, there was no curtained bedchamber. Genji had Koremitsu put up screens and curtains, sent someone else to the east wing for bedding, and lay down. Though trembling violently, the girl managed to keep from sobbing aloud.

'I always sleep with Shōnagon,' she said softly in childish accents.

'Imagine a big girl like you still sleeping with her nurse.'

Weeping quietly, the girl lay down.

Shōnagon sat up beside them, looking out over the garden as dawn came on. The buildings and grounds were magnificent, and the sand in the garden was like jewels. Not used to such affluence, she was glad there were no other women in this west wing. It was here that Genji received occasional callers. A few guards beyond the blinds were the only attendants.

They were speculating on the identity of the lady he had brought with him. 'Someone worth looking at, you can bet.'

Water pitchers and breakfast were brought in. The sun was

high when Genji arose. 'You will need someone to take care of you. Suppose you send this evening for the ones you like best.' He asked that children be sent from the east wing to play with her. 'Pretty little girls, please.' Four little girls came in, very pretty indeed.

The new girl, his Murasaki, still lay huddled under the singlet he had thrown over her.

'You are not to sulk, now, and make me unhappy. Would I have done all this for you if I were not a nice man? Young ladies should do as they are told.' And so the lessons began.

She seemed even prettier here beside him than from afar. His manner warm and fatherly, he sought to amuse her with pictures and toys he had sent for from the east wing. Finally she came over to him. Her dark mourning robes were soft and unstarched, and when she smiled, innocently and unprotestingly, he had to smile back. She went out to look at the trees and pond after he had departed for the east wing. The flowers in the foreground, delicately touched by frost, were like a picture. Streams of courtiers, of the medium ranks and new to her experience, passed back and forth. Yes, it was an interesting place. She looked at the pictures on screens and elsewhere and (so it is with a child) soon forgot her troubles.

Staying away from court for several days, Genji worked hard to make her feel at home. He wrote down all manner of poems for her to copy, and drew all manner of pictures, some of them very good. 'I sigh, though I have not seen Musashi,'* he wrote on a bit of lavender paper. She took it up, and thought the hand marvelous. In a tiny hand he wrote beside it:

> 'Thick are the dewy grasses of Musashi,
>   Near this grass to the grass I cannot have.'

'Now you must write something.'

'But I can't.' She looked up at him, so completely without affectation that he had to smile.

'You can't write as well as you would like to, perhaps, but it would be wrong of you not to write at all. You must think of me as your teacher.'

*Anonymous, *Kokin Rokujō, Zoku Kokka Taikan* 34353:

> I sigh at its name, though I have not seen Musashi.
> I sigh as if they were mine, those lavender grasses.

It was strange that even her awkward, childish way of holding
the brush should so delight him. Afraid she had made a mistake,
she sought to conceal what she had written. He took it from her.

'I do not know what it is that makes you sigh.
And whatever grass can it be I am so near to?'

The hand was very immature indeed, and yet it had strength,
and character. It was very much like her grandmother's. A touch
of the modern and it would not be at all unacceptable. He ordered
dollhouses and as the two of them played together he found himself for the first time neglecting his sorrows.

Prince Hyōbu went for his daughter on schedule. The women
were acutely embarrassed, for there was next to nothing they
could say to him. Genji wished to keep the girl's presence at Nijō
secret, and Shōnagon had enjoined the strictest silence. They
could only say that Shōnagon had spirited the girl away, they did
not know where.

He was aghast. 'Her grandmother did not want me to have her,
and so I suppose Shōnagon took it upon herself, somewhat sneak-
ily I must say, to hide her away rather than give her to me.' In
tears, he added: 'Let me know if you hear anything.'

Which request only intensified their confusion.

The prince inquired of the bishop in the northern hills and
came away no better informed. By now he was beginning to feel
some sense of loss (such a pretty child); and his wife had overcome
her bitterness and, happy at the thought of a little girl to do with as
she pleased, was similarly regretful.

Presently Murasaki had all her women with her. She was a
bright, lively child, and the boys and girls who were to be her
playmates felt quite at home with her. Sometimes on lonely nights
when Genji was away she would weep for her grandmother. She
thought little of her father. They had lived apart and she scarcely
knew him. She was by now extremely fond of her new father. She
would be the first to run out and greet him when he came home,
and she would climb on his lap, and they would talk happily
together, without the least constraint or embarrassment. He was
delighted with her. A clever and watchful woman can create all
manner of difficulties. A man must be always on his guard, and
jealousy can have the most unwelcome consequences. Murasaki

was the perfect companion, a toy for him to play with. He could not have been so free and uninhibited with a daughter of his own. There are restraints upon paternal intimacy. Yes, he had come upon a remarkable little treasure.

CHAPTER 6
The Safflower

Though the years might forget 'the evening face'* that had been with him such a short time and vanished like the dew, Genji could not. His other ladies were proud and aloof, and her pretty charms were unlike any others he had known. Forgetting that the affair had ended in disaster, he would ask himself if he might not find another girl, pretty and of not too high a place in the world, with whom he might be as happy. He missed no rumor, however obscure, of a well-favored lady, and (for he had not changed) he felt confident in each instance that a brief note from him would not be ignored. The cold and unrelenting ones seemed to have too grand a notion of their place in the world, and when their proud ambition began to fail it failed completely and in the end they made very undistinguished marriages for themselves. His inquiries usually ended after a note or two.

He continued to have bitter thoughts about the governor's wife, the lady of 'the locust shell.'† As for her stepdaughter, he favored her with notes, it would seem, when suitable occasions arose. He would have liked to see her again as he had seen her then, in dishabille by lamplight. He was a man whose nature made it impossible for him to forget a woman.

One of his old nurses, of whom he was only less fond than of Koremitsu's mother, had a daughter named Tayū, a very susceptible young lady who was in court service and from time to time did favors for Genji. Her father belonged to a cadet branch of the royal family. Because her mother had gone off to the provinces with her present husband, the governor of Chikuzen, Tayū lived in her father's house and went each day to court. She chanced to tell Genji that the late Prince Hitachi had fathered a daughter in his old age. The princess had enjoyed every comfort while she had had him to dote upon her, but now she was living a sad, straitened life. Genji was much touched by the story and inquired further.

'I am not well informed, I fear, about her appearance and disposition. She lives by herself and does not see many people. On

*See Chapter 4.
†See Chapters 2 and 3.

evenings when I think I might not be intruding, I sometimes have
a talk with her through curtains and we play duets together. We
have the koto as a mutual friend, you might say.'

'*That* one of the poet's three friends is permitted to a lady, but
not the next.* You must let me hear her play sometime. Her father
was very good at the koto. It does not seem likely that she would
be less than remarkable herself.'

'I doubt, sir, that she could please so demanding an ear.'

'That was arch of you. We will pick a misty moonlit night and
go pay a visit. You can manage a night off from your duties.'

Though she feared it would not be easy, they made their plans,
choosing a quiet spring evening when little was happening at
court. Tayū went on ahead to Prince Hitachi's mansion. Her
father lived elsewhere and visited from time to time.† Not being
on very good terms with her stepmother, she preferred the Hitachi
mansion, and she and the princess had become good friends.

Genji arrived as planned. The moon was beautiful, just past full.

'It seems a great pity,' said Tayū, 'that this should not be the
sort of night when a koto sounds best.'

'Do go over and urge her to play something, anything. Otherwise I will have come in vain.'

She showed him into her own rather cluttered room. She
thought the whole adventure beneath his dignity, but went to the
main hall even so. With the shutters still raised, a delicate fragrance
of plum blossoms was wafted in.

She saw her chance. 'On beautiful nights like this I think of
your koto and wish we might become better acquainted. It seems
a pity that I always have to rush off.'

'I fear that you have heard too much really fine playing. My
own can hardly seem passable to someone who frequents the
palace.'

Yet she reached for her koto. Tayū was very nervous, wondering what marks Genji would give the concert. She played a soft
strain which in fact he found very pleasing. Her touch was not

---

*Po Chū-i's three 'Friends at the North Window' (Collected Works, XXIX) were
the koto, wine, and poetry.

†Tayū's father and Prince Hitachi's daughter seem to share a mansion, but the relationship is not clear. We are told in Chapter 15 that the princess has a brother who
is a priest. No other brother is mentioned.

particularly distinguished, but the instrument was by no means ordinary, and he could see that she had inherited something of her father's talent. She had been reared in old-fashioned dignity by a gentleman of the finest breeding, and now, in this lonely, neglected place, scarcely anything of the old life remained. She must have known all the varieties of melancholy. It was just such a spot that the old romancers chose for their most moving scenes. He would have liked to let her know of his presence, but did not want to seem forward.

A clever person, Tayū thought it would be best not to let Genji hear too much. 'It seems to have clouded over,' she said. 'I am expecting a caller and would not wish him to think I am avoiding him. I will come again and hope for the pleasure of hearing you at more considerable length.' And on this not very encouraging note she returned to her room.

'She stopped just too soon,' said Genji. 'I was not able to tell how good she might be.' He was interested. 'Perhaps if it is all the same you can arrange for me to listen from a little nearer at hand.'

Tayū thought it would be better to leave him as he was, in a state of suspense. 'I fear not, sir. She is a lonely, helpless person, quite lost in her own thoughts. It is all very sad, and I would certainly not want to do anything that might distress her.'

She was right. He must defer to the lady's position. There were ranks and there were ranks, and it was in the lower of them that ladies did not always turn away sudden visitors.

'But do please give her some hint of my feelings.' He had another engagement and went quietly out.

'It amuses me sometimes to think that your royal father believes you to be excessively serious. I doubt that he ever sees you dressed for these expeditions.'

He smiled over his shoulder. 'You do not seem in a very good position to criticize. If this sort of thing requires comment, then what are we to say of the behavior of certain ladies I know?'

She did not answer. Her somewhat indiscriminate ways invited such remarks.

Wondering if he might come upon something of interest in the main hall, he took cover behind a moldering, leaning section of bamboo fence. Someone had arrived there before him. Who might it be? A young gallant who had come courting the lady, no doubt. He fell back into the shadows.

In fact, it was his friend Tō no Chūjō. They had left the palace together that evening. Genji, having abruptly said goodbye, had gone neither to his father-in-law's Sanjō mansion nor to his own at Nijō. Tō no Chūjō followed him, though he had an engagement of his own. Genji was in disguise and mounted on a very unprepossessing horse and, to puzzle his friend further, made his way to this unlikely place. As Tō no Chūjō debated the meaning of these strange circumstances there came the sound of a koto. He waited, thinking that Genji would appear shortly. Genji tried to slip away, for he still did not recognize his friend, and did not want to be recognized himself.

Tō no Chūjō came forward. 'I was not happy to have you shake me off, and so I came to see you on your way.

'Though together we left the heights of Mount Ouchi,*
   This moon of the sixteenth night has secret ways.'

Genji was annoyed and at the same time amused. 'This is a surprise.

'It sheds its rays impartially here and there,
   And who should care what mountain it sets behind?'

'So here we are. And what do we do now? The important thing when you set out on this sort of escapade is to have a proper guard. Do not, please, leave me behind next time. You have no idea what awful things can happen when you go off by yourself in disguise.' And so he made it seem that he was the one privileged to administer reproofs.

It was the usual thing: Tō no Chūjō was always spying out his secrets. Genji thought it a splendid coup on his part to have learned and concealed from his friend the whereabouts of 'the wild carnation.'†

They were too fond of each other to say goodbye on the spot. Getting into the same carriage, they played on their flutes as they made their way under a pleasantly misted moon to the Sanjō mansion. Having no outrunners, they were able to pull in at a secluded gallery without attracting attention. There they sent for court dress. Taking up their flutes again, they proceeded to the

*The palace.
†The daughter of 'the evening faces' of Chapter 4.

main hall as if they had just come from court. The minister, eager
as always for a concert, joined in with a Korean flute.* He was a
fine musician, and soon the more accomplished of the ladies within the blinds had joined them on lutes. There was a most accomplished lady named Nakatsukasa. Tō no Chūjō had designs upon
her, but she had turned him away. Genji, who so rarely came to
the house, had quite won her affections. News of the infatuation
had reached the ears of Princess Omiya, Tō no Chūjō's mother,
who strongly disapproved of it. Poor Nakatsukasa was thus left
with her own sad thoughts, and tonight she sat forlornly apart
from the others, leaning on an armrest. She had considered seeking a position elsewhere, but she was reluctant to take a step that
would prevent her from seeing Genji again.

The two young men were both thinking of that koto earlier in
the evening, and of that strange, sad house. Tō no Chūjō was lost
in a most unlikely reverie: suppose some very charming lady lived
there and, with patience, he were to make her his, and to find her
charming and sad beyond description − he would no doubt be
swept away by very confused emotions. Genji's new adventure
was certain to come to something.

Both seem to have written to the Hitachi princess. There were
no answers. Tō no Chūjō thought this silence deplorable and
incomprehensible. What a man wanted was a woman who
thought impoverished had a keen and ready sensibility and let him
guess her feelings by little notes and poems as the clouds passed
and the grasses and blossoms came and went. The princess had
been reared in seclusion, to be sure, but such extreme reticence
was simply in bad taste. Of the two he was the more upset.

A candid and open sort, he said to Genji: 'Have you had any
answers from the Hitachi lady? I let a drop a hint or two myself,
and I have not had a word in reply.'

So it had happened. Genji smiled. 'I have had none myself, perhaps because I have done nothing to deserve any.'

It was an ambiguous answer which left his friend more restless
than ever. He feared that the princess was playing favorites.

Genji was not in fact very interested in her, though he too
found her silence annoying. He persisted in his efforts all the same.
Tō no Chūjō was an eloquent and persuasive young man, and

*The Korean flute had one more hole than the commoner Chinese flute.

Genji would not want to be rejected when he himself had made the first advances. He summoned Tayū for solemn conference.

'It bothers me a great deal that she should be so unresponsive. Perhaps she judges me to be among the frivolous and inconstant ones. She is wrong. My feelings are unshakable. It is true that when a lady makes it known that she does not trust me I sometimes go a little astray. A lady who does trust me and who does not have a meddling family, a lady with whom I can be really comfortable, is the sort I find most pleasant.'

'I fear, sir, that she is not your "tree in the rain."* She is not, I fear, what you are looking for. You do not often these days find such reserve.' And she told him a little more about the princess.

'From what you say, she would not appear to be a lady with a very grand manner or very grand accomplishments. But the quiet, naïve ones have a charm of their own.' He was thinking of 'the evening face.'

He had come down with malaria,† and it was for him a time of secret longing; and so spring and summer passed.

Sunk in quiet thoughts as autumn came on, he even thought fondly of those fullers' blocks and of the foot pestle that had so disturbed his sleep. He sent frequent notes to the Hitachi princess, but there were still no answers. In his annoyance he almost felt that his honor was at stake. He must not be outdone.

He protested to Tayū. 'What can this mean? I have never known anything like it.'

She was sympathetic. 'But you are not to hold me responsible, sir. I have not said anything to turn her against you. She is impossibly shy, and I can do nothing with her.'

'Outrageously shy – that is what I am saying. When a lady has not reached the age of discretion or when she is not in a position

*"My Lady's Gate,' a Saibara:

> My lady's gate, my lady's gate,
> Is difficult to pass.
> If I hold up my hands to keep off the rain,
> Might she not let me in?
> Like a cuckoo hunting a tree in the rain
> Might I not go within?

†The time is as at the beginning of Chapter 5.

to make decisions for herself, such shyness is not unreasonable. I am bored and lonely for no very good reason, and if she were to let me know that she shared my melancholy I would feel that I had not approached her in vain. If I might stand on that rather precarious veranda of hers, quite without a wish to go further, I would be satisfied. You must try to understand my feelings, though they may seem very odd to you, and take me to her even without her permission. I promise to do nothing that will upset either of you.'

He seemed to take no great interest generally in the rumors he collected, thought Tayū, and yet he seemed to be taking very great interest indeed in at least one of them. She had first mentioned the Hitachi princess only to keep the conversation from lagging.

These repeated queries, so earnest and purposeful, had become a little tiresome. The lady was of no very great charm or talent, and did not seem right for him. If she, Tayū, were to give in and become his intermediary, she might be an agent of great unhappiness for the poor lady, and if she refused she would seem unfeeling.

The house had been forgotten by the world even before Prince Hitachi died. Now there was no one at all to part the undergrowth. And suddenly light had come filtering in from a quite unexpected source, to delight the princess's lowborn women. She must definitely answer him, they said. But she was no maddeningly shy that she refused even to look at his notes.

Tayū made up her mind. She would find a suitable occasion to bring Genji to the princess's curtains, and if he did not care for her, that would be that. If by chance they were to strike up a brief friendship, no one could possibly reprove Tayū herself. She was a rather impulsive and headstrong young woman, and she does not seem to have told even her father.

It was an evening toward the end of the Eighth Month when the moon was late in rising. The stars were bright and the wind sighed through the pine trees. The princess was talking sadly of old times. Tayū had judged the occasion a likely one and Genji had come in the usual secrecy. The princess gazed uneasily at the decaying fence as the moon came up. Tayū persuaded her to play a soft strain on her koto, which was not at all displeasing. If only she could make the princess over even a little more into the hospitable modern sort, thought Tayū, herself so willing in these matters.

There was no one to challenge Genji as he made his way inside. He summoned Tayū.

'A fine thing,' said Tayū, feigning great surprise. 'Genji has come. He is always complaining about what a bad correspondent you are, and I have had to say that there is little I can do. And so he said that he would come himself and give you a lesson in manners. And how am I to answer him now? These expeditions are not easy for him and it would be cruel to send him away. Suppose you speak to him – through your curtains, of course.'

The princess stammered that she would not know what to say and withdrew to an inner room. Tayū thought her childish.

'You are very inexperienced, my lady,' she said with a smile. 'It is all right for people in your august position to make a show of innocence when they have parents and relatives to look after them, but your rather sad circumstances make this reserve seem somehow out of place.'

The princess was not, after all, one to resist very stoutly. 'If I need not speak to him but only listen, and if you will lower the shutters, I shall receive him.'

'And leave him out on the veranda? That would not do at all. He is not a man, I assure you, to do anything improper.' Tayū spoke with great firmness. She barred the doors, having put out a cushion for Genji in the next room.

The lady was very shy indeed. Not having the faintest notion how to address such a fine gentleman, she put herself in Tayū's hands. She sighed and told herself that Tayū must have her reasons.

Her old nurse had gone off to have a nap. The two or three young women who were still with the princess were in a fever to see this gentleman of whom the whole world was talking. Since the princess did not seem prepared to do anything for herself, Tayū changed her into presentable clothes and otherwise got her ready. Genji had dressed himself carefully though modestly and presented a very handsome figure indeed. How she would have liked to show him to someone capable of appreciating him, thought Tayū. Here his charms were wasted. But there was one thing she need not fear: an appearance of forwardness or impertinence on the part of the princess. Yet she was troubled, for she did fear that even as she was acquitted of the delinquency with which Genji was always charging her, she might be doing injury to the princess.

Genji was certain that he need not fear being dazzled – indeed the certainty was what had drawn him to her. He caught a faint, pleasing scent, and a soft rustling as her women urged her forward. They suggested serenity and repose such as to convince him that his attentions were not misplaced. Most eloquently, he told her how much she had been in his thoughts over the months. The muteness seemed if anything more unsettling from near at hand than from afar.

'Countless times your silence has silenced me.
My hope is that you hope for something better.

'Why do you not tell me clearly that you dislike me? "Uncertainty weaves a sadly tangled web." '*

Her nurse's daughter, a clever young woman, finding the silence unbearable, came to the princess's side and offered a reply:

'I cannot ring a bell enjoining silence.
Silence, strangely, is my only answer.'†

The young voice had a touch of something like garrulity in it. Unaware that it was not the princess's, Genji thought it oddly unrestrained and, given her rank, even somewhat coquettish.

'I am quite speechless myself.

'Silence, I know, is finer by far than words.
Its sister, dumbness, at times is rather painful.'

He talked on, now joking and now earnestly entreating, but there was no further response. It was all very strange – her mind did not seem to work as others did. Finally losing patience, he slid the door open.‡ Tayū was aghast – he had assured her that he would behave himself. Though concerned for the poor princess, she slipped off to her own room as if nothing had happened. The princess's young women were less disturbed. Such misdemeanors

---

*Anonymous, *Kokinshū* 1037:

Why will you not clearly tell me that you hate me?
Uncertainty weaves a sadly tangled web.

†The relationship between the bell and silence is unclear, though it may be the bell that signals the end of a sermon.

‡There is an inconsistency, since we have been told that the doors were bolted.

were easy to forgive when the culprit was so uniquely handsome. Their reproaches were not very loud, though they could see that their lady was in a state of shock, so swiftly had it happened. She was incapable now of anything but dazed silence. It was strange and wonderful, thought Genji, that the world still contained such a lady. A measure of eccentricity could be excused in a lady who had lived so sheltered a life. He was both puzzled and sympathetic.

But how, given her limited resources, was the lady to win his affection? It was with much disappointment that he departed late in the night. Though Tayū had been listening carefully, she pretended that she did not know of his departure and did not come out to see him off. He would have had nothing to say to her.

Back at Nijō he lay down to rest, with many a sigh that the world failed to present him with his ideal lady. And it would not be easy to treat the princess as if nothing had happened, for she was after all a princess.

Tō no Chūjō interrupted unhappy thoughts. 'What an uncommonly late sleeper you are. There must be reasons.'

'I was allowing myself a good rest in my lonely bed. Have you come from the palace?'

'I just left. I was told last night that the musicians and dancers for His Majesty's outing had to be decided on today and was on my way to report to my father. I will be going straight back.' He seemed in a great hurry.

'Suppose I go with you.'

Breakfast was brought in. Though there were two carriages, they chose to ride together. Genji still seemed very sleepy, said his friend, and very secretive too. With many details of the royal outing still to be arranged, Genji was at the palace through the day.

He felt somewhat guilty about not getting off a note to the princess, but it was evening when he dispatched his messenger. Though it had begun to rain, he apparently had little inclination to seek again that shelter from the rain. Tayū felt very sorry for the princess as the conventional hour for a note came and went. Though embarrassed, the princess was not one to complain. Evening came, and still there was only silence.

This is what his messenger finally brought:

> 'The gloomy evening mists have not yet cleared,
> And now comes rain, to bring still darker gloom.

'You may imagine my restlessness, waiting for the skies to clear.'

Though surprised at this indication that he did not intend to visit, her women pressed her to answer. More and more confused, however, she was not capable of putting together the most ordinary note. Agreeing with her nurse's daughter that it was growing very late, she finally sent this:

'My village awaits the moon on a cloudy night.
    You may imagine the gloom, though you do not share it.'

She set it down on paper so old that the purple had faded to an alkaline gray. The hand was a strong one all the same, in an old-fashioned style, the lines straight and prim. Genji scarcely looked at it. He wondered what sort of expectations he had aroused. No doubt he was having what people call second thoughts. Well, there was no alternative. He must look after her to the end. At the princess's house, where of course these good intentions were not known, despondency prevailed.

In the evening he was taken off to Sanjō by his father-in-law. Everyone was caught up in preparations for the outing. Young men gathered to discuss them and their time was passed in practice at dance and music. Indeed the house quite rang with music, and flute and flageolet sounded proud and high as seldom before. Sometimes one of them would even bring a drum up from the garden and pound at it on the veranda. With all these exciting matters to occupy him, Genji had time for only the most necessary visits; and so autumn came to a close. The princess's hopes seemed, as the weeks went by, to have come to nothing.

The outing approached. In the midst of the final rehearsals Tayū came to Genji's rooms in the palace.

'How is everything?' he asked, somewhat guiltily.

She told him. 'You have so neglected her that you have made things difficult for us who must be with her.' She seemed ready to weep.

She had hoped, Genji surmised, to make the princess seem remote and alluring, and he had spoiled her plans. She must think him very unfeeling. And the princess, brooding her days away, must be very sad indeed. But there was nothing to be done. He simply did not have the time.

'I had thought to help her grow up,' he said, smiling.

Tayū had to smile too. He was so young and handsome, and at an age when it was natural that he should have women angry at him. It was natural too that he should be somewhat selfish.

When he had a little more time to himself he occasionally called on the princess. But he had found the little girl, his Murasaki, and she had made him her captive. He neglected even the lady at Rokujō, and was of course still less inclined to visit this new lady, much though he felt for her. Her excessive shyness made him suspect that she would not delight the eye in any great measure. Yet he might be pleasantly surprised. It had been a dark night, and perhaps it was the darkness that had made her seem so odd. He must have a look at her face – and at the same time he rather dreaded trimming the lamp.

One evening when the princess was passing the time with her women he stole up to the main hall, opened a door slightly, and looked inside. He did not think it likely that he would see the princess herself. Several ancient and battered curtain frames had apparently been standing in the same place for years. It was not a very promising scene. Four or five women, at a polite distance from their lady, were having their dinner, so unappetizing and scanty that he wanted to look away, though served on what seemed to be imported celadon. Others sat shivering in a corner, their once white robes now a dirty gray, the strings of their badly stained aprons in clumsy knots. Yet they respected the forms: they had combs in their hair, which were ready, he feared, to fall out at any moment. There were just such old women guarding the treasures in the palace sanctuary, but it had not occurred to him that a princess would choose to have them in her retinue.

'What a cold winter it has been. You have to go through this sort of thing if you live too long.'

'How can we possibly have thought we had troubles when your royal father was still alive? At least we had him to take care of us.' The woman was shivering so violently that it almost seemed as if she might fling herself into the air.

It was not right to listen to complaints not meant for his ears. He slipped away and tapped on a shutter as if he had just come up.

One of the women brought a light, raised the shutter, and admitted him.

The nurse's young daughter was now in the service of the high priestess of Kamo. The women who remained with the princess tended to be gawky, untrained rustics, not at all the sort of servants Genji was used to. The winter they had complained of was being very cruel. Snow was piling in drifts, the skies were dark, and the wind raged. When the lamp went out there was no one to relight it. He thought of his last night with the lady of 'the evening faces.' This house was no less ruinous, but there was some comfort in the fact that it was smaller and not so lonely. It was a far from cozy place all the same, and he did not sleep well. Yet it was interesting in its way. The lady, however, was not. Again he found her altogether too remote and withdrawn.

Finally daylight came. Himself raising a shutter, he looked out at the garden and the fields beyond. The scene was a lonely one, trackless snow stretching on and on.

It would be uncivil to go off without a word.

'Do come and look at this beautiful sky. You are really too timid.'

He seemed even younger and handsomer in the morning twilight reflected from the snow. The old women were all smiles.

'Do go out to him. Ladies should do as they are told.'

The princess was not one to resist. Putting herself into some sort of order, she went out. Though his face was politely averted, Genji contrived to look obliquely at her. He was hoping that a really good look might show her to be less than irredeemable.

That was not very kind or very realistic of him. It was his first impression that the figure kneeling beside him was most uncommonly long and attenuated. Not at all promising – and the nose! That nose how dominated the scene. It was like that of the beast on which Samantabhadra rides, long, pendulous, and red. A frightful nose. The skin was whiter than the snow, a touch bluish even. The forehead bulged and the line over the cheeks suggested that the full face would be very long indeed. She was pitifully thin. He could see through her robes how narrow her shoulders were. It now seemed ridiculous that he had worked so hard to see her; and yet the visage was such an extraordinary one that he could not immediately take his eyes away. The shape of the head and the flow of the hair were very good, little inferior, he thought, to those of ladies whom he had held to be great beauties. The hair fanned out over the hem of her robes with perhaps a foot to spare. Though it may not seem in very good taste to dwell upon her dress, it is dress that is always described first in the old romances.

Over a sadly faded singlet she wore a robe discolored with age to a
murky drab and a rather splendid sable jacket, richly perfumed,
such as a stylish lady might have worn a generation or two before.
It was entirely wrong for a young princess, but he feared that she
needed it to keep off the winter cold. He was as mute as she had
always been; but presently he recovered sufficiently to have yet
another try at shaking her from her muteness. He spoke of this and
that, and the gesture as she raised a sleeve to her mouth was somehow stiff and antiquated. He thought of a master of court rituals
taking up his position akimbo. She managed a smile for him,
which did not seem to go with the rest of her. It was too awful.
He hurried to get his things together.

'I fear that you have no one else to look to. I would hope that
you might be persuaded to be a little more friendly to someone
who, as you see, is beginning to pay some attention to you. You
are most unkind.' Her shyness became his excuse.

'In the morning sun, the icicles melt at the eaves.
Why must the ice below refuse to melt?'

She giggled. Thinking that it would be perverse of him to test
this dumbness further, he went out. The gate at the forward gallery, to which his carriage was brought, was leaning dangerously.
He had seen something of the place on his nocturnal visits, but of
course a great deal had remained concealed. It was a lonely, desolate sight that spread before him, like a village deep in the mountains. Only the snow piled on the pine trees seemed warm. The
weed-choked gate of which his friend had spoken that rainy night*
would be such a gate as this. How charming to have a pretty lady
in residence and to think compassionate thoughts and to long each
day to see her! He might even be able to forget his impossible,
forbidden love. But the princess was completely wrong for such a
romantic house. What other man, he asked himself, could be persuaded to bear with her as he had? The thought came to him that
the spirit of the departed prince, worried about the daughter he
had left behind, had brought him to her.

He had one of his men brush the snow from an orange tree.
The cascade of snow as a pine tree righted itself, as if in envy,
made him think of the wave passing over 'famous Sué, the Mount

*See the rainy night discussion in Chapter 2.

of the Pines.'* He longed for someone with whom he might have a quiet, comforting talk, if not an especially intimate or fascinating one. The gate was not yet open. He sent someone for the gatekeeper, who proved to be a very old man. A girl of an age such that she could be either his daughter or his granddaughter, her dirty robes an unfortunate contrast with the snow, came up hugging in her arms a strange utensil which contained the merest suggestion of embers. Seeing the struggle the old man was having with the gate, she tried to help. They were a very forlorn and ineffectual pair. One of Genji's men finally pushed the gate open.

'My sleeves are no less wet in the morning snow
Than the sleeves of this man who wears a crown of snow.'

And he added softly: 'The young are naked, the aged are cold.'†

He thought of a very cold lady with a very warmly colored nose, and he smiled. Were he to show that nose to Tō no Chūjō, what would his friend liken it to? And a troubling thought came to him: since Tō no Chūjō was always spying on him, he would most probably learn of the visit. Had she been an ordinary sort of lady, he might have given her up on the spot; but any such thoughts were erased by the look he had had at her. He was extremely sorry for her, and wrote to her regularly if noncommittally. He sent damasks and cottons and unfigured silks, some of them suited for old women, with which to replace those sables, and was careful that the needs of everyone, high and low, even that aged gatekeeper, were seen to. The fact that no expressions of love accompanied these gifts did not seem to bother the princess and so matters were easier for him. He resolved that he must be her support, in this not very intimate fashion. He even tended to matters

*Tosa, *Gosenshū* 684:

> Am I that famous Sué, the Mount of the Pines?
> Each day comes a wave from the sky to drench my sleeve.

†Po Chü-i, Collected Works, II, the second of 'Ten Poems Composed at Ch'ang-an':

> The young are naked, the aged are cold.
> In the freezing air, sobs sting the nostrils.

which tact would ordinarily have persuaded him to leave private. The profile of the governor's wife as he had seen her over the Go board had not been beautiful, but she had been notably successful at hiding her defects. This lady was certainly not of lower birth. It was as his friend had said that rainy night: birth did not make the crucial difference. He often thought of the governor's wife. She had had considerable charms, of a quiet sort, and he had lost her.

The end of the year approached. Tayū came to see him in his palace apartments. He was on easy terms with her, since he did not take her very seriously, and they would joke with each other as she performed such services as trimming his hair. She would visit him without summons when there was something she wished to say.

'It is so very odd that I have been wondering what to do.' She was smiling.

'What is odd? You must not keep secrets from me.'

'The last thing I would do. You must sometimes think I forget myself, pouring out all my woes. But this is rather difficult.' Her manner suggested that it was very difficult indeed.

'You are always so shy.'

'A letter has come from the Hitachi princess.' She took it out.

'The last thing you should keep from me.'

She was fidgeting. The letter was on thick Michinoku paper* and nothing about it suggested feminine elegance except the scent that had been heavily burned into it. But the hand was very good.

'Always, always my sleeve is wet like these.
Wet because you are so very cold.'

He was puzzled. 'Wet like what?'

Tayū was pushing a clumsy old hamper toward him. The cloth in which it had come was spread beneath it.

'I simply couldn't show it to you. But she sent it especially for you to wear on New Year's Day, and I couldn't bring myself to send it back, she would have been so hurt. I could have kept it to myself, I suppose, but that didn't seem right either, when she sent it especially for you. So I thought may be after I had shown it to you —'

*A thick, furrowed mulberry paper.

'I would have been very sorry if you had not. It is the perfect gift for someone like me, with "no one to help me dry my tear-drenched pillow." '*

He said no more.

It was a remarkable effort at poetry. She would have worked and slaved over it, with no one to help her. The nurse's daughter would no doubt, had she been present, have suggested revisions. The princess did not have the advice of a learned poetry master. Silence, alas, might have been more successful. He smiled at the thought of the princess at work on her poem, putting all of herself into it. This too, he concluded, must be held to fall within the bounds of the admirable. Tayū was crimson.

In the hamper were a pink singlet, of an old-fashioned cut and remarkably lusterless, and an informal court robe of a deep red lined with the same color. Every stitch and line seemed to insist on a peculiar lack of distinction. Alas once more – he could not possibly wear them. As if to amuse himself he jotted down something beside the princess's poem. Tayū read over his shoulder:

'Red is not, I fear, my favorite color.
Then why did I let the safflower stain my sleeve?

A blossom of the deepest hue, and yet –'†

The safflower must signify something, thought Tayū – and she thought of a profile she had from time to time seen in the moonlight.‡ How very wicked of him, and how sad for the princess!

'This robe of pink, but new to the dyer's hand:
Do not soil it, please, beyond redemption.

That would be very sad.'

She turned such verses easily, as if speaking to herself. There was nothing especially distinguished about them. Yet it would help, he thought again and again, if the princess were capable of even such an ordinary exchange. He did not wish at all to defame a princess.

*Anonymous, *Manyōshū* 2321:

O falling snow, fall not today, I pray you.
No one will help me dry my tear-drenched pillow.

†Apparently a poetic reference.
‡The words for 'flower' and 'nose' are homophonous.

Several women came in.

'Suppose we get this out of the way,' he said. 'It is not the sort of thing just anyone would give.'

Why had she shown it to him? Tayū asked herself, withdrawing in great embarrassment. He must think her as inept as the princess.

In the palace the next day Genji looked in upon Tayū, who had been with the emperor.

'Here. My answer to the note yesterday. It has taken a great deal out of me.'

The other women looked on with curiosity.

'I give up the red maid of Mikasa,' he hummed as he went out, 'even as the plum its color.'*

Tayū was much amused.

'Why was he smiling all to himself?' asked one of her fellows.

'It was nothing,' she replied. 'I rather think he saw a nose which on frosty mornings shows a fondness for red. Those bits of verse were, well, unkind.'

'But we have not one red nose among us. It might be different if Sakon or Higo were here.' Still uncomprehending, they discussed the various possibilities.

His note was delivered to the safflower princess, whose women gathered to admire it.

'Layer on layer, the nights when I do not see you.
     And now these garments – layers yet thicker between us?'

It was the more pleasing for being in a casual hand on plain white paper.

On New Year's Eve, Tayū returned the hamper filled with clothes which someone had readied for Genji himself, among them singlets of delicately figured lavender and a sort of saffron. It did not occur to the old women that Genji might not have found the princess's gift to his taste. Such a rich red, that one court robe, not at all inferior to these, fine though they might be.†

'And the poems: our lady's was honest and to the point. His is merely clever.'

Since her poem had been the result of such intense labor, the princess copied it out and put it away in a drawer.

The first days of the New Year were busy ones. Music sounded

---

*Thought to be from a folk song.

†Fashions in Murasaki Shikibu's time seem to have tended toward pale colors.

through all the galleries of the palace, for the carolers were going their rounds this year.* The lonely Hitachi house continued to be in Genji's thoughts. One evening – it was after the royal inspection of the white horses† – he made his excuses with his father and withdrew as if he meant to spend the night in his own rooms. Instead he paid a late call upon the princess.

The house seemed a little more lively and in communication with the world than before, and the princess just a little less stiff. He continued to hope that he might in some degree make her over and looked forward with pleasure to the results. The sun was coming up when, with a great show of reluctance, he departed. The east doors were open. Made brighter by the reflection from a light fall of snow, the sun streamed in unobstructed, the roof of the gallery beyond having collapsed. The princess came forward from the recesses of the room and sat turned aside as Genji changed to court dress. The hair that fell over her shoulders was splendid. If only she, like the year, might begin anew, he thought as he raised a shutter. Remembering the sight that had so taken him aback that other morning, he raised it only partway and rested it on a stool. Then he turned to his toilet. A woman brought a battered mirror, a Chinese comb box, and a man's toilet stand. He thought it very fine that the house should contain masculine accessories. The lady was rather more modish, for she had on all the clothes from that hamper. His eye did not quite take them all in, but he did think he remembered the cloak, a bright and intricate damask.

'Perhaps this year I will be privileged to have words from you. More than the new warbler, we await the new you.'‡

'With the spring come the calls –'**she replied, in a tense, faltering voice.

*On the fourteenth of the First Month a troupe of courtiers sang at several palaces and mansions. Known as Otokotōka, the observance seems to have fallen into disuse late in the tenth century.

†On the seventh day of the First Month.

‡Sosei, *Shūishū* 5:

> This morn we await the call of the new-come warbler,
> Announcing as well the dawn of the new-come year.

**Anonymous, *Kokinshū* 28:

> With the spring come the calls of countless birds.
> Everything is new, and I grow old.

'There, now. That's the style. You have indeed turned over a new leaf.' He went out smiling and softly intoning Narihira's poem about the dream and the snows.*

She was leaning on an armrest. The bright safflower emerged in profile from over the sleeve with which she covered her mouth. It was not a pretty sight.

Back at Nijō, his Murasaki, now on the eve of womanhood, was very pretty indeed. So red could after all be a pleasing color, he thought. She was delightful, at artless play in a soft cloak of white lined with red. Because of her grandmother's conservative preferences, her teeth had not yet been blackened or her eyebrows plucked. Genji had put one of the women to blackening her eyebrows, which drew fresh, graceful arcs. Why, he continued asking himself, should he go seeking trouble outside the house when he had a treasure at home? He helped arrange her doll-houses. She drew amusing little sketches, coloring them as the fancy took her. He drew a lady with very long hair and gave her a very red nose, and though it was only a picture it produced a shudder. He looked at his own handsome face in a mirror and daubed his nose red, and even he was immediately grotesque. The girl laughed happily.

'And if I were to be permanently disfigured?'

'I wouldn't like that at all.' She seemed genuinely worried.

He pretended to wipe vigorously at his nose. 'Dear me. I fear it will not be white again. I have played a very stupid trick upon myself. And what,' he said with great solemnity, 'will my august father say when he sees it?'

Looking anxiously up at him, Murasaki too commenced rubbing at his nose.

'Don't, if you please, paint me a Heichū black†. I think I can endure the red.' They were a charming pair.

The sun was warm and spring-like, to make one impatient for blossoms on branches now shrouded in a spring haze. The swelling

---

*Ariwara Narihira, *Kokinshū* 970 and *Tales of Ise* 83:

> It is like a dream, to see your priestly robes.
> I had not thought to make my way through these snows.

†Heichū, or Taira Sadabumi (?–923), visiting a lady, wetted his cheeks with water to simulate weeping. The lady exposed the fraud by mixing ink with the water.

of the plum buds was far enough advanced that the rose plum beside the roofed stairs, the earliest to bloom, was already showing traces of color.

'The red of the florid nose fails somehow to please,
    Though one longs for red on these soaring branches of plum.

'A pity that it should be so.'
And what might have happened thereafter to our friends?

CHAPTER 7

An Autumn Excursion

The royal excursion to the Suzaku Palace took place toward the middle of the Tenth Month. The emperor's ladies lamented that they would not be present at what was certain to be a most remarkable concert. Distressed especially at the thought that Fujitsubo should be deprived of the pleasure, the emperor ordered a full rehearsal at the main palace. Genji and Tō no Chūjō danced 'Waves of the Blue Ocean.' Tō no Chūjō was a handsome youth who carried himself well, but beside Genji he was like a nondescript mountain shrub beside a blossoming cherry. In the bright evening light the music echoed yet more grandly through the palace and the excitement grew; and though the dance was a familiar one, Genji scarcely seemed of this world. As he intoned the lyrics his auditors could have believed they were listening to the Kalavinka bird of paradise. The emperor brushed away tears of delight, and there were tears in the eyes of all the princes and high courtiers as well. As Genji rearranged his dress at the end of his song and the orchestra took up again, he seemed to shine with an ever brighter light.

'Surely the gods above are struck dumb with admiration,' Lady Kokiden, the mother of the crown prince, was heard to observe. 'One is overpowered by such company.'

Some of the young women thought her rather horrid.

To Fujitsubo it was all like a dream. How she wished that those unspeakable occurrences had not taken place. Then she might be as happy as the others.

She spent the night with the emperor.

'There was only one thing worth seeing,' he said. ' "Waves of the Blue Ocean." Do you not agree?'

'It was most unusual,' she finally replied.

'Nor is Tō no Chūjō a mean dancer. There is something about the smallest gesture that tells of breeding. The professionals are very good in their way – one would certainly not wish to suggest otherwise – but they somehow lack freshness and spontaneity. When the rehearsals have been so fine one fears that the excursion itself will be a disappointment. But I would not for anything have wished you to miss it.'

The next morning she had a letter from Genji. 'And how did it all seem to you? I was in indescribable confusion. You will not welcome the question, I fear, but

'Through the waving, dancing sleeves could you see a heart
  So stormy that it wished but to be still?'

The image of the dancer was so vivid, it would seem, that she could not refuse to answer.

'Of waving Chinese sleeves I cannot speak.
  Each step, each motion, touched me to the heart.

'You may be sure that my thoughts were far from ordinary.'

A rare treasure indeed. He smiled. With her knowledge of music and the dance and even, it would seem, things Chinese, she already spoke like an empress. He kept the letter spread before him as if it were a favorite sutra.

On the day of the excursion the emperor was attended by his whole court, the princes and the rest. The crown prince too was present. Music came from boats rowed out over the lake, and there was an infinite variety of Chinese and Korean dancing. Reed and string and drum echoed through the grounds. Because Genji's good looks had on the evening of the rehearsal filled him with foreboding, the emperor ordered sutras read in several temples. Most of the court understood and sympathized, but Kokiden thought it all rather ridiculous. The most renowned virtuosos from the high and middle court ranks were chosen for the flutists' circle. The director of the Chinese dances and the director of the Korean dances were both guards officers who held seats on the council of state. The dancers had for weeks been in monastic seclusion studying each motion under the direction of the most revered masters of the art.

The forty men in the flutists' circle played most marvelously. The sound of their flutes, mingled with the sighing of the pines, was like a wind coming down from deep mountains. 'Waves of the Blue Ocean,' among falling leaves of countless hues, had about it an almost frightening beauty. The maple branch in Genji's cap was somewhat bare and forlorn, most of the leaves having fallen, and seemed at odds with his handsome face. The General of the Left* replaced it with several chrysanthemums which he brought from

*Otherwise unidentified.

below the royal seat. The sun was about to set and a suspicion of an autumn shower rustled past as if the skies too were moved to tears. The chrysanthemums in Genji's cap, delicately touched by the frosts, gave new beauty to his form and his motions, no less remarkable today than on the day of the rehearsal. Then his dance was over, and a chill as if from another world passed over the assembly. Even unlettered menials, lost among deep branches and rocks, or those of them, in any event, who had some feeling for such things, were moved to tears. The Fourth Prince, still a child, son of Lady Shōkyōden,* danced 'Autumn Winds,' after 'Waves of the Blue Ocean' the most interesting of the dances. All the others went almost unnoticed. Indeed complaints were heard that they marred what would otherwise have been a perfect day. Genji was that evening promoted to the First Order of the Third Rank, and Tō no Chūjō to the Second Order of the Fourth Rank, and other deserving courtiers were similarly rewarded, pulled upwards, it might be said, by Genji. He brought pleasure to the eye and serenity to the heart, and made people wonder what bounty of grace might be his from former lives.

Fujitsubo had gone home to her family. Looking restlessly, as always, for a chance to see her, Genji was much criticized by his father-in-law's people at Sanjō. And rumors of the young Murasaki were out. Certain of the women at Sanjō let it be known that a new lady had been taken in at Nijō. Genji's wife was intensely displeased. It was most natural that she should be, for she did not of course know that the 'lady' was a mere child. If she had complained to him openly, as most women would have done, he might have told her everything, and no doubt eased her jealousy. It was her arbitrary judgments that sent him wandering. She had no specific faults, no vices or blemishes, which he could point to. She had been the first lady in his life, and in an abstract way he admired and treasured her. Her feelings would change, he felt sure, once she was more familiar with his own. She was a perceptive woman, and the change was certain to come. She still occupied first place among his ladies.

Murasaki was by now thoroughly comfortable with him. She was maturing in appearance and manner, and yet there was artless-

*Neither mother nor son figures otherwise in the story.

ness in her way of clinging to him. Thinking it too early to let the people in the main hall know who she was, he kept her in one of the outer wings, which he had had fitted to perfection. He was constantly with her, tutoring her in the polite accomplishments and especially calligraphy. It was as if he had brought home a daughter who had spent her early years in another house. He had studied the qualifications of her stewards and assured himself that she would have everything she needed. Everyone in the house, save only Koremitsu, was consumed with curiosity. Her father still did not know of her whereabouts. Sometimes she would weep for her grandmother. Her mind was full of other things when Genji was with her, and often he stayed the night; but he had numerous other places to look in upon, and he was quite charmed by the wistfulness with which she would see him off in the evening. Sometimes he would spend two and three days at the palace and go from there to Sanjō. Finding a pensive Murasaki upon his return, he would feel as if he had taken in a little orphan. He no longer looked forward to his nocturnal wanderings with the same eagerness. Her granduncle the bishop kept himself informed of her affairs, and was pleased and puzzled. Genji sent most lavish offerings for memorial services.

Longing for news of Fujitsubo, still with her family, he paid a visit. Omyōbu, Chūnagon, Nakatsukasa, and others of her women received him, but the lady whom he really wanted to see kept him at a distance. He forced himself to make conversation. Prince Hyōbu, her brother and Murasaki's father, came in, having heard that Genji was on the premises. He was a man of great and gentle elegance, someone, thought Genji, who would interest him enormously were they of opposite sexes. Genji felt very near this prince so near the two ladies, and to the prince their conversation seemed friendly and somehow significant as earlier conversations had not. How very handsome Genji was! Not dreaming that it was a prospective son-in-law he was addressing, he too was thinking how susceptible (for he was a susceptible man) he would be to Genji's charms if they were not of the same sex.

When, at dusk, the prince withdrew behind the blinds, Genji felt pangs of jealousy. In the old years he had followed his father behind those same blinds, and there addressed the lady. Now she was far away – though of course no one had wronged him, and he had no right to complain.

'I have not been good about visiting you,' he said stiffly as he got up to leave. 'Having no business with you, I have not wished to seem forward. It would give me great pleasure if you would let me know of any services I might perform for you.'

Omyōbu could do nothing for him. Fujitsubo seemed to find his presence even more of a trial than before, and showed no sign of relenting. Sadly and uselessly the days went by. What a frail, fleeting union theirs had been!

Shōnagon, Murasaki's nurse, continued to marvel at the strange course their lives had taken. Perhaps some benign power had arranged it, the old nun having mentioned Murasaki in all her prayers. Not that everything was perfect. Genji's wife at Sanjō was a lady of the highest station, and other affairs, indeed too many of them, occupied him as well. Might not the girl face difficult times as she grew into womanhood? Yet he did seem fond of her as of none of the others, and her future seemed secure. The period of mourning for a maternal grandmother being set at three months, it was on New Year's Eve that Murasaki took off her mourning weeds. The old lady had been for her both mother and grandmother, however, and so she chose to limit herself to pale, unfigured pinks and lavenders and yellows. Pale colors seemed to suit her even better than rich ones.

'And do you feel all grown up, now that a new year has come?' Smiling, radiating youthful charm, Genji looked in upon her. He was on his way to the morning festivities at court.

She had already taken out her dolls and was busy seeing to their needs. All manner of furnishings and accessories were laid out on a yard-high shelf. Dollhouses threatened to overflow the room.

'Inuki knocked everything over chasing out devils last night and broke this.' It was a serious matter. 'I'm gluing it.'

'Yes, she really is very clumsy, that Inuki. We'll ask someone to repair it for you. But today you must not cry. Crying is the worst way to begin a new year.'

And he went out, his retinue so grand that it overflowed the wide grounds. The women watched from the veranda, the girl with them. She set out a Genji among her dolls and saw him off to court.

'This year you must try to be just a little more grown up,' said Shōnagon. 'Ten years old, no, even more, and still you play with dolls. It will not do. You have a nice husband, and you must try to calm down and be a little more wifely. Why, you fly into a tantrum even when we try to brush your hair.' A proper shaming was among Shōnagon's methods.

So she had herself a nice husband, thought Murasaki. The husbands of these women were none of them handsome men, and hers was so very young and handsome. The thought came to her now for the first time, evidence that, for all this play with dolls, she was growing up. It sometimes puzzled her women that she should still be such a child. It did not occur to them that she was in fact not yet a wife.

From the palace Genji went to Sanjō. His wife, as always, showed no suggestion of warmth or affection; and as always he was uncomfortable.

'How pleasant if this year you could manage to be a little friendlier.'

But since she had heard of his new lady she had become more distant than ever. She was convinced that the other was now first among his ladies, and no doubt she was as uncomfortable as he. But when he jokingly sought to make it seem that nothing was amiss, she had to answer, if reluctantly. Everything she said was uniquely, indefinably elegant. She was four years his senior and made him feel like a stripling. Where, he asked, was he to find a flaw in this perfection? Yet he seemed determined to anger her with his other affairs. She was a proud lady, the single and treasured daughter, by a princess, of a minister who overshadowed the other grandees, and she was not prepared to tolerate the smallest discourtesy. And here he was behaving as if these proud ways were his to make over. They were completely at cross purposes, he and she.

Though her father too resented Genji's other affairs, he forgot his annoyance when Genji was here beside him, and no service seemed too great or too small. As Genji prepared to leave for court the next day, the minister looked in upon him, bringing a famous belt for him to wear with his court dress, straightening his train, as much as helping him into his shoes. One almost felt something pathetic in this eagerness.

'I'll wear it to His Majesty's family dinner later in the month,'* said Genji.

'There are other belts that would do far more honor to such an

*The Naien, late in the First Month, graced by the composition of Chinese poetry.

occasion.' The minister insisted that he wear it. 'It is a little unusual, that is all.'

Sometimes it was as if being of service to Genji were his whole life. There could be no greater pleasure than having such a son and brother, little though the Sanjō family saw of him.

Genji did not pay many New Year calls. He called upon his father, the crown prince, the old emperor,* and, finally, Fujitsubo, still with her family. Her women thought him handsomer than ever. Yes, each year, as he matured, his good looks produced a stronger shudder of delight and foreboding. Fujitsubo was assailed by innumerable conflicting thoughts.

The Twelfth Month, when she was to have been delivered of her child, had passed uneventfully. Surely it would be this month, said her women, and at court everything was in readiness; but the First Month too passed without event. She was greatly troubled by rumors that she had fallen under a malign influence. Her worries had made her physically ill and she began to wonder if the end was in sight. More and more certain as time passed that the child was his, Genji quietly commissioned services in various temples. More keenly aware than most of the evanescence of things, he now found added to his worries a fear that he would not see her again. Finally toward the end of the Second Month she bore a prince, and the jubilation was unbounded at court and at her family palace. She had not joined the emperor in praying that she be granted a long life, and yet she did not want to please Kokiden, an echo of whose curses had reached her. The will to live returned, and little by little she recovered.

The emperor wanted to see his little son the earliest day possible. Genji, filled with his own secret paternal solicitude, visited Fujitsubo at a time when he judged she would not have other visitors.

'Father is extremely anxious to see the child. Perhaps I might have a look at him first and present a report.'

She refused his request, as of course she had every right to do. 'He is still very shriveled and ugly.'

There was no doubt that the child bore a marked, indeed a rather wonderful, resemblance to Genji. Fujitsubo was tormented

---

*Perhaps the father of the reigning emperor, he is mentioned nowhere else. The reign of the present emperor seems to have been preceded by that of Fujitsubo's father, now dead.

by feelings of guilt and apprehension. Surely everyone who saw
the child would guess the awful truth and damn her for it. People
were always happy to seek out the smallest and most trivial of misdeeds. Hers had not been trivial, and dreadful rumors must surely
be going the rounds. Had ever a woman been more sorely tried?

Genji occasionally saw Omyōbu and pleaded that she intercede
for him; but there was nothing she could do.

'This insistence, my lord, is very trying,' she said, at his constant and passionate pleas to see the child. 'You will have chances
enough later.' Yet secretly she was as unhappy as he was.

'In what world, I wonder, will I again be allowed to see her?'
The heart of the matter was too delicate to touch upon.

> 'What legacy do we bring from former lives
> That loneliness should be our lot in this one?

'I do not understand. I do not understand at all.'

His tears brought her to the point of tears herself. Knowing
how unhappy her lady was, she could not bring herself to turn him
brusquely away.

> 'Sad at seeing the child, sad at not seeing.
> The heart of the father, the mother, lost in darkness.'*

And she added softly: 'There seems to be no lessening of the
pain for either of you.'

She saw him off, quite unable to help him. Her lady had said
that because of the danger of gossip she could not receive him
again, and she no longer behaved toward Omyōbu with the old
affection. She behaved correctly, it was true, and did nothing that
might attract attention, but Omyōbu had done things to displease
her. Omyōbu was very sorry for them.

In the Fourth Month the little prince was brought to the
palace. Advanced for his age both mentally and physically, he was
already able to sit up and to right himself when he rolled over. He
was strikingly like Genji. Unaware of the truth, the emperor
would say to himself that people of remarkable good looks did
have a way of looking alike. He doted upon the child. He had
similarly doted upon Genji, but, because of strong opposition –
and how deeply he regretted the fact – had been unable to make

See note, page 13.

him crown prince. The regret increased as Genji, now a commoner, improved in looks and in accomplishments. And now a lady of the highest birth had borne the emperor another radiant son. The infant was for him an unflawed jewel, for Fujitsubo a source of boundless guilt and foreboding.

One day, as he often did, Genji was enjoying music in Fujitsubo's apartments. The emperor came out with the little boy in his arms.

'I have had many sons, but you were the only one I paid a great deal of attention to when you were this small. Perhaps it is the memory of those days that makes me think he looks like you. Is it that all children look alike when they are very young?' He made no attempt to hide his pleasure in the child.

Genji felt himself flushing crimson. He was frightened and awed and pleased and touched, all at the same time, and there were tears in his eyes. Laughing and babbling, the child was so beautiful as to arouse fears that he would not be long in this world. If indeed he resembled the child, thought Genji, then he must be very handsome. He must take better care of himself. (He seemed a little self-satisfied at times.) Fujitsubo was in such acute discomfort that she felt herself breaking into a cold sweat. Eager though he had been to see the child, Genji left in great agitation.

He returned to Nijō, thinking that when the agitation had subsided he would proceed to Sanjō and pay his wife a visit. In near the verandas the garden was a rich green, dotted with wild carnations. He broke a few off and sent them to Omyōbu, and it would seem that he also sent a long and detailed letter, including this message for her lady:

> 'It resembles you, I think, this wild carnation,
> Weighted with my tears as with the dew.

' "I know that when it blossoms at my hedge"*– but could any two be as much and as little to each other as we have been?'

Perhaps because the occasion seemed right, Omyōbu showed the letter to her lady.

---

*Anonymous, *Gosenshū* 199:

> I know that when it blossoms at my hedge,
> The wild carnation, I shall think of you.

'Do please answer him,' she said, 'if with something of no more weight than the dust on these petals.'

Herself prey to violent emotions, Fujitsubo did send back an answer, a brief and fragmentary one, in a very faint hand:

'It serves you ill, the Japanese carnation,
  To make you weep. Yet I shall not forsake it.'

Pleased with her success, Omyōbu delivered the note. Genji was looking forlornly out at the garden, certain that as always there would be silence. His heart jumped at the sight of Omyōbu and there were tears of joy in his eyes.

This moping, he decided, did no good. He went to the west wing in search of company. Rumpled and wild-haired, he played a soft strain on a flute as he came into Murasaki's room. She was leaning against an armrest, demure and pretty, like a wild carnation, he thought, with the dew fresh upon it. She was charming.

Annoyed that he had not come immediately, she turned away.

'Come here,' he said, kneeling at the veranda.

She did not stir. ' "Like the grasses at full tide," '* she said softly, her sleeve over her mouth.

'That was unkind. So you have already learned to complain? I would not wish you to tire of me, you see, as they say the fishermen tire of the sea grasses at Ise.'†

He had someone bring a thirteen-stringed koto.

'You must be careful. The second string breaks easily and we would not want to have to change it.' And he lowered it to the *hyōjō* mode.‡

After plucking a few notes to see that it was in tune, he pushed it toward her. No longer able to be angry, she played for him, briefly and very competently. He thought her delightful as she leaned forward to press a string with her left hand. He took out a

*Sakanoue no Iratsume, *Manyōshū* 1394:

> Are you hidden like the grasses at full tide,
> That so often I sigh for you, so seldom see you?

†Anonymous, *Kokinshū* 683:

> I would not have you see too much of me,
> As at Ise they see each day the same sea grasses.

‡The tonic is E.

flute and she had a music lesson. Very quick, she could repeat a difficult melody after but a single hearing. Yes, he thought, she was bright and amiable, everything he could have wished for. 'Hosoroguseri' made a pretty duet, despite its outlandish name.* She was very young but she had a fine sense for music. Lamps were brought and they looked at pictures together. Since he had said that he would be going out, his men coughed nervously, to warn him of the time. If he did not hurry it would be raining, one of them said. Murasaki was suddenly a forlorn little figure. She put aside the pictures and lay with her face hidden in a pillow.

'Do you miss me when I am away?' He stroked the hair that fell luxuriantly over her shoulders.

She nodded a quick, emphatic nod.

'And I miss you. I can hardly bear to be away from you for a single day. But we must not make too much of these things. You are still a child, and there is a jealous and difficult lady whom I would rather not offend. I must go on visiting her, but when you are grown up I will not leave you ever. It is because I am thinking of all the years we will be together that I want to be on good terms with her.'

His solemn manner dispelled her gloom but made her rather uncomfortable. She did not answer. Her head pillowed on his knee, she was presently asleep.

He told the women that he would not after all be going out. His retinue having departed, he ordered dinner and roused the girl.

'I am not going,' he said.

She sat down beside him, happy again. She ate very little.

'Suppose we go to bed, then, if you aren't going out.' She was still afraid he might leave her.

He already knew how difficult it would be when the time came for the final parting.

Everyone of course knew how many nights he was now spending at home. The intelligence reached his father-in-law's house at Sanjō.

'How very odd. Who might she be?' said the women. 'We have not been able to find out. No one of very good breeding, you may be sure, to judge from the way she clings to him and

*It is the name of a plumed grass.

presumes upon his affection. Probably someone he ran into at court and lost his senses over, and now he has hidden her away because he is ashamed to have people see her. But the oddest thing is that she's still a child.'

'I am sorry to learn that the Minister of the Left is unhappy with you,' the emperor said to Genji. 'You cannot be so young and innocent as to be unaware of all he has done for you since you were a very small boy. He has been completely devoted to you. Must you repay him by insulting him?'

It was an august reproach which Genji was unable to answer.

The emperor was suddenly sorry for him. It was clear that he was not happy with his wife. 'I have heard no rumors, it is true, that you are promiscuous, that you have scattered your affections too liberally here at court and elsewhere. He must have stumbled upon some secret.'

The emperor still enjoyed the company of pretty women. He preferred the pretty ones even among chambermaids and seamstresses, and all the ranks of his court were filled with the best-favored women to be found. Genji would joke with one and another of them, and few were of a mind to keep him at a distance. Someone among them would remark coyly that perhaps he did not like women; but, no doubt because she offered no novelty, he would answer so as not to give offense and refuse to be tempted. To some this moderation did not seem a virtue.

There was a lady of rather advanced years called Naishi. She was wellborn, talented, cultivated, and widely respected; but in matters of the heart she was not very discriminating. Genji had struck up relations, interested that her wanton ways should be so perdurable, and was taken somewhat aback at the warm welcome he received. He continued to be interested all the same and had arranged a rendezvous. Not wanting the world to see him as the boy lover of an aged lady, he had turned away further invitations. She was of course resentful.

One morning when she had finished dressing the emperor's hair and the emperor had withdrawn to change clothes, she found herself alone with Genji. She was bedecked and painted to allure, every detail urging him forward. Genji was dubious of this superannuated coquetry, but curious to see what she would do next. He tugged at her apron. She turned around, a gaudy fan hiding her face, a sidelong glance – alas, the eyelids were dark and muddy – emerging from above it. Her hair, which of course the fan could

not hide, was rough and stringy. A very poorly chosen fan for an
old lady, he thought, giving her his and taking it from her. So
bright a red that his own face, he was sure, must be red from the
reflection, it was decorated with a gold painting of a tall grove. In
a corner, in a hand that was old-fashioned but not displeasingly so,
was a line of poetry: 'Withered is the grass of Oaraki.'* Of all the
poems she could have chosen!

'What you mean, I am sure, is that your grove is summer lodging for the cuckoo.'†

They talked for a time. Genji was nervous lest they be seen, but
Naishi was unperturbed.

> 'Sere and withered though these grasses be,
>   They are ready for your pony, should you come.'

She was really too aggressive.

> 'Were mine to part the low bamboo at your grove,
>   It would fear to be driven away by other ponies.

'And that would not do at all.'

He started to leave, but she caught at his sleeve. 'No one has
ever been so rude to me, no one. At my age I might expect a little
courtesy.'

These angry tears, he might have said, did not become an old
lady.

'I will write. You have been on my mind a great deal.' He tried
to shake her off but she followed after.

' "As the pillar of the bridge —" '‡ she said reproachfully.

*Anonymous, *Kokinshū* 892:

> Withered is the grass of Oaraki,
> No pony comes for it, no harvester.

†Saneakira, in his 'private collection':

> The cuckoo calls, to tell us that the grove
> Of Oaraki is its summer lodging.

‡Anonymous, *Shinchokusenshū* 1285:

> Rotting as the pillar of the bridge,
> I think of you, and so the years go by.

Having finished dressing, the emperor looked in from the next room. He was amused. They were a most improbable couple.

'People complain that you show too little interest in romantic things,' he laughed, 'but I see that you have your ways.'

Naishi, though much discommoded, did not protest with great vehemence. There are those who do not dislike wrong rumors if they are about the right men.

The ladies of the palace were beginning to talk of the affair, a most surprising one, they said. Tō no Chūjō heard of it. He had thought his own affairs varied, but the possibility of a liaison with an old woman had not occurred to him. An inexhaustibly amorous old woman might be rather fun. He arranged his own rendezvous. He too was very handsome, and Naishi thought him not at all poor consolation for the loss of Genji. Yet (one finds it hard to condone such greed) Genji was the one she really wanted.

Since Tō no Chūjō was secretive, Genji did not know that he had been replaced. Whenever Naishi caught sight of him she showered him with reproaches. He pitied her in her declining years and would have liked to do something for her, but was not inclined to trouble himself greatly.

One evening in the cool after a shower he was strolling past the Ummeiden Pavilion. Naishi was playing on her lute, most appealingly. She was a unique mistress of the instrument, invited sometimes to join men in concerts before the emperor. Unrequited love gave her playing tonight an especial poignancy.

'Shall I marry the melon farmer?'* she was singing, in very good voice.

Though not happy at the thought of having a melon farmer supplant him, he stopped to listen. Might the song of the maiden of E-chou, long ago, have had the same plaintive appeal?† Naishi seemed to have fallen into a meditative silence. Humming 'The

---

*'Yamashiro,' a Saibara:

> The melon farmer wants me for his wife.
> Shall I marry the melon farmer
> Before the melons grow?

†Po Chü-i, Collected Works, X, 'On Hearing a Song in the Night.'

Eastern Cottage,'* he came up to her door. She joined in as he sang: 'Open my door and come in.' Few women would have been so bold.

'No one waits in the rain at my eastern cottage.
  Wet are the sleeves of the one who waits within.'

It did not seem right, he thought, that he should be the victim of such reproaches. Had she not yet, after all these years, learned patience?

'On closer terms with the eaves of your eastern cottage
  I would not be, for someone is there before me.'

He would have preferred to move on, but, remembering his manners, decided to accept her invitation. For a time they exchanged pleasant banter. All very novel, thought Genji.

Tō no Chūjō had long resented Genji's self-righteous way of chiding him for his own adventures. The proper face Genji showed the world seemed to hide rather a lot. Tō no Chūjō had been on the watch for an opportunity to give his friend a little of what he deserved. Now it had come. The sanctimonious one would now be taught a lesson.

It was late, and a chilly wind had come up. Genji had dozed off, it seemed. Tō no Chūjō slipped into the room. Too nervous to have more than dozed off, Genji heard him, but did not suspect who it would be. The superintendent of palace repairs, he guessed, was still visiting her. Not for the world would he have had the old man catch him in the company of the old woman.

'This is a fine thing. I'm going. The spider surely told you to expect him,† and you didn't tell me.'

He hastily gathered his clothes and hid behind a screen. Fighting back laughter, Tō no Chūjō gave the screen an unnecessarily loud thump and folded it back. Naishi had indulged her amorous

---

*A Saibara:

> He: I am wet from the rain from the eaves of your eastern cottage.
>   Will you not open the door and let me in?
> She: I would lock it if I had a bolt and lock.
>   Open my door and come in. I am your wife.

†A busy spider was thought to give tidings of the approach of a lover.

ways over long years and had had similarly disconcerting experiences often enough before. What did this person have in mind? What did he mean to do to her Genji? She fluttered about seeking to restrain the intruder. Still ignorant of the latter's identity, Genji thought of headlong flight; but then he thought of his own retreating figure, robes in disorder, cap all askew. Silently and wrathfully, Tō no Chūjō was brandishing a long sword.

'Please, sir, please.'

Naishi knelt before him wringing her hands. He could hardly control the urge to laugh. Her youthful smartness had taken a great deal of contriving, but she was after all nearly sixty. She was ridiculous, hopping back and forth between two handsome young men. Tō no Chūjō was playing his role too energetically. Genji guessed who he was. He guessed too that this fury had to do with the fact that he was himself known. It all seemed very stupid and very funny. He gave the arm wielding the sword a stout pinch and Tō no Chūjō finally surrendered to laughter.

'You are insane,' said Genji. 'And these jokes of yours are dangerous. Let me have my clothes, if you will.'

But Tō no Chūjō refused to surrender them.

'Well, then, let's be undressed together.' Genji undid his friend's belt and sought to pull off his clothes, and as they disputed the matter Genji burst a seam in an underrobe.

'Your fickle name so wants to be known to the world
  That it bursts its way through this warmly disputed garment.

'It is not your wish, I am sure, that all the world should notice.'*
Genji replied:

'You taunt me, sir, with being a spectacle
  When you know full well that your own summer robes are
    showy.'

Somewhat rumpled, they went off together, the best of friends. But as Genji went to bed he felt that he had been the loser, caught in such a very compromising position.

*Anonymous, *Kokin Rokujō, Zoku Kokka Taikan* 34107:

> I keep them out of sight, my robes of crimson,
> It is not my wish that all the world should notice.

An outraged Naishi came the next morning to return a belt and a pair of trousers. She handed Genji a note:

'I need not comment now upon my feelings.
      The waves that came in together went out together,

leaving a dry river bed.'

It was an inappropriate reproof after the predicament in which she had placed him, thought Genji, and yet he could imagine how upset she must be. This was his reply:

'I shall not complain of the wave that came raging in,
      But of the welcoming strand I must complain.'

The belt was Tō no Chūjō's, of a color too dark to go with Genji's robe. He saw that he had lost a length of sleeve. A most unseemly performance. People who wandered the way of love found themselves in mad situations. With that thought he quelled his ardor.

On duty in the palace, Tō no Chūjō had the missing length of sleeve wrapped and returned, with the suggestion that it be restored to its proper place. Genji would have liked to know when he had succeeded in tearing it off. It was some comfort that he had the belt.

He returned it, wrapped in matching paper, with this poem:

'Not to be charged with having taken your take,
      I return this belt of indigo undamaged.'

An answer came immediately:

'I doubted not that you took my indigo belt,
      And charge you now with taking the lady too.

You will pay for it, sir, one day.'

Both were at court that afternoon. Tō no Chūjō had to smile at Genji's cool aloofness as he sorted out petitions and orders, and his own business-like efficiency was as amusing to Genji. They exchanged frequent smiles.

Tō no Chūjō came up to Genji when no one else was near. 'You have had enough, I hope,' he said, with a fierce sidelong glance, 'of these clandestine adventures?'

'Why, pray, should I? The chief hurt was to you who were not invited – and it matters a great deal, since you do so love each other.'* And they made a bond of silence, a vow that they would behave like the Know-Nothing River.†

Tō no Chūjō lost no opportunity to remind Genji of the incident. And it had all been because of that troublesome old woman, thought Genji. He would not again make such a mistake. It was a trial to him that she continued, all girlishly, to make known her resentment. Tō no Chūjō did not tell his sister, Genji's wife, of the affair, but he did want to keep it in reserve. Because he was his father's favorite, Genji was treated respectfully even by princes whose mothers were of the highest rank, and only Tō no Chūjō refused to be awed by him. Indeed he was prepared to contest every small point. He and his sister, alone among the minister's children, had the emperor's sister for their mother. Genji belonged, it was true, to the royal family, but the son of the emperor's sister and of his favorite minister did not feel that he had to defer to anyone; and it was impossible to deny that he was a very splendid young gentleman. The rivalry between the two produced other amusing stories, I am sure, but it would be tedious to collect and recount them.

In the Seventh Month, Fujitsubo was made empress. Genji was given a seat on the council of state. Making plans for his abdication, the emperor wanted to name Fujitsubo's son crown prince. The child had no strong backing, however. His uncles were all princes of the blood, and it was not for them to take command of public affairs. The emperor therefore wanted Fujitsubo in an unassailable position from which to promote her son's career.

Kokiden's anger, most naturally, reached new peaks of intensity.

'You needn't be in such a stir,' said the emperor. 'Our son's day is coming, and no one will be in a position to challenge you.'

As always, people talked. It was not an easy thing, in naming an empress, to pass over a lady who had for more than twenty years

---

*Apparently a deliberate misquotation of a poem by Ise, *Kokin Rokujō, Zoku Kokka Taikan* 32960:

> The rumors are thick as the sea grass the fishermen gather.
> It matters not, for we do so love each other.

†Anonymous, *Kokinshū* 1108:

> If they should ask about us, O Know-Nothing River,
> Be true to your name, and merely say: 'I wonder.'

been the mother of the crown prince. Genji was in attendance the night Fujitsubo made her formal appearance as empress. Among His Majesty's ladies she alone was the daughter of an empress, and she was herself a flawless jewel; but for one man, at least, it was not an occasion for gladness. With anguish he thought of the lady inside the ceremonial palanquin. She would now be quite beyond his reach.

> 'I see her disappear behind the clouds
>   And am left to grope my way through deepest darkness.'

The days and months passed, and the little prince was becoming the mirror image of Genji. Though Fujitsubo was in constant terror, it appeared that no one had guessed the truth. How, people asked, could someone who was not Genji yet be as handsome as Genji? They were, Genji and the little prince, like the sun and moon side by side in the heavens.

CHAPTER 8

The Festival of the Cherry Blossoms

Towards the end of the Second Month, the festival of the cherry blossoms took place in the Grand Hall. The empress and the crown prince were seated to the left and right of the throne. This arrangement of course displeased Kokiden, but she put in an appearance all the same, unable to let such an occasion pass. It was a beautiful day. The sky was clear, birds were singing. Adepts at Chinese poetry, princes and high courtiers and others, drew lots to fix the rhyme schemes for their poems.

'I have drawn "spring," ' said Genji, his voice finely resonant in even so brief a statement.

Tō no Chūjō might have been disconcerted at something in the eyes of the assembly as they turned from Genji to him, but he was calm and poised, and his voice as he announced his rhyme was almost as distinguished as Genji's. Several of the high courtiers seemed reluctant to follow the two, and the lesser courtiers were more reluctant still. They came stiffly out into the radiant garden, awed by the company in which they found themselves – for both the emperor and the crown prince were connoisseurs of poetry, and it was a time when superior poets were numerous. To produce a Chinese poem is never an easy task, but for them it seemed positive torture. Then there were the great professors who took such occasions in their stride, though their court dress may have been a little shabby. It was pleasant to observe the emperor's interest in all these varied sorts of people.

The emperor had of course ordered the concert to be planned with the greatest care. 'Spring Warbler,' which came as the sun was setting, was uncommonly fine. Remembering how Genji had danced at the autumn excursion, the crown prince himself presented a spring of blossoms for his cap and pressed him so hard to dance that he could not refuse. Though he danced only a very brief passage, the quiet waving of his sleeves as he came to the climax was incomparable. The Minister of the Left forgot his anger at his negligent son-in-law. There were tears in his eyes.

'Where is Tō no Chūjō?' asked the emperor. 'Have him come immediately.'

Tō no Chūjō, whose dance was 'Garden of Willows and

Flowers,' danced with more careful and deliberate art than had Genji, perhaps because he had been prepared for the royal summons. It was so interesting a performance that the emperor presented him with a robe – a most gratifying sign of royal approval, everyone agreed.

Other high courtiers danced, in no fixed order, but as it was growing dark one could not easily tell who were the better dancers. The poems were read. Genji's was so remarkable that the reader paused to comment upon each line. The professors were deeply moved. Since Genji was for the emperor a shining light, the poem could not fail to move him too. As for the empress, she wondered how Kokiden could so hate the youth – and reflected on her own misfortune in being so strangely drawn to him.

> 'Could I see the blossom as other blossoms,
>   Then would there be no dew to cloud my heart.'

She recited it silently to herself. How then did it go the rounds and presently reach me?

The festivities ended late in the night.

The courtiers went their ways, the empress and the crown prince departed, all was quiet. The moon came out more brightly. It wanted proper appreciation, thought Genji. The ladies in night attendance upon the emperor would be asleep. Expecting no visitors, his own lady might have left a door open a crack. He went quietly up to her apartments, but the door of the one whom he might ask to show him in was tightly closed. He sighed. Still not ready to give up, he made his way to the gallery by Kokiden's pavilion. The third door from the north was open. Kokiden herself was with the emperor, and her rooms were almost deserted. The hinged door at the far corner was open too. All was silent. It was thus, he thought, that a lady invited her downfall. He slipped across the gallery and up to the door of the main room and looked inside. Everyone seemed to be asleep.

' "What can compare with a misty moon of spring?" '* It was a

*Oe Chisato, *Shinkokinshū* 55:

> What can vie with a misty moon of spring,
>   Shining dimly, yet not clouded over?

The poem has been misquoted, probably intentionally, to make it sound less Chinese and therefore more feminine.

sweet young voice, so delicate that its owner could be no ordinary serving woman.

She came (could he believe it?) to the door. Delighted, he caught at her sleeve.

'Who are you?' She was frightened.

'There is nothing to be afraid of.

> 'Late in the night we enjoy a misty moon.
> There is nothing misty about the bond between us.'

Quickly and lightly he lifted her down to the gallery and slid the door closed. Her surprise pleased him enormously.

Trembling, she called for help.

'It will do you no good. I am always allowed my way. Just be quiet, if you will, please.'

She recognized his voice and was somewhat reassured. Though of course upset, she evidently did not wish him to think her wanting in good manners. It may have been because he was still a little drunk that he could not admit the possibility of letting her go; and she, young and irresolute, did not know how to send him on his way. He was delighted with her, but also very nervous, for dawn was approaching. She was in an agony of apprehension lest they be seen.

'You must tell me who you are,' he said. 'How can I write to you if you do not? You surely don't think I mean to let matters stand as they are?'

> 'Were the lonely one to vanish quite away,
> Would you go to the grassy moors to ask her name?'

Her voice had a softly plaintive quality.

'I did not express myself well.

> 'I wish to know whose dewy lodge it is
> Ere winds blow past the bamboo-tangled moor.*

'Only one thing, a cold welcome, could destroy my eagerness to visit. Do you perhaps have some diversionary tactic in mind?'

They exchanged fans and he was on his way. Even as he spoke a stream of women was moving in and out of Kokiden's rooms. There were women in his own rooms too, some of them still

---

*'I would like to know who you are now, before rumors spread abroad.'

awake. Pretending to be asleep, they poked one another and exchanged whispered remarks about the diligence with which he pursued these night adventures.

He was unable to sleep. What a beautiful girl! One of Kokiden's younger sisters, no doubt. Perhaps the fifth or sixth daughter of the family, since she had seemed to know so little about men? He had heard that both the fourth daughter, to whom Tō no Chūjō was uncomfortably married, and Prince Hotaru's wife were great beauties,* and thought that the encounter might have been more interesting had the lady been one of the older sisters. He rather hoped she was not the sixth daughter, whom the minister had thoughts of marrying to the crown prince. The trouble was that he had no way of being sure. It had not seemed that she wanted the affair to end with but the one meeting. Why then had she not told him how he might write to her? These thoughts and others suggest that he was much interested. He thought too of Fujitsubo's pavilion, and how much more mysterious and inaccessible it was, indeed how uniquely so.

He had a lesser spring banquet with which to amuse himself that day. He played the thirteen-stringed koto, his performance if anything subtler and richer than that of the day before. Fujitsubo went to the emperor's apartments at dawn.

Genji was on tenterhooks, wondering whether the lady he had seen in the dawn moonlight would be leaving the palace. He sent Yoshikiyo and Koremitsu, who let nothing escape them, to keep watch; and when, as he was leaving the royal presence, he had their report, his agitation increased.

'Some carriages that had been kept out of sight left just now by the north gate. Two of Kokiden's brothers and several other members of the family saw them off; so we gathered that the ladies must be part of the family too. They were ladies of some importance, in any case – that much was clear. There were three carriages in all.'

How might he learn which of the sisters he had become friends with? Supposing her father were to learn of the affair and welcome him gladly into the family – he had not seen enough of the lady to be sure that the prospect delighted him. Yet he did want very much to know who she was. He sat looking out at the garden.

*The crown prince, Genji, and Prince Hotaru are all brothers.

Murasaki would be gloomy and bored, he feared, for he had not visited her in some days. He looked at the fan he had received in the dawn moonlight. It was a 'three-ply cherry.'* The painting on the more richly colored side, a misty moon reflected on water, was not remarkable, but the fan, well used, was a memento to stir longing. He remembered with especial tenderness the poem about the grassy moors.

He jotted down a poem beside the misty moon:

> 'I had not known the sudden loneliness
> Of having it vanish, the moon in the sky of dawn.'

He had been neglecting the Sanjō mansion of his father-in-law for rather a long time, but Murasaki was more on his mind. He must go comfort her. She pleased him more, she seemed prettier and cleverer and more amiable, each time he saw her. He was congratulating himself that his hopes of shaping her into his ideal might not prove entirely unrealistic. Yet he had misgivings – very unsettling ones, it must be said – lest by training her himself he put her too much at ease with men. He told her the latest court gossip and they had a music lesson. So he was going out again – she was sorry, as always, to see him go, but she no longer clung to him as she once had.

At Sanjō it was the usual thing: his wife kept him waiting. In his boredom he thought of this and that. Pulling a koto to him, he casually plucked out a tune. 'No nights of soft sleep,'† he sang, to his own accompaniment.

The minister came for a talk about the recent pleasurable events.

'I am very old, and I have served through four illustrious reigns, but never have I known an occasion that has added so many years to my life. Such clever, witty poems, such fine music and dancing

---

*A somewhat mysterious object. One theory holds it to have had three-ply end ribs covered with pink paper.

†'The River Nuki,' a Saibara:

> No nights of soft sleep,
> Soft as the reed pillow,
> The waves of the river Nuki.
> My father comes between us.

– you are on good terms with the great performers who so abound in our day, and you arrange things with such marvelous skill. Even we aged ones felt like cutting a caper or two.'

'The marvelous skill of which you speak, sir, amounts to nothing at all, only a word here and there. It is a matter of knowing where to ask. 'Garden of Willows and Flowers' was much the best thing, I thought, a performance to go down as a model for all the ages. And what a memorable day it would have been, what an honor for our age, if in the advancing spring of your life you had followed your impulse and danced for us.'

Soon Tō no Chūjō and his brothers, leaning casually against the veranda railings, were in fine concert on their favorite instruments.

The lady of that dawn encounter, remembering the evanescent dream, was sunk in sad thoughts. Her father's plans to give her to the crown prince in the Fourth Month were a source of great distress. As for Genji, he was not without devices for searching her out, but he did not know which of Kokiden's sisters she was, and he did not wish to become involved with that unfriendly family.

Late in the Fourth Month the princes and high courtiers gathered at the mansion of the Minister of the Right, Kokiden's father, for an archery meet. It was followed immediately by a wisteria banquet. Though the cherry blossoms had for the most part fallen, two trees, perhaps having learned that mountain cherries do well to bloom late,* were at their belated best. The minister's mansion had been rebuilt and beautifully refurnished for the initiation ceremonies of the princesses his granddaughters. It was in the ornate style its owner preferred, everything in the latest fashion.

Seeing Genji in the palace one day, the minister had invited him to the festivities. Genji would have preferred to stay away, but the affair seemed certain to languish without him. The minister sent one of his sons, a guards officer, with a message:

> 'If these blossoms of mine were of the common sort,
>   Would I press you so to come and look upon them?'

Genji showed the poem to his father.

---

*Ise, *Kokinshū* 68:

> These mountain cherries with no one to look upon them:
>   Might they not bloom when all the others have fallen?

'He seems very pleased with his flowers,' laughed the emperor. 'But you must go immediately. He has, after all, sent a special invitation. It is in his house that the princesses your sisters are being reared. You are scarcely a stranger.'

Genji dressed with great care. It was almost dark when he finally presented himself. He wore a robe of a thin white Chinese damask with a red lining and under it a very long train of magenta. Altogether the dashing young prince, he added something new to the assembly that so cordially received him, for the other guests were more formally clad. He quite overwhelmed the blossoms, in a sense spoiling the party, and played beautifully on several instruments. Late in the evening he got up, pretending to be drunk. The first and third princesses were living in the main hall. He went to the east veranda and leaned against a door. The shutters were raised and women were gathered at the southwest corner, where the wisteria was in bloom. Their sleeves were pushed somewhat ostentatiously out from under blinds, as at a New Year's poetry assembly. All rather overdone, he thought, and he could not help thinking too of Fujitsubo's reticence.

'I was not feeling well in the first place, and they plied me with drink. I know I shouldn't, but might I ask you to hide me?' He raised the blind at the corner door.

'Please, dear sir, this will not do. It is for us beggars to ask such favors of you fine gentlemen.' Though of no overwhelming dignity, the women were most certainly not common.

Incense hung heavily in the air and the rustling of silk was bright and lively. Because the princesses seemed to prefer modern things, the scene may perhaps have been wanting in mysterious shadows.

The time and place were hardly appropriate for a flirtation, and yet his interest was aroused. Which would be the lady of the misty moon?

'A most awful thing has happened,' he said playfully. 'Someone has stolen my fan.'* He sat leaning against a pillar.

*An oblique reference, the words for 'fan' and 'sash' being similar, to the Saibara 'Ishikawa':

> A most awful thing has happened.
> Someone has stolen my sash.
> 'Tis the Korean of Ishikawa.

'What curious things that Korean does do.' The lady who thus deftly returned his allusion did not seem to know about the exchange of fans.

Catching a sigh from another lady, he leaned forward and took her hand.

'I wander lost on Arrow Mount and ask:
    May I not see the moon I saw so briefly?

'Or must I continue to wander?'

It seemed that she could not remain silent:

'Only the flighty, the less than serious ones,
    Are left in the skies when the longbow moon is gone.'*

It was the same voice. He was delighted. And yet –

*Both poems contain elaborate allusions to archery.

CHAPTER 9

Heartvine

With the new reign Genji's career languished, and since he must be the more discreet about his romantic adventures as he rose in rank, he had less to amuse him. Everywhere there were complaints about his aloofness.

As if to punish him, there was one lady who continued to cause him pain with her own aloofness. Fujitsubo saw more of the old emperor, now abdicated, than ever. She was always at his side, almost as if she were a common housewife. Annoyed at this state of affairs, Kokiden did not follow the old emperor when he left the main palace. Fujitsubo was happy and secure. The concerts in the old emperor's palace attracted the attention of the whole court, and altogether life was happier for the two of them than while he had reigned. Only one thing was lacking: he greatly missed the crown prince, Fujitsubo's son, and worried that he had no strong backers. Genji, he said, must be the boy's adviser and guardian. Genji was both pleased and embarrassed.

And there was the matter of the lady at Rokujō. With the change of reigns, her daughter, who was also the daughter of the late crown prince, had been appointed high priestess of the Ise Shrine. No longer trusting Genji's affections, the Rokujō lady had been thinking that, making the girl's youth her excuse, she too would go to Ise.

The old emperor heard of her plans. 'The crown prince was so very fond of her,' he said to Genji, in open displeasure. 'It is sad that you should have made light of her, as if she were any ordinary woman. I think of the high priestess as one of my own children, and you should be good to her mother, for my sake and for the sake of the dead prince. It does you no good to abandon yourself to these affairs quite as the impulse takes you.'

It was perfectly true, thought Genji. He waited in silence.

'You should treat any woman with tact and courtesy, and be sure that you cause her no embarrassment. You should never have a woman angry with you.'

What would his father think if he were to learn of Genji's worst indiscretion? The thought made Genji shudder. He bowed and withdrew.

The matter his father had thus reproved him for did no good for either of them, the woman or Genji himself. It was a scandal, and very sad for her. She continued to be very much on his mind, and yet he had no thought of making her his wife. She had grown cool toward him, worried about the difference in their ages. He made it seem that it was because of her wishes that he stayed away. Now that the old emperor knew of the affair the whole court knew of it. In spite of everything, the lady went on grieving that he had not loved her better.

There was another lady, his cousin Princess Asagao.* Determined that she would not share the plight of the Rokujō lady, she refused even the briefest answer to his notes. Still, and he thought her most civil for it, she was careful to avoid giving open offense.

At Sanjō, his wife and her family were even unhappier about his infidelities, but, perhaps because he did not lie to them, they for the most part kept their displeasure to themselves. His wife was with child and in considerable distress mentally and physically. For Genji it was a strange and moving time. Everyone was delighted and at the same time filled with apprehension, and all manner of retreats and abstinences were prescribed for the lady. Genji had little time to himself. While he had no particular wish to avoid the Rokujō lady and the others, he rarely visited them.

At about this time the high priestess of Kamo resigned. She was replaced by the old emperor's third daughter, whose mother was Kokiden. The new priestess was a favorite of both her brother, the new emperor, and her mother, and it seemed a great pity that she should be shut off from court life; but no other princess was qualified for the position. The installation ceremonies, in the austere Shinto tradition, were of great dignity and solemnity. Many novel details were added to the Kamo festival in the Fourth Month, so that it was certain to be the finest of the season. Though the number of high courtiers attending the princess at the lustration† was limited by precedent, great care was taken to choose handsome men of good repute. Similar care was given to their uniforms and to the uniform trappings of their horses. Genji was among the attendants, by special command of the new emperor. Courtiers and ladies had readied their carriages far in advance, and Ichijō was

*She first appears in Chapter 2.

†At the Kamo River, some days in advance of the festival.

a frightening crush, without space for another vehicle. The stands along the way had been appointed most elaborately. The sleeves that showed beneath the curtains fulfilled in their brightness and variety all the festive promise.

Genji's wife seldom went forth on sightseeing expeditions and her pregnancy was another reason for staying at home.

But her young women protested. 'Really, my lady, it won't be much fun sneaking off by ourselves. Why, even complete strangers – why, all the country folk have come in to see our lord! They've brought their wives and families from the farthest provinces. It will be too much if you make us stay away.'

Her mother, Princess Omiya, agreed. 'You seem to be feeling well enough, my dear, and they will be very disappointed if you don't take them.'

And so carriages were hastily and unostentatiously decked out, and the sun was already high when they set forth. The waysides were by now too crowded to admit the elegant Sanjō procession. Coming upon several fine carriages not attended by grooms and footmen, the Sanjō men commenced clearing a space. Two palm-frond carriages remained, not new ones, obviously belonging to someone who did not wish to attract attention. The curtains and the sleeves and aprons to be glimpsed beneath them, some in the gay colors little girls were, were in very good taste.

The men in attendance sought to defend their places against the Sanjō invaders. 'We aren't the sort of people you push around.'

There had been too much drink in both parties, and the drunken ones were not responsive to the efforts of their more mature and collected seniors to restrain them.

The palm-frond carriages were from the Rokujō house of the high priestess of Ise. The Rokujō lady had come quietly to see the procession, hoping that it might make her briefly forget her unhappiness. The men from Sanjō had recognized her, but preferred to make it seem otherwise.

'They can't tell us who to push and not to push,' said the more intemperate ones to their fellows. 'They have General Genji to make them feel important.'

Among the newcomers were some of Genji's men. They recognized and felt a little sorry for the Rokujō lady, but, not wishing to become involved, they looked the other way. Presently all the Sanjō carriages were in place. The Rokujō lady, behind the lesser ones, could see almost nothing. Quite aside from her natural distress at the insult, she was filled with the bitterest chagrin that, having refrained from display, she had been recognized. The stools for her carriage shafts had been broken and the shafts propped on the hubs of perfectly strange carriages, a most undignified sight. It was no good asking herself why she had come. She thought of going home without seeing the procession, but there was no room for her to pass; and then came word that the procession was approaching, and she must, after all, see the man who had caused her such unhappiness. How weak is the heart of a woman! Perhaps because this was not 'the bamboo by the river Hinokuma,'* he passed without stopping his horse or looking her way; and the unhappiness was greater than if she had stayed at home.

Genji seemed indifferent to all the grandly decorated carriages and all the gay sleeves, such a flood of them that it was as if ladies were stacked in layers behind the carriage curtains. Now and again, however, he would have a smile and a glance for a carriage he recognized. His face was solemn and respectful as he passed his wife's carriage. His men bowed deeply, and the Rokujō lady was in misery. She had been utterly defeated.

She whispered to herself:

'A distant glimpse of the River of Lustration.
His coldness is the measure of my sorrow.'

She was ashamed of her tears. Yet she thought how sorry she would have been if she had not seen that handsome figure set off to such advantage by the crowds.

The high courtiers were, after their several ranks, impeccably dressed and caparisoned and many of them were very handsome; but Genji's radiance dimmed the strongest lights. Among his special attendants was a guards officer of the Sixth Rank, though attendants of such standing were usually reserved for the most splendid royal processions. His retinue made such a fine procession itself that every tree and blade of grass along the way seemed to bend forward in admiration.

*Anonymous, *Kokinshū* 1080:

In the bamboo by the river Hinokuma,
Stop that your horse may drink, and I may see you.

It is not on the whole considered good form for veiled ladies of no mean rank and even nuns who have withdrawn from the world to be jostling and shoving one another in the struggle to see, but today no one thought it out of place. Hollow-mouthed women of the lower classes, their hair tucked under their robes, their hands brought respectfully to their foreheads, were hopping about in hopes of catching a glimpse. Plebeian faces were wreathed in smiles which their owners might not have enjoyed seeing in mirrors, and daughters of petty provincial officers of whose existence Genji would scarcely have been aware had set forth in carriages decked out with the most exhaustive care and taken up posts which seemed to offer a chance of seeing him. There were almost as many things by the wayside as in the procession to attract one's attention.

And there were many ladies whom he had seen in secret and who now sighed more than ever that their station was so out of keeping with his. Prince Shikibu viewed the procession from a stand. Genji had matured and did indeed quite dazzle the eye, and the prince thought with foreboding that some god might have noticed, and was making plans to spirit the young man away. His daughter, Princess Asagao, having over the years found Genji a faithful correspondent, knew how remarkably steady his feelings were. She was aware that attentions moved ladies even when the donor was a most ordinary man; yet she had no wish for further intimacy. As for her women, their sighs of admiration were almost deafening.

No carriages set out from the Sanjō mansion on the day of the festival proper.

Genji presently heard the story of the competing carriages. He was sorry for the Rokujō lady and angry at his wife. It was a sad fact that, so deliberate and fastidious, she lacked ordinary compassion. There was indeed a tart, forbidding quality about her. She refused to see, though it was probably an unconscious refusal, that ladies who were to each other as she was to the Rokujō lady should behave with charity and forbearance. It was under her influence that the men in her service flung themselves so violently about. Genji sometimes felt uncomfortable before the proud dignity of the Rokujō lady, and he could imagine her rage and humiliation now.

He called upon her. The high priestess, her daughter, was still with her, however, and, making reverence for the sacred *sakaki* tree* her excuse, she declined to receive him.

She was right, of course. Yet he muttered to himself: 'Why must it be so? Why cannot the two of them be a little less prickly?'

It was from his Nijō mansion, away from all this trouble, that he set forth to view the festival proper. Going over to Murasaki's rooms in the west wing, he gave Koremitsu instructions for the carriages.

'And are all our little ladies going too?' he asked. He smiled with pleasure at Murasaki, lovely in her festive dress. 'We will watch it together.' He stroked her hair, which seemed more lustrous than ever. 'It hasn't been trimmed in a very long time. I wonder if today would be a good day for it.' He summoned a soothsayer and while the man was investigating told the 'little ladies' to go on ahead. They too were a delight, bright and fresh, their hair all sprucely trimmed and flowing over embroidered trousers.

He would trim Murasaki's hair himself, he said. 'But see how thick it is. The scissors get all tangled up in it. Think how it will be when you grow up. Even ladies with very long hair usually cut it here at the forehead, and you've not a single lock of short hair. A person might even call it untidy.'

The joy was more than a body deserved, said Shōnagon, her nurse.

'May it grow to a thousand fathoms,' said Genji.

> 'Mine it shall be, rich as the grasses beneath
> The fathomless sea, the thousand-fathomed sea.'

Murasaki took out brush and paper and set down her answer:

> 'It may indeed be a thousand fathoms deep.
> How can I know, when it restlessly comes and goes?'

She wrote well, but a pleasant girlishness remained.

Again the streets were lined in solid ranks. Genji's party pulled up near the cavalry grounds, unable to find a place.

'Very difficult,' said Genji. 'Too many of the great ones hereabouts.'

---

*A glossy-leafed tree related to the camellia. Its branches are used in Shinto ritual.

A fan was thrust from beneath the blinds of an elegant ladies' carriage that was filled to overflowing.

'Suppose you pull in here,' said a lady. 'I would be happy to relinquish my place.'

What sort of adventuress might she be? The place was indeed a good one. He had his carriage pulled in.

'How did you find it? I am consumed with envy.'

She wrote her reply on a rib of a tastefully decorated fan:

'Ah, the fickleness! It summoned me
    To a meeting, the heartvine now worn by another.*

'The gods themselves seemed to summon me, though of course I am not admitted to the sacred precincts.'

He recognized the hand: that of old Naishi,† still youthfully resisting the years.

Frowning, he sent back:

'Yes, fickleness, this vine of the day of meeting,
    Available to all the eighty clans.'

It was her turn to reply, this time in much chagrin:

'Vine of meeting indeed! A useless weed,
    A mouthing, its name, of empty promises.'

Many ladies along the way bemoaned the fact that, apparently in feminine company, he did not even raise the blinds of his carriage. Such a stately figure on the day of the lustration – today it should have been his duty to show himself at his ease. The lady with him must surely be a beauty.

A tasteless exchange, thought Genji. A more proper lady would have kept the strictest silence, out of deference to the lady with him.

For the Rokujō lady the pain was unrelieved. She knew that she could expect no lessening of his coldness, and yet to steel her-

*The *aoi*, a vine the heart-shaped leaves of which are a common decorative motif, was a symbol of the Kamo festival. Because of its sound, *aoi* being also 'day of meeting,' it was much used in poetry to signify a rendezvous. This exchange of poems gives the chapter its title, and from the chapter title, in turn, comes the name Aoi, by which Genji's wife has traditionally been known.

†See Chapter 7.

self and go off to Ise with her daughter – she would be lonely, she knew, and people would laugh at her. They would laugh just as heartily if she stayed in the city. Her thoughts were as the fisherman's bob at Ise.* Her very soul seemed to jump wildly about, and at last she fell physically ill.

Genji discounted the possibility of her going to Ise. 'It is natural that you should have little use for a reprobate like myself and think of discarding me. But to stay with me would be to show admirable depths of feeling.'

These remarks did not seem very helpful. Her anger and sorrow increased. A hope of relief from this agony of indecision had sent her to the river of lustration, and there she had been subjected to violence.

At Sanjō, Genji's wife seemed to be in the grip of a malign spirit. It was no time for nocturnal wanderings. Genji paid only an occasional visit to his own Nijō mansion. His marriage had not been happy, but his wife was important to him and now she was carrying his child. He had prayers read in his Sanjō rooms. Several malign spirits were transferred to the medium and identified themselves, but there was one which quite refused to move. Though it did not cause great pain, it refused to leave her for so much as an instant. There was something very sinister about a spirit that eluded the powers of the most skilled exorcists. The Sanjō people went over the list of Genji's ladies one by one. Among them all, it came to be whispered, only the Rokujō lady and the lady at Nijō seemed to have been singled out for special attentions, and no doubt they were jealous. The exorcists were asked about the possibility, but they gave no very informative answers. Of the spirits that did announce themselves, none seemed to feel any deep enmity toward the lady. Their behavior seemed random and purposeless. There was the spirit of her dead nurse, for instance, and there were spirits that had been with the family for generations and had taken advantage of her weakness.

The confusion and worry continued. The lady would sometimes weep in loud wailing sobs, and sometimes be tormented by nausea and shortness of breath.

*Anonymous, *Kokinshū* 509:

> Has my heart become the fisherman's bob at Ise?
> It jumps and bobs and knows not calm or resolve.

The old emperor sent repeated inquiries and ordered religious services. That the lady should be worthy of these august attentions made the possibility of her death seem even more lamentable. Reports that they quite monopolized the attention of court reached the Rokujō mansion, to further embitter its lady. No one can have guessed that the trivial incident of the carriages had so angered a lady whose sense of rivalry had not until then been strong.

Not at all herself, she left her house to her daughter and moved to one where Buddhist rites would not be out of place.* Sorry to hear of the move, Genji bestirred himself to call on her. The neighborhood was a strange one and he was in careful disguise. He explained his negligence in terms likely to make it seem involuntary and to bring her forgiveness, and he told her of Aoi's† illness and the worry it was causing him.

'I have not been so very worried myself, but her parents are beside themselves. It has seemed best to stay with her. It would relieve me enormously if I thought you might take a generous view of it all.' He knew why she was unwell, and pitied her.

They passed a tense night. As she saw him off in the dawn she found that her plans for quitting the city were not as firm as on the day before. Her rival was of the highest rank and there was this important new consideration; no doubt his affections would finally settle on her. She herself would be left in solitude, wondering when he might call. The visit had only made her unhappier. In upon her gloom, in the evening, came a letter.

'Though she had seemed to be improving, she has taken a sudden and drastic turn for the worse. I cannot leave her.'

The usual excuses, she thought. Yet she answered:

'I go down the way of love and dampen my sleeves,
And go yet further, into the muddy fields.

A pity the well is so shallow.'‡

---

*They were out of place in the house of a Shinto priestess.
†Genji's wife's. See note*, page 173.
‡Anonymous, *Kokin Rokujō, Zoku Kokka Taikan* 31863:

A pity the mountain well should be so shallow.
I seek to take water and only wet my sleeves.

The hand was the very best he knew. It was a difficult world, which refused to give satisfaction. Among his ladies there was none who could be dismissed as completely beneath consideration and none to whom he could give his whole love.

Despite the lateness of the hour, he got off an answer: 'You only wet your sleeves – what can this mean? That your feelings are not of the deepest, I should think.

> 'You only dip into the shallow waters,
>   And I quite disappear into the slough?

'Do you think I would answer by letter and not in person if she were merely indisposed?'

The malign spirit was more insistent, and Aoi was in great distress. Unpleasant rumors reached the Rokujō lady, to the effect that it might be her spirit or that of her father, the late minister. Though she had felt sorry enough for herself, she had not wished ill to anyone; and might it be that the soul of one so lost in sad thoughts went wandering off by itself? She had, over the years, known the full range of sorrows, but never before had she felt so utterly miserable. There had been no release from the anger since the other lady had so insulted her, indeed behaved as if she did not exist. More than once she had the same dream: in the beautifully appointed apartments of a lady who seemed to be a rival she would push and shake the lady, and flail at her blindly and savagely. It was too terrible. Sometimes in a daze she would ask herself if her soul had indeed gone wandering off. The world was not given to speaking well of people whose transgressions had been far slighter. She would be notorious. It was common enough for the spirits of the angry dead to linger on in this world. She had thought them hateful, and it was her own lot to set a hateful example while she still lived. She must think no more about the man who had been so cruel to her. But so to think was, after all, to think.*

The high priestess, her daughter, was to have been presented at court the year before, but complications had required postponement. It was finally decided that in the Ninth Month she would go from court to her temporary shrine. The Rokujō house was thus busy preparing for two lustrations, but its lady, lost in thought, seemed strangely indifferent. A most serious state of affairs – the

---

*A poetic allusion, apparently, but none has been satisfactorily identified.

priestess's attendants ordered prayers. There were no really alarming symptoms. She was vaguely unwell, no more. The days passed. Genji sent repeated inquiries, but there was no relief from his worries about another invalid, a more important one.

It was still too early for Aoi to be delivered of her child. Her women were less than fully alert; and then, suddenly, she was seized with labor pains. More priests were put to more strenuous prayers. The malign spirit refused to move. The most eminent of exorcists found this stubbornness extraordinary, and could not think what to do. Then, after renewed efforts at exorcism, more intense than before, it commenced sobbing as if in pain.

'Stop for a moment, please. I want to speak to General Genji.'

It was as they had thought. The women showed Genji to a place at Aoi's curtains. Thinking – for she did seem on the point of death – that Aoi had last words for Genji, her parents withdrew. The effect was grandly solemn as priests read from the Lotus Sutra in hushed voices. Genji drew the curtains back and looked down at his wife. She was heavy with child, and very beautiful. Even a man who was nothing to her would have been saddened to look at her. Long, heavy hair, bound at one side, was set off by white robes, and he thought her lovelier than when she was most carefully dressed and groomed.

He took her hand. 'How awful. How awful for you.' He could say no more.

Usually so haughty and forbidding, she now gazed up at him with languid eyes that were presently filled with tears. How could he fail to be moved? This violent weeping, he thought, would be for her parents, soon to be left behind, and perhaps, at this last leave-taking, for him too.

'You mustn't fret so. It can't be as bad as you think. And even if the worst comes, we will meet again. And your good mother and father: the bond between parents and children lasts through many lives. You must tell yourself that you will see them again.'

'No, no. I was hurting so, I asked them to stop for a while. I had not dreamed that I would come to you like this. It is true: a troubled soul will sometimes go wandering off.' The voice was gentle and affectionate.

'Bind the hem of my robe, to keep it within,
The grieving soul that has wandered through the skies.'*

*Tying the skirt of a robe was a device for keeping an errant spirit at home.

It was not Aoi's voice, nor was the manner hers. Extraordinary – and then he knew that it was the voice of the Rokujō lady. He was aghast. He had dismissed the talk as vulgar and ignorant fabrication, and here before his eyes he had proof that such things did actually happen. He was horrified and repelled.

'You may say so. But I don't know who you are. Identify yourself.'

It was indeed she. 'Aghast' – is there no stronger word? He waved the women back.

Thinking that these calmer tones meant a respite from pain, her mother came with medicine; and even as she drank it down she gave birth to a baby boy. Everyone was delighted, save the spirits that had been transferred to mediums. Chagrined at their failure, they were raising a great stir, and all in all it was a noisy and untidy scene. There was still the afterbirth to worry about. Then, perhaps because of all the prayers, it too was delivered. The grand abbot of Hiei and all the other eminent clerics departed, looking rather pleased with themselves as they mopped their foreheads. Sure that the worst was past after all the anxious days, the women allowed themselves a rest.

The prayers went on as noisily as ever, but the house was now caught up in the happy business of ministering to a pretty baby. It hummed with excitement on each of the festive nights.* Fine and unusual gifts came from the old emperor and from all the princes and high courtiers. Ceremonies honoring a boy baby are always interesting.

The Rokujō lady received the news with mixed feelings. She had heard that her rival was critically ill, and now the crisis had passed. She was not herself. The strangest thing was that her robes were permeated with the scent of the poppy seeds burned at exorcisms. She changed clothes repeatedly and even washed her hair, but the odor persisted. She was overcome with self-loathing. And what would others be thinking? It was a matter she could discuss with no one. She could only suffer in distraught silence.

Somewhat calmer, Genji was still horrified at the unsolicited remarks he had had from the possessive spirit. He really must get off a note to the Rokujō lady. Or should he have a talk with her?

*There were celebrations on the third, fifth, seventh, and ninth nights.

He would find it hard to be civil, and he did not wish to hurt her. In the end he made do with a note.

Aoi's illness had been critical, and the strictest vigil must be continued. Genji had been persuaded to stop his nocturnal wanderings. He still had not really talked to his wife, for she was still far from normal. The child was so beautiful as to arouse forebodings, and preparations were already under way for a most careful and elaborate education. The minister was pleased with everything save the fact that his daughter had still not recovered. But he told himself that he need not worry. A slow convalescence was to be expected after so serious an illness.

Especially around the eyes, the baby bore a strong resemblance to the crown prince, whom Genji suddenly felt an intense longing to see. He could not sit still. He had to be off to court.

'I have been neglecting my duties,' he said to the women,' and am feeling rather guilty. I think today I will venture out. It would be good if I might see her before I go. I am not a stranger, you know.'

'Quite true, sir. You of all people should be allowed near. She is badly emaciated, I fear, but that is scarcely a reason for her to hide herself from you.'

And so a place was set out for him at her bedside. She answered from time to time, but in a very weak voice. Even so little, from a lady who had been given up for dead, was like a dream. He told her of those terrible days. Then he remembered how, as if pulling back from a brink, she had begun talking to him so volubly and so eagerly. A shudder of revulsion passed over him.

'There are many things I would like to say to you, but you still seem very tired.'

He even prepared medicine for her. The women were filled with admiration. When had he learned to be so useful?

She was sadly worn and lay as if on the border of death, pathetic and still lovely. There was not a tangle in her lustrous hair. The thick tresses that poured over her pillows seemed to him quite beyond compare. He gazed down at her, thinking it odd that he should have felt so dissatisfied with her over the years.

'I must see my father, but I am sure I will not be needed long. How nice if we could always be like this. But your mother is with you so much, I have not wanted to seem insistent. You must get back your strength and move back to your own rooms. Your mother pampers you too much. That may be one reason why you are so slow getting well.'

As he withdrew in grand court dress she lay looking after him as she had not been in the habit of doing.

There was to be a conference on promotions and appointments. The minister too set off for court, in procession with all his sons, each of them with a case to plead and determined not to leave his side.

The Sanjō mansion was almost deserted. Aoi was again seized with a strangling shortness of breath; and very soon after a messenger had been sent to court she was dead. Genji and the others left court, scarcely aware of where their feet were taking them. Appointments and promotions no longer concerned them. Since the crisis had come at about midnight there was no possibility of summoning the grand abbot and his suffragans. Everyone had thought that the worst was over, and now of course everyone was stunned, dazed, wandering aimlessly from room to room, hardly knowing a door from a wall. Messengers crowded in with condolences, but the house was in such confusion that there was no one to receive them. The intensity of the grief was almost frightening. Since malign spirits had more than once attacked the lady, her father ordered the body left as it was for two or three days in hopes that she might revive. The signs of death were more and more pronounced, however, and, in great anguish, the family at length accepted the truth. Genji, who had private distress to add to the general grief, thought he knew as well as anyone ever would what unhappiness love can bring. Condolences even from the people most important to him brought no comfort. The old emperor, himself much grieved, sent a personal message; and so for the minister there was new honor, happiness to temper the sorrow. Yet there was no relief from tears.

Every reasonable suggestion was accepted toward reviving the lady, but, the ravages of death being ever more apparent, there was finally no recourse but to see her to Toribe Moor. There were many heartrending scenes along the way. The crowds of mourners and priests invoking the holy name quite overflowed the wide moor. Messages continued to pour in, from the old emperor, of course, and from the empress and crown prince and all the great houses as well.

The minister was desolate. 'Now in my last years to be left

behind by a daughter who should have had so many years before her.' No one could see him without sharing his sorrow.

Grandly the services went on through the night, and as dawn came over the sky the mourners turned back to the city, taking with them only a handful of ashes. Funerals are common enough, but Genji, who had not been present at many, was shaken as never before. Since it was late in the Eighth Month a quarter moon still hung in a sky that would have brought melancholy thoughts in any case; and the figure of his father-in-law, as if groping in pitch darkness, seemed proper to the occasion and at the same time indescribably sad.

A poem came to his lips as he gazed up into the morning sky:

'Might these clouds be the smoke that mounts from her pyre?
They fill my heart with feelings too deep for words.'

Back at Sanjō, he was unable to sleep. He thought over their years together. Why had he so carelessly told himself that she would one day understand? Why had he allowed himself silly flirtations, the smallest of them sure to anger her? He had let her carry her hostility to the grave. The regrets were strong, but useless.

It was as if in a trance that he put on the dull gray mourning robes. Had she outlived him, it occurred to him, hers would have been darker gray.*

'Weeds obey rules. Mine are the shallower hue.
But tears plunge my sleeves into the deepest wells.'

He closed his eyes in prayer, a handsomer man in sorrow than in happiness. He intoned softly: 'Hail, Samantabhadra, in whose serene thoughts all is contained.'† The invocation seemed more powerful than from the mouth of the most reverend priest.

There were tears in his eyes as he took the little boy up in his arms. 'What would we have to remember her by?'‡ he whispered to himself. The sorrow would be worse if he did not have this child.

*A widow wore darker mourning than a widower.
†The source of the invocation is unknown.
‡The nurse of Kanetada's mother, *Gosenshū* 1188:

> What would we have to remember our lady by
> Were it not for this keepsake, this child she left behind?

Princess Omiya took to her bed in such a sad state that services were now commenced for her. The preparations for memorial rites were the sadder for the fact that there had been so little warning. Parents grieve at the loss of the most ill-favored child, and the intensity of the grief in this case was not to be wondered at. The family had no other daughters. It was as if – it was worse than if the jewels upon the silken sleeve had been shattered to bits.*

Genji did not venture forth even to Nijō. He passed his days in tears and in earnest prayer. He did, it is true, send off a few notes. The high priestess of Ise had moved to a temporary shrine in the guards' quarters of the palace. Making the girl's ritual purity her excuse, the Rokujō lady refused to answer. The world had not been kind to him, and now, gloomier than ever, he thought that if he had not had this new bond with the world he would have liked to follow what had for so long been his deepest inclinations and leave it entirely behind. But then he would think of the girl Murasaki at Nijō. He slept alone. Women were on duty nearby, but still he was lonely. Unable to sleep, he would say to himself: 'In autumn, of all the seasons.'† Summoning priests of good voice, he would have them chant the holy name; and the dawn sky would be almost more than he could bear.

In one of those late-autumn dawns when the very sound of the wind seems to sink to one's bones, he arose from a lonely, sleepless bed to see the garden enshrouded in mist. A letter was brought in, on dark blue-gray paper attached to a half-opened bud of chrysanthemum. In the best of taste, he thought. The hand was that of the Rokujō lady.

'Do you know why I have been so negligent?

'I too am in tears, at the thought of her sad, short life.
Moist the sleeves of you whom she left behind.

'These autumn skies make it impossible for me to be silent.'

The hand was more beautiful than ever. He wanted to fling the note away from him, but could not. It seemed to him altogether too disingenuous. Yet he could not bring himself to sever rela-

---

*Apparently a quotation, but the source has not been identified.
†Mibu Tadamine, *Kokinshū* 839:

> Why did he die in autumn, of all the seasons?
> In autumn one grieves for those who yet remain.

tions. Poor woman, she seemed marked for notoriety. No doubt Aoi had been fated to die. But anger rose again. Why had he seen and heard it all so clearly, why had it been paraded before him? Try though he might, he could not put his feelings toward the woman in order. He debated at great length, remembering too that perhaps he should hold his tongue out of respect for the high priestess.

But he finally decided that the last thing he wanted was to seem cold and insensitive. His answer was on soft, quiet purple. 'You for your part will understand, I am sure, the reasons for this inexcusably long silence. You have been much on my mind, but I have thought it best to keep my distance.

'We go, we stay, alike of this world of dew.
We should not let it have such a hold upon us.

'You too should try to shake loose. I shall be brief, for perhaps you will not welcome a letter from a house of mourning.'

Now back at Rokujō, she waited until she was alone to read the letter. Her conscience told her his meaning all too clearly. So he knew. It was too awful. Surely no one had been more cruelly treated by fate than herself. What would the old emperor be thinking? He and her late husband, the crown prince, were brothers by the same mother, and they had been very close. The prince had asked his protection for their daughter, and he had replied that he would look upon the girl as taking the place of her father. He had repeatedly invited the lady and her daughter to go on living in the palace, but she held to a demanding view of the proprieties. And so she had found herself in this childish entanglement, and had succeeded in making a very bad name for herself. She was still not feeling well.

In fact, the name she had made for herself was rather different. She had long been famous for her subtlety and refinement, and when her daughter moved to another temporary shrine, this one to the west of the city, all the details were tasteful and in the latest fashion. Genji was not surprised to hear that the more cultivated of the courtiers were making it their main business to part the dew-drenched grasses before the shrine. She was a lady of almost too good taste. If, wanting no more of love, she were to go with her daughter to Ise, he would, after all, miss her.

The memorial services were over, but Genji remained in

seclusion for seven weeks. Pitying him in the unaccustomed tedium, Tō no Chūjō would come and divert him with the latest talk, serious and trivial; and it seems likely that old Naishi was cause for a good laugh now and then.

'You mustn't make fun of dear old Granny,' said Genji; but he found stories of the old lady unfailingly amusing.

They would go over the list of their little adventures, on the night of a misty autumn moon, just past full, and others; and their talk would come around to the evanescence of things and they would shed a few tears.

On an evening of chilly autumn rains, Tō no Chūjō again came calling. He had changed to lighter mourning and presented a fine, manly figure indeed, enough to put most men to shame. Genji was at the railing of the west veranda, looking out over the frostbitten garden. The wind was high and it was as if his tears sought to compete with the driven rain.

'Is she the rain, is she the clouds? Alas, I cannot say.'*

He sat chin in hand. Were he himself the dead lady, thought Tō no Chūjō, his soul would certainly remain bound to this world. He came up to his friend. Genji, who had not expected callers, quietly smoothed his robes, a finely glossed red singlet under a robe of a deeper gray than Tō no Chūjō's. It was the modest, conservative sort of dress that never seems merely dull.

Tō no Chūjō too looked up at the sky.

'Is she the rain? Where in these stormy skies,
  To which of these brooding clouds may I look to find her?

Neither can I say,' he added, as if to himself.

'It is a time of storms when even the clouds
  To which my lady has risen are blotted away.'

Genji's grief was clearly unfeigned. Very odd, thought Tō no Chūjō. Genji had so often been reproved by his father for not being a better husband, and the attentions of his father-in-law had made him very uncomfortable. There were circumstances, having largely to do with his nearness to Princess Omiya, which kept him from leaving Aoi completely; and so he had continued to wait upon her, making little attempt to hide his dissatisfaction. Tō no

*More than one Chinese source has been averred.

Chūjō had more than once been moved to pity him in this unhappy predicament. And now it seemed that she had after all had a place in his affections, that he had loved and honored her. Tō no Chūjō's own sorrow was more intense for the knowledge. It was as if a light had gone out.

Gentians and wild carnations peeped from the frosty tangles. After Tō no Chūjō had left, Genji sent a small bouquet by the little boy's nurse, Saishō, to Princess Omiya, with this message:

> 'Carnations at the wintry hedge remind me
> Of an autumn which we leave too far behind.

Do you not think them a lovely color?'

Yes, the smiling little 'wild carnation' he now had with him was a treasure.

The princess, less resistant to tears than the autumn leaves to the winds, had to have someone read Genji's note to her.

She sent this answer:

> 'I see them, and my sleeves are drenched afresh,
> The wild carnations at the wasted hedge.'

It was a dull time. He was sure that his cousin Princess Asagao, despite her past coolness, would understand his feelings on such an evening. He had not written in a long time, but their letters had always been irregularly spaced. His note was on azure Chinese paper.

> 'Many a desolate autumn have I known,
> But never have my tears flowed as tonight.

Each year brings rains of autumn.'*

His writing was more beautiful all the time, said her women, and see what pains he had taken. She must not leave the note unanswered.

She agreed. 'I knew how things must be on Mount Ouchi,† but what was I to say?

> 'I knew that the autumn mists had faded away,
> And looked for you in the stormy autumn skies.'

*Probably a poetic allusion.

†The palace.

That was all. It was in a faint hand which seemed to him – his imagination, perhaps – to suggest deep, mysterious things. We do not often find in this world that the actuality is better than the anticipation, but it was Genji's nature to be drawn to retiring women. A woman might be icy cold, he thought, but her affections, once awakened, were likely to be strengthened by the memory of the occasions that had called for reluctant sympathy. The affected, overrefined sort of woman might draw attention to herself, but it had a way of revealing flaws she was herself unaware of. He did not wish to rear his Murasaki after such a model. He had not forgotten to ask himself whether she would be bored and lonely without him, but he thought of her as an orphan he had taken in and did not worry himself greatly about what she might be thinking or doing, or whether she might be resentful of his outside activities.

Ordering a lamp, he summoned several of the worthier women to keep him company. He had for some time had his eye on one Chūnagon, but for the period of mourning had put away amorous thoughts. It seemed most civilized of him.

He addressed them affectionately, though with careful politeness. 'I have felt closer to you through these sad days. If I had not had you with me I would have been lonelier than I can think. We need not brood over what is finished, but I fear that difficult problems lie ahead of us.'

They were in tears. 'It has left us in the blackest darkness,' said one of them, 'and the thought of how things will be when you are gone is almost too much to bear.' She could say no more.

Deeply touched, Genji looked from one to another. 'When I am gone – how can that be? You must think me heartless. Be patient, and you will see that you are wrong. Though of course life is very uncertain.' Tears came to his eyes as he looked into the lamplight. They made him if anything handsomer, thought the women.

Among them was a little girl, an orphan, of whom Aoi had been especially fond. He quite understood why the child should now be sadder than any of the others. 'You must let me take care of you, Ateki.' She broke into a violent sobbing. In her tiny singlet, a very dark gray, and her black cloak and straw-colored trousers, she was a very pretty little thing indeed.

Over and over again he asked the women to be patient. 'Those of you who have not forgotten – you must bear the loneliness and do what you can for the boy. I would find it difficult to come visiting if you were all to run off.'

They had their doubts. His visits, they feared, would be few and far between. Life would indeed be lonely.

Avoiding ostentation, the minister distributed certain of Aoi's belongings to her women, after their several ranks: little baubles and trinkets, and more considerable mementos as well.

Genji could not remain forever in seclusion. He went first to his father's palace. His carriage was brought up, and as his retinue gathered an autumn shower swept past, as if it knew its time, and the wind that summons the leaves blew a great confusion of them to the ground; and for the sorrowing women the sleeves that had barely had time to dry were damp all over again. Genji would go that night from his father's palace to Nijō. Thinking to await him there, his aides and equerries went off one by one. Though this would not of course be his last visit, the gloom was intense.

For the minister and Princess Omiya, all the old sorrow came back. Genji left a note for the princess: 'My father has asked to see me, and I shall call upon him today. When I so much as set foot outside this house, I feel new pangs of grief, and I ask myself how I have survived so long. I should come in person to take my leave, I know, but I fear that I would quite lose control of myself. I must be satisfied with this note.'

Blinded with tears, the princess did not answer.

The minister came immediately. He dabbed at his eyes, and the women were weeping too. There seemed nothing in the least false about Genji's own tears, which gave an added elegance and fineness of feature.

At length controlling himself, the minister said: 'An old man's tears have a way of gushing forth at the smallest provocation, and I am unable to stanch the flow. Sure that I must seem hopelessly senile and incontinent, I have been reluctant to visit your royal father. If the subject arises, perhaps you can explain to him how matters are. It is painful, at the end of your life, to be left behind by a child.' He spoke with great difficulty.

Genji was weeping only less openly. 'We all of course know the way of the world, that we cannot be sure who will go first and who will remain behind, but the shock of the specific instance is all the same hard to bear. I am sure that my father will understand.'

'Well, then, perhaps you should go before it is too dark. There seems to be no letting up of the rain.'

Genji looked around at the rooms he was about to leave. Behind curtains, through open doors, he could see some thirty women in various shades of gray, all weeping piteously.

'I have consoled myself,' said the minister, 'with the thought that you are leaving someone behind in this house whom you cannot abandon, and that you will therefore find occasion to visit in spite of what has happened; but these not very imaginative women are morbid in their insistence that you are leaving your old home for good. It is natural that they should grieve for the passing of the years when they have seen you on such intimate and congenial terms, indeed that they should grieve more than for the loss of their lady. You were never really happy with her, but I was sure that things would one day improve, and asked them to hope for the not perhaps very hopeful. This is a sad evening.'

'You have chosen inadequate grounds for lamenting, sir. I may once have neglected you and your good lady, in the days when I too thought that a not very happy situation would improve. What could persuade me to neglect you now? You will see presently that I am telling you the truth.'

He left. The minister came back into the house. All the furnishings and decorations were as they had been, and yet everything seemed lifeless and empty. At the bed curtains were an inkstone which Genji had left behind and some bits of paper on which he had practiced his calligraphy. Struggling to hold back the tears, the minister looked at them. There were, it seemed, some among the younger women who were smiling through their tears. Genji had copied and thrown away highly charged passages from old poems, Chinese and Japanese, in both formal and cursive scripts. Magnificent writing, thought the minister, looking off into space. It was cruel that Genji should now be a stranger.

'The old pillow, the old bed: with whom shall I share them now?' It was a verse from Po Chü-i.* Below it Genji had written a verse of his own:

> 'Weeping beside the pillow of one who is gone,
> I may not go, so strong the ties, myself.'

*From a Japanized version of 'The Song of Everlasting Sorrow.'

'The flower is white with frost.' It was another phrase from the same poem, and Genji had set down another of his own:

'The dust piles on the now abandoned bed.
How many dew-drenched nights have I slept alone!'

With these jottings were several withered carnations, probably from the day he had sent flowers to Princess Omiya.

The minister took them to her. 'The terrible fact, of course, is that she is gone, but I tell myself that sad stories are far from unheard of in this world. The bond between us held for such a short time that I find myself thinking of the destinies we bring with us into this world. Hers was to stay a short time and to cause great sorrow. I have somehow taken comfort in the thought. But I have missed her more each day, and now the thought that he will be no more than a stranger is almost too much to bear. A day or two without him was too much, and now he has left us for good. How am I to go on?'

He could not control the quaver in his voice. The older of the women had broken into unrestrained sobbing. It was in more ways than one a cold evening.

The younger women were gathered in clusters, talking of things which had somehow moved them. No doubt, they said, Genji was right in seeking to persuade them of the comfort they would find in looking after the boy. What a very fragile little keepsake he was, all the same. Some said they would go home for just a few days and come again, and there were many emotional scenes as they said goodbye.

Genji called upon his father, the old emperor.

'You have lost a great deal of weight,' said the emperor, with a look of deep concern. 'Because you have been fasting, I should imagine.' He pressed food on Genji and otherwise tried to be of service. Genji was much moved by these august ministrations.

He then called upon the empress, to the great excitement of her women.

'There are so many things about it that still make me weep,' she sent out through Omyōbu. 'I can only imagine how sad a time it has been for you.'

'One knows, of course,' he sent back, 'that life is uncertain; but one does not really know until the fact is present and clear. Your several messages have given me strength.' He seemed in great anguish, the sorrow of bereavement compounded by the sorrow he always felt in her presence. His dress, an unpatterned robe and a gray singlet, the ribbons of his cap tied up in mourning, seemed more elegant for its want of color.

He had been neglecting the crown prince. Sending in apologies, he made his departure late in the night.

The Nijō mansion had been cleaned and polished for his return. The whole household assembled to receive him. The higher-ranking ladies had sought to outdo one another in dress and grooming. The sight of them made him think of the sadly dejected ladies at Sanjō. Changing to less doleful clothes, he went to the west wing. The fittings, changed to welcome the autumn, were fresh and bright, and the young women and little girls were all very pretty in autumn dress. Shōnagon had taken care of everything.

Murasaki too was dressed to perfection. 'You have grown,' he said, lifting a low curtain back over its frame.

She looked shyly aside. Her hair and profile seemed in the lamplight even more like those of the lady he so longed for.

He had worried about her, he said, coming nearer. 'I would like to tell you everything, but it is not a very lucky sort of story. Maybe I should rest awhile in the other wing. I won't be long. From now on you will never be rid of me. I am sure you will get very bored with me.'

Shōnagon was pleased but not confident. He had so many well-born ladies, another demanding one was certain to take the place of the one who was gone. She was a dry, unsentimental sort.

Genji returned to his room. Asking Chūjō to massage his legs, he lay down to rest. The next morning he sent off a note for his baby son. He gazed on and on at the answer, from one of the women, and all the old sadness came back.

It was a tedious time. He no longer had any enthusiasm for the careless night wanderings that had once kept him busy. Murasaki was much on his mind. She seemed peerless, the nearest he could imagine to his ideal. Thinking that she was no longer too young for marriage, he had occasionally made amorous overtures; but she had not seemed to understand. They had passed their time in games of Go and *hentsugi*.* She was clever and she had many

---

*Or *hentsuki*. Guessing concealed parts of Chinese characters.

delicate ways of pleasing him in the most trivial diversions. He had not seriously thought of her as a wife. Now he could not restrain himself. It would be a shock, of course.

What had happened? Her women had no way of knowing when the line had been crossed. One morning Genji was up early and Murasaki stayed on and on in bed. It was not at all like her to sleep so late. Might she be unwell? As he left for his own rooms, Genji pushed an inkstone inside her bed curtains.

At length, when no one else was near, she raised herself from her pillow and saw beside it a tightly folded bit of paper. Listlessly she opened it. There was only this verse, in a casual hand:

> 'Many have been the nights we have spent together
> Purposelessly, these coverlets between us.'

She had not dreamed he had anything of the sort on his mind. What a fool she had been, to repose her whole confidence in so gross and unscrupulous a man.

It was almost noon when Genji returned. 'They say you're not feeling well. What can be the trouble? I was hoping for a game of Go.'

She pulled the covers over her head. Her women discreetly withdrew. He came up beside her.

'What a way to behave, what a very unpleasant way to behave. Try to imagine, please, what these women are thinking.'

He drew back the covers. She was bathed in perspiration and the hair at her forehead was matted from weeping.

'Dear me. This does not augur well at all.' He tried in every way he could think of to comfort her, but she seemed genuinely upset and did not offer so much as a word in reply.

'Very well. You will see no more of me. I do have my pride.'

He opened her writing box but found no note inside. Very childish of her – and he had to smile at the childishness. He stayed with her the whole day, and he thought the stubbornness with which she refused to be comforted most charming.

Boar-day sweets* were served in the evening. Since he was still in mourning, no great ceremony attended upon the observance.

---

*Eaten on the first Day of the Boar in the Tenth Month, to insure good health, and perhaps too by way of prayer for a fruitful marriage, the wild boar being a symbol of fertility.

Glancing over the varied and tastefully arranged foods that had been brought in cypress boxes to Murasaki's rooms only, Genji went out to the south veranda and called Koremitsu.

'We will have more of the same tomorrow night,' he said, smiling, 'though not in quite such mountains. This is not the most propitious day.'

Koremitsu had a quick mind. 'Yes, we must be careful to choose lucky days for our beginnings.' And, solemnly and deliberately: 'How many rat-day sweets am I asked to provide?'*

'Oh, I should think one for every three that we have here.'†

Koremitsu went off with an air of having informed himself adequately. A clever and practical young fellow, thought Genji.

Koremitsu had the nuptial sweets prepared at his own house. He told no one what they signified.

Genji felt like a child thief. The role amused him and the affection he now felt for the girl seemed to reduce his earlier affection to the tiniest mote. A man's heart is a very strange amalgam indeed! He now thought that he could not bear to be away from her for a single night.

The sweets he had ordered were delivered stealthily, very late in the night. A man of tact, Koremitsu saw that Shōnagon, an older woman, might make Murasaki uncomfortable, and so he called her daughter.

'Slip this inside her curtains, if you will,' he said, handing her an incense box.‡ 'You must see that it gets to her and to no one else. A solemn celebration. No carelessness permitted.'

She thought it odd. 'Carelessness? Of that quality I have had no experience.'

'The very word demands care. Use it sparingly.'

Young and somewhat puzzled, she did as she was told. It would seem that Genji had explained the significance of the incense box to Murasaki.

*There were no 'rat-day sweets.' The words for 'rat' and 'sleep' being homophonous, and the Day of the Rat following the Day of the Boar, Koremitsu refers obliquely to the nuptial bed.

†This statement was treated by early commentators as one of the 'great *Genji* riddles.' The number three seems to be crucial, since the bridegroom ate three ritual cakes on the third night of a marriage.

‡Probably to disguise the contents.

The women had no warning. When the box emerged from the curtains the next morning, the pieces of the puzzle began to fall into place. Such numbers of dishes – when might they have been assembled? – and stands with festooned legs, bearing sweets of a most especial sort. All in all, a splendid array. How very nice that he had gone to such pains, thought Shōnagon. He had overlooked nothing. She wept tears of pleasure and gratitude.

'But he really could have let us in on the secret,' the women whispered to one another. 'What can the gentleman who brought them have thought?'

When he paid the most fleeting call on his father or put in a brief appearance at court, he would be impossibly restless, overcome with longing for the girl. Even to Genji himself it seemed excessive. He had resentful letters from women with whom he had been friendly. He was sorry, but he did not wish to be separated from his bride for even a night. He had no wish to be with these others and let it seem that he was indisposed.

'I shall hope to see you when this very difficult time has passed.'

Kokiden took note of the fact that her sister Oborozukiyo, the lady of the misty moon, seemed to have fond thoughts of Genji.

'Well, after all,' said her father, the Minister of the Right, 'he has lost the lady most important to him. If what you suggest with such displeasure comes to pass, I for one will not be desolate.'

'She must go to court,' thought Kokiden. 'If she works hard, she can make a life for herself there.'

Genji had reciprocated the fond thoughts and was sorry to hear that she might be going to court; but he no longer had any wish to divide his affections. Life was short, he would settle them upon one lady. He had aroused quite enough resentment in his time.

As for the Rokujō lady, he pitied her, but she would not make a satisfactory wife. And yet, after all, he did not wish a final break. He told himself that if she could put up with him as he had been over the years, they might be of comfort to each other.

No one even knew who Murasaki was. It was as if she were without place or identity. He must inform her father, he told himself. Though avoiding display, he took great pains with her initiation ceremonies. She found this solicitude, though remarkable, very distasteful. She had trusted him, she had quite entwined herself about him. It had been inexcusably careless of her. She now refused to look at him, and his jokes only sent her into a more sullen silence. She was not the old Murasaki. He found the change both sad and interesting.

'My efforts over the years seem to have been wasted. I had hoped that familiarity would bring greater affection, and I was wrong.'

On New Year's Day he visited his father and the crown prince. He went from the palace to the Sanjō mansion. His father-in-law, for whom the New Year had not brought a renewal of spirits, had been talking sadly of things gone by. He did not want this kind and rare visit to be marred by tears, but he was perilously near weeping. Perhaps because he was now a year older, Genji seemed more dignified and mature, and handsomer as well. In Aoi's rooms the unexpected visit reduced her women to tears. The little boy had grown. He sat babbling and laughing happily, the resemblance to the crown prince especially strong around the eyes and mouth. All the old fears came back which his own resemblance to the crown prince had occasioned. Nothing in the rooms had been changed. On a clothes rack, as always, robes were laid out for Genji; but there were none for Aoi.

A note came from Princess Omiya. 'I had become rather better at controlling my tears, but this visit has quite unsettled me. Here are your New Year robes. I have been so blinded with tears these last months that I fear the colors will not please you. Do, today at least, put them on, inadequate though they may be.'

Yet others were brought in. A good deal of care had clearly gone into the weaving and dyeing of the singlets which she wished him to wear today. Not wanting to seem ungrateful, he changed into them. He feared that she would have been very disappointed if he had not come.

'I am here,' he sent back, 'that you may see for yourself whether or not spring has come. I find myself reduced to silence by all the memories.

'Yet once again I put on robes for the new,
And tears are falling for all that went with the old.

I cannot contain them.'

She sent back:

'The New Year brings renewal, I know, and yet
The same old tears still flow from the same old woman.'

The grief was still intense for both of them.

CHAPTER 10

The Sacred Tree

The Rokujō lady was more and more despondent as the time neared for her daughter's departure. Since the death of Aoi, who had caused her such pain, Genji's visits, never frequent, had stopped altogether. They had aroused great excitement among her women and now the change seemed too sudden. Genji must have very specific reasons for having turned against her – there was no explaining his extreme coldness otherwise. She would think no more about him. She would go with her daughter. There were no precedents for a mother's accompanying a high priestess to Ise, but she had as her excuse that her daughter would be helpless without her. The real reason, of course, was that she wanted to flee these painful associations.

In spite of everything, Genji was sorry when he heard of her decision. He now wrote often and almost pleadingly, but she thought a meeting out of the question at this late date. She would risk disappointing him rather than have it all begin again.

She occasionally went from the priestess's temporary shrine to her Rokujō house, but so briefly and in such secrecy that Genji did not hear of the visits. The temporary shrine did not, he thought, invite casual visits. Although she was much on his mind, he let the days and months go by. His father, the old emperor, had begun to suffer from recurrent aches and cramps, and Genji had little time for himself. Yet he did not want the lady to go off to Ise thinking him completely heartless, nor did he wish to have a name at court for insensitivity. He gathered his resolve and set off for the shrine.

It was on about the seventh of the Ninth Month. The lady was under great tension, for their departure was imminent, possibly only a day or two away. He had several times asked for a word with her. He need not go inside, he said, but could wait on the veranda. She was in a torment of uncertainty but at length reached a secret decision: she did not want to seem like a complete recluse and so she would receive him through curtains.

It was over a reed plain of melancholy beauty that he made his way to the shrine. The autumn flowers were gone and insects hummed in the wintry tangles. A wind whistling through the pines brought snatches of music to most wonderful effect, though so distant that he could not tell what was being played. Not wishing to attract attention, he had only ten outrunners, men who had long been in his service, and his guards were in subdued livery. He had dressed with great care. His more perceptive men saw how beautifully the melancholy scene set him off, and he was having regrets that he had not made the journey often. A low wattle fence, scarcely more than a suggestion of an enclosure, surrounded a complex of board-roofed buildings, as rough and insubstantial as temporary shelters.

The shrine gates, of unfinished logs, had a grand and awesome dignity for all their simplicity, and the somewhat forbidding austerity of the place was accentuated by clusters of priests talking among themselves and coughing and clearing their throats as if in warning. It was a scene quite unlike any Genji had seen before. The fire lodge* glowed faintly. It was all in all a lonely, quiet place, and here away from the world a lady already deep in sorrow had passed these weeks and months. Concealing himself outside the north wing, he sent in word of his arrival. The music abruptly stopped and the silence was broken only by a rustling of silken robes.

Though several messages were passed back and forth, the lady herself did not come out.

'You surely know that these expeditions are frowned upon. I find it very curious that I should be required to wait outside the sacred paling. I want to tell you everything, all my sorrows and worries.'

He was right, said the women. It was more than a person could bear, seeing him out there without even a place to sit down. What was she to do? thought the lady. There were all these people about, and her daughter would expect more mature and sober conduct. No, to receive him at this late date would be altogether too undignified. Yet she could not bring herself to send him briskly on his way. She sighed and hesitated and hesitated again, and it was with great excitement that he finally heard her come forward.

'May I at least come up to the veranda?' he asked, starting up the stairs.

*There are several theories about the use of this building. The most likely are that it was for preparing offerings and that it was for lighting torches and flares.

The evening moon burst forth and the figure she saw in its light was handsome beyond describing.

Not wishing to apologize for all the weeks of neglect, he pushed a branch of the sacred tree* in under the blinds.

> 'With heart unchanging as this evergreen,
> This sacred tree, I enter the sacred gate.'

She replied:

> 'You err with your sacred tree and sacred gate.
> No beckoning cedars stand before my house.'†

And he:

> 'Thinking to find you here with the holy maidens,
> I followed the scent of the leaf of the sacred tree.'

Though the scene did not encourage familiarity, he made bold to lean inside the blinds.

He had complacently wasted the days when he could have visited her and perhaps made her happy. He had begun to have misgivings about her, his ardor had cooled, and they had become the near strangers they were now. But she was here before him, and memories flooded back. He thought of what had been and what was to be, and he was weeping like a child.

She did not wish him to see her following his example. He felt even sadder for her as she fought to control herself, and it would seem that even now he urged her to change her plans. Gazing up into a sky even more beautiful now that the moon was setting, he poured forth all his pleas and complaints, and no doubt they were enough to erase the accumulated bitterness. She had resigned herself to what must be, and it was as she had feared. Now that she was with him again she found her resolve wavering.

Groups of young courtiers came up. It was a garden which aroused romantic urges and which a young man was reluctant to leave.

Their feelings for each other, Genji's and the lady's, had run the whole range of sorrows and irritations, and no words could suffice

Sakaki, related to the camellia. See note, page 172.

†Anonymous, *Kokinshū* 982:

> Should you seek my house at the foot of Mount Miwa,
> You need only look for the cedars by the gate.

for all they wanted to say to each other. The dawn sky was as if made for the occasion. Not wanting to go quite yet, Genji took her hand, very gently.

'A dawn farewell is always drenched in dew,
    But sad is the autumn sky as never before.

A cold wind was blowing, and a pine cricket* seemed to recognize the occasion. It was a serenade to which a happy lover would not have been deaf. Perhaps because their feelings were in such tumult, they found that the poems they might have exchanged were eluding them.

At length the lady replied:

'An autumn farewell needs nothing to make it sadder.
    Enough of your songs, O crickets on the moors!'

It would do no good to pour forth all the regrets again. He made his departure, not wanting to be seen in the broadening daylight. His sleeves were made wet along the way with dew and with tears.

The lady, not as strong as she would have wished, was sunk in a sad reverie. The shadowy figure in the moonlight and the perfume he left behind had the younger women in a state only just short of swooning.

'What kind of journey could be important enough, I ask you,' said one of them, choking with tears, 'to make her leave such a man?'

His letter the next day was so warm and tender that again she was tempted to reconsider. But it was too late: a return to the old indecision would accomplish nothing. Genji could be very persuasive even when he did not care a great deal for a woman, and this was no ordinary parting. He sent the finest travel robes and supplies, for the lady and for her women as well. They were no longer enough to move her. It was as if the thought had only now come to her of the ugly name she seemed fated to leave behind.

The high priestess was delighted that a date had finally been set. The novel fact that she was taking her mother with her gave rise to

---

Matsumushi. It seems to have been what is today called 'bell cricket,' suzumushi. See note, page 14.

talk, some sympathetic and some hostile. Happy are they whose place in the world puts them beneath such notice! The great ones of the world live sadly constricted lives.

On the sixteenth there was a lustration at the Katsura River, splendid as never before. Perhaps because the old emperor was so fond of the high priestess, the present emperor appointed a retinue of unusually grand rank and good repute to escort her to Ise. There were many things Genji would have liked to say as the procession left the temporary shrine, but he sent only a note tied with a ritual cord.* 'To her whom it would be blasphemy to address in person,' he wrote on the envelope.

'I would have thought not even the heavenly thunderer strong enough.†

 'If my lady the priestess, surveying her manifold realms,
  Has feelings for those below, let her feel for me.

'I tell myself that it must be, but remain unconvinced.'

There was an answer despite the confusion, in the hand of the priestess's lady of honor:

 'If a lord of the land is watching from above,
  This pretense of sorrow will not have escaped his notice.'

Genji would have liked to be present at the final audience with the emperor, but did not relish the role of rejected suitor. He spent the day in gloomy seclusion. He had to smile, however, at the priestess's rather knowing poem. She was clever for her age, and she interested him. Difficult and unconventional relationships always interested him. He could have done a great deal for her in earlier years and he was sorry now that he had not. But perhaps they would meet again – one never knew in this world.‡

A great many carriages had gathered, for an entourage presided over by ladies of such taste was sure to be worth seeing. It entered

---

*Yū, a cord of paper mulberry used by Shinto priests and priestesses to tie up their sleeves.

†Anonymous, *Kokinshū* 701:

  Is even the rage of the heavenly thunderer,
  Stamping and storming, enough to keep us apart?

‡It was common for a high priestess to be replaced at the beginning of a new reign.

the palace in midafternoon. As the priestess's mother got into her
state palanquin, she thought of her late father, who had had ambitious plans for her and prepared her with the greatest care for the
position that was to be hers; and things could not have gone more
disastrously wrong. Now, after all these years, she came to the
palace again. She had entered the late crown prince's household at
sixteen and at twenty he had left her behind; and now, at thirty,
she saw the palace once more.

> 'The things of the past are always of the past.
>   I would not think of them. Yet sad is my heart.'

The priestess was a charming, delicate girl of fourteen, dressed
by her mother with very great care. She was so compelling a little
figure, indeed, that one wondered if she could be long for this
world. The emperor was near tears as he put the farewell comb in
her hair.

The carriages of their ladies were lined up before the eight
ministries to await their withdrawal from the royal presence. The
sleeves that flowed from beneath the blinds were of many and
marvelous hues, and no doubt there were courtiers who were
making their own silent, regretful farewells.

The procession left the palace in the evening. It was before
Genji's mansion as it turned south from Nijō to Dōin. Unable to
let it pass without a word, Genji sent out a poem attached to a
sacred branch:

> 'You throw me off; but will they not wet your sleeves,
>   The eighty waves of the river Suzuka?'*

It was dark and there was great confusion, and her answer, brief
and to the point, came the next morning from beyond Osaka
Gate.

> 'And who will watch us all the way to Ise,
>   To see if those eighty waves have done their work?'

Her hand had lost none of its elegance, though it was a rather
cold and austere elegance.

---

*In Ise. *Suzu* means 'bell' and the swinging of a bell suggests rejection or shaking off.

The morning was an unusually sad one of heavy mists. Absently he whispered to himself:

'I see her on her way. Do not, O mists,
This autumn close off the Gate of the Hill of Meeting.'*

He spent the day alone, sunk in a sad reverie entirely of his own making, not even visiting Murasaki. And how much sadder must have been the thoughts of the lady on the road!

From the Tenth Month alarm for the old emperor spread through the whole court. The new emperor called to inquire after him. Weak though he was, the old emperor asked over and over again that his son be good to the crown prince. And he spoke too of Genji:

'Look to him for advice in large things and in small, just as you have until now. He is young but quite capable of ordering the most complicated public affairs. There is no office of which he need feel unworthy and no task in all the land that is beyond his powers. I reduced him to common rank so that you might make full use of his services. Do not, I beg of you, ignore my last wishes.'

He made many other moving requests, but it is not a woman's place to report upon them. Indeed I feel rather apologetic for having set down these fragments.

Deeply moved, the emperor assured his father over and over again that all of his wishes would be respected. The old emperor was pleased to see that he had matured into a man of such regal dignity. The interview was necessarily a short one, and the old emperor was if anything sadder than had it not taken place.

The crown prince had wanted to come too, but had been persuaded that unnecessary excitement was to be avoided and had chosen another day. He was a handsome boy, advanced for his years. He had longed to see his father, and now that they were together there were no bounds to his boyish delight. Countless emotions assailed the old emperor as he saw the tears in Fujitsubo's eyes. He had many things to say, but the boy seemed so very young and helpless. Over and over again he told Genji what he must do, and the well-being of the crown prince dominated his

*Osaka means 'hill of meeting.'

remarks. It was late in the night when the crown prince made his departure. With virtually the whole court in attendance, the ceremony was only a little less grand than for the emperor's visit. The old emperor looked sadly after the departing procession. The visit had been too short.

Kokiden too wanted to see him, but she did not want to see Fujitsubo. She hesitated, and then, peacefully, he died. The court was caught quite by surprise. He had, it was true, left the throne, but his influence had remained considerable. The emperor was young and his maternal grandfather, the Minister of the Right, was an impulsive, vindictive sort of man. What would the world be like, asked courtiers high and low, with such a man in control? For Genji and Fujitsubo, the question was even crueler. At the funeral no one thought it odd that Genji should stand out among the old emperor's sons, and somehow people felt sadder for him than for his brothers. The dull mourning robes became him and seemed to make him more deserving of sympathy than the others. Two bereavements in successive years had informed him of the futility of human affairs. He thought once more of leaving the world. Alas, too many bonds still tied him to it.

The old emperor's ladies remained in his palace until the forty-ninth-day services were over. Then they went their several ways. It was the twentieth of the Twelfth Month, and skies which would in any case have seemed to mark the end of things were for Fujitsubo without a ray of sunlight. She was quite aware of Kokiden's feelings and knew that a world at the service of the other lady would be difficult to live in. But her thoughts were less of the future than of the past. Memories of her years with the old emperor never left her. His palace was no longer a home for his ladies, however, and presently all were gone.

Fujitsubo returned to her family palace in Sanjō. Her brother, Prince Hyōbu, came for her. There were flurries of snow, driven by a sharp wind. The old emperor's palace was almost deserted. Genji came to see them off and they talked of old times. The branches of the pine in the garden were brown and weighed down by snow.

The prince's poem was not an especially good one, but it suited the occasion and brought tears to Genji's eyes:

'Withered the pine whose branches gave us shelter?
Now at the end of the year its needles fall.'

The pond was frozen over. Genji's poem was impromptu and not, perhaps, among his best:

'Clear as a mirror, these frozen winter waters.
The figure they once reflected is no more.'

This was Omyōbu's poem:

'At the end of the year the springs are silenced by ice.
And gone are they whom we saw among the rocks.'

There were other poems, but I see no point in setting them down. The procession was as grand as in other years. Perhaps it was only in the imagination that there was something forlorn and dejected about it. Fujitsubo's own Sanjō palace now seemed like a wayside inn. Her thoughts were on the years she had spent away from it.

The New Year came, bringing no renewal. Life was sad and subdued. Sadder than all the others, Genji was in seclusion. During his father's reign, of course, and no less during the years since, the New Year appointments had brought such streams of horses and carriages to his gates that there had been room for no more. Now they were deserted. Only a few listless guards and secretaries occupied the offices. His favorite retainers did come calling, but it was as if they had time on their hands. So, he thought, life was to be.

In the Second Month, Kokiden's sister Oborozukiyo, she of the misty moon, was appointed wardress of the ladies' apartments, replacing a lady who in grief at the old emperor's death had become a nun. The new wardress was amiable and cultivated, and the emperor was very fond of her.

Kokiden now spent most of her time with her own family. When she was at court she occupied the Plum Pavilion. She had turned old Kokiden Pavilion over to Oborozukiyo, who found it a happy change from her rather gloomy and secluded rooms to the north. Indeed it quite swarmed with ladies-in-waiting. Yet she could not forget that strange encounter with Genji, and it was on her initiative that they still kept up a secret correspondence. He was very nervous about it, but excited (for such was his nature) by the challenge which her new position seemed to offer.

Kokiden had bided her time while the old emperor lived, but she was a willful, headstrong woman, and now it seemed that she meant to have her revenge. Genji's life became a series of defeats and annoyances. He was not surprised, and yet, accustomed to being the darling of the court, he found the new chilliness painful and preferred to stay at home. The Minister of the Left, his father-in-law, was also unhappy with the new reign and seldom went to court. Kokiden remembered all too well how he had refused his daughter to the then crown prince and offered her to Genji instead. The two ministers had never been on good terms. The Minister of the Left had had his way while the old emperor lived, and he was of course unhappy now that the Minister of the Right was in control. Genji still visited Sanjō and was more civil and attentive than ever to the women there, and more attentive to the details of his son's education. He went far beyond the call of ordinary duty and courtesy, thought the minister, to whom he was as important as ever. His father's favorite son, he had had little time to himself while his father lived; but it was now that he began neglecting ladies with whom he had been friendly. These flirtations no longer interested him. He was soberer and quieter, altogether a model young man.

The good fortune of the new lady at Nijō was by now well known at court. Her nurse and others of her women attributed it to the prayers of the old nun, her grandmother. Her father now corresponded with her as he wished. He had had high hopes for his daughters by his principal wife, and they were not doing well, to the considerable chagrin and envy, it seems, of the wife. It was a situation made to order for the romancers.

In mourning for her father, the old emperor, the high priestess of Kamo resigned and Princess Asagao took her place. It was not usual for the granddaughter rather than the daughter of an emperor to hold the position, but it would seem that there were no completely suitable candidates for the position. The princess had continued over the years to interest Genji, who now regretted that she should be leaving his world. He still saw Chūjō, her woman, and he still wrote to the princess. Not letting his changed circumstances worry him unnecessarily, he sought to beguile the tedium by sending off notes here and there.

The emperor would have liked to follow his father's last injunctions and look to Genji for support, but he was young and docile and unable to impose his will. His mother and grandfather had their way, and it was not at all to his liking.

For Genji one distasteful incident followed another. Oborozukiyo relieved the gloom by letting him know that she was still fond of him. Though fraught with danger, a meeting was not difficult to arrange. Homage to the Five Lords* was to begin and the emperor would be in retreat. Genji paid his visit, which was like a dream. Chūnagon contrived to admit him to the gallery of the earlier meeting. There were many people about and the fact that he was nearer the veranda than usual was unfortunate. Since women who saw him morning and night never tired of him, how could it be an ordinary meeting for one who had seen so little of him? Oborozukiyo was at her youthful best. It may be that she was not as calm and dignified as she might have been, but her young charms were enough to please him all the same.

It was near dawn. Almost at Genji's elbow a guardsman announced himself in loud, vibrant tones. Another guardsman had apparently slipped in with one of the ladies hereabouts and this one had been dispatched to surprise him. Genji was both amused and annoyed. 'The first hour of the tiger!'† There were calls here and there as guardsmen flushed out intruders.

The lady was sad, and more beautiful for the sadness, as she recited a poem:

'They say that it is dawn, that you grow weary.
I weep, my sorrows wrought by myself alone.'

He answered:

'You tell me that these sorrows must not cease?
My sorrows, my love will neither have an ending.'

He made his stealthy way out. The moon was cold in the faint beginnings of dawn, softened by delicate tracings of mist. Though in rough disguise, he was far too handsome not to attract attention. A guards officer, brother of Lady Shōkyōden,‡ had emerged from

---

*Vidhyārāja, Japanese Myō-ō. Their blessings were invoked on such special occasions as the beginning of a new reign.

†About four in the morning.

‡One of the emperor's concubines, and an ally of the Minister of the Right.

the Wisteria Court and was standing in the shadow of a latticed fence. If Genji failed to notice him, it was unfortunate.

Always when he had been with another lady he would think of the lady who was so cold to him. Though her aloofness was in its way admirable, he could not help resenting it. Visits to court being painful, Fujitsubo had to worry from afar about her son the crown prince. Though she had no one to turn to except Genji, whom she depended on for everything, she was tormented by evidence that his unwelcome affections were unchanged. Even the thought that the old emperor had died without suspecting the truth filled her with terror, which was intensified by the thought that if rumors were to get abroad, the results, quite aside from what they might mean for Fujitsubo herself, would be very unhappy for the crown prince. She even commissioned religious services in hopes of freeing herself from Genji's attentions and she exhausted every device to avoid him. She was appalled, then, when one day he found a way to approach her. He had made his plans carefully and no one in her household was aware of them. The result was for her an unrelieved nightmare.

The words with which he sought to comfort her were so subtle and clever that I am unable to transcribe them, but she was unmoved. After a time she was seized with sharp chest pains. Omyōbu and Ben hurried to her side. Genji was reeling from the grim determination with which she had repulsed him. Everything, past and future, seemed to fall away into darkness. Scarcely aware of what he was doing, he stayed on in her apartments even though day was breaking. Several other women, alerted to the crisis, were now up and about. Omyōbu and Ben bundled a half-conscious Genji into a closet. They were beside themselves as they pushed his clothes in after him. Fujitsubo was now taken with fainting spells. Prince Hyōbu and her chamberlain were sent for. A dazed Genji listened to the excitement from his closet.

Towards evening Fujitsubo began to feel rather more herself again. She had not the smallest suspicion that Genji was still in the house, her women having thought it best to keep the information from her. She came out to her sitting room. Much relieved, Prince Hyōbu departed. The room was almost empty. There were not many women whom she liked to have in her immediate presence and the others kept out of sight. Omyōbu and Ben were wondering how they might contrive to spirit Genji away. He must not be allowed to bring on another attack.

The closet door being open a few inches, he slipped out and made his way between a screen and the wall. He looked with wonder at the lady and tears came to his eyes. Still in some pain, she was gazing out at the garden. Might it be the end? she was asking herself. Her profile was lovely beyond description. The women sought to tempt her with sweets, which were indeed most temptingly laid out on the lid of a decorative box, but she did not look at them. To Genji she was a complete delight as she sat in silence, lost in deeply troubled meditations. Her hair as it cascaded over her shoulders, the lines of her head and face, the glow of her skin, were to Genji irresistibly beautiful. They were very much like each other, she and Murasaki. Memories had dimmed over the years, but now the astonishing resemblance did a little to dispel his gloom. The dignity that quite put one to shame also reminded him of Murasaki. He could hardly think of them as two persons, and yet, perhaps because Fujitsubo had been so much in his thoughts over the years, there did after all seem to be a difference. Fujitsubo's was the calmer and more mature dignity. No longer in control of himself, he slipped inside her curtains and pulled at her sleeve. So distinctive was the fragrance that she recognized him immediately. In sheer terror she sank to the floor.

If she would only look at him! He pulled her towards him. She turned to flee, but her hair became entangled in her cloak as she tried to slip out of it. It seemed to be her fate that everything should go against her!

Deliriously, Genji poured forth all the resentment he had kept to himself; but it only revolted her.

'I am not feeling well. Perhaps on another occasion I will be better able to receive you.'

Yet he talked on. Mixed in with the flow were details which did, after all, seem to move her. This was not of course their first meeting, but she had been determined that there would not be another. Though avoiding explicit rejoinder, she held him off until morning. He could not force himself upon her. In her quiet dignity, she left him feeling very much ashamed of himself.

'If I may see you from time to time and so drive away a little of the gloom, I promise you that I shall do nothing to offend you.'

The most ordinary things have a way of moving people who

are as they were to each other, and this was no ordinary meeting.
It was daylight. Omyōbu and Ben were insistent and Fujitsubo
seemed barely conscious.

'I think I must die,' he said in a final burst of passion. 'I cannot
bear the thought of having you know that I still exist. And if I die
my love for you will be an obstacle on my way to salvation.

'If other days must be as this has been,
    I still shall be weeping two and three lives hence.

And the sin will be yours as well.'
    She sighed.

'Remember that the cause is in yourself
    Of a sin which you say I must bear through lives to come.'

She managed an appearance of resignation which tore at his
heart. It was no good trying her patience further. Half distraught,
he departed. He would only invite another defeat if he tried to see
her again. She must be made to feel sorry for him. He would not
even write to her. He remained shut up at Nijō, seeing neither the
emperor nor the crown prince, his gloom spreading discomfort
through the house and making it almost seem that he had lost the
will to live. 'I am in this world but to see my woes increase.'* He
must leave it behind – but there was the dear girl who so needed
him. He could not abandon her.

Fujitsubo had been left a near invalid by the encounter.
Omyōbu and Ben were saddened at Genji's withdrawal and refusal
to write. Fujitsubo too was disturbed: it would serve the crown
prince badly if Genji were to turn against her, and it would be a
disaster if, having had enough of the world, he were to take holy
orders. A repetition of the recent incident would certainly give
rise to rumors which would make visits to the palace even more
distasteful. She was becoming convinced that she must relinquish
the title that had aroused the implacable hostility of Kokiden. She
remembered the detailed and emphatic instructions which the old
emperor had left behind. Everything was changed, no shadow

*Anonymous, *Kokinshū* 951:

    I am in this world but to see my woes increase.
    I shall go beyond the crags of Yoshino.

remained of the past. She might not suffer quite as cruel a fate as Lady Ch'i,* but she must doubtless look forward to contempt and derision. She resolved to become a nun. But she must see the crown prince again before she did. Quietly, she paid him a visit.

Though Genji had seen to all her needs in much more complicated matters than this one, he pleaded illness and did not accompany her to court. He still made routine inquiries as civility demanded. The women who shared his secret knew that he was very unhappy, and pitied him.

Her little son was even prettier than when she had last seen him. He clung to her, his pleasure in her company so touching that she knew how difficult it would be to carry through her resolve. But this glimpse of court life told her more clearly than ever that it was no place for her, that the things she had known had vanished utterly away. She must always worry about Kokiden, and these visits would be increasingly uncomfortable; and in sum everything caused her pain. She feared for her son's future if she continued to let herself be called empress.

'What will you think of me if I do not see you for a very long time and become very unpleasant to look at?'

He gazed up at her. 'Like Shikibu?' He laughed. 'But why should you ever look like her?'

She wanted to weep. 'Ah, but Shikibu is old and wrinkled. That is not what I had in mind. I meant that my hair would be shorter and I would wear black clothes and look like one of the priests that say prayers at night. And I would see you much less often.'

'I would miss you,' he said solemnly, turning away to hide his tears. The hair that fell over his shoulders was wonderfully lustrous and the glow in his eyes, warmer as he grew up, was almost enough to make one think he had taken Genji's face for a mask. Because his teeth were slightly decayed, his mouth was charmingly dark when he smiled. One almost wished that he had been born a girl. But the resemblance to Genji was for her like the flaw in the gem. All the old fears came back.

Genji too wanted to see the crown prince, but he wanted also to make Fujitsubo aware of her cruelty. He kept to himself at

---

*A concubine of the emperor Kao-tsu who was murdered by his widow.

Nijō. Fearing that his indolence would be talked about and thinking that the autumn leaves would be at their best, he went off to the Ujii Temple, to the north of the city, over which an older brother of his late mother presided. Borrowing the uncle's cell for fasting and meditation, he stayed for several days.

The fields, splashed with autumn color, were enough to make him forget the city. He gathered erudite monks and listened attentively to their discussions of the scriptures. Though he would pass the night in the thoughts of the evanescence of things to which the setting was so conducive, he would still, in the dawn moonlight, remember the lady who was being so cruel to him. There would be a clattering as the priests put new flowers before the images, and the chrysanthemums and the falling leaves of varied tints, though the scene was in no way dramatic, seemed to offer asylum in this life and hope for the life to come. And what a purposeless life was his!

'All who invoke the holy name shall be taken unto Lord Amitābha and none shall be abandoned,'* proclaimed Genji's uncle in grand, lingering tones, and Genji was filled with envy. Why did he not embrace the religious life? He knew (for the workings of his heart were complex) that the chief reason was the girl at Nijō.

He had been away from her now for an unusually long time. She was much on his mind and he wrote frequently. 'I have come here,' he said in one of his letters, 'to see whether I am capable of leaving the world. The serenity I had hoped for eludes me and my loneliness only grows. There are things I have yet to learn. And have you missed me?' It was on heavy Michinoku paper. The hand, though casual, was strong and distinguished.

'In lodgings frail as the dew upon the reeds
 I left you, and the four winds tear at me.'

It brought tears to her eyes. Her answer was a verse on a bit of white paper:

'Weak as the spider's thread upon the reeds,
 The dew-drenched reeds of autumn, I blow with the winds.'

He smiled. Her writing had improved. It had come to resemble

*From what was to become one of the main texts of the Pure Land Sect.

his, though it was gentler and more ladylike. He congratulated himself on having such a perfect subject for his pedagogical endeavors.

The Kamo Shrines were not far away. He got off a letter to Princess Asagao, the high priestess. He sent it through Chūjō, with this message for Chūjō herself: 'A traveler, I feel my heart traveling yet further afield; but your lady will not have taken note of it, I suppose.'

This was his message for the princess herself:

'The gods will not wish me to speak of them, perhaps,
But I think of sacred cords of another autumn.

"Is there no way to make the past the present?" '*

He wrote as if their relations might permit of a certain intimacy. His note was on azure Chinese paper attached most solemnly to a sacred branch from which streamed ritual cords.

Chūjō's answer was courteous and leisurely. 'We live a quiet life here, and I have time for many stray thoughts, among them thoughts of you and my lady.'

There was a note from the princess herself, tied with a ritual cord:

'Another autumn – what can this refer to?
A secret hoard of thoughts of sacred cords?

And in more recent times?'†

The hand was not perhaps the subtlest he had seen, but it showed an admirable mastery of the cursive style, and interested him. His heart leaped (most blasphemously) at the thought of a beauty of feature that would doubtless have outstripped the beauty of her handwriting.

He remembered that just a year had passed since that memorable night at the temporary shrine of the other high priestess, and (blasphemously again) he found himself berating the gods, that the fates of his two cousins should have been so strangely similar. He

---

*Tales of Ise 32:

> Is there no way to make the past the present,
> To wind and unwind it like a ball of yarn?

†Very cryptic. Apparently a poetic allusion.

had had a chance of successfully wooing at least one of the ladies who were the subjects of these improper thoughts, and he had procrastinated; and it was odd that he should now have these regrets. When, occasionally, Princess Asagao answered, her tone was not at all unfriendly, though one might have taxed her with a certain inconsistency.

He read the sixty Tendai fascicles and asked the priests for explanations of difficult passages. Their prayers had brought this wondrous radiance upon their monastery, said even the lowliest of them, and indeed Genji's presence seemed to bring honor to the Blessed One himself. Though he quietly thought over the affairs of the world and was reluctant to return to it, thoughts of the lady at Nijō interfered with his meditations and made it seem useless to stay longer. His gifts were lavish to all the several ranks in the monastery and to the mountain people as well; and so, having exhausted the possibilities of pious works, he made his departure. The woodcutters came down from the hills and knelt by the road to see him off. Still in mourning, his carriage draped in black, he was not easy to pick out, but from the glimpses they had they thought him a fine figure of a man indeed.

Even after this short absence Murasaki was more beautiful and more sedately mature. She seemed to be thinking about the future and what they would be to each other. Perhaps it was because she knew all about his errant ways that she had written of the 'reeds of autumn.' She pleased him more and more and it was with deeper affection than ever that he greeted her.

He had brought back autumn leaves more deeply tinted by the dews than the leaves in his garden. Fearing that people might be remarking upon his neglect of Fujitsubo, he sent a few branches as a routine gift, and with them a message for Omyōbu:

'The news, which I received with some wonder, of your lady's visit to the palace had the effect of making me want to be in retreat for a time. I have rather neglected you, I fear. Having made my plans, I did not think it proper to change them. I must share my harvest with you. A sheaf of autumn leaves admired in solitude is like "damasks worn in the darkness of the night."* Show them to your lady, please, when an occasion presents itself.'

*Ki no Tsurayuki, *Kokinshū* 297:

> Autumn leaves which fall in distant mountains
> Are damasks worn in the darkness of the night.

They were magnificent. Looking more closely, Fujitsubo saw hidden in them a tightly folded bit of paper. She flushed, for her women were watching. The same thing all over again! So much more prudent and careful now, he was still capable of unpleasant surprises. Her women would think it most peculiar. She had one of them put the leaves in a vase out near the veranda.

Genji was her support in private matters and in the far more important matter of the crown prince's well-being. Her clipped, businesslike notes left him filled with bitter admiration at the watchfulness with which she eluded his advances. People would notice if he were suddenly to terminate his services, and so he went to the palace on the day she was to return to her family.

He first called on the emperor, whom he found free from court business and happy to talk about recent and ancient events. He bore a strong resemblance to their father, though he was perhaps handsomer, and there was a gentler, more amiable cast to his features. The two brothers exchanged fond glances from time to time. The emperor had heard, and himself had had reason to suspect, that Genji and Oborozukiyo were still seeing each other. He told himself, however, that the matter would have been worth thinking about if it had only now burst upon the world, but that it was not at all strange or improper that old friends should be interested in each other. He saw no reason to caution Genji. He asked Genji's opinion about certain puzzling Chinese texts, and as the talk naturally turned to little poems they had sent and received he remarked on the departure of the high priestess for Ise. How pretty she had been that day! Genji told of the dawn meeting at the temporary shrine.

It was a beautiful time, late in the month. A quarter moon hung in the sky. One wanted music on nights like this, said the emperor.*

'Her Majesty is leaving the palace this evening,' said Genji, 'and I was thinking of calling on her. Father left such detailed instructions and there is no one to look after her. And then of course there is the crown prince.'

'Yes, Father did worry a great deal about the crown prince. Indeed one of his last requests was that I adopt him as my own son.

---

*Music is forbidden because the court is in mourning.

He is, I assure you, much on my mind, but one must worry about
seeming partial and setting a precedent. He writes remarkably well
for his age, making up for my own awkward scrawl and general
incompetence.'

'He is a clever child, clever beyond his years. But he is very
young.'

As he withdrew, a nephew of Kokiden happened to be on his
way to visit a younger sister. He was on the winning side and saw
no reason to hide his light. He stopped to watch Genji's modest
retinue go by.

'A white rainbow crosses the sun,' he grandly intoned. 'The
crown prince trembles.'*

Genji was startled but let the matter pass. He was aware that
Kokiden's hostility had if anything increased, and her relatives had
their ways of making it known. It was unpleasant, but one was
wise to look the other way.

'It is very late, I fear,' he sent in to Fujitsubo. 'I have been with
the emperor.'

On such nights his father's palace would have been filled with
music. The setting was the same, but there was very little left by
which to remember the old reign.

Omyōbu brought a poem from Fujitsubo:

'Ninefold mists have risen and come between us.
    I am left to imagine the moon beyond the clouds.'

She was so near that he could feel her presence. His bitterness
quite left him and he was in tears as he replied:

'The autumn moon is the autumn moon of old.
    How cruel the mists that will not let me see it.

The poet has told us that mists are as unkind as people, and so I suppose
that I am not the first one so troubled.'†

She had numerous instructions for her son with which to delay
her farewell. He was too young to pay a great deal of attention,

---

*A treasonous prince in the *Shih Chi* was persuaded by a white rainbow passing
through the sun that a plot against Ch'in Shih-huang-ti would not succeed. The
implication seems to be that Genji, an ally of the crown prince, is disloyal to the
emperor.

†The poet has not been identified.

however, and she drew little comfort from this last interview. Though he usually went to bed very early, tonight he seemed determined to stay up for her departure. He longed to go with her, but of course it was impossible.

That objectionable nephew of Kokiden's had made Genji wonder what people really thought of him. Life at court was more and more trying. Days went by and he did not get off a note to Oborozukiyo. The late-autumn skies warned of the approach of winter rains. A note came from her, whatever she may have meant by thus taking the initiative:

> 'Anxious, restless days. A gust of wind,
>   And yet another, bringing no word from you.'

It was a melancholy season. He was touched that she should have ventured to write. Asking the messenger to wait, he selected a particularly fine bit of paper from a supply he kept in a cabinet and then turned to selecting brush and ink. All very suggestive, thought the women. Who might the lady be?

'I had grown thoroughly weary of a one-sided correspondence, and now – "So long it has been that you have been waiting too?"*

> 'Deceive yourself not into thinking them autumn showers,
>   The tears I weep in hopeless longing to see you.

'Let our thoughts of each other drive the dismal rains from our minds.'

One may imagine that she was not the only lady who tried to move him, but his answers to the others were polite and perfunctory.

Fujitsubo was making preparations for a solemn reading of the Lotus Sutra, to follow memorial services on the anniversary of the old emperor's death. There was a heavy snowfall on the anniversary, early in the Eleventh Month.

This poem came from Genji:

'We greet once more the day of the last farewell,
  And when, in what snows, may we hope for a day of meeting?'

*Anonymous, *Gosenshū* 1261:

> Sadly I wait in a silence not of my making.
> So long it has been that you have been waiting too?

It was a sad day for everyone.

This was her reply:

'To live these months without him has been sorrow.
But today seems to bring a return of the days of old.'

The hand was a casual one, and yet – perhaps he wished it so –
he thought it uniquely graceful and dignified. Though he could
not expect from her the bright, modern sort of elegance, he
thought that there were few who could be called her rivals. But
today, with its snow and its memories, he could not think of her.
He lost himself in prayer.

The reading took place toward the middle of the Twelfth
Month. All the details were perfection, the scrolls to be dedicated
on each of the several days, the jade spindles, the mountings of
delicate silk, the brocade covers. No one was surprised, for she was
a lady who on far less important occasions thought no detail too
trivial for her attention. The wreaths and flowers, the cloths for
the gracefully carved lecterns – they could not have been outdone
in paradise itself. The reading on the first day was dedicated to her
father, the late emperor, on the second to her mother, the empress,
and on the third to her husband. The third day brought the reading of the climactic fifth scroll. High courtiers gathered in large
numbers, though aware that the dominant faction at court would
not approve. The reader had been chosen with particular care, and
though the words themselves, about firewood and the like,* were
familiar, they seemed grander and more awesome than ever
before. The princes made offerings and Genji seemed far handsomer than any of his brothers. It may be that I remark too frequently upon the fact, but what am I to do when it strikes me
afresh each time I see him?

On the last day, Fujitsubo offered prayers and vows of her own.
In the course of them she announced her intention of becoming a
nun. The assembly was incredulous. Prince Hyōbu and Genji were
visibly shaken. The prince went into his sister's room even before
the services were over. She made it very clear, however, that her
decision was final. In the quiet at the end of the reading she summoned the grand abbot of Hiei and asked that he administer the

*Among the menial tasks which the Buddha in a former incarnation performed that
he might receive the Lotus Sutra was the cutting of firewood.

vows. As her uncle, the bishop of Yokawa, approached to trim her hair, a stir spread through the hall, and there were unpropitious sounds of weeping. It is strangely sad even when old and unremarkable people leave the world, and how much sadder the sudden departure of a lady so young and beautiful. Her brother was sobbing openly. Saddened and awed by what had just taken place, the assembly dispersed. The old emperor's sons, remembering what Fujitsubo had been to their father, offered words of sympathy as they left. For Genji it was as if darkness had settled over the land. Still in his place, he could think of nothing to say. He struggled to control himself, for an excess of sorrow was certain to arouse curiosity. When Prince Hyōbu had left he went in to speak to Fujitsubo. The turmoil was subsiding and the women, in little clusters, were sniffling and dabbing at their eyes. The light from a cloudless moon flooded in, silver from the snow in the garden.

Genji somehow managed to fight back the tears that welled up at the memories the scene brought back. 'What are you thinking of, taking us so by surprise?'

She replied, as always, through Omyōbu: 'It is something on which I deliberated for a very long time. I did not want to attract attention. It might have weakened my resolve.'

From her retreat came poignant evidence of sorrow. There was a soft rustling of silk as her women moved diffidently about. The wind had risen. The mysterious scent of 'dark incense'* drifted through the blinds, to mingle with the fainter incense from the altars and Genji's own perfume and bring thoughts of the Western Paradise.

A messenger came from the crown prince. At the memory of their last interview her carefully maintained composure quite left her, and she was unable to answer. Genji set down an answer in her place. It was a difficult time, and he was afraid that he did not express himself well.

'My heart is with her in the moonlight above the clouds,
    And yet it stays with you in this darker world.

'I am making excuses. Such resolve leaves me infinitely dissatisfied with myself.'

---

*A mixture of cloves, aloes, and other perfumes.

That was all. There were people about, and he could not even begin to describe his turbulent thoughts.

Fujitsubo sent out a note:

'Though I leave behind a world I cannot endure,
My heart remains with him, still of that world.

And will be muddied by it.'

It would seem to have been largely the work of her sensitive women. Numb with sorrow, Genji made his way out.

Back at Nijō he withdrew to his own rooms, where he spent a sleepless night. In a world that had become in every way distasteful, he too still thought of the crown prince. The old emperor had hoped that at least the boy's mother would stay with him, and now, driven away, she would probably feel constrained to relinquish her title as well. What if Genji were to abandon the boy? All night the question chased itself through his mind.

He turned to the work of fitting out the nunnery and hurried to have everything ready by the end of the year. Omyōbu had followed her lady in taking vows. To her too, most feelingly, he sent gifts and assurances of his continuing esteem.

A complete description of such an event has a way of seeming overdone, and much has no doubt been left out; which is a pity, since many fine poems are sure to be exchanged at such times.

He felt more at liberty now to call on her, and sometimes she would come out and receive him herself. The old passions were not dead, but there was little that could be done to satisfy them now.

The New Year came. The court was busy with festive observances, the emperor's poetry banquet and the carols.* Fujitsubo devoted herself to her beads and prayers and tried to ignore the echoes that reached her. Thoughts of the life to come were her strength. She put aside all the old comforts and sorrows. Leaving her old chapel as it was, she built a new one some distance to the south of the west wing, and there she took up residence, and lost herself in prayer and meditation.

The Naien and the Otokotōka respectively. See note, page 145, and note*, page 137.

Genji came calling and saw little sign that the New Year had brought new life. Her palace was silent and almost deserted. Only her nearest confidantes were still with her, and even they (or perhaps it was his imagination) seemed downcast and subdued. The white horses,* which her entire household came out to see, brought a brief flurry of the old excitement. High courtiers had once gathered in such numbers that there had seemed room for no more, and it was sad though understandable that today they gathered instead at the mansion of the Minister of the Right, across the street. Genji was as kind and attentive as ever, and to the women, shedding unnoticed tears, he seemed worth a thousand of the others.

Looking about him at these melancholy precincts, Genji was at first unable to speak. They had become in every way a nunnery: the blinds and curtains, all a drab gray-green, glimpses of gray and yellow sleeves – melancholy and at the same time quietly, mysteriously beautiful. He looked out into the garden. The ice was melting from the brook and pond, and the willow on the bank, as if it alone were advancing boldly into spring, had already sent out shoots. 'Uncommonly elegant fisherfolk,'† he whispered, himself an uncommonly handsome figure.

> 'Briny my sleeves at the pines of Urashima
> As those of the fisherfolk who take the sea grass.'

Her reply was faint and low, from very near at hand, for the chapel was small and crowded with holy objects:

> 'How strange that waves yet come to Urashima,
> When all the things of old have gone their way.'

He tried not to weep. He would have preferred not to show his tears to nuns who had awakened to the folly of human affairs. He said little more.

*After being reviewed by the emperor, on the seventh day of the First Month, ceremonial horses were reviewed by other members of the royal family.

†Sosei, *Gosenshū* 1094:

> Long have I heard of the pines of Urashima.
> Uncommonly elegant fisherfolk dwell among them.

Ama means both 'fisherman' and 'nun.' The pun is repeated in Genji's poem.

'What a splendid gentleman he has become,' sobbed one of the old women. 'Back in the days when everything was going his way, when the whole world seemed to be his, we used to hope that something would come along to jar him just a little from his smugness. But now look at him, so calm and sober and collected. There is something about him when he does the smallest little thing that tugs at a person's heart. It's all too sad.'

Fujitsubo too thought a great deal about the old days.

The spring promotions were announced, and they brought no happiness to Fujitsubo's household. Promotions that should have come in the natural order of things or because of her position were withheld. It was unreasonable to argue that because she had become a nun she was no longer entitled to the old emoluments; but that was the argument all the same. For her people, the world was a changed place. Though there were times when she still had regrets, not for herself but for those who depended upon her, she turned ever more fervently to her prayers, telling herself that the security of her son was the important thing. Her secret worries sometimes approached real terror. She would pray that by way of recompense for her own sufferings his burden of guilt be lightened, and in the prayer she would find comfort.

Genji understood and sympathized. The spring lists had been no more satisfying for his people than for hers. He remained in seclusion at Nijō.

And it was a difficult time for the Minister of the Left. Everything was changed, private and public. He handed in his resignation, but the emperor, remembering how his father had looked to the minister as one of the men on whom the stability of the reign depended and how just before his death he had asked especially that the minister's services be retained, said that he could not dispense with such estimable services. He declined to accept the resignation, though it was tendered more than once. Finally the minister withdrew to the seclusion of his Sanjō mansion, and the Minister of the Right was more powerful and prosperous every day. With the retirement of a man who should have been a source of strength, the emperor was helpless. People of feeling all through the court joined him in his laments.

Genji's brothers-in-law, the sons of the Minister of the Left, were all personable and popular young men, and life had been pleasant for them. Now they too were in eclipse. On Tō no

Chūjō's rare visits to his wife, the fourth daughter of the Minister of the Right, he was made to feel all too clearly that she was less than delighted with him and that he was not the minister's favorite son-in-law. As if to emphasize the point, he too was omitted from the spring lists. But he was not one to fret over the injustice. Genji's setbacks seemed to him evidence enough that public life was insecure, and he was philosophic about his own career. He and Genji were constant companions in their studies and in such diversions as music. Now and then something of their madcap boyhood rivalry seemed almost to come back.

Genji paid more attention than in other years to the semiannual readings of holy scriptures and commissioned several unscheduled readings as well. He would summon learned professors who did not have much else to do and beguile the tedium of his days composing Chinese poetry and joining in contests of rhyme guessing and the like. He seldom went to court. This indolent life seems to have aroused a certain amount of criticism.

On an evening of quiet summer rain when the boredom was very great, Tō no Chūjō came calling and brought with him several of the better collections of Chinese poetry. Going into his library, Genji opened cases he had not looked into before and chose several unusual and venerable collections. Quietly he sent out invitations to connoisseurs of Chinese poetry at court and in the university. Dividing them into teams of the right and of the left, he set them to a rhyme-guessing contest. The prizes were lavish. As the rhymes became more difficult even the erudite professors were sometimes at a loss, and Genji would dazzle the assembly by coming up with a solution which had eluded them. The meeting of so many talents in one person – it was the wonder of the day, and it told of great merits accumulated in previous lives.

Two days later Tō no Chūjō gave a banquet for the victors. Though it was a quiet, unostentatious affair, the food was beautifully arranged in cypress boxes. There were numerous gifts and there were the usual diversions, Chinese poetry and the like. Here and there below the veranda a solitary rose was coming into bloom, more effective, in a quiet way, than the full bloom of spring or autumn. Several of the guests presently took up instruments and began an impromptu concert. One of Tō no Chūjō's little sons, a boy of eight or nine who had just this year been admitted to the royal presence, sang for them in fine voice and played on the *shō* pipes. A favorite of Genji, who often joined him in a duet, the boy was Tō no Chūjō's second son and a grandson of the Minister of the Right. He was gifted and intelligent and very handsome as well, and great care had gone into his education. As the proceedings grew noisier he sang 'Takasago'* in a high, clear voice. Delighted, Genji took off a singlet and presented it to him. A slight flush from drink made Genji even handsomer than usual. His skin glowed through his light summer robes. The learned guests looked up at him from the lower tables with eyes that had misted over. 'I might have met the first lily of spring' – the boy had come to the end of his song. Tō no Chūjō offered Genji a cup of wine and with it a verse:

> 'I might have met the first lily of spring, he says.
> I look upon a flower no less pleasing.'

Smiling, Genji took the cup:

> 'The plant of which you speak bloomed very briefly.
> It opened at dawn to wilt in the summer rains,

and is not what it used to be.'

Though Tō no Chūjō did not entirely approve of this garrulity, he continued to press wine upon his guest.

There seem to have been numerous other poems; but Tsurayuki has warned that it is in bad taste to compose under the influence of alcohol and that the results are not likely to have much merit,† and so I did not trouble myself to write them down. All the poems, Chinese and Japanese alike, were in praise of Genji. In fine form, he said as if to himself: 'I am the son of King Wen, the brother of King Wu.' It was magnificent. And what might he have meant to add about King Ch'eng?‡ At that point, it seems, he

---

*A congratulatory Saibara, which is little more than a listing of flora.

†The warning is not to be found in Tsurayuki's surviving works.

‡'I am the son of King Wen, the brother of King Wu, and the uncle of King Ch'eng,' says the Duke of Chou in the *Shih Chi*.

thought it better to hold his tongue. Prince Sochi,* who could always be counted upon to enliven these gatherings, was an accomplished musician and a witty and good-humored adversary for Genji.

Oborozukiyo was spending some time with her family. She had had several attacks of malaria and hoped that rest and the services of priests might be beneficial. Everyone was pleased that this treatment did indeed prove effective. It was a rare opportunity. She made certain arrangements with Genji and, though they were complicated, saw him almost every night. She was a bright, cheerful girl, at her youthful best, and a small loss of weight had made her very beautiful indeed. Because her sister, Kokiden, also happened to be at home, Genji was in great apprehension lest his presence be detected. It was his nature to be quickened by danger, however, and with elaborate stealth he continued his visits. Although it would seem that, as the number increased, several women of the house began to suspect what was happening, they were reluctant to play informer to the august lady. The minister had no suspicions.

Then one night toward dawn there came a furious thunderstorm. The minister's sons and Kokiden's women were rushing about in confusion. Several women gathered trembling near Oborozukiyo's bed curtains. Genji was almost as frightened, for other reasons, and unable to escape. Daylight came. He was in a fever, for a crowd of women had by now gathered outside the curtains. The two women who were privy to the secret could think of nothing to do.

The thunder stopped, the rain quieted to showers. The minister went first to Kokiden's wing and then, his approach undetected because of the rain on the roof, to Oborozukiyo's. He marched jauntily up the gallery and lifted a blind.

'How did you come through it all? I was worried about you and meant to look in on you. Have the lieutenant† and Her Majesty's vice-chamberlain been here?'

---

*Both Murasaki's father and one of Genji's brothers, Prince Hotaru, are sometimes called Prince Sochi. This could be either, though it is more probably the latter.
†One of his sons.

A cascade of words poured forth. Despite the precariousness of his situation, Genji could not help smiling at the difference between the two ministers. The man could at least have come inside before he commenced his speech.

Flushed and trembling, Oborozukiyo slipped through the bed curtains. The minister feared that she had had a relapse.

'My, but you do look strange. It's not just malaria, it's some sort of evil spirit, I'm sure of it, a very stubborn one. We should have kept those priests at it.'

He caught sight of a pale magenta sash entwined in her skirts. And something beside the curtain too, a wadded bit of paper on which he could see traces of writing.

'What might *this* be?' he asked in very great surprise. 'Not at all something that I would have expected to find here. Let me have it. Give it to me, now. Let me see what it is.'

The lady glanced over her shoulder and saw the incriminating objects. And now what was she to do? One might have expected a little more tact and forbearance from a man of parts. It was an exceedingly difficult moment, even if she was his own daughter. But he was a headstrong and not very thoughtful man, and all sense of proportion deserted him. Snatching at the paper, he lifted the bed curtains. A gentleman was lying there in dishabille. He hid his face and sought to pull his clothes together. Though dizzy with anger, the minister pulled back from a direct confrontation. He took the bit of paper off to the main hall.

Oborozukiyo was afraid she would faint and wished she might expire on the spot. Genji was of course upset too. He had gone on permitting himself these heedless diversions and now he faced a proper scandal. But the immediate business was to comfort the lady.

It had always been the minister's way to keep nothing to himself, and now the crotchetiness of old age had been added in ample measure to this effusiveness. Why should he hold back? He poured out for Kokiden the full list of his complaints.

'It is Genji's handwriting,' he said, after describing what he had just seen. 'I was careless and I let it all get started several years ago. But Genji is Genji, and I forgave everything and even hoped I might have him as a son-in-law. I was not happy of course that he did not seem to take her very seriously, and sometimes he did things that seemed completely outrageous; but I told myself that these things happen. I was sure that His Majesty would overlook a little blemish or two and take her in, and so I went back to my original plan and sent her off to court. I wasn't happy – who would have been? – that the affair had made him feel a little odd about her and kept her from being one of his favorites. And now I really do think I've been misused. Boys will do this sort of thing, I know, but it's really too much. They say he's still after the high priestess of Kamo and gets off secret letters to her, and something must be going on there too. He is a disgrace to his brother's reign and a disgrace in general, to himself and everyone else too. But I would have expected him to be cleverer about it. One of the brighter and more talented people of our day, everyone says. I simply would not have expected it of him.'

Of an even more choleric nature, Kokiden spoke in even stronger terms. 'My son is emperor, to be sure, but no one has ever taken him seriously. The old Minister of the Left refused to let him have that prize daughter of his and then gave her to a brother who was hardly out of swaddling clothes and wasn't even a prince any more. And my sister: we had thought of letting His Majesty have her, and did anyone say anything at all to Genji when he had everyone laughing at the poor thing? Oh, no – he was to be just everyone's son-in-law, it seemed. Well, we had to make do and found a place for her. I was sorry, of course, but I hoped she might work hard and still make a decent career, and someday teach that awful boy a lesson. And now see what she has done. She has let him get the better of her. I think it very likely indeed that something is going on between him and the high priestess. The sum and substance of it all is that we must be careful. He is waiting very eagerly for the next reign to come.'

The minister was beginning to feel a little sorry for Genji and to regret that he had come to her with his story. 'Well, be that as it may, I mean to speak to no one else of what has happened. You would be wise not to tell His Majesty. I imagine she is presuming on his kindness and is sure he will forgive even this. Tell her to be more careful, and if she isn't, well, I suppose I'll have to take responsibility.'

But it did not seem that he had quieted her anger. 'That awful boy' had come into a house where she and her sister were living side by side. It was a deliberate insult. She was angrier and angrier. It would seem that the time had come for her to lay certain plans.

CHAPTER 11

The Orange Blossoms

Genji's troubles, which he had brought upon himself, were nothing new. There was already gloom enough in his public and private life, and more seemed to be added each day. Yet there were affairs from which he could not withdraw.

Among the old emperor's ladies had been one Reikeiden. She had no children, and after his death her life was sadly straitened. It would seem that only Genji remembered her. A chance encounter at court, for such was his nature, had left him with persistent thoughts of her younger sister. He paid no great attention to her, however, and it would seem that life was as difficult for her as for her sister. Now, in his own despondency, his thoughts turned more fondly to the girl, a victim if ever there was one of evanescence and hostile change. Taking advantage of a rare break in the early-summer rains, he went to call on her.

He had no outrunners and his carriage and livery were unobtrusive. As he crossed the Inner River and left the city he passed a small house with tasteful plantings. Inside someone was playing a lively strain on a Japanese koto accompanied by a thirteen-stringed Chinese koto of good quality. The house being just inside the gate, he leaned from his carriage to survey the scene. The fragrance that came on the breeze from a great laurel tree* made him think of the Kamo festival. It was a pleasant scene. And yes – he had seen it once before, a very long time ago. Would he be remembered? Just then a cuckoo called from a nearby tree, as if to urge him on. He had the carriage turned so that he might alight. Koremitsu, as always, was his messenger.

> 'Back at the fence where once it sang so briefly,
>   The cuckoo is impelled to sing again.'

The women seemed to be near the west veranda of the main building. Having heard the same voices on that earlier occasion, Koremitsu coughed to attract attention and handed in his message.

*Katsura, *Cercidiphyllum japonicum*, more properly a Judas tree.

There seemed to be numbers of young women inside and they at first seemed puzzled to know who the sender might be.

This was the answer:

> 'It seems to be a cuckoo we knew long ago.
> But alas, under rainy skies we cannot be sure.'

Koremitsu saw that the bewilderment was only pretended. 'Very well. The wrong trees, the wrong fence.'* And he went out.

And so the women were left to nurse their regrets. It would not have been proper to pursue the matter, and that was the end of it. Among women of their station in life, he thought first of the Gosechi dancer, a charming girl, daughter of the assistant viceroy of Kyushu.† He went on thinking about whatever woman he encountered. A perverse concomitant was that the women he went on thinking about went on thinking about him.

The house of the lady he had set out to visit was, as he had expected, lonely and quiet. He first went to Reikeiden's apartments and they talked far into the night. The tall trees in the garden were a dark wall in the light of the quarter moon. The scent of orange blossoms drifted in, to call back the past. Though no longer young, Reikeiden was a sensitive, accomplished lady. The old emperor had not, it is true, included her among his particular favorites, but he had found her gentle and sympathetic. Memory following memory, Genji was in tears. There came the call of a cuckoo – might it have been the same one? A pleasant thought, that it had come following him. 'How did it know?'‡ he whispered to himself.

> 'It catches the scent of memory, and favors
> The village where the orange blossoms fall.**

*Apparently a reference to a poem or proverb.

†The episode dangles curiously. The Gosechi dancer appears in the next chapter and is not to be identified with this lady.

‡Anonymous, *Kokin Rokujō, Zoku Kokka Taikan* 33650:

> We talk of things of old and – how did it know? –
> The cuckoo calls in a voice known long ago.

**Anonymous, *Kokinshū* 139:

> At the scent of orange blossoms, awaiting the Fifth Month,
> One thinks of a scented sleeve of long ago.

'I should come to you often, when I am unable to forget those years. You are a very great comfort, and at the same time I feel a new sadness coming over me. People change with the times. There are not many with whom I can exchange memories, and I should imagine that for you there are even fewer.'

He knew how useless it was to complain about the times, but perhaps he found something in her, an awareness and a sensitivity, that set off a chain of responses in himself.

'The orange blossoms at the eaves have brought you
To a dwelling quite forgotten by the world.'

She may not have been one of his father's great loves, but there was no doubt that she was different from the others.

Quietly he went to the west front and looked in on the younger sister. He was a rare visitor and one of unsurpassed good looks, and it would seem that such resentment as had been hers quite faded away. His manner as always gentle and persuasive, it is doubtful that he said anything he did not mean. There were no ordinary, common women among those with whom he had had even fleeting affairs, nor were there any among them in whom he could find no merit; and so it was, perhaps, that an easy, casual relationship often proved durable. There were some who changed their minds and went on to other things, but he saw no point in lamenting what was after all the way of the world. The lady behind that earlier fence would seem to have been among the changeable ones.

CHAPTER 12

Suma

For Genji life had become an unbroken succession of reverses and afflictions. He must consider what to do next. If he went on pretending that nothing was amiss, then even worse things might lie ahead. He thought of the Suma coast. People of worth had once lived there, he was told, but now it was deserted save for the huts of fishermen, and even they were few. The alternative was worse, to go on living this public life, so to speak, with people streaming in and out of his house. Yet he would hate to leave, and affairs at court would continue to be much on his mind if he did leave. This irresolution was making life difficult for his people.

Unsettling thoughts of the past and the future chased one another through his mind. The thought of leaving the city aroused a train of regrets, led by the image of a grieving Murasaki. It was very well to tell himself that somehow, someday, by some route they would come together again. Even when they were separated for a day or two Genji was beside himself with worry and Murasaki's gloom was beyond describing. It was not as if they would be parting for a fixed span of years; and if they had only the possibility of a reunion on some unnamed day with which to comfort themselves, well, life is uncertain, and they might be parting forever. He thought of consulting no one and taking her with him, but the inappropriateness of subjecting such a fragile lady to the rigors of life on that harsh coast, where the only callers would be the wind and the waves, was too obvious. Having her with him would only add to his worries. She guessed his thoughts and was unhappy. She let it be known that she did not want to be left behind, however forbidding the journey and life at the end of it.

Then there was the lady of the orange blossoms. He did not visit her often, it is true, but he was her only support and comfort, and she would have every right to feel lonely and insecure. And there were women who, after the most fleeting affairs with him, went on nursing their various secret sorrows.

Fujitsubo, though always worried about rumors, wrote frequently. It struck him as bitterly ironical that she had not returned his affection earlier, but he told himself that a fate which they had shared from other lives must require that they know the full range of sorrows.

He left the city late in the Third Month. He made no announcement of his departure, which was very inconspicuous, and had only seven or eight trusted retainers with him. He did write to certain people who should know of the event. I have no doubt that there were many fine passages in the letters with which he saddened the lives of his many ladies, but, grief-stricken myself, I did not listen as carefully as I might have.

Two or three days before his departure he visited his father-in-law. It was sad, indeed rather eerie, to see the care he took not to attract notice. His carriage, a humble one covered with cypress basketwork, might have been mistaken for a woman's. The apartments of his late wife wore a lonely, neglected aspect. At the arrival of this wondrous and unexpected guest, the little boy's nurse and all the other women who had not taken positions elsewhere gathered for a last look. Even the shallowest of the younger women were moved to tears at the awareness he brought of transience and mutability. Yūgiri, the little boy, was very pretty indeed, and indefatigably noisy.

'It has been so long. I am touched that he has not forgotten me.' He took the boy on his knee and seemed about to weep.

The minister, his father-in-law, came in. 'I know that you are shut up at home with little to occupy you, and I had been thinking I would like to call on you and have a good talk. I talk on and on when once I let myself get started. But I have told them I am ill and have been staying away from court, and I have even resigned my offices; and I know what they would say if I were to stretch my twisted old legs for my own pleasure. I hardly need to worry about such things any more, of course, but I am still capable of being upset by false accusations. When I see how things are with you, I know all too painfully what a sad day I have come on at the end of too long a life. I would have expected the world to end before this was allowed to happen, and I see not a ray of light in it all.'

'Dear sir, we must accept the disabilities we bring from other lives. Everything that has happened to me is a result of my own inadequacy. I have heard that in other lands as well as our own an offense which does not, like mine, call for dismissal from office is thought to become far graver if the culprit goes on happily living his old life. And when exile is considered, as I believe it is in my case, the offense must have been thought more serious. Though I know I am innocent, I know too what insults I may look forward to if I stay, and so I think that I will forestall them by leaving.'

Brushing away tears, the minister talked of old times, of Genji's father, and all he had said and thought. Genji too was weeping. The little boy scrambled and rolled about the room, now pouncing upon his father and now making demands upon his grandfather.

'I have gone on grieving for my daughter. And then I think what agony all this would have been to her, and am grateful that she lived such a short life and was spared the nightmare. So I try to tell myself, in any event. My chief sorrows and worries are for our little man here. He must grow up among us dotards, and the days and months will go by without the advantage of your company. It used to be that even people who were guilty of serious crimes escaped this sort of punishment; and I suppose we must call it fate, in our land and other lands too, that punishment should come all the same. But one does want to know what the charges are. In your case they quite defy the imagination.'

Tō no Chūjō came in. They drank until very late, and Genji was induced to stay the night. He summoned Aoi's various women. Chūnagon was the one whom he had most admired, albeit in secret. He went on talking to her after everything was quiet, and it would seem to have been because of her that he was prevailed upon to spend the night. Dawn was at hand when he got up to leave. The moon in the first suggestions of daylight was very beautiful. The cherry blossoms were past their prime, and the light through the few that remained flooded the garden silver. Everything faded together into a gentle mist, sadder and more moving than on a night in autumn. He sat for a time leaning against the railing at a corner of the veranda. Chūnagon was waiting at the door as if to see him off.

'I wonder when we will be permitted to meet again.' He paused, choking with tears. 'Never did I dream that this would happen, and I neglected you in the days when it would have been so easy to see you.'

Saishō, Yūgiri's nurse, came with a message from Princess Omiya. 'I would have liked to say goodbye in person, but I have waited in hope that the turmoil of my thoughts might quiet a little. And now I hear that you are leaving, and it is still so early. Everything seems changed, completely wrong. It is a pity that you cannot at least wait until our little sleepyhead is up and about.'

Weeping softly, Genji whispered to himself, not precisely by way of reply:

'There on the shore, the salt burners' fires await me.
Will their smoke be as the smoke over Toribe Moor?

Is this the parting at dawn we are always hearing of? No doubt there are those who know.'

'I have always hated the word "farewell,"' said Saishō, whose grief seemed quite unfeigned. 'And our farewells today are unlike any others.'

'Over and over again,' he sent back to Princess Omiya, 'I have thought of all the things I would have liked to say to you; and I hope you will understand and forgive my muteness. As for our little sleepyhead, I fear that if I were to see him I would wish to stay on even in this hostile city, and so I shall collect myself and be on my way.'

All the women were there to see him go. He looked more elegant and handsome than ever in the light of the setting moon, and his dejection would have reduced tigers and wolves to tears. These were women who had served him since he was very young. It was a sad day for them.

There was a poem from Princess Omiya:

'Farther retreats the day when we bade her goodbye,
For now you depart the skies that received the smoke.'

Sorrow was added to sorrow, and the tears almost seemed to invite further misfortunes.

He returned to Nijō. The women, awake the whole night through, it seemed, were gathered in sad clusters. There was no one in the guardroom. The men closest to him, reconciled to going with him, were making their own personal farewells. As for other court functionaries, there had been ominous hints of sanctions were they to come calling, and so the grounds, once crowded with horses and carriages, were empty and silent. He knew again what a hostile world it had become. There was dust on the tables, cushions had been put away. And what would be the extremes of waste and the neglect when he was gone?

He went to Murasaki's wing of the house. She had been up all night, not even lowering the shutters. Out near the verandas little girls were noisily bestirring themselves. They were so pretty in their night dress – and presently, no doubt, they would find the loneliness too much, and go their various ways. Such thoughts had not before been a part of his life.

He told Murasaki what had kept him at Sanjō. 'And I suppose you are filled with the usual odd suspicions. I have wanted to be with you every moment I am still in the city, but there are things that force me to go out. Life is uncertain enough at best, and I would not want to seem cold and unfeeling.'

'And what should be "odd" now except that you are going away?'

That she should feel these sad events more cruelly than any of the others was not surprising. From her childhood she had been closer to Genji than to her own father, who now bowed to public opinion and had not offered a word of sympathy. His coldness had caused talk among her women. She was beginning to wish that they had kept him in ignorance of her whereabouts.

Someone reported what her stepmother was saying: 'She had a sudden stroke of good luck, and now just as suddenly everything goes wrong. It makes a person shiver. One after another, each in his own way, they all run out on her.'

This was too much. There was nothing more she wished to say to them. Henceforth she would have only Genji.

'If the years go by and I am still an outcast,' he continued, 'I will come for you and bring you to my "cave among the rocks."* But we must not be hasty. A man who is out of favor at court is not permitted the light of the sun and the moon, and it is thought a great crime, I am told, for him to go on being happy. The cause of it all is a great mystery to me, but I must accept it as fate. There seems to be no precedent for sharing exile with a lady, and I am sure that to suggest it would be to invite worse insanity from an insane world.'

He slept until almost noon.

Tō no Chūjō and Genji's brother, Prince Hotaru, came calling.

*Anonymous, *Kokinshū* 952:

> Where shall I go, to what cave among the rocks,
> To be free of tidings of this gloomy world?

Since he was now without rank and office, he changed to informal dress of unfigured silk, more elegant, and even somehow grand, for its simplicity. As he combed his hair he could not help noticing that loss of weight had made him even handsomer.

'I am skin and bones,' he said to Murasaki, who sat gazing at him, tears in her eyes. 'Can I really be as emaciated as this mirror makes me? I am a little sorry for myself.

> 'I now must go into exile. In this mirror
> An image of me will yet remain beside you.'

Huddling against a pillar to hide her tears, she replied as if to herself:

> 'If when we part an image yet remains,
> Then will I find some comfort in my sorrow.'

Yes, she was unique – a new awareness of that fact stabbed at his heart.

Prince Hotaru kept him affectionate company through the day and left in the evening.

It was not hard to imagine the loneliness that brought frequent notes from the house of the falling orange blossoms. Fearing that he would seem unkind if he did not visit the ladies again, he resigned himself to spending yet another night away from home. It was very late before he gathered himself for the effort.

'We are honored that you should consider us worth a visit,' said Lady Reikeiden – and it would be difficult to record the rest of the interview.

They lived precarious lives, completely dependent on Genji. So lonely indeed was their mansion that he could imagine the desolation awaiting it once he himself was gone; and the heavily wooded hill rising dimly beyond the wide pond in misty moonlight made him wonder whether the 'cave among the rocks' at Suma would be such a place.

He went to the younger sister's room, at the west side of the house. She had been in deep despondency, almost certain that he would not find time for a visit. Then, in the soft, sad light of the moon, his robes giving off an indescribable fragrance, he made his way in. She came to the veranda and looked up at the moon. They talked until dawn.

'What a short night it has been. I think how difficult it will be for us to meet again, and I am filled with regrets for the days I wasted. I fear I worried too much about the precedents I might be setting.'

A cock was crowing busily as he talked on about the past. He made a hasty departure, fearful of attracting notice. The setting moon is always sad, and he was prompted to think its situation rather like his own. Catching the deep purple of the lady's robe, the moon itself seemed to be weeping.*

'Narrow these sleeves, now lodging for the moonlight.
Would they might keep a light which I do not tire of.'

Sad himself, Genji sought to comfort her.

'The moon will shine upon this house once more.
Do not look at the clouds which now conceal it.'

'I wish I were really sure it is so, and find the unknown future clouding my heart.'

He left as dawn was coming over the sky.

His affairs were in order. He assigned all the greater and lesser affairs of the Nijō mansion to trusted retainers who had not been swept up in the currents of the times, and he selected others to go with him to Suma. He would take only the simplest essentials for a rustic life, among them a book chest, selected writings of Po Chü-i and other poets, and a seven-stringed Chinese koto. He carefully refrained from anything which in its ostentation might not become a nameless rustic.

Assigning all the women to Murasaki's west wing, he left behind deeds to pastures and manors and the like and made provision for all his various warehouses and storerooms. Confident of Shōnagon's perspicacity, he gave her careful instructions and put stewards at her disposal. He had been somewhat brisk and businesslike toward his own serving women, but they had had security – and now what was to become of them?

'I shall be back, I know, if I live long enough. Do what you can in the west wing, please, those of you who are prepared to wait.'

And so they all began a new life.

*Ise, *Kokinshū* 756:

Catching the drops on my sleeves as I lay in thought,
The moonlight seemed to be shedding tears of its own.

To Yūgiri's nurse and maids and to the lady of the orange blossoms he sent elegant parting gifts and plain, useful everyday provisions as well.

He even wrote to Oborozukiyo. 'I know that I have no right to expect a letter from you; but I am not up to describing the gloom and the bitterness of leaving this life behind.

'Snagged upon the shoals of this river of tears,
 I cannot see you. Deeper waters await me.

'Remembering is the crime to which I cannot plead innocent.'

He wrote nothing more, for there was a danger that his letter would be intercepted.

Though she fought to maintain her composure, there was nothing she could do about the tears that wet her sleeves.

'The foam on the river of tears will disappear
 Short of the shoals of meeting that wait downstream.'

There was something very fine about the hand disordered by grief.

He longed to see her again, but she had too many relatives who wished him ill. Discretion forbade further correspondence.

On the night before his departure he visited his father's grave in the northern hills. Since the moon would be coming up shortly before dawn, he went first to take leave of Fujitsubo. Receiving him in person, she spoke of her worries for the crown prince. It cannot have been, so complicated were matters between them, a less than deeply felt interview. Her dignity and beauty were as always. He would have liked to hint at old resentments; but why, at this late date, invite further unpleasantness, and risk adding to his own agitation?

He only said, and it was reasonable enough: 'I can think of a single offense for which I must undergo this strange, sad punishment, and because of it I tremble before the heavens. Though I would not care in the least if my own unworthy self were to vanish away, I only hope that the crown prince's reign is without unhappy event.'

She knew too well what he meant, and was unable to reply. He was almost too handsome as at last he succumbed to tears.

'I am going to pay my respects at His Majesty's grave. Do you have a message?'

She was silent for a time, seeking to control herself.

'The one whom I served is gone, the other must go.
Farewell to the world was no farewell to its sorrows.'

But for both of them the sorrow was beyond words.
He replied:

'The worst of grief for him should long have passed.
And now I must leave the world where dwells the child.'*

The moon had risen and he set out. He was on horseback and had only five or six attendants, all of them trusted friends. I need scarcely say that it was a far different procession from those of old. Among his men was that guards officer who had been his special attendant at the Kamo lustration services.† The promotion he might have expected had long since passed him by, and now his right of access to the royal presence and his offices had been taken away. Remembering that day as they came in sight of the Lower Kamo Shrine, he dismounted and took Genji's bridle.

'There was heartvine in our caps. I led your horse.
And now at this jeweled fence I berate the gods.'

Yes, the memory must be painful, for the young man had been the most resplendent in Genji's retinue. Dismounting, Genji bowed toward the shrine and said as if by way of farewell:

'I leave this world of gloom. I leave my name
To the offices of the god who rectifies.'‡

The guards officer, an impressionable young man, gazed at him in wonder and admiration.

Coming to the grave, Genji almost thought he could see his father before him. Power and position were nothing once a man was gone. He wept and silently told his story, but there came no answer, no judgement upon it. And all those careful instructions and admonitions had served no purpose at all?

Grasses overgrew the path to the grave, the dew seemed to

*Konoyo means both 'this world' and 'the world of the child.'
†See Chapter 9.
‡Tadasu no kami, 'the god who rectifies,' has his abode in the Lower Kamo Shrine.

gather weight as he made his way through. The moon had gone
behind a cloud and the groves were dark and somehow terrible. It
was as if he might lose his way upon turning back. As he bowed in
farewell, a chill came over him, for he seemed to see his father as
he once had been.

> 'And how does he look upon me? I raise my eyes,
>   And the moon now vanishes behind the clouds.'

Back at Nijō at daybreak, he sent a last message to the crown
prince. Tying it to a cherry branch from which the blossoms had
fallen, he addressed it to Omyōbu, whom Fujitsubo had put in
charge of her son's affairs. 'Today I must leave. I regret more than
anything that I cannot see you again. Imagine my feelings, if you
will, and pass them on to the prince.

> 'When shall I, a ragged, rustic outcast,
>   See again the blossoms of the city?'

She explained everything to the crown prince. He gazed at her
solemnly.

'How shall I answer?' Omyōbu asked.

'I am sad when he is away for a little, and he is going so far, and
how – tell him that, please.'

A sad little answer, thought Omyōbu.*

All the details of that unhappy love came back to her. The two
of them should have led placid, tranquil lives, and she felt as if she
and she alone had been the cause of all the troubles.

'I can think of nothing to say.' It was clear to him that her
answer had indeed been composed with great difficulty. 'I passed
your message on to the prince, and was sadder than ever to see
how sad it made him.

> 'Quickly the blossoms fall. Though spring departs,
>   You will come again, I know, to a city of flowers.'

There was sad talk all through the crown prince's apartments in
the wake of the letter, and there were sounds of weeping. Even
people who scarcely knew him were caught up in the sorrow. As
for people in his regular service, even scullery maids of whose

---

*The crown prince's answer breaks into seven-syllable lines, as if he were trying to
compose a poem.

existence he can hardly have been aware were sad at the thought that they must for a time do without his presence.

So it was all through the court. Deep sorrow prevailed. He had been with his father day and night from his seventh year, and, since nothing he had said to his father had failed to have an effect, almost everyone was in his debt. A cheerful sense of gratitude should have been common in the upper ranks of the court and the ministries, and omnipresent in the lower ranks. It was there, no doubt; but the world had become a place of quick punishments. A pity, people said, silently reproving the great ones whose power was now absolute; but what was to be accomplished by playing the martyr? Not that everyone was satisfied with passive acceptance. If he had not known before, Genji knew now that the human race is not perfect.

He spent a quiet day with Murasaki and late in the night set out in rough travel dress.

'The moon is coming up. Do please come out and see me off. I know that later I will think of any number of things I wanted to say to you. My gloom strikes me as ridiculous when I am away from you for even a day or two.'

He raised the blinds and urged her to come forward. Trying not to weep, she at length obeyed. She was very beautiful in the moonlight. What sort of home would this unkind, inconstant city be for her now? But she was sad enough already, and these thoughts were best kept to himself.

He said with forced lightness:

'At least for this life we might make our vows, we thought.
And so we vowed that nothing would ever part us.

How silly we were!'

This was her answer:

'I would give a life for which I have no regrets
If it might postpone for a little the time of parting.'

They were not empty words, he knew; but he must be off, for he did not want the city to see him in broad daylight.

Her face was with him the whole of the journey. In great sorrow he boarded the boat that would take him to Suma. It was a long spring day and there was a tail wind, and by late afternoon he had reached the strand where he was to live. He had never before been on such a journey, however short. All the sad, exotic things along the way were new to him. The Oe station* was in ruins, with only a grove of pines to show where it had stood.

> 'More remote, I fear, my place of exile
> Than storied ones in lands beyond the seas.'

The surf came in and went out again. 'I envy the waves,' he whispered to himself.† It was a familiar poem, but it seemed new to those who heard him, and sad as never before. Looking back toward the city, he saw that the mountains were enshrouded in mist. It was as though he had indeed come 'three thousand leagues.'‡ The spray from the oars brought thoughts scarcely to be borne.

> 'Mountain mists cut off that ancient village.
> Is the sky I see the sky that shelters it?'

Not far away Yukihira had lived in exile, 'dripping brine from the sea grass.'** Genji's new house was some distance from the coast, in mountains utterly lonely and desolate. The fences and everything within were new and strange. The grass-roofed cottages, the reed-roofed galleries – or so they seemed – were interesting enough in their way. It was a dwelling proper to a remote littoral, and different from any he had known. Having once had a taste for out-of-the-way places, he might have enjoyed this Suma had the occasion been different.

Yoshikiyo had appointed himself a sort of confidential steward. He summoned the overseers of Genji's several manors in the region and assigned them to necessary tasks. Genji watched

---

*In the heart of the present Osaka. It was used by high priestesses on their way to and from Ise.

†*Tales of Ise* 7, attributed to Ariwara Narihira:

> Strong my yearning for what I have left behind.
> I envy the waves that go back whence they came.

‡Po Chü-i, Collected Works, XIII, 'Lines Written on the Winter Solstice, in the Arbutus Hall.'

**Ariwara Yukihira, *Kokinshū* 962:

> If someone should inquire for me, reply:
> 'He idles at Suma, dripping brine from the sea grass.'

admiringly. In very quick order he had a rather charming new house. A deep brook flowed through the garden with a pleasing murmur, new plantings were set out; and when finally he was beginning to feel a little at home he could scarcely believe that it all was real. The governor of the province, an old retainer, discreetly performed numerous services. All in all it was a brighter and livelier place than he had a right to expect, although the fact that there was no one whom he could really talk to kept him from forgetting that it was a house of exile, strange and alien. How was he to get through the months and years ahead?

The rainy season came. His thoughts traveled back to the distant city. There were people whom he longed to see, chief among them the lady at Nijō, whose forlorn figure was still before him. He thought too of the crown prince, and of little Yūgiri, running so happily, that last day, from father to grandfather and back again. He sent off letters to the city. Some of them, especially those to Murasaki and to Fujitsubo, took a great deal of time, for his eyes clouded over repeatedly.

This is what he wrote to Fujitsubo:

'Bring our sleeves on the Suma strand; and yours
In the fisher cots of thatch at Matsushima?*

'My eyes are dark as I think of what is gone and what is to come, and "the waters rise." '†

His letter to Oborozukiyo he sent as always to Chūnagon, as if it were a private matter between the two of them. 'With nothing else to occupy me, I find memories of the past coming back.

'At Suma, unchastened, one longs for the deep-lying sea pine.
And she, the fisher lady burning salt?'

I shall leave the others, among them letters to his father-in-law and Yūgiri's nurse, to the reader's imagination. They reached their several destinations and gave rise to many sad and troubled thoughts.

---

*A very common pun makes Matsushima 'the isle of the one who waits.'
†Anonymous, *Kokin Rokujō, Zoku Kokka Taikan* 33193:

> The sorrow of parting brings such floods of tears
> That the waters of this river must surely rise.

Murasaki had taken to her bed. Her women, doing everything they could think of to comfort her, feared that in her grief and longing she might fall into a fatal decline. Brooding over the familiar things he had left behind, the koto, the perfumed robes, she almost seemed on the point of departing the world. Her women were beside themselves. Shōnagon sent asking that the bishop, her uncle, pray for her. He did so, and to double purpose, that she be relieved of her present sorrows and that she one day be permitted a tranquil life with Genji.

She sent bedding and other supplies to Suma. The robes and trousers of stiff, unfigured white silk brought new pangs of sorrow, for they were unlike anything he had worn before. She kept always with her the mirror to which he had addressed his farewell poem, though it was not acquitting itself of the duty he had assigned to it. The door through which he had come and gone, the cypress pillar at his favorite seat – everything brought sad memories. So it is even for people hardened and seasoned by trials, and how much more for her, to whom he had been father and mother!' 'Grasses of forgetfulness'* might have sprung up had he quite vanished from the earth; but he was at Suma, not so very far away, she had heard. She could not know when he would return.

For Fujitsubo, sorrow was added to uncertainty about her son. And how, at the thought of the fate that had joined them, could her feelings for Genji be of a bland and ordinary kind? Fearful of gossips, she had coldly turned away each small show of affection, she had become more and more cautious and secretive, and she had given him little sign that she sensed the depth of his affection. He had been uncommonly careful himself. Gossips are cruelly attentive people (it was a fact she knew too well), but they seemed to have caught no suspicion of the affair. He had kept himself under tight control and preserved the most careful appearances. How then could she not, in this extremity, have fond thoughts for him?

Her reply was more affectionate than usual.

> 'The nun of Matsushima burns the brine
>   And fuels the fires with the logs of her lamenting,
>
> now more than ever.'

Wasuregusa, day lilies.

Enclosed with Chūnagon's letter was a brief reply from Oboro-zukiyo:

'The fisherwife burns salt and hides her fires
And strangles, for the smoke has no escape.

'I shall not write of things which at this late date need no saying.'

Chūnagon wrote in detail of her lady's sorrows. There were tears in his eyes as he read her letter.

And Murasaki's reply was of course deeply moving. There was this poem:

'Taking brine on that strand, let him compare
His dripping sleeves with these night sleeves of mine.'

The robes that came with it were beautifully dyed and tailored. She did everything so well. At Suma there were no silly and frivolous distractions, and it seemed a pity that they could not enjoy the quiet life together. Thoughts of her, day and night, became next to unbearable. Should he send for her in secret? But no: his task in this gloomy situation must be to make amends for past misdoings. He began a fast and spent his days in prayer and meditation.

There were also messages about his little boy, Yūgiri. They of course filled him with longing; but he would see the boy again one day, and in the meantime he was in good hands. Yet a father must, however he tries, 'wander lost in thoughts upon his child.'*

In the confusion I had forgotten: he had sent off a message to the Rokujō lady, and she on her own initiative had sent a messenger to seek out his place of exile. Her letter was replete with statements of the deepest affection. The style and the calligraphy, superior to those of anyone else he knew, showed unique breeding and cultivation.

'Having been told of the unthinkable place in which you find yourself, I feel as if I were wandering in an endless nightmare. I should imagine that you will be returning to the city before long, but it will be a very long time before I, so lost in sin, will be permitted to see you.

'Imagine, at Suma of the dripping brine,
The woman of Ise, gathering briny sea grass.

See note, page 13.

And what is to become of one, in a world where everything conspires to bring new sorrow?' It was a long letter.

> 'The tide recedes along the coast of Ise.
> No hope, no promise in the empty shells.'

Laying down her brush as emotion overcame her and then beginning again, she finally sent off some four or five sheets of white Chinese paper. The gradations of ink were marvelous. He had been fond of her, and it had been wrong to make so much of that one incident. She had turned against him and presently left him. It all seemed such a waste. The letter itself and the occasion for it so moved him that he even felt a certain affection for the messenger, an intelligent young man in her daughter's service. Detaining him for several days, he heard about life at Ise. The house being rather small, the messenger was able to observe Genji at close range. He was moved to tears of admiration by what he saw.

The reader may be left to imagine Genji's reply. He said among other things: 'Had I known I was destined to leave the city, it would have been better, I tell myself in the tedium and loneliness here, to go off with you to Ise.

> 'With the lady of Ise I might have ridden small boats
> That row the waves, and avoided dark sea tangles.*

> 'How long, dripping brine on driftwood logs,
> On logs of lament, must I gaze at this Suma coast?

'I cannot know when I will see you again.'

But at least his letters brought the comfort of knowing that he was well.

There came letters, sad and yet comforting, from the lady of the orange blossoms and her sister.

> 'Ferns of remembrance weigh our eaves ever more,
> And heavily falls the dew upon our sleeves.'

---

*"Men of Ise,' a 'vulgar song' (*fūzokuuta*):

> Oh, the men of Ise are strange ones.
> How so? How are they strange?
> They ride small boats that row the waves,
> That row the waves, they do.

There was no one, he feared, whom they might now ask to clear away the rank growth. Hearing that the long rains had damaged their garden walls, he sent off orders to the city that people from nearby manors see to repairs.

Oborozukiyo had delighted the scandalmongers, and she was now in very deep gloom. Her father, the minister, for she was his favorite daughter, sought to intercede on her behalf with the emperor and Kokiden. The emperor was moved to forgive her. She had been severely punished, it was true, for her grave offense, but not as severely as if she had been one of the companions of the royal bedchamber. In the Seventh Month she was permitted to return to court. She continued to long for Genji. Much of the emperor's old love remained, and he chose to ignore criticism and keep her near him, now berating her and now making impassioned vows. He was a handsome man and he groomed himself well, and it was something of an affront that old memories should be so much with her.

'Things do not seem right now that he is gone,' he said one evening when they were at music together. 'I am sure that there are many who feel the loss even more strongly than I do. I cannot put away the fear that I have gone against Father's last wishes and that it is a dereliction for which I must one day suffer.' There were tears in his eyes and she too was weeping. 'I have awakened to the stupidity of the world and I do not feel that I wish to remain in it much longer. And how would you feel if I were to die? I hate to think that you would grieve less for me gone forever than for him gone so briefly such a short distance away. The poet who said that we love while we live did not know a great deal about love.'* Tears were streaming from Oborozukiyo's eyes. 'And whom might you be weeping for? It is sad that we have no children. I would like to follow Father's instructions and adopt the crown prince, but people will raise innumerable objections. It all seems very sad.'

There were some whose ideas of government did not accord with his own, but he was too young to impose his will. He passed his days in helpless anger and sorrow.

At Suma, melancholy autumn winds were blowing. Genji's house was some distance from the sea, but at night the wind that

---

*The poet has not been satisfactorily identified.

blew over the barriers, now as in Yukihira's day, seemed to bring the surf to his bedside. Autumn was hushed and lonely at a place of exile. He had few companions. One night when they were all asleep he raised his head from his pillow and listened to the roar of the wind and of the waves, as if at his ear. Though he was unaware that he wept, his tears were enough to set his pillow afloat.* He plucked a few notes on his koto, but the sound only made him sadder.

'The waves on the strand, like moans of helpless longing.
The winds – like messengers from those who grieve?'

He had awakened the others. They sat up, and one by one they were in tears.

This would not do. Because of him they had been swept into exile, leaving families from whom they had never before been parted. It must be very difficult for them, and his own gloom could scarcely be making things easier. So he set about cheering them. During the day he would invent games and make jokes, and set down this and that poem on multicolored patchwork, and paint pictures on fine specimens of figured Chinese silk. Some of his larger paintings were masterpieces. He had long ago been told of this Suma coast and these hills and had formed a picture of them in his mind, and he found now that his imagination had fallen short of the actuality. What a pity, said his men, that they could not summon Tsunenori and Chieda† and other famous painters of the day to add colors to Genji's monochromes. This resolute cheerfulness had the proper effect. His men, four or five of whom were always with him, would not have dreamed of leaving him.

There was a profusion of flowers in the garden. Genji came out, when the evening colors were at their best, to a gallery from which he had a good view of the coast. His men felt chills of apprehension as they watched him, for the loneliness of the setting made him seem like a visitor from another world. In a dark robe tied loosely over singlets of figured white and aster-colored trousers, he announced himself as 'a disciple of the Buddha' and

*This extravagant figure of speech is to be found in *Kokin Rokujō, Zoku Kokka Tai-kan* 34087.

†Tsunenori seems to have been active some three quarters of a century before; so too, presumably, was Chieda.

slowly intoned a sutra, and his men thought that they had never heard a finer voice. From offshore came the voices of fishermen raised in song. The barely visible boats were like little seafowl on an utterly lonely sea, and as he brushed away a tear induced by the splashing of oars and the calls of wild geese overhead, the white of his hand against the jet black of his rosary was enough to bring comfort to men who had left their families behind.

> 'Might they be companions of those I long for?
> Their cries ring sadly through the sky of their journey.'

This was Yoshikiyo's reply:

> 'I know not why they bring these thoughts of old,
> These wandering geese. They were not then my comrades.'

And Koremitsu's:

> 'No colleagues of mine, these geese beyond the clouds.
> They chose to leave their homes, and I did not.'

And that of the guards officer who had cut such a proud figure on the day of the Kamo lustration:

> 'Sad are their cries as they wing their way from home.
> They still find solace, for they still have comrades.

It is cruel to lose one's comrades.'

His father had been posted to Hitachi, but he himself had come with Genji. He contrived, for all that must have been on his mind, to seem cheerful.

A radiant moon had come out. They were reminded that it was the harvest full moon. Genji could not take his eyes from it. On other such nights there had been concerts at court, and perhaps they of whom he was thinking would be gazing at this same moon and thinking of him.

'My thoughts are of you, old friend,' he sang, 'two thousand leagues away.'* His men were in tears.

His longing was intense at the memory of Fujitsubo's farewell poem, and as other memories came back, one after another, he had

---

*Po Chü-i, Collected Works, XIV, 'On the Evening of the Full Moon of the Eighth Month.'

to turn away to hide his tears. It was very late, said his men, but still he did not come inside.

'So long as I look upon it I find comfort,
The moon which comes again to the distant city.'

He thought of the emperor and how much he had resembled their father, that last night when they had talked so fondly of old times. 'I still have with me the robe which my lord gave me,'* he whispered, going inside. He did in fact have a robe that was a gift from the emperor, and he kept it always beside him.

'Not bitter thoughts alone does this singlet bring.
Its sleeves are damp with tears of affection too.'

The assistant viceroy of Kyushu was returning to the capital. He had a large family and was especially well provided with daughters, and since progress by land would have been difficult he had sent his wife and the daughters by boat. They proceeded by easy stages, putting in here and there along the coast. The scenery at Suma was especially pleasing, and the news that Genji was in residence produced blushes and sighs far out at sea. The Gosechi dancer† would have liked to cut the tow rope and drift ashore. The sound of a koto came faint from the distance, the sadness of it joined to a sad setting and sad memories. The more sensitive members of the party were in tears.

The assistant viceroy sent a message. 'I had hoped to call on you immediately upon returning to the city from my distant post, and when, to my surprise, I found myself passing your house, I was filled with the most intense feelings of sorrow and regret. Various acquaintances who might have been expected to come from the city have done so, and our party has become so numerous that it would be out of the question to call on you. I shall hope to do so soon.'

His son, the governor of Chikuzen, brought the message. Genji had taken notice of the youth and obtained an appointment for him in the imperial secretariat. He was sad to see his patron in such straits, but people were watching and had a way of talking, and he stayed only briefly.

*Sugawara Michizane, 'The Tenth of the Ninth Month,' in *Last Poems* (*Kanke Kōsō*).
†See Chapter 11.

'It was kind of you to come,' said Genji. 'I do not often see old friends these days.'

His reply to the assistant viceroy was in a similar vein. Everyone in the Kyushu party and in the party newly arrived from the city as well was deeply moved by the governor's description of what he had seen. The tears of sympathy almost seemed to invite worse misfortunes.

The Gosechi dancer contrived to send him a note.

'Now taut, now slack, like my unruly heart,
    The tow rope is suddenly still at the sound of a koto.

'Scolding will not improve me.'*

He smiled, so handsome a smile that his men felt rather inadequate.

'Why, if indeed your heart is like the tow rope,
    Unheeding must you pass this strand of Suma?

'I had not expected to leave you for these wilds.'†

There once was a man who, passing Akashi on his way into exile, brought pleasure into an innkeeper's life with an impromptu Chinese poem.‡ For the Gosechi dancer the pleasure was such that she would have liked to make Suma her home.

As time passed, the people back in the city, and even the emperor himself, found that Genji was more and more in their thoughts. The crown prince was the saddest of all. His nurse and Omyōbu would find him weeping in a corner and search helplessly for ways to comfort him. Once so fearful of rumors and their possible effect on this child of hers and Genji's, Fujitsubo now grieved that Genji must be away.

In the early days of his exile he corresponded with his brothers and with important friends at court. Some of his Chinese poems were widely praised.

*Anonymous, *Kokinshū* 508:

> My heart is like a ship upon the seas.
> I am easily moved. Scolding will not improve me.

†Ono no Takamura, *Kokinshū* 961:

> I had not expected to leave you for these wilds.
> A fisherman's net is mine, an angler's line.

‡The exile was Sugawara Michizane. The incident is recorded in the *Okagami*.

Kokiden flew into a rage. 'A man out of favor with His Majesty is expected to have trouble feeding himself. And here he is living in a fine stylish house and saying awful things about all of us. No doubt the grovelers around him are assuring him that a deer is a horse.*

And so writing to Genji came to be rather too much to ask of people, and letters stopped coming.

The months went by, and Murasaki was never really happy. All the women from the other wings of the house were now in her service. They had been of the view that she was beneath their notice, but as they came to observe her gentleness, her magnanimity in household matters, her thoughtfulness, they changed their minds, and not one of them departed her service. Among them were women of good family. A glimpse of her was enough to make them admit that she deserved Genji's altogether remarkable affection.

And as time went by at Suma, Genji began to feel that he could bear to be away from her no longer. But he dismissed the thought of sending for her: this cruel punishment was for himself alone. He was seeing a little of plebeian life, and he thought it very odd and, he must say, rather dirty. The smoke near at hand would, he supposed, be the smoke of the salt burners' fires. In fact, someone was trying to light wet kindling just behind the house.

'Over and over the rural ones light fires.
Not so unflagging the urban ones with their visits.'

It was winter, and the snowy skies were wild. He beguiled the tedium with music, playing the koto himself and setting Koremitsu to the flute, with Yoshikiyo to sing for them. When he lost himself in a particularly moving strain the others would fall silent, tears in their eyes.

He thought of the lady the Chinese emperor sent off to the Huns.† How must the emperor have felt, how would Genji

---

*It is recorded in the *Shih Chi* chronicle of the reign of Ch'in Shih-huang-ti that a eunuch planning rebellion showed the high courtiers a deer and required them to call it a horse, and so assured himself that they feared him.

†Wang Chao-chün was dispatched to the Huns from the harem of the Han emperor Yüan-ti because she had failed to bribe the artists who did portraits of court ladies, and the emperor therefore thought her ill favored.

himself feel, in so disposing of a beautiful lady? He shuddered, as if some such task might be approaching, 'at the end of a frosty night's dream.'*

A bright moon flooded in, lighting the shallow-eaved cottage to the farthest corners. He was able to imitate the poet's feat of looking up at the night sky without going to the veranda.† There was a weird sadness in the setting moon. 'The moon goes always to the west,'‡ he whispered.

'All aimless is my journey through the clouds.
    It shames me that the unswerving moon should see me.'

He recited it silently to himself. Sleepless as always, he heard the sad calls of the plovers in the dawn and (the others were not yet awake) repeated several times to himself:

'Cries of plovers in the dawn bring comfort
    To one who awakens in a lonely bed.'

His practice of going through his prayers and ablutions in the deep of night seemed strange and wonderful to his men. Far from being tempted to leave him, they did not return even for brief visits to their families.

The Akashi coast was a very short distance away. Yoshikiyo remembered the daughter of the former governor, now a monk, and wrote to her. She did not answer.

'I would like to see you for a few moments sometime at your convenience,' came a note from her father. 'There is something I want to ask you.'

Yoshikiyo was not encouraged. He would look very silly if he went to Akashi only to be turned away. He did not go.

The former governor was an extremely proud and intractable man. The incumbent governor was all-powerful in the province, but the eccentric old man had no wish to marry his daughter to such an upstart. He learned of Genji's presence at Suma.

'I hear that the shining Genji is out of favor,' he said to his wife,

---

*From a Chinese poem about Miss Wang in the *Wakan Rōeishū*, by Oe no Asatsuna.
†In another Chinese poem in the *Wakan Rōeishū*, Miyoshi Kiyoyuki so describes a view of the night sky from within a ruined palace.
‡Sugawara Michizane, 'To the Moon,' in *Last Poems*.

'and that he has come to Suma. What a rare stroke of luck – the chance we have been waiting for. We must offer our girl.'

'Completely out of the question. People from the city tell me that he has any number of fine ladies of his own and that he has reached out for one of the emperor's. That is why the scandal. What interest can he possibly take in a country lump like her?'

'You don't understand the first thing about it. My own views couldn't be more different. We must make our plans. We must watch for a chance to bring him here.' His mind was quite made up, and he had the look of someone whose plans were not easily changed. The finery which he had lavished upon house and daughter quite dazzled the eye.

'He may be ever so grand a grand gentleman,' persisted the mother, 'but it hardly seems the right and sensible thing to choose of all people a man who has been sent into exile for a serious crime. It might just possibly be different if he were likely to look at her – but no. You must be joking.'

'A serious crime! Why in China too exactly this sort of thing happens to every single person who has remarkable talents and stands out from the crowd. And who do you think he is? His late mother was the daughter of my uncle, the Lord Inspector. She had talent and made a name for herself, and when there wasn't enough of the royal love to go around, the others were jealous, and finally they killed her. But she left behind a son who was a royal joy and comfort. Ladies should have pride and high ambitions. I may be a bumpkin myself, but I doubt that he will think her entirely beneath contempt.'

Though the girl was no great beauty, she was intelligent and sensitive and had a gentle grace of which someone of far higher rank would have been proud. She was reconciled to her sad lot. No one among the great persons of the land was likely to think her worth a glance. The prospect of marrying someone nearer her station in life revolted her. If she was left behind by those on whom she depended, she would become a nun, or perhaps throw herself into the sea.

Her father had done everything for her. He sent her twice a year to the Sumiyoshi Shrine, hoping that the god might be persuaded to notice her.

The New Year came to Suma, the days were longer, and time went by slowly. The sapling cherry Genji had planted the year before sent out a scattering of blossoms, the air was soft and warm, and memories flooded back, bringing him often to tears. He thought longingly of the ladies for whom he had wept when, toward the end of the Second Month the year before, he had prepared to depart the city. The cherries would now be in bloom before the Grand Hall. He thought of that memorable cherry-blossom festival, and his father, and the extraordinarily handsome figure his brother, now the emperor, had presented, and he remembered how his brother had favored him by reciting his Chinese poem.*

A Japanese poem formed in his mind:

> 'Fond thoughts I have of the noble ones on high,
> And the day of the flowered caps has come again.'

Tō no Chūjō was now a councillor. He was a man of such fine character that everyone wished him well, but he was not happy. Everything made him think of Genji. Finally he decided that he did not care what rumors might arise and what misdeeds he might be accused of and hurried off to Suma. The sight of Genji brought tears of joy and sadness. Genji's house seemed very strange and exotic. The surroundings were such that he would have like to paint them. The fence was of plaited bamboo and the pillars were of pine and the stairs of stone.† It was a rustic, provincial sort of dwelling, and very interesting.

Genji's dress too was somewhat rustic. Over a singlet dyed lightly in a yellowish color denoting no rank or office‡ he wore a hunting robe and trousers of greenish gray. It was plain garb and intentionally countrified, but it so became the wearer as to bring an immediate smile of pleasure to his friend's lips. Genji's personal utensils and accessories were of a make-shift nature, and his room was open to anyone who wished to look in. The gaming boards and stones were also of rustic make. The religious objects that lay about told of earnest devotion. The food was very palatable and very much in the local taste. For his friend's amusement, Genji had fishermen bring fish and shells. Tō no Chūjō had them questioned

---

*See Chapter 8, in which, however, there is no mention of this mark of the royal favor. Seven years have passed.

†Giving the house a Chinese aspect.

‡Probably a pink touched with yellow.

about their maritime life, and learned of perils and tribulations. Their speech was as incomprehensible as the chirping of birds, but no doubt their feelings were like his own. He brightened their lives with clothes and other gifts. The stables being nearby, fodder was brought from a granary or something of the sort beyond, and the feeding process was as novel and interesting as everything else. Tō no Chūjō hummed the passage from 'The Well of Asuka'* about the well-fed horses.

Weeping and laughing, they talked of all that had happened over the months.

'Yūgiri quite rips the house to pieces, and Father worries and worries about him.'

Genji was of course sorry to hear it; but since I am not capable of recording the whole of the long conversation, I should perhaps refrain from recording any part of it. They composed Chinese poetry all through the night. Tō no Chūjō had come in defiance of the gossips and slanderers, but they intimidated him all the same. His stay was a brief one.

Wine was brought in, and their toast was from Po Chü-i:†

'Sad topers we. Our springtime cups flow with tears.'

The tears were general, for it had been too brief a meeting.
A line of geese flew over in the dawn sky.

'In what spring tide will I see again my old village?
I envy the geese, returning whence they came.'

Sorrier than ever that he must go, Tō no Chūjō replied:

'Sad are the geese to leave their winter's lodging.
Dark my way of return to the flowery city.'

He had brought gifts from the city, both elegant and practical. Genji gave him in return a black pony, a proper gift for a traveler.

'Considering its origins, you may fear that it will bring bad luck; but you will find that it neighs into the northern winds.'‡

See note, page 36.
†Recollections of meetings with Yüan Chen, *Collected Works*, XVII.
‡'Old Poem,' *Wen-hsüan*:

The Tartar pony faces towards the north.
The Annamese bird nests on the southern branch.

It was a fine beast.

'To remember me by,' said Tō no Chūjō, giving in return what was recognized to be a very fine flute. The situation demanded a certain reticence in the giving of gifts.

The sun was high, and Tō no Chūjō's men were becoming restive. He looked back and looked back, and Genji almost felt that no visit at all would have been better than such a brief one.

'And when will we meet again? It is impossible to believe that you will be here forever.'

> 'Look down upon me, cranes who skim the clouds,
> And see me unsullied as this cloudless day.

'Yes, I do hope to go back, someday. But when I think how difficult it has been for even the most remarkable men to pick up their old lives, I am no longer sure that I want to see the city again.'

> 'Lonely the voice of the crane among the clouds.
> Gone the comrade that once flew at its side.

'I have been closer to you than ever I have deserved. My regrets for what has happened are bitter.'

They scarcely felt that they had had time to renew their friendship. For Genji the loneliness was unrelieved after his friend's departure.

It was the day of the serpent, the first such day in the Third Month.

'The day when a man who has worries goes down and washes them away,' said one of his men, admirably informed, it would seem, in all the annual observances.

Wishing to have a look at the seashore, Genji set forth. Plain, rough curtains were strung up among the trees, and a soothsayer who was doing the circuit of the province was summoned to perform the lustration.

Genji thought he could see something of himself in the rather large doll being cast off to sea, bearing away sins and tribulations.

> 'Cast away to drift on an alien vastness,
> I grieve for more than a doll cast out to sea.'

The bright, open seashore showed him to wonderful advantage. The sea stretched placid into measureless distances. He thought of all that had happened to him, and all that was still to come.

> 'You eight hundred myriad gods must surely help me,
> For well you know that blameless I stand before you.'

Suddenly a wind came up and even before the services were finished the sky was black. Genji's men rushed about in confusion. Rain came pouring down, completely without warning. Though the obvious course would have been to return straightway to the house, there had been no time to send for umbrellas. The wind was now a howling tempest, everything that had not been tied down was scuttling off across the beach. The surf was biting at their feet. The sea was white, as if spread over with white linen. Fearful every moment of being struck down, they finally made their way back to the house.

'I've never seen anything like it,' said one of the men. 'Winds do come up from time to time, but not without warning. It is all very strange and very terrible.'

The lightning and thunder seemed to announce the end of the world, and the rain to beat its way into the ground; and Genji sat calmly reading a sutra. The thunder subsided in the evening, but the wind went on through the night.

'Our prayers seem to have been answered. A little more and we would have been carried off. I've heard that tidal waves do carry people off before they know what is happening to them, but I've not seen anything like this.'

Towards dawn sleep was at length possible. A man whom he did not recognize came to Genji in a dream.

'The court summons you.' He seemed to be reaching for Genji. 'Why do you not go?'

It would be the king of the sea, who was known to have a partiality for handsome men. Genji decided that he could stay no longer at Suma.

CHAPTER 13

Akashi

The days went by and the thunder and rain continued. What was Genji to do? People would laugh if, in this extremity, out of favor at court, he were to return to the city. Should he then seek a mountain retreat? But if it were to be noised about that a storm had driven him away, then he would cut a ridiculous figure in history.

His dreams were haunted by that same apparition. Messages from the city almost entirely ceased coming as the days went by without a break in the storms. Might he end his days at Suma? No one was likely to come calling in these tempests.

A messenger did come from Murasaki, a sad, sodden creature. Had they passed in the street, Genji would scarcely have known whether he was man or beast, and of course would not have thought of inviting him to come near. Now the man brought a surge of pleasure and affection – though Genji could not help asking himself whether the storm had weakened his moorings.

Murasaki's letter, long and melancholy, said in part: 'The terrifying deluge goes on without a break, day after day. Even the skies are closed off, and I am denied the comfort of gazing in your direction.

'What do they work, the sea winds down at Suma?
At home, my sleeves are assaulted by wave after wave.'

Tears so darkened his eyes that it was as if they were inviting the waters to rise higher.

The man said that the storms had been fierce in the city too, and that a special reading of the Prajñāpāramitā Sutra had been ordered. 'The streets are all closed and the great gentlemen can't get to court, and everything has closed down.'

The man spoke clumsily and haltingly, but he did bring news. Genji summoned him near and had him questioned.

'It's not the way it usually is. You don't usually have rain going on for days without a break and the wind howling on and on. Everyone is terrified. But it's worse here. They haven't had this hail beating right through the ground and thunder going on and on and not letting a body think.' The terror written so plainly on his face did nothing to improve the spirits of the people at Suma.

Might it be the end of the world? From dawn the next day the wind was so fierce and the tide so high and the surf so loud that it was as if the crags and the mountains must fall. The horror of the thunder and lightning was beyond description. Panic spread at each new flash. For what sins, Genji's men asked, were they being punished? Were they to perish without another glimpse of their mothers and fathers, their dear wives and children?

Genji tried to tell himself that he had been guilty of no misdeed for which he must perish here on the seashore. Such were the panic and confusion around him, however, that he bolstered his confidence with special offerings to the god of Sumiyoshi.

'O you of Sumiyoshi who protect the lands about: if indeed you are an avatar of the Blessed One, then you must save us.'

His men were of course fearful for their lives; but the thought that so fine a gentleman (and in these deplorable circumstances) might be swept beneath the waters seemed altogether too tragic. The less distraught among them prayed in loud voices to this and that favored deity, Buddhist and Shinto, that their own lives be taken if it meant that his might be spared.

They faced Sumiyoshi and prayed and made vows: 'Our lord was reared deep in the fastnesses of the palace, and all blessings were his. You who, in the abundance of your mercy, have brought strength through these lands to all who have sunk beneath the weight of their troubles: in punishment for what crimes do you call forth these howling waves? Judge his case if you will, you gods of heaven and earth. Guiltless, he is accused of a crime, stripped of his offices, driven from his house and city, left as you see him with no relief from the torture and the lamentation. And now these horrors, and even his life seems threatened. Why? we must ask. Because of sins in some other life, because of crimes in this one? If your vision is clear, O you gods, then take all this away.'

Genji offered prayers to the king of the sea and countless other gods as well. The thunder was increasingly more terrible, and finally the gallery adjoining his rooms was struck by lightning. Flames sprang up and the gallery was destroyed. The confusion was immense; the whole world seemed to have gone mad. Genji was moved to a building out in back, a kitchen or something of the sort it seemed to be. It was crowded with people of every station and rank. The clamor was almost enough to drown out the lightning and thunder. Night descended over a sky already as black as ink.

Presently the wind and rain subsided and stars began to come out. The kitchen being altogether too mean a place, a move back to the main hall was suggested. The charred remains of the gallery were an ugly sight, however, and the hall had been badly muddied and all the blinds and curtains blown away. Perhaps, Genji's men suggested somewhat tentatively, it might be better to wait until dawn. Genji sought to concentrate upon the holy name, but his agitation continued to be very great.

He opened a wattled door and looked out. The moon had come up. The line left by the waves was white and dangerously near, and the surf was still high. There was no one here whom he could turn to, no student of the deeper truths who could discourse upon past and present and perhaps explain these wild events. All the fisherfolk had gathered at what they had heard was the house of a great gentleman from the city. They were as noisy and impossible to communicate with as a flock of birds, but no one thought of telling them to leave.

'If the wind had kept up just a little longer,' someone said, 'absolutely everything would have been swept under. The gods did well by us.'

There are no words – 'lonely' and 'forlorn' seem much too weak – to describe his feelings.

'Without the staying hand of the king of the sea
The roar of the eight hundred waves would have taken us under.'

Genji was as exhausted as if all the buffets and fires of the tempest had been aimed at him personally. He dozed off, his head against some nondescript piece of furniture.

The old emperor came to him, quite as when he had lived. 'And why are you in this wretched place?' He took Genji's hand and pulled him to his feet. 'You must do as the god of Sumiyoshi tells you. You must put out to sea immediately. You must leave this shore behind.'

'Since I last saw you, sir,' said Genji, overjoyed, 'I have suffered an unbroken series of misfortunes. I had thought of throwing myself into the sea.'

'That you must not do. You are undergoing brief punishment for certain sins. I myself did not commit any conscious crimes

while I reigned, but a person is guilty of transgressions and oversights without his being aware of them. I am doing penance and
have no time to look back towards this world. But an echo of your
troubles came to me and I could not stand idle. I fought my way
through the sea and up to this shore and I am very tired; but now
that I am here I must see to a matter in the city.' And he disappeared.

Genji called after him, begging to be taken along. He looked
around him. There was only the bright face of the moon. His
father's presence had been too real for a dream, so real that he
must still be here. Clouds traced sad lines across the sky. It had
been clear and palpable, the figure he had so longed to see even in
a dream, so clear that he could almost catch an afterimage. His
father had come through the skies to help him in what had seemed
the last extremity of his sufferings. He was deeply grateful, even to
the tempests; and in the aftermath of the dream he was happy.

Quite different emotions now ruffled his serenity. He forgot his
immediate troubles and only regretted that his father had not
stayed longer. Perhaps he would come again. Genji would have
liked to go back to sleep, but he lay wakeful until daylight.

A little boat had pulled in at the shore and two or three men
came up.

'The revered monk who was once governor of Harima has
come from Akashi. If the former Minamoto councillor, Lord
Yoshikiyo, is here, we wonder if we might trouble him to come
down and hear the details of our mission.'

Yoshikiyo pretended to be surprised and puzzled. 'He was once
among my closer acquaintances here in Harima, but we had a falling out and it has been some time since we last exchanged letters.
What can have brought him through such seas in that little boat?'

Genji's dream had given intimations. He sent Yoshikiyo down
to the boat immediately. Yoshikiyo marveled that it could even
have been launched upon such a sea.

These were the details of the mission, from the mouth of the
old governor: 'Early this month a strange figure came to me in a
dream. I listened, though somewhat incredulously, and was told
that on the thirteenth there would be a clear and present sign. I
was to ready a boat and make for this shore when the waves subsided. I did ready a boat, and then came this savage wind and lightning. I thought of numerous foreign sovereigns who have received

instructions in dreams on how to save their lands, and I concluded that even at the risk of incurring his ridicule I must on the day appointed inform your lord of the import of the dream. And so I did indeed put out to sea. A strange jet blew all the way and brought us to this shore. I cannot think of it except as divine intervention. And might I ask whether there have been corresponding manifestations here? I do hate to trouble you, but might I ask you to communicate all of this to your lord?'

Yoshikiyo quietly relayed the message, which brought new considerations. There had been these various unsettling signs conveyed to Genji dreaming and waking. The possibility of being laughed at for having departed these shores under threat now seemed the lesser risk. To turn his back on what might be a real offer of help from the gods would be to ask for still worse misfortunes. It was not easy to reject ordinary advice, and personal reservations counted for little when the advice came from great eminences. 'Defer to them; they will cause you no reproaches,' a wise man of old once said.* He could scarcely face worse misfortunes by deferring than by not deferring, and he did not seem likely to gain great merit and profit by hesitating out of concern for his brave name. Had not his own father come to him? What room was there for doubts?

He sent back his answer: 'I have been through a great deal in this strange place, and I hear nothing at all from the city. I but gaze upon a sun and moon going I know not where as comrades from my old home; and now comes this angler's boat, happy tidings on an angry wind.† Might there be a place along your Akashi coast where I can hide myself?'

The old man was delighted. Genji's men pressed him to set out even before sunrise. Taking along only four or five of his closest attendants, he boarded the boat. That strange wind came up again and they were at Akashi as if they had flown. It was very near, within crawling distance, so to speak; but still the workings of the wind were strange and marvelous.

---

*Lao-tze, say early commentaries; but the advice is not to be found in his extant writings.

†Ki no Tsurayuki, *Gosenshū* 1225:

> An angler's boat upon the waves that pound us,
> Happy tidings on an angry wind.

The Akashi coast was every bit as beautiful as he had been told it was. He would have preferred fewer people, but on the whole he was pleased. Along the coast and in the hills the old monk had put up numerous buildings with which to take advantage of the four seasons: a reed-roofed beach cottage with fine seasonal vistas; beside a mountain stream a chapel of some grandeur and dignity, suitable for rites and meditation and invocation of the holy name; and rows of storehouses where the harvest was put away and a bountiful life assured for the years that remained. Fearful of the high tides, the old monk had sent his daughter and her women off to the hills. The house on the beach was at Genji's disposal.

The sun was rising as Genji left the boat and got into a carriage. This first look by daylight at his new guest brought a happy smile to the old man's lips. He felt as if the accumulated years were falling away and as if new years had been granted him. He gave silent thanks to the god of Sumiyoshi. He might have seemed ridiculous as he bustled around seeing to Genji's needs, as if the radiance of the sun and the moon had become his private property; but no one laughed at him.

I need not describe the beauty of the Akashi coast. The careful attention that had gone into the house and the rocks and plantings of the garden, the graceful line of the coast – it was infinitely pleasanter than Suma, and one would not have wished to ask a less than profoundly sensitive painter to paint it. The house was in quiet good taste. The old man's way of life was as Genji had heard it described, hardly more rustic than that of the grandees at court. In sheer luxury, indeed, he rather outdid them.

When Genji had rested for a time he got off messages to the city. He summoned Murasaki's messenger, who was still at Suma recovering from the horrors of his journey. Loaded with rewards for his services, he now set out again for the city. It would seem that Genji sent off a description of his perils to priests and others of whose services he regularly made use,* but he told only Fujitsubo how narrow his escape had in fact been. He repeatedly laid down his brush as he sought to answer that very affectionate letter from Murasaki.

'I feel that I have run the whole gamut of horrors and then run

---

*The commentators inform us that these men are probably a part of Genji's spy system.

it again, and more than ever I would like to renounce the world;
but though everything else has fled away, the image which you
entrusted to the mirror has not for an instant left me. I think that I
might not see you again.

> 'Yet farther away, upon the beach at Akashi,
>   My thoughts of a distant city, and of you

'I am still half dazed, which fact will I fear be too apparent in
the confusion and disorder of this letter.'

Though it was true that his letter was somewhat disordered, his
men thought it splendid. How very fond he must be of their lady!
It would seem that they sent off descriptions of their own perils.

The apparently interminable rains had at last stopped and the
sky was bright far into the distance. The fishermen radiated good
spirits. Suma had been a lonely place with only a few huts scattered among the rocks. It was true that the crowds here at Akashi
were not entirely to Genji's liking, but it was a pleasant spot with
much to interest him and take his mind from his troubles.

The old man's devotion to the religious life was rather wonderful. Only one matter interfered with it: worry about his daughter.
He told Genji a little of his concern for the girl. Genji was sympathetic. He had heard that she was very handsome and wondered
if there might not be some bond between them, that he should
have come upon her in this strange place. But no; here he was in
the remote provinces, and he must think of nothing but his own
prayers. He would be unable to face Murasaki if he were to depart
from the promises he had made her. Yet he continued to be interested in the girl. Everything suggested that her nature and appearance were very far from ordinary.

Reluctant to intrude himself, the old man had moved to an
outbuilding. He was restless and unhappy when away from Genji,
however, and he prayed more fervently than ever to the gods and
Buddhas that his unlikely hope might be realized. Though in his
sixties he had taken good care of himself and was young for his
age. The religious life and the fact that he was of proud lineage
may have had something to do with the matter. He was stubborn
and intractable, as old people often are, but he was well versed in
antiquities and not without a certain subtlety. His stories of old
times did a great deal to dispel Genji's boredom. Genji had been
too busy himself for the sort of erudition, the lore about customs

and precedents, which he now had in bits and installments, and he told himself that it would have been a great loss if he had not known Akashi and its venerable master.

In a sense they were friends, but Genji rather overawed the old man. Though he had seemed so confident when he told his wife of his hopes, he hesitated, unable to broach the matter, now that the time for action had come, and seemed capable only of bemoaning his weakness and inadequacy. As for the daughter, she rarely saw a passable man here in the country among people of her own rank; and now she had had a glimpse of a man the like of whom she had not suspected to exist. She was a shy, modest girl, and she thought him quite beyond her reach. She had had hints of her father's ambitions and thought them wildly inappropriate, and her discomfort was greater for having Genji near.

It was the Fourth Month. The old man had all the curtains and fixtures of Genji's rooms changed for fresh summery ones. Genji was touched and a little embarrassed, feeling that the old man's attentions were perhaps a bit overdone; but he would not have wished for the world to offend so proud a nature.

A great many messages now came from the city inquiring after his safety. On a quiet moonlit night when the sea stretched off into the distance under a cloudless sky, he almost felt that he was looking at the familiar waters of his own garden. Overcome with longing, he was like a solitary, nameless wanderer. 'Awaji, distant foam,'* he whispered to himself.

'Awaji: in your name is all my sadness,
And clear you stand in the light of the moon tonight.'

He took out the seven-stringed koto, long neglected, which he had brought from the city and spread a train of sad thoughts through the house as he plucked out a few tentative notes. He exhausted all his skills on 'The Wide Barrow,'† and the sound reached the house in the hills on a sighing of wind and waves.

*The name Awaji suggests both *awa*, 'foam,' and *aware*, an ejaculation of vague and undefined sadness. Oshikōchi Mitsune, *Shinkokinshū* 1513:

> Awaji in the moonlight, like distant foam:
> From these cloudly sovereign heights it seems so near.

†A Chinese composition, apparently, which does not survive.

Sensitive young ladies heard it and were moved. Lowly rustics, though they could not have identified the music, were lured out into the sea winds, there to catch cold.

The old man could not sit still. Casting aside his beads, he came running over to the main house.

'I feel as if a world I had thrown away were coming back,' he said, breathless and tearful. 'It is a night such as to make one feel that the blessed world for which one longs must be even so.'

Genji played on in a reverie, a flood of memories of concerts over the years, of this gentleman and that lady on flute and koto, of voices raised in song, of times when he and they had been the center of attention, recipients of praise and favors from the emperor himself. Sending to the house on the hill for a lute and a thirteen-stringed koto, the old man now seemed to change roles and become one of these priestly mendicants who make their living by the lute. He played a most interesting and affecting strain. Genji played a few notes on the thirteen-stringed koto which the old man pressed on him and was thought an uncommonly impressive performer on both sorts of koto. Even the most ordinary music can seem remarkable if the time and place are right; and here on the wide seacoast, open far into the distance, the groves seemed to come alive in colors richer than the bloom of spring or the change of autumn, and the calls of the water rails were as if they were pounding on the door and demanding to be admitted.

The old man had a delicate style to which the instruments were beautifully suited and which delighted Genji. 'One likes to see a gentle lady quite at her ease with a koto,' said Genji, as if with nothing specific in mind.

The old man smiled. 'And where, sir, is one likely to find a gentler, more refined musician than yourself? On the koto I am in the third generation from the emperor Daigo. I have left the great world for the rustic surroundings in which you have found me, and sometimes when I have been more gloomy than usual I have taken out a koto and picked away at it; and, curiously, there has been someone who has imitated me. Her playing has come quite naturally to resemble my master's. Or perhaps it has only seemed so to the degenerate ear of the mountain monk who has only the pine winds for company. I wonder if it might be possible to let you hear a strain, in the greatest secrecy of course.' He brushed away a tear.

'I have been rash and impertinent. My playing must have sounded like no playing at all.' Genji turned away from the koto. 'I do not know why, but it has always been the case that ladies have taken especially well to the koto. One hears that with her father to teach her the fifth daughter of the emperor Saga was a great master of the instrument, but it would seem that she had no successors. The people who set themselves up as masters these days are quite ordinary performers with no real grounding at all. How fascinating that someone who still holds to the grand style should be hidden away on this coast. Do let me hear her.'

'No difficulty at all, if that is what you wish. If you really wish it, I can summon her. There was once a poet, you will remember, who was much pleased at the lute of a tradesman's wife.* While we are on the subject of lutes, there were not many even in the old days who could bring out the best in the instrument. Yet it would seem that the person of whom I speak plays with a certain sureness and manages to affect a rather pleasing delicacy. I have no idea where she might have acquired these skills. It seems wrong that she should be asked to compete with the wild waves, but sometimes in my gloom I do have her strike up a tune.'

He spoke with such spirit that Genji, much interested, pushed the lute toward him.

He did indeed play beautifully, adding decorations that have gone out of fashion. There was a Chinese elegance in his touch, and he was able to induce a particularly solemn tremolo from the instrument. Though it might have been argued that the setting was wrong, an adept among his retainers was persuaded to sing for them about the clean shore of Ise.† Tapping out the rhythm, Genji would join in from time to time, and the old man would pause to offer a word of praise. Refreshments were brought in, very prettily arranged. The old man was most assiduous in seeing that the cups were kept full, and it became the sort of evening when troubles are forgotten.

*Po Chü-i, Collected Works, XII, 'The Lutist.'
†'The Sea of Ise,' a Saibara:

> On the clean shore of Ise,
> Let us gather shells in the tide.
> Let us gather shells and jewels.

Late in the night the sea breezes were cool and the moon seemed brighter and clearer as it sank towards the west. All was quiet. In pieces and fragments the old man told about himself, from his feelings upon taking up residence on this Akashi coast to his hopes for the future life and the prospects which his devotions seemed to be opening. He added, unsolicited, an account of his daughter. Genji listened with interest and sympathy.

'It is not easy for me to say it, sir, but the fact that you are here even briefly in what must be for you strange and quite unexpected surroundings, and the fact that you are being asked to undergo trials new to your experience – I wonder if it might not be that the powers to whom an aged monk has so fervently prayed for so many years have taken pity on him. It is now eighteen years since I first prayed and made vows to the god of Sumiyoshi.* I have had certain hopes for my daughter since she was very young, and every spring and autumn I have taken her to Sumiyoshi. At each of my six daily services, three of them in the daytime and three at night, I have put aside my own wishes for salvation and ventured a suggestion that my hopes for the girl be noticed. I have sunk to this provincial obscurity because I brought an unhappy destiny with me into this life. My father was a minister, and you see what I have become. If my family is to follow the same road in the future, I ask myself, then where will it end? But I have had high hopes for her since she was born. I have been determined that she go to some noble gentleman in the city. I have been accused of arrogance and unworthy ambitions and subjected to some rather unpleasant treatment. I have not let it worry me. I have said to her that while I live I will do what I can for her, limited though my resources may be; and that if I die before my hopes are realized she is to throw herself into the sea.' He was weeping. It had taken great resolve for him to speak so openly.

Genji wept easily these days. 'I had been feeling put upon, bundled off to this strange place because of crimes I was not aware of having committed. Your story makes me feel that there is a bond between us. Why did you not tell me earlier? Nothing has seemed quite real since I came here, and I have given myself up to prayers to the exclusion of everything else, and so I fear that I will

---

*There is a chronological difficulty, since by this account the girl would be about nine when, in Chapter 5, she is reported to be turning away suitors.

have struck you as spiritless. Though reports had reached me of the lady of whom you have spoken, I had feared that she would want to have nothing to do with an outcast like myself. You will be my guide and intermediary? May I look forward to company these lonely evenings?'

The old man was thoroughly delighted.

'Do I catch, as I gaze into unresponsive skies,' — 'Do you too know the sadness of the nights On the shore of Akashi with only thoughts for companions?

'Imagine, if you will, how it has been for us through the long months and years.' He faltered, though with no loss of dignity, and his voice was trembling.

'But you, sir, are used to this seacoast.

'The traveler passes fretful nights at Akashi. The grass which he reaps for his pillow reaps no dreams.'

His openness delighted the old man, who talked on and on – and became rather tiresome, I fear. In my impatience I may have allowed inaccuracies to creep in, and exaggerated his eccentricities.

In any event, he felt a clean happiness sweep over him. A beginning had been made.

At about noon the next day Genji got off a note to the house on the hill. A real treasure might lie buried in this unlikely spot. He took a great deal of trouble with his note, which was on a fine saffron-colored Korean paper.

'Do I catch, as I gaze into unresponsive skies, A glimpse of a grove of which I have had certain tidings?

'My resolve has been quite dissipated.'*

And was that all? one wonders.

The old man had been waiting. Genji's messenger came staggering back down the hill, for he had been hospitably received.

But the girl was taking time with her reply. The old man rushed to her rooms and urged haste, but to no avail. She thought her hand quite unequal to the task, and awareness of the difference

*Anonymous, *Kokinshū* 503:

> Resolve that I would keep them to myself,
> These thoughts of you, has been quite dissipated.

in their stations dismayed her. She was not feeling well, she said, and lay down.

Though he would certainly have wished it otherwise, the old man finally answered in her place. 'Her rustic sleeves are too narrow to encompass such awesome tidings, it would seem, and indeed she seems to have found herself incapable of even reading your letter.

'She gazes into the skies into which you gaze.
May they bring your thoughts and hers into some accord.

'But I fear that I will seem impertinent and forward.'

It was in a most uncompromisingly old-fashioned hand, on sturdy Michinoku paper; but there was something spruce and dashing about it too. Yes, 'forward' was the proper word. Indeed, Genji was rather startled. He gave the messenger a 'bejeweled apron,' an appropriate gift, he thought, from a beach cottage.*

He got off another message the next day, beautifully written on soft, delicate paper. 'I am not accustomed to receiving letters from ladies' secretaries.

'Unwillingly reticent about my sorrows
'I still must be – for no one makes inquiry.

'Though it is difficult to say just what I mean.'

There would have been something unnatural about a girl who refused to be interested in such a letter. She thought it splendid, but she also thought it impossibly out of her reach. Notice from such supreme heights had the perverse effect of reducing her to tears and inaction.

She was finally badgered into setting something down. She chose delicately perfumed lavender paper and took great care with the gradations of her ink.

'Unwillingly reticent – how can it be so?
How can you sorrow for someone you have not met?'

The diction and the handwriting would have done credit to any of the fine ladies at court. He fell into a deep reverie, for he

---

*There is a pun on *tamamo*, 'jeweled apron' (an elegant word for 'apron') and a kind of seaweed.

was reminded of days back in the city. But he did not want to attract attention, and presently shook it off.

Every other day or so, choosing times when he was not likely to be noticed, and when he imagined that her thoughts might be similar to his – a quiet, uneventful evening, a lonely dawn – he would get off a note to her. There was a proud reserve in her answers which made him want more than ever to meet her. But there was Yoshikiyo to think of. He had spoken of the lady as if he thought her his property, and Genji did not wish to contravene these long-standing claims. If her parents persisted in offering her to him, he would make that fact his excuse, and seek to pursue the affair as quietly as possible. Not that she was making things easy for him. She seemed prouder and more aloof than the proudest lady at court; and so the days went by in a contest of wills.

The city was more than ever on his mind now that he had moved beyond the Suma barrier. He feared that not even in jest* could he do without Murasaki. Again he was asking himself if he might not bring her quietly to Akashi, and he was on the point of doing just that. But he did not expect to be here very much longer, and nothing was to be gained by inviting criticism at this late date.

In the city it had been a year of omens and disturbances. On the thirteenth day of the Third Month, as the thunder and winds mounted to new fury, the emperor had a dream. His father stood glowering at the stairs to the royal bedchamber and had a great deal to say, all of it, apparently, about Genji. Deeply troubled, the emperor described the dream to his mother.

'On stormy nights a person has a way of dreaming about the things that are on his mind,' she said. 'If I were you I would not give it a second thought.'

Perhaps because his eyes had met the angry eyes of his father, he came down with a very painful eye ailment. Retreat and fasting were ordered for the whole court, even Kokiden's household. Then the minister, her father, died. He was of such years that his death need have surprised no one, but Kokiden too was unwell, and worse as the days went by; and the emperor had a great deal to

*Anonymous, *Kokinshū* 1025:

> I wondered if even in jest I could do without you.
> I gave it a try, to which I proved unequal.

worry about. So long as an innocent Genji was off in the wilderness, he feared, he must suffer. He ventured from time to time a suggestion that Genji be restored to his old rank and offices.

His mother sternly advised against it. 'People will tax you with shallowness and indecision. Can you really think of having a man go into exile and then bringing him back before the minimum three years have gone by?'

And so he hesitated, and he and his mother were in increasingly poor health.

At Akashi it was the season when cold winds blow from the sea to make a lonely bed even lonelier.

Genji sometimes spoke to the old man. 'If you were perhaps to bring her here when no one is looking?'

He thought that he could hardly be expected to visit her. She had her own ideas. She knew that rustic maidens should come running at a word from a city gentleman who happened to be briefly in the vicinity. No, she did not belong to his world, and she would only be inviting grief if she pretended that she did. Her parents had impossible hopes, it seemed, and were asking the unthinkable and building a future on nothing. What they were really doing was inviting endless trouble. It was good fortune enough to exchange notes with him for so long as he stayed on this shore. Her own prayers had been modest: that she be permitted a glimpse of the gentleman of whom she had heard so much. She had had her glimpse, from a distance, to be sure, and, brought in on the wind, she had also caught hints of his unmatched skill (of this too she had heard) on the koto. She had learned rather a great deal about him these past days, and she was satisfied. Indeed a nameless woman lost among the fishermen's huts had no right to expect even this. She was acutely embarrassed at any suggestion that he be invited nearer.

Her father too was uneasy. Now that his prayers were being answered he began to have thoughts of failure. It would be very sad for the girl, offered heedlessly to Genji, to learn that he did not want her. Rejection was painful at the hands of the finest gentleman. His unquestioning faith in all the invisible gods had perhaps led him to overlook human inclinations and probabilities.

'How pleasant,' Genji kept saying, 'if I could hear that koto to the singing of the waves. It is the season for such things. We should not let it pass.'

Dismissing his wife's reservations and saying nothing to his disciples, the old man selected an auspicious day. He bustled around making preparations, the results of which were dazzling. The moon was near full. He sent off a note which said only: 'This night that should not be wasted.'* It seemed a bit arch, but Genji changed to informal court dress and set forth late in the night. He had a carriage decked out most resplendently, and then, deciding that it might seem ostentatious, went on horseback instead. The lady's house was some distance back in the hills. The coast lay in full view below, the bay silver in the moonlight. He would have liked to show it to Murasaki. The temptation was strong to turn his horse's head and gallop on to the city.

'Race on through the moonlit sky, O roan-colored horse,
    And let me be briefly with her for whom I long.'†

The house was a fine one, set in a grove of trees. Careful attention had gone into all the details. In contrast to the solid dignity of the house on the beach, this house in the hills had a certain fragility about it, and he could imagine the melancholy thoughts that must come to one who lived here. There was sadness in the sound of the temple bells borne in on pine breezes from a hall of meditation nearby. Even the pines seemed to be asking for something as they sent their roots out over the crags. All manner of autumn insects were singing in the garden. He looked about him and saw a pavilion finer than the others. The cypress door upon which the moonlight seemed to focus was slightly open.

He hesitated and then spoke. There was no answer. She had resolved to admit him no nearer. All very aristocratic, thought Genji. Even ladies so wellborn that they were sheltered from sudden visitors usually tried to make conversation when the visitor was Genji. Perhaps she was letting him know that he was under a cloud. He was annoyed and thought of leaving. It would run against the mood of things to force himself upon her, and on the other hand he would look rather silly if it were to seem that she

---

*Minamoto Nobuakira, *Gosenshū* 103:

> If only I could show them to someone who knows,
>   This moon, these flowers, this night that should not be wasted.

†A play on words gives a roan horse a special affinity with moonlight.

had bested him at this contest of wills. One would indeed have wished to show him, the picture of dejection, 'to someone who knows.'

A curtain string brushed against a koto, to tell him that she had been passing a quiet evening at her music.

'And will you not play for me on the koto of which I have heard so much?

'Would there were someone with whom I might share my thoughts
And so dispel some part of these sad dreams.'

'You speak to one for whom the night has no end.
How can she tell the dreaming from the waking?'

The almost inaudible whisper reminded him strongly of the Rokujō lady.

This lady had not been prepared for an incursion and could not cope with it. She fled to an inner room. How she could have contrived to bar it he could not tell, but it was very firmly barred indeed. Though he did not exactly force his way through, it is not to be imagined that he left matters as they were. Delicate, slender – she was almost too beautiful. Pleasure was mingled with pity at the thought that he was imposing himself upon her. She was even more pleasing than reports from afar had had her. The autumn night, usually so long, was over in a trice. Not wishing to be seen, he hurried out, leaving affectionate assurances behind.

He got off an unobtrusive note later in the morning. Perhaps he was feeling twinges of conscience. The old monk was equally intent upon secrecy, and sorry that he was impelled to treat the messenger rather coolly.

Genji called in secret from time to time. The two houses being some distance apart, he feared being seen by fishermen, who were known to relish a good rumor, and sometimes several days would elapse between his visits. Exactly as she had expected, thought the girl. Her father, forgetting that enlightenment was his goal, quite gave his prayers over to silent queries as to when Genji might be expected to come again; and so (and it seems a pity) a tranquillity very laboriously attained was disturbed at a very late date.

Genji dreaded having Murasaki learn of the affair. He still loved her more than anyone, and he did not want her to make even joking reference to it. She was a quiet, docile lady, but she had

more than once been unhappy with him. Why, for the sake of
brief pleasure, had he caused her pain? He wished it were all his to
do over again. The sight of the Akashi lady only brought new
longing for the other lady.

He got off a more earnest and affectionate letter than usual, at
the end of which he said: 'I am in anguish at the thought that,
because of foolish occurrences for which I have been responsible
but have had little heart, I might appear in a guise distasteful to
you. There has been a strange, fleeting encounter. That I should
volunteer this story will make you see, I hope, how little I wish to
have secrets from you. Let the gods be my judges.

'It was but the fisherman's brush with the salty sea pine
    Followed by a tide of tears of longing.'

Her reply was gentle and unreproachful, and at the end of it she
said: 'That you should have deigned to tell me a dreamlike story
which you could not keep to yourself calls to mind numbers of
earlier instances.

'Naïve of me, perhaps; yet we did make our vows.
And now see the waves that wash the Mountain of Waiting!'*

It was the one note of reproach in a quiet, undemanding letter.
He found it hard to put down, and for some nights he stayed away
from the house in the hills.

The Akashi lady was convinced once more that her fears had
become actuality. Now seemed the time to throw herself into the
sea. She had only her parents to turn to and they were very old.
She had had no ambitions for herself, no thought of making a
respectable marriage. Yet the years had gone by happily enough,
without storms or tears. Now she saw that the world can be very
cruel. She managed to conceal her worries, however, and to do
nothing that might annoy Genji. He was more and more pleased
with her as time went by.

---

*Anonymous, *Kokinshū* 1093:

> On the day that I am unfaithful to my vows,
>   May the waves break over the Mountain of Waiting of Sué.

A very common pun makes Matsuyama, 'Mount of the Pines,' also 'Mountain
of Waiting.' See also note*, page 133.

But there was the other, the lady in the city, waiting and waiting for his return. He did not want to do anything that would make her unhappy, and he spent his nights alone. He sent sketchbooks off to her, adding poems calculated to provoke replies. No doubt her women were delighted with them; and when the sorrow was too much for her (and as if by thought transference) she too would make sketches and set down notes which came to resemble a journal.

And what did the future have in store for the two of them?

The New Year came, the emperor was ill, and a pall settled over court life. There was a son, by Lady Shōkyōden, daughter of the Minister of the Right,* but the child was only two, far too young for the throne. The obvious course was to abdicate in favor of the crown prince. As the emperor turned over in his mind the problem of advice and counsel for his successor, he thought it more than ever a pity that Genji should be off in the provinces. Finally he went against Kokiden's injunctions and issued an amnesty. Kokiden had been ill from the previous year, the victim of a malign spirit, it seemed, and numerous other dire omens had disturbed the court. Though the emperor's eye ailment had for a time improved, perhaps because of strict fasting, it was worse again. Late in the Seventh Month, in deep despondency, he issued a second order, summoning Genji back to the city.

Genji had been sure that a pardon would presently come, but he also knew that life is uncertain. That it should come so soon was of course pleasing. At the same time the thought of leaving this Akashi coast filled him with regret. The old monk, though granting that it was most proper and just, was upset at the news. He managed all the same to tell himself that Genji's prosperity was in his own best interest. Genji visited the lady every night and sought to console her. From about the Sixth Month she had shown symptoms such as to make their relations more complex. A sad, ironical affair seemed at the same time to come to a climax and to disintegrate. He wondered at the perverseness of fates that seemed always to be bringing new surprises. The lady, and one could scarcely have blamed her, was sunk in the deepest gloom. Genji had set forth on a strange, dark journey with a comforting

*Later to be the father-in-law of Tamakazura. See Chapter 31.

certainty that he would one day return to the city; and he now lamented that he would not see this Akashi again.

His men, in their several ways, were delighted. An escort came from the city, there was a joyous stir of preparation, and the master of the house was lost in tears. So the month came to an end. It was a season for sadness in any case, and sad thoughts accosted Genji. Why, now and long ago, had he abandoned himself, heedlessly but of his own accord, to random, profitless affairs of the heart?

'What a great deal of trouble he does cause,' said those who knew the secret. 'The same thing all over again. For almost a year he didn't tell anyone and he didn't seem to care the first thing about her. And now just when he ought to be letting well enough alone he makes things worse.'

Yoshikiyo was the uncomfortable one. He knew what his fellows were saying: that he had talked too much and started it all.

Two days before his departure Genji visited his lady, setting out earlier than usual. This first really careful look at her revealed an astonishingly proud beauty. He comforted her with promises that he would choose an opportune time to bring her to the city. I shall not comment again upon his own good looks. He was thinner from fasting, and emaciation seemed to add the final touches to the picture. He made tearful vows. The lady replied in her heart that this small measure of affection was all she wanted and deserved, and that his radiance only emphasized her own dullness. The waves moaned in the autumn winds, the smoke from the salt burners' fires drew faint lines across the sky, and all the symbols of loneliness seemed to gather together.

'Even though we now must part for a time,
  The smoke from these briny fires will follow me.'

'Smoldering thoughts like the sea grass burned on these shores.
  And what good now to ask for anything more?'

She fell silent, weeping softly, and a rather conventional poem seemed to say a great deal.

She had not, through it all, played for him on the koto of which he had heard so much.

'Do let me hear it. Let it be a memento.'

Sending for the seven-stringed koto he had brought from the city, he played an unusual strain, quiet but wonderfully clear on the midnight air. Unable to restrain himself, the old man pushed a thirteen-stringed koto toward his daughter. She was apparently in a mood for music. Softly she tuned the instrument, and her touch suggested very great polish and elegance. He had thought Fujitsubo's playing quite incomparable. It was in the modern style, and enough to bring cries of wonder from anyone who knew a little about music. For him it was like Fujitsubo herself, the essence of all her delicate awareness. The koto of the lady before him was quiet and calm, and so rich in overtones as almost to arouse envy. She left off playing just as the connoisseur who was her listener had passed the first stages of surprise and become eager attention. Disappointment and regret succeeded pleasure. He had been here for nearly a year. Why had he not insisted that she play for him, time after time? All he could do now was repeat the old vows.

'Take this koto,' he said, 'to remember me by. Someday we will play together.'

Her reply was soft and almost casual:

'One heedless word, one koto, to set me at rest.
In the sound of it the sound of my weeping, forever.'

He could not let it pass.

'Do not change the middle string* of this koto.
Unchanging I shall be till we meet again.

'And we will meet again before it has slipped out of tune.'

Yet it was not unnatural that the parting should seem more real than the reunion.

On the last morning Genji was up and ready before daybreak. Though he had little time to himself in all the stir, he contrived to write to her:

'Sad the retreating waves at leaving this shore.
Sad I am for you, remaining after.'

'You leave, my reed-roofed hut will fall to ruin.
Would that I might go out with these waves.'

---

*There are several theories as to what the expression might mean. The most likely of them has it referring not to the seven-stringed but to the thirteen-stringed koto.

It was an honest poem, and in spite of himself he was weeping. One could, after all, become fond of a hostile place, said those who did not know the secret. Those who did, Yoshikiyo and others, were a little jealous, concluding that it must have been a rather successful affair.

There were tears, for all the joy; but I shall not dwell upon them.

The old man had arranged the grandest of farewell ceremonies. He had splendid travel robes for everyone, even the lowliest footmen. One marveled that he had found time to collect them all. The gifts for Genji himself were of course the finest, chests and chests of them, borne by a retinue which he attached to Genji's. Some of them would make very suitable gifts in the city. He had overlooked nothing.

The lady had pinned a poem to a travel robe:

'I made it for you, but the surging brine has wet it.
    And might you find it unpleasant and cast it off?'

Despite the confusion, he sent one of his own robes in return, and with it a note:

'It was very thoughtful of you.

'Take it, this middle robe, let it be the symbol
    Of days uncounted but few between now and then.'

Something else, no doubt, to put in her chest of memories. It was a fine robe and it bore a most remarkable fragrance. How could it fail to move her?

The old monk, his face like one of the twisted shells on the beach, was meanwhile making some of the younger people smile. 'I have quite renounced the world,' he said, 'but the thought that I may not see you back to the city –

'Though weary of life, seasoned by salty winds,
    I am not able to leave this shore behind,

and I wander lost in thoughts upon my child.* Do let me see you at least as far as the border. It may seem forward of me, but if something should from time to time call up thoughts of her, do please let her hear from you.'

See note, page 13.

'It is an impossibility, sir, for very particular reasons, that I can ever forget her. You will very quickly be made to see my real intentions. If I seem dispirited, it is only because I am sad to leave all this behind.

'I wept upon leaving the city in the spring.
I weep in the autumn on leaving this home by the sea.

'What else can I do?' And he brushed away a tear.

The old man seemed on the point of expiring.

The lady did not want anyone to guess the intensity of her grief, but it was there, and with it sorrow at the lowly rank (she knew that she could not complain) that had made this parting inevitable. His image remained before her, and she seemed capable only of weeping.

Her mother tried everything to console her. 'What could we have been thinking of? You have such odd ideas,' she said to her husband, 'and I should have been more careful.'

'Enough, enough. There are reasons why he cannot abandon her. I have no doubt that he has already made his plans. Stop worrying, mix yourself a dose of something or other. This wailing will do no good.' But he was sitting disconsolate in a corner.

The women of the house, the mother and the nurse and the rest, went on charging him with unreasonable methods. 'We had hoped and prayed over the years that she might have the sort of life any girl wants, and things finally seemed to be going well – and now see what has happened.'

It was true. Old age suddenly advanced and subdued him, and he spent his days in bed. But when night came he was up and alert.

'What can have happened to my beads?'

Unable to find them, he brought empty hands together in supplication. His disciples giggled. They giggled again when he set forth on a moonlight peregrination and managed to fall into the brook and bruise his hip on one of the garden stones he had chosen so carefully. For a time pain drove away, or at least obscured, his worries.

Genji went through lustration ceremonies at Naniwa and sent a messenger to Sumiyoshi with thanks that he had come thus far and a promise to visit at a later date in fulfillment of his vows. His retinue had grown to an army and did not permit side excursions. He made his way directly back to the city. At Nijō the reunion was like a dream. Tears of joy flowed so freely as almost to seem inauspicious. Murasaki, for whom life had come to seem of as little value as her farewell poem had suggested it to be, shared in the joy. She had matured and was more beautiful than ever. Her hair had been almost too rich and thick. Worry and sorrow had thinned it somewhat and thereby improved it. And now, thought Genji, a deep peace coming over him, they would be together. And in that instant there came to him the image of the one whom he had not been ready to leave. It seemed that his life must go on being complicated.

He told Murasaki about the other lady. A pensive, dreamy look passed over his face, and she whispered, as if to dismiss the matter: 'For myself I do not worry.'*

He smiled. It was a charmingly gentle reproof. Unable to take his eyes from her now that he had her before him, he could not think how he had survived so many months and years without her. All the old bitterness came back. He was restored to his former rank and made a supernumerary councillor. All his followers were similarly rehabilitated. It was as if spring had come to a withered tree.

The emperor summoned him and as they made their formal greetings thought how exile had improved him. Courtiers looked on with curiosity, wondering what the years in the provinces would have done to him. For the elderly women who had been in service since the reign of his late father, regret gave way to noisy rejoicing. The emperor had felt rather shy at the prospect of receiving Genji and had taken great pains with his dress. He seemed pale and sickly, though he had felt somewhat better these last few days. They talked fondly of this and that, and presently it was night. A full moon flooded the tranquil scene. There were tears in the emperor's eyes.

'We have not had music here of late,' he said, 'and it has been a very long time since I last heard any of the old songs.'

Genji replied:

---

*Ukon, *Shūishū* 870:

> For myself, who am forgotten, I do not worry,
> But for him who vowed fidelity while he lived.

> 'Cast out upon the sea, I passed the years
> As useless as the leech child of the gods.'*

The emperor was touched and embarrassed.

> 'The leech child's parents met beyond the pillar.
> We meet again to forget the spring of parting.'

He was a man of delicate grace and charm.

Genji's first task was to commission a grand reading of the Lotus Sutra in his father's memory. He called on the crown prince, who had grown in his absence, and was touched that the boy should be so pleased to see him. He had done so well with his studies that there need be no misgivings about his competence to rule. It would seem that Genji also called on Fujitsubo, and managed to control himself sufficiently for a quiet and affectionate conversation.

I had forgotten: he sent a note with the retinue which, like a returning wave, returned to Akashi. Very tender, it had been composed when no one was watching.

> 'And how is it with you these nights when the waves roll in?

> 'I wonder, do the morning mists yet rise,
> There at Akashi of the lonely nights?'

The Kyushu Gosechi dancer had had fond thoughts of the exiled Genji, and she was vaguely disappointed to learn that he was back in the city and once more in the emperor's good graces. She sent a note, with instructions that the messenger was to say nothing of its origin:

> 'There once came tidings from a boat at Suma,
> From one who now might show you sodden sleeves.'

Her hand had improved, though not enough to keep him from guessing whose it was.

> 'It is I, not you, from whom the complaints should come.
> My sleeves have refused to dry since last you wrote.'

*In one of the Nihongi versions of the creation myth, the leech child, among the Sun Goddess's siblings, lives approximately the period of Genji's exile before being cast out to sea. It is at a pillar (see the emperor's answering poem) that both the leech and the Sun Goddess are conceived.

He had not seen enough of her, and her letter brought fond memories. But he was not going to embark upon new adventures.

To the lady of the orange blossoms he sent only a note, cause more for disappointment than for pleasure.

CHAPTER 14
Channel Buoys

Unable to forget that almost too vivid dream of his father and wanting somehow to lighten the penance, Genji immediately set about plans for a reading of the Lotus Sutra. It was to be in the Tenth Month. Everyone at court helped with the arrangements. The spirit of cooperation was as before Genji fell into disfavor.

Though seriously ill, Kokiden was still an enemy, angry that she had not succeeded in crushing him completely. The emperor had been convinced that he must pay the penalty for having gone against his father's wishes. Now that he had had Genji recalled, he was in greatly improved spirits, and the eye ailment that had so troubled him had quite gone away. Melancholy forebodings continued to be with him, however. He frequently sent for Genji, who was now in his complete confidence. Everyone thought it splendid that he was at last having his way.

The day appointed for his abdication drew near. It grieved him to think of the precarious position in which it would leave Oborozukiyo.

'Your father is dead,' he said to her, 'and my mother is in worse health all the time. I doubt that I have much longer to live and fear that everything will change once I am gone. I know that there is someone you have long preferred to me; but it has been a way of mine to concentrate upon one object, and I have thought only of you. Even if the man whom you prefer does as you wish him to, I doubt that his affection can match my own. The thought is too much for me.' He was in tears.

She flushed and turned away. An irresistible charm seemed to flow from her, to make him forget his grievances.

'And why have you not had a child? It seems such a pity. No doubt you will shortly have one by the man with whom you seem to have the stronger bond, and that will scarcely be to my taste. He is a commoner, you know, and I suppose the child must be reared as a commoner.'

These remarks about the past and about the future so shamed her that she could not bring herself to look at him. He was a handsome, civil man, and his behavior over the years had told of a deepening affection; and so she had come to understand, as she had become more alive to these subtleties, that Genji, for all his good looks and gallantry, had been less than ideally devoted to her. Why had she surrendered to childish impulses and permitted a scandal which had seriously damaged her name and done no good for his? These reminders of the past brought her untold pain.

In the Second Month of the following year initiation ceremonies were held for the crown prince. He was eleven, tall and mature for his age, and the very image of Genji. The world marveled at the almost blinding radiance, but it was a source of great trepidation for Fujitsubo. Very pleased with his successor, the emperor in a most gentle and friendly way discussed plans for his own abdication.

He abdicated that same month, so suddenly that Kokiden was taken by surprise.

'I know that it will be as a person of no importance,' he said, seeking to calm her, 'but I hope that I will see you rather more frequently and at my leisure.'

His son by Lady Shōkyōden was made crown prince. Everything had changed overnight, causes for rejoicing were innumerable. Genji was made a minister. As the number of ministers is limited by the legal codes and there were at the time no vacancies, a supernumerary position was created for him. It was assumed that his would be the strongest hand in the direction of public affairs.

'I am not up to it,' he said, deferring to his father-in-law, who was persuaded to come out of retirement and accept appointment as regent.

'I resigned because of poor health,' protested the old man, 'and now I am older and even more useless.'

It was pointed out, however, that in foreign countries statesmen who in time of civil disorder have withdrawn to deep mountain retreats have thought it no shame, despite their white beards, to be of service once peace has been restored. Indeed they have been revered as the true saints and sages. The court and the world at large agreed that there need be no obstacle whatever to resuming upon recovery offices resigned because of illness. Unable to persist in his refusal, he was appointed chancellor. He was sixty-three. His retirement had been occasioned in part by the fact that affairs of state were not going as he wished, but now all was in order. His sons, whose careers had been in eclipse, were also brought back. Most striking was the case of Tō no Chūjō, who was made a supernumerary councillor. He had been especially careful about the training of his daughter, now twelve, by Kokiden's sister, and was hoping to send her to court. The boy who had sung 'Takasago' so nicely* had come of age and was the sort of son every father wished for. Indeed Tō no Chūjō had a troop of sons by his various ladies which quite filled Genji with envy.

Genji's own Yūgiri was as handsome a boy as any of them. He served as page for both the emperor and the crown prince. His grandparents, Princess Omiya and the chancellor, continued to grieve for their daughter. But she was gone, and they had Genji's prosperity to take their minds from their sorrow; and it seemed that the gloomy years of Genji's exile had vanished without a trace. Genji's devotion to the family of his late wife was as it had always been. He overlooked no occasion that seemed to call for a visit, or for gifts to the nurse and the others who had remained faithful through the bad years. One may be sure that there were many happy women among them.

At Nijō too there were women who had awaited his return. He wished to do everything possible to make up for the sorrows that must have been theirs, and upon such women as Chūjō and Nakatsukasa, appropriately to their station in life, he bestowed a share of his affection. This left him no time for women outside the house. He had most splendidly remodeled the lodge to the east of his mansion. He had inherited it from his father, and his plan was that it be home for the lady of the orange blossoms and other neglected favorites.

I have said nothing about the Akashi lady, whom he had left in such uncertainty. Busy with public and private affairs, he had not been able to inquire after her as he would have wished. From about the beginning of the Third Month, though he told no one, she was much on his mind, for her time must be approaching. He sent off a messenger, who very soon returned.

'A girl was safely delivered on the sixteenth.'

It was his first daughter. He was delighted – but why had he not brought the lady to have her child in the capital?

'You will have three children,' a fortuneteller had once told him. 'Two of them are certain to become emperor and empress. The least of the three will become chancellor, the most powerful man in the land.' The whole of the oracle seemed by way of coming true.

He had consulted physiognomists in large numbers and they had been unanimous in telling him that he would rise to grand heights and have the world to do with as he wished; but through the unhappy days he had dismissed them from his thoughts. With the commencement of the new reign it seemed that his most extravagant hopes were being realized. The throne itself lay beyond his reach. He had been his father's favorite over his many brothers, but his father had determined to reduce him to common status, and that fact made it apparent that the throne must not be among his ambitions. Although the reasons were of course secret, the accession of the new emperor seemed evidence enough that the fortuneteller had not deceived him. As for future prospects, he thought that he could see the god of Sumiyoshi at work. Had it been foreordained that someone from Akashi was meant for remarkable things, and was it for that reason that her eccentric father had had what had seemed preposterous plans? Genji had done badly in letting his daughter be born in a corner of the provinces. He must send for mother and daughter as soon as the proprieties allowed, and he gave orders that the remodeling of the east lodge be hurried.

Capable nurses would be difficult to find, he was afraid, in Akashi. He remembered having heard the sad story of a woman whose mother had been among the old emperor's private secretaries and whose father had been a chamberlain and councillor. The parents both dead and the lady herself in straitened circumstances, she had struck up an unworthy liaison and had a child as a result. She was young and her prospects were poor, and she did not hesitate at the invitation to quit a deserted and ruinous mansion, and so the contract was made. By way of some errand or other, in the greatest secrecy, Genji visited her. Though she had made the commitment, she had been having second thoughts. The honor of the visit quite removed her doubts.

'I shall do entirely as you wish.'

Since it was a propitious day, he sent her off immediately.

'You will think it selfish and unfeeling of me, I am sure; but I have rather special plans. Tell yourself that there is a precedent for being sent off to a hard life in a strange land, and put up with it for a time.' And he told her in detail of her duties.

Since she had been at court, he had occasionally had a glimpse of her. She was thinner now. Her once fine mansion was sadly neglected, and the plantings in the garden were rank and over-grown. How, he wondered, had she endured such a life?

'Suppose we call it off,' he said jokingly, 'and keep you here.' She was such a pretty young woman that he could not take his eyes from her.

She could not help thinking that, if it was all the same, she would prefer serving him from somewhat nearer at hand.

'I have not, it is true, been so fortunate as to know you,
    But sad it is to end the briefest friendship.

'And so perhaps I should go with you.'

She smiled.

'I do not trust regrets at so quick a farewell.
    The truth has to do with someone you wish to visit.'

It was nicely done.

She left the city by carriage. He assigned as escort men whom he trusted implicitly and enjoined them to the strictest secrecy. He sent with her a sword for the little girl and other appropriate gifts and provisions, in such quantities that the procession was in danger of falling behind schedule. His attentions to the newly appointed nurse could not have been more elaborate.

He smiled to think what this first grandchild would mean to the old man, how busy and self-important he would be. No doubt it told of events in a former life (and the thought brought twinges of conscience), that she meant so much to Genji himself. Over and over again he told the nurse that he would not be quick to forgive lapses and oversights.

'One day this sleeve of mine shall be her shelter
    Whose years shall be as the years of the angel's rock.'*

They hurried to the Harima border by boat and thence by horse. The old man was overjoyed and there was no end to his

---

*'May she live a *kalpa*.' Among the definitions of a *kalpa* is the time required for brushes of an angel's wing once a millennium to wear away a rock several billion cubic miles in volume.

awed gratitude. He made obeisance in the direction of the capital. At this evidence that the little girl was important to Genji he began to feel rather in awe of her too. She had an unearthly, almost ominous sort of beauty, to make the nurse see that the fuss and bother had not after all been overdone. There had been something horrible about this sudden removal to the countryside, but now it was as if she were awakening from a nightmare into broad sunlight. She already adored the little girl.

The Akashi lady had been in despair. She had decided as the months went by that life was without meaning. This evidence of Genji's good intentions was comforting. She bestirred herself to make the guests from the city feel welcome.

The escort was in a hurry to return. She set down something of her feelings in a letter to Genji, to which she added this poem:

'These sleeves are much too narrow to offer protection.
The blossom awaits those all-encompassing ones.'*

Genji was astonished at himself, that his daughter should be so much on his mind and that he should so long to see her.

He had said little to Murasaki of the events at Akashi, but he feared that she might have the story from someone else. 'And that would seem to be the situation,' he said, concluding his account. 'Somehow everything has gone wrong. I don't have children where I really want them, and now there is a child in a very unlikely place. And it is a girl. I could of course simply disown her, but that is the sort of thing I do not seem capable of. I will bring her here one of these days and let you have a look at her. You are not to be jealous, now.'

Murasaki flushed. 'How strange you are. You make me dislike myself, constantly assigning traits which are not mine at all. When and by whom, I wonder, shall I begin to have lessons in jealousy?'

Genji smiled, and tears came to his eyes. 'When indeed, pray. You are very odd, my dear. Things come into your mind that would not occur to anyone else.'

*Anonymous, *Gosenshū* 64:

> They need, these blossoms of spring, assailed by the winds,
> An all-encompassing sleeve to close off the skies.

She thought of their longing for each other through the years apart, of letters back and forth, and his delinquencies and her resentment seemed like a silly joke.

'There are very special reasons for it all,' he continued, 'that she should be so much on my mind, and that I should be so diligent in my inquiries. But I fear that it is too soon to tell you of them. You would not understand. I think that the setting may have been partly responsible.'

He had told of her of the lines of smoke across the Akashi sky that last evening, and, though with some understatement, perhaps, of the lady's appearance and of her skill on the koto. And so while she herself had been lost in infinite sadness, thought Murasaki, he had managed to keep himself entertained. It did not seem right that he should have allowed himself even a playful glance at another woman.

If he had his ways, she would have hers. She looked aside, whispering as if to herself: 'There was a time when we seemed rather a nicely matched couple.

> 'I think I shall be the first to rise as smoke,
>   And it may not go the direction of that other.'

'What a very unpleasant thing to say.

> 'For whom, in mountains, upon unfriendly seas,
>   Has the flow of my tears been such as to sweep me under?

'I wish you could understand me, but of course it is not the way of this world that we are ever completely understood. I would not care or complain except for the fact that I do so love you.'

He took out a koto and tuned it and pushed it towards her; but, perhaps somewhat displeased at his account of the other lady's talents, she refused to touch it. She was a calmly, delightfully gentle lady, and these small outbursts of jealousy were interesting, these occasional shows of anger charming. Yes, he thought, she was someone he could be with always.

His daughter would be fifty days old on the fifth of the Fifth Month. He longed more than ever to see her. What a splendid affair the fiftieth-day celebrations would be if they might take place in the city! Why had he allowed the child to be born in so unseemly a place? If it had been a boy he would not have been so concerned, but for a girl it was a very great disability not to be born in the city. And she seemed especially important because his unhappiness had had so much to do with her destinies.

He sent off messengers with the strictest orders to arrive on that day and no other. They took with them all the gifts which the most fertile imagination could have thought of for such an occasion, and practical everyday supplies as well.

This was Genji's note:

> 'The sea grass, hidden among the rocks, unchanging,
>   Competes this day for attention with the iris.*

'I am quite consumed with longing. You must be prepared to leave Akashi. It cannot be otherwise. I promise you that you have not the smallest thing to worry about.'

The old man's face was a twisted shell once more, this time, most properly, with joy. Very elaborate preparations had been made for the fiftieth-day ceremonies, but had these envoys not come from Genji they would have been like brocades worn in the night.†

The nurse had found the Akashi lady to her liking, a pleasant companion in a gloomy world. Among the women whom the lady's parents, through family connections, had brought from the city were several of no lower standing than the nurse; but they were all aged, tottering people who could no longer be used at court and who had in effect chanced upon Akashi in their search for a retreat among the crags. The nurse was at her elegant best. She gave this and that account, as her feminine sensibilities led her, of the great world, and she spoke too of Genji and how everyone admired him. The Akashi lady began to think herself important for having had something to do with the little memento he had left behind. The nurse saw Genji's letter. What extraordinary good fortune the lady did have, she had been thinking, and how unlucky she had been herself; and Genji's inquiries made her feel important too.

The lady's reply was honest and unaffected.

Ayame, 'iris,' also suggests 'attention.' The fifth of the Fifth Month is the day of the iris (more properly, sweet-flag) festival.

†The *Shih Chi* informs us that to be rich and powerful and not to display that fact in one's native village is to wear brocades in pitch darkness. See also note*, page 212.

'The crane is lost on an insignificant isle.
Not even today do you come to seek it out.

'I cannot be sure how long a life darkened by lonely rever-
ies and brightened by occasional messages from outside can be
expected to continue, and must beg of you that the child be freed
of uncertainty the earliest day possible.'

Genji read the letter over and over again, and sighed.

'The distant boat more distant.'* Murasaki looked away as she
spoke, as if to herself, and said no more.

'You do make a large thing of it. Myself, I make no more of it
than this: sometimes a picture of that seacoast comes into my
mind, and memories come back, and I sigh. You are very attentive, not to miss the sigh.'

He let her see only the address. The hand would have done
honor to the proudest lady at court. She could see why the Akashi
lady had done so well.

It was sad that his preoccupation with Murasaki had left him no
time for the lady of the orange blossoms. There were public affairs
as well, and he was now too important to wander about as he
would wish. It seemed that all was quiet in that sector, and so he
gave little thought to it. Then came the long rains of early summer
to lay a pall over things and bring a respite from his duties. He
roused himself for a visit.

Though she saw little of him, the lady was completely dependent on him; but she was not of the modern sort, given to outpourings of resentment. He knew that she would not make him
uncomfortable. Long neglected, her house now wore a weirdly
ruinous aspect. As usual, he first looked in on her sister, and late in
the night moved on to the lady's own rooms. He was himself
weirdly beautiful in the misty moonlight. She felt very inadequate,
but she was waiting for him out near the veranda, in meditative
contemplation of the night. Her refusal to let anything upset her
was remarkable.

From nearby there came the metallic cry of a water rail.

*Ise, *Shinkokinshū* 1048:

> You seem more distant than the distant boat
> More distant yet as it rows out from Kumano.

'Did not this bird come knocking at my door,
What pretext would I find to admit the moon?'

Her soft voice, trailing off into silence, was very pleasing. He
sighed, almost wishing it were not the case that each of his ladies
had something to recommend her. It made for a most complicated
life.

'You respond to the call of every water rail?
You must find yourself admitting peculiar moons.

'I am worried.'
Not of course that he really suspected her of indiscretion. She
had waited for him and she was very dear to him.

She reminded him of his farewell admonition not to look at the
cloudy moon. 'And why,' she said, gently as always, 'should I have
thought then that I was unhappy? It is no better now.'

He made the usual points (one wondered that they came so
effortlessly) as he sought to comfort her.

He had not forgotten the Kyushu Gosechi dancer. He would
have liked to see her again, but a clandestine meeting was
altogether too difficult to arrange. He dominated her thoughts, so
much so that she had turned away all the prospective bridegrooms
who interested her father and had decided that she would not
marry. Genji's plans were that once his east lodge had been redone,
all cheerfully and pleasantly, he would gather just such ladies there,
and, should a child be born who required careful upbringing, ask
them to take charge of it. The new house compared very well
indeed with the old, for he had assigned officials of intelligence
and good taste to the work of remodeling.

He had not forgotten Oborozukiyo. He let her know that that
unfortunate event had not stilled his ardor. She had learned her
lesson, however, and so for Genji an affair that had never been
really successful had become a complete failure.

Life was pleasant for the retired emperor, who had taken up
residence in the Suzaku Palace. He had parties and concerts as the
seasons went by and was in generally good spirits. Various ladies
were still with him. The mother of the crown prince was the
exception. Not especially conspicuous among them, she had been
no match for Oborozukiyo. Now she had come into her own. She
left the emperor's side to manage the crown prince's affairs. Genji

now occupied his mother's rooms at the palace. The crown prince was in the Pear Pavilion, which adjoined them, and Genji was his companion and servant.

Though Fujitsubo could not resume her former titles, she was given the emoluments of a retired emperor. She maintained a full household and pursued her religious vocation with solemn grandeur. Factional politics had in recent years made it difficult for her to visit the palace, and she had grieved at not being able to see her son. Now everything was as she would have wished it, and the time had come for Kokiden to be unhappy with the world. Genji was scrupulously attentive to Kokiden's needs. This fact did nothing to change her feelings towards him, which were the subject of unfriendly criticism.

Prince Hyōbu, Murasaki's father, had sought during the bad years to please the dominant faction. Genji had not forgotten. Genji's conduct was on the whole not vengeful, but he was sometimes openly unfriendly to the prince. Fujitsubo saw and was unhappy.

The conduct of public affairs was now divided between Genji and his father-in-law, to pursue as they wished. The ceremonies when Tō no Chūjō's daughter entered court in the Eighth Month were magnificent, under the energetic direction of the chancellor himself. It was known that Prince Hyōbu had been putting all his time and wealth into preparing his second daughter for court service. Genji made it clear that the girl was not to be so honored, and what was the prince to do?

In the autumn Genji made a pilgrimage to Sumiyoshi. It was a brilliant progress, in thanks for the granting of his prayers. By the merest chance, it came on the day the Akashi lady had chosen for her own pilgrimage, a semiannual observance which this time had a special purpose, to apologize for her not having been able to present herself the year before or earlier this year. She came by ship. As the ship pulled in, a gorgeous array of offerings was being laid out on the beach. The shrine precincts rang with the shouts of bearers and there were uniformed dancers, all very good-looking.

'And whose party might it be?' asked one of her men.

The very inferior footman to whom the query was made laughed heartily. 'You mean there is someone who does not know that the Genji minister has come because of his vows?'

The lady was stunned. To have chosen this day of all days, to be among the distant onlookers – her own inferiority could not have been emphasized more painfully. She was, in spite of it, tied to him by some bond or other, and here were these underlings, completely pleased with themselves, reflecting his glory. Why, because of what crimes and sins, should she, who never ceased thinking of him, have made this journey to Sumiyoshi on this day without catching an echo of it all? She could only turn away and try to hide her sorrow.

Genji's attendants were numberless, their robes of deep hues and brilliant hues like maple leaves and cherry blossoms against the deep green of the pine groves. Among the courtiers of the Sixth Rank, the yellow-green of the imperial secretariat stood out. The man who had on an earlier day had bitter words for the sacred fence of Kamo was among them. Also holding a guards commission, he had an imposing retinue of his own. Yoshikiyo too was a guards officer. He seemed especially proud of himself, and indeed his scarlet robe was very grand. All the men she had known at Akashi were scattered among the crowds, almost unrecognizable in their finery, the picture of prosperity. The young courtiers had even sought to outdo one another in caparisoning their horses, and for the rustics from Akashi it was a very fine show.

For the lady it was torment to see all the splendor and not to see Genji himself. Like the Kawara minister,* he had been granted a special honor guard of page boys, ten of them, all very pretty, of uniform height, and resplendently decked out, the cords that bound up their hair in the pageboy style a most elegant blending from white to deep purple. Yūgiri, whom Genji denied nothing, had put even his stableboys into livery.

The Akashi lady felt as if she were gazing at a realm beyond the clouds. Her own child seemed so utterly insignificant. She bowed to the shrine and prayed more fervently.

The governor of the province came to greet Genji, and no doubt the repast he had made ready was finer than for most ministers.

The lady could bear no more. 'If I were to go up with my miserable little offerings, the god would scarcely notice, and

---

*Minamoto Tōru. It is recorded that certain high courtiers received page-boy guards as a mark of special favor, but it is not recorded that Tōru was ever so honored.

would not think I had done much by way of keeping my promises. But the whole trip would be pointless if we were to turn and go home.' She suggested that they put in at Naniwa and there commission lustration ceremonies.

Not dreaming what had happened, Genji passed the night in entertainments sure to please the god. He went beyond all his promises in the novelty and ingenuity of the dances. His nearest retainers, men like Koremitsu, knew how much the god had done for them. As Genji came unannounced from the shrine, Koremitsu handed him a poem:

'These pines of Sumiyoshi make me think
    Of days when we were neighbors to this god.'

Very apt, thought Genji.

'Remembering those fearful winds and waves,
    Am I to forget the god of Sumiyoshi?'

'Yes, it has without question been through his intervention.' There was solemn gratitude in the words.

Genji was greatly upset when Koremitsu told him that a boat had come from Akashi and been turned away by the crowds on the beach. Again the god of Sumiyoshi seemed to be at work. The lady would surely regret having chosen this day. He must at least get off a note. Leaving Sumiyoshi, he made excursions to other famous places in the region and had grand and solemn lustrations performed on the seven strands of Naniwa. 'The waves of Naniwa,'* he said to himself (though with no real thought, one may imagine, of throwing himself in) as he looked out over the buoys that marked the Horie channel.

Koremitsu, who was among his mounted attendants, overheard. Always prepared for such an exigency, he took out a short writing brush and handed it to Genji.

*Prince Motoyoshi, *Shūishū* 766:

> The waves of Naniwa: if I throw myself in,
>   As the channel buoys suggest, perhaps we shall meet.

Miotsukushi, 'channel buoys,' suggests bringing one's affairs to an end, being done with it all. There were 'seven strands' at which lustrations were performed in Kyoto, but the meaning of 'the seven strands of Naniwa' is unclear.

A most estimable servant, thought Genji, jotting down a poem on a sheet of paper he had at hand.

'Firm the bond that brings us to Naniwa,
  Whose channel buoys invite me to throw myself in.'

Koremitsu sent it to the lady by a messenger who was familiar with the events at Akashi. She wept tears of joy at even so small a favor. A line of horsemen was just then passing by.

This was her reply, to which she tied sacred cords for the lustration at Tamino:*

'A lowly one whose place is not to demand,
  To what purpose, at Naniwa, should I cast myself in?'

It was evening, and the scene was a lovely one, with the tide flooding in and cranes calling ceaselessly from the shallows. He longed to see her, whatever these crowds might think.

'My sleeves are wet as when I wandered these shores.
  The Isle of the Raincoat does not fend off the dews.'†

To joyous music, he continued his round of the famous places, but his thoughts were with the Akashi lady.

Women of pleasure‡ were in evidence. It would seem that there were susceptible young men even among the highest ranks. Genji looked resolutely away. It was his view that one should be moved only by adequate forces, and that frivolous claims were to be rejected even in the most ordinary affairs. Their most seductive and studied poses had no effect upon him.

His party moved on. The next day being a propitious one, the Akashi lady made offerings at Sumiyoshi, and so, in keeping with her more modest station, acquitted herself of her vows. The incident had only served to intensify her gloom. A messenger came from Genji even before he could have returned to the city. He meant very shortly to send for her, he said. She was glad, and yet she hesitated, fearing the uncertainties of sailing off beyond the islands to a place she could not call home. Her father too was

---

*In the heart of Osaka, the Naniwa of the tale.

†Tamino means 'field of the rain cloak.' Genji's poem is an acrostic, with the name Naniwa buried in it.

‡*Asobi*. This is the only hint in the tale that such a class existed.

uneasy. But life in Akashi would be even more difficult than in earlier years. Her reply was obedient but indecisive.

I had forgotten: a new high priestess had been appointed for the Ise Shrine, and the Rokujō lady had returned to the city with her daughter. Genji's attentions, his inquiries as to her needs, were as always very thorough, but she remembered his coldness in other years and had no wish to call back the old sorrow and regret. She would treat him as a distant friend, no more. For his part, he made no special effort to see her. The truth was that he could not be sure of his own feelings, and his station in life was now such that he could not pursue sundry love affairs as he once had. He had no heart for importuning the lady. He would have liked all the same to see what the years had done to her daughter, the high priestess. The Rokujō house had been kept in good repair. As always, she selected only ladies of the finest taste and endowments to be with her, and the house was once more a literary and artistic salon. Though her life was in many ways lonely, there were ample pleasures and distractions.

Suddenly she fell ill. Troubled by feelings of guilt that she had spent those years in Ise, so remote from the Good Law, she became a nun.

Genji canceled all his appointments and rushed to her side. The old passion had departed, but she had been important to him. His commiserations were endless. She had had a place set out for him near her pillows. Raising herself to an armrest, she essayed her own answers. She seemed very weak, and he wept to think that she might die before he was able to let her know how fond he had been of her. It moved her deeply to think that now, when everything else seemed to be going, he should still care.

She spoke to him of her daughter. 'She will have no one to turn to when I am gone. Please do count her among those who are important to you. She has been the unluckiest of girls, poor dear. I am a useless person and I have done her no good, but I tell myself that if my health will only hold out a little longer I may look after her until she is better able to look after herself.' She was weeping, and life did indeed seem to be leaving her.

'You speak as if we might become strangers. It could not have happened, it would have been quite impossible, even if you had not said this to me. I mean to do everything I can for her. You must not worry.'

'It is all so difficult. Even when a girl has a father to whom she can look with complete confidence, the worst thing is to lose her mother. Life can be dreadfully complicated when her guardian is found to have thoughts not becoming a parent. Unfortunate suspicions are sure to arise, and other women will see their chance to be ugly. These are distasteful forebodings, I know. But please do not let anything of the sort come into your relations with her. My life has been an object lesson in uncertainty, and my only hope now is that she be spared it all.'

She need not be *quite* so outspoken, thought Genji; but he replied calmly enough. 'I am a steadier and soberer person than I used to be, and it astonishes me that you still think me a trifler. One of these days the true state of affairs will be apparent even to you.'

It was dark outside her curtains, through which came suggestions of lamplight. Was it just possible? He slid forward and looked through an opening in the curtains. He saw her dimly, leaning against an armrest, so beautiful with her hair cut short that he wished he might ask someone to do her likeness. And the one beyond, to the east of the bed curtains, would be the priestess. Her curtain frames had been pushed casually to one side. She sat chin in hand, in an attitude of utter despondency. Though he could not see her well, she seemed very beautiful. There was great dignity in the flow of her hair down over her shoulders and in the shape of her head, and he could see that, for all the nobility, it was also a winsome and delicate sort of beauty. He felt certain stirrings of the heart, and remembered her mother's worries.

'I am feeling much worse,' said the lady, 'and fear I may be guilty of rudeness if you stay longer.' A woman helped her into bed.

'How happy I would be if this visit might bring some sign of improvement. What exactly is the nature of the illness?'

She had sensed that she was being seen. 'I must look like a witch. There is a very strong bond between us — it must be so — that you should have come to me now. I have been able to tell you a little of what has been on my mind, and I am no longer afraid to die.'

'It moves me deeply that you should have thought me worthy. I have many brothers, but I have never felt close to them. My father looked upon the high priestess as one of his daughters, and to me she shall be a sister. I have no daughters of my own. She will fill an emptiness in my life.'

His inquiries were warm and frequent, but a week or so later she died. Aware all over again of the uncertainty of life, Genji gave orders for the funeral and went into retreat. The priestess's stewards could have seen to them after a fashion, but he was her chief support.

He paid a visit. She replied, through her lady of honor, that she was feeling utterly lost and helpless.

'Your mother spoke about you, and left instructions, and it would be a great satisfaction if I might have your complete confidence.'

Her women found him such a source of strength and comfort that they thought he could be forgiven earlier derelictions.

The services were very grand, with numerous people from Genji's house to help.

Still in retreat, he sent frequently to inquire after her. When presently she had regained a measure of composure, she sent her own replies. She was far from easy about being in correspondence with him, but her nurse and others insisted that it would be rude to use an intermediary.

It was a day of high winds and driving snow and sleet. He thought how much more miserable the weather must seem to her.

'I can imagine,' he wrote, 'what these hostile skies must do to you, and yet –

'From skies of wild, unceasing snow and sleet
    Her spirit watches over a house of sorrow.'

He had chosen paper of a cloudy azure, and taken pains with all the details which he thought might interest a young girl.

She was hard put to reply, but her women again insisted that secretaries should have no part in these matters. She finally set down a poem on a richly perfumed gray paper, relying on the somber texture to modulate the shadings of her ink.

'I wish to go, but, blind with tears, am helpless
    As snows which were not asked where they would fall.'

It was a calm, reserved hand, not remarkably skilled, but with a pleasantly youthful quality about it and much that told of good breeding. She had had a particular place in his thoughts ever since her departure for Ise, and now of course nothing stood in his way. But, as before, he reconsidered. Her mother had had good reason for her fears, which worried him less, it must be added, than the rumors that were even now going the rounds. He would behave in quite the opposite manner. He would be a model of propriety and parental solicitude, and when the emperor was a little older and better equipped to understand, he would bring her to court. With no daughters on hand to make life interesting, he would look after her as if she were his daughter. He was most attentive to her needs and, choosing his occasions well, sometimes visited her.

'You will think it forward of me to say so, but I would like nothing better than to be thought a substitute for your mother. Every sign that you trust me will please me enormously.'

She was of a very shy and introspective nature, reluctant even to let him hear her voice. Her women were helpless to overcome this extreme reticence. She had in her service several minor princesses whose breeding and taste were such, he was sure, that she need not feel at all uncomfortable or awkward at court. He wanted very much to have a look at her and see whether his plans were well grounded – evidence, perhaps, that his fatherly impulses were not unmixed. He could not himself be sure when his feelings would change, and he let fall no hint of his plans. The princess's household felt greatly in his debt for his careful attention to the funeral and memorial services.

The days went by in dark procession. Her retainers began to take their leave. Her house, near the lower eastern limits of the city, was in a lonely district of fields and temples where the vesper bells often rang an accompaniment to her sobs. She and her mother had been close as parent and child seldom are. They had not been separated even briefly, and it had been without precedent for a mother to accompany a high priestess to Ise. She would have begged to be taken on this last journey as well, had it been possible.

There were men of various ranks who sought to pay court through her women. Quite as if he were her father, Genji told the women that none of them, not even the nurse, should presume to take matters into her own hands. They were very careful, for they would not want damaging reports to reach the ears of so grand a gentleman.

The Suzaku emperor still had vivid memories of the rites in the

Grand Hall upon her departure for Ise, and of a beauty that had seemed almost frightening.

'Have her come to me,' he had said to her mother. 'She shall live exactly as my sisters, the high priestess of Kamo and the others.'

But the Rokujō lady had misgivings and managed to evade the august invitation. The Suzaku emperor already had several well-born consorts, and her daughter would be without strong backing. He was not in good health, moreover, and she feared that to her own misfortune might be added her daughter's. With the Rokujō lady gone, the priestess's women were more acutely aware than ever of the need for strong backing. The Suzaku emperor repeated his invitation.

Genji learned of his brother's hopes. It would be altogether too high-handed to spirit the princess away, and on the other hand Genji would have strong regrets at letting such a beautiful lady go. He decided that he must consult Fujitsubo, the mother of the new emperor.

He told her of all that was troubling him. 'Her mother was a careful, thoughtful lady. My loose ways were responsible for all the trouble. I cannot tell you how it hurts me to think that she came to hate me. She died hating me; but as she lay dying she spoke to me about her daughter. Enough had been said about me, I gather, to convince her that I was the one to turn to, and so she controlled her anger and confided in me. The thought of it makes me want to start weeping again. I would find it difficult to ignore such a sad case even if it were not my personal concern, and I want to do all I can to put the poor lady's soul at rest and persuade her to forgive me. His Majesty is mature for his age, but he is still very young, and I often think how good it would be if he had someone with him who knew a little about the world. But of course the decision must be yours.'

'This is very thoughtful and understanding of you. One does not wish to be unkind to the Suzaku emperor, of course, but perhaps, taking advantage of the Rokujō lady's instructions, you could pretend to be unaware of his wishes. He seems in any case to have given himself over to his prayers, and such concerns can scarcely matter very much any more. I am sure that if you explain the situation to him he will not harbor any deep resentment.'

'If you agree, then, and are kind enough to number her among the acceptable candidates, I shall say a word to her of your decision. I have thought a great deal about her interests and have at length come to the conclusion I have just described to you. The gossips do upset me, of course.'

He would do as she suggested. Pretending to be unaware of the Suzaku emperor's hopes, he would take the girl into the Nijō mansion.

He told Murasaki of this decision. 'And,' he added, 'she is just the right age to be a good companion.'

She was delighted. He pushed ahead with his plans.

Fujitsubo was concerned about her brother, Prince Hyōbu, who was in a fever, it seemed, to have his own daughter received at court. He and Genji were not on good terms. What did Genji propose to do in the matter?

Tō no Chūjō's daughter, now a royal consort, occupied the Kokiden apartments, and made a good playmate for the emperor. She had been adopted by her grandfather, the chancellor, who denied her nothing. Prince Hyōbu's daughter was about the same age as the emperor, and Fujitsubo feared that they would make a rather ridiculous couple, as if they were playing house together. She was delighted at the prospect of having an older lady with him, and she said as much. Genji was untiring in his services, advising him in public matters, of course, to the great satisfaction of Fujitsubo, and managing his private life as well. Fujitsubo was ill much of the time. Even when she was at the palace she found it difficult to be with her son as much as she wished. It was quite imperative that he have an older lady to look after him.

CHAPTER 15
The Wormwood Patch

In those days of sea grass steeped in brine,* many ladies had lamented Genji's absence and hoped he would soon be back in the city. For ladies like Murasaki, whose place in his life was secure, there were at least letters (though of course they did not completely deaden the pain) to inform them that he was well. Though he wore the plainer clothes of exile, Murasaki found comfort, in a gloomy world, in making sure that they followed the seasons. There were less fortunate ones whom he had not openly recognized and who, not having seen his departure into exile, could only imagine how it must have been.

The safflower princess had lived a very straitened life after the death of her father, Prince Hitachi. Then had come that windfall. For Genji it had been the merest trifle, but for her, whose sleeves were so pitifully narrow, it was as if all the stars had suddenly fallen into her bowl. And then had come the days when the whole world had seemed to turn against him. Genji did not have time for everyone, and after his removal to distant Suma he did not or could not take the trouble to write. The princess wept for a time, and lived a loveless and threadbare existence after the tears had dried.

'Some people seem to have done all the wrong things in their other lives,' grumbled one of her old women. 'As if he had not been unkind enough already, the Blessed One all of a sudden brings a bit of pleasure – rather more than a bit, actually – and then takes it away again. How nice it was! The way of the world, you might say, that it should all disappear – and a body is expected to go on living.'

Yes, it had been very perverse of the Blessed One. A lady grows used to hunger and deprivation, but when they have been absent for a time they no longer seem like proper and usual conditions. Women who could be useful to her had somehow of their own accord come into her ken, and one by one they went away again; and so, as the months passed, her house was lonelier and lonelier.

*See note**, page 241.

Her gardens, never well tended, now offered ample cover for foxes and other sinister creatures, and owls hooted in unpruned groves morning and night. Tree spirits are shy of crowds, but when people go away they come forward as if claiming sovereignty. Frightening apparitions were numberless.

'Really, my lady, we cannot go on this way,' said one of the few women who still remained with her. 'There are governors of this and that province who have a taste for old parks and who have set their eyes on these woods and grounds and asked through neighbors if you might not be persuaded to let them go. Please, my lady, do consider selling. Do let us move to a place where we need not be constantly looking over our shoulders. We have stayed with you, but we cannot be sure how much longer we will be able to.'

'You must not say such things. What will people think? Can you really believe that I would sell Father's house? I agree with you that we have not kept it up very well, and sometimes I find myself looking over my shoulder too. But it is home for me and it was home for Father and I somehow feel that he is still here.' She wept and refused to listen.

The furnishings were old but of the finest workmanship, exactly the sort that collectors like best. Word got out that this and that piece was by this and that master, and the collectors were sure that the impoverished Hitachi house would be an easy target.

'But, my lady, everyone does it. Why should we pretend to be different?' When their lady was not looking, they sought to make their own accommodations.

She was very angry when she detected what was happening. 'Father had them made for us and no one else. How can you dream of having those awful people paw at them? It would kill me to think he might be watching.'

There was no one now to whom she might turn for help. It is true that her older brother, a monk, would stop by when he chanced to be in the city; but he had no part in practical or elegant affairs. Even among his colleagues he had a name for saintly unworldliness. He did not seem to notice that the wormwood was asking to be cut back. The rushes were so thick that one could not be sure whether they grew from land or water. Wormwood touched the eaves, bindweed had firmly barred the gates. This last fact would perhaps have given comfortable feelings of security had it not been for the fact that horses and cattle had knocked over the fences and worn paths inside. Still more impolite were the boys who in spring and summer deliberately drove their herds through. In the Eighth Month one year a particularly savage typhoon blew down all the galleries and stripped the servants' quarters to bare frames, and so the servants left. No smoke rose from the kitchen. Things had, in a word, come to a sorry pass. A glance at the brambles convinced robbers that the place was not worth looking into. But the furnishings and decorations in the main hall were as they had always been. There was no one to clean and polish them, of course; but if the lady lived among mountains of dust it was elegant and orderly dust.

She might have beguiled the loneliness of her days with old songs and poems, but she really did not have much feeling for such things. It is usual for young ladies who, though not remarkably subtle, have time on their hands to find amusement through the passing seasons in exchanging little notes and poems with kindred spirits; but, faithful to the principles by which her father had reared her, she did not welcome familiarity, and remained aloof even from people who might have enjoyed an occasional note. Sometimes she would open a scarred bookcase and take out an illustrated copy of *The Bat, The Lady Recluse,* or *The Bamboo Cutter.*[*]

Old poems bring pleasure when they are selected with taste and discrimination, with fine attention to author and occasion and import; but there can be little to interest anyone in random, hackneyed poems set down on yellowing business paper or portentously furrowed Michinoku. Yet it was just such collections that she would browse through when the loneliness and the gloom were too much for her. The sacred texts and rites to which most recluses turn intimidated her, and as for rosaries, she would not have wished, had there been anyone to see, to be seen with one. It was a very undecorated life she lived.

Only Jijū, her old nurse's daughter, was unable to leave. The high priestess of Kamo,[†] whose house she had frequented, was no longer living, and life was very difficult and uncertain.

---

[*]Only the last survives. The text has *karamori* for the first. There is evidence that it is a miscopying for *Kōmori.*

[†]See Chapter 6.

There was a lady, the princess's maternal aunt, who had fallen in the world and married a provincial governor. She was devoted to her daughters, into whose service she had brought numbers of not at all contemptible women. Jijū occasionally went to visit, for after all a house so close to her family was more inviting than a house of strangers.

The princess, of an extremely shy and retiring nature, had never warmed to her aunt, and there had been some petulance on the part of the latter.

'I know that my sister thought me a disgrace to the family,' she would say; 'and that is why, though I feel very sorry indeed for your lady, I am able to offer neither help nor sympathy.'

She did, however, write from time to time.

The sons and daughters of provincial governors are sometimes nobler than the high nobility, as they imitate their betters; and a child of the high nobility can sometimes sink to a lamentable commonness. So it was with the aunt, a drab, vulgar sort of person. She herself had come to be looked down upon, and now that her sister's house was in ruins she would have loved to hire her niece as governess. The princess was rather old-fashioned, it was true, but she could be depended upon.

'Do come and see us occasionally,' wrote the aunt. 'There are several people here who long to hear your koto.'

Jijū kept at her lady to accept the invitation; but, less from any wish to resist than from extreme and incurable shyness, the princess remained aloof, and the aunt's resentment unalloyed.

Her husband was presently appointed assistant viceroy of Kyushu. Making suitable arrangements for her daughters, she set off with him for his new post.

She was eager to take her niece along. 'I will be very far away,' she would say, always plausibly. 'I have not inquired after you as frequently as I would have wished, but I have had the comfort of knowing you are near, and I do hate to leave you behind.'

She was noisily angry when the princess refused again. 'A *most* unpleasant person. She has made up her mind that she is better than the rest of us. Well, I doubt that the Genji general will come courting the princess of the wormwood patch.'

And then the court was astir with the news that Genji would return to the city. The competition was intense, in high places and low, to demonstrate complete and unswerving loyalty. Genji learned a great deal about human nature. In these busy, unsettled times he apparently did not think of the safflower princess. It was the end of all hope, she thought. She had grieved for him in his misfortune and prayed that happy spring would come. Now all the clods in the land were rejoicing, and she heard of all the joy from afar, as if he were a stranger. She had asked herself, in the worst days, whether some change had perhaps been wrought by herself upon the world.* It had all been to no purpose. Sometimes, when she was alone, she wept aloud.

The aunt thought her a proper fool. It was just as she had said it would be. Could anyone possibly pay court to a person who lived such a beggarly existence, indeed such a ridiculous existence? It is said that the Blessed One bestows his benign grace upon those who are without sin – and here the princess was, quite unapologetic, pretending that matters were as they had been while her royal father and her good mother lived. It was rather sad, really.

The aunt sent another plausible note. 'Please do make up your mind and come with us. The poet said that in bad times a person wants a trip to the mountains.† Nothing very dreadful is going to happen to you if you come with us.'

The princess was the despair of her women. 'Why will she not listen? She doesn't know which way to turn, and yet she manages to go on being stubborn. How can you account for it?'

Jijū had been successfully wooed by a nephew, perhaps it was, of the new assistant viceroy. Her bridegroom would not dream of leaving her, and so, reluctantly, she determined to go. She pleaded with her lady to go too. It would be a terrible worry, she said, if her lady were to stay behind all alone. But the princess still put her faith in Genji, who had neglected her for so long. The years might pass, she told herself, but the day would come when he would remember her. He had made such affectionate, earnest promises, and though it now seemed her fate to have been forgotten, it would not always be so. He would one day have, upon some wind, tidings of her, and when he did he would come to her. So

*Anonymous, *Kokinshū* 948:

> Is the world a sadder place than once it was?
> And has the change been wrought by me alone?

†See note*, page 208.

she had made her way through the weeks and months. Though her mansion fell into deeper ruin, she resolutely clung to her treasures, and insisted on living as she always had. The world seemed darker and darker, and she wept and wept, and her nose was as if someone had affixed a bright berry to it. As for her profile, only someone with more than ordinary affection for her could have borne to look at it. But I shall not go into the details. I am a charitable person, and would not wish for the world to seem malicious.

Winter came and the days passed in forlorn procession. The lady had literally nothing to cling to. Genji commissioned a reading of the Lotus Sutra* which was the talk of the court. Making it known that he would have no ordinary clerics among the officiants, he summoned venerable and erudite sages who could be counted on to know what to do. Among them was the brother of the safflower princess.

On his return to the monastery he came by to see his sister. 'It was all very grand, so lavish and in such impeccable taste that it made one think that the Pure Land had come down to this world. Genji must be an incarnation of a Blessed One or perhaps a messiah even. How can such a man have been born into this world of sin and corruption?' And he was on his way.

They were an unusually taciturn brother and sister, unable to exchange the most idle remarks. Yet his words had made an impression. A Blessed One, a messiah, indeed! A fine messiah, taking no notice at all of her misery and peril. She understood at last. She would never see him again.

The aunt came busily in upon the worst of the gloom. Although she had not been close to the princess, she came laden with gifts, hoping that even now she might lure the princess off to the provinces. Her carriage a grand one, she came quite without forewarning, obviously satisfied with the course her career was taking. She was shocked at the desolation that lay before her. The gates were coming unhinged and leaning precariously, and resisted all the grunting efforts to open them. Even the 'three paths'† had disappeared in the undergrowth. The carriage forced its way to a raised shutter at the south front. The princess, though offended,

---

*See the preceding chapter.

†In Chinese folklore there are three paths through a hermit's garden.

had Jijū receive the visitor from behind yellowing curtains. The
years were catching up with Jijū. She was thin and dispirited. She
still retained enough of her old elegance, however, that the aunt,
inappropriate though it would of course have been to say so,
would have preferred having her for a niece.

'So I am off, and I must leave you to this. I have come for Jijū.
I know that you dislike me and would not consider making a trip
around the corner with me, but perhaps you might at least permit
me to have Jijū. You poor thing, how can you stand it?' She was
trying very hard to weep, but the triumphant smile of the assistant
viceroy's wife was not very well hidden. 'To the end of his days
your royal father looked upon me as a disgrace to the family. But I
do not hold grudges, and so here I am. Thanks to Genji there was
a time when you might have hoped to go on living like a princess.
I would not have dreamed of trying to insinuate my way into your
royal presence. But these things pass. Sometimes the underdog
wins. The mighty sometimes fall, and a person does after all have
to feel sorry for them. I have not been very diligent about keeping
in touch, I know, but I have had the comforting knowledge that
you are near. Now I am going off to the provinces. I can hardly
bear to think of leaving you all alone.'

The princess offered a few stiff words in reply. 'It is kind of you
to have invited me. I fear that I would not be good company. I
shall stay where I am, thank you very much, and that will be that.'

'No doubt. I do have to admire you. Not everyone would have
the courage. I am sure Genji could make this place over into a
gleaming palace in a minute if he chose to. But they tell me he
finds time these days for Prince Hyōbu's daughter and no one else.
He has always had an eye for the ladies, I'm told, but they come
and they go, and the ones that used to please him don't any more.
Do you think he will be grateful to you for watching over the
wormwood?'

The princess was in tears. Though the aunt was right, of course,
she spent a whole day in futile argument.

'Well, let me have Jijū then.' It was evening, and she was in a
hurry to be off.

Forced at last to take a stand, Jijū was weeping copiously. 'I will
just see your aunt on her way, then, my lady, as she has urged me
to. I think that what she says is quite true,' she added in a whisper,
'and at the same time I think it quite understandable that you can-

not find it in yourself to agree. I am put in a very difficult position.'

So Jijū too was leaving. The princess could only weep. The everyday robes she might have offered as farewell presents were yellow and stained. And what else was there, what token of her gratitude for long years of service? She remembered that she had collected her own hair as it had fallen, rather wonderful, ten feet or so long. She now put it into a beautifully fabricated box, and with it a jar of old incense.

'I had counted upon them not to slacken or give,
    These jeweled strands – and far off now they are borne.

'I am a useless person, I know, but there were your mama's last instructions, and I had thought you would stay with me.' She was weeping bitterly. 'You must go, of course. And what am I to do without you?'

Jijū could scarcely reply. 'Yes, of course, there was Mama. Don't, please, remind me of her, my lady. We have been through a great deal together, and I am not asking them to take me away from you.

'The jeweled strands may snap, but I swear by the gods,
    The gods of the road, that I will not cast them off.

Though I cannot of course be sure how long I shall live.'

Meanwhile the aunt was grumbling. 'Can't you hurry just a little? It's getting dark.'

In a daze, Jijū was urged into the carriage. She looked back and looked back again as it pulled away.

The princess was lonelier than ever. She had said goodbye to the last of them. Jijū had not left her side through all the difficult years.

'She was quite right to go. How could she have stayed? It is getting to be more than we ourselves can stand.' Even old women whose remaining task was to die were looking for better positions.

The princess only hoped that no one heard their complaining.

There was a great deal of snow and sleet as winter came. In other gardens it melted, but in hers there were weeds to protect it, until presently one was reminded of White Mountain in Etchū. The princess gazed out at a garden without gardeners. The last friend with whom she could exchange an occasional pleasantry had left her. She passed lonely days and nights in a dusty boudoir.

Genji, having been away for so long, was completely occupied at Nijō. He had no time to visit ladies of lesser importance. He did from time to time think of the safflower princess and wonder whether she would still be among the living. He had no great wish to seek her out, however; and so the year came to an end.

In the Fourth Month he thought of the lady of the orange blossoms. Telling Murasaki that he had an errand to do, he slipped out of the Nijō house. A light rain was falling, the end of several days' rain. The moon came out just as the clouds were breaking. He was sunk in thoughts of other secret expeditions as he made his way through the soft evening moonlight. He passed a house so utterly ruinous, a garden so rank, that he almost wondered whether human beings had ever broken the wild forest. Wisteria blossoms, trailing from a giant pine, waved gently in the moonlight. The breeze brought in a vague, nostalgic perfume, similar to but somehow different from orange blossoms. He leaned from his carriage. Without support from the crumbling earthen wall, the branches of a willow dropped to the ground in great disorder. He had been here before. Yes – Prince Hitachi's mansion. He had his carriage stopped, and inquired of Koremitsu, who was always with him on these expeditions, whether it was indeed Prince Hitachi's.

'It is, my lord.'

'What an awful time the poor princess was having. I wonder if she still lives here. I had been thinking about her, but you know what people would say if I tried to see her. An opportunity it would be wrong to let pass. Go inside, please, and ask. But be very sure of yourself before you do. We would look very silly if we found ourselves with the wrong person.'

Though he did not know it, he had chosen a moment of heightened feeling. She had been napping and she had dreamed of her father. Afterwards, as if on his order, she set someone to mopping the rainwater that had leaked into a penthouse, and someone else to rearranging cushions, and in general it seemed as if she had resumed housekeeping.

> 'My sleeves still wet from tears for him who died
> Are wetter yet from rain through ruined eaves.'

It was just at this moment. Koremitsu was wandering about

seeking traces of human occupancy. He found none. He had
passed the house on earlier occasions and looked in. It had seemed
quite deserted. The moon burst forth brightly as he turned to
leave. He saw that a pair of shutters was raised and a blind was
moving slightly. Though this first sign of life was a little frightening, he approached and cleared his throat to announce his
presence.

After a cough, a fearfully aged voice replied: 'Who is that out
there? Who are you?'

Koremitsu identified himself. 'I would like to speak to Jijū,
please, if I may.'

'Jijū's gone away and left us. But there's someone here you
might call just the same as Jijū.' The voice was a very, very ancient
one. He thought he had heard it before.

Suddenly, without warning, from nowhere, a gentleman in
travel dress, to all appearances courteous and civil. No longer
accustomed to receiving visitors, the old woman wondered if it
might be a fox or some equally perverse and mischievous creature.

He came nearer. 'I must beg to be told exactly how things are
with you. If your lady has not changed, then my lord's wishes to
call upon her have not changed either. He found that he could not
pass you by, and had his carriage stopped outside. What shall I tell
him? You have nothing to be afraid of.'

There was uncertain laughter, and a woman answered haltingly:
'Do you think that if she had changed she would not have moved
away from this jungle? Please imagine for yourself, sir, the situation of which you inquire, and report it to your lord. We who
should be used to it by now think it most extraordinary. We ask
ourselves how many other examples there can possibly be in the
whole world.'

'I see. I will tell him.' Fearing he might have a longer answer
than he wished, Koremitsu returned to Genji's carriage.

'You took your time,' said Genji. 'And what did you find? You
must have had to cut away a great deal of underbrush to find anything.'

Koremitsu described the search that had taken him so long. 'I
spoke to Jijū's aunt, the old lady called Shōshō. I would have
recognized her voice anywhere.'

'What a way to live.' Genji was sorry he had so neglected his
safflower. 'What shall I do? It has been a very long time. These

secret travels are not easy for me, and if I let this opportunity pass there is not likely to be another. If she hasn't changed –'

It seemed rather inelegant just to walk in. He would have liked to send in a clever note. But he remembered how slow she was with her answers. Unless she had gained momentum Koremitsu might expect to be kept waiting all night.

'It is very wet, sir. Suppose you wait until I have shaken a little of it away.'

> 'Myself will I break a path through towering weeds
> And ask: does a constant spirit dwell within?'

Genji spoke as if to himself, and despite Koremitsu's warnings got from his carriage.

Koremitsu beat at the grass with a horsewhip. The drops from the trees were like a chilly autumn shower.

'I have an umbrella,' said Koremitsu. 'These groves shed the most fearful torrents.'*

Genji's feet and ankles were soaking. Even in the old days the passage through the south gallery had been more obstacle than passage. Now the gallery had caved in, and Genji's entry was a most ungraceful one. He was glad there were no witnesses.

Having waited so long, clinging to the hope that he would come someday, the princess was of course delighted. Yet she regretted that he must see her in these circumstances. The various robes that were gifts from the assistant viceroy's wife had been put aside, for she did not like the giver. The old women had put them in a scented Chinese chest. Now they came out again, pleasantly scented. The princess let herself be dressed and received Genji from behind the yellow curtains of the last interview with her aunt.

'Although we have seen so little of each other,' said Genji, 'I have not ceased to think of you all this time. I have waited impatiently for some sign that you too still care. Although I did not detect any welcoming cedars this evening,† I did somehow feel these groves pulling at me. And so you have won the game.'

---

*Anonymous, *Kokinshū* 1091:

> Your master, good sirs, must not be without an umbrella.
> These groves at Miyagino shed the most fearful torrents.

†See note†, page 197.

He pushed the curtain slightly aside. She was as shy and with-drawn as ever, he could see, and she was not immediately able to answer. Finally, impressed that he should have made his way through the undergrowth, she gathered courage for a few tentative syllables.

'I can imagine that it has been uncommonly difficult for you these last few years,' said Genji. 'I myself seem incapable of chang-ing and forgetting, and it would interest me to know how it strikes you that I should have come swimming through these grasses, with no idea at all whether you yourself might have changed. Per-haps I may ask you to forgive the neglect. I have neglected every-one, not only you. I shall consider myself guilty of breach of promise if I ever again do anything to displease you.'

The warmly affectionate utterances came forth in far larger numbers than he had any real feeling for. Everything urged against spending the night here. Having made excuses, he was about to leave. The pine tree was not one which he himself had planted, but someone had planted it, many years ago – years that seemed like a dream.

'I obey the waving summons of wisteria
Because it flows, at your gate, from the waiting tree.'

'Yes, it has been many years. Things have changed, not always for the better. Someday I must tell you of my struggles with the fisherman's net and the angler's line.* Another thing that seems strange, now that I think of it, is my complete confidence that you would refuse to tell anyone else the story of your unhappy springs and autumns.'

'I have waited and waited, to no avail, it seems.
Wisteria, not the waiting pine, has brought you.'

The faint stirring behind the curtains, the faint perfume that came to him from her sleeves, made him feel that she had perhaps improved a little with age. The setting moon streamed unob-structed through the open doors, both the gallery and the eaves having collapsed. He could see to the farthest corners of the room. The furnishings which she kept as they had always been made it seem a much finer house than the roof sagging under the weight of

*See note†, page 250.

ferns would have led him to imagine. She was very unlike – and the contrast was touching – the princess in the old romance who destroyed the tower.* Her stoicism in the face of poverty gave her a certain dignity. It had made her worth remembering. He hated to think of his own selfishness through the years.

Nor could the lady of the orange blossoms have been described as a bright, lively, modern sort. The difference between the two ladies, indeed, as he saw them in quick succession, did not seem very great; and the safflower princess's defects were minimized.

Gifts always poured in as the Kamo festival approached. He distributed them among his several ladies as seemed appropriate, taking care this time that Prince Hitachi's mansion was not slighted. He set stewards and artisans who had his confidence to replacing the decayed earthen walls with a sturdy wooden fence. Genji himself stayed away, fearing derisive rumors about his diligence in having searched her out. He sent many an earnest and affectionate note, however. He was remodeling a house very near his own Nijō mansion, he said, and he thought she might wish to move into it. Perhaps she could be thinking about presentable maids and footmen and the like. The wormwood patch now seemed to choke with gratitude. Looking off in Genji's direction, the Hitachi household offered thanks.

People had always said that Genji chose superior women to spend even a single night with. It was very odd: everything suggested that the Hitachi princess in no respect even rose to mediocrity. What could explain it? A bond tied in a former life, no doubt.

Most of the princess's women, whatever their stations in life, had dismissed her as beyond redemption and scrambled over one another in search of better places. Now the direction of the scramble was reversed. The princess, gentle and retiring to a fault, had spoiled them. Life in the service of provincial governors was unpleasantly different from what she had accustomed them to. A certain crassness was apparent in the haste with which they returned.

Ever more prosperous and powerful, Genji was more thoughtful as well. His instructions had been very detailed, and the prin-

---

*The romance has been lost, but the destruction of the tower would seem to have been a symbol of unfilial conduct.

cess's mansion came back to life. People were seen at the gates and in the garden, the brook was cleared, the wormwood was cut away so that breezes passed once more. Among Genji's lesser stewards were men who had not yet succeeded in catching his eye. He seemed to care about the Hitachi place. It offered the opportunity they had been looking for.

The princess stayed there for two years, after which he moved her to the east lodge at Nijō. Now he could visit her in the course of ordinary business. It could no longer be said that he treated her badly.

Though no one has asked me to do so, I should like to describe the surprise of the assistant viceroy's wife at this turn of events, and Jijū's pleasure and guilt. But it would be a bother and my head is aching; and perhaps – these things do happen, they say – something will someday remind me to continue the story.

CHAPTER 16

The Gatehouse

The vice-governor of Iyo had the year after the death of Genji's father become vice-governor of Hitachi. His wife, the lady of the locust shell,* had gone with him to his post. In that distant part of the realm she heard of Genji's exile. One is not to imagine that she was unconcerned, but she had no way of writing to him. The winds blowing down over Tsukuba† were not to be trusted, it seemed, and reports from the city were few; and so the months and years went by. Although the period of his exile had not been fixed, he did finally return to the city. A year later the vice-governor of Hitachi also returned to the city.

It happened that on the day the Hitachi party came to Osaka barrier, Genji had set off on a pilgrimage of thanksgiving to Ishiyama. The former governor of Kii and others had come from the city to meet the Hitachi party. They brought news of Genji's excursion. Thinking how enormous the confusion was likely to be if the two parties met, the vice-governor set out at dawn. The women's carriages moved slowly, however, and soon the sun was high. As they reached Uchidenohama, on the coast of Lake Biwa, Genji's outrunners were already clearing the road. He himself was just entering the hills east of the city, they said. The vice-governor pulled his carriages in under the cedars at the top of the barrier rise. Unhitching the oxen, the coachmen knelt respectfully for Genji to pass. Though spaced at intervals along the road, the Hitachi procession was impressive. The ladies' sleeves and skirts protruding gaily from the blinds of perhaps ten of the carriages seemed not at all frowsy or countrified. Genji thought of the carriages awaiting the high priestess's departure for Ise. In wave upon wave, his attendants turned to admire the sleeves and skirts.

It being the end of the Ninth Month, the autumn leaves, some crimson and some but gently tinted, and the grasses and flowers touched lightly by the frost were very beautiful indeed; and Genji's men, pouring past the gatehouse in travel livery, damasks and dappled prints, added yet more color. His blinds lowered, Genji sent for Kogimi, the lady's brother, now a guards officer.

*See Chapters 2 and 3.

†The highest mountain in Hitachi, to the northeast of the present Tokyo.

'See, I have come all the way to the barrier. Should this not tell her something?'

Affectionate memories came flooding back, but he had to make do with this most ordinary of greetings.

The lady too was assailed by memories, of events which she had kept to herself all these years.

> 'It flowed as I went, it flows as I return,
> The steady crystal spring at the barrier rise.'

There was no point in trying to explain what she meant.

Kogimi went out to meet Genji on the return from Ishiyama and to apologize for not having stayed with him that earlier day. He had been a favorite with Genji, whose patronage had seen him as far as the Fifth Rank. Fearing at the time of Genji's exile that the association would be damaging, he had gone off to Hitachi with his sister and brother-in-law. If, in the years since, Genji had been somewhat less fond of him, there was no sign of that fact in his behavior now. Though things could not be quite the same again, of course, Genji still thought the youth rather promising. The governor of Kii had since become governor of Kawachi. His younger brother, a guards officer, had been stripped of his commission and had gone into exile with Genji, and now he was being richly rewarded. Regret was usual among those who in those difficult days had given way to the pressures of the times.

Genji gave Kogimi a message for his sister. How very attentive he was to these details, thought Kogimi, when no one need have been surprised if he had forgotten everything.

'I wonder if it occurred to you the other day,' said Genji's note, 'how strong a bond there must be between us.

> 'By chance we met, beside the gate of meeting.
> A pity its fresh waters should be so sterile.*

'How I envy the occupant of the gatehouse. It all comes back, after years of silence. I have a way of looking back upon things of long ago as if they were of this very moment. Will you once again accuse me of promiscuity?'

The youth respectfully undertook to deliver it. 'I do think you should let him have an answer,' he said to his sister. 'I would not have been surprised if he had shown a certain hostility, but he was as civil and polite as ever. I could not have been more grateful. It

---

*There is a pun on *kai nashi*, which means both 'fruitless' and 'without seashells.' The 'occupant of the gatehouse' is the lady's husband, the returning vice-governor.

does a man no good to be an intermediary in these matters, but I could not say no to him. You are a woman, and no one will reprove you, I think, if you concede a point and answer him.'

The lady had become more reticent with the years, but she was unable to ignore so remarkable a message.

'The gate of meeting, atop the barrier rise,
Is shaded by impassable wailing groves.

'It is all like a dream.'

Touching things, annoying things, Genji could forget none of them. From time to time he got off notes to the lady which he hoped would interest and excite her.

Now an old man, her husband was ill much of the time. He talked of her to his sons.

'Please, I beseech you, do not refuse her anything. Treat her exactly as if I were still alive.' No hour of the day passed without his renewing the plea.

She had not been lucky, thought the lady, and if now she were left a widow, what sort of ruin might lie ahead? He knew what she was thinking; but life is not ours to cling to as we will, however strong the determination. If only he could send an angel down to watch over her! They were his sons, but his confidence in them was far from complete. He continued to hand down injunctions and to worry; and then, for all his will to live, he was dead.

For a time the sons seemed to honor his last wishes. The appearance of affection and concern was superficial, however, a fact which circumstances were quick enough to establish. It was the way of the world, and though she lamented her misfortune she did not complain. The governor of Kawachi, always an amorous sort, showed an extra measure of solicitude.

'Father spoke of you so constantly,' he would say. 'You must not feel shy about asking me for things. Ask me for anything, useless though you may find me.'

His intentions were apparent, and shocking to so proper a lady. She could not think, were she to go on as she was, what tangles she might find herself enmeshed in. Her mind was made up. Consulting no one, she became a nun.

Her women were of course upset, and the governor was somewhat disappointed, and discommoded that she should have found him so little to her liking. He wondered how she meant to make her way through the long years ahead.

Not that the problem was his to worry about.

CHAPTER 17

A Picture Contest

Fujitsubo was most eager that Akikonomu, the former high priestess of Ise, be received at court. Genji knew that Akikonomu had no strong and reliable backer but, not wanting to alienate the Suzaku emperor, had decided not to bring her to Nijō. Making every effort to appear withdrawn and impartial, he took general responsibility for the proceedings and stood in the place of the girl's father.

The Suzaku emperor knew of course that it would not do to write to her of his disappointment. On the day of her presentation at court he sent magnificent robes and other gifts as well, wonderfully wrought cases and vanity chests and incense coffers, and incomparable incenses and sachets, so remarkable that they could be detected even beyond the legendary hundred paces. It may have been that the very special attention he gave to his gifts had to do with the fact that Genji would see them.

Akikonomu's lady of honor showed them to Genji. He took up a comb box of the most remarkable workmanship, endlessly fascinating in its detail. Among the rosettes on the box of decorative combs was a poem in the Suzaku emperor's own hand:

> 'I gave you combs and sent you far away.
> The god now sends me far away from you?'

Genji almost felt as if he were guilty of sacrilege and blasphemy. From his own way of letting his emotions run wild, he could imagine Suzaku's feelings when the priestess had departed for Ise, and his disappointment when, after years of waiting, she had returned to the city and everything had seemed in order, and this new obstacle had intervened. Would bitterness and resentment mar the serenity of his retirement? Genji knew that he himself would have been very much upset indeed. And it was he who had brought Akikonomu to the new emperor at the cost of hurting the retired emperor. There had been a time, of course, when he had felt bitter and angry at Suzaku; but he had known through it all that his brother was of a gentle, sensitive nature. He sat lost in thought.

'And how does she mean to answer? Have there been other letters? What have they said?'

But the lady of honor showed no disposition to let him see them.

Akikonomu was not feeling well and would have preferred not to answer.

'But you must, my lady.' Genji could hear the discussion through blinds and curtains. 'You know that you owe him a little respect.'

'They are quite right,' said Genji. 'It will not do at all. You must let him have something, if only a line or two.'

Though the inclination not to answer was very strong, Akikonomu remembered her departure for Ise. Gently, softly handsome, the emperor had wept that she must leave. Though only a child, she had been deeply touched. And she remembered her dead mother, then and on other occasions. This (and only this?) was the poem which she finally set down:

> 'Long ago, one word you said: Away!
> Sorry now am I that I paid no heed.'

She rewarded Suzaku's messenger lavishly. Genji would have liked to see her reply, but could hardly say so. He was genuinely troubled. Suzaku was so handsome a man that one could imagine falling in love with him were he a woman, and Akikonomu was by no means an ill match for him. Indeed they would have been a perfect couple. And the present emperor was still a boy. Genji wondered whether Akikonomu herself might not feel uneasy at so incongruous a match. But it was too late now to halt the proceedings.

He gave careful instructions to the superintendent of palace repairs. Not wishing the Suzaku emperor to think that he was managing the girl's affairs, he paid only a brief courtesy call upon her arrival at court. She had always been surrounded by gifted and accomplished women, and now that the ones who had gone home were back with her she had easily the finest retinue at court. Genji thought of the Rokujō lady, her dead mother. With what feelings of pride would she now be overseeing her daughter's affairs! He would have thought her death a great loss even if he had not loved her. She had had few rivals. Her tastes had been genuinely superior, and she was much in his thoughts these days.

Fujitsubo was also at court. The emperor had heard that a fine new lady had arrived, and his eagerness was most charming.

'Yes, she is splendid,' said his mother. 'You must be on your best behavior when you meet her.'

He feared that a lady of such advanced years might not be easy to talk to. It was late in the night when she made her appearance. She was small and delicately molded, and she seemed quiet and very much in control of herself, and in general made a very good impression on the emperor. His favorite companion was Tō no Chūjō's little daughter, who occupied the Kokiden apartments. The new arrival, so calm and self-possessed, did make him feel on the defensive, and then Genji behaved towards her with such solemnity that the emperor was lured into rather solemn devoirs. Though he distributed his nights impartially between the two ladies, he preferred the Kokiden apartments for diurnal amusements. Tō no Chūjō had ambitious plans for his daughter and was worried about this new competitor.

The Suzaku emperor had difficulty resigning himself to what had happened. Genji came calling one day and they had a long and affectionate talk. The Suzaku emperor, who had more than once spoken to Genji of the priestess's departure for Ise, mentioned it again, though somewhat circumspectly. Genji gave no open indication that he knew what had happened, but he did discuss it in a manner which he hoped would elicit further remarks from his brother. It was clear that the Suzaku emperor had not ceased to love the girl, and Genji was very sorry for him indeed. He knew and regretted that he could not see for himself the beauty which seemed to have such a powerful effect upon everyone who did see it. Akikonomu permitted not the briefest glimpse. And so of course he was fascinated. He saw enough to convince him that she must be very near perfection.

The emperor had two ladies and there was no room for a third. Prince Hyōbu's plans for sending his daughter to court had foundered. He could only hope that as the emperor grew older he would be in a more receptive mood.

The emperor loved art more than anything else. He loved to look at paintings and he painted beautifully. Akikonomu was also an accomplished artist. He went more and more frequently to her apartments, where the two of them would paint for each other. His favorites among the young courtiers were painters and students of painting. It delighted him to watch this new lady, so beautiful and so elegant, casually sketching a scene, now and again pulling back to think the matter over. He liked her much better now.

Tō no Chūjō kept himself well informed. A man of affairs who had strong competitive instincts, he was determined not to lose this competition. He assembled master painters and he told them exactly what he wanted, and gave them the best materials to work with. Of the opinion that illustrations for the works of established authors could always be counted on, he chose his favorites and set his painters to illustrating them. He also commissioned paintings of the seasons and showed considerable flair with the captions. The emperor liked them all and wanted to share his pleasure with Akikonomu; but Tō no Chūjō objected. The paintings were not to leave the Kokiden apartments.

Genji smiled. 'He was that way when he was a boy, and in many ways he still is a boy. I do not think it a very deft way to manage His Majesty. I'll send off my whole collection and let him do with it as he pleases.'

All the chests and bookcases at Nijō were ransacked for old paintings and new, and Genji and Murasaki sorted out the ones that best suited current fancies. There were interesting and moving pictures of those sad Chinese ladies Yang Kuei-fei and Wang Chao-chün.* Genji feared, however, that the subjects were inauspicious.

Thinking this a good occasion to show them to Murasaki, he took out the sketchbooks and journals of his exile. Any moderately sensitive lady would have found tears coming to her eyes. For Murasaki those days had been unrelieved pain, not easily forgotten. Why, she asked, had he not let her see them before?

'Better to see these strands where the fishermen dwell
Than far away to weep, all, all alone.

'I think the uncertainty might have been less cruel.'
It was true.

'Now more than in those painful days I weep
As tracings of them bring them back to me.'

He must let Fujitsubo see them. Choosing the more presentable scrolls, the ones in which life upon those shores came forward

*See note†, page 251.

most vividly, he could almost feel that he was back at Akashi once more.

Hearing of Genji's activities, Tō no Chūjō redoubled his own efforts. He quite outdid himself with all the accessories, spindles and mountings and cords and the like. It was now the middle of the Third Month, a time of soft, delicious air, when everyone somehow seemed happy and at peace. It was also a quiet time at court, when people had leisure for these avocations. Tō no Chūjō saw a chance to bring the young emperor to new raptures. He would offer his collection for the royal review.

Both in the Kokiden apartments and in Akikonomu's Plum Pavilion there were paintings in endless variety. Illustrations for old romances seemed to interest both painter and viewer. Akikonomu rather preferred secure and established classics, while the Kokiden girl chose the romances that were the rage of the day. To the casual observer it might have seemed perhaps that her collection was the brighter and the more stylish. Connoisseurs among the court ladies had made the appraisal of art their principal work.

Fujitsubo was among them. She had had no trouble giving up most pleasures, but a fondness for art had refused to be shaken off. Listening to the aesthetic debates, she hit upon an idea: the ladies must divide into two sides.

On the left was the Plum Pavilion or Akikonomu faction, led by Heinaishinosuke, Jijū no Naishi, and Shōshō no Myōbu; and in the right or Kokiden faction, Daini no Naishinosuke, Chūjō no Myōbu, and Hyōe no Myōbu. Fujitsubo listened with great interest as each gave forth with her opinions.

The first match was between an illustration for *The Bamboo Cutter*, the ancestor of all romances, and a scene centering upon Toshikage from *The Tale of the Hollow Tree*.

From the left came this view: 'The story has been with us for a very long time, as familiar as the bamboo growing before us, joint upon joint. There is not much in it that is likely to take us by surprise. Yet the moon princess did avoid sullying herself with the affairs of this world, and her proud fate took her back to the far heavens; and so perhaps we must accept something august and godly in it, far beyond the reach of silly, superficial women.'

And this from the right: 'It may be as you say, that she returned to a realm beyond our sight and so beyond our understanding. But this too must be said: that in our world she lived in a stalk of bamboo, which fact suggests rather dubious lineage. She exuded a radiance, we are told, which flooded her stepfather's house with light; but what is that to the light which suffuses these many-fenced halls and pavilions? Lord Abe threw away a thousand pieces of gold and another thousand in a desperate attempt to purchase the fire rat's skin, and in an instant it was up in flames – a rather disappointing conclusion. Nor is it very edifying, really, that Prince Kuramochi, who should have known how well informed the princess was in these matters, should have forged a jeweled branch and so made of himself a forgery too.'

The *Bamboo Cutter* illustration, by Kose no Omi* with a caption by Ki no Tsurayuki, was mounted on cerise and had a spindle of sandalwood – rather uninteresting, all in all.

'Now let us look at the other. Toshikage was battered by tempests and waves and swept off to foreign parts, but he finally came home, whence his musical activities sent his fame back across the waters and down through the centuries. This painting successfully blends the Chinese and the Japanese and the new and the old, and I say that it is without rival.'

On stiff white paper with a blue mounting and a spindle of yellow jade, it was the work of Tsunenori and bore a caption by Michikaze.† The effect was dazzlingly modern. The left had to admit defeat.

The Tales of Ise was pitted against *The Tale of Jōsammi.*‡ No decision was forthcoming. The picture offered by the right was again a bright, lively painting of contemporary life with much, including details of the palace itself, to recommend it.

> 'Shall we forget how deep is the sea of Ise
> Because the waves have washed away old tracks?'

It was Heinaishinosuke, pleading the cause of the left, though without great fire or eloquence. 'Are the grand accomplishments

---

*A son of Kose no Kanaoka, active early in the tenth century.

†For Tsunenori, see note†, page 247. Ono no Michikaze, or Dōfū, active in the early and middle tenth century, is commonly called one of the three great calligraphers of the Heian Period. Murasaki Shikibu seems to be setting the episode some three quarters of a century before the time of writing.

‡The latter has been lost.

of Lord Narihira to be dwarfed by a little love story done with a
certain cleverness and plausibility?'

> 'To this Jōsammi, high above august clouds,
>   The thousand-fathomed sea seems very shallow.'

It was Daini, speaking for the right.

Fujitsubo offered an opinion. 'However one may admire the
proud spirit of Lady Hyōe, one certainly would not wish to malign
Lord Narihira.

> 'At first the strands of sea grass may seem old,
>   But the fisherfolk of Ise are with us yet.'

And so poem answered poem in an endless feminine dispute.
The younger and less practiced women hung upon the debate as if
for their very lives; but security precautions had been elaborate,
and they were permitted to see only the smallest part of the riches.

Genji stopped by and was much diverted. If it was all the same,
he said, why not make the final judgments in the emperor's
presence? He had had a royal inspection in mind from the start,
and so had taken very great pains with his selections, which
included a scroll of his own Suma and of his Akashi paintings. Nor
was Tō no Chūjō to be given low marks for effort. The chief business at court these days had become the collecting of evocative
paintings.

'I think it spoils the fun to have them painted specially,' said
Genji. 'I think we should limit ourselves to the ones we have had
all along.'

He was of course referring to Tō no Chūjō and his secret stu-
dio.

The Suzaku emperor heard of the stir and gave Akikonomu
paintings of his own, among them representations of court festivals
for which the emperor Daigo had done the captions; and on a
scroll depicting events from his own reign was the scene, for him
unforgettable, of Akikonomu's departure for Ise. He himself had
carefully gone over the sketches, and the finished painting, by
Kose no Kimmochi,* quite lived up to his hopes. It was in a box,
completely modern, of pierced aloeswood with rosettes that quietly
enhanced its beauty. He sent a verbal message through a guards

---

*A grandson of Kanaoka.

captain on special assignment to Suzaku, setting down only this verse, beside a painting of the solemn arrival at the Grand Hall:

> 'Though now I dwell beyond the sacred confines,
>   My heart is there committing you to the gods.'

It required an answer. Bending a corner of one of the sacred combs, she tied a poem to it and wrapped it in azure Chinese paper:

> 'Within these sacred precincts all has changed.
>   Fondly I think of the days when I served the gods.'

She rewarded the messenger very elegantly.

The Suzaku emperor was deeply moved and longed to return to his days on the throne. He was annoyed at Genji, and perhaps was now having a gentle sort of revenge. It would seem that he sent large numbers of pictures through his mother to the Kokiden lady. Oborozukiyo, another fancier of painting, had also put together a distinguished collection.

The day was appointed. The careful casualness of all the details would have done justice to far more leisurely preparations. The royal seat was put out in the ladies' withdrawing rooms, and the ladies were ranged to the north and south. The seats of the court-iers faced them on the west. The paintings of the left were in boxes of red sandalwood on sappanwood stands with flaring legs. Purple Chinese brocades were spread under the stands, which were covered with delicate lavender Chinese embroidery. Six little girls sat behind them, their robes of red and their jackets of white lined with red, from under which peeped red and lavender. As for the right or Kokiden side, the boxes were of heavy aloes and the stands of lighter aloes. Green Korean brocades covered the stands, and the streamers and the flaring legs were all in the latest style. The little page girls wore green robes and over them white jackets with green linings, and their singlets were of a grayish green lined with yellow. Most solemnly they lined up their treasures. The emperor's own women were in the uniforms of the two sides.

Genji and Tō no Chūjō were present, upon royal invitation. Prince Hotaru, a man of taste and cultivation and especially a con-noisseur of painting, had taken an inconspicuous place among the courtiers. Perhaps Genji had suggested inviting him. It was the emperor's wish that he act as umpire. He found it almost impossible to hand down decisions. Old masters had painted cycles of the four seasons with uncommon power, fluency, and grace, and a rather wonderful sense of unity; but they sometimes seemed to run out of space, so that the observer was left to imagine the grandeur of nature for himself. Some of the more superficial pictures of our own day, their telling points in the dexterity and ingenuity of the strokes and in a certain impressionism, did not seem markedly their inferior, and sometimes indeed seemed ahead of them in brightness and good spirits. Several interesting points were made in favor of both.

The doors to the breakfast suite, north of the ladies' withdrawing rooms, had been slid open so that Fujitsubo might observe the proceedings. Having long admired her taste in painting, Genji was hoping that she might be persuaded to give her views. When, though infrequently, he was not entirely satisfied with something Prince Hotaru said and offered an opinion of his own, he had a way of sweeping everything before him.

Evening came, and still Prince Hotaru had not reached a final decision. As its very last offering Akikonomu's side brought out a scroll depicting life at Suma. Tō no Chūjō was startled. Knowing that the final inning had come, the Kokiden faction too brought out a very remarkable scroll, but there was no describing the sure delicacy with which Genji had quietly set down the moods of those years. The assembly, Prince Hotaru and the rest, fell silent, trying to hold back tears. They had pitied him and thought of themselves as suffering with him; and now they saw how it had really been. They had before their eyes the bleakness of those nameless strands and inlets. Here and there, not so much open description as poetic impressions, were captions in cursive Chinese and Japanese. There was no point now in turning to the painting offered by the right. The Suma scroll had blocked everything else from view. The triumph of the left was complete.

Dawn approached and Genji was vaguely melancholy. As the wine flagons went the rounds he fell into reminiscence.

'I worked very hard at my Chinese studies when I was a boy, so hard that Father seemed to fear I might become a scholar. He thought it might be because scholarship seldom attracts wide acclaim, he said, that he had rarely seen it succeed in combining happiness with long life. In any event, he thought it rather pointless in my case, because people would notice me whether I knew anything or not. He himself undertook to tutor me in pursuits not related to the classics. I don't suppose I would have been called remarkably inept in any of them, but I did not really excel in any of them either. But there was painting. I was the merest dabbler, and yet there were times when I felt a strange urge to do something really good. Then came my years in the provinces and leisure to examine that remarkable seacoast. All that was wanting was the power to express what I saw and felt, and that is why I have kept my inadequate efforts from you until now. I wonder,' he said, turning to Prince Hotaru, 'if my presuming to bring them out might set some sort of precedent for impertinence and conceit.'

'It is true of every art,' said the prince, 'that real mastery requires concentrated effort, and it is true too that in every art worth mastering (though of course that word "mastering" contains all manner of degrees and stages) the evidences of effort are apparent in the results. There are two mysterious exceptions, painting* and the game of Go, in which natural ability seems to be the only thing that really counts. Modest ability can of course be put to modest use. A rather ordinary person who has neither worked nor studied so very hard can paint a decent picture or play a decent game of Go. Sometimes the best families will suddenly produce someone who seems to do everything well.' He was now speaking to Genji. 'Father was tutor for all of us, but I thought he took himself seriously only when you were his pupil. There was poetry, of course, and there was music, the flute and the koto. Painting seemed less study than play, something you let your brush have its way with when poetry had worn you out. And now see the results. See all of our professionals running off and hiding their faces.'

The prince may have been in his cups. In any event, the thought of the old emperor brought a new flood of tears.

A quarter moon having risen, the western sky was silver. Musical instruments were ordered from the royal collection. Tō no Chūjō chose a Japanese koto. Genji was generally thought the finest musician in court, but Tō no Chūjō was well above the ordinary. Genji chose a Chinese koto, as did Prince Hotaru, and

*'The taking of the brush,' which also covers calligraphy.

Shōshō no Myōbu took up a lute. Courtiers with a good sense of rhythm were set to marking time, and all in all it was a very good concert indeed. Faces and flowers emerged dimly in the morning twilight, and birds were singing in a clear sky. Gifts were brought from Fujitsubo's apartments. The emperor himself bestowed a robe on Prince Hotaru.

Examination and criticism of Genji's journals had become the main business of the court. He asked that his paintings of the seacoast be given to Fujitsubo. She longed to see what went before and came after, but he said only that he would in due course show her everything. The pleasure which he had given the emperor was pleasure for Genji himself. It worried Tō no Chūjō that Genji should so favor Akikonomu. Was her triumph to be complete? He comforted himself with the thought that the emperor would not have forgotten his own early partiality for the Kokiden girl. Surely she would not be cast aside.

Genji had a strong sense of history and wanted this to be one of the ages when things begin. Very great care therefore went into all the fetes and observances. It was an exciting time.

But he was also obsessed with evanescence. He was determined to withdraw from public affairs when the emperor was a little older. Every precedent told him that men who rise to rank and power beyond their years cannot expect long lives. Now, in this benign reign, perhaps by way of compensation for the years of sorrow and disgrace, Genji had an abundance, indeed a plethora, of rank and honor. Further glory could only bring uncertainty. He wanted to withdraw quietly and make preparations for the next life, and so add to his years in this one. He had purchased a quiet tract off in a mountain village and was putting up a chapel and collecting images and scriptures. But first he must see that no mistake was made in educating his children. So it was that his intentions remained in some doubt.

CHAPTER 18

The Wind in the Pines

The east lodge at Nijō was finished, and the lady of the orange blossoms moved in. Genji turned the west wing and adjacent galleries into offices and reserved the east wing for the Akashi lady. The north wing was both spacious and ingeniously partitioned, so that he might assign its various rooms to lesser ladies who were dependent on him, and so make them happy too. He reserved the main hall for his own occasional use.

He wrote regularly to Akashi. The time had come, he said firmly, for the lady's removal to the city. She was painfully aware of her humble station, however, and she had heard that he made even ladies of the highest rank more unhappy by his way of behaving coolly but correctly than if he had simply dismissed them. She feared that she could expect little attention from him. Her rank could not be hidden, of course, and her daughter would suffer for it. And how painful it would be, and what an object of derision she herself would be, if she had to sit waiting for brief and stealthy visits. But there was the other side of the matter: it would not do for her daughter to grow up in the remote countryside, a child of the shadows. So she could not tell Genji that he had behaved badly and be finished with him. Her parents understood, and could only add their worries to hers. The summons from their noble visitor only made them unhappier.

The old man remembered that his wife's grandfather, Prince Nakatsukasa, had had a villa on the river Oi to the west of the city. There had been no one to take charge after his death and it had been sadly neglected. He summoned the head of the family that had assumed custody.

'I had quite given up my ambitions and fallen quietly into country life, and now in my declining years something rather unexpected has come up. I must have a residence in the city once more. It would be too much of a change to move back into the great world immediately. The noise and the bustle would be very upsetting for a rustic like me. I need a sort of way station, a familiar place that has been in the family. Might you see to repairs and make the place reasonably livable? I will of course take care of all the expenses.'

'It has been deserted for so long that it is the worst tangle you can imagine. I myself patched up one of the outbuildings to live in. Since this spring there has been a real commotion, you never saw the likes of it. The Genji minister has been putting up a temple, several very big halls, and the place is swarming with carpenters. If it's quiet you're looking for, then I'm afraid this is not what you want.'

'It makes no difference at all. As a matter of fact, I'm rather counting on the minister for certain favors. I'll of course take care of all the expenses, the fittings and decorations and all. Just make it your business, please, to have it ready for occupancy as soon as you possibly can.'

'It's true that I've never had clear title, but there wasn't really anyone else to take over. We've just been following our quiet country ways over the years. The fields and the rest were going to waste, absolutely to ruin. So I paid the late Mimbu no Tayū what seemed like a reasonable amount and got his permission, and I've been working the fields ever since.' He was obviously worried about his crops. His nose and then the whole of his wary, bewhiskered face was crimson, and his mouth was twisted as if in a growl.

'It is not your fields I am concerned with. You can go on working them as you always have. I have a great many deeds and titles and the like, but I've rather lost track of them these last years. I'll look into them.'

The hint that Genji was an indirect party to the negotiations warned the man that he might be inviting trouble. The recompense being ample, he made haste to get the house in order.

Genji had been puzzled and upset by the lady's reluctance to move. He did not want people to associate his daughter with Akashi. Presently the Oi house was ready and he learned of it. Now he understood: the lady had been frightened at the thought of the great city. These precautions had been reasonable and indeed laudable.

He sent off Lord Koremitsu, his usual adviser and agent in confidential matters, to scout the grounds and see if further preparations were necessary.

'The setting is very good,' said Koremitsu. 'I was reminded a little of Akashi.'

Nothing could be better. The temple which Genji was putting up was to the south of the Daikakuji, by a mountain cascade which rivaled that of the Daikakuji itself.* The main hall of the Oi villa was simple and unpretentious, almost like a farmhouse, in a grove of magnificent pines beside the river. Genji himself saw to all the furnishings. Very quietly, he sent off trusted retainers to be the lady's escort.

So there was no avoiding it. The time had come to leave the familiar coast. She wept for her father and the loneliness he must face, and for every small detail of her old home. She had known all the sorrows, and would far rather that this manna had never fallen.

The hope that had been with the old man, waking and sleeping, for all these years was now to be realized, but the sadness was more than he would have thought possible now that the time had come. He would not see his little granddaughter again. He sat absently turning the same thought over and over again in his mind.

His wife was as sad. She had lived more with her daughter than her husband, and she would go with her daughter. One becomes fond, after a time, of sea and strand,† and of the chance acquaintance. Her husband was a strange man, not always, she had thought, the firmest support, but the bond between them had held. She had been his wife, and Akashi had become for her the place to live and to die. The break was too sudden and final.

The young women were happy enough to be finished with country life, which had been mostly loneliness and boredom, but this coast did after all have a hold on them. With each advancing wave they wept that it would return, but they would not.

It was autumn, always the melancholy season. The autumn wind was chilly and the autumn insects sang busily as the day of the departure dawned. The Akashi lady sat looking out over the sea. Her father, always up for dawn services, had arisen deep in the night, much earlier than usual. He was weeping as he turned to his prayers. Tears were not proper or auspicious on such an occasion, but this morning they were general. The little girl was a delight, like the jade one hears of which shines in darkness. He had not

---

*There is evidence here that the action is set some decades before the time of writing, since the cascade of the great Daikakuji, to the west of Kyoto, is known to have disappeared by Murasaki Shikibu's day.

†Probably a poetic allusion.

once let her out of his sight, and here she was again, scrambling all over him, so very fond of him. He had great contempt for people who renounce the world and then appear not to have done so after all. But she was leaving him.

> 'The old weep easily, and I am weeping
> As I pray that for her the happy years stretch on.

'I am very much ashamed of myself.' He drew a sleeve over his eyes.

No one could have thought it odd that his wife too was weeping.

> 'Together we left the city. Alone I return,
> To wander lost over hill and over moor?'

The reasons did not seem adequate that she should be leaving him after they had been together so long.

The lady was begging her father to go with them as far as Oi, if only by way of escort.

> 'When do you say that we shall meet again,
> Trusting a life that is not ours to trust?'

He counted over once more his reasons for refusing, but he seemed very apprehensive. 'When I gave up the world and settled into this life, it was my chief hope that I might see to your needs as you deserved. Aware that I had not been born under the best of stars, I knew that going back to the city as another defeated provincial governor I would not have the means to put my hut in order and clear the weeds from my garden. I knew that in my private life and my public life I would give them all ample excuse to laugh, and that I would be a disgrace to my dead parents; and so I decided from the outset, and it seemed to be generally understood, that when I left the city I was leaving all that behind. And indeed I did rather effectively leave the world in the sense of giving up worldly ambitions. But then you grew up and began to see what was going on around you, and in the darkness that is the father's heart* I was not for one moment free from a painful question: why was I hiding my most precious brocade in a wild corner of the provinces? I kept my lonely hopes and prayed to the gods and the blessed ones

See note, page 13.

that it not be your fate, because of an unworthy father, to spend your life among these rustics. Then came that happy and unexpected event, which had the perverse effect of emphasizing our low place in life. Determined to believe in the bond of which our little one here is evidence, I could see too well what a waste it would be to have you spend your days on this seacoast. The fact that she seems meant for remarkable things makes all the more painful the need to send her away. No, enough, I have left it all. You are the ones whose light will bathe the world. You have brought pleasure to us country people. We are told in the scriptures of times when celestial beings descend to ugly worlds. The time is past, and we must part.

'Do not worry about services when word reaches you that I have died. Do not trouble yourself over what cannot be avoided.' He seemed to have finished his farewells. Then, his face twisted with sorrow, he added: 'Thoughts of our little one will continue to bring regrets until the evening when I too rise as smoke.'

A single progress by land, the escort said, would be unmanageable, and a succession of convoys would only invite trouble. So it had been decided that so far as possible the journey would be an unobtrusive one by boat. The party set sail at perhaps seven or eight in the morning.

The lady's boat disappeared among the mists that had so saddened the poet.* The old man feared that his enlightened serenity had left him forever. As if in a trance, he gazed off into the mists. The old woman's thoughts upon leaving home were in sad confusion.

> 'I want to be a fisherwife upon
> A far, clean shore, and now my boat turns back.'

Her daughter replied:

> 'How many autumns now upon this strand?
> So many, why should this flotsam now return?'

A steady seasonal wind was blowing and they reached Oi on schedule, very careful not to attract attention on the land portion

---

*Anonymous, *Kokinshū* 409:

> Sad am I as the boat puts out from Akashi
> And disappears among the island mists.

of the journey. They found the Oi villa very much to their taste, so like Akashi, indeed, that it soothed the homesickness, though not, of course, dispelling it completely. Thoughts of the Akashi years did after all come back. The new galleries were in very good taste, and the garden waters pleasant and interesting. Though the repairs and fittings were not yet complete, the house was eminently livable.

The steward, one of Genji's more trusted retainers, did everything to make them feel at home. The days passed as Genji cast about for an excuse to visit. For the Akashi lady the sorrow was yet more insistent. With little to occupy her, she found her thoughts running back to Akashi. Taking out the seven-stringed Chinese koto which Genji had left with her, she played a brief strain as fancy took her. It was the season for sadness, and she need not fear that she was being heard; and the wind in the pines struck up an accompaniment.

Her mother had been resting.

'I have returned alone, a nun, to a mountain village,
And hear the wind in the pines of long ago.'

The daughter replied:

'I long for those who know the country sounds,
And listen to my koto, and understand.'

Uneasy days went by. More restless than when she had been far away, Genji could contain himself no longer. He did not care what people would think. He did not tell Murasaki all the details, but he did send her a note. Once again he feared that reports would reach her from elsewhere.

'I have business at Katsura which a vague apprehension tells me I have neglected too long. Someone to whom I have made certain commitments is waiting there. And my chapel too, and those statues, sitting undecorated. It is quite time I did something about them. I will be away perhaps two or three days.'

This sudden urge to visit Katsura and put his chapel in order made her suspect his actual motives. She was not happy. Those two or three days were likely to become days enough to rot the handle of the woodcutter's ax.*

---

*A Chinese woodcutter named Wang Chih found that his ax had rotted away as he stood watching a supernatural game of Go.

'I see you are being difficult again.' He laughed. 'You are in a small minority, my dear, for the whole world agrees that I have mended my ways.'

The sun was high when he finally set out.

He had with him a very few men who were familiar with the situation at Oi. Darkness was falling when he arrived. The lady had thought him quite beyond compare in the rough dress of an exile, and now she saw him in court finery chosen with very great care. Her gloom quite left her.

And the daughter whom he was meeting for the first time – how could she fail to be a treasure among treasures? He was angry at each of the days and months that had kept them apart. People said that his son, the chancellor's grandson, was a well-favored lad, but no doubt an element of sycophancy entered into the view. Nothing of the sort need obscure his view of the bud before him now. The child was a laughing, sparkling delight.

Her nurse was much handsomer than when she had left for Akashi. She told Genji all about her months on the seashore. Genji felt somewhat apologetic. It had been because of him that she had had to live among the salt burners' huts.

'You are still too far away,' he said to the lady, 'and it will not be easy for me to see you. I have a place in mind for you.'

'When I am a little more used to it all.' Which was not unreasonable of her.

They passed the night in plans and promises.

Genji gave orders for finishing the house. Since word had been sent that he would be at his Katsura villa, people had gathered from all his nearby manors, and presently sought him out at Oi. He set them to clearing the garden.

'What a jumble. It could be a rather distinguished garden – but why take the trouble? It is not as if you meant to spend the rest of your life here, and you know better than most what a mistake it is to get too attached to a place.'

He was so open, so sure of himself. She was more in love with him than ever.

The old nun grinned upon them. All her worries had departed. Personally supervising the work of clearing the brook that ran from under the east gallery, Genji had thrown off his cloak. The old lady thought him charming in his undersleeves. The holy vessels reminded him that she too had come. He was being rude. He sent immediately for his cloak.

'I am sure it is your prayers that have made our little girl into such perfection,' he said, coming up to her curtains. 'I am very grateful. And I must thank you too, most sincerely, that you have left peace and serenity for what must be the ugliest sort of confusion. You left your saintly husband behind, all by himself, with nothing to occupy him but thoughts of you. It must have been very difficult.'

'Yes, I thought I had given all this up, and it *was* a little confusing. But your kindness and understanding make me feel that I am being rewarded for having lived so long.' There were tears in her voice. 'I worried about the seedling pine on those unfriendly coasts. Its prospects have improved enormously, and yet I am afraid. Its roots are so very shallow.' She spoke in soft, courtly tones.

He asked her about the villa as it had been in Prince Nakatsukasa's day. The brook, now cleared of weeds and litter, seemed to have found the moment to announce itself.

'The mistress, long gone, is lost upon her return
  To find that the brook has quite usurped her claims.'

A voice can seem affected as it trails off at the end of a poem, but the old nun's was genteel and courtly.

'Clean waters, bringing back the distant past
  To one who comes to them in somber habit.'

As he stood gazing meditatively out over the scene, he seemed to the old nun the ultimate in noble dignity.

Going on to his chapel, he ordered bimonthly services in honor of Amitābha, Sākyamuni, and Samantabhadra, and interim services as well, and gave instructions for decorating the chapel and the images. He returned to Oi by moonlight.

Memories of similar nights in Akashi must not go unaccompanied. The lady brought out the Chinese koto he had given her. He plucked out a strain as he gave himself up to the memories. The tuning, as when he had given it to her, took him back to those days and to Akashi.

'Unchanged it is when now we meet again.
  And do you not see changelessness in me?'

'Your promise not to change was my companion.
I added my sighs to those of the wind in the pines.'

She held her own very well in these exchanges, evidence, he
thought, that she had been meant for unusual things. She had
improved in looks and in bearing since last he had seen her. He
could not take his eyes from the child. And what now? The
mother *was* of inferior birth, and the disability must not be passed
on to the daughter. It could be overcome if he were to take her to
Nijō and see to her needs as he wished. Yet there were the feelings
of the mother to be considered and of them he was uncertain.
Choking with tears, he tried to bring the matter up.

The little girl, no more than a baby, was shy at first, but soon
they were friends, and she was gurgling more happily and prettily
all the time. Her mother meanwhile sat in mute gratitude. The
future seemed to open limitlessly.

He overslept the next morning, when he was to return to the
city. He had meant to go directly back, but great crowds had
gathered at the Katsura villa, and several men from the city had
even made their way to Oi.

'How very inconvenient and embarrassing,' he muttered as he
dressed. 'I had meant it to be rather more of a retreat.'

He had no choice but to go off with them. He stood in the
doorway fondling the little girl, who was in her nurse's arms.

'It is very selfish of me, but I can see that I won't be able to let
her out of my sight. What am I to do? Must you be so far away?'

'Yes,' said the nurse, 'the fact that you are nearer only makes
things worse.'

In her arms, the child was straining towards him.

'There seems to be no end to my troubles. I hate the thought of
being away from you for even a minute, my sweet. But just look
at this. You are sorry to see me go, but your mother does not seem
to be. She could comfort me a little, if she chose.'

The nurse smiled and transmitted the message.

The lady hung back. This morning's farewell seemed more
difficult than all the years away from him. There was just a little
too much of the grand lady in this behavior, thought Genji. Her
women, urging her on, had to agree. Finally she came forward.
Her profile, half hidden by the curtain, was wonderfully soft and
gentle. She might have been a princess. He pulled the curtain back

and offered some last affectionate words of farewell. His men were in a great hurry to be off, and he was about to follow. He looked back again. Though she was remarkably good at hiding her emotions, she was gazing at him now with open regret. He seemed even handsomer than at Akashi. Then he had seemed a little slender for his height. He had filled out, and no one could have found fault with his proportions or his manner, the essence of mature dignity. Perfection from head to foot, she thought – though she may have been a prejudiced observer.

The young guards officer whose fortunes had sunk and risen with Genji's – he who had had reproachful words for the god of Kamo* – now wore the cap of the Fifth Rank, and was in his glory. Waiting to take Genji's sword, he spied a woman inside the blinds.

'It may seem that I have forgotten the old days,' he said, rather self-importantly, one may have thought, 'but that is because I have been on good behavior. The breezes that awoke me this morning seemed very much like the sea breezes at Akashi. I looked in vain for a way to tell you so.'

'This mountain village, garlanded in eightfold mists, is not inferior, we have found, to that where the boat disappears among the island mists. All that had seemed wanting was that the pines were not the pines of old. It is a comfort to find that there is one who has not forgotten.'†

Scarcely what he had hoped for – and he had been fond of her. 'I will see you again,' he said, and returned to Genji's side.

Genji walked off to his carriage amid the shouts of his outrunners. He invited Tō no Chūjō and Hyōe no Kami‡ to ride with him.

'You cannot know what a disappointment it is,' he said, in genuine annoyance, 'to have people pour in on what you had hoped would be a hideaway.'

'Nor can you know our disappointment, my lord, at not being permitted to share the moon with you last night. That is why we

---

*See Chapters 12 and 14.

†These remarks are very 'poetic.' See, for instance, note*, page 336. The word *matsu* is commonly used in the double sense captured also in the English 'pine.'

‡Neither appears elsewhere. The former cannot be the Tō no Chūjō who is Genji's great friend.

fought our way through the autumn mists. Though the journey did have its pleasures. The autumn leaves are not quite at their best, perhaps, but the autumn flowers were very beautiful.' He went on to describe a falconing expedition that was keeping certain of his friends longer than they had planned.

'And so we must go to Katsura, I suppose,' said Genji, to the modest consternation of the stewards, who now had to put together an impromptu banquet.

The calls of the cormorant fishermen made him think of the fishermen at Akashi, their speech as incomprehensible as the chirping of birds. Back from their night upon the moors, the young falconers offered a sampling of their take, tied to autumn reeds. The flagons went the rounds so frequently that a river crossing seemed out of the question, and so of course a day of roistering must be passed at Katsura. Chinese poems were tossed back and forth. As moonlight flooded the scene the music was more boisterous, dominated by the flute, there being several fine flutists in the company. The stringed instruments were quieter, only the Japanese koto and the lute. The flute is an autumn instrument, at its best in the autumn breezes. Every detail of the riverbank rose clear and high and clean in the moonlight. A new party arrived from the palace, from the royal presence itself, indeed. The emperor had been much disappointed that Genji had not called at the end of the week-long retreat from which the court had just emerged. There was music once more, and surely, thought the emperor, Genji would appear. This was the emperor's personal message, delivered by a secretary after Genji had offered suitable excuses:

> 'Cleaner, more stately the progress of the moon
> Through regions beyond the river Katsura.*

'I am envious.'

Genji repeated his apologies, most elaborately. But this somehow seemed a better place for music than even the palace. They abandoned themselves to music and to wine.

The Katsura villa being inadequately supplied, Genji sent to Oi to see if there might not be quietly elegant cloths and garments

---

*A *katsura*, 'Judas tree,' was thought to grow on the moon.

with which to reward the messengers. Two chests came back from the Oi closets. There was a set of women's robes for the royal envoy, who returned immediately to the city.

Genji's reply to the emperor was an oblique hint that a royal visit would be welcomed:

> 'It is not true to its name, this Katsura.
> There is not moon enough to dispel the mists.'

'Katsura, at the heart of the eternal moon,'* he added softly; and he thought too of Mitsune's 'Awaji in the moonlight.'†

> 'So near and clear tonight, is it the moon
> Of far Awaji? We both have come back.'

This was the reply:

> 'All should now be peace. Then lost in clouds
> The moon sends forth again its radiance.'

Sadaiben, an older official who had been in close attendance upon Genji's father, also had a poem:

> 'The midnight moon should still be in the heavens.
> Gone is its radiance – hidden in what valley?'

There would seem to have been poems and poems, but I did not have the patience to set them all down. I could have enjoyed a millennium of Genji's company, however, so serene and sure did he seem.

Today they must definitely go back, said Genji, and soon. No rotting ax handles, please.

Gifts were distributed as became the several ranks, and the waves of courtiers, coming and going, disappearing and reappearing in the morning mists, were like banks of autumn flowers. Some of the warrant officers were good poets and singers. Rather bored with elegance, they had moved on to ribaldry. Someone

---

*Ise, *Kokinshū* 968:

> Katsura, at the heart of the eternal moon –
> Yet one looks elsewhere for eternal light.

†See note*, page 265.

sang 'Oh My Pony,'* so successfully that courtier after courtier was seen stripping off robes and pressing them upon him. It was as if the wind had spread a brocade of autumn leaves over the garden. Echoes of this noisy departure reached Oi, and a sad lady. Genji was sorry that he had not been able to get off a letter.

Back at Nijō, he rested for a time and went to tell Murasaki of the excursion.

'I must apologize for having stayed away longer than I had planned. They hunted me down and dragged me off with them. I am exhausted.' He tried to be casual about what was too obvious, that she was not happy. 'You have a way, my dear, of comparing yourself with people who simply are not in your class. Give yourself your just due, if you will.'

About to leave for court that evening, he turned his attention from her to his writing desk. She knew which lady demanded being written to, and could see that the letter was full of warm avowals.

He returned to Nijō late that night. Usually he would have spent the night at court, but he was worried about Murasaki. An answer had come from Oi which he could not hide from her. Fortunately it was a decorous one.

'Tear it up and throw it away if you will, please,' he said, leaning against an armrest. 'I am too old to leave this sort of thing scattered around the house.' He gazed into the lamplight, and his thoughts were in Oi.

Though he had spread the letter before her, Murasaki did not look at it.

He smiled. 'You are very funny when you are pretending not to want to see.' He came nearer, quite exuding charm. 'As a matter of fact, the child is a very pretty little girl, if you wish to know. I cannot help feeling that there is a legacy of some sort from another life, and that it is not to be dismissed. But I am worried. She has so much against her. Put yourself in my place, if you will, and make the decision for me. What do you think? Will you perhaps take her in? She has reached the years of the leech child,† but

*A Kagura:

> My pony, oh my pony, she wants feed.
> I give her hay, I give her hay and water.

†See note*, page 282.

I cannot quite bring myself to behave as the leech child's parents did. She is still in diapers, one might say, and if they do not repel you, might I perhaps ask you to see to pinning them up?'

'If I sometimes sulk, it is because you ask me to, and I would not think of refusing.' She was smiling now. 'I will love her, I am sure I will. Just at the dearest age.' She did love children, and longed even now to have the girl in her arms.

Genji was still worried. Should he bring her to Nijō? It was not easy for him to visit Oi. His chapel would offer the occasion for no more than two visits a month. Though better off, perhaps, than Princess Tanabata,* the Akashi lady was certain to be unhappy.

*Of the Tanabata legend, who meets her lover but once a year.

CHAPTER 19

A Rack of Cloud

Life was sadder on the banks of the Oi as winter came on.

'This cannot continue,' said Genji. 'You must move nearer.'

But the Akashi lady did not want to observe at close hand the coldness of which she had heard from afar. It would be the end of everything.

'I must make arrangements for the child, then. I have plans for her, and they would come to nothing if I were to leave her here. I have discussed the matter with the lady in the west wing at Nijō, who is most anxious to see her.' Murasaki might be asked, he said, to arrange unostentatiously for the ritual bestowing of trousers.

The Akashi lady had long known that something of the sort was on his mind. This declaration brought matters to a climax, while adding greatly to the uncertainty. 'I have no doubt that you mean to treat her as if her mother were the noblest of your ladies, but of course people are sure to know who she really is, and behave accordingly.'

'You need not have the slightest fear that she will be mistreated. It is a matter of very great unhappiness for the lady at Nijō that after all these years she has no children of her own. The former high priestess of Ise is already a grown lady, and yet the Nijō lady insists on treating her like a child. She is sure to adore your little girl. That is her way.' He perhaps exaggerated Murasaki's maternal tendencies a little.

Rumors of his amorous adventuring had reached Akashi, where there had been speculation upon the sort of grand love affair that might finally bring it to an end. Now it did seem to have vanished without a trace. The bond from an earlier life must be a very strong one, and the lady herself a paragon. She would think it most impertinent of the Akashi lady to come forward. Well, thought the latter, she must drive her own affairs from her mind, and think only of the child, whose future lay before her. In that Murasaki was best qualified to advise. Genji had said that the humane thing would be to take the child away while she was still an infant, and no doubt he was right. Yet she would worry, she knew, and what would she now have to relieve the tedium of her days? What reason would Genji have to pay her the briefest and rarest visit? The only thing which seemed certain in this web of uncertainty was that she had been born under unhappy stars.

She consulted her mother, a very wise old lady.

'You fret over things that are so simple. It will not be easy to live without her, I know, but it is her interest we must consider, and it is her interest, I have no doubt at all, that His Lordship is most concerned about. You must put your trust in him and let her go. Even when a child has the emperor himself for its father, the mother's station in life makes all the difference. Look at the case of His Lordship. He was the handsomest and the most gifted of them all, and still he was made a commoner. His maternal grandfather was just not important enough, and his mother was one of the lesser ladies at court. And if there are these distinctions among princes, think how much more extreme they are among us commoners. Even the daughter of a prince or a minister is at a great disadvantage if her mother's family does not have influence. Her father cannot do the things that one might expect from his rank. Your own little girl can look forward to only one thing if a daughter is born to one of the grand ladies: she will be forgotten. The ones with a chance in the world are the ones whose parents give them that chance. I don't care how much we spend on her, no one is going to pay the slightest attention off here in the hills. No, you must turn her over to His Lordship and see what he means to do for her.'

Through well-placed friends she consulted renowned fortune-tellers and it was their uniform opinion, to her considerable distress, that the child should be put in Murasaki's charge. Genji had of course long been of that opinion, but had not wished to seem unreasonable or importunate.

What did she propose, asked Genji, in the matter of the bestowing of trousers?

'It is of course as you say. It would be quite unfair to leave the child with a useless person like myself. And yet I fear for her. Might they not make fun of her if you were to take her away with you?'

He felt very sorry for her indeed.

He had a propitious day selected and quietly saw to arrangements for the move. The thought of giving up the child was almost more than the lady could bear, but she held herself under

tight control, trying to keep everything from her mind but the
future that was spreading before the child.

'And so you must leave?' she said to the nurse. 'You have been
my comfort through the loneliness and boredom. I shall be quite
lost without you.'

The nurse too was in tears. 'We must reconcile ourselves, my
lady, to what must be. I shall not forget your unfailing kindness
since we came together so unexpectedly, and I know that we shall
continue to think of each other. I refuse to accept it as a final parting. The prospect of going out among strangers is very frightening,
and my comfort will be the thought that we will soon be near each
other again.'

The Twelfth Month came.

There were snow and sleet to add to the gloom. What sort of
legacy was hers from other lives, asked the lady, that she must put
up with so much in this one? She spent more time than ever with
the little girl, combing her hair, changing her clothes. On a dark
morning of drifting snows she went to the veranda and gazed out
at the ice on the river, and thought of what was past and what was
to come. It was not like her to expose herself so. She preferred the
inner rooms of the house. Warmed by several soft white robes, she
sat lost in thought; and the molding of her head and the flow of
her hair and robes made her women feel sure that the noblest lady
in the land could not be lovelier.

She brushed away a tear and said to the nurse: 'This sort of
weather will be even more trying now.

'These mountain paths will be closed by snow and clouds.
Do not, I pray you, let your tracks be lost.'

The nurse replied:

'And were you to move to deepest Yoshino,
I still would find you, through unceasing snow.'

The snow had melted a little when Genji paid his next visit. She
would have been delighted except for the fact that she knew its
purpose. Well, she had brought it on herself. The decision had been
hers to make. Had she refused he would not have forced her to give
up the child. She had made a mistake, but would not risk seeming
mercurial and erratic by trying to rectify it at this late date.

The child was sitting before her, pretty as a doll. Yes, she was meant for unusual things, one could not deny it. Since spring her hair had been allowed to grow, and now, thick and flowing, it had reached the length that would be usual for a nun. I shall say nothing of the bright eyes and the glowing, delicately carved features. Genji could imagine the lady's anguish at sending her child off to a distant foster mother. Over and over again he sought to persuade her that it was the only thing to do.

'Please, you needn't. I will be happy if you see that she becomes something more than I have been myself.' But for all her valiant efforts at composure she was in tears.

The little girl jumped innocently into the waiting carriage, the lady having brought her as far as the veranda to which it had been drawn up. She tugged at her mother's sleeves and in charming baby talk urged her to climb in too.

'It is taken away, the seedling pine, so young.
When shall I see it grandly shading the earth?'

Her voice broke before she had come to the end.

She had every right to weep, thought Genji.

'A seedling, yes, but with the roots to give
The thousand years of the pines of Takekuma.*

'You must be patient.'

He was right, of course. She resumed the struggle, which was not entirely successful, to control herself.

Only the nurse and a very personable young woman called Shōshō got into the little girl's carriage, taking with them the sword which Genji had sent to Akashi† and a sacred guardian doll. In a second carriage were several other handsome women and some little page girls. And so the Akashi lady saw them off.

Knowing how lonely she would be, Genji asked himself whether he was committing a crime for which he would one day be summoned to do penance. It was dark when they reached Nijō. He had feared that the suddenly lavish surroundings would intimidate these provincial women, but Murasaki had gone to a

---

*Twin pines often mentioned in poetry. It is doubtful where they grew, though it is thought to have been somewhere in northeastern Japan.

†See Chapter 14.

great deal of trouble. The west room of her west wing had been fitted most charmingly to resemble a doll's house. She assigned the nurse a room on the north side of the adjoining gallery.

The girl had slept most of the way. She did not weep as she was taken from the carriage. When sweets had been set before her, she looked around and saw that her mother was not with her. The puckered little face was very pretty. Her nurse sought to comfort her.

Genji's thoughts were on that mountain dwelling, where the gloom and tedium must be next to unbearable. But he had the child's education to think about. A little jewel, quite flawless – and why had such a child not been born at Nijō?

She wept and hunted for her mother; but she was of a docile, affectionate nature, and soon she had quite taken to Murasaki. For Murasaki it was as if her last wish had been granted. She was always taking the child in her arms, and soon she and the nurse were very close friends. A second nurse, a woman of good family, had by now joined the household.

Though no very lavish preparations were made for bestowing the trousers, the ceremony became of its own accord something rather special. The appurtenances and decorations were as if for the finest doll's house in the world. The stream of congratulatory visitors made no distinction between day and night – though one might not have found it remarkably different from the stream that was always pouring in and out of the Nijō mansion. The trousers cord,* everyone said, was the most charming little detail of all.

The Akashi lady went on thinking that she had brought gratuitous sorrow upon herself. Her mother had been so brave and confident; but old people weep easily, and she was weeping, though pleased at news that the child was the center of such attention. What could they send by way of congratulation? They contented themselves with robes for the nurse and the other women, hoping that the colors gave them a certain distinction.

Oi continued to be much on Genji's mind. It was just as she had thought it would be, the lady was no doubt saying to herself; and so he paid a quiet visit late in the year. Oi was a lonely place at best, and she had lost her dearest treasure. He wrote constantly.

---

*Tasuki, which today would be a cord for tying up kimono sleeves. The meaning in the present context is uncertain.

Murasaki's old bitterness had left her. She had the child, and the account was settled.

The New Year came. The skies were soft and pleasant and nothing seemed wanting at the Nijō mansion, which had been refurbished for the holidays. On the seventh day there was a continious stream of venerable and eminent callers, and younger people too, all the picture of prosperity. No doubt there were dissatisfactions beneath the surface, but it was a surface of contentment and pleasure.

The lady of the orange blossoms was very happy indeed in the east lodge. Her retinue was efficient and well mannered and the mere fact of being near Genji had changed her life enormously. Sometimes when he had nothing else to do he would look in on her, though never with the intention of staying the night. She was an undemanding creature, and she asked nothing more. Her life was quiet, remarkably free of unsettling events, and as the seasonal observances came and went she had no reason to think that she was being slighted. In point of smooth and efficient service, indeed, she perhaps had the better of it over Murasaki.

He continued to worry about Oi and his inability to visit. Choosing a time when little was happening at court and taking more than usual care with his dress, he set off. His underrobes were beautifully dyed and scented, and over them he had thrown an informal court robe of white lined with red. Looking after him as he came to say goodbye, his radiance competing with the evening sunlight, Murasaki felt vaguely apprehensive.

The little girl clung to his trousers and seemed prepared to go with him.

'I've a twenty-acre field,' he sang, looking fondly down at her, 'and I'll be back tomorrow.'*

*From the Saibara 'Cherry-Blossom Girl.' The allusion is doubly appropriate because a white robe lined with red was known as a cherry blossom.

> *The man:* Stop that boat, cherry-blossom girl.
> I will row out to the island.
> I've a twenty-acre field,
> And I'll be back tomorrow.
>
> *The woman:* You say you'll be back tomorrow.
> You've a woman over there.
> You won't be back tomorrow.
> No, you won't be back tomorrow.

Chūjō was waiting in the gallery with a poem from her mistress:

'We shall see if you are back tomorrow,
If no one there essays to take your boat.'

Chūjō's elocution was beautiful. He smiled appreciatively.

'I go but for a while, and shall return
Though she may wish I had not come at all.'

Murasaki no longer really thought a great deal about her rival. The little girl, scampering and tumbling about, quite filled her thoughts. Yet she did feel for the Akashi lady, knowing how desperate her own loneliness would be in such circumstances. Taking the little girl in her arms, she playfully offered one of her own small breasts. It was a charming scene. What had gone wrong? asked her women. Why was Genji's daughter not hers? But such was the way of the world.

Life at Oi was quiet and dignified. The house was pleasing as country houses can be, and each time he saw the lady Genji thought how little there was to distinguish her from ladies of the highest rank. Judged by themselves her appearance and manner were beyond reproach. By herself she could compete – such things did happen – with the best of them, even though she had that very odd father.* He wished he might find time someday for a really satisfying visit. 'A bridge that floats across dreams?'† he whispered, reaching for a koto. Always at such times their last night at Akashi came back to him. Diffidently she took up the lute which he pushed towards her, and they played a brief duet. He marveled again that her accomplishments should be so varied. He told her all about the little girl. Sometimes, though a great deal argued against it, he would take a light supper and stay the night. Katsura and his chapel provided the excuse. His manner toward the lady was not, it is true, his most gallant, but neither was it chilly or uncivil. One might have classed it as rather above the ordinary in warmth and tenderness. She understood and was content, and was careful to seem neither forward nor obsequiously deferential. She wanted to be what he wanted her to be, and she succeeded. Rumor had told

---

*The passage is obscure. This is only a guess at the meaning.
†Clearly a poetic reference, but one that has not been satisfactorily identified.

her that he was stiffer and more formal with most women, and the wiser course seemed to be to keep her distance. If she were nearer she would be vulnerable, too easy a target for the other ladies. She would count it her good fortune that he troubled himself to visit her occasionally, and ask no more.

Her father had told her that last day that he was no longer a part of her life. Yet he worried, and from time to time he would send off a retainer to make quiet inquiry about Genji's behavior. Some of the reports disturbed him, some pleased him.

At about this time Aoi's father died. He had been a loyal and useful public servant, and the emperor was deeply grieved. He had been much missed when he retired from court even briefly, and now he was gone forever. Genji was sadder than anyone. He had had time for himself because he had shared the business of government with his father-in-law. Now it would all be his.

The emperor was mature for his age and his judgment was to be trusted. Yet he did need support and advice. To whom was he to look besides Genji? Sadly, Genji concluded that his plans for a life of quiet meditation would have to be deferred. He was even more attentive than the chancellor's sons to the details of the funeral and memorial services.

It was a time of bad omens, erratic movements of the celestial bodies and unsettling cloud formations. The geomancers and soothsayers issued portentous announcements. Genji had his own very private reasons for disquiet.

Fujitsubo had been ill from early in the year, and from the Third Month her condition was grave. Her son, the emperor, called upon her. He had been very young when his father died and had understood little of what was happening. Now his sorrow made his mother grieve as if it were for someone else.

'I had been sure,' she said, her voice very weak, 'that this would be a bad year for me.* I did not feel so very ill at first, and did not wish to be one of those for whom the end always seems to be in sight. I asked for no prayers or services besides the usual ones. I must call on you, I kept telling myself, and have a good talk about the old days. But it has been so seldom these last weeks that I have really felt myself. And so here we are.'

She seemed much younger than her thirty-seven years. It was even sadder, because she was so youthful, that she might be dying.

---

*The thirty-seventh year, by the Oriental count, was held to be a dangerous one.

As she had said, it was a dangerous year. She had been aware for some weeks of not being well but she had contented herself with the usual penances and retreats. Apologizing for his negligence, the emperor ordered numerous services.

Genji was suddenly very worried. She had always been sickly, and he had thought it just another of her indispositions.

Protocol required that the emperor's visit be a short one. He returned to the palace in great anguish. His mother had been able to speak to him only with very great difficulty. She had received the highest honors which this world can bestow, and her sorrows and worries too had been greater than most. That the emperor must remain ignorant of them added to the pain. He could not have dreamed of the truth, and so the truth must be the tie with this world which would keep her from repose in the other.

Genji shared in the public concern at this succession of misfortunes in high places, and of course his private feelings were deep and complex. He overlooked nothing by way of prayer and petition. He must speak to her once again of what had been given up so long before. Coming near her curtains, he asked how she was feeling. In tears, one of her women gave an account.

'All through her illness she has not for a moment neglected her prayers. They have only seemed to make her worse. She will not touch the tiniest morsel of food, not the tiniest bit of fruit. We are afraid that there is no hope.'

'I have been very grateful,' she said to Genji, 'for all the help you have been to the emperor. You have done exactly as your father asked you to do. I have waited for an opportunity to thank you. My gratitude is far beyond the ordinary, and now I fear it is too late.'

He could barely catch the words and was too choked with tears to answer. He would have preferred not to exhibit his tears to her women. The loss would have been a grievous one even if she had been, all these years, no more than a friend. But life is beyond our control, and there was nothing he could do to keep her back, and no point in trying to describe his sorrow.

'I have not been a very effective man, I fear, but I have tried, when I have seen a need, to be of use to him. The chancellor's death is a great blow, and now this – it is more than I can bear. I doubt that I shall be in this world much longer myself.'

And as he spoke she died, like a dying flame. I shall say no more of his grief.

Among persons of the highest birth whose charity and benevolence seem limitless there have been some who, sheltered by power and position, have been unwitting agents of unhappiness. Nothing of the sort was to be detected in the comportment of the dead lady. When someone had been of service to her she went to no end of trouble to avoid the sort of recompense that might indirectly have unfortunate consequences. Again, there have since the day of the sages been people who have been misled into extravagant and wasteful attentions to the powers above. Here too matters were quite different with the dead lady. Her faith and devotion complete, she offered only what was in her heart to offer, always within her means. The most ignorant and insensitive of mendicant mountain priests regretted her passing.

Her funeral became the only business of court, where grief was universal. The colors of late spring gave way to unrelieved gray and black. Gazing out at his Nijō garden, Genji thought of the festivities that spring a dozen years before.* 'This year alone,'† he whispered. Not wanting to be seen weeping, he withdrew to the chapel, and there spent the day in tears. The trees at the crest of the ridge stood clear in the evening light. Wisps of cloud trailed below, a dull gray. It was a time when the want of striking color had its own beauty.

> 'A rack of cloud across the light of evening
>   As if they too, these hills, wore mourning weeds.'

There was no one to hear.

The memorial rites were over, and the emperor still grieved. There was an old bishop who had had the confidence of successive empresses since Fujitsubo's mother. Fujitsubo herself had been very close to him and valued his services highly, and he had been the emperor's intermediary in solemn vows and offerings. A saintly man, he was now seventy. He had been in seclusion, making his own final preparations for the next life, but he had come down

---

*See Chapter 8.

†Kanzuke Mineo, *Kokinshū* 832.

> If you have hearts, O cherries of Fukakusa,
> This year alone send forth your flowers in black.

from the mountains to be at Fujitsubo's side. The emperor had kept him on at the palace.

Genji too had pressed him to stay with the emperor through the difficult time and see to his needs as in the old days. Though he feared, replied the bishop, that he was no longer capable of night attendance, he was most honored by the invitation and most grateful that he had been permitted to serve royal ladies for so long.

One night, in the quiet before dawn, between shifts of courtiers on night duty, the bishop, coughing as old people will, was talking with the emperor about matters of no great importance.

'There is one subject which I find it very difficult to broach, Your Majesty. There are times when to speak the truth is a sin, and I have held my tongue. But it is a dilemma, since your august ignorance of a certain matter might lead to unknowing wrong. What good would I do for anyone if I were to die in terror at meeting the eye of heaven? Would it have for me the scorn which it has for the groveling dissembler?'

What might he be referring to? Some bitterness, some grudge, which he had not been able to throw off? It was unpleasant to think that the most saintly of hearts can be poisoned by envy.

'I have kept nothing from you since I learned to talk,' said the emperor, 'and I shall not forgive easily if now you are keeping something from me.'

'It is wrong, I know, Your Majesty. You must forgive me. You have been permitted to see into depths which are guarded by the Blessed One, and why should I presume to keep anything from you? The matter is one which can project its unhappy influence into the future. Silence is damaging for everyone concerned. I have reference to the late emperor, to your late mother, and to the Genji minister.

'I am old and of no account, and shall have no regrets if I am punished for the revelation.

'I humbly reveal to you what was first revealed to me through the Blessed One himself. There were matters that deeply upset your mother while she was carrying you within her. The details were rather beyond the grasp of a simple priest like myself. There was that unexpected crisis when the Genji minister was charged with a crime he had not committed. Your royal mother was even more deeply troubled, and I undertook yet more varied and

elaborate services. The minister heard of them and on his own initiative commissioned the rites which I undertook upon Your
Majesty's accession.' And he described them in detail.

It was a most astounding revelation. The terror and the sorrow
were beyond describing. The emperor was silent for a time. Fearing that he had given offense, the old man started from the room.

'No, Your Reverence. My only complaint is that you should
have concealed the matter for so long. Had I gone to my grave
ignorant of it, I would have had it with me in my next life. And is
there anyone else who is aware of these facts?'

'There are, I most solemnly assure you, two people and two
people only who have ever known of them, Omyōbu and myself.
The fear and the awe have been all the worse for that fact. Now
you will understand, perhaps, the continuing portents which have
had everyone in such a state of disquiet. The powers above held
themselves in abeyance while Your Majesty was still a boy, but
now that you have so perfectly reached the age of discretion they
are making their displeasure known. It all goes back to your
parents. I had been in awful fear of keeping the secret.' The old
man was weeping. 'I have forced myself to speak of what I would
much prefer to have forgotten.'

It was full daylight when the bishop left.

The emperor's mind was in turmoil. It was all like a terrible
dream. His reputed father, the old emperor, had been badly
served, and the emperor was serving his real father badly by letting
him toil as a common minister. He lay in bed with his solitary
anguish until the sun was high. A worried Genji came making
inquiries. His arrival only added to the confusion in the emperor's
mind. He was in tears. More tears for his mother, surmised Genji,
it being a time when there was no respite from tears. He must
regretfully inform the emperor that Prince Shikibu* had just died.
Another bit of the pattern, thought the emperor. Genji stayed
with him all that day.

'I have the feeling,' said the emperor, in the course of quiet,
intimate talk, 'that I am not destined to live a long life. I have a
feeling too which I cannot really define that things are wrong, out
of joint. There is a spirit of unrest abroad. I had not wished to

*Genji's uncle, the father of the high priestess of Kamo.

upset my mother by subjecting her and all of you to radical change, but I really do think I would prefer a quieter sort of life.'

'It is out of the question. There is no necessary relationship between public order and the personal character of a ruler. In ages past we have seen the most deplorable occurrences in the most exemplary reigns. In China there have been violent upheavals during the reigns of sage emperors. Similar things have happened here. People whose time has come have died, and that is all. You are worrying yourself about nothing.'

He described many precedents which it would not be proper for me to describe in my turn.

In austere weeds of mourning, so much more subdued than ordinary court dress, the emperor looked extraordinarily like Genji. He had long been aware of the resemblance, but his attention was called to it more forcibly by the story he had just heard. He wanted somehow to hint of it to Genji. He was still very young, however, and rather awed by Genji and fearful of embarrassing or displeasing him. Though it turned on matters far less important, their conversation was unusually warm and affectionate.

Genji was too astute not to notice and be puzzled by the change. he did not suspect, however, that the emperor knew the whole truth.

The emperor would have liked to question Omyōbu; but somehow to bring her into this newest secret seemed a disservice to his mother and the secret she had guarded so long and so well. He thought of asking Genji, as if by way of nothing at all, whether his broad knowledge of history included similar examples, but somehow the occasion did not present itself. He pursued his own studies more diligently, going through voluminous Chinese and Japanese chronicles. He found great numbers of such irregularities in Chinese history, some of which had come to the public notice and some of which had not. He could find none at all in Japanese history – but then perhaps they had been secrets as well guarded as this one. He found numerous examples of royal princes who had been reduced to common status and given the name of Genji and who, having become councillors and ministers, had been returned to royal status and indeed named as successors to the throne. Might not Genji's universally recognized abilities be sufficient reason for relinquishing the throne to him? The emperor turned the matter over and over in his mind, endlessly.

He had reached one decision, consulting no one: that Genji's appointment as chancellor would be on the autumn lists. He told Genji of his secret thoughts about the succession.

So astonished that he could scarcely raise his eyes, Genji offered the most emphatic opposition. 'Father, whatever may have been his reasons, favored me above all his other sons, but never did he consider relinquishing the throne to me. What possible reason would I now have for going against his noble intentions and taking for myself a position I have never coveted? I would much prefer to follow his clear wishes and be a loyal minister, and when you are a little older, perhaps, retire to the quiet pursuits I really wish for.'

To the emperor's very great disappointment, he was adamant in his refusal.

Then came the emperor's wish to appoint him chancellor. Genji had reasons for wishing to remain for a time a minister, however, and the emperor had to be content with raising him one rank and granting him the special honor of bringing his carriage in through the Great South Gate. The emperor would have liked to go a little further and restore him to royal status, but Genji's inclinations were against that honor as well. As a prince he would not have the freedom he now had in advising the emperor, and who besides him was to perform that service? Tō no Chūjō was a general and councillor. When he had advanced a step or two Genji might safely turn everything over him to him and, for better or worse, withdraw from public life.

But there was something very odd about the emperor's behavior. Suspicions crossed Genji's mind. If they were valid, then they had sad implications for the memory of Fujitsubo, and they suggested secret anguish on the part of the emperor. Genji was overwhelmed by feelings of awed guilt. Who could have let the secret out?

Having become mistress of the wardrobe, Omyōbu was now living in the palace. He went to see her.

Had Fujitsubo, on any occasion, allowed so much as a fragment of the secret to slip out in the emperor's presence?

'Never, my lord, never. She lived in constant terror that he might hear of it from someone else, and in terror of the secret itself, which might bring upon him the disfavor of the powers above.'

Genji's longing for the dead lady came back anew.

Meanwhile Akikonomu's performance at court was above reproach. She served the emperor well and he was fond of her. She could be given perfect marks for her sensitivity and diligence, which to Genji were beyond pricing. In the autumn she came to Nijō for a time. Genji had had the main hall polished and refitted until it quite glittered. He now stood unapologetically in the place of her father.

A gentle autumn rain was falling. The flower beds near the veranda were a riot of color, softened by the rain. Genji was in a reminiscent mood and his eyes were moist. He went to her apartments, a figure of wonderful courtliness and dignity in his dark mourning robes. The recent unsettling events had sent him into retreat. Though making no great show of it, he had a rosary in his hand. He addressed her through only a curtain.

'And so here are the autumn flowers again with their ribbons all undone. It has been a rather dreadful year, and it is somehow a comfort that they should come back, not one of them forgetting its proper time.'

Leaning against a pillar, he was very handsome in the evening light. 'When I think of her'* – was the princess too thinking of her mother? He told her of the memories that had been so much with him these last days, and especially of how reluctant he had been to leave the temporary shrine that morning shortly before their departure for Ise. He heard, and scarcely heard at all, a soft movement behind the curtains, and guessed that she was weeping. There was a touching delicacy in it. Once more he regretted that he was not permitted to look at her. (It is not entirely admirable, this sort of regret.)

'All my life I have made trouble for myself which I could have avoided, and gone on worrying about ladies I have been fond of. Among all the affairs in which, I fear, my impulsiveness has brought pain to others, two have continued to trouble me and refused to go away.

'One was the case of your late mother. To the end she seems to have thought my behavior outrageous, and I have always known that to the end I shall be sorry. I had hoped that my being of service to you and enjoying your confidence as I hope I do might have comforted her. But it would seem that in spite of

*Obviously a poetic allusion. More than one poem has been suggested.

everything the smoke refused to clear, and I must continue to live with it.'

Two affairs, he had said; but he did not elaborate upon the second.

'There were those years when I was lost to the world. Most of the unfinished business which I took with me has since been put in order, after a fashion. There is the lady in the east lodge, for instance: she has been rescued from her poverty and is living in peace and security. Her amiable ways are well known to everyone, most certainly to me, and I should say that in that quarter mutual understanding prevails. That I am back in the city and able to be of some service to His Majesty is not, for me, a matter that calls for very loud congratulation. I am still unable to fight back the unfortunate tendencies of my earlier years as I would have wished. Are you aware, I wonder, that my services to you, such as they have been, have required no little self-control? I should be very disappointed indeed if you were to leave me with the impression that you have not guessed.'

A heavy silence succeeded these remarks.

'You must forgive me.' And he changed the subject. 'How I wish that, for the remaining years that have been granted me, I might shut myself up in some retreat and lose myself in quiet preparations for the next world. My great regret would be that I would leave so little behind me. There is, as you may know, a girl, of such mean birth that the world cannot be expected to notice her. I wait with great impatience for her to grow up. I fear that it will seem inappropriate of me to say so, but it would give me much comfort to hope that you might number the prosperity of this house among your august concerns, and her, after I am gone, among the people who matter to you.'

Her answer was but a word, so soft and hesitant that he barely caught it. He would have liked to take her in his arms. He stayed on, talking affectionately until it was quite dark.

'But aside from house and family, it is nature that gives me the most pleasure, the changes through the seasons, the blossoms and leaves of autumn and spring, the shifting patterns of the skies. People have always debated the relative merits of the groves of spring and the fields of autumn, and had trouble coming to a conclusion. I have been told that in China nothing is held to surpass the brocades of spring, but in the poetry of our own country the preference would seem to be for the wistful notes of autumn. I watch them come and go and must allow each its points, and in the end am unable to decide between song of bird and hue of flower. I go further: within the limits allowed by my narrow gardens, I have sought to bring in what I can of the seasons, the flowering trees of spring and the flowering grasses of autumn, and the humming of insects that would go unnoticed in the wilds. This is what I offer for your pleasure. Which of the two, autumn or spring, is your own favorite?'

He had chosen another subject which produced hesitation, but one on which silence would seem merely rude.

'If your Lordship finds it difficult to hand down a decision, how much more do I. It is as you say: some are of the one opinion and some of the other. Yet for me the autumn wind which poets have found so strange and compelling – in the dews I sense a fleeting link with my mother.'*

He found the very muteness and want of logic deeply touching.

'Then we two feel alike. You know my secret:
For me it is the autumn winds that pierce.

'There are times when I find them almost more than I can bear.'

How was she to answer? She made it seem that she had not understood. Somehow he was in a complaining mood this evening. He caught himself just short of further indiscretion. She had every right to be unhappy with him, for he was behaving like a silly stripling. He sighed a heavy sigh, and even that rather put her off with its intrusive elegance. She seemed to be inching away from him.

'I have displeased you, and am sorry – though I doubt that most people of feeling would have been quite as displeased. Well, do not let the displeasure last. It could be very trying.'

He went out. Even the perfume that lingered on upset her.

'What a scent he did leave on these cushions – just have a whiff. I can't find words to describe it.' Her women were lowering the shutters. 'He brings everything all together in himself, like

---

*Akikonomu means 'to prefer the autumn.' The sobriquet derives from this episode.

a willow that is all of a sudden blooming like a cherry. It sets a person to shivering.'

He went to Murasaki's wing of the house. He did not go inside immediately, but, choosing a place on the veranda as far as possible from the lamps, lay for a time in thought. He exchanged desultory talk with several of her women. He was thinking of love. Had those wild impulses still not left him? He was too old for them, and angry with himself for the answer which the question demanded. He had misbehaved grievously, but he had been young and unthinking, and was sure that he would by now have been forgiven. So he sought to comfort himself; and there was genuine comfort in the thought that he was at least more aware of the dangers than he once had been.

Akikonomu was sorry that she had said as much as she had. Her remarks about the autumn must have sounded very poetic, and she should have held her tongue. She was so unhappy with herself that she was feeling rather tired. Genji's robustness had not seemed to allow for fatigue. He was behaving more all the time as if he were her father.

He told Murasaki of this newly discovered preference for the autumn. 'Certainly I can appreciate it. With you it is the early spring morning, and that too I understand. We must put together a really proper entertainment sometime to go with the blossoms and the autumn leaves. But I have been so busy. Well, it will not always be so. I will have what I want most, the life of the recluse. And will you be lonely, my dear? The possibility that you might is what really holds me back.'

He still thought a great deal about the Akashi lady, but his life was so constricted that he could not easily visit her. She seemed to have concluded that the bond between them meant nothing. By what right? Her refusal to leave the hills for a more conventional abode seemed to him a touch haughty. Yet he pitied her, and took every opportunity to attend services in his new chapel. Oi only seemed sadder as she came to know it better, the sort of place that must have a melancholy effect on even the chance visitor. Genji's visits brought contradictory feelings: the bond between them was a powerful one, obviously, and it had meant unhappiness. She might have been better off without it. These are the sad thoughts which most resist consolation.

The torches of the cormorant fishermen through the dark groves were like fireflies on a garden stream.

'For someone not used to living beside the water,' said Genji, 'I think it must be wonderfully strange and different.'

> 'The torches bobbing with the fisher boats
> Upon those waves have followed me to Oi.

'The torches and my thoughts are now as they were then.'
And he answered:

> 'Only one who does not know deep waters
> Can still be bobbing, dancing on those waves.

'Who, I ask you, has made whom unhappy?' So he turned her gentle complaint against her.

It was a time of relative leisure when Genji could turn his thoughts to his devotions. Because his visits were longer, the Akashi lady (or so one hears) was feeling somewhat happier with her lot.

CHAPTER 20

The Morning Glory

The high priestess of Kamo, Princess Asagao, resigned her position upon the death of her father. Never able to forget ladies who had interested him, Genji had sent frequent inquiries after her health. Her answers were always very stiff and formal. She was determined never again to be the subject of rumors. He was of course not happy.

He learned that she had returned to her father's Momozono Palace in the Ninth Month. The Fifth Princess, younger sister of the old emperor and aunt of Asagao and of Genji as well, was also in residence at Momozono. Genji paid a visit, making the Fifth Princess his excuse. The old emperor had been very fond of his sister and niece, and Genji could say that he had inherited a responsibility. They occupied the east and west wings of the palace, which already showed signs of neglect and wore a most melancholy aspect.

The Fifth Princess received him. She seemed to have aged and she coughed incessantly. Princess Omiya, the mother of Genji's dead wife, was her older sister, but the two were very different. Princess Omiya had retained her good looks to the end. A husky-voiced, rather gawky person, the Fifth Princess had somehow never come into her own.

'The world has seemed such a sad place since your father died. I spend my old age sniffling and sobbing. And now Prince Shikibu has left me too. I was sure that no one in the world would even remember me, and here you are. Your kind visit has done a great deal to dispel the gloom.'

Yes, she had aged. He addressed her most courteously. 'Everything seemed to change when Father died. There were those years when with no warning and for no reason that I could see I languished in the provinces. Then when my good brother saw fit to call me back and I was honored with official position once more, I found that I had little time of my own, and I fear that I have neglected you inexcusably. I have so often thought that I would like to call and have a good talk about old times.'

'As you say, it has been a very uncertain and disorderly world. Everywhere I look I see something more to upset me. And I have lived through it all quite as if I were no part of it. No one should be asked to live so long – but now that I see you back where you should be, I remember how I hated the thought of dying while you were still away.' Her voice cracked and wavered. 'Just see what a handsome gentleman you have become. You were so pretty when you were little that it was hard to believe you were really meant for this world, and each time since I have had the same thought, that you might have been meant for somewhere else. They say that His Majesty looks just like you, but I don't believe it. There can't be two such handsome men.'

He smiled. She might have waited until he was out of earshot. 'You praise me too highly. I neglected myself when I was in the provinces and I fear I have not shaken off the countrified look. As for His Majesty, there has been no one, past or present, to rival him in good looks. You are quite right when you say that there cannot be two such handsome men.'

'I think I may expect to live awhile longer if I may be honored from time to time with a visit like this. It is as if both years and sorrows were leaving me.' There was a pause for tears. 'I was, I must admit it, envious of Princess Omiya that she had succeeded in establishing such close relations with you. There was evidence that Prince Shikibu was envious too.'

The conversation had taken an interesting turn. 'A bond with Prince Shikibu's house,' he said somewhat sardonically, 'would have been an honor and a pleasure. But I fear that I was not made to feel exactly wanted.'

His eye had been wandering in the direction of the other wing. The withered garden had a monochrome beauty all its own. He was restless. What would this quiet seclusion have done to Asagao?

'I think I will just look in at the other wing. She would think it rude of me not to.'

He passed through a gallery. In the gathering darkness he could still see somber curtains of mourning beyond blinds trimmed in dark gray. A wonderfully delicate incense came drifting towards him.

He was invited into the south room, for it would not do to leave him on the veranda. Asagao's lady of honor came with a message.

'So you still treat me as if I were a headstrong boy. I have waited so long that I have come to think myself rather venerable, and would have expected the privilege of the inner rooms.'

'I feel as if I were awakening from a long dream,' the princess sent back, 'and I must ask time to deliberate the patience of which you speak.'

Yes, thought Genji, the world was an uncertain, dreamlike place.

'One does indeed wait long and cheerless months
In hopes the gods will someday give their blessing.

'And what divine command do you propose to invoke this time? I have thought and felt a great deal, and would take comfort from sharing even a small part of it with you.'

The princess sensed cool purpose in the old urgency and impetuosity. He had matured. Yet he still seemed much too young for the high office he held.

'The gods will tell me I have broken my vows
For having had the briefest talk with you.'

'What a pity. I would have thought them prepared to let the gentle winds take these things away.'

There really was no one else like him. But she was in grim earnest, refusing to be amused when her lady of honor suggested that the god of Kamo was likely to take her no more seriously than he had taken Narihira.* The years only seemed to have made her less disposed to welcome gallantry. Her women were much distressed by her coldness.

'You have given the interview quite the wrong turn.' Genuinely annoyed, he got up to leave. 'We seem to grow older for purposes of suffering more massive indignities. Is it your purpose to reduce me to the ultimate in abjection?'

The praise was thunderous (it always had been) when he was gone. It was a time when the skies would have brought poignant thoughts in any case, and a falling leaf could take one back to things of long ago. The women exchanged memories of his attentions in matters sad and joyous.

He lay awake with his disappointment. He had the shutters raised early and stood looking out at the morning mist. Trailing

*Ariwara Narihira, *Tales of Ise* 65:

> For an end of love I prayed at the Mitarashi.
> It seems that the gods declined to hear my prayer.

over the withered flowers was a morning glory that still had one or two sad, frostbitten little blooms. He broke it off and sent it to Asagao.*

'You turned me away in shame and humiliation, and the thought of how the rout must have pleased you is not comfortable.

'I do not forget the morning glory I saw.
Will the years, I wonder, have taken it past its bloom?

'I go on, in spite of everything, hoping that you pity me for the sad thoughts of so many years.'

It was a civil sort of letter which it would be wrong to ignore, said her women, pressing an inkstone upon her.

'The morning glory, wholly changed by autumn,
Is lost in the tangle of the dew-drenched hedge.

'Your most apt simile brings tears.'

It could not have been called a very interesting or encouraging reply, but he was unable to put it down. Perhaps it was the elegance of the handwriting, on soft gray-green paper, that so held him.

Sometimes, in an exchange of this sort, one is deluded by rank or an elegant hand into thinking that everything is right, and afterwards, in attempting to describe it, made to feel that it was not so at all. It may be that I have written confidently and not very accurately.

Not wishing to seem impulsive, he was reluctant to reply; but the thought of all the months and years through which she had managed to be cold and yet keep him interested brought some of his youthful ardor back. He wrote a most earnest letter, having summoned her messenger to the east wing, where they would not be observed. Her women tended to be of an easygoing sort, less than firm even towards lesser men, and their noisy praise had put her on her guard. She herself had always been uncompromising, and now she thought that they were too old and too conspicuous, he and she, for such flirtations. The most routine and perfunctory exchange having to do with the flowers and grasses of the seasons seemed likely to invite criticism. The years had not changed her.

*Asagao means 'morning glory' in modern Japanese. The name derives from this chapter. See note†, page 44.

In annoyance and admiration, he had to admit that she was unusual.

Word that he had seen her got abroad in spite of everything. It was said that he was sending her very warm letters. The Fifth Princess, among others, was pleased. They did seem such a remarkably well-matched pair. The rumor presently reached Murasaki, who at first told herself that he would not dream of keeping such a secret from her. Then, watching him closely, she could not dismiss the evidences which she found of restlessness. So he was serious about something which he had treated as a joke. She and Asagao were both granddaughters of emperors, but somehow the other lady had cut the grander figure. If Genji's intentions proved serious Murasaki would be in a very unhappy position indeed. Perhaps, too confident that she had no rivals, she had presumed too much upon his affections. It did not seem likely that he would discard her, at least in the immediate future, but it was quite possible that they had been together too long and that he was taking her for granted. Though in matters of no importance she could scold him most charmingly, she gave no hint of her concern when she was really upset. He spent much of his time these days gazing into the garden. He would spend several nights at court and on his return busy himself with what he called official correspondence, and she would conclude that the rumors were true. Why did he not say something? He seemed like a stranger.

There were no festivals this year.* Bored and fidgety, he set off for Momozono again one evening. He had taken the whole day with his toilet, choosing pleasantly soft robes and making sure that they were well perfumed. The weaker sort of woman would have had even fewer defenses against his charms than usual.

He did, after all, think it necessary to tell Murasaki. 'The Fifth Princess is not well. I must look in upon her.'

He waited for a reply, but she was busying herself with the little girl. Her profile told him that all was not well.

'You seem so touchy these days. I cannot think why. I have not wanted to be taken for granted, like a familiar and rumpled old robe, and so I have been staying away a little more than I used to. What suspicions are you cherishing this time?'

*The court is in mourning.

'Yes, it is true. One does not enjoy being wearied of.' She turned away and lay down.

He did not want to leave her, but he had told the Fifth Princess that he would call, and really must be on his way.

So this, thought Murasaki, was marriage. She had been too confident.

Mourning robes have their own beauty, and his were especially beautiful in the light reflected from the snow. She could not bear to think that he might one day be leaving her for good.

He took only a very few intimate retainers with him. 'I have reached an age,' he said, very plausibly, 'when I do not want to go much of anywhere except to the palace. But they are having a rather sad time of it at Momozono. They had Prince Shikibu to look after them, and now it seems very natural, and very sad too, that they should turn to me.'

Murasaki's women were not convinced. 'It continues to be his great defect that his attention wanders. We only hope that no unhappiness comes of it.'

At Momozono the traffic seemed to be through the north gate. It would have been undignified for Genji to join the stream, and so he sent one of his men in through the great west gate. The Fifth Princess, who had not expected him so late on a snowy evening, made haste to order the gate opened. A chilly-looking porter rushed out. He was having trouble and there was no one to help him.

'All rusty,' he muttered. Genji felt rather sorry for him.

And so thirty years had gone by,* like yesterday and today. It was a fleeting, insubstantial world, and yet the temporary lodgings which it offered were not easy to give up. The grasses and flowers of the passing seasons continued to pull at him.

> 'And when did wormwood overwhelm this gate,
>   This hedge, now under snow, so go to ruin?'

Finally the gate was opened and he made his way in.

The Fifth Princess commenced talking, as always, of old times. She talked on and on, and Genji was drowsy. She too began to yawn.

---

*Some texts say three years. 'Thirty years' could refer to Genji's age. 'Three years' would seem to refer to nothing at all.

'I get sleepy of an evening. I'm afraid I'm not the talker I used to be.'

The sounds which then began to emerge from her may have been snores, but they were unlike any he had heard before.

Delighted at this release, he started off. But another woman had taken over, coughing a very aged cough. 'I had ventured to hope that you might remember me, but I see that you no longer count me among the living. Your late father used to call me Granny* and have a good laugh over me.'

She identified herself and he remembered. It was old Naishi. He had heard that she had become a nun and that she and the old princess kept religious company, but it astonished him to learn that she was still alive.

'It seems a very long time since my father died. Even to think of those days somehow makes me sad. What a pleasure it is to hear your voice. You must be kind to me, as you would be kind to a fatherless wanderer.'†

Evidence that he had settled down again and that she had his attention seems to have swept her back to the old years, and all the old coquettishness came forth anew. It was too evident, from the imperfect articulation, that the playful words came from a toothless old mouth. 'Even as I spoke,'‡ she said, and it seemed rather too much. He was both amused and saddened at the suggestion that old age had come upon her suddenly and undetected.

Of the ladies who had competed for the old emperor's affections when Naishi was in her prime, some were long dead, and no doubt others had come upon sad days at the end of long lives. What a short life Fujitsubo had lived! A world which had already seemed uncertain enough was making another display of cruel uncertainty. Here serenely pursuing her devotions was a woman who had seemed ready for death even then and who had never had a great deal to recommend her.

---

*There is no earlier mention of his having done so.

†Prince Shōtoku, *Shūishū* 1350:

> Weep for the fatherless wanderer starving and dying
> On Mount Kataoka of the terraced fields.

‡A poetic allusion, apparently. The following sentence suggests that the poem, which has not been identified, speaks of the sudden onset of old age.

Pleased that she had had an effect upon him, she moved on to other playful endeavors.

'I do not forget that bond, though years have passed,
For did you not choose to call me Mother's mother?'

It was a bit extreme.

'Suppose we wait for another world to tell us
Of instances of a child's forgetting a parent.

'Yes, it does seem a most durable bond. We must have a good talk about it sometime.'
And he left.

A few shutters were still open along the west wing, as if the princess did not want to make him feel completely unwelcome. The moon had come out and was shining upon the snow to turn the evening into a suddenly beautiful one. Such encounters as the one from which he had just emerged were held by the world to be inept examples of something or other.

His manner was very sober and proper this evening. 'If I could have a single word directly from you expressing your dislike for me, then I might resign myself to what must be.'

But she was disinclined to grant him even this. Young indiscretion can be forgiven, and she had sensed that her late father was not ill disposed toward him; but she had rejected him, and that was that. At their age it was all most unseemly. The prospect of the single word he asked for left her in acute embarrassment. He thought her a very cold lady indeed, and she for her part wished he would give her credit for trying, through her intermediary, not to seem inhospitable. It was late and the wind was high and cold.

Though feeling very sorry for himself, he managed a certain elegance as he brushed away a tear.

'Long years of coldness have not chastened me,
And now I add resentment to resentment.

Though of course it is true that I came asking for it.'
He spoke as if to himself, and once again her women were noisy in agreeing that he was not being treated well.
She sent out an answer:

'I could not change if I wished at this late date.
I know that others do, but I cannot.

I leave things exactly as I find them.'

He did not wish to go storming out like an angry boy. 'This must be kept secret,' he said in the course of whispered consultation with the woman who brought her messages. 'I would not want to set a ridiculous example. It is of course not you but your lady – you must think it rather coy of me – to whom I should be commending the river Isara as a model.'*

Her women were agreed that he had not been treated well. 'Such a fine gentleman. Why must she be so stubborn? He seems incapable of the tiniest rudeness or recklessness.'

She knew well enough that he was a most admirable and interesting man, but she wanted no remark from her to join the anthems she heard all about her. He was certain to conclude that she too had succumbed – he was so shamelessly handsome. No, an appearance of warmth and friendliness would not serve her purposes. Always addressing him through an intermediary, she expressed herself carefully and at careful intervals, just short of what he might take for final silence. She wanted to lose herself in her devotions and make amends for her years away from the Good Law, but she did not want the dramatics of a final break. They too would amuse the gossips. Not trusting even her own women, she withdrew gradually into her prayers. Prince Shikibu had had numerous children, her mother only one. She was not close to her half brothers and sisters. The Momozono Palace was neglected and her retinue was small. Now came this fine gentleman with his impassioned suit, in which everyone in sight seemed to be joining.

It is not to be imagined that Genji had quite lost his heart to the princess. It was rather that her coldness put him on his mettle. He did not wish to admit defeat. He was extremely careful these days about his behavior, which left no room for criticism. He knew how happy people were to pass judgment in such matters and he was no longer the Genji of the youthful indiscretions. He was not at this late date going to admit scandal into his life. Yet rejected suitors did look rather ridiculous.

Isaya means something like 'I have no idea.' In *Kokinshū* 1108 the river Isaya, in Omi, is offered as the proper reply to inquiries into a certain secret. 'Isara' is probably a miscopying. See note†, page 157.

His nights away from Nijō were more frequent. 'I wonder if even in jest,'* said Murasaki to herself. The tears would come, however she tried to hold them back.

'You are not looking well,' he said, stroking her hair. 'What can be the trouble?' He gazed affectionately at her, and they seemed such a perfect pair that one would have wished to do a likeness of them. 'The emperor has been very despondent since his mother's death, and now that the chancellor is gone there is no one but me who can really make decisions. I have been terribly busy. You are not used to having me away so much, and it is very natural that you should be unhappy; but you have nothing at all to worry about. You are no longer a girl, and this refusal to understand is rather funny.' He smoothed the hair at her forehead, matted with tears. She looked away. 'Who can have been responsible for your education, that you refuse to grow up?'

It was an uncertain and capricious world, and he grieved that anything at all should come between them. 'I wonder if you might possibly have misconstrued the little notes I have sent to the high priestess of Kamo. If so, then you are very far from the mark. You will see for yourself one of these days. She has always been such a cold one. I have sought to intimidate her with what might be taken for love notes. Life is dull for her, it would seem, and sometimes she has answered. Why should I come crying to you with the answers when they mean so little to me? I must assure you once more that you have nothing to worry about.' He spent the whole day in her rooms.

There was a heavy fall of snow. In the evening there were new flurries. The contrast between the snow on the bamboo and the snow on the pines was very beautiful. Genji's good looks seemed to shine more brightly in the evening light.

'People make a great deal of the flowers of spring and the leaves of autumn, but for me a night like this, with a clear moon shining on snow, is the best – and there is not a trace of color in it. I cannot describe the effect it has on me, weird and unearthly somehow. I do not understand people who find a winter evening forbidding.' He had the blinds raised.

The moon turned the deepest recesses of the garden a gleaming white. The flower beds were wasted, the brook seemed to send up

See note, page 271.

a strangled cry, and the lake was frozen and somehow terrible. Into this austere scene he sent little maidservants, telling them that they must make snowmen. Their dress was bright and their hair shone in the moonlight. The older ones were especially pretty, their jackets and trousers and ribbons trailing off in many colors, and the fresh sheen of their hair black against the snow. The smaller ones quite lost themselves in the sport. They let their fans fall most immodestly from their faces. It was all very charming. Rather outdoing themselves, several of them found that they had a snowball which they could not budge. Some of their fellows jeered at them from the east veranda.

'I remember a winter when they made a snow mountain for your aunt, the late empress. There was nothing remarkable about it, but she had a way of making the smallest things seem remarkable. Everything reminds me of her. I was kept at a distance, of course, and did not have the good fortune to observe her closely, but during her years at court she was good enough to take me into her confidence. In my turn I looked to her for advice. She was always very quiet and unassertive, but I always came away feeling that I had been right to ask her. I think I never came away without some small thing that seemed very precious. I doubt that we will see anyone quite like her again. She was a gentle lady and even a little shy, and at the same time she had a wonderful way of seeing to the heart of things. You of course wear the same colors,* but I do sometimes find that I must tax you with a certain willfulness.

'The Kamo priestess is another matter. With time on our hands and no real business, we have exchanged notes. I should say that she is the one who puts me to the test these days.'

'But the most elegant and accomplished one of them all, I should think, is Lady Oborozukiyo. She seemed like caution incarnate and yet those strange things did happen.'

'If you are naming the beautiful and interesting ones, she must be among them. It does seem a pity that there should have been that incident. A wild youth is not an easy thing to have on one's conscience – and mine was so much tamer than most.' The thought of Oborozukiyo brought a sigh. 'Then there is the lady off in the hills of whom you have such a low opinion. She is more sensitive and accomplished than one might expect from her rank.

Murasaki and *fuji* are both shades of purple.

She demands rather special treatment and so I have chosen to
overlook a tendency not to be as aware as she might of her place in
the world. I have never taken charge of a lady who has had nothing at all to recommend her. Yet the really outstanding ones are
rare indeed. The lady in the east lodge here is an example of complete devotion and dependability. I undertook to look after her
when I saw her finer qualities, and I have found absolutely nothing
in her behavior which I might call forward or demanding. We
have become very fond of each other, and would both, I think, be
sad at the thought of parting.' So they passed the night.

The moon was yet brighter, the scene utterly quiet.

'The water is stilled among the frozen rocks.
A clear moon moves into the western sky.'*

Bending forward to look out at the garden, she was incomparably lovely. Her hair and profile called up most wonderfully the
image of Fujitsubo, and his love was once again whole and
undivided.

There was the call of a waterfowl.

'A night of drifting snow and memories
Is broken by another note of sadness.'

He lay down, still thinking of Fujitsubo. He had a fleeting
dream of her. She seemed angry.

'You said that you would keep our secret, and it is out. I am
unable to face the world for the pain and the shame.'

He was about to answer, as if defending himself against a sudden, fierce attack.

'What is the matter?'

It was Murasaki's voice. His longing for the dead lady was indescribable. His heart was racing and in spite of himself he was weeping. Murasaki gazed at him, fear in her eyes. She lay quite still.

'A winter's night, I awaken from troubled sleep.
And what a brief and fleeting dream it was!'

Arising early, sadder than if he had not slept at all, he commissioned services, though without explaining his reasons. No doubt

*The mobile moon is Genji, the static water Murasaki herself.

she did blame him for her sufferings. She had tried very hard, it seemed, to do penance for her sins, but perhaps the gravest of them had remained with her. The thought that there are laws in these matters filled him with a sadness almost unbearable. He longed, by some means, to visit her where she wandered alone, a stranger, and to take her sins for his own. He feared that if he made too much of the services he would arouse suspicions. Afraid that a suspicion of the truth might even now be disturbing the emperor, he gave himself over to invoking the holy name.

If only they might share the same lotus in another world.

'I fear, in my longing, to go in search of her
And find not her shade on the banks of the River of Death.'

These are the thoughts, one is told, with which he tormented himself.

CHAPTER 21

The Maiden

The New Year came, and the end of mourning for Fujitsubo. Mourning robes were changed for the bright robes of ordinary times. It was as if the warm, soft skies of the Fourth Month and the Kamo festival had everywhere brought renewal. For Asagao, however, life was sad and dull. The wind rustling the laurels* made her think of the festival and brought countless memories to her young women as well.

On the day of the Kamo lustration a note came from Genji. It was on lavender paper folded with formal precision and attached to a spray of wisteria. 'I can imagine the quiet memories with which you are passing this day.

'I did not think that when the waters returned
It would be to take away the weeds of mourning.'

It was a time of memories. She sent off an answer:

'How quick the change. Deep mourning yesterday,
Today the shallow waters of lustration.

'Everything seems fleeting and insubstantial.'

Brief and noncommittal though it was, Genji could not put it down.

His gifts, addressed to her lady of honor, quite overflowed her wing of the Momozono Palace. She hated to have it seem that he was treating her as one of his ladies. If she had been able to detect anything which struck her as in the least improper she could have sent them back; but she had had gifts from him before, on suitable occasions, and his letter was most staid and proper. She could not think how to answer.

He was also very particular on such occasions about writing to the Fifth Princess.

'It seems like only yesterday that he was a little boy, and here he is so gallant and polite. He is the handsomest man I have ever seen, and so good-natured too, much nicer than any other young gentleman I know.' The young women were much amused.

*Sprays of *katsura*, more properly 'Judas tree,' were worn in the hair by participants in the Kamo festival.

Asagao was always the recipient of an outmoded description of things when she saw her aunt. 'Such lovely notes as the Genji minister is always writing. No, please, now – whatever you say you can't pretend that he's only just now come courting. I remember how disappointed your father was when he married the other lady and we did not have the pleasure of welcoming him here. All your fault, your father was always saying. Your unreasonable ways lost us our chance. While his wife was still alive, I was not able to support my brother in his hopes, because after all she was my niece too. Well, she had him and now she's gone.* What possible reason can there be for not doing as your father wanted you to do? Here he is courting you again as if nothing ever happened. I think it must be your fate to marry him.'

'I seemed stubborn while Father was alive. How would I seem now if I were suddenly to accede to your wishes?'

The subject was obviously one which distressed her, and the old lady pursued it no further.

Poor Asagao lived in constant trepidation, for not only her aunt but everyone in the Momozono Palace seemed to be on his side. Genji, however, having made the sincerity of his affections clear, seemed prepared to wait for a conciliatory move on her part. He was not going to demand a confrontation.

Though it would have been more convenient to have Yūgiri's initiation ceremonies at Nijō, the boy's grandmother, Princess Omiya, naturally wanted to see them. So it was decided that they would take place at Sanjō. His maternal uncles, Tō no Chūjō and the rest, were now all very well placed and in the emperor's confidence. They vied with one another in being of service to Genji and his son. Indeed the whole court, including people whose concern it need not have been, had made the ceremony its chief business.

Everyone expected that Yūgiri would be promoted to the Fourth Rank. Genji deliberated the possibility and decided that rapid promotions when everyone knew they could be as rapid as desired had a way of seeming vulgar. Yūgiri looked so forlorn in his blue robes that Princess Omiya was angry for him. She demanded an explanation of Genji.

'We need not force him into adult company. I have certain thoughts in the matter. I think he should go to the university, and

---

*It is ten years since Aoi died.

so we may think of the next few years as time out, a vacation from all these promotions. When he is old enough to be of real service at court it will be soon enough. I myself grew up at court, always at Father's side. I did not know what the larger world was like and I learned next to nothing about the classics. Father himself was my teacher, but there was something inadequate about my education. What I did learn of the classics and of music and the like did not have a broad grounding.

'We do not hear in our world of sons who excel inadequate fathers, and over the generations the prospect becomes one of sad decline. I have made my decision. A boy of good family moves ahead in rank and office and basks in the honors they bring. Why, he asks, should he trouble himself to learn anything? He has his fun, he has his music and other pleasures, and rank and position seem to come of their own accord. The underlings of the world praise him to his face and laugh at him behind his back. This is very well while it lasts – he is the grand gentleman. But changes come, forces shift. Those who can help themselves do so, and he is left behind. His affairs fall into a decline and presently nothing is left.

'No, the safe thing is to give him a good, solid fund of knowledge. It is when there is a fund of Chinese learning that the Japanese spirit* is respected by the world. He may feel dissatisfied for a time, but if we give him the proper education for a minister of state, then I need not worry about what will happen after I am gone. He may not be able to spread his wings for a time, but I doubt that, given the house he comes from, people will sneer at him as a threadbare clerk.'

The princess sighed. 'Yes, I suppose you are right. I hadn't thought things through quite so far. My sons have said that you are being very strict with him, and he did seem so very forlorn when all the cousins he has looked down on have moved from blue to brighter colors. I had to feel sorry for him.'

Genji smiled. 'He is very grown-up for his age.' In fact, he thought Yūgiri's behavior rather endearing. 'But he'll get over it when they've put a little learning into his head.'

The matriculation ceremonies were held in the east lodge at Nijō, the east wing of which was fitted out for the occasion. It was

---

*Yamatodamashii. The only appearance of the word in the tale, and its first known appearance anywhere.

a rare event. Courtiers crowded round to see what a matriculation might be like. The professors must have been somewhat
astonished.

'You are to treat him exactly as the rules demand,' said Genji.
'Make no exceptions.'

The academic assembly was a strange one, solemn of countenance, badly fitted in borrowed clothes, utterly humorless of word
and manner, yet given to jostling for place. Some of the younger
courtiers were laughing. Fearing that that would be the case, Genji
had insisted that the professorial cups be kept full by older and
better-controlled men. Even so, Tō no Chūjō and Prince Mimbu*
were reprimanded by the learned gentlemen.†

'Most inadequate, these libation pourers. Do they propose to
conduct the affairs of the land without the advice of the sages?
Most inadequate indeed.'

There came gusts of laughter.

'Silence, if you please. Silence is called for. Such improprieties
are unheard of. We must ask your withdrawal.'

Everyone thought the professors rather fun. For courtiers who
had themselves been to the university the affair was most satisfying. It was very fine indeed that Genji should see fit to give his
son a university education. The professors put down merriment
with a heavy hand and made unfavorable note of other departures
from strict decorum. Yet as the night wore on, the lamps revealed
something a little different, a little clownish, perhaps, or forlorn,
under the austere professorial masks. It was indeed an unusual
assembly.

'I am afraid, sirs, that I am the oaf you should be scolding,' said
Genji, withdrawing behind a blind. 'I am quite overcome.'

Learning that there had not been places enough for all the
scholars, he had a special banquet laid out in the angling pavilion.

He invited the professors and several courtiers of a literary bent
to stay behind and compose Chinese poems. The professors were
assigned stanzas of four couplets, and the amateurs, Genji among
them, were allowed to make do with two. The professors assigned
titles. Dawn was coming on when the reading took place, with

*Otherwise unidentified.

†The following remarks have a stilted, Confucian tone, and include several words
which appear nowhere else in the tale.

Sachūben* the reader. He was a man of imposing manner and fine looks, and his voice as he read took on an almost awesome grandeur. Great things were to be expected from him, everyone said. The poems, all of them interesting, brought in numerous old precedents by way of celebrating so laudable an event, that a young man born to luxury and glory should choose to make the light of the firefly his companion, the reflection from the snow his friend.† One would have liked to send them for the delectation of the land across the sea. They were the talk of the court.

Genji's poem was particularly fine. His paternal affection showed through and brought tears from the company. But it would not be seemly for a woman to speak in detail of these scholarly happenings, and I shall say no more.

Then came the formal commencement of studies. Genji assigned rooms in the east lodge, where learned tutors were put at Yūgiri's disposal. Immersed in his studies, he rarely went to call on his grandmother. He had been with her since infancy, and Genji feared that she would go on pampering him. Quiet rooms near at hand seemed appropriate. He was permitted to visit Sanjō some three times a month.

Shut up with musty books, he did think his father severe. His friends, subjected to no such trials, were moving happily from rank to rank. He was a serious lad, however, not given to frivolity, and soon he had resolved that he would make quick work of the classics and then have his career. Within a few months he had finished *The Grand History*. Genji conducted mock examinations with the usual people in attendance, Tō no Chūjō, Sadaiben, Shikibu no Tayū, Sachūben,‡ and the rest. The boy's chief tutor was invited as well. Yūgiri was asked to read passages from *The Grand History* on which he was likely to be challenged. He did so without hesitation, offering all the variant theories as to the meaning, and leaving no smudgy question marks behind. Everyone was delighted, and indeed tears of delight might have been observed. It had been an outstanding performance, though not at all unex-

*Otherwise unidentified.

†Two impoverished scholars of the Ch'in period studied by the light of the firefly and the reflection from the snow.

‡The last three are otherwise unknown, although a Sadaiben is mentioned on page 343.

pected. How he wished, said Tō no Chūjō, that the old chancellor could have been present.

Genji was not completely successful at hiding his pride. 'There is a sad thing that I have more than once witnessed, a father who grows stupider as his son grows wiser. So here it is happening to me, and I am not so very old. It is the way of the world.' His pleasure and pride were a rich reward for the tutor.

The drinks which Tō no Chūjō pressed on this gentleman seemed to make him ever leaner. He was an odd man whose scholarly attainments had not been put to proper use, and life had not been good to him. Sensing something unusual in him, Genji had put him in charge of Yūgiri's studies. These rather over-whelming attentions made him feel that life had begun again, and no doubt a limitless future seemed to open for him.

On the day of the examination the university gates were jammed with fine carriages. It was natural that no one, not even people who had no real part in the proceedings, should wish to be left out. The young candidate himself, very carefully dressed and surrounded by solicitous retainers, was so handsome a figure that people were inclined to ask again what he was doing here. If he looked a little self-conscious taking the lowest seat as the company assembled, that too was natural. Again stern calls to proper deport-ment emerged from the professors, but he read without misstep to the end.

It was a day to make one think of the university in its finest age. People high and low now competed to pursue the way of learning, and the level of official competence rose. Yūgiri got through his other examinations, the literary examination and the rest, with no trouble. He quite immersed himself in his studies, spurring his tutors to new endeavors. Genji arranged composition meets at Nijō from time to time, to the great satisfaction of the scholars and poets. It was a day when their abilities were recognized.

The time had come to name an empress. Genji urged the case of Akikonomu, reminding everyone of Fujitsubo's wishes for her son. It would mean another Genji* empress, and to that there was opposition. And Tō no Chūjō's daughter had been the first of the emperor's ladies to come to court. The outcome of the debate remained in doubt.

*The expression seems here to mean 'non-Fujiwara.'

Murasaki's father, Prince Hyōbu, was now a man of importance, the maternal uncle of the emperor. He had long wanted to
send a daughter to court and at length he had succeeded, and so
two of the principal contenders were royal granddaughters. If
the choice was to be between them, people said, then surely the
emperor would feel more comfortable with his mother's niece.
He could think of her as a substitute for his mother. But in the
end Akikonomu's candidacy prevailed. There were many remarks
upon the contrast between her fortunes and those of her late
mother.

There were promotions, Genji to chancellor and Tō no Chūjō
to Minister of the Center. Genji left the everyday conduct of government to his friend, a most honest and straightforward man who
had also a bright side to his nature. He was very intelligent and he
had studied hard. Though he could not hold his own with Genji
in rhyme-guessing contests, he was a gifted administrator. He had
more than a half score of sons by several ladies, all of them growing or grown and making names for themselves. It was a good day
for his house. He had only one daughter, Kumoinokari, besides
the lady who had gone to court. It could not have been said, since
her mother came from the royal family, that she was the lesser of
the two daughters, but the mother had since married the Lord
Inspector and had a large family of her own. Not wishing to leave
the girl with her stepfather, Tō no Chūjō had brought her to
Sanjō and there put her in Princess Omiya's custody. Though he
paid a good deal more attention to the other daughter, Kumoinokari was a pretty and amiable child. She and Yūgiri grew up like
brother and sister in Princess Omiya's apartments. Tō no Chūjō
separated them when they reached the age of ten or so. He knew
that they were fond of each other, he said, but the girl was now
too old to have male playmates. Yūgiri continued to think of her,
in his boyish way, and he was careful to notice her when the
flowers and grasses of the passing seasons presented occasions, or
when he came upon something for her dollhouses. She was not at
all shy in his presence. They were so young, said her nurses, and
they had been together so long. Why must the minister tear them
apart? Yet one had to grant him a point in suspecting that, despite
appearances, they might no longer be children.

In any event the separation upset them. Their letters, childish
but showing great promise, were always falling into the wrong

hands, for they were as yet not very skilled managers. But if some of her women knew what was going on, they saw no need to tell tales.

The round of congratulatory banquets was over. In the quiet that followed, Tō no Chūjō came visiting his mother. It was an evening of chilly showers and the wind sent a sad rustling through the reeds. He summoned Kumoinokari for a lesson on the koto. Princess Omiya, a fine musician, was the girl's teacher.

'A lady is not perhaps seen at her most graceful when she is playing the lute, but the sound is rather wonderful. You do not often hear a good lute these days. Let me see now.' And he named this prince and that commoner who were good lutists. 'I have heard from the chancellor that the lady he has out in the country is a very good hand at it. She comes from a line of musicians, but the family is not what it once was, and she has been away for a very long time. It is surprising that she should be so good. He does seem to have a high regard for her, to judge from the way he is always talking about her. Music is not like other things. It requires company and concerts and a familiarity with all the styles. You do not often hear of a self-taught musician.' He urged a lute upon his mother.

'I don't even know where to put the bridge any more.' Yet she took the instrument and played very commendably indeed. 'The lady you mention would seem to have a great deal to distinguish her besides her good luck. She gave him the daughter he has always wanted. He was afraid the daughter would be handicapped by a rustic mother, they tell me, and gave her to a lady of quite unassilable position. I hear that she is a little jewel.' She had put the instrument down.

'Yes, you are right, of course. It was more than luck that got her where she is. But sometimes things don't seem entirely fair. I cannot think of any respect in which the girl I sent to court is inferior to her rivals, and I gave her every skill she could possibly need to hold her own. And all of a sudden someone emerges from an unexpected quarter and overtakes her. I hope that nothing of the sort happens to this other one. The crown prince will soon be coming of age and I have plans. But do I once again see unexpected competition?' He sighed. 'Once the daughter of this most fortunate Akashi lady is at court she seems even more likely than the empress to have everything her way.'

The old lady was angry with Genji for what had happened. 'Your father was all wrapped up in his plans to send your little girl to court, and he thought it extremely unlikely that an empress would be named from any house but ours. It is an injustice which would not have been permitted if he had lived.'

Tō no Chūjō gazed proudly at Kumoinokari, who was indeed a pretty little thing, in a still childish way. As she leaned over her koto the hair at her forehead and the thick hair flowing over her shoulders seemed to him very lovely. She turned shyly from his gaze, and in profile was every bit as charming. As she pushed at the strings with her left hand, she was like a delicately fashioned doll. The princess too was delighted. Gently tuning the koto, the girl pushed it away.

Tō no Chūjō took out a Japanese koto and tuned it to a minor key,* and so put an old-fashioned instrument to modern uses. It was very pleasing indeed, the sight of a grand gentleman at home with his music. All eager to see, the old women were crowding and jostling one another behind screens.

' "The leaves await the breeze to scatter them," ' he sang. ' "It is a gentle breeze."† My koto does not, I am sure, have the effect of that Chinese koto, but it is a strangely beautiful evening. Would you let us have another?'

The girl played 'Autumn Winds,'‡ with her father, in fine voice, singing the lyrics. The old lady looked affectionately from the one to the other.

Yūgiri came in, as if to add to the joy.

'How very nice,' said Tō no Chūjō, motioning him to a place at the girl's curtains. 'We do not see as much of you these days as we would like. You are so fearfully deep in your studies. Your father knows as well as I do that too much learning is not always a good thing, but I suppose he has his reasons. Still it seems a pity that you should be in solitary confinement. You should allow yourself diversions from time to time. Music too has a proper and venerable tradition, you know.' He offered Yūgiri a flute.

There was a bright, youthful quality about the boy's playing.

*Ritsu, apparently held to have a bright, modern sound.

†Lu Chi, 'The Hero.' Tō no Chūjō's next remark alludes to the same poem, in which a seven-stringed Chinese koto has an effect upon the leaves.

‡Originally Chinese, but Japanized in the eighth century.

Tō no Chūjō put his koto aside and quietly beat time with a fan. 'My sleeves were stained from the *hagi*,'* he hummed.

'Your father so loves music. He has abandoned dull affairs of state. Life is a gloomy enough business at best, and I would like to follow his lead and do nothing that I do not want to.'

He ordered wine. Presently it was dark. Lamps were lighted and dinner was brought.

He sent Kumoinokari off to her rooms. Yūgiri had not even been permitted to hear her koto. No good would come of these stern measures, the old women whispered.

Pretending to leave, Tō no Chūjō went to call on a lady to whom he was paying court. When, somewhat later, he made his stealthy way out, he heard whispering. He stopped to listen. He himself proved to be the subject.

'He thinks he is so clever, but he is just like any other father. Unhappiness will come of it all, you can be very sure. The ancients did not know what they were talking about when they said that a father knows best.'†

They were nudging one another to emphasize their points.

Well, now. Most interesting. He had not been without suspicions, but he had not been enough on his guard. He had said that they were still children. It was a complicated world indeed. He slipped out, giving no hint of what he had heard and surmised.

The women were startled by the shouts of outrunners. 'Just leaving? Where can he have been hiding himself? A little old for such things, I would have thought.'

The whisperers were rather upset. 'There was that lovely perfume,' said one of them, 'but we thought it would be the young gentleman. How awful. You don't suppose he heard? He can be difficult.'

Tō no Chūjō deliberated the problem as he rode home. A marriage between cousins was not wholly unacceptable, of course, but

---

*'Autumn Robes' (Koromogae), a Saibara:

> A change to autumn dress, my lads.
> While I wandered the meadows and groves
> My thoughts on that unkind girl,
> My sleeves were stained from the *hagi* they brushed against.

†The statement is to be found in both the *Shih Chi* and the *Nihongi*.

people would think it at best uninteresting. It had not been pleasant to have his other daughter so unconditionally defeated by Genji's favorite, and he had been telling himself that this one must be a winner. Though he and Genji were and had long been good friends, echoes of their old rivalry persisted. He spent a sleepless night. His mother no doubt knew what was going on and had let her darlings have their way. He had overheard enough to be angry. He had a straightforward masculinity about him and the anger was not easy to control.

Two days later he called on his mother. Delighted to be seeing so much of him, she had someone touch up her nun's coiffure and chose her cloak with great care. He was such a handsome man that he made her feel a little fidgety, even though he was her own son, and she let him see her only in profile.

He was very much out of sorts. 'I know what your women are saying and I do not feel at all comfortable about visiting you. I am not a man of very great talent, I know, but I had thought that as long as I lived I would do what I could for you. I had thought that we would always be close and that I would always keep watch over your health and comfort.' He brushed away a tear. 'Now it has become necessary for me to speak about a matter that greatly upsets me. I would much prefer to keep it to myself.'

Omiya gazed at him in astonishment. Under her powder she changed color. 'Whatever can it be? Whatever can I have done in my old age to make you so angry?'

He felt a little less angry but went on all the same. 'I have grievously neglected her ever since she was a tiny child. I have thought that I could leave everything to you. I have been worried about the not entirely happy situation of the girl in the palace and have busied myself doing what I can for her, confident that I could leave the other to you. And now something very surprising and regrettable has come to my attention. He may be a talented and erudite young man who knows more about history than anyone else at court, but even the lower classes think it a rather dull and common thing for cousins to marry. It will do him no more good than her. He would do far better to find a rich and stylish bride a little farther afield. I am sure that Genji will be no more pleased than I am. In any event, I would have been grateful if you had kept me informed. Do please try a little harder to keep us from looking ridiculous. I must emphasize my astonishment that you have been so careless about letting them keep company.'

This was news to Omiya. 'You are right to be annoyed. I had not suspected anything, and I am sure that I have a right to feel even more put upon than you do. But I do not think you should accuse me of collusion. I have been very fond of the children ever since you left them with me, and I have worked very hard to bring out fine points that you yourself might not be entirely aware of. They are children, and I have not, I must assure you, been blinded by affection into wanting to rush them into each other's arms. But be that as it may, who can have told you such awful things? I do not find it entirely admirable of you to gather common gossip and make a huge issue of it. Nothing so very serious has happened, of that I am sure, and you are doing harm to the girl's good name.'

'Not quite nothing. All of your women are laughing at us, and I do not find it pleasant.' And he left.

The better-informed women were very sorry for the young people. The whisperers were of course the most upset of all.

Tō no Chūjō looked in on his daughter, whom he found at play with her dolls, so pretty that he could not bring himself to scold her. 'Yes,' he said to her woman, 'she is still very young and innocent; but I fear that in my own innocence, making my own plans for her, I failed to recognize the degree of her innocence.'

They defended themselves, somewhat uncertainly. 'In the old romances even the emperor's daughter will sometimes make a mistake. There always seems to be a lady-in-waiting who knows all the secrets and finds ways to bring the young people together. Our case is quite different. Our lady has been with the two of them morning and night over all these years, and it would not be proper for us to intrude ourselves and try to separate them more sternly than she has seen fit to, and so we did not worry. About two years ago she does seem to have changed to a policy of keeping them apart. There are young gentlemen who take advantage of the fact that people still think them boys and do odd and mischievous things. But not the young master. There has not been the slightest suggestion of anything improper in his behavior. What you say comes as a surprise to us.'

'Well, what is done is done. The important thing now is to see that the secret does not get out. These things are never possible to keep completely secret, I suppose, but you must pretend that it is a matter of no importance and that the gossips do not know what they are talking about. I will take the child home with me. My mother is the one I am angry with. I do not imagine that any of you wanted things to turn out as they have.'

It was sad for the girl, thought the women, but it could have been worse. 'Oh, yes, sir, you may be sure that you can trust us to keep the secret. What if the Lord Inspector were to hear? The young master is a very fine boy, but it is not after all as if he were a prince.'

The girl still seemed very young indeed. However many stern injunctions he might hand down, it did not seem likely that she would see their real import. The problem was to protect her. He discussed it with her women, and his anger continued to be at his mother.

Princess Omiya was fond of both her grandchildren, but it seems likely that the boy was her favorite. She had thought his attentions toward his cousin altogether charming, and here Tō no Chūjō was talking as if they were a crime and a scandal. He understood nothing, nothing at all. He had paid very little attention to the girl and it was only after Omiya herself had done so much that he had commenced having grand ideas about making her crown princess. If his plans went astray and the girl was after all to marry a commoner, where was she likely to find a better one? Where indeed, all through the court, was his equal in intelligence and looks? No, the case was the reverse of what her good son took it to be: the boy was the one who, if he chose, could marry into the royal family. Wounded affection now impelled her to return her son's anger in good measure. He would no doubt have been even angrier if he had known what she was thinking.

Ignorant of this commotion, Yūgiri came calling. He chose evening for his visit. There had been such a crowd that earlier evening that he had been unable to exchange words with Kumoi-nokari, and so his longing was stronger.

His grandmother was usually all smiles when she received him, but this evening she was stern. 'I have been put in a difficult position because your uncle is displeased with you,' she said, after solemn prefatory remarks. 'You have brought trouble because it seems you have ambitions which it would not do for people to hear about. I would have preferred not to bring the matter up, but it seems necessary to ask whether you have anything on your conscience.'

He flushed scarlet, knowing at once what she was referring to. 'What could it be? I wonder. I have been shut up with my books and I have seen no one. I cannot think of anything that might have upset him.'

He was unable to look at her. She thought his confusion both sad and endearing. 'Very well. But do be careful, please.' And she moved on to other matters.

He saw that it would be difficult even to exchange notes with his cousin. Dinner was brought but he had no appetite. He lay down in his grandmother's room, unable to sleep. When all was quiet he tried the door to the girl's room. Unlocked most nights, it was tightly locked tonight. No one seemed astir. He leaned against the door, feeling very lonely. She too was awake, it seemed. The wind rustled sadly through the bamboo thickets and from far away came the call of a wild goose.

'The wild goose in the clouds – as sad as I am?'* Her voice, soft and girlish, spoke of young longing.

'Open up, please. Is Kojijū there?' Kojijū was her nurse's daughter.

She had hidden her face under a quilt, embarrassed that she had been overheard. But love, relentless pursuer, would be after her however she might try to hide. With her women beside her she was afraid to make the slightest motion.

> 'The midnight call to its fellows in the clouds
> Comes in upon the wind that rustles the reeds,

and sinks to one's very bones.'

Sighing, he went back and lay down beside his grandmother. He tried not to move lest he awaken her.

Not up to conversation, he slipped back to his own room very early the next morning. He wrote a letter to the girl but was unable to find Kojijū and have it delivered, and of course he was unable to visit the girl's room.

Though vaguely aware of the reasons for the whole stir, the girl was not greatly disturbed about her future or about the gossip. Pretty as ever, she could not bring herself to do what seemed to be asked of her and dislike her cousin. She did not herself think that

*The poems quoted in early commentaries are not otherwise known. Kumoinokari means 'the wild goose in the clouds.' The name of course comes from this episode.

she had behaved so dreadfully, but with these women so intent on exaggerating everything she could not write. An older boy would have found devices, but he was even younger than she, and could only nurse his wounds in solitude.

There had been no more visits from the minister, who was still very displeased with his mother. He said nothing to his wife. Looking vaguely worried, he did speak to her of his other daughter.

'I am very sad for her indeed. She must feel uncertain and very much out of things, what with all these preparations to proclaim the new empress. I think I will ask if we may bring her home for a while. She is with the emperor constantly in spite of everything, and some of her women have told me what a strain it is on all of them.' And very abruptly she was brought home.

The emperor was reluctant to let her go, but Tō no Chūjō insisted.

'I fear you will be bored,' he said to her. 'Suppose we ask your sister to come and keep you company. I know that her grand-mother is taking fine care of her, but there is that boy, growing up too fast for his own good. They are at a dangerous age.' And with equal abruptness he sent for Kumoinokari.

Omiya was naturally upset. 'I did not know what to do with myself when your sister died, and I couldn't have been happier when you let me have the girl. I thought that I would always have her with me, a comfort in my declining years. I would not have thought you capable of such cruelty.'

He answered most politely. 'I have informed you of certain matters that have been troubling me. I do not think I have done anything that might be described as cruel. The other girl is under-standably upset at what is happening at court and so she came home a few days ago. And now that she is there I am afraid she finds precious little to keep her entertained. I thought the two of them might think of things, music and the like. That is all. I mean to have her with me for only a very short time. I certainly do not wish to minimize your services in taking care of her all these years and making her into the fine young lady she is.'

Seeing that his mind was made up and that nothing she said was likely to change it, she shed tears of sorrow and chagrin. 'People can be cruel. In this way and that the young people have not been good to me. But one expects such things of the young. You ought to be more understanding, but you go blaming me for everything, and now you are taking her away from me. Well, we will see whether she is safer under your watchful eye.'

Yūgiri picked this unfortunate time to come calling. He called frequently these days, hoping for a few words with Kumoinokari. He saw Tō no Chūjō's carriage and slipped guiltily off to his own room.

Tō no Chūjō had several of his sons with him, but they were not permitted access to the women's quarters. The late chancellor's sons by other ladies continued to be attentive, and various grandsons were also frequent callers. None of them rivaled Yūgiri in looks. He was her favorite grandchild. Now that he had been taken away Kumoinokari was the one she kept beside her. And Kumoinokari too was being taken away. The loneliness would be too much.

'I must look in at the palace,' said Tō no Chūjō. 'I will come for her in the evening.'

He was beginning to think that he must act with forbearance and presently let the two have their way. But he was angry. When the boy had advanced somewhat in rank and presented a somewhat more imposing figure, he might see whether they were still as fond of each other. Then, if he chose to give his permission, he would arrange a proper wedding. In the meantime he could not be sure – for children were not to be trusted – that his orders would be obeyed, and he had no confidence in his mother. So, with the other daughter his main material, he put together a case which he argued before his wife and his mother, and brought Kumoinokari home.

Omiya sent a note to her granddaughter: 'Your father may be angry with me, but you will understand my feelings. Do let me have another look at you.'

Beautifully dressed, she came to her grandmother's apartments. She was fourteen, still a child but already endowed with a most pleasing calm and poise.

'You have been my little plaything all these mornings and nights. I have scarcely let you out of my sight. I will be very lonely without you.' She was weeping. 'I have thought a great deal about what is to come and who will see you through it all. I am sorry for you. Who will you have now that they are taking you away?'

Also in tears and much embarrassed, the girl was unable to look at her grandmother.

Saishō, the boy's nurse, came in. 'I had thought of myself as serving both of you,' she said softly. 'I am very sorry indeed that you are leaving. Whatever plans your esteemed father may have for marrying you to someone else, do not let him have his way.'

Yet more acutely embarrassed, Kumoinokari looked at the floor.

'We must not speak of such difficult things,' said Omiya. 'Life is uncertain for all of us.'

'That is not the point, my lady,' replied Saishō indignantly. 'His Lordship dismisses the young master as beneath his contempt. Well, let him go asking whether anyone is thought better.'

Yūgiri was observing what he could from behind curtains. Usually he would have been afraid of being apprehended, but today sorrow had overcome caution. He dabbed at his eyes.

It was all too sad, thought Saishō. With Omiya's connivance, she took advantage of the evening confusion to arrange one last meeting.

They sat for a time in silent tears, suddenly shy before each other.

'Your father is being very strict. I will do as he wishes. But I know I will be lonely without you. Why did you not let me see more of you when it was possible?'

'I only wish I had.'

'Will you think of me?' There was an engaging boyishness in the gently bowed figure.

Lamps were lighted. A great shouting in the distance proclaimed that the minister was on his way back from court. Women darted here and there preparing to receive him. The girl was trembling.

If they wanted to be so noisy, thought the boy, let them; but he would defend her.

Her nurse found him in this defiant attitude. Outrageous – and Princess Omiya had without a doubt known of it.

'It will not do, my lady,' she said firmly. 'Your father will be furious. Your young friend here may have many excellent qualities. Of them I do not know. I do know that you were meant for someone better than a page boy dressed in blue.'

A page boy in blue! Anger drove away a part of the sorrow. 'You heard that?

'These sleeves are crimson, dyed with tears of blood.
How can she say that they are lowly blue?

It was very unkind.'

> 'My life is dyed with sorrows of several hues.
> Pray tell me which is the hue of the part we share.'

She had scarcely finished when her father came to take her away.

Yūgiri was very angry and very unhappy. He went to his own room and lay down. Three carriages hurried off into the distance, the shouting somewhat more deferential than before. He was unable to sleep, but when his grandmother sent for him he sent back that he had retired for the night.

It was a tearful night. Early in the morning, while the ground was still white with frost, he hurried back to Nijō. He did not want anyone to see his red eyes, and he was sure that his grandmother would be after him again. He wanted to be alone. All the way home his thoughts were of the troubles he had brought upon himself. It was not yet full daylight. The sky had clouded over.

> 'It is a world made grim by frost and ice,
> And now come tears to darken darkened skies.'

Genji was this year to provide a dancer for the Gosechi dances.* It was a task of no very great magnitude, but as the day approached, his women were busy with robes for the little flower girls and the like. The women in the east lodge were making clothes for the presentation at court. More general preparations were left to the main house, and the empress was very kind in seeing to the needs of the retinue. Indeed it seemed, so lavish were the preparations, that Genji might be trying to make up for the fact that there had been no dances the year before. The patrons of the dancers, among them a brother of Tō no Chūjō, the Lord Inspector, and, on a somewhat less exalted level, Yoshikiyo, now governor of Omi and a Moderator of the Left, so vied with one another that their endeavors were the talk of the whole court. The emperor had deigned to give orders that the dancers this year be taken into the court service. As his own dancer Genji had chosen one of Koremitsu's daughters, said to be among the prettiest and most talented girls in the city. Koremitsu, now governor of Settsu and of the western ward of the city as well, was somewhat abashed

*At the harvest festival in the Eleventh Month.

at the proposal, but people pointed out that the Lord Inspector was offering a daughter by an unimportant wife and so there was no need at all to feel reticent. Meaning to send the girl to court in any case, he concluded that she might as well make her debut through the Gosechi dances. She practiced diligently at home, her retinue was chosen with great care, and on the appointed day he escorted her to Nijō.

The retinue came from the households of Genji's various ladies, and to be selected was thought a considerable honor. Genji ordered a final rehearsal for the presentation at court. He said he could not possibly rank them one against the others, they were all so pretty and so well dressed. The pity was, he laughed, that he did not have more than one dancer to patronize. Gentleness of nature and delicacy of manner had had a part in the selection.

Yūgiri had quite lost his appetite. He lay brooding in his room and the classics were neglected. Wanting a change of air, he slipped out and wandered quietly through the house. He was well dressed and very good-looking, and calm and self-possessed for his age. The young women who saw him were entranced. He went to Murasaki's wing of the house but was not permitted near her blinds. Remembering his own past behavior, Genji was taking precautions. Yūgiri lived in the east lodge and was not on intimate terms with Murasaki's women; but today he took advantage of the excitement to slip into her part of the house, where he stood watching from behind a screen or blind of some sort.

The Gosechi dancer was helped from her carriage to an enclosure of screens that had been put up near the veranda. Yūgiri made his way behind a screen. Apparently tired, she was leaning against an armrest. She was about the same height as Kumoinokari, or perhaps just a little taller. She may have been just a little prettier. He could not say, for the light was not good; but she did so remind him of his love that, though it would have been an exaggeration to say that he transferred his affections on the spot, he found himself strongly drawn to her. He reached forward and tugged at a sleeve. She was startled, by the tugging and by the poem which followed:

'The lady who serves Toyooka in the heavens
    Is not to forget that someone thinks of her here.*

*The goddess of Toyooka has been identified, though inconclusively, with the Sun Goddess.

'I have long been looking through the sacred fence.'

It was a pleasant young voice, but she could not identify it. She was frightened. Just then her women came in to retouch her face, and he reluctantly withdrew.

Ashamed of his blue robes and in general feeling rather out of things, he had been staying away from court. For the festivities, however, regulations assigning colors to ranks had been relaxed. He was mature for his years, and as he strolled around the palace in his bright robes he was perhaps the most remarked-upon lad present. Even the emperor noticed him.

The dancers were at their best for the formal presentation, but everyone said that Genji's dancer and the Lord Inspector's were the prettiest and the best dressed. It was very difficult to choose between the two of them, though perhaps a certain dignity gave the nod to Koremitsu's daughter. She was so lavishly and stylishly dressed that one would have been hard put to guess her origins. The dancers being older than in most years, the festival seemed somehow grander.

Genji remembered a Gosechi dancer to whom he had once been attracted.* After the dances he got off a note to her. The reader will perhaps guess its contents, which included this poem:

'What will the years have done to the maiden, when he
Who saw her heavenly sleeves is so much older?'

It was a passing thought as he counted over the years, but she was touched that he should have felt constrained to write.

This was her reply:

'Garlands in my hair, warm sun to melt the frost,
So very long ago. It seems like yesterday.'

The blue paper was the blue of the dancers' dress, and the hand, subtly shaded in a cursive style to conceal the identity of the writer, was better than one would have expected from so modest a rank.

That glimpse of Koremitsu's daughter had excited Yūgiri. He wandered about with certain thoughts in his mind, but was not permitted near. Still too young to devise stratagems for breaching the blockade, he felt very sorry for himself. She was pretty indeed and could be a consolation for the loss of Kumoinokari.

*See Chapters 11 and 12.

It has already been said that the dancers were to stay on in court service. Today, however, they went back to their families. In the recessional the competition was also intense. Yoshikiyo's daughter went off to Karasaki for her lustration, Koremitsu's to Naniwa. The inspector had already arranged for his daughter's return to court. People criticized Tō no Chūjō's brother for having offered a daughter unworthy of the occasion, but she was received into court service with the others.

There being a vacancy on the empress's staff, Koremitsu asked Genji whether his daughter might not be favored with appointment. Genji said that he would see what could be done. This was disappointing news for Yūgiri. She was being taken beyond his reach. Though the disappointment was not of a really devastating sort, new sorrow was added to old.

The girl had a brother who was a court page. Yūgiri had occasionally made use of his services.

One day Yūgiri addressed him in a friendlier manner than usual. 'And when may we hope to see your sister at court?'

'By the end of the year, I am told.'

'I thought her very pretty. I envy you, able to see her whenever you want to. Do you suppose I might ask you to let me see her myself sometime?'

'I am afraid it would be very difficult. I am her brother and even I am kept at a distance. I am afraid it would be very difficult indeed.'

'At least give her this letter.'

The boy had long been under very stern instructions to have no part in such maneuvers, but Yūgiri was insistent.

The Gosechi dancer, perhaps a little precocious, was delighted with the letter, which was on delicate blue paper very tastefully folded with papers of several colors. The hand, though young, showed great promise.

'Were you aware of it as you danced in the sunlight,
    The heart that was pinned upon the heavenly sleeves?'

Koremitsu came in as they were admiring it.

'What's this? Who's it from?' They flushed. There had been no time to hide it. 'You know very well that I do not permit this sort of thing.'

He blocked the boy's escape.

'The chancellor's son asked me to deliver it.'

'Well, now. What an amusing little prank. You are the same age, and I only wish you had a few of his talents.' His anger having quite left him, he went off to show the letter to his wife. 'If he is still interested when he is a little older, she would be better off in his hands than at court. I know His Lordship well. Once a woman has attracted his attention he never forgets her. This could be a very good thing. Look at the Akashi lady.'

But they could think of little these days except preparations for sending the girl to court.

Yūgiri was filled with thoughts of the far better placed young lady to whom he could not write. His longing grew. Would he ever see her again? He no longer enjoyed visiting his grandmother and kept to himself at Nijō. He remembered the room that had been his for so long, the room where they had played so happily together. The very thought of the Sanjō house became oppressive.

Genji asked the lady of the orange blossoms to look after the boy. 'His grandmother does not have a great many years ahead of her. The two of you have known each other so long – might I ask you to take over?'

It was her way to do everything Genji asked of her. Gently but with complete dedication she put herself into the work of keeping house for Yūgiri.

He would sometimes catch a glimpse of her. She was not at all beautiful, and yet his father had been faithful to her. Was it merely silly, his own inability to forget the beauty of a girl who was being unkind to him? He should look for someone of a similarly compliant nature. Not, however, someone who was positively repulsive. Though Genji had kept the lady of the orange blossoms with him all these years, he seemed quite aware of her defects. When he visited her he was always careful to see that she was as fully ensheathed as an amaryllis bud, and that he was spared the need to look upon her. Yūgiri understood. He had an eye for these things that would have put the adult eye to shame. His grandmother was still very beautiful even now that she had become a nun. Surrounded from infancy by beautiful women, he naturally took adverse notice of a lady who, not remarkably well favored from the start, was past her prime, a bit peaked and thin of hair.

The end of the year approached. Omiya occupied herself with his New Year robes to the exclusion of everything else. They were very splendid and very numerous, but they only added to his gloom.

'I don't see why you're going to so much trouble. I'm not at all sure that I will even go to court.'

'Whatever are you talking about? You are behaving like a defeated old man.'

'I may not be old,' he said to himself, brushing away a tear, 'but I certainly am defeated.'

His grandmother wanted to weep with him. She knew too well what was troubling him.

'They say that a man is only as low as his thoughts. You must pull yourself out of it. All this mooning, I can't think what good it will ever do you.'

'You needn't worry. But I know that people are calling me the unpromoted marvel, and I don't enjoy going to court. If Grandfather were still alive they wouldn't be laughing at me. Father is Father, I know, and I know I should be going to him with my problems. But he is so stiff and remote and he doesn't come to the east lodge all that often. The lady there is very good to me, but I do wish sometimes that I had a mother of my own.'

He was trying to hide his tears, and she was now weeping openly. 'It is sad for anyone, I don't care who, to lose his mother, but people do grow up and follow their own destinies, and these little stings and smarts go away. You must not take them so seriously. I agree that it would have been nice if your grandfather had lived a little longer. Your father should be doing just as much for you, but in some ways he does rather leave something to be desired. People say what a fine figure of a man your uncle, the minister, is, but I only think myself that he is less and less like the boy I used to know. When I see you so unhappy, and your whole future ahead of you, I wonder if I haven't lived too long. You are letting yourself get worked up over nothing at all, I know, but I do get angry for you.'

His presence not being required at court, Genji spent a pleasant New Year at home. He followed the precedent of Chancellor Yoshifusa* and reviewed the white horses on his own Nijō grounds, where the observances were no less grand than at court. Some of the details even went beyond what precedent required.

*He lived from 804 to 872.

Late in the Second Month the emperor paid a visit to the Suzaku Palace of the retired emperor. The full bloom of the cherries would have coincided with the anniversary of Fujitsubo's death, but the early blossoms were very beautiful. The Suzaku Palace had been carefully repaired and redecorated. The court, even princes of the blood, wore uniform dress, green over white lined with red. The emperor wore red, as did Genji, present by royal summons. People seemed to carry themselves with greater dignity than on most occasions. The two of them, emperor and chancellor, looked so radiantly alike that they could almost have been mistaken for each other. The Suzaku emperor had improved with age. He had a soft, gentle sort of grace that was all his own.

Though no professed men of letters had been invited, ten and more university scholars were present, young men who were already making their marks as poets. The emperor assigned subjects from the official examinations. It was a mock examination for the benefit of the chancellor's son, people suspected. Fidgeting nervously, the scholars were sent off to deliberate on their topics, each in a separate boat on the lake. They seemed to be having trouble. Musicians were rowed out on the lake as the sun was setting. A sudden wind came down from the hills to enliven the tuning of the instruments. Yūgiri was angry with the world. Only he was forbidden to sing and to joke.

'Spring Warbler' brought back memories of a spring festival many years before.*

'I wonder if we will ever again see such an affair,' said the Suzaku emperor.

Genji was lost in memories of his father's reign. When the dance was over he offered a cup to the Suzaku emperor, and with it a verse:

'The warblers are today as long ago,
  But we in the shade of the blossoms are utterly changed.'

The Suzaku emperor replied:

'Though kept by mists from the ninefold-garlanded court,
  I yet have warblers to tell me spring has come.'

Prince Hotaru filled the emperor's cup and offered this poem:

*The now famous one in Chapter 8.

'The tone of the flute is as it always has been,
  Nor do I detect a change in the song of the warbler.'

It was very thoughtful and tactful of him to suggest that not all was decline.

With awesome dignity, the emperor replied:

'The warbler laments as it flies from tree to tree –
  For blossoms whose hue is paler than once it was?'

And that I have no more poems to set down – is it because, the occasion being a formal one, the flagons did not make the complete rounds? Or is it that our scrivener overlooked some of them? The concert being at such a distance that the emperor could not hear very well, instruments were brought into the royal presence: a lute for Prince Hotaru, a Japanese koto for Tō no Chūjō, for the retired emperor a thirteen-stringed Chinese koto, and for Genji, as always, a seven-stringed Chinese koto. They must all play for him, said the emperor. They were accomplished musicians and they outdid themselves, and the concert could not have been finer. Numerous courtiers were happy to sing the lyrics, 'How Grand the Day'* and 'Cherry-Blossom Girl' and the rest. A misty moon came up, flares were set out on the island, and the festivities came to an end.

Though it was very late, the emperor thought it would be rude to ignore Lady Kokiden, the Suzaku emperor's mother. He looked in on her as he started back for the palace.† Genji was with him. An old lady now, she was very pleased. Genji thought of Fujitsubo. It seemed wrong that of his father's ladies the one should be living so long and the other should have died so soon.‡

'I am old and forgetful,' said Kokiden, weeping, 'but your kind visit brings everything back.'

'Having lost the ones whom I so depended upon,' the emperor replied, 'I have scarcely been able to detect the arrival of spring, but this interview quite restores my serenity. I shall call upon you from time to time, if I may.'

A Saibara, remarking happily upon the company that has assembled. For 'Cherry-Blossom Girl,' see note, page 351.
†Some texts say 'in the Kaeden,' a part of the Suzaku Palace.
‡It may be that these thoughts are the emperor's.

Genji too said that he would call again. Kokiden was disconcerted by the grandeur of the procession as they made a somewhat hasty departure. What sort of memories would Genji have of her and her better days? She was sorry now for what she had done. It had been his destiny to rule, and she had been able to change nothing. Her sister Oborozukiyo, with little else to occupy her thoughts, found them turning to the past, in which there was much to muse upon and be moved by. It would seem that she still contrived, on this occasion and that, to get off a note to Genji. Kokiden was always finding fault with the management of her stipends and allowances, and grumbling about her misfortune in having lived on into so inferior a reign. She complained so much, indeed, that not even her son could bear her company.

Yūgiri's graduation poem was proclaimed a masterpiece and he received his degree. Only the most advanced and promising scholars were permitted to take the examinations and only three of them passed. At the autumn levy he was promoted to the Fifth Rank and made a chamberlain. Kumoinokari was never out of his thoughts, but he was not prepared to take the extreme measures that would be necessary to elude her watchful father. He was unhappy, of course, and so was she.

Genji had been thinking that he needed more room for the leisurely life which was now his. He wanted to have everyone near him, including the people who were still off in the country. He had bought four parks in Rokujō, near the eastern limits of the city and including the lands of the Rokujō lady.

Prince Hyōbu, Murasaki's father, would be fifty next year. She busied herself with preparations for the event. Genji had concluded that further aloofness would be mean-spirited. He gave orders that his new Rokujō place be finished in time for the celebrations.

With the New Year they occupied still more of Murasaki's time. There was a division of effort, Genji troubling himself with dancing and music for the banquet after the religious services and Murasaki concentrating on the services themselves, the decorations for the scriptures and images, the robes, the offerings, and the like. The lady of the orange blossoms was a great help to her. On better terms than ever, they kept up a lively and elegant correspondence.

Prince Hyōbu presently heard of these preparations, of which everyone was talking. Though Genji was generally thought to be a kind and thoughtful man, his kindness had thus far not reached the prince. Indeed, Genji seemed almost to devise occasions for humiliating him and his family. Unpleasantness followed unpleasantness until the prince had to conclude that Genji harbored singularly durable grudges. It was good all the same that Murasaki should be his favorite. Not much of the glory brushed off on the prince, but still she *was* his daughter. And now all this, the whole world was talking. It was an unexpected honor in his declining years.

His wife was not so easily pleased. Indeed, she was more resentful than ever. Her own daughter had gone to court, and what had Genji done for her?

The new Rokujō mansion was finished in the Eighth Month and people began moving in. The southwest quarter, including her mother's lands, was assigned to Akikonomu as her home away from the palace. The northeast quarter was assigned to the lady of the orange blossoms, who had occupied the east lodge at Nijō, and the northwest quarter to the lady from Akashi. The wishes of the ladies themselves were consulted in designing the new gardens, a most pleasant arrangement of lakes and hills.

The hills were high in the southeast quarter, where spring-blossoming trees and bushes were planted in large numbers. The lake was most ingeniously designed. Among the plantings in the forward parts of the garden were cinquefoil pines, maples, cherries, wisteria, *yamabuki,** and rock azalea, most of them trees and shrubs whose season was spring. Touches of autumn too were scattered through the groves.

In Akikonomu's garden the plantings, on hills left from the old garden, were chosen for rich autumn colors. Clear spring water went singing off into the distance, over rocks designed to enhance the music. There was a waterfall, and the whole expanse was like an autumn moor. Since it was now autumn, the garden was a wild profusion of autumn flowers and leaves, such as to shame the hills of Oi.

In the northeast quarter there was a cool natural spring and the plans had the summer sun in mind. In the forward parts of the

---

*Kerria japonica, a yellow-flowering shrub related to the rose.

garden the wind through thickets of Chinese bamboo would be cool in the summer, and the trees were deep and mysterious as mountain groves. There was a hedge of mayflower,* and there were oranges to remind the lady of days long gone. There were wild carnations and roses and gentians† and a few spring and autumn flowers as well. A part of the quarter was fenced off for equestrian grounds. Since the Fifth Month would be its liveliest time, there were irises along the lake. On the far side were stables where the finest of horses would be kept.

And finally the northwest quarter: beyond artificial hillocks to the north were rows of warehouses, screened off by pines which would be beautiful in new falls of snow. The chrysanthemum hedge would bloom in the morning frosts of early winter, when also a grove of 'mother oaks'‡ would display its best hues. And in among the deep groves were mountain trees which one would have been hard put to identify.

The move was made at about the time of the equinox. The plan was that everyone would move together, but Akikonomu was loath to make such an occasion of it and chose to come a few days later. The lady of the orange blossoms, docile and unassertive as ever, moved on the same evening as Murasaki.

Murasaki's spring garden was out of its season but very beautiful all the same. There were fifteen women's carriages in her procession. The attendants, in modest numbers, were of the Fourth and Fifth ranks and less prominently of the Sixth Rank, all of them men who had long been close to Genji and his house. Genji did not want to be criticized for extravagance or ostentation, and the arrangements were generally austere. The two ladies were given virtually the same treatment, with Yūgiri seeing to the needs of the lady of the orange blossoms. Everyone thought this most proper.

The women's rooms were appointed with great care, down to the smallest details. How nice everything was, they said, and their own arrangements were the nicest of all.

Akikonomu moved into her new lodgings five or six days later. Though she had specified that the arrangements be simple, they

*Unohana, Deutzia crenata.

†Kutani. The word does not survive in modern Japanese, and there is doubt as to the meaning. One theory has it a peony.

‡Hahaso, thought to cover several varieties of oak.

were in fact rather grand. She had of course been singled out for
remarkable honors, but she was of a calm and retiring nature,
much esteemed by the whole court.

There were elaborate walls and galleries with numerous pas-
sageways this way and that among the several quarters, so that the
ladies could live apart and still be friendly.

The Ninth Month came and Akikonomu's garden was resplendent with autumn colors. On an evening when a gentle wind
was blowing she arranged leaves and flowers on the lid of an
ornamental box and sent them over to Murasaki. Her messenger
was a rather tall girl in a singlet of deep purple, a robe of lilac lined
with blue, and a gossamer cloak of saffron. She made her practiced
way along galleries and verandas and over the soaring bridges that
joined them, with the dignity that became her estate, and yet so
pretty that the eyes of the whole house were upon her. Everything
about her announced that she had been trained to the highest service.

This was Akikonomu's poem, presented with the gift:

'Your garden quietly awaits the spring.
Permit the winds to bring a touch of autumn.'

The praise which Murasaki's women showered on the messenger did not at all displease her. Murasaki sent back an arrangement of moss on the same box, with a cinquefoil pine against
stones suggesting cliffs. A poem was tied to a branch of the pine:

'Fleeting, your leaves that scatter in the wind.
The pine at the cliffs is forever green with the spring.'

One had to look carefully to see that the pine was a clever fabrication. Akikonomu was much impressed that so ingenious a
response should have come so quickly. Her women were speechless.

'I think you were unnecessarily tart,' said Genji to Murasaki.
'You should wait until your spring trees are in bloom. What will
the goddess of Tatsuta think when she hears you belittling the best
of autumn colors? Reply from strength, when you have the force
of your spring blossoms to support you.' He was looking wonderfully young and handsome.

There were more such exchanges, in this most tasteful of
houses.

The Akashi lady thought that she should wait until the grand ladies had moved and then make her own quiet move. She did so in the Tenth Month. With an eye on his daughter's future, Genji took great care that nothing about her retinue or the appointments of her rooms suggest inferiority.

CHAPTER 22

The Jeweled Chaplet

The years passed, and Genji had not forgotten the dew upon the evening faces he had seen so briefly. As he came to know a variety of ladies, he only regretted the more strongly that the lady of the evening faces had not lived.

Ukon, her woman, was not of very distinguished lineage, but Genji was fond of her, and thought of her as a memento of her dead lady. She was now one of the older women in his household. He had transferred everyone to Murasaki's wing of the Nijō house when he left for Suma, and there she had stayed. Murasaki valued her as a quiet, good-natured servant. Ukon could only think with regret that if her own lady had lived she would now be honored with treatment similar at least to that accorded the Akashi lady. Genji was a generous man and he did not abandon women to whom he had been even slightly drawn; and the lady of the evening faces, if not perhaps one of the really important ones, would surely have been in the company that recently moved to Rokujō.

Ukon had not made her whereabouts known to the little girl, the lady's daughter, left with her nurse in the western part of the city. Genji had told her that she must keep the affair to herself and that nothing was to be gained by letting his part in it be known at so late a date. She had made no attempt to find the nurse. Presently the nurse's husband had been appointed deputy viceroy of Kyushu and the family had gone off with him to his post. The girl was four at the time. They had prayed for information of any sort about the mother. Day and night, always in tears, they had looked for her where they thought she might possibly be. The nurse finally decided that she would keep the child to remember the mother by. Yet it was sad to think of taking her on a hard voyage to a remote part of the land. They debated seeking out her father, Tō no Chūjō, and telling him of her whereabouts. When no good entree presented itself, they gathered in family council: it would be difficult to tell him, since they did not know what had happened to the mother; life would be hard for the girl, introduced so young to a father who was a complete stranger; and if he knew that she was his daughter he was unlikely to let her go. She was a pretty child, already showing signs of distinction, and it was very sad indeed to take her off in a shabby boat.

'Are we going to Mother's?' she asked from time to time.

The nurse and her daughters wept tears of nostalgia and regret. But they must control themselves. Tears did not bode well for the journey.

The scenery along the way brought memories. 'She was so young and so alive to things – how she would have loved it all if she could have come with us. But of course if she were alive we would still be in the city ourselves.'

They were envious of the waves, returning whence they had come.*

'Sadly, sadly we have journeyed this distance,'† came the rough voices of the sailors.

The nurse's daughters looked at each other and wept.

> 'To whom might it be that the thoughts of these sailors turn,
> Sadly singing off the Oshima strand?'‡

> 'Here on the sea, we know not whence or whither,
> Or where to look in search of our lost lady.

'I had not expected to leave her for these wilds.'**

'We will not forget' was the refrain when the ship had passed Cape Kane;†† and when they had made land, tears welled up again, in the awareness of how very far they had come.

They looked upon the child as their lady. Sometimes, rarely, one of them would dream of the dead mother. She would have with her a woman who might have been her twin, and afterwards the dreamer would fall ill. They had to conclude that she was no longer living.

Years passed, and the deputy viceroy's term of service was over. He thought of returning to the city, but hesitated, for he was a man of no great influence even off in that remote land. He was

---

*See note†, page 241.

†Apparently from a sea chantey, though the diction seems somewhat elegant.

‡In the province of Chikuzen, where the viceroy had his seat.

**See note†, page 250.

††Also in Chikuzen. The ship probably sails between Oshima and Cape Kane and so into Hakata Bay.

still hesitating when he fell seriously ill. On the point of death, he looked up at the girl, now ten, and so beautiful that he feared for her.

'What difficult times you will face if I leave you! I have thought it a shameful waste that you should grow up so far from everything, and I have wanted to get you back to the city as soon as I possibly can. I have wanted to present you to the right people and leave you to whatever destinies may be yours, and I have been making my preparations. The capital is a large place and you would be safe there. And now it seems that I must end my days here.'

He had three sons. 'You must give first priority to taking her back. You need not worry about my funeral.'

No one outside of his immediate family knew who the girl was. He had let it be known that she was a grandchild whom, for certain reasons, it had fallen his lot to rear, and he had let no one see her. He had done what he could, and now, suddenly, he was dying. The family went ahead with preparations for the return. There were many in the region who had not been on good terms with the deputy viceroy, and life was full of perils. The girl was even prettier than her mother, perhaps because her father's blood also flowed in her veins. Delicate and graceful, she had a quiet, serene disposition. One would have had to look far to find her equal.

The young gallants of the region heard about her and letters came pouring in. They produced only grim and irritable silence.

'You wouldn't call her repulsive, exactly,' the nurse said to people, 'but she has a most unfortunate defect that makes it impossible for her to marry. She is to become a nun and stay with me as along as I live.'

'A sad case,' they all said, in hushed tones as of something dark and ominous. 'Did you hear? The old deputy's granddaughter is a freak.'

His sons were determined to take the girl back to her father. He had seemed so fond of her when she was little. It was most unlikely that he would disown her now. They prayed to all the various native and foreign gods.

But presently they and their sisters married into provincial families, and the return to the city, once so devoutly longed for, receded into the distance. Life was difficult for the girl as she came to understand her situation a little better. She made her retreats three times a year. Now she was twenty, and she had attained to a perfection wasted in these harsh regions.

The family lived in the province of Hizen. The local gentry continued to hear rumors and to pay court. The nurse only wished they would go away.

There was an official of the Fifth Rank who had been on the viceroy's staff and who was a member of a large clan scattered over the province of Higo. He was something of a local eminence, a warrior of very considerable power and influence. Though of an untamed nature, he did have a taste for the finer things, and among his avocations was the collecting of elegant ladies.

He heard of the girl. 'I don't care if she is the worst sort of freak. I'll just shut my eyes.' His suit was earnest and a little threatening too.

'It is quite impossible,' the nurse sent back. 'Tell him that she is to become a nun.'

The man came storming into Hizen and summoned the nurse's sons for conference. If they did what he wanted, they would be his allies. He could do a great deal for them. The two young sons were inclined to accede.

'It is true that we did not want her to marry beneath her. But he *will* be a strong ally, and if we make an enemy of him we will have to pack up and leave. Yes, she is very wellborn. That we do not deny – but what good does it do when her father doesn't recognize her and no one even knows she exists? She is lucky he wants her. She is probably here because she was meant all along to marry someone like him. There's no point in trying to hide. He is a determined and ruthless man, and he will do anything if he is crossed.'

But the oldest brother, who was vice-governor of Bungo, disagreed. 'It is out of the question. Have you forgotten Father's instructions? I must get her back to the capital.'

Tearfully, the daughters supported him. The girl's mother had wandered off and they had quite lost track of her, but they would think themselves sufficiently repaid for their worries if they could make a decent life for the girl. They most certainly did not want to see her marry the Higo man.

Confident of his name and standing and unaware of this disagreement, the man showered her with letters, all of them on good Chinese paper, richly colored and heavily perfumed. He wrote a not at all contemptible hand, but his notion of the courtly was very provincial. Having made an ally of the second son, he came calling. He was about thirty, tall and powerfully built, not unpleasant to look at. Perhaps it was only in the imagination that his vigorous manner was a little intimidating. He glowed with health and had a deep, rough voice and a heavy regional accent that made his speech seem as alien as bird language. Lovers are called 'night crawlers,' one hears, but he was different. He came of a spring evening, victim, it would seem, of the urgings which the poet felt more strongly on autumn evenings.*

Not wishing to offend him, the 'grandmother' came out.

'The late deputy was a great man and he understood things. I wanted to be friends with him and I'm sorry he died. Now I want to make up for it. I got my courage up and came to see the little lady. She's too good for me, but that's all right. I'll look up to her and be her servant. I hear Your Grace doesn't want me to have her. Maybe because of all my other women? Don't worry. She won't be one of them. She'll be the queen.' It was a very forceful statement.

'Thank you very much. It is gratifying to hear of your interest. But she has been unlucky. To our great regret we must keep her out of sight and do not find it possible to let her marry. It is all very sad.'

'Oh, come on. I don't care if she's blind and has a club foot. I swear it by all the gods.'

He asked that a day be named when he might come for her. The nurse offered the argument often heard in the region that the end of the season was a bad time to marry.

He seemed to think that a farewell poem was called for. He deliberated for rather a long time.

'I vow to the Mirror God of Matsura:
    If I break it he can do what he wants with me.

'Pretty good.' He smiled.

Poetry was not perhaps what he had had most experience with. The nurse was by this time too nervous to answer, and her

*Anonymous, *Kokinshū* 546:

> There are no nights when I am free of longing,
> But even to me it seems excessive in autumn.

daughters protested that they were in an even worse state. Time ran on. Finally she sent back the first verse that came into her head.

'It will be for us to reproach the Mirror God
If our prayers of so many years remain unanswered.'

Her voice trembled.

'What's that? How's that?'

He seemed about to attack them frontally. The nurse blanched. Despite her agitation, one of the daughters managed a brave laugh. 'Our niece is not normal. That is I'm sure what she meant to say, and we would be very unhappy if she had bad luck in the matter of your kind proposal. Poor Mother. She is very old, and she is always saying unfortunate things about her gods.'

'I see, I see.' He nodded. 'A very good poem. You may look down on us country people, but what's so great about city people? Anyone can come up with a poem. Don't think I can't do as well as the next one.'

He seemed to think demonstration called for, but it refused to take shape. He left.

With her second son gone over to the enemy, the old woman was terrified. She urged her oldest son to action.

'But what can I do? There is no one I can go to for help. I don't have all that many brothers, and they have turned against me. Life will be impossible if we make an enemy of the man, and if I try something bold I will only make things worse.'

But he agreed that death would be better for the girl than marriage to such a man. He gathered his courage and they set sail. His sisters left their husbands.* The one who had as a child been called Ateki was now called Hyōbu. She slipped off in the night and boarded ship with her lady.

The man had gone home to Higo, to return on the day appointed, late in the Fourth Month. The older of the nurse's daughters had a large family of her own and was unable to join them. The farewells were tearful, for it seemed unlikely that the family would ever be united again. They had no very great love for Hizen, in which they had lived for so long, but the departing

*The text clearly says 'sisters,' but it soon becomes equally clear that only Hyōbu returns to the capital. Perhaps another sister goes part of the way.

party did look back in sorrow at the shrine of Matsura. They were leaving dear ones in its charge.

'Shores of trial, now gloomy Ukishima.
On we sail. Where next will be our lodging?'

'We sail vast seas and know not where we go,
Floating ones, abandoned to the winds.'*

The girl sat weeping, the picture of the sad uncertainty which her poem suggested.

If news that they had left reached the Higo man, he was certain to come in pursuit. They had provided themselves with a fast boat and the winds did good service, and their speed was almost frightening. They passed Echo Bay in Harima.

'See the little boat back there, almost flying at us. A pirate, maybe?'

The brother thought he would prefer the cruelest pirate to the Higo man. There was nothing to be done, of course, but sail on.

'The echoes of Echo Bay are slight and empty
Beside the tumult I hear within myself.'

Then they were told that the mouth of the river Yodo lay just ahead. It was as if they had returned from the land of the dead.

'Past Karadomari we row, past Kawajiri.'† It was a rough song, but pleasing. The vice-governor hummed with special feeling the passage about dear wives and children left behind. Yes, it had been a step, leaving them all behind. What disasters would now be overtaking them? He had brought with him everyone in the province who might have been thought an ally, and what sort of revenge would the Higo person be taking? It had been reckless, after all these years. In the calm following the crisis he began to think once more of his own affairs, and everything now seemed rash and precipitate. He collapsed in weak tears. 'We have left our wives and children in alien lands,'‡ he intoned softly.

His sister Hyōbu heard. She now feared that she had behaved very strangely, turning against her husband of so many years and flying off in the night. What would he be thinking?

*Ukishima, in the province of Suō, can be either 'Sad Island' or 'Floating Island.'
†Probably another sea chantey. Both places are in the province of Harima.
‡Po Chü-i, Collected Works, III, 'Prisoners' Song.'

They had no house and no friends in the city. Because of the girl, they had left behind a province which over the years had become home and put themselves at the mercy of wind and waves. They could not think what to do next, nor had they any clear notion of what was to be done for the girl. But there was no point in hesitating. They hurried on to the city.

The vice-governor searched out an old acquaintance who was still living at Kujō. It was to be sure within the city limits, but not a place where gentlemen lived; a gloomy place, rather, of tradesmen and peddlers. Autumn came, amid thoughts of what had been and what was to be. The vice-governor was like a seabird cast ashore. He was without employment in a strange new world and unable to return to the old. The whole party was now having regrets. Some left to take positions sought out through this and that acquaintance, others to return to Kyushu.

The old nurse wept at this inability to find a new foothold.

Her son, the vice-governor, did what he could to comfort her. 'I am not in the least worried. I have been prepared to risk everything for our lady and what does it matter that I am not doing so very well at the moment? What comfort would wealth and security have been if they had meant marrying her to that man? Our prayers will be answered and she will be put back in her rightful place someday, you may be sure of it. Hachiman, now, just over there. Our lady prayed to Hachiman at Matsura and Hakozaki just before we left. Now that you are safely back, my lady, you must go and thank him.' And he sent the girl off to the Iwashimizu Hachiman Shrine.

He had learned that an eminent cleric whom his father had known was among the Buddhist priests in service at the shrine. The man undertook to be her guide.

'And then,' said the vice-governor, 'there is Hatsuse. It is known even in China as the Japanese temple among them all that gets things done. It can't help doing something for a poor lady back after all those years so far away.' And this time he sent her to Hatsuse.

The pilgrimage was to be on foot. Though not used to walking, the girl did as she was told. What sort of crimes had she been guilty of, she was asking, that she must be subjected to such trials? She prayed that the powers above, if they pitied her, take her to whatever world her mother might be in. If her mother was living, please, then, just a glimpse of her. The girl could not remember her mother. She had thought how happy she would be if only she had a mother. Now the problem was a much more immediate one. Late on the morning of the fourth day, barely alive, they arrived at Tsubaichi, just below Hatsuse.

Though they had come very slowly, the girl was so footsore when they reached Tsubaichi that they feared she could not go on. Led by the former vice-governor, the party included two bowmen, three or four grooms and pages, three women, heavily veiled, and a pair of ancient scullery women. Every effort had been made not to attract attention. Darkness came on as they were replenishing their stock of candles and the like.

The monk who kept the way station was very uncivil, grumbling about arrangements that had been made without consulting him. 'Who are these people? We have some others coming. Stupid women, they've botched it again.'

A second party did just then come up, also on foot, including two women who seemed to be of considerable standing and a number of attendants, men and women. Four or five of the men were on horseback. Though display was obviously being avoided, the horses were nicely caparisoned. The monk paced the floor and scratched his head and generally made himself objectionable. He was determined to accommodate the second party. Well, he would not insist that the others move on, but he would put the menials out in back and divide the room with curtains.

Though respectable, the second party did not seem to be of the most awesome rank. Both parties were polite and deferential, and all was presently quiet.

In fact, the principal pilgrim in the second party was that Ukon who had never ceased weeping for the lady of the evening faces. In all the uncertainties of her life, she had long been in the habit of making pilgrimages to Hatsuse. She was used to travel, but the walk was exhausting even so. She was resting when the vice-governor came up to the curtains, evidently with food for his lady.

'Give this to her, if you will, please. I know of course that she is not used to such rough service.'

Obviously a lady of higher rank than the others, thought Ukon, going over to look through an opening in the curtains. She had seen the man before, she was sure, but could not think where. Someone she had known when he was young, and much less stout and sunburned, and much better dressed. Who might he be?

'Sanjō. Our lady wants you.'

She knew the woman who came forward at this summons: a lesser attendant upon the lady of the evening faces, with them in the days of hiding. It was like a dream. Ukon longed to see the lady they were in attendance upon, but she remained out of sight. Now Ukon thought she knew the man too. Yes, without question, the one they had called Hyōtōda. Perhaps the girl would be with them. Unable to sit still, she went again to the curtain and called to Sanjō, who was just inside. Sanjō was not easily torn from her meal. It was a little arbitrary of Ukon, perhaps, to think this an impertinence.

At length Sanjō presented herself. 'It can't be me you want. I'm a poor woman who's been off in Kyushu these twenty years and more, and I doubt there would be anyone here who would know me. It must be a mistake.' She had on a somewhat rustic robe of fulled silk and an unlined jacket, and she had put on a great deal of weight.

'Look at me,' said Ukon, hating to think how she herself must have changed. 'Don't you recognize me?'

Sanjō clapped her hands. 'It's you! It's you! Where did you come from? Is our lady with you?' And she was weeping convulsively.

Ukon too was in tears. She had known this woman as a girl. So many months and years had passed!

'And is my lady's nurse with you? And what has happened to the little girl? And Ateki?' She said nothing for her part about the lady of the evening faces.

'They are here. The little girl is a fine young lady. I must go tell Nurse.' And she withdrew to the back of the room.

'It is like a dream,' said the nurse. 'Ukon, you say? We have every right to be furious with Ukon.' But she went up to the curtains.

She was at first too moved to speak.

'And what has happened to my lady?' she asked finally. 'I have prayed and prayed for so many years that I might be taken wherever she is. I have wanted to go to her, even if it be in a dream. And then I had to suffer in a place so far away that not even the winds brought word of her. I have lived too long. But thoughts of

the little girl have kept me tied to this world and made it difficult
for me to go on to the next one. And so, as you see, I have come
limping along.'

Ukon almost wished she were back in the days when she had
not been permitted to speak. 'There is no point in talking of our
lady. She died long ago.'

And the three of them gave themselves up to tears.

It was now quite dark. Ready for the walk up to the temple,
the men were urging them on. The farewells were confused.
Ukon suggested that they go together, but the sudden friendship
might seem odd. It had not been possible to take even the former
vice-governor into their confidence. Quietly the two parties set
forth. Ukon saw ahead of her a beautiful and heavily veiled figure.
The hair under what would appear to be an early-summer singlet
was so rich that it seemed out of place. A flood of affection and
pity swept over Ukon.

Used to walking, she reached the temple first. The nurse's
party, coaxing and helping the girl on, arrived in time for the
evening services. The temple swarmed with pilgrims. A place had
been set out for Ukon almost under the right hand of the Buddha.
Perhaps because their guide was not well known at Hatsuse, the
Kyushu party had been assigned a place to the west, behind the
Buddha and some distance away. Ukon sent for them. They must
not be shy, she said. Leaving the other men and telling the vice-
governor what had happened, they accepted the invitation.

'I am not one who matters,' said Ukon, 'but I work in the
Genji chancellor's house. Even when I come with the few attendants you see, I can be sure that nothing will happen to me. You
can never be sure what country people will do, and I would hate
to have anything unpleasant happen to our lady.'

She would have liked to continue, but the noise was over-
whelming. She turned to her prayers. What she had prayed longest
for had been granted. She had sensed that Genji too continued to
think about the girl, and her prayer now was that, informed of her
whereabouts, he would make her happiness his concern.

Among the pilgrims, from all over the land, was the wife of the
governor of the province.

Sanjō was dazzled and envious. She brought her hands to her
forehead. 'O Lord of Great Mercy,' she proclaimed, 'I have no
prayer but this, that if my lady cannot be the wife of the assistant

viceroy you let her marry the greatest one in this province. My name is Sanjō. If you find decent places for us, then I will come and thank you. I promise I will.'

Ukon would have hoped that Sanjō might aim a little higher. 'You have a great deal to learn. But you must know, and you must have known in the old days, that Lord Tō no Chūjō was meant for great things. He is a grand minister now and he has everything his way. Our lady comes from the finest family, and here you are talking about marrying her off to a governor.'

'Oh, hush. You and your ministers and lordships. You just ought to see the lady from the assistant viceroy's house when she goes off to Kiyomizu. Why, the emperor himself couldn't put on a better show. So just hush, please.' And she continued her peroration, hands pressed always to forehead.

The Kyushu party planned to stay three days. Ukon had not thought of staying so long, but this seemed the opportunity for a good talk. She informed one of the higher priests of a sudden wish to go into retreat. He knew what she would need, votive lights and petitions and the like. She described her reasons.

'I have come as usual in behalf of Lady Tamakazura* of the Fujiwara. Pray well for her, if you will. I have recently been informed of her whereabouts, and I wish to offer thanks.'

'Excellent. Our prayers over the years have been heard.'

Services went on through the night, very noisily indeed.

In the morning they all went to the cell of Ukon's eminent acquaintance. The talk was quite uninhibited. The lady was very beautiful, and rather shy in her rough travel dress.

'I have been privileged to know ladies so grand that few people ever see them. In the ordinary course of events they would have been kept out of my sight. I have thought for a very long time that Lady Murasaki, the chancellor's lady, couldn't possibly have a rival. But then someone came along who could almost compete with her. It needn't have surprised anyone, of course. The chancellor's daughter is growing up into a very beautiful lady indeed. He has done everything for her. And just see what we have here, so quiet and unassuming. She's every bit as pretty.

*Ukon actually calls the girl 'Lady Ruri,' a childhood name, apparently, not used elsewhere; but it seems convenient here to introduce the name by which she is most commonly known.

'The chancellor has seen them all, ever since the reign of his late father, all the consorts and the other royal ladies. I once heard him say to Lady Murasaki that the word "beautiful" must have been invented for the late empress and his own daughter. I never saw the late empress and so I cannot say, and the other is still a child, and a person can only imagine how beautiful she will be someday. But Lady Murasaki herself: really she doesn't have a rival even now. I'm sure he just didn't want to speak of her own beauty right there in front of her. He most certainly is aware of it. I once heard him say – he was joking, of course – that she should know better than to take her place beside a handsome man like him. You should see the two of them! The sight of them makes you think years have been added to your life, and you wonder if anywhere else in the world there is anything like it. But just see what we have here, just look at this lady. She could hold her own with no trouble. You don't go looking for a halo with even the most raving beauty, but if you want the next-best thing –'

She smiled at Tamakazura, and the old nurse was grinning back. 'Just a little longer and she would have been wasted on Kyushu. I couldn't stand the idea, and so I threw away pots and pans and children and came running back to the city. It might as well have been the capital of a foreign country. Take her to something better, please, as soon as you possibly can. You are in one of the great houses and you know everyone. Do please think of some way to tell her father. Make him count her among his children.'

The girl looked away in embarrassment.

'No, it is true. I don't amount to anything, but His Lordship has seen fit to call me into his presence from time to time, and once when I said I wondered what had happened to the child he said that he wondered too and I must let him know if I heard anything.'

'Yes, of course, he is a very fine gentleman. But he already has all those other fine ladies. I would feel a little more comfortable, I think, if you were to inform her father.'

Ukon told her about the lady of the evening faces. 'His Lordship took it very hard. He said he wanted the little girl to remember her by. He said then and he went on saying that he had so few children of his own, he could tell people he had found a lost daughter. I was young and inexperienced and unsure of myself, and I was afraid to go looking for her. I recognized the name of your good husband when he was appointed deputy viceroy. I even caught a glimpse of him when he came to say goodbye to His Lordship. I thought you might have left the child behind at the house where I last saw you. Suppose she had spent the rest of her life in Kyushu – the very thought of it makes me shiver.'

They looked down upon streams of pilgrims. The river before them was the Hatsuse.

'Had I not come to the place of cedars twain,*
How should I have met you here beside the old river?'

said Ukon. 'I am very happy.'

Tamakazura replied:

'I know little, I fear, about the swift old river,
But I know the flow of tears of happiness.'

She was indeed weeping, and very beautiful.

Astonishingly so – a jewel quite unblemished by rough provincial life. The old nurse had worked wonders, and Ukon was deeply grateful. The girl's mother had been such a quiet little child of a thing, completely gentle and unresisting. The girl herself seemed proud and aloof by comparison; and there was something else, something quietly mysterious about her, suggestive of great depths. Kyushu must be a remarkable place – and yet look at these others, very countrified indeed.

In the evening they all went up to the main hall, and the next day was a quiet one of prayers and rites.

The autumn wind blowing up from the valley was cold, but they did not let it trouble them. They had other concerns. For the Kyushu people despair had suddenly given way to talk of Tō no Chūjō and the careers he had made for the least likely of his children by his several ladies. It seemed possible that the sunlight would reach even to this undermost leaf. Fearing that they might once more lose track of each other, Ukon and the nurse exchanged addresses before they left the temple. Ukon's family lived not far from the Rokujō mansion, a fact that gave a comforting sense of nearness and accessibility.

When she was next on duty at Rokujō, Ukon looked for a chance to tell Genji a little of what had happened. As her carriage

*See note†, page 197.

was pulled inside the gate she had a sudden feeling of vast spaces, and all the grand carriages coming and going made her marvel that she too was in attendance at the jeweled pavilion. No occasion presented itself that evening. She went restlessly to bed with her problem. The next day he summoned her by name. It was a great honor, for numbers of women, old and important and young and obscure, had the evening before come back from vacation.

'And why did you stay so long? But you have changed. The old stiffness has given way to a more yielding quality, might we say? Something interesting has surely happened.'

'I was gone for about a week, just wasting my time. But I did come on someone rather interesting off in the hills.'

'Yes?'

She preferred that Murasaki hear, lest she later be taxed with secretiveness.

Other women came up. Lamps were lighted, and Genji and Murasaki were pleasing indeed as they settled down for a quiet evening. Now in her late twenties, Murasaki was at her best. It seemed to Ukon that even in the brief time she had been away her lady had improved. And Tamakazura was almost as beautiful – and perhaps it was only Ukon's imagination that there was a small difference to be observed between the more and the less fortunate.

Ukon was summoned to massage Genji's legs.

'The young ones hate to do it,' he laughed. 'We oldsters get on best.'

'Really, sir, who would hate to do anything for you?' said one of the younger women. 'You do make the worst jokes.'

'Even we oldsters must be careful. There is jealousy abroad. We are in danger.' He could be very amusing.

Having relieved himself of the heavier business of government, he was able to relax with the women. Even an aging woman like Ukon was not ignored.

'Now, then, who is this interesting person in the hills? A well-endowed hermit you have come to an understanding with?'

'Please, sir, someone might hear you. I have found a lady who is not unrelated to those evening faces. Do you remember? The ones that faded so quickly.'

'Ah, yes, memories do come back. Where has she been all this time?'

Ukon did not know how to begin. 'She has been very far away. Some of the people who were with her then are still with her. We talked about the old days. It was so sad.'

'Do remember, please, that we have an uninformed audience.'

'You needn't worry,' said Murasaki, covering her ears. 'Your audience is too sleepy to care in the least.'

'Is she as pretty as her mother?'

'I wouldn't have thought she could possibly be, but she has grown into a very beautiful young lady indeed.'

'How interesting. Would you compare her with our lady here?'

'Oh, sir, hardly.'

'But you seem confident enough. Does she look like me? If so, then I can be confident too.'

He was already talking as if he were her father.

He called Ukon off by herself. 'You must bring her here. I have thought of her so often. I am delighted at this news and sorry that we lost her for so long. She must not be kept away any longer. Why should we tell her father? His house swarms with children. I am afraid the poor little thing would be overwhelmed. And I have so few myself – we can say that I have come upon a daughter in a most unexpected place. She will be our treasure. We will have all the young gallants eager to meet her.'

'I leave everything to your judgment, sir. If her father is to know, then you must be the one to tell him. I am sure that any little gesture in memory of the lady we lost will lighten the burden of sin.'

'The burden is mine, you are saying?' He smiled, but he was near tears. 'I have thought so often what a sad, brief affair it was. I have all the ladies you see here, and I doubt that I have ever felt toward any of them quite that intensity of affection. Most of them have lived long enough to see that I am after all a steady sort, and she vanished so quickly, and I have had only you to remember her by. I have not forgotten her. It would be as if all my prayers had been answered if you were to bring the girl here.'

He got off a letter. Yet he was a little worried, remembering the safflower princess. Ladies were not always what one hoped they would be, and this was a lady who had had a hard life.

His letter was most decorous. At the end of it he said: 'And as to my reasons for writing,

'You may not know, but presently you will,
    Where leads the line of rushes at Mishimae.'*

Ukon delivered it and gave an account of their conversation. She brought all manner of garments for the lady herself and for the others. Genji had told Murasaki the whole story and gone through his warehouses for the best of everything, and very different it all was from what they had been used to in Kyushu.

Tamakazura suggested that the delight would be more considerable if there were word from her father. She saw no reason to go and live with a stranger.

Ukon set about making her think otherwise. 'Your father is sure to hear of you once you are set up in a decent sort of life. The bond between parent and child is not so easily broken. I am nobody, and I found you because of my prayers. There can be no other explanation. These things happen if we live long enough. You must get off an answer.'

The girl was timid, sure that any answer from her would seem hopelessly countrified. She chose richly perfumed Chinese paper and wrote only this, in a faint, delicate hand:

'You speak of lines and rushes – and by what line
    Has this poor rush taken root in this sad world?'

The hand was immature, but it showed character and breeding. Genji was more confident.

The problem now was where to put her. There was no room in the several wings of Murasaki's southeast quarter. It was the grandest part of the house and all its apartments were in use, and it was so much frequented that a new presence would very probably be noticed. Akikonomu's southwest quarter was quiet and in many ways suitable, but Genji would not have wished Tamakazura to be taken for one of the empress's attendants. Though a little gloomy and remote, there was the west wing of the northeast quarter, now being used as a library. Genji ordered the books and papers moved. The lady of the orange blossoms had already been assigned the northeast quarter, but she was a gentle, amiable person who would be good company for the new lady.

*Mishimae, near the present Osaka, and *mikuri*, here translated 'rushes,' are associated for purposes of euphony and assonance. The use of *mikuri* is otherwise obscure, though it would seem to suggest continuity and lineage.

He had told Murasaki the whole ancient story. She chided him for having kept it so long a secret.

'Please, my dear – why should I have offered it to you all gratuitously? I would have been reluctant to tell such a story even if it had been about someone you know. I am telling you now because you mean so very much to me.' He was in a reminiscent mood. 'I have seen and heard of so many cases in which I have not myself been involved. I have seen and heard how strong a woman's feelings can be in the most casual affair, and I have not wanted that sort of thing in my own life. But one's wishes are not always consulted in these matters. I have had numbers of affairs that might be called illicit, but I doubt that any of them has had quite that gentle sort of pull on me. I think that if she were still living I would be doing at least as much for her as for the lady in the northwest quarter. No one in this world is quite like anyone else. She may not have been the most intelligent and accomplished person, but she did have a way about her, and she was pretty.'

'I doubt very much indeed that she would be a rival of the lady in the northwest quarter.' Evidently there was still resentment.

But here was the little Akashi girl, listening to the conversation with such charming unconcern. Murasaki thought she could see why he had a high regard for the mother.

It was the Ninth Month. Tamakazura's move was no routine affair. Superior women must be found to wait on her. Through various offices a retinue of women who had drifted down from the capital had been put together in Kyushu, but the suddenness of the departure had made it impossible to bring them along. The city was a vast place. Tradeswomen could be helpful in these matters. Quietly, not letting the girl's identity be known, the Kyushu people moved in with Ukon's family. Finally everything was ready. In the Tenth Month they moved to Rokujō.

Genji had taken the lady of the orange blossoms into his confidence. 'Someone I was once fond of was having a difficult time and ran off into the mountains. I hunted and hunted, but I did not find the daughter until she was quite grown-up. Even then it was only by accident that I learned a little about her. I do not think it is too late. Might I bring her here? The mother is no longer living. I think I might without imposing too dreadfully ask you to do for her as you have done for Yūgiri. She grew up in the country, and no doubt you will find a great deal that does not entirely please you. Do give her the benefit of your advice.' He was very polite and attentive to detail.

She agreed most generously. 'I had not dreamed of such a thing. How very nice for you. You have been lonely with just the one little girl.'

'Her mother was a gentle, amiable young lady. It has all worked out so nicely. You are such an amiable lady yourself.'

'I shall be delighted. I have so little to do.'

He had only a few words for the other women.

'And what will he have come up with this time? Such a bothersome collector as he is!'

There were three carriages for the move. Ukon managed to cover the more obvious appearances of rusticity. Genji sent a large supply of damasks and other figured cloths. Promptly that evening he paid a visit. The Kyushu women had long known of 'the shining Genji,' but his radiance had come to seem very far off. And here it was, dimming the lamplight through openings in curtains, almost frightening.

Ukon went to admit him. 'One comes through this door,' he said, laughing, 'with wildly palpitating heart.' He took a seat in an outer room. 'A very soft and suggestive sort of light. I was told that you wished to see your father's face. Is that not the case?' He pushed the curtain aside.

She looked away, but he had seen enough to be very pleased.

'Can't we have a little more light? This is really *too* suggestive.'

Ukon trimmed a lamp and brought it near.

'Now we are being bold.'

Yes, she was very beautiful, and she reminded him of her mother.

'There was no time through all those years when you were out of my thoughts, and now that we are together it is all like a dream.' His manner was intimate, as if he were her father. 'I am overwhelmed and reduced to silence.' He was in fact deeply moved, and he brushed away a tear as he counted up the years. 'How very sad it has been. I doubt that many fathers and daughters are kept apart for so long. But come: you are too old for this bashfulness, and there are so many things we must talk about. You must not treat me like a stranger.'

She could not look at him. Finally she replied in a voice which he could barely hear but which, as it trailed off into silence, reminded him very much of her mother. 'I was like the leech child when they took me away.* I could not stand up. Afterwards I was hardly sure whether it was happening to me or not.'

He smiled. It was a most acceptable answer. 'And now who besides me is to pity you for all the wasted years?'

He gave Ukon various instructions and left.

Pleased that she had passed the test so nicely, he went to tell Murasaki. 'I had felt for her, in a lofty, abstract sort of way; and now I find her so much in control of herself that she almost makes me uncomfortable. I must let everyone know that I have taken her in, and we shall watch the pulses rise as Prince Hotaru and the rest come peeking through my fences. We have seen composed and sedate countenances all around us, and that has been because we have not had the means for creating disturbances. Now we shall improve our service and see who among them is the most unsettled.'

'What a very odd sort of father, thinking first how to lead them all into temptation.'

'If I had been sufficiently alive to these things,' he said, 'I might have been similarly thoroughgoing in my management of your affairs. I did not consider all the possibilities.'

She flushed, as young and beautiful as ever.

He reached for an inkstone and jotted down a verse:

'With unabated longing I sought the other.
What lines have drawn me to the jeweled chaplet?†

'It is all so very affecting,' he added, as if to himself.

Yes, thought Murasaki, he would seem to have found a memento of someone very important to him.

He told Yūgiri that he must be good to the girl.

'Not that I could have done very much,' Yūgiri said to her solemnly, 'but I am the one you should have come to. I must apologize for not having been present to receive you.'

The situation was somewhat embarrassing to those who shared the secret.

The house in Kyushu had seemed the ultimate in luxury and elegance, but now she could see that it had been hopelessly

---

See note, page 282.

†*Tamakazura.* It is from this poem that the girl takes her name.

provincial. Here every detail was in the latest fashion, and every member of the family (she was received as one of the family) was very prepossessing indeed. The woman Sanjō was now able to put the assistant viceroy in his place, and as for the hot-blooded person from Higo, the very thought of him repelled her. Tamakazura and Ukon knew how much they owed the nurse's son, the former vice-governor of Bungo. Genji chose Tamakazura's stewards with the greatest care, for he wanted no laxness in the management of her household. The nurse's son was among them. He would not in ordinary circumstances have had entree to so grand a mansion, and the change after all those years in the provinces was almost too sudden. Here he was among the great ones, coming and going, morning and night. It was a singular honor. Genji was almost too attentive to all the housekeeping details.

With the approach of the New Year he turned his attention to festive dress and appurtenances, determined that nothing suggest less than the highest rank. Though the girl had been a pleasant surprise thus far, he made allowances for rustic tastes. He himself reviewed all the colors and cuts upon which the finest craftsmen had concentrated their skills.

'Vast numbers of things,' he said to Murasaki. 'We must see that they are divided so that no one has a right to feel slighted.'

He had everything spread before him, the products of the offices and of Murasaki's personal endeavors as well. Such sheens and hues as she had wrought, displaying yet another of her talents! He would compare what the fullers had done to this purple and that red, and distribute them among chests and wardrobes, with women of experience to help him reach his decisions.

Murasaki too was with him. 'A very hard choice indeed. You must always have the wearer in mind. The worst thing is when the clothes do not suit the lady.'

Genji smiled. 'So it is a matter of cool calculation? And what might my lady's choices be for herself?'

'My lady is not confident,' she replied, shyly after all, 'that the mirror can give her an answer.'

For Murasaki he selected a lavender robe with a clear, clean pattern of rose-plum blossoms and a singlet of a fashionable lavender.* For his little daughter there was a white robe lined with red

---

*There are doubts about several of the colors. Here, for instance, the original says only 'a stylish color.' Purple or red is most likely.

and a singlet beaten to a fine glow. For the lady of the orange blossoms, a robe of azure with a pattern of seashells beautifully woven in quiet colors, and a crimson singlet, also fulled to a high sheen. For the new lady, a cloak of bright red and a robe of russet lined with yellow. Though pretending not to be much interested, Murasaki was wondering what sort of lady would go with these last garments. She must resemble her father, a man of fine and striking looks somewhat lacking in the gentler qualities. It was clear to Genji that despite her composure she was uneasy.

'But it is not fair to compare them by their clothes,' he said. 'There is a limit to what clothes can do, and the plainest lady has something of her own.'

He chose for the safflower princess a white robe lined with green and decorated profusely with Chinese vignettes. He could not help smiling at its vivacity. And there were garments too for the Akashi lady: a cloak of Chinese white with birds and butterflies flitting among plum branches and a robe of a rich, deep, glossy purple. Its proud elegance immediately caught the eye – and seemed to Murasaki somewhat overdone. For the lady of the locust shell, now a nun, he selected a most dignified habit of a deep blue-gray, a yellow singlet of his own, and a lavender jacket. He sent around messages that everyone was to be in full dress. He wanted to see how well, following Murasaki's principle, he had matched apparel and wearer.

All the ladies took great pains with their answers and with gifts for the messengers. The safflower lady, left behind in the east lodge at Nijō, might have had certain feelings of deprivation, but she was not one to neglect ceremony. She gave the messenger a yellow lady's robe rather discolored at the sleeves – a hollow locust shell, so to speak. Her note was on official stationery, heavily scented and yellow with age.

'Your gifts bring boundless sorrow.

'Tearfully I don this Chinese robe,
   And having dampened its sleeves, I now return it.'

The hand was very old-fashioned. Smiling, he read and reread the poem. Murasaki wondered what had so taken his fancy.

The messenger slipped away, fearing that Genji might be amused as well at the bounty he had received. The women were all whispering and laughing. The safflower princess, so inflexibly conservative in her ways, could be discommodingly polite.

'A most courtly and elegant lady,' said Genji. 'Her conservative style is unable to rid itself of Chinese robes and wet sleeves. I am a rather conservative person myself, and must somewhat grudgingly admire this tenacious fidelity. Hers is a style which considers it mandatory to mention 'august company' whenever royalty is in the vicinity, and when the exchange is of a romantic nature a reference to fickleness can always be counted on to get one over the caesura. 'He was still smiling. 'One reads all the handbooks and memorizes all the gazetteers, and chooses an item from this and an item from that, and what is wanting is originality. She once showed me her father's handbooks. You can't imagine all the poetic marrow and poetic ills I found in them. Somewhat intimidated by these rigorous standards, I gave them back. But this does seem a rather wispy product from so much study and erudition.'

He was a little too amused, thought Murasaki, who answered most solemnly: 'And why did you send them back? We could have made copies and given them to the little girl. I used to own some handbooks too, but I'm afraid I let the worms have them. I'm not the student of poetry some people are.'

'I doubt that they would have contributed to the girl's education. Girls should not be too intense. Ignorance is not to be recommended, of course, but a certain tact in the management of learning is.'

He did not seem disposed to answer the safflower princess.

'She speaks of returning your gifts. You must let her have something in return for her poem.'

Essentially a kind man, Genji agreed. He dashed off an answer. This would seem to be what he sent:

' "Return," you say – ah, "turn," I see you mean,
     Your Chinese robe, prepared for lonely slumber.*

'I understand completely.'

*There was a popular belief that a robe turned inside out brought dreams of one's lover.

CHAPTER 23

The First Warbler

New Year's Day was cloudless. There is joy inside the humblest of hedges as the grass begins to come green among patches of snow and there is a mist of green on the trees while the mists in the air tell of the advent of spring. There was great joy in the jeweled precincts of Genji's Rokujō mansion, where every detail of the gardens was a pleasure and the ladies' apartments were perfection.

The garden of Murasaki's southeast quarter was now the most beautiful. The scent of plum blossoms, wafting in on the breeze and blending with the perfumes inside, made one think that paradise had come down to earth. Murasaki may have had her small worries, but she lived in peace and security. She had assigned the prettier of her young women to the service of Genji's little daughter, and kept in her own service older women whose beauty was in fact of a statelier sort and who were extremely particular about their dress and grooming. They were gathered in little groups, helping the New Year with its 'teething,'* taking New Year's cakes, and otherwise welcoming another year of the thousand which they laughingly appropriated for themselves. Genji came in. They had been caught with their ribbons undone, so to speak, and they quickly brought themselves to order.

'And are all these congratulations for me?' He smiled. 'But you must have little wishes of your own. Tell me what they are, and I will then think of some that you forgot.' He seemed the very incarnation of New Year gladness.

Chūjō thought herself privileged to speak. 'Assured by the mirror cake† that ten centuries are in store for your august lordship, how should I think of anything for myself?'

Yowai means both 'tooth' and 'year.' The taking of certain New Year delicacies was therefore called 'the firming of the teeth.'

†Decorative New Year rice cakes were and are still called 'mirror cakes.' The mirror is in numerous ways a felicitous symbol of the New Year. Otomo Kuronushi, *Kokinshū* 1086:

> Looking to the Mirror Mountains of Omi,
> We see ten centuries for this august reign.

All morning, callers streamed in and out of the Rokujō mansion. Genji dressed with great care for a round of calls upon his ladies. One would not have easily wearied of looking at him when his preparations were finished. 'Your women were having such a good time that they made me envious,' he said to Murasaki. 'Let us now have a congratulatory note for ourselves.

'The mirror of this lake, now freed from ice,
Offers an image of utter peace and calm.'

And indeed it did reflect an image of very great beauty and felicity.

'Upon the cloudless mirror of this lake,
Clear is the image, for ten thousand years.'

Everything about the scene seemed to make manifest a bond that was meant to last a thousand years – and New Year's Day this year fell on the Day of the Rat.*

He went to his daughter's rooms. Her page girls and young serving women were out on the hill busying themselves with seedling pines, too intoxicated with the occasion, it would seem, to stay inside. The Akashi lady – it was clear that she had gone to enormous trouble – had sent over New Year delicacies in 'bearded baskets'† and with them a warbler on a very cleverly fabricated pine branch:

'The old one's gaze rests long on the seedling pine,
Waiting to hear the song of the first warbler,

in a village where it does not sing.'‡

Yes, thought Genji, it was a lonely time for her. One should not weep on New Year's Day, but he was very close to tears.

---

*Because of the homophonous 'rat' and 'root,' seedling pines were set out on the Day of the Rat as tokens of longevity.

†Baskets with the ends of the woven strands left untrimmed.

‡The *uguisu*, warbler, is usually associated with the plum. By attaching an artificial warbler to an artificial pine branch, the lady makes use of the usual pun on *matsu*, 'pine' and 'wait,' to convey her longing for her daughter. The words following her poem are apparently a quotation, but the poem quoted in old commentaries is not otherwise known.

'You must answer her yourself,' he said to his daughter. 'You are surely not the sort to begrudge her that first song.' He brought ink and brush.

She was so pretty that even those who were with her day and night had to smile. Genji was feeling guilty for the years he had kept mother and daughter apart.

Cheerfully, she jotted down the first poem that came to her:

> 'The warbler left its nest long years ago,
>   But cannot forget the roots of the waiting pine.'

He went to the summer quarter of the lady of the orange blossoms. There was nothing in her summer gardens to catch the eye, nothing that was having its moment, and yet everything was quietly elegant. They were as close as ever, she and Genji, despite the passage of the years. It was an easy sort of intimacy which he would not have wished to change. They had their talks, pleasant and easy as talks between husband and wife seldom are. He pushed the curtain between them slightly aside. She made no effort to hide herself. Her azure robe was as quietly becoming as he had hoped it would be. Her hair had thinned sadly. He rather wished she might be persuaded to use a switch, though not so considerable a one as to attract notice. He knew that no other man was likely to have been as good to her, and in the knowledge was one of his private pleasures. What misfortunes might she not have brought upon herself had she been a less constant sort! Always when he was with her he thought first of his own dependability and her undemanding ways. They were a remarkable pair. They talked quietly of the year that had passed, and he went on to see Tamakazura.

She was not yet really at home, but her rooms were in very good taste. She had a large retinue of women and pretty little girls. Though much still needed to be done by way of furnishing and decorating, the rooms already wore an air of clean dignity. Even more striking was the elegance of their occupant. She seemed to enhance the glow of her yellow dress and send it into the deepest corners of the room, taking away the last gloomy shadow. It was a scene, he thought, which could never seem merely ordinary. Perhaps because of her trials, her hair was just a little sparse at the edges. The casual flow drew wonderfully clean lines down over her skirts. And what might have happened to her if he had not brought her here? (The question may have suggested that he was already thinking of certain changes.) There was no barrier between them, though she was very much on her guard. It was a strange situation with a certain dreamlike quality about it that both interested and amused him.

'I feel as if you had been with us for years. Everything seems so cozy. I could not wish for more. I hope that by now you are feeling quite at home. Today you might just possibly want to go over to the southeast quarter, where you will find a young lady at her New Year's music lesson. You need not have the slightest fear that anyone will say anything unpleasant about you.'

'I shall do exactly as you wish me to.'

In the circumstances, a most acceptable answer.

He went in the evening to the northwest quarter and called on the Akashi lady. He was greeted by the perfume from within her blinds, a delicate mixture that told of the most refined tastes. And where was the lady herself? He saw notebooks and the like disposed around an inkstone. He took one up, and another. A beautifully made koto lay against the elaborate fringe of a cushion of white Loyang damask, and in a brazier of equally fine make she had been burning courtly incenses, which mingled with the perfume burnt into all the furnishings to most wonderful effect. Little practice notes lay scattered about. The hand was a superior and most individual one, in an easy cursive style that allowed no suggestion of pretense or imposture. Pleased at having heard from her daughter, it would seem, she had been amusing herself with jottings from the anthologies.

And there was a poem of her own:

'Such happiness! The warbler among the blossoms
  Calls across the glen to its old nest.'

'I had waited so long,' she had added; and, to comfort herself: ' "I dwell upon a hill of blossoming plums." '*

He smiled one of his most radiant smiles.

He had just taken up a brush when the lady came in. Luxury had not made her any less modest or retiring. Yes, she was differ-

---

*Anonymous, *Manyōshū* 1820:

I dwell upon a hill of blossoming plums.
Often and often I hear the call of the warbler.

ent. Her dark tresses gleamed against the white of her robe, not so thick that they might have seemed assertive. He decided to spend the night with her, though sorry indeed if in other quarters the New Year must begin with spasms of jealousy. She was dear to him in a very special way, he thought somewhat uneasily. In Murasaki's quarter he may have been the object of sterner reproaches than he had for himself.

It was not yet full daylight when he left. He might, thought the Akashi lady, have awaited a more seemly hour. In the southeast quarter he sensed that the welcome was mixed.

'I dozed off, and there I was sleeping like a baby, and no one woke me.' He was charmingly ingenuous, but Murasaki pretended to be asleep.

He lay down beside her. The sun was high when he arose.

New Year's callers kept him busy that day and were his excuse for avoiding a confrontation. The whole court came. There was music and there were lavish gifts. Each of the guests was determined to cut the finest figure, though in fact (I say it regretfully) no one could challenge the host. By themselves they were strong enough lights, but Genji dimmed them all. The lowliest among them made sure that he was looking his best when he came to Rokujō, and the highest seemed to have something new and original on his mind. A quiet breeze coaxed perfume from the flowers and especially from the plums just coming into bloom at the veranda. 'How grand this house:' the festivities were at a climax, and came to an end with 'the three-branched *sakigusa*.'* Genji himself helped with the concluding passages. Restrained though his part might be, it always seemed to make a very great difference.

In all the other quarters, there were only distant echoes of horse and carriage, to make the ladies feel that they were living in an outer circle of paradise where the lotuses were slow to open. The east lodge at Nijō was of course even farther away. Life may have been a little uneventful for the ladies there, but they were spared the more bitter trials of the world, and would have thought it out of place to complain. Neglected they unquestionably were, and they might have wished for something different; but their lives were calm and comfortable and secure. The nun could pursue her

---

*The beginning and end of the Saibara 'This House.' The *sakigusa* has not been identified.

prayers and the connoisseur her poetry texts and neither need fear distraction.

When the busy days were over he went calling, with careful ceremony, for the safflower princess was after all a princess. Her hair had been her principal and indeed her only charm when she was young, but now the flow was a white trickle, and her profile was better not seen. He looked tactfully away. The white robe which he had sent had, he feared, been rather better by itself. She seemed quite congealed in a frosting of white over something of a dark, dull gray so stiff that it rustled dryly. And was there nothing else, no underclothing to keep her warm? The safflower nose was aglow all the same, bright through the densest mists. He sighed and rearranged her curtains, and she seemed not to guess why. He could not help being touched at the pleasure which the visit, evidence that he still thought of her, so obviously gave. Poor, lonely thing, he must do something for her from time to time. She too was rather special – leastways one did not often see her like. Her voice too seemed congealed.

He was concerned. 'Who is in charge of your wardrobe? You live a rather informal life here, and I should think that informal dress might be called for. Quilted garments, for instance, have much to recommend them. You worry too much about appearances.'

She managed a short laugh. 'I have my brother to look after, the priest at Daigo, and I have no time to think about my own clothes. I do get a little chilly. I let him have my sable.'

Yes, she had a sable. And a brother, also the possessor of a safflower nose. She was an honest lady but not a very practical one. He felt very honest himself when he was with her, away from the niceties and deceptions of the elegant life.

'I think you did well to let him have your sable. It rains a great deal off in the mountains, and I am sure he needs a raincoat. But what of yourself? You need some underclothing, really you do. Pile it on, seven and eight layers of it. I am sometimes forgetful in these matters, and you must keep reminding me. You must not put up with my obtuseness.'

He sent to the Nijō warehouses for plain and figured silks. The Nijō mansion could not have been called neglected or run-down, but a silence had settled over it with his removal to Rokujō. Yet the plantings were fine. It seemed a pity that there was no one to appreciate the rose plum, just coming into bloom.

      'I stop to look at the groves of my old village,
      And the blossom I see reminds me of a safflower.'

He spoke very softly. It is unlikely that the princess caught the full implications.

He next looked in upon the lady of the locust shell. She was living very modestly, the larger part of her rooms given over to sacred images. He found the evidences of the religious life very moving. The scrolls and the decorations and utensils down to the least of the fonts showed very good taste indeed. She was a refined and cultivated lady. Only her sleeves showed modest and ladylike through the ingenious arrangement of gray curtains behind which she had hidden herself.

'I should perhaps have been satisfied,' he said, almost in tears, 'with seeing Urashima from a distance.* Things have never been easy between us, and I should hope that we might go on having as much as we have now.'

She too seemed deeply moved. 'It can have been no weak bond that has made me put my trust in you.'

'Considerable wrongs, I should think, call for considerable acts of contrition. Am I not right? Perhaps you see now that not everyone would have been as honest with you as I have been.'

She could not look at him. He was obviously referring to her stepson's lamentable behavior.† 'My contrition is in showing myself to you as I am, and in having you see me thus to the end.'

She seemed ever calmer and more serene, and the fact that she had become a nun made him feel more strongly that he must keep her with him. But it was not the time to say so. The talk might be of the present or of the past, but it must be in generalities. How good, he thought, glancing in the direction of the safflower princess's rooms, to be with someone who could talk at all.

He was seeing to the needs of others in this same matter-of-fact way. He looked in on all of them.

'I may seem negligent at times, but I have not forgotten. Nor will I forget, though life is uncertain, and final goodbyes must presently come.'

---

*See note†, page 219.

†At the end of Chapter 16.

He addressed each of them most gently and courteously, and indeed he was fond of them all, after their several stations. They could not have complained whatever he chose to do with them, but he was moderation itself, allowing no suggestion of the haughty or arbitrary. His attentions were for them the chief comfort in life.

The carolers were out this year.* They went from the main palace to the Suzaku Palace of the retired emperor and thence to Rokujō. The way being a long one, it was dawn when they arrived. A moon hung in a cloudless sky and a light fall of snow set the garden off to weirdly delicate effect. Everyone wanted to be his best when he came to Rokujō. It was an age well provided with fine musicians, and the sound of flute rang high through the grounds. Genji had invited all his ladies to watch, and there they all were along the east and west wings and galleries. Tamakazura had been invited to the south front of the main hall, where she was introduced to Genji's daughter. Murasaki watched from behind a curtain.

Dawn was already coming on as the carolers did honor to Kokiden, the mother of the Suzaku emperor. There should have been only light refreshments at Rokujō, but Genji had in fact had an elaborate banquet set out. The moon was almost too bright in the dawn sky and there were snow flurries. A wind came down through the tall pines. The soft yellow-greens and whites of the carolers did nothing to break the cold, white calm, and the cloth posies in their caps, far from seeming to intrude with too much color, moved over the scene with a light grace such as to make the onlookers feel that years were being added to their lives. Yūgiri and Tō no Chūjō's sons were the handsomest and proudest of the carolers. Day broke amid new flurries of snow, 'Bamboo River'† fell on freezing air, and the dancing and the singing – I longed to paint the scene, though certain that my efforts must fall short of the actuality.

See note, page 137.

†A Saibara:

> Let me go among the flowers, among the flowers,
> Beside the bridge, beside the bridge,
> Beside the Bamboo River,
> That I may be with the maiden.

The sleeves emerging from the blinds as each of the ladies sought to outdo all the others made one think of a tapestry spread out in a spring haze. It was all quite magical, if in a very slightly unsettling way, the high caps so far from the ordinary and the noisy congratulations and all the trappings and appurtenances. The carolers went off in full daylight, bearing as always the evidences of Genji's munificence. The ladies dispersed. Genji lay down to rest, and arose when the sun was high.

'Yūgiri may have sung a little less well than Kōbai,'* he said to Murasaki, 'but only a very little. Ours is a good day for music. The ancients may have been better at scholarship and learning, but I think we more than hold our own in the gentler pursuits. I wanted to make a sober public servant of him and to keep him from wasting his time on the frivolities that took up so much of my own. But it is right that he should find time for them too. Unrelieved sobriety is itself an excess.'

In obvious pleasure at his son's performance, he interrupted himself to hum 'The Delight of Ten Thousand Springs.'†

'We must arrange a day of music for ourselves. Our own private recessional.'‡

He carefully undid the fine cloths in which the instruments had been stored away, and dusted and tuned them; and it would seem that the ladies were already hard at practice.

---

*Tō no Chūjō's second son, famous for his voice. He has already appeared in Chapter 10.

†The refrain to a chant, in Chinese, that was a part of the Otokotkaōa carols.

‡Goen, a court banquet some weeks after the carols. Genji is treating the musicale he proposes with mock dignity.

CHAPTER 24

Butterflies

It was late in the Third Month. Murasaki's spring garden was coming ever more to life with blossoms and singing birds. Elsewhere spring had departed, said the other ladies, and why did it remain here? Genji thought it a pity that the young women should have only distant glimpses of the moss on the island, a deeper green each day. He had carpenters at work on Chinese pleasure boats, and on the day they were launched he summoned palace musicians for water music. Princes and high courtiers came crowding to hear.

Akikonomu was in residence at Rokujō. Now was the time, thought Murasaki, for a proper answer to the poem about the garden that 'awaits the spring.'* Genji agreed. It would have been good to show these spring blossoms to the empress herself, but casual visits were out of the question for one in her position. Numbers of her young women who were thought likely to enjoy such an outing were therefore rowed out over the south lake, which ran from her southwest quarter to Murasaki's southeast, with a hillock separating the two. The boats left from the hillock. Murasaki's women were stationed in the angling pavilion at the boundary between the two quarters.

The dragon and phoenix boats were brilliantly decorated in the Chinese fashion. The little pages and helmsmen, their hair still bound up in the page-boy manner, wore lively Chinese dress, and everything about the arrangements was deliciously exotic, to add to the novelty, for the empress's women, of this southeast quarter. The boats pulled up below a cliff at an island cove, where the smallest of the hanging rocks was like a detail of a painting. The branches caught in mists from either side were like a tapestry, and far away in Murasaki's private gardens a willow trailed its branches in a deepening green and the cherry blossoms were rich and sensuous. In other places they had fallen, but here they were still at their smiling best, and along the galleries wisteria was beginning to send forth its lavender. Yellow *yamabuki* reflected on the lake as if about to join its own image. Waterfowl swam past in amiable pairs, and

*At the end of Chapter 21.

flew in and out with twigs in their bills, and one longed to paint the mandarin ducks as they coursed about on the water. Had that Chinese woodcutter been present, he might well have gazed on until his ax handle rotted away. Presently it was evening.

'The breezes blow, the wave flowers brightly blossom.
 Will it be the Cape of Yamabuki?'*

'Is this the lake where flows the River of Ide,†
 That *yamabuki* should plunge into its depths?'

'There is no need to visit Turtle Mountain.‡
 "Ageless" shall be the name of our pleasure boats.'

'Our boats row out into the bright spring sun,
 And water drops from the oars like scattering petals.'

Poem followed poem. The young women seemed to forget that the day must end and they must go home.

In the gathering twilight, to the sonorous strains of 'The Royal Deer,'** the boats were pulled up once more at the angling pavilion and the women reluctantly disembarked. It was a building of simple but very great elegance. The lengths to which the competitive young women had gone with their dress and grooming made one think of a tapestry upon which blossoms had fallen. The music, all very novel, went on and on, for Genji had chosen musicians whose repertory did not permit of monotony.

It was night, and they seemed indefatigable. Flares having been put out in the garden, they were invited to the moss carpet below the verandas, and the princes and high courtiers had places above with the kotos and flutes in which they took such pride. The most accomplished of the professional flutists struck up a melody in the *sōjō* mode,†† in which the courtiers joined most brilliantly with their kotos, and as they moved on to 'How Grand the Day'‡‡

---

*Thought to have been in the province of Omi.

† A famous place for *yamabuki*, in Yamashiro.

‡Mythical.

**_Ojō_, a Chinese dance.

††Based on G.

‡‡See note*, page 402.

even the most ignorant of the footmen off among the horses and carriages seemed to respond. The sky and the music, the spring modes and echoes, all seemed better here – no one could fail to see the difference. The night was passed in music. With 'Joy of Spring'* the mode shifted to an intimate minor. Prince Hotaru twice sang 'Green Willow,'† in very good voice. Genji occasionally joined in.

Morning came. From behind her fences Akikonomu listened to the morning birds and feared that her autumn garden had lost the contest.

Though a perpetual spring radiance seemed to hang over this Rokujō mansion, there were those who had complained of a want of interesting young ladies. Now the rumors were of a new lady in the northeast quarter, and how pretty she was and how attentive Genji seemed to be. The anticipated stream of letters had commenced. Several of those whose station in life made them confident that their candidacy was acceptable already had their intermediaries at work. Others seemed to be keeping their ardor rather more to themselves. It is to be imagined that several of the suitors, Tō no Chūjō's son, for instance, would have dropped their suits if they had known who she really was.

Prince Hotaru, Genji's brother, had lost his wife of some years and for three years had been living a lonely bachelor's life. He was now quite open with his suit. Pretending to be hopelessly drunk, he was very amusing indeed as he gamboled about all willow-like with a spray of wisteria in his cap.‡ Quite as expected, thought Genji, though he gave no sign that he noticed.

The wine flagon came around once more and the prince pretended to be in great discomfort. 'If there were not something rather special to keep me here, I think I would be trying to escape. It is too much, oh, really too much.' He refused to drink any more.

---

*Chinese. It does not survive.

†A Saibara.

> The green willow, the green willow.
> The warbler makes a cup of its twigs,
> A plum-blossom cap it makes.

‡Lavender is the color of affinity, and so the wisteria is suggestive of his interest in Tamakazura.

'Lavender holds me and puts me in mind of things.
I mean, let them say what they will, to throw myself in.'

He generously divided his wisteria and put a sprig in Genji's cap.
Genji smiled broadly.

'Please hold yourself in abeyance beneath these flowers,
To judge if the plunge would have the proper effect.'

The prince accepted this suggestion, it seemed, and stayed on.
The morning concert was if anything livelier than the evening
concert had been.

Today there was to be a reading of the Prajñāpāramitā Sutra
commissioned by Empress Akikonomu. Many of the guests had
been given rooms in which to change to formal dress. Though
some had previous engagements and excused themselves, Genji's
prestige had removed any doubt that it would be a grand and solemn occasion. He led the assembly to Akikonomu's quarter at
noon.

Murasaki had prepared the floral offerings. She chose eight of
her prettiest little girls to deliver them, dressing four as birds and
four as butterflies. The birds brought cherry blossoms in silver
vases, the butterflies *yamabuki* in gold vases. In wonderfully rich
and full bloom, they completed a perfect picture. As the party
rowed out from the hillock to Akikonomu's end of the lake, a
breeze came up to scatter a few cherry petals. The skies were clear
and happy, and the little girls were charming in the delicate spring
haze. Akikonomu had declined Murasaki's offer of awnings and
had instead put out seats for the orchestra in one of the galleries
adjoining her main hall. The little girls came to the stairs with
their flowers. Incense bearers received them and set them out
before the holy images.

Yūgiri delivered this poem from Murasaki:

'Low in your grasses the cricket awaits the autumn
And views with scorn these silly butterflies.'

Akikonomu smiled, recognizing an answer to her poem about
the autumn leaves.

'No, Your Majesty, nothing surpasses that garden,' said one of
the women, still drunk with the joys of the day before.

The music for the dance of the Kalavinka bird rang forth to the singing of warblers, to which the waterfowl on the lake added their clucks and chirps, and it was with very great regret that the audience saw the dance come to an end. The butterflies seemed to fly higher than the birds as they disappeared behind a low fence over which poured a cascade of *yamabuki*. Akikonomu's assistant chamberlain asked that courtiers of appropriate rank distribute gifts: to the birds, white robes lined with red, and to the butterflies robes of pale russet lined with yellow. It would seem that Akikonomu had made careful preparations. Then came gifts for the musicians, white singlets and bolts of cloth. Yūgiri received a lady's ensemble, most conspicuously a lavender robe lined with blue.

This was Akikonomu's reply:

'I weep in my longing to follow your butterflies.
You put up fences of *yamabuki* between us.'

Are the grand ones of the realm consistently good at poetry? One is sometimes disappointed.

I had forgotten: Murasaki had had lavish gifts for her guests too. But I fear that the details would be tiresome. In any event, there were tasteful diversions morning and night to keep the least of the serving women happy, and there were these poetic exchanges.

Murasaki and Tamakazura sometimes wrote to each other, now that they had been introduced. It was too early perhaps to know whether Tamakazura was a comrade to turn to for help, but she did seem to be quietly good-natured and not the sort to cause trouble. People were on the whole favorably disposed towards her. She had many suitors by now, but it did not seem that Genji was ready for a decision. Perhaps not quite sure, indeed, that he wished to be consistent in the role of the good parent, he considered telling her father everything.

Yūgiri was permitted to approach her curtains and she favored him with direct replies. She was uncomfortable at the need to do so, but her women quite approved. He was always very solemn and proper. Tō no Chūjō's sons, who were his constant companions, were seen sighing and mooning about the house, and now and again they dropped hints of their interest. She was much disturbed, not because she disliked them but because they were victims of false appearances. It was not a matter she could discuss openly with Genji, however. He was charmed at the evidences, shy and girlish, that she considered him her guardian. He could not have said that she looked very much like her mother, but there was an indefinable resemblance in tone and manner. She was clearly the more intelligent of the two.

The Fourth Month came, and the change to bright summer clothes. Even the skies seemed to favor the occasion. Genji passed his spare time, of which he had a great deal, in music and the like. It was as he had expected: the flood of love letters was rising. Looking them over as he visited her apartments, he encouraged her to answer the more likely ones. These promptings had the effect of putting her on guard.

Prince Hotaru was already describing the torments of unrequited love.

Genji smiled. 'He was my favorite brother when we were boys. We kept nothing from each other. Or rather he kept one thing from me, his romantic life. He was very secretive about that. It is interesting and at the same time a little sad that he should still burn with such a youthful flame. You must answer. When a lady really matters to him, there is no one quite like him, I often think, for letting her know it. And he is most amusing company.'

He made his brother seem very attractive, but she looked away in embarrassment.

General Higekuro* was on the whole a very earnest and serious man, but he seemed bent on illustrating the truth that even the most superior of men, even Confucius himself, can stumble as he makes his way through the wilderness of love. Yet his letters were interesting.

Genji's attention was caught by a bit of azure Chinese paper gently but richly perfumed and folded into a tiny knot.

'You haven't even opened it,' he said, undoing the knot himself. The hand was a strong one in the modern style. This was the poem:

'You cannot know how deep my feelings are.
    Their colors are hidden, like waters among the rocks.'

'And whose feelings might they be?' he asked. Her answer was evasive.

He summoned Ukon. 'You must rate them carefully and have her answer the ones that seem deserving. The dissolute gallants of

---

*The crown prince's uncle, probably the most important statesman in the land after Genji and Tō no Chūjō.

our day are capable of anything, but sometimes they are not wholly to blame. My own experience has been that a lady can at the outset seem cold and unfeeling and unaware of the gentler things, and if she is of no importance I can call her impertinent and forget about her. Yet in idle exchanges about birds and flowers the lady who teases with silence can seem very interesting. If the man does forget, then of course part of the responsibility is hers; but a lady is not well advised to answer by return messenger a note that has not meant a great deal to the man who sent it, and profuse answers all saturated with sensibility can come to seem very tiresome. But Prince Hotaru and General Higekuro are grown men who know what they are doing. Your lady should not risk giving them the impression that she is unfeeling and unsympathetic. When it comes to lesser people, you must judge each on his own merits. Some may be serious and some may not. The genuine should be recognized.'

Tamakazura was very beautiful as she listened with averted gaze to this long discourse. Her dress was dignified and fashionable, a robe of pink lined with blue and a singlet that caught the colors of the season.* She had had a certain air of rustic stolidity, but, though traces remained, it was rapidly giving way to a subtler, more delicate sort of calm. No one could have found fault with her dress, and her beauty seemed to glow ever more brightly. Genji was beginning to think that she was too good to let go.

Ukon looked smilingly from the one to the other. He was much too youthful for the role of father. They were far more like husband and wife.

'I have not delivered letters from anyone else,' said Ukon. 'I did accept the few which you have seen. It seemed altogether too rude to turn them back. My lady has answered only the ones which you have specifically told her to answer, and those very reluctantly.'

'And whose is the one in the boyish little knot?' He was smiling. 'The hand is very good.'

'He was very insistent indeed. Captain Kashiwagi, the minister's son. He has known our Miruko for a rather long time and is making use of her services. I gather that there is no one else he can ask.'

---

*The white unohana, Deutizia crenata, was the flower of the Fourth Month.

'Charming. He may not be very important yet, but he is not to be dismissed. In some ways he is as highly thought of as the best of them, and he is a good deal more dependable than his brothers. He will eventually learn the truth, but for the moment it seems best to keep him in ignorance. Yes, he does write a very good hand.' He examined it admiringly. 'You may think it strange of me,' he said to Tamakazura, 'but I think you would have a difficult time if you were dropped down in that enormous family of your father's, all of them as good as strangers. The time will come, when you have found a place for yourself. Prince Hotaru is a bachelor at the moment, but he is, I fear, a promiscuous sort, and the gossips associate him with innumerable women, some of whom are called ladies-in-waiting and others of whom go by less dignified names. A lady of tolerance and very great skill might possibly steer her way through, but the first sign of jealousy would be fatal. It is all in all a situation calling for tact and caution.

'There is General Higekuro. He has been married for some years but it appears that he is not at all happy with his wife, and so he has turned to you. There are people who do not look favorably upon his suit. I can quite see the arguments, and am reluctant to hand down an opinion. You might not find it easy to tell your own father how you feel, but you are no longer a child and I see no reason why you should not presently come to your own conclusions. Perhaps you can think of me as a sort of substitute for your mother and we can tell ourselves that we have gone back to the old days. The last thing I would wish is to make you unhappy.' He looked at her solemnly.

She was extremely uncomfortable and would have preferred not to answer; but she was, as he said, no longer a child. 'I have been an orphan ever since I can remember,' she said quietly, 'and I fear that I have no thoughts in the matter.'

He could see her point. 'Well, as they say, a foster parent sometimes does better than a real parent.* You will find me an unusually devoted foster parent.' He preferred not to say what he was really thinking. Though he had dropped a hint or two, she had pretended not to notice. He sighed and went out.

He paused to admire a luxuriant new growth of Chinese bamboo swaying in the breeze.

*There is a popular saying to this effect.

'The bamboo so firmly rooted within our hedges
Will send out distant shoots to please its convenience?'

He raised the blind. She slipped away, but not before she had given him an answer:

'Why should the young bamboo at this late date
Go forth in search of roots it has left behind,

and make trouble for itself?'

He had to feel sorry for her.

She was by no means as much at home as her poem suggested. She longed to announce herself to her father. Yet she knew, from what she had read and seen, and she was seeing more, that the father from whom she had been separated from infancy was not likely to be as thoughtful as Genji had been. She held her tongue, increasingly aware of how difficult it would be to do otherwise.

She pleased him more and more. 'There is something singularly appealing about her,' he said to Murasaki. 'Her mother was a little too solemn and humorless. She is very quick and bright, and somehow a person immediately wants to be friends with her. I am very sure now that she will not be an embarrassment.'

Familiar with his inability to let well enough alone, she had guessed what was happening. 'It must be rather difficult for her not to have any secrets and to be so completely dependent on you.'

'And why should she not be dependent on me?'

She smiled. 'Can you think that I have forgotten all the sighs and pains your way of doing things produced in my own younger years?'

How quick she was! 'You find very odd and foolish things to worry about. Do you think she would permit anything of the sort?' He changed the subject; but she had surveyed the scene and come to her conclusions, and he had to admit that there were matters on his conscience.

He thought a great deal about Tamakazura. He often visited her and he was of service to her in many ways. One quiet evening after a rainfall, when the green of the maples and oaks was clean and rich, he looked up into a singularly affecting twilight sky and intoned a phrase from Po Chü-i: 'It is gentle, it is fresh.'* At such

*Po Chü-i, Collected Works, XIX, 'To the Minister of Transport.'

times it was more than anything the fresh glow of the new lady that he was thinking of. He slipped quietly away to her apartments. At her writing desk, she bowed courteously and turned shyly away, very beautiful indeed. Suddenly, gently, she was exactly like her mother. He wanted to weep.

'You must forgive me, but I cannot help it. When I first saw you I did not think you looked so very much like her, and yet there have been times when I could have mistaken you for her. Yūgiri is not in the least like me and so I had come to think that children do not on the whole resemble parents. And then I come on an instance like this.'

There was an orange in the fruit basket before her.

'Scented by orange blossoms long ago,
    The sleeve she wore is surely the sleeve you wear.*

'So many years have gone by, and through them all I have been unable to forget. Sometimes I feel as if I might be dreaming – and as if the dream were too much for me. You must not dismiss me for my rudeness.'

And he took her hand.

Nothing like this had happened to her before. But she must not lose her composure.

'The sleeve bears the scent of that blossom long ago .
    Then might not the fruit as quickly vanish away?'

He found this quiet confusion delightful. She sat with bowed head, unable to think what to make of his behavior and what to do next. The hand in his was soft, her skin smooth and delicate. He had made his confession because beauty and pain had suddenly come to seem very much alike. She was trembling.

'Am I so objectionable, then? I have worked hard to keep our secret, and you must help me. You have always been important to me. Now you are important in a new way. I wonder if there has ever been anything quite like it. I can think of no reason that you should prefer those others to me. I cannot imagine feelings deeper than my own, and I cannot bear the thought of passing you on to them and their frivolity.'

It all seemed rather beyond the call of paternal duty.

---

*The orange blossom was the flower of remembrance. See note**, page 228.

The night was a lovely one. The breeze was rustling the bamboo,* the wind had stopped, and a bright moon had come out. Her women had tactfully withdrawn. Though he saw a great deal of her, a better opportunity did not seem likely to present itself. From the momentum, perhaps, which his avowal had given him, he threw off his robe with practiced skill – it was a soft one that made no sound – and pulled her down beside him.

She was stunned. What would her women think? She was sobbing helplessly. Her father might treat her coldly, but at least he would protect her from such outrages.

Yes, of course: she had a right to weep. He turned to the work of calming her. 'So you reject me. I am shattered. Ladies must often depend on men who are nothing to them – it is the way of the world – and I should have thought that I was rather a lot to you, at least in terms of what I have done for you. This unfriendliness is not at all easy to accept. But enough. It will not happen again. My comfort will be in heaping restraint upon virtuous restraint.'

She was so like her mother that the resemblance was scarcely to be borne. He knew that this impetuous behavior did not become his age and eminence. Collecting himself, he withdrew before the lateness of the hour brought her women to mistaken conclusions.

'It will not be easy to forget that I have caused such revulsion. You may be very sure that you will not succeed in driving anyone else quite so thoroughly mad, and that my limitless, bottomless feelings for you will keep me from doing anything unseemly in the future. A quiet talk for old times' sake is all I ask. Can you not be persuaded to grant me that much?'

She was unable to reply.

'Such coldness, I would not have thought you capable of it. You do seem to hate me most extravagantly.' He sighed. 'We must let no one guess what has happened.' And he left.

She was no child, but among ladies her age she was remarkable in not having had the company of anyone of even modest experience. She could not imagine a worse outrage, or a stranger fate than hers had been. Her women thought she must be ill and could not think what to suggest.

'His Lordship has done so much for us,' whispered Hyōbu.

Another reference to the Po Chü-i poem in note, on page 448.

'Really more than we deserve. I doubt that even your honorable father could be kinder and more considerate.'

She wanted to reply that his kindness had taken a curious turn. Her lot was a very strange one!

A letter came from him early in the morning. She was still in bed and said that she was not feeling well; but with her women pressing ink and brush on her she reluctantly looked at it. Though it seemed very prim on white paper, the contents were rather different.

'You have cut so deeply that I shall never be whole again. And what, I wonder, will they all be thinking?

'Although I scarcely saw the tender grasses,
They look as if I had tied them all in knots.

'Which seems silly of them.'

Even here he somehow managed a suggestion of the avuncular. He was impossible! But her women would think it odd if she did not answer. She finally wrote this and no more on a sheet of thick, businesslike Michinoku paper:

'I have noted the contents of your letter, and must apologize for being too unwell to reply.'

He smiled. She had a certain flair.

One might have hoped that he would pursue the matter no further; but he had made his confession and was not 'the pine of Ota'* he once had been. He quite overwhelmed her with letters. She felt as if the trap were closing and closing, and finally she took to her bed, physically ill. There were very few who knew the truth, and outsiders as well as people who might have been called part of the family seemed to think him a model father. How they would all laugh when they learned the truth! And her real father, to whom she was nothing, would doubtless laugh more derisively than the rest. She had nowhere to turn.

Hotaru and Higekuro had sensed that Genji considered them acceptable candidates and were energetically pleading their cases; and one hears that the water among the rocks, similarly if obliquely encouraged, and still ignorant of the true state of affairs, was complaining at great length and very nervously.

*Though the poem quoted in early commentaries is otherwise unknown, the pine of Ota would seem to signify silent and patient yearning.

CHAPTER 25

Fireflies

Genji was famous and life was secure and peaceful. His ladies had in their several ways made their own lives and were happy. There was an exception, Tamakazura, who faced a new crisis and was wondering what to do next. She was not as genuinely frightened of him, of course, as she had been of the Higo man; but since few people could possibly know what had happened, she must keep her disquiet to herself, and her growing sense of isolation. Old enough to know a little of the world, she saw more than ever what a handicap it was not to have a mother.

Genji had made his confession. The result was that his longing increased. Fearful of being overheard, however, he found the subject a difficult one to approach, even gingerly. His visits were very frequent. Choosing times when she was likely to have few people with her, he would hint at his feelings, and she would be in an agony of embarrassment. Since she was not in a position to turn him away, she could only pretend that she did not know what was happening.

She was of a cheerful, affectionate disposition. Though she was also of a cautious and conservative nature, the chief impression she gave was of a delicate, winsome girlishness.

Prince Hotaru continued to pay energetic court. His labors had not yet gone on for very long when he had the early-summer rains to be resentful of.

'Admit me a little nearer, please,' he wrote. 'I will feel better if I can unburden myself of even part of what is in my heart.'

Genji saw the letter. 'Princes,' he said, 'should be listened to. Aloofness is not permitted. You must let him have an occasional answer.' He even told her what to say.

But he only made things worse. She said that she was not feeling well and did not answer.

There were few really highborn women in her household. She did have a cousin called Saishō, daughter of a maternal uncle who had held a seat on the council. Genji had heard that she had been having a difficult time since her father's death, and had put her in Tamakazura's service. She wrote a passable hand and seemed generally capable and well informed. He assigned her the task of composing replies to gentlemen who deserved them. It was she whom he summoned today. One may imagine that he was curious to see all of his brother's letters. Tamakazura herself had been reading them with more interest since that shocking evening. It must not be thought that she had fallen in love with Hotaru, but he did seem to offer a way of evading Genji. She was learning rapidly.

Unaware that Genji himself was eagerly awaiting him, Hotaru was delighted at what seemed a positive invitation and quietly came calling. A seat was put out for him near the corner doors, where she received him with only a curtain between them. Genji had given close attention to the incense, which was mysterious and seductive — rather more attention, indeed, than a guardian might have felt that his duty demanded. One had to admire the results, whatever the motive. Saishō was at a loss to reply to Hotaru's overtures. Genji pinched her gently to remind her that her mistress must not behave like an unfeeling lump, and only added to her discomfiture. The dark nights of the new moon were over and there was a bland quarter-moon in the cloudy sky. Calm and dignified, the prince was very handsome indeed. Genji's own very special perfume mixed with the incense that drifted through the room as people moved about. More interesting than he would have expected, thought the prince. In calm control of himself all the while (and in pleasant contrast to certain other people), he made his avowals.

Tamakazura withdrew to the east penthouse and lay down. Genji followed Saishō as she brought a new message from the prince.

'You are not being kind,' he said to Tamakazura. 'A person should behave as the occasion demands. You are unnecessarily coy. You should not be sending a messenger back and forth over such distances. If you do not wish him to hear your voice, very well, but at least you should move a little nearer.'

She was in despair. She suspected that his real motive was to impose himself upon her, and each course open to her seemed worse than all the others. She slipped away and lay down at a curtain between the penthouse and the main hall.

She was sunk in thought, unable to answer the prince's outpourings. Genji came up beside her and lifted the curtain back over its frame. There was a flash of light. She looked up startled.

Had someone lighted a torch? No – Genji had earlier in the evening put a large number of fireflies in a cloth bag.* Now, letting no
one guess what he was about, he released them. Tamakazura
brought a fan to her face. Her profile was very beautiful.

Genji had worked everything out very carefully. Prince Hotaru†
was certain to look in her direction. He was making a show of
passion, Genji suspected, because he thought her Genji's daughter,
and not because he had guessed what a beauty she was. Now he
would see, and be genuinely excited. Genji would not have gone
to such trouble if she had in fact been his daughter. It all seems
rather perverse of him.

He slipped out through another door and returned to his part
of the house.

The prince had guessed where the lady would be. Now he
sensed that she was perhaps a little nearer. His heart racing, he
looked through an opening in the rich gossamer curtains. Suddenly, some six or seven feet away, there was a flash of light – and
such beauty as was revealed in it! Darkness was quickly restored,
but the brief glimpse he had had was the sort of thing that makes
for romance. The figure at the curtains may have been indistinct
but it most certainly was slim and tall and graceful. Genji would
not have been disappointed at the interest it had inspired.

'You put out this silent fire to no avail.
Can you extinguish the fire in the human heart?

'I hope I make myself understood.'
Speed was the important thing in answering such a poem.

'The firefly but burns and makes no comment.
Silence sometimes tells of deeper thoughts.'

It was a brisk sort of reply, and having made it, she was gone.
His lament about this chilly treatment was rather wordy, but he
would not have wished to overdo it by staying the night. It was
late when he braved the dripping eaves (and tears as well) and
went out. I have no doubt that a cuckoo sent him on his way, but
did not trouble myself to learn all the details.

So handsome, so poised, said the women – so very much like

*Kata, perhaps a miscopying for kami, 'paper.'
†'The Firefly Prince.' He is so called from this chapter.

Genji. Not knowing their lady's secret, they were filled with gratitude for Genji's attentions. Why, not even her mother could have
done more for her.

Unwelcome attentions, the lady was thinking. If she had been
recognized by her father and her situation were nearer the ordinary, then they need not be entirely unwelcome. She had had
wretched luck, and she lived in dread of rumors.

Genji too was determined to avoid rumors. Yet he continued
to have his ways. Can one really be sure, for instance, that he no
longer had designs upon Akikonomu? There was something different about his manner when he was with her, something especially charming and seductive. But she was beyond the reach of
direct overtures. Tamakazura was a modern sort of girl, and
approachable. Sometimes dangerously near losing control of himself, he would do things which, had they been noticed, might have
aroused suspicions. It was a difficult and complicated relationship
indeed, and he must be given credit for the fact that he held back
from the final line.

On the fifth day of the Fifth Month, the Day of the Iris, he
stopped by her apartments on his way to the equestrian grounds.

'What happened? Did he stay late? You must be careful with
him. He is not to be trusted – not that there are very many men
these days a girl really can trust.'

He praised his brother and blamed him. He seemed very young
and was very handsome as he offered this word of caution. As for
his clothes, the singlets and the robe thrown casually over them
glowed in such rich and pleasing colors that they seemed to brim
over and seek more space. One wondered whether a supernatural
hand might not have had some part in the dyeing. The colors
themselves were familiar enough, but the woven patterns were as
if everything had pointed to this day of flowers.* The lady was sure
she would have been quite intoxicated with the perfumes burned
into them had she not had these worries.

A letter came from Prince Hotaru, on white tissue paper in a
fine, aristocratic hand. At first sight the contents seemed very
interesting, but somehow they became ordinary upon repeating.

Ayame means both 'iris' (more properly, 'sweet flag') and 'patterns.' The pun is
repeated several times in the following passage, as for instance in Hotaru's poem, in
which *ayame* suggests something like 'discernment.'

'Even today the iris is neglected.
Its roots, my cries, are lost among the waters.'*

It was attached to an iris root certain to be much talked of.
'You must get off an answer,' said Genji, preparing to leave.
Her women argued that she had no choice.

Whatever she may have meant to suggest by it, this was her answer, a simple one set down in a faint, delicate hand:

'It might have flourished better in concealment,
The iris root washed purposelessly away.

'Exposure seems rather unwise.'

A connoisseur, the prince thought that the hand could just possibly be improved.

Gifts of medicinal herbs in decorative packets† came from this and that well-wisher. The festive brightness did much to make her forget earlier unhappiness and hope that she might come uninjured through this new trial.

Genji also called on the lady of the orange blossoms, in the east wing of the same northeast quarter.

'Yūgiri is to bring some friends around after the archery meet. I should imagine it will still be daylight. I have never understood why our efforts to avoid attention always end in failure. The princes and the rest of them hear that something is up and come around to see, and so we have a much noisier party than we had planned on. We must in any event be ready.'

The equestrian stands were very near the galleries of the northeast quarter.

'Come, girls,' he said. 'Open all the doors and enjoy yourselves. Have a look at all the handsome officers. The ones in the Left Guards are especially handsome, several cuts above the common run at court.'

They had a delightful time. Tamakazura joined them. There were fresh green blinds all along the galleries, and new curtains too, the rich colors at the hems fading, as is the fashion these days, to white above. Women and little girls clustered at all the doors. The girls in green‡ robes and trains of purple gossamer seemed to

*There is a pun on ne, 'root' and 'cry' or 'sob.'
†Conventional on the Day of the Iris.
‡There are doubts about several of the colors.

be from Tamakazura's wing. There were four of them, all very pretty and well behaved. Her women too were in festive dress, trains blending from lavender at the waist down to deeper purple and formal jackets the color of carnation shoots.

The lady of the orange blossoms had her little girls in very dignified dress, singlets of deep pink and trains of red lined with green. It was very amusing to see all the women striking new poses as they draped their finery about them. The young courtiers noticed and seemed to be striking poses of their own.

Genji went out to the stands toward midafternoon. All the princes were there, as he had predicted. The equestrian archery was freer and more varied than at the palace. The officers of the guard joined in, and everyone sat entranced through the afternoon. The women may not have understood all the finer points, but the uniforms of even the common guardsmen were magnificent and the horsemanship was complicated and exciting. The grounds were very wide, fronting also on Murasaki's southeast quarter, where young women were watching. There was music and dancing, Chinese polo music and the Korean dragon dance.* As night came on, the triumphal music rang out high and wild. The guardsmen were richly rewarded according to their several ranks. It was very late when the assembly dispersed.

Genji spent the night with the lady of the orange blossoms.

'Prince Hotaru is a man of parts,' he said. 'He may not be the handsomest man in the world, but everything about him tells of breeding and cultivation, and he is excellent company. Did you chance to catch a glimpse of him? He has many good points, as I have said, but it may be that in the final analysis there is something just a bit lacking in him.'

'He is younger than you but I thought he looked older. I have heard that he never misses a chance to come calling. I saw him once long ago at court and had not really seen him again until today. He has improved. Prince Sochi† is a very fine gentleman too, but somehow he does not quite look like royalty.'

Genji smiled. Her judgment was quick and sure. But he kept his own counsel. This sort of open appraisal of people still living was not to his taste. He could not understand why the world had

---

*Tagyūraku and Rakuson.

†A brother of Genji and Prince Hotaru who does not appear elsewhere.

such a high opinion of Higekuro and would not have been pleased to receive him into the family, but these views too he kept to himself.

They were good friends, he and she, and no more, and they went to separate beds. Genji wondered when they had begun to drift apart. She never let fall the tiniest hint of jealousy. It had been the usual thing over the years for reports of such festivities to come to her through others. The events of the day seemed to bring new recognition to her and her household.

She said softly:

'You honor the iris on the bank to which
No pony comes to taste of withered grasses?'*

One could scarcely have called it a masterpiece, but he was touched.

'This pony, like the love grebe, wants a comrade.
Shall it forget the iris on the bank?'

Nor was his a very exciting poem.

'I do not see as much of you as I would wish, but I do enjoy you.' There was a certain irony in the words, from his bed to hers, but also affection. She was a dear, gentle lady. She had let him have her bed and spread quilts for herself outside the curtains. She had in the course of time come to accept such arrangements as proper, and he did not suggest changing them.

The rains of early summer continued without a break, even gloomier than in most years. The ladies at Rokujō amused themselves with illustrated romances. The Akashi lady, a talented painter, sent pictures to her daughter.

Tamakazura was the most avid reader of all. She quite lost herself in pictures and stories and would spend whole days with them. Several of her young women were well informed in literary matters. She came upon all sorts of interesting and shocking incidents (she could not be sure whether they were true or not), but she found little that resembled her own unfortunate career. There was *The Tale of Sumiyoshi*, popular in its day, of course, and still well thought of. She compared the plight of the heroine, within a hair-

See note, page 152.

breadth of being taken by the chief accountant,* with her own escape from the Higo person.

Genji could not help noticing the clutter of pictures and manuscripts. 'What a nuisance this all is,' he said one day. 'Women seem to have been born to be cheerfully deceived. They know perfectly well that in all these old stories there is scarcely a shred of truth, and yet they are captured and made sport of by the whole range of trivialities and go on scribbling them down, quite unaware that in these warm rains their hair is all dank and knotted.'

He smiled. 'What would we do if there were not these old romances to relieve our boredom? But amid all the fabrication I must admit that I do find real emotions and plausible chains of events. We can be quite aware of the frivolity and the idleness and still be moved. We have to feel a little sorry for a charming princess in the depths of gloom. Sometimes a series of absurd and grotesque incidents which we know to be quite improbable holds our interest, and afterwards we must blush that it was so. Yet even then we can see what it was that held us. Sometimes I stand and listen to the stories they read to my daughter, and I think to myself that there certainly are good talkers in the world. I think that these yarns must come from people much practiced in lying. But perhaps that is not the whole of the story?'

She pushed away her inkstone. 'I can see that that would be the view of someone much given to lying himself. For my part, I am convinced of their truthfulness.'

He laughed. 'I have been rude and unfair to your romances, haven't I. They have set down and preserved happenings from the age of the gods to our own. *The Chronicles of Japan* and the rest are a mere fragment of the whole truth. It is your romances that fill in the details.

'We are not told of things that happened to specific people exactly as they happened; but the beginning is when there are good things and bad things, things that happen in this life which one never tires of seeing and hearing about, things which one cannot bear not to tell of and must pass on for all generations. If the storyteller wishes to speak well, then he chooses the good things; and if he wishes to hold the reader's attention he chooses bad things, extraordinarily bad things. Good things and bad things alike, they are things of this world and no other.

*There is no such incident in the version which survives today.

'Writers in other countries approach the matter differently. Old stories in our own are different from new. There are differences in the degree of seriousness. But to dismiss them as lies is itself to depart from the truth. Even in the writ which the Buddha drew from his noble heart are parables, devices for pointing obliquely at the truth. To the ignorant they may seem to operate at cross purposes. The Greater Vehicle is full of them, but the general burden is always the same. The difference between enlightenment and confusion is of about the same order as the difference between the good and the bad in a romance. If one takes the generous view, then nothing is empty and useless.'

He now seemed bent on establishing the uses of fiction.

'But tell me: is there in any of your old stories a proper, upright fool like myself?' He came closer. 'I doubt that even among the most unworldly of your heroines there is one who manages to be as distant and unnoticing as you are. Suppose the two of us set down our story and give the world a really interesting one.'

'I think it very likely that the world will take notice of our curious story even if we do not go to the trouble.' She hid her face in her sleeves.

'Our curious story? Yes, incomparably curious, I should think.' Smiling and playful, he pressed nearer.

'Beside myself, I search through all the books,
And come upon no daughter so unfilial.

'You are breaking one of the commandments.'

He stroked her hair as he spoke, but she refused to look up. Presently, however, she managed a reply:

'So too it is with me. I too have searched,
And found no cases quite so unparental.'

Somewhat chastened, he pursued the matter no further. Yet one worried. What was to become of her?

Murasaki too had become addicted to romances. Her excuse was that Genji's little daughter insisted on being read to.

'Just see what a fine one this is,' she said, showing Genji an illustration for *The Tale of Kumano*.* The young girl in tranquil and confident slumber made her think of her own younger self. 'How

*Or *The Tale of Komano*. It does not survive.

precocious even very little children seem to have been. I suppose I might have set myself up as a specimen of the slow, plodding variety. I would have won that competition easily.'

Genji might have been the hero of some rather more eccentric stories.

'You must not read love stories to her. I doubt that clandestine affairs would arouse her unduly, but we would not want her to think them commonplace.'

What would Tamakazura have made of the difference between his remarks to her and these remarks to Murasaki?

'I would not of course offer the wanton ones as a model,' replied Murasaki, 'but I would have doubts too about the other sort. Lady Atemiya in *The Tale of the Hollow Tree*, for instance. She is always very brisk and efficient and in control of things, and she never makes mistakes; but there is something unwomanly about her cool manner and clipped speech.'

'I should imagine that it is in real life as in fiction. We are all human and we all have our ways. It is not easy to be unerringly right. Proper, well-educated parents go to great trouble over a daughter's education and tell themselves that they have done well if something quiet and demure emerges. It seems a pity when defects come to light one after another and people start asking what her good parents can possibly have been up to. Yet the rewards are very great when a girl's manner and behavior seem just right for her station. Even then empty praise is not satisfying. One knows that the girl is not perfect and looks at her more critically than before. I would not wish my own daughter to be praised by people who have no standards.'

He was genuinely concerned that she acquit herself well in the tests that lay before her.

Wicked stepmothers are of course standard fare for the romancers, and he did not want them poisoning relations between Murasaki and the child. He spent a great deal of time selecting romances he thought suitable, and ordered them copied and illustrated.

He kept Yūgiri from Murasaki but encouraged him to be friends with the girl. While he himself was alive it might not matter a great deal one way or the other, but if they were good friends now their affection was likely to deepen after he was dead. He permitted Yūgiri inside the front room, though the inner rooms were forbidden. Having so few children, he had ample time for Yūgiri, who was a sober lad and seemed completely dependable. The girl was still devoted to her dolls. They made Yūgiri think of his own childhood games with Kumoinokari. Sometimes as he waited in earnest attendance upon a doll princess, tears would come to his eyes. He sometimes joked with ladies of a certain standing, but he was careful not to lead them too far. Even those who might have expected more had to make do with a joke. The thing that really concerned him and never left his mind was getting back at the nurse who had sneered at his blue sleeves. He was fairly sure that he could better Tō no Chūjō at a contest of wills, but sometimes the old anger and chagrin came back and he wanted more. He wanted to make Tō no Chūjō genuinely regretful for what he had done. He revealed these feelings only to Kumoinokari. Before everyone else he was a model of cool composure.

Her brothers sometimes thought him rather conceited. Kashiwagi, the oldest, was greatly interested these days in Tamakazura. Lacking a better intermediary, he came sighing to Yūgiri. The friendship of the first generation was being repeated in the second.

'One does not undertake to plead another's case,' replied Yūgiri quietly.

Tō no Chūjō was a very important man, and his many sons were embarked upon promising careers, as became their several pedigrees and inclinations. He had only two daughters. The one who had gone to court had been a disappointment. The prospect of having the other do poorly did not of course please him. He had not forgotten the lady of the evening faces. He often spoke of her, and he went on wondering what had happened to the child. The lady had put him off guard with her gentleness and appearance of helplessness, and so he had lost a daughter. A man must not under any circumstances let a woman out of his sight. Suppose the girl were to turn up now in some outlandish guise and stridently announce herself as his daughter – well, he would take her in.

'Do not dismiss anyone who says she is my daughter,' he told his sons. 'In my younger days I did many things I ought not to have done. There was a lady of not entirely contemptible birth who lost patience with me over some triviality or other, and so I lost a daughter, and I have so few.'

There had been a time when he had almost forgotten the lady. Then he began to see what great things his friends were doing for their daughters, and to feel resentful that he had been granted so few.

One night he had a dream. He called in a famous seer and asked for an interpretation.

'Might it be that you will hear of a long-lost child who has been taken in by someone else?'

This was very puzzling. He could think of no daughters whom he had put out for adoption. He began to wonder about Tamakazura.

CHAPTER 26

Wild Carnations

It was a very hot day. Genji was cooling himself in the angling pavilion of the southeast quarter. Yūgiri and numerous friends of the middle court ranks were with him. They had offered to roast trout which had been brought from the Katsura and goby from nearer streams.* Several of Tō no Chūjō's sons, his constant companions, were among them.

'You came at a very good time,' said Genji. 'I was feeling bored and sleepy.' Wine and ice water and other refreshments were brought, and it had become a very lively picnic. Though a pleasant wind was blowing, the air was heavy and the sun seemed to move more slowly than usual through a cloudless sky. The shrilling of cicadas was intense, almost oppressive. 'It does not do us much good to be on top of the water. I am going to be rude.' He lay down. 'Not even music helps in weather like this, and yet it is not very satisfying to go through a whole day doing nothing at all. You youngsters must have a hard time of it in your offices. Here at least you can undo yourselves and relax and bring me up on all the amusing gossip. I am old and out of things, and I must look to you to keep me informed and drive away the yawns.'

It seemed a heavy responsibility. Most of them had withdrawn to the verandas, where it was cooler.

He turned to Kōbai, Tō no Chūjō's second son. 'Where did I hear – I can't think – that your father had found a stray daughter and is all in a ferment over her? Is it true?'

'Oh, I don't think it's a very interesting piece of news, really. There was a woman, it is true, who got wind of a dream Father had this spring and made it known that she had certain relevant matters to bring to his attention. My brother Kashiwagi went to see her and asked what evidence she had to support her claims. I am afraid I have not kept myself very well informed of all the details, though it does seem to be true, as you suggest, sir, that rather a big thing is made of it all. I do not think myself that it brings great honor to Father or to the family.'

Ayu and *haze*.

So it was true. 'Very greedy of him, going out after stray geese when the flock is so large already. My own is so small that I would be delighted to learn of strays. Perhaps my humble status discourages people from coming to me with similar claims. I have detected none, in any event. But isn't it like your father?' He smiled. 'He has stirred the waters rather a lot in his time, and one expects to find a muddy moon reflected from them.'

Yūgiri, who had heard the whole story, was smiling. Tō no Chūjō's sons seemed to be in some discomfort.

'How about it, my young lord?' said Genji to Yūgiri. 'Suppose you go pick up this fallen leaf. It would be better to have something in your bonnet than to be known as a complete failure. After all, she is one of us.'

Genji and Tō no Chūjō had always maintained an appearance of close friendship, but their differences were of long standing. Genji did not at all like the way Yūgiri had been treated, and would have been pleased to have Kōbai take home reports which would annoy his father. Genji was sure that Tamakazura would be received courteously and properly honored if Tō no Chūjō were to learn of her presence. He was a strong, decisive man, very definite in his opinions and inclined to be more emphatic than most in praising good and castigating evil. He would be severe in his judgment of Genji, but he would not turn away the daughter who suddenly presented herself to him. He was certain to treat her with the most scrupulous ceremony.

A cool breeze informed them that evening was finally at hand. The young men were reluctant to leave.

'Well, let us all have a good time. I am at an age when I fear I am not welcome in such company.' Genji started for Tamakazura's northeast quarter.

They all followed, dressed very much alike and almost indistinguishable one from another in the twilight.

'Suppose you come out toward the veranda just a little,' he said, going in and addressing her in intimate tones not likely to be overheard. 'Kōbai and several of his brothers have come with me. They are all mad for introductions, and our staid and opprobrious Yūgiri does nothing at all for them. Even a very undistinguished young lady, you know, can expect suitors while she is still under her father's wing. Somehow everything in this house gets wildly blown up and exaggerated. We have not had young ladies to arouse their interest, and in my boredom I have thought it might be fun to see you at work on them. You have not disappointed me.'

He had avoided showy plantings in this northeast quarter, but the choicest of wild carnations caught the evening light beneath low, elegant Chinese and Japanese fences. The young men seemed very eager to step down and pluck them (and the flower within as well).

'They are knowledgeable, well-bred young men, all of them. They of course have their various ways. That is as it should be, and I find nothing to take serious exception to. Kashiwagi is perhaps the most serious of them. Indeed he sometimes makes me feel a little uncomfortable. Has he written to you? You must not be unkind to him.'

Yūgiri stood out even in so fine an assembly.

'I cannot think why my friend the minister dislikes him. Does he have such a high regard for his own proud name that he looks down on us offshoots of the royal family?'

' "Come and be my bridegroom,"* everyone is saying. Or so I am told.'

'I do not ask that he be invited in for a banquet, only that he be admitted inside. A clean and innocent attachment is being frustrated, and that I do not like. Is it that the boy does not yet amount to much? That is a problem which he can safely leave to me.'

These matters seemed to complicate the girl's life yet further. When, she wondered, would she be permitted to meet her own father?

There was no moon. Lamps were brought in.

'Not so close, please. Why don't we have flares down in the garden?'

Taking out a Japanese koto and finding it satisfactorily tuned, he plucked out a few notes. The tone was splendid.

'If you have disappointed me at all, it has been because you have shown so little interest in music. Might I recommend the Japanese koto, for instance? It is a surprisingly bright and up-to-date sort of instrument when you play it with no nonsense and let it join the crickets in the cool moonlight of an autumn evening.

See note, page 45. Tamakazura refers to the staid first half of the Saibara, and leaves the ribald second half to Genji.

For some reason it does not always seem entirely at home in a formal concert, but it goes very well with other instruments even so. A crude domestic product if you will – but just see how cleverly it is put together. It is for ladies who do not set much stock by foreign things. I warmly recommend it if you think you might want to begin taking music lessons. You must always look for new ways to make it go with other instruments. The basic techniques may seem simple, and indeed they are; but to put them to really good use is another matter. There is no better hand in the whole court than your father, the minister. He has only to give it the slightest muted pluck* and there they all are, the grand, high tones of all the imported kotos.'

Already somewhat familiar with the instrument, she was eager to hear more. 'Do you suppose we might have a concert here sometime and ask him to join us? It is the instrument all the country people play, and I had thought that there was not a great deal to it.' She did seem to be most eager. 'You are right, of course. It is very different in the hands of someone who knows what he is doing.'

'It is also called the eastern koto, you know, and that brings up thoughts of the wild frontier. But when there is a concert at the palace the Japanese koto is always the first instrument His Majesty sends for. I do not know much about other countries, but in our own it must be called the grandfather of all the instruments, and you could not possibly find a better teacher than the minister. We see him here from time to time, but the trouble is that he is rather shy about playing. The really good ones always are. But you will have your chance to hear him one of these days.'

He played a few strains, the tone richer and cleaner than anything she had heard before. She wondered how her father could possibly be a better musician, and she longed more than ever to meet him, and to see him thus at home with his koto.

'Soft as the reed pillow,' he sang, very gently, 'the waves of the river Nuki.'† He smiled as he came to the passage about the uncooperative parent. There was wonderful delicacy in the muted chord‡ with which he brought it to a conclusion.

Sugagaki. There are several theories as to the meaning.

†See note†, page 163.

‡*Sugagaki* once more.

'Now we must hear from you. In artistic matters modesty is not a virtue. I have, it is true, heard of ladies who keep "I Long for Him"* to themselves, but in other matters openness never seems brazen.'

But she had had lessons in the remote countryside from an old woman who said, though she gave no details, that she had been born in the capital and had royal blood in her veins. Such credentials did not inspire confidence, and the girl refused to touch the instrument.

'No, let me hear just a little more, and perhaps I will be clever enough to imitate it.' And so the Japanese koto brought her close to him when other devices had failed. 'Is it the wind that accounts for that extraordinary tone?' He thought her quite ravishing as she sat in the dim torchlight as if seeking an answer to her question.

'An extraordinary wind,' he said, smiling, 'demonstrating that you are not after all deaf.'

He pushed the koto towards her, but he had given her reason to be out of sorts; and besides, her women were listening.

'And what of our young men? They did not pay proper attention to our wild carnations.' He was in a meditative mood. 'I really must show this garden to my friend the minister sometime. Life is uncertain, of course. We are gone tomorrow. And yet all those years since he and I talked of your mother, and you yourself were our wild carnation – somehow an eternity can seem like nothing at all.

'Were he to see its gentle hues unchanging,
    Would he not come to the hedge of the wild carnation?

'And that would complicate matters, and so I have kept you in a cocoon. I fear you have found it constraining.'

Brushing away a tear, she replied:

'Who would come to seek the wild carnation
    That grew at such a rough and rustic hedge?'

The note of self-effacement made her seem very young and gentle.

---

*Sōfuren, a Chinese melody which seems to have been originally not about love but about lotuses. Ren, Chinese lien, signifies either.

'If he does not come,'* whispered Genji, by no means sure how much longer he could control himself.

Uncomfortable about the frequency of his visits, he took to writing letters, which came in a steady stream. She was never out of his thoughts. Why, he asked himself, did he become so engrossed in matters which should not have concerned him? He knew that to let his feelings have their way would be to give himself a name for utter frivolity, and of course to do the girl great harm. He knew further that though he loved her very much she would never be Murasaki's rival. What sort of life would she have as one of the lesser ladies? He might be the grandest statesman in the land, but a lesser lady was still a lesser lady. She would be better off as the principal wife of some middling councillor. Should he then let Hotaru or Higekuro have her? He might succeed in resigning himself to such an arrangement. He would not be happy, but – or so he sometimes thought – it might perhaps after all be best. And then he would see her, and change his mind.

He still visited her frequently. The Japanese koto was his excuse. Embarrassed at first to find herself his pupil, she presently began to feel that he did not mean to take advantage of her, and came to accept the visits as normal and proper. Rather prim and very careful to avoid any suggestion of coquetry, she pleased him more and more. Matters could not be left as they were.

Suppose then that he were to find her a bridegroom but keep her here at Rokujō, where he could continue to see her, clandestinely, of course. She knew nothing of men, and his overtures disturbed her. He had to feel sorry for her; but once she was better informed he would make his way past the most unblinking of gatekeepers and have his way with her. These thoughts may not seem entirely praiseworthy. The longing and fretfulness increased and invited trouble – it was a very difficult relationship indeed.

Tō no Chūjō had learned that his new daughter had not really been accepted as one of the family and that people thought her rather funny. Kōbai remarked in the course of a conversation that Genji had inquired about her.

'I have indeed brought home a daughter whom I allowed to grow up in the hills.† I am not surprised that Genji asked about

---

*A poetic reference, apparently. None has been identified.

†It may seem odd that Tō no Chūjō is telling the youth about his own half sister, but half siblings could be complete strangers to each other.

her. He seldom has a bad word for anyone, but for me and my family he has a few bad words on every occasion. We are much honored.'

'He has a new lady at Rokujō, you know, and everything suggests that she is a beauty, the next thing to perfection. Prince Hotaru seems very much interested in her. The gossip suggests that he has every right to be.'

'Oh, yes, I am sure everyone is interested in her. But that is only because she is Genji's daughter. So it goes. I doubt that she is so very special, really. If she were he would have found her long before this. Yes, the great Genji, not a fleck of dust on his name and fame, much too good, everyone says, for our degenerate age. It seems a pity that his favorite lady, a perfect jewel, has no children. He must feel rather badly served. He seems to have ambitious plans for the little Akashi girl, even though her mother leaves something to be desired. Well, what will be will be. As for the new lady, a suspicious and cynical person might wonder whether she is in fact his daughter. He is a fine man but he has his little eccentricities, and it might all be sham and playacting.'

'I wonder what plans he has for the new lady, and how Prince Hotaru might figure in them. They have been the closest of brothers, and I should think they would get on very well as father and son.'

Tō no Chūjō continued to be unhappy with Kumoinokari. He would have liked to make her the belle of the day, the rage of the court. Infatuated with a minor courtier like Yūgiri, she was not being cooperative. Perhaps if Genji were to step in with repeated and earnest supplications Tō no Chūjō could graciously give his consent. Yūgiri's coolness and imperturbability did not help matters.

Tō no Chūjō went unannounced to Kumoinokari's rooms. She was napping, very small and pretty, and managing to look cool in spite of the heat. Her skin was a soft glow through a gossamer singlet. One hand still held a fan most prettily, and her head was cradled on an arm. The hair that flowed behind her in natural tresses was neither too long nor troublesomely thick, and beautifully combed. Her women too were asleep, behind blinds and screens. They were not easily awakened. She looked innocently up at him as he tapped with his fan, her eyes round and startled, and the flush that came over her face delighted him.

'So here you are sleeping, and I have told you I can't think how many times that constant vigilance is one of the marks of a lady. There is not a vigilant eye in this room. You are all looking very abandoned indeed. Not of course that I would want you to storm and glower. Vigilance is not to be recommended when it merely puts people off.

'They tell me that Genji is going to enormous trouble with the girl he means to send to court. He seems to have embarked upon a liberal and expansive program, giving her something of everything and not letting her specialize, seeing that she is ignorant of nothing and not asking that she be an expert. A very liberal sort of education. Yet we do all have our preferences, and no doubt hers will emerge as she gets older. I am eagerly awaiting the day when she appears at court.

'You have not made things easy for me, my dear, but do at least try to keep people from laughing at us. I have given very careful attention to reports about a number of young gentlemen. It is still too early for you to accept the tender pleas of any one of them. You must leave that to me.'

All the while he was lecturing he was thinking how pretty she was.

She was very sorry for the trouble she had caused, and would not for the world have wanted to seem unapologetic. She could not look at him. Her grandmother, Princess Omiya, complained of neglect, but it was just such paternal reproaches as these that made it difficult for her to visit the old lady.

Tō no Chūjō had been very happy at finding a daughter off in Omi, and he would not seem his usual sensible self if now that she had become a public joke he were to send her back again. Nor was the alternative very pleasing, to keep her here and make it seem that he had serious plans for her. Perhaps his daughter at court could use her, and everyone could have a good laugh over her. She was not so impossibly ill favored that she must be kept out of sight.

'I will make you a gift of her,' he said to the other daughter. 'If she seems too completely silly, you can tell your older women that they have someone to educate, and maybe you can keep the younger ones from laughing unmercifully. I must admit that she does at times seem a little flighty.'

'Oh, surely she is not as bad as all that. Kashiwagi led us to have high hopes for her, and it may be that she has not entirely lived up

to them.' She was rather splendid. 'Don't you suppose it embarrasses the poor thing to be the center of so much attention?'

Though not the reigning beauty of the day, this other daughter
had elegance and dignity and a pleasantly gentle manner. She was
like a plum blossom opening at dawn. Her father loved the way
she had of making it seem that a great deal was being left unsaid.

'Kashiwagi is young and naïve, and he halted his investigations
before he had come upon the obvious.' He was not being very
kind to his new daughter.

He thought he would look in on her, since her room was not
far away. He found her, blinds raised high, at a contest of backgammon.

Her hands at her forehead in earnest supplication, she was rattling off her prayer at a most wondrous speed. 'Give her a deuce,
give her a deuce.' Over and over again. 'Give her a deuce, give
her a deuce.'

This really was rather dreadful. Motioning his attendants to
silence, he slipped behind a hinged door from which the view was
unobstructed through sliding doors beyond.

'Revenge, revenge,' shrieked Gosechi, the clever young
woman who was her opponent. Gosechi was not to be outdone in
earnestness or shrillness. She shook and shook the dicebox and was
not quick to make her throw.

If either of them had anything at all in her empty mind she was
not showing it. The Omi daughter was small* and pretty and had
beautiful hair, and could by no means have been described as an
unrelieved scandal – though a narrow forehead and a too exuberant and indeed a torrential way of speaking canceled out her good
points. No beauty, certainly, and yet it was impossible not to recognize immediately whose daughter she was. It made Tō no
Chūjō uncomfortable to realize that he might have been looking
at his own mirror image.

'Are you feeling quite at home?' he presently asked. 'Are they
being good to you? I am very busy, I fear, and do not see you as
often as I would wish.'

'Just being here is enough. No complaints, not a one.' The
speed was undiminished. 'All those years I just wanted to see your

*Hijijika. It appears only here, and the meaning can only be hazarded.

face. That's all I wanted, all those years. But I still get the bad throws. I don't get to look at you very much.'

'I am genuinely sorry. I rather keep to myself, and I had hoped that we would have a great deal of time for each other. But things have not so arranged themselves. You will have seen that ordinary ladies rather tend to get lost in the crowd, and it does not matter very much how they behave. That is very nice for them. But it sometimes happens that a lady comes from such a good family that people are always pointing her out, and it sometimes happens that she does not do full honor to the family name, and –'

The full significance of the final conjunction was lost upon the lady. 'Oh no oh no. I don't care if I don't stand out in a crowd. I just tell myself family makes trouble and keep out of sight. Give me the chamber pot to empty and I'll do it.'

A guffaw emerged from the minister. 'Oh, that won't be necessary, I think. But if you do wish to demonstrate your keen sense of duty, then see if you can't manage to let your words have a little more room. Space them a little more generously. Let them be drawn out a little more and I will feel that the years of my life are being drawn out with them.' He smiled at his little joke.

'I've always had the fastest tongue. Mother scolded me for it, way back when I was a baby. The steward of the Myōhōji Temple, she said, it was all his fault. He was there when I was born way out in Omi, and he had the fastest tongue too, and that was where I got it. I'll see what I can do about it.' She said it most solemnly, as if prepared to sacrifice anything in the cause of filial duty.

He was touched. 'He did you a disservice, the good steward, in presiding at your birth. He sounds like someone who has much to atone for. The Lotus Sutra tells us that dumbness and stammering are punishment for blasphemy.'

He was in some awe of his daughter at court, and was having second thoughts about letting her see this new sister. The mistake had been Kashiwagi's, in bringing the strange creature home before he knew what she was. People were laughing, and there was nothing to be done.

'Your sister is with us at the moment. Watch her carefully, and see how she behaves. Good manners have a way of spreading out from the center. Think of it that way, and see what she has to teach you.'

'I'd be delighted. Morning and night it's the thing I asked for, just to be one of them and make them take me as one of them. Morning and night and months and years it's what I've wanted. Just tell her to make them make me one of them and I'll do anything she tells me. I'll bring in the water. I'll bring it in on my head.' She had gathered such momentum that she was next to incomprehensible and somewhat intimidating.

'Oh, I doubt that she will ask you to cut the kindling. What will be asked of you is that you rid yourself of the good steward and find yourself a new model.'

She was not as alive as she might have been to irony, nor did she seem aware what a great man she was addressing. She did not share in the general awe.

'So when shall I go see her?'

'Suppose we pick a lucky day. No, we needn't make such a thing of it. Just drop in on her when you feel like it, today if you wish.' And he went out.

Just see what a father she had found for herself. An ordinary turn around the house, and just look at all the Fourth Rankers and Fifth Rankers he had with him. 'And I'm his own little girl. Why did I have to grow up in Omi?'

'Too fine a papa, really,' said Gosechi. 'Don't you think you might have been better off with an ordinary one who cared a little about you?'

'There you go. You always make everything turn out wrong. Well, just you remember something. You're with your betters, and don't you forget it. I've got big things ahead of me.'

One could not be angry with her. Commonness and honest, sturdy indignation could be charming. The trouble was with her speech. She had grown up among country people, and it was very inelegant. Pure, precise speech can give a certain distinction to rather ordinary remarks. An impromptu poem, for instance, if it is spoken musically, with an air at the beginning and end as of something unsaid, can seem to convey worlds of meaning, even if upon mature reflection it does not seem to have said much of anything at all. Torrential remarks have the opposite effect: the distinguished seems flat and vulgar. The overemphatic Omi speech patterns made everything seem less than serious. She had acquired them at her nurse's breast and was not shy about using them; and they were all wrong. Yet she did have her little accomplishments. She could without warning rattle off poem after poem of approximately the right length, and if the top half did not seem to go with the bottom half, that was all right too.

'Father says I must go see Sister, and so that's just what I'll do. Wouldn't want to disappoint him. Maybe I'll go right away. No, maybe I'll wait till dark. I'm Father's own little pet, but that won't do me much good if we're not chums, me and all the rest of them.'

The rest of them did not seem to be so eager.

She immediately set about composing a letter to her sister.

'Though here beside your fence of rushes,* the fact I have not had the happiness of stepping on your shadow might be from a gate which says "Come not my way."† It may be rude to mention Musashi when we haven't been introduced yet‡ but forgive me.' This last was followed by several ditto marks, and there were underlinings. Then there was a 'please turn over,' and: 'Yes, I forgot. I may come see you this evening because unfriendliness intensifies my longing.** I'm all in a dither and writing poorly, very poorly. It must be I am like the Minase.'†† And there was a poem, and one final remark:

'Cape How of the grassy pastures of Hitachi
Says how can the waves of Farmer Beach come see you.

*Anonymous, *Kokinshū* 506:

I linger here beside your fence of rushes,
So near, and why is there no chance of meeting?

†The Lady of Kohachijō, *Gosenshū* 683:

Though not so near as to step upon your shadow,
I face a gate which says: 'Come not my way.'

‡See note*, page 116.
**Anonymous, *Gosenshū* 609:

Unfriendliness intensifies my longing.
How then are we to put an end to it?

††Ki no Tomonori, *Kokinshū* 607:

Underground and silent, the Minase,
And underground and silent flows my love.

'And the waves of the river broad.'*

It was on a single sheet of green paper in a somewhat impatient style, the style of what master one could not easily have said. Given to wanderings and extensions, it seemed in spite of everything much pleased with itself, though asking for a larger piece of paper. She smiled at her composition and, folding it into a demure little knot, fastened it to a wild carnation. For her messenger she chose a little scullery maid, pretty and confident though new to the service.

'This is for *her*,' said the messenger, marching in upon the ladies-in-waiting.

'A letter has come from the north wing.' The woman who took it recognized her and opened the letter.

Another woman, called Chūnagon, glanced curiously at the minister's daughter, who smiled as she put it down. 'It looks like a most stylish sort of letter.'

'I do not seem to be very good at the cursive style,' said the lady, handing it to her. 'I can't somehow quite get the thread of it. But she will look down upon me if I do not answer in a similarly sophisticated and literary vein. Work up a draft for me, if you will, please.'

The younger women were giggling.

'It was not easy,' said Chūnagon, presenting her draft, 'to maintain the graceful, poetic tone. And we would not wish to insult her with anything from the hand of a scrivener.'

She had made it seem that the answer had come from the hand of the lady herself:

'It does indeed seem cruel that I should not have the pleasure of your company when you are so near.

> 'You waves of the Suma coast of Suruga—
> Hitachi, the pine of Hakosaki waits.'

'Oh, no! Everyone will think I wrote it.'

'Few will make that mistake, my lady.'

And so it was put in an envelope and sent off.

*Another poetic allusion, obviously. Perhaps a garbling of *Kokinshū* 699, anonymous:

> Wisteria flows beside the Yoshino.
> Think you my love so broad and generous?

'What a nice poem,' said the Omi lady. 'What a nice poem. And she's waiting for me, she says.'

She scented and rescented her robes, though the first scenting made them insistent, and put on crimson rouge and brushed furiously at her hair. Her completed toilet was very gay and rather charming.

No doubt there was a certain boldness too in her address.

CHAPTER 27

Flares

Everyone was talking about the minister's new daughter from Omi, and most of the talk was not kind.

'I do not like it,' said Genji. 'She should have been kept out of sight, and here for no reason at all he brings her grandly into his house and lets the whole world laugh at her. He has always been quick to take a stand, and he probably sent for her without finding out much of anything about her, and when he saw that she was not what he wanted he did what he has done. These things should be managed quietly.'

Tamakazura could see now that she had after all been lucky. Tō no Chūjō was her father, to be sure, but if she had gone to him as a stranger, quite ignorant of his thoughts and feelings over the years, she might have been subjected to similar humiliations. Ukon was of the same view, and said so. Genji did, it was true, show regrettable tendencies, but he kept himself under control and seemed to have become genuinely fond of Tamakazura. Her fright had left her and she had settled happily into life at Rokujō.

It was autumn. The first touch of the autumn breezes brought vague feelings of loneliness. Genji was always going off to Tamakazura's northeast quarter and spending whole days there, large parts of them in music lessons.

The new moon was quick to set. The sky had clouded delicately over and the murmur of the rushes was sadder. They lay down side by side with their heads pillowed against the koto. He stayed very late, sighing and asking whether anywhere else in the world there were attachments quite like this one. Reluctantly, fearful of gossip, he was about to leave. Noticing that the flares in the garden were low, he sent a guards officer to stir and refuel them.

They had been set out, not too brightly, under a spindle tree* that arched gracefully over the cool waters of the brook, far enough from the house so that they too seemed cool and gentle. In the soft light the lady was more beautiful than ever. The touch of her hair was coolly elegant, and a certain shyness and diffidence added to her charm. He did not want to leave.

*Mayumi, *Evonymus sieboldianus.*

'You should always have flares,' he said. 'An unlighted garden on a moonless summer night can almost be frightening.

> 'They burn, these flares and my heart, and send off smoke.
> The smoke from my heart refuses to be dispersed.

'For how long?'
Very strange, she was thinking.

> 'If from your heart and the flares the smoke is the same,
> Then one might expect it to find a place in the heavens.

'I am sure that we are the subject of much curious comment.'
'You wish me to go?' But someone in the other wing had taken up a flute, someone who knew how to play, and there was a Chinese koto too. 'Yūgiri is at it again with those inseparable companions of his. This one will be Kashiwagi.' He listened for a time. 'There is no mistaking Kashiwagi.'

He sent over to say that the light of the flares, cool and hospitable, had kept him on. Yūgiri and two friends came immediately.

'I felt the autumn wind in your flute and had to ask you to join me.'

His touch on the koto was soft and delicate, and Yūgiri's flute, in the *banjiki* mode,* was wonderfully resonant. Kashiwagi could not be persuaded to sing for them.

'You must not keep us waiting.'

His brother, less shy, sang a strain and repeated it, keeping time with his fan, and one might have taken the low, rich tones for a bell cricket.† Kashiwagi was now persuaded to play something on the koto. His touch was very little if at all inferior to his father's.

'I believe there is someone inside with an ear for these things,' said Genji. 'I must be abstemious. Old men have a way of saying things they regret when they drink too much.'

Tamakazura was indeed listening, and with complex feelings which the guests, her own brothers, could not have imagined. Kashiwagi was of the two the more strongly drawn to her. Indeed, he seemed in danger of falling in love with her. In his playing, however, there was not the smallest suggestion of disorder.

---

*Based on B.
†Probably the pine cricket, *Madasumma marmorata*, of today.

CHAPTER 28

The Typhoon

In Akikonomu's autumn garden the plantings were more beautiful by the day. All of the autumn colors were gathered together, and emphasized by low fences of black wood and red.* Though the flowers were familiar, they somehow seemed different here. The morning and evening dews were like gem-studded carpets. So wide that it seemed to merge with the autumn fields, this autumn garden made the women forget Murasaki's spring garden, which had so pleased them a few months before. They quite lost themselves in its cool beauties. The autumn side has always had the larger number of adherents in the ancient debate over the relative merits of spring and autumn. Women who had been seduced by the spring garden (so it is in this world) were now seduced by the autumn.

Akikonomu was in residence. Music seemed called for, but the anniversary of her father's death came this Eighth Month. Though she was fearful for the well-being of her flowers as autumn deepened, they seemed only to be brighter and fresher. But then came a typhoon, more savage than in most years. Falling flowers are always sad, but to see the dews scatter like jewels from a broken strand was for her almost torment. The great sleeve which the poet had wanted as a defense against the spring winds† she wanted against those of the autumn. The storm raged into the night, dark and terrible. Behind lowered shutters Akikonomu worried about her autumn flowers.

Murasaki's southeast garden had been pruned and otherwise readied for winter, but the wind was more than 'the little *hagi*'‡ had been waiting for. Its branches turned and twisted and offered no place for the raindrops. Murasaki came out to the veranda. Genji was with his daughter. Approaching along the east gallery, Yūgiri saw over a low screen that a door was open at a corner of

*Wood with and without bark, respectively.

†See note*, page 289.

‡Anonymous, *Kokinshū* 694:

> I wait, as dew-laden on Miyagino,
> The little *hagi* awaits the call of the winds.

the main hall. He stopped to look at the women inside. The screens having been folded and put away, the view was unobstructed. The lady at the veranda – it would be Murasaki. Her noble beauty made him think of a fine birch cherry* blooming through the hazes of spring. It was a gentle flow which seemed to come to him and sweep over him. She laughed as her women fought with the unruly blinds, though he was too far away to make out what she said to them, and the bloom was more radiant. She stood surveying the scene, seeing what the winds had done to each of the flowers. Her women were all very pretty too, but he did not really look at them. It almost frightened him to think why Genji had so kept him at a distance. Such beauty was irresistible, and just such inadvertencies as this were to be avoided at all costs.

As he started to leave, Genji came through one of the doors to the west, separating Murasaki's rooms from his daughter's.

'An irritable, impatient sort of wind,' he said. 'You must close your shutters. There are men about and you are very visible.'

Yūgiri looked back. Smiling at Murasaki, Genji was so young and handsome that Yūgiri found it hard to believe he was looking at his own father. Murasaki too was at her best. Nowhere could there be a nearer approach to perfection than the two of them, thought Yūgiri, with a stabbing thrill of pleasure. The wind had blown open the shutters along the gallery to make him feel rather exposed. He withdrew. Then, going up to the veranda, he coughed as if to announce that he had just arrived.

'See,' said Genji, pointing to the open door. 'You have been quite naked.'

Nothing of the sort had been permitted through all the years. Winds can move boulders and they had reduced the careful order to disarray, and so permitted the remarkable pleasure that had just been Yūgiri's.

Some men had come up to see what repairs were needed. 'We are in for a real storm,' they said. 'It's blowing from the northeast and you aren't getting the worst of it here. The stables and the angling pavilion could blow away any minute.'

'And where are you on your way from?' Genji asked Yūgiri.

'I was at Grandmother's, but with all the talk of the storm I was

---

Kabazakura. The word, which seems to refer to a wild cherry, is not found in the modern language.

worried about you. But they're worse off at Sanjō than you are here. The roar of the wind had Grandmother trembling like a child. I think perhaps if you don't mind I'll go back.'

'Do, please. It doesn't seem fair that people should be more childish as they get older, but it is what we all have to look forward to.'

He gave his son a message for the old lady: 'It is a frightful storm, but I am sure that Yūgiri is taking good care of you.'

Though the winds were fierce all the way to Sanjō, Yūgiri's sense of duty prevailed. He looked in on his father and his grandmother every day except when the court was in retreat. His route, even when public affairs and festivals were keeping him very busy, was from his own rooms to his father's and so to Sanjō and the palace. Today he was even more dutiful, hurrying around under black skies as if trying to keep ahead of the wind.

His grandmother was delighted. 'In all my long years I don't think I have ever seen a worse storm.' She was trembling violently.

Great branches were rent from trees with terrifying explosions. Tiles were flying through the air in such numbers that the roofs must at any moment be stripped bare.

'It was very brave of you.'

Yūgiri had been her chief comfort since her husband's death. Little was left for her of his glory. Though one could not have said that the world had forgotten her, it does change and move on. She felt closer to Yūgiri than to her son, Tō no Chūjō.

Yūgiri was jumpy and fretful as he sat listening to the howl of the wind. That glimpse of Murasaki had driven away the image that was so much with him. He tried to think of other things. This would not do, indeed it was rather terrible. But the same image was back again a moment after he had driven it away. There could have been few examples in the past of such beauty, nor were there likely to be many in the future. He thought of the lady of the orange blossoms. It was sad for her, but comparison was not possible. How admirable it had been of Genji not to discard so ill-favored a lady! Yūgiri was a very staid and sober young man who did not permit himself wanton thoughts, but he went on thinking wistfully of the years it would add to a man's life to be with such beauty day and night.

The storm quieted toward dawn, though there were still intermittent showers. Reports came that several of the outbuildings at

Rokujō had collapsed. Yūgiri was worried about the lady of the orange blossoms. The Rokujō grounds were vast and the buildings grand, and Genji's southeast quarter would without question have been well guarded. Less well guarded, the lady of the orange blossoms must have had a perilous time in her northeast quarter. He set off for Rokujō before it was yet full daylight. The wind was still strong enough to drive a chilly rain through the carriage openings. Under unsettled skies, he felt very unsettled himself, as if his spirit had flown off with the winds. Another source of disquiet had been added to what had seemed sufficient disquiet already, and it was of a strange and terrible kind, pointing the way to insanity.

He went first to the northeast quarter, where he found the lady of the orange blossoms in a state of terror and exhaustion. He did what he could to soothe her and gave orders for emergency repairs. Then he went to Genji's southeast quarter. The shutters had not yet been raised. Leaning against the balustrade of the veranda, he surveyed the damage. Trees had been uprooted on the hillocks and branches lay strewn over the garden. The flowers were an almost complete loss. The garden was a clutter of shingles and tiles and shutters and fences. The wan morning light was caught by raindrops all across the sad expanse. Black clouds seethed and boiled overhead. He coughed to announce his presence.

'Yūgiri is with us already.' It was Genji's voice. 'And here it is not yet daylight.'

There was a reply which Yūgiri did not catch, and Genji laughed and said: 'Not even in our earliest days together did you know the parting at dawn so familiar to other ladies. You may find it painful at first.'

This sort of bedroom talk had a very disturbing effect on a young man. Yūgiri could not hear Murasaki's answers, but Genji's jocular manner gave a sense of a union so close and perfect that no wedge could enter.

Genji himself raised the shutters. Yūgiri withdrew a few steps, not wishing to be seen quite so near at hand.

'And how were things with your grandmother? I imagine she was very pleased to see you.'

'She did seem pleased. She weeps much too easily, and I had rather a time of it.'

Genji smiled. 'She does not have many years left ahead of her. You must be good to her. She complains about that son of hers.

He lacks the finer qualities of sympathy and understanding, she says. He does have a flamboyant strain and a way of brushing things impatiently aside. When it comes to demonstrating filial piety he puts on almost too good a show, and one senses a certain carelessness in the small things that really matter. But I do not wish to speak ill of him. He is a man of superior intelligence and insight, and more talented than this inferior age of ours deserves. He can be a bother at times, but there are not many men with so few faults. But what a storm. I wonder if Her Majesty's men took proper care of her.'

He sent Yūgiri with a message. 'How did the screaming winds treat you? I had an attack of chills* just as they were their lunatic worst, and so the hours went by and I was not very attentive. You must forgive me.'

Yūgiri was very handsome in the early-morning light as he made his way along a gallery and through a door to Akikonomu's southwest quarter. He could see from the south veranda of the east wing that two shutters and several blinds had been raised at the main hall. Women were visible in the dim light beyond. Two or three had come forward and were leaning against the balustrades. Who might they be? Though in casual dress, they managed to look very elegant in multicolored robes that blended pleasantly in the twilight. Akikonomu had sent some little girls to lay out insect cages in the damp garden. They had on robes of lavender and pink and various deeper shades of purple, and yellow-green jackets lined with green, all appropriately autumnal hues. Disappearing and reappearing among the mists, they made a charming picture. Four and five of them with cages of several colors were walking among the wasted flowers, picking a wild carnation here and another flower there for their royal lady. The wind seemed to bring a scent from even the scentless asters, most delightfully, as if Akikonomu's own sleeves had brushed them. Thinking it improper to advance further without announcing himself, Yūgiri quietly made his presence known and stepped forward. The women withdrew inside, though with no suggestion of surprise or confusion. Still a child when Akikonomu had gone to court, he had had the privilege of her inner chambers. Even now her women did not treat

---

*Okoriai, meaning unclear. It could be almost anything from a fit of sneezing to a seizure of malaria.

him as an outsider. Having delivered Genji's message, he paused to talk of more personal matters with such old friends as Saishō and Naishi. For all the informality, Akikonomu maintained proud and strict discipline, the palpable presence of which made him think of the ladies who so occupied and disturbed his thoughts.

The shutters had meanwhile been raised in Murasaki's quarter. She was looking out over her flowers, the cause of such regrets the evening before and now quite devastated.

Coming up to the stairs before the main hall, Yūgiri delivered a message from Akikonomu.

'Her Majesty was sure that you would protect her from the winds,' he said to Genji, 'and thought it very foolish that she should be feeling sorry for herself. She added that your inquiries brought great comfort.'

'It is true that she has a timid strain in her. I imagine that she felt very badly protected with only women around her – and rather resentful too.'

As Genji raised the blinds to go inside and change into court dress that he might call on her, Yūgiri saw sleeves under a low curtain very near at hand. He knew whose they would be. His heart raced. Ashamed of himself, he looked away.

'See how handsome he is in the morning light,' Genji said softly to Murasaki as he knelt before a mirror. 'We all know how badly illuminated a father's heart is,* and no doubt I have my blind spots. Yet I do think he is rather pleasant to look at. He is still a boy, of course.'

Probably he was thinking that for all the accumulated years he was still rather pleasant to look at himself. He was feeling a little nervous. 'I am always on my mettle when I call upon Her Majesty. There is nothing exactly intimidating about her, but she always seems to have so much in reserve. That gentle surface conceals a very firm core.'

Coming out, he found Yūgiri sunk in thought and not immediately aware of his presence. Very much alive to such details, he went inside again.

'Do you suppose he might have seen you in the confusion last night? The corner door was open, you know.'

See note, page 13.

'How could he possibly have?' Murasaki flushed. 'I am very sure that there was no one outside.'

Very strange all the same, thought Genji.

While he was having his audience with Akikonomu, Yūgiri made light talk with the women who had gathered at the gallery door. They thought him unusually subdued.

Genji next went to inquire after the Akashi lady. Though she had not summoned her steward, there were competent gardeners among her women. They were down tending the flowers. Little girls, very pretty in informal dress, were righting the trellises over which her favored gentians and morning glories had been trained. She was at the veranda playing an impromptu elegy on her koto. He took note of her admirable attention to the proprieties: hearing him come up, she reached for a cloak on a nearby rack and slipped it over her soft robes. He sat down beside her and made his inquiries and was on his way once more.

She whispered to herself:

'Even the wind that rustles the leaves of the reeds
    Is with me longer in my lonely vigil.'

In terror through much of the night, Tamakazura had slept late and was just now at her morning toilet. Genji silenced his men and came softly up beside her. Screens and other furnishings were stacked untidily in a corner and the rooms were in considerable disarray. The sunlight streamed in upon almost startlingly fresh beauty. Genji sat down to make his inquiries, and it annoyed her that he managed to give even them a suggestive note.

'Your behavior,' she said, 'has been such that I rather hoped last night to be carried off by the wind.'

Genji was amused. 'How rash of you – though I have no doubt that you had a particular destination in mind. So I displease you more and more all the time, do I? Well, that is as it should be.'

Her thoughts exactly. She too had to smile, a glowing smile that was very lovely indeed. A glow like a *hōzuki* berry* came through rich strands of hair. If he had been searching for faults, he might have pointed out that she smiled too broadly; but it was a very small fault.

---

*Physalis alkekengi, sometimes called 'Japanese lantern.'

Waiting through this apparently intimate tête-à-tête, Yūgiri caught sight of a somewhat disarranged curtain behind the corner blinds. Raising it over the frame, he found that he had a clear view deep into the room. He was rather startled at what he saw. They were father and daughter, to be sure, but it was not as if she were an infant for Genji to take in his arms, as he seemed about to do. Though on ready alert lest he be detected, Yūgiri was spellbound. The girl turned away and sought to hide behind a pillar, and as Genji pulled her towards him her hair streamed over her face, hiding it from Yūgiri's view. Though obviously very uncomfortable, she let him have his way. They seemed on very intimate terms indeed. Yūgiri was a little shocked and more than a little puzzled. Genji knew all about women, there could be no question of that. Perhaps because he had not had her with him to fret and worry over since girlhood it was natural that he should feel certain amorous impulses towards her. It was natural, but also repellent. Yūgiri felt somehow ashamed, as if it were in a measure his responsibility. She was a half sister and not a full sister and he saw that he could himself be tempted. She was very tempting. She was not perhaps the equal of the other lady of whom he had recently had a glimpse, but she brought a smile of pleasure all the same. She would not have seemed in hopeless competition with Murasaki. He thought of a rich profusion of *yamabuki* sparkling with dew in the evening twilight. The image was of spring and not autumn, of course, but it was the one that came to him all the same. Indeed she might be thought even more beautiful than the *yamabuki*, which after all has its ragged edges and untidy stamens.

They seemed to be talking in whispers, unaware, of course, that they were being observed.

Suddenly very serious, Genji stood up. He softly repeated a poem which the girl had recited in tones too low for Yūgiri to hear:

'The tempest blows, the maiden flower has fears
That the time has come for it to fade and die.'

It brought both revulsion and fascination. But he could stay no longer.

He hoped he had misunderstood his father's answer:

'If it gives itself up to the dew beneath the tree,
It need not fear, the maiden flower, the winds.

'It should look to the example of the pliant bamboo.'

He went next to see the lady of the orange blossoms. Perhaps because the weather had suddenly turned chilly and she had not been expecting guests, her older women were at their sewing and her younger women were pressing bolts of cotton on long, narrow boxes of some description. Scattered about the room were red silks beaten to a soft luster and gossamers of a delicate saffron.

'Underrobes for Yūgiri? What a pity that you should have gone to so much trouble when the royal garden party is sure to be called off. Everything has been blown to pieces. We are going to have a wasted and unlovely sort of autumn.'

The fabrics were very beautiful indeed. She was every bit as accomplished at this sort of thing as Murasaki. A cloth with a floral pattern, just out of the dyeing vats, was to become an informal court robe for Genji himself. The dyes, from new flowers, were excellent.

'It would suit Yūgiri better,' he said as he left. 'It is a little too youthful for me.'

Yūgiri was not happy at being taken on this round of calls. There was a letter which he wished to get off and soon it would be noon.

He went to his sister's rooms.

'She is over in the other wing,' said her nurse. 'She was so frightened at the storm that we could not get her out of bed this morning.'

'It was an awful storm. I meant to stay with you, but my grandmother was in such a state that I really couldn't. And how did our dollhouses come through?'

The women laughed. 'Even the breeze from a fan sends her into a terror, and last night we thought the roof would come down on us any minute. The dollhouses required a great deal of battening and shoring.'

'Do you have a scrap of paper? Anything will do. And maybe I could borrow an inkstone from one of you?'

A woman went to one of her mistress's cupboards and came back with several rolls of paper laid out on a writing box.

'This is too good.' But he thought of the Akashi lady and decided that he need not feel overawed. He wrote his letter, choosing a purple tissue paper. He ground the ink carefully and was very handsome as he gazed meditatively at the tip of his brush. Yet his poem had a somewhat stiff and academic sound to it:

'Even on a night of raging tempests
I did not forget the one whom I do not forget.'

He tied it to a rush broken by the wind.

'The lieutenant of Katano,'* said the women, 'was always careful to have the flower or the grass match the paper.'

'I do not seem up to these fine distinctions. What flower or
grass would you suggest?' He had few words for these women and
kept them at a distance.

He wrote another note and gave both to a cavalry officer who
in turn passed them on, with whispered instructions, to a pretty
little page and a guardsman accustomed to such services. The
young women were overcome with curiosity.

They were busy getting the rooms in order, for word had come
that their mistress was returning. After the other beauties he had
seen in recent hours, Yūgiri wondered what floral image his sister
would call to mind. She had not much interested him, but now he
took a crouched position behind a swinging door and, pulling a
blind over himself, looked through an opening in the curtains. She
came into the room. He was annoyed at the furniture that stood in
the way and at all the women passing back and forth. But she was
charming, a tiny thing in a lavender robe, her hair, which did not
yet reach to her feet, spreading out like a fan. She had blossomed
wonderfully in the two years since he had last seen her. What a
beauty she would presently be! He had likened the other two
ladies to the cherry and the *yamabuki* – and might he liken his sister to the wisteria? There was just such elegance in wisteria trailing
from a high tree and waving in the breeze. How good if he could
look upon these ladies quite as he wished, morning and night. He
saw no reason why he should not, since it was all in the family, but
Genji had other ideas and was very strict about keeping him away
from them – and so created restless yearnings in this most proper
of young men.

Going now to Sanjō, he found his grandmother at her devotions. The young women who waited upon her were far above the
ordinary, but in manner and appearance they could not compete
with the women at Rokujō. Yet a nunnery could have its own sort
of somber beauty.

*The hero of a lost romance.

Lamps were lighted. Tō no Chūjō came for a quiet talk with his mother.

Everything made the old lady weep. 'It seems altogether too much that you should keep Kumoinokari from me.'

'I will have her come and see you very soon. She is all tangled up in problems of her own making and has lost so much weight that we worry about her. I often think that a man does better not to have daughters. Everything they do brings new worries.'

He seemed to have an old grievance in mind. His mother concluded sadly that it would be well not to pursue the matter.

'I have found another daughter,' he smiled, 'a somewhat outlandish and unmanageable one.'

'How very curious. I would certainly not have expected you to produce that sort of daughter.'

'I do have my troubles,' he replied (or so one is told). 'I must arrange for you to meet your new granddaughter one of these days.'

CHAPTER 29
The Royal Outing

Genji would have liked to put Tamakazura's affairs in order, but the Silent Waterfall* of his longing produced complications. It was beginning to seem that Murasaki's fears had been well founded and that Genji would be the subject of scandalous rumors. Tō no Chūjō was a man who liked to have things clear and in the open. He could not bear subterfuge. How sheepish a son-in-law he himself would be, thought Genji, on the day when everything was revealed to his friend!

In the Twelfth Month there was a royal outing to Oharano.† Like everyone else, the ladies of Rokujō set out in their carriages to watch. The procession, very splendid even for a royal outing, left the palace early in the morning and proceeded south along Suzaku and west on Gojō. Carriages lined the streets all the way to the river Katsura. The princes and high officials were beautifully fitted out. Their guards and grooms, very good-looking and of generally matching heights, were in the finest of livery. All the ministers and councillors and indeed the whole court had turned out for the occasion, the higher ranks dressed uniformly in yellow-green robes and lavender singlets. Even the skies seemed intent on favoring the occasion, for there were flurries of snow. The princes and high courtiers in charge of the falcons were in fine hunting dress. The falconers from the guards were even more interesting, all in printed robes of most fanciful design. Everything was very grand and very novel, and the carriages of the spectators fought for places. Some among the spindly carriages of the lesser ladies emerged from the struggle with broken wheels. The better carriages had gathered at the approaches to the floating bridge.

Tamakazura was among the spectators. As she surveyed the splendid courtiers in such intense competition, it was her verdict that no one compared with the emperor in his red robes. He looked neither to the right nor to the left. Then there was her own

---

*Apparently a poetic allusion. There are several waterfalls called 'silent,' one of them within the limits of the present city.

†To the west of the old city.

father, Tō no Chūjō (almost no one knew that he was her father). He was handsome and dignified, in the prime of manhood, though of course circumscribed in his dress by the codes relating to his office. He was quite the finest of the courtiers – but her eye returned to the royal palanquin. The generals and captains and other high officials who had most of the young women swooning interested her very little. Yes, the emperor was the best of them – though Genji so resembled him that they might have been mistaken for each other. Perhaps it was only her imagination that the emperor was a shade the grander of the two. She was sure that she would have to look very far, in any case, to find their equal. She had thought, because of Genji and Yūgiri, that men of good family were all endowed with superior looks, but the competition today exacted casualties in such numbers that she was inclined to dismiss most of the men she saw as scarcely human. Prince Hotaru was present, as also was General Higekuro, always very solemn and important, and today in very grand uniform, quiver and all. His face was dark and his beard heavy, and she did not think him pleasing – though it would have been too much to expect his roughness to meet the standards of carefully tended femininity. She sniffed contemptuously. Genji had suggested that she go to court. She had heard much about the embarrassments and insults which a court lady must be prepared to put up with, but now she wondered whether it might not after all be rather nice to serve His Majesty, though not as one of the ladies of the bedchamber.

The procession reached Oharano, where awnings had been put out. The high courtiers changed to informal court dress and hunting dress. Refreshments were brought from Genji's Rokujō mansion. The emperor had invited Genji to join the hunt, but Genji had replied that a defilement made it impossible for him to go out. By a guards officer the emperor sent a brace of pheasants tied to a leafy branch. I shall not seek to record the contents of the royal letter, but this was the poem:

'Deep in the snows of this Mount Oshio
Are ancient pheasant tracks. Would you might see them.'*

But I wonder if in fact precedent can be found for inviting a chancellor to be in attendance upon a royal hunt.

*That is: 'You should follow precedent and join us.' Mount Oshio is also to the west of the old city.

Genji received the messenger very ceremoniously and sent back this answer:

> 'The snows beneath the pines of Oshio
> Have never known so mighty a company.'*

These are the bits I gathered, and I may not have recorded them accurately.

Genji wrote to Tamakazura the next day. 'I suppose you saw the emperor? Did you find yourself inclining a little in the direction I have suggested?'

It was a cozy, friendly sort of note on prim white paper, containing none of the usual innuendos. It pleased her and yet she smiled wryly. He had been very clever at reading her thoughts.

'It was all rather confused and unclear,' she wrote back.

> 'Amid deep snows upon a day of clouds
> How does one see the radiance far above?'

Genji showed the letter to Murasaki. 'I have, as you see, suggested that she go to court, but I already have the empress there and should perhaps refrain from sending another lady so soon. And if I were to reveal the secret to her father he would be faced with complications because of his other daughter. A girl who can do as she pleases is of course very eager to go to court once she has had a glimpse of His Majesty.'

'Don't you think,' she said, smiling, 'that however handsome His Majesty may be, it is good for girls to be a little less forward?'

'You may say so, but I should imagine that you yourself would be first in line.'

He got off an answer:

> 'The crimson glow is there in a cloudless sky.
> Have you let yourself be blinded by the snow?

'You must make up your mind.'

There was first the matter of her initiation ceremonies. He was already making preparations, collecting the masterpieces of the finest craftsmen in the land. Ceremonies in which he had a part had a way of becoming very grand even when he did not pay

---

*The snow flurries have been very obliging, making it possible to introduce *miyuki*, 'deep snows' and 'royal progress,' into this poem and the two poems following.

much attention to them, and he was paying a great deal of attention to these, which were to be his occasion for informing Tō no Chūjō.

They were set for the Second Month. Even after a lady has reached adulthood and attracted considerable attention, it is not necessary, so long as she is living a quiet life at home, that she step forward and announce herself to the gods, and so Tamakazura's position had remained ambiguous. But now, if Genji's plans were to be realized, there was a danger of offending the god of Kasuga, patron of the Fujiwara family. Her true identity must be revealed. Not wishing to leave behind a name for furtiveness and duplicity because he had kept the secret so long, Genji even now considered alternative measures. Adoptions were not at all unusual these days among commoners. He finally decided, however, that the bond between parent and child is not easily severed and that Tō no Chūjō must be told everything. He wrote asking that Tō no Chūjō do him the honor of tying the ceremonial apron. The answer came back that Princess Omiya had been ill since late the preceding year and was not improving and that it would be unseemly for Tō no Chūjō to make ceremonial appearances. Yūgiri was, moreover, living at Sanjō to be with his grandmother and would not find it convenient to divide his attentions.

And so what was to be done? Life is uncertain. Princess Omiya might die, and Tamakazura would be guilty of sacrilege if she did not go into mourning for her grandmother. The princess must be informed. Genji set out for Sanjō, ostensibly to inquire after her health.

It was no longer possible for him to go out inconspicuously. His excursions these days tended to be even grander than royal outings. At the sight of him, so handsome that he scarcely seemed of this world, Princess Omiya felt her afflictions leave her. She got out of bed to receive him. She was very weak and needed the support of an armrest, but her speech was clear.

'What a pleasure it is to see that you are not as ill as I had feared,' said Genji. 'My informant seems to have been an alarmist. He led me to fear the very worst. I do not even go to court these days except on very special occasions. I stay shut up at home quite as if I had no public duties, and lead an indolent, useless existence. Some men go on working when they are so bent with age that they can hardly carry themselves about. I was not born with great talents, and now I have added laziness to my disabilities.'

'It is a very long time since I first became aware that old age had overtaken me,' replied the princess, 'but since the beginning of the year I have felt that I do not have much longer to live. It has made me very sad to think that I might not see you again. And here you are, and death does not seem so near after all. I have lived a long life and have no very great wish to live longer. The dearest ones have gone on ahead of me, and the others seem intent on showing me what a mistake it is to live so long. I have been quietly making my preparations. Yūgiri has been the exception. He is wonderfully kind and attentive. His problems have held me back and made me want to live on.'

Her voice was trembling. Her remarks might have sounded like the empty complaining of a dotard, but to Genji they seemed genuine. He was deeply moved.

They talked of many things, ancient and recent.

'I suppose your son comes to see you every day. It would please me enormously if he were to come today. There is something I have been wanting to speak to him about, but it is not easy to arrange a meeting when I do not have important business.'

'I do not see a great deal of him, I fear, perhaps because he does not have an overwhelming sense of filial duty. What might you wish to speak to him about? Yūgiri has his just grievances. I say to my son that however matters may once have been, rumors that have escaped do not come meekly home again. Nothing is to be gained at this late date by keeping the two apart. The end result could be to make us all look ridiculous. But he has never been an easy man to talk to, and I am by no means sure that he sees the point.'

Genji smiled. She always thought first of Yūgiri. 'But I had heard that your good son was prepared to accept the facts. I made bold to drop a few hints of my own, and afterwards rather wished that I hadn't, because they only got the boy a scolding. Things eventually come out clean in the wash, they say, and I have wondered why he has not seen fit to let the water do its work. But of course that is not entirely true. There are things that no amount of laundering does much for. They get worse the longer you wait. I am sorry for the damage that has already been done.

'But as a matter of fact,' he said, turning to his main business. 'As a matter of fact, there is a girl who should have been his responsibility but who quite by accident has become mine. I did not at first know the truth and I was not as diligent as I might have been in seeking it out. Having so few children of my own, I convinced the girl in question that it need make no difference if she thought of herself as one of them. I did not try as hard as I might have to make her feel like one of the family, and time passed. Then one day – I cannot think how he heard about her – there was a summons from His Majesty.

'He told me very confidentially that he was concerned about the inner palace. If the ladies' apartments do not have a competent wardress the ladies are left without proper guidance. There are two elderly assistant wardresses and there are other candidates as well, all of them most eagerly desiring the appointment, but His Majesty is not enthusiastic about any of them. It has been the practice to appoint someone of good birth who is not unduly encumbered by family problems. He could, he said, consider intelligence and attainments and promote someone who has served long and faithfully, but in the absence of remarkable promise he would prefer a younger lady who is beginning to attract favorable notice.

'I thought immediately of the young lady I have mentioned, and wondered how your son would feel about proposing her as a candidate. Ladies who go to court, whatever their rank, find themselves in competition for His Majesty's affection, and the more prosaic work of seeing that the palace continues to function does not seem very attractive or challenging. But I have come to think myself that whether it is or is not depends on the lady whose responsibility it is. Having made further inquiry about the lady I had taken under my protection, I had concluded that her age identified her as someone who should more properly be under your son's protection. I would like to discuss the matter quite frankly with him. I do not want anything as grand as a formal conference. I hoped I had found the occasion for informing him, but when I wrote inviting him to be present he was not enthusiastic and wrote back that your illness made it necessary for him to decline. I had to agree that my timing was less than ideal. But now I see that you are not as ill as my informant had led me to fear, and so I think I must insist. Could you so inform him, please?'

'How very interesting, and how very unlikely. I know that he has been rather indiscriminately collecting children who have claimed to be his. It is astonishing that this one went to the wrong father. Was she herself misinformed?'

'There is an explanation. I am sure that he will be familiar with the details. It is the sort of thing that happens in the untidy lives of the lower classes and is always being talked about. I have not told even Yūgiri. I hope that you will be as careful as I have been.'

Tō no Chūjō heard with surprise of Genji's visit. 'But they have far too few people at Sanjō to receive such a guest. Who will be looking after his men and seeing that he is properly entertained himself? I imagine Yūgiri will be with him.' He immediately sent off a few sons and several of their friends. 'I ought to go myself, but I would not want to make too elaborate an affair of it.'

A letter came from Princess Omiya. 'The Rokujō minister has been kind enough to inquire after my health. We are badly under-staffed and cannot be making a good impression. Do you suppose I might ask you to come, as quietly as possible, without having it seem that I sent for you? He has said that there is something he wishes to speak to you about.'

What would it be? Yet more about Yūgiri? Princess Omiya did not have much longer to live and was making strong pleas in Yūgiri's behalf. If Genji were to lodge a protest Tō no Chūjō would have great trouble turning it away. Tō no Chūjō had been thinking how unfortunate it would be to learn at this late date that Yūgiri's ardor had died. He must find an occasion to let it be known that he might consider acceding to the young people's wishes. If Genji and the princess were in collusion he would have very great trouble answering their arguments. He was a stubborn man, however, and a rather perverse man as well, and he did not want to surrender without a fight.

His mother had sent for him, and Genji would be waiting. He did not want to offend either of them. He would see what they had to say. He dressed very carefully and ordered a modest retinue, and presented a very grand figure as he set forth surrounded by sons. He was tall and strongly built and carried himself with magisterial dignity. In purple trousers surmounted by a very long train of white lined with red, he might almost have been accused of overdressing. By contrast, the easy informality of Genji's dress, a robe of white Chinese brocade lined with red over several red singlets, suggested a prince who has ample time to cultivate his sensibilities. It might have been said that Genji had the finer material to work with and Tō no Chūjō worked harder with what he had.*

His sons were also very handsome. He had two brothers with him, men of considerable eminence, a grand councillor and a chamberlain to the crown prince. Though he did not wish to seem ostentatious, he had in his retinue upwards of ten middle-ranking courtiers of unexceptionable name and family and very good taste, including two privy secretaries, two guards officers, and a moderator, and there were lesser courtiers in large numbers.

The wine flowed freely and pleasant intoxication was general, and the talk was of what a fortunate lady the old princess was.

It was also of course reminiscent, for Genji and Tō no Chūjō had not met in a very long time. When they did not see each other they were always finding themselves at odds over things that did not matter, but when they were together all the solid reasons for friendship reasserted themselves. They talked of happenings old and recent, and presently it was evening. Tō no Chūjō continued to press wine on his mother's guests.

'I have hesitated to visit Mother without an invitation. And what would you have said if I had known you were here and not come?'

'Nothing at all, except to apologize for my own remissness – though I have at times, you know, had reason to be annoyed with you.'†

The troublesome matter of the younger generation, thought Tō no Chūjō, retreating into polite silence.

'In the old days,' said Genji, 'I never felt comfortable unless I had your opinion on every matter, public and private, large and small, and the two of us in His Majesty's service seemed like two wings serving one bird. As the years went by there were from time to time things that rather went against my wishes. They were private. In matters of public policy I have never doubted our being on the same side, and I do not doubt it now. I find my thoughts

---

*The statement is obscure, and there are variant texts. Some texts seem to give Genji the better of it, some Tō no Chūjō.

†There is a textual difficulty. It may be that the second clause essentially repeats the first.

turning more to the past, and I also find that we see less and less of each other. It is entirely proper that you should stand on the dignity of your office, and yet I do sometimes wish that in private matters ceremony might be dispensed with. There have been times when I have wished that you might come calling.'

'Yes, it is as you say. In the old days you must have thought it ill-mannered and inconsiderate of me to make such demands on your time. I had no secrets from you and I profited enormously from your advice. You praise me too highly when you suggest that I have ever performed as your companion wing. I have made use of your enormous abilities to support my own inadequate ones and so I have been privileged to be of service to His Majesty. You must not for a moment think that I am ungrateful. But it is once again as you say: we see far too little of each other.'

Genji presently found a chance to turn to his main subject.

'How perfectly extraordinary.' Tō no Chūjō was in tears. 'I believe that my feelings once got the better of me and I told you of my search for the girl. As I have risen to my modest position in the world I have gathered my stupid daughters around me, not omitting the least-favored of them. They have found ways to make themselves known. And when I think of the lost ones, it is she who comes first to mind.'

As they remembered the confessions made and the conclusions reached that rainy night, they laughed and wept and the earlier stiffness disappeared. It was very late when they went their separate ways.

'The sight of you brings fond memories,' said Genji, 'and I do not at all want to leave.' It was not like him to weep so easily. Perhaps he had had too much to drink.

Princess Omiya was weeping copiously. The sight of Genji, so much handsomer and grander than in the old years, made her think of her late daughter. It does seem to be true that a nun's habit and briny waters have an affinity for each other.*

Genji let the opportunity pass to touch upon Yūgiri's affairs. It would have been in bad taste to introduce so clear a case of injustice on Tō no Chūjō's part, and Tō no Chūjō himself thought the

---

*Because of the common pun on *ama*, 'nun' and 'fisherman,' nuns are associated with brine.

matter one for Genji to bring up. And so the tension between them was not after all completely dispelled.

'I know that I should see you home,' said Tō no Chūjō, 'but you gave me such short notice, and I would not want to attract attention. I will call on you soon to tell you again how grateful I am for this visit.'

Genji replied that it had been a joy to find Omiya less ill than he had feared and that he would hold Tō no Chūjō most firmly to his engagement to bestow the ceremonial train.

They parted in the best of spirits, on the surface at least. Their retinues were very grand. The various sons and brothers in attendance would have liked very much to know what had been discussed. Both Genji and Tō no Chūjō seemed happy with the discussion, and so who might be expected to resign what office now, and in favor of whom? No one suspected what had in fact been the reason for the meeting.

Tō no Chūjō was badly unsettled. There were difficulties in the way of taking Tamakazura into his house immediately. It seemed highly unlikely, everything considered, that Genji had sought the girl out and brought her into his house and then left her quite untouched. Out of regard for his other ladies, Genji had probably refrained from adding her openly and formally to the company. Probably he was finding the clandestine affair unmanageable and was worried about gossip, and so had chosen to let Tō no Chūjō in on the secret. It was a pity, of course, but the girl's reputation need not be thought irreparably damaged. People could hardly criticize Tō no Chūjō if he were to let Genji keep her. Genji's suggestion that she be sent to court opened the possibility of unpleasantness for the sister already there. But he would respect Genji's wishes, whatever Genji decided to do.

The meeting just described took place early in the Second Month. The sixteenth, at the beginning of the equinoctial services,* was found to be a propitious day for initiation ceremonies. The soothsayers advised indeed that no better day would come for some time, and Princess Omiya's illness did not at the moment seem serious.

In the course of the preparations Genji told Tamakazura in great detail of his conversation with her father. Genji's kindness

*Higan, a Buddhist festival, probably of Shinto origins, in the spring and autumn.

could not have been greater, she thought, if he had been her father, and at the same time she was delighted at the prospect of meeting her real father.

Genji took Yūgiri into his confidence. The pieces fell into place, numbers of puzzles were solved. Yūgiri now thought Tamakazura in pleasing contrast to the cold lady upon whom he had set his affections, and he thought himself very obtuse for not having guessed earlier. He was an honest and sensible boy, and he told himself that the possibilities introduced by the new situation must be dismissed from his mind.

On the day of the ceremony a secret messenger arrived bringing gifts from Princess Omiya. Despite the shortness of the notice, the princess had put together a fine collection of comb boxes and the like.

'Nuns do not write letters,' she said, 'and so I shall be brief. I hope that I may persuade you to follow my example in living a long and full life. Perhaps it is improper of me to confess how deeply moved I was to learn of your circumstances. I would not wish in any way to offend you, but

> 'Whatever lid the jeweled comb box bears,
> I still shall think it no one's box but mine.'*

It was in a tremulous old-fashioned hand. Busy with last-minute preparations and instructions, Genji was in Tamakazura's rooms when it arrived.

'Yes, it is a little old-fashioned,' he said, 'but it is very touching all the same. She has aged, poor thing. She used to write a very fine hand. See how it shakes and wanders.' He read it again and yet again, and laughed quietly. 'One might charge her with making too much of her boxes. A box per line – I doubt that it would be possible to write a more box-filled poem.'

Akikonomu sent formal robes, a white train and a Chinese jacket and the rest, and other gifts as well, all of superb quality. There were combs for the formal coiffure and, as always, the best of Chinese perfumes in a variety of jars. And there were robes for

*The princess is saying that she looks upon Tamakazura as her granddaughter whether Tamakazura's father is Genji or Tō no Chūjō. As Genji's next remarks suggest, her poem is highly contrived, containing a large number of 'associative words' having to do with combs and boxes.

Tamakazura from the other ladies at Rokujō, and combs and fans and the like for her attendants, all of them showing very clearly the tastes of the several ladies. One would have found it quite impossible to say that any one gift was superior to the others. A competition among ladies of taste can produce a most marvelous display.

Though the ladies in the east lodge at Nijō also heard of the preparations, it did not seem their place to offer congratulations. The safflower princess was the exception. Inflexible in her allegiance to good form, she must not let the occasion pass or have it seem that she was unconcerned — and one had to grant that such punctiliousness was in its way admirable. She sent a robe of a greenish drab, lined trousers of a dusty rose or some such color much admired by the ancients, and a faded purple jacket of a minute weave, all in a beautifully wrought wardrobe and elaborate wrapping.

Her letter was expansive. 'I do not hope to make your acquaintance, but I would not for the world want it to seem that I am ignoring you. These poor garments will doubtless seem beneath your notice. If, however, you find an attendant who might be able to use them, please pass them on to her.'

Genji saw it and grimaced. 'She is a strange old thing. It would be far better for us all if she were to let her shyness have its way and keep to herself. I fear I am blushing. You must answer, I suppose. She will be upset if you don't. When I remember how fond her father was of her I find it impossible not to be kind to her.'

Attached to the jacket was a poem which showed the usual obsession with clothing.

'How very unhappy I am, for my Chinese sleeves
  Cannot be friends with the sleeves of your Chinese robe.'

The hand was, as always, rather dreadful, cramped and rocklike and stiff and angular. Though discommoded, Genji could not help being amused as well. 'I imagine that it took a great deal out of her. She has even less assistance in these endeavors than she used to have. I think I will compose your answer for you, busy though I am.'

'How very observant you are,' he wrote. 'You notice things which escape the ordinary eye. Indeed I might almost wish you were a little less so.

'A Chinese robe, a Chinese robe once more,
And yet again a Chinese Chinese robe.'

'It pleases her to make these avowals,' he said, showing it to Tamakazura, 'and I defer to her tastes.'

She laughed brightly. 'Dare I suspect unkind wit?'

But I have lost myself in trivialities.

Tō no Chūjō had not been much interested in the ceremonies, but now he was very eager indeed to see the girl. He arrived early. Aware of and grateful for all the trouble Genji had gone to, he thought it rather odd even so. Late in the evening he was admitted to his daughter's apartments. Refreshments were served. The lights were somewhat brighter than one might have expected, and the smallest detail was in careful order. The ritual did not permit more than a glimpse of his daughter, but he could hardly keep himself from staring openly as he bestowed the train.

'We shall not speak of things long over and done with,' said Genji, 'and we would do well not to let the secret out quite yet. Please try to make it all seem as routine as possible.'

'I cannot thank you enough,' said Tō no Chūjō, raising his cup. 'There can be no precedent for such kindness. And yet I must register a brief complaint that you have kept the secret so long.

'Bitter, bitter, that the fisherfolk
So long have hidden the treasures of the sea.'

It was accompanied by an illustrative shedding of tears.

The company of two such splendid gentlemen had reduced Tamakazura to silence. The answering poem came from Genji:

'The fisherfolk refusing to take them in,
The grasses drifted ashore as best they might.

'Your objection is not well taken, sir.'

Tō no Chūjō had to grant the truth in it. He had no answer.

The whole court was in attendance, including several of Tamakazura's suitors. It struck them as odd that Tō no Chūjō should stay so long behind her curtains. Of his sons, only Kashiwagi and Kōbai had some glimmering of the truth. They were disappointed and pleased, disappointed because they had themselves had certain designs upon the girl.

'I certainly am glad that I did not give myself away,' whispered Kōbai.

'Genji has his own way of doing things,' said someone else. 'Do you suppose he means to do for her what he did for the empress?'

'We must be careful that we do not emerge in an unfavorable light,' said Genji, overhearing. 'People who are unencumbered with rank and office do all manner of strange things, I am sure, but we are vulnerable. We must let matters take their course until people are prepared to accept them for what they are.'

'I shall follow your wishes unquestioningly,' replied Tō no Chūjō. 'There must have been some bond between the two of you from another life, that you should have found her and taken care of her with no help at all from me.'

He was of course richly and imaginatively rewarded for his services. As for the other gifts, Genji managed to add original touches to what precedent and regulation demanded. They were very splendid indeed. Because of Princess Omiya's illness the concert after the ceremonies was simple.

Prince Hotaru so descended from his dignity as to plead his case openly. 'The excuses which you have made,' he said, 'would no longer seem to hold.'

'We have had overtures from His Majesty. We shall let you have an answer when we know what his reaction has been to our having felt constrained to decline so august an invitation.'

Tō no Chūjō was consumed with curiosity and impatience. He had had a glimpse of his daughter and he wanted a good, clear look at her. He was sure that if she had any serious defects Genji would not have gone to troubles that seemed almost exaggerated. In any event, that strange dream was now explained.

Tō no Chūjō took the daughter at court into his confidence. They did what they could to keep the secret, but gossip is what people like best. Rumors spread and presently reached the ears of his more unruly daughter.

'So Father has a new girl. Isn't that nice. So she has both of them to look after her, Father and Genji. Just imagine. So her mother's a poor thing like my own.'

Her sister could think of nothing to say.

'I have no doubt,' said Kashiwagi, 'that she deserves all the attention she is getting. But you should not be quite so open about it, my dear. Does it not occur to you that people might be listening?'

'Oh, do be quiet, please. I know as much about it as the next one. I know that Father's going to send her to the palace and make her the grand high wardress. I've worked and slaved and hoped he would do something like that for me. I've done things when everybody else said no. And see how my own sister treats me.'

They had to smile. 'I thought of asking for the position myself when it came vacant. But don't you think it is rather bold of you to announce your candidacy so openly?'

The Omi lady was very annoyed indeed. 'I know I don't belong in this fine company. You. You're the one. You came hunting me out and now you make fun of me. How can a body *be* in a place like this? Terrible is what it is. Terrible, terrible.' She withdrew to a corner of the room, whence she sent sidelong glances in the direction of her brothers. They may not have been spiteful glances, exactly, but they did suggest someone with strong opinions and purposes.

Kashiwagi no longer felt quite so amused. She was right: it would have been better for everyone if he had left her in Omi.

'I don't think that anyone is making fun of you,' said Kōbai, standing up to leave. 'We do appreciate you. You are such a good worker. Just quietly bide your time. That is all you have to do. With your energy you should have no trouble making snow of the largest boulder. I am sure that all your prayers will be answered.'

'Though perhaps it might be better to stay shut up in your cave in the meantime,'* said Kashiwagi, also getting up to leave.

'Terrible, terrible.' She was shedding angry tears. 'My very own brothers. But I am working and slaving for you,' she said, turning to her sister. 'You understand even if they don't.'

And indeed she did work very hard, plunging into tasks from which the lowest menials tended to pull back. She dashed here and dashed there and quite lost herself in her labors. She once more announced her availability should the emperor wish to appoint her wardress of the ladies' apartments. Her sister wondered whether she could be serious. Tō no Chūjō laughed merrily when he heard of it.

'How would it be if we were to summon our Omi friend?' he said one day, in the course of a conversation with her sister.

'Oh, just fine,' said the lady herself, emerging noisily.

*Both the reduction to powder and the retreat into the cave are from the story of the Sun Goddess in the *Nihon Shoki*.

'I can see that you work hard and I think you would be a valuable addition to any office. Why did you not tell me of your wish to become wardress?'

He said it most solemnly. The lady was delighted. 'I did want to feel you out. I was sure I could count* on Sister here. But they say somebody else might get it. When I heard about it I felt like somebody that got rich and then found out it was a dream. But I have my fingers crossed.'† There was no suggestion that she lacked confidence.

'As always, you are too self-effacing.' He tried not to smile. 'If you had only told me, I would have made certain that your candidacy came first to His Majesty's ears. It is true that the chancellor has a daughter, but I feel certain that His Majesty would not turn away a warm recommendation from me, whatever fine ladies might be in the running. It is still not too late. You must compose your formal application, making sure that it is in the most exalted language. In verse, perhaps. He could not possibly ignore a long poem, and he holds accomplished verse in the highest esteem.'

He was not being a very good father.

'I'm not much of a poet but I'll give it a try. Just tell me in a general way what to put into it. I'll put the meat on the bones.‡ We'll be partners, you and me.' She brought her hands together by way of concluding the contract.

The women behind the curtains were choking and strangling. Some had to withdraw lest they disgrace themselves. The sister flushed scarlet.

'We can always count on our Omi lady to drive away the gloom,' said Tō no Chūjō.

People suspected that he was trying to conceal his discomfiture over the affairs of yet another daughter.

---

*She uses an expression which appears nowhere else.

†Literally: 'I have my hand pressed against my breast,' probably with reference to a superstition.

‡Another expression which appears nowhere else.

CHAPTER 30

Purple Trousers

Everyone was urging Tamakazura to become wardress of the ladies' apartments, but she did not feel safe even from Genji, who had put himself in charge of her affairs. She feared that she would be helpless if untoward incidents were to arise at court and that she would be an embarrassment to the sister already there. She still did not know either of the two gentlemen, Genji or Tō no Chūjō, well enough to feel that she could count on him. The world did not hold her in such high esteem that it would refrain from laughing if irregularities were to be detected in her affairs. Everywhere she looked she saw difficulties. Old enough to be aware of all the implications, she felt completely alone.

It was true that Genji was treating her well enough, but the difficulties in her relations with him were enormous. She only hoped that she might emerge unscathed from arrangements that must seem very odd to everyone.

Out of deference to Genji, Tō no Chūjō did not seem prepared to assume paternal responsibilities. There were difficulties on both sides, and so it seemed that romantic tangles and gossip must be her lot. The fact that her real father now knew of her circumstances seemed to have released her foster father from his inhibitions and so made matters worse.

She had no mother to whom she might have revealed at least a part of her troubles. Genji and Tō no Chūjō were so grand and remote that they had little time for her. She was very beautiful indeed as she sat out near the veranda looking up into a sad evening sky, lost in thought about her remarkably complex problems. She was in light-gray mourning,* her beauty the more striking for the want of color. Her women smiled with pleasure.

Yūgiri came calling, very handsome in informal court robes of a somewhat deeper gray. The ribbons of his cap were tied up in sign of mourning. She had been friendly enough in the days when he had thought her his sister, and it did not seem right to be suddenly cool and distant. She received him at her curtains as before

*We learn later that Princess Omiya died in the Third Month.

and dispensed with the services of an intermediary. He had been sent by Genji with a message from the emperor.

She was friendly but cautious, ladylike though mindful of her own interests. He had not forgotten the glimpse he had had of her the morning after the typhoon. At the time he had not thought it proper to be interested in her, but now the situation seemed to demand action. He could not understand why Genji wanted her to go to court. Perhaps her beauty was causing difficulties here at Rokujō.*

He managed to hide his excitement. 'I was informed that the matter must be considered highly confidential,' he said, looking pointedly at the women, who looked away as they withdrew behind curtains.

In great detail and very plausibly, he gave instructions from Genji which in fact he had made up. The emperor, he said, had intentions against which she must be on her guard. He thought her sighs charming, indeed irresistible, as she sought in vain for an answer.

'We were to come out of mourning this month, but it seems that examination of the almanacs did not yield an auspicious day. Father has said that he means to go to the river on the thirteenth and end his own mourning. I am to go along.'

'I think it would perhaps attract attention if I were to go with you. Perhaps I should arrange my own services, as quietly as possible.' She was being very careful indeed, not yet wanting to make public avowal of her reasons for having gone into mourning.

'You are too cautious. But I hate the thought myself of changing these dark clothes. They are reminders of a lady who was very dear to me. I must confess that I do not know why you are still living here. If you were not in mourning I might not know even now whose daughter you are.'

'I am not very quick at these things and I am sure that I am more puzzled than you are. Dark clothes do bring on sad thoughts.' She seemed more subdued than usual. She delighted him.

---

*The passage is obscure. It may be that the jealousy among his ladies has forced the emperor himself to give her up.

Perhaps thinking that there would not be another occasion to let her know of his interest, he had come provided with a fine bouquet of 'purple trousers.'*

'We may find in these flowers a symbol of the bond between us.' He pushed them under her curtains and caught at her sleeve as she reached for them.

> 'Dew-drenched purple trousers: I grieve as you do.
> And long for the smallest hint that you understand.'

Was this his own hint that he hoped for a union at 'journey's end?'† Not wanting to show her displeasure openly, she pretended that she did not understand and withdrew a little deeper into the room.

> 'It grew, if you ask, in the dews of a distant moor.
> That purple is false which tells of anything nearer.

'I think perhaps this conversation will mark our nearest approach.'

He smiled, 'You are a lady of discrimination. The fact is that I have held myself back because I feared full knowledge of the truth would make you more difficult. The truth is that not even the august summons to court has been enough to quell my ardor. Perhaps I should follow the suggestion of the channel buoys.‡

'Did you know that Kashiwagi was interested in you? And can you have thought that his interest did not interest me? Now that our positions are reversed I feel quite powerless, and rather envious of him, free to see you for a friendly talk whenever he wishes. Do at least pity me.'

Fujibakama, Eupatorium fortunei. Related to the aster and the chrysanthemum, it produces clusters of pink or lavender flowers in the autumn. Lavender, in general the color of affinity, here also suggests Tamakazura's family, the Fujiwara (*fuji*, 'wisteria'), and the mourning robes (*fujigoromo*, 'wisteria robes') which both are wearing.

†Anonymous, *Shinkokinshū* 1052:

> The sash is bound at Hitachi, at journey's end.
> I long for a hint of even so distant a union.

The tying of a ceremonial sash at the Kashima Shrine in Hitachi, on the remote eastern frontier, signified betrothal.

‡See note*, page 296.

He said a great deal more, but of such a questionable nature that I shall not try to describe it.

She withdrew yet further into the room.*

'This is very unfriendly of you. You must know that I am not a man to do anything rash.' Though he had not finished, she said that she was not feeling well and withdrew. With many a deep sigh he left.

He was beginning to fear that he had overreached himself. What a pleasure, he thought wistfully as he went to Genji's rooms, if even through curtains he might hear the voice of the lady more beautiful even than Tamakazura.

'I rather think,' said Genji, 'that Prince Hotaru was making progress. He is a very experienced man and he seems to have pleaded his case very eloquently. In any event, she had not been enthusiastic about going to court. And so he is to be disappointed? A pity; but that glimpse of His Majesty seems to have changed her mind completely. A glimpse is enough to convince any young lady that she *must* go to court. I thought it might be so when I made these arrangements for her.'

'Which of the two solutions would best fit her temperament? I wonder. Her Majesty has no real competition for His Majesty's affections, and the other lady is in a very strong position because of her father. I really doubt very much that Tamakazura can make enough of an impression on His Majesty to join in the competition. Prince Hotaru does seem to be very much drawn to her, and people are saying what a pity it would be if anything were to come between two brothers as close as you and he. They expect him to be very disappointed indeed even if she does not become one of the ladies of the bedchamber.' These were very mature remarks from so young a gentleman.†

'It is very difficult. Higekuro seems to be annoyed with me too, quite as if her arrangements were mine to make. Her life is very complicated and I thought I should do what I could for her. And the result is that I am unjustly reproached by both of them. I should have been more careful. I could not forget her mother's last request, and one day I heard that she was off in the far provinces.

---

*Tamakazura is here called 'the wardress of the ladies' apartments.' It would seem that the appointment has already been made.

†He is sixteen by the Oriental count.

When she said that her father refused to listen to her troubles, I had to feel sorry for her and offer to help her. I think her father is finally beginning to treat her like a human being because of the interest I have taken in her.' It was a consistent enough account of what had happened.

'I think she might make my brother a good wife,' he continued. 'She is a lively, modern sort of girl, much too clever to make any serious mistakes. They would get on very well together, I am sure. And on the other hand she seems beautifully qualified for service at court. She is pretty and efficient and even-tempered and well informed in matters of ceremony and precedent – exactly what His Majesty is looking for.'

Yūgiri wished to probe further. 'People seem a little curious about your reasons for being so good to her. Even her father hinted to a messenger from General Higekuro at what he thought might be your deeper reasons.'

Genji smiled. 'People imagine too much. I shall defer entirely to her father's wishes. I shall be quite happy if he sends her to court, and if he finds a husband for her that will be splendid too. A woman must obey three men in her life, and it would not do for her to get the order wrong.'*

'Someone I know was saying the other day that Tō no Chūjō is filled with secret admiration at the way you have arranged things. You have several ladies whose place in your life cannot be challenged, he seems to be thinking, and it would not do to add to their number at this late date; and so you mean to get her an appointment at court and still keep her for yourself.' He could not have been accused of indirection.

So matters would doubtless seem to Tō no Chūjō. Genji was sorry that it should be so.

'He has a suspicious sort of mind, probably because it is at the same time such a thorough mind. But he will see the truth soon enough if we let things take their course. Yes, a very thorough-going sort of man.'

Though his father's manner was cheerfully open, Yūgiri still had doubts. Genji himself could not dismiss the problem quite as easily as he pretended. It would serve neither Tamakazura's interests nor his own to play the role which rumor had evidently

*A woman obeys in succession her father, her husband, and her son.

assigned him. He must find an opportunity to assure Tō no Chūjō of his real intentions. And he was uncomfortable that Tō no Chūjō had guessed certain of his reasons for leaving Tamakazura's position at court somewhat equivocal and badly defined.

She had emerged from mourning. Since the Ninth Month would not be propitious for her court debut,* a date in the Tenth Month was fixed upon. The emperor was very impatient and her suitors were beside themselves. Tearfully, they besought their intermediaries to forestall the event. They might as well have requested the damming of Yoshino Falls.† Word came back that the prospect was next to hopeless.

Regretting his earlier loquacity, Yūgiri had made Tamakazura's business his own. He hoped that impersonal services, a wide variety of which he now undertook, would correct the unfavorable impression he must surely have made. He was in firm control of himself. No indiscretion would be permitted.

Her brothers were of course no longer among her suitors. They waited impatiently for her appearance at court, when they might be of service to her. The change in Kashiwagi, until but yesterday the picture of desolate yearning, amused her women. He came calling one moonlit night and took shelter under a laurel tree,‡ no public announcement having yet been made of her identity, as he sent in word that he had brought a message from his father. Received at the south door, he smiled wryly as he thought how she had refused even to accept his letters. She was still shy about addressing him, however, and sent back her answers through Saishō.

'I rather think that Father expected the message to go directly to my sister and not to travel these impossible distances. Why otherwise would he have chosen me for his messenger? You must forgive me if I seem insistent. I may not be a very important man, but it is a well-known fact that the bond between us is one which

---

*The First, Fifth, and Ninth months were considered unpropitious for such glad events as a first appearance at court. The reason may have been that religious observances were frequent.

†In *Kokin Rokujō, Zoku Kokka Taikan* 33083, the damming of Yoshino Falls is given as a simile for the impossible.

‡*Katsura*, more properly Judas tree. The *katsura* is associated with moonlight because one was thought to grow on the moon.

we could not cut even if we wished to. But enough. I sound like a complaining old man. Let me only add that your lady has been important to me.'

Again the answer came back through Saishō. 'Yes, it would have been good to have a long talk about things that have happened over the years. Unfortunately I have not been feeling well these last few days and would not be good company if I were to drag myself out and receive you. You *are* being rather insistent, and you make me feel shy and uncomfortable.'

'If you are ill, may I not come to your bedside? But you are right: I must watch my manners.' He lowered his voice as he transmitted his father's message. Saishō did not think that he compared at all badly with her suitors. 'Though Father is not as well informed as he might be in the matter of your court appointment, there are perhaps confidential matters which you will wish to discuss with him. He feels that he is being watched, he says, and that it would be even more difficult than it might once have been to see you.' And he added a few words of his own: 'I shall not forget myself again, even though your refusal to be friendly bothers me a great deal. Look at us now, for instance. I should have hoped for the privilege of your north porch at least, where I might have made the acquaintance of some of your less well-known ladies, however odd Saishō might have thought me. Where do you find a precedent for this unfriendliness? We are, after all, fairly close to each other.'

Saishō found his complaints rather endearing. She liked his bemused way of cocking his head to one side as he contemplated his unhappiness. She passed the message on to her lady.

'It is as you have suggested.' The answer was to the point. 'Too long an interview would without doubt attract attention, and so I must for the moment forgo the pleasure of a long conversation about my years of obscurity.'

Somewhat intimidated, he offered only a verse in reply:

'I did not know it was Sibling Mountain we climbed,
And came to a halt on hostile Odae Bridge.'*

---

*Imoseyama, 'Brother-Sister Mountain,' and Odaenohashi, 'the Bridge of Interruption,' were much used in poetry. There was more than one Imoseyama. Odaenohashi, was in the northern province of Mutsu.

It was a futile complaint about unhappiness of his own making. This was her answer:

> 'Not knowing that you did not know, I found
>   Your tracks up Sibling Mountain strange indeed.'

'Your remarks seem to have puzzled my lady,' said Saishō. 'She is very much concerned about appearances. Though I do not doubt that matters will presently change, she finds it impossible to speak with you further.'

She was right, of course. 'Yes, I suppose it is still too early for a good conversation,' he said, getting up to leave. 'I shall come again when a complaint about the debt for my accumulated services seems called for.'

There was a bright moon high in the sky, which was a lovely one. He was very handsome in lively, informal court dress. Though not perhaps as handsome as Yūgiri, said the women, he was certainly handsomer than most of them. Such remarkable good looks as did run in that family!

An officer in the guards division of which Higekuro was the commander, Kashiwagi was constantly being summoned for solemn conferences and had presented Higekuro's suit to Tō no Chūjō. Higekuro was a man of the finest character, certain to become one of the most important statesmen in the land. Though Tō no Chūjō did not think that Tamakazura was likely to do better, he would defer to Genji's wishes. Genji must have his reasons, some of them, perhaps, of a highly personal nature.

Higekuro was the crown prince's maternal uncle, lower in the royal esteem only than Genji and Tō no Chūjō. In his early thirties, he was married to the eldest daughter of Prince Hyōbu and so was Murasaki's brother-in-law. It need not have been cause for embarrassment that his wife was three or four years his senior, but for some reason he had never been really fond of her. He called her 'the old woman' and would have been happy enough to divorce her. It was for this reason, perhaps, that Genji did not welcome his suit and thought that Tamakazura would be making a mistake to encourage it. Higekuro was not of an amorous nature and no scandal had been associated with his name; but now he had lost his senses over Tamakazura. Tō no Chūjō did not think him at all beneath contempt and Tamakazura did not seem enthusiastic about going to court. Higekuro had a good informant who kept him apprised of these matters in considerable detail.

'Genji does not seem to like me,' he said to Bennomoto, one of her women, who had become his agent. 'We must see that the wishes of her real father are respected.'

The Ninth Month came. On that magically beautiful morning of the first frost the usual notes were brought in by the usual women, messengers for her several suitors. She had them read to her.

This one was from Higekuro:

'Hateful the Long Month* to those who are sure of themselves. I hang, as if for my life, on each fleeting day.

'The days upon which I had fastened my hopes pass in empty futility and the autumn skies bring the most intense anxiety.'

He thus made it clear that he was keeping himself well informed.

And this from Prince Hotaru: 'There is no point in questioning a firm and final decision, and yet,

> 'Warm though it be in the radiant morning sun,
>   Let the jeweled bamboo not forget the frost beneath.†

'A word of reassurance and understanding would suffice to quiet the turmoil of my thoughts.'

It was attached to a sprig of bamboo curled by the frost which still lay upon it. The choice of a messenger had been as careful.‡

Murasaki had a brother who held a guards commission. On friendly terms with the Rokujō house, he too had informed himself well of Tamakazura's affairs and was much disappointed by the turn they were taking. Among his rather lengthy complaints was this poem:

> 'Difficult it is to try to forget.
>   What shall I do about you, about myself?'

Each of these several notes was superior in all of its details, the color of the paper, the perfume that had been burned into it, the modulations of the ink. Such gentlemen, said her women, must be kept interested.

---

*The Ninth Month.

†The poem is an extremely contrived one, containing at least three poetic allusions.

‡Or perhaps, though it seems somewhat sportive for the occasion: 'The messenger was as dry and bent as the bamboo.'

Whatever she may have had in mind, Tamakazura replied briefly to Prince Hotaru's letter only.

> 'Not the sunflower, choosing to follow the sun,
> Forgets so soon the morning frost beneath.'

The faint, delicate hand quite fascinated him. Though as fragile as the dew, it was at least favorable notice.

There is nothing further to record, save that the complaining went on.

And, one is told, both ministers, her real father and her foster father, thought her behavior a model which other ladies would do well to imitate.

CHAPTER 31

The Cypress Pillar

'I dread having His majesty hear of it,' said Genji. 'Suppose we try to keep it secret for a while.'

But the gentleman in question was not up to such restraint. Though several days had passed since the successful conclusion to his suit, Tamakazura did not seem happy with him, and it pained him to note that she still seemed to think her lot a sad one. Yet he could tell himself that the bond between them had been tied in a former life, and he shuddered to think how easily a lady who more nearly approached his ideal each time he saw her might have gone to another. He must offer thanks to Bennomoto even as to the Buddha of Ishiyama. Bennomoto had so incurred the displeasure of her lady that she had withdrawn to the privacy of her room;* and it must indeed have been through the intervention of the Buddha that, having made so many men unhappy, the lady had gone to a man for whom she had no great affection.

Genji too was unhappy. He was sorry that she had done as she had, but of course helpless to change things. Since everyone had apparently acquiesced in the match, he would only be insulting Higekuro if at this late date he gave any sign of disapproval. He personally saw to arrangements for the nuptials, which were magnificent.

Higekuro wanted to take her home with him as soon as possible. Genji suggested, however, that haste might seem to show an inadequate regard for her rank and position, and pointed out that a lady who could hardly be expected to give her a warm welcome was already in residence there.

'Tact and deliberation are called for if you are to escape the reproaches of the world.'

'It is perhaps after all the less difficult course,' Tō no Chūjō was meanwhile saying to himself. 'I had had misgivings about sending her to court. A lady without the support of influential relatives can

---

*An obscure sentence. Another possible meaning is that Higekuro, of the successful conclusion to whose courtship we are being circumspectly informed, is staying away from court.

have a difficult time in competition for the royal affections. I would have wanted to help her, of course, but what could I have done with another daughter there ahead of her?'

And indeed it would have been unkind to send her to court when the prospect was that she would join the ranks of lesser ladies and see the emperor infrequently.

Tō no Chūjō was most pleased with the reports he had of the third-night ceremonies.

Though no formal announcement was made, the marriage was the talk of the day.

The emperor heard of it. 'A pity. But she seems to have been meant for him. She does still seem to be interested in her work. Perhaps if I make it clear that I have no personal designs upon her –'

It was now the Eleventh Month, a time of Shinto festivals, which kept her busy. She had offices at Rokujō, where she was visited by a steady stream of chamberlains and ladies-in-waiting. His Excellency the general,* hoping that he was not making a nuisance of himself, spent his days with her. She did in fact think him rather a nuisance.

Prince Hotaru and her other suitors were of course unhappy. Murasaki's brother was the unhappiest of all, for the gossips were having malicious fun over the affairs of another sister, Higekuro's wife. But he told himself that a confrontation with Higekuro would do him no good.

Higekuro had been offered as a model of sobriety, a man who had not been known to lose his head over a woman. Now see him, delirious with joy, a changed man! Stealing in and out of Tamakazura's rooms in the evening and morning twilight, he was the very model of youthful infatuation. The women were vastly amused.

There was little sign these days of Tamakazura's essentially cheerful nature. She had withdrawn into a brooding silence and seemed intent on making it clear to the world that her husband had not been her first choice. What would Genji be thinking of it all? And Prince Hotaru, who had been so friendly and attentive? She had never shown much warmth toward Higekuro, and in that regard she had not changed.

*Perhaps ironical.

Genji stood acquitted of the charges that had been leveled against him. Reviewing the record, he could tell himself that he had shown very little interest, really, in amorous dalliance.

'You did not have enough faith in me,' he said to Murasaki.

It would invite a proper scandal if now he were to surrender to temptation. There had been times when he had thought he would do anything to have the girl, and it was not easy to give her up.

He called on her one day when Higekuro was out. So despondent that she was feeling physically ill, she did not want to see him. Half concealed behind curtains, she sought to compose herself for an interview. Genji addressed her most ceremoniously and they talked for a time of things that did not greatly interest them. The company of a plainer sort of man made her see more than ever what a surpassingly handsome and elegant man Genji was. Yes, her lot had been and continued to be a sad one. She was in tears, which she sought to hide from him.

As the conversation moved to more intimate topics he leaned forward and looked through an opening in the curtains. She was more beautiful, he thought, for being thinner. It had been very careless of him to let her go.

> 'I made no move myself to try the river,
>   But I did not think to see you cross with another.

'It is too unbelievably strange.' He brushed away a tear. She turned away and hid her face.

> 'I wish I might vanish as foam on a river of tears.
>   Before I come to the river Mitsuse.'*

'Not the river I would choose myself,' he said, smiling. 'There is no detour around the other, I am told, and I had hoped that I might take you gently by the hand and help you. I am joking, but I am sure that you now see the truth. Few men can have been as harmlessly silly as I was. I think you see, and I take comfort in the thought.'

He changed the subject, fearing that she saw all too well. 'It is sad that His Majesty should still be asking for you. Perhaps you should make a brief appearance at court. The general seems to

---

*Both poems refer to the river Mitsuse, in the land of the dead. A lady expected to be helped across by her first love.

think you his property, to do with as he pleases, and so I suppose it will not be possible to put you in the royal service. Things have not turned out quite as I had hoped. His Lordship at Nijō* seems satisfied, however, and that is the important thing.'

He said much that amused her and also embarrassed her. She could only listen. He was sorry for her, and gave no hint of the improper designs which he had not quite put aside. He offered many helpful suggestions for her work at court. It seemed that he did not want her to go immediately to Higekuro's house.

Higekuro was not pleased at the thought of having her in court service. Then it occurred to him, though such deviousness went against his nature, that a brief appearance at court might be just what he wanted. He could take her from the palace to his house. He set about redecorating it and restoring rooms that had been allowed to decay and gather dust over the years. He was quite indifferent to the effect of all this activity upon his wife, and thought nothing at all of the effect on his dear children. A man of feeling and sensitivity thinks first of others, but he was an obstinate, unswerving sort of man, whose aggressiveness was constantly giving offense. His wife was not a woman to be made light of. She was the pampered daughter of a royal prince, comely and well thought of. For some years a malign and strangely tenacious power had made her behavior eccentric in the extreme and not infrequently violent. Though he no longer had much affection for her, he still considered her his principal wife, unchallenged in her claim to that position. Now, suddenly, there was another lady, superior in every respect. More to the point, the shadows and suspicions surrounding this second lady had been dispelled. She had become a perfectly adequate object for his affections, which were stronger every day.

'And so you are to live miserably off in a corner of the house,' said Prince Hyōbu, her father, 'while a fashionable young lady takes over the rest? What will people say when they hear of *that* arrangement? No. While I am alive I will not permit them to laugh at you.'

He had redecorated the east wing of his house and wanted her to come home immediately. The thought of going as a discarded wife so distressed her that the fits of madness became more frequent. She took to her bed. She was of a quiet, pleasant nature,

*Tō no Chūjō.

almost childishly docile and amiable in her saner moments, and people would have enjoyed her company if it had not been for her great disability. Because of it she had so neglected herself that she could hardly expect to please a man who was used to the best. Yet they had been together for many years and he would be sorry in spite of everything to have her go.

'People of taste and sensibility see even their casual affairs through to a proper conclusion. You have not been well, and I have not wanted to bring the matter up – but you should give a thought to the promises we made. We meant them to last, I think. I have put up with your rather unusual illness for a very long time and I have meant to take care of you to the end, and now it seems that you are prepared to forestall me. You must think of the children, and you could think of me too. I doubt very much that I have behaved improperly. You are emotional, as all women are, and you are angry with me. It is quite understandable that you should be. You cannot of course know my real feelings and intentions. But do please reserve judgment for a little while longer. Your father is being rash and reckless, taking you off the minute he hears that something is wrong. Of course I cannot be sure whether he is serious or whether he wants to frighten me.'

He permitted himself a tentative smile, which did not please her. Even those of her women whom he had especially favored, Moku and Chūjō among them, thought and said, with proper deference, that he was behaving badly. The lady herself, whom he had found in one of her lucid moments, wept quietly.

'I cannot complain that you do not find my stupidity and eccentricities to your taste. But it does not seem fair that you should bring Father into the argument. It is not his fault, poor man, that I am what I am. But I am used to your arbitrary ways, and do not propose to do anything about them.'

She was still handsome as she turned angrily away. She was a slight woman and illness made her seem even more diminutive. Her hair, which had once been long and thick, now looked as if someone had been pulling it out by the roots. It was wild from long neglect and dank and matted from weeping, altogether a distressing sight. Though no one could have described her as a great beauty, she had inherited something of her father's courtliness, badly obscured now by neglect and illness. There was scarcely a trace left of youthful freshness.

'Can you really think I mean to criticize your father? The suggestion is ill advised in the extreme and could lead to serious misunderstanding. The Rokujō house is such perfection that it makes a plain, rough man like me feel very uncomfortable. I want to have her here where I can be more comfortable, that is all. Genji is a very important man, but that is not the point. You should think rather of yourself and what they will say if word gets to that beautifully run house of the unpleasantness and disorder here. Do try to control yourself and be friendly to her. If you insist on going, then you may be sure that I will not forget you. My love for you will not vanish and I will not join in the merriment – indeed it will make me very sad – when the world sees you making a fool of yourself. Let us be faithful to our vows and try to help each other.'

'I am not worried about myself. You may do with me as you wish. It is Father I am thinking of. He knows how ill I am and it upsets him enormously that after all these years people should be talking about us. I do not see how I can face him. And you are surely aware of another thing, that Genji's wife is not exactly a stranger to me. It is true that Father did not have responsibility for her when she was a girl, but it hurts him that she should now have made herself your young lady's sponsor. It is no concern of mine, of course. I but observe.'

'Most perceptively. But I fear that once again you are a victim of delusions. Do you think that a sheltered lady like her could know about the affairs of the lady of whom you are so comtemptuous? I do not think that your father is being very fatherly and I would hate to have these allegations reach Genji.'

They argued until evening. He grew impatient and fretful, but unfortunately a heavy snow was falling, which made it somewhat awkward for him to leave. If she had been indulging in a fit of jealousy he could have said that he was fighting fire with fire and departed. She was calmly lucid, and he had to feel sorry for her. What should he do? He withdrew to the veranda, where the shutters were still raised.

She almost seemed to be urging him on his way. 'It must be late, and you may have trouble getting through the snow.'

It was rather touching – she had evidently concluded that nothing she said would detain him.

'How can I go out in such weather? But things will soon be

different. People do not know my real intentions, and they talk, and the talk gets to Genji and Tō no Chūjō, who of course are not pleased. It would be wrong of me not to go. Do please try to reserve judgment for a time. Things will be easier once I have brought her here. When you are in control of yourself you drive thoughts of other people completely from my mind.'

'It is worse for me,' she said quietly, 'to have you here when your thoughts are with someone else. An occasional thought for me when you are away might do something to melt the ice on my sleeves.'*

Taking up a censer, she directed the perfuming of his robes. Though her casual robes were somewhat rumpled and she was looking very thin and wan, he thought the all too obvious melancholy that lay over her features both sad and appealing. The redness around her eyes was not pleasant, but when as now he was in a sympathetic mood he tried not to notice. It was rather wonderful that they had lived together for so long. He felt a little guilty that he should have lost himself so quickly and completely in a new infatuation. But he was more and more restless as the hours went by. Making sure that his sighs of regret were audible, he put a censer in his sleeve and smoothed his robes, which were pleasantly soft. Though he was of course no match for the matchless Genji, he was a handsome and imposing man.

His attendants were nervous. 'The snow seems to be letting up a little,' said one of them, as if to himself. 'It is very late.'

Moku and Chūjō and the others sighed and lay down and whispered to one another about the pity of it all. The lady herself, apparently quite composed, was leaning against an armrest. Suddenly she stood up, swept the cover from a large censer, stepped behind her husband, and poured the contents over his head. There had been no time to restrain her. The women were stunned.

The powdery ashes bit into his eyes and nostrils. Blinded, he tried to brush them away, but found them so clinging and stubborn that he had to throw off even his underrobes. If she had not had the excuse of her derangement he would have marched from

---

*Anonymous, *Gosenshū* 482:

> I lie awake all through the winter night.
> The fire of my thoughts does not melt the ice on my sleeves.

her presence and vowed never to return. It was a very perverse sort of spirit that possessed her.

The stir was enormous. He was helped into new clothes, but it was as if he had had a bath of ashes. There were ashes deep in his side whiskers. Clearly he was in no condition to appear in Tamakazura's elegant rooms.

Yes, she was ill, he said angrily. No doubt about that – but what an extraordinary way to be ill! She had driven away the very last of his affection. But he calmed himself. A commotion was the last thing he wanted at this stage in his affairs. Though the hour was very late, he called exorcists and set them at spells and incantations. The groans and screams were appalling.

Pummeled and shaken by the exorcists as they sought to get at the malign spirit, she screamed all through the night. In an interval of relative calm he got off a most earnest letter to Tamakazura.

'There has been a sudden and serious illness in the house and it has not seemed right to go out in such difficult weather. As I have waited in hopes of improvement the snow has chilled me body and soul. You may imagine how deeply troubled I am, about you, of course, and about your women as well, and the interpretation they may be placing on it all.

'I lie in the cold embrace of my own sleeves.
Turmoil in the skies and in my heart.

'It is more than a man should be asked to endure.'

On thin white paper, it was not a very distinguished letter. The hand was strong, however. He was not a stupid or uncultivated man. His failure to visit had not in the least upset Tamakazura. She did not look at his letter, the product of such stress and turmoil, and did not answer it. He passed a very gloomy day.

The ravings were so violent that he ordered prayers. He was praying himself that her sanity be restored even for a little while. It was all so horrible. Had he not known what an essentially gentle creature she was, he would not have been able to endure it so long.

He hurried off in the evening. He was always grumbling, for his wife paid little attention to his clothes, that nothing fitted or looked right, and indeed he was a rather strange sight. Not having a change of court dress at hand, he was sprinkled with holes from the hot ashes and even his underrobes smelled ominously of smoke. Tamakazura would not be pleased at this too clear evidence of his wife's fiery ways. He changed underrobes and had another bath and otherwise did what he could for himself.

Moku perfumed the new robes. A sleeve over her face, she whispered:

'Alone with thoughts which are too much for her,
She has let unquenchable embers do their work.'

And she added: 'You are so unlike your old self that not even we underlings can watch in silence.'

The eyebrows over the sleeve were very pretty, but he was asking himself, rather unfeelingly, one must say, how such a woman could ever have interested him.

'These dread events so fill me with rage and regret
That I too choke from the fumes that rise within me.

'I will be left with nowhere to turn if word of them gets out.'
Sighing, he departed.

He thought that Tamakazura had improved enormously in the one night he had been away. He could not divide his affections. He stayed with her for several days, hoping to forget the disturbances at home and fearful of incidents that might damage his name yet further. The exorcists continued to be busy, he heard, and malign spirits emerged noisily from the lady one after another. On occasional trips home he avoided her rooms and saw his children, a daughter twelve or thirteen and two younger sons, in another part of the house. He had seen less and less of his wife in recent years, but her position had not until now been challenged. Her women were desolate at the thought that the final break was approaching.

Her father sent for her again. 'It is very clear that he is abandoning you. Unless you wish to look ridiculous you cannot stay in his house. There is no need for you to put up with this sort of thing so long as I am here to help you.'

She was somewhat more lucid again. She could see that her marriage was a disaster and that to stay on until she was dismissed would be to lose her self-respect completely. Her oldest brother was in command of one of the guards divisions and likely to attract attention. Her younger brothers, a guards captain, a chamberlain, and an official in the civil affairs ministry, came for her in three carriages. Her women had known that a final break was unavoidable, but they were sobbing convulsively. She was returning to a house she had left many years before and to less spacious rooms. Since it was clear that she would not be able to take all of her women with her, some of them said that they would go home and return to her service when her affairs were somewhat more settled. They went off taking their meager belongings with them. The lamentations were loud as the others saw to the cleaning and packing as became their several stations.

Her children were too young to understand the full proportions of the disaster that had overtaken them.

'I do not care about myself,' she said to them, weeping. 'I will face what comes, and I do not care whether I live or die. It is you I am sad for. You are so very young and now you must be separated and scattered.* You, my dear,' she said to her daughter, 'must stay with me whatever happens. It may be even worse for you,' she said to the boys. 'He will not be able to avoid seeing you, of course, but he is not likely to trouble himself very much on your account. You will have someone to help you while Father lives, but Genji and Tō no Chūjō control the world. The fact that you are my children will not make things easier for you. I could take you out to wander homeless, of course, but the regrets would be so strong that I would have them with me in the next world.'

They were sobbing helplessly.

She summoned their nurses. 'It is the sort of thing that happens in books. A perfectly good father loses his head over a new wife and lets her dominate him and forgets all about his children. But he has been a father in name only. He forgot about them long ago. I doubt that he can be expected to do much for them.'

It was a forbidding night, with snow threatening. Her brothers tried to hurry her.

'A really bad storm might be blowing up.'

They brushed away tears as they looked out into the garden. Higekuro had been especially fond of his daughter. Fearing that she would never see him again, she lay weeping and wondering how she could possibly go.

'Do you so hate the thought of going with me?' said her mother.

*There are two allusions in this passage to Sugawara Michizane's departure into exile.

The girl was hoping to delay their departure until her father came home, but there was little likelihood that he would leave Tamakazura at so late an hour. Her favorite seat had been beside the cypress pillar in the east room. Now it must go to someone else. She set down a poem on a sheet of cypress-colored notepaper and thrust a bodkin through it and into a crack in the pillar. She was in tears before she had finished writing.

> 'And now I leave this house behind forever.
>   Do not forget me, friendly cypress pillar.'

'I do not share these regrets,' said her mother.

> 'Even if it wishes to be friends,
>   We may not stay behind at this cypress pillar.'

The women were sobbing as they took their farewells of trees and flowers to which they had not paid much attention but which they knew they would remember fondly.

Moku, being in Higekuro's service, would stay behind. This was Chūjō's farewell poem:

> 'The waters, though shallow, remain among the rocks,
>   And gone is the image of one who would stay beside them.

'I had not dreamed that I would have to go.'
'What am I to say?' replied Moku.

> 'The water among the rocks has clouded over.
>   I do not think my shadow long will linger.'

More aware than ever of the uncertainty of life, the lady looked back at a house she knew she would not see again. She gazed at each twig and branch until house and garden were quite out of sight. Though it was not as if she were leaving a place she loved, there are always regrets for a familiar house.

If it was an angry father who awaited her, it was a still angrier mother. The princess had not paused to catch her breath as she told her husband how she felt about it all. 'You seem very proud to have Genji for a son-in-law. He was born our enemy, I say, and the strength of his hostility has never ceased to amaze me. He loses no chance to make things difficult for our girl at court. You have said that he will change once he has taught us a lesson for not helping him during his troubles. Other people have said so too. I say it is odd if he is so fond of his Murasaki that he doesn't have a thought for her family now and then. But that's only the beginning. At his age he takes in a stray he knows nothing about and to keep on the right side of his Murasaki he finds an honest upright man no breath of scandal has ever touched and marries her off to him.'

'I must ask you to hold your tongue. The world has only good things to say of Genji and you may not permit yourself the luxury of abusing him. I am sure you are right when you say that he wanted to get even. It was my bad luck to give him cause. I can see that in his quiet way he has been very efficient and intelligent about handing out rewards and punishments, and if my punishment has been especially severe it is because we are especially close. You will remember what an occasion he made of my fiftieth birthday some years ago. It was more than I deserved, the talk of the whole court. I count it among the great honors of my life.'

But she was a strong-minded woman and he only made her angrier. Her language was more and more abusive.

Higekuro learned that his wife had left him. One might have expected such behavior, he said, from a rather younger wife. But he did not blame her. Prince Hyōbu was an impetuous man, and it had all been his doing. Higekuro was sure that left to herself she would have thought of the children and tried to keep up appearances.

'A fine thing,' he said to Tamakazura. 'It will make things easier for us, of course, but I fear I miscalculated. She is a gentle soul and I was sure she would just keep to herself in her corner of the house. That headstrong father of hers is behind it all. I must go and see what has happened. I will seem completely irresponsible if I do not.'

He was handsome and dignified in a heavy robe, a singlet of white lined with green, and gray-green brocade trousers. The women thought that their lady had not done at all badly for herself, but this new development did nothing to give her a happier view of her marriage. She did not even glance at him.

He stopped by his house on his way to confront Prince Hyōbu. Moku and the others told him what had happened. He tried manfully to control himself but their description of his daughter reduced him to tears.

'Your lady does not seem to see that it has been good of me to put up with her strange ways for so long. A less indulgent man would not have been capable of it. But we need not discuss her case further. She seems beyond helping. The question is what she means to do with the children.'

They showed him the slip of paper at the cypress pillar. Though the hand was immature the poem touched him deeply. He wept all the way to Prince Hyōbu's, where it was not likely that he would be permitted to see the girl.

'He has always been good at ingratiating himself with the right people,' said the prince to his daughter, and there was much truth in it. 'I do not think that we need be surprised. I heard several years ago that he had lost his senses over that girl. It would be utter self-deception to hope for a recovery. You will only invite further insults if you stay with him.' In this too there was much truth.

He did not find Higekuro's addresses convincing.

'This does not seem a very civilized way to behave,' said Higekuro. 'I cannot apologize enough for my own inadequacy. I was quite confident that she would stay with me because of the children, and that was very stupid of me. But might you not be a little more forbearing and wait until it comes to seem that I have left her no alternative?'

He asked, though not hopefully, to see his daughter. The older son was ten and in court service, a most likable boy. Though not remarkably good-looking, he was intelligent and popular, and old enough to have some sense of what was happening. The other son was a pretty child of eight or so. Higekuro wept and stroked his hair and said that he must come home and help them remember his sister, whom he resembled closely.

Prince Hyōbu sent someone out to say that he seemed to be coming down with a cold and could not receive guests. It was an awkward situation.

Higekuro presently departed, taking the boys with him. All the way back to his house, where he left them, for he could not after all take them to Rokujō, he gave them his side of the story.

'Just pretend that nothing is amiss. I will look in on you from time to time. It will be no trouble at all.'

They were yet another weight on his spirits, which revived considerably, however, at the sight of his new wife, in such contrast to the queer old wife who had left him.

He made Prince Hyōbu's hostility his excuse for not writing. The prince thought it rather exaggerated and extreme.

'I think it very unfair of her to be angry with me,' said Murasaki.

'It is difficult for all of us,' said Genji. 'Tamakazura has always been an unmanageable young lady, and now she has won me the emperor's displeasure. I understand that Prince Hotaru has been very angry. But he is a reasonable man, and the signs are that he has accepted my explanations. Romantic affairs cannot be kept secret, whatever precautions we may take. I am glad that I have nothing on my conscience.'

The excitement she had caused did nothing to dispel Tamakazura's gloom, which was more intense as time went by. Higekuro was worried: the emperor was likely to hold him responsible for the abrupt change in her plans, and Genji and Tō no Chūjō would doubtless have thoughts in the matter. It was not unprecedented for an official to have a wife in the royal service, and so he presented her at court just before the New Year caroling parties.* The presentation ceremonies were very grand, having behind them, besides Higekuro's own efforts, all the prestige of the two ministers, her foster father and her real father. Yūgiri busied himself most energetically in her behalf and her brothers were in lively competition to win her favor.

She was assigned apartments on the east side of the Shōkyōden Pavilion. Prince Hyōbu's daughter occupied the west rooms of the same building and only a gallery separated them. In spirit they were very far apart indeed. It was an interesting and lively time, a time of considerable rivalry among the emperor's ladies. Besides Empress Akikonomu, they included Tō no Chūjō's daughter, this daughter of Prince Hyōbu, and the daughter of the Minister of the Left.† As for the lesser ranks that so often figure in untidy incidents, there were only the daughters of two councillors.

The caroling parties were very gay, all the ladies having invited their families to be present. The array of festive sleeves was dazzling as each lady tried to outdo the others. The crown prince was still very young, but his mother‡ was a lady of fashion who saw to

The Otokotōka, in the middle of the First Month. See note, page 137.
†Not otherwise identified.
‡Higekuro's sister.

it that his household was no duller than the others. The carolers visited the emperor, the empress, and the Suzaku emperor in that order. Having had to omit Rokujō, they returned from the Suzaku Palace to sing for the crown prince. Some of them were rather drunk when, in the beautiful beginnings of dawn, they came to 'Bamboo River.'* Among the courtiers of the middle ranks Tō no Chūjō's sons, some four or five of them, were especially good-looking and talented. His eighth son, by his principal wife, was one of his favorites, very pretty indeed in page's livery. Tamakazura was delighted with him, standing beside Higekuro's older son, and of course she could hardly think him a stranger. She had already given her rooms at court a fashionable elegance with which the better-established ladies found it hard to compete. She had not ventured any startlingly new color schemes but she managed to give a remarkable freshness to the familiar ones.

Now that she was at court she hoped to enjoy herself, and in this hope she had the enthusiastic support of her women. The bolts of cloth with which she rewarded the carolers were similar to those offered by the other ladies and yet subtly different. Though she was expected to offer only light refreshments, her rooms seemed more festive than any of the others; and though precedent and regulation were carefully honored, great attention had gone into all of the details, none of which was merely routine. Higekuro had taken an active part in the arrangements.

He sent repeated messengers from his offices, all with the same message: 'We will leave together as soon as it is dark. I do not want you to make this your occasion for establishing residence here. Indeed I would be very upset.'

She did not answer.

'The Genji minister,' argued her women, 'says that we needn't be in such a hurry. He says that His Majesty has seen little of us and it is our duty to let him see more. Don't you think it would be rather abrupt and even a little rude if we were to slip off this very night?'

'I plead with her and plead with her,' said Higekuro, 'and seem to have no effect at all.'

Though Prince Hotaru had come for the carols, his attention was chiefly on Tamakazura. Unable to restrain himself, he got off

*See note†, page 438.

a message. Higekuro was on duty in the guards quarter. It was
from his offices, said the women, that the note had come. She
glanced at it.

> 'You fly off wing to wing through mountain forests,
>   And in this nest of mine it is lonely spring.

'I hear distant, happy singing.'

She flushed, fearing that she had not been kind to the prince.
And how was she to answer? Just then the emperor came calling.
He was unbelievably handsome in the bright moonlight, and the
very image of Genji. It seemed a miracle that there should be two
such men in the world. Genji had been genuinely fond of her, she
was sure, but there had been those unfortunate complications.
There were none in the emperor's case. Gently, he reproved her
for having gone against his wishes. She hid her face behind a fan,
unable to think of an answer.

'How silent you are. I would have expected you to be grateful
for these favors. Are you quite indifferent?

> 'Why should I be drawn to lavender
>   So utterly remote and uncongenial?'

'Are we likely to be treated to deeper shades of purple?'

She found his good looks intimidating, but told herself that he
was really no different from Genji. And her answer – is it to be
interpreted as thanks for having been promoted to the Third Rank
before she had done anything to deserve the honor?

> 'I know not the meaning of this lavender,
>   Though finding in it marks of august grace.

'I shall do everything to show that I am grateful.'

He smiled. 'Suppose I summon a qualified judge to tell us
whether it is not perhaps a little late to be donning the colors of
gratitude.'

She was silent. She did not wish to seem coy, but she was confused at evidences that he shared certain tendencies with lesser
men. She did not seem very friendly, he was thinking, but doubtless she would change as time went by.

Higekuro was very restless indeed. She must go away with him
immediately, he said. Somewhat concerned about appearances

herself, she contrived a plausible excuse with the expert assistance of her father and others and was at length able to leave.

'Goodbye, then.' The emperor seemed genuinely regretful. 'Do not let anyone tell you that because this has happened you must not come again. I was the first to be interested in you and I let someone else get ahead of me. It does not seem fair that he should remain unchallenged. But there we are. I can think of precedents.'*

She was far more beautiful than distant rumor had made her. Any man would have regretted seeing her go, and he was in a sense a rejected suitor. Not wishing her to think him light-headed and frivolous, he addressed her most earnestly and did everything he could to make her feel comfortable. She understood and, though awed, wished she could stay with him.

He was still at her side when a hand carriage was brought up to take her away. Her father's men were waiting and Higekuro was making a nuisance of himself.

'You are guarded too closely,' said the emperor.

> 'Invisible beyond the ninefold mists,
> May not the plum blossom leave its scent behind?'

It may have been that the emperor's good looks made his poem seem better than it was.

'Enamored of the fields, I had hoped to stay the night,'† he continued, 'but I find someone impatiently reaching to pluck the flowers. How shall I write to you?'

Sorry to have made him unhappy, she replied:

> 'I count not myself among the finer branches,
> Yet hope that the fragrance may float upon the breeze.'

He looked back time after time as he finally made his exit.

Higekuro had meant all along to take her with him but had kept his plans secret, lest Genji oppose them.

---

*Unclear, although he seems to have a specific precedent in mind. Early commentators offer the instance of Taira Sadabumi, who had his wife taken by Fujiwara Tokihira.

†Yamanoe Akahito, *Manyōshū* 1424:

> I only went to gather violets,
> Then stayed the night, enamored of the fields.

'I seem to be coming down with a cold,' he said to the emperor, as if no further explanation were necessary. 'I think I should take care of myself, and would not want to have her away from me.'

Though Tō no Chūjō thought it all rather sudden and unceremonious, he did not want to risk offending Higekuro. 'Do as you see fit,' he said. 'I have not had a great deal to do with her plans.'

Genji was startled but helpless. The lady was a little startled herself at the direction in which the smoke was blowing.* Higekuro was enjoying the role of lady stealer.†

She thought he had behaved very badly, showing his jealousy of the emperor so openly. A coarse, common sort of man – she made less attempt than ever to hide her distaste.

Prince Hyōbu and his wife, who had spoken of him in such strong terms, were beginning to wish that he would come visiting. But his life was full. His days and nights were dedicated to his new lady.

The Second Month came. It had been cruel of her, Genji was thinking. She had caught him off guard. He thought about her a great deal and wondered what people would be saying. It had all been fated, no doubt, and yet he could not help thinking that he had brought it on himself. Higekuro was so unsubtle a man that Genji feared venturing even a playful letter. On a night of boredom when a heavy rain was falling, however, he remembered that on other such nights he had beguiled the tedium by visiting her, and got off a note. He sent it secretly to Ukon. Not sure what view she would take of it, he limited himself to commonplaces.

'A quiet night in spring. It rains and rains.
    Do your thoughts return to the village you left behind?

'It is a dull time, and I grumble – and no one listens.'

Ukon showed it to Tamakazura when no one else was near. She wept. He had been like a father, and she longed to see him. But it was, as he suggested, impossible. She had not told Ukon

---

*Tales of Ise 112:

> At Suma the fishermen are burning salt.
>
> The winds bear it off in a rather surprising direction.

†Probably a reference to Tales of Ise 6, in which an empress is kidnapped.

how unseemly his behavior had sometimes been and she now had
no one with whom to share her feelings. Ukon had suspicions of
the truth, but they were not very precise.

'It embarrasses me to write to you,' Tamakazura sent back, 'but
I am afraid that you might be worried. As you say, it is a time of
rainy boredom.

> 'It rains and rains. My sleeves have no time to dry.
> Of forgetfulness there comes not the tiniest drop.'

She concluded with conventional remarks of a daughterly sort.

Genji was near tears as he read it, but did not wish to treat these
women to a display of jewel-like teardrops. As the rising waters
threatened to engulf him, he thought of how, all those years ago,
Kokiden had kept him from seeing her sister Oborozukiyo. Yet so
novel was the Tamakazura affair that it seemed without precedents. Men of feeling did have a way of sowing bitter herbs. He
tried to make himself accept the plain facts, that the lady was not a
proper object for his affections and that these regrets came too
late. He took out a Japanese koto, and it too brought memories.
What a gentle touch she had had! He plucked a note or two* and,
trying to make it sound lighthearted, sang 'The Jeweled Grasses'†
to himself. It is hard to believe that the lady for whom he longed
would not have pitied him if she could have seen him.

Nor was the emperor able to forget the beauty and elegance he
had seen so briefly. 'Off she went, trailing long red skirts behind
her.'‡ It was not a very refined old poem, but he found it somehow comforting when his thoughts turned to her. He got off a
secret note from time to time.

Sugagaki, meaning unclear.

†'Kōzuke,' a 'popular song' (*fūzokuuta*):

> Do not pull up the jeweled grasses
> Of Hara Pond,
> Where come the ducks, the ducklings, the mandarins and mallards.
> Let them spread, the jeweled grasses, spread and grow.

‡Anonymous, *Manyōshū* 2550:

> Off she went, trailing long red skirts behind her.
> I wake, I sleep, the image is with me always.

These attentions gave her no pleasure. Still lamenting her sad fate, she did not reply. Genji and his kindness were much on her mind.

The Third Month came. Wisteria and *yamabuki* were in brilliant flower. In the evening light they brought memories of a beautiful figure once seated beneath them. Genji went to the northeast quarter, where Tamakazura had lived. A clump of *yamabuki* grew untrimmed in a hedge of Chinese bamboo, very beautiful indeed. 'Robes of gardenia, the silent hue,'* he said to himself, for there was no one to hear him.

> 'The *yamabuki* wears the hue of silence,
> So sudden was the parting at Idé road.†

'I still can see her there.'

He seemed to know for the first time – how strange! – that she had left him.

Someone having brought in a quantity of duck's eggs, he arranged them to look like oranges and sent them off to her with a casual note which it would not have embarrassed him to mislay.

'Through the dull days and months I go on thinking resentfully of your strange behavior. Having heard that someone else had a hand in the matter, I can only regret my inability to see you unless some very good reason presents itself.' He tried to make it seem solemnly parental.

> 'I saw the duckling hatch and disappear.
> Sadly I ask who may have taken it.'

Higekuro smiled wryly. 'A lady must have very good reasons for visiting even her parents. And here is His Lordship pretending that he has some such claim upon your attentions and refusing to accept the facts.'

---

*Anonymous, *Kokin Rokujō, Zoku Kokka Taikan* 34356:

> I shall put on robes of gardenia, the silent hue,
> And let them speak of my love with words of silence.

A yellow dye was made from the seeds of the gardenia, which the Japanese call 'the mouthless flower.'

†Idé, in the province of Yamashiro, was known for its *yamabuki*.

She thought it unpleasant of him. 'I do not know how to answer.'

'Let me answer for you.' Which suggestion was no more pleasing.

'Off in a corner not counted among the nestlings,
   It was hidden by no one. It merely picked up and left.

'Your question, sir, seems strangely out of place. And please, I beg of you, do not treat this as a billet-doux.'

'I have never seen him in such a playful mood,' said Genji, smiling. In fact, he was hurt and angry.

The divorce had been a cruel wrench for Higekuro's wife, whose lucid moments were rarer. He continued to consider himself responsible for her, however, and she was as dependent upon him as ever. He was very mindful of his duties as a father. Prince Hyōbu still refused to allow him near his daughter, Makibashira,* whom he longed to see. Young though she was, she thought that they were being unfair to him, and did not see why she should be so closely guarded.

Her brothers went home frequently and of course brought back reports of his new lady. 'She seems very nice. She is always thinking of new games.'

She longed to go with them. Boys were the lucky ones, free to go where they pleased.

Tamakazura had a strange talent for disturbing people's lives.

In the Eleventh Month she had a son, a very pretty child. Higekuro was delighted. The last of his hopes had been realized. As for the general rejoicing, I shall only say that her father, Tō no Chūjō, thought her good fortune not at all surprising. She seemed in no way inferior to the daughters on whom he had lavished such attention. Kashiwagi, who still had not entirely freed himself of unbrotherly feelings, wished that she had gone to court as planned.

'I have heard His Majesty lament that he has no sons,' he said, and one may have thought it a little impertinent of him, when he saw what a fine child it was. 'How pleasing for all of us if it were a little prince.'

Makibashira means 'cypress pillar,' from her poem upon leaving home.

She continued to serve as wardress of the ladies' apartments, though it was not reasonable to expect that she would again appear at court.

I had forgotten about the minister's other daughter, the ambitious one who had herself been desirous of appointment as wardress. She was a susceptible sort of girl and she was restless. The minister did not know what to do with her. The sister at court lived in dread of scandal.

'We must not let her out where people will see her,' said the minister.

But she was not easily kept under cover.

One evening, I do not remember exactly when, though it must have been at the loveliest time of autumn, several fine young gentlemen were gathered in the sister's rooms. There was music of a quiet, undemanding sort. Yūgiri was among them, more jocular than usual.

'Yes, he *is* different,' said one of the women.

The Omi lady pushed herself to the fore. They tried to restrain her but she turned defiantly on them and would not be dislodged.

'Oh, *there* he is,' she said in a piercing whisper of that most proper young man. '*There's* the one that's different.'

Now she spoke up, offering a poem in firm, clear tones:

'If you're a little boat with nowhere to go,
     Just tell me where you're tied. I'll row out and meet you.

'Excuse me for asking, but are you maybe the open boat that comes back again and again?'*

He was startled. One did not expect such blunt proposals in these elegant rooms. But then he remembered a lady who was much talked about these days.

'Not even a boatman driven off course by the winds
     Would wish to make for so untamed a shore.'

She could not think how to answer – or so one hears.

See note, page 107.

CHAPTER 32

A Branch of Plum

Genji was immersed in preparations for his daughter's initiation ceremonies. Similar ceremonies were to be held for the crown prince in the Second Month. The girl was to go to court immediately afterwards.

It was now the end of the First Month. In his spare time Genji saw to blending the perfumes she would take with her. Dissatisfied with the new ones that had come from the assistant viceroy of Kyushu,* he had old Chinese perfumes brought from the Nijō storehouses.

'It is with scents as with brocades: the old ones are more elegant and congenial.'

Then there were cushions for his daughter's trousseau, and covers and trimmings and the like. New fabrics did not compare with the damasks and red and gold brocades which an embassy had brought from Korea early in his father's reign. He selected the choicest of them and gave the Kyushu silks and damasks to the serving women.

He laid out all the perfumes and divided them among his ladies. Each of them was to prepare two blends, he said. At Rokujō and elsewhere people were busy with gifts for the officiating priests and all the important guests. Every detail, said Genji, must be of the finest. The ladies were hard at work at their perfumes, and the clatter of pestles was very noisy indeed.

Setting up his headquarters in the main hall, apart from Murasaki, Genji turned with great concentration to blending two perfumes the formulas for which – how can they have come into his hands? – had been handed down in secret from the day of the emperor Nimmyō.† In a deeply curtained room in the east wing Murasaki was at work on blends of her own, after the secret Hachijō tradition.‡ The competition was intense and the security very strict.

*Otherwise unidentified.
†Ninth century.
‡Perfected by Prince Motoyasu, a son of Nimmyō.

'Let the depths and shallows be sounded,' said Genji solemnly, 'before we reach our decisions.' His eagerness was so innocent and boyish that few would have taken him for the father of the initiate.

The ladies reduced their staffs to a minimum and let it be known that they were not limiting themselves to perfumes but were concerned with accessories too. They would be satisfied with nothing but the best and most original jars and boxes and censers.

They had exhausted all their devices and everything was ready. Genji would review the perfumes and seal the best of them in jars.

Prince Hotaru came calling on the tenth of the Second Month. A gentle rain was falling and the rose plum near the veranda was in full and fragrant bloom. The ceremonies were to be the next day. Very close since boyhood, the brothers were admiring the blossoms when a note came attached to a plum branch from which most of the blossoms had fallen. It was from Princess Asagao, said the messenger. Prince Hotaru was very curious, having heard rumors.

'I made certain highly personal requests of her,' said Genji, smiling and putting the letter away. 'I am sure that as always she has complied with earnest efficiency.'

The princess had sent perfumes kneaded into rather large balls in two jars, indigo and white, the former decorated with a pine branch and the latter a branch of plum. Though the cords and knots were conventional, one immediately detected the hand of a lady of taste. Inspecting the gifts and finding them admirable, the prince came upon a poem in faint ink which he softly read over to himself.

'Its blossoms fallen, the plum is of no further use.
Let its fragrance sink into the sleeves of another.'

Yūgiri had wine brought for the messenger and gave him a set of lady's robes, among them a Chinese red lined with purple.

Genji's reply, tied to a spray of rose plum, was on red paper.

'And what have you said to her?' asked the prince. 'Must you be so secretive?'

'I would not dream of having secrets from you.'

This, it would seem, is the poem which he jotted down and handed to his brother:

'The perfume must be hidden lest people talk,
But I cannot take my eye from so lovely a blossom.'

'This grand to-do may strike you as frivolous,' said Genji, 'but a man does go to very great troubles when he has only one daughter. She is a homely little thing whom I would not wish strangers to see, and so I am keeping it in the family by asking the empress to officiate. The empress is a lady of very exacting standards, and even though I think of her as one of the family I would not want the smallest detail to be wrong.'

'What better model could a child have than an empress?'

The time had come to review the perfumes.

'It should be on a rainy evening,' said Genji. 'And you shall judge them. Who if not you?'*

He had censers brought in. A most marvelous display was ranged before the prince, for the ladies were determined that their manufactures be presented to the very best advantage.

'I am hardly the one who knows,' said the prince.

He went over them very carefully, finding this and that delicate flaw, for the finest perfumes are sometimes just a shade too insistent or too bland.

Genji sent for the two perfumes of his own compounding. It being in the old court tradition to bury perfumes beside the guardsmen's stream, he had buried them near the stream that flowed between the main hall and the west wing. He dispatched Koremitsu's son, now a councillor, to dig them up. Yūgiri brought them in.

'You have assigned me a most difficult task,' said the prince. 'I fear that my judgment may be a bit smoky.'

The same tradition had in several fashions made its way down to the several contestants. Each had added ingeniously original touches. The prince was faced with many interesting and delicate problems.

Despite Asagao's self-deprecatory poem, her 'dark' winter incense was judged the best, somehow gentler and yet deeper than the others. The prince decided that among the autumn scents, the 'chamberlain's perfumes,' as they are called, Genji's had an intimacy which however did not insist upon itself. Of Murasaki's three, the plum or spring perfume was especially bright and original, with a tartness that was rather daring.

*Ki no Tomonori, *Kokinshū* 38:

> Who shall judge the color, the scent of the plum?
> Who if not you? The one who knows best knows best.

'Nothing goes better with a spring breeze than a plum blossom,' said the prince.

Observing the competition from her summer quarter, the lady of the orange blossoms was characteristically reticent, as inconspicuous as a wisp of smoke from a censer. She finally submitted a single perfume, a summer lotus-leaf blend with a pungency that was gentle but firm. In the winter quarter the Akashi lady had as little confidence that she could hold her own in such competition. She finally submitted a 'hundred pace'* sachet from an adaptation of Minamoto Kintada's† formula by the earlier Suzaku emperor,‡ of very great delicacy and refinement.

The prince announced that each of the perfumes was obviously the result of careful thought and that each had much to recommend it.

'A harmless sort of conclusion,' said Genji.

The moon rose, there was wine, the talk was of old times. The mistenshrouded moon was weirdly beautiful, and the breeze following gently upon the rain brought a soft perfume of plum blossoms. The mixture of scents inside the hall was magical.

It was the eve of the ceremony. The stewards' offices had brought musical instruments for a rehearsal. Guests had gathered in large numbers and flute and koto echoed through all the galleries. Kashiwagi, Kōbai, and Tō no Chūjō's other sons stopped by with formal greetings. Genji insisted that they join the concert. For Prince Hotaru there was a lute, for Genji a thirteen-stringed koto, for Kashiwagi, who had a quick, lively touch, a Japanese koto. Yūgiri took up a flute, and the high, clear strains, appropriate to the season, could scarcely have been improved upon. Beating time with a fan, Kōbai was in magnificent voice as he sang 'A Branch of Plum.'** Genji and Prince Hotaru joined him at the climax. It was

---

*Hyperbolic, suggesting the distance at which it could be detected.

†Kintada was a grandson of the emperor Kōkō, who reigned late in the ninth century.

‡Probably Uda, 867-931, the first of the 'cloistered emperors.'

**A Saibara:

> The warbler in the plum tree
> Sings all through the spring.
> But here it is already,
> And snow is falling and falling.

Kōbai who, still a court page, had sung 'Takasago' at the rhyme-guessing contest so many years before.* Everyone agreed that though informal it was an excellent concert.

Prince Hotaru intoned a poem as wine was brought in:

'The voice of the warbler lays a deeper spell
    Over one already enchanted by the blossoms.

'For a thousand years, if they do not fall?'†
Genji replied:

'Honor us by sharing our blossoms this spring
    Until you have taken on their hue and fragrance.'

Kashiwagi recited this poem as he poured for Yūgiri:

'Sound your bamboo flute all through the night
    And shake the plum branch where the warbler sleeps.'

Yūgiri replied:

'I thought we wished to protect them from the winds,
    The blossoms you would have me blow upon madly.

'Most unthinking of you, sir.' There was laughter.
This was Kōbai's poem:

'Did not the mists intercede to dim the moonlight
    The birds on these branches might burst into joyous blossom.'

And indeed music did sound all through the night, and it was dawn when Prince Hotaru made ready to leave. Genji had a set of informal court robes and two sealed jars of perfume taken out to his carriage.

'If she catches a scent of blossoms upon these robes,
    My lady will charge me with having misbehaved.'

'How very sad for you,' said Genji, coming out as the carriage was being readied.

*See Chapter 10.
†Sosei, *Kokinshū* 96:

How long shall I wander enchanted over these fields?
A thousand years, if these blossoms do not fall?

'I should have thought your lady might be pleased
   To have you come home all flowers and brocades.

'She can scarcely be witness to such a sight every day.'
The prince could not immediately think of an answer.*

There were modest but tasteful gifts, ladies' robes and the like,
for all the other guests.

Genji went to the southwest quarter early that evening. A
porch at the west wing, where Akikonomu was in residence, had
been fitted out for the ceremony. The women whose duty it
would be to bind up the initiate's hair were already in attendance.
Murasaki thought it a proper occasion to visit Akikonomu. Each
of the two ladies had a large retinue with her. The ceremonies
reached a climax at about midnight with the tying of the ceremonial train. Though the light was dim, Akikonomu could see that
the girl was very pretty indeed.

'Still a gawky child,' said Genji. 'I am giving you this glimpse
of her because I know you will always be good to her. It awes me
to think of the precedent we are setting.'

'Do I make a difference?' replied Akikonomu, very young and
pretty herself. 'None at all, I should have thought.'

Such a gathering of beauty, said Genji, was itself cause for jubilation.

The Akashi lady was of course sad that she would not see her
daughter on this most important of days. Genji debated the possibility of inviting her but concluded that her presence would make
people talk and that the talk would do his daughter no good.

I shall omit the details. Even a partial account of a most ordinary ceremony in such a house can be tedious at the hands of an
incompetent narrator.

The crown prince's initiation took place later in the month. He
was mature for his years and the competition to enter his service
should have been intense. It seemed to the Minister of the Left,†
however, that Genji's plans for his daughter made the prospects
rather bleak for other ladies. Colleagues with nubile daughters
tended to agree, and kept the daughters at home.

'How petty of them,' said Genji. 'Do they want the prince to

---

*The exchange is ironical, Prince Hotaru being a widower and a rejected suitor.
†Otherwise unidentified.

be lonely? Don't they know that court life is only interesting when all sorts of ladies are in elegant competition?'

He postponed his daughter's debut. The Minister of the Left presently relented and dispatched his third daughter to court. She was called Reikeiden.

It was now decided that Genji's daughter would go to court in the Fourth Month. The crown prince was very impatient. The hall in which Genji's mother had lived and Genji had had his offices was now assigned to his daughter. The finest craftsmen in the land were busy redecorating the rooms, which it might have seemed were splendid enough already. Genji himself went over the plans and designs.

And there was her library, which Genji hoped would be a model for later generations. Among the books and scrolls were masterpieces by calligraphers of an earlier day.

'We live in a degenerate age,' said Genji. 'Almost nothing but the "ladies' hand" seems really good. In that we do excel. The old styles have a sameness about them. They seem to have followed the copybooks and allowed little room for original talent. We have been blessed in our own day with large numbers of fine calligraphers. Back when I was myself a student of the "ladies' hand" I put together a rather distinguished collection. The finest specimens in it, quite incomparable, I thought, were some informal jottings by the mother of the present empress. I thought that I had never seen anything so fine. I was so completely under their spell that I behaved in a manner which I fear did damage to her name. Though the last thing I wanted to do was hurt her, she became very angry with me. But she was a lady of great understanding, and I somehow feel that she is watching us from the grave and knows that I am trying to make amends by being of service to her daughter. As for the empress herself, she writes a subtle hand, but' – and he lowered his voice – 'it may sometimes seem a little weak and wanting in substance.

'Fujitsubo's was another remarkable hand, remarkable and yet perhaps just a little uncertain, and without the richest overtones. Oborozukiyo is too clever, one may think, and somewhat given to mannerism; but among the ladies still here to please us she has only two rivals, Princess Asagao and you yourself, my dear.'

'The thought of being admitted to such company overwhelms me,' said Murasaki.

'You are too modest. Your writing manages to be gentle and intimate without ever losing its assurance. It is always a pleasant surprise when someone who writes well in the Chinese style moves over to the Japanese and writes that just as well.'

He himself had had a hand in designing the jackets and bindings for several booklets which still awaited calligraphers. Prince Hotaru must copy down something in one of them, he said, and another was for a certain guards commander, and he himself would see to putting something down in one or two others.

'They are justly proud of their skills, but I doubt that they will leave me any great distance behind.'

Selecting the finest inks and brushes, he sent out invitations to all his ladies to join in the endeavor. Some at first declined, thinking the challenge too much for them. Nor were the 'young men of taste,' as he called them, to be left out. Yūgiri, Murasaki's oldest brother, and Kashiwagi, among others, were supplied with fine Korean papers of the most delicate hues.

'Do whatever you feel like doing, reed work* or illustrations for poems or whatever.'

The competition was intense. Genji secluded himself as before in the main hall. The cherry blossoms had fallen and the skies were soft. Letting his mind run quietly through the anthologies, he tried several styles with fine results, formal and cursive Chinese and the more radically cursive Japanese 'ladies' hand.' He had with him only two or three women whom he could count on for interesting comments. They ground ink for him and selected poems from the more admired anthologies. Having raised the blinds to let the breezes pass, he sat out near the veranda with a booklet spread before him, and as he took a brush meditatively between his teeth the women thought that they could gaze at him for ages on end and not tire. His brush poised over papers of clear, plain reds and whites, he would collect himself for the effort of writing, and no one of reasonable sensitivity could have failed to admire the picture of serene concentration which he presented.

'His Highness Prince Hotaru.'

Shaking himself from his reverie and changing to informal court dress, Genji had a place readied for his guest among the

---

*A highly mannered style in which the calligraphic strokes merge into a landscape painting.

books and papers. As the prince came regally up the stairs the women were delighted anew. The two brothers carried themselves beautifully as they exchanged formal greetings.

'My seclusion from the world had begun to be a little trying. It was thoughtful of you to break in upon the tedium.'

The prince had come to deliver his manuscript. Genji read through it immediately. The hand could not have been called strikingly original, but of its sort it was disciplined and orderly. The prince had chosen poems from the older anthologies and set each of them down in three short lines. The style was a good cursive that made spare use of Chinese characters.

'I had not expected anything half so good,' said Genji. 'You leave me with no recourse but to break my brushes and throw them all away.'

'I do at least give myself high marks for the boldness that permitted me to enter such a competition.'

Genji could not very well hide the manuscript he had been at work on himself. They went over it together. The cursive Chinese characters on unusually stiff Chinese paper were very good indeed. As for the passages in the 'ladies' hand,' they were superb, gently flowing strokes on the softest and most delicately tinted of Korean papers. A flow of admiring tears threatened to join the flow of ink. The prince thought that he could never tire of such pleasures. On bright, bold papers made by the provisioner for our own royal court Genji had jotted down poems in a whimsical cursive style, the bold abandon of which was such as to make the prince fear that all the other manuscripts must seem at best inoffensive.

The guards commander had also hoped to give an impression of boldness, but a certain muddy irresolution was hidden, or rather an attempt had been made to hide it, by mere cleverness. The selection of poems, moreover, left him open to charges of affectation.

Genji was more secretive with the ladies' manuscripts and especially Princess Asagao's.

The 'reed work' was very interesting, each manuscript different from the others. Yūgiri had managed to suggest the flow of water in generous, expansive strokes, and his vertical strokes called to mind the famous reeds of Naniwa. The joining of reeds and water was accomplished very deftly. There were sudden and bold variations, so that, turning a page, the reader suddenly came upon craggy, rocklike masses.

'Very fine indeed,' said the prince, a man of wide and subtle interests. 'He has obviously taken it very seriously and worked very hard.'

As the conversation ranged over the varieties of calligraphy and manuscripts, Genji brought out several books done in patchwork with old and new papers. The prince sent his son the chamberlain to bring some scrolls from his own library, among them a set of four on which the emperor Saga had copied selections from the *Manyōshū*, and a *Kokinshū* at the hand of the emperor Daigo, on azure Chinese papers with matching jade rollers, intricate damask covers of a darker blue, and flat Chinese cords in multicolored checkers. The writing was art of the highest order, infinitely varied but always gently elegant. Genji had a lamp brought near.

'I could look at them for weeks and always see something new. Who in our own day can do more than imitate the smallest fragment?'

They were for Genji's daughter, said the prince. 'Even if I had a daughter of my own, I would want to be very sure that she was capable of appreciating them. As it is, they would rot ignominiously away.'

Genji gave the chamberlain a fine Korean flute and specimens of Chinese patchwork in a beautifully wrought aloeswood box.

He now immersed himself in study of the cursive Japanese styles. Having made the acquaintance of the more notable calligraphers, he commissioned from each a book or scroll for his daughter's library, into which only the works of the eminent and accomplished were to be admitted. In the assembled collection there was not an item that could have been called indifferent, and there were treasures that would have filled gaps in the great court libraries across the seas. Young people were begging to see the famous patchwork. There were paintings too. Genji wanted his own Suma diary to go to his descendants, but decided that his daughter was perhaps still a little young for it.

Tō no Chūjō caught distant echoes of the excitement and was resentful. His daughter Kumoinokari was being wasted in the full bloom of her youth. Her gloom and boredom weighed on his own spirits — and Yūgiri seemed quite unconcerned. Tō no Chūjō knew that he would look ridiculous if he were suddenly to admit defeat. He was beginning to regret that he had not grandly nodded his acquiescence back in the days when Yūgiri was such an earnest plaintiff. He kept these thoughts to himself, and he was too honest with himself to be angry with the boy. Yūgiri was aware of them, but the people around Kumoinokari had once treated him with contempt and he was not going to give them the satisfaction of seeming eager. Yet he showed that he was still interested by not being even slightly interested in other ladies. These were matters which he could not treat of even in jest.* It may have been that he was seeking a chance to show his councillor's robes to the nurse who had had such contempt for the humbler blue.

Genji thought it time he was married. 'If you no longer want the minister's daughter, then Prince Nakatsukasa and the Minister of the Right† have both let it be known that they would welcome a proposal. Suppose you were to take one of their daughters.'

Yūgiri listened respectfully but did not answer.

'I did not pay a great deal of attention to my father's advice and so I am in no position to lecture to you. But I am old enough now to see what an unerring guide he would have been if I had chosen to listen.

'People think there is something odd about you because you are not married, and if in the end it seems to have been your fate to disappoint us, well, we can only say that you once showed promise. Do please always be on guard against the possibility that you are throwing yourself away because your ambitions have proven unreal.

'I grew up at court and had little freedom. I was very cautious, because the smallest mistake could make me seem reckless and giddy. Even so, people said that I showed promiscuous tendencies. It would be a mistake for you to think that because you are still relatively obscure you can do as you please. The finest of men – it was true long ago and it is still true today – can disgrace themselves because they do not have wives to keep them from temptation. A man never recovers from a scandal, nor does the woman he has let himself become involved with. Even a difficult marriage can be made to work. A man may be unhappy with his wife, but if he tries hard he can count on her parents to help him. If she has none, if she is alone in the world and without resources, then pity for her

See note, page 271.

†Both are otherwise unidentified.

can make him see her good points. The man of discrimination makes the best of the possibilities before him.'

It was when he had little else to do that he offered such advice.

But for Yūgiri the thought of taking another wife was not admissible. Kumoinokari was not comfortable with his attentions these days because she knew how disturbed and uncertain her father was. She was sorry for herself too, but tried to hide her gloom. Sometimes, when the longing was too much for Yūgiri, there would be an impassioned letter. A more experienced lady, though aware that there was no one except the man himself to question about his intentions, might have suspected posing and posturing. She found only sentiments that accorded with her own.

Her women were talking. 'It seems that Prince Nakatsukasa has reached a tacit understanding with Genji and is pushing ahead with the arrangements.'

Tō no Chūjō was troubled. There were tears in his eyes when, very gently, he told Kumoinokari what he had heard. 'It seems very unkind of the boy. I suppose that Genji is trying to get back at me. I cannot give my consent now without looking ridiculous.'

Intensely embarrassed, she too was weeping. He thought her charming as she turned away to hide her tears. He left feeling more uncertain than ever. Should he make new attempts to learn what they all were thinking?

Kumoinokari went out to the veranda. Why was it, she asked herself, that the tide of tears must be forever waxing and joy forever on the wane? And what would her poor father be thinking?

A letter from Yūgiri came in upon the gloom. She opened it, and could detect no change in his manner.

'This coldness takes you the usual way of the world.
Am I the deviant, that I cannot forget you?'

She did not like this calm refusal to say anything of his new affair. Yet she answered.

'You cannot forget, and now you have forgotten.
You are the one who goes the way of the world.'

That was all. What could she possibly mean? He looked at it from this angle and that – so one is told – and could make no sense of it.

CHAPTER 33

Wisteria Leaves

Yūgiri thought himself odd that he should be so gloomy when everyone else was so caught up in the excitement. His singleness of purpose had come to seem obsessive. Now there appeared a possibility that Tō no Chūjō was prepared to look the other way – and so why did he not slip through? But no. An air of cool indifference had served him well thus far and it must be maintained to the end. It cost him a great deal. As for Kumoinokari, she feared that if the rumors her father had brought were true, then this indifference was not feigned; and so even as they turned from each other they went on thinking about each other.

Calm and resolute on the surface, Tō no Chūjō suspected that he was no longer in control of his daughter's affairs. If on the assumption that the reports about Prince Nakatsukasa's daughter were true he were to begin thinking of other arrangements for Kumoinokari, the man to whom he turned would hardly feel flattered, nor was Tō no Chūjō's own dignity likely to emerge unimpaired. There would be talk and there might be incidents. Well, he had made a mistake, and that fact could not be kept secret. He must surrender and hope to do so with some dignity.

But he must wait for the proper occasion. He could not step forth and make a great show of welcoming Yūgiri as his own. That would be too utterly ridiculous. The time would come, however. A surface calm hid these tensions.

The anniversary of Princess Omiya's death fell on the twentieth of the Third Month. Tō no Chūjō attended memorial services at the Gokurakuji Temple, south of the city. All of his sons were with him, a very grand entourage indeed. As handsome as any of them, Yūgiri was also of the party. Though he had avoided Tō no Chūjō since the days when the latter had treated him so badly, he had not let the smallest sign of his resentment show. Tō no Chūjō was increasingly aware of it all the same.

Genji too commissioned memorial services, and Yūgiri solemnly busied himself with services of his own.

As they returned from the Gokurakuji in the evening, cherry petals were drifting through the spring haze. In a reminiscent mood, Tō no Chūjō intoned lines from the anthologies. Yūgiri was no less moved by the beauty of the evening. It looked like rain, someone said. Yūgiri did not seem to hear.

Tō no Chūjō (one may imagine that it was with some apprehension) tugged at his sleeve.

'Why are you angry with me? Might this not be the occasion to forgive me, whatever I may have done? I think I have a right myself to complain, that you should have cast me aside in my declining years.'

'Grandmother's last instructions,' said Yūgiri, very politely, 'were that I look to you for advice and support. But you have not seemed to welcome my presence.'

Suddenly there was a downpour. They hurried home in twos and threes.

What could have produced this sudden change? The words themselves had seemed casual enough, but they came from a man before whom Yūgiri seldom felt comfortable. He lay awake all night asking what they could mean.

Perhaps his patience had been rewarded. Tō no Chūjō seemed to be relenting. He continued to seek a proper occasion, neither too ostentatious nor too casual, for a reconciliation.

Early in the Fourth Month the wisteria at Tō no Chūjō's veranda came into profuse bloom, of a subtly richer hue than most wisteria. He arranged a concert, thinking that it must not go unnoticed. As the colors mounted richer in the twilight, he sent Kashiwagi with a note.

'It was a pity that we were not permitted a more leisurely talk under the cherry blossoms. If you are free, I would be most honored to see you.

'Come join me in regrets for the passing of spring
  And wisteria now aglow in the evening light.'

It was attached to a magnificent spray of the flower.

Restraining his excitement at the letter awaited so long, Yūgiri sent back a polite answer:

'I grope my way through the gathering shades of evening
  With no great hopes of coming upon wisteria.'

'I am not sure I have struck the right note,' he said to Kashiwagi. 'Would you look it over, please?'

'All that is required of you is that you come with me.'

'You are far too grand an escort.'

He sent Kashiwagi ahead and went to show Genji the letter.

'I think he must have his reasons,' said Genji, who seemed pleased with himself. 'I had thought that he was not showing proper respect towards his late mother, but this changes things.'

'I doubt that it is so very important. Everyone says that his wisteria is very fine this year. I imagine that he was bored and arranged a concert in its honor.'

'He sent a very special messenger, in any event. You must go.'

And so a nervous Yūgiri had his father's blessing.

'It would not do to overdress,' Genji continued. 'A magenta would be all right, I suppose, if you were not yet on the council or if you were between offices. Do please dress very carefully.' He sent one of Yūgiri's men with a fine robe and several singlets from his own wardrobe.

Yūgiri did take great care with his dress. Tō no Chūjō had begun to grow restless when finally he arrived. Seven or eight of Tō no Chūjō's sons, led by Kashiwagi, came out to receive him. They were all very handsome, but Yūgiri was even handsomer, with a calm dignity that rather put them to shame. Tō no Chūjō showed him to his place. It was clear that the preparations for receiving him had been thorough.

'Be sure that you get a good look at him,' Tō no Chūjō had said to his wife and her young women as he changed to formal dress. 'He is completely in control of himself. In that respect I think he is more than his father's equal, though of course Genji is so handsome that a smile from him can make you think all the world's problems have been solved. I doubt that anyone minds very much if he sometimes seems a little flippant in his treatment of public affairs. Yūgiri is a sterner sort and he has studied hard. I for one would have trouble finding anything wrong with him, and I suspect that most people would have the same trouble.'

Dispensing with the stiffer formalities, he turned immediately to the matter of honoring his wisteria.

'There is much to be said for cherry blossoms, but they seem so flighty. They are so quick to run off and leave you. And then just when your regrets are the strongest the wisteria comes into bloom, and it blooms on into the summer. There is nothing quite like it. Even the color is somehow companionable and inviting.' He was still a very handsome man. His smile said a great deal.

Though the lavender was not very apparent in the moonlight, he worked hard at admiring it. The wine flowed generously and there was music. Pretending to be very drunk and to have lost all thought for the proprieties, he pressed wine upon Yūgiri, who, though sober and cautious as always, found it hard to refuse.

'Everyone agrees that your learning and accomplishments are more than we deserve in this inferior day of ours. I should think you might have the magnanimity to put up with old dotards like myself. Do you have in your library a tract you can refer to in the matter of filial piety? I must lodge a complaint that you who are so much better informed than most about the teachings of the sages should in your treatment of me have shown indifference to their high principles.' Through drunken tears – might one call them? – came these adroit hints.

'You do me a very grave injustice, sir. I think of you as heir to all the ages, and so important that no sacrifice asked of me could be too great. I am a lazy, careless man, but I cannot think what I might have done to displease you.'

The moment had come, thought Tō no Chūjō. 'Underleaves of wisteria,' he said, smiling.* Kashiwagi broke off an unusually long and rich spray of wisteria and presented it to Yūgiri with a cup of wine. Seeing that his guest was a little puzzled, Tō no Chūjō elaborated upon the reference with a poem of his own:

'Let us blame the wisteria, of too pale a hue,
    Though the pine has let itself be overgrown.'

Taking a careful though elegant sip from the cup that was pressed upon him, Yūgiri replied:

'Tears have obscured the blossoms these many springs,
    And now at length they open full before me.'

He poured for Kashiwagi, who replied:

'Wisteria is like the sleeve of a maiden,
    Lovelier when someone cares for it.'

---

*Anonymous, Gosenshū 100:

    Underleaves of wisteria in the spring:
    If they augur honesty I shall be honest with you.
  The underleaves, *uraba*, are echoed by *uratokete*, 'being honest.'

Cup followed cup, and it would seem that poem followed poem with equal rapidity; and in the general intoxication none were superior to these.

The light of the quarter-moon was soft and the pond was a mirror, and the wisteria was indeed very beautiful, hanging from a pine of medium height that trailed its branches far to one side. It did not have to compete with the lusher green of summer.

Kōbai, in his usual good voice, sang 'The Fence of Rushes,'* very softly.

'What an odd one to have chosen,' Tō no Chūjō said, laughing. Also in fine voice, he joined in the refrain, changing the disturbed house into 'a house of eminence.' The merriment was kept within proper bounds and all the old enmity vanished.

Yūgiri pretended to be very drunk. 'I am not feeling at all well,' he said to Kashiwagi, 'and doubt very much that I can find my way home. Let me borrow your room.'

'Find him a place to rest, my young lord,' said Tō no Chūjō. 'I am afraid that in these my declining years I do not hold my liquor well and may create a disturbance. I shall leave you.' He withdrew.

'Are you saying that you mean to pass one night among the flowers?' said Kashiwagi. 'It is a difficult task you assign your guide.'

'The fickle flowers, watched over by the steadfast pine? Please, sir – do not let any hint of the inauspicious creep into the conversation.'

Kashiwagi was satisfied, though he did not think that he had risen to the occasion as wittily as he might have. He had a very high opinion of Yūgiri and would not have wished the affair to end otherwise. With no further misgivings he showed his friend to Kumoinokari's room.

For Yūgiri it was a waking dream. He had waited, long and well. Kumoinokari was very shy but more beautiful than when, all those years before, he had last seen her. He too was satisfied.

*A Saibara:

> Parting the fence of rushes,
> Making her way through the fence,
> Someone has spoken to Father,
> Spoken to Father of you.
> The house is in an uproar.
> It was my brother's wife!

'I knew that people were laughing,' he said, 'but I let them laugh, and so here we are. Your chief claim to distinction through it all, if I may say so, has been your chilliness. You heard the song your brother was singing, I suppose. It was not kind of him. The fence of rushes – I would have liked to answer with the one about the Kawaguchi Barrier.'*

This, she thought, required comment: 'Deplorable.

'So shallow a river, flowing out to sea.
Why did so stout a fence permit it to pass?'

He thought her delightful.

'Shallowness was one, but only one,
Among the traits that helped it pass the barrier.

'The length of the wait has driven me mad, raving mad. At this point I understand nothing.' Intoxication was his excuse for a certain fretful disorderliness. He appeared not to know that dawn was approaching.

The women were very reluctant to disturb him.

'He seems to sleep a confident and untroubled sleep,' said Tō no Chūjō.

He did, however, leave before it was full daylight. Even his yawns were handsome.

His note was delivered later in the morning with the usual secrecy. She had trouble answering. The women were poking one another jocularly and the arrival of Tō no Chūjō added to her embarrassment. He glanced at the note.

'Your coldness serves to emphasize my own inadequacy, and makes me feel that the best solution might be to expire.

'Do not reprove me for the dripping sleeves
The whole world sees. I weary of wringing them dry.'

*The Saibara 'Kawaguchi' ('Rivermouth'):

> The stout fence at Kawaguchi,
> At Rivermouth Barrier,
> Has a guard to guard it.
> But I have made my way through,
> Come through and made my bed,
> Through the stout fence at Kawaguchi.

It may have seemed somewhat facile.

'How his writing has improved.' Tō no Chūjō smiled. The old resentments had quite disappeared. 'He will be impatient for an answer, my dear.'

But he saw that his presence had an inhibiting effect and withdrew.

Kashiwagi ordered wine and lavish gifts for the messenger, an assistant guards commander who was among Yūgiri's most trusted attendants. He was glad that he no longer had to do his work in secret.

Genji thought his son more shiningly handsome* than ever this morning. 'And how are you? Have you sent off your letter? The most astute and sober of men can stumble in the pursuit of a lady, and you have shown your superiority in refusing to be hurried or to make a nuisance of yourself. Tō no Chūjō was altogether too stern and uncompromising. I wonder what people are saying now that he has surrendered. But you must not gloat and you must be on your best behavior. You may think him a calm, unruffled sort of man, but he has a strain of deviousness that does not always seem entirely manly and does not make him the easiest person in the world to get along with.' Genji went on giving advice, it will be seen, though he was delighted with the match.

They looked less like father and son than like brothers, the one not a great deal older than the other. When they were apart people were sometimes not sure which was which, but when they were side by side distinctive traits asserted themselves. Genji was wearing an azure robe and under it a singlet of a Chinese white with the pattern in clear relief, sprucely elegant as always. Yūgiri's robe was of a somewhat darker blue, with a rich saffron and a softly figured white showing at the sleeves. No bridegroom could have been more presentable.

A procession came in bearing a statue of the infant Buddha.† It was followed somewhat tardily by priests. In the evening little girls brought offerings from the several Rokujō ladies, as splendid as anything one would see at court. The services too were similar,

---

Hikari soite. The word *hikari* is used to describe only Genji, Reizei, Yūgiri, and Murasaki (the last when she lies dead).

†On the Buddha's birthday, the eighth of the Fourth Month.

the chief difference being the rather curious one that more care and expense would seem to have gone into these at Rokujō.

Yūgiri was impatient to be on his way. He dressed with very great care. He had had his little dalliances, it would seem, none of them very important to him, and there were ladies who felt pangs of jealousy as they saw him off. But he had been rewarded for years of patience, and the match was of the sort the poet called 'watertight.'* Tō no Chūjō liked him much better now that he was one of the family. It was not pleasant to have been the loser, of course, but his extraordinary fidelity over the years made it difficult to hold grudges. Kumoinokari was now in a position of which her sister at court might be envious. Her stepmother could not, it is true, restrain a certain spitefulness, but it was not enough to spoil the occasion. Her real mother, now married to the Lord Inspector, was delighted.

The presentation of the Akashi girl at court had been fixed for late in the Fourth Month.

Murasaki went with Genji to the Miare festival, which preceded the main Kamo festival. She invited the other Rokujō ladies to join them, but they declined, fearing that they might look like servants. Her procession was rather quiet and very impressive for the fact, twenty carriages simply appointed and a modest number of outrunners and guards. She paid her respects at the shrine very early on the morning of the festival proper and took a place in the stands. The array of carriages was imposing, large numbers of women having come with her from the other Rokujō households. Guessing from considerable distances whose lady she would be, people looked on in wondering admiration.

Genji remembered another Kamo festival and the treatment to which the Rokujō lady, mother of the present empress, had been subjected. 'My wife was a proud and willful woman who proved to be wanting in common charity. And see how she suffered for her pride – how bitterness was heaped upon her.' He drew back from speaking too openly about the horrible conclusion to the rivalry. 'The son of the one lady is crawling ahead in the ordinary service, and the heights to which the daughter of the other has

*Tales of Ise 28:

> We plighted our troth. It was to be watertight.
> And now, alas, it has become a sieve.

risen bring on an attack of vertigo. Life is uncertain for all of us. We can only hope to have things our way for a little while. I worry about you, my dear, and how it will be for you when I am gone.'

He went to speak to some courtiers of the higher ranks who had gathered before the stands. They had come from Tō no Chūjō's mansion with Kashiwagi, who represented the inner guards. Kore-mitsu's daughter too had come as a royal legate. A much admired young lady, she was showered with gifts from the emperor, the crown prince, and Genji, among others. Yūgiri managed to get a note through the cordons by which she was surrounded. He had seen her from time to time and she had been pained to learn of his marriage to so fine a lady.

'This sprig of — what is it called? — this sprig in my cap.
  So long it has been, I cannot think of the name.'

One wonders what it may have meant to her. She answered, even in the confusion of being seen into her carriage.

'The scholar armed with laurel should know its name.
  He wears it, though he may not speak of it.

'Not everyone, perhaps — but surely an erudite man like you?'*
Not a very remarkable poem, he thought, but better than his own.

Rumor had it that they were still meeting in secret.

It was assumed that Murasaki would go to court with the Akashi girl. She could not stay long, however, and she thought that the time had come for the girl's real mother to be with her. It was sad for them both, mother and daughter, that they had been kept apart for so long. The matter had been on Murasaki's conscience and she suspected that it had been troubling the girl as well.

'Suppose you send the Akashi lady with the child,' she said to Genji. 'She is still so very young. She ought to have an older woman with her. There are limits to what a nurse can do, and I would be much happier about leaving her if I knew that her mother would be taking my place.'

---

*The *katsura*, here translated 'laurel,' was a symbol of scholarship. It was also, with the *aoi*, 'vine of meeting' or 'heartvine,' a symbol of the Kamo festival. See note*, page 173. It is the name *aoi* which Yūgiri here pretends to have forgotten.

How very thoughtful of her, thought Genji. The Akashi lady was of course delighted at the suggestion. Her last wish was being granted. She threw herself into the preparations, none of the other ladies more energetically. The long separation had been especially cruel for the girl's grandmother, the old Akashi nun. The pleasure of watching the girl grow up, her last attachment to this life, had been denied her.

It was late in the night when the Akashi girl and Murasaki rode to court in a hand-drawn carriage. The Akashi lady did not want to follow on foot with the lesser ladies. She was not concerned for her own dignity, but feared that an appearance of inferiority would flaw the gem which Genji had polished so carefully. Though Genji had wanted the ceremonies to be simple, they seemed to take on brilliance of their own accord. Murasaki must now give up the child who had been her whole life. How she wished that she had had such a daughter, someone to be with in just such circumstances as these! The same thought was for Genji and Yūgiri the only shadow upon the occasion.

Leaving on the third day, Murasaki met the Akashi lady, who had come to replace her.

'You see what a fine young lady she has become,' said Murasaki, 'and the sight of her makes you very aware, I am sure, of how long I have had her with me. I hope that we shall be friends.'

It was the first note of intimacy between them. Murasaki could see why Genji had been so strongly drawn to the Akashi lady, and the latter was thinking how few rivals Murasaki had in elegance and dignity. She quite deserved her place of eminence. It seemed to the Akashi lady the most remarkable good fortune that she should be in such company. The old feelings of inferiority came back as she saw Murasaki leave court in a royal carriage, as if she were one of the royal consorts.

The girl was like a doll. Gazing upon her as if in a dream, the Akashi lady wept, and could not agree with the poet that tears of joy resemble tears of sorrow.* It had seemed all these years that she had been meant for sorrow. Now she wanted to live on for joy. The god of Sumiyoshi had been good to her.

---

*Anonymous, *Gosenshū* 1189:

> Joy and sorrow are very much the same.
> The tears for the one are as the tears for the other.

The girl was very intelligent and the most careful attention had been given to her education, and the results were here for the world to admire. The crown prince, in his boyish way, was delighted with her. Certain rivals made sneering remarks about her mother, but she did not let them bother her. Alert and discerning, she brought new dignity to the most ordinary occasion. Her household offered the young gallants new challenges, for not one of her women was unworthy to be in her service.

Murasaki visited from time to time. She and the Akashi lady were now on the best of terms, though no one could have accused the latter of trying to push herself forward. She was always a model of reserve and diffidence.

Genji had numbered the girl's presentation at court among the chief concerns of his declining years, which he feared might not be numerous. Now her position was secure. Yūgiri, who had seemed to prefer the unsettled bachelor's life, was most happily married. The time had come, thought Genji, to do what he wanted most to do. Though it saddened him to think of leaving Murasaki, she and Akikonomu were good friends and she was still the most important person in the Akashi girl's life. As for the lady of the orange blossoms, her life was not perhaps very exciting, but Yūgiri could be depended on to take care of her. Everything seemed in order.

Genji would be forty next year. Preparations were already under way at court and elsewhere to celebrate the event. In the autumn he was accorded benefices equivalent to those of a retired emperor. His life had seemed full enough already and he would have preferred to decline the honor. All the old precedents were followed,* and he was so hemmed in by retainers and formalities that it became almost impossible for him to go to court. The emperor had his own secret reason for dissatisfaction: public opinion apparently would not permit him to abdicate in favor of Genji.

Tō no Chūjō now became chancellor and Yūgiri was promoted to middle councillor. He so shone† with youthful good looks when he went to thank the emperor that Tō no Chūjō was coming to think Kumoinokari, away from the cruel competition at court, the most fortunate of his daughters.

Yūgiri had not forgotten her nurse's scorn for his blue sleeves.

*It is interesting to note that there were no real precedents, although a dowager empress was similarly honored in Murasaki Shikibu's own day.

†See note*, page 557.

One day he handed the nurse a chrysanthemum delicately tinged by frost.

> 'Did you suspect by so much as a mist of dew
>   That the azure bloom would one day be a deep purple?

'I have not forgotten,' he added with a bright, winning smile. She was both pleased and confused.

> 'What mist of dew could possibly fail to find it,
>   Though pale its hue, in so eminent a garden?'

She was now behaving, one might almost have said, like his mother-in-law.

His new circumstances had made the Nijō house seem rather cramped. He moved into his grandmother's Sanjō house, which was of course a place of fond memories. It had been neglected since her death and extensive repairs were necessary. His grandmother's rooms, redecorated, became his own personal rooms. The garden badly needed pruning. The shrubbery was out of control and a 'sheaf of grass'* did indeed threaten to take over the garden. He had the weeds cleared from the brook, which gurgled pleasantly once more.

He was sitting out near the veranda with Kumoinokari one beautiful evening. Memories of their years apart were always with them, though she, at least, would have preferred not to remember that all these women had had their thoughts in the matter. Yūgiri had summoned various women who had lived in odd corners of the house since Princess Omiya's death. It was for them a very happy reunion.

Said Yūgiri:

> 'Clearest of brooks, you guard these rocks, this house.
>   Where has she gone whose image you once reflected?'

And Kumoinokari:

> 'We see the image no more. How is it that
>   These pools among the rocks yet seem so happy?'

Having heard that the garden was in its autumn glory, Tō no

---

*Miharu Arisuke, *Kokinshū* 853:

> You set out a sheaf of grass. It has become
> An autumn field alive with insect voices.

Chūjō stopped by on his way from court. New life had come to the sedate old house, not much changed from his mother's day. A slight flush on his cheeks, Yūgiri too was thinking of the old princess. Yes, said Tō no Chūjō to himself, they were a well-favored pair, one of them, he might add, more so than the other. While Kumoinokari was distinguished but not unique, Yūgiri was without rivals. The old women were having a delightful time, and the conversation flowed on and on.

Tō no Chūjō looked at the poems that lay scattered about. 'I would like to ask these same questions of your brook,' he said, brushing away a tear, 'but I rather doubt that you would welcome my senile meanderings.

'The ancient pine is gone. That need not surprise us —
For see how gnarled and mossy is its seedling.'

Saishō, Yūgiri's old nurse, was not quite ready to forget old grievances. It was with a somewhat satisfied look that she said:

'I now am shaded by two splendid trees
Whose roots were intertwined when they were seedlings.'

It was an old woman's poem. Yūgiri was amused, and Kumoinokari embarrassed.

The emperor paid a state visit to Rokujō late in the Tenth Month. Since the colors were at their best and it promised to be a grand occasion, the Suzaku emperor accepted the invitation of his brother, the present emperor, to join him. It was a most extraordinary event, the talk of the whole court. The preparations, which occupied the full attention of everyone at Rokujō, were unprecedented in their complexity and in the attention to brilliant detail.

Arriving late in the morning, the royal party went first to the equestrian grounds, where the inner guards were mustered for mounted review in the finery usually reserved for the iris festival. There were brocades spread along the galleries and arched bridges and awnings over the open places when, in early afternoon, the party moved to the southeast quarter. The royal cormorants had been turned out with the Rokujō cormorants on the east lake, where there was a handsome take of small fish. Genji hoped that he was not being a fussy and overzealous host, but he did not want a single moment of the royal progress to be dull. The autumn leaves were splendid, especially in Akikonomu's southwest garden. Walls had been taken down and gates opened, and not so much as an autumn mist was permitted to obstruct the royal view. Genji showed his guests to seats on a higher level than his own. The emperor ordered this mark of inferiority dispensed with, and thought again what a satisfaction it would be to honor Genji as his father.

The lieutenants of the inner guards advanced from the east and knelt to the left and right of the stairs before the royal seats, one presenting the take from the pond and the other a brace of fowl taken by the royal falcons in the northern hills. Tō no Chūjō received the royal command to prepare and serve these delicacies. An equally interesting repast had been laid out for the princes and high courtiers. The court musicians took their places in late afternoon, by which time the wine was having its effect. The concert was quiet and unpretentious and there were court pages to dance for the royal guests. It was as always the excursion to the Suzaku Palace so many years before that people remembered.* One of Tō no Chūjō's sons, a boy of ten or so, danced 'Our Gracious Monarch' most elegantly. The emperor took off a robe and laid it over his shoulders, and Tō no Chūjō himself descended into the garden for ritual thanks.

Remembering how they had danced 'Waves of the Blue Ocean' on that other occasion, Genji sent someone down to break off a chrysanthemum, which he presented to his friend with a poem:

'Though time has deepened the hue of the bloom at the hedge,
I do not forget how sleeve brushed sleeve that autumn.'

He himself had done better than most, thought Tō no Chūjō, but Genji had no rivals. No doubt it had all been fated. An autumn shower passed, as if sensing that the moment was right.

'A purple cloud is this chrysanthemum,
A beacon star which shines upon us all.

And grows brighter and brighter.'

The evening breeze had scattered leaves of various tints to

*See Chapter 7.

make the ground a brocade as rich and delicate as the brocades along the galleries. The dancers were young boys from the best families, prettily dressed in coronets and the usual gray-blues and roses, with crimsons and lavenders showing at their sleeves. They danced very briefly and withdrew under the autumn trees, and the guests regretted the approach of sunset. The formal concert, brief and unassuming, was followed by impromptu music in the halls above, instruments having been brought from the palace collection. As it grew livelier a koto was brought for each of the emperors and a third for Genji. The Suzaku emperor was delighted to hear 'the Uda monk'* again after so many years and be assured that its tone was as fine as ever.

'This aged peasant has known many autumn showers
And not before seen finer autumn colors.'

This suggestion that the day was uniquely glorious must not, thought the emperor, go unchallenged:

'Think you these the usual autumn colors?
Our garden brocade imitates an earlier one.'

He was handsomer as the years went by, and he and Genji might have been mistaken for twins. And here was Yūgiri beside them – one stopped in amazement upon seeing the same face yet a third time. Perhaps it was one's imagination that Yūgiri had not quite the emperor's nobility of feature. His was in any event the finer glow of youth.

He was unsurpassed on the flute. Among the courtiers who serenaded the emperors from below the stairs Kōbai had the finest voice. It was cause for general rejoicing that the two houses should be so close.

---

*A famous koto that belonged to the emperor Uda.

CHAPTER 34

New Herbs: Part One

The Suzaku emperor had been in bad health since his visit to Rokujō. Always a sickly man, he feared that this illness might be his last. Though it had long been his wish to take holy orders and retire from the world, he had not wanted to do so while his mother lived.

'My heart seems to be urging me in that direction – and in any event I fear I am not long for this world.' And he set about making the necessary preparations.

Besides the crown prince he had four children, all girls. The mother of the Third Princess had herself been born a royal princess, the daughter of the emperor who had preceded Genji's father.* She had been reduced to commoner status and given the name Genji. Though she had come to court when the Suzaku emperor was still crown prince and might one day have been named empress, her candidacy had no powerful backers. Her mother, of undistinguished lineage, was among the emperor's lesser concubines, and not among the great and brilliant ladies at court. Oborozukiyo had been brought to court by her powerful sister, Kokiden, the Suzaku emperor's mother, and had had no rival for his affection; and so the mother of the Third Princess had had a sad time of it. The Suzaku emperor was sorry and did what he could for her, but after he left the throne it was not a great deal. She died an obscure and disappointed lady. The Third Princess was the Suzaku emperor's favorite among his children.

She was now some thirteen or fourteen. The Suzaku emperor worried about her more than about any of the others. To whom could she look for support when he finally withdrew from the world?

He had chosen his retreat, a temple in the western hills, and now it was ready. He was busy both with preparations for the move and with plans for the Third Princess's initiation. He gave her his most prized treasures and made certain that everything she had, even the most trifling bauble, was of the finest quality. Only

*And therefore a sister of Fujitsubo and Murasaki's father.

when his best things had gone to her did he turn to the needs of his other daughters.

Knowing of course that his father was ill and learning of these new intentions, the crown prince paid a visit. His mother was with him. Though she had not been the Suzaku emperor's favorite among his ladies, she could not, as mother of the crown prince, be ignored. They had a long talk about old times. The Suzaku emperor offered good advice on the management of public affairs when presently his son's time on the throne should begin. The crown prince was a sober, mature young man and his mother's family was powerful. So far as his affairs were concerned, the Suzaku emperor could retire with no worries.

'It is your sisters. I fear I must worry about them to the end. I have heard, and thought it a great pity, that women are shallow, careless creatures who are not always treated with complete respect. Please do not forget your sisters. Be good to them when your day comes. Some of them have reliable enough sponsors. But the Third Princess — it is she I worry about. She is very young and she has been completely dependent on me. And now I am abandoning her.' He brushed away a tear. 'What will happen to the poor child?'

He also asked the crown prince's mother to be good to her. He had been rather less fond of her than of the Third Princess's mother, however, and there had been resentments and jealousies back in the days when his several ladies were competing for his attention. Though he surmised that no very deep rancor persisted, he knew that he could not expect her to trouble herself greatly in the Third Princess's behalf.

Seriously ill as the New Year approached, he no longer ventured from behind his curtains. He had had similar attacks before, but they had not been so frequent or stubborn. He feared that the end might be near. It was true that he had left the throne, but he continued to be of service to the people he had once favored, and their regrets were genuine. Genji made frequent inquiries, and, to the sick man's very great pleasure, proposed a visit.

Yūgiri came with the news and was invited behind the royal curtains for an intimate talk.

'During his last illness Father gave me all manner of advice and instructions. He seemed to worry most about your father and about the present emperor. There is a limit, I fear, to what a reigning monarch can do. My affection for your father continued to be as it had always been, but a silly little incident provoked me to behavior which I fear he has not been able to forgive. But I only suspect this to be the case. He has not through all the long years let slip a single word of bitterness. In happier times than these the wisest of men have sometimes let personal grievances affect their impartiality and cloud their judgment until a wish to even scores has lured them from the straight way of justice. People have watched him carefully, wondering when his bitterness might lead him similarly astray, but not for a moment has he ever lost control of himself. It would seem that he has the warmest feelings towards the crown prince. Nothing could please me more than the new bond between them. I am not a clever man, and we all know what happens to a father when he starts thinking about his children.* I have rather withdrawn from the crown prince's affairs, not wanting to make a fool of myself, and left them to your father.

'I do not think that I went against Father's wishes in my behavior towards the emperor, whose radiance will shine through the ages and perhaps make future generations overlook my own misrule. I am satisfied. When I saw your father last autumn a flood of memories came back. It would please me enormously if I might see him again. We have innumerable things to talk about.' There were tears in his eyes. 'Do insist that he come.'

'I fear that I am not as well informed as I might be on what happened long ago, but since I have been old enough to be of some service I have tried this way and that to inform myself in the ways of the world. Father and I sometimes have a good talk about important things and about trivialities as well, but I may assure you that I have not once heard him suggest that he was a victim of injustice. I have occasionally heard him say that since he retired from immediate service to the emperor and turned to the quiet pursuits he has always enjoyed most, he has become rather self-centered and has not been at all faithful to the wishes of your royal father. While Your Majesty was on the throne he was still young and inexperienced, he has said, and there were many more eminent and talented men than he, and so his accomplishments fell far short of his hopes. Now that he has withdrawn from public affairs he would like nothing better than a free and open interview with

See note, page 13.

Your Majesty. Unfortunately his position makes it difficult for him to move about, and so time has gone by and he has neglected you sadly.'

Not yet twenty, Yūgiri was in the full bloom of youth, a very handsome boy indeed. The Suzaku emperor looked at him thoughtfully, wondering whether he might not offer a solution to the problem of the Third Princess.

'They tell me that you are now a member of the chancellor's family. It worried me to see the matter so long in abeyance, and I was enormously relieved at news of your marriage. And yet it would be less than candid of me not to acknowledge that I felt certain regrets at the same time.'

What could this mean? Then Yūgiri remembered rumors about the Suzaku emperor's concern for the Third Princess, and his wish to find a good husband for her before he took holy orders.

But to let it appear that he had guessed with no trouble at all might not be good manners. 'I am not much of a prize,' he said as he took his leave, 'and I fear that I was not very eagerly sought after.'

The women of the house had all gathered for a look at him.

'What a marvelous young man. And see how beautifully he carries himself.'

This sort of thing from the younger ones. The older ones were not so sure. 'You should have seen his father when he was that age. He was so handsome that he left you quite giddy.'

The Suzaku emperor overheard them. 'Yes, Genji was unique. But why do you say "that age"? He has only improved as the years have gone by. I often say to myself that the word "radiant" was invented especially for him. In grand matters of public policy we all fall silent when he speaks, but he has another side too, a gentle sense of humor that is irresistible. There is no one quite like him. I sometimes wonder what he can have been in his other lives. He grew up at court and he was our father's favorite, the joy and treasure of his life. Yet he was always a model of quiet restraint. When he turned twenty, I seem to remember, he was not yet even a middle councillor. The next year he became councillor and general. The fact that his son has advanced more rapidly is evidence, I should think, that the family is well thought of. Yūgiri's advice in official matters has always been careful and solid. I may be mistaken, but I doubt that he does less well in that respect than his father.'

The Third Princess was a pretty little thing, still very young in her ways and very innocent. 'How nice,' said the Suzaku emperor, 'if we could find a good, dependable man to look after you. Someone who would see to your education too. There are so many things you need to know.'

He summoned her nurses and her more knowledgeable attendants for a conference about the initiation ceremonies. 'It would be quite the best thing if someone could be persuaded to do for her what Genji did for Prince Hyōbu's daughter. I can think of no one in active court service. His Majesty has the empress, and his other ladies are all so very well favored that I would fear for her in the competition and worry about her lack of adequate support. I really should have dropped a hint or two while Yūgiri was still single. He is young but extremely gifted, and he would seem to have a brilliant future.'

'But he is such a steady, proper young man. Through all those years he thought only of the girl who is now his wife, and nothing could pull him away from her. He will doubtless be even more unbudgeable now that they are married. I should think that the chances might be better with his father. It would seem that Genji still has the old acquisitive instincts and that he is always on the alert for ladies of really good pedigree. I am told that he still thinks of the former high priestess of Kamo and sometimes gets off a letter to her.'

'But that is exactly what worries me – his eagerness for the hunt.'

Yet it would seem that the Suzaku emperor's thoughts were running in much the same direction. There might be unpleasantness of some description, since there were all those other ladies; but he could do worse than ask that Genji take in the Third Princess much as he might have brought home a daughter.

'I'm sure that everyone with a marriageable daughter has the same thought, that when all is said and done Genji would not be a bad son-in-law. Life is short and a man wants to do what he can with it. If I had been born a woman I suspect I might have been drawn to him in a not too sisterly fashion. I used to think so when we were boys, and I have never been surprised at all when I have seen a lady losing her senses over him.'

It may have been that he was thinking of his own Oborozukiyo.

Among the princess's nurses was a woman of good family whose elder brother was a moderator of the middle rank. He had long been among Genji's more trusted followers and he had been of good service to the Third Princess as well. One day when he was with her his sister told him of the Suzaku emperor's remarks.

'Perhaps you might find occasion to speak to His Lordship. It is a common enough thing for princesses to remain single, but it is good all the same when one of them finds a man who is fond of her and will look after her. My poor lady, only her father really cares about her. Except for us, of course – and what can *we* do? As a matter of fact, I would feel better if I were the only one concerned. There are other women with her, and one of them could easily bring about her ruin. It would be an enormous relief if something could be arranged while her father is still with us. Even a princess may be fated for unhappy things, and I do worry most inordinately. There are jealousies because she is her father's favorite. I only wish it were in my power to protect her.'

'Genji is a more reliable man than you would imagine. When he has had an affair, even the most lighthearted sort of adventure, he ends up by taking the lady in and making her one of his own. The result is that he has a large collection. But no man can distribute his affections indefinitely, and it would seem that there is one lady who dominates them. I should imagine, though I cannot be sure, that there are numbers of ladies who feel rather neglected as a result. But if it should be the princess's fate to marry him, I doubt that the one lady need be a dangerous threat to her. I must admit all the same that I have misgivings. I have heard him say, without making a great point of it, that his life has been too well favored in an otherwise poorly favored day, and that it would be greedy and arrogant of him to want more, but that he himself and others too have thought that in his relations with women he has not been completely successful. I think I can see what he means. Not one of his ladies need be ashamed of her family, and not one of them is of really the very best. They are all in some measure his inferior. I should think that your lady might be exactly what is needed.'

The nurse found occasion to speak of these matters to the Suzaku emperor. 'My brother says that His Lordship at Rokujō would without question be friendly to a proposal from Your Majesty. He would see in it the fulfillment of all his wishes. With Your Majesty's concurrence my brother would be happy to transmit a proposal. Yet we have misgivings. His Lordship is very kind to them all, after their various stations, but even a commoner who does not have her royal dignity to worry about finds it unpleasant to be one of many wives. I wonder if the strain on my lady might not perhaps be too much. I gather that she has other suitors. I hope that Your Majesty will consider all the possibilities very carefully before coming to a decision. Ladies tend these days to think first about their own convenience and to be indifferent to the claims of high birth. My own lady is really so very innocent and inexperienced, astonishingly so, indeed, and there is a limit to what we others can do for her. When we are conscientious we do our work under direction, and we find ourselves helpless if it begins to weaken.'

'I have worried a great deal, and think I am aware of all the arguments and considerations. It may be the more prudent course for a princess to remain single. The claims of birth cannot be relied upon to protect a marriage from bitterness and unhappiness. They are certain to come. And on the other hand there are unmarried princesses who suddenly find themselves alone in the world, quite without protection. In the old days people were diffident and respectful and would not have dreamed of violating the proprieties, but in our own day the most determined and purposeful lady cannot be sure that she is not going to be insulted. Such, in any event, has been the purport of the various discussions I have overheard. A lady who was until yesterday guarded by worthy and influential parents today finds herself involved in a scandal with an adventurer of no standing at all and brings dishonor upon her dead parents. Such instances are constantly coming to my attention. And so there are arguments on both sides. The fact that a lady was born a princess is no guarantee that things will go well for her. You cannot imagine how I have worried.

'When a lady has put herself in the hands of those who ought to know best, then she can resign herself to what must be, and if it is not happy then at least she does not have herself to blame. Or if she is not that sort of lady, affairs may shape themselves so that in the end she may congratulate herself upon her independence. Even then the initial secrecy and the affront to her parents and advisers are not good. They do injury to her name from which it is not easy to recover. What a silly, heedless girl, people say, even of a commoner. Or if a lady's wishes should have been consulted but she finds herself joined to a man who does not please her, and people are heard to say that it is just as they thought it would be – then her advisers may be taxed with carelessness. I have reason to believe that the Third Princess is not at all reliable in these matters, and that you people are reaching out and taking her affairs into your own hands. If it were to become known that that is the case, the results could easily be disastrous.'

These troubled meditations, as he prepared to leave the world, did not make things easier for the princess's women.

'I think I have been rather patient,' continued the Suzaku emperor, 'waiting for her to grow up and become just a little more aware of things, but now I begin to fear that my deepest wish may be denied me. I can wait no longer.

'It is true that Genji has other ladies, but he is a sober and intelligent man, indeed a tower of strength. Let us not worry about the others. She must make a place for herself. It would be hard to think of a more dependable man.

'But let us consider the other possibilities.

'There is my brother, Prince Hotaru. He is a thoroughly decent man and certainly no stranger, nor is he someone we may consider we have any right to look down upon. But I sometimes think that his preoccupation with deportment rather diminishes his stature and even makes him seem less than completely serious. I doubt that we can depend on him in such an important matter.

'I have heard that the Fujiwara councillor* would like to manage her affairs. I have no doubt that he would be a very loyal servant, and yet – might one not hope for a less ordinary sort of man? The precedents all suggest that true eminence is what matters, and that an eagerness to be of service is not quite enough.

'There is Kashiwagi. Oborozukiyo† tells me that he suffers from secret longings. Perhaps he might someday do, but he is still very young and rather obscure. I am told that he has remained single because he wants the very best. No one else has been so dedicated to such high ambitions. He has studied hard, and I have no doubt that he will one day be among the most useful of public servants. But I doubt that he is quite what we want at the moment.'

No one troubled him with the affairs of his other daughters,

*Otherwise unidentified.

†Kashiwagi's maternal aunt.

who worried him much less. It was strange how reports of his secret anxiety had so spread that it had become a matter of public concern.

It came to the attention of Tō no Chūjō, who presented his addresses through Oborozukiyo, his sister-in-law. 'Kashiwagi is still single because he is determined to marry a princess and no one else. You might point this fact out to the Suzaku emperor when he is making final plans for his daughters. If Kashiwagi were to be noticed I would feel greatly honored myself.'

Oborozukiyo did what she could to advance her nephew's cause.

Prince Hotaru, having been rejected by Tamakazura, was determined to show her that he could do even better. It was not likely that the affairs of the Third Princess had escaped his notice. Indeed, he was very restless.

The Fujiwara councillor was very close to the Suzaku emperor, whose chief steward he had been for many years. With his master's retirement from the world his prospects were bleak. It would seem that he was trying to call the Suzaku emperor's attention to his claims as the man most competent to manage the princess's affairs.

Yūgiri had of course been taken into the royal confidence. It excited him, apparently, to think that the Suzaku emperor, having said so much, could not shrug off a proposal from him. But Kumoinokari had joined her destinies to his. He had been steadfast through all the unfriendly years and could not admit the possibility of making her unhappy now. And of course marriage to the chancellor's daughter limited his options. Action on two fronts, so to speak, could be very exacting and very unpleasant. Always the most prudent of young men, he kept his own counsel. Yet he watched each new development with great interest, and he was not at all sure that he would not be disappointed when a husband was finally chosen for the princess.

The crown prince too was well informed. He offered it as his view that one must be very careful about setting precedents. 'You must deliberate on every facet of the case. However excellent a man may be, a commoner is still a commoner. But if Genji is to be your choice, then I think he should be asked to look after her as a father looks after a daughter.'

'I quite agree. I can see that you have thought the matter over carefully.'

Increasingly enthusiastic about Genji's candidacy, the Suzaku emperor summoned the moderator, brother of the Third Princess's nurse, and asked that Genji be made aware of his thoughts.

Genji was of course very much aware of them already. 'I am sorry to hear it. He may fear that he has not much longer to live, but how can he be sure that I will outlive him? If we could be sure to die in the order in which we were born, then of course I might expect to be around for a little while yet. But I can look after her without marrying her. I could hardly be indifferent towards any of his children. If he is especially concerned about the Third Princess, then I will want to respect his wishes. Though of course nothing in this world is certain.

'I am overwhelmed by these evidences of trust and affection. But supposing I were to follow her father's example and retire to a hermitage myself – would that not be sad for her? And she would be a strong bond tying me to a world I wish to leave.

'What of Yūgiri? He is still young and not very important, I know, but he will someday be one of the grand ministers. He has all the qualifications. If the Suzaku emperor is so inclined, I am not being frivolous, I most emphatically assure you, when I commend Yūgiri to his attention. Perhaps he has held back because he knows that the boy is a monogamous sort and that he already has his wife.'

Genji seemed to be withdrawing his candidacy. Knowing that the Suzaku emperor's decision had not been hasty, the moderator was much distressed. He described all the deliberations in great detail.

Genji smiled. 'Yes, he is very fond of her, and I can imagine how he must worry. But there is one unassailable way to end his worries: make her one of the emperor's ladies. He has numbers of fine ladies already, I know, but they need not be a crucial consideration. It is by no means a firm rule that ladies who come to court later are at a disadvantage. He has only to look back to the days of our late father. The dowager empress was his first wife. She came to court when he was still crown prince and she seemed to have everything her way, and yet there were the years when she was quite overshadowed by Fujitsubo, the very last of his ladies. Your princess's mother was, I believe, Fujitsubo's sister, only less well endowed, people tell me, than she. With such fine looks on both sides of the family it cannot be doubted that your princess is very lovely.'

The Suzaku emperor took the last remark as evidence that Genji was himself not uninterested.

The year drew to an end. The Suzaku emperor made haste to get his affairs in order. The plans for the Third Princess's initiation were so grand that it seemed likely to oust all other such affairs from the history books. The west room of the Oak Pavilion was fitted out for the ceremonies. Only the most resplendent imported brocades were used for hangings and cushions, and the results would have pleased a Chinese empress.

Suzaku had long before asked Tō no Chūjō to bestow the ceremonial train. He was such a busy man that one was reluctant to make demands upon his time, but he had never turned away a request from Suzaku. The other two ministers and all the high courtiers were also present, even some who had had previous engagements. Indeed the whole court was present, including the whole of the emperor's private household and that of the crown prince. Eight royal princes were among the guests. For the emperor and the crown prince and many others too there was sadness mingled with the joy. It would be the last such affair arranged by the Suzaku emperor. The warehouses and supply rooms were searched for the most splendid of imported gifts. A large array of equally splendid gifts came from Rokujō, some in Genji's own name and some in that of the Suzaku emperor. It was Genji who saw that Tō no Chūjō was properly rewarded for his services.

From Akikonomu came robes and combs and the like, all of them selected with the greatest care. She got out combs and bodkins from long ago* and made sure that the necessary repairs did not obscure their identity. On the evening of the ceremony she dispatched them by her assistant chamberlain, who also served in the Suzaku Palace, with instructions that they be delivered directly to the Third Princess. With them was a poem:

'I fear these little combs are scarred and worn.
I have used them to summon back an ancient day.'

The Suzaku emperor chanced to be with the princess when the gift was delivered. The memories were poignant. Perhaps Akikonomu meant to share some of her own good fortune with the prin-

---

*Presented to her by the Suzaku emperor upon her departure for Ise.

cess. It was a beautiful gift in any case. He got off a note of thanks from which he tried to exclude his own feelings:

> 'I only hope that she may be as you,
> All through the myriad years of the boxwood comb.'

It was with a considerable effort of the will that he was present at the ceremonies, for he was in great pain. Three days later he took the tonsure. Even an ordinary man leaves grief and regret behind him, and in his case the regret was boundless.

Oborozukiyo refused to leave his side.

'My worries about my daughters may come to an end,' he said, 'but how can I stop worrying about you?'

He forced himself to sit up. The grand abbot of Hiei shaved his head and there were three eminent clerics to administer the vows. The final renunciation, symbolized by the change to somber religious habit, was very sad indeed. Even the priests, who should long ago have left sorrow behind them, were unable to hold back their tears. As for the Suzaku emperor's daughters and ladies and attendants high and low, the halls and galleries echoed with their laments. And even now, he sighed, he could not have the peace he longed for. The Third Princess was still too much on his mind.

He was of course showered with messages, from the emperor and from the whole court.

Hearing that he was a little better, Genji paid a visit. Genji's allowances were now those of a retired emperor, but he was determined to avoid equivalent ceremony. He rode in a plain carriage and kept his retinue to a minimum, and preferred a carriage escort to the more ostentatious mounted guard. Delighted at the visit, the Suzaku emperor braved very great discomfort to receive him. He shared Genji's wishes that the visit be informal and had places set out in his private parlor. Genji was shocked and saddened at the change in his brother. A shadow seemed to sweep over the past and on into the future, and he was in tears.

'Father's death more than anything made me aware of impermanence and change. I resolved that I must leave the world. But I have never had much will power, and I have delayed, and so you see me unable to raise my head before you who have done the great thing first. I have known how much easier it should be for me than for you and I have made the resolve over and over again, and somehow regret for the world has always been stronger.'

The Suzaku emperor was also weeping. In an uncertain voice he talked of old and recent happenings. 'For years I have had a persistent feeling that I would not last the night, and still the years have gone by. Fearing that I might die without accomplishing the first of my resolves, I have finally taken the step. Now that I have changed to these dark robes I know more than ever how little time I have ahead of me. I fear that I shall not go far down the way I have chosen. I must be satisfied with the easier route. I shall calm my thoughts for a time and invoke the holy name, and that will be all. I am not a man of very grand and rare substance, and I cannot think that I was meant for anything different. I must reprove myself for the years of lazy indecision.'

He described his plans and hopes and managed to touch upon the matter that worried him most. 'I am sad for all of my daughters, but most of all for the most inadequately protected of them.'

Genji was sad for his brother, and in spite of everything rather interested in the Third Princess. 'Yes, the higher a lady's standing, the sadder it is for her to be without adequate defenses. I am very much aware that our crown prince is among our greatest blessings. The whole world looks upon him as more than this inferior day of ours has any right to expect, and I know perhaps better than anyone how unlikely he is to refuse Your Majesty's smallest request. There is no cause for concern, none at all. Yet it is as Your Majesty has said: there is a limit to what even he can do. When his day comes he may be able to manage public affairs quite as he wishes, but there is no assurance that he can arrange things ideally for his own sisters. Yes, the safest thing by far would be to find someone whom the Third Princess can depend upon in everything. Let the vows be exchanged and the man charged with responsibilities he cannot deny. If Your Majesty will insist upon worrying about the whole of the vast, distant future, then a decision must be made and a suitable guardian chosen, promptly but quietly.'

'I quite agree. But it is by no means easy. Many princesses have been provided with suitable husbands while their fathers have still occupied the throne. The matter is more urgent for my own poor girl, and her affairs are the last which I still think of as my own. Promptly and quietly, you say — but they remain beyond my power either to ignore or to dispose of. And as I have worried my health has deteriorated, and days and weeks which will not return have gone by to no purpose.

'It is not easy for me to make the request, and no easier for you, I am sure, to be the object – but might I ask that you take the girl in your very special charge and, quite as you think appropriate, find a husband for her? I should have made a proposal to your son while he was still single, and it is a great source of regret that I was anticipated by the chancellor.'

'He is a serious, dependable lad, but he is still very young and inexperienced. It may seem presumptuous of me – but let us suppose that I were myself to take responsibility. Her life need not be much different from what it is now, though there is the disquieting consideration that I am no longer young, and the time may come when I can no longer be of service to her.'

And so the contract was made.

In the evening there was a banquet, for Genji's party and the Suzaku household. The priest's fare was unpretentious but beautifully prepared and served. The tableware and the trays of light aloeswood also suggested the priestly vocation and brought tears to the eyes of the guests. The melancholy and moving details were innumerable, but I fear that they would clutter my story.

It was late in the night when Genji and his men departed, the men bearing lavish gifts. The Fujiwara councillor was among those who saw them off. There had been a fall of snow and the Suzaku emperor had caught cold. But he was happy. The future of the Third Princess seemed secure.

Genji was worried. Murasaki had heard vague rumors, but she had told herself that it could not be. Genji had once been very serious about the high priestess of Ise, it seemed, but in the end he had held himself back. She had not worried a great deal, and asked no questions.

How would she take this news? Genji knew that his feelings towards her would not change, or if they did it would be in the direction of greater intensity. But only time could assure her of that fact, and there would be cruel uncertainty in the meantime. Nothing had been allowed to come between them in recent years, and the thought of having a secret from her for even a short time made him very unhappy.

He said nothing to her that night.

The next day was dark, with flurries of snow.

'I went yesterday to call on the Suzaku emperor. He is in very poor health indeed.' It was in the course of a leisurely conversation that Genji brought the matter up. 'He said many sad things, but what seems to trouble him most as he goes off to his retreat is the future of the Third Princess.' And he described that part of the interview. 'I was really so extremely sorry for him that I found it impossible to refuse. I suppose people will make a great thing of it. The thought of taking a bride at my age has seemed so utterly preposterous that I have tried through this and that intermediary to suggest a certain want of ardor. But to see him in person and have it directly from him — I simply could not bring myself to refuse. Do you think that when the time does finally come for him to go off into the mountains we might have her come here? Would that upset you terribly? Please do not let it. Trust me, and tell yourself what is the complete truth, that nothing is going to change. She has more right to feel insecure than you do. But I am sure that we can arrange things happily enough for her too.'

She was always torturing herself over the smallest of his affairs, and he had dreaded telling her of this one.

But her reply was quiet and unassertive. 'Yes, it is sad for her. The only thing that worries me is the possibility that she might feel less than completely at home. I shall be very happy if our being so closely related persuades her that I am no stranger.'

'How silly that this very willingness to accept things should bother me. But it does. It makes me start looking for complications, and I am sure I will feel guiltier as the two of you get used to each other. You must pay no attention to what people say. Rumors are strange things. It is impossible to know where they come from, but there they are, like living creatures bent on poisoning relations between a man and a woman. You must listen only to yourself and let matters take their course. Do not start imagining things, and do not torture yourself with empty jealousies.'

It was a tempest out of the blue which there was no escaping. Murasaki was determined that she would not complain or give any hint of resentment. She knew that neither her wishes nor her advice would have made any difference. She did not want the world to think that she had been crushed by what had to come. There was her sharp-tongued stepmother, so quick to blame and to gloat — she had even held Murasaki responsible for the curious solution to the Tamakazura problem. She was certain to gloat over this, and to say that Murasaki deserved exactly what had come to her. Though very much in control of herself, Murasaki was prey to these worries. The very durability of her relations with Genji was sure to make people laugh harder. But she gave no hint of her unhappiness.

The New Year came, and at the Suzaku Palace the Third Princess's wedding plans kept people busy. Her several suitors were deeply disappointed. The emperor, who had let it be known that he would welcome her at court, was among them.

It was Genji's fortieth year,* to which the court could not be indifferent and which had long promised to send gladness ringing through the land. With his dislike for pomp and ceremony, Genji only hoped that the rejoicing would not be too loud.

The Day of the Rat fell on the twenty-third of the First Month. Tamakazura came with the new herbs that promise long life. She came very quietly, not letting anyone know of her intentions. Faced with an accomplished fact, Genji could hardly turn her and her gifts away. She too disliked ceremony, but the movements of so important a lady† were certain to be noticed.

A west room of the main southeast hall was made ready to receive her. New curtains were hung and new screens set out, as were forty cushions, more comfortable and less ostentatious, thought Genji, than ceremonial chairs. In spite of the informality, the details were magnificent. Wardrobes were laid out upon four cupboards inlaid with mother-of-pearl, and there was a fine though modest array of summer and winter robes, incense jars, medicine and comb boxes, inkstones, vanity sets, and other festive paraphernalia. The stands for the ritual chaplets‡ were of aloeswood and sandalwood, beautifully carved and fitted in the modern manner, with metal trimmings in several colors. Tamakazura's touch was apparent everywhere. She was a lady of refinement and sensibility, and when she exerted herself the results were certain to be memorable – though she agreed with Genji that lavish display was in poor taste.

The party assembled and Genji and Tamakazura exchanged greetings, formal but replete with memories. Genji seemed so

---

*'Fortieth birthday' would not be a proper translation, since the Oriental count is of course being followed. We are not told when his birthday falls, but on it he is thirty-nine by the 'full' Occidental count.

†She is the daughter of the chancellor and the wife of his most likely successor.

‡Artificial flowers the theoretical purpose of which was to hide age.

youthful that one wondered whether he might not have miscalculated his age. He looked more like her bridegroom than her foster father. She was shy at first, not having seen him in a very long time, but determined not to raise unnecessary barriers. She had brought her two sons with her, very pretty boys indeed. It rather embarrassed her to have had two sons in such quick succession, but Higekuro, her husband, had said that they must be introduced to Genji, and that there was not likely to be a better occasion. They were in identical dress, casual and boyish, and they still wore their hair in the page-boy fashion, parted in the middle.

'I try not to worry about my age,' said Genji, 'and to pretend that I am still a boy, and it gives me pause to be presented with the new generation. Yūgiri has children, I am told, but he makes a great thing of not letting me see them. This day which you were the first to remember does after all bring regrets. I had hoped to forget my age for a little while yet.'

Tamakazura was very much the matron, in an entirely pleasant way. Her congratulatory poem was most matronly:

'I come to pray that the rock may long endure
And I bring with me the seedling pines from the field.'

Genji went through the ceremony of sampling the new herbs, which were arranged in four aloeswood boxes. He raised his cup.

'Long shall be the life of the seedling pines –
To add to the years of the herbs brought in from the fields?'

There was a large assembly of high officials in the south room. Prince Hyōbu had been of two minds about coming. He finally decided, at about noon, that to stay away would be to attract attention to his daughter's misfortunes. Yes, of course it was annoying that Higekuro should be making such a show of his close relations with Genji, but his other children, Prince Hyōbu's grandchildren, were doubly close to Genji, through their mother and through their stepmother, and had been assigned a conspicuous part in the celebrations.

There were forty baskets of fruit and forty boxes of food, presented by as many courtiers, with Yūgiri leading the procession. Genji poured wine for his guests and sampled a broth from the new herbs. Before him were four aloeswood stands, laid out with the finest tableware in the newest fashion.

Out of respect for the ailing Suzaku emperor, no musicians had been summoned from the palace. Tō no Chūjō had brought wind instruments, taking care from far in advance to choose only the best. 'There is not likely to be another banquet so splendid,' he said.

It was an easy, informal concert. Tō no Chūjō had also brought the Japanese koto that was among his most prized treasures. He was one of the finest musicians of the day, and when he put himself out no one was his equal – certainly no one was eager to take up the Japanese koto when he had finished. At Genji's insistence Kashiwagi did finally venture a strain, and everyone agreed that he was very little if at all his father's inferior. There was something almost weirdly beautiful about his playing, to make people exclaim in wonder that though of course talent could be inherited no one would have expected so original a style to be handed from father to son. There is perhaps nothing so very mysterious about the secret Chinese repertory, for all its variety. The scores may be secret but they are fixed and not hard to read. It is rather the Japanese koto, the improvising after the dictates of one's fancy, all the while deferring to the requirements of other instruments, that fills the listener with wonder. His koto tuned very low, Tō no Chūjō managed an astonishingly rich array of overtones. Kashiwagi chose a higher, more approachable tuning. Not informed in advance that he had such talents, the audience, princes and all, was mute with admiration.

Genji's brother, Prince Hotaru, chose a seven-stringed Chinese koto, a palace treasure rich in associations, having been handed down from emperor to emperor. In his last years Genji's father had given it to his eldest daughter, who numbered it among her dearest treasures. Tō no Chūjō had asked for it especially to honor the occasion. Prince Hotaru, who had drunk rather freely and was in tears, glanced tentatively at Genji and pushed the koto towards him. All this gaiety seemed to demand novel music, and though both Tamakazura and Genji had wished to avoid ostentation it was in the end a most remarkable concert. The singers, gathered at the south stairway, were all in fine voice. They presently shifted to a minor key, to announce that the hour was late and the music should be more familiar and intimate. 'Green Willow'* was

*See note†, page 442.

enough to make the warblers start from their roosts. Since the affair was deemed exempt from public sumptuary regulations, the gifts were of astonishing richness and variety, for Tamakazura and for all the other guests. She made ready to leave at dawn.

'I live quite apart from the world,' said Genji, 'and I find myself losing track of time. Your very courteous reminder is also a melancholy one. Do stop by occasionally to see how I have aged. It is a great pity that an elder statesman cannot move about as he would wish, and so I do not see you often.'

Yes, the associations were both melancholy and happy. He thought it a pity that she must leave so soon, nor did she want to go. She honored her real father in a formal and perfunctory way, but it was to Genji that she owed the larger debt. He had taken her in and made a place for her, and her gratitude increased as the years went by.

The Third Princess came to Rokujō towards the middle of the Second Month. The preparations to receive her were elaborate. The west room of the main southeast hall in which Genji had sampled the new herbs became her boudoir. Very great attention had been given to appointing her women's rooms as well, in the galleries and two wings to the west. The trousseau was brought from the Suzaku Palace with all the ceremony of a presentation at court, and it goes without saying that similar pomp accompanied the formal move to Rokujō. Her retinue was enormous, led by the highest courtiers. Among them was a reluctant one, the Fujiwara councillor who had hoped to take charge of her affairs. Genji broke with precedent by himself coming out to receive her. Certain limitations were imposed upon a commoner, and she was after all neither going to court nor receiving a prince as a bridegroom; and all in all it was a most unusual event.

Through the three days following, the nuptial ceremonies, arranged by the Suzaku and Rokujō households, were of very great dignity and elegance.

It was an unsettling time for Murasaki. No doubt Genji was giving an honest view of the matter when he said that she would not be overwhelmed by the Third Princess. Yet for the first time in years she felt genuinely threatened. The new lady was young and, it would seem, rather showy in her ways, and of such a rank that Murasaki could not ignore her. All very unsettling; but she gave no hint of her feelings, and indeed helped with all the arrangements. Genji saw more than ever that there was really no one like her.

The Third Princess was, as her father had said, a mere child. She was tiny and immature physically, and she gave a general impression of still greater, indeed quite extraordinary, immaturity. He thought of Murasaki when he had first taken her in. She had even then been interesting. She had had a character of her own. The Third Princess was like a baby. Well, thought Genji, the situation had something to recommend it: she was not likely to intrude and make Murasaki unhappy with fits of jealousy. Yet he did think he might have hoped for someone a *little* more interesting. For the first three nights he was faithfully in attendance upon her. Murasaki was unhappy but said nothing. She gave herself up to her thoughts and to such duties, now performed with unusual care, as scenting his robes. He thought her splendid. Why, he asked himself, whatever the pressures and the complications, had he taken another wife? He had been weak and he had given an impression of inconstancy, and brought it all upon himself. Yūgiri had escaped because the Suzaku emperor had seen what an unshakable pillar of fidelity he was.

Genji was near tears. 'Please excuse me just this one more night. I have no alternative. If after this I neglect you, then you may be sure that I will be angrier with myself than you can ever be with me. We do have to consider her father's feelings.'

'Do not ask us bystanders,' she said, a faint smile on her lips, 'to tell you how to behave.'

He turned away, chin in hand, to hide his confusion.

'I had grown so used to thinking it would not change.
And now, before my very eyes, it changes.'

He took up the paper on which she had jotted down old poems that fitted her mood as well as this poem of her own. It was not the most perfect of poems, perhaps, but it was honest and to the point.

'Life must end. It is a transient world.
The one thing lasting is the bond between us.'

He did not want to leave, but she said that he was only making things more difficult for her. He was wearing the soft robes which she had so carefully scented. She had over the years seen new threats arise only to be turned away, and she had finally come to think that there would be no more. Now this had happened, and everyone was talking. She knew how susceptible he had been in his earlier years, and now the whole future seemed uncertain. It was remarkable that she showed no sign of her disquiet.

Her women were talking as of the direst happenings.

'Who would have expected it? He has always kept himself well supplied with women, but none of them has seemed the sort to raise a challenge. So things have been quiet. I doubt that our lady will let them defeat her – but we must be careful. The smallest mistake could make things very difficult.'

Murasaki pretended that nothing at all was amiss. She talked pleasantly with them until late in the night. She feared that silence on the most important subject might make it seem more important than it was.

'I am so glad that she has come to us. We have had a full house, but I sometimes think he has been a little bored with us, poor man. None of us is grand enough to be really interesting. I somehow hope that we will be the best of friends. Perhaps it is because they say that she is still a mere child. And here you all are digging a great chasm between us. If we were of the same rank, or perhaps if I had some slight reason to think myself a little her superior, then I would feel that I had to be careful. But as it is – you may think it impertinent of me to say so – I only want to be friendly.'

Nakatsukasa and Chūjō exchanged glances. 'Such kindness,' one of them, I do not know which, would seem to have muttered. They had once been recipients of Genji's attentions but they had been with Murasaki for some years now, and they were among her firmer allies.

Inquiries came from the ladies in the other quarters, some of them suggesting that they who had long ago given up their ambitions might be the more fortunate ones. Murasaki sighed. They meant to be kind, of course, but they were not making things easier. Well, there was no use in tormenting herself over things she could not change, and the inconstancy of the other sex was among them.

Her women would think it odd if she spent the whole night talking with them. She withdrew to her boudoir and they helped her into bed. She was lonely, and the presence of all these women did little to disguise the fact. She thought of the years of his exile.

She had feared that they would not meet again, but the agony of waiting for word that he was still alive was in itself a sort of distraction from the sorrow and longing. She sought to comfort herself now with the thought that those confused days could so easily have meant the end of everything.

The wind was cold. Not wanting her women to know that she could not sleep, she lay motionless until she ached from the effort. Still deep in the cold night, the call of the first cock seemed to emphasize the loneliness and sorrow.

She may not have been in an agony of longing, but she was deeply troubled, and perhaps for that reason she came to Genji in his dreams. His heart was racing. Might something have happened to her? He lay waiting for the cock as if for permission to leave, and at its first call rushed out as if unaware that it would not yet be daylight for some time. Still a child, the princess kept her women close beside her. One of them saw him out through a corner door. The snow caught the first traces of dawn, though the garden was still dark. 'In vain the spring night's darkness,'* whispered her nurse, catching the scent he had left behind.

The patches of snow were almost indistinguishable from the white garden sands. 'There is yet snow by the castle wall,'† he whispered to himself as he came to Murasaki's wing of the house and tapped on a shutter. No longer in the habit of accommodating themselves to nocturnal wanderings, the women let him wait for a time.

'How slow you are,' he said, slipping in beside her. 'I am quite congealed, as much from terror as from cold. And I have done nothing to deserve it.'

He thought her rather wonderful. She did nothing at all, and yet, hiding her wet sleeves, she somehow managed to keep him at a distance. Not even among ladies of the highest birth was there anyone quite like her. He found himself comparing her with the little princess he had just left.

*Oshikōchi Mitsune, *Kokinshū* 40:

> In vain the spring night's darkness accosts the plum,
> Destroying the color but not the scent of its blossoms.

†Po Chü-i, Collected Works, XVI, 'Dawn from Yü Hsin's Tower.'

He spent the day beside her, going over their years together, and charging her with evasion and deviousness.

He sent a note saying that he would not be calling on the princess that day. 'I seem to have caught a chill from the snow and think I would be more comfortable here.'

Her nurse sent back tartly by word of mouth that the note had been passed on to her lady. Not a very amiable sort, thought Genji.

He did not want the Suzaku emperor to know of his want of ardor, but he did not seem capable even of maintaining appearances. Things could scarcely have been worse. For her part, Murasaki feared that the Suzaku emperor would hold her responsible.

Waking this time in the familiar rooms, he got off another note to the princess. He took great trouble with it, though he was not sure that she would notice. He chose white paper and attached it to a sprig of plum blossom.

'Not heavy enough to block the way between us,
    The flurries of snow this morning yet distress me.'

He told the messenger that the note was to be delivered at the west gallery.*

Dressed in white, a sprig of plum in his hand, he sat near the veranda looking at patches of snow like stragglers waiting for their comrades to return.† A warbler called brightly from the rose plum at the eaves. 'Still inside my sleeve,'‡ he said, sheltering the blossom in his hand and raising a blind for a better look at the snow. He was so youthfully handsome that no one would have taken him for one of the great men of the land and the father of a grown son.

Sure that he could expect no very quick answer from the princess, he went to show Murasaki his sprig of plum. 'Blossoms

---

*His reasons are not clear. There is a theory that he does not want Murasaki to see, but it is not very tenable.

†Ki no Tsurayuki, Gosenshū 472:

> Black was my hair, and now it is white and whiter,
>   Like snows that wait for their comrades to return.

‡Anonymous, Kokinshū 32:

> So noisy the warbler! Does it think from the scent
>   That I still have the plum blossom here inside my sleeve?

should have sweet scents. Think what the cherry blossom would be if it had the scent of the plum – we would have an eye for no other blossom. The plum comes into bloom when there is no contest. How fine if we could see it in competition with the cherry.'

An answer did presently come. It was on red tissue paper and folded neatly in an envelope. He opened it with trepidation, hoping that it would not be too irredeemably childish. He did not want to have secrets from Murasaki, and yet he did not want her to see the princess's hand, at least for a time. To display the princess in all her immaturity seemed somehow insulting. But it would be worse to make Murasaki yet unhappier. She sat leaning against an armrest. He laid the note half open beside her.

'You do not come. I fain would disappear,
A veil of snow upon the rough spring winds.'

It was every bit as bad as he had feared, scarcely even a child's hand – and of course in point of years she was not a child at all. Murasaki glanced at it and glanced away as if she had not seen it. He would have offered it up for what it was, evidence of almost complete uselessness, had it been from anyone else.

'So you see that you have nothing to worry about,' he said.

He paid his first daytime call upon the princess. He had dressed with unusual care and no doubt his good looks had an unusually powerful effect on women not used to them. For the older and more experienced of them, the nurse, for instance, the effect was of something like apprehension. He was so splendid that they feared complications. Their lady was such a pretty little child of a thing, reduced to almost nothing at all by the brilliance of her surroundings. It was as if there were no flesh holding up the great mounds of clothing. She did not seem shy before him, and if it could have been said that her openness and freedom from mannerism were for purposes of putting him at his ease, then it could also have been said that they succeeded very well. Her father was not generally held to be a virile sort of man, but no one denied his superior taste and refinement, and the mystery was that he had done so little by way of training her. And of course Genji, like everyone else, knew that she was his favorite, and that he worried endlessly about her. It all seemed rather sad. The other side of the matter was that she did undeniably have a certain girlish charm. She listened quietly and answered with whatever came into her

mind. He must be good to her. In his younger days his disappointment would have approached contempt, but he had become more
tolerant. They all had their ways, and none was enormously superior to the others. There were as many sorts of women as there
were women. A disinterested observer would probably have told
him that he had made a good match for himself. Murasaki was the
only remarkable one among them all, more remarkable now than
ever, he thought, and he had known her very well for a very long
time. He had no cause for dissatisfaction with his efforts as guardian and mentor. A single morning or evening away from her and
the sense of deprivation was so intense as to bring a sort of foreboding.

The Suzaku emperor moved into his temple that same month.
Numbers of emotional letters came to Rokujō, for Genji and of
course for the princess. He said several times that Genji must not
think about him but must follow his own judgment in his treatment of the princess. He could not even so hide his disquietude.
She was so very young and defenseless.

He also wrote to Murasaki. 'I fear I have left an unthinking
child on your hands. Do please be tolerant. I venture to comfort
myself with the thought that the close relationship between you
will make it difficult for you to reject her.

    'Deep into these mountains I would go,
      But thoughts of one I leave still pull me back.

'If I express myself foolishly it is because the heart of a father is
darkness.* You must forgive me.'

Genji was with her when it was delivered. It showed deep feeling, he said, and must be treated with respect. He ordered wine
for the messenger.

Murasaki did not know how to reply. A long and elaborate letter somehow did not seem appropriate. She finally made do with
an impromptu poem:

    'If your thoughts are upon the world you leave behind,
      You should not make a point of cutting your ties.'

She gave the messenger a set of women's robes.
So fine was her handwriting that it set the Suzaku emperor to

See note, page 13.

worrying anew. He should not have left his artless daughter in a house where the other ladies were so subtle.

There were sad farewells now that the time had come for his ladies to go their several ways. Oborozukiyo moved into Kokiden's Nijō mansion. After the Third Princess she had been most on the Suzaku emperor's mind. She thought of becoming a nun, but he dissuaded her, saying that a great rush to holy orders would be unseemly. She devoted more and more of her time to collecting holy images and otherwise preparing for the religious vocation.

The disastrous conclusion to their affair had made it impossible for Genji to forget her. He wanted very much to see her again. Their positions were such, however, that they must always be on good behavior, and the memory of the disaster was still vivid. He kept his wishes to himself. But he did want very much to know something of her thoughts now that she had cut the old entanglements. Though quite aware of the impropriety, he wrote to her from time to time, pretending that his letters, in fact rather warm, were routine inquiries after her health. Because they were no longer young, she sometimes answered. He could tell that she was much improved, and now he did want very much to see her. From time to time he got off a sad petition to her woman Chūnagon.

He summoned Chūnagon's brother, the former governor of Izumi, and addressed him as if they were young adventurers again. 'There is something I want very much to speak to your sister's lady about. Something confidential. You must arrange a secret interview. I no longer go off keeping lighthearted rendezvous, and I am sure that she is as careful as I am, and that we need not worry about being detected.'

But she answered sadly that she could not even consider receiving him. As she had grown in her understanding of the world she had come to see rather better that she had been badly treated. And what had they to talk about now, save regret that the Suzaku emperor was leaving them? Yes, a meeting might be kept secret — but what was she to tell her own conscience?

She had welcomed his advances, however, back in the days when they had presented far greater difficulties. Though her solicitude for the Suzaku emperor, now off in his hermitage, was without doubt genuine, she could hardly say that she and Genji had been nothing to each other. She might now make a great thing of her chastity, but the telltale flock of birds, as the poet said,* would not come back. He summoned his courage and hoped that he might rely for shelter on the grove of Shinoda.†

'The Hitachi lady in the east lodge at Nijō has not been well,' he said to Murasaki. 'I have been too busy to look in on her, and I have been feeling guilty. It would not do to raise a great stir in the middle of the day. I think a quiet evening visit is what is called for, something no one even need know about.'

She thought him improbably nervous about visiting a lady who had never meant a great deal to him. But a certain reserve had grown up between them and she let his explanation pass.

As for the Third Princess, he made do with an exchange of notes. He spent the whole day scenting his robes. It was well after dark when he set off with four or five close retainers. His carriage was a plain one covered with woven palm fronds, putting one in mind of his youthful exploits. The governor of Izumi had been sent ahead to announce his approach.

Oborozukiyo's women informed her in whispers, and she was aghast. 'What can the governor have told him?'

'You must receive him politely, my lady, and send him on his way. You have no alternative.'

Reluctantly, she had him shown in.

After inquiring about her health, he asked that intermediaries be dispensed with. 'I will not object if you keep curtains between us, and I assure you that I am no longer the unthinking boy you once knew.'

She sighed and came forward. So, in spite of everything, she was not completely unapproachable – and they had known each other well enough that a certain excitement communicated itself through the barred door behind which she sat at the southeast corner of the west wing.

'Remember, please, that you have been in my thoughts for a sum of years which I can reckon up very easily. Do not be so girlish.'

*Anonymous, *Kokinshū* 674:

> Rumors have flown and spread. I may no more
> Entice them back than I might a flock of birds.

†An Izumi place name much used in poetry. It is introduced here because the former governor of Izumi is Genji's intermediary.

It was very late. The call of a waterfowl and the answering call of its mate were like reminders of the old affair. The house, once so crowded and noisy, was almost deserted. He could not be accused of wishing to imitate Heichū as he brushed away a tear.* He spoke with a calm self-possession of which he would not earlier have been capable, and yet he rattled irritably at the door.

'So many years, and we meet at Meeting Barrier.
A barrier it remains, but not to my tears.'

'Though tears may flow as the spring at Meeting Hill,
The road between us was long ago blocked off.'

She knew that she was not being very friendly. Memories came back and she asked herself who had been chiefly responsible for their misfortunes. It was not wrong of him to want to see her. She had become more aware of her own inadequacies as she had come to know more of the world. In public life and in private the occasions for guilt and regret had been numberless and had turned her more and more strongly in upon herself. Now the old affair seemed suddenly very near, and she was not capable of treating him coldly. She seemed as young and engaging as ever, and her very great reticence gave her a charm as fresh as upon their first meeting. He found it very difficult to leave her. Birds were already singing in an unusually beautiful dawn. The cherry blossoms had fallen and new leaves were a pale green through morning mists. He remembered a wisteria party long ago,† at just this time of the year. All the years since seemed to come flooding back at once.

Chūnagon saw him off. He turned back as he started to leave.

'How can wisteria be so beautiful? Just see what a magical color it is – and I must leave it.'

The morning sun was now pouring over the hills. He had always been a dazzlingly handsome man, thought Chūnagon, and the years had only improved him. Why could he and her lady not have come together? Life at court was difficult and constricting and her lady had not reached the highest position. Kokiden had insisted on having things her own way, and the scandal had served no purpose at all. Nothing had come of her lady's love for Genji.

*See note†, page 138.
†Chapter 8.

Many things had still been left unsaid, but he was not master of his own movements. He feared prying eyes as the sun rose higher, and his men, who had had his carriage brought up to a gallery, were coughing politely but nervously. He had one of them break off a spray of wisteria.

'I have not forgotten the depths into which I plunged,
    And now these waves of wisteria seek to engulf me.'

Chūnagon was very sorry for him, leaning against a balustrade in an attitude of utter dejection. Though even more fearful than he of being seen, Oborozukiyo felt constrained to answer.

'No waves at all of which to be so fearful.
    My heart, unchastened, sends out waves to join them.'

Genji regretted the harm his youthful heedlessness had done, and yet, perhaps encouraged by evidences that her gate was not very closely guarded, he took his leave only after she had promised to see him again. Why, after all, should he deny his feelings? She had been important to him, and the affair had been brief.

A very sleepy Genji returned to Rokujō. It was not hard for Murasaki to guess what had happened, but she gave no hint of her suspicions. Her silence was more effective than the most violent tantrum, and made Genji feel a little sorry for himself. Did she no longer care what he did? His avowals of undying love were more fervent than ever, and he so rejected the claims of secrecy, which he quite recognized, as to tell her a little of what had happened the night before. There had been a very short interview through screens, he said, and it had left him far from satisfied. He hoped that another might be arranged, so tastefully and discreetly that no one could reprove him for it.

A suggestion of a smile came to her lips. 'Such a marvel of rejuvenation.' But her voice trembled as she went on: 'An ancient affair is superimposed on a new one, and I am caught beneath.'

She was never lovelier than when on the verge of tears.

'Sulking is the one thing I cannot bear. Pinch me and beat me and pour out all your anger, but do not sulk. It is not what I trained you for.'

And presently, it would seem, the whole story came forth.

He was in no hurry to visit the Third Princess. She did not seem to care a great deal whether he came or not, but her women were unhappy. If she had made trouble he would probably have been more worried about her than about Murasaki; but as it was she worried him no more than a pretty, harmless toy.

Genji's daughter, the crown princess,* had not yet been permitted to come home from court. Young and pampered, she needed a rest, and as the warm weather came she began feeling unwell and thought it unkind of the crown prince not to let her go. Her condition was for the crown prince a most interesting and indeed exciting one. She was still very young, rather too young, people thought, to have children. Finally her request was granted and she came home to Rokujō.

She was given rooms on the east side of the main southeast hall, where the Third Princess was also living. Her mother, now blissfully happy, was with her.

Murasaki was to come calling. 'Perhaps we might open the doors to the princess's rooms,' she suggested to Genji, 'and I can introduce myself. I have been looking for an occasion. I do want to be friendly, and I think it might please her.'

Genji smiled. 'Nothing could please me more. You will find her a mere child. Perhaps you can make us all happy by being her teacher.'

As she sat before her mirror she was less worried about the princess than about the Akashi lady. She washed her hair and brushed it carefully and took very great pains with her dress. Genji thought her incomparably lovely.

He went to the princess's rooms. 'The lady in the east wing will be going to see the lady who has just come from court, and she has said that she thinks it a good opportunity for the two of you to become friends. I hope you will see her. She is a very good lady, and so young that you should have no trouble finding things to talk about.'

'I'm sure I will be very tongue-tied. Tell me what to say.'

'You will think of things. Just let the conversation take its course. You needn't feel shy.'

He wanted the two of them to like each other. He was embarrassed that the princess should be so immature for her years, but very pleased that Murasaki had suggested a meeting.

---

*The designation is a convenience in translating. There was no such position. Ladies were named empress but not crown princess.

And so she was being received in audience, thought Murasaki – but was she really so much the princess's inferior? Genji had come upon her in unfortunate circumstances, and that was the main difference between them. Calligraphy was her great comfort when she was in low spirits. She would take up a brush and jot down old poems as they came to her, and the unhappiness in them would speak to her very directly.

Back from seeing the other two ladies, his daughter and his new wife, Genji was filled with wonder at this more familiar lady. They had been together for so many years, and here she was delighting him anew. She managed with no loss of dignity – and it was a noble sort of dignity – to be bright and humorous. He counted over the several aspects of beauty and found them here gathered together; and she was at her loveliest. But then she always seemed her loveliest, more beautiful each year than the year before, today than yesterday. It was her power of constant renewal that most filled him with wonder.

She slipped her jottings under an inkstone. He took them up. The writing was not perhaps her very best, but it had great charm and subtlety.

'I detect a change in the green upon the hills.
Is autumn coming to them? Is it coming to me?'

He wrote beside it, as if he too were at writing practice:

'No change do we see in the white of the waterfowl.
Not so constant the lower leaves of the *hagi*.'

She might write of her unhappiness, but she did not let it show. He thought her splendid.

Free this evening of obligations at Rokujō, he decided to hazard another secret visit to Nijō. Self-loathing was not enough to overcome temptation.

To the crown princess, Murasaki was more like a mother than her real mother. Murasaki thought her even prettier than when they had last met. They talked with all the old ease and intimacy.

Murasaki then went to see the Third Princess. Yes indeed – still very much a child. Murasaki addressed her in a motherly fashion and reminded her what close relatives they were.

She turned to the princess's nurse, Chūnagon. 'It will seem impertinent of me to say so, but we do after all "wear the same garlands."* I have been very slow about introducing myself, I am afraid, but I will hope to see a great deal of you, and I hope too that you will let me know immediately of any derelictions and oversights of which I am guilty.'

'You are very kind. My lady has been feeling rather disconsolate without her father, and nothing could be more comforting. It was his hope as he prepared to leave the world that you would not turn away from her, but would look upon her, still very much a child, as someone to educate and improve. My lady is being very quiet, but I know that she shares these hopes.'

'Ever since the Suzaku emperor honored me with a letter I have wanted to do something; but I have found, alas, that I am capable of so very little.'

Gently, she sought to draw the princess into conversation about illustrated romances and the like. Even at her age, she said, she still played with dolls. She left the princess feeling, in a childish, half-formed way, that this was a kind and gentle lady, not so old in heart and manner as to make a young person feel uncomfortable. Genji had been right. They frequently exchanged notes and from time to time Murasaki joined her in her games.

The world has an unpleasant way of gossiping about people in high places. How, everyone asked, was Murasaki responding to it all? Some lessening of Genji's affection seemed inevitable, and some loss of place and prestige. When it became clear beyond denying that his affection had if anything increased, there were those who said that he really ought to be nicer to his princess. Finally it became clear that the two ladies were getting on very well together, and the world had to look elsewhere for its gossip.

In the Tenth Month, Murasaki made offerings in Genji's honor, choosing a temple in Saga, to the west of the city. She had meant to respect his distaste for ceremony, but the images and sutras, the latter in wonderfully wrought boxes and covers, made one think of an earthly paradise. She commissioned a reading, very solemn and grand, of the sutras for the protection of the realm. The temple was a large one and the congregation was enormous and included most of the highest officials, in part, perhaps, because the

*Ise, *Gosenshū* 810:

> Should anyone come to Yoshino asking for me,
> It will be seen that the two of us wear the same garlands.

fields and moors were at their autumn best. Already the carriages and horses sent up a wintry rustling through the dry grasses.

The other ladies at Rokujō also commissioned holy readings, each one seeking to outdo her fellows.

Genji ended his fast on the twenty-third.* Unlike the other Rokujō ladies, Murasaki still thought of Nijō as her real home. It was there that she arranged a banquet. She herself saw to the arrangements, the festive dress and the like. The other ladies all volunteered their services. The occupants of the outer wings at Nijō were temporarily moved elsewhere and their rooms refitted to accommodate the important guests and their retinues, down to grooms and footmen. The chair of honor, decorated with mother-of-pearl, was put out on a porch before the main hall. Twelve wardrobe stands, on which were the usual summer and winter robes and quilts and spreads, were set out in the west room – though the observer was left to guess what might lie beneath the rich covers of figured purple. Before the chair of honor were two tables spread with a Chinese silk of a gradually deeper hue towards the fringes. The ceremonial chaplet was on an aloeswood stand with flared legs and decorations in metal appliqué, gold birds in silver branches, designed by the Akashi lady and in very good taste indeed. The four screens behind, commissioned by Prince Hyōbu, were excellent. Convention required landscapes of the four seasons, but he had been at pains to insure that they be more than routine. The array of treasures on four tiered stands along the north wall quite suited the occasion. The highest-ranking guests, the ministers and Prince Hyōbu and the others, had seats near the south veranda of the main hall. As for the lower ranks, almost no one failed to appear. Awnings had been set out for the musicians in the garden, to the left and right of the dance platform. Gifts for the guests were laid out along the southeast verandas, viands in eighty boxes and robes in forty Chinese chests.

The musicians took their places in early afternoon. There were dances which one is not often privileged to see, 'Myriad Years' and 'The Royal Deer,' and, as sunset neared, the Korean dragon dance, to flute and drum. Yūgiri and Kashiwagi went out to dance the closing steps. The image of the two of them under the autumn

---

*Perhaps his birthday. It is interesting to note that Tamakazura's banquet fell on the twenty-third of the First Month.

leaves seemed to linger on long afterwards. For the older members of the audience it was joined to the image of a dance long before, 'Waves of the Blue Ocean,' at the Suzaku Palace, in the course of that memorable autumn excursion. In face and manner and general repute the sons seemed very little if at all inferior to the fathers. Indeed, their careers were advancing rather more briskly. And how many years had it been since that autumn excursion? That the friendship of the first generation should be repeated in the second told of very close ties from other worlds. Genji was in tears as memories flooded back.

In the evening the musicians withdrew along the lake and hillock. The white robes which Murasaki's stewards had given them from the Chinese chests were draped over their shoulders, and one thought of the white cranes that promise ten thousand years of life.

And now the guests began their own concert, and it too was very fine. The crown prince had provided the instruments, including a lute and a seven-stringed koto that had belonged to his father, the Suzaku emperor, all of them heirlooms with rich associations. It was long since Genji had last enjoyed such a concert, and each turn and phrase brought memories of his years at court. If only Fujitsubo had lived to permit him the pleasure of arranging just such a concert for her! He somehow felt that he had let her die without knowing what she had meant to him.

The emperor often thought of his mother, and his longing for her was intensified by the fact – indeed it was the great unhappiness of his life – that he was unable to do filial honor to his real father. He had hoped that the festivities might accommodate another royal progress to Rokujō, but finally acceded to Genji's repeated orders that no one was to be inconvenienced.

Back at Rokujō towards the end of the year, Akikonomu arranged the final jubilee observances, readings at the seven great Nara temples and forty temples in and near the capital. To the former she sent forty bolts of cotton and to the latter four hundred double bolts of silk. She was much in Genji's debt, and never again would she have such an opportunity to show her gratitude. She wanted everything to be as her late mother and father would have had it; but since Genji's wish to avoid display had frustrated even the emperor's hopes, she limited herself to a small part of what she would have wished to do.

'I have seen it happen so often,' said Genji. 'People make a great thing of fortieth birthdays and promptly they die. Let us speak softly this time, and wait for something really memorable.'

But she was, after all, empress, and what she arranged was inevitably magnificent. She was hostess at a banquet in the main hall of her southwest quarter, similar in most of its details to Murasaki's Nijō banquet. The gifts for the important guests were as at a state banquet. For royal princes there were sets of ladies' robes, very imaginatively chosen, and, after their several ranks, the other guests received white robes, also for ladies, and bolts of cloth. Among the fine old objects (it was like a display of the very finest) were some famous belts and swords which she had inherited from her father and which were so laden with memory that several of the guests were in tears. We have all read romances which list every gift and offering at such affairs, but I am afraid that they rather bore me; nor am I able to provide a complete guest list.

The emperor still wanted a part in the festivities. A general having resigned because of ill health, he proposed a special jubilee appointment for Yūgiri. Genji replied that he was deeply grateful, and only hoped that Yūgiri was not too young for the honor.

And so there was another banquet, this time in the northeast quarter, where Yūgiri's foster mother, the lady of the orange blossoms, was in residence. It was to be a small, private affair, but like the others it took on magnificence quite of its own accord. Under the personal supervision of the imperial secretariat and upon royal command, supplies were brought from the palace granaries and storehouses. Five royal princes were among the guests, as were both of the ministers and ten councillors, two of the first and three of the middle rank. Neither the crown prince nor the Suzaku emperor was present, but they sent most of their personal aides, and the court attended en masse. By royal command, Tō no Chūjō, the chancellor, was also present, and he had earlier given his attention to the table settings and decorations. It was a very special honor, for which Genji was deeply grateful. He and Tō no Chūjō sat opposite each other in the main hall. Tō no Chūjō was a tall, strongly built man who carried himself with all the dignity of his high office. And Genji was still the shining Genji.

Again there were screens for the four seasons. The polychrome paintings, on figured Chinese silk of a delicate lavender, were very fine, of course, but the superscriptions, by the emperor himself, were superb. (Or did they so dazzle because one knew from whose hand they had come?) The imperial secretariat had provided tiered stands on which were arranged musical instruments and other treasures attesting to Yūgiri's new eminence. Darkness was falling as forty guardsmen lined up forty royal horses for review. The dances, 'Myriad Years' and 'Our Gracious Monarch,' were brief but by no means casual, for they did honor to the chancellor as royal emissary. Prince Hotaru took up his favored lute, and his mastery of the instrument was as always impressive. Genji chose a seven-stringed Chinese koto and the chancellor a Japanese koto. Genji had not heard his friend play in a very long time, and thought that he had improved. He kept back few of his own secret skills on the Chinese koto. There was talk of old times. They had been boyhood friends and there were new ties between them, and the cordiality could scarcely have been greater. The wine cups went the rounds time after time, the impromptu concert was an unmixed delight, and pleasant intoxication brought happy tears which no one tried very hard to hold back.

Genji gave Tō no Chūjō a fine Japanese koto, a Korean flute that was among his particular favorites, and a sandalwood book chest filled with Japanese and Chinese manuscripts. They were taken out to Tō no Chūjō's carriage as he prepared to leave. There was a Korean dance by officials of the Right Stables to signify grateful acceptance of the horses. Yūgiri had gifts for the guardsmen. Once again Genji had asked that unnecessary display be avoided, but of course the emperor, the crown prince, the Suzaku emperor, and the empress were all very close to his house, and the splendor of the arrangements seemed in the end to have taken little account of his wishes.

He had only one son, but such a son, an excellent young man whom everyone admired, that he had little right to feel deprived. He thought again of the bitterness between the two mothers, Akikonomu's and Yūgiri's, and the fierceness of their rivalry. Fate had unexpected ways of working itself out.

This time the lady of the orange blossoms chose the festive robes and the like, entrusting many of the details to Kumoinokari. She had always felt somehow left out of family gatherings, and she had been a little frightened at the prospect of receiving such an array of grandees. Here they were and here she was, and it was all because of Yūgiri.

The New Year came and the crown princess's time drew near.

There were continuous prayers at Nijō and services were commissioned at numerous shrines and temples. Remembering Aoi's last days, Genji was in terror. He had of course wanted Murasaki to have children, but at the same time he had been happy that she was spared the danger. The crown princess was very young and very delicate, a worry to everyone. She fell ill in the Second Month. The soothsayers ordered an immediate change of air. Not wanting to send her a great distance away, Genji moved her to the Akashi lady's northwest quarter. It had two large wings and several galleries along which altars were put up. Prayers and incantations echoed solemnly through the quarter as famous and successful liturgists set about their work. The Akashi lady was perhaps the most apprehensive of all, for her whole past and future seemed to be coming up for judgment.

The birth of a great-grandchild was for the old Akashi nun a dream breaking in upon the slumbers of old age. She came immediately to the crown princess's side and refused to leave. The princess had of course known the company of her mother over the years, but the Akashi lady had had little to say of the past. And here was this old woman, obviously very happy, talking on and on in a tearful, quavering voice. At first the girl gazed at her in distaste and surprise, but then she remembered hints from her mother that there was such a person at Rokujō. Tears streaming from her eyes, the old nun told of Genji's stay on the Akashi coast and of the crown princess's birth.

'We were at wits' end when he left us and came back to the city. That was that, we said. Fate had been good to us up to a point and no further. But it brought you to redeem us all. Isn't that a lovely thought?'

The girl too was in tears. Without the old lady to tell her, she might never have learned of those sad events so long ago. She began to see that she had no right to consider herself better than her rivals. Murasaki had prepared her for the competition. Otherwise she would not have escaped their open contempt. She had thought herself the grandest of them all, far and away the grandest. The others had scarcely seemed worth the trouble of a sneer. And what must they have been thinking of her all the while! Now she knew the whole truth. She had known that her mother was not of the best lineage, but she had not known that she herself had been born in a remote corner of the provinces. How stupid of her not to have inquired! (One must join her in these reproaches. She really should have been more curious.) She had much to think about: the sad story of her grandmother, for instance, now quite cut off from the world.

Her mother found her lost in these painful thoughts. The liturgists, in small groups, had resoundingly begun their noonday rites. There were few women in immediate attendance on the princess. The old nun had quite taken charge of her.

'But can't you be just a little more careful? The wind is blowing a gale, and you might at least have had them bring something up to close the gaps in the curtains. And here you are hanging over her as if you were her doctor! Don't you know that old people are supposed to keep out of sight?'

Though the old nun must have realized that she had outdone herself, she only cocked her head to one side as if trying to hear a little better. She was not as old as her daughter's remarks suggested, only in her middle sixties. Her nun's habit was in very good taste. Her tearful countenance informed her daughter, who was not at all pleased, that she had been dwelling upon the past.

'I suppose she has been rambling on about things that happened a very long time ago. She has a way of remembering things that never happened at all. Sometimes it all seems like a fantastic dream.'

She smiled down at the girl, who was very pretty and who seemed rather more pensive than usual. She could scarcely believe that anyone so charming could be her own daughter – and the old nun would seem to have upset her with sad talk of the past. It had been the lady's intention to tell the whole story when the final goal was in sight. She doubted that anything the old nun had said could destroy the girl's confidence, but she saw all the same that the conversation had been unsettling.

The holy men having left, the Akashi lady brought in sweets and urged her daughter to take just a morsel. So beautiful and so gentle, the girl brought a new flood of tears from the old nun. A smile suddenly cut a great gap across the aged face, still shining with tears. The Akashi lady tried to signal that the effect was less than enchanting, but to no avail.

'Old waves come upon a friendly shore.
A nun's sleeves dripping brine – who can object?

'It used to be the thing, or so I am told, to be tolerant of old people and their strange ways.'

The crown princess took up paper and a brush from beside her inkstone.

'The weeping nun must take me over the waves
To the reed-roofed cottage there upon the strand.'

Turning away to hide her own tears, the Akashi lady set down a poem beside it:

'An old man leaves the world, and in his heart
Is darkness yet,* there on the Akashi strand.'

How the princess wished that she could remember the morning of their departure!

For all the worry and confusion, the birth, towards the middle of the month, was easy. And the child was a boy. Genji was enormously pleased and relieved. This northwest quarter seemed rather cramped and secluded for the celebrations that would follow, though no doubt it was for the old nun 'a friendly shore.' The princess was soon moved back to the southeast quarter. Murasaki was with her, very beautiful, all in white, the baby in her arms as if she were its grandmother. She had no children of her own, nor had she ever before been present at a childbirth. It was all very new and wonderful. She kept the baby with her through the dangerous and troublesome early days. Quite giving over custody, the Akashi lady busied herself with arrangements for the natal bath. The crown prince was represented by his lady of honor, who watched the Akashi lady carefully and was most favorably impressed. She had known in a general way of the lady's circumstances and had thought how unfortunate it would be for the crown princess to be burdened with an unacceptable mother. Everything convinced her that the lady had been meant for high honors. Natal ceremonies should be familiar enough that I need not go into the details.

It was on the sixth day that the princess was moved back to the southeast quarter. Gifts and other provisions for the seventh-night ceremonies came from the palace. Perhaps because the Suzaku emperor, the little prince's grandfather, was in seclusion and could

See note, page 13, once more.

not do the honors, the emperor sent a secretary as his special emissary* and with him gifts of unprecedented magnificence. The empress too sent gifts, robes and the like, more lavish than if the event had taken place at the palace, and princes and ministers seemed to have made the selection of gifts their principal work. No exhortations to frugality came from Genji this time. The pomp and splendor seem so to have dazzled the guests that they failed to notice the gentler, more courtly details that are really worth remembering.

'I have other grandchildren,' said Genji, taking the little prince in his arms, 'but my good son refuses to let me see them. And now I have this pretty little one to make up for his niggardliness.' And indeed the child was pretty enough to justify all manner of boasting.

He grew rapidly, almost perceptibly, as if some mysterious force were giving him its special attention. The selection of nurses and maids had proceeded with great care and deliberation. Only cultivated women of good family were allowed near him.

The Akashi lady kept herself unobtrusively occupied. She knew when to stay in the background, and everyone thought her conduct unexceptionable. Murasaki saw her informally from time to time. Thanks to the little prince, the resentment of the earlier years had quite disappeared, and the Akashi lady was now among her more valued friends. Always fond of children, she made little guardian dolls for the child and more lighthearted playthings too. She seemed very young as she busied herself seeing to his needs.

It was the old nun, the baby's great-grandmother, who felt badly treated. The brief glimpse she had had, she said, threatened to kill her with longing.

The news reached Akashi, where an enlightened old man still had room in his heart for mundane joy. Now, he said to his disciples, he could withdraw from the world in complete peace and serenity. He turned his seaside house into a temple with fields nearby to support it, and appointed for his new retreat certain lands he had acquired deep in a mountainous part of the province, where no one was likely to disturb him. His seclusion would be complete. There would be no more letters and he would see no one. Various small concerns had held him back, and now, with

---

*This is probably Kōbai, Tō no Chūjō's second son.

gods native and foreign to give him strength, he would make his way into the mountains.

He had in recent years dispatched messengers to the city only on urgent business, and when a messenger came from his wife he would send back a very brief note. Now he got off a long letter to his daughter.

'Though we live in the same world, you and I, it has been as if I had been reborn in another. I have sent and received letters only on very rare occasions. Personal messages in intimate Japanese are a waste of time, I have thought. They contribute nothing to and indeed distract from my devotions. I have been overjoyed all the same at news I have had of the girl's career at court. Now she is the mother of a little prince. It is not for me, an obscure mountain hermit, to claim credit or to seek glory at this late date, but I may say that you have been constantly on my mind, and in my prayers morning and night your affairs have taken precedence over my own trivial quest for a place in paradise.

'One night in the Second Month of the year you were born I had a dream. I supported the blessed Mount Sumeru in my right hand. To the left and right of the mountain the moon and the sun poured a dazzling radiance over the world. I was in the shadow of the mountain, not lighted by the radiance. The mountain floated up from a vast sea, and I was in a small boat rowing to the west. That was my dream.

'From the next day I began to have ambitions of which I should not have been worthy. I began to wonder what the extraordinary dream could signify for one like myself. Your good mother became pregnant. I did not cease looking through texts in the true Buddhist writ and elsewhere for an explanation of the dream. I came upon strong evidence that dreams are to be taken seriously, and, as I have said, I began to have ambitions that might have seemed wholly out of keeping with my lowly station. Your future became my whole life. I withdrew to the countryside because there was a limit to what I could do in the city. Not even the waves of old age, I resolved, would be permitted to sweep me back. I passed long years here by the sea because my hopes were in you. I made many secret vows in your behalf, and the time has now come to fulfill them. Because your daughter is to be mother to the nation you must make pilgrimages to Sumiyoshi and the other shrines. What doubts need we have? My very last wish for the girl is certain to be granted, and I know beyond doubt that it too will be granted, my prayer to be reborn in the highest circle of the paradise to the west of the ten million realms. I await the day when I am summoned to my place on the lotus. Until then I shall devote myself to prayers among clean waters and grasses deep in the mountains. To them I now shall go.

'The dawn is at hand. The radiance soon will pour forth.
I turn from it to speak of an ancient dream.'

He had affixed the date, after which there was a postscript: 'Do not be disturbed when my last day comes. Do not put on the mourning robes which have so long been customary. You must think of yourself as an avatar and offer a prayer or two, no more, for the repose of the soul of an aged monk. Do not, all the same, let the pleasures and successes of this world distract your attention from the other. We are certain to meet again in the realm to which we all seek admission. It will not be long, you must tell yourself, until we meet there on the far shore, having left these sullied shores behind us.'

For his wife there was only a short note: 'On the fourteenth I shall leave this grass hut behind and go off into the mountains. I shall give my useless self to the bears and wolves. Live on, and see our hopes to their conclusion. We shall meet in the radiant land.'

The messenger, a priest, filled in some of the details. 'The third day after he wrote the letter he went off into the mountains. We went with him as far as the foothills, where he made us turn back. Only a priest and two acolytes went on with him. I had thought when I saw him take his first vows that I knew the deepest possible sorrow, but still deeper sorrow lay ahead. He took up the koto and the lute that had kept him company through the years and played on them one last time, and when he said his last prayers in the chapel he left them there. He left most of his other personal possessions there too, after choosing several mementos, in keeping with our several ranks, for us who had joined him in taking holy orders. There were about sixty of us, all very close to him. The rest of his things have come to you here. And so we saw him off into the clouds and mists, and mourn for him in the house he left behind.'

The messenger had gone to Akashi as a boy. Still in Akashi, he was now an old man. It is not likely that he exaggerated his account of the sorrow and loneliness.

The most enlightened disciples of the Buddha himself, converted by the Hawk Mountain Sermon, were plunged into grief when finally the flame of his life went out. The old nun's grief was limitless.

The Akashi lady slipped away from the southeast quarter when she heard what sort of letter had come. Her new eminence made it impossible for her to see as much of her mother as in earlier years, but she had to find out for herself what sad news had come. The old nun seemed heartbroken. The lady had a lamp brought near and read the letter, and she too was soon weeping helplessly.

She thought of little things that had happened over the years, things that could have meant nothing to anyone else, and her longing for her father was intense. She would not see him again. She now understood: he had put his faith in a dream as the true and sacred word. It had become an obsession, and a source of great unhappiness and embarrassment for the lady herself. She had feared at times that she might go mad – and now she saw that the cause of it all was one insubstantial dream.

The old nun at length controlled her weeping. 'Because of you, we have had blessings and honors quite beyond anything we deserved. The sorrows and trials have been large in proportion. Though I certainly was not a person of any great distinction, I thought that our decision to leave the familiar city and live in Akashi was itself somehow a mark of distinction. I did not expect that I would be as I am now, a widow and not a widow. I had thought that we would be together in this world and that we would share the same lotus in the next world, where my chief hopes lay. Then your own life took that extraordinary turn and I was back in a city I thought I had left forever. I was happy for you and I grieved for him. And now I learn that we are not to meet again. Everyone thought him a very eccentric and unsociable man even before he left court, but two young people are a support for each other and the bond between us was unusally strong. We had faith in each other. We are still almost within calling distance of each other, and we are kept apart. Why should it be?' The old lady's face was twisted with grief.

Her daughter too was weeping bitterly. 'What good are promises of great things? I do not consider myself worthy of any great honors, but it does seem too sad that he should end his days like a forgotten exile. It is easy to say that what must be must be.

He has gone off into those wild mountains, and we cannot any of us be sure how long we will live. It all seems so empty and useless.'

They gave the night over to sad talk.

'Genji knows that I was in the southeast quarter last night,' said the lady. 'I am afraid he will think it rude and selfish of me to have come away without leave. I do not care about myself, but I have her to think of.' She returned at dawn.

'And how is the baby?' asked her mother. 'Don't you suppose they might let me see him?'

'Oh, I am sure of it. You'll see him before long. The princess speaks very fondly of you, and Genji remarked by way of something or other that if things go well — it was inviting bad luck to make distant predictions, he said, but if things go well he hopes that you will be here to enjoy them. I cannot be sure, of course, what he had in mind.'

The old lady smiled. 'There you have it. For better or for worse, I seem to have been meant for peculiar things.'

The Akashi lady had someone take the letter box to the southeast quarter.

The crown prince was impatient to have the princess back at court. There were repeated summonses.

'I quite understand,' said Murasaki. 'Such a happy event, and he is being left out of it.' She got the baby ready for a quiet visit to his father.

The princess had hoped for a longer stay at Rokujō. She was seldom permitted to leave court, and it had been a frightening experience for so young a lady. She was even prettier for the loss of weight.

'You have been kept so busy,' said her mother. 'You need a good, quiet rest.'

'But I think he should see her before she begins putting on weight again,' said Genji. 'He is sure to like her even better.'

In the evening, when Murasaki had returned to her wing of the house and the crown princess's rooms were quiet, the lady spoke to her daughter of the box that had come from Akashi. 'I should wait until everything is completely in order, I suppose, and all our hopes have been realized. But life is uncertain and I may die, and I am not of such rank that I can be sure of a final interview. It seems best to tell you of these trivialities while I still have my wits about me. You will find that his vows are in a cramped and ugly hand, I fear, but do please glance over them. Keep them in a drawer beside you, and when the time seems right go over them again and see that all the promises are kept. Do not, please, speak of them to anyone who is not likely to understand. Now that your affairs seem in order, I too should think of leaving the world. I somehow feel that time is running out. Do not – and this I most genuinely beg of you – do not ever let anything come between you and the lady in the east wing. I have come to know what an extraordinarily gentle and thoughtful person she is and I pray that she will live a much longer life than I. It was clear from the outset that I would only do you harm by being with you, and so I let her have you. I worried, of course, because stepmothers are not famous for their kindness, but I finally came to see that I had nothing to worry about.'

It had been for her a long speech. She had always been very formal even with her daughter. The girl was in tears. The old man's letter was indeed difficult. The five or six sheets of furrowed Michinoku paper were stiff and discolored with age, but they had been freshly scented. She turned half away. Her hair, now shining with tears, framed a lovely profile.

Genji came in from the Third Princess's rooms. There was no time to hide the letter, but the lady pulled up a curtain frame and half hid herself.

'And is he awake? I want to rush back for another look at him when I have been away even a few minutes.'

The princess did not answer. Murasaki had taken the child, said her mother.

'You must not let her monopolize it. She is always carrying it around and so she is always having to change to dry clothes. She can come here if she wants to see it.'

'You are being unkind, and I do not think you have thought things through very carefully. I would have no doubts at all about letting her take a little girl off with her, and we can be much bolder with little boys even when they are princes. Is it your wise view that the two of them should be kept apart?'

'I shall defer to your wiser view, though not before protesting your treatment of me. I have no doubt that I am a pompous old fool, but you need not make me so aware of that fact by leaving me out of things and talking behind my back. I have no doubt that you say the most dreadful things about me.'

He pulled aside the curtain and found her leaning against a pillar, dignified and elegantly dressed. The box was beside her. She had not wished to attract his attention to it by pushing it out of sight.

'And what is this? Something of profound significance, no doubt. An endless poem from a lovelorn gentleman, all locked up in a strong box?'

'Again you are being unkind. You seem very young these days, and sometimes your humor is beyond the reach of the rest of us.'

She was smiling, but it was clear that something had saddened her. He was so openly curious, his head cocked inquiringly to one side, that she thought an explanation necessary.

'My father has sent a list of prayers and vows from his cave in Akashi. He thought that I might perhaps ask you to look at them sometime. But not quite yet, I think, if you don't mind.'

'I can only imagine how hard he has worked at his devotions and what enormous wisdom and grace he must have accumulated over the years. I sometimes hear of a priest who has made a most awesome name for himself, and find on looking into the matter a little more closely that he still smells rather strongly of the world. Erudition is not enough, and in the matter of sheer dedication and concentration your father is, I am sure, ahead of all the others, and besides his learning and wisdom he has a feeling for the gentler things. And through it all he is a very modest man who makes no great show of his virtues. I thought when I knew him that he did not live in the same world as the rest of us, and now he is throwing off the last traces of our world and finding true liberation. How I would love to go off and have a quiet talk with him!'

'I am told that he has left the seacoast and gone off into mountains so deep that no birds fly singing overhead.'*

'And this is his last will and testament? Have you had a letter from him? And your mother – what does she think of it all?' His voice trembled. 'The bond between husband and wife is often stronger than that between parent and child. As the years have gone by and I have come to know a little of the world, I have felt

*Anonymous, *Kokinshū* 535:

> I beg to inform you that I go off into mountains
> So deep that no birds fly singing overhead.

strangely near him. I can only try to imagine what that stronger bond must be.'

The part about the dream, she thought, might interest him. 'It is in an outlandish hand – it might almost be Sanskrit. Perhaps certain passages might be worth glancing at. I thought I was saying goodbye to it all, but there are some things, it would seem, that I did not after all leave behind.'

'It is a fine hand, still very young and strong.' In tears, he lingered over the description of the dream. 'He is a very learned and a very talented man, and all that has been lacking is a certain political sense, a flair for making his way ahead in the world. There was a minister in your family, an extremely earnest and intelligent man, I have always heard. People who speak of him in such high terms have always asked what misstep may have been responsible for bringing his line to an end – though of course we have you, and even though you are a lady we cannot say that his line has come to a complete end. No doubt your father's piety and devotion are being rewarded.'

The old man had been thought impossibly eccentric and wholly unrealistic in his ambitions. Genji had been in bad conscience about the whole Akashi episode. The crown princess's birth had seemed to tell of a bond from a former life, but the future had seemed very uncertain all the same. He now saw how much that one fragile dream had meant to the old man. It had fed the apparently wild ambition to have Genji as a son-in-law. Genji had suffered in exile, it now seemed, that the crown princess might be born. And what sort of vows might the old man have made? Respectfully, he looked through the contents of the box.

'I have papers that might go with them,' he said to his daughter. 'I must show them to you.' After a time he continued: 'Now you know the truth, or most of it, I should think. You are not to let what you have learned make any difference in your relations with the lady in the east wing. A little kindness or a word of affection from an outsider can sometimes mean more than all the natural affection between husband and wife or parent and child. And in her case it has been far more. She took responsibility for you when she saw that everything was already in perfectly capable hands, and her affection has not wavered. The wise ones of the world have always taken it upon themselves to see that we are aware of pretense. There may be stepmothers, they tell us, who seem kind and well-meaning, but this is the worst sort of pretense. But even when a stepmother does in fact have sinister intentions a child can sometimes overcome them by the simple device of not seeing them, of behaving with quite open and unfeigned affection. What a horrid person she has been, says the stepmother of herself, and so she resolves to do better. There are basic and ancient hostilities, of course, that nothing can overcome, but most disagreements are the result of no great wrongdoing on either side. All that is needed for reconciliation is an acceptance of that fact. The most tiresome thing is to raise a great stir over nothing, to fume and complain when the sensible thing would have been to look the other way. I cannot pretend that my observations have been very wide and diverse, but I would give it to you as my conclusion that there is a level of competence to which most of us can attain and which is quite high enough. We all have our strong points – or in any event I have never myself seen anyone with none at all. Yet when you are looking for someone to fill your whole life there are not many who seem right. For me there has been the lady in the east wing, the perfect partner in everything. And it is unfortunately the case that even a lady of the most unassailable birth can sometimes seem a little wispy and undependable.' He left her to guess whom he might have in mind.

Speaking now in softer tones, he turned to the Akashi lady. 'I know that your discernment and understanding leave nothing to be desired. The two of you must be the best of friends as you look after our princess here.'

'You need not even say it. I have been only too aware of her kindness, and I am always speaking of it. She could so easily have taken my presence as an affront and had nothing to do with me, but in fact her kindness has been almost embarrassing. It is she who has covered my inadequacies.'

'No very special kindness on her part, I should say. She has wanted to have someone with the girl, and that is all. You have not chosen to stand on your rights as a mother and that has helped a great deal. I have nothing to complain or worry about. It is amazing the damage that obtuseness and ill temper can do, and I cannot tell you how grateful I am that these lamentable qualities are alien to both of you.'

He went back to the east wing, and the Akashi lady was left to meditate upon the interview. Yes, modesty and self-effacement had brought their rewards. As for Murasaki, she seemed to claim more and more of his attention, and her charms and attainments were such that one could not be surprised or wish it otherwise. His relations with the Third Princess seemed quite correct, and yet something was missing. He did not visit her as frequently as might have been expected – and she was after all a princess. She and Murasaki were very closely related, though her standing was perhaps just a little the higher. How sad for her. But all of this the Akashi lady kept to herself. She did not gossip and she did not complain. She knew that she had done very well. Things did not always go ideally well for princesses even, and she was certainly no princess. Her only sorrow was for her father, now off in the mountain wilds. As for the old nun, she put her faith in 'the seed that falls upon good ground.'* She gave up thoughts of this world for thoughts of the next.

The Third Princess had not been beyond Yūgiri's reach, and her marriage to Genji and her presence so close at hand had an unsettling effect on him. Performing this and that routine service for her, he was coming to see what sort of lady she was. She was very young and rather quiet, and that was all. Genji seemed determined to do what the world expected of him, but it was hard to believe that she really interested him very much. Nor did there seem to be women of substance among her attendants. Yūgiri thought them a flock of pretty young things forever preening themselves and chatting and playing games. It was a happy enough household, but if it contained women of a serious, meditative bent the outsider did not see them. The most melancholy of women would have been painted over with the same cheerful brush. Genji might not be enormously pleased at the sight of all these little girls at their games the whole day through, but he was by nature neither an uncharitable man nor a reformer, and he did not interfere. He did, however, give some attention to training the princess herself, and she was beginning to seem a little less heedless and immature.

Not many women, thought Yūgiri, were perfect. Only Murasaki had over the years seemed beyond criticism. She had quietly lived her own life and no scandal had touched her. She had treated

*Apparently a poetic allusion.

no one maliciously or arrogantly, and had herself always been a model of graceful and courtly demeanor. He could not forget the one glimpse he had had of her. Kumoinokari, his own wife, was certainly pretty and pleasing enough, but she was in a way rather ordinary. She was without strong traits or remarkable accomplishments. Now that he had no more worries in that quarter he found his excitement waning and his interest moving back to Rokujō, where so many fine ladies, each outstanding in her way, were gathered together. The Third Princess's pedigree was certainly the finest, but it seemed equally certain that Genji gave her a lower rating as a person than some of the others and was but keeping up appearances. Yūgiri was not exactly consumed with longing and curiosity, but he did hope that he might sometime have a glimpse of her too.

A frequenter of the Suzaku Palace, Kashiwagi had known all about the Third Princess and the Suzaku emperor's worries. He had offered himself as a candidate for her hand. His candidacy had not been dismissed, and then, suddenly and to his very great disappointment, she had gone to Genji. He still could not reconcile himself to what had happened. He seems to have taken some comfort in exchanging reports with women whom he had known in her maiden days. He of course heard what everyone else heard, that she was no great competitor for Genji's affection.

He was forever complaining to Kojijū, her nurse's daughter. 'I am much beneath her, I know, but I would have made her happy. I know of course that she was meant for someone far grander.'

Nothing in this world is permanent, and Genji might one day make up his mind to leave it. Kashiwagi kept after Kojijū.

Prince Hotaru and Kashiwagi came calling at Rokujō one pleasant day in the Third Month. Genji received them.

'Life is quiet these days, and rather dull, I fear. My affairs public and private go almost too smoothly. So how shall we amuse ourselves today? Yūgiri is devoted to that small-bow of his, and never misses a chance to take it out, and that would be a possibility. Where might he be? He had a collection of eminent young archers with him. Was he so unwise as to let them go?' He was told that Yūgiri and his friends, a large band of them, were at football in the northeast quarter. 'Not a very genteel pastime, perhaps, but something to wake you up and keep you on the alert. Send for him, please.'

The summons was delivered and Yūgiri came bringing numbers of young gentlemen with him.

'Did you bring your ball? And who are all of you?'

Yūgiri gave the names.

'Fine. Let us see what you can do.'

The crown princess and her baby had gone back to the palace. Genji was in her rooms, now almost deserted. The garden was level and open where the brooks came together. It seemed both a practical and an elegant place for football. Tō no Chūjō's sons, Kashiwagi and the rest, some grown men and some still boys, rather dominated the gathering. The day was a fine, windless one. It was late afternoon. Kōbai at first seemed to stand on his dignity, but he quite lost himself in the game as it gathered momentum.

'Just see the effect it has on civil office,' said Genji. 'I would expect you guardsmen to be jumping madly about and letting your commissions fall where they may. I was always among the spectators myself, and now I genuinely wish I had been more active. Though as I have said it may not be the most genteel pursuit in the world.'

Taking their places under a fine cherry in full bloom, Yūgiri and Kashiwagi were very handsome in the evening light. Genji's less than genteel sport – such things do happen – took on something of the elegance of the company and the place. Spring mists enfolded trees in various stages of bud and bloom and new leaf. The least subtle of games does have its skills and techniques, and each of the players was determined to show what he could do. Though Kashiwagi played only briefly, he was clearly the best of them all. He was handsome but retiring, intense and at the same time lively and expansive. Though the players were now under the cherry directly before the south stairs, they had no eye for the blossoms. Genji and Prince Hotaru were at a corner of the veranda.

Yes, there were many skills, and as one inning followed another a certain abandon was to be observed and caps of state were pushed rather far back on noble foreheads. Yūgiri could permit himself a special measure of abandon, and his youthful spirits and vigor were infectious. He had on a soft white robe lined with red. His trousers were gently taken in at the ankles, but by no means untidy. He seemed very much in control of himself despite the abandon, and cherry petals fell about him like a flurry of snow. He broke off a twig from a dipping branch and went to sit on the stairs.

'How quick they are to fall,' said Kashiwagi, coming up behind him. 'We much teach the wind to blow wide and clear.'*

He glanced over toward the Third Princess's rooms. They seemed to be in the usual clutter. The multicolored sleeves pouring from under the blinds and through openings between them were like an assortment of swatches to be presented to the goddess of spring. Only a few paces from him a woman had pushed her curtains carelessly aside and looked as if she might be in a mood to receive a gentleman's addresses. A Chinese cat, very small and pretty, came running out with a larger cat in pursuit. There was a noisy rustling of silk as several women pushed forward to catch it. On a long cord which had become badly tangled, it would not yet seem to have been fully tamed. As it sought to free itself the cord caught in a curtain, which was pulled back to reveal the women behind. No one, not even those nearest the veranda, seemed to notice. They were much too worried about the cat.

A lady in informal dress stood† just inside the curtains beyond the second pillar to the west. Her robe seemed to be of red lined with lavender, and at the sleeves and throat the colors were as bright and varied as a book of paper samples. Her cloak was of white figured stain lined with red. Her hair fell as cleanly as sheaves of thread and fanned out towards the neatly trimmed edges some ten inches beyond her feet. In the rich billowing of her skirts the lady scarcely seemed present at all. The white profile framed by masses of black hair was pretty and elegant – though unfortunately the room was dark and he could not see her as well in the evening light as he would have wished. The women had been too delighted with the game, young gentlemen heedless of how they scattered the blossoms, to worry about blinds and concealment. The lady turned to look at the cat, which was mewing piteously,

*Fujiwara Yoshikaze, *Kokinshū* 85:

> Blow wide and clear, spring wind, of the cherry blossoms.
> Let us see if they will fall of their own accord.

†The verb is important. Well-behaved ladies did not permit themselves to be seen standing.

and in her face and figure was an abundance of quiet, unpretend-
ing young charm.

Yūgiri saw and strongly disapproved, but would only have
made matters worse by stepping forward to lower the blind. He
coughed warningly. The lady slipped out of sight. He too would
have liked to see more, and he sighed when, the cat at length
disengaged, the blind fell back into place. Kashiwagi's regrets were
more intense. It could only have been the Third Princess, the lady
who was separated from the rest of the company by her informal
dress. He pretended that nothing had happened, but Yūgiri knew
that he had seen the princess, and was embarrassed for her. Seeking
to calm himself, Kashiwagi called the cat and took it up in his
arms. It was delicately perfumed. Mewing prettily, it brought the
image of the Third Princess back to him (for he had been ready to
fall in love).

'This is no place for our young lordships to be wasting
their time,' said Genji. 'Suppose we go inside.' He led the way to
the east wing, where he continued his conversation with Prince
Hotaru.

Still excited from the game, the younger men found places on
the veranda, where they were brought simple refreshments, pears
and oranges and camellia cakes,* and wine and dried fish and the
like to go with it.

Kashiwagi was lost in thought. From time to time he would
look vacantly up at the cherries.

Yūgiri thought he understood. His friend must agree, he was
also thinking, that it was unseemly for so fine a lady to step forward into such an exposed position. Murasaki would never have
been so careless. Yūgiri could see, he feared, why Genji's esteem
for the princess seemed to fall rather short of that of the world in
general. This childlike insouciance was no doubt charming, but it
might cause trouble.

Kashiwagi was not thinking about the princess's defects. He
had seen her accidentally and very briefly, to be sure, but he had
most certainly seen her. He was telling himself that there had to be
a bond between them and that the steadfastness of his devotion
was being rewarded.

*Rice pounded into dumplings, sweetened, and served between camellia leaves. A
sporting delicacy.

'Tō no Chūjō and I were always in competition,' said Genji, in a reminiscent mood, 'and football was the one thing I never succeeded in besting him at. It may seem flippant to speak of a football heritage, but I really believe that there must be such a thing, unusual talent handed down in a family. You quite dazzled us, sir.'

Kashiwagi smiled. 'I doubt that the honor will mean very much to our descendants.'

'Surely you are wrong. Everything that is genuinely outstanding deserves to be chronicled. This would be a most interesting and edifying item for a family chronicle.'

Kashiwagi was wondering what sort of charms would be required to impress the wife of a man so youthful and handsome, to win her pity and sympathy. He was overwhelmed by sudden and hopeless feelings of inferiority.

He and Yūgiri left in the same carriage.

'We were right to pay our visit,' said Yūgiri. 'I fear the poor man is bored. We must find time for another before the blossoms have fallen. Do come again and bring your bow with you, and help us enjoy the last of the spring.'

They agreed upon a day.

'I gather that your father spends most of his time in the east wing. His regard for the lady there seems really extraordinary.' And Kashiwagi went on to say perhaps more than he should have. 'What effect do you suppose it has on the Third Princess? She has always been her father's favorite. It must be a new experience for her.'

'Nonsense. It is true that the lady in the east wing has a rather particular place in his life, but that is because he took her in when she was still a child. But he is very good to the princess.'

'You needn't try to distort the facts. I know quite well enough what they are. People tell me that she has a sad time of it. Nothing in her background can have prepared her.

'The generous warbler, moving from tree to tree,
Neglects the cherry alone among them all.'

And he added softly: 'And the cherry, among them all, seems right for the bird of spring.'*

---

*The rhythm of the last sentence suggests that he may be improvising or quoting a poem.

This seemed downright impertinent, though Yūgiri did think he understood his friend's reasons.

'The cuckoo building its nest in mountain depths
Does not, be assured, neglect the cherry blossom.

'Surely, sir, you are not asking that he give her the whole of his attention?'

Wishing to hear no more, he changed the subject, and presently they went their separate ways.

Kashiwagi still lived alone in the east wing of his father's mansion. He had had his hopes, and though he remained a bachelor by his own choice he was sometimes bored and unhappy. He was good enough, he had still been able to tell himself, to have the lady he wanted if he only waited long enough. But now he was in anguish. When might he again see the Third Princess, even as briefly as on the evening of the football match? A lesser lady might have found an excuse for leaving the house, a taboo or something of the sort. But she was a princess, and he must contrive to send word of his longing through thick walls and curtains.

He settled upon the usual note to Kojijū. 'The winds the other day blew me in upon your premises, to increase your lady's hostility, no doubt. Since that evening I have been in deep despondency. I brood my days away for no good reason.*

'The trees of sorrow seem denser from near at hand,
And my yearning grows for those blossoms in the twilight.'

Not knowing what 'blossoms in the twilight' he had reference to, Kojijū thought him a very moody young man indeed.

Choosing a time when the princess had few people with her, she delivered the note. 'He seems a rather sticky sort,' she smiled. 'I do not know why I take him seriously.'

'Aren't you funny,' said the princess, glancing at the note, which Kojijū had opened for her.

Immediately recognizing the allusion and the incident upon which it was based, she flushed scarlet. And she thought of some-

---

*Ariwara Narihira, Kokinshū 476 and Tales of Ise 99:

I brood my days away for no good reason,
Less that I do not see than that I see poorly.

thing else, how Genji was always reproving her for just such carelessness.

'You must not let Yūgiri see you,' he would say. 'You are very
young and you may not pay a great deal of attention to these
things. But you really should.'

She was terrified. Had Yūgiri seen and told Genji? Would
Genji scold her? She was indeed a child, that fear of Genji should
come first.

Finding her lady even more unresponsive than usual, Kojijū did
not press the matter. When she was alone she got off the usual sort
of answer in a flowing, casual hand.

'Away you went, so very coolly. I was incensed. And what do
you mean by suggesting that you see poorly? These innuendos are
almost insulting.

> 'Do not let it be known, I pray of you,
> That your eye has fallen on the mountain cherry.

'It will never do, never.'

CHAPTER 35

New Herbs: Part Two

Kojijū's answer was not unreasonable, and yet it seemed rather brusque. Was there to be nothing more? Might he not hope for some word from the princess herself? He seemed in danger of doing grave disservice to Genji, whom he so liked and admired.

On the last day of the Third Month there was a large gathering at the Rokujō mansion. Kashiwagi did not want to attend, but presently decided that he might feel a little less gloomy under the blossoms where the Third Princess lived. There was to have been an archery meet in the Second Month, but it had been canceled, and in the Third Month the court was in retreat. Everyone was always delighted to hear that something was happening at Rokujō. The two generals, Higekuro and Yūgiri, were of course present, both of them being very close to the Rokujō house, and all their subordinates were to be present as well. It had been announced as a competition at kneeling archery, but events in standing archery were also included, so that several masters of the sport who were to be among the competitors might show their skills. The bowmen were assigned by lot to the fore and after sides. Evening came, and the last of the spring mists seemed somehow to resent it. A pleasant breeze made the guests even more reluctant to leave the shade of the blossoms. It may have been that a few of them had had too much to drink.

'Very fine prizes,' said someone. 'They show so nicely the tastes of the ladies who chose them. And who really wants to see a soldier battering a willow branch with a hundred arrows in a row?* We much prefer a mannerly meet of the sort we are here being treated to.'

The two generals, Higekuro and Yūgiri, joined the other officers in the archery court. Kashiwagi seemed very thoughtful as he took up his bow. Yūgiri noticed and was worried. He could not, he feared, tell himself that the matter did not concern him. He and Kashiwagi were close friends, alive to each other's moods as

---

*There is an account of such an exploit in the *Shih Chi*.

friends seldom are. One of them knew immediately when the smallest shadow had crossed the other's spirits.

Kashiwagi was afraid to look at Genji. He knew that he was thinking forbidden thoughts. He was always concerned to behave with complete correctness and much worried about appearances. What then was he to make of so monstrous a thing as this? He thought of the princess's cat and suddenly longed to have it for himself. He could not share his unhappiness with it, perhaps, but he might be less lonely. The thought became an obsession. Perhaps he could steal it — but that would not be easy.

He visited his sister at court, hoping that she would help him forget his woes. She was an extremely prudent lady who allowed him no glimpse of her. It did seem odd that his own sister should be so careful to keep up the barriers when the Third Princess had let him see her; but his feelings did not permit him to charge her with loose conduct.

He next called on the crown prince, the Third Princess's brother. There must, he was sure, be a family resemblance. No one could have called the crown prince devastatingly handsome, but such eminence does bestow a certain air and bearing. The royal cat had had a large litter of kittens, which had been put out here and there. One of them, a very pretty little creature, was scampering about the crown prince's rooms. Kashiwagi was of course reminded of the Rokujō cat.

'The Third Princess has a really fine cat. You would have to go a very long way to find its rival. I only had the briefest glimpse, but it made a deep impression on me.'

Very fond of cats, the crown prince asked for all the details. Kashiwagi perhaps made the Rokujō cat seem more desirable than it was.

'It is a Chinese cat, and Chinese cats are different. All cats have very much the same disposition, I suppose, but it does seem a little more affectionate than most. A perfectly charming little thing.'

The crown prince made overtures through the Akashi princess and presently the cat was delivered. Everyone was agreed that it was a very superior cat. Guessing that the crown prince meant to keep it, Kashiwagi waited a few days and paid a visit. He had been a favorite of the Suzaku emperor's and now he was close to the crown prince, to whom he gave lessons on the koto and other instruments.

'Such numbers of cats as you do seem to have. Where is my own special favorite?'

The Chinese cat was apprehended and brought in. He took it in his arms.

'Yes, it is a handsome beast,' said the crown prince, 'but it does not seem terribly friendly. Maybe it is not used to us. Do you really think it so superior to our own cats?'

'Cats do not on the whole distinguish among people, though perhaps the more intelligent ones do have the beginnings of a rational faculty. But just look at them all, such swarms of cats and all of them such fine ones. Might I have the loan of it for a few days?'

He was afraid that he was being rather silly. But he had his cat. He kept it with him at night, and in the morning would see to its toilet and pet it and feed it. Once the initial shyness had passed it proved to be a most affectionate animal. He loved its way of sporting with the hem of his robe or entwining itself around a leg. Sometimes when he was sitting at the veranda lost in thought it would come up and speak to him.

'What an insistent little beast you are.' He smiled and stroked its back. 'You are here to remind me of someone I long for, and what is it you long for yourself? We must have been together in an earlier life, you and I.'

He looked into its eyes and it returned the gaze and mewed more emphatically. Taking it in his arms, he resumed his sad thoughts.

'Now why should a cat all of a sudden dominate his life?' said one of the women. 'He never paid much attention to cats before.'

The crown prince asked to have the cat back, but in vain. It had become Kashiwagi's constant and principal companion.

Tamakazura still felt closer to Yūgiri than to her brothers and sisters. She was a sensitive and affectionate lady and when he came calling she received him without formality. He particularly enjoyed her company because his sister, the crown princess, rather put him off. Higekuro was devoted to his new wife and no longer saw his old wife, Prince Hyōbu's daughter. Since Tamakazura had no daughters, he would have liked to bring Makibashira into the house, but Prince Hyōbu would not hear of it. Makibashira at least must not become a laughingstock. Prince Hyōbu was a highly respected man, one of the emperor's nearest advisers,* and no request of his was refused. A vigorous man with lively modern tastes, he stood so high in the general esteem that he was only less in demand than Genji and Tō no Chūjō. It was commonly thought that Higekuro would be equally important one day. People were of course much interested in his daughter, who had many suitors. The choice among them would be Prince Hyōbu's to make. He was interested in Kashiwagi and thought it a pity that Kashiwagi should be less interested in Makibashira than in his cat. She was a bright, modern sort of girl. Because her mother was still very much at odds with the world, she turned more and more to Tamakazura, her stepmother.

Prince Hotaru was still single. The ladies he had so energetically courted had gone elsewhere. He had lost interest in romantic affairs and did not want to invite further ridicule. Yet bachelorhood was too much of a luxury. He let it be known that he was not uninterested in Makibashira.

'I think he would do nicely,' said Prince Hyōbu. 'People generally say that the next-best thing after sending a daughter to court is finding a prince for her. I think it rather common and vulgar, the rush these days to marry daughters off to mediocrities who have chiefly their seriousness to recommend them.' He accepted Prince Hotaru's proposal without further ado.

Prince Hotaru was somewhat disappointed. He had expected more of a challenge. Makibashira was not a lady to be spurned, however, and it was much too late to withdraw his proposal. He visited her and was received with great ceremony by Prince Hyōbu's household.

'I have many daughters,' said Prince Hyōbu, 'and they have caused me nothing but trouble. You might think that by now I would have had enough. But Makibashira at least I must do something for. Her mother is very odd and only gets odder. Her father has not been allowed to manage her affairs and seems to want no part of them. It is all very sad for her.'

He supervised the decorations and went to altogether more trouble than most princes would have thought necessary.

Prince Hotaru had not ceased to grieve for his dead wife. He had hoped for a new wife who looked exactly like her.

*They are uncle and nephew.

Makibashira was not unattractive, but she did not resemble the other lady. Perhaps it was because of disappointment that he so seldom visited her.

Prince Hyōbu was surprised and unhappy. In her lucid moments, the girl's mother could see what was happening, and sigh over their sad fate, hers and her daughter's. Higekuro, who had been opposed to the match from the outset, was of course very displeased. It was as he had feared and half expected. Prince Hotaru had long been known for a certain looseness and inconstancy. Now that she had evidence so near at hand, Tamakazura looked back to her maiden days with a mixture of sadness and amusement, and wondered what sort of troubles Genji and Tō no Chūjō would now be facing if she had accepted Hotaru's suit. Not that she had had much intention of doing so. She had seemed to encourage him only because of his very considerable ardor, and it much shamed her to think that she might have seemed even a little eager. And now her stepdaughter was his wife. What sort of things would he be telling her? But she did what she could for the girl, whose brothers were in attendance on her as if nothing had gone wrong.

Prince Hotaru for his part had no intention of abandoning her, and he did not at all like what her sharp-tongued grandmother was saying.

'One marries a daughter to a prince in the expectation that he will give her his undivided attention. What else is there to make up for the fact that he does not amount to much?'

'This seems a bit extreme,' said Prince Hotaru, missing his first wife more than ever. 'I loved her dearly, and yet I permitted myself an occasional flirtation on the side, and I do not remember that I ever had to listen to this sort of thing.'

He withdrew more and more to the seclusion of his own house, where he lived with memories.

A year passed, and two years. Makibashira was reconciled to her new life. It was the marriage she had made for herself, and she did not complain.

And more years went by, on the whole uneventfully. The reign was now in its eighteenth year.*

The emperor had no sons. He had long wanted to abdicate and had not kept the wish a secret. 'A man never knows how many

---

*Genji is now forty-six by the Oriental count. He was forty-one when last seen.

years he has ahead of him. I would like to live my own life, see the people I want to see and do what I want to do.'

After some days of a rather painful indisposition he suddenly abdicated. It was a great pity, everyone said, that he should have taken the step while he was still in the prime of life; but the crown prince was now a grown man and affairs of state passed smoothly into his hands.

Tō no Chūjō submitted his resignation as chancellor and withdrew to the privacy of his own house. 'Nothing in this world lasts forever,' he said, 'and when so wise an emperor retires no one need have any regrets at seeing an old graybeard turn in his badge and keys.'

Higekuro became Minister of the Right, in effective charge of the government. His sister would now be the empress-mother if she had lived long enough. She had not been named empress and she had been overshadowed by certain of her rivals. The eldest son of the Akashi princess* was named crown prince. The designation was cause for great rejoicing, though no one was much surprised. Yūgiri was named a councillor of the first order. He and the new minister were the closest of colleagues and the best of friends.

Genji lamented in secret that the abdicated emperor, who now moved into the Reizei Palace, had no sons. Genji's worries had passed and his great sin had gone undetected, and he stood in the same relationship to the crown prince as he would have stood to a Reizei son. Yet he would have been happier if the succession had gone through the Reizei emperor. These regrets were of course private. He shared them with no one.

The Akashi princess had several children and was without rivals for the emperor's affection. There was a certain dissatisfaction abroad that yet another Genji† lady seemed likely to be named empress.

Akikonomu was more grateful to Genji as the years went by, for she knew that without him she would have been nothing. It was now much easier for the Reizei emperor to see Genji, and he was far happier than when he had occupied the throne.

---

*She does not automatically become empress upon her husband's succession, but must wait to see which of his wives is chosen for the honor.

†The expression means 'non-Fujiwara.' Two of the preceding three empresses have come from the royal family.

The new emperor was most solicitous of the Third Princess, his sister. Genji paid her due honor, but his love was reserved for Murasaki, in whom he could see no flaw. It was an ideally happy marriage, closer and fonder as the years went by.

Yet Murasaki had been asking most earnestly that he let her become a nun. 'My life is a succession of trivialities. I long to be done with them and turn to things that really matter. I am old enough to know what life should be about. Do please let me have my way.'

'I would not have thought you heartless enough to suggest such a thing. For years now I have longed to do just that, but I have held back because I have hated to think what the change would mean to you. Do try to imagine how things would be for you if I were to have my way.'

The Akashi princess was fonder of Murasaki than of her real mother, but the latter did not complain. She was an undemanding woman and she knew that her future would be peaceful and secure in quiet service to her daughter. The old Akashi nun needed no encouragement to weep new tears of joy. Red from pleasant weeping, her eyes proclaimed that a long life could be a happy one.

The time had come, thought Genji, to thank the god of Sumiyoshi. The Akashi princess too had been contemplating a pilgrimage. Genji opened the box that had come those years before from Akashi. It was stuffed with very grand vows indeed. Towards the prosperity of the old monk's line the god was to be entertained every spring and autumn with music and dancing. Only someone with Genji's resources could have seen to fulfilling them all. They were written in a flowing hand which told of great talent and earnest study, and the style was so strong and bold that the gods native and foreign must certainly have taken notice. But how could a rustic hermit have been so imaginative? Genji was filled with admiration, even while thinking that the old man had somewhat overreached himself. Perhaps a saint from a higher world had been fated to descend for a time to this one. He could not find it in him to laugh at the old man.

The vows were not made public. The pilgrimage was announced as Genji's own. He had already fulfilled his vows from those unsettled days on the seacoast, but the glory of the years since had not caused him to forget divine blessings. This time he would take Murasaki with him. He was determined that the arrangements be as simple as possible and that no one be inconvenienced. There were limits, however, to the simplicity permitted one of his rank, and in the end it proved to be a very grand progress. All the high-ranking courtiers save only the ministers were in attendance. Guards officers of fine appearance and generally uniform height were selected for the dance troupe. Among those who did not qualify were some who thought themselves very badly used. The most skilled of the musicians for the special Kamo and Iwashimizu festivals were invited to join the orchestra. There were two famed performers from among the guards musicians as well, and there was a large troupe of Kagura dancers. The emperor, the crown prince, and the Reizei emperor all sent aides to be in special attendance on Genji. The horses of the grandees were caparisoned in infinite variety and all the grooms and footmen and pages and miscellaneous functionaries were in livery more splendid than anyone could remember.

The Akashi princess and Murasaki rode in the same carriage. The next carriage was assigned to the Akashi lady, and her mother was quietly shown to the place beside her. With them was the nurse of the Akashi days. The retinues were very grand, five carriages each for Murasaki and the Akashi princess and three for the Akashi lady.

'If your mother is to come with us,' said Genji, 'then it must be with full honors. We shall see to smoothing her wrinkles.'

'Are you quite sure you should be showing yourself on such a public occasion?' the lady asked her mother. 'Perhaps when the very last of our prayers has been answered.'*

But they could not be sure how long she would live, and she did so want to see everything. One might have said that she was the happiest of them all, the one most favored by fortune. For her the joy was complete.

It was late in the Tenth Month. The vines† on the shrine fence were red and there were red leaves beneath the pine trees as well,

*'When the Akashi princess has been named empress.'

†*Kuzu*, sometimes translated 'arrowroot': *Pueraria lobata*.

so that the services of the wind were not needed to tell of the advent of autumn.* The familiar eastern music† seemed friendlier than the more subtle Chinese and Korean music. Against the sea winds and waves, flutes joined the breeze through the high pines of the famous grove with a grandeur that could only belong to Sumiyoshi. The quiet clapping that went with the koto was more moving than the solemn beat of the drums. The bamboo of the flutes had been stained to a deeper green, to blend with the green of the pines.‡ The ingeniously fabricated flowers in all the caps seemed to make a single carpet with the flowers of the autumn fields.

'The One I Seek'** came to an end and the young courtiers of the higher ranks all pulled their robes down over their shoulders as they descended into the courtyard, and suddenly a dark field seemed to burst into a bloom of pink and lavender. The crimson sleeves beneath, moistened very slightly by a passing shower, made it seem for a moment that the pine groves had become a grove of maples and that autumn leaves were showering down. Great reeds that had bleached to a pure white swayed over the dancing figures, and the waves of white seemed to linger on when the brief dance was over and they had returned to their places.

For Genji, the memory of his time of troubles was so vivid that it might have been yesterday. He wished that Tō no Chūjō had come with him. There was no one else with whom he could exchange memories. Going inside, he took out a bit of paper and quietly got off a note to the old nun in the second carriage.

'You and I remember – and who else?
Only we can address these godly pines.'

Remembering that day, the old lady was in tears. That day:

*Ki no Yoshimochi, *Kokinshū* 251:

There are no autumn leaves upon these hills
Forever green. The wind announces autumn.

The same poem is attributed to Onakatomi Yoshinobu in the *Shūishū*.
†*Azumaasobi*, folk music of eastern Japan.
‡One theory has it that there was a pattern of green bamboo on the musicians' robes.
**'Motomego,' an *Azumaasobi* thought to have varied with the occasion.

Genji had said goodbye to the lady who was carrying his daughter, and they had thought that they would not see him again. And the old lady had lived for this day of splendor! She wished that her husband could be here to share it, but would not have wanted to suggest that anything was lacking.

> 'The aged fisherwife knows as not before
> That Sumiyoshi is a place of joy.'

It was a quick and spontaneous answer, for it would not do on such an occasion to seem sluggish. And this was the poem that formed in her heart:

> 'It is a day I never shall forget.
> This god of Sumiyoshi brings me joy.'

The music went on through the night. A third-quarter moon shone clear above and the sea lay calm below; and in a heavy frost the pine groves too were white. It was a weirdly, coldly beautiful scene. Though Murasaki was of course familiar enough with the music and dance of the several seasons, she rarely left the house and she had never before been so far from the city. Everything was new and exciting.

> 'So white these pines with frost in the dead of night.
> Bedecked with sacred strands by the god himself?'

She thought of Takamura musing upon the possibility that the great white expanse of Mount Hira had been hung out with sacred mulberry strands.* Was the frost a sign that the god had acknowledged their presence and accepted their offerings?

This was the princess's poem:

> 'Deep in the night the frost has added strands
> To the sacred branches with which we make obeisance.'

And Nakatsukasa's:†

> 'So white the frost, one takes it for sacred strands
> And sees in it a sign of the holy blessing.'

---

*One no Takamura was active in the early ninth century. The reference is not to be found in his surviving works.

†Nakatsukasa is one of Murasaki's women.

There were countless others, but what purpose would be served by setting them all down? Each courtier thinks on such occasions that he has outdone all his rivals – but is it so? One poem celebrating the thousand years of the pine is very much like another.

There were traces of dawn and the frost was heavier. The Kagura musicians had had such a good time that response was coming before challenge. They were perhaps even funnier than they thought they were. The fires in the shrine courtyard were burning low. 'A thousand years' came the Kagura refrain, and 'Ten thousand years,' and the sacred branches waved to summon limitless prosperity for Genji's house. And so a night which they longed to stretch into ten thousand nights came to an end. It seemed a pity to all the young men that the waves must now fall back towards home. All along the line of carriages curtains fluttered in the breeze and the sleeves beneath were like a flowered tapestry spread against the evergreen pines. There were numberless colors for the stations and tastes of all the ladies. The footmen who set out refreshments on all the elegant stands were fascinated and dazzled. For the old nun there was ascetic fare on a tray of light aloeswood spread with olive drab. People were heard to whisper that she had been born under happy stars indeed.

The progress to Sumiyoshi had been laden with offerings, but the return trip could be leisurely and meandering. It would be very tiresome to recount all the details. Only the fact that the old Akashi monk was far away detracted from the pleasure. He had braved great difficulties and everyone admired him, but it is probable that he would have felt sadly out of place. His name had become synonymous with high ambitions, and his wife's with good fortune. It was she whom the Omi lady called upon for good luck in her gaming. 'Akashi nun!' she would squeal as she shook her dice. 'Akashi nun!'

The Suzaku emperor had given himself up most admirably to the religious vocation. He had dismissed public affairs and gossip from his life, and it was only when the emperor, his son, came visiting in the spring and autumn that memories of the old days returned. Yet he did still think of his third daughter. Genji had taken charge of her affairs, but the Suzaku emperor had asked his son to help with the more intimate details. The emperor had named her a Princess of the Second Rank and increased her emoluments accordingly, and so life was for her ever more cheerful.

Murasaki looked about her and saw how everyone seemed to be moving ahead, and asked herself whether she would always have a monopoly on Genji's affections. No, she would grow old and he would weary of her. She wanted to anticipate the inevitable by leaving the world. She kept these thoughts to herself, not wanting to nag or seem insistent. She did not resent the fact that Genji divided his time evenly between her and the Third Princess. The emperor himself worried about his sister and would have been upset by any suggestion that she was being neglected. Yet Murasaki could not help thinking that her worst fears were coming true. These thoughts too she kept to herself. She had been given charge of the emperor's daughter, his second child after the crown prince. The little princess was her great comfort on nights when Genji was away, and she was equally fond of the emperor's other children.

The lady of the orange blossoms looked on with gentle envy and was given a child of her own, one of Yūgiri's sons, by the daughter of Koremitsu. He was a pretty little boy, advanced for his age and a favorite of Genji's. It had been Genji's chief lament that he had so few children, and now in the third generation his house was growing and spreading. With so many grandchildren to play with he had no excuse to be bored.

Genji and Higekuro were better friends now, and Higekuro came calling more frequently. Tamakazura had become a sober matron. No longer suspicious of Genji's intentions, she too came calling from time to time. She and Murasaki were very good friends.

The Third Princess was the one who refused to grow up. She was still a little child. Genji's own daughter was now with the emperor. He had a new daughter to worry about.

'I feel that I have very little time left,' said the Suzaku emperor. 'It is sad to think about dying, of course, but I am determined not to care. My only unsatisfied wish is to see her at least once more. If I do not I shall continue to have regrets. Perhaps I might ask that without making a great show of it she come and see me?'

Genji thought the request most reasonable and set about preparations. 'We really should have sent you without waiting for him to ask. It seems very sad that he should have you so on his mind even now.'

But they had to have a good reason – a casual visit would not do. What would it be? He remembered that the Suzaku emperor would soon be entering his fiftieth year, and an offering of new herbs seemed appropriate. He gave orders for dark robes and other things a hermit might need and asked the advice of others on how to arrange something worthy of the occasion. The Suzaku emperor had always been fond of music and so Genji began selecting dancers and musicians. Two of Higekuro's sons and three of Yūgiri's, including one by Koremitsu's daughter, had passed the age of seven and gone to court. There were young people too in Prince Hotaru's house and other eminent houses, princely and common, and there were young courtiers distinguished for good looks and graceful carriage. Everyone was happy to make an extra effort for so festive an event. All the masters of music and dance were kept busy.

The Suzaku emperor had given the Third Princess lessons on the seven-stringed Chinese koto. She was still very young when she left him, however, and he wondered what progress she might have made.

'How good if she could play for me. Perhaps in that regard at least she has grown up a little.'

He quietly let these thoughts be known and the emperor heard of them. 'Yes, I should think that with the koto at least she should have made progress. How I wish I might be there.'

Genji too heard of them. 'I have done what I can to teach her,' he said. 'She has improved a great deal, but I wonder whether her playing is really quite good enough yet to delight the royal ear. If she goes unprepared and has to play for him, she might have a very uncomfortable time of it.'

Turning his attention now to music lessons, he kept back none of his secrets, none of the rare strains, complex medleys, and seasonal variations and tunings. She seemed uncertain at first but presently gathered confidence.

'There are always such crowds of people around in the daytime,' he said. 'You have your left hand poised over the koto and are wondering what to do with it, and along comes someone with a problem. The evening is the time. I will come in the evening when it is quiet and teach you everything I know.'

He had given neither Murasaki nor the Akashi princess lessons on the seven-stringed koto. They were most anxious to hear what must certainly be unusual playing. The emperor was always reluctant to let the Akashi princess leave court, but he did finally give permission for a visit, which must, he said, be a brief one. She would soon have another child – she had two sons and was five months pregnant – and the danger of defiling any one of the many Shinto observances was her excuse for leaving. In the Twelfth Month there were repeated messages from the emperor urging her return. The nightly lessons in the Third Princess's rooms fascinated her and aroused a certain envy. Why, she asked Genji, had he not taken similar troubles with her?

Unlike most people, Genji loved the cold moonlit nights of winter. With deep feeling he played several songs that went well with the snowy moonlight. Adepts among his men joined him on lute and koto. In Murasaki's wing of the house preparations were afoot for the New Year. She made them her own personal concern.

'When it is warmer,' she said more than once, 'you really must let me hear the princess's koto.'

The New Year came.

The emperor was determined that his father's jubilee year begin with the most solemn and dignified ceremony. A visit from the Third Princess would complicate matters, and so a date towards the middle of the Second Month was chosen. All the musicians and dancers assembled for rehearsals at Rokujō, which went on and on.

'The lady in the east wing has long been after me to let her hear your koto,' said Genji to the Third Princess. 'I think a feminine concert on strings is what we want. We have some of the finest players of our day right here in this house. They can hold their own, I am sure of it, with the professionals. My own formal training was neglected, but when I was a boy I was eager to learn what was to be learned. I had lessons from the famous masters and looked into the secret traditions of all the great houses. I came upon no one who exactly struck me dumb with admiration. It is even worse today. Young people dabble at music and pick up mannerisms, and what passes for music is very shallow stuff indeed. You are almost alone in your attention to this seven-stringed koto. I doubt that we could find your equal all through the court.'

She smiled happily at the compliment. Though she was in her early twenties and very pretty, she was tiny and fragile and still very much a child. He wished that she might at least look a little more grown-up.

'Your royal father has not seen you in years,' he would say. 'You must show him what a fine young lady you have become.'

Her women silently thanked him. That she had grown up at all was because of the trouble he had taken with her.

Late in the First Month the sky was clear and the breeze was warm, and the plums near the veranda were in full bloom. In delicate mists, the other flowering trees were coming into bud.

'From the first of the month we will be caught up in our final rehearsals,' said Genji, inviting Murasaki to the Third Princess's rooms. 'The confusion will be enormous, and we would not want it to seem that you are getting ready to go with us on the royal visit. Suppose we have our concert now, while it is still fairly quiet.'

All her women wanted to come with her, but she selected only those, including some of rather advanced years, whose aptitude for music had been shaped by serious study. Four of her prettiest little girls were also with her, all of them in red robes, cloaks of white lined with red, jackets of figured lavender, and damask trousers. Their chemises were also red, fulled to a high sheen. They were as pretty and stylish as little girls can be. The apartments of the Akashi princess were more festive than usual, bright with new spring decorations. Her women quite outdid themselves. Her little girls too were in uniform dress, green robes, cloaks of pink lined with crimson, trousers of figured Chinese satin, and jackets of a yellow Chinese brocade. The Akashi lady had her little girls dressed in quiet but unexceptionable taste: two wore rose plum* and two were in white robes lined with red, and all four had on celadon-green cloaks and purple jackets and chemises aglow with the marks of the fulling blocks.

The Third Princess, upon being informed that she was to be hostess to such a gathering, put her little girls into robes of a rich yellowish green, white cloaks lined with green, and jackets of magenta. Though there was nothing overdone about this finery, the effect was of remarkable richness and elegance.

The sliding doors were removed and the several groups separated from one another by curtains. A cushion had been set out for Genji himself at the very center of the assembly. Out near the veranda were two little boys charged with setting the pitch, Tamakazura's elder son on the *shō* pipes and Yūgiri's eldest on the

---

*There are doubts about some of the colors.

flute. Genji's ladies were behind blinds with their much-prized instruments set out before them in fine indigo covers, a lute for the Akashi lady, a Japanese koto for Murasaki, a thirteen-stringed Chinese koto for the Akashi princess. Worried lest the Third Princess seem inadequate, Genji himself tuned her seven-stringed koto for her.

'The thirteen-stringed koto holds its pitch on the whole well enough,' he said, 'but the bridges have a way of slipping in the middle of a concert. Ladies do not always get the strings as tight as they should. Maybe we should summon Yūgiri. Our pipers are rather young, and they may not be quite firm enough about bringing things to order.'

Yūgiri's arrival put the ladies on their mettle. With the single exception of the Akashi lady they were all Genji's own treasured pupils. He hoped that they would not shame him before his son. He had no fears about the Akashi princess, whose koto had often enough joined others in His Majesty's own presence. It was the Japanese koto that was most likely to cause trouble. He felt for Murasaki, whose responsibility it would be. Though it is a rather simple instrument, everything about it is fluid and indefinite, and there are no clear guides. All the instruments of spring* were here assembled. It would be a great pity if any of them struck a sour note.

Yūgiri was in dashingly informal court dress, the singlets and most especially the sleeves very nicely perfumed. It was evening when he arrived, looking a little nervous. The plums were so heavy with blossom in the evening light that one might almost have thought that a winter snow had refused to melt. Their fragrance mixed on the breeze with the wonderfully delicate perfumes inside the house to such enchanting effect that the spring warbler might have been expected to respond immediately.

'I know I should let you catch your breath,' said Genji, pushing a thirteen-stringed koto towards his son, 'but would you be so kind as to try this out and see that it is in tune? There are no strangers here before whom you need feel shy.'

Bowing deeply (his manners were always perfect), Yūgiri tuned the instrument in the *ichikotsu*† mode and waited politely for further instructions.

*Haru no koto, meaning unclear. There are variant texts.
†Based on D.

'You must get things started for us,' said Genji. 'No false notes, if you please.'

'I fear I do not have the qualifications to join you.'

'I suppose not,' smiled Genji. 'But would you wish to have it said that a band of ladies drove you away?'

Yūgiri played just enough to make quite sure the instrument was in tune and pushed it back under the blinds.

The little boys were very pretty in casual court dress. Their playing was of course immature, but it showed great promise.

The stringed instruments were all in tune and the concert began. Each of the ladies did beautifully, but the lute somehow stood out from the other instruments, sedately and venerably quiet and yet with great authority. Yūgiri was listening especially for the Japanese koto. The tone was softly alluring and the plectrum caught at the strings with a vivacity which seemed to him very novel. None of the professed masters could have done better. He would not have thought that the Japanese koto had such life in it. Clearly Murasaki had worked hard, and Genji was pleased and satisfied.

The thirteen-stringed Chinese koto, a gentle, feminine sort of instrument, takes its place hesitantly and deferentially among the other instruments. As for the seven-stringed koto, the Third Princess was not quite a complete master yet, but her playing had an assurance that did justice to her recent labors. Her koto took its place very comfortably among the other instruments. Yes, thought Yūgiri, who beat time and sang the lyrics, she had acquired a most admirable touch. Sometimes Genji too would beat time with his fan and sing a brief passage. His voice had improved with the years, filled out and taken on a dignity it had not had before. Yūgiri's voice was almost as good. I would be very hard put indeed to describe the pleasures of the night, which was somehow quieter as it filled with music.

It was the time of the month when the moon rises late. The flares at the eaves were just right, neither too dim nor too strong. Genji glanced at the Third Princess. She was smaller than the others, so tiny indeed that she seemed to be all clothes. Hers was not a striking sort of beauty, but it was marked by very great refinement and delicacy. One thought of a willow sending forth its first shoots toward the end of the Second Month, so delicate that the breeze from the warbler's wing seems enough to disarrange them. The hair flowing over a white robe lined with red also suggested the trailing strands of a willow. One knew that she was the most wellborn of ladies. Beside her the Akashi princess seemed gentle and delicate in a livelier, brighter way, and somehow deeper and subtler too, trained to greater diversity. One might have likened her to a wisteria in early morning, blooming from spring into summer with no other blossoms to rival it. She was heavy with child and seemed uncomfortable. She pushed her koto away and leaned forward on an armrest which, though the usual size, seemed too large for her. Genji would have liked to send for a smaller one. Her hair fell thick and full over rose plum. She had a most winning charm in the soft, wavering light from the eaves.

Over a robe of pink Murasaki wore a robe of a rich, deep hue, a sort of magenta, perhaps. Her hair fell in a wide, graceful cascade. She was of just the right height, so beautiful in every one of her features that they added up to more than perfection. A cherry in full bloom – but not even that seemed an adequate simile.

One would have expected the Akashi lady to be quite overwhelmed by such company, but she was not. Careful, conservative taste was evident in her grooming and dress. One sensed quiet depths, and an ineffable elegance which was all her own. She had on a figured 'willow' robe, white lined with green, and a cloak of a yellowish green, and as a mark of respect for the other ladies, a train of a most delicate and yielding gossamer. Everything about her emphasized her essential modesty and unassertiveness, but there was much that suggested depth and subtlety as well. Again as a mark of respect, she knelt turned somewhat away from the others with her lute before her and only her knees on the green Korean brocade with which the matting was fringed. She guided her plectrum with such graceful assurance through a quiet melody that it was almost more of a pleasure to the eye than to the ear. One thought of fruit and flowers on the same orange branch, 'awaiting the Fifth Month.'*

Everything he heard and saw told Yūgiri of a most decorous and formal assembly. He would have liked to look inside the blinds, most especially at Murasaki, who would doubtless have taken on a calmer and more mature beauty since he had had that one glimpse of her. As for the Third Princess, only a slight shift of

*See note**, page 228.

fate and she might have been his rather than his father's. The Suzaku emperor had more than once hinted at something of the sort of Yūgiri himself and mentioned the possibility to others. Yūgiri should have been a little bolder. Yet it was not as if he had lost his senses over the princess. Certain evidences of immaturity had had the effect not exactly of cheapening her in his eyes but certainly of cooling his ardor. He could have no possible designs on Murasaki. She had through the years been a remote and lofty symbol of all that was admirable. He only wished that he had some way of showing, some disinterested, gentlemanly way, how very high was his regard for her. He was a model of prudence and sobriety and would not have dreamed of doing anything unseemly.

It was late and rather chilly when the first rays of 'the moon for which one lies in wait'* came forth.

'The misty moon of spring is not the best, really,' said Genji. 'In the autumn the singing of the insects weaves a fabric with the music. The combination is rather wonderful.'

'It is true,' replied Yūgiri, 'that on an autumn night there is sometimes not a trace of a shadow over the moon and the sound of a koto or a flute can seem as high and clear as the night itself. But the sky can have a sort of put-on look about it, like an artificial setting for a concert, and the autumn flowers insist on being gazed at. It is all too pat, too perfect. But in the spring – the moon comes through a haze and a quiet sound of flute joins it in a way that is not possible in the autumn. No, a flute is not really its purest on an autumn night. It has long been said that it is the spring night to which the lady is susceptible, and I am inclined to accept the statement. The spring night is the one that brings out the quiet harmonies.'

'The ancients were unable to resolve the dispute, and I think it would be presumptuous of their inferior descendants to seek to do so. It is a fact that the major modes of spring are commonly given precedence over the minor modes of autumn, and so you may be right.

'His Majesty from time to time has the famous masters in to play for him, and the conclusion seems to be that the ones who deserve the name are fewer and fewer. Am I wrong in suspecting that a person has less to learn from them? Our ladies here may not

*The moon of the nineteenth night of the lunar month.

be on the established list of masters, but I doubt that they would seem hopelessly out of place. Of course, it may be that I have been away from things for so long that I no longer have a very good ear. That would be a pity. Yet I do sometimes find myself marveling that a little practice in this house brings out such talents. How does what you have heard tonight compare with what is chosen for His Majesty to hear?'

'I am very badly informed,' said Yūgiri, 'but I do have a thought or two in the matter. It may be a confession of ignorance of the great tradition to say that Kashiwagi on the Japanese koto and Prince Hotaru on the lute are to be ranked among the masters. I had thought them quite without rivals, but this evening I have been forced to change my mind. I am filled with astonishment at what I have heard. Might it be that I had been prepared for something more casual, more easygoing? You have asked me to be voice and percussion, and I have felt very inadequate indeed. Lord Tō no Chūjō is said to be the best of them all on the Japanese koto, the one who has the widest and subtlest variety of touches to go with the seasons. It is true that one rarely hears anything like his koto, but I confess that tonight I have been treated to skills that seem to me every bit as remarkable.'

'Oh, surely you exaggerate.' Genji was smiling proudly. 'But I do have a fine set of pupils, do I not? I cannot claim credit for the lute, but even there I think residence in this house has made a difference. I thought it most extraordinary off in the hinterlands and I think it has improved since it came to the city.'

The women were exchanging amused glances that he should be claiming credit even for the Akashi lady.

'It is very difficult indeed to master any instrument,' he continued. 'The possibilities seem infinite and nothing seems complete and finished. But there are few these days who even try, and I suppose it should be cause for satisfaction when someone masters any one small aspect. The sevenstringed koto is the unmanageable one. We are told that in ancient times there were many who mastered the whole tradition of the instrument, and made heaven and earth their own, and softened the hearts of demons and gods. Taking into this one instrument all the tones and overtones of all the others,* they found joy in the depths of sorrow and transformed

*An obscure statement.

the base and mean into the fine and proud, and gained wealth and universal fame. There was a time, before the tradition had been established in Japan, when the most enormous trouble was required of anyone who sought to learn the art. He must spend years in strange lands and give up everything, and even then only a few came back with what they had gone out to seek. In the old chronicles there are stories of musicians who moved the moon and the stars and brought unseasonal snows and frosts and conjured up tempests and thunders. In our day there is scarcely anyone who has even mastered the whole of the written lore, and the full possibilities are enormous. So little these days seems to make even a beginning – because the Good Law is in its decline, I suppose.

'It may be that people are intimidated. The seven-stringed koto was the instrument that moved demons and gods, and inadequate mastery had correspondingly unhappy results. What other instrument is to be at the center of things, setting the tone for all the others? Ours is a day of very sad decline. Only a madman, we say, would be so obsessed with an art as to abandon parents and children and go wandering off over Korea and China. But we need not make quite such extreme sacrifices. Keeping within reasonable bounds, why should we not try to make the beginning that seems at least possible? The difficulties in mastering a single mode are indescribable, and there are so many modes and so many complicated melodies. Back in the days when I was a rather enthusiastic student of music, I went through the scores that have been preserved in this country, and presently there was no one to teach me. Yet I know that I am infinitely less competent than the old masters; and it is sad to think that no one is prepared to learn from me even the little that I know, and so the decline must continue.'

It was true, thought Yūgiri, feeling very inadequate.

'If one or another of my princely grandchildren should live up to the promise he shows now and I myself still have a few years before me, then perhaps by the time he is grown I can pass on what I know. It is very little, I am afraid. I think that the Second Prince shows very considerable promise.'

It pleased the Akashi lady to think that she had had a part in this glory.

As she lay down to rest, the Akashi princess pushed her koto towards Murasaki, who relinquished hers to Genji. They played an intimate sort of duet, the Saibara 'Katsuragi,'* very light and happy. In better voice than ever, Genji sang the lyrics over a second time. The moon rose higher and the color and scent of the plum blossoms seemed to be higher and brighter too. The Akashi princess had a most engagingly girlish touch on the thirteen-stringed koto. The tremolo, bright and clear, had in it something of her mother's style. Murasaki's touch, strangely affecting, seemed quiet and solemn by comparison, and her cadenzas† were superb. For the envoi there was a shift to a minor mode, somehow friendlier and more approachable. In 'The Five Airs' the touch of the plectrum against the fifth and sixth strings of the seven-stringed koto is thought to present the supreme challenge, but the Third Princess had a fine sureness and lucidity.‡ One looked in vain for signs of immaturity. The mode an appropriate one for all the strains of spring and autumn, she did not let her attention waver and she gave evidence of real understanding. Genji felt that he had won new honors as a teacher.

The little pipers had been charming, most solemnly attentive to their responsibilities.

'You must be sleepy,' said Genji. 'It seemed as if we had only begun and I wanted to hear more and more. It was silly of me to think of picking the best when everything was so good, and so the night went by. You must forgive me.'

He urged a sip of wine on the little *shō* piper and rewarded him with a singlet, one of his own favorites. A lady had something for the little flutist, a pair of trousers and a lady's robe cut from an unassuming fabric. The Third Princess offered a cup to Yūgiri and presented him with a set of her own robes.

'Now this seems very strange and unfair,' said Genji. 'If there are to be such grand rewards, then surely the teacher should come first. You are all very rude and thoughtless.'

A flute, a very fine Korean one, was pushed towards him from beneath the Third Princess's curtains. He smiled as he played a few notes. The guests were beginning to leave, but Yūgiri took up his

See note, page 100.
†*Rin no te*, meaning unclear.
‡The passage is very obscure. It is not known whether 'The Five Airs' are in fact melodies or modes, and the seven-stringed koto is not commonly played with a plectrum.

son's flute and played a strain marvelous in its clean strength. They were all his very own pupils, thought Genji, to whom he had taught his very own secrets, and they were all accomplished musicians. He knew of course that he had had superior material to work with.

The moon was high and bright as Yūgiri set off with his sons. The extraordinary sound of Murasaki's koto was still with him. Kumoinokari, his wife, had had lessons from their late grandmother, but had been taken away before she had learned a great deal. She quite refused to let him hear her play. She was a sober, reliable sort of lady whose family duties took all her time. To Yūgiri she seemed somewhat backward in the gentler accomplishments. She was her most interesting when, as did sometimes happen, she allowed herself a fit of temper or jealousy.

Genji returned to the east wing. Murasaki stayed behind to talk with the Third Princess and it was daylight when she too returned. They slept late.

'Our princess has developed into a rather good musician, I think. How did she seem to you?'

'I must confess that I had very serious doubts when I caught the first notes. But now she is very good indeed, so good that I can scarcely believe it is the same person. Of course I needn't be surprised, seeing how much of your time it has taken.'

'It has indeed. I am a serious teacher and I have led her every step of the way. The seven-stringed koto is such a bother that I would not try to teach it to just anyone, but her father and brother seemed to be saying that I owed her at least that much. I was feeling a little undutiful at the time, and I thought I should do something to seem worthy of the trust.

'Back in the days when you were still a child I was busy with other things and I am afraid I neglected your lessons. Nor have I done much better in recent years. I have frittered my time away and gone on neglecting you. You did me great honor last night. It was beautiful. I loved the effect it had on Yūgiri.'

Murasaki was now busy being grandmother to the royal children. She did nothing that might have left her open to charges of bad judgment. Hers was a perfection, indeed, that was somehow ominous. It aroused forebodings. The evidence is that such people are not meant to have long lives. Genji had known many women and he knew what a rarity she was. She was thirty-seven this year.*

He was thinking over the years they had been together. 'You must be especially careful this year. You must overlook none of the prayers and services. I am very busy and sometimes careless, and I must rely on you to keep track of things. If there is something that calls for special arrangements I can give the orders. It is a pity that your uncle, the bishop, is no longer living. He was the one who really knew about these things.

'I have always been rather spoiled and there can be few precedents for the honors I enjoy. The other side of the story is that I have had more than my share of sorrow. The people who have been fond of me have left me behind one after another, and there have been events in more recent years that I think almost anyone would call very sad. As for nagging little worries, it almost seems as if I were a collector of them. I sometimes wonder if it might be by way of compensation that I have lived a longer life than I would have expected to. You, on the other hand – I think that except for our years apart you have been spared real worries. There are the troubles that go with the glory of being an empress or one of His Majesty's other ladies. They are always being hurt by the proud people they must be with and they are engaged in a competition that makes a terrible demand on their nerves. You have lived the life of a cloistered maiden, and there is none more comfortable and secure. It is as if you had never left your parents. Have you been aware, my dear, that you have been luckier than most? I know that it has not been easy for you to have the princess move in on us all of a sudden. We sometimes do not notice the things that are nearest to us, and you may not have noticed that her presence has made me fonder of you. But you are quick to see these things, and perhaps I do you an injustice.'

'You are right, of course. I do not much matter, and it must seem to most people that I have been more fortunate than I deserve. And that my unhappiness should sometimes have seemed almost too much for me – perhaps that is the prayer that has sustained me.'† She seemed to be debating whether to go on. He

*She should be thirty-nine or forty. The thirty-seventh year by the Oriental count was thought a dangerous one. It was then that Fujitsubo died.
†The remark has been interpreted in several ways. Perhaps the most interesting interpretation takes it to be ironical.

thought her splendid. 'I doubt that I have much longer to live. Indeed, I have my doubts about getting through this year if I pretend that no changes are needed. It would make me very happy if you would let me do what I have so long wanted to do.'

'Quite out of the question. Do you think I could go on without you? Not very much has happened these last years, I suppose, but knowing that you are here has been the most important thing. You must see to the end how very much I have loved you.'

It was the usual thing, all over again.

A very little more and she would be in tears, he could see. He changed the subject.

'I have not known enormous numbers of women, but I have concluded that they all have their good points, and that the genuinely calm and equable ones are very rare indeed.

'There was Yūgiri's mother. I was a mere boy when we were married and she was one of the eminences in my life, someone I could not think of dismissing. But things never went well. To the end she seemed very remote. It was sad for her, but I cannot convince myself that the fault was entirely mine. She was an earnest lady with no faults that one would have wished to single out, but it might be said that she was the cold intellectual, the sort you might turn to for advice and find yourself uncomfortable with.

'There was the Rokujō lady, Akikonomu's mother. I remember her most of all for her extraordinary subtlety and cultivation, but she was a difficult lady too, indeed almost impossible to be with. Even when her anger seemed justified it lasted too long, and her jealousy was more than a man could be asked to endure. The tensions went on with no relief, and the reservations on both sides made easy companionship quite impossible. I stood too much on my dignity, I suppose. I thought that if I gave in she would gloat and exult. And so it ended. I could see how the gossip hurt her and how she condemned herself for conduct which she thought unworthy of her position, and I could see that difficult though she might be I was at fault myself. It is because I have so regretted what finally happened that I have gone to such trouble for her daughter. I do not claim all the credit, of course. It is obvious that she was meant all along for important things. But I made enemies for myself because of what I did for her, and I like to think that her mother, wherever she is, has forgiven me. I have on the impulse of the moment done many things I have come to regret. It was true long ago and it is true now.' By fits and starts, he spoke of his several ladies.

'There is the Akashi lady. I looked down upon her and thought her no more than a plaything. But she has depths. She may seem docile and uncomplicated, but there is a firm core underneath it all. She is not easily slighted.'

'I was not introduced to the other ladies and can say nothing about them,' replied Murasaki. 'I cannot pretend to know very much about the Akashi lady either, but I have had a glimpse of her from time to time, and would agree with you that she has very great pride and dignity. I often wonder if she does not think me a bit of a simpleton. As for your daughter, I should imagine that she forgives me my faults.'

It was affection for the Akashi princess, thought Genji, that had made such good friends of Murasaki and a lady she had once so resented. Yes, she was splendid indeed.

'You may have your little blank spots,' he said, 'but on the whole you manage things as the people and the circumstances demand. I have as I have said known numbers of ladies and not one of them has been quite like you. Not' – he smiled – 'that you always keep your feelings to yourself.'

In the evening he went off to the main hall. 'I must commend the princess for having carried out her instructions so faithfully.'

Immersed in her music, she was as youthful as ever. It did not seem to occur to her that anyone might be less than happy with her presence.

'Let me have a few days off,' said Genji, 'and you take a few off too. You have quite satisfied your teacher. You worked hard and the results were worthy of the effort. I have no doubts now about your qualifications.' He pushed the koto aside and lay down.

As always when he was away, Murasaki had her women read stories to her. In the old stories that were supposed to tell what went on in the world, there were men with amorous ways and women who had affairs with them, but it seemed to be the rule that in the end the man settled down with one woman. Why should Murasaki herself live in such uncertainty? No doubt, as Genji had said, she had been unusually fortunate. But were the ache and the scarcely endurable sense of deprivation to be with her to the end? She had much to think about and went to bed very late, and towards daylight she was seized with violent chest pains.

Her women were immediately at her side. Should they call Genji? Quite out of the question, she replied. Presently it was daylight. She was running a high fever and still in very great pain. No one had gone for Genji. Then a message came from the Akashi princess and she was informed of Murasaki's illness, and in great trepidation sent word to Genji. He immediately returned to Murasaki's wing of the house, to find her still in great pain.

'And what would seem to be the matter?' He felt her forehead. It was flaming hot.

He was in terror, remembering that only the day before he had warned her of the dangerous year ahead. Breakfast was brought but he sent it back. He was at her side all that day, seeing to her needs. She was unable to sit up and refused even the smallest morsel of fruit.

The days went by. All manner of prayers and services were commissioned. Priests were summoned to perform esoteric rites. Though the pain was constant, it would at times be of a vague and generalized sort, and then, almost unbearable, the chest pains would return. An endless list of abstinences was drawn up by the soothsayers, but it did no good. Beside her all the while, Genji was in anguish, looking for the smallest hopeful sign, the barely perceptible change that can brighten the prospects in even the most serious illness. She occupied the whole of his attention. Preparations for the visit to the Suzaku emperor, who sent frequent and courteous inquiries, had been put aside.

The Second Month was over and there was no improvement. Thinking that a change of air might help, Genji moved her to his Nijō mansion. Anxious crowds gathered there and the confusion was enormous. The Reizei emperor was much troubled and Yūgiri even more so. There were others who were in very great disquiet. Were Murasaki to die, then Genji would almost certainly follow through with his wish to retire from the world. Yūgiri saw to the usual sort of prayers and rites, of course, and extraordinary ones as well.

'Do you remember what I asked for?' Murasaki would say when she was feeling a little more herself. 'May I not have it even now?'

'I have longed for many years to do exactly that,' Genji would reply, thinking that to see her even briefly in nun's habit would be as painful as to know that the final time had come. 'I have been held back by the thought of what it would mean to you if I were to insist on having my way. Can you now think of deserting me?'

But it did indeed seem that the end might be near. There were repeated crises, each of which could have been the last. Genji no longer saw the Third Princess. Music had lost all interest and koto and flute were put away. Most of the Rokujō household moved to Nijō. At Rokujō, where only women remained, it was as if the fires had gone out. One saw how much of the old life had depended on a single lady.

The Akashi princess was at Genji's side.

'But whatever I have might take advantage of your condition,' said Murasaki, weak though she was. 'Please go back immediately.'

The princess's little children were with them, the prettiest children imaginable. Murasaki looked at them and wept. 'I doubt that I shall be here to see you grow up. I suppose you will forget all about me?'

The princess too was weeping.

'You must not even think of it,' said Genji. 'Everything will be all right if only we manage to think so. When we take the broad, easy view we are happy. It may be the destiny of the meaner sort to rise to the top, but the fretful and demanding ones do not stay there very long. It is the calm ones who survive. I could give you any number of instances.'

He described her virtues to all the native and foreign gods and told them how very little she had to atone for. The venerable sages entrusted with the grander services and the priests in immediate attendance as well, including the ones on night duty, were sorry that they seemed to be accomplishing so little. They turned to their endeavors with new vigor and intensity. For five and six days there would be some improvement and then she would be worse again, and so time passed. How would it all end? The malign force that had taken possession of her refused to come forth. She was wasting away from one could not have said precisely what ailment, and there was no relief from the worry and sorrow.

I have been neglecting Kashiwagi. Now a councillor of the middle rank, he enjoyed the special confidence of the emperor and was one of the more promising young officials of the day. But fame and honor had done nothing to satisfy the old longing. He took for his bride the Second Princess, daughter of the Suzaku emperor by a low-ranking concubine. It must be admitted that he thought her less than the very best he could have found. She was an agreeable lady whose endowments were far above the ordinary, but she was not capable of driving the Third Princess from his thoughts. He did not, to be sure, treat her like one of the old women who are cast out on mountainsides to die, but he was not as attentive as he might have been.

The Kojijū to whom he went with the secret passion he was unable to quell was a daughter of Jijū, the Third Princess's nurse. Jijū's elder sister was Kashiwagi's own nurse, and so he had long known a great deal about the princess. He had known when she was still a child that she was very pretty and that she was her father's favorite. It was from these early beginnings that his love had grown.

Guessing that the Rokujō mansion would be almost deserted, he called Kojijū and warmly pleaded his case. 'My feelings could destroy me, I fear. You are my tie with her and so I have asked you about her and hoped that you might let her know something of my uncontrollable longing. You have been my hope and you have done nothing. Someone was saying to her royal father that Genji had many ladies to occupy his attention and that one of them seemed to have monopolized it, and the Third Princess was spending lonely nights and days of boredom. It would seem that her father might have been having second thoughts. If his daughters had to marry commoners, he said, it would be nice if they were commoners who had a little time for them. Someone told me that he might even think the Second Princess the more fortunate of the two. She is the one who has long years of comfort and security ahead of her. I cannot tell you how it all upsets me.' He sighed. 'They are daughters of the same royal father, but the one is the one and the other is the other.'

'I think, sir, that you might be a little more aware of your place in the world. You have one princess and you want another? Your greed seems boundless.'

He smiled. 'Yes, I suppose so. But her father gave me some encouragement and so did her brother. Though it may be, as you say, that I am not as aware of my place in the world as I should be, I have let myself think of her. Both of them found occasion to say that they did not consider me so very objectionable. You are the one who is at fault – you should have worked just a little harder.'

'It was impossible. I have been told that there is such a thing as fate. It may have been fate which made Genji ask for her so earnestly and ceremoniously. Do you really think His Majesty's affection for you such that, had you made similar overtures, they would have prevailed over His Lordship's? It is true that you have a little more dignity and prestige now than you had then.'

He did not propose to answer this somewhat intemperate outburst. 'Let us leave the past out of the matter. The present offers a rare opportunity. There are very few people around her and you can, if you will, contrive to admit me to her presence and let me tell her just a little of what has been on my mind. As for the possibility of my doing anything improper – look at me, if you will, please. Do I seem capable of anything of the sort?'

'This is preposterous, utterly preposterous. The very thought of it terrifies me. Why did I even come?'

'Not entirely preposterous, I think. Marriage is an uncertain arrangement. Are you saying that these things never under any circumstances happen to His Majesty's own ladies? I should think that the chances might be more considerable with someone like the princess. On the surface everything may seem to be going beautifully, but I should imagine that she has her share of private dissatisfactions. She was her father's favorite and now she is losing out to ladies of no very high standing. I know everything. It is an uncertain world we live in and no one can legislate to have things exactly as he wants them.'

'You are not telling me, are you, that she is losing out to others and so she must make fine new arrangements for herself? The arrangements she has already made for herself are rather fine, I should think, and of a rather special nature. Her royal father would seem to have thought that with His Lordship to look after her as if she were his daughter she would have no worries. I should imagine that they have both of them accepted the relationship for what it is. Do you think it is quite your place to suggest changes?'

He must not let her go away angry. 'You may be sure that I am aware of my own inadequacy and would not dream of exposing myself to the critical eye of a lady who is used to the incomparable Genji. But it would not be such a dreadful thing, I should think, to approach her curtains and speak with her very briefly? It is not considered such a great sin, I believe, for a person to speak the whole truth to the powers above.'

He seemed prepared to swear by all the powers, and she was young and somewhat heedless, and when a man spoke as if he were prepared to throw his life away she could not resist forever.

'I will see what I can do if I find what seems the right moment. On nights when His Lordship does not come the princess has swarms of women in her room, and always several of her favorites right beside her, and I cannot imagine what sort of moment it will be.'

Frowning, she left him.

He was after her constantly. The moment finally came, it seemed, and she got off a note to him. He set out in careful disguise, delighted but in great trepidation. It did not occur to him that a visit might only add to his torments. He wanted to see a little more of her whose sleeves he had glimpsed that spring evening. If he were to tell her what was in his heart, she might pity him, she might even answer him briefly.

It was about the middle of the Fourth Month, the eve of the lustration for the Kamo festival. Twelve women from the Third Princess's household were to be with the high priestess, and girls and young women of no very high rank who were going to watch the procession were busy at their needles and otherwise getting ready. No one had much time for the princess. Azechi, one of her most trusted intimates, had been summoned by the Minamoto captain with whom she was keeping company and had gone back to her room. Only Kojijū was with the princess. Sensing that the time was right, she led him to a seat in an east corner of the princess's boudoir. And was that not a little extreme?

The princess had gone serenely off to bed. She sensed that a man was in her room and thought that it would be Genji. But he seemed rather too polite – and then suddenly he put his arms around her and took her from her bed. She was terrified. Had some evil power seized her? She forced herself to look up and saw that it was a stranger. And here he was babbling complete nonsense. She called for her women, but no one came. She was trembling and bathed in perspiration. Though he could not help feeling sorry for her, he thought this agitation rather charming.

'I know that I am nothing, but I would not have expected quite such unfriendliness. I once had ambitions that were perhaps too grand for me. I could have kept them buried in my heart, I suppose, eventually to die there, but I spoke to someone of a small part of them and they came to your father's attention. I took courage from the fact that he did not seem to consider them entirely beneath his notice, and I told myself that the regret would be worse than anything if a love unique for its depth and intensity should come to nothing, and my low rank and only that must be held responsible. It was a very deep love indeed, and the sense of regret, the injury, the fear, the yearning, have only grown stronger as time has gone by. I know that I am being reckless and I am very much ashamed of myself that I cannot control my feelings and must reveal myself to you as someone who does not know his proper place. But I vow to you that I shall do nothing more. You will have no worse crimes to charge me with.'

She finally guessed who he was, and was appalled. She was speechless.

'I know how you must feel; but it is not as if this sort of thing had never happened before. Your coldness is what has no precedent. It could drive me to extremes. Tell me that you pity me and that will be enough. I will leave you.'

He had expected a proud lady whom it would not be easy to talk to. He would tell her a little of his unhappiness, he had thought, and say nothing he might later regret. But he found her very different. She was pretty and gentle and unresisting, and far more graceful and elegant, in a winsome way, than most ladies he had known. His passion was suddenly more than he could control. Was there no hiding place to which they might run off together?

He presently dozed off (it cannot be said that he fell asleep) and dreamed of the cat of which he had been so fond. It came up to him mewing prettily. He seemed to be dreaming that he had brought it back to the princess. As he awoke he was asking himself why he should have done that. And what might the dream have meant?*

The princess was still in a state of shock. She could not believe that it had all happened.

'You must tell yourself that there were ties between us which we could not escape. I am in as much of a daze as you can possibly be.'

He told her of the surprising event that spring evening, of the

---

*Early commentaries say, though there is no other documentary evidence, that a dream of a cat was thought to signify the conception of a child.

cat and the cord and the raised blind. So it had actually happened! Sinister forces seemed to preside over her affairs. And how could she face Genji? She wept like a little child and he looked on with respectful pity. Brushing away her tears, he let them mingle with his own.

There were traces of dawn in the sky. He felt that he had nowhere to go and that it might have been better had he not come at all. 'What am I to do? You seem to dislike me most extravagantly, and I find it hard to think of anything more to say. And I have not even heard your voice.'

He was only making things worse. Her thoughts in a turmoil, she was quite unable to speak.

'This muteness is almost frightening. Could anything be more awful? I can see no reason for going on. Let me die. Life has seemed to have some point and so I have lived, and even now it is not easy to think that I am at the end of it. Grant me some small favor, some gesture, anything at all, and I will not mind dying.'

He took her in his arms and carried her out. She was terrified. What could he possibly mean to do with her? He spread a screen in a corner room and opened the door beyond. The south door of the gallery, through which he had come the evening before, was still open. It was very dark. Wanting to see her face, even dimly, he pushed open a shutter.

'This cruelty is driving me mad. If you wish to still the madness, then say that you pity me.'

She did want to say something. She wanted to say that his conduct was outrageous. But she was trembling like a frightened child. It was growing lighter.

'I would like to tell you of a rather startling dream I had, but I suppose you would not listen. You seem to dislike me very much indeed. But I think it might perhaps mean something to you.'

The dawn sky seemed sadder than the saddest autumn sky.

'I arise and go forth in the dark before the dawn.
  I know not where, nor whence came the dew on my sleeve.'

He showed her a moist sleeve.

He finally seemed to be leaving. So great was her relief that she managed an answer:

'Would I might fade away in the sky of dawn,
  And all of it might vanish as a dream.'

She spoke in a tiny, wavering voice and she was like a beautiful child. He hurried out as if he had only half heard, and felt as if he were leaving his soul behind.

He went quietly off to his father's house, preferring it to his own and the company of the Second Princess. He lay down but was unable to sleep. He did not know what if anything the dream had meant. He suddenly longed for the cat – and he was frightened. It was a terrible thing he had done. How could he face the world? He remained in seclusion and his secret wanderings seemed to be at an end. It was a terrible thing for the Third Princess, of course, and for himself as well. Supposing he had seduced the emperor's own lady and the deed had come to light – could the punishment be worse? Even if he were to avoid specific punishment he did not know how he could face a reproachful Genji.

There are wellborn ladies of strongly amorous tendencies whose dignity and formal bearing are a surface that falls away when the right man comes with the right overtures. With the Third Princess it was a matter of uncertainty and a want of firm principles. She was a timid girl and she felt as vulnerable as if one of her women had already broadcast her secret to the world. She could not face the sun. She wanted to brood in darkness.

She said that she was unwell. The report was passed on to Genji, who came hurrying over. He had thought that he already had worries enough. There was nothing emphatically wrong with her, it would seem, but she refused to look at him. Fearing that she was out of sorts because of his long absence, he told her about Murasaki's illness.

'It may be the end. At this time of all times I would not want her to think me unfeeling. She has been with me since she was a child and I cannot abandon her now. I am afraid I have not had time these last months for anyone else. It will not go on forever, and I know that you will presently understand.'

She was ashamed and sorry. When she was alone she wept a great deal.

For Kashiwagi matters were worse. The conviction grew that it would have been better not to see her. Night and day he could only lament his impossible love. A group of young friends, in a hurry to be off to the Kamo festival, urged him to go with them, but he pleaded illness and spent the day by himself. Though correct in his behavior toward the Second Princess, he was not really fond of her. He passed the tedious hours in his own rooms. A little girl came in with a sprig of *aoi*, the heartvine of the Kamo festival.

'In secret, without leave, she brings this heartvine.
A most lamentable thing, a blasphemous thing.'

He could think only of the Third Princess. He heard the festive roar in the distance as if it were no part of his life and passed a troubled day in a tedium of his own making.

The Second Princess was used to these low spirits. She did not know what might be responsible for them, but she felt unhappy and inadequate. She had almost no one with her, most of the women having gone off to the festival. In her gloom she played a sad, gentle strain on a koto. Yes, she was very beautiful, very delicate and refined; but had the choice been his he would have taken her sister. He had not, of course, been fated to make the choice.

'Laurel branches twain, so near and like.
Why was it that I took the fallen leaf?'*

It was a poem he jotted down to while away the time – and not very complimentary to the Second Princess.

Though Genji was in a fever of impatience to be back at Nijō, he so seldom visited Rokujō that it would be bad manners to leave immediately.

A messenger came. 'Our lady has expired.'

He rushed off. The road was dark before his eyes, and ever darker. At Nijō the crowds overflowed into the streets. There was weeping within. The worst did indeed seem to have happened. He pushed his way desperately through.

'She had seemed better these last few days,' said one of the women, 'and now this.'

The confusion was enormous. The women were wailing and asking her to take them with her. The altars had been dismantled and the priests were leaving, only the ones nearest the family remaining behind. For Genji it was like the end of the world.

He set about quieting the women. 'Some evil power has made

*The Second Princess is often called Ochiba, 'Fallen Leaf.' The appellation comes from this poem.

it seem that she is dead. Nothing more. Certainly this commotion does not seem called for.'

He made vows more solemn and detailed than before and summoned ascetics known to have worked wonders.

'Even if her time has come and she must leave us,' they said, 'let her stay just a little longer. There was the vow of the blessed Acala.* Let her stay even that much longer.'

So intense and fevered were their efforts that clouds of black smoke seemed to coil over their heads.

Genji longed to look into her eyes once more. It had been too sudden, he had not even been allowed to say goodbye. There seemed a possibility – one can only imagine the dread which it inspired – that he too was on the verge of death.

Perhaps the powers above took note. The malign spirit suddenly yielded after so many tenacious weeks and passed from Murasaki to the little girl who was serving as medium, and who now commenced to thresh and writhe and moan. To Genji's joy and terror Murasaki was breathing once more.

The medium was now weeping and flinging her hair madly about. 'Go away, all of you. I want a word with Lord Genji and it must be with him alone. All these prayers and chants all these months have been an unrelieved torment. I have wanted you to suffer as I have suffered. But then I saw that I had brought you to the point of death and I pitied you, and so I have come out into the open. I am no longer able to seem indifferent, though I am the wretch you see. It is precisely because the old feelings have not died that I have come to this. I had resolved to let myself be known to no one.'

He had seen it before. The old terror and anguish came back. He took the little medium by the hand lest she do something violent.

'Is it really you? I have heard that foxes and other evil creatures sometimes go mad and seek to defame the dead. Tell me who you are, quite plainly. Or give me a sign, something that will be meaningless to others but unmistakable to me. Then I will try to believe you.'

---

*Early commentaries say that Acala vowed to give six more months of life to those of the faithful who wished it, but the source in the writ is not known.

Weeping copiously and speaking in a loud wail, the medium seemed at the same time to cringe with embarrassment.

'I am horribly changed, and you pretend not to know me. You are the same. Oh dreadful, dreadful.'

Even in these wild rantings there was a suggestion of the old aloofness. It added to the horror. He wanted to hear no more.

But there was more. 'From up in the skies I saw what you did for my daughter and was pleased. But it seems to be a fact that the ways of the living are not the ways of the dead and that the feeling of mother for child is weakened. I have gone on thinking you the cruelest of men. I heard you tell your dear lady what a difficult and unpleasant person you once found me, and the resentment was worse than when you insulted me to my face and finally abandoned me. I am dead, and I hoped that you had forgiven me and would defend me against those who spoke ill of me and say that it was none of it true. The hope was what twisted a twisted creature more cruelly and brought this horror. I do not hate her; but the powers have shielded you and only let me hear your voice in the distance. Now this has happened. Pray for me. Pray that my sins be forgiven. These services, these holy texts, they are an unremitting torment, they are smoke and flames, and in the roar and crackle I cannot hear the holy word. Tell my child of my torments. Tell her that she is never to fall into rivalries with other ladies, never to be a victim of jealousy. Her whole attention must go to atoning for the sins of her time at Ise, far from the Good Law. I am sorry for everything.'

It was not a dialogue which he wished to pursue. He had the little medium taken away and Murasaki quietly moved to another room.

The crowds swarming through the house seemed themselves to bode ill. All the high courtiers had been off watching the return procession from the Kamo Shrine and it was on their own way home that they heard the news.

'What a really awful thing,' said someone, and there was no doubting the sincerity of the words. 'A light that should for every reason have gone on shining has been put out, and we are left in a world of drizzling rain.'

But someone else whispered: 'It does not do to be too beautiful and virtuous. You do not live long. "Nothing in this world would be their rival," the poet said.* He was talking about cherry blossoms, of course, but it is so with her too. When such a lady lives to know all the pleasures and successes, her fellows must suffer. Maybe now the Third Princess will enjoy some of the attention that should have been hers all along. She has not had an easy time of it, poor thing.'

Not wanting another such day, Kashiwagi had ridden off with several of his brothers to watch the return procession. The news of course came as a shock. They turned towards Nijō.

'Nothing is meant in this world to last forever,'† he whispered to himself. He went in as if inquiring after her health, for it had after all been only a rumor. The wailing and lamenting proclaimed that it must be true.

Prince Hyōbu had arrived and gone inside and was too stunned to receive him. A weeping Yūgiri came out.

'How is she? I heard these awful reports and was unable to believe them, though I had of course known of her illness.'

'Yes, she has been very ill for a very long time. This morning at dawn she stopped breathing. But it seems to have been a possession. I am told that although she has revived and everyone is enormously relieved the crisis has not yet passed. We are still very worried.'

His eyes were red and swollen. It was his own unhappy love, perhaps, that made Kashiwagi look curiously at his friend, wondering why he should grieve so for a stepmother of whom he had not seen a great deal.

'She was dangerously ill,' Genji sent out to the crowds. 'This morning quite suddenly it appeared that she had breathed her last. The shock, I fear, was such that we were all quite deranged and given over to loud and unbecoming grief. I have not myself been as calm and in control of things as I ought to have been. I will thank you properly at another time for having been so good as to call.'

*Anonymous, *Kokinshū* 70:

> If cherry blossoms waited at our command,
> Nothing in this world would be their rival.

†*Tales of Ise* 82:

> The cherry blossom is dearest when it falls.
> Nothing is meant in this world to last forever.

It would not have been possible for Kashiwagi to visit Rokujō except in such a crisis. He was in acute discomfort even so – evidence, no doubt, of a very bad conscience.

Genji was more worried than before. He commissioned numberless rites of very great dignity and grandeur. The Rokujō lady had done terrible things while she lived, and what she had now become was utterly horrible. He even felt uncomfortable about his relations with her daughter, the Reizei empress. The conclusion was inescapable: women were creatures of sin. He wanted to be done with them. He could not doubt that it was in fact the Rokujō lady who had addressed him. His remarks about her had been in an intimate conversation with Murasaki overheard by no one. Disaster still seemed imminent. He must do what he could to forestall it. Murasaki had so earnestly pleaded to become a nun. He thought that tentative vows might give her strength and so he permitted a token tonsure and ordered that the five injunctions be administered. There were noble and moving phrases in the sermon describing the admirable power of the injunctions. Weeping and hovering over Murasaki quite without regard for appearances, Genji too invoked the holy name. There are crises that can unsettle the most superior of men. He wanted only to save her, to have her still beside him, whatever the difficulties and sacrifices. The sleepless nights had left him dazed and emaciated.

Murasaki was better, but still in pain through the Fourth Month. It was now the rainy Fifth Month, when the skies are their most capricious. Genji commissioned a reading of the Lotus Sutra in daily installments and other solemn services as well towards freeing the Rokujō lady of her sins. At Murasaki's bedside there were continuous readings by priests of good voice. From time to time the Rokujō lady would make dolorous utterances through the medium, but she refused all requests that she go away.

Murasaki was troubled with a shortness of breath and seemed even weaker as the warm weather came on. Genji was in such a state of distraction that Murasaki, ill though she was, sought to comfort him. She would have no regrets if she were to die, but she did not want it to seem that she did not care. She forced herself to take broth and a little food and from the Sixth Month she was able to sit up. Genji was delighted but still very worried. He stayed with her at Nijō.

The Third Princess had been unwell since that shocking visitation. There were no specific complaints or striking symptoms. She felt vaguely indisposed and that was all. She had eaten very little for some weeks and was pale and thin. Unable to contain himself, Kashiwagi would sometimes come for visits as fleeting as dreams. She did not welcome them. She was so much in awe of Genji that to rank the younger man beside him seemed almost blasphemous. Kashiwagi was an amiable and personable young man, and people who were no more than friends were quite right to think him superior; but she had known the incomparable Genji since she was a child and Kashiwagi scarcely seemed worth a glance. She thought herself very badly treated indeed that he should be the one to make her unhappy. Her nurse and a few others knew the nature of her indisposition and grumbled that Genji's visits were so extremely infrequent. He did finally come to inquire after her.

It was very warm. Murasaki had had her hair washed and otherwise sought renewal. Since she was in bed with her hair spread about her, it was not quick to dry. It was smooth and without a suggestion of a tangle to the farthest ends. Her skin was lovely, so white that it almost seemed iridescent, as if a light were shining through. She was very beautiful and as fragile as the shell of a locust.

The Nijō mansion had been neglected and was somewhat run-down, and compared to the Rokujō mansion it seemed very cramped and narrow. Taking advantage of a few days when she was somewhat more herself, Genji sent gardeners to clear the brook and restore the flower beds, and the suddenly renewed expanse before her made Murasaki marvel that she should be witness to such things. The lake was very cool, a carpet of lotuses. The dew on the green of the pads was like a scattering of jewels.

'Just look, will you,' said Genji. 'As if it had a monopoly on coolness. I cannot tell you how pleased I am that you have improved so.' She was sitting up and her pleasure in the scene was quite open. There were tears in his eyes. 'I was almost afraid at times that I too might be dying.'

She was near tears herself.

'It is a life in which we cannot be sure
Of lasting as long as the dew upon the lotus.'

And he replied:

'To be as close as the drops of dew on the lotus
   Must be our promise in this world and the next.'

Though he felt no great eagerness to visit Rokujō, it had
been some time since he had learned of the Third Princess's
indisposition. Her brother and father would probably have heard
of it too. They would think his inability to leave Murasaki rather
odd and his failure to take advantage of a break in the rains even
odder.

The princess looked away and did not answer his questions.
Interpreting her silence as resentment at his long absence, he set
about reasoning with her.

He called some of her older women and made detailed
inquiries about her health.

'She is in an interesting condition, as they say.'

'Really, now! And at this late date! I couldn't be more surprised.'

It was his general want of success in fathering children that
made the news so surprising. Ladies he had been with for a very
long while had remained childless. He thought her sweet and
pathetic and did not pursue the matter. Since it had taken him so
long to collect himself for the visit, he could not go back to Nijō
immediately. He stayed with her for several days. Murasaki was
always on his mind, however, and he wrote her letter after letter.

'He certainly has thought of a great deal to say in a very short
time,' grumbled a woman who did not know that her lady was the
more culpable party. 'It does not seem like a marriage with the
firmest sort of foundations.'

Kojijū was frantic with worry.

Hearing that Genji was at Rokujō, Kashiwagi was a victim of a
jealousy that might have seemed out of place. He wrote a long
letter to the Third Princess describing his sorrows. Kojijū took
advantage of a moment when Genji was in another part of the
house to show her the letter.

'Take it away. It makes me feel worse.' She lay down and
refused to look at it.

'But do just glance for a minute at the beginning here.' Kojijū
unfolded the letter. 'It is very sad.'

Someone was coming. She pulled the princess's curtains closed
and went off.

It was Genji. In utter confusion, the princess had time only to push it under the edge of a quilt.

He would be going back to Rokujō that evening, said Genji. 'You do not seem so very ill. The lady in the other house is very ill indeed and I would not want her to think I have deserted her. You are not to pay any attention to what they might be saying about me. You will presently see the truth.'

So cheerful and even frolicsome at other times, she was subdued and refused to look at him. It must be that she thought he did not love her. He lay down beside her and as they talked it was evening. He was awakened from a nap by a clamor of evening cicadas.

'It will soon be dark,' he said, getting up to change clothes.

'Can you not stay at least until you have the moon to guide you?'*

She seemed so very young. He thought her charming. At least until then – it was a very small request.

'The voice of the evening cicada says you must leave.
"Be moist with evening dews," you say to my sleeves?'

Something of the cheerful innocence of old seemed to come back. He sighed and knelt down beside her.

'How do you think it sounds in yonder village,
    The cicada that summons me there and summons me here?'

He was indeed pulled in two directions. Finally deciding that it would be cruel to leave, he stayed the night. Murasaki continued to be very much on his mind. He went to bed after a light supper.

He was up early, thinking to be on his way while it was still cool.

'I left my fan somewhere. This one is not much good.' He searched through her sitting room, where he had had his nap the day before.

He saw a corner of pale-green tissue paper at the edge of a slightly disarranged quilt. Casually he took it up. It was a note in a man's hand. Delicately perfumed, it somehow had the look of a

*Oyakeme of Buzen, *Manyōshū* 709, with variations in other anthologies:

> Dark the way and dangerous. Can you not stay
> At least until you have the moon to guide you?

rather significant document. There were two sheets of paper covered with very small writing. The hand was without question Kashiwagi's.

The woman who opened the mirror for him paid little attention. It would of course be a letter he had every right to see. But Kojijū noted with horror that it was the same color as Kashiwagi's of the day before. She quite forgot about breakfast. It could not be. Nothing so awful could have been permitted to happen. Her lady absolutely *must* have hidden it.

The princess was still sleeping soundly. What a child she was, thought Genji, not without a certain contempt. Supposing someone else had found the letter. That was the thing: the heedlessness that had troubled him all along.

He had left and the other women were some distance away. 'And what did you do with the young gentleman's letter?' asked Kojijū. 'His Lordship was reading a letter that was very much the same color.'

The princess collapsed in helpless weeping.

Kojijū was sorry for her, of course, but shocked and angry too. 'Really, my lady – where *did* you put it? There were others around and I went off because I did not want him to think we were conspiring. That was how *I* felt. And you had time before he came in. Surely you hid it?'

'He came in on me while I was reading it. I didn't have time. I slipped it under something and forgot about it.'

Speechless, Kojijū went to look for the letter. It was of course nowhere to be found.

'How perfectly, impossibly awful. The young gentleman was terrified of His Lordship, terrified that the smallest word might reach him. And now this has happened, and in no time at all. You are such a child, my lady. You let him see you, and he could not forget you however many years went by, and came begging to me. But that we should lose control of things so completely – it just did not seem possible. Nothing could be worse for either of you.'

She did not mince words. The princess was too good-natured and still too much of a child to argue back. Her tears flowed on.

She quite lost her appetite. Her women thought Genji cruel and unfeeling. 'She is so extremely unwell, and he ignores her. He gives all his attention to a lady who has quite recovered.'

Genji was still puzzled. He read the letter over and over again. He tested the hypothesis that one of her women had deliberately set about imitating Kashiwagi's hand. But it would not do. The idiosyncrasies were all too clearly Kashiwagi's. He had to admire the style, the fluency and clear detail with which Kashiwagi had described the fortuitous consummation of all his hopes, and all his sufferings since. But Genji had felt contemptuous of the princess and he must feel contemptuous of her young friend too. A man simply did not set these matters down so clearly in writing. Kashiwagi was a man of discernment and some eminence, and he had written a letter that could easily embarrass a lady. Genji himself had in his younger years never forgotten that letters have a way of going astray. His own letters had always been laconic and evasive even when he had longed to make them otherwise. Caution had not always been easy.

And how was he to behave towards the princess? He understood rather better the reasons for her condition. He had come upon the truth himself, without the aid of informers. Was there to be no change in his manner? He would have preferred that there be none but feared that things could not be the same again. Even in affairs which he had not from the outset taken seriously, the smallest evidence that the lady might be interested in someone else had always been enough to kill his own interest; and here he had more, a good deal more. What an impertinent trifler the young man was! It was not unknown for a young man to seduce even one of His Majesty's own ladies, but this seemed different. A young man and lady might in the course of their duties in the royal service find themselves favorably disposed towards each other and do what they ought not to have done. Such things did happen. Royal ladies were, after all, human. Some of them were not perhaps as sober and careful as they might be and they made mistakes. The man would remain in the court service and unless there was a proper scandal the mistake might go undetected. But this – Genji snapped his fingers in irritation. He had paid more attention to the princess than the lady he really loved, the truly priceless treasure, and she had responded by choosing a man like Kashiwagi!

He thought that there could be no precedent for it. Life had its frustrations for His Majesty's ladies when they obediently did their duty. There might come words of endearment from an honest man and there might be times when silence seemed impossible, and in a lady's answers would be the start of a love affair. One did not condone her behavior but one could understand it. But Genji thought himself neither fatuous nor conceited in wondering how the Third Princess could possibly have divided her affections between him and a man like Kashiwagi.

Well, it was all very distasteful. But he would say nothing. He wondered if his own father had long ago known what was happening and said nothing. He could remember his own terror very well, and the memory told him that he was hardly the one to reprove others who strayed from the narrow path.

Despite his determined silence, Murasaki knew that something was wrong. She herself had quite recovered, and she feared that he was feeling guilty about the Third Princess.

'I really am very much better. They tell me that Her Highness is not well. You should have stayed with her a little longer.'

'Her Highness — it is true that she is indisposed, but I cannot see that there is a great deal wrong with her. Messenger after messenger has come from court. I gather that there was one just today from her father. Her brother worries about her because her father worries about her, and I must worry about both of them.'

'I would worry less about them than about the princess herself if I thought she was unhappy. She may not say very much, but I hate to think of all those women giving her ideas.'

Genji smiled and shrugged his shoulders. 'You are the important one and you have no troublesome relatives, and you think of all these things. I think about her important brother and you think about her women. I fear I am not a very sensitive man.' But of her suggestion that he return to Rokujō he said only: 'There will be time when you are well enough to go with me.'

'I would like to stay here just a little while longer. Do please go ahead and make her happy. I won't be long.'

And so the days went by. The princess was of course in no position to charge him with neglect. She lived in dread lest her father get some word of what had happened.

Letter after passionate letter came from Kashiwagi. Finally, pushed too far, Kojijū told him everything. He was horrified. When had it happened? It had been as if the skies were watching him, so fearful had he been that something in the air might arouse Genji's suspicions. And now Genji had irrefutable evidence. It was a time of still, warm weather even at night and in the morning, but he felt as if a cold wind were cutting through him. Genji had singled him out for special favors and made him a friend and adviser, and for all this Kashiwagi had been most grateful. How could he now face Genji – who must think him an intolerable upstart and interloper! Yet if he were to avoid Rokujō completely people would notice and think it odd, and Genji would of course have stronger evidence than before. Sick with worry, Kashiwagi stopped going to court. It was not likely that he would face specific punishment, but he feared that he had ruined his life. Things could not be worse. He hated himself for what he had let happen.

Yes, one had to admit that the princess was a scatterbrained little person. The cat incident should not have occurred. Yūgiri had made his feelings in the matter quite clear, and Kashiwagi was beginning to share them. It may be that he was now trying to see the worst in the princess and so to shake off his longing. Gentle elegance was no doubt desirable, but it could go too far and become a kind of ignorance of the everyday world. And the princess had not surrounded herself with the right women. The results were too apparent, disaster for the princess and disaster for Kashiwagi himself. Yet he could not help feeling sorry for her.

She was very pretty, and she was not well. Genji pitied her too. He might tell himself that he was dismissing her from his thoughts, but the facts were rather different. To be dissatisfied with her did not mean to commence disliking her. He would be so sorry for her when he saw her that he could hardly speak. He commissioned prayers and services for her safe delivery. His outward attentions were as they had always been, and indeed he seemed more solicitous than ever. Yet he was very much aware of the distance between them and had to work hard to keep people from noticing. He continued to reprove her in silence and she to suffer agonies of guilt; and that the silence did nothing to relieve the agonies was perhaps another mark of her immaturity, which had been the cause of it all. Innocence can be a virtue, but when it suggests a want of prudence and caution it does not inspire confidence. He began to wonder about other women, about his own daughter, for instance. She was almost too gentle and good-natured, and a man who was drawn to her would no doubt lose his head as completely as Kashiwagi had. Aware of and feeling a certain easy contempt for evidence of irresolution, a man sometimes sees possibilities in a lady who should be far above him.

He thought of Tamakazura. She had grown up in straitened circumstances with no one really capable of defending her interests. She was quick and shrewd, however, and an adroit manipulator. Genji had made the world think he was her father and had caused her problems which a real father would not have. She had turned them smoothly away, and when Higekuro had found an accomplice in one of her serving women and forced his way into her presence she had made it clear to everyone that she had had no say in the matter, and then made it equally clear that her acceptance of his suit was for her a new departure; and so she had emerged unscathed. Genji saw more than ever what a virtuoso performance it had been. No doubt something in earlier lives had made it inevitable that she and Higekuro come together and live together, but it would have done her no good to have people look back on the beginnings of the affair and say that she had led him on. She had managed very well indeed.

Genji thought too of Oborozukiyo. It had come to seem that she had been more accessible than she should have been. He was very sorry to learn that she had finally become a nun. He got off a long letter describing his pain and regret.

'I should not care that now you are a nun?
My sleeves were wet at Suma – because of you!

'I know that life is uncertain, and I am sorry that I have let you anticipate me and at the same time hurt that you have cast me aside. I take comfort in the hope that you will give me precedence in your prayers.'

It was he who had kept her from becoming a nun long before. She mused upon the cruel and powerful bond between them. Weeping at the thought that this might be his last letter, the end of a long and difficult correspondence, she took great pains with her answer. The hand and the gradations of the ink were splendid.

'I had thought that I alone knew the uncertainty of it all. You say that I have anticipated you, but

'How comes it that the fisherman of Akashi
Has let the boat make off to sea without him?

'As for my prayers, they must be for everyone.'

It was on deep green-gray paper attached to a branch of anise,* not remarkably original or imaginative and yet obviously done with very great care. And the hand was as good as ever.

Since there could be no doubt that this was the end of the affair, he showed the letter to Murasaki.

'Her point is well taken,' he said. 'I should not have let her get ahead of me. I have known many sad things and lived through them all. The detached sort of friend with whom you can talk about the ordinary things that interest you and you think might interest her too – I have had only Princess Asagao and this lady, and now they both are nuns.† I understand that the princess has quite lost herself in her devotions and has no time for anything else. I have known many ladies, personally and by repute, and I think I have never known anyone else with quite that combination of earnestness and gentle charm.

'It is not easy to rear a daughter. You cannot know what conditions she has brought with her from earlier lives and so cannot be sure of always having your way. She requires endless care and attention as she grows up. I am glad now that I was spared great numbers of them. In my young and irresponsible days I used to lament that I had so few and to think that a man could not have too many. Endless care and attention – they are what I must ask of you in the case of your little princess. Her mother is young and inexperienced and busy with other things, and I am sure there is a great deal that she is just not up to. I would be much upset if anyone were to find fault with my royal granddaughter. I hope she will have everything she needs to make her way smoothly through life. Ladies of lower rank can find husbands to look after them, but it is not always so with a princess.'

'I certainly mean to do what I can for as long as I can. But,' she added wistfully, 'I am not sure that it will be very much.' She envied these other ladies, free to lose themselves in religion.

'Nun's dress must feel rather new to her and she may not have caught the knack quite yet. Might I ask you to have something done for her? Surplices and that sort of thing – how do you go about making them? Do what you can, in any event, and I will ask the lady in the northeast quarter at Rokujō to see what she can do.

---

*Shikimi, *Illicium anisatum*, often used to decorate altars.

†We are here informed for the first time that Asagao has become a nun.

Nothing too elaborate, I should think. Something tasteful and womanly all the same.'

Murasaki now turned her attention to green-drab robes, and needlewomen were summoned from the palace and put to quiet but carefully supervised work on the cushions and quilts and curtains a nun should have.

The visit to the Suzaku emperor had been postponed until autumn. Since the anniversary of Princess Omiya's death came in the Eighth Month, Yūgiri had no time for musicians and rehearsals. In the Ninth Month came the anniversary of the death of Kokiden, the Suzaku emperor's mother. So the Tenth Month had been fixed upon. The Third Princess was not well, however, and another postponement was necessary.

The Second Princess, Kashiwagi's wife, did that month visit her father. Tō no Chūjō, now the retired chancellor, saw to it that the arrangements outdid all precedents. Kashiwagi was now almost an invalid, but he forced himself to go along.

The Third Princess too had been in seclusion, alone with her troubles. It was perhaps in part because of them that she was having a difficult pregnancy. Genji could not help worrying about her, so tiny and fragile. He began almost to fear the worst. It had been for him a year of prayers and religious services.

Reports of the Third Princess had reached her father's mountain retreat. He longed to see her. Someone told him that Genji was living at Nijō and rarely visited her. What could it mean? He was deeply troubled and knew again how uncertain married life can be. Reports that Genji had quite refused to leave Murasaki's side all through her illness had upset the Suzaku emperor, and now he learned that Murasaki had recovered and Genji still saw little of the Third Princess. Had something happened, not by the princess's own choice but through the machinations of women in her household? During his years at court ugly rumors had sometimes disturbed the decorous life of the women's quarters. Perhaps his daughter was the victim of something of the sort? He had dismissed worldly trivia from his life, but he was still a father.

He wrote to the Third Princess in long and troubled detail. 'I have neglected you because I have had no reason to write, and I hate to think how much time has gone by. I have heard that you are not well. You are in my thoughts even when they should be on my prayers. And how in fact are you? You must be patient, whatever happens and however lonely you may be. It is unseemly to show displeasure when the facts of a matter are less than clear.'

'How sad,' said Genji, who chanced to be with her.

The Suzaku emperor could not possibly have learned the horrid secret. He must have Genji's negligence in mind.

'And how do you mean to answer?' asked Genji after a time. 'I am very sorry indeed to have such melancholy tidings. I may have certain causes for dissatisfaction but I think I may congratulate myself on having said nothing about them. Where can his information have come from?'

The princess looked away in embarrassment. Though she had lost weight because of her worries, she was more delicately beautiful than ever.

'He worries about leaving you behind when you are so very young and innocent. I fear that I worry too. I hope that you are being careful. I say so because I am very sorry indeed that things may not seem to be going as he would have wished and because I want at least you to understand. You are not as self-reliant as you might be and you are easily influenced, and so you may think that I have not behaved well. And of course – of this I have no doubt – I am much too old to be very interesting. Neither of these facts makes me happy, but neither of them should keep you from putting up with me for as long as your father lives. And perhaps you can try not to be too contemptuous of the old man who was, after all, your father's choice.

'Women are commonly thought to be weak and undependable, but women have preceded me down the road I have long wanted to go. However slow and indecisive I may be, there is not much that need hold me back. But I was moved and pleased that I should have been your father's choice when he resolved to leave the world. If now I should seem to be following his precedent I am sure I will stand charged with failing to respect his wishes.

'No one among the other ladies who have been important to me need stand in my way. I do not of course know with certainty how things will be for my daughter, but she is having children one after another, and if I see to her needs for as long as I can, I need have no fear about what will happen to her afterwards. My other ladies are all at an age when they need arouse no very sharp regrets if after their several conveniences they too leave the world. I find myself without worries in that regard.

'It does not seem likely that your father will live a great deal longer. He has always been a sickly man and he has recently been in poor spirits as well, and I hope you will be careful that no unpleasant rumors come to him at this late date to disturb his retirement. We shall not worry too much about this world, for it is not worth worrying about. But it would be a terrible sin to stand in the way of his salvation.'

Though he had spoken with careful indirection, tears were streaming from her eyes and she was in acute discomfort. Presently Genji too was in tears. And he was beginning to feel a little ashamed of himself.

'Senile meanderings. I am unhappy when I have them from other people and here I am making you listen to them. You must think me a noisy, tiresome old fool.'

He pushed an inkstone towards her and himself ground the ink and chose the paper on which she was to reply to her father. Her hand was trembling so violently that she could not write. He doubted that she had had such difficulty in replying to the long and detailed letter he had discovered. Though no longer very sorry for her, he told her what to say.

'And your visit? We are almost at the end of the month and your sister has already paid what I am told was a very elaborate visit. I should imagine that in your present condition you will invite unfortunate comparisons. I have memorial services coming up next month and the end of the year is always busy and confused. He may be upset when he sees you, but we cannot put it off forever. Do please try to look a little more cheerful and a little less tired.'

She was in spite of everything very pretty.

Genji had always sent for Kashiwagi when something interesting or important came up, but in recent months there had been no summonses. Though Genji feared that people would think his silence odd, he squirmed at the thought of appearing before the man who had cuckolded him and doubted that he would be able to conceal his distaste. He was by no means unhappy that Kashiwagi stayed away. The rest of the court thought only that Kashiwagi was not well and that there had been no good parties at Rokujō recently. Yūgiri alone suspected that something was amiss. He suspected that Kashiwagi, a susceptible youth, had not been able to suppress the excitement aroused by the view that spring evening to which Yūgiri had also been treated. He did not of course know that anything so extremely scandalous had occurred.

The Twelfth Month came and the visit was scheduled for the middle of the month. The Rokujō mansion echoed with music. Eager to see the rehearsals, Murasaki returned from Nijō. The Akashi princess, who had had another son, was also at Rokujō. Passing whole days with his grandchildren, delightful little creatures all of them, Genji had ample reason to think that a long life can be happy. Tamakazura too came for the rehearsals. Since Yūgiri had been conducting preliminary rehearsals in the northeast quarter, the lady of the orange blossoms did not feel left out of things.

The affair would not be complete without Kashiwagi, and his absence would seem very strange indeed. He at first declined Genji's invitation on grounds of poor health. Nerves, thought Genji, hearing that there were no very clear symptoms and sending off a warmer and more intimate invitation.

'You are refusing?' said Tō no Chūjō. 'But he will think it unfriendly of you, and you do not seem so very unwell. You must go, even if it takes a little out of you.'

Reluctantly, when these urgings had been added to several invitations from Rokujō, Kashiwagi set out.

The most important guests had not yet arrived. He was as always admitted to Genji's drawing room. He looked every bit as ill as reports had him. He had always been a solemn, melancholy youth, overshadowed by his lively brothers. Today he was quieter than usual. Most people would have said that he was in every way qualified to be a royal son-in-law, but to Genji (and he felt rather the same about the princess) he was a callow young person who did not know how to behave.

Though Genji turned on him what seemed a strong eye, the words were gentle enough. 'It has been a very long time. I have had nothing to ask your advice about and we have had sick people on our hands. Indeed, I have had little time for anything else. Our princess here has all along thought of doing something in honor of her father, but we have had delay after delay and now the year is almost over. Though not at all what we would really like to do, we hope to put together a minor sort of banquet in keeping with his new position. No, that is too grand a word for it – but we do have our little princes to show off, and so we have had them at dance practice. In that, at least, we should not disappoint him. I have thought and thought and been able to think of no one but you to take charge of the rehearsals. And so I shall not scold you for having neglected me so.'

There was nothing in Genji's manner to suggest innuendos and hidden meanings. Kashiwagi was acutely uncomfortable all the same, and afraid that his embarrassment might show.

'I was much troubled,' he finally managed to say, 'at the news that first one of your ladies and then another was ill, but since spring I have had such trouble with my legs* that I have hardly been able to walk. It has been worse all the time and I have been living like a hermit and not even going to court. Now we have the Suzaku emperor's jubilee. Father says, quite rightly, that the event should be of more concern to us than anyone else. He has resigned his offices and should not be indulging in ceremonies and celebrations, he says, but in spite of my own insignificance we must give some evidence that my gratitude is as deep as his own. And so I forced myself to go with the rest of them.

'His Majesty has withdrawn more and more from the vulgar world and we were sure that he would not welcome an elaborate display. The simple, intimate sort of visit you have in mind seems to me exactly the right thing.'

Genji thought it well mannered of him not to dwell on the details of the Second Princess's visit, which he knew had been more than elaborate.

'You can see how little we mean to do. I had feared that people might think us wanting in respect and esteem, and to have the approval of the one who understands these things best is very reassuring. Yūgiri seems to be doing modestly well with his work, but he would seem by nature to be little inclined toward the more elegant things. As for the Suzaku emperor, there is not a single one of them at which he is not an expert, but music has always been his chief love and there is little that he does not know about it. He has as you say left the vulgar world behind and it would seem that he has given up music too, but I think that precisely because of the quiet and serenity in which it will be received we must give most careful attention to what we offer. Do please add your efforts to Yūgiri's and see that the lads are well prepared and in a proper

---

*Kakubyō, which includes but does not seem to have been limited to beriberi.

frame of mind as well. I do not doubt that the professionals know
what they are doing, but somehow the last touch seems missing.'

He could not have been more courteous and friendly, and
Kashiwagi was of course grateful; but he was in acute discomfort
all the same. He said little and wanted only to escape. It was far
from the easy and pleasant converse of other years, and he did
presently slip away.

In the northeast quarter he had suggestions to make about the
costumes and the like which Yūgiri had chosen. Though in many
ways they already exhausted the possibilities, he showed that he
deserved Genji's high praise by adding new touches.

It was only a rehearsal, but Genji did not want his ladies to be
disappointed. On the day of the visit itself the dancers were to
wear red robes and lavender singlets. Today they wore green singlets and pink robes lined with red. Seats for thirty musicians,
all dressed in white, had been put out on the gallery which led
to the angling pavilion, to the southeast of the main buildings.
The dancers emerged from beyond the hillock to the strains of
'The Misty Hermitage.' There were a few flakes of snow but
spring had 'come next door.'* The plums smiled with their first
blossoms. Genji watched through blinds with only Prince Hyōbu and
Higekuro beside him. The lesser courtiers were on the veranda.
Since it was an informal affair there was only a light supper.

Higekuro's fourth son, Yūgiri's third son, and two of Prince
Hotaru's sons danced 'Myriad Years.' They were very pretty and
even now they carried themselves like little aristocrats. Graceful
and beautifully fitted out, they were (was a part of it in the eye of
the observer?) elegance incarnate. Yūgiri's second son, by the
daughter of Koremitsu, and a grandson of Prince Hyōbu, son of
the guards officer called the Minamoto councillor, danced 'The
Royal Deer.' Higekuro's third son did a masked dance about a
handsome Chinese general† and Yūgiri's oldest son the Korean
dragon dance. And then the several dancers, all of them close

*Kiyowara Fukayabu, *Kokinshū* 1021:

> Though it is winter, spring has come next door.
> Petals and snow fall over the wall between.

†Ranryōō or Raryōō. About one General Ling, who was so handsome that he went
masked into battle to avoid disconcerting his own troops.

relatives, did 'Peace' and 'Joy of Spring' and numbers of other dances. As evening came on, Genji had the blinds raised, and as the festivities reached a climax his little grandchildren showed most remarkable grace and skill in several plain, unmasked dances. Their innate talents had been honed to the last delicate edge by their masters. Genji was glad that he did not have to say which was the most charming. His aging friends were all weeping copiously and Prince Hyōbu's nose had been polished to a fine, high red.

'An old man does find it harder and harder to hold back drunken tears,' said Genji. He looked at Kashiwagi. 'And just see our young guardsman here, smiling a superior smile to make us feel uncomfortable. Well, he has only to wait a little longer. The current of the years runs only in one direction, and old age lies downstream.'

Pretending to be drunker than he was, Genji had singled out the soberest of his guests. Kashiwagi was genuinely ill and quite indifferent to the festivities. Though Genji's manner was jocular each of his words seemed to Kashiwagi a sharper blow than the one before. His head was aching. Genji saw that he was only pretending to drink and made him empty the wine cup under his own careful supervision each time it came around. Kashiwagi was the handsomest of them even in his hour of distress. So ill that he left early, he was feeling much worse when he reached home. He could not understand himself. He had in spite of everything remained fairly sober – and he sometimes drank himself senseless. Had his frayed nerves caused his blood to rise? But he was not such a weakling. It had all been a lamentable and most unbecoming performance in any case.

The aftereffects were not of a sort to disappear in a day. He was seriously ill. His parents, in great alarm, insisted that he come home. The Second Princess was very reluctant to let him go. Through the dull days she had told herself that their relations must surely improve, and though it could not have been said that they were a devoted couple she could not bear to say goodbye. She feared that she would not see him again. He was very sorry, and thought himself guilty of very great disrespect to leave a royal princess in forlorn solitude.

Her mother, one of the Suzaku emperor's lesser ladies, was more vocally grieved. 'Parents should not come between husband and wife, I do not care what sort of crisis it might be. I cannot even think of having you away for such a long time. Until you have recovered, they say – but suppose you have a try at recovering here.' She addressed him through only a curtain.

'There is much in what you say. I am not an important man and I received august permission to marry far beyond my station. I had hoped to show my gratitude by living a long life and reaching a position at least a little more worthy of the honor. And now this has happened, and perhaps I will in the end not be able to show even the smallest part of my true feelings. I fear that I am not long for this world. The thought suddenly makes the way into the next world seem very dark and difficult.'

They were both in tears. He was persuaded that he really could not leave.

But his mother, desperately worried, sent for him again. 'Why do you refuse to let me even see your face? When I am feeling a little unhappy or indisposed it is you among them all that I want to see first. This is too much.'

And of course this position too was thoroughly tenable.

'Maybe it is because I am the oldest that I have always been her favorite. Even now I am her special pet. She says that she is not herself when I am away for even a little while. And now I am ill, it may be critically, and I fear it would be a very grave offense to stay away. Come to me quietly, please, if you hear that the worst is at hand. I know that we will meet again. I am a stupid, indecisive sort, and no doubt you have found me most unsatisfactory. I had not expected to die quite so soon. I had thought that we had many years ahead of us.'

He was in tears as he left the house. The princess, now alone, was speechless with grief and unrequited affection.

In Tō no Chūjō's house there was a great stir to receive him. The illness was not sudden and it had not seemed serious. He had gradually lost his appetite and now he was eating almost nothing. It was as if some mysterious force were pulling him in. That so erudite and discriminating a young man should have fallen into such a decline was cause for lamenting all through the court. Virtually the whole court came around to inquire after him and there were repeated messages from the emperor and the retired emperors, whose concern compounded the worries of his parents. Genji too was surprised and upset and sent many earnest messages to Tō no Chūjō. Yūgiri, perhaps Kashiwagi's closest friend, was constantly at his side.

The visit to the Suzaku emperor was set for the twenty-fifth. With such a worthy young man so seriously ill and the whole eminent clan in a turmoil, the timing seemed far from happy. The visit had already been postponed too long and too often, however, and to cancel it at this late date seemed out of the question. Genji felt very sorry indeed for the Third Princess.

As is the custom on such occasions, sutras were read in fifty temples. At the temple in which the Suzaku emperor was living, the sutra to Great Vairocana.*

*The chapter ends in midsentence in a cadence suggesting poetry.

CHAPTER 36

The Oak Tree

The New Year came and Kashiwagi's condition had not improved. He knew how troubled his parents were and he knew that suicide was no solution, for he would be guilty of the grievous sin of having left them behind. He had no wish to live on. Since his very early years he had had high standards and ambitions and had striven in private matters and public to outdo his rivals by even a little. His wishes had once or twice been thwarted, however, and he had so lost confidence in himself that the world had come to seem unrelieved gloom. A longing to prepare for the next world had succeeded his ambitions, but the opposition of his parents had kept him from following the mendicant way through the mountains and over the moors. He had delayed, and time had gone by. Then had come events, and for them he had only himself to blame, which had made it impossible for him to show his face in public. He did not blame the gods. His own deeds were working themselves out. A man does not have the thousand years of the pine, and he wanted to go now, while there were still those who might mourn for him a little, and perhaps even a sigh from *her* would be the reward for his burning passion. To die now and perhaps win the forgiveness of the man who must feel so aggrieved would be far preferable to living on and bringing sorrow and dishonor upon the lady and upon himself. In his last moments everything must disappear. Perhaps, because he had no other sins to atone for, a part of the affection with which Genji had once honored him might return.*

The same thoughts, over and over, ran uselessly through his mind. And why, he asked himself in growing despair, had he so deprived himself of alternatives? His pillow threatened to float away on the river of his woes.

He took advantage of a slight turn for the better, when his parents and the others had withdrawn from his bedside, to get off a letter to the Third Princess.

'You may have heard that I am near death. It is natural that you should not care very much, and yet I am sad.' His hand was so

*The soliloquy contains allusions to at least five poems.

uncertain that he gave up any thought of saying all that he would have wished to say.

'My thoughts of you: will they stay when I am gone
Like smoke that lingers over the funeral pyre?

'One word of pity will quiet the turmoil and light the dark road I am taking by my own choice.'

Unchastened, he wrote to Kojijū of his sufferings, at considerable length. He longed, he said, to see her lady one last time. She had from childhood been close to his house, in which she had near relatives.* Although she had strongly disapproved of his designs upon a royal princess who should have been far beyond his reach, she was extremely sorry for him in what might be his last illness.

'Do answer him, please, my lady,' she said, in tears. 'You must, just this once. It may be your last chance.'

'I am sorry for him, in a general sort of way. I am sorry for myself too. Any one of us could be dead tomorrow. But what happened was too awful. I cannot bear to think of it. I could not possibly write to him.'

She was not by nature a very careful sort of lady, but the great man to whom she was married had terrorized her with hints, always guarded, that he was displeased with her.

Kojijū insisted and pushed an inkstone towards her, and finally, very hesitantly, she set down an answer which Kojijū delivered under cover of evening.

Tō no Chūjō had sent to Mount Katsuragi for an ascetic famous as a worker of cures, and the spells and incantations in which he immersed himself might almost have seemed overdone. Other holy men were recommended and Tō no Chūjō's sons would go off to seek in mountain recesses men scarcely known in the city. Mendicants quite devoid of grace came crowding into the house. The symptoms did not point to any specific illness, but Kashiwagi would sometimes weep in great, racking sobs. The soothsayers were agreed that a jealous woman had taken possession of him. They might possibly be right, thought Tō no Chūjō. But whoever she was she refused to withdraw, and so it was that the search for healers reached into these obscure corners. The ascetic from

---

*Kashiwagi's nurse is her aunt.

Katsuragi, an imposing man with cold, forbidding eyes, intoned mystic spells in a somewhat threatening voice.

'I cannot stand a moment more of it,' said Kashiwagi. 'I must have sinned grievously. These voices terrify me and seem to bring death even nearer.'

Slipping from bed, he instructed the women to tell his father that he was asleep and went to talk with Kojijū. Tō no Chūjō and the ascetic were conferring in subdued tones. Tō no Chūjō was robust and youthful for his years and in ordinary times much given to laughter. He told the holy man how it had all begun and how a respite always seemed to be followed by a relapse.

'Do please make her go away, whoever she might be,' he said entreatingly.

A hollow shell of his old self, Kashiwagi was meanwhile addressing Kojijū in a faltering voice sometimes interrupted by a suggestion of a laugh.

'Listen to them. They seem to have no notion that I might be ill because I misbehaved. If, as these wise men say, some angry lady has taken possession of me, then I would expect her presence to make me hate myself a little less. I can say that others have done much the same thing, made mistakes in their longing for ladies beyond their reach, and ruined their prospects. I can tell myself all this, but the torment goes on. I cannot face the world knowing that he knows. His radiance dazzles and blinds me. I would not have thought the misdeed so appalling, but since the evening when he set upon me I have so lost control of myself that it has been as if my soul were wandering loose. If it is still around the house somewhere, please lay a trap for it.'*

She told him of the Third Princess, lost in sad thoughts and afraid of prying eyes. He could almost see the forlorn little figure. Did unhappy spirits indeed go wandering forth disembodied?

'I shall say no more of your lady. It has all passed as if it had never happened at all. Yet I would be very sorry indeed if it were to stand in the way of her salvation. I have only one wish left, to

*Tales of Ise 110:

> In longing my soul has ventured forth alone.
> If you see it late in the night, please seek to trap it.

There were ways of catching errant spirits.

know that the consequences of the sad affair have been disposed of safely. I have my own interpretation of the dream I had that night and have had very great trouble keeping it to myself.'

Kojijū was frightened at the inhuman tenacity which these thoughts suggested. Yet she had to feel sorry for him. She was weeping bitterly.

He sent for a lamp and read the princess's note. Though fragile and uncertain, the hand was interesting. 'Your letter made me very sad, but I cannot see you. I can only think of you. You speak of the smoke that lingers on, and yet

'I wish to go with you, that we may see
   Whose smoldering thoughts last longer, yours or mine.'

That was all, but he was grateful for it.

'The smoke – it will follow me from this world. What a useless, insubstantial affair it was!'

Weeping uncontrollably, he set about a reply. There were many pauses and the words were fragmentary and disconnected and the hand like the tracks of a strange bird.

'As smoke I shall rise uncertainly to the heavens,
   And yet remain where my thoughts will yet remain.

'Look well, I pray you, into the evening sky. Be happy, let no one reprove you; and, though it will do no good, have an occasional thought for me.'

Suddenly worse again, he made his way tearfully back to his room. 'Enough. Go while it is still early, please, and tell her of my last moments. I would not want anyone who already thinks it odd to think it even odder. What have I brought from other lives, I wonder, to make me so unhappy?'

Usually he kept her long after their business was finished, but today he dismissed her briefly. She was very sorry for him and did not want to go.

His nurse, who was her aunt, told Kojijū of his illness, weeping all the while.

Tō no Chūjō was in great alarm. 'He had seemed better these last few days. Why the sudden change?'

'I cannot see why you are surprised,' replied his son. 'I am dying. That is all.'

That evening the Third Princess was taken with severe pains.

Guessing that they were birth pangs, her women sent for Genji in great excitement. He came immediately. How vast and unconditional his joy would be, he thought, were it not for his doubts about the child. But no one must be allowed to suspect their existence. He summoned ascetics and put them to continuous spells and incantations, and he summoned all the monks who had made names for themselves as healers. The Rokujō mansion echoed with mystic rites. The princess was in great pain through the night and at sunrise was delivered of a child. It was a boy. Most unfortunate, thought Genji. It would not be easy to guard the secret if the resemblance to the father was strong. There were devices for keeping girls in disguise and of course girls did not have to appear in public as did boys. But there was the other side of the matter: given these nagging doubts from the outset, a boy did not require the attention which must go into rearing a girl.

But how very strange it all was! Retribution had no doubt come for the deed which had terrified him then and which he was sure would go on terrifying him to the end. Since it had come, all unexpectedly, in this world, perhaps the punishment would be lighter in the next.

Unaware of these thoughts, the women quite lost themselves in ministering to the child. Because it was born of such a mother in Genji's late years, it must surely have the whole of his affection.

The ceremonies on the third night were of the utmost dignity and the gifts ranged out on trays and stands showed that everyone thought it an occasion demanding the best. On the fifth night the arrangements were Akikonomu's. There were robes for the princess and, after their several ranks, gifts for her women too, all of which would have done honor to a state occasion. Ceremonial repast was laid out for fifty persons and there was feasting all through the house. The staff of the Reizei Palace, including Akikonomu's personal chamberlain, was in attendance. On the seventh day the gifts and provisions came from the emperor himself and the ceremony was no less imposing than if it had taken place at court. Tō no Chūjō should have been among the guests of honor, but his other worries made it impossible for him to go beyond general congratulations. All the princes of the blood and court grandees were present. Genji was determined that there be no flaw in the observances, but he was not happy. He did not go out of his way to make his noble guests feel welcome, and there was no music.

The princess was tiny and delicate and still very frightened. She quite refused the medicines that were pressed upon her. In the worst of the crisis she had hoped that she might quietly die and so make her escape. Genji behaved with the strictest correctness and was determined to give no grounds for suspicion. Yet he somehow thought the babe repellent and was held by certain of the women to be rather chilly.

'He doesn't seem to like it at all.' One of the old women interrupted her cooings. 'And such a pretty little thing too. You're almost afraid for it. And so late in his life, when he has had so few.'

The princess caught snatches of their conversation and seemed to see a future of growing coldness and aloofness. She knew that she too was to blame and she began to think of becoming a nun. Although Genji paid an occasional daytime visit, he never stayed the night.

'I feel the uncertainty of it all more than ever,' he said, pulling her curtains back. 'I sometimes wonder how much time I have left. I have been occupied with my prayers and I have thought that you would not want to see people and so I have stayed away. And how are you? A little more yourself again? You have been through a great deal.'

'I almost feel that I might not live.' She raised her head from her pillow. 'But I know that it would be a very grave sin to die now.* I rather think I might like to become a nun. I might begin to feel better, and even if I were to die I might be forgiven.' She seemed graver and more serious than before, and more mature.

'Quite out of the question – it would only invite trouble. What can have put the idea into your head? I could understand if you really were going to die, but of course you are not.'

But he was thinking that if she felt constrained to say such things, then the generous and humane course might be to let her become a nun. To require that she go on living as his wife would be cruel, and for him too things could not be the same again. He might hurt her and word of what he had done might get abroad and presently reach her royal father. Perhaps she was right: the present crisis could be her excuse. But then he thought of the long life ahead of her, as long as the hair which she was asking to have

---

*It was thought a grave sin to die in childbirth.

cut – and he thought that he could not bear to see her in a nun's drab robes.

'No, you must be brave,' he said, urging medicine upon her. 'There is nothing wrong with you. The lady in the east wing has recovered from a far worse illness. We really did think she was dead. The world is neither as cruel nor as uncertain as we sometimes think it.'

There was a rather wonderful calm in the figure before him, pale and thin and quite drained of strength. Her offense had been a grave one, but he thought that he had to forgive her.

Her father, the Suzaku emperor, heard that it had been an easy birth and longed to see her. His meditations were disturbed by reports that she was not making a good recovery.

She ate nothing and was weaker and more despondent. She wept as she thought of her father, whom she longed to see more intensely than at any time since she had left his house. She feared that she might not see him again. She spoke of her fears to Genji, who had an appropriate emissary pass them on to the Suzaku emperor. In an agony of sorrow and apprehension and fully aware of the impropriety, he stole from his mountain retreat under cover of darkness and came to her side.

Genji was surprised and awed by the visit.

'I had been determined not to have another glance at the vulgar world,' said the emperor, 'but we all know how difficult it is for a father to throw off thoughts of his child.* So I have let my mind wander from my prayers. If the natural order of things is to be reversed and she is to leave me, I have said to myself, then I must see her again. Otherwise the regret would be always with me. I have come in spite of what I know they all will say.'

There was quiet elegance in his clerical dress. Not wanting to attract attention, he had avoided the livelier colors permitted a priest. A model of clean simplicity, thought Genji, who had long wanted to don the same garb. Tears came easily, and he was weeping again.

'I do not think it is anything serious,' he said, 'but for the last month and more she has been weak and has eaten very little.' He had a place set out for the emperor before the princess's curtains. 'I only wish we were better prepared for such an august visit.'

See note, page 13.

Her women dressed her and helped her to sit up.

'I feel like one of the priests you have on night duty,' said the emperor, pulling her curtains slightly aside. 'I am embarrassed that my prayers seem to be having so little effect. I thought you might want to see me, and so here I am, plain and undecorated.'

She was weeping. 'I do not think I shall live. May I ask you, while you are here, to administer vows?'

'A most admirable request, if you really mean it. But the fact that you are ill does not mean that you will die. Sometimes when a lady with years ahead of her takes vows she invites trouble, and the blame that is certain to go with it. We must not be hasty.' He turned to Genji. 'But she really does seem to mean it. If this is indeed her last hour, we would certainly not want to deny her the support and comfort of religion, however briefly.'

'She has been saying the same thing for some days now, but I have suspected that an outside force has made her say it. And so I have refused to listen.'

'I would agree if the force seemed to be pulling in the wrong direction. But the pain and regret of refusing a last wish – I wonder.'

He had had unlimited confidence in Genji, thought the emperor, and indications that Genji had no deep love for the princess had been a constant worry. Even now things did not seem to be going ideally well. He had been unable to discuss the matter with Genji. But now – might not a quiet separation be arranged, since there were no signs of a bitterness likely to become a scandal? Genji had no thought of withdrawing his support, it seemed clear, and so, taking his apparent willingness as the mark of his fidelity and himself showing no sign of resentment, might the emperor not even now make plans for disposing of his property, and appoint for her residence the fine Sanjō mansion which he had inherited from his father? He would know before he died that she had settled comfortably into the new life. However cold Genji might be he surely would not abandon her.

These thoughts must be tested.

'Suppose, then, while I am here, I administer the preliminary injunctions and give her the beginnings of a bond with the Blessed One.'

Regret and sorrow drove away the last of Genji's resentment. He went inside the princess's curtains. 'Must you think of leaving me when I have so little time before me? Do please try to bear with me a little longer. You must take your medicine and have something to eat. What you propose is very admirable, no doubt, but do you think you are up to the rigors it demands? Wait until you are well again and we will give it a little thought.'

But she shook her head. He was making things worse.

Though she said nothing, he could imagine that he had hurt her deeply, and he was very sorry. He remonstrated with her all through the night and presently it was dawn.

'I do not want to be seen by daylight,' said the Suzaku emperor. He summoned the most eminent of her priests and had them cut her hair. And so they were ravaged, the thick, smooth tresses now at their very best. Genji was weeping bitterly. She was the emperor's favorite, and she had been brought to this. His sleeves were wet with tears.

'It is done,' he said. 'Be happy and work hard at your prayers.'

The sun would be coming up. The princess still seemed very weak and was not up to proper farewells.

'It is like a dream,' said Genji. 'The memory of an earlier visit comes back and I am extremely sorry not to have received you properly. I shall call soon and offer apologies.'

He provided the emperor with an escort for the return journey.

'Fearing that I might go at any time,' said the emperor, 'and that awful things might happen to her, I felt that I had to make provision for her. Though I knew that I was going against your deeper wishes in asking you to take responsibility, I have been at peace since you so generously agreed to do so. If she lives, it will not become her new vocation to remain in such a lively establishment. Yet I suspect that she would be lonely in a mountain retreat like my own. Do please go on seeing to her needs as seems appropriate.'

'It shames me that you should find it necessary at this late date to speak of the matter. I fear that I am too shaken to reply.' And indeed he did seem to be controlling himself only with difficulty.

In the course of the morning services the malignant spirit emerged, laughing raucously. 'Well, here I am. You see what I have done. I was not at all happy, let me tell you, to see how happy you were with the lady you thought you had taken from me. So I stayed around the house for a while to see what I could do. I have done it and I will go.'

So she still had not left them! Genji was horrified, and regretted that they had let the princess take her vows. Though she now seemed a little more her old self she was very weak and not yet out of danger. Her women sighed and braced themselves for further efforts. Genji ordered that there be no slackening of the holy endeavors, and in general saw that nothing was left undone.

News of the birth seemed to push Kashiwagi nearer death. He was very sad for his wife, the Second Princess. It would be in bad taste for her to come visiting, however, and he feared that, whatever precautions were taken, she might suffer the embarrassment of being seen by his parents, who were always with him. He said that he would like to visit her, but they would not hear of it. He asked them, and others, to be good to her.

His mother-in-law had from the start been unenthusiastic about the match. Tō no Chūjō had pressed the suit most energetically, however, and, sensing ardor and sincerity, she had at length given her consent. After careful consideration the Suzaku emperor had agreed. Back in the days when he had been so worried about the Third Princess he had said that the Second Princess seemed nicely taken care of. Kashiwagi feared that he had sadly betrayed the trust.

'I hate to think of leaving her,' he said to his mother. 'But life does not go as we wish it. Her resentment at the promises I have failed to keep must be very strong. Do please be good to her.'

'You say such frightening things. How long do you think I would survive if you were to leave me?'

She was weeping so piteously that he could say no more, and so he tried discussing the matter of the Second Princess with his brother Kōbai.* Kashiwagi was a quiet, well-mannered youth, more father than brother to his youngest brothers, who were plunged into the deepest sorrow by these despairing remarks. The house rang with lamentations, which were echoed all through the court. The emperor ordered an immediate promotion to councillor of the first order.

'Perhaps,' he said, 'he will now find strength to visit us.'

The promotion did not have that happy effect, however. He could only offer thanks from his sickbed. This evidence of the royal esteem only added to Tō no Chūjō's sorrow and regret.

---

*Textual difficulties make it possible that this is either Kōbai or a younger brother.

A worried Yūgiri came calling, the first of them all to offer congratulations. The gate to Kashiwagi's wing of the house was jammed with carriages and there were crowds of well-wishers in his antechambers. Having scarcely left his bed since New Year, he feared that he would look sadly rumpled in the presence of such finery. Yet he hated to think that he might not see them again.

Yūgiri at least he must see. 'Do come in,' he said, sending the priests away. 'I know you will excuse my appearance.'

The two of them had always been the closest of friends, and Yūgiri's sorrow was as if he were a brother. What a happy day this would have been in other years! But of course these wishful thoughts accomplished nothing.

'Why should it have happened?' he said, lifting a curtain. 'I had hoped that this happy news might make you feel a little better.'

'I am very sorry indeed that I do not. I do not seem to be the man for such an honor.' Kashiwagi had put on a formal cap. He tried to raise his head but the effort was too much for him. He was wearing several pleasantly soft robes and lay with a quilt pulled over him. The room was in simple good taste and incenses and other details gave it a deep, quiet elegance. Kashiwagi was in fact rather carefully dressed, and great attention had obviously gone into all the appointments. One expects an invalid to look unkempt and even repulsive, but somehow in his case emaciation seemed to give a new fineness and delicacy. Yūgiri suffered with him as he struggled to sit up.

'But what a pleasant surprise,' said Yūgiri (though brushing away a tear). 'I would have expected to find you much thinner after such an illness. I actually think you are better-looking than ever. I had assumed, somehow, that we would always be together and that we would go together, and now this awful thing has happened. And I do not even know why. We have been so close, you and I – it upsets me more than I can say to know nothing about the most important matter.'

'I could not tell you if I wanted to. There are no marked symptoms. I have wasted away in this short time and scarcely know what is happening. I fear that I may no longer be in complete control of myself. I have lingered on, perhaps because of all the prayers of which I am so unworthy, and in my heart I have only wanted to be done with it all.

'Yet for many reasons I find it hard to go. I have only begun to do something for my mother and father, and now I must cause them pain. I am also being remiss in my duties to His Majesty. And as I look back over my life I feel sadder than I can tell you to think how little I have accomplished, what a short distance I have come. But there is something besides all this that has disturbed me very much. I have kept it to myself and doubt that I should say anything now that the end is in sight. But I must. I cannot keep it to myself, and how am I to speak of it if not to you? I do have all these brothers, but for many reasons it would do no good even to hint of what is on my mind.

'There was a matter which put me at cross purposes with your esteemed father and for which I have long been making secret apology. I did not myself approve of what I had done and I fell into a depression that made me avoid people, and finally into the illness in which you now see me. It was all too clear on the night of the rehearsal at Rokujō that he had not forgiven me. I did not see how it would be possible to go on living with his anger. I rather lost control of myself and began having nervous disturbances, and so I have become what you see.

'I am sure that I never meant very much to him, but I for my part have been very dependent on him since I was very young. Now a fear of the slanders he may have heard is my strongest bond with this world and may be the greatest obstacle on my journey into the next. Please remember what I have said and if you find an opportunity pass on my apologies to him. If after I am gone he is able to forgive whatever I have done, the credit must be yours.'

He was speaking with greater difficult. Yūgiri could think of details that seemed to fit into the story, but could not be sure exactly what the story had been.

'You are morbidly sensitive. I can think of no indication of displeasure on his part, and indeed he has been very worried about you and has said how he grieves for you. But why have you kept these things to yourself? I should surely have been the one to convey apologies in both directions, and now I suppose it is too late.' How he wished that they could go back a few years or months!

'I had long thought that when I was feeling a little better I must speak to you and ask your opinion. But of course it is senseless to go on thinking complacently about a life that could end today or tomorrow. Please tell no one of what I have said. I have spoken to you because I have hoped that you might find an opportunity to speak to him, very discreetly, of course. And if you would occasionally look in on the Second Princess. Do what you can, please, to keep her father from worrying about her.'

He wanted to say more, it would seem, but he was in ever greater pain. At last he motioned that he wanted Yūgiri to leave him. The priests and his parents and numerous others returned to his bedside. Weeping, Yūgiri made his way out through the confusion.

Kashiwagi's sisters, one of them married to Yūgiri and another to the emperor, were of course deeply concerned. He had a sort of fraternal expansiveness that reached out to embrace everyone. For Tamakazura he was the only one in the family who really seemed like a brother. She too commissioned services.

They were not the medicine he needed.* He went away like the foam upon the waters.

The Second Princess did not after all see him again. He had not been deeply in love with her, not, indeed, even greatly attached to her. Yet his behavior had been correct in every detail. He had been a gentle, considerate husband, making no demands upon her and giving no immediate cause for anger. Thinking sadly over their years together, she thought it strange that a man doomed to such a short life should have shown so little inclination to enjoy it. For her mother, the very worst had happened, though she had in a way expected it. Her daughter had married a commoner, and now everyone would find her plight very amusing.

Kashiwagi's parents were shattered. The cruelest thing is to have the natural order upset. But of course it had happened, and complaining did no good. The Third Princess, now a nun, had thought him impossibly presumptuous and had not joined in the prayers, but even she was sorry. Kashiwagi had predicted the birth of the child. Perhaps their strange, sad union had been joined in

*Anonymous, *Shūishū* 665:

> My sickness comes from unrequited longing.
> The medicine I need is brewed from heartvine.

There is the usual pun on *aoi*, 'heartvine' and 'day of meeting,' and there is the further association with the Kamo festival, which provided the occasion, in the preceding chapter, for Kashiwagi's first meeting with the Third Princess.

another life. It was a depressing chain of thoughts, and she was soon in tears.

The Third Month came, the skies were pleasant and mild, and the little boy reached his fiftieth day. He had a fair, delicate skin and was already showing signs of precociousness. He was even trying to talk.

Genji came visiting. 'And have you quite recovered? Whatever you say, it is a sad thing you have done. The occasion would be so much happier if you had not done it.' He seemed near tears. 'It was not kind of you.'

He now came to see her every day and could not do enough for her.

'What are you so worried about?' he said, seeing that her women did not seem to know how fiftieth-day ceremonies should be managed in a nun's household. 'If it were a girl the fact that the mother is a nun might seem to invite bad luck and throw a pall over things. But with a boy it makes no difference.'

He had a little place set out towards the south veranda of the main hall and there offered the ceremonial rice cakes. The nurse and various other attendants were in festive dress and the array of baskets and boxes inside the blinds and out covered the whole range of colors – for the managers of the affair were uninhibited by a knowledge of the sad truth. They were delighted with everything, and Genji smarted and squirmed.

Newly risen from her sickbed, the princess found her heavy hair very troublesome and was having it brushed. Genji pulled her curtains aside and sat down. She turned shyly away, more fragile than ever. Because there had been such regrets for her lovely hair only a very little had been cut away, and only from the front could one see that it had been cut at all. Over several grayish singlets she wore a robe of russet. The profile which she showed him was charming, in a tiny, childlike way, and not at all that of a nun.

'Very sad, really,' said Genji. 'A nun's habit is depressing, there is no denying the fact. I had thought I might find some comfort in looking after you as always, and it will be a very long time before my tears have dried. I had thought that it might help to tax myself with whatever unwitting reasons I may have given you for dismissing me. Yes, it is very sad. How I wish it were possible to go back.

'If you move away I shall have to conclude that you really do reject me, with all your heart, and I do not see how I shall be able to face you again. Do please have a thought for me.'

'They tell me that nuns tend to be rather withdrawn from ordinary feelings, and I seem to have been short on them from the start. What am I to say?'

'You are not fair to yourself. We have had ample evidence of your feelings.' He turned to the little boy.

The nurse and the other attendants were all handsome, well-born women whom Genji himself had chosen. He now summoned them for a conference.

'What a pity that I should have so few years left for him.'

He played with the child, fair-skinned and round as a ball, and bubbling with good spirits. He had only very dim memories of Yūgiri as a boy, but thought he could detect no resemblance. His royal grandchildren of course had their father's blood in their veins and even now carried themselves with regal dignity, but no one would have described them as outstandingly handsome. This boy was beautiful, there was no other word for it. He was always laughing, and a very special light would come into his eyes which fascinated Genji. Was it Genji's imagination that he looked like his father? Already there was a sort of tranquil poise that quite put one to shame, and the glow of the skin was unique.

The princess did not seem very much alive to these remarkable good looks, and of course almost no one else knew the truth. Genji was left alone to shed a tear for Kashiwagi, who had not lived to see his own son. How very unpredictable life is! But he brushed the tear away, for he did not want it to cloud a happy occasion.

'I think upon it in quiet,' he said softly, 'and there is ample cause for lamenting.'*

His own years fell short by ten of the poet's fifty-eight, but he feared that he did not have many ahead of him. 'Do not be like your father':† this, perhaps, was the admonition in his heart. He

---

*Po Chü-i, Collected Works, XXVIII, on the birth of a son in his old age:

> I think upon it in quiet. There is ample cause for joy,
> And ample cause for lamenting.

†From the same poem.

wondered which of the women might be in the princess's confidence. He could not be sure, but they were no doubt laughing at him, whoever they were. Well, he could bear the ridicule, and a discussion of his responsibilities and hers in the sad affair would be more distressing for her than for him. He would say nothing and reveal nothing.

The little boy was charming, especially the smiling, happy eyes and mouth. Would not everyone notice the resemblance to the father? Genji thought of Kashiwagi, unable to show this secret little keepsake to his grieving parents, who had longed for at least a grandchild to remember him by. He thought how strange it was that a young man so composed and proud and ambitious should have destroyed himself. His resentment quite left him, and he was in tears.

'And how does he look to you?' Genji had taken advantage of a moment when there were no women with the princess. 'It is very sad to think that in rejecting me you have rejected him too.'

She flushed.

'Yes, very sad,' he continued softly.

'Should someone come asking when the seed was dropped,
What shall it answer, the pine among the rocks?'

She lay with her head buried in a pillow. He saw that he was hurting her, and fell silent. But he would have liked to know what she thought of her own child. He did not expect mature discernment of her, but he would have liked to think that she was not completely indifferent. It was very sad indeed.

Yūgiri was sadder than the dead man's brothers. He could not forget that last interview and the mysterious matters which Kashiwagi had been unable to keep to himself. What had he been trying to say? Yūgiri had not sought to press for more. The end had been in sight, and it would have been too unfeeling. Though not seriously ill, it would seem, the princess had simply and effortlessly taken her vows. Why, and why had Genji permitted them? On the very point of death Murasaki had pleaded that he let her become a nun, and he had quite refused to listen. So Yūgiri went on sifting through such details as he had. More than once he had seen Kashiwagi's feelings go out of control. Kashiwagi had been calmer and more careful and deliberate than most young men, so quietly in possession of himself, indeed, that his reserve had made people uncomfortable. But he had had his weak side too. Might an excess of gentleness have been at the root of the trouble? Yūgiri found it hard to understand any excess that could make a man destroy himself. Kashiwagi had not done well by the princess, but for Yūgiri the wrong was of a more general nature. Perhaps there were conditions which Kashiwagi had brought with him from former lives – but Yūgiri found such a loss of control difficult to accept even so. He kept his thoughts to himself, saying nothing even to his wife, Kashiwagi's sister. He wanted very much to see what effect those oblique hints might have on Genji, but found no occasion.

Tō no Chūjō and his wife seemed barely conscious of the passing days. All the details of the weekly memorial services, clerical robes and the like, were left to their sons. Kōbai, the oldest, gave particular attention to images and scriptures. When they sought to arouse their father for the services, his reply was as if he too might be dying.

'Do not come to me. I am as you see me, lost to this world. I would be an obstacle on his way through the next.'

For the Second Princess there was the added sorrow of not having been able to say goodbye. Sadly, day after day, she sat looking over the wide grounds of her mother's Ichijō house, now almost deserted. The men of whom Kashiwagi had been fondest did continue to stop by from time to time. His favorite grooms and falconers seemed lost without him. Even now they were wandering disconsolately over the grounds. The sight of them, and indeed every small occurrence, summoned back the unextinguishable sadness. Kashiwagi's belongings gathered dust. The lute and the Japanese koto upon which he had so often played were silent and their strings were broken. The very air of the place spoke of sorrow and neglect. The princess gazed sadly out at the garden, where the trees wore the green haze of spring. The blossoms had none of them forgotten their proper season.

Late one morning, as dull as all the others, there was a vigorous shouting of outrunners and a procession came up to the gate.

'We had forgotten,' said one of the women. 'It almost seemed for a moment that His Lordship had come back.'

The princess's mother had thought that it would be one or more of Kashiwagi's brothers, who were frequent callers, but the caller was in fact more stately and dignified than they. It was

Yūgiri. He was offered a seat near the south veranda of the main hall. The princess's mother herself came forward to receive him – it would have been impolite to send one of the women.

'I may assure you,' said Yūgiri, 'that I have been sadder than if he were my brother. But there are restraints upon an outsider and I was able to offer only the most perfunctory condolences. He said certain things at the end that have kept your daughter very much on my mind. It is not a world in which any of us can feel secure, but until the day when it becomes clear which of us is to go first, I mean to exert myself in your behalf and hers in every way I can think of. Too much has been going on at court to let me follow my own inclinations and simply withdraw from things, and it would not have been very satisfying to look in on you and be on my way again. And so the days have gone by. I have heard that Tō no Chūjō is quite insane with grief. My own grief has only been less than his, and it has been deepened by the thought of the regret with which my friend must have left your daughter behind.'

His words were punctuated from time to time by a suggestion of tears. The old lady thought him very courtly and dignified and at the same time very approachable.

There were tears in her voice too, and when she had finished speaking she was weeping openly. 'Yes, the sad thing is that it should all be so uncertain and fleeting. I am old and I have tried to tell myself that worse things have happened. But when I see her lost in grief, almost out of her mind, I cannot think what to do. It almost comes to seem that I am the really unlucky one, destined to see the end of two brief lives.

'You were close to him and you may have heard how little inclined I was to accept his proposal. But I did not want to go against his father's wishes, and the emperor too seemed to have decided that he would make her a good husband. So I told myself that I must be the one who did not understand. And now comes this nightmare, and I must reprove myself for not having been truer to my very vague feelings. They did not of course lead me to expect anything so awful.

'I had thought, in my old-fashioned way, that unless there were really compelling reasons it was better that a princess not marry. And for her, poor girl, a marriage that should never have been has come to nothing. It would be better, I sometimes think, and people would not judge her harshly, if she were to let the smoke from her funeral follow his. Yet the possibility is not easy to accept, and I go on looking after her. It has been a source of very great comfort in all the gloom to have reports of your concern and sympathy. I do most sincerely thank you. I would not have called him an ideal husband, but it moves me deeply to learn that because you were so close to him you were chosen to hear his dying words, and that there were a few for her mixed in among them.'

She was weeping so piteously that Yūgiri too was in tears. 'It may have been because he was strangely old for his years that he came at the end to seem so extremely despondent. I had been foolish enough to fear that too much enlightenment might destroy his humanity and to caution him against letting it take the joy out of him. I fear that I must have given him cause to think me superficial. But it is your daughter I am saddest for, though you may think it impertinent of me to say so.' His manner was warm and open. 'Her grief and the waste seem worse than anything.'

This first visit was a short one.

He was five or six years younger than Kashiwagi, but a youthful receptivity had made Kashiwagi a good companion. Yūgiri had almost seemed the maturer of the two and certainly he was the more masculine, though his extraordinary good looks were also very youthful. He gave the young women who saw him off something happy to think about after all the sorrow.

There were cherry blossoms in the forward parts of the garden. 'This year alone'* – but the allusion did not seem a very apt one. 'If we wish to see them,'† he said softly, and added a poem of his own, not, however, as if he had a specific audience in mind.

> 'Although a branch of this cherry tree has withered,
>   It bursts into new bloom as its season comes.'

The old lady was prompt with her answer, which was sent out to him as he was about to leave:

> 'The willow shoots this spring, not knowing where
>   The petals may have fallen, are wet with dew.'

---

*See note†, page 355.

†Anonymous, *Kokinshū* 97:

> We may be sure that the cherries will come again.
> If we wish to see them we have but to stay alive.

She had not perhaps been the deepest and subtlest of the Suzaku emperor's ladies, but her talents had been much admired, and quite properly so, he thought.

He went next to Tō no Chūjō's mansion, where numerous sons were gathered. After putting himself in order Tō no Chūjō received him in the main drawing room. Sorrow had not destroyed his good looks, though his face was thin and he wore a bushy beard, which had been allowed to grow all during his son's illness. He seemed to have been more affected by his son's death than even by his mother's. The sight of him came near reducing Yūgiri to tears, but he thought weeping the last thing the occasion called for. Tō no Chūjō was less successful at controlling his tears, for Yūgiri and the dead youth had been such very close friends. The talk was of the stubborn, lingering sadness, and as it moved on to other matters Yūgiri told of his interview with the Second Princess's mother. This time the minister's tears were like a sudden spring shower. Yūgiri took out a piece of notepaper on which he had jotted down the old lady's poem.

'I'm afraid I can't make it out,' said Tō no Chūjō, trying to see through his tears. The face once so virile and proud had been softened by grief. Though the poem was not a particularly distinguished one the image about the dew on the willow shoots seemed very apt and brought on a new flood of tears.

'The autumn your mother died I thought that sorrow could not be crueler. But she was a woman, and one does not see very much of women. They tend to have few friends and to stay out of sight. My sorrow was an entirely private matter. My son was not a remarkably successful man, but he did attract the emperor's gracious notice and as he grew older he rose in rank and influence, and more and more people looked to him for support. After their various circumstances they were all upset by his death. Not of course that my grief has to do with prestige and influence. It is rather that I remember him before all this happened, and see what a dreadful loss it is. I wonder if I will ever be the same again.'

Looking up into an evening sky which had misted over a dull gray, he seemed to notice for the first time that the tips of the cherry branches were bare. He jotted down a poem on the same piece of notepaper, beside that of the princess's mother.

'Drenched by the fall from these trees, I mourn for a child
   Who should in the natural order have mourned for me.'

Yūgiri answered:

> 'I doubt that he who left us wished it so,
> That you should wear the misty robes of evening.'

And Kashiwagi's brother Kōbai:

> 'Bitter, bitter – whom can he have meant
> To wear the misty robes ere the advent of spring?'

The memorial services were very grand. Kumoinokari, Yūgiri's wife, helped with them, of course, and Yūgiri made them his own special concern.

He frequently visited the Ichijō mansion of the Second Princess. There was something indefinably pleasant about the Fourth Month sky and the trees were a lovely expanse of new green; but the house of sorrows was quiet and lonely, and for the ladies who lived there each new day was a new trial.

It was in upon this sadness that he came visiting. Young grasses had sprung up all through the garden, and in the shade of a rock or a tree, where the sand covering was thin, wormwood and other weeds had taken over as if asserting an old claim. The flowers that had been tended with such care were now rank and overgrown. He thought how clumps of grass now tidy and proper in the spring would in the autumn be a dense moor humming with insects,* and he was in tears as he parted the dewy tangles and came up to the veranda. Rough blinds of mourning were hung all along the front of the house. Through them he could see gray curtains newly changed for the season. He had glimpses too of skirts that told of the presence of little page girls, very pretty and at the same time incongruously drab. A place was set out for him on the veranda, but the women protested that he should be treated with more ceremony. Vaguely unwell, the princess's mother had been resting. He looked out into the garden as he talked with her women, and the indifference of the trees brought new pangs of sorrow. Their branches intertwined, an oak† and a maple seemed younger than the rest.

See note, page 562.

†*Kashiwagi, Quercus dentata.* The name by which the dead man has been traditionally known derives from this passage. Kashiwagi held a commission in the guards, of which the *kashiwagi* was a symbol.

'How reassuring. What bonds from other lives do you suppose have brought them together?' Quietly, he came nearer the blinds.

'By grace of the tree gold let the branch so close
    To the branch that withered be close to the branch that lives.

'I think it very unkind of you to keep me outdoors.' He leaned forward and put a hand on the sill.

The women were in whispered conversation about the gentler Yūgiri they were being introduced to. Among them was one Shōshō,* through whom came the princess's answer.

'There may not be a god protecting the oak.
    Think not, even so, its branches of easy access.

'There is a kind of informality that can suggest a certain shallowness.'

He smiled. It was a point well taken. Sensing that her mother had come forward, he brought himself to attention.

'My days have been uninterrupted gloom, and that may be why I have not been feeling well.' She did indeed seem to be unwell. 'I have been unable to think what to do next. You are very kind to come calling so often.'

'Your grief is quite understandable, but you should not let it get the better of you. Everything is determined in other lives, everything has its time and goes.'

The princess seemed to be a more considerable person than he had been led to expect. She had had wretched luck, belittled in the first instance for having married beneath her and now for having been left a widow. He thought he might find her interesting, and questioned the mother with some eagerness. He did not expect great beauty, but one could be fond of any lady who was not repulsively ugly. Beauty could sometimes make a man forget himself, and the more important thing was an equable disposition.

'You must learn to tell yourself that I am as near as he once was.' His manner fell short of the insinuating, perhaps, but his earnestness did carry overtones all the same.

He was very imposing and dignified in casual court dress.

'His Lordship had a gentle sort of charm,' one of the women would seem to have whispered to another. 'There was no one

---

*We learn later that she is the princess's maternal cousin.

quite like him, really, for quiet charm and elegance. But just see this gentleman, so vigorous and manly, all aglow with good looks. You want to squeal with delight the minute you set eyes on him. There was no one like the other gentleman and there can't be many like this one either. If we need someone to look after us, well, we couldn't do much better.'

'The grass first greens on the general's grave,'* he said to himself, very softly.

There was no one, in a world of sad happenings near and remote, who did not regret Kashiwagi's passing. Besides the more obvious virtues, he had been possessed of a most extraordinary gentleness and sensitivity, and even rather improbable courtiers and women, even very old women, remembered him with affection and sorrow. The emperor felt the loss very keenly, especially when there were concerts. 'If only Kashiwagi were here.' The remark became standard on such occasions. Genji felt sadder as time went by. For him the little boy was a memento he could share with no one else. In the autumn the boy began crawling about on hands and knees.†

---

*A reference, say early commentaries, to an elegy by Ki no Arimasa which does not survive.

†Some texts conclude the chapter with a description of Genji's growing affection for the child.

CHAPTER 37

The Flute

Many still mourned Kashiwagi, who had vanished before his time. Genji tended to feel very deeply the deaths even of people who had been nothing to him, and he had been fond of Kashiwagi and had made him a constant companion. It is true that he had good reason to be angry, but the fond memories were stronger than the resentment. He commissioned a sutra reading on the anniversary of the death. And he was consumed with pity for the little boy, whose agent he secretly thought himself as he made a special offering of a hundred pieces of gold.* Tō no Chūjō was very grateful, though of course he did not know Genji's real reasons.

Yūgiri too made lavish offerings and commissioned his own memorial services. He was especially attentive to the Second Princess, more so, indeed, than her brothers-in-law. How generous he was, said Kashiwagi's parents, far more generous than they had any right to expect. But these evidences of the esteem in which the world had held their dead son only added to the bitterness of the regret.

The Suzaku emperor now worried about his second daughter, whose plight was no doubt the object of much malicious laughter. And his third daughter had become a nun, and cut herself off from the pleasures of ordinary life. The disappointment was in both cases very cruel. He had resolved, however, to concern himself no more with the affairs of this vulgar world, and he held his peace. He would think, in the course of his devotions, that the Third Princess would be at hers. Since she had taken her vows he had found numerous small occasions for writing to her. Thinking the mountain harvests rather wonderful, the bamboo shoots that thrust their way up through the undergrowth of a thicket near his retreat, the taro root from deeper in the mountains, he sent them off to the Third Princess with an affectionate letter at the end of which he said:

'My people make their way with great difficulty through the misty spring hills, and here, the merest token, is what I asked them to gather for you.

*Some three and a half pounds.

> 'Away from the world, you follow after me,
>   And may we soon arrive at the same destination.*

'It is not easy to leave the world behind.'

Genji came upon her in tears. He wondered why she should have these bowls ranged before her, and then saw the letter and gifts. He was much moved. The Suzaku emperor had written most feelingly of his longing and his inability, when life was so uncertain, to see her as he would wish. 'May we soon arrive at the same destination.' He would not have called it a notable statement, but the priestly succinctness was very effective all the same. Evidences of Genji's indifference had no doubt added to the emperor's worries.

Shyly the Third Princess set about composing her answer. She gave the messenger a figured blue-gray robe. Genji took up a scrap of paper half hidden under her curtains and found something written on it in a childlike, uncertain hand.

> 'Longing for a place not of this world,
>   May I not join you in your mountain dwelling?'

'He worries so about you,' said Genji. 'It is not kind of you to say these things.'

She turned away from him. The still-rich hair at her forehead and the girlish beauty of her profile seemed very sad. Because the sadness was urging him towards something he might regret and be taken to task for, he pulled a curtain between them, trying very hard all the same not to seem distant or chilly.

The little boy, who had been with his nurse, emerged from her curtains. Very pretty indeed, he tugged purposefully at Genji's sleeve. He was wearing a robe of white gossamer and a red chemise of a finely figured Chinese weave. All tangled up in his skirts, he seemed bent on divesting himself of these cumbersome garments and had stripped himself naked to the waist. Though of course it is the sort of thing all little children do, he was so pretty in his dishabille that Genji was reminded of a doll carved from a newly stripped willow. The shaven head had the blue-black tinge of the dewflower,† and the lips were red and full. Already there

---

*There is a pun on *tokoro*, 'taro root' and 'place.' It is repeated in the princess's poem.

†*Tsuyukusa.*

was a sort of quelling repose about the eyes. Genji was strongly reminded of Kashiwagi, but not even Kashiwagi had had such remarkable good looks. How was one to explain them? There was scarcely any resemblance at all to the Third Princess. Genji thought of his own face as he saw it in the mirror, and was not sure that a comparison of the two was ridiculous. Able to walk a few steps, the boy tottered up to a bowl of bamboo shoots. He bit at one and, having rejected it, scattered them in all directions.

'What vile manners! Do something, someone. Get them away from him. These women are not kind, sir, and they will already be calling you a little glutton. Will that please you?' He took the child in his arms. 'Don't you notice something rather different about his eyes? I have not seen great numbers of children, but I would have thought that at his age they are children and no more, one very much like another. But he is such an individual that he worries me. We have a little princess in residence, and he may be her ruination and his own. Will I live, I wonder, to watch them grow up? "If we wish to see them we have but to stay alive." '* He was gazing earnestly at the little boy.

'Please, my lord. That is as good as inviting bad luck,' said one of the women.

Just cutting his teeth, the boy had found a good teething object. He dribbled furiously as he bit at a bamboo shoot.

'I see that his desires take him in a different direction,' Genji said, laughing.

'We cannot forget unpleasant associations.
We do not discard the young bamboo even so.'

He parted child and bamboo, but the boy only laughed and went on about his business.

He was more beautiful by the day, so beautiful that people were a little afraid for him. Genji was beginning to think that it might in fact be possible to 'forget unpleasant associations.' It had been predestined, no doubt, that such a child be born, and there had been no escaping them. But so often in his life thoughts about predestination had failed to make actual events more acceptable. Of all the ladies in his life the Third Princess had had the most to

*See note†, page 697.

recommend her. The bitterness surged forward once more and the transgression seemed very hard to excuse.

Yūgiri still thought a great deal about Kashiwagi's last words. He wanted to see how they might affect Genji. But of course he had very little to go on, and it would not be easy to think of the right questions. He could only wait and hope that he might one day have the whole truth, and a chance to tell Genji of Kashiwagi's dying thoughts.

On a sad autumn evening he visited the Second Princess. She had apparently been having a quiet evening with her music. He was shown to a south room where instruments and music still lay scattered about. The rustling of silk and the rich perfume as a lady who had been out near the south veranda withdrew to the inner rooms had a sort of mysterious elegance that he found very exciting. It was the princess's mother who as usual came out to receive him. For a time they exchanged reminiscences. Yūgiri's own house was noisy and crowded and he was used to troops of unruly children. The Ichijō house was by contrast quiet and even lonely. Though the garden had been neglected, an air of courtly refinement still hung over house and garden alike. The flower beds caught the evening light in a profusion of bloom and the humming of autumn insects was as he had imagined it in an earlier season.* He reached for a Japanese koto. Tuned now to a minor key, it seemed to have been much favored and still held the scent of the most recent player. This was no place, he thought, for the impetuous sort of young man. Unworthy impulses could too easily have their way, and the gossips something to amuse themselves with. Very competently, he played a strain on the koto he had so often heard Kashiwagi play.

'What a delight it was to hear him,' he said to the princess's mother. 'Dare I imagine that an echo of his playing might still be in the instrument, and that Her Highness might be persuaded to bring it out for us?'

'But the strings are broken,† and she seems to have forgotten all that she ever knew. I am told that when His Majesty had his

See note, page 533.
†Probably a literary reference. A poem in the *Kagerō Nikki* and a neo-Taoist tale have been averred.

daughters at their instruments he did not think her the least talented of them. But so much time has gone by since she last had much heart for music, and I am afraid that it would only be cause to remember.'*

'Yes, one quite understands. "Were it a world which puts an end to sorrow." '† Looking out over the garden, he pushed the koto towards the old lady.

'No, please. Let me hear more, so that I may decide whether an echo of his playing does indeed still remain in the instrument. Let it take away the unhappy sounds of more recent days.'

'But it is the sound of the middle string‡ that is important. I cannot hope to have it from my own hand.'

He pushed the koto under the princess's blinds, but she did not seem inclined to take it. He did not press her.

The moon had come out in a cloudless sky. And what sad, envious thoughts would the calls of the wild geese, each wing to wing with its mate, be summoning up? The breeze was chilly. In the autumn sadness she played a few notes, very faintly and tentatively, on a Chinese koto. He was deeply moved, but wished that he had heard more or nothing at all. Taking up a lute, he softly played the Chinese lotus song with all its intimate overtones.**

'I would certainly not wish to seem forward, but I had hoped that you might have something to say in the matter.'

But it was a melody that brought inhibitions, and she kept her sad thoughts to herself.

> 'There is a shyness which is more affecting
> Than any sound of word or sound of koto.'††

---

*Another unidentified reference, apparently. That there should be two such references in a single speech suggests that the old lady wishes to sound literary and is letting her references fall where they may.

†Sakanoe Korenori, *Kokin Rokujō, Zoku Kokka Taikan* 33417:

> Were it a world which puts an end to sorrow,
> Then ours by now should surely have had an end.

‡An obscure pun, signifying on the one hand a marriage and on the other a koto string. The difficulty is that the expression seems to have been part of the jargon associated with a variety of Chinese koto, but not with the Japanese koto.

**See note*, page 468.

††*Koto* also means 'word.'

Her response was to play the last few measures of the Chinese song. She added a poem:

'I feel the sadness, in the autumn night.
How can I speak of it if not through the koto?'

He was resentful that he had heard so little. The solemn tone of the Japanese koto, the melody which the one now gone had so earnestly taught her, were as they had always been, and yet there was something chilling, almost menacing in them.

'Well, I have plucked away on this instrument and that and kept my feelings no secret. My old friend is perhaps reproving me for having enjoyed so much of the autumn night with you. I shall come again, though you may be sure that I shall do nothing to upset you. Will you leave our koto as it is until then? People do have a way of thinking thoughts about a koto and about a lady.' And so he left hints, not too extremely broad, behind him.

'I doubt,' said the old lady, 'that anyone could reprove us for enjoying ourselves this evening. You have made the evening seem short with honest talk of the old days. I am sure that if you were to let me hear more of your playing it would add years to my life.'

She gave him a flute as he left.

'It is said to have a rich past. I would hate to have it lost among these tangles of wormwood. You must play on it as you leave and drown out the calls of your runners. That would give me great pleasure.'

'Far too valuable an addition to my retinue.'

It did indeed have a rich past. It had been Kashiwagi's favorite. Yūgiri had heard him say more than once that it had possibilities he had never done justice to, and that he wanted it to have an owner more worthy of it. Near tears once more, he blew a few notes in the *banjiki* mode,* but did not finish the melody he had begun.

'My inept pluckings on the koto may perhaps be excused as a kind of memorial, but this flute leaves me feeling quite helpless, wholly inadequate.'

The old lady sent out a poem:

'The voices of insects are unchanged this autumn,
Rank though the grasses be round my dewy lodging.'

*Based on B.

He sent back:

> 'The melody is as it always was.
> The voices that mourn are inexhaustible.'

Though it was very late, he left with great reluctance.

His house was firmly barred and shuttered, and everyone seemed to be asleep. Kumoinokari's women had suggested that his kindness to the Second Princess was more than kindness, and she was not pleased to have him coming home so late at night. It is possible that she was only pretending to be asleep.

'My mountain girl and I,'* he sang, in a low but very good voice.

'This place is locked up like a fort. A dark hole of a place. Some people do not seem to appreciate moonlight.'

He had the shutters raised and himself rolled up the blinds. He went out to the veranda.

'Such a moon, and there are people sound asleep? Come on out. Be a little more friendly.'

But she was unhappy and pretended not to hear. Little children were sprawled here and there, sound asleep, and there were clusters of women, also asleep. It was a thickly populated scene, in sharp contrast to the mansion from which he had just come. He blew a soft strain on his new flute. And what would the princess be thinking in the wake of their interview? Would she indeed, as he had requested, leave the koto and the other instruments in the same tuning? Her mother was said to be very good on the Japanese koto. He lay down. In public Kashiwagi had shown his wife all the honors due a princess, but they had seemed strangely hollow. Yūgiri wanted very much to see her, and at the same time feared that he would be disappointed. One was often disappointed when the advance reports were so interesting. His thoughts turned to his own marriage. All through the years he had given not the smallest cause for jealousy. He had given his wife ample cause, perhaps, to be somewhat overbearing.

*"My Girl and I,' a Saibara:

> My mountain girl and I
> Must avoid the mountain magnolias.
> The scent upon our sleeves
> Is strong enough already.

He dozed off and dreamed that Kashiwagi was beside him, dressed as on their last meeting. He had taken up the flute. How unsettling, Yūgiri said to himself, still dreaming, that his friend should still be after the flute.

'If it matters not which wind sounds the bamboo flute,
  Then let its note be forever with my children.

'I did not mean it for you.'

Yūgiri was about to ask for an explanation when he was awakened by the screaming of a child. It was screaming very lustily, and vomiting. The nurse was with it, and Kumoinokari, sending for a light and pushing her hair roughly behind her ears, had taken it in her arms. A buxom lady, she was offering a well-shaped breast. She had no milk, but hoped that the breast would have a soothing effect. The child was fair-skinned and very pretty.

'What seems to be the trouble?' asked Yūgiri, coming inside.

The noise and confusion had quite driven away the sadness of the dream. One of the women was scattering rice to exorcise malign spirits.

'We have a sick child on our hands and here you are prancing and dashing about like a young boy. You open the shutters to enjoy your precious moonlight and let in a devil or two.'

He smiled. She was still very young and pretty. 'They have found an unexpected guide. I suppose if it had not been for me they would have lost their way? A mother of many children acquires great wisdom.'

'Go away, if you will, please.' He was so handsome that she could think of nothing more severe to say. 'You should not be watching.'

She did indeed seem to find the light too strong. Her shyness was not at all unattractive.

The child kept them awake the whole night.

Yūgiri went on thinking about the dream. The flute was threatening to raise difficulties. Kashiwagi was still attached to it, and so perhaps it should have stayed at Ichijō. It should not, in any case, have been passed on to Yūgiri by a woman. But what had Kashiwagi meant, and what would he be thinking now? Because of the regret and the longing he must wander in stubborn darkness, worrying about trifles. One did well to avoid such entanglements.

He had services read on Mount Otagi* and at a temple favored by Kashiwagi. But what to do about the flute? It had a rich history, the old lady had said. Offered immediately to a temple it might do a little toward the repose of Kashiwagi's soul. Yet he hesitated.

He visited Rokujō.

Genji, he was told, was with his daughter.

Murasaki had been given charge of the Third Prince, now three, the prettiest of Genji's royal grandchildren. He came running up.

'If you're going over there, General, take my royal highness with you.'

Yūgiri smiled at this immodest language. 'If you wish to go. But am I to walk past a lady's curtains without a by-your-leave? That would be very rude.' He took the little prince in his arms.

'No one will see. Look, I'll cover your face. Let's go, let's go.'

He was charming as he covered Yūgiri's face with his sleeves. The two of them went off to the Akashi princess's apartments. The Second Prince was there, as was Genji's little son. Genji was fondly watching them at play. Yūgiri deposited the Third Prince in a corner, where the Second Prince discovered him.

'Carry me too, General,' he commanded.

'He's my general,' objected the Third Prince, refusing to dismiss him.

'Don't you have any manners, the two of you?' said Genji. 'He is supposed to guard your father, and you are appropriating him for yourselves. And you, young sir,' he said to the Third Prince, 'are just a little too pushy. You are always trying to get the best of your brother.'

'And the other one,' said Yūgiri, 'is very much the big brother, always willing to give way if it seems the right thing. Such a fine young gentleman that I'm already a little afraid of him.'

Genji smiled. They were both of them very fine lads indeed. 'But come. This is no place for an important official to be wasting his time.'

He started off towards the east wing, trailing children behind him. His own little boy ought not to be so familiar with the princes – but the usual awareness of such things told him that any sort of discrimination would hurt the Third Princess. She had a bad

*Crematory grounds to the east of the city.

conscience and was easily hurt. He too was a very pretty boy, and Genji had grown fond of him.

Yūgiri had seen very little of the boy. Picking up a fallen cherry branch he motioned towards the blinds. The boy came running out. He had on but a single robe, of a deep purple. The fair skin glowed, and there was in the round little figure something, an extraordinary refinement, that rather out did the princes. Perhaps, thought Yūgiri, he had chanced to catch an unusual angle; but it did seem to him that there was remarkable strength in the eyes, and the arch of the eyebrows reminded him very much of Kashiwagi. And that sudden glow when he laughed – perhaps, thought Yūgiri, he had caught a very rare moment – but Genji must surely have noticed. He really must do a bit of probing.

The princes were princes, already proud and courtly, but they had the faces of pretty children, no more. The other boy, he thought, looking from one child to another, had a most uncommon face and manner. How very sad. Tō no Chūjō, half lost to the world, kept asking why no one came demanding to be recognized as Kashiwagi's son, why there were no keepsakes. If Yūgiri's suspicions were well founded, then to keep the secret from the bereaved grandfather would be a sin. But Yūgiri could not be sure. He still had no real solution to the puzzle, nothing to go on. He was delighted with the child, who seemed unusually gentle and affectionate.

They talked quietly on and it was evening. Genji listened smiling to Yūgiri's account of his visit to Ichijō the evening before.

'So she played the lotus song. That is the sort of thing a lady with the old graces would do. Yet one might say that she allowed an ordinary conversation to take an unnecessarily suggestive turn. You behaved quite properly when you told her that you wished to carry out the wishes of a dead friend and be of assistance to her. The important thing is that you continue to behave properly. Both of you will find the clean, friendly sort of relationship the more rewarding.'

Yes, thought Yūgiri, his father had always been ready with good advice. And how would Genji himself have behaved in the same circumstances?

'How can you even suggest that there has been anything improper? I am being kind to her because her marriage lasted such a tragically short time, and what suspicions would it give rise to if my kindness were to be equally short-lived? Suggestive, you say. I might have been tempted to use the word if she had offered the lotus song on her own initiative. But the time was exactly right, and the gentle fragment I heard seemed exactly right too. She is not very young any more, and I think I am a rather steady sort, and so I suppose she felt comfortable with me. Everything tells me that she is a gentle, amiable sort of lady.'

The moment seemed ripe. Coming a little closer, he described his dream. Genji listened in silence and was not quick to answer. It did of course mean something to him.

'Yes, there are reasons why I should have the flute. It belonged to the Yōzei emperor and was much prized by the late Prince Shikibu.* Remarking upon Kashiwagi's skills, the prince gave it to him one day when we had gathered to admire the *hagi*. I should imagine that the princess's mother did not quite know what she was doing when she gave it to you.'

He understood Kashiwagi's reference to his own descendants. He suspected that Yūgiri was too astute not to have understood also.

The expression on Genji's face made it difficult for Yūgiri to proceed, but having come this far, he wanted to tell everything. Hesitantly, as if he had just this moment thought of something else, he said: 'I went to see him just before he died. He gave me a number of instructions, and said more than once that he had reasons for wanting very much to apologize to you. I have fretted a great deal over the remark, and even now I cannot imagine what he may have had in mind.'

He spoke very slowly and hesitantly. Genji was convinced that he did indeed know the truth. Yet there seemed no point in making a clean breast of things long past.

After seeming to turn the matter over in his mind for a time, he replied: 'I must on some occasion have aroused his resentment by seeming to reveal sentiments which in fact were not mine. I can-

---

Shikibukyō no miya, literally 'the princely minister of rites.' Murasaki's father and Asagao's father both held the position, though if it is the former we should have been told of his death, which would have put Murasaki's part of the Rokujō house into mourning. Another theory is that since the Yōzei emperor is a historical personage (he died in 949), so is this prince. Yōzei in fact had a younger brother who was minister of rites.

not think when it might have been. I shall give some quiet thought to that dream of yours, and of course I shall let you know if I come upon anything that seems significant. I have heard women say that it is unlucky to talk about dreams at night.'

It had not been a very satisfying answer. One is told that Yūgiri was left feeling rather uncomfortable.

CHAPTER 38

The Bell Cricket

In the summer, when the lotuses were at their best, the Third Princess dedicated holy images for her chapel. All the chapel fittings to which Genji had given such careful attention were put to use. There were soft, rich banners of an unusual Chinese brocade which were Murasaki's work, and the covers for the votive stands were of a similarly rich material, tie-dyed in subtle and striking colors. The curtains were raised on all four sides of the princess's bedchamber, at the rear of which hung a Lotus Mandala. Proud blossoms of harmonious colors had been set out in silver vases, while a 'hundred pace' Chinese incense spread through the chapel and beyond. The main image, an Amitābha, and the two attendants were graceful and delicately wrought, and all of sandalwood. The fonts, also small and delicate, held lotuses of white, blue, and purple.* Lotus-leaf pellets compounded with a small amount of honey had been crushed to bits, to give off a fragrance that blended with the other to most wondrous effect.

The princess had had scrolls of the holy writ copied for each of the Six Worlds.† Genji himself had copied a sutra for her own personal use, and asked in the dedication that, having thus plighted their troth, they be permitted to go hand in hand down the way to the Pure Land. He had also made a copy of the Amitābha Sutra. Fearing that Chinese paper might begin to crumble after frequent use, he had ordered a fine, unmarked paper from the royal provisioner. He had been hard at work since spring and the results quite justified his labors. A glimpse of an unrolled corner was enough to tell the most casual observer that it was a masterpiece. The gilt lines were very good, but the sheen of the black ink and the contrast with the paper were quite marvelous. I shall not attempt to describe the spindle, the cover, and the box, save to say that they were all of superb workmanship. On a new aloeswood stand with flared legs, it occupied a central place beside the holy trinity.

---

*The colors suggest that they are artificial.

†Between heaven and hell, the worlds of starving demons, beasts, Asura, and men.

The chapel thus appointed, the officiants took their places and the procession assembled. Genji looked in upon the west antechamber, where the princess was in temporary residence. It seemed rather small, now crowded with some fifty or sixty elaborately dressed women, and rather warm as well. Indeed some of the little girls had been pushed out to the north veranda.

The censers were being tended so assiduously that the room was dark with their smoke. 'An incense is sometimes more effective,' said Genji, thinking that these giddy novices needed advice, 'when one can scarcely tell where it is coming from. This is like a smoldering Fuji. And when we gather for these ceremonies we like to get quietly to the heart of the matter, and would prefer to be without distractions. Too emphatic a rustling of silk, for instance, gives an unsettling awareness of being in a crowd.'

Tiny and pretty and overwhelmed by the crowd, the princess was leaning against an armrest.

'The boy is likely to be troublesome,' he added. 'Suppose you have someone put him out of sight.'

Blinds hung along the north side of the room in place of the sliding doors, and it was there that the women were gathered. Asking for quiet, he gave the princess necessary instructions, politely and very gently. The sight of her bedchamber now made over into a chapel moved him to tears.

'And so here we are, rushing into monkish ceremonies side by side. Who would have expected it? Let us pray that we will share blossomstrewn lodgings in the next world.'

Borrowing her inkstone, he wrote a poem on her cloves-dyed fan:

'Separate drops of dew on the leaf of the lotus,
We vow that we will be one, on the lotus to come.'

She answered:

'Together, you say, in the lotus dwelling to come.
But may you not have certain reservations?'

'And so my proposal is rejected, and I am castigated for it?' He was smiling, but it was a sad, meditative smile.

There were as usual large numbers of princes in the congregation. The other Rokujō ladies had sought to outdo one another in the novelty and richness of their offerings, which quite overflowed the princess's rooms. Murasaki had seen to the most essential provisions, robes for the seven officiants and the like. They were all of brocade, and people with an eye for such things could see that every detail, the most inconspicuous seam of a surplice, for instance, was of unusually fine workmanship. I feel compelled to touch upon very small details myself.

The sermon, by a most estimable cleric, described the significance of the occasion. It was entirely laudable, and food for profound thought, he said, that so young and lovely a lady should renounce the world and seek to find in the Lotus Sutra her future for all the lives to come. A gifted and eloquent man, he quite outdid himself today and had the whole congregation in tears.

Genji had wanted the dedication of the chapel and its images to be quiet and unpretentious, but the princess's brother and father had word of the preparations and sent representatives, and the proceedings suddenly became rather elaborate. Ceremonies which Genji sought to keep simple had a way of becoming elaborate from the outset, and the brilliance of these added offerings made one wonder what monastery would be large enough to accommodate them.

Genji's feelings for the princess had deepened since she had taken her vows. He was endlessly solicitous. Her father had indicated a hope that she might one day move to the Sanjō mansion, which he was giving her, and suggested that appearances might best be served if she were to go now.

'I would prefer otherwise,' said Genji. 'I would much prefer to have her here with me, so that I can look after her and ask her this and tell her that – I would feel sadly deprived if she were to leave me. No one lives forever and I do not expect to live much longer. Please do not deny me the pleasure while I am here.'

He spared no expense in remodeling the Sanjō mansion, where he made arrangements for storing the finest produce of her fields and pastures. He had new storehouses built and saw that all her treasures, gifts from her father and the rest, were put under heavy guard. He himself would be responsible for the general support of her large and complex household.

In the autumn he had the garden to the west of the main hall at Rokujō* done over to look like a moor. The altar and all the

---

*The princess has rooms at the west side of the main hall of the southeast quarter, the garden of which is best in the spring.

votive dishes were in gentle, ladylike taste. The princess readily agreed that the older of her women, her nurse among them, follow her in taking vows. Among the younger ones she chose only those whose resolve seemed firm enough to last out their lives. All of the others, caught up in a certain contagion, were demanding that they be admitted to the company.

Genji did not at all approve of this flight to religion. 'If any of you, I don't care how few, are not ready for it, you are certain to cause mischief, and the world will say that you have been rash and hasty.'

Only ten or so of them finally took vows.

Genji had autumn insects released in the garden moor, and on evenings when the breeze was cooler he would come visiting. The insect songs his pretext, he would make the princess unhappy by telling her once again of his regrets. He seemed to have forgotten her vows, and in general his behavior was not easily condoned. It was proper enough when there were others present, but he managed to make it very clear to her that he knew of her misdeeds. It was chiefly because she found his attentions so distasteful that she had become a nun. She had hoped that she might now find peace – and here he was with endless regrets. She longed to withdraw to a retreat of her very own, but she was not one to say so.

On the evening of the full moon, not yet risen, she sat near the veranda of her chapel meditatively invoking the holy name. Two or three young nuns were arranging flowers before the holy images. The sounds of the nunnery, so far from the ordinary world, the clinking of the sacred vessels and the murmur of holy water, were enough to induce tears.

Genji paid one of his frequent visits. 'What a clamor of insects you do have!' He joined her, very softly and solemnly, in the invocation to Amitābha.

None was brighter and clearer among the insects than the bell cricket, swinging into its song.*

'They all have their good points, but Her Majesty† seems to prefer the pine cricket. She sent some of her men a great distance

---

*There is a pun on *furiidetaru*, which suggests the swinging of a bell. The bell cricket and pine cricket of the Heian Period seem to have had their names reversed in the centuries since.

†Akikonomu.

to bring them in from the moors, but when she had them in her garden only a very few of them sang as sweetly for her as they had sung in the wilds. One would expect them to be as durable as pines, but in fact they seem to have short lives. They sing very happily off in forests and mountains where no one hears them, and that seems unsociable of them. These bell crickets of yours are so bright and cheerful.'

'The autumn is a time of deprivation,
    I have thought – and yet have loved this cricket.'

She spoke very softly and with a quiet, gentle elegance.
'What can you mean, "deprivation"?'

'Although it has chosen to leave its grassy dwelling,
    It cannot, this lovely insect, complain of neglect.'

He called for a koto and treated her to a rare concert. She quite forgot her beads. The moon having come forth in all its radiance, he sat gazing up at it, lost in thoughts of his own. What a changeable, uncertain world it is, he was thinking. His koto seemed to plead in sadder tones than usual.

Prince Hotaru, his brother, came calling, having guessed that on such an evening there would be music. Yūgiri was with him, and they were well and nobly attended. The sound of the koto led them immediately to the princess's rooms.

'Please do not call it a concert; but in my boredom I thought I might have a try at the koto I have so long neglected. Here I am playing for myself. It was good of you to hear and to come.'

He invited the prince inside.

One after another the high courtiers came calling. There was to have been a moon-viewing fete at the palace, but it had been canceled, to their very great disappointment. Then had come word that people were gathering at Rokujō.

There were judgments upon the relative merits of the insect songs.

'One is always moved by the full moon,' said Genji, as instrument after instrument joined the concert, 'but somehow the moon this evening takes me to other worlds. Now that Kashiwagi is no longer with us I find that everything reminds me of him. Something of the joy, the luster, has gone out of these occasions. When we were talking of the moods of nature, the flowers and the birds, he was the one who had interesting and sensitive things to say.'

The sound of his own koto had brought him to tears. He knew that the princess, inside her blinds, would have heard his remarks about Kashiwagi.

The emperor too missed Kashiwagi on nights when there was music.

Genji suggested that the whole night be given over to admiring the bell cricket. He had just finished his second cup of wine, however, when a message came from the Reizei emperor. Disappointed at the sudden cancellation of the palace fete, Kōbai and Shikibu no Tayū* had appeared at the Reizei Palace, bringing with them some of the more talented poets of the day. They had heard that Yūgiri and the others were at Rokujō.

'It does not forget, the moon of the autumn night,
    A corner remote from that realm above the clouds.

'Do please come, if you have no other commitments.'

Even though he in fact had few commitments these days and the Reizei emperor was living in quiet retirement, Genji seldom went visiting. It was sad that the emperor should have found it necessary to send for him. Despite the suddenness of the invitation he immediately began making ready.

'In your cloud realm the moonlight is as always,
    And here we see that autumn means neglect.'

It was not a remarkable poem, but it was honest, speaking of past intimacy and recent neglect. The messenger was offered wine and richly rewarded.

The procession, led by numerous outrunners and including Yūgiri and his friends Saemon no Kami and Tōsaishō,† formed in order of rank, and so Genji gave up his quiet evening at home. Long trains gave a touch of formality to casual court dress. It was late and the moon was high, and the young men played this and that air on their flutes as the spirit moved them. It was an unobtrusively elegant progress. Bothersome ceremony always went with a formal meeting, and Genji wished this one to take them back to

*Otherwise unknown, but probably another of Tō no Chūjō's sons.

†The former is certainly, and the latter probably, among Tō no Chūjō's many sons.

days when he had been less encumbered. The Reizei emperor was delighted. His resemblance to Genji was more striking as the years went by. The emperor had chosen to abdicate when he still had his best years ahead of him, and had found much in the life of retirement that pleased him.

The poetry, in Chinese and Japanese, was uniformly interesting and evocative, but I have fallen into an unfortunate habit of passing on but a random sampling of what I have heard, and shall say no more. The Chinese poems were read as dawn came over the sky, and soon afterwards the visitors departed.

Genji called on Akikonomu before returning to Rokujō.

'Now that you are not so busy,' he said, 'I often think how good it would be to pass the time of day with you and talk of the things one does not forget. But I am neither in nor out of the world, a very tiresome position. My meditations on the uselessness of it all are unsettled by an awareness of how many people younger than I are moving ahead down the true path; and so I want more and more to find myself a retreat away from everything. I have asked you to look after the one I would be leaving behind. I am sure that I can count on you.'

'I almost think that you are more inaccessible than when all those public affairs stood between us.' She managed, as always, to seem both youthful and wise. 'The thought that I would no longer have your kind advice and attention has been my chief reason for not following the example of so many others in renouncing the world. I have been very dependent on you and it is a painful thought.'

'I awaited with the greatest pleasure the visits which protocol allowed you to make, and know that I should not expect to see much of you now. It is an uncertain and unreliable world, and yet one is attached to it, and unless there are very compelling reasons cannot easily give it up. Even when the right time seems to have come and everything seems in order, the ties still remain. It must be with you as with everyone else, and if you join the competition for salvation which we see all around us you may be sure that your detractors will put the wrong light upon your conduct. I do hope that you can be persuaded to give up all thought of it.'

She feared that he did not, after all, understand. And in what smokes of hell would her poor mother be wandering? Genji had told no one that the vengeful spirit of the Rokujō lady had paid yet another visit. People will talk, however, and reports had presently reached Akikonomu, to make the whole world seem harsh and inhospitable. She wanted to hear her mother's exact words, or at least a part of them, but she could not bring herself to ask.

'I have been told, though I have no very precise information, that my mother died carrying a heavy burden of sin. Everything I know convinces me that it is true, but I fear I have been feeling too sorry for myself to do very much for her. I have been feeling very guilty and apologetic. I have become more and more convinced that I must find a holy man and ask him to be my guide in doing what should be done toward dispelling the smokes and fires.'

Genji was deeply moved. He quite understood her feelings. 'Most of us face those same fires, and yet a life as brief as the time of the morning dew continues to make its demands on us. We are told that among the disciples of the Blessed One there was a man who found immediate help in this world for a mother suffering in another,* but it is an achievement which few of us can hope to imitate. Regrets would remain for the jeweled tresses which you propose to cut. No, what you must do is strengthen yourself in the faith and pray that the flames are extinguished. I have had the same wishes, and still the days have gone purposelessly by, and the quiet for which I long seems very far away. In the quiet I could add prayers for her to prayers for myself, and these delays seem very foolish.'

So they talked of a world which, for all its trials and uncertainties, is not easy to leave.

What had begun as a casual visit had attracted the notice of the whole court, and courtiers of the highest ranks were with Genji when he left in the morning.

He had no worries for the Akashi princess, so responsive to all his hopes and efforts, or for Yūgiri, who had attained to remarkable eminence for his age. He thought rather more about the Reizei emperor than about either of them. It was because he had wanted to be master of his own time and to see more of Genji that the Reizei emperor had been so eager to abdicate.

---

*Maudgalyāyana, Japanese Mokuren, was given instruction by the Buddha himself on how to obtain his mother's release from one of the several hells.

Akikonomu found it harder than ever to visit Rokujō. She was now beside her husband like any ordinary housewife. There were concerts and other pleasures, and life was in many ways more interesting than before, the serenity disturbed only by fears for her mother. She turned more and more to her prayers, but had little hope that the Reizei emperor would let her become a nun. Prayers for her mother made her more aware than ever of the evanescence of things.*

---

*Some texts conclude with a brief reference to Genji's own efforts in behalf of the Rokujō lady.

CHAPTER 39

Evening Mist

Making full use of his name for probity and keeping to himself the fact he thought the Second Princess very interesting, Yūgiri let it seem to the world that he was only being faithful to an old friendship. He paid many a solemn visit, and came to feel more and more as the weeks and months went by that the situation was a little ridiculous. The princess's mother thought him the kindest of gentlemen. He provided the only relief from the loneliness and monotony of her life. He had given no hint of romantic intentions, and it would not do to proclaim himself a suitor. He must go on being kind, and the time would come, perhaps, when the princess would invite overtures. He took careful note, whenever an occasion presented itself, of her manners and tastes.

He was still awaiting his chance when her mother, falling into the clutches of an evil and very stubborn possession, moved to her villa at Ono. A saintly priest who had long guided her devotions and who had won renown as a healer had gone into seclusion on Mount Hiei and vowed never to return to the city. He would, however, come down to the foot of the mountain, and it was for that reason that she had moved to Ono. Yūgiri provided the carriage and escort for the move. Kashiwagi's brothers were too busy with their own affairs to pay much attention. Kōbai, the oldest of them, had taken an interest in the princess, but the bewilderment with which she had greeted evidence that it might be more than brotherly had made him feel unwelcome. Yūgiri had been cleverer, it would seem, keeping his intentions to himself. When there were religious services he would see to the vestments and offerings and all the other details. The old lady was too ill to thank him.

The women insisted that, given his stern devotion to the proprieties, he would not be pleased with a note from a secretary. The princess herself must answer. And so she did presently get off an answer. The hand was good, and the single line of poetry* was quietly graceful. The rest of the letter was gentle and amiable and

---

*This is conjecture. There is no specific statement that the 'single line' is poetry.

convinced him more than ever that he must see her. He wrote frequently thereafter. But Kumoinokari was suspicious and raising difficulties, and it was by no means easy for him to visit Ono.

The Eighth Month was almost over. At Ono the autumn hills would be at their best.

'That priest of hers, what is his name,' he said nonchalantly, 'has come down from the mountains. There is something I absolutely must talk to him about, and it is a rare opportunity. He comes so seldom. And her mother has not been at all well, and I have been neglecting her.'

He had with him five or six favored guardsmen, all in travel dress. Though the road led only through the nearer hills, the autumn colors were good, especially at Matsugasaki, in gently rolling country.

The Ono villa had an air of refinement and good taste that would have distinguished the proudest mansion in the city. The least conspicuous of the wattled fences was done with a flair which showed that a temporary dwelling need not be crude or common. A detached room at the east front of what seemed to be the main building had been fitted out as a chapel. The mother's room faced north and the princess had rooms to the west.

These evil spirits are greedy and promiscuous, the mother had said, begging the princess to stay behind in the city. But the princess had insisted upon coming. How could she bear to be so far from her mother? She was forbidden access to the sickroom, however.

Since they were not prepared to receive guests, Yūgiri was shown to a place at the princess's veranda, whence messages were taken to her mother.

'You are very kind indeed to have come such a distance. You make me feel that I must live on – how else can I thank you for the extraordinary kindness?'

'I had hoped that I myself might be your escort, but my father had things for me to do. My own trivial affairs have occupied me since, and so I have neglected you. I should be very sorry indeed if at any time it might have seemed to you that I did not care.'

Behind her curtains, the princess listened in silence. He was aware of her presence, for the blinds were flimsy and makeshift. An elegant rustling of silk told him what part of the room to be interested in. He used the considerable intervals between messages from the old lady to remonstrate with Koshōshō and the others.

'It has been some years now since I began visiting you and trying to be of service. This seems like a very chilly reception after such a record. I am kept outside and allowed only the diluted conversation that is possible through messengers. It is not the sort of thing my experience has prepared me for. Though of course it may be my lack of experience that is responsible. If I had been a trifling sort in my younger years I might possibly have learned to avoid making myself look silly. There can be few people my age who are so stupidly, awkwardly honest.'

Yes, some of the women were whispering. He had every right to complain, and he was not the sort of underling one treated so brusquely.

'It will be embarrassing, my lady, if you try to put him off. You will seem obtuse and insensitive.'

'I am very sorry indeed that she seems too ill to answer your kind inquiry in the way that it deserves,' the princess finally sent out. 'I shall try to answer for her. Whatever spirit it is that has taken possession of her, it seems to be of an unusually baneful sort, and so I have come from the city to be her nurse. I almost feel that I am no longer among the living myself. I fear you will think this no answer at all.'

'These are her own words?' he said, bringing himself to attention. 'I have felt, all through this sad illness, as if I myself were the victim. And do you know what that has been? It may seem rude and impertinent of me to say so, but until she has fully and happily recovered, the most important thing to all of us is that you yourself remain healthy and in good spirits. It is you I have been thinking of. If you have been telling yourself that my only concern is for your mother, then you have failed to sense the depth and complexity of my feelings.'

True, perfectly true, said the women.

Soon it would be sunset. Mists were rising, and the mountain fastnesses seemed already to be receding into night. The air was heavy with the songs of the evening cicadas. Wild carnations at the hedge and an array of autumn flowers near the veranda caught the evening light. The murmur of waters was cool. A brisk wind came down from the mountain with a sighing of deep pine forests. As bells announced that a new relay of priests had come on duty, the solemnity of the services was redoubled, new voices joined to the old. Every detail strengthened the spell that was falling over him.

He wanted to stay on and on. The voice of the priest who had come down from the mountain was grander and more solemn than the rest.

Someone came to inform them that the princess's mother was suddenly in great pain. Women rushed to her side, and so the princess, who had brought few women with her in any event, was almost alone. She said nothing. The time for an avowal seemed to have arrived.

A bank of mist came rolling up to the very eaves.

'What shall I do?' he said. 'The road home is blocked off.

'An evening mist – how shall I find my way? –
  Makes sadder yet a lonely mountain village.'*

'The mists which enshroud this rustic mountain fence
  Concern him only who is loathe to go.'

He found these soft words somewhat encouraging and was inclined to forget the lateness of the hour.

'What a foolish predicament. I cannot see my way back, and you will not permit me to wait out the mists here at Ono. Only a very naïve man would have permitted it to happen.'

Thus he hinted at feelings too strong to control. She had pretended to be unaware of them and was greatly discommoded to have them stated so clearly. Though of course he was not happy with her silence, he was determined to seize the opportunity. Let her think him frivolous and rude. She must be informed of the feelings he had kept to himself for so long. He quietly summoned one of his attendants, a junior guards officer who had not long before received the cap of the Fifth Rank.

'I absolutely must speak to His Reverence, the one who has come down from the mountain. He has been wearing himself out praying for her, and I imagine he will soon be taking a rest. The best thing would be to stay the night and try to see him when the evening services are over.'

He gave instructions that the guard go to his Kurusuno villa, not far away, and see to feeding the horses.

'I don't want a lot of noise. It will do no good to have people know we are here.'

Sensing hidden meanings, the man bowed and withdrew.

---

*Yūgiri means 'evening mist.' The appellation derives from this poem.

'I would doubtless lose my way if I tried to go home,' Yūgiri continued unconcernedly. 'Perhaps there are rooms for me somewhere hereabouts? This one here by your curtains – may I ask you to let me have the use of it? I must see His Reverence. He should be finishing his prayers very shortly.'

She was most upset. This insistent playfulness was not like him. She did not want to offend him, however, by withdrawing pointedly to the sickroom. He continued his efforts to coax her from her silence, and when a woman went in with a message he followed after.

It was still daylight, but the mists were heavy and the inner rooms were dark. The woman was horrified at having thus become his guide. The princess, sensing danger, sought to make her escape through the north door, to which, with sure instinct, he made his way. She had gone on into the next room, but her skirts trailed behind, making it impossible for her to bar the door. Drenched in perspiration, she sat trembling in the half-open door. Her women could not think what to do. It would not have been impossible to bar the door from the near side, but that would have meant dragging him away by main force, and one did not lay hands upon such a man.

'Sir, sir. We would not have dreamed that you could even think of such a thing.'

'Is it so dreadful that I am here beside her? I may not be the most desirable man in the world – indeed I am as aware as anyone that I am far from it.' He spoke slowly and with quiet emphasis. 'But after all this time she can scarcely call me a stranger.'

She was not prepared to listen. He had taken advantage of her, and there was nothing she wished to say.

'You are behaving like a selfish child. My crime has been to have feelings which I have kept to myself but which I cannot control. I promise you that I will do nothing without your permission. You have shattered my heart, and am I to believe that you do not know it? I am here because you have kept me at a distance and maintained this impossible pretense of ignorance – because I have had no alternative. I have risked being thought a boorish upstart because my sorrows would mean nothing if you did not know of them. Your coldness could make me angry, but I respect your position too much to speak of it.'

It would have been easy to force the door open, but that would have destroyed the impression of solemn sincerity which he had been at such pains to create.

'How touching,' he said, laughing. 'This thin little line between us seems to mean so much to you.'

She was a sweet, gentle lady, in spite of everything. Perhaps it was her worries that made her seem so tiny and fragile. Her sleeves, pleasantly soft and rumpled – for she had not been expecting guests – gave off a friendly sort of perfume, and indeed everything about her was gently, quietly pleasing.

In upon a sighing wind came the sounds of the mountain night, a humming of insects, the call of a stag, the rushing of a waterfall. It was a scene that would have made the most sluggish and insensitive person postpone his rest. As the moon came over the mountain ridge he was almost in tears.

'If you wish your silence to suggest unplumbed depths you may be assured that it is having the opposite effect. You do not seem to know that I am utterly harmless, and so without pretense that I am easily made a victim of. People who feel free to deal in rumors laugh mightily at me. Are you one of them? If so, I really must beg your leave to be angry. You cannot pretend not to know about these things.'

She was wretched, hating especially the hints that her experience should direct her towards easy acceptance. She had been very unlucky, and she wished she might simply vanish away.

'I am sure I have been guilty of errors in judgment, but nothing has prepared me for this.' Her voice, very soft, seemed on the edge of tears.

'Weeping and weeping, paraded before the world,
    The one and only model of haplessness?'

She spoke hesitantly, as if to herself. He repeated the poem in a whisper. She wished she had kept it to herself.

'I am sorry. I should not have said it.

'Had I not come inspiring all these tears,
    The world would not have noticed your misfortunes?

'Come, now.' She sensed that he was smiling. 'A show of resolve is what is called for.'

He tried to coax her out into the moonlight, but she held stubbornly back. He had no trouble taking her in his arms.

'Cannot this evidence of my feeling persuade you to be a little more companionable? But you may be assured that I shall do nothing without your permission.'

Dawn was approaching. The mists had lifted and moonlight flooded the room, finding the shallow eaves of the west veranda scarcely a hindrance at all. She tried to hide her face and he thought her charming. He spoke briefly of Kashiwagi. Quietly, politely, he reproved her for holding him so much the inferior of his dead friend.

She was as a matter of fact comparing them. Although Kashiwagi had still been a minor and rather obscure official, everyone had seemed in favor of the marriage and she too had come to accept it; and once they were married he had shown that astonishing indifference. Now came scandalous insinuations on the part of a man who was as good as one of the family. How would they appear to her father-in-law – and to the world in general – and to her own royal father? It was too awful. She might fight him off with her last ounce of strength, but the world was not likely to give her much credit. And to keep her mother in ignorance seemed a very grave delinquency indeed. What a dunce her mother would think her when presently she learned of it all!

'Do please leave before daylight.' She had nothing more to say to him.

'This is very odd. You know the interpretation which the dews are likely to put upon a departure at this hour. You shall have your way all the same; but please remember this: I have let you see what a fool I am, and if you gloat over what you have done I shall not hold myself responsible for the extremes I may be driven to.'

He was feeling very inadequate to the situation and would have liked to persist further; but for all his inexperience he knew that he would regret having forced himself upon her. For her sake and for his own he made his way out under the cover of the morning mists.

> 'Wet by dew-laden reeds beneath your eaves,
> I now push forth into the eightfold mists?

'And do you think that your own sleeves will be dry?* You must pay for your arbitrary ways.'

Nureginu means both 'wet robes' and 'damaged reputation.'

Though she could do little about rumors, she was determined not to face the reproaches of her own conscience.

'I think I have not heard the likes of it,' she replied, more icily than before.

> 'Because these dewy grasses wet your sleeves
> I too shall have wet sleeves – is that your meaning?'

She was delightful. He felt sorry for her and ashamed of himself, that having so distinguished himself in her service and her mother's he should suddenly take advantage of her and propose a rather different sort of relationship. Yet he would look very silly if he were to bow and withdraw.

He left in great uncertainty. The weed-choked path to the city resembled his thoughts. These nocturnal wanderings were novel and exciting, but they were very disturbing too. His damp sleeves would doubtless be matter for speculation if he returned to Sanjō, and so he went instead to the northeast quarter at Rokujō. Morning mists lay heavy over the garden – and how much heavier must they be at Ono!

The women were whispering. It was not the sort of thing they expected of him. The lady of the orange blossoms always had a change of clothing ready, fresh and elegant and in keeping with the season. When he had had breakfast he went to see his father.

He got off a note to the princess, but she refused to look at it. She was very upset at this sudden aggressiveness. She did not want to tell her mother, but it would be even worse if her mother were to have vague suspicions or to hear the story from one of the women. It was a world which refused to keep secrets. Perhaps, after all, the best thing – it would upset her mother of course, but that could not be helped – would be to have her women transmit the whole story, complete and without distortion. They were close even for mother and daughter, and there had not been the smallest secret between them. The romancers tell us of daughters who keep secrets from their parents even when the whole world knows, but the possibility did not occur to the princess.

'There is not the slightest indication,' said one of the women, 'that her mother knows anything. It is much too soon for the poor girl to begin worrying.'

They were beside themselves with curiosity about the unopened letter.

'It will seem very odd, my lady, if you do not answer. Odd and, I should say, rather childish.' And they opened it for her.

'It was entirely my fault,' said the princess. 'I was not as careful as I should have been and so he caught a glimpse of me. Yet I do think it inconsiderate of him, shockingly so. Tell him, please, that I could not bring myself to read it.' Desperately lonely, she turned away from them.

The letter was warm but inoffensive, so much of it as they were able to see.

> 'My heart is there in the sleeve of an unkind lady,
>   Quite without my guidance. I am helpless.

'That is nothing unique, I tell myself. We all know what happens when a heart is left to its own devices. I do think all the same that it has been very badly misled.'*

It was a long letter, but this was all the women were able to read. They were puzzled. It did not sound like a nuptial letter, and yet – they were sad for their lady, so visibly upset, and they were troubled and curious too. He had been so very kind, and if she were to let him have his way he might be disappointed in her. The future seemed far from secure.

The sick lady knew nothing of all this. The evil spirit continued to torment her, though there were intervals when she was more herself.

The noontide services were over and she had only her favorite priest beside her.

'Unless the blessed Vairocana is deceiving us,' he said, overjoyed to see that she was resting comfortably, 'I have every reason to believe that my humble efforts are succeeding. These spirits can be very stubborn, but they are lost souls, no more, doing penance for sins in other lives.' He had a gruff voice and an abrupt manner. He added, apropos of nothing: 'General Yūgiri – how long has he been keeping company with our princess?'

'Company? You are suggesting – but there has been nothing of the sort. He and my late son-in-law were the closest of friends, and he has been very kind, most astonishingly kind, and that is all. He has come to inquire after me and I am very grateful.'

---

*The letter contains at least three poetic allusions.

'Now this is strange. I am a humble man from whom you need not hide the truth. As I was going in for the early services I saw a very stylish gentleman come out through the door there at the west corner. The mists were heavy and I was not able to make out his features, but some of my colleagues were saying that it was definitely the general. He sent his carriage away yesterday evening, they said, and stayed the night. I did catch a very remarkable scent. It almost made me dizzy. Yes, said I, it had to be the general. He does have such a scent about him always. My own feeling is that you should not be exactly overjoyed. He knows a great deal, there is no doubt about that. His grandmother was kind enough to have me read scriptures for him when he was a boy, and whenever it has been within my humble power I have continued to be of service to him since. I do not think that there are advantages in the match for your royal daughter. His lady has an iron will and very great influence, and her family is at the height of its power. She has seven or eight children. I think it most doubtful that your daughter has much chance of supplanting her. Women are weak creatures, born with sinful inclinations, and just such missteps as this leave them wandering in darkness all the long night through. If she angers the other lady she will have much to do penance for. No, my lady, no. I cannot be held responsible.' Not one to mince words, he concluded with an emphatic shake of the head.

'It is, as you say, strange. There has been no indication, not the slightest, of anything of the sort. The women said that he was upset to find me so ill, and that after he had rested a little he would try to see me. Don't you suppose that is why he stayed the night? He is the most proper and honest of gentlemen.'

She pretended to disagree, but his observations made sense. There had from time to time been signs of an uncommon interest. But Yūgiri was such an earnest, scholarly sort, so very attentive to the proprieties, so concerned to avoid scandal. She had felt sure that nothing would happen without her daughter's permission. Had he taken advantage of the fact that she was so inadequately attended?

She summoned Koshōshō when the priest had taken his leave. 'What did in fact happen?' she asked, describing his view of the case. 'Why didn't she tell me? But it can't really be so bad.'

Though sorry for the princess, Koshōshō described everything she knew in very great detail. She told of the impression made by the letter that morning, of what she had seen and the princess had hinted at.

'Don't you suppose he made a clean breast of his feelings? That and no more? He showed the most extraordinary caution and left before the sun was up. What have the others told you?'

She did not suspect who the real informer was. The old lady was silent, tears streaming over her face. Koshōshō wished she had not been so frank. She feared the effect of so highly charged a revelation on a lady already dangerously ill.

'But the door was barred,' she said, trying to repair the damage a little.

'Maybe it was. But she let him see her, nothing alters that horrid fact. She may be blameless otherwise, but if the priests and the wretched urchins they brought with them have had something to say, can you imagine that they will have no more? Can you expect outsiders to make apologies for her and to protect and defend her?' And she added: 'We have such a collection of incompetents around us.'

Poor, poor lady, Koshōshō was thinking – in torment already, and now this shocking news. She had wanted for her daughter the elegant and courtly seclusion that becomes a princess, and just think what the world would be saying about her!

'Please tell her,' said the old lady, drying her tears, 'that I am feeling somewhat better and would like to see her. She will understand, I am sure, why I cannot call on her, as I know I should. It seems such a very long time.'

Koshōshō went for the princess, saying only that her mother wanted to see her. The princess brushed her hair, wet from weeping, and changed to fresh clothes. Still she hesitated. What would these women be thinking? And her mother – her mother could know nothing as yet, and would be hurt if hints were to come from someone else.

'I am feeling dreadful,' she said, lying down again. 'It would be better for everyone if I were not to recover. Something seems to be attacking my legs.'

She had one of the women massage it away, a force, probably, that had taken advantage of the confusion to mount through the extremities.

'Someone has been telling your good mother stories,' said Koshōshō. 'She asked me about last night and I told her everything. I insisted on your innocence by making the door seem a little firmer than it was. If she should ask you, please try to make your story match mine.' She did not say how upset the old lady had been.

So it was true. Utterly miserable, the princess wept in silence. Then and now – she had had two suitors, both of them unwelcome. Both had caused her poor mother pain. As for the princess herself, she seemed to face a future of limitless trials. There would be further overtures. She had resisted, and that was some small comfort; but for a princess to have exposed herself as she had was inexcusably careless.

Presently it was evening.

'Do please come,' said her mother.

She made her way in through a closet. The old lady sat up, ill though she was, and omitted none of the amenities. 'I must look a fright. Do please excuse me. It has only been a few days and it seems like an eternity. We cannot know that we will meet in another world, and we cannot be sure that we will recognize each other if we meet again in this one. Perhaps it was a mistake to become so fond of each other. Such a very short time together and we must say goodbye.' She was weeping.

The princess could only gaze at her in silence. Always a quiet, reserved girl, she knew nothing of the comforts of confession. The mother could not bring herself to ask questions. She ordered lights and had dinner brought for the two of them. Having heard from Koshōshō that the princess was not eating, she arranged the meal in the way the princess liked best, but to no avail. The princess was pleased all the same to see her mother so improved.

A letter came from Yūgiri. A woman who knew nothing of what had happened took it. 'From the general,' she said, 'for Koshōshō.'

How unfortunate, thought Koshōshō. Very deferentially, the mother asked what might be in it. Resentment was giving way to anticipation and a hope that Yūgiri might again come visiting. Indeed, the possibility that he might not was emerging as her chief worry.

'You really must answer him,' she said to the princess. 'You may proclaim to the world that you are clean and pure, but how many will believe you? Let him have a good-natured answer and let things go on very much as they are. That will be the best thing. You will not want him to think you an ill-mannered flirt.'

Reluctantly Koshōshō gave up the letter.

'You may be sure that evidence of your unconscionable hostility will have the effect of arousing me further.

> 'Shallow it is, for all these efforts to dam it.
> You cannot dam and conceal so famous a flow.'

It was a long letter, but the old lady read no more. It seemed to her the worst sort of sophistry, and the implied reason for his failure to visit seemed pompous and wholly unacceptable. Kashiwagi had not been the best of husbands, but he had behaved correctly and never made the princess feel threatened or insecure. The old lady had not been happy with him – and Yūgiri's behavior was far worse. What would Tō no Chūjō and his family be thinking, what would they be saying?

But she must try to learn more of Yūgiri's intentions. Drying her tears and struggling to quiet her thoughts, she set about composing a letter. The hand was like the strange tracks of a bird.

'When she came inquiring about my health, which is in a sorry state, I urged that she reply to your letter. I could see that she was not at all well herself, and I felt that some sort of reply was required of someone.

> 'You stay a single night. It means no more,
> This field of sadly fading maiden flowers?'

It was a much shorter note than she would have wished. She folded it formally and lay down, suddenly worse. Her women were greatly alarmed. The evil spirit had lulled her into a moment of inattention and taken advantage of it. The more famous healers were put to work again and the house echoed with their prayers and incantations. The princess must return at once to her rooms, insisted the women. She refused absolutely. If her mother was to die she wished to die also.

Yūgiri returned to his Sanjō mansion at about noon. He knew what almost no one else did, that nothing had happened, and he would have felt rather foolish running off to Ono again in the evening. This victory for restraint, however, increased his longing a thousand times over. Kumoinokari had sensed in a general way what was happening and was of course not pleased, but with so many children to look after she had no trouble feigning ignorance. She was resting in her parlor.

It was dark when the old lady's letter arrived. In that strange hand, like the tracks of a bird, it was next to illegible. He brought it close to a lamp.

Kumoinokari came lurching through her curtains and snatched it from over his shoulder.

'And why did you do that? It is a note from the lady at Rokujō. She was coming down with a cold this morning and feeling wretched. I meant to look in on her when I left Father, but something came up, and so I got off a note instead. Read it, if you are so curious. Does it look like a love letter? It seems rather common of you to want to. You treat me more like a child the longer we are together. Have you thought of the effect it may have on me?'

He did not try to recover the note, nor could she quite bring herself to read it.

'It is your own conduct,' she said, 'which makes you feel that I do not do sufficient honor to your maturity.'

Though she found his self-possession somewhat daunting, she answered with a brisk youthfulness that was not at all unconvincing.

'You may be right. But there is one matter of which you seem to be unaware, that this sort of thing happens all the time. What is unique, I suspect, is the case of a man who reaches a certain station in life and continues to be unwaveringly faithful to one lady. You have heard of henpecking, perhaps? People always seem to find it very funny. And I should point out that the wife of so stodgy a man tends not to seem very exciting herself. Think how her reputation rises, how the wrinkles go away, how interesting and amusing life is, when she is first among a multitude of ladies. What fun is it and what satisfaction does it give to be like the old dotard, what's his name, hanging on to his Lady Something-or-other?'*

It seemed to be his purpose, while pretending that the letter was nothing, to get it back.

She smiled a bright and pretty smile. 'But you are so young all of a sudden that you make me very much aware of my wrinkles.†

---

*The reference is as obscure as it sounds. Several Chinese sources have been averred.
†She is some two years older than he.

And the novelty will take some getting used to. I have not had the proper education.'

A complaining wife, he thought, can sometimes be rather charming.

'Oh, you see a change in me? That surprises and upsets me. It shows that we no longer understand each other as we once did. Has someone been talking about me? Someone, perhaps, who long ago found me unacceptable? Who has failed to note that my sleeves are no longer blue,* and still wishes to interfere? But whoever she may be, an innocent princess is being wronged.' He was not feeling in the least apologetic, and did not wish to argue the matter.

Tayū squirmed but was no more prepared to argue than he. The discussion went on for a time, during which Kumoinokari managed to hide the letter. Pretending not to care very much, he went to bed. But he was very excited and very eager to have it back. He had guessed that it was from the princess's mother. And what might it say? He lay sleepless, and when Kumoinokari was asleep probed under her quilts. He found nothing. How had she been able to hide it?

He lay in bed after the sun was up and after Kumoinokari had been summoned to work by the children. As if putting himself in order for the day, he probed yet further, and still found no trace of it. Persuaded that it was indeed an innocent sort of letter, the busy Kumoinokari had forgotten about it. The children were chasing one another and ministering to their dolls and having their time at reading and calligraphy. The baby had come crawling up and was tugging at her sleeves. She had no thought for the letter. Yūgiri could think of nothing else. He must get off an answer, but he did not know what he would be answering. The old lady would conclude that her letter had been lost if his seemed irrelevant.

After breakfast there came a lull of sorts and he felt that he could wait no longer.

'What was in the letter last night? Do you propose to keep it secret? I ought to go see her again today, but I am not feeling at all well myself. So I ought to get off a note.'

He did not seem to care a great deal, and she was beginning to feel a little foolish.

*In Chapter 21, her nurse Tayū objected to his humble rank.

'Oh, think up some elegant excuse. Tell her you went hiking in the mountains and caught cold.'

'That was not funny, and I see no need for elegance. You think I am like all the others, do you? Our friends here have always thought me a queer old stick, and these insinuations must strike them as rather far from the mark. But the letter – where is it?'

She was in no hurry. They talked of this and that, and had their naps, and it was evening. Awakened by the evening cicadas he thought again of the gloomy mountain mists. What a wretched business! And he still had not answered. Deliberately, he got ink and brush ready, and considered how to answer an unseen letter. His eyes lighted on a cushion that seemed to bulge along the far edge – and there it was! The obvious places were the ones a person overlooked. He smiled, and immediately was serious again. It was deeply distressing. The old lady was assuming that something of significance had occured. How very unfortunate – and his failure to visit the night before must have been for her a disaster. He had not even written. No ordinary sort of disquiet could explain such a chaotic hand.

Nothing could be done now to repair the damage. He was angry with Kumoinokari. Her playfulness could have done no good even if it had done no damage. But no, the fault was his. He had not trained her properly. He was so angry with her and with himself that he wanted to weep.

Perhaps he should go immediately to Ono. He could expect the princess to be no friendlier than before. But how was he to explain the mother's apparent sense of crisis? It was moreover a very unlucky day, not the sort on which a man went forth in the expectation of having a bride bestowed upon him. He must be calm and take the longer view. He set about an answer.

'I was surprised and for many reasons pleased to have your letter. Yet it is somehow accusing. What can have aroused your suspicions?

'Although I made my way through thick autumn grasses,
    I wove no pillow of grass for vagrant sleep.

'Apologies are not always to the point, even when silence might seem to speak of something.'*

---

*The remark is very obscure. Several interpretations are possible.

There was a long message for the princess as well. Ordering a fast horse, he summoned the guards officer of the last Ono visit and, with whispered instructions, sent him off to Ono once more.

'Say that I have been at Rokujō all day and have just come home.'

The princess's mother had been persuaded by his apparent coldness to dispatch a resentful note, and there had been no answer. What utter insolence! It was evening once more and she was in despair and in even greater pain. The princess, for her part, did not find his behavior even mildly surprising. Her only concern was that she had let him see her. Her mother's apparent view of the case embarrassed her acutely and left her more inarticulate than ever. Poor child, the mother was thinking. Misfortune heaped upon misfortune.

'I do not wish to seem querulous, my dear, but your astonishing innocence makes it difficult for me to resign myself to what has happened. You have left yourself exposed. There is nothing to be done now, but do please try to be more careful. I do not count, I know, but I have tried to do my best. I would have thought that you had reached an age when you could be expected to know about men. I have hoped that I might be a little more confident. But I see that you are still as easily persuaded as a child, and pray that I may live a little longer.

'Wellborn ladies, even if they are not princesses, do not have two husbands. And you are a princess, and should above everything guard against appearing to be within easy reach. Things went so badly the first time and I worried so about you. But it was meant to be, and there is no point in complaining. Your royal father seemed to find him acceptable, and he seems to have had his father's permission too, and so I told myself that I must be the one who did not understand. I watched it all, knowing that you had done nothing wrong and that I might as well complain to the skies.* This new affair will bring no great honor to either of you, but if it leads to the usual sort of relationship, well, time will go by and we can try not to listen to the gossips, and perhaps learn to live with it. Or so I had concluded.' She was weeping. 'So I had concluded before I discovered what sort of man he is.'

---

*Probably a literary allusion, though none has been satisfactorily identified.

A gently, forlornly elegant little figure, the princess could only weep with her.

'Certainly there is nothing wrong with your appearance,' continued the mother, gazing at her, 'nothing that singles you out as remarkably inferior. What can you have done in other lives that you should have no happiness in this one?'

She was suddenly in very great pain. Malevolent spirits have a way of seizing upon a crisis. She fell into a coma and was growing colder by the moment. The priests offered the most urgent supplications. For her favorite priest there was a special urgency. He had compromised his vows, and it would be a cruel defeat to take down his altar and, having accomplished nothing at all, wander back up the mountain. Surely he deserved better treatment at the hands of the Blessed One.

The princess was beside herself.

In the midst of all the confusion a letter arrived from Yūgiri. The old lady, now dimly aware of what was happening, took it as evidence that another night would pass without a visit. Worse and worse – nothing now could keep her daughter from being paraded before the world as an utter simpleton. And she herself – what could have persuaded her to write so damaging a letter?

These were her last thoughts. She was no more.

I need not describe the grief and desolation she left behind. She had been ill much of the time, victim of a malign possession, and more than once they had thought that she was dying. It had been assumed that this was another such seizure, and the priests had been feverishly at work. But it was soon apparent that the end had come. The princess clung to her, longing to go wherever she had gone.

'We must accept the inevitable, my lady.' The women offered the usual platitudes. 'Of course you are sad, but she has gone the way from which there is no returning. However much you may wish to go with her, it is not possible.' They pulled her from her mother's side. 'You are inviting bad luck, and your dear mother will have much to reprove you for. Do please come with us.'

But the girl seemed to waste away before their eyes, and to understand nothing of what was said to her.

The altar was taken down. Two and three at a time, the priests were departing. Intimates of the family remained, as might have been expected, but everything was over, and the house was still and lonely. Messages of condolence were already coming in, for the news had spread swiftly. A dazed Yūgiri was among the first to send condolences. There were messages from Genji and Tō no Chūjō and many others.

There was an especially touching letter from the princess's father, the Suzaku emperor. The princess forced herself to read it.

'I had known of her illness for some time, but I had known too, of course, that she had long been in bad health. I see now that I was not as worried as I should have been. But that is over and finished, and what concerns us now is your own state of mind. Please be sure, if it is any comfort, that I am grieving with you, and please try to take some comfort from the thought that everything must pass.'

Through her tears, she set down an answer.

The old lady had left instructions that the funeral take place that same day. Her nephew, the governor of Yamato, had charge of the arrangements. The princess asked for a last silent interview with her mother, but of course it accomplished nothing. The arrangements were soon in order.

At the worst possible moment Yūgiri appeared.

'I must go to Ono today,' he had said as he left Sanjō. 'If I don't go today I don't know when I can go. The next few days are bad.' The image of the grieving princess was before his eyes.

'Please, my lord,' said the women. 'You should not seem to be in such a hurry.'

But he insisted.

The journey to Ono was a long one and a house of grief awaited him at the end of it. Gloomy screens and awnings kept the funeral itself from his view. He was shown to the princess's room, where the governor of Yamato, in tears, thanked him for his visit. Leaning against a corner railing, he asked that one or two of the princess's women be summoned. They were none of them in a state to receive him, but Koshōshō did presently come in. Though he was not an emotional man, what he had seen of the house and its occupants so moved him that he was at first unable to speak. Generalizations about the evanescence of things were suddenly particular and immediate.

'I had allowed myself to be persuaded that she was recovering,' he said, controlling himself with difficulty. 'It always takes time to awaken, as they say,* and this has been so sudden.'

*Probably a literary allusion.

The cause of her mother's worst torments, thought the princess, was here before her. She knew about inevitability and all that sort of thing. But how cruel they were, the ties that bound her to him! She could not bring herself to send out an answer.

'And what may we tell him you have said, my lady? He is an important man and he has come running all this distance to see you. Do not, please, make it seem that you are unaware of his kindness.'

'Imagine how I feel and say what seems appropriate. I cannot think of anything myself.' And she went to bed.

Her women quite understood. 'Poor lady, she is half dead herself,' said one of them. 'I have told her that you are here.'

'There is nothing more I can say. I shall come again when I am a little more in control of myself and when your lady is somewhat more composed. But why did it happen so suddenly?'

With many pauses and with some understatement, Koshōshō described the old lady's worries. 'I fear I will seem to be accusing you of something, my lord. This dreadful business has left us somewhat distraught, and it may be that I have been guilty of inaccuracies. My lady seems only barely alive, but these things too must end, and when she is a little more herself perhaps I can describe things a little more clearly and listen more carefully to whatever you may wish to say to her.'

She did not seem to be exaggerating her grief. There was little more to be said.

'Yes, we are all wandering in pitch-blackness. Please do try to comfort her, and if there should be the briefest answer —'

He did not want to go, but it was a delicate situation and he had his dignity to consider. It had not occurred to him that the funeral would take place this very evening. Though the arrangements had been hurried, they did not seem in any way inadequate. He left various instructions with the people from his manors and started for the city. Ceremonies which because of the haste might have been almost perfunctory were both grand and well attended.

'Extraordinarily kind of Your Lordship,' said the governor of Yamato.

And so it was all over, and the princess was quite alone. She was convulsed with grief, but of course nothing was to be done. It went against nature, thought the women, to become so strongly attached to anyone, even a mother.

'You cannot stay here by yourself,' insisted the governor, busy with the last details. 'If you are ever to find comfort it must be back in the city.'

But the princess insisted that she would live out her days at Ono, with the mountain mists to remember her mother by. The priests who were to preside over the mourning had put up temporary cells in the east rooms and galleries and certain of the east outbuildings. One hardly knew that they were still on the premises. The last traces of color had been stripped from the princess's rooms.

The days went by, though she was scarcely able to distinguish day from night, and it was the Ninth Month.

Harsh winds came down from the mountains, the trees were stripped bare, and it was the melancholy time of the year. The princess's spirits were as black as the skies. She wanted to die, but not even that was permitted her.* The gloom was general, though Yūgiri's gifts brightened the lives of the priests a little. There were daily messages for the princess which combined the most eloquent condolences with chidings for her aloofness. She refused to look at them. She was still living her mother's last days. It was as if her mother, wasting away, were still here beside her, seeing everything in the worst light, convinced that no other interpretation was possible. The resentment would most certainly be an obstacle on the way into the next world. The briefest of his messages repelled her and brought on new floods of tears. The women could not think what to do for her.

Yūgiri at first attributed the silence to grief. But too much time went by and he was becoming resentful. Grief must end, after all. She was being unkind, obtuse even, and indeed he was coming to think it a rather childish performance. If his notes had been full of flowers and butterflies and all the other fripperies, she would have been right to ignore them; but he made it quite clear that he felt her grief as his own.

He remembered his grandmother's death. It had seemed to him that Tō no Chūjō was inadequately grief-stricken and too easily philosophical, and that the memorial services were more for the public than for the dead lady herself. He had been deeply grateful to Genji, on the other hand, for going beyond what was asked of

*Another unidentified allusion, apparently.

an outsider, and he had felt very close to Kashiwagi. Of a quiet, meditative nature, Kashiwagi had seemed the most lovable of them all, the most sensitive to the sorrows of things. And so he felt very keenly for the bereaved princess.

What did it all mean? Kumoinokari was asking. He had not seemed on such very good terms with the dead lady, nor had their correspondence been of the most flourishing.

One evening as he lay gazing up at the sky she sent one of her little boys with a note on a rather ordinary bit of paper.

'Which emotion demands my sympathy,
    Grief for the one or longing for the other?

'The uncertainty is most trying.'

He smiled. She had a lively imagination, though he did not think the reference to the princess's mother in very good taste. Coolly he dashed off a reply.

'I do not know the answer to your question.
    The dew does not rest long upon the leaves.

'My feelings are for the world in general.'

She wished he might be a little more communicative. It was not the fleeting dews that worried her.

He set off for Ono once more. He had thought to wait until the mourning was over but could no longer contain his impatience. The princess's reputation was beyond saving in any event, and he might as well do what other men did and have his way with her. He did not try very hard to persuade Kumoinokari that her suspicions were groundless. For all the princess's determination to be unfriendly, he had a weapon to use against her, the old lady's reproof at his failure to come visiting that second evening.

It was the middle of the Ninth Month, a time when not even the most insensitive of men can be unaware of the mountain colors. The autumn winds tore at the trees and the leaves of the vines* seemed fearful of being left behind. Someone far away was reading a sutra, and someone was invoking the holy name, and for the rest Ono seemed deserted. Indifferent to the clappers meant to frighten them from the harvests, the deer that sought shelter by the garden fences were somber spots among the hues of autumn. A

---

*Kuzu, often translated 'arrowroot.'

stag bayed plaintively, and the roar of a waterfall was as if meant to
break in upon sad thoughts. Insect songs, less insistent, among the
brown grasses, seemed to say that they must go but did not know
where. Gentians peered from the grasses, heavy with dew, as if
they alone might be permitted to stay on. The sights and sounds of
autumn, ordinary enough, but recast by the occasion and the place
into a melancholy scarcely to be borne.

In casual court robes, pleasantly soft, and a crimson singlet
upon which the fulling blocks had beaten a delicate pattern, he
stood for a time at the corner railing. The light of the setting sun,
almost as if directed upon him alone, was so bright that he raised a
fan to his eyes, and the careless grace would have made the
women envious had he been one of their number. But alas, they
could not have imitated it. He smiled, so handsome a smile that it
must bring comfort to the cruelest grief, and asked for Koshōshō.

'Come closer, please.' Though she was already very near, he
sensed that there were others behind the blinds. 'I would expect at
least you to be a little friendlier. The mists are thick enough to
hide you, if you are afraid of being seen.' He glanced up at them,
though not as if reposing great faith in them. 'Do please come
out.'

She gathered her skirts and took a place behind a curtain of
mourning which she had set out just beyond the blinds. A younger
sister of the governor of Yamato, she had been taken in by her
aunt and reared with the Second Princess, almost as a sister. She
had therefore put on the most somber of mourning robes.

He was soon in tears. 'To a grief that refuses to go away is
added a sense of injury quite beyond describing, enough to take all
the meaning from life. Everywhere I look I encounter expressions
of amazement that it should be so.' He spoke too of the mother's
last letter.

Koshōshō was sobbing. 'When you did not write she withdrew into her thoughts as if she did not mean to come out again.
She seemed to go away with the daylight. I could see that the
evil spirit, whatever it may have been, was behaving as usual,
taking advantage of her weakness. I had seen it happen many
times during our troubles with the young master. But she
always seemed to rally, with a great effort of will, when she saw
that the princess was as unhappy as she and needed comforting.
The princess, poor thing, has been in a daze.' There were many

pauses, as if it had all been more than she could reconcile herself to.

'That is exactly what I mean. She must pull herself together and make up her mind. You may think it impertinent of me to say so, but I am all she has left. Her father is a complete recluse. She cannot expect messages to come very often from those cloudy peaks. Do, please, have a word with her. What must be must be. She may not want to live on, but we cannot have our way in these matters. If we could, then of course these cruel partings would not occur.'

Koshōshō did not seek to interrupt. A stag called out from just beyond the garden wall.

'I would not be outdone.*

'I push my way through tangled groves to Ono.
Shall my laments, O stag, be softer than yours?'

Koshōshō replied:

'Dew-drenched wisteria robes† in autumn mountains.
Sobs to join the baying of the stag.'

It was no masterpiece, but the hushed voice and the time and place were right.

He sent in repeated messages to the princess. A single answer came back, so brief that it was almost curt. 'It is like a nightmare. I shall try to thank you when I am a little more myself.'

What uncommon stubbornness! The thought of it rankled all the way back to the city. Though the autumn skies were sad, the moon, near full, saw him safely past Mount Ogura.‡ The princess's Ichijō mansion wore an air of neglect and disrepair. The southwest corner of the garden wall had collapsed. The shutters were drawn and the grounds were deserted save for the moon, which had quite taken possession of the garden waters. He thought how Kashiwagi's flute would have echoed through these same grounds on such a night.

*Anonymous, *Kokinshū* 582:

> I would not be outdone by the baying stags,
> My only comrades in these autumn mountains.

†Mourning weeds were called 'wisteria robes.'

‡Mount Ogura lies to the west of the city, and therefore not along his route. It is introduced because the name suggests darkness.

'No shadows now of them whom once I knew.
Only the autumn moon to guard the waters.'

Back at Sanjō he gazed up at the moon as if his soul had abandoned him and gone wandering through the skies.

'Never saw anything like it,' said one of the women. 'He always used to be so well behaved.'

Kumoinokari was very unhappy indeed. He seemed to have lost his head completely. Perhaps he had been observing the ladies at Rokujō, long used to this sort of thing, and had concluded that she was worse than uninteresting. Well, it might be that his dissatisfaction should be directed at himself. Life might have been better for her if he had been a Genji. Everyone seemed to agree that she was married to a model of decorum and that her marriage had been ordained by the happiest fates. And was it to end in scandal?

Dawn was near. Sleepless, they were alone with their separate thoughts. He was as always in a rush to get off a letter, even before the morning mists had lifted. Disgusting, thought she, though she did not this time try to take it from him. It was a long letter, and when he had finished he read certain favored passages over to himself, softly but quite audibly.

'It falls from above.*

'Waking from the dream of an endless night
You said – and when may I pay my visit?'

'And what am I to do?' he added in a whisper as he folded it into an envelope and sent for a messenger.

She would have liked to know what else was in it and hoped that she might have a glimpse of the reply. It was all most unsettling.

The sun was high when the reply came. On paper of a dark purple, it was as usual from Koshōshō, and, as usual, short and businesslike.

'She made a few notes at the end of your letter. Feeling a little sorry for you and thinking them better than nothing, I gathered them and herewith smuggle them to you.'

So the princess had seen his letter! His delight was perhaps a little too open. There were indeed scraps of paper, fragmentary and disconnected, some of which he reassembled into a poem:

*Unclear. Probably a poetic allusion.

'Morning and night, laments sound over Mount Ono
And Silent Waterfall – a flow of tears?'

There were also fragments from the anthologies, in a very good hand.

He had always thought that there was something wrong with a man who could lose his senses over a woman, and here he was doing it himself. How strange it was, and how extremely painful. He tried to shake himself back into sanity, but without success.

Genji learned of the affair. The calm, sober Yūgiri, about whom there had never been a whisper of scandal, an edifying contrast with the Genji of the days when he had seemed rather too susceptible – here Yūgiri was making two women unhappy. And he was Tō no Chūjō's son-in-law and nephew, certainly no stranger to the family. But Yūgiri must know what he was doing. No doubt it had all been fated, and Genji was in no position to offer advice. He felt very sorry for the women, and he thought of Murasaki and how unhappy he had made her. Each time a new rumor reached him he would tell her how he worried about her and the life that awaited her when he was gone.

It was not kind of him, she thought, flushing, to have plans for leaving her. Such a difficult, constricted life as a woman was required to live! Moving things, amusing things, she must pretend to be unaffected by them. With whom was she to share the pleasure and beguile the tedium of this fleeting world? Since it chose to look upon women as useless, unfeeling creatures, should it not pity the fathers who went to such trouble rearing them? Like the mute prince who was always appearing in sad parables,* a woman should be sensitive but silent. The balance was certainly very difficult to maintain – and the little girl in her care, Genji's granddaughter, must face the same difficulties.

Genji found occasion, on one of Yūgiri's visits, to seek further information. 'I suppose the mourning for the Ichijō lady will soon be over. It was only yesterday, you think, and already thirty years and more have gone by.† That is the sort of world we live in, and we cling to a life that is no more substantial than the evening dew.

---

*There are several references in Buddhist writ to a prince who remained mute through childhood because he had learned the advantages of silence in earlier lives.
†Perhaps a proverb. Some texts say 'three years,' in which case the reference is perhaps to Kashiwagi's death.

I have wanted for a very long time to leave it all behind, and it does not seem right that I should go on living this comfortable life.'

'It is true,' said Yūgiri. 'The very least of us clings to his tiny bit of life. The governor of Yamato saw to the memorial services without the help of anyone. It was rather pathetic, somehow. You sensed how little the poor lady had behind her. There was an appearance of solidity while she lived and then it was gone.'

'I suppose there have been messages from the Suzaku emperor? I can imagine how things must be with the princess. I did not know them well, but there have been reports in recent years suggesting what a superior person the dead lady was. We all feel the loss. The ones we need are the ones who go away. It must have been a dreadful blow to the Suzaku emperor. I am told that the Second Princess is his favorite after the Third Princess here. Everyone says that she is most attractive.'

'But what about her disposition? I wonder. The mother was, as you suggest, a lady whom no one could find fault with. I did not know her well, but I did see her a few times, on this occasion and that.'

He obviously did not propose to give himself away. Genji held his peace. One did not question the feelings of a man so admirably in control of himself, nor did one expect to be listened to.

Yūgiri himself had in fact taken responsibility for the memorial services. Such matters do not remain secret, and reports reached Tō no Chūjō. Knowing Yūgiri, he put the whole blame on the princess and concluded that she must be a frivolous, flighty little thing. His sons were all present at the services, and Tō no Chūjō himself sent lavish offerings. In the end, because no one wished to be outdone, they were services worthy of the highest statesman in the land.

The princess had said that she would end her days at Ono. Her father learned of these intentions and sought to remonstrate with her.

'It will not do. You are right to want to avoid complications, but it sometimes happens that when a lady alone in the world seeks to withdraw from it completely she finds that just the opposite has happened. She finds herself involved in scandal, and therefore in the worst position, neither in the world nor out of it. I have become a priest and your sister has followed me and become a nun, and people seem to think my line rather unproductive. I know that in theory I should not care what they say, but I must admit that it is not the most pleasing sight, my daughters racing one another into a nunnery. No, my dear – the world may seem too much for you, but when you run impulsively away from it you sometimes find that it is with you more than ever. Do please wait a little while and have a calm look at things when you are in better spirits.'

It seemed that he had heard of Yūgiri's activities. People would not make charitable judgments, he feared. They would say that she had been jilted. Though he would not think it entirely dignified of her to appear before the world as one of Yūgiri's ladies, he did not want to embarrass her by saying so. He should not even have heard of the affair and he had no right to an opinion. He said not a word about it.

Yūgiri was feeling restless and inadequate. His petitions were having no effect at all. Nor did it seem likely that persistence would accomplish anything. If he could only think how, he might let it be known that the mother had accepted his suit. He might risk doing slight discredit to the dead lady's name by making it seem that the affair had begun rather a long time before, he scarcely knew when. He would feel very silly, in any event, going through the tears and supplications all over again.

Choosing a propitious day for taking her back to Ichijō, he instructed the governor of Yamato to make the necessary preparations. He also gave instructions for cleaning and repairing the Ichijō mansion. It was a fine house, a suitable dwelling for royalty, but the women she had left behind could scarcely see out through the weeds that had taken over the garden. When he had everything cleaned and polished he turned to preparations for the move itself, asking the governor to put his craftsmen to work on screens and curtains and cushions and the like.

On the appointed day he went to Ichijō and sent carriages and an escort to Ono. The princess quite refused to leave. Her women noisily sought to persuade her, as did the governor of Yamato.

'I am near the end of my patience, Your Highness. I have felt sorry for you and done everything I could think of to help you, even at the cost of neglecting my official duties. I absolutely must go down to Yamato and see to putting things in order again. I would not want to send you back to Ichijō all by yourself, but we have the general taking care of everything. I have to admit that when I give a little thought to these arrangements I do not find them ideal for a princess, but we have examples enough of far worse things. Are you under the impression that you alone may escape criticism? A very childish impression indeed. The strongest and most forceful lady cannot put her life in order without some-one to help her, someone to make the arrangements and box the corners. Much the wiser thing would be to accept help where it is offered. And you,' he said to Koshōshō and Sakon. 'You have not given her good advice, and your behavior has not been above reproach.'

They stripped her of mourning and brought out fresh, bright robes and brushed the hair she had resolved to cut. It was a little thinner, but still a good six feet long and the envy of them all. Yet she went on telling herself that she looked dreadful, that she must not be seen, that no one had ever been more miserable than she.

'We are late, my lady.' Her women accosted her one after another. 'We are very late.'

There was a sudden and violent rain squall.

'My choice would be to rise with the smoke from the peaks,
Which might perhaps not go in a false direction.'*

Knowing of her wish to become a nun, they had hidden the knives and scissors. All very unnecessary. She no longer cared in the least what happened to her, and she would not have been so childish, nor would she have wished people to think her so obsti-nate, as to cut her hair in secret.†

Everyone was in a great hurry. All manner of combs and boxes and chests and bulging bags had already been sent off to the city. The house was bare, she could not stay on alone. In tears, she was finally shown into a carriage, and beside her was the empty seat that had been her mother's. On the journey to Ono her mother, desperately ill, had stroked her hair and gently sought to comfort her, and on their arrival had insisted that she dismount first. She had her talisman sword beside her as always, and a sutra box inlaid with mother-of-pearl, a memento of her mother.

See note, page 534.

†The passage is unclear, and there are variant texts. It may be that she is thinking specifically of her father.

'A small bejeweled box, now wet with tears,
To help me remember and seek elusive solace.'

She had kept it back from the offerings in memory of her mother. The black sutra box she had ordered for herself was not yet ready.

She felt like the son of Urashima,* returning to an utterly changed world. The Ichijō house, now buzzing with life, was scarcely recognizable. She found it somehow frightening, and at first refused to leave the carriage, which had been pulled up at a veranda. What a foolish child, said her women, who could not think what to do.

Yūgiri had taken the main room of the east wing for his own use. There were whispers of astonishment back at Sanjō. 'When can it all have begun?'

This most proper of gentlemen was showing unexpected tendencies. Everyone concluded that he must have kept the affair secret for months and years. It did not occur to people that in fact the princess was still defending her virtue. The gossip and Yūgiri's continuing attentions made her very unhappy indeed.

It was not the best possible time for nuptial measures, but he proceeded to the princess's rooms when dinner was over and the house was quiet, and demanded that Koshōshō admit him.

'Please, sir. If your affection seems likely to last awhile longer, please do her the kindness of waiting a day or two. It may seem to you that she has come home, but she feels utterly lost and is lying there as if she might be on the point of expiring. She tells me I am being heartless when I try to rouse her. I would find it almost impossible to say more than I have already said even if I were arguing my own case.'

'How very strange. She is a sillier goose than I had imagined.' All over again, he assured Koshōshō that his motives were unassailable.

'Please, sir, I beg of you. I do almost fear that I might have another dead lady on my hands, and your reasoned arguments are beyond me. Please, please do nothing rash or violent.'

'Now this is a unique situation. I have been put at the bottom of the list, and I would like to call in judges and ask whether I deserve to be there.' He fell silent.

*The Japanese Rip van Winkle.

Koshōshō smiled. 'If you think it unique, then you are confessing that you have not had much experience in these matters. We must by all means call in judges.'

This jocularity hid very great uneasiness, for she was powerless to restrain him. He marched in ahead of her and made his way through unfamiliar rooms to the princess's side. She was stunned. She would not have thought him capable of such impetuosity. She still had a device or two, however, and they could all scream to the world, if they wished, that she was being childish. She locked herself in a closet and prepared to spend the night there. She still felt far from secure, and she was very angry with Koshōshō and the rest, who seemed to find his advances pleasing and exciting.

Yūgiri too was angry, but he persuaded himself to take the longer view. Like the mountain pheasant, he spent the night alone.*

Daylight came and the impasse remained.

'Open the door just a crack,' he said over and over again. There was no answer.

> 'My sorrows linger as the winter night.
> The stony barrier gate is as slow to open.

'O cruelest of ladies!' In tears, he made his way out.

He rested for a time at Rokujō.

'We have heard from Tō no Chūjō's people,' said the lady of the orange blossoms, 'that you have moved the Second Princess back to Ichijō. What can it mean?' He could see her, calm and gentle, through the curtains.

'Yes, it is the sort of thing people like to talk about. Her mother quite refused to agree to anything of the sort, but towards the end she let it be known – possibly her resolution had weakened, or possibly the thought of leaving the princess all alone was too much for her – she let it be known that I was the one the princess was to turn to. These thoughts fitted perfectly with my own intentions. And so I suppose each of the gossips has his own conclusion to the story.' He laughed. 'How righteous and confident people can be in disposing of these trivialities. The princess herself says only that she wants to become a nun. I have very little hope of dissuading her. The rumors will go on in any event, and I

---

*The *yamadori, Syrmaticus soemmerringii,* was thought to roost away from its mate.

only hope that my fidelity to her mother's dying wishes outlasts them. So I have made such arrangements as I have made. When you next see Father you might try to explain all of this to him. I have managed to keep his respect over the years, I think, and I would hate to lose it now.' He lowered his voice. 'It is curious how irrelevant all the advice and all the promptings of your own conscience can sometimes seem.'

'I had not believed it. There is nothing so unusual about it, I suppose, though I do feel sorry for your lady at Sanjō. She has had such a good life all these years.'

' "Your lady" – that is kind of you. "Your ogre" might be more to the point. But surely you cannot imagine that I would not do the right thing? You will think it impertinent of me to say so, but consider for a moment the arrangements you have here at Rokujō. Yes, the tranquil life is what we all want. A man may dodge a noisy woman and make all the allowances, but in the end he wants to be quietly rid of her. The noise may die down but the irritation remains. Murasaki seems in many ways a very rare sort of lady. And when it comes to sweetness and docility you do not have many rivals yourself.'

She smiled. 'This sort of praise makes me feel that my short-comings must show very clearly. One thing does strike me as odd: your good father seems to think that no one has the smallest suspicion of his own delinquencies, and that yours give him a right to lecture when you are here and criticize when you are not. We have heard of sages whose wisdom does not include themselves.'

'Yes, he does lecture, indefatigably. And I am a rather careful person even in the absence of his wise advice.'

He went to Genji's rooms. Genji too had heard of these new developments, but he saw no point in saying so. Waiting for Yūgiri to speak, he did not see how anyone could reprove such a handsome young man, at the very best time of life, for occasionally misbehaving. Surely the most intolerant of the powers above must feel constrained to forgive him. And he was not a child. His younger years had been blameless, and, yes, he could be forgiven these little affairs. The remarkable thing, if Genji did say so about his own son, was that the image he saw in the mirror did not give him the urge to go out and make conquest after conquest.

It was midmorning when Yūgiri returned to Sanjō. Pretty little boys immediately commenced climbing all over him. Kumoinokari

was resting and did not look up when he came behind her curtains. He could see that she was very much put out with him. She
had every right to be, but he could only pretend that he had nothing to be ashamed of.

'Do you know where you are?' she said finally. 'You are in hell.
You have always known that I am a devil, and I have merely come
home.'

'In spirit worse than a devil,' he replied cheerfully, 'but in
appearance not at all unpleasant.'

She snorted and sat up. 'I know that I do not go very well with
your own fine looks, and I would prefer just to be out of sight. I
have wasted so many years. Please do not remember me as I am
now.'

He thought her anger, which had turned her a fresh, clean scarlet, very charming.

'I am used to you and am not at all terrified of you. Indeed, I
might almost wish for something a little more awesome.'

'That will do. Just disappear, please, if you do not mind, and I
will hurry and do the same. I do not like the sight of you and I do
not like the sound of you. My only worry is that I may die first
and leave you happily behind.'

He found her more and more amusing. 'Oh, but you would
still hear about me. How do you propose to avoid that unpleasantness? Is the point of your remarks that there would seem to be a
strong bond between us? It will hold, I think. We are fated to
move on to another world in quick succession.'

He sought to dismiss it as an ordinary marital spat. She was a
good-natured lady in spite of everything, youthful and forgiving,
and though she knew very well what he was doing her anger presently left her.

He was sorry for her, to the extent that his unsettled state of
mind permitted. The princess did not strike him as a willful or
arbitrary sort, but if she were this time to insist on having her way
and become a nun he would look very silly indeed. He must not
let her spend many nights alone, he nervously concluded. Evening
approached, and again it became apparent that he would not hear
from her. Dinner was brought in. Kumoinokari ate very little, and
Yūgiri himself had eaten nothing at all since the day before.

'I remember all the years when I thought of no one but you,
and your father would not have me. Thanks to him the whole

world was laughing at me. But I persevered and bore the unbearable, and refused all the other young ladies who were offered to
me. I remember how my friends all laughed. Not even a woman
was expected to be so constant and steadfast, they all said. And
indeed I can see that my solemn devotion must have been rather
funny. You may be angry with me at the moment, but before you
think of leaving me think of all the little ones you can have no
intention of leaving. They are threatening to crowd us out of the
house. You are not that angry, surely?' He dabbed at his eyes. 'Do
give the matter a moment's thought. Life is very uncertain.'

She thought how remarkably happy their marriage had been,
and concluded that they must indeed have brought a strong bond
from other lives.

He changed his rumpled house clothes for exquisitely perfumed new finery. Seeing him off, a dazzlingly handsome figure in
the torchlight, she burst into tears and reached for one of the
singlets he had discarded.

> 'I do not complain that I am used and rejected.
> Let me but go and join them at Matsushima.*

'I do not think I can possibly be expected to continue as I am.'
Though she spoke very softly, he heard and turned back.
'You do seem to be in a mood.

> 'Robes of Matsushima, soggy and worn,
> For even them you may be held to account.'

It was an impromptu effort and not a very distinguished one.
Again he found the princess locked in a closet.
'What a silly child you are,' said one of her women. 'People
will think it very, very strange. Do please come out and receive
him in a more conventional sort of room.

She knew that they were right, but she hated him for the
unhappiness he had caused and for all the gossip to come. She had
not asked for these attentions, and she hated them. She spent
another night in her closet.

'Astounding,' said he. 'At first I thought you were joking.'
Her women agreed with him completely. 'She says, my lord,

---

*'Let me become a nun.' *Ama* means both 'nun' and 'fisherman,' and Matsushima is
a fishing port.

that she is certain to feel a little more herself one of these days, and perhaps she can talk with you then if you still wish it. She is much concerned, however, that nothing be allowed to disturb the period of mourning. She knows that unpleasant rumors seem to be making the rounds, and they have upset her enormously.'

'My feelings and intentions are such that she has no right to feel upset in the least. Please ask her to come out of that closet. She can keep curtains between us if she insists. I am prepared to wait years and years.' His petition was lengthy but unsuccessful.

'It is unkind of you to add to my troubles,' she sent back. 'The rumors are sensational. They make me unhappy, but I must grant that they are well founded. Your behavior is indefensible.'

He must act. The rumors were not at all surprising, and he was beginning to feel uncomfortable before these women.

'Let us consider another possibility,' he said to Koshōshō. 'Let us make it seem that she has accepted me, even though we are guilty of deception. People must be very curious to know whether she has or has not. And think how much worse the damage would be from her point of view if I were to stop coming. This grim determination is both sad and foolish.'

Koshōshō agreed, and could not hold out against so ill-used and so estimable a gentleman. The closet had a back door through which servants were admitted. She led him to it.

The princess was angry and bewildered, and helpless. Such was human nature, it appeared. No doubt she could expect even worse in the future.

Sometimes eloquently and sometimes jokingly, he sought to teach her the natural and, he should have thought, universally recognized ways of the world. But she was very angry and very sorry for herself.

'You have put me in my place. I only wish I had been cool enough to see from the outset what an unlikely affection it was. But here we are. What good is your proud name now? Forget about it, please, and accept what must be. One hears of people who in desperation throw themselves into the deep. Think of it as a simile: my love is a deep pool into which you may throw yourself.'

She sat with her face in her hands and a singlet pulled over her head and bowed shoulders. Far from being 'proud,' she was utterly forlorn, capable only of weeping aloud. He looked at her in wonderment, unable to do more. It was a fine predicament. Why did she so dislike him? They had long passed the point at which an ordinary woman would have given in, however much she disliked a man. The princess was as unyielding as a rock or a tree. He had heard that these antipathies are sometimes formed in other lives. Might it be so with the princess?

He thought of Kumoinokari, for whom it would be a lonely night, and all their years together. Their marriage had been a remarkably peaceful one, and they had been nearer than most husbands and wives. And now this predicament, which he could so easily have avoided. He gave up trying to prevail upon the princess and spent the night with his sighs.

To flee from this ridiculous situation would only be to make it worse. He spent the day quietly at Ichijō.

What brazen impudence, the princess was thinking. She wished she had never seen him. And he for his part, half angry and half apologetic, was thinking what a very silly child she was.

The closet was bare save for a perfume chest and a cupboard. They had been pushed aside and simple curtains put up to make a semblance of a boudoir. The morning light somehow came seeping in. He pulled away the quilts and smoothed her tangled hair, and so had his first good look at her. She was very pretty, delicate and ladylike. He himself was handsomer in casual dress than in full court regalia. She remembered how even in her better days with Kashiwagi he had lost no opportunity to make her feel inferior. And here she was, wan and emaciated, exposed to the gaze of this extraordinarily handsome man. He would glance at her a single time, surely, and cast her away. She tried to sort out her thoughts and make some sense of them. She feared she was guilty of all the misdeeds with which the world seemed to be charging her, and her timing could not have been worse.

She returned to her sitting room and, having seen to her toilet, ordered breakfast. The somber mourning fixtures being ill-omened and inappropriate for such an occasion, there were screens along the east side and cloves-dyed curtains of saffron at the main parlor.* The tiered stands of unlacquered wood, plain but tasteful,

*The arrangements of the rooms are obscure, but it seems likely that the main parlor is to the south, and that there is another room, along which screens are arranged, to the east.

had with the other furnishings been provided by the governor of Yamato. The women in attendance at breakfast were in yellows and reds and greens and purples, neither dull nor ostentatious, and there were lavender trains and yellow-greens to break the neutral tones of mourning.* The princess's housekeeping arrangements had been rather loose and disorganized since Kashiwagi's death, and only the governor of Yamato had sought to discipline the few stewards and chamberlains she had left. Stewards who had been off about their own business came running back at news of this eminent guest. They all seemed very busy.

Yūgiri wished to make it appear that he had established residence at Ichijō, and Kumoinokari, though she tried to tell herself that it could not be so, concluded that all was over between them. She had heard that when honest, serious men change they change completely. It did seem to be true, she sighed, going over her stock of nuptial lore. Wanting to avoid further insults and armed with a convenient taboo, she went home to her father's house. Her sister, one of the Reizei emperor's ladies, happened to be there too. With such interesting company she was not in her usual hurry to be back at Sanjō.

Yūgiri heard the news. It was as he had feared. She was a flighty and somewhat choleric lady, perhaps having inherited these traits from her father, never as calm a man as one might have wished. No doubt each of them was now busy strengthening the other's view that he had behaved outrageously and would be doing them a great favor if he were to disappear.

He hurried back to Sanjō. She had taken her daughters with her and left behind all her sons but the youngest. It was a touching reunion. The boys clambered all over him in their delight to see him, though some were also calling for their mother.

He sent messages and emissaries, but there was no reply. He was angry now – such blind obstinacy as he had allied himself to! Waiting for darkness, he went to see what thoughts her father might have in the matter.

Their lady was in the main hall, said the women. The children were with their nurse.

He sent over a stern message. 'We are a little old, I should

*The passage is obscure, and it is not possible to know the precise functions of all the several colors.

think, for this sort of thing. There you are by yourself, having left a trail of children behind you, here and at Sanjō. I have found much in your nature that does not ideally suit me, but I have been fated to stay with you. And now – these swarms of children convince me that the time for desertion has passed. Your behavior seems ridiculously dramatic and overdone.'

' "And now." Yes,' she sent back, 'you have "now" quite lost patience, and so I suppose that matters are "now" beyond repair. And what then are we to do? It will give me some comfort if you find it possible to stay with these little ragamuffins.'

'Thank you – such a sweet answer. And whose is the more sorrowfully injured name? I wonder.'* He did not insist that she come to him, and spent the night alone.

Lying down among the children, he surveyed the confusion he had managed to create in both houses. The Second Princess must be utterly bewildered. What man in his right mind could think these affairs interesting or amusing? He had had enough of them.

At dawn he sent over another indignant message. 'Everything people see and hear must strike them as infantile. If you wish this to be the end, well, let us have a try at it and see how it suits us. Though I am sure that the children at Sanjō are very touching as they ask where we may be, I am sure too that you had your reasons for bringing some with you and leaving others behind. I do not find it possible to play favorites myself. I shall go on doing everything I can for all of them.'

Always quick with her judgments, she saw in the message a threat to take the girls away and hide them from her.

'Come with me,' he said to one of them, a very pretty little thing. 'It will not be easy for me to visit you here, and I must think of your brothers too. I want you all to be together. You must not listen to what your mother says about me. She doesn't understand me very well.'

Tō no Chūjō had heard of these events and was much disturbed. 'You should not have been so hasty,' he said to his daughter. 'There is probably an explanation, and this is the sort of thing that gives a woman a bad name. But what is done is done. You have made your position quite clear and there is no need for

---

*Probably a poetic allusion.

you to rush home again now that you are here. His position should soon be clearer.'

He sent one of his sons with a note for the Second Princess.

'A bond from another life yet holds us together?
Fond thoughts I have, disquieting reports.

'Nor, I should imagine, will you have forgotten us.'

The young man came marching in. The princess's women received him at the south veranda but could think of nothing to say. The princess was even more uncomfortable. He was one of Tō no Chūjō's handsomer sons, and they were all very handsome, and he carried himself well. As he looked calmly about him, he seemed to be remembering the past.

'I feel as if I belonged here,' he said. It had the sound of an innuendo. 'You must not treat me like a stranger.'

The princess sent back that he had found her in a very unsettled state and that she could not, she feared, give his father a proper answer.

'This is no way for a grown woman to behave,' said one of the women who crowded about her. 'And it will seem very rude if one of us tries to answer in your place.'

How she wished that her mother were here, to protect her and explain away everything, even details of which she might not approve. Tears fell to mix with the ink.

She finally managed to set down a verse, though it had a fragmentary and unfinished look about it.

'Disquieting reports, resentful thoughts –
Of one who does not matter in the least?'

She folded it into an envelope.

'You may expect to see a great deal more of me,' said the young man to the women. 'I would feel much more comfortable inside the house. Yes, the ties are strong, and I shall come often. I shall tell myself that because of my services over the years I have been given the freedom of the house.' It was all most suggestive.

Yūgiri could think of nothing to do. The princess's hostility quite baffled him.

Still with her father, Kumoinokari was more and more unhappy.

Rumors reached Koremitsu's daughter, who thought of the haughty disdain with which Kumoinokari had treated her in other years. Kumoinokari had found her equal this time! Koremitsu's daughter had written occasionally and now got off a note.

'The gloom I would know were I among those who matter
I see from afar. I weep in sympathy.'

A bit impertinent, thought Kumoinokari. But she was lonely and bored, and here, if not of the most satisfying kind, was sympathy. She sent off an answer.

'Many unhappy marriages I have seen,
And never felt them as I feel my own.'

It seemed honest and unaffected. The other lady had been the sole and secret object of Yūgiri's attentions in the days when Kumoinokari was refusing him. Though he had turned away from her after his marriage, she had borne several of his children. Kumoinokari was the mother of his first, third, fifth, and sixth sons and second, fourth, and fifth daughters; the other lady, of his first, third, and sixth daughters and second and fourth sons.* They were all fine children, healthy and pretty, but Koremitsu's grandchildren were perhaps the brightest and prettiest. The lady of the orange blossoms had been given the third daughter and second son to rear, and they had the whole of her attention. Genji had become very much attached to them.

Yūgiri's affairs, one is told, were very complicated indeed.

---

*Some texts apportion the children differently. This is the most likely apportionment, giving Koremitsu's daughter the oldest child.

CHAPTER 40

The Rites

Murasaki had been in uncertain health since her great illness. Although there were no striking symptoms and there had been no recurrence of the crisis that had had her near death, she was progressively weaker. Genji could not face the thought of surviving her by even a day. Murasaki's one regret was that she must cause him pain and so be unfaithful to their vows. For the rest, she had no demands to make upon this world and few ties with it. She was ready to go, and wanted only to prepare herself for the next world. Her deepest wish, of which she sometimes spoke, had long been to give herself over entirely to prayers and meditations. But even now Genji refused to hear of it.

Yet he had for some time had similar wishes. Perhaps the time had come and they should take their vows together. He would permit himself no backward glances, however, once the decision was made. They had promised, and neither of them doubted, that they would one day have their places side by side upon the same lotus, but they must live apart, he was determined, a peak between them even if they were on the same mountain, once they had taken their vows. They would not see each other again. The sight of her now, ravaged with illness, made him fear that the final separation would be too much for him. The clear waters of their mountain retreat would be muddied. Years went by, and he had been left far behind by people who, their conversion far from thorough, had taken holy orders heedlessly and impulsively.

It would have been ill mannered of Murasaki to insist on having her way, and she would be running against her own deeper wishes if she opposed his; and so resentment at his unyielding ways was tempered by a feeling that she might be at fault herself.

For some years now she had had scriveners at work on the thousand copies of the Lotus Sutra that were to be her final offering to the Blessed One. They had their studios at Nijō, which she still thought of as home. Now the work was finished, and she made haste to get ready for the dedication. The robes of the seven priests were magnificent, as were all the other details. Not wanting to seem insistent, she had not asked Genji's help, and he had stayed discreetly in the background. No other lady, people said, could have arranged anything so fine. Genji marveled that she should be so conversant with holy ritual, and saw once again that nothing which she set her mind to was beyond her. His own part in the arrangements had been of the most general and perfunctory sort. Yūgiri gave a great deal of time and thought to the music and dancing. The emperor, the empresses,* the crown prince, and the ladies at Rokujō limited themselves to formal oblations, and even these threatened to overflow the Nijō mansion. There were others as well, all through the court, who wanted some small part in the ceremonies, which in the end were so grand that people wondered when she might have commenced laying her plans. They suggested a holy resolve going back through all the ages of the god of Furu.† The lady of the orange blossoms and the lady of Akashi were among those who assembled at Nijō. Murasaki's place was in a walled room to the west of the main hall, sequestered but for doors at the south and east opening upon the ceremonies. The other ladies were in the northern rooms, separated from the altar by screens.

It was the tenth day of the Third Month. The cherries were in bloom and the skies were pleasantly clear. One felt that Amitābha's paradise could not be far away, and for even the less than devout it was as if a burden of sin were being lifted. At the grand climax the voices of the brushwood bearers and of all the priests rose to describe in solemn tones the labors of the Blessed One,‡ and then there was silence, more eloquent than the words. It spoke to the least sensitive of those present, and it spoke worlds to her for whom everything these days was vaguely, delicately sad.

She sent a poem to the Akashi lady through little Niou, the Third Prince:

---

*Akikonomu and Genji's daughter. This is our first word that the latter has been named empress.

†Because *furu* means 'to grow old' and 'to elapse,' the name of this deity is much used in punning.

‡At a climactic point in readings of the Lotus Sutra, a procession of marchers bearing brushwood intoned a poem attributed to Gyōgi, *Shūishū* 1346, describing the labors of Gautama in a former life that he might obtain the sutra.

> I brought in water, gathered herbs and brushwood.
> My recompense was the Lotus of the Law.

'I have no regrets as I bid farewell to this life.
Yet the dying away of the fire is always sad.'*

If the lady's answer seemed somewhat cool and noncommittal, it may have been because she wished above all to avoid theatrics:

'Our prayers, the first of them borne in on brushwood,
Shall last the thousand years of the Blessed One's toils.'†

The chanting went on all through the night, and the drums beat intricate rhythms. As the first touches of dawn came over the sky the scene was is if made especially for her who so loved the spring. All across the garden cherries were a delicate veil through spring mists, and bird songs rose numberless, as if to outdo the flutes. One would have thought that the possibilities of beauty were here exhausted, and then the dancer on the stage became the handsome General Ling,‡ and as the dance gathered momentum and the delighted onlookers stripped off multicolored robes and showered them upon him, the season and the occasion brought a yet higher access of beauty. All the finest performers among the princes and grandees had quite outdone themselves. Looking out upon all this joy and beauty, Murasaki thought how little time she had left.

She was almost never up for a whole day, and today** she was back in bed again. These were the familiar faces, the people who had gathered over the years. They had delighted her one last time with flute and koto. Some had meant more to her than others. She gazed intently at the most distant of them and thought that she could never have enough of those who had been her companions at music and the other pleasures of the seasons. There had been rivalries, of course, but they had been fond of one another. All of them would soon be gone, making their way down the unknown road, and she must make her lonely way ahead of them.

---

*The image is taken from the description in the Lotus Sutra of Gautama's death.

†The labors of Gautama to obtain the Lotus Sutra lasted a thousand years.

‡See note*, page 675.

**The time sequence is obscure. If the services last several days, as would be necessary if there is a complete reading of the Lotus Sutra, then this is probably the second or fourth day, Murasaki having been out of bed on either the first day or the climactic third day, when the march of the brushwood bearers takes place. If they last but a single day, the reference is probably to the following day.

The services were over and the other Rokujō ladies departed.
She was sure that she would not see them again. She sent a poem
to the lady of the orange blossoms:

'Although these holy rites must be my last,
The bond will endure for all the lives to come.'

This was the reply:

'For all of us the time of rites is brief.
More durable by far the bond between us.'

They were over, and now they were followed by solemn and
continuous readings from the holy writ, including the Lotus Sutra.
The Nijō mansion had become a house of prayers. When they
seemed to do no good for its ailing lady, readings were commissioned at favored temples and holy places.

Murasaki had always found the heat very trying. This summer
she was near prostration. Though there were no marked symptoms
and though there was none of the unsightliness that usually goes
with emaciation, she was progressively weaker. Her women saw
the world grow dark before their eyes as they contemplated the
future.

Distressed at reports that there was no improvement, the
empress visited Nijō. She was given rooms in the east wing and
Murasaki waited to receive her in the main hall. Though there was
nothing unusual about the greetings, they reminded Murasaki, as
indeed did everything, that the empress's little children would
grow up without her. The attendants announced themselves one
by one, some of them very high courtiers. A familiar voice,
thought Murasaki, and another. She had not seen the empress in a
very long while and hung on the conversation with fond and eager
attention.

Genji looked in upon them briefly. 'You find me disconsolate
this evening,' he said to the empress, 'a bird turned away from its
nest. But I shall not bore you with my complaints.' He withdrew.
He was delighted to see Murasaki out of bed, but feared that the
pleasure must be a fleeting one.

'We are so far apart that I would not dream of troubling you to
visit me, and I fear that it will not be easy for me to visit you.'*

*The speaker may be either Murasaki or the empress.

After a time the Akashi lady came in. The two ladies addressed each other affectionately, though Murasaki left a great deal unsaid. She did not want to be one of those who eloquently prepare the world to struggle along without them. She did remark briefly and quietly upon the evanescence of things, and her wistful manner said more than her words.

Genji's royal grandchildren were brought in.

'I spend so much time imagining futures for you, my dears. Do you suppose that I do after all hate to go?'

Still very beautiful, she was in tears. The empress would have liked to change the subject, but could not think how.

'May I ask a favor?' said Murasaki, very casually, as if she hesitated to bring the matter up at all. 'There are numbers of people who have been with me for a very long while, and some of them have no home but this. Might I ask you to see that they are taken care of?' And she gave the names.

Having commissioned a reading from the holy writ, the empress returned to her rooms.

Little Niou, the prettiest of them all, seemed to be everywhere at once. Choosing a moment when she was feeling better and there was no one else with her, she seated him before her.

'I may have to go away. Will you remember me.'

'But I don't want you to go away.' He gazed up at her, and presently he was rubbing at his eyes, so charming that she was smiling through her tears. 'I like my granny,* better than Father and Mother. I don't want you to go away.'

'This must be your own house when you grow up. I want the rose plum and the cherries over there to be yours. You must take care of them and say nice things about them, and sometimes when you think of it you might put flowers on the altar.'†

He nodded and gazed up at her, and then abruptly, about to burst into tears, he got up and ran out. It was Niou and the First Princess whom Murasaki most hated to leave. They had been her special charges, and she would not live to see them grow up.

The cool of autumn, so slow to come, was at last here. Though far from well, she felt somewhat better. The winds were still

---

*Haha, the most common word for 'mother.' Some commentators argue for baba, 'old woman' or 'grandmother.'

†She is probably asking him to pray for her after her death.

gentle, but it was a time of heavy dews all the same. She would have liked the empress to stay with her just a little while longer but did not want to say so. Messengers had come from the emperor, all of them summoning the empress back to court, and she did not want to put the empress in a difficult position. She was no longer able to leave her room, however much she might want to respect the amenities, and so the empress called on her. Apologetic and at the same time very grateful, for she knew that this might be their last meeting, she had made careful preparations for the visit.

Though very thin, she was more beautiful than ever – one would not have thought it possible. The fresh, vivacious beauty of other years had asked to be likened to the flowers of this earth, but now there was a delicate serenity that seemed to go beyond such present similes. For the empress the slight figure before her, the very serenity bespeaking evanescence, was utter sadness.

Wishing to look at her flowers in the evening light, Murasaki pulled herself from bed with the aid of an armrest.

Genji came in. 'Isn't this splendid? I imagine Her Majesty's visit has done wonders for you.'

How pleased he was at what was in fact no improvement at all – and how desolate he must soon be!

> 'So briefly rests the dew upon the *hagi*.
> Even now it scatters in the wind.'

It would have been a sad evening in any event, and the plight of the dew even now being shaken from the tossing branches, thought Genji, must seem to the sick lady very much like her own.

> 'In the haste we make to leave this world of dew,
> May there be no time between the first and last.'

He did not try to hide his tears.

And this was the empress's poem:

> 'A world of dew before the autumn winds.
> Not only theirs, these fragile leaves of grass.'

Gazing at the two of them, each somehow more beautiful than the other, Genji wished that he might have them a thousand years just as they were; but of course time runs against these wishes. That is the great, sad truth.

'Would you please leave me?' said Murasaki. 'I am feeling rather worse. I do not like to know that I am being rude and find myself unable to apologize.' She spoke with very great difficulty.

The empress took her hand and gazed into her face. Yes, it was indeed like the dew about to vanish away. Scores of messengers were sent to commission new services. Once before it had seemed that she was dying, and Genji hoped that whatever evil spirit it was might be persuaded to loosen its grip once more. All through the night he did everything that could possibly be done, but in vain. Just as light was coming she faded away. Some kind power above, he thought, had kept the empress with her through the night. He might tell himself, as might all the others who had been with her, that these things have always happened and will continue to happen, but there are times when the natural order of things is unacceptable. The numbing grief made the world itself seem like a twilight dream. The women tried in vain to bring their wandering thoughts together. Fearing for his father, more distraught even than they, Yūgiri had come to him.

'It seems to be the end,' said Genji, summoning him to Murasaki's curtains. 'To be denied one's last wish is a cruel thing. I suppose that their reverences will have finished their prayers and left us, but someone qualified to administer vows must still be here. We did not do a great deal for her in this life, but perhaps the Blessed One can be persuaded to turn a little light on the way she must take into the next. Tell them, please, that I want someone to give the tonsure. There is still someone with us who can do it, surely?'

He spoke with studied calm, but his face was drawn and he was weeping.

'But these evil spirits play very cruel tricks,' replied Yūgiri, only slightly less benumbed than his father. 'Don't you suppose the same thing has happened all over again? Your suggestion is of course quite proper. We are told that even a day and a night of the holy life brings untold blessings. But suppose this really is the end – can we hope that anything we do will throw so very much light on the way she must go? No, let us come to terms with the sorrow we have before us and try not to make it worse.'

But he summoned several of the priests who had stayed on, wishing to be of service through the period of mourning, and asked them to do whatever could still be done.

He could congratulate himself on his filial conduct over the years, upon the fact that he had permitted himself no improper thoughts; but he had had one fleeting glimpse of her, and he had gone on hoping that he might one day be permitted another, even as brief, or that he might hear her voice, even faintly. The second hope had come to nothing, and the other – if he did not see her now he never would see her. He was in tears himself, and the room echoed with the laments of the women.

'Do please try to be a little quieter, just for a little while.' He lifted the curtains as he spoke, making it seem that Genji had summoned him. In the dim morning twilight Genji had brought a lamp near Murasaki's dead face. He knew that Yūgiri was beside him, but somehow felt that to screen this beauty from his son's gaze would only add to the anguish.

'Exactly as she was,' he whispered. 'But as you see, it is all over.'

He covered his face. Yūgiri too was weeping. He brushed the tears away and struggled to see through them as the sight of the dead face brought them flooding back again. Though her hair had been left untended through her illness, it was smooth and lustrous and not a strand was out of place. In the bright lamplight the skin was a purer, more radiant white than the living lady, seated at her mirror, could have made it. Her beauty, as if in untroubled sleep, emptied words like 'peerless' of all content. He almost wished that the spirit which seemed about to desert him might be given custody of the unique loveliness before him.

Since Murasaki's women were none of them up to such practical matters, Genji forced himself to think about the funeral arrangements. He had known many sorrows, but none quite so near at hand, demanding that he and no one else do what must be done. He had known nothing like it, and he was sure that there would be nothing like it in what remained of his life.

Everything was finished in the course of the day. We are not permitted to gaze upon the empty shell of the locust. The wide moor was crowded with people and carriages. The services were solemn and dignified, and she ascended to the heavens as the frailest wreath of smoke. It is the way of things, but it seemed more than anyone should be asked to endure. Helped to the scene by one or two of his men, he felt as if the earth had given way beneath him. That such a man could be so utterly defeated, thought the onlookers; and there was no one among the most insensitive of menials who was not reduced to tears. For Murasaki's women, it was as if they were wandering lost in a nightmare. Threatening to fall from their carriages, they put the watchfulness of the grooms to severe test. Genji remembered the death of his first wife, Yūgiri's mother. Perhaps he had been in better control of himself then – he could remember that there had been a clear moon that night. Tonight he was blinded with tears. Murasaki had died on the fourteenth and it was now the morning of the fifteenth.* The sun rose clear and the dew had no hiding place. Genji thought of the world he must return to, bleak and comfortless. How long must he go on alone? Perhaps he could make grief his excuse for gratifying the old, old wish and leaving the world behind. But he did not want to be remembered as a weakling. He would wait until the immediate occasion had passed, he decided, his heart threatening to burst within him.

Yūgiri stayed at his father's side all through the period of mourning. Genuinely concerned, he did what he could for the desperately grieving Genji. A high wind came up one evening, and he remembered with a new onset of sorrow an evening of high winds long before. He had seen her so briefly, and at her death that brief glimpse had been like a dream. Invoking the name of Lord Amitābha, he sought to drive away these almost unbearable memories – and to let his tears lose themselves among the beads of his rosary.

'I remember an autumn evening long ago
As a dream in the dawn when we were left behind.'

He† set the reverend gentlemen to repeating the holy name and to reading the Lotus Sutra, very sad and very moving. Still Genji's tears flowed on. He thought back over his life. Even the face he saw in the mirror had seemed to single him out for unusual honors, but there had very early been signs that the Blessed One meant him more than others to know the sadness and evanescence of things. He had made his way ahead in the world as if he had not learned the lesson. And now had come grief which surely did

---

*There is doubt as to whether it is the fifteenth, the day of the full moon, or the sixteenth.

†Perhaps Genji is the subject.

single him out from all men, past and future. He would have nothing more to do with the world. Nothing need stand in the way
of his devotions. Nothing save his uncontrollable grief, which
he feared would not permit him to enter the path he so longed to
take. He prayed to Amitābha for even a small measure of forgetfulness.

Many had come in person to pay condolences, and there had
been messages from the emperor and countless others, all of them
going well beyond conventional expressions of sympathy. Though
he had no heart for them, he did not want the world to think him
a ruined old man. He had had a good and eventful life, and he did
not want to be numbered among those who were too weak to go
on. And so to grief was added dissatisfaction at his inability to follow his deepest wishes.

There were frequent messages from Tō no Chūjō, who always
did the right thing on sad occasions and who was honestly saddened that such loveliness should have passed so swiftly. His sister,
Yūgiri's mother, had died at just this time of the year, and so many
of the people who had sent condolences then had themselves died
since. There was so very little time between the first and last.* He
gazed out into the gathering darkness and presently set down his
thoughts in a long and moving letter which he had delivered to
Genji by one of his sons and which contained this poem:

> 'It is as if that autumn had come again
>   And tears for the one were falling on tears for the other.'

This was Genji's answer:

> 'The dews of now are the dews of long ago,
>   And autumn is always the saddest time of all.'

'It is very kind of you to write so often,' he added, not wanting
his perceptive friend to guess how thoroughly the loss had undone

---

*These thoughts would seem to echo Genji's last poem to Murasaki, which presum-
ably Tō no Chūjō has not seen; but both the thoughts and the poem echo Henjō,
Shinkokinshū 757:

> Above, below, the dew falls soon and late,
>   As if to tell us the story of the world.

him. He wore darker mourning than the gray weeds of that other autumn.*

The successful and happy sometimes arouse envy, and sometimes they let pride and vanity have their way and bring unhappiness to others. It was not so with Murasaki, whom the meanest of her servants had loved and the smallest of whose acts had seemed admirable. There was something uniquely appealing about her, having to do, perhaps, with the fact that she always seemed to be thinking of others. The wind in the trees and the insect songs in the grasses brought tears this autumn to the eyes of many who had not known her, and her intimates wondered when they might find consolation. The women who had long been with her saw the life they must live without her as utter bleakness. Some of them, wishing to be as far as possible from the world, went off into remote mountain nunneries.

There were frequent messages from Akikonomu, seeking to describe an infinite sorrow.

'I think that now, finally, I understand.

'She did not like the autumn, that I knew –
Because of the wasted moors that now surround us?'

Hers were the condolences that meant most, the letters that spoke to Genji through the numbness of his heart. He wept quietly on, lost in a sad reverie, and took a very long time with his answer.

'Look down upon me from your cloudy summit,
Upon the dying autumn which is my world.'

He folded it into an envelope and still held it in his hand. He had taken residence in the women's quarters, not wanting people to see what a useless dotard he had become. A very few women with him, he lost himself in prayer. He and Murasaki had exchanged their vows for a thousand years, and already she had left him. His thoughts must now be on that other world. The dew upon the lotus: it was what he must strive to become, and nothing must be allowed to weaken the resolve. Alas, he did still worry about the name he had made for himself in this world.

*See his poem upon Aoi's death, Chapter 9.

Yūgiri took charge of the memorial services. If they had been left to Genji they would have been managed far less efficiently. He would take his vows today, Genji told himself; he would take his vows today. Dream-like, the days went by.

The empress too remained inconsolable.

CHAPTER 41
The Wizard

Bright spring was dark this year. There was no relief from the sadness of the old year. Genji had callers as always, but he said that he was not well and remained in seclusion. He made an exception for his brother, Prince Hotaru, whom he invited behind his curtains.

'And why has spring so graciously come to visit
A lodging where there is none to admire the blossoms?'

The prince was in tears as he replied:

'You take me for the usual viewer of blossoms?
If that is so, I seek their fragrance in vain.'

He went out to admire the rose plum, and Genji was reminded of other springs. And who indeed was there to admire these first blossoms? He had arranged no concerts this year. In very many ways it was unlike the springs of other years.

The women who had been longest in attendance on Murasaki still wore dark mourning, and acceptance and resignation still eluded them. Their one real comfort was that Genji had not gone back to Rokujō. He was still here at Nijō, for them to serve. Although he had had no serious affairs with any of them, he had favored one and another from time to time. He might have been expected, in his loneliness, to favor them more warmly now, but the old desires seemed to have left him. Even the women on night duty slept outside his curtains. Sometimes, to break the tedium, he would talk of the old years. He would remember, now that romantic affairs meant so little to him, how hurt Murasaki had been by involvements of no importance at all. Why had he permitted himself even the trivial sort of dalliance for which he had felt no need to apologize? Murasaki had been too astute not to guess his real intentions; and yet, though she had been quick to recover from fits of jealousy which were never violent in any event, the fact was that she had suffered. Each little incident came back, until he felt that he had no room in his heart for them all. Sometimes a woman would comment briefly on an incident to

which she had been witness, for there were women still with him
who had seen everything.

Murasaki had given not the smallest hint of resentment when
the Third Princess had come into the house. He had known all the
same that she was upset, and he had been deeply upset in his turn.
He remembered the snowy morning, a morning of dark, rolling
clouds, when he had been kept waiting outside her rooms until he
was almost frozen. She had received him quietly and affectionately
and tried to hide her damp sleeves. All through the wakeful nights
he thought of her courage and strength and longed to have them
with him again, even in a dream.

'Just see what a snow we have had!' One of the women seemed
to be returning to her own room. It was snowy dawn, just as then,
and he was alone. That was the tragic difference.

'The snow will soon have left this gloomy world.
My days must yet go on, an aimless drifting.'

Having finished his ablutions, he turned as usual to his prayers.
A woman gathered embers from the ashes of the night before and
another brought in a brazier. Chūnagon and Chūjō were with
him.*

'Every night is difficult when you are alone, but last night was
worse than most of them. I was a fool not to leave it all behind
long ago.'

How sad life would be for these women if he were to renounce
the world! His voice rising and falling in the silence of the chapel
as he read from a sutra had always had a strange power to move,
unlike any other, and for the women who served him it now
brought tears that were not to be held back.

'I have always had everything,' he said to them. 'That was the
station in life I was born to. Yet it has always seemed that I was
meant for sad things too. I have often wondered whether the
Blessed One was not determined to make me see more than others
what a useless, insubstantial world it is. I pretended that I did not
see the point, and now as my life comes to a close I know the
ultimate in sorrow. I see and accept my own inadequacies and the

---

*Ladies by these names have appeared in early chapters, but, although the names are
here introduced as if we should already be familiar with them, the earlier ladies
would by now be very old.

disabilities I brought with me from other lives. There is nothing, not the slenderest bond, that still ties me to the world. No, that is not true: there are you who seem so much nearer than when she was alive. It will be very hard to say goodbye.'

He dried his tears and still they flowed on. The women were weeping so piteously that they could not tell him what sorrow it would be to leave him.

In sad twilight in the morning and evening he would summon the women who had meant most to him. He had known Chūjō since she was a little girl, and would seem to have favored her with discreet attentions. She had been too fond of Murasaki to let the affair go on for very long, and he thought of her now, with none of the old desire, as one of Murasaki's favorites, a sort of memento the dead lady had left behind. A pretty, good-natured woman, she was, so to speak, a yew tree* nearer the dead lady's grave than most.

He saw only the closest intimates. His brothers, good friends among the high courtiers – they all came calling, but for the most part he declined to see them. Try though he might to control himself, he feared that his senility and his crankish ways would shock callers and be what future generations would remember him by. People might assume, of course, that his retirement was itself evidence of senility, and that would be a pity; but it could be far worse to have people actually see him. Even Yūgiri he addressed through curtains and blinds. He had decided that he would bide his time until talk of the change in him had stopped and then take holy orders. He paid very brief calls at Rokujō, but because the flow of tears was only more torrential he was presently neglecting the Rokujō ladies.

The empress, his daughter, returned to court, leaving little Niou to keep him company. Niou remembered the instructions his 'granny' had left and was most solicitous of the rose plum at the west wing. Genji thought it very kind of him, and completely charming. The Second Month had come, and plum trees in bloom and in bud receded into a delicate mist. Catching the bright song of a warbler in the rose plum that had been Murasaki's especial favorite, Genji went out to the veranda.

*Unaimatsu, a pine planted beside a grave.

'The warbler has come again. It does not know
That the mistress of its tree is here no more.'

It was high spring and the garden was as it had always been. He tried not to remember, but everything his eye fell on brought such trains of memory that he longed to be off in the mountains, where no birds sing.* Tears darkened the yellow cascade of *yamabuki*. In most gardens the cherry blossoms had fallen. Here at Nijō the birch cherry† followed the double cherries and presently it was time for the wisteria. Murasaki had brought all the spring trees, early and late, into her garden, and each came into bloom in its turn.

'*My* cherry,' said Niou. 'Can't we do something to keep it going? Maybe if we put up curtains all around and fasten them down tight. Then the wind can't get at it.'

He was so pretty and so pleased with his proposal that Genji had to smile. 'You are cleverer by a great deal than the man who wanted to cover the whole sky with his sleeve.'‡ Niou was his one companion.

'It may be that we can't go on being friends much longer,' he continued, feeling as always that tears were not far away. 'We may not be able to see each other, even if it turns out that I still have some life left in me.'

The boy tugged uncomfortably at his sleeve and looked down. 'Do you have to say what Granny said?'

At a corner balustrade, or at Murasaki's curtains, Genji would sit gazing down into the garden. Some of the women were still in dark weeds, and those who had changed back to ordinary dress limited themselves to somber, unfigured cloths. Genji was in subdued informal dress. The rooms were austerely furnished and the house was hushed and lonely.

'Taking the final step, I must abandon
The springtime hedge that meant so much to her.'

No one was hurrying him off into a cell. It would be his own doing, and yet he was sad.

With time heavy on his hands, he visited the Third Princess.

See note, page 611.

†*Kabazakura*. Murasaki was likened to one in Chapter 28.

‡See note*, page 289.

Niou and his nurse came along. As usual, Niou was everywhere, and the company of Kaoru, the princess's little boy, seemed to make him forget his fickle cherry blossoms. The princess was in her chapel, a sutra in her hands. Genji had never found her very interesting or exciting, but he had to admire this quiet devotion, untouched, apparently, by regrets for the world and its pleasures. How bitterly ironical that this shallow little creature should have left him so far behind!

The flowers on the altar were lovely in the evening light.

'She is no longer here to enjoy her spring flowers, and I am afraid that they do very little for me these days. But if they are beautiful anywhere it is on an altar.' He paused. 'And her *yamabuki* – it is in bloom as I cannot remember having seen it before. The sprays are gigantic. It is not a flower that insists on being admired for its elegance, and that may be why it seems so bright and cheerful. But why do you suppose it chose this year to come into such an explosion of bloom? – almost as if it wanted us to see how indifferent it is to our sorrows.'

'Spring declines to come to my dark valley,'* she replied, somewhat nonchalantly.

Hardly an appropriate allusion. Even in the smallest matters Murasaki had seemed to know exactly what was wanted of her. So it had been to the end. And in earlier years? All the images in his memory spoke of sensitivity and understanding in mood and manner and words. And so once again he was letting one of his ladies see him in maudlin tears.

Evening mists came drifting in over the garden, which was very beautiful indeed.

He went to look in on the Akashi lady. She was startled to see him after such a long absence, but she received him with calm dignity. Yes, she was a superior lady. And Murasaki's superiority had been of a different sort. He talked quietly of the old years.

'I was very soon taught what a mistake it is to be fond of anyone. I tried to make sure that I had no strong ties with the world. There was that time when the whole world seemed to turn against me. If it did not want me, I had nothing to ask of it. I could

*Kiyowara Fukayabu, *Kokinshū* 967:

> Spring declines to come to my dark valley.
> I hear no laments for blossoms so quick to fall.

see no reason why I should not end my days off in the mountains. And now the end is coming and I still have not freed myself of the old ties. I go on as you see me. What a weakling I do seem to be.'

He spoke only indirectly of the matter most on his mind, but she understood and sympathized. 'Even people whom the world could perfectly well do without have lingering regrets, and for you the regrets must be enormous. But I think that if you were to act too hastily the results might be rather unhappy. People will think you shallow and flighty and you will not be happy with yourself. I should imagine that the difficult decisions are the firmest once they are made. I have heard of so many people who have thrown away everything because of a little surprise or setback that really has not mattered in the least. That is not what you want. Be patient for a time, and if your resolve has not weakened when your grandchildren are grown up and their lives seem in order – I shall have no objections and indeed I shall be happy for you.'

It was good advice. 'But the caution at the heart of the patience you recommend is perhaps even worse than shallowness.'

He spoke of the old days as memories came back. 'When Fujitsubo died I thought the cherry trees should be in black.* I had had so much time when I was a boy to admire her grace and beauty, and it may have been for that reason that I seemed to be the saddest of all when she died. Grief does not correspond exactly with love. When an old and continuous relationship comes to an end, the sorrow is not just for the relationship itself. The memory of the girl who was presently a woman and of all the years until suddenly at the end of your own life you are alone – this is too much to be borne. It is the proliferation of memories, some of them serious and some of them amusing, that makes for the deepest sorrow.'

He talked on into the night of things old and new, and was half inclined to spend the night with her; but presently he made his departure. She looked sadly after him, and he was puzzled at his own behavior.

Alone once more, he continued his devotions on through the night, resting only briefly in his drawing room. Early in the morning he got off a letter to the Akashi lady, including this poem:

*See note†, page 355.

'I wept and wept as I made my slow way homewards.
It is a world in which nothing lasts forever.'

Though his abrupt departure had seemed almost insulting, she was in tears as she thought of the dazed, grieving figure, somehow absent, so utterly unlike the old Genji.

'The wild goose has flown, the seedling rice is dry.
Gone is the blossom the water once reflected.'*

The hand was as always beautiful. He remembered Murasaki's resentment towards the Akashi lady. They had in the end become good friends, and yet a certain stiffness had remained. Murasaki had kept her distance. Had anyone except Genji himself been aware of it? He would sometimes look in on the Akashi lady when the loneliness was too much for him, but he never stayed the night.

It was time to change into summer robes. New robes came from the lady of the orange blossoms, and with them a poem:

'It is the day of the donning of summer robes,
And must there be a renewal of memories?'

He sent back:

'Thin as the locust's wing, these summer robes,
Reminders of the fragility of life.'

The Kamo festival seemed very remote indeed from the dullness of his daily round.

'Suppose you all have a quiet holiday,' he said to the women, fearing that the tedium must be even more oppressive today than on most days. 'Go and see what the people at home are up to.'

Chūjō was having a nap in one of the east rooms. She sat up as he came in. A small woman, she brought a sleeve to her face, bright and lively and slightly flushed. Her thick hair, though somewhat tangled from sleep, was very beautiful. She was wearing a singlet of taupe-yellow, dark-gray robes, and saffron trousers, all of them just a little rumpled, and she had slipped off her jacket and train. She now made haste to put herself in order. Beside her was a sprig of heartvine.

*Kari, which indicated transience in Genji's poem, becomes 'wild goose' in the lady's. It is the season when the wild geese fly over on their way north.

'It is so long since I have had anything to do with it,' he said, picking it up, 'that I have even forgotten the name.'

She thought it a somewhat suggestive remark.

'With heartvine we garland our hair – and you forget!
All overgrown the urn, so long neglected.'*

Yes, he had neglected her, and he was sorry.

'The things of this world mean little to me now,
And yet I find myself reaching to break off heartvine.'

There still seemed to be one lady to whom he was not indifferent.

The rainy Fifth Month was a difficult time.

Suddenly a near-full moon burst through a rift in the clouds. Yūgiri chanced to be with him at this beautiful moment. The white of the orange blossoms leaped forward in the moonlight and on a fresh breeze the scent that so brings memories came wafting into the room. But it was for only a moment. The sky darkened even as they awaited, 'unchanged a thousand years, the voice of the cuckoo.'† The wind rose and almost blew out the eaves lamp, rain pounded on the roof, and the sky was black once more.

'The voice of rain at the window,'‡ whispered Genji. It was not a very striking or novel allusion, but perhaps because it came at the right moment Yūgiri wished it might have been heard 'at the lady's hedge.'**

'I know I am not the first man who has had to live alone,' said Genji, 'but I do find myself restless and despondent. I should imagine that after this sort of thing a mountain hermitage might come as a relief. Bring something for our guest,' he called to the women. 'I suppose it is too late to send for the men.'

---

*There is a complex pun on *yorube*, a ritual vessel the sound of whose name suggests reliance or dependence.

†Anonymous, *Gosenshū* 186:

> Year after year, unchanged, the orange blossom.
> Unchanged a thousand years, the voice of the cuckoo.

‡Po Chü-i, Collected Works, III, 'Sardonic Injunction, 3.'

**The poem cited in early commentaries is otherwise unknown. The meaning seems to be that Murasaki, not Yūgiri, should have been the one to hear.

Yūgiri wished that his father were not forever gazing up into the sky as if looking for someone there.* This inability to forget must surely stand in the way of salvation. But if he himself was unable to forget the one brief glimpse he had had of her, how could he reprove his father?

'It seems like only yesterday, and here we are at the first anniversary. What plans do you have for it?'

'Only the most ordinary sort. This is the time, I think, to dedicate the Paradise Mandala she had done, and of course she had a great many sutras copied. The bishop, I can't think of his name, knows exactly what she wanted. He should be able to give all the instructions.'

'Yes, she seems to have thought about these things a great deal, and I am sure that they are a help to her wherever she is now. We know, of course, what a fragile bond she had with this world, and the saddest thing is that she had no children.'

'There are ladies with stronger bonds who still have not done very well in the matter of children. It is you who must see that our house grows and prospers.'

Not wanting it to seem that he did nothing these days but weep, Genji said little of the past.

Just then, faintly – how can it have known?† – there came the call of the cuckoo for which they had been waiting.

'Have you come, O cuckoo, drenched in nighttime showers,
    In memory of her who is no more?'

And still he was gazing up into the sky.
Yūgiri replied:

'Go tell her this, O cuckoo: the orange blossoms
    Where once she lived are now their loveliest.'

The women had poems too, but I shall not set them down.

Yūgiri, who often kept his father company through the lonely nights, spent this night too with him. The sorrow and longing

---

*Sakai Hitozane, *Kokinshū* 743:

> The heavens vast – are they to remember her by,
> That each time I think of her I gaze at them?

†See note‡, page 228.

were intense at the thought that the once-forbidden rooms were so near and accessible.

One very hot summer day Genji went out to cool himself beside a lotus pond, now in full bloom. 'That there should be so very many tears':* it was the phrase that first came into his mind. He sat as if in a trance until twilight. What a useless pursuit it was, listening all by himself to these clamorous evening cicadas and gazing at the wild carnations in the evening light.

> 'I can but pass a summer's day in weeping.
> Is that your pretext, O insects, for weeping too?'

Presently it was dark, and great swarms of fireflies were wheeling about. 'Fireflies before the pavilion of evening' – this time it was a Chinese verse† that came to him.

> 'The firefly knows that night has come, and I –
> My thoughts do not distinguish night from day.'

The Seventh Month came, and no one seemed in a mood to honor the meeting of the stars.‡ There was no music and there were no guests. Deep in the night Genji got up and pushed a door open. The garden below the gallery was heavy with dew. He went out.

> 'They meet, these stars, in a world beyond the clouds.
> My tears but join the dews of the garden of parting.'

Already at the beginning of the Eighth Month the autumn winds were lonely. Genji was busy with preparations for the memorial services. How swiftly the months had gone by! Everyone went through fasting and penance and the Paradise Mandala was dedicated. Chūjō as usual brought holy water for Genji's vesper devotions. He took up her fan, on which she had written a poem:

---

*Ise, *Kokin Rokujō, Zoku Kokka Taikan* 33325:

> The sorrow grows and grows. How strange it is
> That there should be so very many tears.

†From 'The Song of Everlasting Sorrow.'
‡Tanabata, the seventh of the Seventh Month.

'This day, we are told, announces an end to mourning.
How can it be, when there is no end to tears?'

He wrote beside it:

'The days are numbered for him who yet must mourn.
And are they numbered, the tears that yet remain?'

Early in the Ninth Month came the chrysanthemum festival. As always, the festive bouquets were wrapped in cotton to catch the magic dew.

'On other mornings we took the elixir together.
This morning lonely sleeves are wet with dew.'

The Tenth Month was as always a time of gloomy winter showers. Looking up into the evening sky, he whispered to himself: 'The rains are as the rains of other years.'* He envied the wild geese overhead, for they were going home.

'O wizard flying off through boundless heavens,
Find her whom I see not even in my dreams.'†

The days and months went by, and he remained inconsolable.

Presently the world was buzzing with preparations for the harvest festival and the Gosechi dances. Yūgiri brought two of his little boys, already in court service, to see their grandfather. They were very nearly the same age, and very pretty indeed. With them were several of their uncles, spruce and elegant in blue Gosechi prints, a very grand escort indeed for two little boys. At the sight of them all, so caught up in the festive gaiety, Genji thought of memorable occurrences on ancient festival days.

'Our lads go off to have their Day of Light.‡
For me it is as if there were no sun.'

And so he had made his way through the year, and the time had come to leave the world behind. He gave his attendants, after their several ranks, gifts to remember him by. He tried to avoid grand

---

*Probably a poetic allusion.

†In 'The Song of Everlasting Sorrow' the emperor sends a wizard in search of the dead Yang Kuei-fei. In Chapter 1, Genji's grieving father is put in mind of the same passage. The word *maboroshi*, 'wizard,' occurs in the tale only these two times.

‡Toyonoakari, the day following the harvest festival proper.

farewells, but they knew what was happening, and the end of the year was a time of infinite sadness. Among his papers were letters which he had put aside over the years but which he would not wish others to see. Now, as he got his affairs in order, he would come upon them and burn them. There was a bundle of letters from Murasaki among those he had received at Suma from his various ladies. Though a great many years had passed, the ink was as fresh as if it had been set down yesterday. They seemed meant to last a thousand years. But they had been for him, and he was finished with them. He asked two or three women who were among his closest confidantes to see to destroying them. The handwriting of the dead always has the power to move us, and these were not ordinary letters. He was blinded by the tears that fell to mingle with the ink until presently he was unable to make out what was written.

'I seek to follow the tracks of a lady now gone
    To another world. Alas, I lose my way.'

Not wanting to display his weakness, he pushed them aside.

The women were permitted glimpses of this and that letter, and the little they saw was enough to bring the old grief back anew. Murasaki's sorrow at being those few miles from him now seemed to remove all bounds to their own sorrow. Seeking to control a flow of tears that must seem hopelessly exaggerated, Genji glanced at one of the more affectionate notes and wrote in the margin:

'I gather sea grasses no more, nor look upon them.
    Now they are smoke, to join her in distant heavens.'

And so he consigned them to flames.

In the Twelfth Month the clanging of croziers as the holy name was invoked was more moving than in other years, for Genji knew that he would not again be present at the ceremony. These prayers for longevity – he did not think that they would please the Blessed One. There had been a heavy fall of snow, which was now blowing into drifts. The repast in honor of the officiant was elaborate and Genji's gifts were even more lavish than usual. The holy man had often presided over services at court and at Rokujō. Genji was sorry to see that his hair was touched with gray. As always, there were numerous princes and high courtiers in the congregation. The plum trees, just coming into bloom, were lovely in the snow.

There should have been music, but Genji feared that this year music would make him weep. Poems were read, in keeping with the time and place.

There was this poem as Genji offered a cup of wine to his guest of honor:

'Put blossoms in your caps today. Who knows
That there will still be life when spring comes round?'

This was the reply:

'I pray that these blossoms may last a thousand springs.
For me the years are as the deepening snowdrifts.'

There were many others, but I neglected to set them down.

It was Genji's first appearance in public. He was handsomer than ever, indeed almost unbelievably handsome. For no very good reason, the holy man was in tears.

Genji was more and more despondent as the New Year approached.

Niou scampered about exorcising devils, that the New Year might begin auspiciously.

'It takes a lot of noise to get rid of them. Do you have any ideas?'

Everything about the scene, and especially the thought that he must say goodbye to the child, made Genji fear that he would soon be weeping again.

'I have not taken account of the days and months.
The end of the year – the end of a life as well?'

The festivities must be more joyous than ever, he said, and his gifts to all the princes and officials, high and low – or so one is told – quite shattered precedent.

CHAPTER 42

His Perfumed Highness

The shining Genji was dead, and there was no one quite like him. It would be irreverent to speak of the Reizei emperor. Niou, the third son of the present emperor, and Kaoru, the young son of Genji's Third Princess, had grown up in the same house* and were both thought by the world to be uncommonly handsome, but somehow they did not shine with the same radiance. They were but sensitive, cultivated young men, and the fact that they were rather more loudly acclaimed than Genji had been at their age was very probably because they had been so close to him. They were in any event very well thought of indeed. Niou had been reared by Murasaki, her favorite among Genji's grandchildren, and still had her Nijō house for his private residence. If the crown prince was because of his position the most revered of the royal children, Niou was his parents' favorite. They would have liked to have him with them in the palace, but he found life more comfortable in the house of the childhood memories. Upon his initiation he was appointed minister of war.†

The First Princess, his sister, lived in the east wing of Murasaki's southeast quarter at Rokujō. It was exactly as it had been at Murasaki's death, and everything about it called up memories. The Second Prince had rooms in the main hall of the same quarter and spent much of his spare time there. The Plum Court was his palace residence. He was married to Yūgiri's second daughter and was of such high character and repute that he was widely expected to become crown prince when the next reign began.

Yūgiri had numerous daughters. The oldest was married to the crown prince and had no rival for his affections. It had been generally assumed that the younger daughters would be married to royal princes in turn. The Akashi empress, Yūgiri's sister, had put in a good word for them. Niou, however, had thoughts of his own. He was a headstrong young man who did exactly what he wanted to do. Yūgiri told himself that there were after all no laws in these

---

*Presumably in Genji's Rokujō mansion.

†Hyōbukyō, a position commonly assigned to young princes of the blood and held by both Murasaki's father and Prince Hotaru.

matters, meanwhile making sure that his daughters had every advantage and letting it be known that princes who came paying court would not be turned away. Princes and high courtiers who flattered themselves that they were among the eligible had very exciting reports about the sixth daughter.

Genji's various ladies tearfully left Rokujō for the dwellings that would be their last. Genji had given the lady of the orange blossoms the east lodge at Nijō. Kaoru's mother lived in her own Sanjō mansion. With the Akashi empress now in residence at the palace, Rokujō had become a quiet and rather lonely place. Yūgiri had observed — it had been true long ago and it was still true — how quickly the mansions of the great fall into ruin. Enormous expense and attention went into them, and one could almost see the beginning of the process when their eminent masters were dead, and so they became the most poignant reminders of evanescence. He did not want anything of the sort to happen at Rokujō. He was determined that there would be life in the mansion and the streets around it while he himself was still alive. He therefore installed Kashiwagi's widow, the Second Princess, in the northeast quarter, where he had lived as the foster son of the lady of the orange blossoms. He was very precise and impartial in his habits, spending alternate nights there and at his Sanjō residence, where Kumoinokari lived.

Genji had polished the Nijō house to perfection, and then the southeast quarter at Rokujō had become the jeweled pavilion, the center of life and excitement. Now it was as if they had been meant all along for one among his ladies and for her grandchildren. There it was that the Akashi lady ministered to the needs of the empress's children. Making no changes in the ordering of the two households, Yūgiri treated Genji's several ladies as if he were the son of them all. His strongest regret was that Murasaki had not lived to see evidences of his esteem. After all these years he still grieved for her.

And the whole world still mourned Genji. It was as if a light had gone out. For his ladies, for his grandchildren, for others who had been close to him, the sadness was of course more immediate and intense, and they were constantly being reminded of Murasaki too. It is true, they all thought: the cherry blossoms of spring are loved because they bloom so briefly.

Genji had asked the Reizei emperor to watch over Kaoru. The

emperor was faithful to the trust, and his empress, Akikonomu, sad
that she had no children of her own, found her greatest pleasure in
being of service to him. His initiation ceremonies, when he was
fourteen, were held in the Reizei Palace. In the Second Month
he was made a chamberlain and in the autumn Captain of the
Right Guards. This rapid promotion was at the behest of the Reizei emperor, who seemed to have his own reasons for haste. So it
was that Kaoru was a man of importance at a very early age. He
was given rooms in the Reizei Palace and the Reizei emperor
made it his personal business to see that all the ladies-in-waiting
and even the maids and page girls were the prettiest and ablest to
be had. Similar attention went into fitting the rooms, which
would not have offended the sensibilities of the most refined and
demanding princess. Indeed, the Reizei emperor and his empress
forwent the services of the most accomplished women in their
own retinue, that Kaoru might be more elegantly served. They
wanted him to be happy at Reizei and could not have been more
attentive to his needs if he had been their son. The Reizei
emperor had only one child, a princess by a daughter of Tō no
Chūjō. There was of course nothing that he was not ready and
eager to do for her. Perhaps it was because his love for Akikonomu
had deepended over the years that he was equally solicitous of
Kaoru. There were some, indeed, who did not quite understand
this partiality.

Kaoru's mother had quite given herself up to her devotions.
She spared herself no expense in arranging the monthly invocation
of the holy name and the semiannual reading of the Lotus Sutra
and all the other prescribed rites. Her son's visits were her chief
pleasure. Sometimes he almost seemed more like a father than a
son – a fact which he was aware of and thought rather sad. He was
a constant companion of both the reigning emperor and the
retired emperor, and was much sought after by the crown prince
and other princes too, until he sometimes wished that he could be
in two places at once. From his childhood there had been things,
chance remarks, brief snatches of an overheard conversation, that
had upset him and made him wish that there were someone to
whom he could go for an explanation. There was no one. His
mother would be distressed at any hint that he had even these
vague suspicions. He could only brood in solitude and ask what
missteps in a former life might explain the painful doubts with

which he had grown up – and wish that he had the clairvoyance of a Prince Rāhula,* who instinctively knew the truth about his own birth.

'Whom might I ask? Why must it be
That I do not know the beginning or the end?'

But of course there was no one he could go to for an answer.

These doubts were with him most persistently when he was unwell. His mother, taking the nun's habit when still in the flush of girlhood – had it been from a real and thorough conversion? He suspected rather that some horrible surprise had overtaken her, something that had shaken her to the roots of her being. People must surely have heard about it in the course of everyday events, and for some reason had felt constrained to keep it from him.

His mother was at her devotions, morning and night, but he thought it unlikely that the efforts of a weak and vacillating woman could transform the dew upon the lotus into the bright jewel of the law. A woman labors under five hindrances, after all.† He wanted somehow to help her towards a new start in another life.

He thought too of the gentleman who had died so young.‡ His soul must still be wandering lost, unable to free itself of regrets for this world. How he wished that they could meet – there would be other lives in which it might be possible.

His own initiation ceremonies interested him not in the least, but he had to go through with them. Suddenly he found himself a rather conspicuous young man, indeed the cynosure of all eyes. This new eminence only made him withdraw more resolutely into himself.

The emperor favored him because they were so closely related, but a quite genuine regard had perhaps more to do with the matter. As for the empress, her children had grown up with him and he still seemed almost one of them. She remembered how Genji had sighed at the unlikelihood that he would live to see this child

---

*A son of the Buddha who was himself able to dispose of doubts about his paternity. Some texts here have Kui Taishi, others Zengyō Taishi. Though these have traditionally been taken to designate Rāhula, it is by no means certain that they do.

†The Lotus Sutra lists five degrees of Buddhahood to which women may not attain.

‡Kashiwagi.

of his late years grown into a man, and felt that Genji's worries had added to her own responsibilities. Yūgiri was more attentive to Kaoru than to his own sons.

The shining Genji had been his father's favorite child, and there had been jealousy. He had not had the backing of powerful maternal relatives, but, blessed with a cool head and mature judgment, he had seen the advantages of keeping his radiance somewhat dimmed, and so had made his way safely through a crisis that might have been disastrous for the whole nation. So it had been too with preparations for the world to come: everything in its proper time, he had said, going about the matter carefully and unobtrusively. Kaoru had received too much attention while still a boy, and it may have been charged against him that he was not sufficiently aware of his limitations. Something about him did make people think of avatars and suspect that perhaps a special bounty of grace set him apart from the ordinary run of men. There was nothing in his face or manner, to be sure, that brought people up short, but there was a compelling gentleness that was unique and suggested limitless depths.

And there was the fragrance he gave off, quite unlike anything else in this world. Let him make the slightest motion and it had a mysterious power to trail behind him like a 'hundred-pace incense.' One did not expect young aristocrats to affect the plain and certainly not the shabby. The elegance that is the result of a careful toilet was the proper thing. Kaoru, however, wished often enough that he might be free of this particular mark of distinction. He could not hide. Let him step behind something in hopes of going unobserved, and that scent would announce his presence. He used no perfume, nor did he scent his robes, but somehow a fragrance that had been sealed deep inside a Chinese chest would emerge the more ravishing for his presence. He would brush a spray of plum blossoms below the veranda and the spring rain dripping from it would become a perfume for others who passed. The masterless purple trousers* would reject their own perfume for his.

Niou was his rival in everything and especially in the competition to be pleasantly scented. The blending of perfumes would

*Sosei, *Kokinshū* 241:

> Purple trousers – left behind by whom? –
> Give sweetly forth the scent of an unknown master.

become his work for days on end. In the spring he would gaze inquiringly up at the blossoming plum, and in the autumn he would neglect the maiden flower of which poets have made so much and the *hagi* beloved of the stag, and instead keep beside him, all withered and unsightly, the chrysanthemum 'heedless of age'* and purple trousers, also sadly faded, and the burnet that has so little to recommend it in the first place. Perfumes were central to his pursuit of good taste. There were those who accused him of a certain preciosity. Genji, they said, had managed to avoid seeming uneven.

Kaoru was always in Niou's apartments, and music echoed through the halls and galleries as their rivalry moved on to flute and koto. They were rivals but they were also the best of friends. Everyone called them (sometimes it was a little tiresome) 'his perfumed highness' and 'the fragrant captain.'† No father of a pretty and nubile daughter was unaware of their existence or lost an opportunity to remind them that there were young ladies to be had. Niou would get off notes to such of them as seemed worthy of his attention and gather pertinent information about them, but no lady could thus far have been said to excite him unduly. Or rather, there was one: the Reizei princess, who aroused thoughts of eventual marriage. Her maternal grandfather had been a very important man, and she was reputed to be something of a treasure. Women who had been briefly in her service would add to his store of information, until presently he was very excited indeed.

Kaoru was a different sort of young man. He already knew what an empty, purposeless world it is, and was reluctant to commit himself any more firmly than seemed quite necessary. He did not want the final renunciation to be difficult. Some thought him rather ostentatiously enlightened in his disdain for amorous things, and it seemed wholly unlikely that he would ever urge himself upon a lady against her wishes.

*Ki no Tsurayuki, *Kokin Rokujō, Zoku Kokka Taikan* 31072:

> Chrysanthemums, they say, are heedless of age
> And brush aside a century in an instant.

†Niou Hyōbukyō and Kaoru Chūjō. The names, or designations, by which the two have traditionally been known derive from this passage.

He held the Third Rank and a seat on the council, still keeping his guards commission, when he was only nineteen. The esteem of the emperor and empress had already made him an extraordinary sort of commoner; but the old doubts persisted, and with them a strain of melancholy that kept him from losing himself in romantic dalliance. Nothing seemed capable of penetrating his reserve. To some, his precocious maturity seemed a little daunting.

He had rooms in the Reizei Palace of the princess who so interested Niou and had no trouble gathering intelligence about her. All of it suggested that she was a very unusual lady, indeed a lady in whom, were he interested in marriage himself, he might find the most fascinating possibilities. In all else completely open and unreserved, the Reizei emperor chose to surround his daughter with stern barriers. Kaoru thought this not at all unreasonable of him, and made no effort to force his way through. He was a very prudent young man who did not choose to risk unpleasantness for himself or for a lady.

Because he was so universally admired, ladies were not on the whole disposed to ignore his notes. Indeed, the response was usually immediate, and so he had in the course of time had numerous little affairs, all of them very fleeting. He always managed to seem interested but not fascinated. Perversely, any suggestion that he was not wholly indifferent had a most heady effect, and so his mother's Sanjō mansion swarmed with comely young serving women. His aloofness did not please them, of course, but the prospect of removing themselves from his presence was far worse. Numbers of ladies whom one would have thought too good for domestic service had come to put their trust in a rather improbable relationship. He was not very cooperative, perhaps, but there was no denying that he was a courteous gentleman of more than ordinary good looks. Ladies who had had a glimpse of him seemed to make careers of deceiving themselves.

It would be his first duty for so long as his royal mother lived, he often said, to be her servant and protector.

Though Yūgiri went on thinking how fine it would be to offer a daughter to Niou and another to Kaoru, he kept his own counsel. Marriage to a near relative is not usually held to be very interesting, but he did not think he would find more desirable sons-in-law if he searched through the whole court. His sixth daughter, a grandchild of Koremitsu, was more beautiful than any of Kumoinokari's daughters, and she had outdistanced them too in the polite accomplishments. He was determined to make up for the fact that the world seemed to look down upon her because of her mother, and so he had made her the ward of the Second Princess, Kashiwagi's widow, lonely and bored with no children of her own. A casual hint to Niou or Kaoru was not likely to go unnoticed, he thought – for she was a young lady of remarkable endowments. He had chosen not to keep her behind the deepest of curtains, but had encouraged her to maintain a bright and lively salon, echoes of which were certain to reach the ear of an alert young gentleman.

The victory banquet following the New Year's archery meet was to be at Rokujō this year. The preparations were elaborate, for it was assumed that the royal princes would all attend. And indeed those among them who had come of age did accept the invitation. Niou was the handsomest of the empress's sons, all of whom were handsome. Hitachi, the Fourth Prince, was the son of a lesser concubine, and it may have been for that reason that people thought him rather ill favored. The Left Guards won easily, as usual, and the meet was over early in the day. Starting back for Rokujō, Yūgiri invited Niou, Hitachi, and the Fifth Prince, also a son of the empress, to ride with him. Kaoru, who had been on the losing side, was making a quiet departure when Yūgiri asked him to join them. It was a large procession, including numbers of high courtiers and several of Yūgiri's sons – a guards officer, a councillor of the middle order, a moderator of the first order – that set off for Rokujō. The way was a long one, made more beautiful by flurries of snow. Soon the high, clear tone of a flute was echoing through Rokujō, that place of delights for the four seasons, outdoing, one sometimes thought, all the many paradises.

As protocol required, the victorious guards officers were assigned places facing south in the main hall, and the princes and important civil officials sat opposite them facing north. Cups were filled and the party became noisier, and several guards officers danced 'The One I Seek.'* Their long, flowing sleeves brought the

---

*An 'eastern song.' To judge from the quotation in the last sentence of the chapter, there is a confusion with a *fūzokuuta*, 'vulgar song,' called 'Eight Maidens.'

scent of plum blossoms in from the veranda, and as always it took on a kind of mysterious depth as it drifted past Kaoru.

'The darkness may try to keep us from seeing,' said one of the women lucky enough to have a good view of the proceedings, 'but it can't keep the scent away. And I must say there is nothing quite like it.'

Yūgiri was thinking how difficult it would be to find fault with Kaoru's looks and manners.

'And now you must sing it for us,' he said. 'Remember that you are a host and not a guest, and it is your duty to be entertaining.'

Kaoru obeyed, but not as if to join in the roistering. 'Where dwell the gods' – they were the grandest words of his song, but what went before had the same quiet dignity.

CHAPTER 43

The Rose Plum

Kōbai, the oldest surviving son of the late Tō no Chūjō, was now Lord Inspector. He was an energetic, clever, open man who from his boyhood had shown great promise. He had reached considerable eminence, of course, and was well thought of and a great favorite with the emperor. Upon his first wife's death he married Makibashira, daughter of Higekuro, the chancellor. It was she who had such strong regrets for the cypress pillar when her mother left her father's house.* Her grandfather had arranged for her to marry Prince Hotaru, who had left her a widow. The inspector favored her with clandestine attentions after Prince Hotaru's death, and would seem to have concluded that it was a sufficiently distinguished liaison to be made public. Having been left with two children, both daughters, he prayed to the gods native and foreign that his second wife bear him a son. The prayer was soon granted. Makibashira had brought with her a daughter by Prince Hotaru.

Kōbai was scrupulously impartial in his treatment of the three girls, but malicious, troublemaking women are to be found in most important households and his was no exception. There were unpleasant incidents, most of which, however, Makibashira, a cheerful, amiable lady, managed to smooth over so that no one was left feeling aggrieved. She did not let the princess's claims influence her unduly, and it was on the whole a harmonious household over which she presided.

In rapid succession there were initiation ceremonies for the three girls. Kōbai built a spacious new hall, a beam span wider in either direction than most. To his older daughter he assigned the south rooms, to his younger the west, and to the prince's daughter the east. The outsider is likely to pity the fatherless daughter among stepsisters but the princess had come into a good inheritance from both sides of her family and was able to indulge her tastes and interests quite as she wished, on festive occasions and at ordinary times as well.

*See Chapter 31.

Young ladies who enjoy such advantages are certain to be noticed, and as each of the girls reached maturity she was noticed by even the emperor and the crown prince, who sent inquiries. The empress so dominated court life, however, that Kōbai was uncertain how to reply. Presently he was able to persuade himself that a refusal to face competition is the worst possible thing for a young lady's prospects. Yūgiri's daughter, already married to the crown prince, would be the most formidable of competition, but the superior man did not let such difficulties control his life. An attractive young lady should not be wasted at home. So he gave his older daughter to the crown prince. She was seventeen or eighteen, very pretty and vivacious.

The second girl had, it was reported, a graver, deeper sort of beauty. Kōbai was most reluctant to give her in marriage to a commoner. Might Prince Niou perhaps be interested?

Niou was fond of joking with Kōbai's young son when the two of them were at court together. The boy had artistic talents and a countenance that suggested considerable intellectual endowments as well.

'Tell your father,' said Niou, 'that I am annoyed with him for keeping the rest of the family out of sight. You are surely not its most interesting member?'

The boy passed the remark on, and Kōbai was all smiles. There were times when it was good to have a daughter or two.

'It might not be a bad idea, you know. The competition at court is fierce, and a pretty daughter could do worse than marry one of the younger princes. The idea is rather exciting, now that I give it a little thought.'

This happened while he was getting his older daughter ready for presentation at court. He had been reminding the god of Kasuga that empresses were supposed to come from the Fujiwara family. It was the god's own promise, and Tō no Chūjō had been badly used in the days when the Reizei emperor was preparing to name his consort. Perhaps something might be done now to make amends.

Court gossip had it that the older daughter was doing well in the competition for the crown prince's affection. Knowing how strange and difficult court life can be, Kōbai sent Makibashira to be with her. Makibashira was a most admirable guardian and adviser, but Kōbai was bored without her, and the younger daughter was very much at loose ends. Prince Hotaru's daughter did not choose, in this difficult time, to stand on her dignity, and the two girls often spent the night together, passing the time at music and more frivolous pursuits. Kōbai's daughter accepted the other as her mentor and they got on very well together. The princess was an extremely retiring young lady, not completely open even with her own mother. It was indeed a degree of reserve that attracted unfavorable comment, though it stopped short of positive eccentricity. She was, as a matter of fact, a rather charming girl in her way, far better favored, certainly, than most.

Kōbai was feeling guilty about his stepdaughter, left out of all the excitement.

'You must make certain decisions,' he said to Makibashira. 'I will do everything for her that I would do for one of my own daughters.'

'She seems to be completely without the hopes and plans one expects a young girl to have,' said Makibashira, brushing away a tear. 'I certainly would not want to insist upon them. I suppose I must call it fate and keep her with me. She will have problems when I am gone, I am afraid, but perhaps people won't laugh at her if she becomes a nun.' And she added that in spite of everything the girl had a great deal to recommend her.

Kōbai was determined to be a good father, and he wished that the girl would cooperate at least to the extent of letting him see her.

'It is not kind of you to insist upon hiding yourself.' He had taken to stealing up to her curtains and searching for a hole or a gap, but he always went away disappointed.

'I want to be father and mother to you,' he continued, having posted himself firmly before her curtains, 'and I am hurt that you should treat me like a stranger.'

Her answers, in very soft tones, suggested great elegance, as indeed did everything about her. He wanted more than ever to see her. He was not prepared to admit that his own daughters were not the finest young ladies in the land, but he suspected that the princess might outshine them. The world was too wide and varied, that was the trouble. A man might think he had a peerless daughter, and somewhere a lovelier lady was almost certain to appear. Yes, he really must have a look at the princess.

'It has been a month and more since I last had the pleasure of hearing you play. Things have been in such a frightful stir. The girl in the west rooms is absolutely mad about the lute, you know. Do you think she has possibilities? The lute should be left alone unless it is played well. Give her a lesson or two, please, if you have nothing better to do. I am not the man I once was, and I never had regular lessons, but I was a passable musician in my day. I can still tell good from bad on almost any instrument. You are very parsimonious with your playing, but I do occasionally catch an echo, and it brings back old memories. Lord Yūgiri is still with us, of course, to keep the Rokujō tradition alive. Then there is his brother, the middle councillor,* and there is Prince Niou. I am sure that they could have held their own against the best of the old masters. I am told that they are very serious about their music, though they may not have quite Yūgiri's confident touch. Each time I hear your own lute I think how much it resembles his. People are always saying that the most important thing is tact and forbearance in the use of the left hand. That is important, of course, but a misplaced bridge can be a disaster, and for a lady a gentle touch with the right hand is very important too. Come, now, let me hear you play. A lute, someone!'

Her women were on the whole much less reticent than she, though one of them, very young and from a very good family, had annoyed him by withdrawing to a distant corner.

'Just see my lady, will you, way off over there. Who has she been led to think she is?'

His son came in, wearing casual court dress, more becoming, Kōbai thought, than full regalia.

He gave the boy a message for the daughter at court. 'I cannot be with you this evening. You must do without me. Perhaps you can say that I am not feeling well.' That business out of the way, he smiled and turned to other business. 'Bring your flute with you one of these days. It may be what your sister here needs to encourage her. Do you ever play for His Majesty? And do you please him, in your infantile way?'

He set the boy to a strain in the sōjō mode,† which he managed very commendably.

'Good, very good. I can see that you have profited from our

*This is our first word that Kaoru has been promoted to chūnagon.
†Based on G.

little musicales. And now you must join him,' he said to the princess.

She played with obvious reluctance and declined to use a plectrum, but the brief duo was very pleasing indeed. Kōbai whistled an accompaniment, rich and full.

He looked out at a rose plum in full bloom just below this east veranda.

'Magnificent. Am I right in thinking that Prince Niou is living in the palace these days? Take him a branch – the one who knows best knows best.* How well I remember the days when Genji was young. They called him 'the shining one.' It would have been when he was a guards commander, and I was a page, as you are now. I was lucky enough to attract his attention, and I never shall forget the pleasure it gave me. They talk about Prince Niou and his good friend Kaoru, and indeed they have become very fine young gentlemen. I may have been heard to say that they are not like Genji, really not like him at all, but that is because for me there can never be another Genji. I find myself choking up at the thought that I once stood there beside him. And I was never so very close to him. For those that were it must seem as if something had gone very wrong, that they should be here without him.' His voice had become somewhat husky. Seeking to control himself, he broke off a plum branch and, handing it to the boy, pushed him towards the door. 'Prince Niou is the only one left who reminds me of him. When the Blessed One died his disciples thought they saw something of his radiance in Prince Ananda, and ventured to hope that he had come back. For me Prince Niou is the light in all the darkness.'

Full of youthful good spirits once more, he dashed off a poem on a bit of scarlet paper and folded it inside a sheet of notepaper the boy chanced to have with him.

'A purposeful breeze wafts forth the scent of our plum.
Will not the warbler be first to heed the summons?'

The boy rushed off to the palace, delighted at the prospect of seeing Niou, whom he found emerging from the empress's audience chamber. Niou singled him out among the throngs in her anterooms.

See note, page 541.

'Why did you have to run off in such a hurry last night? How long have you been here this evening?'

'I was sorry I had to go. I came early this evening because they said you might still be here.' He spoke as one man to another.

'You must come and see me at Nijō sometime. It is a more comfortable sort of place, and it seems to attract young people, I don't really know why.'

The stir had subsided. Sensing an intimate tête-à-tête, the throngs were withdrawing.

'So my brother, the crown prince, is letting you have a little time of your own for a change? It used to be that he had to have you with him every moment of the day. Does it make you a little jealous, that your sister is occupying so much of his attention?'

'You are not to think I wanted it that way. If it had been you, now —' Confidently he took a seat beside the prince.

'They insist on treating me like a child. If that is their view of me, there is not much that I can do about it. Yet I cannot help being annoyed. Perhaps you might remind another sister, the one whose rooms face east, I am told, that we come from the same worn-out old family,* and so perhaps we might be friends.'

It was the boy's opportunity to present the plum branch.

Niou smiled. 'I am glad it is not a peace offering.' He was delighted with it. The scent and color and the distribution of the blossoms surpassed anything he had seen in the palace gardens.

'I've heard it said that the rose plum puts everything into its color and lets the white plum have all the perfume, but here we have color and perfume all in the same blossoms.'

The plum blossom had always been among his favorites. The boy was delighted to have brought such pleasure.

'You are on duty this evening, I believe? Why don't you stay here with me?'

And so the boy was not after all able to call on the crown prince. The scent of the plum blossoms was rather overwhelmed by the scent from Niou's robes. Lying beside him, the boy thought he had never met a more charming gentleman.

---

*He is a son and the princess a granddaughter of an emperor. The remark has ironic reference to the low regard in which the royal family was held by the Fujiwara. Kōbai is a Fujiwara.

'And my cousin, the mistress of your plums?* Was she not invited to come into the crown prince's service?'

'I don't think I've ever heard anyone mention it – but I did hear my father say that the one who knows best knows best.'

Niou's informants had apprised him of the fact that Kōbai was more concerned about his own daughter than Prince Hotaru's. Since she did not happen to be Niou's favorite, he did not immediately answer Kōbai's poem.

Early the next morning he did have a poem ready for the boy to take with him. It was not perhaps a very warm one.

> 'If I were one who followed inviting scents
> Perhaps I might be summoned by the wind.'

'Do not let yourself become involved in talks with the aged,' he said more than once to the boy. 'Have a quiet talk with someone nearer your own age.'

These remarks had the effect of making the boy feel responsible for his royal sister. His father's daughters were more open with him and seemed more like sisters, and his childish view of the princess was almost worshipful. Yes, he must find her a good husband. He wished well for all his sisters, and the tasteful gaiety of the crown prince's household made him think that the royal one among them had had very bad luck. How good it would be to see her at Niou's side! The branch of plum blossoms had produced most encouraging hints.

He delivered Niou's poem to his father.

'Not very friendly, I must say. But it is amusing to see what a prim and proper face he is putting on for us. I suppose he is aware that Yūgiri and all the rest of us think him a little too much of a ladies' man. The primness does not accord very well with his talents in that direction.'

If he was annoyed he quickly recovered, and today again got off a friendly note:

> 'Ever fragrant, the royal sleeves touch the blossoms
> And bring them into higher and higher repute.

'I must ask to be forgiven if I seem frivolous.'

---

*Prince Hotaru's daughter.

Perhaps, thought Niou, it was worth taking seriously. He answered:

'Were I to follow the fragrance of the blossoms,
Might I not be accused of wantonness?'

Kōbai thought it a bit stiff, when things had been going so well. Makibashira came home from court. 'The boy seems to have spent a night at the palace not long ago. When he left the next morning everyone was admiring the marvelous perfume. "Aha," said the crown prince, "he has been with my brother Niou." The crown prince is very quick in these things. And that, he said, was why he was being neglected himself. We all thought it very amusing. Had you written to Prince Niou? Somehow it didn't seem as if you had.'

'I had indeed. He has always been fond of plum blossoms, and the rose plum is so unusually fine this year that I could not let the opportunity pass. I broke off a branch and sent it to him. He gives off such an extraordinary scent himself. I doubt that you could find in all the wardrobes of all the grand ladies a robe with a finer scent burnt into it. With Lord Kaoru it all comes naturally. He seems to have no interest at all in perfumes. It is very curious, really – what do you suppose he has been up to in other lives? One plum blossom may go by the same name as another, but it's the roots that make all the difference. Prince Niou was kind enough to praise this one of ours, and I must say that it deserves to be praised.' So the plum became his excuse for discussing Niou.

Prince Hotaru's daughter was old enough to know what was expected of young ladies, and she took careful note of what went on around her. She had evidently concluded with some firmness that marriage was not for her. Men are easily swayed by power and prestige, and Kōbai's daughters, with their influential father behind them, had already had many earnest proposals. The princess had lived a quiet, withdrawn sort of life by comparison. But Niou seemed to have decided that she was the one for him. Kōbai's son, now among his regular attendants, was kept busy delivering secret notes.

Kōbai had hopes of his own and watched for evidence that they had been noticed. Indeed he was already making plans.

Makibashira thought him rather pathetic. 'He has it all wrong.

This stream of letters might have some point if the prince were even a little interested.'

Niou was spurred to new efforts by the silence with which his notes were greeted. Makibashira occasionally sought to coax an answer from her daughter. Niou's prospects were bright and a girl could certainly do worse. But the princess found it hard to believe that he was serious. He was known to be keeping up numerous clandestine liaisons, and his trips to Uji did not seem merely frivolous.*

Makibashira got off a quiet letter from time to time. A prince was, after all, a prince.

*This piece of information tells us that the action is concurrent with that of Chapters 47 through 49.

CHAPTER 44

Bamboo River

The story I am about to tell wanders rather far from Genji and his family. I had it unsolicited from certain obscure women who lived out their years in Higekuro's house. It may not seem entirely in keeping with the story of Murasaki, but the women themselves say that there are numerous inaccuracies in the accounts we have had of Genji's descendants, and put the blame on women so old that they have become forgetful. I would not presume to say who is right.

Tamakazura, now a widow, had three sons and two daughters. Higekuro had had the highest ambitions for them, and had waited eagerly for them to grow up; and then, suddenly, he was dead. Tamakazura was lost without him. He had been impatient to see his children in court service and now of course his plans had come to nothing. People go streaming off in the direction of power and prestige, and though the treasures and manors from Higekuro's great days had not been dispersed his house was now still and silent.

Tamakazura came from a large and influential clan, but on such levels people tend to be remote, and Higekuro had been a difficult man, somewhat too open in his likes and dislikes. She found that her brothers kept their distance. Genji's children, on the other hand, continued to treat her as if she were one of them. Only the empress, Genji's daughter, had received more careful attention in his will, and Yūgiri was as friendly and considerate as a brother could possibly have been. He lost no opportunity to call on her or to write to her.

The sons went through their initiation ceremonies. Tamakazura wished very much that her husband were still alive, but no one doubted that they would make respectable careers for themselves all the same. The daughters were the problem. Higekuro had petitioned the emperor to take them into court service, and when the emperor was reminded that sufficient time had elapsed for them to have come of age he sent repeatedly to remind Tamakazura of her husband's wishes. The empress was in a position of such unrivaled influence, however, that the other ladies, waiting far down the line for an occasional sidelong glance, were having a difficult time of it. And on the other hand Tamakazura would not wish it to seem that she did not think her daughters up to the competition.

There were friendly inquiries from the Reizei emperor too. He reminded her that she had long ago disappointed him.

'Perhaps you think me too old to be in the running, but if you were to let me have one of them she would be like a daughter to me.'

Tamakazura hesitated. She had been fated, it seemed, and the matter had always puzzled her, to hurt and disappoint the Reizei emperor. Certainly she had not wanted to. She felt awed and humbled now, and perhaps she was being given a chance to make amends.

Her daughters had acquired a numerous band of suitors. The young lieutenant, son of Yūgiri and Kumoinokari, was his father's favorite, a very fine lad indeed. He was among the more earnest of the suitors. Tamakazura could not refuse him and his brothers the freedom of her house, for there were close connections on both sides of the family.* They had their allies among the serving women and had no trouble making representations. Indeed, they had become rather a nuisance, hovering about the house day and night.

There were letters too from Kumoinokari.

'He is still young and not at all important,' said Yūgiri himself, 'but he does have his good points. Have you perhaps noticed them?'

Tamakazura would not be satisfied with an ordinary marriage for the older girl, but for the younger – well, she asked modest respectability and not much more. She was beginning to be a little afraid of the lieutenant. There were ominous rumblings to the effect that he would make off with one of the girls if he could not have her otherwise. Though his suit was certainly not beneath consideration, it would not help the prospects of one daughter if the other were to be abducted.

'I do not like it at all,' she said to her women. 'You must be very careful.'

---

*Tamakazura is a half sister of the boy's mother, but not, by Heian standards, closely related to his father. Perhaps the point is that she lived for a time in Genji's Rokujō mansion and was thought to be Yūgiri's half sister.

These instructions made it difficult for them to go on delivering his notes.

Kaoru, now fourteen or fifteen, had for some time been so close to the Reizei emperor that they might have been father and son. He was sober and mature for his years, a fine young man for whom everyone expected a brilliant future. Tamakazura would have been happy to list him among the suitors. Her house was very near the Sanjō house where he lived with his mother, and one or another of her sons was always inviting him over for a musical evening. Because of the interesting young ladies known to be in residence, he always found other young men on the premises. They tended to seem foppish and none had his good looks or confident elegance. The lieutenant, Yūgiri's son, was of course always loitering about, his good looks dimmed by Kaoru's. Perhaps because of his nearness to Genji, Kaoru was held in universally high esteem. Tamakazura's young attendants thought him splendid. Tamakazura agreed that he was a most agreeable young man and often received him for a friendly talk.

'Your father was so good to me. The sense of loss is still overpowering, and I find myself looking for keepsakes. There is your brother, the minister, of course, but he is such an important man that I cannot see him unless I have a very good reason.'

She treated him like a brother and it was in that mood that he came visiting. She knew that, unlike other young men, he would do nothing rash or frivolous. His rectitude was such, indeed, that some of the younger women thought him a little prudish. He did not take at all well to their teasing.

Early in the New Year Kōbai came calling. He was Tamakazura's brother, now Lord Inspector, and it was he who had delighted them long before with his rendition of 'Takasago.'* With him were, among others, a son of the late Higekuro who was full brother to Makibashira, now Kōbai's wife. Yūgiri also came calling, a very handsome man in grand ministerial procession, all six of his sons among his attendants. They were all of them excellent young gentlemen and their careers were progressing more briskly than those of most of their colleagues. No cause for self-pity here, one would have said – and yet the lieutenant seemed moody and

*In Chapter 10.

withdrawn. The indications were as always that he was his father's favorite.

Tamakazura received Yūgiri from behind curtains. His easy, casual manner took her back to an earlier day.

'The trouble is that there has to be an explanation for every visit I make. Visits to the palace are an exception, of course, for I must make them; but the most informal call is so hemmed in by ceremony that it hardly seems worth the trouble. I cannot tell you how often I have wanted to come for a talk of old times and have had to reconsider. Please send for these youngsters of mine whenever they can be of service. They have instructions to keep reminding you of their availability.'

'I am as you see me, a recluse quite cut off from the world. Your very great kindness somehow makes me all the more aware of how good your father was to me.' She spoke circumspectly of the messages that had come from the Reizei Palace. 'I have been telling myself that a lady who goes to court without strong allies is asking for trouble.'

'I have had reports that the emperor too has been in communication with you. I scarcely know what to advise. The Reizei emperor is no longer on the throne, of course, and one may say that his great day is over. Yet the years have done nothing at all to his remarkable looks. I count over the list of my own daughters and ask whether one of them might not qualify, and have reluctantly decided not to enter them in such grand competition. You know of course that he has a daughter of his own, and one must always consider her mother's feelings.* Indeed, I have heard that people have been frightened off by exactly that question.'

'Oh, but I may assure you that I am interested in the proposal because she approves very warmly. She has little to occupy her, she has said, and it would be a great pleasure to help the Reizei emperor make a young lady feel at home.'

Tamakazura's house was now thronging with New Year callers. Yūgiri went off to the Sanjō house of the Third Princess, Kaoru's mother. She had no reason to feel neglected, for courtiers who had enjoyed the patronage of her father and brother found it impossible to pass her by. Tamakazura's three sons, a guards captain, a

---

*Tamakazura and the mother of the Reizei emperor's daughter are half sisters.

moderator, and a chamberlain, went with Yūgiri, who presided over an even grander procession than before.

Kaoru called on Tamakazura that evening. The other young gentlemen having left – who could have found serious fault with any of them? – it was as if everything had been arranged to set off his good looks. Yes, he was unique, said the susceptible young women.

'Oh, that Kaoru. Put him beside our young lady here and you would really have something.'

It may have sounded just a little cheeky, but he was young and certainly he was very handsome, and his smallest motion sent forth that extraordinary fragrance. A discerning lady, however deeply cloistered, had to recognize his superiority.

Tamakazura was in her chapel and invited him to join her. He went up the east stairway and took a place just outside the blinds. The plum at the eaves was sending forth its first buds and the warbler was still not quite able to get through its song without faltering. Something about his manner made the women want to joke with him, but his replies were rather brusque.

A woman named Saishō offered a poem:

'Come, young buds – a smile is what we need,
    To tell us that, taken in hand, you would be more fragrant.'

Thinking it good for an impromptu poem, he answered:

'A barren, blossomless tree, I have heard it called.
    At heart it bursts even now into richest bloom.

'Stretch out a hand, if you wish to be sure.'

'Lovely the color, lovelier yet the fragrance.'* And it was indeed as if she meant to find out for herself.

Tamakazura had come forward from the recesses of the chapel. 'What horrid young creatures you are,' she said gently. 'Do you not know that you are in the presence of the most proper of young gentlemen?'

Kaoru knew very well that they called him 'Lord Proper,' and he was not at all proud of the title.

*Anonymous, *Kokinshū* 33:

> This plum in blossom – whose sleeves can it have brushed?
> Lovely the color, lovelier yet the fragrance.

The chamberlain, Tamakazura's youngest son, was not yet on the regular court rosters and had no New Year calls to make. Refreshments were served on trays of delicate sandalwood. Tamakazura was thinking that though Yūgiri looked more and more like Genji as the years went by, Kaoru did not really look like him at all. Yet there was an undeniable nobility in his manner and bearing. Perhaps the young Genji had been like him. It was the sort of thought that always reduced her to pensive silence.

The women were chattering about the remarkable fragrance he had left behind.

No, Kaoru did not really like being Lord Proper. Late in the month the plum blossoms were at their best. Thinking it a good time to show them all that they had misjudged him, he went off to visit the apartments of the young chamberlain, Tamakazura's son. Coming in through the garden gate, he saw that another young gentleman had preceded him. Also in casual court dress, the other did not want to be seen, but Kaoru recognized and hailed him. It was Yūgiri's son the lieutenant, very frequently to be found on the premises. Exciting sounds of lute and Chinese koto were coming from the west rooms. Kaoru was feeling somewhat uncomfortable and somewhat guilty as well. The uninvited guest was not his favorite role.

'Come,' he said, when there was a pause in the music. 'Be my guide. I am a complete stranger.'

Side by side under the plum at the west gallery, they serenaded the ladies with 'A Branch of Plum.'* As if to invite this yet fresher perfume inside, someone pushed open a corner door and there was a most skillful accompaniment on a Japanese koto. Astonished and pleased that a lady should be so adept at a *ryo* key,† they repeated the song. The lute too was delightfully fresh and clear. It seemed to be a house given over to elegant pursuits. Kaoru was less diffident than usual.

A Japanese koto was pushed towards him from under the blinds. Each of the visitors deferred to the other so insistently that the issue was finally resolved by Tamakazura, who sent out to Kaoru through her son:

'I have heard that your playing resembles that of my father, the

*See note**, page 542.

†Resembling the major.

late chancellor, and would like nothing better than to hear it. The warbler has favored us this evening. Can you not be persuaded to do as well?'

He would look rather silly biting his finger like a bashful stripling. Though without enthusiasm, he played a short strain on the koto, from which he coaxed an admirably rich tone.

Tamakazura had not been close to her father, Tō no Chūjō, but she missed him, and trivial little incidents were always reminding her of him. And how very much Kaoru did remind her of her late brother Kashiwagi. She could almost have sworn that it was his koto she was listening to. She was in tears – perhaps they come more easily as one grows older.

The lieutenant continued the concert with 'This House.'* He had a fine voice and he was in very good form this evening. The concert had a gay informality that would not have been possible had there been elderly and demanding connoisseurs in the assembly. Everyone wanted to take part in it, and the music flowed on and on. The chamberlain seemed to resemble his father, Higekuro. He preferred wine to music, at which he was not very good.

'Come, now. Silence is not permitted. Something cheerful and congratulatory.'

And so, with someone to help him, he sang 'Bamboo River.'† Though immature and somewhat awkward, it was a commendable enough performance.

A cup was pushed towards Kaoru from under the blinds. He was in no hurry to take it.

'I have heard it said that people talk too much when they drink too much. Is that what you have in mind?'

She had a New Year's gift for him, a robe and cloak from her own wardrobe, most alluringly scented.

'More and more purposeful,' he said, making as if to return it through her son. 'There were all those other parties for the carolers,'‡ he added, deftly turning aside their efforts to keep him on.

He always got all the attention, thought the lieutenant, looking glumly after him, in an even blacker mood than usual. This is the poem with which, sighing deeply, he made his departure:

A Saibara which appears also in Chapter 23. See note, page 435.

†See note†, page 438.

‡See note*, page 137.

'Everyone is thinking of the blossoms,
And I am left alone in springtime darkness.'

This reply came from one of the women behind the curtains:

'There is a time and place for everything.
The plum is not uniquely worthy of notice.'

The young chamberlain had a note from Kaoru the next morning. 'I fear that I may have been too noisy last night. Was everyone disgusted with me?' And there was a poem in an easy, discursive style, obviously meant for young ladies:

'Deep down in the bamboo river we sang of
Did you catch an echo of deep intentions?'

It was taken to the main hall, where all the women read it.

'What lovely handwriting,' said Tamakazura, who hoped that her children might be induced to improve their own scrawls. 'Name me another young gentleman who has such a wide variety of talents and accomplishments. He lost his father when he was very young and his mother left him to rear himself, and look at him, if you will. There must be reasons for it all.'

The chamberlain's reply was in a very erratic hand indeed. 'We did not really believe that excuse about the carolers.

'A word about a river and off you ran,
And left us to make what we would of unseemly haste.'

Kaoru came visiting again, as if to demonstrate his 'deep intentions,' and it was as the lieutenant had said: he got all the attention. For his part, the chamberlain was happy that they should be so close, he and Kaoru, and only hoped that they could be closer.

It was now the Third Month. The cherries were in bud and then suddenly the sky was a storm of blossoms and falling petals. Young ladies who lived a secluded life were not likely to be charged with indiscretion if at this glorious time of the year they took their places out near the veranda. Tamakazura's daughters were perhaps eighteen or nineteen, beautiful and good-natured girls. The older sister had regular, elegant features and a sort of gay spontaneity which one wanted to see taken into the royal family itself. She was wearing a white cloak lined with red and a robe of russet with a yellow lining. It was a charming combination that went beautifully with the season, and there was a flair even in her way of quietly tucking her skirts about her that made other girls feel rather dowdy. The younger sister had chosen a light robe of pink, and the soft flow of her hair put one in mind of a willow tree. She was a tall, proud beauty with a face that suggested a meditative turn. Yet there were those who said that if an ability to catch and hold the eye was the important thing, then the older sister was the great beauty of the day.

They were seated at a Go board, their long hair trailing behind them. Their brother the chamberlain was seated near them, prepared if needed to offer his services as referee.

His brothers came in.

'How very fond they do seem to be of the child. They are prepared to submit their destinies to his mature judgment.'

Faced with this stern masculinity, the serving women brought themselves to attention.

'I am so busy at the office,' said the oldest brother, 'that I have quite abdicated my prerogatives here at home to our young lord chamberlain.'

'But my duties, I may assure you, are far more arduous,' said the second. 'I am scarcely ever at home, and I have been pushed quite out of things.'

The young ladies were charming as they took a shy recess from their game.

'I often think when I am at work,' said the oldest brother, dabbing at his eyes, 'how good it would be if Father were still with us.' He was twenty-seven or twenty-eight, and very handsome and well mannered. He wanted somehow to pursue his father's plans for the sisters.

Sending one of the women down into the garden, a veritable cherry orchard, he had her break off an especially fine branch.

'Where else do you find blossoms like these?' said one of the sisters, taking it up in her hand.

'When you were children you quarreled over that cherry. Father said it belonged to you' – and he nodded to his older sister – 'and Mother said it belonged to *you*, and no one said it belonged to me. I did not exactly cry myself to sleep but I did feel slighted. It is a very old tree and it somehow makes me aware of how old I am getting myself. And I think of all the people who once looked at it and are no longer living.' By turns jocular and melancholy, the brothers paid a more leisurely visit than usual. The older brothers were married and had things to attend to, but today the cherry blossoms seemed important.

Tamakazura did not look old enough to have such fine sons. Indeed she still seemed in the first blush of maidenhood, not at all different from the girl the Reizei emperor had known. It was nostalgic affection, no doubt, that had led him to ask for one of her daughters.

Her sons did not think the prospect very exciting. 'Present and immediate influence is what matters, and his great day is over. He is still very youthful and handsome, of course – indeed, it is hard to take your eyes from him. But it is the same with music and birds and flowers. Everything has its day, its time to be noticed. The crown prince, now –'

'Yes, I had thought of him,' said Tamakazura. 'But Yūgiri's daughter dominates him so completely. A lady who enters the competition without very careful preparation and very strong backing is sure to find herself in trouble. If your father were still alive – no one could take responsibility for the distant future, of course, but he could at least see that we were off to a good start.' In sum, the prospect was discouraging.

When their brothers had left, the ladies turned again to the Go board. They now made the disputed cherry tree their stakes.

'Best two of three,' said someone.

They came out to the veranda as evening approached. The blinds were raised and each of them had an ardent cheering section. Yūgiri's son the lieutenant had come again to visit the youngest son of the house. The latter was off with his brothers, however, and his rooms were quiet. Finding an open gallery door, the lieutenant peered cautiously inside. An enchanting sight greeted him, like a revelation of the Blessed One himself (and it was rather sad that he should be so dazzled). An evening mist somewhat obscured the scene, but he thought that she in the red-lined robe of white, the 'cherry' as it is called, must be the one who so interested him. Lovely, vivacious – she would be 'a memento when they have fallen.'* He must not let another man

*Ki no Aritomo, *Kokinshū* 66:

> Deeply dyed the hue of the cherry blossoms,
> My sleeves shall be a memento when they have fallen.

have her. The young attendants were also very beautiful in the evening light.

The lady on the right was the victor. 'Give a loud Korean cheer,'* said one of her supporters, and indeed they were rather noisy in their rejoicing. 'It leaned to the west to show that it was ours all along, and you people refused to accept the facts.'

Though not entirely sure what was happening, the lieutenant would have liked to join them. Instead he withdrew, for it would not do to let them know that they had been observed in this happy abandon. Thereafter he was often to be seen lurking about the premises, hoping for another such opportunity.

The blossoms had been good for an afternoon, and now the stiff winds of evening were tearing at them.

Said the lady who had been the loser:

'They did not choose to come when I summoned them,
And yet I tremble to see them go away.'

And her woman Saishō, comfortingly:

'A gust of wind, and promptly they are gone.
My grief is not intense at the loss of such weaklings.'

And the victorious lady:

'These flowers must fall. It is the way of the world.
But do not demean the tree that came to me.'

And Tayū, one of her women:

'You have given yourselves to us, and now you fall
At the water's edge. Come drifting to us as foam.'

A little page girl who had been cheering for the victor went down into the garden and gathered an armful of fallen branches.

'The winds have sent them falling to the ground,
But I shall pick them up, for they are ours.'

And little Nareki, a supporter of the lady who had lost:

---

*At equestrian matches and the like, a 'Korean fanfare' celebrated a victory for the side of the Right.

'We have not sleeves that cover all the vast heavens.
We yet may wish to keep these fragrant petals.*

'Be ambitious, my ladies!'

The days passed uneventfully. Tamakazura fretted and came to no decision, and there continued to be importunings from the Reizei emperor.

An extremely friendly letter came from his consort, Tamakazura's sister. 'You are behaving as if we were nothing to each other. His Majesty is saying most unjustly that I seek to block his proposal. It is not pleasant of him even if he is joking. Do please make up your mind and let her come to us immediately.'

Perhaps it had all been fated, thought Tamakazura – but she almost wished that her sister would dispel the uncertainty by coming out in opposition. She sighed and turned to the business of getting the girl ready, and seeing too that all the women were properly dressed and groomed.

The lieutenant was in despair. He went to his mother, Kumoinokari, who got off an earnest letter in his behalf. 'I write to you from the darkness that obscures a mother's heart.† No doubt I am being unreasonable – but perhaps you will understand and be generous.'

Tamakazura sighed and set about an answer. It was a difficult situation. 'I am in an agony of indecision, and these constant letters from the Reizei emperor do not help at all. I only wish – and it is, I think, the solution least likely to be criticized – that someone could persuade your son to be patient. If he really cares, then someday he will perhaps see that his wishes are very important to me.'

It might have been read as an oblique suggestion that she would let him have her second daughter once the Reizei question had been settled. She did not want to make simultaneous arrangements for the two girls. That would have seemed pretentious, and besides, the lieutenant was still very young and rather obscure. He was not prepared to accept the suggestion that he transfer his affections, however, and the image of his lady at the Go board refused to leave him. He longed to see her again, and was in despair at the thought that there might not be another opportunity.

He was in the habit of taking his complaints to Tamakazura's son the chamberlain. One day he came upon the boy reading a

See note, page 289.
†See note*, page 13.

letter from Kaoru. Immediately guessing its nature, he took it from the heap of papers in which the chamberlain sought to hide it. Not wanting to exaggerate the importance of a rather conventional complaint about an unkind lady, the chamberlain smiled and let him read it.

'The days go by, quite heedless of my longing.
     Already we come to the end of a bitter spring.'

It was a very quiet sort of protest compared to the lieutenant's overwrought strainings, a fact which the women were quick to point out. Chagrined, he could think of little to say, and shortly he withdrew to the room of a woman named Chūjō, who always listened to him with sympathy. There seemed little for him to do but sigh at the refusal of the world to let him have his way. The chamberlain strolled past on his way to consult with Tamakazura about a reply to Kaoru's letter, and the sighs and complaints now rose to a level that taxed Chūjō's patience. She fell silent. The usual jokes refused to come.

'It was a dream that I long to dream again,' he said, having informed her that he had been among the spectators at the Go match. 'What do I have to live for? Not a great deal. Not a great deal is left to me. It is as they say: a person even longs for the pain.'*

She did genuinely pity him, but there was nothing she could say. Hints from Tamakazura that he might one day be comforted did not seem to bring immediate comfort; and so the conclusion must be that the glimpse he had had of the older sister – and she certainly was very beautiful – had changed him for life.

Chūjō assumed the offensive. 'You are evidently asking me to plead your case. You do not see, I gather, what a rogue and a scoundrel you would seem if I did. A little more and I will no longer be able to feel sorry for you. I must be forever on my guard, and it is exhausting.'

'This is the end. I do not care what you think of me, and I do not care what happens to me. I did hate to see her lose that game, though. You should have smuggled me inside where she could see me. I would have given signals and kept her from losing. Ah, what a wretched fate is mine! Everything is against me and yet I go on hating to lose. The one thing I cannot overcome is a hatred of losing.'

*Probably a poetic allusion.

Chūjō had to laugh.

'A nod from you is all it takes to win?
This somehow seems at odds with reality.'

It confirmed his impression of a certain want of sympathy.

'Pity me yet once more and lead me to her,
Assured that life and death are in your hands.'*

Laughing and weeping, they talked the night away.

The next day was the first of the Fourth Month. All his brothers set off in court finery, and he spent the day brooding in his room. His mother wanted to weep. Yūgiri, though sympathetic, was more resigned and sensible. It was quite proper, he said, that Tamakazura should respect the Reizei emperor's wishes.

'I doubt that I would have been refused if I had really pleaded your case. I am sorry.'

As he so often did, the boy replied with a sad poem:

'Spring went off with the blossoms that left the trees.
I wander lost under trees in mournful leaf.'

His agents, among the more important women in attendance upon Tamakazura and her daughters, had not given up. 'I do feel sorry for him,' said Chūjō. 'He says that he is teetering between life and death, and he may just possibly mean it.'

His parents had interceded for him, and Tamakazura had thought of consoling him, inconsolable though he held himself to be, with another daughter. She began to fear that he would make difficulties for the older daughter. Higekuro had said that she should not go to a commoner of however high rank. She was going to a former emperor and even so Tamakazura was not happy. In upon her worries came another letter, delivered by one of the lieutenant's sentimental allies.

Tamakazura had a quick answer:

'At last I understand. This mournful mien
Conceals a facile delight with showy blossoms.'

*The jargon of Go runs through the poem, especially in the imagery of life and death.

'That is not kind, my lady.'

But she had too much on her mind to think of revising it.

The older girl was presented at the Reizei Palace on the ninth of the month. Yūgiri provided carriages and a large escort. Kumoi-nokari was somewhat resentful, but did not like to think that her correspondence with Tamakazura, suddenly interesting and flourishing because of the lieutenant's tribulations, must now be at an end. She sent splendid robes for the ladies-in-waiting and otherwise helped with the arrangements.

'I was mustered into the service of a remarkably shiftless young man,' she wrote, 'and I should certainly have consulted your convenience more thoroughly. Yet I think that you for your part might have kept me better informed.'

It was a gentle and circumspect protest, and Tamakazura had to admit that it was well taken.

Yūgiri also wrote. 'Something has come up that requires me to be in retreat just when I ought to be with you. I am sending sons to do whatever odd jobs need to be done. Please make such use of them as you can.' He dispatched several sons, including two guards officers. She was most grateful.

Kōbai also sent carriages. He was her brother and his wife was her stepdaughter and so relations should have been doubly close. In fact, they were rather distant. One of Makibashira's brothers came, however, to join Tamakazura's sons in the escort. How sad it was for Tamakazura, everyone said, that her husband was no longer living.

From Yūgiri's son the lieutenant there came through the usual agent the usual bombast: 'My life is at an end. I am resigned and yet I am sad. Say that you are sorry. Say only that, and I shall manage to struggle on for a little while yet, I think.'

She found the two sisters together, looking very dejected. They had been inseparable, thinking even a closed door an intolerable barrier; and now they must part. Dressed for her presentation at the Reizei Palace, the older sister was very beautiful. It may have been that she was thinking sadly of the plans her father had had for her. She thought the note rather implausible, coming from someone who still had two parents living, and very splendid parents, too. Yet perhaps he was not merely gesturing and posing.

'Tell him this,' she said, jotting down a poem at the end of his note:

'When all is evanescence we all are sad,
And whose affairs does "sad" most aptly describe?'

'An unsettling sort of note,' she added, 'giving certain hints of what "sad" may possibly mean.'

He shed tears of ecstasy at having something in the lady's own hand – for his intermediary had chosen not to recopy it. 'Do you think that if I die for love . . .?'* he sent back. She did not think it a very well-chosen allusion, and what followed was embarrassing, in view of the fact that she had not expected the woman to pass on her words verbatim:

'How true. We live, we die, not as we ask,
And I must die without that one word "sad."'

'I would hurry to my grave if I thought I might have it there.'

She had only the prettiest and most graceful of attendants. The ceremonies were as elaborate as if she were being presented to the reigning emperor. It was late in the night when the procession, having first looked in on Tamakazura's sister, proceeded to the Reizei emperor's apartments. Akikonomu and the ladies-in-waiting had all grown old in his service, and now there was a beautiful lady at her youthful best. No one was surprised that the emperor doted upon her and that she was soon the most conspicuous lady in the Reizei household. The Reizei emperor behaved like any other husband, and that, people said, was quite as it should be. He had hoped to see a little of Tamakazura and was disappointed that she withdrew after a brief conversation.

Kaoru was his constant companion, almost the favorite that Genji had once been. He was on good terms with everyone in the house, including, of course, the new lady. He would have liked to know exactly how friendly she was. One still, quiet evening when he was out strolling with her brother the chamberlain, they came to a pine tree before what he judged to be her curtains. Hanging from it was a very fine wisteria. With mossy rocks for their seats, they sat down beside the brook.

*Kiyowara Fukayabu, *Kokinshū* 603:

A fleeting world, perhaps. But do you think
That if I die for love there will be no gossip?

There may have been guarded resentment in the poem which Kaoru recited as he looked up at it:

'These blossoms, were they more within our reach,
　　Might seem to be of finer hue than the pine.'

The boy understood immediately, and wished it to be known that he had not approved of the match.

'It is the lavender of all such flowers,
　　And yet it is not as I wish it were.'

He was an honest, warmhearted boy, and he was genuinely sorry that Kaoru had been disappointed – not that Kaoru's disappointment could have been described as bitter.

Yūgiri's son the lieutenant, on the other hand, seemed so completely unhinged that one half expected violence. Some of the older girl's suitors were beginning to take notice of the younger. It was the turn which Tamakazura, in response to Kumoinokari's petitions, had hoped his own inclinations might take, but he had fallen silent. Though the Reizei emperor was on the best of terms with all of Yūgiri's sons, the lieutenant seldom came visiting, and when he did he looked very unhappy and did not stay long.

And so Higekuro's very strongly expressed wishes had come to nothing. Wanting an explanation, the emperor summoned Tamakazura's son the captain.

'He is very cross with us,' said the captain to Tamakazura, and it was evident that he too was much put out. 'I did not keep my feelings to myself, you may remember. I said that people would be very surprised. You did not agree, and I found it very difficult to argue with you. Now we seem to have succeeded in alienating an emperor, not at all a wise thing to do.'

'Once again I do not entirely agree with you,' replied Tamakazura calmly. 'I thought the matter over carefully, and the Reizei emperor was so insistent that I had to feel sorry for him. Your sister would have had a very difficult time at court without your father to help her. She is much better off where she is, of that I feel very sure. I do not remember that you or anyone else tried very hard to dissuade me, and now my brother and all of you are saying that I made a horrible mistake. It is not fair – and we must accept what has happened as fate.'

'The fate of which you speak is not something we see here

before us, and how are we to describe it to the emperor? You
seem to worry a great deal about the empress and to forget that
your own sister is one of the Reizei ladies. And the arrangements
you congratulate yourself upon having made for my sister – I
doubt that they will prove workable. But that is all right. I shall do
what I can for her. There have been precedents enough for sending a lady to court when other ladies are already there, so many
of them, indeed, as to argue that cheerful attendance upon an
emperor has from very ancient times been thought its own justifi-
cation. If there is unpleasantness at the Reizei Palace and my good
aunt is displeased with us, I doubt that we will find many people
rushing to our support.'

Tamakazura's sons were not making things easier for her.

The Reizei emperor seemed more pleased with his new lady as
the months went by. In the Seventh Month she became pregnant.
No one thought it strange that so pretty and charming a lady
should have been plagued by suitors or that the Reizei emperor
should keep her always at his side, a companion in music and other
diversions. Kaoru, also a constant companion, often heard her
play, and his feelings as he listened were far from simple. The
Reizei emperor was especially fond of the Japanese koto upon
which Chūjō had played 'A Branch of Plum.'

The New Year came, and there was caroling. Numbers of
young courtiers had fine voices, and from this select group only
the best received the royal appointment as carolers. Kaoru was
named master of one of the two choruses and Yūgiri's son the
lieutenant was among the musicians. There was a bright, cloudless
moon, almost at full, as they left the main palace for the Reizei
Palace. Tamakazura's sister and daughter were both in the main
hall, where a retinue of princes and high courtiers surrounded the
Reizei emperor. Looking them over, one was tempted to conclude that only Yūgiri and Higekuro had succeeded in producing
really fine sons. The carolers seemed to feel that the Reizei Palace
was even more of a challenge than the main palace. The lieutenant
was very tense and fidgety at the thought that his lady was in the
audience. The test on such occasions is the verve with which a
young man wears the rather ordinary rosette in his cap. They all
looked very dashing and they sang most commendably. As the
lieutenant stepped ceremoniously to the royal staircase and
sang 'Bamboo River,' he was so assailed by memories that he was

perilously near choking and losing his place. The Reizei emperor went with them to Akikonomu's apartments. As the night wore on, the moon was immodestly bright, brighter, it almost seemed, than the noonday sun. A too keen awareness of his audience was making the lieutenant feel somewhat unsteady on his feet. He wished that the wine cups would not come quite so unfailingly in his direction.

Exhausted from the night of caroling, which had taken him back and forth across the city, Kaoru was resting when a summons came from the Reizei Palace.

'Sleep is not permitted?' But though he grumbled he set off once more.

The Reizei emperor wanted to know how the carolers had been received at the main palace.

'Isn't it fine that you were chosen over all the old men to lead one of the choruses.'

He was humming 'The Delight of Ten Thousand Springs'* as he started for his new lady's apartments. Kaoru went with him. Her relatives had come in large numbers to enjoy the caroling and everything was very bright and modish.

Kaoru was engaged in conversation at a gallery door.

'The moon was dazzling last night,' he said, 'but I doubt that moons and laurels† account entirely for an appearance of giddiness on the lieutenant's part. It is just as bright up in the clouds where His Majesty lives, but the palace does not seem to have that effect on him at all.'

The women were feeling sorry for the lieutenant. 'The darkness was completely defeated,'‡ said one of them. 'We thought the moonlight did better by you than by him.'

A bit of paper was pushed from under the curtains.

' "Bamboo River," not my favorite song,**
    But somewhat striking, its effect last night.'

The tears that mounted to Kaoru's eyes may have seemed an exaggerated response to a rather ordinary poem, but they served to demonstrate that he had been fond of the lady.

*Banzuraku. It also appears in Chapter 23.

†See note*, page 342.

‡See note*, page 587.

**There is a pun on fushi, 'melody' and 'joint of bamboo.'

'I looked to the bamboo river. It has run dry
And left an arid, barren world behind it.'

This appearance of forlornness, they thought, only made him handsomer. He did not, like the lieutenant, indulge in a frenzy of grief, but he attracted sympathy.

'I shall leave you. I have said too much.'

He did not want to go, but the Reizei emperor was calling him.

'Yūgiri has told me that when your father was alive the music in the ladies' quarters went on all through the morning, long after the carolers had left. No one is up to that sort of thing any more. What an extraordinary range of talent he did bring together at Rokujō. The least little gathering there must have been better than anything anywhere else.'

As if hoping to bring the good Rokujō days back, the emperor sent for instruments, a Chinese koto for his new lady, a lute for Kaoru, a Japanese koto for himself. He immediately struck up 'This House.'* The new lady had been an uncertain musician, but he had been diligent with his lessons and she had proved eminently teachable. She had a good touch both as soloist and as accompanist, and indeed Kaoru thought her a lady with whom it would be difficult to find fault. He knew of course that she was very beautiful.

There were other such occasions. He managed without seeming querulous or familiar to let her know how she had disappointed him. I have not heard how she replied.

In the Fourth Month she bore a princess. It was not as happy an event as it would have been had the Reizei emperor still been on the throne, but the gifts from Yūgiri and others were lavish. Tama-kazura was forever taking the child up in her arms, but soon there were messages from the Reizei Palace suggesting that its father too would like to see it, and on about the fiftieth day mother and child went back to Reizei. Although, as we have seen, the Reizei emperor already had one daughter, he was delighted with the little princess, who certainly was very pretty. Some of the older princess's women were heard to remark that paternal affection could sometimes seem overdone.

See note, page 435.

The royal ladies did not themselves descend to vulgar invective, but there were unpleasant scenes among their serving women. It began to seem that the worst fears of Tamakazura's sons were coming true. Tamakazura was worried, for such incidents could bring cruel derision upon a lady. It did not seem likely that the Reizei emperor's affection would waver, but the resentment of ladies who had been with him for a very long time could make life very unpleasant for the new lady. There had moreover been suggestions that the present emperor was not happy. Perhaps, thought Tamakazura, casting about for a solution, she should resign her own position at the palace in favor of her younger daughter. It was not common practice to accept resignations in such cases and she had for some years sought unsuccessfully to resign. The emperor remembered Higekuro's wishes, however, and very old precedents were called in, and the resignation and the new appointment were presently ratified. The delay, Tamakazura was now inclined to believe, had occurred because the younger daughter's destinies must work themselves out.

In the matter of the new appointment there yet remained the sad case of the lieutenant. Kumoinokari had supported his suit for the hand of the older daughter. Tamakazura had hinted in reply that she might let him have the younger. What might his feelings be now? She had one of her sons make tactful inquiry of Yūgiri.

'There have been representations from the emperor which have left us feeling somewhat uncertain. We would not wish to seem unduly ambitious.'

'It is only natural that the arrangements you have made for your older sister should not please the emperor. And now he proposes a court appointment for the younger, and one does not dismiss such an honor lightly. I suggest that you accept it, and with the least possible delay.'

Sighing that her husband's death had left her and her daughter so unprotected, Tamakazura decided that she must now see whether the empress would approve of the appointment.

Everything was in order, and the calm, dignified efficiency with which the younger sister, very handsome and very elegant, acquitted herself of her duties soon made the emperor forget his dissatisfaction.

Tamakazura thought that the time had come to enter a nunnery, but her sons disagreed. 'You will not be able to concentrate on your prayers until our sisters are somewhat more settled.'

Occasionally she paid a quiet visit at court, but because the Reizei emperor still seemed uncomfortably fond of her she did not visit his palace even when there were important matters to be discussed. She continued to reprove herself for her behavior long ago, and she had given him a daughter at a risk of seeming too ambitious. Any suggestion, even in jest, that she was now being coquettish would be more than she could bear. She did not explain the reasons for her diffidence, and so the Reizei daughter concluded that her old view of the situation had been correct. Her father had been fond of her but her mother had not. Even in such trivial matters as the contest for the cherry tree her mother had sided with her sister. The Reizei emperor let it be known that he too was resentful. Tamakazura's conduct was not at all hard to understand, he said. A mother who has given a young daughter to a hoary old man prefers to keep her distance. He also let it be known that his affection for his new lady was if anything stronger.

After a few years, to everyone's astonishment, a prince was born. What a fortunate lady, people said. So many of the Reizei ladies were still childless after all these years. The Reizei emperor was of course overjoyed, and only wished that he had had a son before he abdicated. There was so much less now that he could do for the child. He had doted upon one princess and then a second, and now he had a little prince, to delight him beyond measure. Tamakazura's sister, the mother of the older princess, thought he was being a little silly, and she was no longer as tolerant of her niece as she once had been. There were little incidents and presently there was evidence that the two ladies were on rather chilly terms. Whatever her rank, it is always the senior lady in such instances who attracts the larger measure of sympathy. So it was at the Reizei Palace. Everyone, high and low, took the part of the great lady who had been with the Reizei emperor for so long. No opportunity was lost to show the younger lady in an unfavorable light.

'We told you so,' said her brothers, making life yet more difficult for Tamakazura.

'So many girls,' sighed that dowager,* 'live happy, inconspicuous lives, and no one criticizes them. Only a girl who seems

*Ōue. The word occurs only in this chapter.

to have been born lucky should think of going into the royal service.'

The old suitors were meanwhile rising in the world. Several of them would make quite acceptable bridegrooms. Then an obscure chamberlain, Kaoru now had a guards commission and a seat on the council. One rather wearied, indeed, of hearing about 'his perfumed highness' and 'the fragrant captain.' He continued to be a very serious and proper young man and stories were common of the princesses and ministers' daughters whom he had been offered and had chosen not to notice.

'He did not amount to a great deal then,' sighed Tamakazura, 'and look at him now.'

Yūgiri's young son had been promoted from lieutenant to captain. He too was much admired.

'He is so good-looking,' whispered one of the cattier women. 'He would have been a much better catch than an old emperor surrounded by nasty women.'

There was, alas, some truth in it.

The lieutenant, now captain, had lost none of his old ardor. He went on feeling sorry for himself, and though he was now married to a daughter of the Minister of the Left,* he was not a very attentive husband. He was often heard declaiming or setting down in writing certain thoughts about a 'sash of Hitachi.'† Not everyone caught the reference.

Tamakazura's older daughter, exhausted by the complications of life at the Reizei Palace, was now spending most of her time at home, a great disappointment to Tamakazura. The younger daughter was meanwhile doing beautifully. She was a cheerful, intelligent girl, and she presided over a distinguished salon.

The Minister of the Left died. Yūgiri was promoted to Minister of the Left and Kōbai to Minister of the Right.‡ Many others were on the promotion lists, including Kaoru, who became a councillor of the middle order. A young man did well to be born into that family, people said, if he wished to get ahead without delay.

---

*Otherwise unidentified.

†See note†, page 509.

‡These promotions seem to be forgotten in later chapters, a fact which has led to the argument that at least parts of the chapter are spurious.

In the course of the round of calls that followed the appointment, Kaoru called on Tamakazura. He made his formal greetings in the garden below her rooms.

'I see that you have not forgotten these weedy precincts. I am reminded of your late father's extraordinary kindness.'

She had a pleasant voice, soft and gently modulated. And how very youthful she was, thought Kaoru. If she had aged like other women the Reizei emperor would by now have forgotten her. As it was, there were certain to be incidents.

'I do not much care about promotions, but I thought it would be a good excuse to show you that I am still about. When you say I have not forgotten, I suspect you are really saying that I have been very neglectful.'

'I know that this is not the time for senile complaining, but I know too that it is not easy for you to visit me. There are very complicated matters that I really must discuss with you in person. My Reizei daughter is having a very unhappy time of it, so unhappy, indeed, that we cannot think what to do next. I was careful to discuss the matter with the Reizei empress and with my sister, and I was sure that I had their agreement. Now it seems that they both think me an impertinent upstart, and this, as you may imagine, does not please me. My grandchildren have stayed behind, but I asked that my daughter be allowed to come home for a rest. She really was having a most difficult time of it. She is here, and I gather that I am being criticized for that too, and indeed that the Reizei emperor is unhappy. Do you think you might possibly speak to him, not as if you were making a great point of it, in the course of a conversation? I had such high hopes for her, and I did so want her to be on good terms with all of them. I must ask myself whether I should not have paid more attention to my very modest place in the world.' She was trying not to weep.

'You take it too seriously. We all know that life in the royal service is not easy. The Reizei emperor is living in quiet retirement, we may tell ourselves, away from all the noise and bother, and his ladies should be sensible and forbearing. But it is too much to ask that they divest themselves of pride and the competitive instinct. What seems like nothing at all to us on the outside may seem intolerable effrontery to them. Royal ladies, empresses and all the others, are unbelievably sensitive, a fact which you were surely aware of when you made your plans.' She could not have accused him of equivocation. 'The best thing would be to forget the whole problem. It would not do, I think, for me to intercede between the Reizei emperor and one of his ladies.'

She smiled. 'I have entertained you with a list of complaints and you have treated it as it deserves.'

It was hard to believe that anyone so quietly and calmly youthful should be upset about the problems of a married daughter. Probably the daughter was very much like her. Certainly his Uji princess was.* Just such qualities had drawn him to her.

The younger sister had come home from the palace and the house wore that happy air of being lived in. Easy, companionable warmth seemed to come to him through the blinds. The dowager could see that although he was very much in control of himself he was also very much on his mettle, and again she thought what a genuinely satisfactory son-in-law he would make.

Kōbai's mansion was immediately to the east. Young courtiers had gathered in large numbers to help with the grand ministerial banquet. Niou had declined Kōbai's invitation to be present, although he had attended the banquet given by the Minister of the Left after the archery meet and the banquet after the wrestling matches, and it had been hoped that he would lend his radiance to this occasion as well. Kōbai was thinking about the arrangements he must make for his much-loved daughters,† and Niou did not for some reason seem interested. Kōbai and his wife also had their eye on Kaoru, a young gentleman in whom it would be difficult to find a flaw.

The festivities next door, the rumbling of carriages and the shouting of outrunners, brought memories of Higekuro's day of glory. Tamakazura's house was quiet by comparison, and sunk in memories.

'Remember how people talked when Kōbai started visiting her and Prince Hotaru was hardly in his grave. Well, it lasted, as you see, and the talk has come to seem rather beside the point. You

---

*This sentence looks ahead to the next chapter.

†In some texts the word is clearly plural, and in others it could be either singular or plural. If the plural is preferred, then the action seems to precede that of the preceding chapter, in which one of the girls is married.

never can tell. Which sort of lady do you think we should offer as a model?'

Yūgiri's son, newly promoted to captain, came calling that evening, on his way home from the banquet. He knew that the Reizei daughter was at home and he was on unusually good behavior.

'It may be said that I am beginning to matter just a little, perhaps.' He brushed away a tear that may have seemed a trifle forced. 'I am no happier for that fact. The months and years will not take away the knowledge that my deepest wish was refused.'

He was at the very best age, some twenty-seven or twenty-eight years old.

'What a tiresome boy,' said Tamakazura, also in tears. 'Things have come too easily, and so you care nothing about rank and promotion. If my husband were still alive my own boys might be permitted that sort of luxury.'

They were in fact doing rather well. The oldest was a guards commander and the second a moderator, though it pained her that they did not yet have seats on the council. The youngest, until recently a chamberlain, was now a guards captain. He too was doing well enough, but other boys his age were doing better.

Yūgiri's son, the new captain, had many plausible and persuasive things to say.

CHAPTER 45

The Lady at the Bridge

There was in those years a prince of the blood, an old man, left behind by the times. His mother was of the finest lineage. There had once been talk of seeking a favored position for him; but there were disturbances and a new alignment of forces,* at the end of which his prospects were in ruins. His supporters, embittered by this turn of events, were less than steadfast: they made their various excuses and left him. And so in his public life and in his private, he was quite alone, blocked at every turn. His wife, the daughter of a former minister, had fits of bleakest depression at the thought of her parents and their plans for her, now of course in ruins. Her consolation was that she and her husband were close as husbands and wives seldom are. Their confidence in each other was complete.

But here too there was a shadow: the years went by and they had no children. If only there were a pretty little child to break the loneliness and boredom, the prince would think – and sometimes give voice to his thoughts. And then, surprisingly, a very pretty daughter was in fact born to them. She was the delight of their lives. Years passed, and there were signs that the princess was again with child. The prince hoped that this time he would be favored with a son, but again the child was a daughter. Though the birth was easy enough, the princess fell desperately ill soon afterwards, and was dead before many days had passed. The prince was numb with grief. The vulgar world had long had no place for him, he said, and frequently it had seemed quite unbearable; and the bond that had held him to it had been the beauty and the gentleness of his wife. How could he go on alone? And there were his daughters. How could he, alone, rear them in a manner that would not be a scandal? – for he was not, after all, a commoner. His conclusion was that he must take the tonsure. Yet he hesitated. Once he was gone, there would be no one to see to the safety of his daughters.

So the years went by. The princesses grew up, each with her own grace and beauty. It was difficult to find fault with them, they

---

*The reference is to the accession of the Reizei emperor after Genji's return from exile. See Chapter 14.

gave him what pleasure he had. The passing years offered him no opportunity to carry out his resolve.

The serving women muttered to themselves that the younger girl's very birth had been a mistake, and were not as diligent as they might have been in caring for her. With the prince it was a different matter. His wife, scarcely in control of her senses, had been especially tormented by thoughts of this new babe. She had left behind a single request: 'Think of her as a keepsake, and be good to her.'

The prince himself was not without resentment at the child, that her birth should so swiftly have severed their bond from a former life, his and his princess's.

'But such was the bond that it was,' he said. 'And she worried about the girl to the very end.'

The result was that if anything he doted upon the child to excess. One almost sensed in her fragile beauty a sinister omen.

The older girl was comely and of a gentle disposition, elegant in face and in manner, with a suggestion behind the elegance of hidden depths. In quiet grace, indeed, she was the superior of the two. And so the prince favored each as each in her special way demanded. There were numerous matters which he was not able to order as he wished, however, and his household only grew sadder and lonelier as time went by. His attendants, unable to bear the uncertainty of their prospects, took their leave one and two at a time. In the confusion surrounding the birth of the younger girl, there had not been time to select a really suitable nurse for her. No more dedicated than one would have expected in the circumstances, the nurse first chosen abandoned her ward when the girl was still an infant. Thereafter the prince himself took charge of her upbringing.

Much care had gone into the planning of his garden. Though the ponds and hillocks were as they had always been, the prince gazed listlessly out upon a garden returning to nature. His stewards being of a not very diligent sort, there was no one to fight off the decay. The garden was rank with weeds, and creeping ferns took over the eaves as if the house belonged to them. The freshness of the cherry blossoms in spring, the tints of the autumn leaves, had been a consolation in loneliness while he had had his wife with him. Now the beauties of the passing seasons only made him lonelier. It became his compelling duty to see that the chapel was properly appointed, and he spent his days and nights in religious observances. Even his affection for his daughters, because it was a bond with this world, made him strangely fretful. He had to set it down as a mark against him for some misdeed in a former life, the fact that he was not up to following his inclinations and renouncing the world. The possibility that he might bow to custom and remarry seemed more and more remote. Time went by and thoughts of marriage left him. He had become a saint who still wore the robes of this world. His wife was dead and it was unthinkable that anyone should replace her.

'Enough of this, Your Highness,' said the people around him. 'We understand, please believe us, why your grief was what it was when our lady left you. But time passes, grief should not go on forever. Can you not bring yourself to do as others do? And look at this house, if you will, with no one to watch over it. If there were someone, anyone, for us to look to, it would not be the ruin it is.'

So they argued, and he was informed of numerous possible matches; but he would not listen. When he was not at his prayers, his daughters were his companions. They were growing up and they occupied themselves with music and Go, and word games,* and other profitless pastimes. Each had her own individual ways, he was beginning to notice. The older girl was composed and meditative, quick to learn but with a tendency toward moodiness. The younger, though also quiet and reserved, was distinguished by a certain shy and childlike gaiety.

One warm spring day he sat looking out over the garden. Mallards were swimming about on the pond, wing to wing, chattering happily to each other. It was a sight which in earlier years would scarcely have caught the prince's eye, but now he felt something like jealousy toward these mindless creatures, each steadfast to its mate.

He had the girls go over a music lesson, and very appealing they were too, as they bent their small figures to the work. The sound of the instruments was enough to bring tears to his eyes. Softly, he recited a verse, brushing away a tear as he did so.

'She has left behind her mate, and these nestlings too.
Why have they lingered in this uncertain world?'

See note, page 190.

He was an extremely handsome man. Emaciation from years of abstinence only added to the courtliness of his bearing. He had put on a figured robe for the music lesson. Somewhat rumpled, casually thrown over his shoulders, it seemed to emphasize by its very carelessness the nobility of the wearer.

Oigimi,* the older girl, quietly took out an inkstone and seemed about to write a few lines on it.

'Come now. You know better than to write on an inkstone.'†
He pushed a sheet of paper towards her.

'I know now, as I see it leave the nest,
How uncertain is the lot of the waterfowl.'

It was not a masterpiece, but in the circumstances it was very touching. The hand showed promise even though the characters were separated one from another in a still childish fashion.

'And now it is your turn,' he said to Nakanokimi,‡ the younger.

More of a child than her sister, she took longer with her verse:

'Unsheltered by the wing of the grieving father,
The nestling would surely have perished in the nest.'

It saddened him to see the princesses, their robes shabby and wrinkled, no one to take care of them, bored and without hope of relief from boredom – but they were utterly charming on such occasions, each in her own way. He read from the holy text in his hand, sometimes interrupting with a poem. To the older girl he had taught the lute, to the younger the thirteen-stringed koto. When they played duets, of which they were fond, he thought them very satisfactory pupils, if still somewhat immature.

He had early lost his father, the old emperor, and his mother as well. Without the sort of resolute backing necessary for a youth in his position, he tended to neglect serious Chinese studies. Practical matters of state and career were yet further beyond his grasp. He

---

*Oigimi, used here as if it were the girl's name, is actually a common noun designating the oldest of two or more wellborn sisters.

†A superstition apparently arising from the fact that the character for 'inkstone' is a combination of the characters for 'stone' and 'see,' and so writing on an inkstone means slinging ink in an eye.

‡Another common noun, designating a second sister.

was of an elegance extraordinary even for one of his birth, with a soft gentility that approached the womanish; and so the treasures from his ancestors, the fields left by his grandfather the minister, which at the outset had seemed inexhaustible, had presently disappeared, he could not have said where. Only his mansion and its furnishings – fine and numerous, to be sure – remained. The last of his retainers had left him, and the last of those with whom he might find companionship. To relieve the tedium he would summon eminent musicians from the palace and lose himself in impractical pursuits. In the course of time he became as skilled a musician as his teachers.

He was the Eighth Prince, a younger brother of the shining Genji. During the years when the Reizei emperor was crown prince, the mother of the reigning emperor had sought in that conspiratorial way of hers to have the Eighth Prince named crown prince, replacing Reizei. The world seemed hers to rule as she wished, and the Eighth Prince was very much at the center of it. Unfortunately his success irritated the opposing faction. The day came when Genji and presently Yūgiri had the upper hand, and he was without supporters. He had over the years become an ascetic in any case, and he now resigned himself to living the life of the sage and hermit.

There came yet another disaster. As if fate had not been unkind enough already, his mansion was destroyed by fire. Having no other suitable house in the city, he moved to Uji, some miles to the southeast, where he happened to own a tastefully appointed mountain villa. He had renounced the world, it was true, and yet leaving the capital was a painful wrench indeed. With fishing weirs near at hand to heighten the roar of the river, the situation at Uji was hardly favorable to quiet study. But what must be must be. With the flowering trees of spring and the leaves of autumn and the flow of the river to bring repose, he lost himself more than ever in solitary meditation. There was one thought even so that never left his mind: how much better it would be, even in these remote mountains, if his wife were with him!

'She who was with me, the roof above are smoke.
And why must I alone remain behind?'

So much was the past still with him that life scarcely seemed worth living.

Mountain upon mountain separated his dwelling from the larger world. Rough people of the lower classes, woodcutters and the like, sometimes came by to do chores for him.* There were no other callers. The gloom continued day after day, as stubborn and clinging as 'the morning mist on the peaks.'†

There happened to be in those Uji mountains an abbot,‡ a most saintly man. Though famous for his learning, he seldom took part in public rites. He heard in the course of time that there was a prince living nearby, a man who was teaching himself the mysteries of the Good Law. Thinking this a most admirable undertaking, he made bold to visit the prince, who upon subsequent interviews was led deeper into the texts he had studied over the years. The prince became more immediately aware of what was meant by the transience and uselessness of the material world.

'In spirit,' he confessed, quite one with the holy man, 'I have perhaps found my place upon the lotus of the clear pond; but I have not yet made my last farewells to the world because I cannot bring myself to leave my daughters behind.'

The abbot was an intimate of the Reizei emperor and had been his preceptor as well. One day, visiting the city, he called upon the Reizei emperor to answer any questions that might have come to him since their last meeting.

'Your honored brother,' he said, bringing the Eighth Prince into the conversation, 'has pursued his studies so diligently that he has been favored with the most remarkable insights. Only a bond from a former life can account for such dedication. Indeed, the depth of his understanding makes me want to call him a saint who has not yet left the world.'

'He has not taken the tonsure? But I remember now – the young people do call him "the saint who is still one of us."'

Kaoru chanced to be present at the interview. He listened intently. No one knew better than he the futility of this world, and

---

*There is possibly a suggestion that their manner was more familiar than their station should have allowed.

†Anonymous, *Kokinshū* 935:

> My gloomy thoughts run on and on, unbroken
> As the morning mist on the peaks the wild geese pass.

‡*Ajari*. Sanskrit *ācārya*. In general, any monk of sufficient learning to act as a preceptor; and in the Shingon and Tendai sects a specific clerical rank.

yet he passed useless days, his devotions hardly so frequent or intense as to attract public notice. The heart of a man who, though still in this world, was in all other respects a saint – to what might it be likened?

The abbot continued: 'He has long wanted to cut his last ties with the world, but a trifling matter made it difficult for him to carry out his resolve. Now he has two motherless children whom he cannot bring himself to leave behind. They are the burden he must bear.'*

The abbot himself had not entirely given up the pleasures of the world: he had a good ear for music. 'And when their high-nesses deign to play a duet,' he said, 'they bid fair to outdo the music of the river, and put one in mind of the blessed musicians above.'

The Reizei emperor smiled at this rather fusty way of stating the matter. 'You would not expect girls who have had a saint for their principal companion to have such accomplishments. How pleasant to know about them – and what an uncommonly good father he must be! I am sure that the thought of having to leave them is pure torment. It is always possible that I will live longer than he, and if I do perhaps I may ask to be given responsibility for them.'

He was himself the tenth son of the family, younger than his brother at Uji. There was the example of the Suzaku emperor, who had left his young daughter in Genji's charge. Something similar might be arranged, he thought. He would have compan-ions to relieve the monotony of his days.

Kaoru was less interested in the daughters than in the father. Quite entranced with what he had heard, he longed to see for himself that figure so wrapped in the serenity of religion.

'I have every intention of calling on him and asking him to be my master,' he said as the abbot left. 'Might I ask you to find out, unobtrusively, of course, how he would greet the possibility?'

'And tell him, please,' said the Reizei emperor, 'that I have been much affected by your description of his holy retreat.' And he wrote down a verse to be delivered to the Eighth Prince.

---

*The abbot here uses an unusual verb form that apparently gives his speech a some-what stilted or archaic flavor.

'Wearily, my soul goes off to your mountains,
And cloud upon circling cloud holds my person back?'

With the royal messenger in the lead, the abbot set off for Uji,
thinking to visit the Eighth Prince on his way back to the monastery. The prince so seldom heard from anyone that he was overjoyed at these tidings. He ordered wine for his guests and side
dishes peculiar to the region.

This was the poem he sent back to his brother:

'I am not as free as I seem. From the gloom of the world
I retreat only briefly to the Hill of Gloom.'*

He declined to call himself one of the truly enlightened. The
vulgar world still called up regrets and resentments, thought the
Reizei emperor, much moved.†

The abbot also spoke of Kaoru, who, he said, was of a strongly
religious bent. 'He asked me most earnestly to tell you about him:
to tell you that he has longed since childhood to give himself up to
study of the scriptures; that he has been kept busy with inconsequential affairs, public and private, and has been unable to leave
the world; that since these affairs are trivial in any case and no one
could call his career a brilliant one, he could hardly expect people
to notice if he were to lock himself up in prayers and meditation;
that he has had an unfortunate way of letting himself be distracted.
And when he had entrusted me with all this, he added that, having
heard through me of your own revered person, he could not take
his mind from you, and was determined to be your pupil.'

'When there has been a great misfortune,' said the prince, 'when
the whole world seems hostile – that is when most people come to
think it a flimsy façade, and wish to have no more of it. I can only
marvel that a young man for whom everything lies ahead, who has
had everything his way, should start thinking of other worlds.
In my own case, it often seems to me, the powers deliberately

---

*The poem contains a common pun on Uji, which suggests gloom. There is also a
reference to a poem by Kisen, *Kokinshū* 983:

In a hut to the south and east of Miyako I dwell;
The place is known as the Hill of the World of Gloom.

†The Eighth Prince's poem is seen to have reference to the rivalry over the succession.

arranged matters to give my mind such a turn, and so I came to religion as if it were the natural thing. I have managed to find a certain amount of peace, I suppose; but when I think of the short time I have left and of how slowly my preparations creep forward, I know that what I have learned comes to nothing and that in the end it will still be nothing. No, I am afraid I would be a scandalously bad teacher. Let him think of me as a fellow seeker after truth, a very humble one.'

Kaoru and the prince exchanged letters and presently Kaoru paid his first visit.

It was an even sadder place than the abbot's description had led him to expect. The house itself was like a grass hut put up for a few days' shelter, and as for the furnishings, everything even remotely suggesting luxury had been dispensed with. There were mountain villages that had their own quiet charm; but here the tumult of the waters and the wailing of the wind must make it impossible to have a moment free of sad thoughts. He could see why a man on the way to enlightenment might seek out such a place as a means of cutting his ties with the world. But what of the daughters? Did they not have the usual fondness for delicate, ladylike things?

A sliding partition seemed to separate the chapel from their rooms. A youth of more amorous inclinations would have approached and made himself known, curious to see what his reception would be. Kaoru was not above feeling a certain excitement at being so near; but a show of interest would have betrayed his whole purpose, which was to be free of just such thoughts, here in distant mountains. The smallest hint of frivolity would have denied the reason for the visit.

Deeply moved by the saintly figure before him, he offered the warmest avowals of friendship. His visits were frequent thereafter. Nowhere did he find evidence of shallowness in the discourses to which he was treated; nor was there a suggestion of pompousness in the prince's explanations of the scriptures and of his profoundly significant reasons, even though he had stopped short of taking the tonsure, for living in the mountains.

The world was full of saintly and learned men, but the stiff, forbidding bishops and patriarchs* who were such repositories of

*Sōzu, Sōjō.

virtue had little time of their own, and he found it far from easy to approach them with his questions. Then there were lesser disciples of the Buddha. They were to be admired for observing the discipline, it was true; but they tended to be vulgar and obsequious in their manner and rustic in their speech, and they could be familiar to the point of rudeness. Since Kaoru was busy with official duties in the daytime, it was in the quiet of the evening, in the intimacy of his private chambers, that he liked to have company. Such people would not do.

Now he had found a man who combined great elegance with a reticence that certainly was not obsequious, and who, even when he was discussing the Good Law, was adept at bringing plain, familiar similes into his discourse. He was not, perhaps, among the completely enlightened, but people of birth and culture have their own insights into the nature of things. After repeated visits Kaoru came to feel that he wanted to be always at the prince's side, and he would be overtaken by intense longing when official duties kept him away for a time.

Impressed by Kaoru's devotion, the Reizei emperor sent messages; and so the Uji house, silent and forgotten by the world, came to have visitors again. Sometimes the Reizei emperor sent lavish gifts and supplies. In pleasant matters having to do with the seasons and the festivals and in practical matters as well, Kaoru missed no chance to be of service.

Three years went by. It was the end of autumn, and the time had come for the quarterly reading of the scriptures.* The roar of the fish weirs was more than a man could bear, said the Eighth Prince as he set off for the abbot's monastery, there to spend a week in retreat.

The princesses were lonelier than ever. It had been weighing on Kaoru's mind that too much time had passed since his last visit. One night as a late moon was coming over the hills he set out for Uji, his guard as unobtrusive as possible, his caparison of the simplest. He could go on horseback and did not have to worry about a boat, since the prince's villa was on the near side of the Uji River. As he came into the mountains the mist was so heavy and

---

*There was no fixed time for this. The meaning is that winter is coming, and if he does not hurry he will have missed the autumn observances. Autumn (see the next sentence) was the fishing season.

the underbrush so thick that he could hardly make out the path; and as he pushed his way through thickets the rough wind would throw showers of dew upon him from a turmoil of falling leaves. He was very cold, and, though he had no one to blame but himself, he had to admit that he was also very wet. This was not the sort of journey he was accustomed to. It was sobering and at the same time exciting.

> 'From leaves that cannot withstand the mountain wind
> The dew is falling. My tears fall yet more freely.'

He forbade his outrunners to raise their usual cries, for the woodcutters in these mountains could be troublesome. Brushing through a wattle fence, crossing a rivulet that meandered down from nowhere, he tried as best he could to silence the hoofs of his colt. But he could not keep that extraordinary fragrance from wandering off on the wind, and more than one family awoke in surprise at 'the scent of an unknown master.'*

As he drew near the Uji house, he could hear the plucking of he did not know what instrument, unimaginably still and lonely. He had heard from the abbot that the prince liked to practice with his daughters, but somehow had not found occasion to hear that famous koto. This would be his chance. Making his way into the grounds, he knew that he had been listening to a lute, tuned to the *ōjiki* mode.† There was nothing unusual about the melody. Perhaps the strangeness of the setting had made it seem different. The sound was cool and clean, especially when a string was plucked from beneath. The lute fell silent and there were a few quiet strokes on a koto. He would have liked to listen on, but he was challenged by a man with a somewhat threatening manner, one of the guards, it would seem.

The man immediately recognized him and explained that, for certain reasons, the prince had gone into seclusion in a mountain monastery. He would be informed immediately of the visit.

'Please do not bother,' said Kaoru. 'It would be a pity to interrupt his retreat when it will be over soon in any case. But do tell the ladies that I have arrived, sodden as you see me, and must go back with my mission unaccomplished; and if they are sorry for me that will be my reward.'

See note, page 792.

†Or *ōshiki*. The tonic is A.

The rough face broke into a smile. 'They will be informed.'

But as he turned to depart, Kaoru called him back. 'No, wait a minute. For years I have been fascinated by stories I have heard of their playing, and this is my chance. Will there be somewhere that I might hide and listen for a while? If I were to rush in on them they would of course stop, and that would be the last thing I would want.'

His face and manner were such as to quell even the most untamed of rustics. 'This is how it is. They are at it morning and night when there is no one around to hear. But let someone come from the city even if he is in rags, and they won't let you have a twang of it. No one's supposed to know they even exist. That's how His Highness wants it.'

Kaoru smiled. 'Now there is an odd sort of secret for you. The whole world knows that two specimens of the rarest beauty are hidden here. But come. Show me the way. I have all the best intentions. That is the way I am, I assure you.' His manner was grave and courteous. 'It is hard to believe that they can be less than perfect.'

'Suppose they find out, sir. I might be in trouble.'

Nonetheless he led Kaoru to a secluded wing fenced off by wattled bamboo and the guards to the west veranda, where he saw to their needs as best he could.

A gate seemed to lead to the princesses' rooms. Kaoru pushed it open a little. The blind had been half raised to give a view of the moon, more beautiful for the mist. A young girl, tiny and delicate, her soft robe somewhat rumpled, sat shivering at the veranda. With her was an older woman similarly dressed. The princesses were farther inside. Half hidden by a pillar, one had a lute before her and sat toying with the plectrum.* Just then the moon burst forth in all its brilliance.

'Well, now,' she said. 'This does quite as well as a fan for bringing out the moon.' The upraised face was bright and lively.

The other, leaning against an armrest, had a koto before her. 'I have heard that you summon the sun with one of those objects,†

---

*This is a much debated passage. We have been told that the older sister is a master of the lute, the younger of the koto; but the description of the girl with the plectrum seems to fit the younger girl better.

†This is obviously an allusion, but it has not been traced.

but you seem to have ideas of your own on how to use it.' She was smiling, a melancholy, contemplative sort of smile.

'I may be asking too much, I admit, but *you* have to admit that lutes and moons are related.'*

It was a charming scene, utterly unlike what Kaoru had imagined from afar. He had often enough heard the young women of his household reading from old romances. They were always coming upon such scenes, and he had thought them the most unadulterated nonsense. And here, hidden away from the world, was a scene as affecting as any in a romance. He was dangerously near losing control of himself. The mist had deepened until he could barely make out the figures of the princesses. Summon it forth again, he whispered – but a woman had come from within to tell them of the caller. The blind was lowered and everyone withdrew to the rear of the house. There was nothing confused, nothing disorderly about the withdrawal, so calm and quiet that he caught not even a rustling of silk. Elegance and grace could at times push admiration to the point of envy.

He slipped out and sent someone back to the city for a carriage.

'I was sorry to find the prince away,' he said to the man who had been so helpful, 'but I have drawn some consolation from what you have been so good as to let me see. Might I ask you to tell them that I am here, and to add that I am thoroughly drenched?'

The ladies were in an agony of embarrassment. They had not dreamed that anyone would be looking in at them – and had he even overheard that silly conversation? Now that they thought of it, there had been a peculiar fragrance on the wind; but the hour was late and they had not paid much attention. Could anything be more embarrassing? Impatient at the woman assigned to deliver his message – she did not seem to have the experience for the task – Kaoru decided that there was a time for boldness and a time for reserve; and the mist was in his favor. He advanced to the blind that had been raised earlier and knelt deferentially before it. The countrified maids had not the first notion of what to say to him. Indeed they seemed incapable of so ordinary a courtesy as inviting him to sit down.

---

*There are three sound holes on the face of a *biwa* lute, two known as half-moons, the other as the full or 'hidden' moon.

'You must see how uncomfortable I am,' he said quietly. 'I have come over steep mountains. You cannot believe, surely, that a man with improper intentions would have gone to the trouble. This is not the reward I expected. But I take some comfort in the thought that if I submit to the drenching time after time your ladies may come to understand.'

They were young and incapable of a proper answer. They seemed to wither and crumple. It was taking a great deal of time to summon a more experienced woman from the inner chambers. The prolonged silence, Oigimi feared, might make it seem that they were being coy.

'We know nothing, nothing. How can we pretend otherwise?' It was an elegantly modulated voice, but so soft that he could scarcely make it out.

'One of the more trying mannerisms of this world, I have always thought, is for people who know its cruelties to pretend that they do not. Even you are guilty of the fault, which I find more annoying than I can tell you. Your honored father has gained deep insights into the nature of things. You have lived here with him. I should have thought that you would have gained similar insights, and that they might now demonstrate their worth by making you see the intensity of my feelings and the difficulty with which I contain them. You cannot believe, surely, that I am the usual sort of adventurer. I fear that I am of a rather inflexible nature and refuse to wander in that direction even when others try to lead me. These facts are general knowledge and will perhaps have reached your ears. If I had your permission to tell you of my silent days, if I could hope to have you come forward and seek some relief from your solitude – I cannot describe the pleasure it would give me.'

Oigimi, too shy to answer, deferred to an older woman who had at length been brought from her room.

There was nothing reticent about *her*. 'Oh no! You've left him out there all by himself! Bring him in this minute. I simply do not understand young people.' The princesses must have found this as trying as the silence. 'You see how it is, sir. His Highness has decided to live as if he did not belong to the human race. No one comes calling these days, not even people you'd think would never forget what they owe him. And here you are, good enough to come and see us. I may be stupid and insensitive, but I know when to be grateful. So do my ladies. But they are so shy.'

Kaoru was somewhat taken aback. Yet the woman's manner suggested considerable polish and experience, and her voice was not unpleasant.

'I had been feeling rather unhappy,' he said, 'and your words cheer me enormously. It is good to be told that they understand.'

He had come inside. Through the curtains, the old woman could make him out in the dawn light. It was as she had been told: he had discarded every pretense of finery and come in rough travel garb, and he was drenched. A most extraordinary fragrance – it hardly seemed of this world – filled the air.

'I would not want you to think me forward,' she said, and there were tears in her voice; 'but I have hoped over the years that the day might come when I could tell you a little, the smallest bit, of a sad story of long ago.' Her voice was trembling. 'In among my other prayers I have put a prayer that the day might come, and now it seems that the prayer has been answered. How I have longed for this moment! But see what is happening. I am all choked up before I have come to the first word.'

He had heard, and it had been his experience, that old people weep easily. This, however, was no ordinary display of feeling.

'I have fought my way here so many times and not known that a perceptive lady like yourself was in residence. Come, this is your chance. Do not leave anything out.'

'This is my chance, and there may not be another. When you are my age you can't be sure that you will last the night. Well, let me talk. Let me tell you that this old hag is still among the living. I have heard somewhere that Kojijū, the one who waited upon your revered mother – I have heard that she is dead. So it goes. Most of the people I was fond of are dead, the people who were young when I was young. And after I had outlived them all, certain family ties* brought me back from the far provinces, and I have been in the service of my ladies these five or six years. None of this, I am sure, will have come to your attention. But you may have heard of the young gentleman who was a guards captain when he died. I am told that his brother is now a grand councillor.† It hardly seems possible that we have had time to dry our

*The old woman, Bennokimi, is a first cousin both of Kojijū and of the Eighth Prince's deceased wife.

†Kashiwagi and Kōbai.

tears, and yet I count on my fingers and I see that there really have been years enough for you to be the fine young gentleman you are. They seem like a dream, all those years.

'My mother was his nurse. I was privileged myself to wait upon him. I did not matter, of course, but he sometimes told me secrets he kept from others, let slip things he could not keep to himself. And as he lay dying he called me to his side and left a will, I suppose you might call it. There were things in it I knew I must tell you of someday. But no more. You will ask why, having said this much, I do not go on. Well, there may after all be another chance and I can tell you everything. These youngsters are of the opinion that I have said too much already, and they are right.' She was a loquacious old person obviously, but now she fell silent.

It was like a story in a dream, like the unprompted recital of a medium in a trance. It was too odd – and at the same time it touched upon events of which he had long wanted to know more. But this was not the time. She was right. Too many eyes were watching. And it would not do to surrender on the spot and waste a whole night on an ancient story.

'I do not understand everything you have said, I fear, and yet your talk of old times does call up fond thoughts. I shall come again and ask you to tell me the rest of the story. You see how I am dressed, and if the mist clears before I leave I will disgrace myself in front of the ladies. I would like to stay longer but do not see how I can.'

As he stood up to leave, the bell of the monastery sounded in the distance. The mist was heavy. The sadness of these lives poured in upon him, of the isolation enforced by heavy mountain mists. They were lives into which the whole gamut of sorrows had entered, he thought, and he thought too that he understood why they preferred to live in seclusion.

'How very sad.

> 'In the dawn I cannot see the path I took
> To find Oyama of the Pines in mist.'*

He turned away, and yet hesitated. Even ladies who saw the great gentlemen of the capital every day would have found him remarkable, and he quite dazzled these rustic maids. Oigimi,

*A mountain in the vicinity of Uji.

knowing that it would be too much to ask one of them to deliver it for her, offered a reply, her voice soft and shy as before, and with a hint of a sigh in it.

> 'Our mountain path, enshrouded whatever the season,
>   Is now closed off by the deeper mist of autumn.'

The scene itself need not have detained him, but these evidences of loneliness made him reluctant to leave. Presently, uncomfortable at the thought of being seen in broad daylight, he went to the west veranda, where a place had been prepared for him, and looked out over the river.

'To have spoken so few words and to have had so few in return,' he said as he left the princesses' wing of the house, 'makes it certain that I shall have much to think about. Perhaps when we are better acquainted I can tell you of it. In the meantime, I shall say only that if you think me no different from most young men, and you do seem to, then your judgment in such matters is not what I would have hoped it to be.'

His men had become expert at presiding over the weirs. 'Listen to all the shouting,' said one of them. 'And they don't seem to be exactly boasting over what they've caught. The fish* are not cooperating.'

Strange, battered little boats, piled high with brush and wattles, made their way up and down the river, each boatman pursuing his own sad, small livelihood at the uncertain mercy of the waters. 'It is the same with all of us,' thought Kaoru to himself. 'Am I to boast that I am safe from the flood, calm and secure in a jeweled mansion?'

Asking for brush and ink, he got off a note to Oigimi: 'It is not hard to guess the sad thoughts that must be yours.

> 'Wet are my sleeves as the oars that work these shallows,
>   For my heart knows the heart of the lady at the bridge.'†

Hiuo, literally 'ice fish.' The young of the *ayu*.

†Anonymous, *Kokinshū* 689:

> Cloak spread for lonely sleep, does she await me,
>   The lady at the Uji Bridge tonight?

The lady is generally taken to be the tutelary goddess of the Uji Bridge.

He sent it in through the guard of the night before. Red from the cold, the man presently returned with an answer. The princess was not proud of the paper, perfumed in a very undistinguished way, but speed seemed the first consideration.

'I have wet sleeves, and indeed my whole being is at the mercy of the waters.

'With sodden sleeves the boatman plies the river.
So too these sleeves of mine, at morn, at night.'

The writing was confident and dignified. He had not been able to detect a flaw in the lady. But here were these people rushing him on, telling him that his carriage had arrived from the city.

He called the guard aside. 'I shall most certainly come again when His Highness has finished his retreat.' Changing to court dress that had come with the carriage, he gave his wet traveling clothes to the man.

The old woman's remarks were very much on his mind after his return to the city, and the princesses were still before his eyes, more beautiful and reposed than he would have thought possible.

'And so,' he thought, 'Uji will not, after all, be my renunciation of the world.'

He sent off a letter, taking care that every detail distinguished it from an ordinary love note: the paper was white and thick and firmly rectangular, the brush strong yet pliant, the ink shaded with great subtlety.

'It seems a great pity,' he wrote, 'that my visit was such a short one, and that I held back so much I would have liked to say; but the last thing I wanted was to be thought forward. I believe I mentioned a hope that in the future I might appear freely before you. I have made note of the day on which your honored father's retreat is to end, and I hope that by then the gloomy mists will have dissipated.'

The letter showed great restraint and avoided any suggestion of romantic intent. The guards officer who was his messenger was instructed to seek out the old woman and give it to her along with certain gifts. He remembered how the watchman had shivered as he made the rounds, and sent lavish gifts for him too, food in cypress boxes and the like.

The following day he dispatched a messenger to the temple to which the prince had withdrawn. 'I have no doubt,' said the letter that accompanied numerous bolts of cotton and silk, 'that the priests will be badly treated by the autumn tempests, and that you will want to leave offerings.'

The prince was making preparations to depart, his retreat having ended the evening before. He gave silk and cotton cloth as well as vestments to the priests who had been of service.

The garments of which that watchman had been the recipient – a most elegant hunting robe and a fine singlet of white brocade – were further remarkable for their softness and fragrance. Alas, the man could not change the fact that he had not been born for such finery. It was the same everywhere he went: no one could resist praising him or chiding him for the fragrance. He came to regret just a little that he had accepted the gift. It restricted his movements, for he dreaded the astonishment each new encounter produced. If only he could have the robes without the odor – but no amount of scrubbing would take it away. The gift had, after all, been from a gentleman renowned for just that fragrance.

Kaoru was much pleased at the graceful and unassuming answer he had had from Oigimi.

'What is this?' said her father, shown a copy of Kaoru's letter. 'Such a chilly reception cannot have at all the effect we want. You must bring yourselves to see that he is different from the triflers the world seems to produce these days. I have no doubt that his thoughts have turned to you because I once chanced to hint at a hope that he would watch over you after my death.' He too got off a letter, his thanks for the stream of gifts that had flooded the monastery.

Kaoru began to think of another visit. He thought too of Niou, always mooning over the possibility of finding a great beauty lost away in the mountains. Well, he had a story that would interest his friend.

One quiet evening he went calling. In the course of the usual court gossip, he mentioned the prince at Uji, and went on to describe in some detail what had taken place in the autumn dawn.

He was not disappointed. 'A masterpiece!' said Niou.

He added yet further exciting details.

'But what of the letter? You said there was a letter, and you haven't shown it to me. That is not kind of you. You know that I would hold nothing back if I were in your place.'

'Oh, to be sure. All those letters you've had from all those ladies and you have not shown me the smallest scrap. But I know that something of this sort is not for the weak and obscure of the world to have all to themselves. I would like to take you for a look sometime, I most definitely would; but it is out of the question. I could not think of taking such an important man to such a place. We who are not too burdened with glory are in the happier position. We have our affairs as we want to have them. But think: there must be *hundreds* of beauties hidden away from us all. There they are, poor dears, cut off from the world, hidden behind this and that mountain, waiting for us to find them. As a matter of fact, I had for a number of years known of princesses off in the Uji mountains, but the thought of them had only made me shudder. A man knows, after all, the effect of saintliness on women. But if the sun sets them off as the moon did, then it would be hard to ask for more.'

By the time he had finished, his companion was honestly jealous. Kaoru was not one to be drawn to any ordinary woman. There must be something truly remarkable here. Niou longed to have a look for himself.

'Do, please, investigate further,' he said, openly impatient with his rank, which made such expeditions difficult.

And he had not even seen the ladies, thought Kaoru, smiling to himself. 'Come, now. Women aren't worth the trouble. I must be serious: I had reasons for wanting to get my mind off of my own affairs, and I especially wanted to avoid the sort of frivolity that so excites you. And if my feelings were to pull me against my resolve – you cannot tell me, can you, that any good would come of it.'

'Fine!' Niou said, laughing. 'Another sermon. Let us all fall silent and hear what our saint has to say. But no. I think we have had enough.'

It was with longing and dismay that Kaoru thought of the events the old woman's story had hinted at. He had never been very strongly drawn even to women of uncommon charm and talent, and now they interested him still less.

On about the fifth or sixth day of the Tenth Month he paid his next visit to Uji. He must make it a point to have a look at the weirs, said his men. It was the season when they were at their most interesting.

He would prefer not to, he replied. 'A fly having a look at the fish* – a pretty picture.'

To present as austere a figure as possible, he rode in a carriage faced with palmetto fronds, such as a woman might use, and ordered a cloak and trousers of coarse, unfigured material.

Delighted to see him, the prince arranged a most tasteful banquet from dishes for which the region was known. In the evening, under the lamps, they listened to a discourse on some of the more difficult passages in scriptures they had been over together. The abbot was among those invited down from the monastery. Sleep was out of the question. The roar of the waters and the whipping of leaves and branches in the violent river winds, which in lesser degree might have moved one to a pleasant awareness of the season, invited gloom and even despair. Dawn would be approaching, thought Kaoru, and the koto strain he had heard that other morning came back to him.

He guided the conversation to the delights of koto and lute. 'On my last visit, as the morning mist was rolling in, I was lucky enough to hear a short melody, a most extraordinary one. It was over in a few seconds, and since then I have not been able to think of anything except how I might hear more.'

'The hues and the scents of the world are nothing to me now,' said the prince, 'and I have forgotten all the music I ever knew.' Even so he sent a woman for the instruments. 'No, I am afraid it will not be right. But perhaps – if I had someone to follow, a little might come back?' He pressed a lute upon Kaoru.

'Can it be,' said Kaoru, tuning the instrument, 'that this is the one I heard the other morning? I had thought that there must be something rather special about the instrument itself, but now I see that there is another explanation for that remarkable music.' He addressed himself to the lute, but in a manner somewhat bemused.

'You must not make sport of us, sir. Where can music likely to catch your ear have come from? You speak of the impossible.'

The prince's koto had a clearness and strength that were almost chilling. Perhaps it borrowed overtones from 'the wind in the

---

*There is a pun here on *hio* (a variant of *hiuo*), literally 'ice fish,' and *hiomushi*, 'mayfly.'

mountain pines.'* He pretended to falter and forget, and pushed the instrument away when he had finished the first strain. The brief performance had suggested great subtlety and discernment.

'Sometimes, without warning, I do hear in the distance a strain such as to make me think that one of my daughters has acquired some notion of what real music is; but they have had little training, and it has been a very long time since I last made much effort to teach them. As the mood takes them, they play a tune or two, and they have only the river to accompany them. It is most unlikely that their twanging would be of any interest to a musician like you. But suppose,' he called to them, 'you were to have a try at it.'

'It was bad enough to be overheard when we thought we were alone.'

'I would disgrace myself.'

And so he was rebuffed by both his daughters. He did not give up easily, but, to Kaoru's great disappointment, they would have nothing of the proposal.

The prince was deeply shamed that his daughters should thus announce themselves as rustic wenches, out of touch with the ways of the world.

'They have lived in such seclusion that their very existence is a secret. I have wished it to be so; but now, when I think how little time I have left, when I think that I may be gone tomorrow, I find that resignation eludes me. They have their whole lives yet to live, and might they not end their years as drifters and beggars? A fear of that possibility will be the one bond holding me to the world when my time comes.'

'It would not be honest of me to enter into a firm commitment,' said Kaoru, deeply moved; 'but you are not to think, because I say so, that I am in the least cool or indifferent to what you have said. Though I cannot be sure that I will survive you for very long, I mean to be true to every syllable I have spoken.'

'You are very kind, very kind indeed.'

When the prince had withdrawn for matins, Kaoru summoned the old woman. Her name was Bennokimi, and the Eighth Prince had her in constant attendance upon his daughters. Though in her

---

*Saigū, *Shūishū* 451:

> The wind in the mountain pines is like a koto.
> Whence, from what hill, what strings, can it have come?

late fifties, she was still favored with the graces of a considerably younger woman. Her tears flowing liberally, she told him of what an unhappy life 'the young captain,' Kashiwagi, had led, of how he had fallen ill and presently wasted away to nothing.

It would have been a very affecting tale of long ago even if it had been about a stranger. Haunted and bewildered through the years, longing to know the facts of his birth, Kaoru had prayed that he might one day have a clear explanation. Was it in answer to his prayers that now, without warning, there had come a chance to hear of these old matters, as if in a sad dream? He too was in tears.

'It is hard to believe – and I must admit that it is a little alarming too – that someone who remembers those days should still be with us. I suppose people have been spreading the news to the world – and I have had not a whisper of it.'

'No one knew except Kojijū and myself. Neither of us breathed a word to anyone. As you can see, I do not matter; but it was my honor to be always with him, and I began to guess what was happening. Then sometimes – not often, of course – when his feelings were too much for him, one or the other of us would be entrusted with a message. I do not think it would be proper to go into the details. As he lay dying, he left the testament I have spoken of. I have had it with me all these years – I am no one, and where was I to leave it? I have not been as diligent with my prayers as I might have been, but I have asked the Blessed One for a chance to let you know of it; and now I think I have a sign that he is here with us. But the testament: I must show it to you. How can I burn it now? I have not known from one day to the next when I might die, and I have worried about letting it fall into other hands. When you began to visit His Highness I felt somewhat better again. There might be a chance to speak to you. I was not merely praying for the impossible, and so I decided that I must keep what he had left with me. Some power stronger than we has brought us together.' Weeping openly now, she told of the illicit affair and of his birth, as the details came back to her.

'In the confusion after the young master's death, my mother too fell ill and died; and so I wore double mourning. A not very nice man who had had his eye on me took advantage of it all and led me off to the West Country, and I lost all touch with the city. He too died, and after ten years and more I was back in the city again, back from a different world. I have for a very long time had

the honor to be acquainted indirectly with the sister of my young
master, the lady who is a consort of the Reizei emperor, and it
would have been natural for me to go into her service. But there
were those old complications, and there were other reasons too.
Because of the relationship on my father's side of the family* I
have been familiar with His Highness's household since I was a
child, and at my age I am no longer up to facing the world. And so
I have become the rotted stump you see,† buried away in the
mountains. When did Kojijū die? I wonder. There aren't many left
of the ones who were young when I was young. The last of them
all; it isn't easy to be the last one, but here I am.'

Another dawn was breaking.

'We do not seem to have come to the end of this old story of
yours,' said Kaoru. 'Go on with it, please, when we have found a
more comfortable place and no one is listening. I do remember
Kojijū slightly. I must have been four or five when she came down
with consumption and died, rather suddenly. I am most grateful to
you. If it hadn't been for you I would have carried the sin‡ to my
grave.'

The old woman handed him a cloth pouch in which several
mildewed bits of paper had been rolled into a tight ball.

'Take these and destroy them. When the young master knew
he was dying, he got them together and gave them to me. I told
myself I would give them to Kojijū when next I saw her and ask
her to be sure that they got to her lady. I never saw her again. And
so I had my personal sorrow and the other too, the knowledge that
I had not done my duty.'

With an attempt at casualness, he put the papers away. He was
deeply troubled. Had she told him this unsolicited story, as is the
way with the old, because it seemed to her an interesting piece of
gossip? She had assured him over and over again that no one else
had heard it, and yet – could he really believe her?

---

*Her father was the uncle of the Eighth Prince's wife.

†Kengei, *Kokinshū* 875:

> The form is a rotted stump, in mountains deep;
> You can, if you try, make the heart come back to life.

‡The sin of not having properly honored his real father.

After a light breakfast he took his leave of the prince. 'Yesterday was a holiday because the emperor was in retreat, but today he will be with us again. And then I must call on the Reizei princess, who is not well, and there will be other things to keep me busy. But I will come again soon, before the autumn leaves have fallen.'

'For me, your visits are a light to dispel in some measure the shadows of these mountains.'

Back in the city, Kaoru took out the pouch the old woman had given him. The heavy Chinese brocade bore the inscription 'For My Lady.'* It was tied with a delicate thread and sealed with Kashiwagi's name. Trembling, Kaoru opened it. Inside were multi-hued bits of paper, on which, among other things, were five or six answers by his mother to notes from Kashiwagi.

And, on five or six sheets of thick white paper, apparently in Kashiwagi's own hand, like the strange tracks of some bird, was a longer letter: 'I am very ill, indeed I am dying. It is impossible to get so much as a note to you, and my longing to see you only increases. Another thing adds to the sorrow: the news that you have withdrawn from the world.

'Sad are you, who have turned away from the world,
But sadder still my soul, taking leave of you.

I have heard with strange pleasure of the birth of the child. We need not worry about him, for he will be reared in security. And yet –

'Had we but life, we could watch it, ever taller,
The seedling pine unseen among the rocks.'

The writing, fevered and in disarray, went to the very edge of the paper. The letter was addressed to Kojijū.

The pouch had become a dwelling place for worms and smelled strongly of mildew; and yet the writing, in such compromising detail, was as clear as if it had been set down the day before. It would have been a disaster if the letter had fallen into the hands of outsiders, he thought, half in sorrow and half in alarm. He was so haunted by this strange affair, stranger than any

---

*It bears the character for 'up' or 'over' (*ue*). There are several theories as to what it might mean, of which this seems the most credible.

the future could possibly bring, that he could not persuade himself to set out for court. Instead he went to visit his mother. Youthful and serene, she had a sutra in her hand, which she put shyly out of sight upon his arrival. He must keep the secret to himself, he thought. It would be cruel to let her know of his own new knowledge. His mind jumped from detail to detail of the story he had heard.

CHAPTER 46

Beneath the Oak

On about the twentieth of the Second Month, Niou made a pilgrimage to Hatsuse. Perhaps the pleasant thought of stopping in Uji on the return from Hatsuse made him seek now to honor a vow he had made some years before. The fact that he should be so interested in a place the name of which tended to call up unpleasant associations* suggested a certain frivolity. Large numbers of the highest-ranking officials were in his retinue, and as for officials of lower ranks, scarcely any were left in the city. On the far bank of the river Uji stood a large and beautifully appointed villa which Yūgiri, Minister of the Right,† had inherited from his father, Genji. Yūgiri ordered that it be put in readiness for the prince's visit. Protocol demanded that he go himself to receive Niou on the return journey from Hatsuse, but he begged to be excused. Certain occurrences had required him to consult soothsayers, who had replied that he must spend some time in retreat and abstinence. Niou was vaguely displeased; but when he heard that Kaoru would be meeting him he decided that this breach of etiquette was in fact a piece of good luck. He need feel no reticence about sending Kaoru to look into the situation on the opposite bank of the Uji, where the Eighth Prince lived. There was, in any case, something too solemn about Yūgiri, a stiffness that invited an answering stiffness in Niou himself.

Several of Yūgiri's sons were in Kaoru's retinue: a moderator of the first order, a chamberlain, a captain, and two lesser guards officers. Because he was the favorite of his royal parents, Niou's prestige and popularity were enormous; and for even the humblest and least influential of Genji's retainers he was 'our prince.' The apartments in which he and his attendants meant to rest were fitted out with the greatest care, in a manner that put the advantages of the setting to the best possible use. The gaming boards were brought

---

See note, page 839.

†Here and elsewhere, the promotions in Chapter 44 seem to be forgotten. See note‡, page 828.

out, Go and backgammon and *tagi** and the rest, and the men
settled down for trials of strength as fancy took them. Not used to
travel and persuaded by something more than fatigue, Niou
decided that it would be a pleasant spot for a night's lodging. After
resting for a time, he had instruments brought out. It was late
afternoon. As so often happens far away from the noisy world, the
accompaniment of the water seemed to give the music a clearer,
higher sound.

The Eighth Prince's villa was across the river, a stone's throw
away. The sound came over on the breeze to make him think of
old days at court.

'What a remarkable flutist that is,' said the prince to himself.
'Who might it be? Genji played an interesting flute, a most charming flute; but this is somehow different. It puts me in mind of the
music we used to hear at the old chancellor's, bold and clear, and
maybe just a little haughty.† It has been a very long time indeed
since I myself took part in such a concert. The months and the
years have gone by like waking dead!'

Pity for his daughters swept over him. If there were only a way
to get them out of these mountains! Kaoru was exactly what he
hoped a son-in-law might be, but Kaoru seemed rather wanting in
amorous urges. How could he think of handing his daughters over
to trifling young men of the sort the world seemed to produce
these days? The worries chased each other through his mind, and
the spring night, endless for someone lost in melancholy thought,
went on and on. Beyond the river, the travelers were enjoying
themselves quite without reserve, and for them, in their fuddle-
ment, the spring night was all too quick to end. It seemed a pity,
thought Niou, to start for home so soon.

The high sky with fingers of mist trailing across it, the cherries
coming into bloom and already shedding their blossoms,‡ 'the

---

*'Tiddlywinks' has been suggested as a translation. The object, however, was not to
flip the pieces into a container but to strike the opponent's pieces ranged on the
opposite side of a ridged board.

†The implication seems to be that blood will make itself known. Although it is not
clear who is playing the flute, Tō no Chūjō, 'the old chancellor,' has numbers of
descendants across the river: most of Yūgiri's sons are his grandsons, and Kaoru,
though known to the world as Genji's son, is in fact Tō no Chūjō's grandson.

‡Probably an allusion.

willows by the river,'* their reflections now bowing and now soaring as the wind caught them – it was a novel sight for the visitor from the city, and one he was reluctant to leave.

Kaoru was thinking what a pity it would be not to call on the Eighth Prince. Could he avoid all these inquiring eyes and row across the river? Would he be thought guilty of indiscretion? As he was debating the problem, a poem was delivered from the prince:

'Parting the mist, a sound comes in on the wind,
But waves of white, far out on the stream, roll between us.'

The writing, a strong, masculine hand, was most distinguished.

Well, thought Niou – from precisely the place that had been on his mind. He himself would send an answering poem:

'On far shore and near, the waves may keep us apart.
Come in all the same, O breeze of the river Uji!'

Kaoru set out to deliver it. In attendance upon him were men known to be particularly fond of music. Summoning up all their artistry, the company played 'The River Music'† as they were rowed across. The landing that had been put out from the river pavilion of the prince's villa, and indeed the villa itself, seemed in the best of taste, again quite in harmony with the setting. Cleaned and newly appointed in preparation for a distinguished visit, it was a house of a very different sort from the one in which they had passed the night. The furnishings, screens of wattled bamboo and the like, simple and yet in very good taste, were right for a mountain dwelling. Unostentatiously, the Eighth Prince brought out antique kotos and lutes of remarkable timbre. The guests, tuning their instruments to the *ichikotsu* mode,‡ played 'Cherry-Blossom

---

*A congratulatory poem attributed to the emperor Kenzō in the *Nihon Shoki* seems to have been popular in the Heian Period, and makes more than one reappearance in somewhat modified form:

The willows by the river, they bow, they soar,
As the waters pass; and still their roots are firm.

†Or perhaps 'The Tipsy Music.' *Kansuiraku.*

‡D is the tonic, unusually low for the piece being rendered, perhaps to accord with the serenity of the setting.

Girl,'* and when they had finished they pressed their host to favor them with something on that famous seven-stringed koto of his. He was diffident, and only joined in with a short strain from time to time. Perhaps because it was a style they were not used to, the young men found that it had a somewhat remote sound to it, a certain depth and mystery, strangely moving.

As for the repast to which they were treated, it was most tasteful in an old-fashioned way, exactly what the setting asked for, and much superior to what they would have expected. There were in the neighborhood numbers of elderly people who, though not of royal blood, came from gentle families, and some who were distant relatives of the emperor himself. They had long wondered what the prince would do if such an occasion were to arise, and as many of them as were able came to help; and the guests found that their cups were being kept full by attendants who, though not perhaps dressed in the latest fashions, could hardly have been called rustic. No doubt there were a number of youngsters whose hearts were less than calm at the thought of ladies' apartments. Matters were even worse for Niou. How constricting it was, to be of a rank that forbade lighthearted adventures! Unable to contain himself, he broke off a fine branch of cherry blossoms and, an elegantly attired page boy for his messenger, sent it across the river with a poem:

> 'I have come, the mountain cherries at their best,
> To break off sprays of blossom for my cap.'

And it would seem that he added: 'Then stayed the night, enamored of the fields.'†

What could they send by way of answer? The princesses were at a loss. But they must send something, that much was sure, said the old women. This was hardly the occasion for a really formal poem, and it would be rude to wait too long. Finally Oigimi composed a reply and had Nakanokimi set it down for her:

'It is true that you have fought your way through the mountain tangles, and yet

> 'For sprays to break, the springtime wanderer pauses
> Before the rustic fence, and wanders on.'

See note, page 351.
†See note†, page 533.

The hand was subtle and delicate.

And so music answered music across the river. It was as Niou had requested, the wind did not propose to keep them apart. Presently Kōbai arrived, upon order of the emperor; and with great crowds milling about Niou made a noisy departure. His attendants looked back again, and he promised himself that he would find an excuse for another visit. The view was magical, with the blossoms at their best and layers of mist trailing among them. Many were the poems in Chinese and in Japanese that the occasion produced, but I did not trouble myself to ask about them.

Niou was unhappy. In the confusion he had not been able to convey the sort of message he had wished to. He sent frequent letters thereafter, not bothering to ask the mediation of Kaoru.

'You really should answer,' said the Eighth Prince. 'But be careful not to sound too serious. That would only excite him. He has his pleasure-loving ways, and you are a pleasure he is not likely to forgo.'

Though with this caveat, he encouraged replies. It was Nakanokimi who set them down. Oigimi was much too cautious and deliberate to let herself become involved in the least significant of such exchanges.

The prince, ever deeper in melancholy, found the long, uneventful spring days harder to get through than other days. The beauty and grace of his daughters, more striking as the years went by, had the perverse effect of intensifying the melancholy. If they were plain little things, he said to himself, then it might not matter so much to leave them in these mountains. His mind ran the circle of worries and ran it again, day and night. Oigimi was now twenty-five, Nakanokimi twenty-three.

It was a dangerous year for him.* He was more assiduous than ever in his devotions. Because his heart was no longer in this world, because he was intent on leaving it behind as soon as possible, the way down the cool, serene path seemed clear. But there was one obstacle, worry about the future of his daughters.

'When he puts himself into his studies,' said the people around him, 'his will power is extraordinary. But don't you suppose he'll

---

*Certain years of one's life were thought to be especially perilous. This is probably his sixty-first year by the Oriental count, or the year in which his sixtieth birthday occurs.

weaken when the final test comes? Don't you suppose his worries about our ladies will be too much for him?'

If only there were *someone*, he thought – someone not perhaps up to the standard he had always set, but still, after his fashion, of a rank and character that would not be demeaning, and someone who would undertake in all sincerity to look after the princesses – then he would be inclined to give his tacit blessing. If even one of the girls could find a secure place in the world, he could without misgivings leave the other in her charge. But thus far no one had come forward with what could be described as serious intentions. Occasionally, on some pretext, there would be a suggestive letter, and occasionally too some fellow, in the lightness of his young heart, stopping on his way to or from a temple, would show signs of interest. But there was always something insulting about these advances, some hint that the man looked down upon ladies left to waste away in the mountains. The prince would not permit the most casual sort of reply.

And now came Niou, who said that he could not rest until he had made the acquaintance of the princesses. Was this ardor a sign of a bond from a former life?

In the autumn Kaoru was promoted to councillor of the middle order.* The distinction of his manner and appearance was more pronounced as he rose in rank and office, and the thoughts that tormented him made similar gains. They were more tenacious than when the doubts about his birth had still been vague and unformed. As he tried to imagine how it had been in those days, so long ago now, when his father had sickened and died, he wanted to lose himself in prayers and rites of atonement.† He had been strongly drawn to the old woman at Uji, and he tried circumspectly to let her know of his feelings.

It was now the Seventh Month. He had been away from Uji, he thought, for a very long while.

Autumn had not yet come to the city, but by the time he reached Mount Otowa the breeze was cool, and in the vicinity of Mount Oyama autumn was already at the tips of the branches. The

*See note†, page 858.

†On behalf of Kaoru himself for having failed to minister to the posthumous needs of his real father, and Kashiwagi for having fallen into adultery.

shifting mountain scenery delighted him more and more as he approached Uji.

The prince greeted him with unusual warmth, and talked on and on of the melancholy thoughts that were so much with him.

'If you should find reasonable occasion, after I am gone,' he said, guiding the conversation to the problem of his daughters, 'do please come and see them from time to time. Put them on your list, if you will, of the people you do not mean to forget.'

'You may remember that you have already brought the matter up once or twice before, and you have my word that I shall not forget. Not that you can expect a great deal of me, I am afraid. All my impulses are to run away from the world, and it does not seem to have very strong hopes for me in any case. No, I do not hold a great deal in reserve. But for as long as I live, my determination will not waver.'

The prince was much relieved. A late moon, breaking through the clouds with a soft, clean radiance, seemed about to touch the western hills. Having said his prayers, to which the scene lent an especial dignity, he turned to talk of old times.

'How is it at court these days? On autumn nights people used to gather in His Majesty's chambers. There was always something a little too good, a little ostentatious – or it so seemed to me – about the way the famous musicians lent their presence to this group and the next one. What was really worth notice was the way His Majesty's favorites and the ladies of the bedchamber and the rest would be chatting away as pleasantly as you could wish, and all the while you knew that they were in savage competition. And then, as quiet came over the palace, you would have the real music, leaking out from their several rooms. Each strain seemed to be pleading its own special cause.

'Women are the problem, good for a moment of pleasure, offering nothing of substance. They are the seeds of turmoil, and it is not hard to see why we are told that their sins are heavy. I wonder if you have ever tried to imagine what a worry a child is for its father. A son is no problem. But a daughter – there is a limit to worrying, after all, and the sensible thing would be to recognize the hopeless for what it is. But fathers will go on worrying.'

He spoke as if in generalities; but could there be any doubt that he was really speaking of himself and his daughters?

'I have told you of my feelings about the world,' said Kaoru. 'One result of them has been that I have not mastered a single art worthy of the name. But music – yes, I know how useless it is, and still I have had a hard time giving it up. I do have a good precedent, after all. You will remember that music made one of the apostles* jump up and dance.'

He had been longing, he continued, to have more of the music of which he had caught that one tantalizing snatch. The prince thought this might be the occasion for a sort of introduction. He went to the princesses' rooms. There came a soft strain on a koto, and that was all. The light, impromptu melody, here where it was always quiet and where now there was not one other human sound, with the sky beginning to take on the colors of dawn, quite entranced Kaoru. But the princesses could not be persuaded to give more.

'Well,' said their father, going to the altar, 'I have done what I can to bring you together. You have years ahead of you, and I must leave the rest to you.

> 'I go, this hut of grass will dry and fall.
> But this solemn undertaking must last forever.

'Something tells me that we will not meet again.' He was in tears. 'You must think me an insufferable complainer.'

> 'Your "hut of grass" has sealed a pledge eternal.
> It will not fall, though ages come and go.

'The wrestling meet will keep me busy for a while, but I will see you again when it is out of the way.'

The prince having withdrawn to his prayers, Kaoru called Ben-nokimi to another room and asked for details of the story she had told. The dawn moon flooded the room, setting him off through the blinds to most wonderful effect. Silently, the princesses withdrew behind deeper curtains. Yet he did seem to be unlike most young men. His way of speaking was quiet and altogether serious. Oigimi occasionally came forth with an answer. Kaoru thought of his friend Niou and the rapidity with which he had been drawn to the princesses. Why must he himself be so different? Their father

---

*Kāsyapa, one of the ten great disciples of the original Buddha. The incident is to be found in the *Hokke mongu* or *Fa-hua-wên-chü*, a Tendai text composed in China.

had as good as offered them to him; and why did he not rush forward to claim them? It was not as if he found the thought of having one of them for his wife quite out of the question. That they were ladies of discernment and sensibility they had shown well enough in tests such as this evening's, and in exchanges having to do with the flowers of spring and the leaves of autumn and other such matters. In a sense, indeed, he thought of them as already in his possession. It would be a cruel wrench if fate should give them to others.

He started back before daylight, his thoughts on the prince and his apparent conviction that death was near. When the round of court duties was over, thought Kaoru, he would come again.

Niou was hoping that the autumn leaves might be his excuse for another visit to Uji. He continued to write to the princesses. Thinking these advances no cause for concern, they were able to answer from time to time in appropriately casual terms.

With the deepening of autumn, the prince's gloom also deepened. Concluding that he must withdraw to some quiet refuge where nothing would upset his devotions, he left behind various admonitions.

'Parting is the way of the world. It cannot be avoided: but the grief is easier to bear when you have a companion to share it with. I must leave it to your imagination – for I cannot tell you – how hard it is for me to go off without you, knowing that you are alone. But it would not do to wander lost in the next world because of ties with this one. Even while I have been here with you, I have as good as run away from the world; and it is not for me to say how it should be when I am gone. But please remember that I am not the only one. You have your mother to think of too. Please do nothing that might reflect on her name. Men who are not worthy of you will try to lure you out of these mountains, but you are not to yield to their blandishments. Resign yourselves to the fact that it was not meant to be – that you are different from other people and were meant to be alone – and live out your lives here at Uji. Once you have made up your minds to it, the years will go smoothly by. It is good for a woman, even more than for a man, to be away from the world and its slanders.'

The princesses were beyond thinking about the future. It was beyond them, indeed, to think how they would live if they were to survive their father by so much as a day. These gloomy and ominous instructions left them in the cruelest uncertainty. He had in effect renounced the world already, but for them, so long beside him, to be informed thus suddenly of a final parting – it was not from intentional cruelty that he had done it, of course, and yet in such cases a certain resentment is inevitable.

On the evening before his departure he inspected the premises with unusual care, walking here, stopping there. He had thought of this Uji villa as the most temporary of dwellings, and so the years had gone by. Everything about him suggesting freedom from worldly taints, he turned to his devotions, and thoughts of the future slipped in among them from time to time. His daughters were so very much alone – how could they possibly manage after his death?

He summoned the older women of the household.

'Do what you can for them, as a last favor to me. The world does not pay much attention when an ordinary house goes to ruin. It happens every day. I don't suppose people pay so very much attention when it happens to one like ours. But if fate seems to have decided that the collapse is final, a man does feel ashamed, and wonders how he can face his ancestors. Sadness, loneliness – they are what life brings. But when a house is kept in a manner that becomes its rank, the appearances it maintains, the feelings it has for itself, bring their own consolation. Everyone wants luxury and excitement; but you must never, even if everything fails – you must never, I beg of you, let them make unsuitable marriages.'

As the moonlight faded in the dawn, he went to take leave of his daughters. 'Do not be lonely when I am gone. Be happy, find ways to occupy yourselves. One does not get everything in this world. Do not fret over what has to be.'

He looked back and looked back again as he started up the path to the monastery.

The girls were lonely indeed, despite these admonitions. What would the one do if the other were to go away? The world offers no security in any case; and what could they possibly do for themselves if they were separated? Smiling over this small matter, sighing over that rather more troublesome detail, they had always been together.

It was the morning of the day when the prince's meditations were to end. He would be coming home. But in the evening a message came instead: 'I have been indisposed since this morning.

A cold, perhaps – whatever it is, I am having it looked after. I long more than ever to see you.'

The princesses were in consternation. How serious would it be? They hastened to send quilted winter garments. Two and three days passed, and there was no sign of improvement. A messenger came back. The ailment was not of a striking nature, he reported. The prince was generally indisposed. If there should be even the slightest improvement he would brave the discomfort and return home.

The abbot, in constant attendance, sought to sever the last ties with this world. 'It may seem like the commonest sort of ailment,' he said, 'but it could be your last. Why must you go on worrying about your daughters? Each of us has his own destiny, and it does no good to worry about others.' He said that the prince was not to leave the temple under any circumstances.

It was about the twentieth of the Eighth Month, a time when the autumn skies are conducive to melancholy in any case. For the princesses, lost in their own sad thoughts, there was no release from the morning and evening mists. The moon was bright in the early-morning sky, the surface of the river was clear and luminous. The shutters facing the mountain were raised. As the princesses gazed out, the sound of the monastery bell came down to them faintly – and, they said, another dawn was upon them.

But then came a messenger, blinded with tears. The prince had died in the night.

Not for a moment had the princesses stopped thinking of him; but this was too much of a shock, it left them dazed. At such times tears refuse to come. Prostrate, they could only wait for the shock to pass. A death is sad when, as is the commoner case, the survivors have a chance to make proper farewells. For the princesses, who did not have their father with them, the sense of loss was even more intense. Their laments would not have seemed excessive if they had wailed to the very heavens. Reluctant to accept the thought of surviving their father by a day, they asked what they were to do now. But he had gone a road that all must take, and weeping did nothing to change that cruel fact.

As had been promised over the years, the abbot arranged for the funeral. The princesses sent word that they would like to see their father again, even in death. And what would be accomplished? replied the holy man. He had trained their father to acceptance of the fact that he would not see them again, and now it was their turn. They must train their hearts to a freedom from binding regrets. As he told of their father's days in the monastery, they found his wisdom somewhat distasteful.

It had long been their father's most fervent wish to take the tonsure, but in the absence of someone to look after his daughters he had been unable to turn his back on them. Day after day, so long as he had lived, this inability had been at the same time the solace of a sad life and the bond that tied him to a world he wished to leave. Neither to him who had now gone the inevitable road nor to them who must remain behind had fulfillment come.

Kaoru was overcome with grief and regret. There were so many things left to talk about if only they might have another quiet evening together. Thoughts about the impermanence of things chased one another through his mind, and he made no attempt to stop the flow of tears. The prince had said, it was true, that they might not meet again; but Kaoru had so accustomed himself over the years to the mutability of this world, to the way morning has of becoming evening, that thoughts 'yesterday, today' had not come to him.* He sent long and detailed letters to the abbot and the princesses. Having received no other such message, the princesses, though still benumbed with grief, knew once again what kindness they had known over the years. The loss of a father is never easy, thought Kaoru, and it must be very cruel indeed for two ladies quite alone in the world. He had had the foresight to send the abbot offerings and provisions for the services, and he also saw, through the old woman, that there were ample offerings at the Uji villa.

The rest of the month was one long night for the princesses, and so the Ninth Month came. The mountain scenery seemed more capable than ever of summoning the showers that dampen one's sleeves, and sometimes, lost in their tears, they could almost imagine that the tumbling leaves and the roaring water and the cascade of tears had become one single flow.

Near distraction themselves, their women thought to dislodge them even a little from their grief. 'Please, my ladies. If this goes

*Ariwara Narihira, *Kokinshū* 861:

> A road, I knew, that all must one day go.
> But not so soon as yesterday, today.

on you will soon be in your own graves. Our lives are short enough in any case.'

Priests were charged with memorial services at the villa as well as at the monastery. With holy images to remind them of the dead prince, the women who had withdrawn into deepest mourning kept constant vigil.

Niou too sent messages, but they were not of a sort that the princesses could bring themselves to answer.

'My friend gets different treatment,' he said, much chagrined. 'Why am I the one they will have nothing to do with?'

He had thought that Uji with the autumn leaves at their best might feed his poetic urges, but now, regretfully, he had to conclude that the time was inappropriate. He did send a long letter. The initial period of mourning* was over, he thought, and there must be an end to grief and a pause in tears. Dispatching his letter on an evening of chilly showers, he had this to say, among many other things:

> 'How is it in yon hills where the hart calls out
>   On such an eve, and dew forms on the *hagi*?

I cannot think how on an evening like this you can be indifferent to melancholy like mine. Autumn brings an unusual sadness over Onoe Moor.'†

'He is right,' said Oigimi, urging her sister on. 'We do let these notes pile up, and I'm sure he thinks us very rude and unfeeling. Do get something off to him.'

Enduring the days since her father's death, thought Nakanokimi, had she once considered taking up brush again? How cruel those days had been! Her eyes clouded over, and she pushed the inkstone away.

'I cannot do it,' she said, weeping quietly. 'I have come this far, you say, and sorrow has to end? No – the very thought of it makes me hate myself.'

Oigimi understood, and urged her no further.

---

*Usually the first forty-nine days, but such a protracted lapse of time would push the chronology askew. Perhaps thirty days of lustration.

†Prince Tomohira, *Shinsenzaishū* 526:

> Sere and sad, from the lower leaves of the *hagi*,
>   Onoe Moor stretches on, where dwell the deer.

The messenger had left the city at dusk and arrived after dark. How could they send him back at this hour? They told him he must stay the night. But no: he was going back, he said, and he hurried to get ready.

Though no more in control of herself than her sister, Oigimi wished to detain him no longer, and composed a stanza for him to take back:

'A mist of tears blots out this mountain village,
    And at its rustic fence, the call of the deer.'

Scarcely able to make out the ink, dark in the night, against dark paper, she wrote with no thought for the niceties. She folded her note into a plain cover and sent it out to the man.

It was a black, gusty night. He was uneasy as he made his way through the wilds of Kohata; but Niou did not pick men who were noted for their timidity. He spurred his horse on, not allowing it to pause even for the densest bamboo thickets, and reached Niou's mansion in remarkably quick time. Seeing how wet he was, Niou gave him a special bounty for his services.

The hand, a strange one, was more mature than the one he was used to, and suggestive of a deeper mind. Which princess would be which? he wondered, gazing and gazing at the note. It was well past time for him to be in bed.

They could see why he would wish to wait up until an answer came, whispered the women, but here he was still mooning over it. The sender must be someone who interested him greatly. There was a touch of asperity in these remarks, as of people who wished they were in bed themselves.

The morning mists were still heavy as he arose to prepare his answer:

'The call of the hart whose mate has strayed away
 In the morning mist – are there those whom it leaves unmoved?*

My own wails are no less piercing.'

'He is likely to be a nuisance if he thinks we understand too well,' said Oigimi, always withdrawn and cautious in these

*Ki no Tomonori, *Gosenshū* 372:

> I cry aloud, though not the stricken hart
> Whose mate is lost among the autumn mists.

matters. 'Before Father died we had him to protect us. We did not want to outlive him, but here we are. He thought of us to the last, and now we must think of him. The slightest little misstep would hurt him.' She would not permit an answer. Yet she did not take the view of Niou that she did of most men. His writing and choice of words, even at their most casual, had an elegance and originality which seemed to her, though she had not had letters from many men, truly superior. But to answer even such subtle letters was inappropriate for a lady in her situation. If the world disagreed, she had no answer: she would live out her life as a rustic spinster, and the world need not think about her.

Kaoru's letters, on the other hand, were of such an earnest nature that she answered them freely. He came calling one day, even before the period of deepest mourning was over. Approaching the lower part of the east room,* where the princesses were still in mourning, he summoned Bennokimi. Wanderers in darkness, they found this sudden burst of light quite blinding. Their own somber garments were too sharp a contrast. They were unable to send out an answer.

'Do they have to go on treating me like a stranger? Have they completely forgotten their father's last wishes? The most ordinary sort of conversation, now and then, would be such a pleasure. I have not mastered the methods of suitors and it does not seem at all natural to have to use a messenger.'

'We have lived on, as you see,' Oigimi finally managed to send back, 'although I do not remember that anyone asked our wishes. It has been one long nightmare. I doubt if our wishes matter much more even now. Everything tells us to stay out of the light, and I must ask you not to ask the impossible.'

'You are being much too conservative. If you were to come marching gaily out into the sunlight or the moonlight of your own free will, now – but you are only creating difficulties. Acquaint me with the smallest particle of what you are thinking and, who knows, I might have a small bit of comfort to offer.'

'How nice,' said the women of the house. 'Here you are floundering and helpless, and here he is trying to help you.'

---

*An ascetic way of life, out of respect to their father, is indicated, but the details are unclear. Perhaps the princesses are doing without mats or cushions.

Oigimi, despite her protestations, was recovering from her grief. She remembered his repeated kindnesses (though one might have said that any good friend would have done as much), and she remembered how, over the years, he had made his way through the high grasses to this distant moor. She moved a little nearer. In the gentlest and friendliest way possible, he told how he had felt for them in their grief, and how he had made certain promises to their father. There was nothing insistent in his manner, and she felt neither constraint nor apprehension. Yet he was not, after all, a real intimate; and now, to have him hear her voice – and her thoughts were further confused by the memory of how, over the weeks, she had come to look to him vaguely for support – no, it was still too painful. She was unable to speak. From what little he had heard he knew that she had scarcely begun to pull herself from her grief, and pity welled up afresh. It was a sad figure that he now caught a glimpse of through a gap in the curtains. It suggested all too poignantly the unrelieved gloom of her days; and he thought of the figure he had seen faintly in the autumn dawn.

As if to himself, he recited a verse:

'The reeds, so sparse and fragile, have changed their color,
To make me think of sleeves that now are black.'

And she replied:

'Upon this sleeve, changed though its color be,
The dew finds refuge; there is no refuge for me.

"The thread from these dark robes of mourning" –'* But she could not go on. Her voice wavered and broke in midsentence, and she withdrew deeper into the room.

He did not think it proper to call her back. Instead he found himself talking to the old woman. An improbable substitute, she still had many sad and affecting things to say about long ago and yesterday. She had been witness to it all, and he could not dismiss her as just another tiresome old crone.

'I was a mere boy when Lord Genji died,' he said, 'and that was my first real introduction to the sorrows of the world. And then as

*Mibu Tadamine, *Kokinshū* 841:

The thread I pull from these dark robes of mourning:
Upon it I shall string my tears of grief.

I grew up it seemed to me that rank and office and glory meant less than nothing. And the prince, who had found repose here at Uji – when he was taken away so suddenly, I thought I had the last word about the futility of things. I wanted to get away from the world, leave it completely behind. You will think, perhaps, that I have found a good excuse when I say that your ladies are pulling me back again. But I do not want to recant a word of that last promise I made to him. Now there is your story from all those years ago, pulling in the other direction.'

He was in tears, and the old woman was so shaken with sobs that she could not answer. He was so like his father! Memories of things long forgotten came back to her, flooding over more recent sorrows; but she was not up to telling of them.

She was the daughter of Kashiwagi's nurse, and her father, a moderator of the middle rank at his death, was an uncle of the princesses' mother. Back in the capital after her father's death and some years in the far provinces, she found that she had grown away from the family of her old master; and so, answering an inquiry from the Eighth Prince, she had taken service here. It could not have been said that she was a woman of unusual accomplishments, and she showed the effects of having been too much in the service of others; but the prince saw that she was not devoid of taste and made her a sort of governess to his daughters. Although she had been with them night and day over the years and had become their closest friend, this one ancient secret she had kept locked within herself. Kaoru found cause for doubt and shame even so: she might not have scattered the news lightheartedly to all comers, but unsolicited stories from old women were standard the world over; and, since his presence had the apparent effect of sending the princesses deep into their shells, he feared that she might have passed it on at least to them. He seemed to find here another reason for not letting them go.

He no longer wanted to spend the night. He thought, as he got ready to leave, how the prince had spoken of their last meeting as if it might indeed be their last, and how, confidently looking forward to the continued pleasure of the prince's company, he had dismissed the possibility. Was it not still the same autumn? Not so many days had passed, and the prince had vanished, no one could say where. Though his had always been the most austere of houses, quite without the usual conveniences, it had been clean and appointed in simple but good taste. The ritual utensils were as they had always been, but now the priests, bustling in and out of the house and busily screening themselves from one another, announced that the sacred images would be taken off to the monastery. Kaoru tried to imagine how it would now be for the princesses, left behind after even such excitement as the priests had offered was gone.

He interrupted these sad thoughts, on the urgings of an attendant who pointed out that it was very late, and got up to leave; and a flock of wild geese flew overhead.

'As I gaze at an autumn sky closed off by mists,
    Why must these birds proclaim that the world is fleeting?'

Back in the city, he called on Niou. The conversation moved immediately to the Uji princesses. The time had come, thought Niou, sending off a warm letter. But the ladies still found the most casual sort of reply next to impossible. He was one of the better-known young gallants, and his intentions were clearly romantic. Could a note thrust from the underbrush in which they themselves lurked strike him as other than clumsy and comically out of date?

They worried and fretted, and their tears had no time to dry. And with what cruel speed the days went by! They had not thought that their father's life, fleeting though it must be, was a matter of 'yesterday, today.'* He had taught them an awareness of evanescence, but it had been as if he were speaking of a general principle. They had not considered the possibility of outliving him by even hours or minutes. They looked back over the way they had come. It had, to be sure, had its uncertainties, but they had traveled it with serenity and without fear or shame or any thought that such a disaster might one day come. And now the wind was roaring, strangers were pounding to be admitted. The panic, the terror, the loneliness, worse each day, were almost beyond endurance.

In this season of snow and hail, the roar of the wind was as always and everywhere, and yet they felt for the first time that they knew the sadness of these mountains. Well, the saddest year was over, said some of their women, refusing to give up hope. Let the New Year bring an end to it all. The chances were not good, thought the princesses.

See note, page 869.

Because the prince had gone there for his retreats, an occasional
messenger came down from the monastery and, rarely, there was a
note from the abbot himself, making general inquiries about their
health. He no longer had reason to call in person. Day by day the
Uji villa was lonelier. It was the way of the world, but they were
sad all the same. Occasionally one or two of the village rustics
would look in on them. Such visits, beneath their notice while
their father was alive, became breaks in the monotony. Mountain
people would bring in firewood and nuts, and the abbot sent char-
coal and other provisions.

'One is saddened to think that the generous flow of gifts may
have ceased forever,' said the note that came with them.

It was a timely reminder: their father had made it a practice to
send the abbot cottons and silks against the winter cold. The princesses made haste to do as well.

Sometimes they would go to the veranda and watch in tears as
priests and acolytes, now appearing among the drifts and now
disappearing again, made their way up towards the monastery.
Even though their father had quite renounced the world, callers
would be more numerous if he were still with them. They might
be lonely, but it would not be the final loneliness of knowing they
would not see him again.

'For him, the mountain path has now been cut.
How can we look on the pine we watched as we waited?'

And Nakanokimi replied:

'Away in the hills, the snow departs from the pines
But comes again. Ah, would it were so with him!'

As if to mock her, the snow came again and again.

Kaoru paid his visit late in the year. The New Year would be
too busy to allow the briefest of visits. With the snow so deep, it
was unusual for the ladies to receive even an ordinary caller. That
he, a ranking courtier, should have set out on such a journey as if
he made one every day was the measure of his kindness. They
were at greater pains than usual to receive him. They had taken
out and dusted a brazier of a color gayer than this house of mourning had been used to. Their women chattered about how happy
his visits had made the prince. Though shy, the princesses did
not want to seem rude or unkind. They did at length essay to

address him from behind screens. The conversation could hardly have been called lively or intimate, but Oigimi managed to put together, for her, an uncommon number of words. Kaoru was pleased and surprised. Perhaps the time had come, he thought, for a sally. (It would seem that the best of men are sometimes untrue to their resolves.)

'My friend Niou is irritated with me, and I have trouble understanding why. It is just possible that I let something slip, or it may be that he guessed it all – he does not miss very much. In any event, he knows about your father's last request, and I have orders to tell you about him. Indeed, I have already told you, and you have not been very cooperative. And so he keeps complaining about what an incompetent messenger I am. The charge comes as something of a surprise, considering all I have done, and at the same time I have to admit that I have made myself his "guide to your seashore."* Must you be so remote and haughty?

'It is true, I know, that the gossips have given him a certain name, but beneath the rakish exterior are depths that would surprise you. It is said that he prefers not to spend his time with women who come at his beck and call. Then there are women who take things as they are. What the world does is what the world does, they say, and they do not care a great deal whether they find husbands or not. If someone comes along who is neither entirely pleasing nor entirely repulsive, well, such is life. They make good wives, rather better than you might think. And then, as the poet said, the bank begins to give way, and what is left is a muddy Tatsuta.† You must have heard of such cases – the last of the old love gone down the stream.

'But there is another possibility. Supposing he finds someone who follows him because she agrees with him, because she cannot

---

*Ono no Komachi, *Kokinshū* 727:

> Of hamlets where fishermen dwell I know but little.
> Must you insist that I be your guide to the seashore?

†Takamuku Kusaharu, *Shūishū* 389:

> Our Tatsuta is muddied. At Kannabi
> Of Mimuro the banks will have given way.

The Tatsuta is a river in the province of Yamato.

find it in her heart to do otherwise. I do not think that he would deal lightly with such a one. He would make his commitments and stand by them. I know, because I am in a position to tell you of things he has not let other people see. Give me the signal, and I will do everything I can to help you. I will dash back and forth between Uji and the city until my feet are stumps.'

It had been an earnest discourse. Unable to think that it had reference to herself, Oigimi wondered whether it might now be her duty to take the place of her father. But she did not know what to say.

'Words fail me.' Her reply to the discourse was a quiet laugh, which was not at all unpleasant. 'This sort of thing is, well, rather suggestive, I'm sure you will admit, and does not simplify the hunt for an answer.'

'Your own situation has nothing to do with the matter. Just take these tidings I bring through the snowdrifts as an older sister might be expected to. He is thinking not of you but of – someone else. I have had vague reports that there have been letters, but there again it is hard to know the truth. Which of you was it that answered?'

Oigimi fell silent. This last question was more embarrassing than he could have intended it to be. It would have been nothing to answer Niou's letters, but she had not been up to the task, even in jest; and an answer to Kaoru's question was quite beyond her.

Presently she pushed a verse from under her curtains:

> 'Along the cliffs of these mountains, locked in snow,
> Are the tracks of only one. That one is you.'

'A sort of sophistry that does not greatly improve things.

> 'My pony breaks the ice of the mountain river
> As I lead the way with tidings from him who follows.

"No such shallowness,"* is it not apparent?'

More and more uncomfortable, she did not answer.

She was not remote to excess, he would have said, and on the other hand she had none of the coyness one was accustomed to in young women. A quiet, elegant lady, in sum – as near his ideal as any lady he could remember having met. But whenever he

See note, page 104.

became forward, however slightly, she feigned deafness. He turned to inconsequential talk of things long past.

His men were coughing nervously. It was late, the snow was deep, and the sky seemed to be clouding over again.

'I can see that you have not had an easy time of it,' he said as he got up to leave. 'It would please me enormously if I could prevail on you to leave Uji behind you. I can think of places that are far more convenient and just as quiet.'

Some of the women overheard, and were delighted. How very pleasant if they could move to the city!

But Nakanokimi thought otherwise. It was not to be, she said.

Fruit and sweets, most tastefully arranged, were brought out for Kaoru, and, in equally good taste, there were wine and side dishes for his men. Kaoru thought of the watchman, the man he had made such a celebrity of with that perfume. Of unlovely mien, he was known as Wigbeard. To Kaoru he seemed an uncertain support for sorely tried ladies.

'I imagine that things have been lonely since His Highness died.'

A scowl spread over the man's face, and soon he was weeping. 'I had the honor of his protection for more than thirty years and now I have nowhere to go. I could wander off into the mountains, I suppose, but "the tree denies the fugitive its shelter." '* Tears did not improve the rough face.

Kaoru asked Wigbeard to open the prince's chapel. The dust lay thick, but the images,† decorated as proudly as ever, gave evidence that the princesses had not been remiss with their devotions. The prayer dais had been taken away and the floor carefully dusted, cleaned of the marks it had left. Long ago, the prince had promised that they would be companions in prayer if Kaoru were to renounce the world.

---

*Henjō, *Kokinshū* 292:

> The tree denies the fugitive its shelter.
> It sheds its scarlet leaves, and so rebuffs him.

The man would not seem to be a completely unlettered rustic.

†This would seem to conflict (see page 875) with the announced intention of the priests to take the images to their monastery.

'Beneath the oak I meant to search for shade.
Now it has gone, and all is vanity.'

Numerous eyes were upon him as he stood leaning meditatively against a pillar. The young maidservants thought they had never seen anyone so handsome.

As it grew dark, his men sent to certain of his manors for fodder. Not having been warned, he was much discommoded by the noisy droves of country people the summonses brought, and tried to make it seem that he had come to see the old woman. They must be of similar service to the princesses in the future, he said as he left.

The New Year came, the skies were soft and bright, the ice melted along the banks of the pond. The princesses thought how strange it was that they should so long have survived their father. With a note saying that he had had them gathered in the melting snow, the abbot sent cress from the marshes and fern shoots from the mountain slopes. Country life did have its points, said the women as they cooked the greens and arranged them on pilgrims' trays. What fun it was, really, to watch the days and months go by with their changing grasses and trees.

They were easily amused, thought the princesses.

'If he were here to pluck these mountain ferns,
Then might we find in them a sign of spring.'

And Nakanokimi:

'Without our father, how are we to praise
The cress that sends its shoots through banks of snow?'

Such were the trifles with which they passed their days. Neither Niou nor Kaoru missed an occasion for greetings. They came in such numbers, indeed, as to be something of a nuisance, and with my usual carelessness I failed to make note of them.

The cherry blossoms were now at their best. 'Sprays of blossom for my cap':* Niou thought of Uji. As if to stir his appetites, the men who had been with him remarked upon the pity of it all, that such a pleasant house should have awaited them in vain.

He sent off a poem to the princesses:

*See Niou's poem on page 861.

'Last year along the way I saw those blossoms.
This year, no mist between, I mean to have them.'

They thought it rather too broadly suggestive. Still, there was little excitement in their lives, and it would be a mistake not to give some slight notice to a poem that had its merits.

'Our house is robed in densest mists of black.
Who undertakes to guide you to its blossoms?'

It did little to assuage his discontent. Sometimes, when it was too much for him, he would descend upon Kaoru. Kaoru had bungled this, made a botch of that. Amused, Kaoru would answer quite as if he had been appointed the princesses' guardian. Occasionally he would take it upon himself to chide his friend for a certain want of steadfastness.

'But it won't go on forever. It's just that I haven't found anyone I really like.'

Yūgiri had for some time wanted to arrange a match between Niou and his daughter Rokunokimi. Niou did not seem interested. There was no mystery, no excitement in the proposal,* and besides, Yūgiri was so stiff and proper and unbending, so quick to raise a stir over each of Niou's venialities.

That year the Sanjō mansion of Kaoru's mother burned to the ground. She moved into Genji's Rokujō mansion. Kaoru was too busy for a visit to Uji. The solemn nature that set him apart from other youths urged that he wait until Oigimi was ready for him, despite the fact that he already thought her his own; and he would be satisfied if she took note of his fidelity to the promise he had made to her father. He would do nothing reckless, nothing likely to offend her.

It was a very hot summer. Suddenly one day the thought came to him that it would be pleasant there by the river. He left the city in the cool of morning, but by the time he reached the Uji villa the sun was blinding. He called Wigbeard to the west room that had been the prince's.† The ladies seemed to be withdrawing to their own rooms from the room immediately to the east of the prince's that had been his chapel. Despite their precautions, for but

---

*Perhaps because they are first cousins.

†It is not clear what Kaoru, having summoned Wigbeard, does with him during the curious events between this point and the end of the chapter.

a single thin partition separated the two rooms, he could hear, or rather sense, the withdrawal. In great excitement, he pulled aside the screen before the partition. He had earlier noticed a small hole beside the latch. Alas, there was a curtain beyond. But as he drew back the wind caught the blind at the front veranda.

'Pull them over, hold it down,' said someone. 'The whole world can see us.'

It was a foolish suggestion, and Kaoru was delighted. The view was now clear. Several curtain frames, high and low, had been moved to the veranda. The princesses were leaving through open doors at the far side of the chapel. The first to enter his range of vision went to the veranda and looked out at his men, who were walking up and down in front of the house, taking the cool of the river breezes. She was wearing a dark-gray singlet and orange trousers. Unusual and surprisingly gay, the combination suggested subtle, careful taste. A scarf* was flung loosely over her shoulders and the ends of a rosary hung from a sleeve. She was slender† and graceful, and her hair, which would perhaps have fallen just short of the hem of a formal robe, was thick and lustrous, with no trace of disorder the whole of its length. Her profile was flawless, her skin fresh and unblemished, and there was pride and at the same time serenity in her manner. He thought of Niou's oldest sister. He had once had a glimpse of her, and the longing it had inspired came back afresh.

The other princess moved cautiously into view.

'That door is absolutely naked.' She looked towards him, everything about her suggesting wariness and reserve. Something in the flow of her hair gave her even more dignity than he had seen in the other lady.

'There's a screen behind it,' said a young serving woman unconcernedly. 'And we won't give him time for a peek.'

'But how awful if he *should* see us.' She looked guardedly back as she made her way to the far door, carrying herself with a pensive grace that few could have imitated. She wore a singlet and a lined robe of the same dark stuff as her sister's, set off in the same combination. Hers was a sadder, quieter beauty which he found

---

*'Apron strings' might be a more accurate translation. The reference is to ribands trailing from the *mo*, a sort of train worn over formal dress.

†Or perhaps 'very tall.'

even more compelling. Her hair was less luxuriant, perhaps from grief and neglect, and the ends were somewhat uneven. Yet it was very lovely, like a cluster of silken threads, and it had the iridescence of 'rainbow tresses,' or the wing of a halcyon. The hand in which she held a purple scroll was smaller and more delicate than her sister's. The younger princess knelt at the far door and looked back smiling. He thought her completely charming.

CHAPTER 47

Trefoil Knots

In the autumn, as the Uji princesses prepared for the anniversary of their father's death, the winds and waters which they had known over the years seemed colder and lonelier than ever. Kaoru and the abbot saw to the general plans. The princesses themselves, with the advice of their attendants, took care of the details, robes for the priests and decorations for the scriptures and the like. They seemed so fragile and sad as they went about the work that one wondered what they would possibly have done without this help from outside. Kaoru made it a point to visit them before the formal end of mourning, and the abbot came down from his monastery.

The riot of threads for decking out the sacred incense led one of the princesses to remark upon the stubborn way their own lives had of spinning on.* Catching sight of a spool through a gap in the curtains, Kaoru recognized the allusion. 'Join my tears as beads,'† he said softly. They found it very affecting, this suggestion that the sorrow of Lady Ise had been even as theirs; yet they were reluctant to answer. To show that they had caught the reference might seem pretentious.‡ But an answering reference immediately came to them: they could not help thinking of Tsurayuki, whose heart had not been 'that sort of thread,' and who had likened it to a thread all the same as he sang the sadness of a parting that was not a

---

*Anonymous, *Kokinshū* 806:

> This life goes on, however sad we are.
> Would that the thread would snap – but still it spins.

†Ise, *Kokin Rokujō, Zoku Kokka Taikan* 33326:

> Make of these laments a thread to join us,
> And add my tears as beads to string upon it.

‡Since the next poem is misquoted, it has been suggested that the princesses' shyness has to do with an uncertain grasp of the classics.

bereavement.* Old poems, they could see, had much to say about the unchanging human heart.

Kaoru wrote out the petition for memorial services, including the details of the scriptures to be read and the deities to be invoked, and while he had brush in hand he jotted down a verse:

> 'We knot these braids in trefoil. As braided threads
> May our fates be joined, may we be together always.'†

Though she thought it out of place, Oigimi managed an answer:

> 'No way to thread my tears, so fast they flow;
> As swiftly flows my life. Can such vows be?'

'But,' he objected, ' "if it cannot be so with us, what use is life?" ‡

She had somehow succeeded in diverting the conversation from the most important point, and she seemed reluctant to say more. And so he began to speak most warmly of his friend Niou: 'I have been watching him very closely. He has had me worried, I must admit. He has a very strong competitive instinct, even when he does not have much at stake, and I was afraid your chilliness might have made it all a matter of pride for him. And so, I admit

---

*Ki no Tsurayuki, *Kokinshū* 415:

> Threads are thin; my heart is no such thread.
> Yet now, as I set forth, it is at the breaking.

The poem is held together by the adjective 'thin.' To be thin-hearted, in Japanese, is to be sad and lonely.

†*Yonu*, 'to twist' and 'to come together.' *Agemaki*, an elaborate three-looped knot into which the braided threads are being tied, also designates a young girl's coiffure, and so, apparently through the following Saibara, calls up romantic associations:

> Well, well, my *agemaki* girl.
> We were two arm's lengths apart when we lay down.
> And then, well, well – we seem to have turned in our sleep,
> And now, well, well, we are lying side by side.

‡Anonymous, *Kokinshū* 483:

> A loose thread here to join to a loose thread there.
> If it cannot be so with us, what use is life?

it, I've been uneasy. But I am sure that this time there is nothing to worry about. It is your turn to do something. Might you just possibly persuade yourself to be a little more friendly? You are not an insensitive lady, I know, and yet you do go on slamming the door. If he resents it, well, so do I. You couldn't be making things more difficult for me if you tried, and I have been very open with you and very willing to take you at your word. I think the time has come for a clear statement from you, one way or the other.'

'How can you say such things? It was exactly because I did *not* want to make things difficult for you that I let you come so near – so near that people must think it very odd. I gather that your view of the matter is different, and I must confess that I am disappointed. I would have expected you to understand a little better. But of course I am at fault too. You have said that I am not an insensitive person, but someone of real sensitivity would by now have thought everything out, even in a mountain hut like this. I have always been slow in these matters. I gather that you are making a proposal. Very well: I shall make my answer as clear as I can. Before Father died, he had many things to say about my future, but not one of them touched even slightly on the sort of thing you suggest. He must have meant that I should be resigned to living out my days alone and away from the world; and so I fear I cannot give you the answer you want, at least so far as it concerns myself. But of course my sister will outlive me, and I have to think of her too. I could not bear to leave her in these mountains like a fallen tree. It would give me great pleasure if something could be arranged for her.'

She fell silent, in great agitation. He regretted having spoken so sternly. For all her air of maturity, he should not have expected her to answer like a woman of the world.

He summoned Bennokimi.

'It was thoughts of the next life that first brought me here; and then, in those last sad days, he left a request with me. He asked me to look after his daughters in whatever way seemed best. I have tried; and now it comes as something of a surprise that they should be disregarding their own father's wishes. Do you understand it any better than I do? I am being pushed to the conclusion that he had hopes for them which they do not share. I know you will have heard about me, what an odd person I am, not much interested in the sort of things that seem to interest everyone else. And now, finally, I have found someone who does interest me, and I am inclined to believe that fate has had a hand in the matter; and I gather that the gossips already have us married. Well, if that is the case – I know it will seem out of place for me to say so – other things being equal, we might as well do as the prince wished us to, and indeed as everyone else does. It would not be the first case the world has seen of a princess married to a commoner.

'And I have spoken more than once about my friend Niou to your other lady. She simply refuses to believe me when I tell her she needn't worry about the sort of husband he is likely to make. I wonder if someone might just possibly be working to turn her against her father's wishes. You must tell me everything you know.'

His remarks were punctuated by many a brooding sigh.

There is a kind of cheeky domestic who, in such situations, assumes a knowing manner and encourages a man in what he wants to believe. Bennokimi was not such a one. She thought the match ideal, but she could not say so.

'My ladies are different from others I have served. Perhaps they were born different. They have never been much interested in the usual sort of thing. We who have been in their service – even while their father was alive, we really had no tree to run to for shelter. Most of the other women decided fairly soon that there was no point in wasting their lives in the mountains, and they went away, wherever their family ties led them. Even people whose families had been close to the prince's for years and years – they were not having an easy time of it, and most of them gave up and went away. And now that he is gone it is even worse. We wonder from one minute to the next who will be left. The ones who have stayed are always grumbling, and I am sure that my ladies are often hurt by the things they say. Back in the days when the prince was still with us, they say, well, he had his old-fashioned notions, and they had to be respected for what they were. My ladies were, after all, royal princesses, he was always saying, and there came a point at which a suitor had to be considered beneath them, and that was that; and so they stayed single. But now they are worse than single, they are completely alone in the world, and it would take a very cruel person to find fault if they were to do what everyone else does. And really, could anyone expect them to go through their lives as they are now? Even the monks who

wander around gnawing pine needles – even they have their different ways of doing things, without forgetting the Good Law.
They cannot deny life itself, after all. I am just telling you what
these women say. The older of my ladies refuses to listen to a word
of it, at least as it has to do with her; but I gather she does hope
that something can be found for her sister, some way to live an
ordinary, respectable life. She has watched you climb over these
mountains year after year and she knows that not many people
would have assumed responsibility as if it were the most natural
thing in the world. I really do think that she is ready to talk of the
details, and all that matters is what you have in mind yourself. As
for Prince Niou, she does not seem to think his letters serious
enough to bother answering.'

'I have told you of her father's last request. I was much moved
by it, and I have vowed to go on seeing them. You might think
that, from my point of view, either of your ladies would do as well
as the other, and I really am very flattered that she should have
such confidence in me. But you know, even a man who doesn't
have much use for the things that excite most people will find
himself drawn to a lady, and when that happens he does not suddenly go running after another – though that would not be too
difficult, I suppose, for the victim of a casual infatuation.

'But no. If only she would stop retreating and putting up walls
between us. If only I could have her here in front of me, to talk to
about the little things that come and go. If so much did not have
to be kept back.

'I am all by myself, and I always have been. I have no brother
near enough my own age to talk to about the amusing things and
the sad things that happen. You will say that I have a sister, but the
things I really want to talk about are always an impossible jumble,
and an empress is hardly the person to go to with them. You will
think of my mother. It is true that she looks young enough to be
my sister, but after all she is my mother. All the others seem so
haughty and so far away. They quite intimidate me. And so I am
by myself. The smallest little flirtation leaves me dumb and paralyzed; and when it seems that the time has come to show my
feelings to someone I really care for, I am not up to the smallest
gesture. I may be hurt, I may be furious, and there I stand like a
post, knowing perfectly well how ridiculous I am.

'But let us talk of Niou. Don't you suppose that problem could be left to me? I promise that I will do no one any harm.'

It would be far better than this lonely life, thought the old woman, wishing she could tell him to go ahead. But they were both so touchy. She thought it best to keep her own counsel.

Kaoru whiled away the time, thinking that he would like to stay the night and perhaps have the quiet talk of which he had spoken. For Oigimi the situation was next to intolerable. Though he had made it known only by indirection, his resentment seemed to be rising to an alarming pitch. The most trivial answer was almost more than she could muster. If only he would stay away from that one subject! In everything else he was a man of the most remarkable sympathy, a fact that only added to her agitation. She had someone open the doors to the chapel and stir the lamps, and withdrew behind a blind and a screen. There were also lights outside the chapel. He had them taken away – they were very unsettling, he said, for they revealed him in shameful disorder – and lay down near the screen. She had fruit and sweets brought to him, arranged in a tasteful yet casual manner. His men were offered wine and very tempting side dishes. They withdrew to a corridor, leaving the two alone for what they assumed would be a quiet, intimate conversation.

She was in great agitation, but in her manner there was something poignantly appealing that delighted and – a pity that it should have been so – excited him. To be so near, separated from her only by a screen, and to let the time go by with no perceptible sign that the goal was near – it was altogether too stupid. Yet he managed an appearance of calm as he talked on of this amusing event and that melancholy one. There was much to interest her in what he said, but from behind her blinds she called to her women to come nearer. No doubt thinking that chaperones would be out of place, they pretended not to hear, and indeed withdrew yet further as they lay down to rest. There was no one to replenish the lamps before the holy images. Again she called out softly, and no one answered.

'I am not feeling at all well,' she said finally, starting for an anteroom. 'I think a little sleep might do me good. I hope you sleep well.'

'Don't you suppose a man who has fought his way over mountains might feel even worse? But that's all right. Just having you here is enough. Don't go off and leave me.'

He quietly pushed the screen aside. She was in precipitous flight through the door beyond.

'So this is what you mean by a friendly talk,' she said angrily as he caught at her sleeve. Far from turning him away, her anger added to the fascination. 'It is not at all what I would have expected.'

'You seem determined not to understand what I mean by friendliness, and so I thought I would show you. Not what you would have expected – and what, may I ask, *did* you expect? Stop trembling. You have nothing to be afraid of. I am prepared to take my vow before the Blessed One here. I have done everything to avoid upsetting you. No one in the world can have dreamed what an eccentric affair this is. But I am an eccentric and a fool myself, and will no doubt continue to be so.'

He stroked the hair that flowed in the wavering light. The softness and the luster were all that he could have asked for. Suppose someone with more active inclinations were to come upon this lonely, unprotected house – there would be nothing to keep him from having his way. Had the visitor been anyone but himself, matters would by now have come to a showdown. His own want of decision suddenly revolted him. Yet here she was, weeping and wringing her hands, quite beside herself. He would have to wait until consent came of its own accord. Distressed at her distress, he sought to comfort her as best he could.

'I have allowed an almost indecent familiarity, and I have had no idea of what was going through your mind; and I may say that you have not shown a great deal of consideration, forcing me to display myself in these unbecoming colors. But I am at fault too. I am not up to what has to be done, and I am sorry for us both.' It was too humiliating, that the lamplight should have caught her in somber, shabby gray.

'Yes, I have been inconsiderate, and I am ashamed and sorry. They give you a good excuse, those robes of mourning. But don't you think you might just possibly be making too much of them? You have seen something of me over the years, and I doubt if mourning gives you a right to act as if we had just been introduced. It is clever of you but not altogether convincing.'

He told her of the many things he had found it so hard to keep to himself, beginning with that glimpse of the two princesses in the autumn dawn. She was in an agony of embarrassment. So he had had this store of secrets all along, and had managed to feign openness and indifference!

He now pulled a low curtain between them and the altar and lay down beside her. The smell of the holy incense, the particularly strong scent of anise, stabbed at his conscience, for he was more susceptible in matters of belief than most people. He told himself that it would be ill considered in the extreme, now of all times, when she was in mourning, to succumb to temptation; and he would be going against his own wishes if he failed to control himself. He must wait until she had come out of mourning. Then, difficult though she was, there would surely be some slight easing of the tensions.

Autumn nights are sad in the most ordinary of places. How much sadder in wailing mountain tempests, with the calls of insects sounding through the hedges. As he talked on of life's uncertain turns, she occasionally essayed an answer. He was touched and pleased. Her women, who had spread their bed-clothes not far away, sensed that a happy arrangement had been struck up and withdrew to inner apartments. She thought of her father's admonitions. Strange and awful things can happen, she saw, to a lady who lives too long. It was as if she were adding her tears to the rushing torrent outside.

The dawn came on, bringing an end to nothing. His men were coughing and clearing their throats, there was a neighing of horses – everything made him think of descriptions he had read of nights on the road. He slid back the door to the east, where dawn was in the sky, and the two of them looked out at the shifting colors. She had come out towards the veranda. The dew on the ferns at the shallow eaves was beginning to catch the light. They would have made a very striking pair, had anyone been there to see them.

'Do you know what I would like? To be as we are now. To look out at the flowers and the moon, and be with you. To spend our days together, talking of things that do not matter.'

His manner was so unassertive that her fears had finally left her. 'And do you know what *I* would like? A little privacy. Here I am quite exposed, and a screen might bring us closer.'

The sky was red, there was a whirring of wings close by as flocks of birds left their roosts. As if from deep in the night, the matin bells came to them faintly.

'Please go,' she said with great earnestness. 'It is almost daylight, and I do not want you to see me.'

'You can't be telling me to push my way back through the morning mists? What would *that* suggest to people? No, make it look, if you will, as if we were among the proper married couples of the world, and we can go on being the curiosities we in fact seem to be. I promise you that I will do nothing to upset you; but perhaps I might trouble you to imagine, just a little, how genuine my feelings are.'

'If what you say is true,' she replied, her agitation growing as it became evident that he was in no hurry to leave, 'then I am sure you will have your way in the future. But please, this morning, let me have *my* way.' She had to admit that there was little she could do.

'So you really are going to send me off into the dawn? Knowing that it is "new to me,"* and that I am sure to lose my way?'

The crowing of a cock was like a summons back to the city.

'The things by which one knows the mountain village
Are brought together in these voices of dawn.'

She replied:

'Deserted mountain depths where no birds sing,
I would have thought. But sorrow has come to visit.'†

Seeing her as far as the door to the inner apartments, he returned by the way he had come the evening before, and lay down; but he was not able to sleep. The memories and regrets were too strong. Had his emotions earlier been toward her as they were now, he would not have been as passive over the months. The prospect of going back to the city was too dreary to face.

Oigimi, in agony at the thought of what her women would have made of it all, found sleep as elusive. A very harsh trial it was, going through life with no one to turn to; and as if that huge uncertainty were not enough, there were these women with all their impossible suggestions. They as good as formed a queue, coming to her with proposals that had nothing to recommend them but the expediency of the moment; and if in a fit of inatten-

*Probably an allusion.
†See note*, page 611.

tion she were to accede to one of them, she would have shame and humiliation to look forward to. Kaoru did not at all displease her. The Eighth Prince had said more than once that if Kaoru should be inclined to ask her hand, he would not disapprove. But no. She wanted to go on as she was. It was her sister, now in the full bloom of youth, who must live a normal life. If the prince's thoughts in the matter could be applied to her sister, she herself would do everything she could by way of support. But who was to be her own support? She had only Kaoru, and, strangely, things might have been easier had she found herself in superficial dalliance with an ordinary man. They had known each other for rather a long time, and she might have been tempted to let him have his way. His obvious superiority and his aloofness, coupled with a very low view of herself, had left her prey to shyness. In timid retreat, it seemed, she would end her days.

She was near prostration, having spent most of the night weeping. She lay down in the far recesses of the room where her sister was sleeping. Nakanokimi was delighted, for she had been disturbed by that odd whispering among the women. She pulled back the coverlet and spread it over Oigimi. She caught the scent of her sister's robes. It was unmistakable, exactly the scent by which poor Wigbeard had been so sorely discommoded. Guessing what Oigimi would be going through, Nakanokimi pretended to be asleep.

Kaoru summoned Bennokimi and had a long talk with her. He permitted no suggestion of the romantic in the note he left for Oigimi.

She would happily have disappeared. There had been that silly little exchange about the trefoil knots. Would her sister think that she had meant by it to beckon him to within 'two arms' lengths'?* Pleading illness, she spent the day alone.

'But the services are almost on us,' said the women, 'and there is no one but you to tend to all these details. Why did you have to pick this particular moment to come down with something?'

Nakanokimi went on preparing the braids; but when it came to the rosettes of gold and silver thread, she had to admit incompetence. She did not even know where to begin. Then night came, and, under cover of darkness, Oigimi emerged, and the two sisters worked together on the intricacies of the rosettes.

*See note†, page 885.

A note came from Kaoru, but she sent back that she had been indisposed since morning. A most unseemly and childish way to behave, muttered her women.

And so they emerged from mourning. They had not wanted to think that they would outlive their father, and, so quickly, a whole year of months and days had passed. How strange, they sighed – and their women had to sigh too – how bleak and grim, that they should have lived on. But the robes of deepest mourning to which they had grown accustomed over the months were changed for lighter colors,* and a freshness as of new life came over the house. Nakanokimi, at the best time of life, was the more immediately appealing of the two. Personally seeing to it that her hair was washed and brushed, Oigimi thought her so delightful that all the cares of these last months seemed to vanish. If only her hopes might be realized, if only Kaoru could be persuaded to look after the girl. Despite his evident reluctance, he was not, if pointed in the girl's direction, likely to find her a disappointment. There being no one else whom she could even consider, and therefore nothing more for her to do, she busied herself with ministering to her sister's needs, quite as if they were mother and daughter.

Kaoru paid a sudden visit. The Ninth Month, when the mourning robes toward which he had been so deferential would surely have been put away, still seemed an unacceptable distance in the future. He sent in word that he hoped as before to be favored with an interview. Oigimi sent back that she had not been well, and must ask to be excused.

He sent in again: 'I had not been prepared for this obstinacy. And what sort of interpretation do you think your women are likely to put upon it?'

'You will understand, I am sure, that when a person comes out of mourning the grief floods back with more force than ever. I really must ask you to excuse me.'

He called Bennokimi and went over the list of his complaints. Since he had all along seemed to the women their one hope in this impossible darkness, they had been telling one another how very nice it would be if he were to answer their prayers and set their lady up in a more becoming establishment. They had plotted ways of admitting him to her boudoir. Though not aware of the details,

---

*They are in half mourning.

Oigimi had certain suspicions: given Kaoru's remarkable fondness for Bennokimi, and indeed their apparent fondness for each other, the old woman might have acquired sinister ideas, and because in old romances wellborn ladies *never* threw themselves at men without benefit of intermediary, her women presented the weakest point in her defenses.

Kaoru was apparently embittered by her own reception of his overtures, and so perhaps the time had come to put her sister decisively forward as a substitute. He did not seem to be one who, properly introduced and encouraged, would incline toward unkindness even when he found himself in the presence of an ill-favored woman; and once he had had a glimpse of the beauty her sister was, he was sure to fall helplessly in love. No man, of course, would want to spring forward at the first gesture, quite as if he had been waiting for an invitation. This apparent reluctance was no doubt partly from a fear of being thought flighty and too susceptible.

Thus she turned the possibilities over in her mind. But would it not be a serious disservice to give Nakanokimi no hint of what she was thinking? In her sister's place, she could see she would be very much hurt indeed. So, in great detail, she offered her view of the matter.

'You will remember of course what Father said. We might be lonely for the rest of our lives, but we were not to demean ourselves and make ourselves ridiculous. We have a great deal to atone for, I think. It was we who kept him from making his peace at the end, and I have no reservations about a single word of his advice. And so loneliness does not worry me at all. But there are these noisy women, not giving me a minute's relief. They chatter on and on about my obstinacy. I must admit that they have a point. I must admit that it would be a tragedy for you to spend the rest of your days alone. If I could only do something for you, my dear – if I only could make a decent match for you – then I could tell myself I had done my duty, and it would not bother me in the least to be alone.'

Nakanokimi replied with some bitterness. Whatever could her sister have in mind? 'Do you really think Father was talking about you? No, I was the one he was worried about. I am the useless one, and he knew what a shambles I would make of things. You are missing the point completely: the point is that we will not be lonely as long as we have each other.'

It was true, thought Oigimi, a wave of affection sweeping over her. 'I'm sorry. I was upset and didn't think. These people say I am so difficult. That is the whole trouble.' And she fell silent.

It was growing dark and Kaoru still had not left. Oigimi was more and more apprehensive. Bennokimi came in and talked on at great length of his perfectly understandable resentment. Oigimi did not answer. She could only sigh helplessly, and ask herself what possible recourse she had. If only she had someone to look to for advice! A father or a mother could have made a match for her, and she would have accepted it as the way of the world. She might have been unable herself to say yes or no,* but that was the nature of things. She would have concealed the unfortunate facts from a world so ready to laugh. But these women – they were old and thought themselves wise. Much pleased with each new discovery, they came to her one after another to tell her how fine a match it promised to be. Was she to take these opinions seriously? No, she was attended by crones, women with obsessions that made no allowance for her own feelings.

As good as clutching her by the hand and dragging her off, they would argue their various cases; and the result was that Oigimi withdrew into increasingly gloomy disaffection. Nakanokimi, with whom she was able to converse so freely on almost every subject, knew even less about this one than she, and, quietly uncomprehending, had no answer. A strange, sad fate ruled over her, Oigimi would conclude, turning away from the company.

Might she not change into robes a little more lively? pleaded her women. She was outraged – it was as if they were intent on pushing her into the man's arms. And indeed what was to keep them from having their way? This tiny house, with everyone jammed in against everyone else, offered no better a hiding place than was granted the proverbial mountain pear.† It had always

*Ise, Gosenshū 938:

> I cannot say yes, I cannot say no; how sad
> That my self cannot go where my heart would lead it.

†Anonymous, Kokin Rokujū, Zoku Kokka Taikan 35111:

> Though cruel the world may be, it is, alas,
> A flower no mountains are deep enough to hide.

Yamanashi, 'there are no mountains,' means also 'pear.'

been Kaoru's apparent intention to make no explicit overtures, inviting the mediation of this or that woman, but to proceed so quietly that people would scarcely know when he had begun. He had thought, and indeed said, that if she was unwilling he was prepared to wait indefinitely. But the old women were whispering noisily into one another's deaf ears. Perhaps they had been somewhat stupid from the outset, perhaps age had dulled their wits. Oigimi found it all very trying in either case.

She sought to communicate something of her distress to Bennokimi. 'He *is* different from other people, I suppose. Father always said so, and that is why we have become so dependent on him since Father died, and allowed him a familiarity that must seem almost improper. And now comes a turn I had not been prepared for. He seems very angry with me, and I cannot for the life of me see why. He must know that if I were in the least interested in the usual things I would most certainly not have tried to put him off. I have always been suspicious of them, and it is a disappointment that he should not seem to understand.' She spoke with great hesitation.

'But there is my sister. It would be very sad if she were to waste the best part of her life. If I sometimes wish this house weren't quite so shabby and cramped, it is only because of her. He says he means to honor Father's wishes. Well, then, he should make no distinction between us. As far as I am concerned we share a single heart, whatever the outward appearances. I will do everything I possibly can. Do you suppose I might ask you to pass this on to him?'

'I have known your feelings all along,' said Bennokimi, deeply moved, 'and I have explained everything to him very carefully. But he says that a man does not shift his affections at will, and he has his friend Niou to think of; and he has offered to do what he can to arrange matters for my younger lady. I must say I think he is behaving very well. Even when they have parents working for them, two sisters cannot reasonably expect to make good matches at the same time; and here you have your chance. I may seem forward when I say so, but you *are* alone in the world, and I worry a great deal about you. It is true that no one can predict what may happen years from now; but at the moment I think both of you have very lucky stars to thank. I certainly would not want to be understood as arguing that you should go against your father's last wishes. Surely he meant no more than that you should not make marriages unworthy of you. He so often said that if the young gentleman should prove willing and he himself might see one of you happily married, then he could die in peace. I have seen so many girls, high and low, who have lost their parents and gone completely to ruin, married to the most impossible men. I wonder if there has been a time in my whole long life when it hasn't been happening somewhere, and no one has ever found it in his heart to poke fun at them. And here you are – a man made to order, a man of the most extraordinary kindness and feeling, comes with a proposal anyone would jump at. If you send him off in the name of this Buddha of yours – well, I doubt that you will be rewarded with assumption into the heavens. You will still have the world to live with.'

She seemed prepared to talk on indefinitely. Angry and resentful, Oigimi lay with her face pressed against a pillow. Nakanokimi led her off to bed, with lengthy commiserations. Bennokimi's remarks had left her feeling threatened, but it was not a house in which she could make a great show of going into retreat. It was, indeed, a house that offered no refuge. Spreading a clean, soft quilt over Nakanokimi, she lay down some slight distance away, the weather still being warm.

Bennokimi told Kaoru of the conversation. What, he asked himself, could have turned a young girl so resolutely away from the world? Was it that she had learned too well from her saintly father the lesson of the futility of things? But they were kindred spirits, he and she, and he could most certainly not accuse her of impertinent trifling.

'And so I suppose from now on I will have trouble even getting permission to speak to her? Take me into her room, just this one evening.'

Having made up her mind to help him, Bennokimi sent most of the other women off to bed. A few of them had been made partners in the conspiracy. As the night drew on, a high wind set the badly fitted shutters to rattling. It was fortunate – not as much stealth was needed as on a quieter night. She led him to the princesses' room. The two were sleeping together; but they always slept together, and she could hardly have separated them for this one night. Kaoru knew them well enough, she was sure, to tell one from the other.

But Oigimi, still awake, sensed his approach, and slipped out through the bed curtains. Poor Nakanokimi lay quietly sleeping. What was to be done? Oigimi was in consternation. If only the two of them could hide together – but she was quaking with fear, and could not bring herself to go back. Then, in the dim light, a figure in a singlet pulled the curtains aside and came into the room quite as if he owned it. Whatever would her hapless sister think if she were to awaken? thought Oigimi, huddled in the cramped space between a screen and a shabby wall. Nakanokimi had rebelled at the very hint that there might be plans for her – and how shocked and resentful she would be if it were to appear now that they had all plotted against her. Oigimi was quite beside herself. It had all happened because they had no one to protect them from a harsh world. Her sorrow and her longing for her father were so intense that it was as if he were here beside her now, exactly as he had made his last farewell in the evening twilight.

Thinking that the old woman had arranged it so, Kaoru was delighted to find a lady sleeping alone. Then he saw that it was not Oigimi. It was a fresher, more winsome, superficially more appealing young lady. Nakanokimi was awake now, and in utter terror. She had been no part of a plot against him, poor girl, it was clear; but pity for her was mixed with anger and resentment at the one who had fled. Nakanokimi was no stranger, of course, but he did not take much comfort from that fact. Mixed with the chagrin was a fear lest Oigimi think he had been less than serious. Well, he would let the night pass, and if it should prove his fate to marry Nakanokimi – she was not, as he had noted, a stranger. Thus composing himself, he lay down beside her, and passed the night much as he had the earlier one with her sister.

Their plans had worked beautifully, said the old woman. But where might Nakanokimi be? It would be odd of her, to say the least, to spend the night with the other two.

'Well, wherever she is, I'm sure she knows what she's doing.'

'Such a fine young gentleman, making our wrinkles go away just by glancing in our direction. He's exactly what every woman has always asked for. Why does she have to be so standoffish?'

'Oh, no reason, really. Something's been at her, as they say. She's hexed.'

Some of the remarks that came from the toothless mouths were not entirely charitable.

They did not pass unchallenged. 'Hexed! Now that's a nice thing to say, as good as asking for bad luck. No, I can tell you what it is. She had a strange bringing up, that's all, way off here in the hills with no one to tell her about things. Men scare her. You'll see – she'll be friendly enough when she gets used to him. It's bound to happen.'

'Let's hope it happens soon, and something good happens to us for a change.'

So they talked on as they got ready for bed, and soon there were loud snores.

Though 'the company'* may not have had a great deal to do with the matter, it seemed to Kaoru that the autumn night had been quick to end.

He was beginning to wonder which of the princesses appealed to him more. If, at his departure, his desires were left unsatisfied, he had no one to blame but himself.

'Remember me,' he said as he left Nakanokimi, 'and do not deceive yourself that she is someone to imitate.' And he vowed that they would meet again.

It had been like a strange dream. Mustering all his self-control, for he wanted to have another try at the icy one, he went back to the room assigned him the night before and lay down.

Bennokimi hurried to the princesses' room. 'Very, very strange,' she said, thinking Oigimi the one she saw there. 'Where will my other lady be?'

Nakanokimi lay consumed with embarrassment. What could it all mean? She was angry, too, reading deep significance into her sister's remarks of the day before.

As the morning grew brighter, the cricket came from the wall.

Oigimi knew what her sister would be thinking, and the pity and the sorrow were too much for her. Neither sister was able to speak. So the last veil had been stripped away, thought Oigimi. One thing was clear: theirs was a world in which not a single unguarded moment was possible.

Bennokimi went to Kaoru's room and at length learned of the uncommon obstinacy of which he had been the victim.

*Oshikōchi Mitsune, *Kokinshū* 636:

> Autumn nights are long? From times of old
> The company has made them long or short.

She was very sorry for him, and she thought he had a right to be angry.

'I have put up with it all because I have thought there might be hope. But after last night, I really feel as if I should jump in the river. The one thing that holds me back is the memory of their father and how he hated to leave them behind. Well, that is that. I shall not bother them again – not, of course, that I am likely to forget the insult. I gather that Niou is forging ahead without a glance to the left or the right. I can understand how a young lady in her place might feel. A man is a man, and she might as well aim for the highest. I think I shall not show myself again for all of you to laugh at. My only request is that you talk about this idiocy as little as possible.'

Today there were no regretful looks backward. How sad, whispered the women, for both of them.

Oigimi too was asking herself what had happened. Supposing his anger now included her sister – what were they to do? And how awful to have all these women with their wise airs, not one of them in fact understanding the slightest part of her confusion. The thoughts were still whirling through her head when a letter came from Kaoru. Surprisingly, she was pleased, more pleased, indeed, than usual. As if he did not know the season, he had attached a leafy branch only one sprig of which had turned crimson. Folded in an envelope, the note was quiet and laconic, and showed little trace of resentment.

'My mountain ladies have dyed it colors twain.
And which of the twain, please tell me, is the deeper?'

He apparently meant to pretend that nothing of moment had occurred. Uncertainty clutched at her once more; and here were these noisy women trying to goad her into a reply. She would have left it to her sister but for a fear that the poor girl was already at the limits of endurance. Finally, after many false starts, she sent back a verse:

'Whatever the "ladies" meant, the answer is clear:
The newer of these hues is far the deeper.'*

It had been jotted down with an appearance of unconcern, and it pleased him. He decided that his resentment was after all finite.

---

*'Clearly my sister is the one for you.'

Two ladies with but a single heart, Bennokimi had told him – there had been more than one hint that Oigimi meant him to have her sister in her place. His refusal to take the hint, it now came to him, accounted for last night's behavior. He had been unkind. A wave of pity came over him. If he had caused her to think him unfeeling, then his hopes would come to nothing. And no doubt Bennokimi, who had been so good about passing his messages on, was beginning to think him untrustworthy. Well, he had let himself be trapped, the mistake had been his own. If people chose to laugh at him as the sort that is constantly forsaking the world, he could only let them laugh. It was worse than they knew. He was a laughable little boat indeed, paddling out only to come back time and time again!*

So he fretted the night away. There was a bright moon in the dawn sky as he went to call on Niou. Upon the burning of his mother's house in Sanjō, he had moved with her to Rokujō. Niou having rooms near at hand,† he was a frequent caller, much, it would seem, to Niou's satisfaction. It was the perfect place to make one forget the troubles of the world. Even the flowers below the verandas were somehow different. The swaying grasses and trees were as elsewhere – and yet they too were different. The clear moon reflected from the brook was as in a picture. Kaoru had expected to find his friend enjoying the moonlight, and he was not disappointed. Startled at the fragrance that came in on the breeze, Niou slipped into casual court dress and otherwise put himself in order. Kaoru had stopped midway up the stairs. Not asking him to come further, Niou stepped out and leaned against the railing, and in these attitudes they talked idly of this and that. The Uji affair always on his mind, he reproved his friend for various inadequacies as a messenger. This was not at all fair, thought Kaoru. He was incapable of seizing the first thing he wanted for himself, and he could hardly be expected to worry about others. But then it occurred to him that his own cause might be advanced if matters were arranged satisfactorily for Niou, and he talked with unusual candor of what he thought might be done.

A mist came in as the dawn brightened. The air was chilly, and

See note, page 107.

†The implication is that Niou also has rooms in Genji's Rokujō mansion. His main residence is at Nijō, where Genji lived before moving to Rokujō.

with the moon now hidden the shade of the trees was dark. It was a pleasant scene despite the gloom.

'The time is coming,' said the prince, 'when you will not get off so easily for leaving me behind.' No doubt the gloom brought sad Uji* very near. Since Kaoru gave no evidence of eagerness, Niou offered a poem:

> 'All the wide field abloom with maiden flowers!
> Why must you string a rope to keep us out?'

In a similarly bantering tone, Kaoru replied:

> 'The maiden flowers on the misty morning field†
> Are set aside for those who bestir themselves.

And,' he said, smiling, 'there are not many such enterprising people.'

'How utterly shameless!'‡

Though long importuned by his friend, Kaoru had wondered whether Nakanokimi could meet this most rigorous of tests. Now he knew that she was at least the equal of her sister. He had feared, too, that her disposition might upon close inspection prove to have its defects, and he was sure now that there was nothing for which he need apologize. Though it might seem cruel to go against Oigimi's wishes, his own affections did not seem prepared to jump lightly to her sister. He must see that Nakanokimi went to his friend. So he would overcome the resentment of both of them, prince and princess.

Unaware of these thoughts, Niou was calling him shameless. It was very amusing.

'We must remember,' said Kaoru, his manner somewhat patronizing, 'that you have given us little cause to admire you for your fidelity.'

'Just you wait and see,' answered Niou most earnestly. 'I have never liked anyone else half as well, I swear it.'

---

*The usual association with *ushi*, 'gloomy,' is implied.

†*Ashitanohara*, 'morning field,' is a place in the province of Yamato famous for *ominaeshi*, 'maiden flowers.'

‡Henjō, *Kokinshū* 1016:

> Voluptuous maiden flowers, on autumn fields,
> So utterly shameless – your day is but a day.

'And I see few signs that they are about to capitulate. You have given me a formidable assignment.'

Yet he proceeded to describe in great detail his thoughts about an expedition to Uji.

The twenty-eighth, when the equinox festival* ended, was a lucky day. With great stealth, including every possible precaution against attracting notice, Kaoru led his friend forth towards Uji. They would be in trouble were Niou's mother, the empress, to learn of the excursion. She would be certain to forbid it. But Niou was determined. Though Kaoru agreed with him in wanting to make it appear that they were off for nowhere at all, the pretense was not a simple one. They would surely be noticed if they tried to cross the Uji River. Forgoing the splendor of Yūgiri's villa on the south bank, therefore, Kaoru left Niou at a manor house he happened to own near the Eighth Prince's villa and went on alone. No one was likely to challenge them now, but it seemed that Kaoru did not want even Wigbeard, who might be patrolling the grounds, to know of Niou's presence.

'His Lordship is here, His Lordship is here!' As usual the women bustled around getting ready to receive him. The princesses were mildly annoyed. But surely, thought Oigimi, she had hinted broadly enough that his affections should rest upon someone other than herself. Nakanokimi, for her part, knew that she was not the one he was attracted to, and that she had nothing to fear from the visit. But since that painful evening she had not felt as close to her sister. A stiff reserve had grown up between them, indeed, and Nakanokimi refused to communicate except through intermediaries. How would it all end? sighed the women who carried her messages.

Niou was led in under cover of darkness.

Kaoru summoned Bennokimi. 'Let me have a single word with the older of your ladies. I know when I have been refused, but I can't very well just run away. And then perhaps, a little later, I may ask you to let me in as you did the other night?'

His manner offered no cause for suspicion. It made little difference, thought the old woman, which of the two girls she took him to. She told Oigimi of the request. Oigimi was pleased and relieved – so his attention had turned to her sister, just as she had

*Higan, centering upon the equinox.

hoped. She closed and barred the door to the veranda, leaving open the door through which he would pass on his way to her sister's; and she was ready to receive him.

'A word is all I need,' he said somewhat testily, 'and it is ridiculous that I must shout it to the whole world. Open the door just a little. Can't you guess how uncomfortable I am out here?'

'I can hear you perfectly well,' she said, leaving the door closed.

Perhaps his affection for her had died and he felt it his duty to say goodbye? They were not, after all, strangers. She must not offend him, she concluded, having come forward a little, but she must watch the time. He clutched at her sleeve through a crack in the door and began railing at her as he pulled her towards him. She was outraged. What was the man not capable of? But she must humor him and hurry him off to her sister. Her innate gentleness came over to him. Quietly and without seeming to insist, she asked that he be to her sister as he had thought of being to herself.

Niou meanwhile was following instructions. He made his way to the door by which Kaoru had entered that other night. He signaled with his fan and Bennokimi came to let him in. How amusing, he thought, that his turn should have come to travel this well-traveled route. In complete ignorance of what was happening, Oigimi still sought to hurry Kaoru on his way. Though he could not keep back a certain exhilaration at being party to such an escapade, he was also moved to pity. He would have no excuse to offer when she learned how effectively she had been duped; and so he said:

'Niou kept pestering me to bring him along, and I couldn't go on saying no. He is here with me. I suspect that by now he will have made his way in. You must forgive him for not having introduced himself. And I rather imagine that talkative old woman of yours will have been asked to show him the way. So here I am left dangling. You can all have a good laugh over me.'

This was a bit more than she had been prepared for. Indeed, she was aghast, and wondered whether her senses might have deserted her. 'Well! I *have* been naïve. Your powers of invention are so far beyond me that I doubt if I could find words to describe them. I have let you see quite through me, and you have learned how stupid and careless I am. This knowledge of your superiority must give you much satisfaction.'

'I have nothing to say. I could apologize all night, and little good it would do me. Pinch me and claw me, if you are so furious. I quite understand. You were aiming high, and you have learned that we are not always masters of our fate. I am inclined to suspect that he has been drawn in another direction all along. I do feel sorry for you, believe me. And, do you know, I feel a little sorry for myself too, left out in the cold with requests that have taken me nowhere at all. But be that as it may, you would do well to accept what has happened, maybe you could even coax forth a thought or two about us, you and me. We may know that your door is locked, but can you imagine that other people will believe in the purity that so distinguishes us? Do you think that my royal friend, for instance, who persuaded me to act as his guide this evening – do you think he can imagine the possibility of such a pointless and useless night?'

He seemed prepared to break the door in. It still seemed best to humor him.

'This "fate" you speak of is not easy to grasp, and I cannot pretend to know much about it. I only know that "tears block off the unknown way ahead."* It is a nightmare, trying to guess what you mean to do next. If people choose to remember my sister and me as some sort of case in point, I am sure it will be to add us to the list of ridiculous women who are always turning up in old stories. And are you prepared to tell me what your friend means to do now that the two of you have been so clever? Please, I beg of you, do not make things worse, do not confuse us further. If I should survive this crisis, and I am not at all sure that I will, I may one day be able to compose myself for a talk with you. At the moment I am feeling very upset and unwell, and think I must rest. Leave me alone, if you do not mind.'

She clearly *was* upset, and that she should be so rational in spite of her distress made him feel his own inadequacy.

'I have done everything imaginable to follow your wishes, and I have made a fool of myself every step of the way. I have done everything, and you seem to find me insufferable. Well, I will go – disappear might be the better expression.' After a moment he con-

---

*Minamoto Wataru, *Gosenshū* 1334:

> I do not know the road down which I go,
> And tears block off the unknown way ahead.

tinued: 'But even if you are not feeling well, we can at least go on talking through the door. Please do not run away.'

He released her sleeve and was delighted to see that she did not withdraw very far. 'Just stay there and be a comfort through the night. I would not dream of asking more.'

It was a difficult, sleepless night. In the roar of the wind and water, which seemed to rise as the night advanced, he was like a pheasant without its mate.*

The first signs of dawn came over the sky, and as always the monastery bells were ringing. His late-sleeping friend had still not left Nakanokimi's side. In some disquiet, Kaoru gave a summoning cough. It was an unusual situation.

'A futile night. The guide of yestereve
Seems doomed to wander lost down the twilight road.

I cannot believe that you have heard of anything quite like it.'

She replied in a voice so low that he could scarcely hear:

'You walk a road you have chosen for yourself,
While helplessly we stumble on in darkness.'

All his impatience came back. 'Can you not be persuaded, please, to dismantle a few of these unnecessary defenses?'

As the sky grew brighter Niou emerged, and with him a quiet fragrance that cast just the right veil of delicacy over the events of the night before. The old women were open-mouthed. But they quickly found comfort. The other young gentleman would surely have all the right motives for his conduct.

Niou and Kaoru hurried back to the city before daylight overtook them. The return journey seemed far longer than had the way to Uji. Always aware of the obstacles that kept a man of his rank from embarking on carefree outings, Niou had already begun to lament 'the nights to come.'† The streets were still deserted when they arrived back at Nijō. Ordering the carriage drawn up at the veranda, they slipped indoors, smiling at the strange, ladylike vehicle that had guarded their incognito.

*The *yamadori* was believed to roost away from its mate.

†Anonymous, *Manyōshū* 2542:

My love and I have had one night together.
May all the nights to come be even thus.

'If you were to ask me, I would say that you had done your duty most admirably,' said Kaoru, letting fall no hint of the grotesque arrangements he himself had made. Niou hurried off to compose a note.

The sisters were in a daze. Nakanokimi was angry and sullen: so her sister had had these plans and had not permitted her an inkling of them. Oigimi, for her part, unable to find a convenient way to protest her innocence, could only sigh at the thought of how just this resentment was. The old women looked from one to the other in search of an explanation for this startling turn of events; but the lady who should have been their strength seemed lost to the world, and they could only go on wondering.

Oigimi opened the note and showed it to her sister, but Nakanokimi lay with her face pressed against her sleeve. 'What a long time they are taking with their answer,' thought the messenger.

This was Niou's verse:

'You cannot think that a trifling urge induced me
To brave, for you, that tangled, dew-drenched path?'

The accomplished hand, ever more remarkable, had delighted them back in the days when it had been of no particular concern to them. Now it was a source of apprehension. Oigimi did not think it seemly to step forward and answer in her sister's place. She limited herself to pressing the claims of propriety, and finally persuaded Nakanokimi to put together a note. They rewarded the messenger with a woman's robe in the wildaster* combination and a pair of doubly lined trousers.† The messenger, a court page whom Niou often made use of and who would be unlikely to attract notice, seemed reluctant to accept the gifts, which they therefore wrapped in a cloth parcel and handed to his man. Having been at such pains to make the mission inconspicuous, Niou was annoyed. He blamed the officious old woman of the evening before.

He asked Kaoru to be his guide again that evening.

---

*Magenta with a green lining.
†*Miegasane no hakama*. This is the only mention in the tale of such a garment, which may be presumed to be a great luxury; hence, in part, the uneasiness with which the messenger receives the gift.

'I am really very sorry, but I have an engagement at the Reizei Palace from which I cannot ask to be excused.'

'So it is with my worthy friend – not at all interested in the most interesting things in life.'

At Uji, Oigimi had been the first to succumb. Could she turn him away on no better grounds than that he was not the suitor she had had in mind for her sister? The house was badly equipped for decking out a nuptial chamber, but she managed to make do rather well with the rustic furnishings at hand. In control of herself once more, she was pleased that Niou should come hurrying down the long road to Uji, and at the same time she could not help wondering that her plans had gone so wildly astray. Nakanokimi, still in a daze, gave herself up to the women who had undertaken to dress her for the night. The sleeves of her crimson robe were damp with tears.

The more composed of the sisters was also in tears. 'I cannot believe I have much longer to live, and I think only of you. These people have worn my ears out telling me what a fine match it is. Well, I have said to myself, they are older and more experienced, and probably they are right, at least as the world sees things. And so I put together a small amount of resolve – not that I pretend to know a great deal – and told myself that I was *not* going to leave you unprotected. But I never dreamed that things could go so horribly awry. People talk about matches that are fated to be, and I suppose this is one of them. I am as upset as you are, you must believe me. When you have calmed yourself a little I shall try to prove that I knew nothing at all about it. Please don't be angry with me. The time will come when you will be sorry if you are.'

She stroked her sister's hair as she spoke. Nakanokimi did not answer. Her mind was jumping from thought to thought. If her sister was so worried about her now, it did not seem likely that she had behaved with any sort of deliberate malice. She herself was only making things worse. They were fools for the world to laugh at, both of them, and there was no point in adding to her sister's unhappiness.

Even in a state of something near shock she had been very beautiful. Tonight, more in possession of herself, she was still more of a delight. Niou's heart ached at the thought of how long, and for him how strewn with obstacles, the road to Uji was. He made promise after promise. Nakanokimi was neither pleased nor moved. She was merely bewildered – men were quite beyond her. All maidens are shy; but shyness has its limits when a maiden, however pampered and sheltered, has lived in a house with brothers. Our princess, though scarcely pampered, had grown up in these secluded mountains, far from the greater world; and the timidity brought on by this unexpected event made it difficult for her to force her way through the tiniest answer. He would think her in every respect queer and countrified, entirely unlike other ladies of his acquaintance; and she was, in every respect, the quicker and more accomplished of the two sisters.

The women reminded them of the rice cakes that are customary on the third night. Yes – it was a form that must be observed, thought Oigimi. She put her sister to work. Nakanokimi was of course a novice in such matters, and Oigimi too, doing her best to play the part of the older sister, felt herself flushing scarlet. How ridiculous they must seem to these women! But in fact the women were entranced. This calm elegance, they thought, was what one expected of an eldest daughter, and at the same time it testified to her concern and affection for her sister.

A letter came from Kaoru, written in a careful cursive hand on rather ordinary Michinoku paper. 'I thought of calling last night, but it is clear that my humble efforts are bringing no rewards. I must confess a certain resentment. I know that there will be all manner of errands to see to this evening, but the memory of the other night leaves me squirming. And so I shall bide my time.'

In several boxes he sent Bennokimi numerous bolts of cloth, for the women, he said. It would seem that, relying on what his mother happened to have at hand, he had not been as lavish as he would have wished to be. Lengths of undyed silk, plain and figured, were hidden beneath two tastefully finished robes and singlets. At the sleeve of a singlet was a poem, somewhat old-fashioned, it might have seemed:

> 'We did not share a bed, I hear you say.
> But we *were* together, that I must insist.'

How very threatening. And yet, in some discomfiture, Oigimi had to grant his point: neither she nor her sister had any defenses left. Some of the messengers ran off* while she was still puzzling

---

*Evidently upon Kaoru's orders. He may have wanted to avoid return gifts, and he may have wanted her to sleep on his 'threatening' note.

over her answer. She detained the lowest-ranking among them until she had a poem to give him.

> 'No barrier, perhaps, between our hearts;
> But say not that our sleeves caress each other.'

It was an ordinary poem, showing, however, traces of her agitation. He was touched. He thought he could see in it honest and unaffected feelings.

Meanwhile Niou was beside himself. He was at the palace and there seemed no chance of escaping. His mother had taken advantage of his presence to chide him for his lengthy absences. 'Here you are still single, and people tell me that you are already beginning to acquire a name for yourself as a lover. I do not like it at all. Do not, if you please, make a career of it. Your father is no happier than I am.'

Niou withdrew to his private chambers. Kaoru came upon him sunk in thought, having finished a letter to Uji. The visit delighted him. Here was someone who understood.

'What am I to do? It is already dark, and – really, *what* am I to do?'

Kaoru saw a chance to explore his friend's intentions. 'We haven't been seeing much of you lately, and your mother will not be at all happy if you go running off again. The ladies have been handing little rumors around. I can already hear the scolding I've let myself in for.'

'Yes, there is the problem of my good mother. She has just annihilated me, as a matter of fact. Those women must be lying to her. What have I done, after all, that the whole world should be criticizing me? Life is not easy when your father wears a crown, that I can tell you.' His sighs did suggest that he found his well-born lot a sad one.

Kaoru was beginning to feel sorry for him. 'Well, you will have a scene on your hands whether you go or whether you stay. If there is to be carnage, I am prepared to immolate myself. Suppose we think of a horse for getting over Mount Kohata. It will attract attention, of course.'*

---

*Manyōshū 2425, from the 'Hitomaro Collection':

> A horse I might have had, to cross Kohata.
> But love would not let me wait. I have come on foot.

Kaoru seems to be saying that for the sake of speed one must go by horse,

The night was blacker and blacker, Niou more and more nervous; but finally he made his departure, on horseback, as Kaoru had suggested.

'I think,' said Kaoru, seeing him off, 'that it would be better for me to stay behind and do what I can to cover the rear.' He went from Niou's apartments to the empress's audience chamber.

'So he has run off again,' said she. 'I cannot understand him. Has he no notion of what people will be thinking? I am the one who will suffer when his father hears of it and concludes that someone has been remiss.'

She was the mother of a considerable band of grown children, and she only seemed younger as the years went by. No doubt her oldest daughter, the First Princess, was very much like her. He thought it a great pity that the occasion had been denied him to approach the daughter, if only to hear her voice, as he was now approaching the mother. It was probably in such a situation, he mused – when the lady was neither distant nor yet near enough to come at a summons – that the amorously inclined young men of the world tended to have improper thoughts. Was there anyone as eccentric as he? And yet even he, once his affections had been engaged, found it impossible to detach them. Here among the empress's attendants was not a single lady who could be called wanting in sensitivity or elegance. Each had her own merits, and several were outstandingly beautiful. But he was propriety itself towards all of them, determined that none should excite him – and this despite the fact that several had made advances. Since the empress held court with such quiet dignity, nothing was allowed to appear on the surface; but women have their ways, and there were those in her retinue who let slip hints that they found him interesting. He for his part was sometimes amused and sometimes touched, and through all these trifling encounters there ran an awareness of evanescence.

Oigimi was in despair. Kaoru had made such a thing of the night before them. The hours passed, and then came his letter. So Niou's fickleness and thoughtlessness were exactly as the world had proclaimed them to be. Then, at about midnight, he came in upon a rising wind, a most pleasing figure enveloped in a rich per-

despite the danger of attracting attention. Or perhaps: rumors are not to be stilled in any case, and horse would be faster than coach.

fume. How could she be angry with him? And the bride herself – unbending a little now, she seemed to understand somewhat better what was expected of her. She was at her most beautiful. He even thought her, carefully groomed for the occasion, an improvement over the night before. Far from disappointing to one who was always surrounded by beauties, her face, her bearing, everything about her seemed more delightful on close inspection – and how could she fail to have these toothless rustic faces wreathed in smiles? She was lovely, the women said to one another, and it would have been a terrible pity had some ordinary man come for her. Fate had finally done them a good turn. And they grumbled that their other lady should still be so unconscionably aloof in her treatment of the other young gentleman. Observing how these persons well past their prime sewed and embroidered bright, flowery things that did not serve their venerable years, how there was not one among them who could escape charges of decking herself out in grotesque brilliance, Oigimi feared that she too was passing her prime. Each day she saw a more emaciated face in her mirror. Who among her women thought herself uncomely? Each of them brushed thin hair over her forehead, unable to observe the strange prospect she afforded from the rear. Each painted herself over with bright cosmetics. Oigimi lay gazing vacantly out at the garden. Was she prey to self-deception when she told herself that she had not decayed to any alarming degree, that her face was still not too sadly changed and wasted? The ordeal of appearing before a fine young gentleman would be worse as time went by, the ravages would be all too evident in a year or two. Youth – how very fleeting and uncertain it was! She looked at her thin hands and wrists, and thought of him and the world and gazed sadly out at the garden.

It had not been easy to win even this small measure of freedom, sighed Niou; and he could expect even less in the future. He told Nakanokimi of his mother's sharp words. 'There may be times when I will not be able to come, however much I may want to, and you are not to let them worry you. Would I have gone to such trouble if I had the slightest intention of neglecting you? I literally threw myself to the winds tonight, and that was because I did not want you to come to the wrong conclusions. Things will not always be this complicated. I will find a way, somehow, to bring you nearer.'

So he said, with apparent sincerity. But here he was already thinking of times, rather extended periods, evidently, when he would not be able to come. Did she not already have a sign that reports about him were true? She was deeply troubled, by his words and by an awareness of how weak her own position was. As dawn began to come over the sky, he opened a side door and invited her out. The layers of mist delighted him even more than in a familiar setting. As always, the little faggot boats rowed out into the mists, leaving faint white traces behind them.* The strangeness of the scene spoke strongly to his refined sensibilities. The sky was lighter at the mountain ridge. The most coddled and pampered of ladies, he thought, could scarcely be the superior of the princess beside him. Perhaps it was family pride that made him think of his own sister, the First Princess. The night, over so quickly, had left him longing to explore these gentle charms more carefully. The roar of the waters was loud, and as the mists cleared from the moldering old bridge the riverbank seemed wilder, more wasted. How had they been able to pass the years in such a place?

Nakanokimi was apologizing inwardly for her rustic dwelling. What had happened was beyond her maddest dreams: before her was every young lady's notion of the ideal prince; and he had made his vows for this life and all the lives to come. Strangely, she felt more at ease with Niou, though she was dazzled, than she had with Kaoru, the only other young man she had known. Kaoru was a chilly young man whose thoughts always seemed to be else-where. She had thought Niou unapproachable because of the dif-ference in their stations, and she had had difficulty answering even the briefest and most casual of his notes. How strange that she should be upset at the prospect of not seeing him again for some days!

His attendants were noisily coughing and clearing their throats in an effort to hasten him on his way. He too was in rather a hurry, for he did not want to arrive home in the middle of the busy day. He told her over and over again how he hated the thought that he would not see her on each of the nights to come.

Turning back in the doorway, he handed her a farewell poem:

*Manzei, *Manyōshū* 351:

> And to what are we to liken this life of ours?
> To white in the wake of the boat rowing out at dawn.

'The lady at the bridge may steep her sleeves
In lonely midnight tears – but not for long.'*

This was the reply:

'That you will come again I do believe.
But must I wait for visits far between?'†

Although she did not complain, her very apparent distress quite stabbed at his heart. He was such a fine figure in the morning sunlight that the young women of the house were near swooning. Having seen him on his way, Nakanokimi had as a secret memento the perfume he had left behind (and perhaps it brought new stirrings of the heart).

The women were taking advantage of this first opportunity to see him in broad daylight. 'The other young gentleman is such a kind soul,' they said, 'but there is something a little withdrawn about him, a little not-quite-there. Of course we *know* that this young gentleman is more important, and we may just possibly be a little partial.'

Remembering Nakanokimi's distress, Niou was seized with an almost uncontrollable urge to turn back. Indeed, his want of composure was almost ludicrously evident to his men. But he had to think of appearances. Once he was back in the city it was not easy for him to get away again. Every day he sent letters to Uji. Oigimi thought his sincerity beyond doubting; and yet, as the days went by and he failed to appear in person, she had to sigh that her sister, whom she had wanted above all to shield from unhappiness, should now be unhappier than herself. She managed an outward calm, for to show her disquiet would be to send her sister into deeper gloom. On one score her resolve was now firm: she would not allow any man to bring this sort of uncertainty into *her* life.

Kaoru kept a close watch over his friend and offered repeated promptings. He knew how things would be at Uji, and much of the responsibility was, after all, his own. But evidence of Niou's concern gradually put his mind at rest.

---

*See note†, page 848.

†There is a verbal flourish missing from the translation: the Uji Bridge is mentioned by way of *jo* or preface to the adjective 'far between.'

The Ninth Month was half over. Those autumn mountains were much on Niou's mind. One evening, as dark clouds brought threats of rain, his restlessness had him on the point (impossible though he knew the thought to be) of setting forth unassisted. Having guessed that this would be the case, Kaoru stopped by to urge him on. 'And how,' he said, 'will things be in rainy Furu?'*

Niou was delighted. Would his friend go with him? They set out as before in a single carriage. How much unhappier Nakano-kimi must be than he himself, said Niou as they fought their way through the mountain tangles. He could talk of nothing but his remorse and his pity for her. Wan twilight enveloped the sere landscape of late autumn, and a chilly rain dampened their clothes; and the fragrance the two of them sent out made the rustics along the way start up in surprise. It was as if from another world. At Uji the old women who had been complaining of Niou's heartlessness were all smiles as they readied a sitting room. Several nieces and daughters who had been in court service had been called in to help. Long contemptuous of the Uji princesses and their countrified way of life, these self-satisfied women were reduced to silence by the wondrous visit. Oigimi too was pleased: they could not have chosen a better moment. At the same time she was embarrassed and somewhat annoyed that Niou's rather pompous friend should have come with him. Then, presently, as she watched the two of them, she had to change her mind in this matter too. Kaoru was a most unusual young man: he had a quiet seriousness that put him in the sharpest contrast with Niou.

Niou was received with elaborate hospitality which made tasteful use of the special resources of the district. Kaoru for his part was happy to be treated as one of the family, though less happy, as the hours passed, at being left in the reception room. Surely, he thought, something cozier might be arranged. Oigimi at length took pity on him and let him speak to her through curtains.

'How long does this have to go on? "I gave it a try, to which I proved unequal." '†

Oigimi had to grant his point; but her sister's predicament had

---

*The name Furu, a hamlet in the province of Yamato, suggests both the falling of rain and the passage of time. Uji lies in the direction of Yamato, and is clearly indicated here.

†See note*, page 271.

left her thinking that relations between husband and wife must be the bleakest the world has to offer. How could she even consider giving herself to a man? The first overtures, capable of arousing such tenderness, must lead to unhappiness later. No, it would be better for them to go on as they were, neither of them demeaning the other and neither going flagrantly against the other's wishes. Her resolve was firmer than ever. He asked how Niou had been comporting himself. Circumspectly, she told him what had taken place. He assured her that his friend's intentions were serious, and that he would keep an alert watch.

'When all of this torment is over, and we have regained our composure,' she said, more affably than was her custom, 'we must have a good talk.'

She did not, it was true, flee from him in the cruelest and most conclusive manner, and yet her door was closed. She would not forgive him easily, he knew, if he tried to break it down. No doubt she had her own counsels to keep, and there was no question whatever of her scattering her favors elsewhere. And so, with his usual self-control, he braved the chill that emanated from her and sought to sooth the turmoil within himself.

'But it is not at all satisfying, you know, to have to talk to a door. Might I just possibly be favored as I was the other night?'

'I am afraid that my mirror offers me "an uglier visage"* each morning. I would not, after all, like to see disgust written large on your own visage. And do you know, I cannot think why that should be.' There was a trace of laughter in her voice which he found wonderfully appealing.

'And so I am to be forever at the mercy of these whims of yours?' Once again they spent the night as do the pheasants.

'I am jealous of him,' said Niou to Nakanokimi, not dreaming that his friend was being treated like the merest lodger, 'throwing himself about as if he owned the place.'

A very curious thing to say, thought Nakanokimi.

It was unfair, Niou was thinking, that he must rush off after having braved such difficulties. Unaware of these regrets, the sisters were left to lament the uncertainty of their situation. They

*Ise, *Kokinshū* 681:

> Each morning an uglier visage in my mirror.
> Not even in your dreams shall you behold me.

would be grateful if they could but escape the ridicule of the world. It was, all in all, a singularly trying and painful relationship, sighed Niou. In the whole capital there was not one spot where he might hide her. Yūgiri occupied the Rokujō mansion and had given evidence of displeasure that the proposed match between his daughter Rokunokimi and Niou, on which he had placed such hopes, seemed to interest Niou not in the slightest. There were signs, too, that Yūgiri was spreading rumors about the boy's waywardness, and had taken his accusations to the emperor and empress themselves; and if Niou were now to present them with a daughter-in-law to whom they had not been introduced, the embarrassment was certain to be extreme. Had she been the object of a passing infatuation, he would happily have installed her as a lady-in-waiting; but this was a far more serious affair. The emperor seemed to be turning the problem of the succession over in his mind, and if all went well Niou would soon be in a position to accord her the highest honors; but he had to live with the knowledge that, whatever bright hopes he might have, he was for the moment powerless.

Kaoru was making plans to bring Oigimi into the city once the Sanjō mansion was rebuilt. Here was poor Niou, so enamored of Nakanokimi, so fearful of spying eyes, chafing so (and she too) at the infrequency of his visits to Uji – the life of the commoner did have its advantages. Kaoru even considered letting the secret out, telling the empress and the rest about Niou's furtive expeditions. There would be a great stir for a time, unfortunate, to be sure, but Nakanokimi would suffer no permanent injury. It was too cruel that Niou could not spend a whole night at Uji – and Nakanokimi deserved, and indeed had every right to demand, a position of dignity. No, he concluded, he did not think it his duty to keep the secret.

Winter was coming on. Winter garments and other provisions against the cold would be needed at Uji, and who if not he could be counted upon to supply them? Without fanfare, he sent off curtains and hangings which he had been collecting for Oigimi's move to Sanjō. A certain need had arisen elsewhere, he told his mother. He also instructed his old nurse and others to prepare garments for the serving women at Uji.

From early in the Tenth Month he began letting fall remarks about the fish weirs at Uji and how they would be at their most interesting, and how Niou owed himself a look at the autumn leaves. Niou hoped to take only his favorite attendants and certain lesser courtiers with whom he was very friendly. His was a station that attracted notice, however, and the retinue grew and grew, until presently it was headed by Yūgiri's son the captain. So he had two eminent courtiers with him, this young man and Kaoru, and of lesser courtiers the number was legion.

Kaoru sent off a long letter to Uji. 'He will of course want to spend a night, and you should be prepared. The men who were with him last year will take advantage of this occasion and of the winter storms to have a look at you.'

They changed the blinds and dusted the rooms, and cleared away a few of the leaves that had collected among the rocks, and grasses from the brook. Kaoru sent the best viands to be had and dispatched servants to help with the preparations. Oigimi would once have found such attentions less than pleasing, but now she sighed and resigned herself to what fate seemed to offer, and went on working.

Music and other exciting sounds came from the boat as it was poled up and down the river. The young women went to the bank for a closer look. They could not make out the figure of the prince himself, but the boat, roofed with scarlet leaves, was like a gorgeous brocade, and the music, as members of the party joined their flutes in this impromptu offering and the next one, came in upon the wind so clearly that it was almost startling. The princesses looked out and made note of the fact that even on what had been announced as a quiet, unobtrusive expedition Niou was the cynosure of numerous eyes; and they told themselves that he was a man a lady would happily await if he deigned to come once a year.*

Knowing that there would be Chinese poems, Niou had brought learned scholars with him. As evening came on, the boat pulled up at the far bank,† and the music and the poetry gathered momentum. Maple branches in their caps, some only tinged with autumn red and some quite saturated, several of Niou's men played 'The Wise Man of the Sea.'‡ Only one member of the party was less

---

*A reference to the meeting of Altair and Vega on Tanabata, the seventh of the Seventh Month.

†At Yūgiri's mansion, where Niou stayed the year before?

‡'Kaisenraku.' Possibly 'The Blue of the Sea.'

than satisfied: Niou himself. His heart like 'the sea of Omi,'* he was in a frenzy of longing as he thought of his princess on the far bank and the disquiet that must be hers. He was quite over-whelmed by Chinese poems appropriate to the season. Kaoru was confident that when the revelry had subsided they could make their visit; but just as he was telling Niou of these hopes, a guards commander who was an elder brother of the captain already in attendance arrived from the city with a large and splendid retinue. He had come at the behest of the empress. Such expeditions might be undertaken surreptitiously, she had said, but they were certain to attract notice and so to become precedents. He had run off without a by-your-leave, very inadequately escorted. She was most displeased. And so Niou had another captain and any number of ranking courtiers on his hands. Kaoru's plans were in ruin, and for the two friends the pleasure of the evening had evaporated. Unaware of this unhappiness, the party drank and sang the night away.

Niou was thinking that he would like to spend the day at Uji. But another horde of courtiers arrived, headed by his mother's chamberlain. They made him no more eager to return to the city.

He sent a note across the river. Eschewing any attempt to be witty or clever, he sought to convey in some detail his honest thoughts. Nakanokimi, knowing that he would be surrounded by prying eyes, did not answer. She knew more than ever how useless it was to think of joining so grand a company. She had been resentful, and with cause, at his prolonged failure to visit her, but she had been able to tell herself that he would one day come; and here he was madly reveling before her very eyes, and he had not a glance for her. She was hurt and she was angry.

Niou's own gloom was almost beyond enduring – and even the fish in the weirs seemed to favor him with their attentions. The catch was large. His men brought it to him, laid out on autumn leaves of various tints. They were delighted, it had been an expedition with something in it to please every one of them. But Niou stood apart, gazing into space, pain clutching at his heart. The trees in the old garden across the river were extraordinarily powerful, strands of ivy, visible even from this distance, adding a venerable melancholy to the evergreens.

*Lake Biwa. Probably a poetic allusion.

Kaoru was thinking that he had not done very well. The ladies would be the more resentful for his having prepared them so carefully. Several among the attendants remembered the cherry blossoms of the year before and remarked to one another on the sad lot of the princesses, now without a father. A few of them seemed to have caught a hint that their master had intended to make a quiet crossing, and even the more obtuse had something to say about the beautiful princesses. Secluded and cloistered though a life may be, word does somehow get around. Truly superior beauties, the talk had it, and superior musicians as well, their princely father having had them at constant practice.

The captain remembered Kaoru's affection for the Eighth Prince:

> 'We saw yon trees in the spring, a blaze of flowers.
> Beneath them too sad autumn now has stolen.'

Kaoru offered this in reply:

> 'With flowers that fade, with leaves that turn, they speak
> Most surely of a world where all is fleeting.'

The newly arrived guards commander also had a poem:

> 'Regretfully, we leave the autumn groves
> Whence autumn, unobserved, has slipped away.'

And the chamberlain:

> 'The vine yet clings to the stone-walled mountain village,
> Longer-lived than he whom once I knew.'

The oldest man in the party, he was in tears, remembering how it had been when the Eighth Prince was young.

And finally Niou, also in tears, had a poem:

> 'Blow not harshly, wind from the mountain pines,
> Through trees where sadness waxes as autumn wanes.'

The men who knew even a little about his feelings made admiring note of their genuineness, and of the trial it must have been for him to let such an opportunity pass. Nothing was to be done: they could not send a grand flotilla out across the river.

The more interesting passages from the Chinese poems were intoned over and over again, and there were a great many Japanese poems as well, inspired by the place and the season; but is anything really original likely to emerge from drunken revelry? The smallest fragment would do injury to my story, I fear, if I were to write it down.

The princesses, their thoughts too deep for words, heard the shouts of the outrunners receding into the distance. Hardly what one would expect from a famous gallant, said the women who had helped with the preparations.

Oigimi's thoughts, indeed, were making her physically ill. It was true, then: he had, after all, the shifting hue of the dew-flower.* She had heard about that. She had heard, albeit in general terms, that men were good at lying, that many a sweet word went into the pretense of love. The rather common women by whom she was surrounded had told her of their ancient affairs. Well of course, she had said to herself: there would be such cads among the men *they* were likely to keep company with. But surely among wellborn people a sense of propriety, a respect for appearances, put limits upon such behavior. She had been wrong. Her father, knowing all about Niou's ways, had rejected him at the outset. And then Kaoru had come along to plead his friend's case with an intensity that should have made them suspicious, and so the impossible had happened. What would Kaoru be thinking now of the sincerity and steadfastness he had proclaimed so energetically? There was no one here at Uji to whom Oigimi need feel at all inferior, but she cringed to think what must be running through the minds of them all. A ridiculous clown indeed, a perfect fool she had made of herself!

And the lady most concerned: on those meetings so few in number he had made the most solemn of pledges, and she had comforted herself with the thought that his absences might be long but he would not abandon her. Even when his apparent neglect had begun to disturb her, she had been able to tell herself that he must have his reasons. It could not have been said, all the same, that his conduct did not trouble her, and now for him to have come so near and passed on again – she was lost in sorrow and chagrin beyond description.

It was apparent to Oigimi that Nakanokimi was crushed, and the pity was almost as difficult to bear as the anger. 'If I had been

*Tsukikusa, or, more commonly today, tsuyukusa.

able to care for her in any ordinary way, if ours had been an ordinary house, she would not have been subjected to such treatment.'

Oigimi was convinced that she would one day find herself in the same predicament. Kaoru had made numerous promises, but he was not to be trusted. However long she might seek to put him off, she would eventually run out of excuses. And her women did not seem to recognize a disaster for what it was. They actually seemed to be asking one another what might be arranged for Oigimi herself, and so she too would presently find herself with an unwanted husband. Against precisely such an eventuality her father had told her over and over again that living alone was far from the worst of fates. They had been born under unlucky stars, that was the first and most essential fact. Why else should their parents have left them behind? They could look forward to being abandoned by their husbands as well. She had made up her mind. If she were to find herself on the list of the world's favorite ninnies, then her father would be the most grievously injured. No, she wanted to die before the worst happened, while the burden of guilt was still relatively light.

The prisoner of these anguished thoughts, she quite refused to eat. She was tormented too by thoughts of her sister, thoughts so painful that it was almost more than she could do to look at the girl. The loneliness would be next to unbearable. The beautiful figure before her, so sadly neglected by the world, had been the secret support of her own existence, the hope of making a decent marriage for her sister had given purpose to her life. And they had found a husband, a man of indisputably good birth, and the marriage had become a cruel joke! It would now be impossible for her sister, the defenseless butt of the joke, to face the world. A decent life was now out of the question. They had been born to no purpose, she and her sister. Life might offer consolation, but not to them.

Back in the city, Niou considered turning around and making another trip, a quiet one this time, to Uji. But the guards captain had already been to the emperor and empress. It was for the secret reasons which he now chose to divulge, he had informed them, that Prince Niou was in the habit of slipping off into the country; and he had added that Prince Niou was conducting himself in a manner altogether irresponsible, of which people were beginning to talk. The empress was much upset, and the emperor too was displeased. It had all happened, he said, because the boy was allowed to live away from the palace. With matters at this difficult pass, Niou was required to take up residence in the palace. He had no wish at all to marry Yūgiri's daughter Rokunokimi, but a consensus had been reached to bestow her upon him.

Kaoru was in dismay. What was to be done now? His own eccentric ways had been to blame – and perhaps fate had stepped in. Unable to forget the Eighth Prince's concern for his daughters, sad that such elegance and beauty, favored by not the smallest stroke of luck, should be wasted, he had been seized by a longing to help them so intense that even to him it had seemed curious. The importunings of his friend had also been hard to resist, and he had found himself in the awkward position of not wanting the one sister when the other did not want him. And so he had made these arrangements, and a fine pass they had come to. No one would have reproved him for making either of the princesses his own. But that was all finished, and what was left was a piece of idiocy to gnash his teeth over at his leisure.

Niou found lighthearted forgetfulness even more elusive. 'If you have someone on your mind,' said his mother time after time, 'bring her here, and settle down to the sort of life people expect of you. We both know very well that you are your father's favorite, and it drives me wild to hear what people are saying about your irresponsible behavior.'

On a quiet day of heavy winter rains he went to call on his sister, the First Princess. She and a few attendants had been looking over a collection of paintings. He addressed her through a curtain. She was among the famous beauties of the day, and yet she preserved a winning girlishness that made him ask whether her rival was to be found anywhere. There was, to be sure, the daughter of the Reizei emperor, her father's joy and pride. What he had heard of her secluded life suggested again a most compelling beauty, but he had no way of approaching her. And there was his own princess at Uji, loveliness itself. With each thought of her the longing grew. By way of distraction he picked up several of the pictures that lay scattered about. They had been painted, and very skillfully, to appeal to womanly tastes.* There was, for instance, a

---

*They are *onna-e*, 'woman pictures.' It has been argued that the expression might refer not to pictures for women, but to pictures of or by women.

lovelorn gentleman, and there was a tasteful mountain villa, and there were numbers of other scenes that seemed to have interested the artists. Several called his own circumstances to mind, and he thought of asking his sister for a few to send to Uji. The illustration for the scene from *Tales of Ise* in which the hero gives his sister a koto lesson* brought him closer to the curtain.

' "A pity indeed if the grasses so sweet, so inviting," ' he whispered, and one may wonder what he had in mind. 'I gather that in those days brother and sister did not have to talk through curtains. You are very remote.'

She asked what picture he was referring to. He rolled it up and pushed it under the curtain, and as she bent to look at it her hair was swept aside and he caught a brief and partial glimpse of her profile. It delighted him. He found himself wishing that she were not his sister. A verse came to his lips:

'I do not propose to sleep among the young grasses,
But ensnared in them I must confess to be.'

Her attendants had withdrawn in embarrassment. A most curious thing to say, thought the princess herself. She did not answer. Her manifest and quite proper discomfort reminded him that the recipient of the old poem had replied in a somewhat inviting manner.†

Murasaki had been fondest of these two, the First Princess and Niou, and of all the royal children they had been the closest. The empress had been especially careful with this oldest daughter, and if anyone among her attendants, who were numerous and all from the best families, was seen to have the slightest flaw, she was very quickly made to feel unwanted.

The volatile Niou moved from one liaison to the next as interesting new ladies appeared, but through them all his heart was

---

*Episode 49. The poem to which Niou alludes has strongly erotic and incestuous overtones:

A pity indeed, if the grasses so sweet, so inviting,
Were taken and bound by another hand than mine.

†Her reply:

Why these words of surprise at the fresh young grasses?
Have they not been wholly yours from the start?

with the princess at Uji. He was a lazy correspondent, however, and so the days went by.

It seemed to the Uji sisters that they had been asked to wait a very long time. It was as she had feared, thought Oigimi; and then Kaoru, having heard that she was not well, came to inquire after her. She was not seriously ill, but she made the indisposition her excuse for not receiving him.

'I have come running all this way,' he said. 'Take me to her room, please, as you did before.'

He seemed so genuinely concerned that someone did presently lead him to her bed curtains. Though she had not wanted to see him, she raised her head and answered civilly enough. He explained that Niou had not had the least intention, on that maple-viewing expedition, of passing them by.

'Do be patient, and try not to worry.'

'My sister does not complain.' There were tears in her voice. 'But what a very unhappy situation it is. I know now what Father was trying to warn us against.'

'The world does not always go as we wish it. You have not had a great deal of experience, and it is natural that you should see things entirely from your own point of view. But try to imagine his, if you will. You have nothing to worry about, not a thing. I would not say so if I were not convinced of it.' How odd, he thought, to have to explain away derelictions that were not his responsibility.

She was in greater discomfort at night. Since her sister was uneasy at having a stranger so near, the women suggested that he remove himself to a detached wing with which he was already familiar.

'I am sick with worry, and I want to be near her. Can you really send me into exile? Can I expect anyone else to do what must be done?'

He summoned Bennokimi and told her that religious services were to be commenced immediately. Oigimi objected, but in silence. She did not want priests to see her in her present condition, and she had no wish that anything be done to prolong her life. She was not up to stating her views, however, and she was touched by these hopes for her recovery.

'Are you feeling a little better?' he asked the next morning. 'Let me talk to you, please, even as briefly as yesterday.'

'I am afraid that time has only made things worse, and I really am very unwell. But do come in anyway.'

He went to her bedside, in great apprehension. This unwonted docility had the effect of making the worst seem at hand. He spoke of this and that trifling matter.

'I am so unwell, I am afraid, that I cannot really talk to you. Perhaps after I have rested.' The sound of her voice, scarcely more than a whisper, only added to his anguish. But he had work to do, and could stay no longer. With the darkest forebodings, he started back for the city.

'Uji is not good for her,' he said to the old woman. 'Don't you suppose we could make this our excuse to find a more hospitable spot?' He left instructions for the abbot to conduct intensive and careful services.

Some of his attendants had become familiar with the young women of the house. 'I hear they have put a stop to Prince Niou's wanderings,' said one of them, idly passing the time of day. 'They have shut him up in the palace. And it seems that they have arranged a match between him and the minister's young daughter. Her family has wanted it for years, and so no one will be inconvenienced. The talk is that they'll be married before the end of the year. Of course he isn't all that enthusiastic. He goes on having little affairs with the ladies-in-waiting. His mother and father haven't had much luck at reforming him. Now if you want a real contrast look at our own master for a minute or two. So serious and self-contained – so queer, really, some might say. People are all agog at his trips here. Some say they're the first real sign of human feeling he has ever shown.'

'That is what he told me.' The woman was quick to pass all this on to her colleagues, and it soon reached the princesses, and did nothing to assuage their distress. Such was the pass they had come to, said Oigimi to herself. It was the end. He had only wanted amusement while he got ready to marry a well-placed lady. With one eye on Kaoru, he had contrived to put together certain words of affection. Beyond thinking further about this duplicity, convinced that the world no longer had a place for her, she lay weeping helplessly. She no longer wished to live. Hers were not women of such rank that she need feel any constraint before them, but the thought of what they would now be saying quite revolted her. She tried to pretend that she had not heard this new report. Her sister was with her, napping as people will who have 'thoughts of things.'* What a dear little creature she was, her long hair flowing over the arm on which her head was pillowed – what remarkable grace and beauty. Oigimi thought of her father and his last admonitions. He would not be in hell of course – but even if he was, could he not summon them to his side? It was too cruel, that he should leave them in these sad straits, refusing to come to them even in a dream.

The evening was dark and rainy and the wind in the trees was a sigh of utter loneliness. For all her worries, Oigimi was a figure of great distinction as she sat leaning against an armrest and thinking of what had been and what was to be. Her hair had long gone untended, and yet not a strand was in disarray as it flowed down over a white robe. The pallor from days of illness gave to her features a certain cast of depth and mystery. The eyes and forehead as she sat gazing out into the dusk – one would have longed to show them to the world of high taste, to connoisseurs of the beautiful.

Nakanokimi started up at a particularly harsh gust of wind. Her robes were a lively combination of yellow and rose,† and her face had a lively glow, a luster as of having been freshly tinted over. There was no trace of worry upon it.

'I dreamed of Father. I saw him for just a second, standing over there. He seemed upset.'

'I have wanted so to see him, even in a dream,' said Oigimi, in a new access of grief, 'and I have not once dreamed of him.'

Both of the girls were in tears. The fact that he had been so much on her mind recently, thought Oigimi, perhaps meant that he was wandering in some limbo.‡ She longed to go to him, wherever he was – not that such a sinful one as she would be permitted to. And so her worries ran on into the other world. There

---

*Anonymous, *Shūishū* 897:

> Mother has said that napping is unseemly.
> But nap one will, when one has thoughts of things.

†The colors have been variously described. All that is really clear is that they are bright.

‡Or: 'It was perhaps because he had been so much on her mind that Nakanokimi had had this glimpse of him.'

was an incense, it was said, which men of a foreign land had used to bring back the dead.* If only she might have a stick of it!

In the evening a letter was delivered from Niou. It came at a difficult time, and should have been some slight comfort to them; but Nakanokimi was in no hurry to look at it.

'You must send off a kind answer, a friendly one,' said Oigimi. 'It worries me a great deal to think that I may die and leave you behind, and some awful man may come along and make things even worse. As long as the prince has an occasional thought for you, the worst sort of man will stay away. It will not be easy, I know, but he *is* a defense of sorts.'

'Do you really think of leaving me? You mustn't even whisper it.' Nakanokimi hid her face.

'We all have to die, and you know how much I hated the idea of living a moment longer than Father. But here I am, with my life still to live out. And who is it that makes me, after all, sorry to leave "a world where no one can be sure of the morrow"?'†

A lamp was brought and they read the letter. It was warm and detailed, as always, and it contained this poem:

'The sky I see is the usual nighttime sky.
    Then why tonight do the showers increase my longing?'

It was so trite and perfunctory, just one more allusion to tear-soaked sleeves. 'Well, that is that,' one could almost hear him saying as he dashed it off. Yet his manner and appearance were enough to make any girl fall in love with him, and he could be completely charming when he wanted to.

Nakanokimi's longing increased as time went by. And there had been those effusive promises, which it was hard to believe he meant to ignore completely. She felt her resentment subside.

The messenger said that he would like to go back that night. Everyone was pressing Nakanokimi for an answer, and finally she produced a poem:

---

*The emperor Wu-ti used this miraculous incense to bring back, albeit faintly, the image of his dead love Madame Li. There is a poem by Po Chü-i on the subject.

†Ki no Tsurayuki, on the death of his cousin Tomonori, *Kokinshū* 838:

> In a world where no one can be sure of the morrow,
> I grieve for him who did not live out the day.

'Here in our hail-flogged village, deep in the mountains,
The skies upon which we gaze are forever cloudy.'

It was late in the Tenth Month, and a whole month had gone
by since Niou's last visit to Uji. He thought nervously each night
of setting forth. But alas, he was 'a small boat caught in reeds,'*
and, with the Gosechi dances coming early this year,† there were
gay events at court to occupy his time. And so the days went by,
and at Uji the wait was increasingly painful. This or that court lady
would briefly catch his eye, but his heart remained with the Uji
princess.

His mother spoke to him again of Yūgiri's daughter. 'When
you have made yourself a good, solid marriage, then you can bring
in anyone who strikes your fancy and set her up wherever it suits
your convenience. But you *must* build yourself a strong base.'

'Wait just a little longer, please. I'm thinking it over.'

At Uji they could not know that it had never been his intention
to hurt them, and each day brought a heavier pall of gloom.

Kaoru meanwhile was wringing his hands. Was his friend less
trustworthy than his observations had led him to believe? Had he
been wrong all along? He rarely visited Niou's apartments these
days, but he sent frequent messengers to inquire after Oigimi's
health. He learned that she had improved somewhat since the first
of the Eleventh Month. It being a season when he had all manner
of business, public and private, he let five or six days go by without further inquiry. Then, suddenly alarmed, he shook off all these
urgent affairs and rushed to Uji.

He had given instructions that the services be continued until
her complete recovery, but she had said that she was much better
and dismissed the abbot. There were very few people in attendance
upon her. He summoned Bennokimi and asked for a full report.

'There are no alarming symptoms, really. It is just that she
refuses to eat. She has always been more delicate than most people,
and you would hardly recognize her now. Ever since the Niou

---

*Hitomaro, *Shūishū* 853:

A small boat caught in reeds as it makes for shore,
I vainly seek to wait upon my love.

†When the Day of the Ox occurred thrice in the Eleventh Month, the dances began
on the second of the three; when twice, on the first.

affair she hasn't let the smallest bit of fruit pass her lips. I am beginning to wonder if anything can save her. I have not had an easy life, and it has gone on too long, that I should live to see these things. I only want to die before she does.' She was in tears, as she had every right to be, even before she had finished speaking.

'But why didn't you tell me? I have been busy at court and at the Reizei Palace and it has worried me terribly that I am not able to look in on her.'

He went to the sickroom and knelt at Oigimi's bedside. She scarcely had strength to answer him.

'No one, no one at all, came to tell me. I have been worried, but what good does that do now?'

He summoned the abbot and other priests whose prayers were in high repute. With rites to begin the following morning, he sent to the city for some of his people, and the Uji villa was alive with courtiers high and low. The women forgot their loneliness. At dusk they brought him a light supper and sought once again to take him to a distant wing of the house. He replied that he wished to be where he could be useful. The priests having occupied the south room, he put up screens in the east room, somewhat nearer Oigimi. Nakanokimi was much upset, but the women, relieved to see that he had not after all abandoned them, had given up their efforts to take him away. Continuous reading of the Lotus Sutra began in the evening, most impressively, twelve priests of the finest voice taking turns. There was a light in Kaoru's room, and the inner room, where Oigimi lay, was dark; and so he raised a curtain and slipped a few inches inside. Two or three women knelt beside her, Nakanokimi having withdrawn to the rear of the room. It was a lonely scene.

'Can't you say just one word to me?'

He took her hand. Startled, she replied in a barely audible whisper. 'I would like very much to speak to you, believe me. But it is such an effort. You had not visited me for so long that I feared I might die without seeing you again.'

'I am furious with myself.' He was sobbing aloud. He felt her brow, which seemed fevered. 'And what sort of misconduct, do you suppose, is responsible for this? Making someone unhappy, perhaps?' He leaned very near and seemed prepared to talk on and on. The merest wisp of a figure, she covered her face. He could not imagine how it would be if she were to die.

'I am sure you are exhausted,' he said to Nakanokimi. 'I am on duty tonight. Suppose you get some rest.'

Hesitantly, Nakanokimi withdrew deeper into the room. Oigimi still hid her face, but he was beside her, and that was some comfort to him. She strove to dispel her embarrassment with the thought that a bond from a former life must account for their being so near. When she compared his calm gentleness with Niou's heartless behavior, she had to admit that the contrast was startling. And she did not want to be remembered for her coldness. She could not send him away. All through the night he had women at work brewing medicines, but she quite refused to take them. He was beside himself. The crisis was real, that much was clear. And what could be done to save her? New lectors came for the matins, and the abbot, who had been present through the night, started up at the fresh resonance and began intoning mystical formulas. His voice was hoarse with age, but it seemed to have in it a store of grace that was enough to bring hope even to this despairing household.

'How did my lady pass the night?' asked the abbot, going on to speak, his voice sometimes wavering, of her father. 'And in which realm will he be now? I wonder. One of peace and serenity, of that I am sure. The other night I dreamed of him. He was wearing secular dress, and he spoke with great clarity. "I had persuaded myself from the depths of my heart to renounce the world," he said, "and had nothing to hold me back. But now a small worry has come up, to ruffle the calm. I must pause on my way to the land where I long to be. It is a cause of great disappointment to me, and I beg you to pray that I soon recover the ground I have lost." I could not immediately think what to do, and so I set five or six of my men to chanting the holy name – it was the one thought that came to me. And then I had another: I sent priests out in the four directions to proclaim the Buddhahood of all men.'*

Kaoru was in tears. Oigimi wanted only to die, at the thought of the burden of sin she must bear for her father's troubles. She

---

*Following the precedent of Sadāparibhūta-bodhisattva (Japanese Jōfugyō), who, in the Lotus Sutra, preserved in telling all and sundry of their Buddhahood even when they beat and stoned him for his troubles.

longed to be with him wherever he was, to join him before his soul had come to its final rest.

After a few words more the abbot withdrew. The priests sent out to proclaim universal Buddhahood had gone to villages near at hand and to the city as well, but presently they were back, for the dawn gales had been cruel.* Seeking out the abbot's room, they prostrated themselves at the garden gate and grandly brought their invocations to an end. Kaoru, whose studies of the Good Law were by now well advanced, was deeply moved.

In painful uncertainty, Nakanokimi came somewhat nearer. Kaoru drew himself up politely as he caught a rustling of silk.

'And how does it seem to you?' he asked. 'These readings may not be the most important things in the world, but they do have a certain dignity.' As if in ordinary conversation, he added a poem:

> 'Forlorn the dawn, when on the frosty bank
> The plovers sound their melancholy notes.'

Something about him reminded her of his cruel friend. But she still found him rather forbidding, and sent her answer through Bennokimi:

> 'The plovers in the dawn, shaking off the frost:
> Do they call to the heart of one now sunk in grief?'

Ill favored though the intermediary was, the poem was delivered gracefully enough.

Nakanokimi seemed very shy, even in these fleeting exchanges, but her gentle replies gave evidence of a sensitive nature he would desperately hate to see leave his life. He thought of the Eighth Prince as the abbot had dreamed of him, and of how it must be to watch all of this from the heavens. He had sutras read at the monastery where the prince had spent his last days and ordered new rites at other temples as well. Taking leave of all his affairs in the city, he set about assuring himself that no device, Buddhist or Shinto, had been overlooked. There were no signs, however, that the sick lady was the victim of a possession, and these varied ministrations seemed to accomplish nothing. Though a prayer in her

---

*The sequence of events is not at all clear. It may be that the abbot has dreamed of the prince during the slumber from which he has just awakened, but if so not much time has been allowed for the invocation of universal Buddhahood.

own behalf might have helped, she saw her chance to die. Kaoru had attached himself to her as if he were her husband. There would be no shaking him off. And if, to push her forebodings further, the emotions that now seemed so powerful were to fade, they would both of them, she and Kaoru, have gloom and uncertainty to look forward to. No, a nun's vows offered the only refuge, and her illness must be her excuse. *Then* they could look forward to long and companionable years together. This one resolve she must carry through.

Hoping that it did not seem pompous, she said to her sister: 'I begin to feel that I am almost beyond help. I have heard that a woman sometimes lives a little longer if she becomes a nun. Might you point this out to the abbot?'

But the house echoed with the objections of her women. 'Absolutely out of the question. Think of the poor young gentleman who has been so kind. Think of the effect it would have on him.'

They refused even to consider telling him of her wishes.

Talk of his retreat was meanwhile going the rounds at court. Several courtiers came to make inquiry. His personal staff and certain stewards and others with whom he was on friendly terms noted that Oigimi's illness seemed important to him, and commissioned services of their own. Back in the city the festival would be reaching its grand and noisy climax. At Uji it was a day of wild storms and winds. It would be more clement in the city, and he could as well have been there. Oigimi was to leave him, it seemed, still a stranger; but something about the fragile figure made him incapable of reproving her for what was over and finished. He was lost in hopeless longing, to see her again, for even a few days, as she once had been, to pour forth before her the whole turbulent flood of his thoughts. Darkness came over an already sunless sky.

He whispered to himself:

'In mountains deep, where clouds turn back the sun,
Each day casts darker shadows upon my heart.'

He seldom left Oigimi's bedside, and his presence was a comfort to the women of the house. The wind was so high that Naka-nokimi was having trouble with her curtains. When she withdrew to the inner rooms the ugly old women followed in some confusion. Kaoru came nearer and spoke to Oigimi. There were tears in his voice.

'And how are you feeling? I have lost myself in prayers, and I fear they have done no good at all. It is too much, that you will not even let me hear your voice. You are not to leave me.'

Though barely conscious, she was still careful to hide her face. 'There are many things I would like to say to you, if I could only get back a little of my strength. But I am afraid – I am sorry – that I must die.'

Tears were painfully near. He must not show any sign of despair – but soon he was sobbing audibly. What store of sins had he brought with him from previous lives, he wondered, that, loving her so, he had been rewarded with sorrow and sorrow only, and that he now must say goodbye? If he could find a flaw in her, he might resign himself to what must be. She became the more sadly beautiful the longer he gazed at her, and the more difficult to relinquish. Though her hands and arms were as thin as shadows, the fair skin was still smooth. The bedclothes had been pushed aside. In soft white robes, she was so fragile a figure that one might have taken her for a doll whose voluminous clothes hid the absence of a body. Her hair, not so thick as to be a nuisance, flowed down over her pillow, the luster as it had always been. Must such beauty pass, quite leave this world? The thought was not to be endured. She had not taken care of herself in her long illness, and yet she was far more beautiful than the sort of maiden who, not for a moment unaware that someone might be looking at her, is forever primping and preening. The longer he looked at her, the greater was the anguish.

'If you leave me, I doubt that I will stay on very long myself. I do not expect to survive you, and if by some chance I do, I will wander off into the mountains. The one thing that troubles me is the thought of leaving your sister behind.'

He wanted somehow to coax an answer from her. At the mention of her sister, she drew aside her sleeve to reveal a little of her face.

'I am sorry that I have been so out of things. I may have seemed rude in not doing as you have wished. I must die, apparently, and my one hope has been that you might think of her as you have thought of me. I have hinted as much, and had persuaded myself that I could go in peace if you would respect this one wish. My one unsatisfied wish, still tying me to the world.'

'There are people who walk under clouds of their own, and I seem to be one of them. No one else, absolutely no one else, has stirred a spark of love in me, and so I have not been able to follow your wishes. I am sorry now; but please do not worry about your sister.'

She was in greater distress as the hours went by. He summoned the abbot and others and had incantations read by well-known healers. He lost himself in prayers. Was it to push a man towards renunciation of the world that the Blessed One sent such afflictions? She seemed to be vanishing, fading away like a flower. No longer caring what sort of spectacle he might make, he wanted to shout out his resentment at his own helplessness. Only half in possession of her senses, Nakanokimi sensed that the last moment had come. She clung to the corpse until that forceful old woman, among others, pulled her away. She was only inviting further misfortunes, they said.

Was it a dream? Kaoru had somehow not accepted the possibility that things would come to this pass. Turning up the light, he brought it to the dead lady's face. She lay as if sleeping, her face still hidden by a sleeve, as beautiful as ever. If only he could go on gazing at her as at the shell of a locust. The women combed her hair preparatory to having it cut, and the fragrance that came from it, sad and mysterious, was that of the living girl. He wanted to find a flaw, something to make her seem merely ordinary. If the Blessed One meant by all this to bring renunciation and resignation, then let him present something repellent, to drive away the regrets. So he prayed; but no relief was forthcoming. Well, he said presently, nothing was left but to commit the body to flames, and so he set about the sad duty of making the funeral arrangements. He walked unsteadily beside the body, scarcely feeling the ground beneath his feet. In a daze, he made his way back to the house. Even the last rites had been faltering, insubstantial; very little smoke had risen from the pyre.

The house was overrun with mourners, and the worst of the loneliness was postponed for a time. Nakanokimi, quite aware of what people would be saying about her predicament, was so sunk in her own sad thoughts that she seemed hardly more alive than her sister. A great many messages of condolence came from Niou; but she had made what now seemed to her a marriage with a curse upon it, Oigimi having gone to her grave unable to forgive him.

Kaoru thought that this ultimate knowledge of evanescence might persuade him to leave the world; but he had his mother's views in the matter to consider, and there was the sad situation in which Nakanokimi had been left. His mind was in a turmoil. Perhaps it would have been better if he had done as Oigimi had suggested, taken her sister in her place. Try though he might to think of them as one, he had not been able to transfer his affections. Rather than invite the despair into which he now was plunged, might he not better have taken Nakanokimi, and sought in his visits to Uji consolation for unrequited love? He did not venture even a brief visit to the city, and his ties with the world were as good as severed. Since it was evident that this had been no ordinary attachment, messages of condolence came in a steady flow, from the palace and from lesser houses.

And so aimless days sped by. On each of the weekly memorial days he had services conducted with unusual solemnity. There was a limit to what an outsider could do, however. He would catch glimpses of the black to which her closest attendants had changed, and regret that custom forbade his changing to black himself.

'Uselessly they fall, these blood-red tears,
    For they do not dye these robes in black remembrance.'

Clean, trim, elegant, he sat gazing out at the garden. His lavender robe had a sheen as of melting ice, and the flow of his tears gave an added luster. The women looked at him admiringly even as they lamented. Their grief over this terrible event aside, they hated to think that the time had come when he must again be a stranger. A heavy burden it was that the fates had asked them to bear! Such a kind gentleman – and neither of their ladies would have him.

'It would be a great comfort,' he said to Nakanokimi, 'if I might talk freely with you, and think of you as a sort of keepsake. Please do not send me away.'

But he was asking too much. She had been born for sorrow and humiliation, of that she was sure. He had always thought her a livelier girl than her sister; but for someone in search of delicacy and gentleness, the older girl had had the stronger appeal.

He spent the whole of one dark, snowy day gazing out upon that dreariest of months – as people will have it – the last of the year. In the evening the moon rose in a clear sky. He went to the veranda and lifted the blinds. The vesper bells came faintly from the monastery. So another day had passed, he said to himself as he listened.

'My heart goes after yon retreating moon.
No home, this world, in which to dwell forever.'

A wind having come up, he went to lower the shutters. In brilliant moonlight, the mountains were reflected in the icy river as in a mirror. However much care might go into his new house, he would be unable to fabricate a scene so lovely. Come back for but a moment, he whispered, and enjoy it with me.

'Deep in the Snowy Mountains* would I vanish,
In search of the brew that is death for those who love.'

If, like the Lad of the Snowy Mountains, he had an accommodating monster of whom he might inquire about a stanza, he would have an excuse to fling himself away.† A less than perfectly enlightened heart our young sage had!

Seemingly unshakable in his serenity, he would talk with the women. The younger ones quite fell in love with him, and the older ones sighed again to think what a hapless lady they had served.

'She lost her grip on herself because she took the prince's odd behavior too seriously. The whole world was laughing at them, she was sure; but she kept it all to herself. She did not want our other lady to know how worried she was. With everything shut up inside her she quietly stopped eating, and that was that. You couldn't always be sure what she was thinking, but there wasn't much that she missed. The beginning of it all was her father, and then there was her sister – she was sure she had done exactly what he had told her not to do.' They would recount little incidents, and at the end of each interview the household was abandoned to tears.

*The Himalayas.

†The 'Sacrifice for a Stanza,' subject of one of the paintings on the Tamamushi Shrine of the Hōryūji. The Boy of the Himalayas (Sessen Dōji), the Buddha in a former life, meets a devil, actually a benevolent power in disguise, and offers to sacrifice himself to learn the second half of a stanza of which his adversary has quoted the first. The episode is in the Mahāparanirvāna Sutra (Daihatsunehangyō).

It had been his fault, thought Kaoru, wishing he had it all to do over again. He lost himself in prayers and turned away from the world.

Suddenly, deep in a sleepless night of freezing snow, there was a loud shouting outside and a neighing of horses. The reverend priests started up in surprise, wondering who could have made his way through such gales in the dead of night. It was Niou, soaking wet, in bedraggled travel dress. For Kaoru the pounding on the door had a familiar sound, and he withdrew to seclusion in one of the inner apartments. Though the mourning was not yet over, an impatient Niou had given a whole night over to his battle with the snows.

The visit should have softened Nakanokimi's resentment at the days of neglect, but she had no wish to receive him. What he had done to her sister seemed inexcusable. He had let her die without a hint of reforming his ways. Perhaps he meant to change now, but it was too late. Her women were determined, however, that she do the sensible thing, and finally she let him address her through curtains. He was profuse with his apologies. She listened quietly, and he sensed that she was still in a daze. Was it possible that she might go the way of her sister? Whatever punishment he might have to face later, he would stay the night.

'You don't of course mean to leave me sitting here?'

But she turned away. 'Perhaps when I am a little more myself.'

Guessing what had happened, Kaoru sent a woman with a secret word of advice. 'You have every right to be angry. From the beginning he behaved in a manner one can only describe as heartless. Scold him if you wish, but not so emphatically as to make him angry in his turn. He is not used to being crossed, and he is easily hurt.'

These sage words only made things worse. She could think of nothing to say.

'You are being rather unpleasant, I must say,' sighed Niou. 'Have you quite forgotten my promises?'

A fierce gale came up in the night. Though he had no one to blame but himself, he was very unhappy. She finally relented and spoke to him, though still through curtains. Calling upon the thousand gods to be his witnesses, he promised that he would be at her side forever. She was not greatly comforted – a most remarkable glibness, she thought. But though his thoughtlessness over the weeks might have seemed too much to excuse, he was with her now, and irresistible. Her bitter resolutions wavering, she said in a whisper:

'Unsure has been the road over which I look back.
What can I know of the road that lies ahead?'

It was not a very inviting or reassuring sort of poem.

'The road ahead must needs be short, you tell me?
Then let us presume upon it while we may.

Life is fleeting, you know, and so is everything in it. Do not make things worse with useless worries.'

Despite his various efforts to please her, she at length said that she was not feeling well and withdrew to an inner room.

He spent a sleepless night, aware that he must seem ridiculous to these women. He understood Nakanokimi's anger, he told himself, shedding bitter tears of his own, but she went too far. Still he could imagine that the resentment he now felt she must have known several times over.

Kaoru seemed to comport himself as if he were master of the place. He treated the domestics like his own, it seemed to Niou, and they trooped off in procession to see that he was comfortable and abundantly fed. Niou was touched and somewhat amused. Kaoru had lost weight and his color was bad; he seemed but half alive to his surroundings. Niou offered genuinely felt condolences. Kaoru longed to talk about the dead girl, knowing well the futility, but he cut himself short, lest he sound like a womanish complainer. The days that had been given over to tears had changed him, but not for the worse. His features were more interesting, more cleanly cut than ever, thought Niou, sure that he himself would find them attractive were he a woman. Further evidence of his deplorable susceptibility, he could see. He turned his thoughts to Nakanokimi. How, without calling down malicious slander upon himself, could he move her to the city? She was being difficult, but to stay another night would certainly mean displeasing his father; and so he started back. He had exhausted his powers of gentle persuasion. Thinking to show him even a little of what aloofness was like, she had been to the end unyielding.

As New Year approaches the skies are forbidding even in civilized regions. Here in the mountains no day passed without storms to heap the snows deeper. The passing days brought no lessening of the sorrow. Niou sent lavish offerings for memorial services. People were beginning to worry about Kaoru, from whom there came hardly a word. Did he mean to weep his way into the New Year? His thoughts were beyond words when finally he left Uji. For the women the sorrow was as great. The house had somehow been alive while he had been with them, and now he was going. The quiet would be even worse than the shock of those first tragic days. He had been with them, so gentle and considerate, so attentive in matters small and large, and they had come to know him far better than in the days of the early visits. They wept as they told themselves that they would see him no more.

A message came from Niou: 'I have concluded that I will find it no easier as time goes by to travel such distances, and have made plans to bring you nearer.'

His mother had apprised herself of all the details, and was sympathetic. If Kaoru was so lost in grief for the older princess, then the younger must also be a rather considerable person. Suppose Niou were to install her in the west wing at Nijō, where he could visit her as he wished. She evidently meant to have it seem that Nakanokimi had entered the service of the First Princess. Still, he must be grateful. Regular visits would now be possible. It was in these circumstances that he sent off his message to Uji.

Kaoru heard of his plans. It had been Kaoru's intention to bring his own love into the city once the Sanjō mansion was finished. He regretted that he had not taken her advice and made Nakanokimi a substitute.

He concluded that it must be his duty to make arrangements for the move to the city. If Niou chose to be suspicious, that was very silly of him.

CHAPTER 48

Early Ferns

The spring sunlight did not discriminate against these 'thickets deep.'*
But Nakanokimi, still benumbed with grief, could only wonder that
so much time had gone by and she had not joined her sister. The two
of them had responded as one to the passing seasons, the color of the
blossoms and the songs of the birds. Some triviality would bring from
one of them a verse, and the other would promptly have a capping
verse. There had been sorrows, there had been times of gloom; but
there had always been the comfort of having her sister beside her.
Something might interest her or amuse her even now, but she had no
one to share it with. Her days were bleak, unbroken solitude. The
sorrow was if anything more intense than when her father had died.
Yearning and loneliness left day scarcely distinguishable from night.
Well, she had to live out her time, and it did little good to complain
that the end did not come at her summons.

There was a letter from the abbot for one of her women: 'And
how will matters be with our lady now that the New Year has
come? I have allowed no lapse in my prayers for her. She is, in fact,
my chief worry. These are the earliest fern shoots, offerings from
certain of our acolytes.' The note came with shoots of bracken and
fern, arranged rather elegantly in a very pretty basket. There was
also a poem, in a bad hand, set apart purposely, it seemed, from the
text of the letter.†

'Through many a spring we plucked these shoots for him.
  Today remembrance bids us do as well.

Please show this to your lady.'

---

*Furu Imamichi, *Kokinshū* 870:

> The sun of spring still favors thickets deep.
> Though Furu is abandoned there still are blossoms.

†Another possible interpretation is that the poem is not written in a cursive script.
The suggestion is clear in any event that the abbot is not accustomed to such frivolities.

Nakanokimi was much moved. The old man was not one to compose poems for every occasion, and these few syllables said more to her than all the splendid words, overlooking no device for pleasing her, of a certain gentleman who, though ardent enough to appearances, did not really seem to care very much. Tears came to her eyes. She sent a reply through one of her women:

'And to whom shall I show these early ferns from the mountain,
    Plucked in remembrance of one who is no more?'

She rewarded the messenger liberally.

Still in the full bloom of her youth, she had lost weight, and the effect was to deepen her beauty, and to remind one of her sister. Side by side, the two sisters had not seemed particularly alike; but now one could almost forget for a moment that Oigimi was dead, so striking was the resemblance. Kaoru had lamented that he could not keep their older lady with him, the women remembered, even as he might have kept a locust shell. Since either of the princesses would have been right for him, it was cruel of fate not to have let him have the younger.

Certain of his men continued to visit Uji, having made the acquaintance of women there. Through them the princess and Kaoru had occasional word of each other. Time had done nothing to dispel his grief, she learned, nor had the coming of the New Year stanched the flow of his tears. It had been no passing infatuation, she could see now. He had been honest in his avowals of love.

Niou was chafing at the restrictions his rank placed upon him, and the evidence was that they would only be more burdensome as time went by. He thought constantly about bringing Nakanokimi to the city.

When the busiest days were over, the time of the grand levee and the like, Kaoru found himself with heavy heart and no one who understood. He paid Niou a visit. It was an evening for melancholy thoughts. Niou was seated at the veranda, gazing out at the garden and plucking a few notes now and then on the koto beside him. He had always loved the scent of plum blossoms. Kaoru broke off an underbranch still in bud and brought it to him, and he found the fragrance so in harmony with his mood that he was stirred to poetry:

'This branch seems much in accord with him who breaks it.
I catch a secret scent beneath the surface.'*

'I should have been more careful with my blossoms.
I offer fragrance, get imputations back.

You do not make things easy for me.'

They seemed the most lighthearted of companions as they
exchanged sallies.

When they settled down to serious matters, they were soon
talking of Uji. And how would Nakanokimi and her women be?
asked Niou. Kaoru told of his own unquenchable sorrow, of the
memories that had tormented him since Oigimi's death, of the
amusing and moving things that had been part of their times
together – of all the laughter and tears, so to speak. And his phil-
andering friend, quicker to weep than anyone even when the matter did not immediately concern him, was now weeping most
generously. He was exactly the sort of companion Kaoru needed.
The sky misted over, as if it too understood. In the night a high
wind came up, and the bite in the air was like a return of winter.
They decided, after the lamp had blown out several times, that
darkness would do as well. Though of course it destroyed the
color of the blossoms,† it did not put an end to the conversation.
The hours passed, and still they had not talked themselves out.

'Ah, yes,' said Niou. 'Yes indeed – purity such as the world is
seldom privileged to behold. But come, now, surely it cannot have
been just that?'

He had a way of assuming that something had been left out, no
doubt because he suspected in others a volatility like his own. Yet
he was a man of sympathy and understanding. So skillfully did he
manage the conversation as he moved from subject to subject,
now seeking to console his friend, now seeking to make him forget, trying this way and that to offer an outlet for the pent-up
anguish – so skillfully that Kaoru, led on step by step, poured forth
the whole store of thoughts that had been too much for him. The
relief was enormous.

Niou told of his plans for bringing Nakanokimi into the city.

*Implying that not everything meets the eye in relations between Kaoru and Naka-
nokimi.

†See note*, page 587.

'I thoroughly approve. As a matter of fact, I had been blaming myself for her difficulties and telling myself that I ought to be looking after her as a sort of legacy of the one – I am repeating myself – I shall go on mourning forever. But it is so easy to be misunderstood.'

He went on to describe briefly how Oigimi had begged him to make no distinction between the two of them, and had asked him to marry her sister. He did not go so far as to speak of the night that called to mind the cuckoo of the grove of Iwase.*

In his heart, all the while, the chagrin and regret were mounting. He should himself have done as Niou was doing with the memento she had left behind. But it was too late. He was skirting dangerous ground, in the direction of which lay unpleasantness for everyone. He tried to think of other matters. Yet there was this consideration: who if not he was to take her father's place in arranging the move to the city? He turned his mind to the preparations.

At Uji, attractive women and girls were being added to Naka-nokimi's retinue, and the air was alive with anticipation. Nakano-kimi alone stood apart from it. Now that the time had come, the thought of abandoning this 'Fushimi' of hers,† letting it go to ruin, seemed intensely sad. Her sorrow would not end, but her pros-pects would be very poor indeed if she were to stand her ground and insist on staying in remote Uji. How could she even think, protested Niou, and there was much to be said for the view, of living in a place where the promises they had made must certainly be broken? It was a dilemma.

Finally the move was set for early in the Second Month. As the day approached, Nakanokimi looked out at the buds on the cherry trees, and thought how very difficult it would be to leave them,

---

*Apparently a poetic allusion. Both Iwase, in the province of Yamato, and the first two syllables of *yobukodori*, 'cuckoo,' can be understood as suggesting direct conver-sation rather than communication through an intermediary. The reference is clearly to the night Kaoru spent with Nakanokimi while Oigimi was playing 'the cricket.'

†Anonymous, *Kokinshū* 981:

> It is decided: here I shall live out my days.
> Else Fushimi of Sugawara will go to ruin.

Fushimi is another Yamato place name.

and the mountain mists too.* And she would be homeless, a lodger at an inn, facing she could not know what humiliation and ridicule. Each new thought, as she brooded the days away, brought new misgivings and reservations. She presently emerged from mourning, and the lustration seemed altogether too cursory and casual. She had not known her mother, and had not mourned for her. She thought how much she would have preferred to put on the deeper weeds with which one mourned a parent, but she kept the thought to herself, for it went against custom. Kaoru sent a carriage and outrunners for the lustration ceremony, and learned soothsayers as well.

He also sent a poem:

'How quickly time does pass. You made and donned
Your mourning robes, and now the blossoms open.'

And he sent numerous flowery robes, for the ceremony and for the move to the city, none of them gaudy or ostentatious, each appropriate to the rank of the recipient.

'You see how it is,' said the women to their mistress. 'He never misses a chance to show us he has not forgotten. How very kind of him. Even if you had a brother, we can assure you, he could not possibly do more for you.'

The older ones, no longer as interested in bright colors as they once had been, were moved by the kindness itself. And the younger ones said: 'He's been coming all these years, and now we're running off. She will miss him, make no mistake about that.'

On the day before the move, early in the morning, Kaoru appeared at Uji. Shown to the usual sitting room, he thought how Oigimi, had she lived, would by now have relented, and he would even now be setting an example for his friend Niou to follow. The image of the dead lady came back, and memories of things she had said. She had not really given herself to him, it was true, but neither had she put him off in a way that could be called cruel or insulting. He must continue to regret that his own eccentricities had helped keep the distance between them.

*Ise, Kokinshū 31:

Wild geese leaving the mists of spring behind them –
Is it that they prefer a blossomless land?

He went to the door and looked for the hole through which he had once peeped in upon the two sisters, but there were blinds and curtains beyond.

In the other room women were weeping softly and exchanging sad memories of their dead lady. The tears flowed on, and especially Nakanokimi's, as if to wash away murky forebodings.

As she lay gazing vacantly out at the garden, a message was brought from Kaoru: 'Memories of these months have no order and form, but they are more than I can keep to myself. It would be a very great comfort to let you have a tiny fragment of them. Do not, please, treat me with the coldness that has been yours in the past. You make me feel as if I had been banished to some remote island.'

'I certainly would not wish you to think me unkind,' she replied, though the effort was almost too much for her; 'but I am really not myself. Indeed, I am so unsettled that I fear I might say things both stupid and rude.'

But her women argued his case, and at length she received him at the door to her room. His good looks had always been somewhat intimidating, and she thought that he had improved and matured in the time since she had last seen him. Along with remarkable grace and elegance, he had an air of composure, of deliberation, such as few men could have imitated. Altogether a remarkable young man, and the knowledge that her sister had meant so much to him made the effect quite overpowering.

'It would be unlucky on such an occasion, I suppose, to speak of the lady I shall go on speaking of forever.' He broke off and began again. 'I shall soon be moving to a house not far from the one where you will be. "Any time of the day or night," the devotees and experts would say – but please do let me see you. I shall want to hear from you whenever I can be of service, and I shall be at your command for as long as I live. No two people are alike, of course, and it is possible that you find the prospect offensive. What might your own thoughts be?'

'I have not wanted to leave home, and I still do not want to. Now that you tell me you are moving too – my thoughts are too much for me. I am afraid I am not making sense.'

Her voice faltered, and her very evident distress so reminded him of her sister that he was left berating himself for having generously handed her over to Niou. But all that was past. He made no mention of their night together, and his frankness in other matters was almost enough to make her think he had forgotten. The scent and color of the rose plum below the veranda brought poignant memories. The warblers seemed unable to pass without a song; and this mark of 'the spring of old'* was the more moving for the memories they shared. The fragrance of the blossoms came in on the breeze to mingle with Kaoru's own fragrance. Orange blossoms could not have been more effective in summoning back the past.† Her sister, she remembered, had been especially fond of the plum blossom, and had made use of it for this or that little pleasantry, and sought consolation from it in difficult times as well. The memories too much for her, she recited a poem in a tiny voice that wavered at the point of disappearing:

'Here where no visitor comes save only the tempest,
    The scent of blossoms brings thoughts of days now gone.'

Kaoru whispered a reply:

'The fragrance lasts of the plum my sleeve has brushed.
    Uprooted now, must it dwell in a distant land?'

He brushed his tears away and left after a few words more. 'There will be chances, I am sure, for a good, quiet talk.'

He went out to give orders for the next day. Wigbeard and others would stay behind as caretakers; and (for nothing escaped his attention) he left orders with the people at his manor to see to their general needs.

Bennokimi had made it known that she would not go along. Through no desire of her own, she had lived this shamefully long life, and the others would think it bad luck to have an old crone with them; and so she had resolved that she was no longer to be considered a part of the world. Kaoru asked to see her. The nun's habit and tonsure again brought him to the point of tears.

They talked of old times. 'I shall of course be stopping by occasionally,' he concluded, his voice faltering, 'and I had feared that

---

*Ariwara Narihira, Kokinshū 747 and Tales of Ise 4:

    The moon, the spring, are the moon and spring of old.
    And only I remain as I was then.

†See note**, page 228.

no one would be here to receive me. I am sorry that you have decided to stay behind, but I know that you will be a great comfort.'

'I have lived too long. Life has a way of becoming more stubborn the more you hate it. I find it hard to forgive my older lady for leaving me behind, and though I know it is wrong of me I am resentful of the whole wide world.'*

She was becoming querulous, pouring forth the complaints as they came to her; but his efforts to comfort her were on the whole successful. Her hair still had traces of its youthful beauty, and her forehead, now shorn, seemed younger than before, and even somewhat distinguished. Overcome with longing for Oigimi, he asked why she could not have stayed with him even thus, as a nun. He might at least have had the comfort of quiet, leisurely conversation. Though the old woman was an improbable object for envy, he was somehow envious of her. He pulled her curtain slightly aside, that she might seem a little nearer. She really was very old, and yet her speech and manner aroused little of the revulsion one expects from advanced age. She must once have been a woman of considerable beauty.

Her face was contorted with sorrow.

'Tears came first. I should have flung myself into
    A stream of tears that would not have left me behind.'

'But that, of course, would have made the sin graver,' said Kaoru. 'People do sometimes reach the far shore, I suppose, but everything considered I doubt that you would have succeeded. We would not want to have lost you in midstream. No, you must remind yourself how empty and useless it all is.

'Deep though one plunges into the river of tears,
    One comes upon occasional snags of remembrance.

'When, I wonder, and where will there be relief?' But he knew the answer: never and nowhere.

He did not want to leave, though it was evening. But an unscheduled night's lodging might arouse suspicions. Presently he set out for the city.

*Ki no Tsurayuki, *Shūishū* 953:

> Left alone to think these dismal thoughts,
> I am resentful of the whole wide world.

She told the other women of his remarks, and her own grief was beyond consoling. She found them engrossed in preparations for their departure, oblivious to the incongruity their twisted old figures emphasized; and her nun's robes seemed drabber for all the happy confusion.

> 'And there they are, so busy getting ready,
>   And wet are the sleeves of the solitary fishwife.'

Nakanokimi answered:

> 'Is it drier, my sleeve, than the brine-wet sleeve of the fishwife?
>   Sodden it is, from the waves upon which it floats.*

'I do not expect to take to this new life. I may well be back after I have given it a try, and so I do not really feel that I am going away. We will meet again. But I do not like the thought of leaving you here by yourself for even a little while. Nuns do not have to cut themselves off completely, you know. Do as all of them do – come and see me occasionally.'

Affection welled up as she spoke. She had arranged to leave behind such of her sister's combs and brushes as she thought a nun could use.

'You seem so much more deeply affected than the others,' she went on. 'It makes me feel sure that there was a bond between us in another life. And you seem even nearer now.'

The old woman was weeping quite helplessly, like a child that has lost its mother.

The rooms were swept, things put away, carriages drawn up. Among the outrunners were numbers of medium-ranking courtiers. Niou had wanted desperately to come for her himself. Since unnecessary display was to be avoided, however, he ordered that the procession be a quiet one, and, intensely impatient, awaited her at Nijō. Kaoru too had sent retainers in large numbers. Niou had taken care of the broader plans and Kaoru of all the small and intimate details. Nakanokimi's women joined the men from the city in warning her that it would soon be dark. Utterly confused, scarcely knowing in which direction the city lay, she finally got into a carriage. She was all alone, and defenseless.

Beside her, a woman called Tayū was smiling happily.

---

*She intimates that she is being borne along by a current (of Niou's engineering) that will presently cast her aside.

'You have lived to come upon these joyous days,
   And are you not glad Old Gloomy* did not get you?'

Nakanokimi was not pleased. What a vast difference, she thought, between this person and the nun Bennokimi.

Another woman had a poem ready:

'We do not forget to look back at one now gone;
   But this day, of all, our hearts must look ahead.'

Both of them had long been in service at Uji, and both had seemed fond of Oigimi. And now they had left her behind. The very fact that they refrained from mentioning her name added to Nakanokimi's bitterness and sorrow. She did not answer.

The road was long and it led through precipitous mountains. She had been deeply resentful of Niou's neglect, but now she began to see why his visits had been infrequent. The bright half-moon was softened and made more mysteriously beautiful by a mist. Unaccustomed to travel, alone with her thoughts, she was soon exhausted.

'The moon comes forth from the mountain upon a world
   That offers no home. It goes again to the mountain.'

The future was too uncertain. What would become of her if anything in this precarious balance should change? She longed to return to days when, she knew now, she had been very silly to feel sorry for herself.

It was late in the night when they arrived at the Nijō mansion. The splendor quite blinded her. The carriage was pulled up at one of the 'threefold, fourfold' halls,† and an impatient Niou came out. Her apartments, she saw, and those of her attendants as well, were beautifully appointed. They had obviously benefited from Niou's personal attention. No detail had been overlooked.

It was matter for much astonishment that he who had been the cause of so many rumors and worries should now, quite suddenly, have found himself a wife. There was nothing ambiguous about what had happened *this* time, people said, hoping for a glimpse of the hidden princess.

---

*The common pun on *ushi*, 'gloomy' and 'Uji.'
†A reference to the Saibara 'This House.' See note*, page 435.

Kaoru was to move into his Sanjō mansion, now near completion, towards the end of the month. He went every day to see how it was progressing. Since Nijō was not far away, he mounted a lookout to see how things would be with Nakanokimi. Presently the men he had sent to Uji came back to report that Niou seemed much taken with the lady, and had been very attentive. Kaoru was pleased, of course; and at the same time he felt a wave of something like resentment. It was senseless, he knew, for his circumstances had, after all, been of his own devising.

'Might I have it back again?'* he whispered to himself.

'The boat setting forth on the undulant Lake of Loons,
    Though badly rigged, did somehow make a landfall.'†

Yūgiri had fixed upon this month for marrying his daughter Rokunokimi to Niou. And now, quite as if to announce that he had priorities of his own, Niou had brought a stranger into his house. Worse, he had stopped calling at Rokujō. Niou felt a little guilty at news of his uncle's displeasure, and sent a note to Rokunokimi from time to time. The whole world knew that plans were being rushed ahead for her initiation, and to postpone it would be to invite derision; and so it took place toward the end of the month. Yūgiri thought of marrying her to Kaoru instead, unexciting though a wedding within the family would be. It seemed a pity to let someone else have him. He was evidently grieving for a lady he had loved in secret over the years. Through a suitable agent, Yūgiri sought to determine how he might respond to a proposal.

The answer was not encouraging. 'I know how useless and insubstantial things are. I have had evidence before my very eyes, such strong evidence that my own existence seems stupid and even revolting.'

Yūgiri was deeply offended. Could the young man not see that the proposal had been a difficult one to make? But Kaoru was not a man with whom even an older brother took liberties, and Yūgiri made no further advances.

*Apparently a poetic allusion.
†A highly contrived and not entirely lucid poem. The Lake of Loons is Biwa. The meaning would seem to be: 'I may not have succeeded in consummating the union, but we did spend that night together.'

Gazing in the direction of the Nijō mansion, where the cherries were in full bloom, Kaoru thought of the cherries, now masterless, at the Uji villa. He might have gone on to ask how they would be responding to the winds, but the old poem* did not offer much comfort.

He went to visit Niou, who was spending most of his time at Nijō and seemed to have settled down happily with his princess. Kaoru had no further cause, it would seem, for worry. That other strange question persisted all the same: why had he brought them together? But his deeper feelings were wholly admirable. He rejoiced that Nakanokimi's affairs had turned out well. The two friends talked of various small matters, and presently, in the evening, servants came to prepare the carriage that was to take Niou to court. A large retinue assembled. Kaoru withdrew to Nakanokimi's wing of the house.

The rude life of the mountain village had been changed for richly curtained luxury. Catching a glimpse of a pretty little girl, Kaoru asked her to convey word of his presence. He was offered a cushion, and a woman apparently familiar with the events at Uji came to bring Nakanokimi's reply.

'I am so near,' he said, admitted to her presence, 'that I was sure it would be like having you beside me all hours of the day and night; but I have had to keep my distance. I have not wanted to intrude, and I have had no real business. Somehow things seem utterly changed. From my garden I look through the mists at the trees in yours, and they bring the fondest memories.'

He fell silent, lost in the memories. It was true, thought Nakanokimi: if Oigimi had lived, they would be visiting each other, she and her sister, and finding their happiness, as the seasons went by, in the same blossoms, the same songs of birds. The sadness, the longing, the regrets were even sharper than they had been at Uji, far away from the world.

'My lady, my lady,' urged her women. 'He is *not* an ordinary guest. He has done everything for you, and now is the time to let him see that you are grateful.'

But Nakanokimi could not bring herself to address him directly.

*Egyō, *Shūishū* 62:

> The cherries in bloom by the house on the sparse-reeded plain
> Are masterless and heedlessly fall in the breeze.

Presently Niou, a splendid figure in full court regalia, came to say goodbye. 'Well, now. There he is sitting outside all by himself. It seems very odd, really after all you owe him. I am the one who should be afraid of him, and here I am telling you how rude and even sinful it is not to invite him inside. Be a little friendlier, have a good talk about the old days.' And abruptly he reversed himself: 'Of course I wouldn't want you to let him have too free a rein. You can never be quite sure what he is up to.'

And so she was left not knowing what to do. She was in Kaoru's debt, that much was clear, for he had been very kind; and she could not dismiss him. He had ventured a hope that she might in some measure fill the emptiness left by her sister. She would ask the same of him. She did want him to know that she understood. But the situation was certainly awkward, with Niou casting these insinuations about.

CHAPTER 49

The Ivy

Among the emperor's consorts was a daughter of a Minister of the Left* who was known as the wisteria lady. She was the earliest of the royal consorts to be presented at court. The emperor, then the crown prince, was very fond of her, even though the more obvious signs of his affection† were somehow wanting. Through the years when his numerous children by the empress‡ were one after another reaching adulthood, she gave birth to only one child, a daughter, who was of course the center of her life. It had been fated that she lose out to a rival, she told herself, and she found consolation in the thought of seeing her daughter succeed where she had failed. The emperor too was fond of the child, a very pretty girl; but the First Princess had a stronger hold on his affection, and this Second Princess** was far from as conspicuous a public figure. Still she had no reason to feel neglected. The legacy from the minister's great days still largely intact, her mother was by no means a pauper. She maintained an elegant and fashionable household, and her women, after their several ranks, dressed for the passing seasons in the most unexceptionable taste.

It was decided that the princess's initiation ceremonies would be held in the early months of her fourteenth year. Plans for them occupied the whole of the mother's attention. She was determined that every detail be correct and yet somehow different. Ancient heirlooms from the late minister's family were brought out and the bustle and stir were such as the house had not seen before. And then in the summer she fell victim to an evil possession, and was gone almost before anyone knew that she was ill. The emperor was desolate, though of course he could do nothing. The grand

---

*Not otherwise identified. The end of Chapter 46 and the beginning of this chapter seem to be synchronous.

†He did not make her his empress.

‡Genji's daughter, Niou's mother.

**Not to be confused with an earlier 'Second Princess,' daughter of the Suzaku emperor and wife of Kashiwagi and Yūgiri.

courtiers agreed that it was a sad loss, for she had been a gentle, sensitive lady; and maids of such low rank that they scarcely had a right to mourn joined the emperor in his grief.

The Second Princess was now alone. The emperor quietly summoned her to the palace when the memorial rites were over, and every day he visited her rooms. The dark robes of mourning and a certain wanness from grief only added to her beauty. Mature for her years, she had a quiet dignity that made her perhaps even a little superior to her mother. And so her position might on the surface have seemed secure. The facts were rather different. She had no maternal uncles to whom she could turn for support. One could find among her mother's half brothers a treasury secretary and a superintendent of palace repairs, but they were very inconspicuous. They would not be much help to the princess in the difficulties that lay ahead, and considerable difficulties they promised to be. The emperor was almost as apprehensive as the princess herself.

He came calling one day when the chrysanthemums, tinged by the frost, were at their best and sad autumn showers were falling. They talked of the wisteria lady. The girl's answers, calm and at the same time very youthful, quite delighted him. Was there no one who was capable of appreciating her many virtues and might be persuaded to look after her? He remembered the deliberations and the final decision when the Suzaku emperor had entrusted his daughter* to Genji. There had been those who argued that it was improper for a princess of the blood to marry a commoner and that she would do better to remain single. And now she had an unusually talented son who was the strongest support a mother could hope for, and no one could have said that she had slipped in the smallest degree from her high position. Had it not been for her marriage to Genji, she might have come upon sad days, no one could guess of what description, and she had her marriage to thank that the world still respected her. Worrying the problem over, the emperor concluded that he must see to the Second Princess's future while he still occupied the throne. And where could he find a more appropriate candidate for her hand than Kaoru, a better

---

*The Third Princess, Kaoru's mother and the present emperor's sister.

solution than to follow in the second generation the precedent of the first? Ranged beside other royal consorts, he would not seem in the least out of place. There did appear, it was true, to be someone of whom he was fond, but he was not a man likely to let any breath of scandal damage his relations with the Second Princess. And of course it was unthinkable that he would remain forever single. He must give some hint of his feelings, the emperor told himself over and over again, before the young man forestalled him by taking a wife.

In the evening, as he and the Second Princess were at a game of Go, a shower passed and the chrysanthemums caught the light of the autumn sunset.

The emperor summoned a page.

'Who is in attendance upon us tonight?'

'His Highness the minister of central affairs, His Highness Prince Kanzuke,* and Lord Minamoto, the councillor, are with us, Your Majesty.'

'Call the last, if you will.'

Kaoru came as ordered. The emperor's choice was not surprising. Everything about the young man was remarkable, even the fragrance that announced his approach.

'Such gentle showers as we are having tonight. They cry out for music; but of course our mourning would not permit it. I can think of no better a pursuit 'for whiling away the days' than a game of Go.'†

He pulled up a Go board. Used to these companionable services, Kaoru settled down for a game.

'There is something I might wager,' said the emperor, 'but I am not quite sure that I have the courage. Let me see, now – what else might there be?'

Immediately guessing what he meant, Kaoru played very soberly. The emperor lost the third game.

---

*Neither of these princes is otherwise identified.

†Po Chü-i, Collected Works, XVI, 'In Idleness':

> We have only wine for sending off the spring.
> There is nothing better than Go for whiling away the days.

'How very disappointing. Well, I will let you break off a blossom.* Go choose one, if you will.'

Kaoru went down into the garden and broke off one of the finer chrysanthemums. Returning, he offered a cautious verse:

'If I had found it at a common hedge,
    I might have plucked it quite to suit my fancy.'

The emperor replied:

'A single chrysanthemum, left in a withered garden,
    Withstands the frost, its color yet unfaded.'

There were such hints from time to time, some through intermediaries. Kaoru was not one to rush in headlong pursuit. He had no compelling desire to marry, and through the years he had turned aside hopeful talk of more than one deprived though attractive young lady. It would not do for the hermit to talk now (an odd way, perhaps, to put the matter) of going back into business; and surely there would be any number of young men willing to brush aside all other commitments in their eagerness to do what they could for a royal princess. He suspected that, in his own case, the conclusions might be somewhat different were the princess one of the empress's daughters; but he quickly put the thought away as unworthy.

Yūgiri had vague reports of what was taking place, and was much annoyed. He had had ideas of his own: Kaoru might not be as consumed with ardor as one might hope, but he could not in the end refuse if Yūgiri were to press his case. And now this strange development. Yūgiri's thoughts turned once again to Niou. It would have been sheer self-deception to credit Niou with great steadfastness, but he had continued all the while to send amusing and interesting little notes to Yūgiri's daughter Rokunokimi. Though people were no doubt right to call him a trifler, fate had dictated stranger things than that he fix his affections upon

*Ki no Tadana, *Wakan Rōeishū* 784, in Chinese:

In yon garden, one hears, are the fairest of flowers.
Allow me to break off a blossom of spring.

Since the 'blossom' is a lady whose hand the poet is seeking, the emperor is offering a very broad hint.

Rokunokimi. Impassioned vows, impermeable, watertight vows,* so to speak, often enough led to disappointment and humiliation when the man was not of grand enough rank.

'What sad days we have come upon,' said Yūgiri. 'Even monarchs must go out begging for sons-in-law. Think how we commoners must worry as we see our daughters passing their prime.'

Though circumspect in his criticism of the emperor, he was otherwise so outspoken with his sister, the empress, that she felt constrained to pass at least a part of his complaints on to Niou:

'I do feel sorry for him, you know. He has been after you for a year and more, knowing quite well what sort of cooperation he can expect from you. You have spent the whole year dashing madly in the other direction, not very good evidence, I must say, of warmth and kindness. And you must remember that a good marriage is very important for someone like you. Your father begins to talk of leaving the throne, and – ordinary people are expected to be satisfied with only one wife, I suppose, but even with them – look at my brother himself, such a model of propriety, and still able to manage two wives without offending anyone. Just let things work themselves out as we hope they will, and you can have any number you like. No one will have the smallest objection.'

She was not a loquacious woman, and it had been a remarkable speech; and it did have a reasonable sound to it.

Never having disliked Rokunokimi, Niou did not want to answer in a way that seemed to slam all the doors; but the prospect of being imprisoned in that excessively decorous household, of forgoing the freedom that was now his, made the proposed match seem unbearably drab. He could not, all the same, deny that his mother's remarks were very sensible, most particularly those about the folly of alienating important people who wished to become one's in-laws. He was caught in a dilemma. And then too there was his tendency to spread his affections generously, and the fact that he still had not found it possible to forget Kōbai's stepdaughter.† As the seasons presented occasions, the flowers of spring and the autumn leaves, he still sent her letters, and he would

See note, page 558.
†See Chapter 43.

have had to include both of them, Rokunokimi and Kōbai's daughter, on the list of those whom he found not uninteresting.

And so the New Year came.* The Second Princess having put away her robes of mourning, there was no longer a need for reticence in the matter of her marriage.

'The indications are,' someone said to Kaoru, 'that the emperor would not be unfriendly to a proposal.'

Kaoru could have feigned ignorance, but he was quite well enough known already for eccentricity and brusqueness. Summoning up his resolve, he found occasion from time to time to hint that he was interested. The emperor of course had no reason to reject these overtures, and presently Kaoru was informed, again through intermediaries, that a date had been set. Though he was altogether in sympathy with the troubled emperor, his life was still haunted by a sense of emptiness, and he still found it impossible to accept the fact that so apparently strong a bond should in the end have snapped like a thread. He knew that he would be drawn to a girl, even a girl of humble birth, who resembled Oigimi. If only he could, like that Chinese emperor,† have a glimpse through magic incense of his lost love! He was in no great rush to wed this royal lady.

Yūgiri *was* in a rush. He suggested to Niou that the Eighth Month might be appropriate for his marriage to Rokunokimi.

So it had happened, thought Nakanokimi, learning of these events. What was she to do? She had passed her days in anticipation of just such gloomy news, which would make her the laughing-stock of the whole world. She had had little confidence in Niou from the start, having heard of his promiscuous ways, and yet when she had come to know him somewhat better she had found him altogether gentle and considerate, and given to the most ardent protestations of eternal love. And now this sudden change – could she be expected to receive it with equanimity? Their union would not be dissolved, obliterated, as she might have had cause to fear had she been of meaner birth, but the future seemed to offer only worries and more worries. No doubt she was fated to go back to the mountains one day. Her thoughts ran on, chasing one another in circles. She was certain that she was at

---

*We are now up to the spring of Chapter 48.

†Han Wu-ti. See note*, page 929.

length facing the punishment she deserved for having gone against her father's wishes and left her mountain home. Better to vanish quite away than to go back now and face the derision of the rustics among whom she had lived. Her sister had seemed weak and indecisive, but a formidable strength had lain beneath the vacillating surface. Though Kaoru seemed to go on grieving, no doubt Oigimi, if she had lived, would have had to face what she herself now faced. Determined that nothing of the sort would happen to her, Oigimi had made use of every possible device, even the threat of becoming a nun, to keep him at a distance. And no doubt she would have carried out the threat. Had hers not been, in retrospect, determination of the very highest order? And so both of them, her father and her sister, thought Nakanokimi, would now be looking down from the heavens and sighing over her stupidity and heedlessness. She was sad and she was ashamed; but it would do no good to show her thoughts. She managed to get through her days with no sign that she had heard the news.

Niou was gentler and more affectionate than ever. At her side constantly, he sought to comfort her. He made promises for this life and for all the lives to come. He had noticed from about the Fifth Month that she was in some physical distress. There were no violent or striking symptoms; but she had little appetite and seemed to spend a great deal of time resting. Not having been familiar with other women in a similar condition, he told himself that the warm weather could be troublesome. Yet certain suspicions did cross his mind.

'Might it just be possible? I believe I have heard descriptions of something of the sort.'

Nakanokimi blushed and insisted that nothing was amiss; and since no one among her women was prepared to step forward with the information he needed, he was left with his own speculations.

The Eighth Month came, and people told her that the day had been set for the wedding. Niou himself had no particular wish to keep the information from her, but each time an opportunity came to tell her he found himself falling mute. His silence made things worse. The whole world knew, and he had not had the courtesy even to inform her of the date. Did she not have a right to be angry? It had been his practice not to spend his nights in the palace unless the findings of the soothsayers or other unusual circumstances made it necessary. Nor had he been busy, as in earlier years, with nocturnal adventures. Now he began to spend an occasional night at court, hoping to prepare her for the absences which the new arrangements would make necessary. This foresight did not make him seem kinder.

Kaoru felt very sorry for her indeed. Niou, given his bright, somewhat showy nature, was certain to be drawn to the more modish and accomplished Rokunokimi, however fond he might be of Nakanokimi. And with that formidable family of hers mounting guard over him, Nakanokimi would be doomed to lonely nights such as she had not known before. An utterly heart-breaking situation, everything considered. And how useless he was himself! Why had he given her away? His spirit had been serene in its renunciation of the world until he had been drawn to Oigimi, and he had let it be stirred and muddied. He had managed to con-trol himself despite the intensity of his devotion, for it would have gone against his original intentions to force himself upon her. He had continued to hope, looking towards a day when he might arouse even a faint response in her and see her heart open even a little. Though everything indicated that her own wishes were very different, he had still found comfort in her apparent inability to send him on his way. She had sought to interest him in her sister, with whom, she had said, she shared a single being. He had sought with unnecessary haste, by way of retaliation, to push Nakanokimi into Niou's arms. In a strong fit of pique he had taken Niou off to Uji and made all the arrangements for him. What an irremediable blunder it had been! And as for Niou — if he remembered a small fraction of Kaoru's troubles in those days, ought he not to be a little concerned about Kaoru's feelings today? Triflers, woman-chasers were not for women to rely upon — not, indeed, for anyone to have much faith in. A farsighted sort of protector Kaoru himself had been! No doubt his way of riveting his attention on a single object seemed strange and reprehensible to most people. Having lost his first love, he was less than delighted at having a bride bestowed upon him by the emperor himself, and every day and every month his longing for Nakanokimi grew. This deplor-able inability to accept his loss had to do with the fact that Oigimi and Nakanokimi had been close as sisters seldom are. With almost her last breath Oigimi had asked him to think of her sister as he had thought of her. She left behind no regrets to tie her to the world, she had said, save that he had gone against her wishes in this one matter. And now, the crisis having come, she would be looking down from the heavens in anger. All through the lonely nights, for which he had no one to blame but himself, he would awaken at the rising of the gentlest breeze, and over and over again he would run through a list of complications from the past and worries for the future that were not, strictly speaking, his own. He had dallied with this or that lady from time to time, and even now there were several in his household whom he had no reason at all to dislike; but not one of them had held his attention for more than a moment. There were others, ladies of royal lineage to whom the times had not been kind and who now lived in poverty and neglect. Several such ladies had been taken in by his mother, but they had not shaken his determination to be without regrets when the time came to leave the world.

One morning, after a more than usually sleepless night, he looked out into the garden, and his eye was caught by morning glories, fragile and uncertain, in among the profusion of dew-soaked flowers at the hedge. 'They bloom for the morning,'* he whispered to himself, the evanescence of the flowers matching his own sense of futility. He lay hoping for a little rest as the shutters were raised, and watched on, alone, as the morning glories opened.

'Please have a carriage brought out, one that won't attract much attention,' he said to a servant. 'I want to go to the Nijō house.'

'But Prince Niou was at the palace all night, my lord. Some men brought his carriage back later in the evening.'

'I want to ask after the princess. I've heard that she is not well. I will be at the palace myself later in the day. Be quick about it, please. I want to get started not too long after sunrise.'

His toilet finished, he stepped down into the garden and wandered among the flowers for a time. There was nothing gaudy or obviously contrived about his dress, but he had a calm dignity that was almost intimidating. It was a manner profoundly his own, for he was not one to strut and preen. Pulling a tendril toward him, he saw that it was still wet with dew.

'It lasts, I know, but as long as the dew upon it.
  Yet am I drawn to the hue that fades with the morning.

*Apparently a poetic allusion.

How very quickly it goes.'

He broke it off to take with him, and left without a glance for the saucy maiden flowers.

The sun was rising as he approached the Nijō mansion, and the skies were hazy from the dew. He began to fear that he had come too early and that the women would still be snoring away. Disliking the thought of anything so unsubtle as coughing to attract attention or pounding on doors or shutters, he sent one of his men to look in at the garden gate. The shutters were up, it seemed, and there were women astir. At the sight of a stately figure approaching through the mists, the women assumed that their master was back from his nocturnal wanderings. But that remarkable scent, made stronger by the dew, quickly informed them of the truth, and soon the younger ones were commenting upon it. Yes, he was terribly nice – but so cool and distant – in that respect not very nice at all, really. They were women who knew what was expected of them, however, and the soft rustle of silk as they pushed a cushion out to him was not unpleasing.

'You almost make me feel like a human being,' he said to Nakanokimi, 'but here I am still on the outside. Try to make me feel a little more at home, or I will not be coming often.'

And what now? the women were asking.

'Might there be a quiet retreat somewhere, perhaps off far in the north, where an old man might take his ease? If something of the sort is what you have in mind, well, so be it.' He was at the door to the inner rooms.

The women persuaded her to go a bit nearer. He had never shown a sign of the impetuousness one expects in young men, and his deportment had of late seemed even calmer and more restrained than before. Her shyness was leaving her. Indeed, they had become rather friendly.

He asked what might be ailing her. The answer came with great hesitation, and a silence that seemed protracted even for her made it easy to guess what the trouble was (and this new knowledge added to the sadness). He set about advising and comforting her, as if he were a brother. Choosing his words very carefully, he told her what marriage is. The voices of the sisters had not seemed alike, but now he found the resemblance astonishing, as if Oigimi had come back. Had it not been for these curious attendants, he would have been tempted to lift the blind and go inside, to be nearer a lady more appealing for the fact that she was unwell. Did no man escape the pangs of love? It was a question that brought its own answer.

'I had always said that a man may not get everything he wants in this world, but he should try to make his way through it without fretting and worrying, without whining about the many frustrations. Now I see that there are defeats and losses that permit no peace, not a moment free of stupid regrets. People who put a high value on rank and position and the like, I can see now, have every right to complain when things are not going well for them. I am sure that my own shortcomigns are worse.'

He gazed at the morning glory, which he had laid on his fan. It took on a reddish tinge as it withered, and a strange new beauty. He thrust it under the blind, and softly recited a poem:

'Should I have taken the proffered morning glory
    With the silver dew, the blessing, still upon it?'

He had made no special effort to preserve the dew, but he was pleased that it should still be there – that the flower should fade away fresh with dew.

'Forlorn the flower that fades with the dew upon it.
    Yet more forlorn the dew that is left behind.

Where would you have me turn?'*

She was so like her sister as she offered this gentlest of reproofs! Her voice trailed into silence.

'It is a sad season, the saddest of the year, I think. I went off to Uji the other day, hoping to shake off a little of the gloom, but it made me even sadder to see how "garden and fence" had gone to ruin.† I was reminded of how it was after my father died. People who had been fond of him would go and look in on the places, the house in Saga‡ and the house in Rokujō and the others, where he

---

*The last words suggest a poetic allusion, but it has not been traced.

†Henjō, *Kokinshū* 248:

> Wasted the dwelling, the dweller left to grow old.
> Garden and fence become an autumn moor.

‡Long thought to have been on the grounds or in the vicinity of the present Daikakuji, which occupies the site of a villa built by the emperor Saga.

was in retirement the last few years of his life. I would go back to Sanjō myself after a look at those trees and grasses, and the tears would be streaming from my eyes. He had been careful to have only sensitive people near him, and the women who had served him were scattered over the city, most of them in seclusion. A few unfortunate ones from the lower classes went quite mad with grief, and ran off into the mountains and forests, where you would not have been able to tell them from mountain people. At Rokujō the "grasses of forgetfulness"* took over. And then my brother, the minister, moved in, and there were princes and princesses there again, and soon it was as lively as ever. I told myself that time took care of everything, that a day would come for the most impossible sorrows to go away; and it did seem to be true that everything had its limits. So I said; but I was young then, and quick to recover. I have now had two great lessons in impermanence, and the more recent one has left a wound I am not likely to recover from. Indeed it makes me rather apprehensive about the world to come. I feel sure I will take along a considerable store of dissatisfaction and regret.'

Tears emphasized his point, as if he had not made it well enough already. Even a lady who had not been close to Oigimi would have found them hard to resist; as for Nakanokimi, the grief and longing and uncertainty she had been so unsuccessful at shaking off quite engulfed her again. She finally succumbed to tears. Far from comforting each other, they only seemed to reopen old wounds.

' "The mountain village is lonely"† – you know the poem they are all so fond of. I never quite saw what it meant. And here I am now, longing for just such a quiet place, away from all this, and I cannot have it. Bennokimi was right to stay behind. How I wish I had had her good sense. The anniversary of Father's death will be coming at the end of the month. It would be so good to hear those bells again. As a matter of fact, I had been thinking I might ask you to take me there for a few days. We needn't tell anyone.'

'I know. You don't want the house going to ruin. But I'm afraid it would be quite impossible. Even a man without baggage

---

*Wasuregusa, day lily.

†Anonymous, Kokinshū 944:

> The mountain village is lonely, that I know,
> But I think it a friendlier world than this world of affairs.

has a time getting over those mountains. Weeks and months go by between my own visits, and I am forever thinking I ought to go. The abbot has all the instructions he needs for the services. But now that you mention it, I had been worrying about the house myself. Would you consider turning it over to the monastery? The sight of it upsets me terribly, and you know how unfortunate attachments of that sort are. Might we get it off our minds? It is for you to decide, of course – your wishes are my own, and my only real wish is for you to be frank with me. Do let me know, please, what you would like to have done.'

Suddenly he had become practical. She had thought, apparently, to offer images and scrolls of her own, and to make the memorial services her excuse for a few quiet days at Uji.

'Impossible, quite impossible. Do, I beg of you, try to keep yourself from worrying about these things.'

The sun was higher, the women were assembling, and if he were to stay longer he would arouse suspicions.

'I am not used to being kept at quite such a distance, and I am not at all comfortable. But I shall come again.'

It would be out of character for Niou not to ask questions. To forestall them, Kaoru looked in upon Niou's chamberlain, who was also one of the city magistrates.

'I had been told that the prince came back from the palace last night, and was disappointed to find him still away. I am going to the palace myself.'

'He left word that he would be back today.'

'I see. I will try to stop by this evening.'

Each interview with Nakanokimi, such a paragon of elegance and sensibility, left him regretting more than ever that he had so freely renounced his claims. Why had he felt constrained to go against Oigimi's wishes? Why had he been so assiduous in seeking out unhappiness, making doubly sure that he had no one to reprove but himself? He turned more than ever to fasting and meditation. His mother, though still girlish and not much given to worry, was upset.

'I do not mean to live forever, as they say,* and it would be a

---

*Anonymous, *Kokinshū* 934:

> I do not mean to live forever; then why
> Must my thoughts be the tangle of weeds the fisherfolk take?

great comfort to see you behaving like other boys. I am a nun and in no position to stop you if you are absolutely set on running away from the world; but I rather imagine that I will have certain regrets when my time comes.'

Not wanting to upset her further, he tried to make it seem that he had not a care in the world.

Yūgiri meanwhile had refurbished the northeast quarter at Rokujō, exhausting his very considerable resources to make it acceptable to the most demanding of bridegrooms. The moon of the sixteenth night had long since risen and still Yūgiri and his family waited. All very embarrassing, thought Yūgiri as he sent off a messenger. The evidence was too clear that the match had failed to delight Niou.

'He left the palace earlier in the evening,' reported the man, 'and it is said that he went back to Nijō.'

Yūgiri was not at all pleased. Ordinary decency asked that this night of all nights the prince put other women from his thoughts. But the world would be all too ready to laugh if they passed the night in waiting, and so he sent off a message to Nijō with one of his sons, a guards captain:

'Even the moon deigns to come to this dwelling of mine.
The night draws on, we await a sign of you.'

Niou had not wished to upset Nakanokimi further by having her see him depart for Rokujō. He therefore sent a message from the palace; but her reply, whatever it might have been, seems to have given him pause. He did, after all, slip off to Nijō. Once there, he felt no need for other company. The captain arrived as the two of them were looking out at the moon and Niou, seeking desperately to comfort her, was pouring forth a stream of vows. Determined not to let her unhappiness show, she managed an appearance of composure and serenity. Her refusal to chide him was far more moving than clear evidence of injured feelings could possibly have been. The arrival of the captain reminded him that the girl at Rokujō might be unhappy too.

'I shall be back in no time. You are not to sit here looking at the moon.* And you must remember how empty the hours will be

*Both Chinese and Japanese authorities confirm that a lady who gazes at the moon invites untimely wrinkles.

until I am with you again.' A most uncomfortable situation, he said to himself as he made his way to the main hall by an inconspicuous route.

Meanwhile, her eyes on the retreating figure, Nakanokimi was telling herself that a lady did not surrender to unworthy emotions. Her pillow might threaten to float away,* but her heart must be kept under tight control.

Fate had been unkind to them, to her sister and her, from the outset. They had had only their father, a man intent upon cutting his ties with the world. Life in the mountains had been lonely and monotonous, but she had not known as she now knew the deep cruelty of the world. There had been the one death and then the other. Not wanting to linger for even a moment after her father and sister, she had deceived herself into thinking that such grief and longing must be unique. But she had lived on, and had come to be treated rather more like a human being than, in the circumstances, one might have expected. Though she had tried to tell herself that this happiness could not last, there Niou had been beside her, the most endearing of men, and the worry and sorrow had gradually subsided. How very ironical that the healing powers of time should have left her all the less prepared for this new shock. It was the end.

Would she not see him from time to time? – for he had not, after all, departed the world. Yet his behavior tonight threw everything, past and future, into a meaningless jumble, and her efforts to find a light through the gloom were unavailing. There would be a change of some sort if she but lived long enough, she told herself over and over again, knowing that to give up would indeed be the end. Her anguish, as the night drew on, had for company the rising moon, the clear moon, 'of the Mount of Women Forsaken.'†

See note, page 247.

†Anonymous, *Kokinshū* 878:

> Beyond consoling, I look upon this moon
> Of the Mount of Women Forsaken, in Sarashina.

Several hills are called Obasuteyama, literally 'the mountain where old women are thrown away.' The most famous is in the Sarashina district of Shinano Province.

To one who knew the wild winds from the mountains of Uji, the pine breeze here was gentleness itself; but tonight she would have preferred the wind through those oaks.

> 'Never, beneath the pines of that mountain village,
>   Did I know the autumn winds to lash at me so.'

So it is that ancient miseries cease to be real.

'Do please come inside, my lady. You mustn't sit there looking up at the moon. And what will become of you if you go on refusing to eat? You haven't touched a thing in days.'

And the women talked among themselves: 'It drives a person frantic. Especially a person that's seen what can happen when a lady won't eat.' Loud sighs punctuated these remarks. 'Things seemed to be going so well. But he won't *leave* her, surely he won't. Yes, I agree with you. Things could be better. But you don't mean to tell me love like that just goes away?'

Nakanokimi heard it all, and wished that they would be quiet. Far better to watch and wait. It may have been, of course, that she did not want to risk diluting her resentment by sharing it with others.

Women who knew of the events leading up to Oigimi's death had cause to wonder at the erratic ways of fate. The other young gentleman had been so good about waiting on their other young lady; and just see how he had been rewarded!

Niou was troubled, but only briefly. Exciting affairs near at hand had the power to distract him, and soon he was lost in preparations to charm his new lady and her family. He had a catching new perfume burnt into his robes, and set forth most grandly. At Rokujō everything was more than ready. Niou's first impression of his bride was that she was rather ample, not at all the fragile thing he had somehow expected. And what of her disposition? Might she be noisy, gaudy, aggressive, a touch masculine, even? None of these qualities would have pleased him. But she proved to be receptive to his attentions, and he became quite engrossed in them. The autumn night (he had been tardy) was over in a trice.

Back at Nijō the next morning, he did not call upon Nakanokimi immediately. After resting for a time in the main hall, he got off the morning-after note that would be expected at Rokujō.

The women were nudging one another. 'You can see he wasn't disappointed. And there *she* is, poor dear, over there all by herself.

For all I know, he may be able to take care of all the women under the sun, but she has real competition on her hands.' They knew the household well, and among them were some who were not prepared to hold back their thoughts about the trials that beset its new mistress.

Niou would have liked to wait in the main hall until a reply came from Rokujō. But he knew that last night would have been far more of a trial for Nakanokimi than his nights at court. He hurried to her wing of the house, a brisk and dashing figure once more, refreshed now from sleep. He found Nakanokimi resting. She raised herself shyly to an elbow. Weeping had added a touch of wistfulness to her beauty. He gazed at her for a time, choked with tears. As she looked away in embarrassment, her hair fell over her shoulders in a strong, graceful flow, lovelier than anything he had ever seen.

He too was somewhat confused, and affectionate words gave way to talk of more practical matters. 'What can be the matter with you? Nothing but the heat, you have said, and so I have waited for the cool weather. Well, here it is, and you still are not yourself. You upset me a great deal, really you do. I have ordered all the prayers that usually work. Maybe we should give them another try. Isn't there a priest somewhere who can give us a guarantee? Maybe we should have that bishop, what was his name, come down and stay with you.'

Yes, he was clever. She was not pleased, but felt that she had to answer. 'I have known all along that I am not like other people. It is nothing new. Give it time, and it will go away.'

'How sure of yourself you are!' He smiled. There was no one like her for delighting with sheer gentleness. And that thought led to a more exciting one, for he had not forgotten his other lady. Yet no one would have judged from the appearances that he was any less fond of Nakanokimi than he had always been. His vows of steadfastness in this life and the next went on and on, and even became somewhat repetitious.

'I shall not stay forever,' she was thinking.* 'Even while I wait

---

*It is possible to argue that she actually gives voice to this and the following thoughts. Whether part of a soliloquy or of a speech, the opening words have reference to a poem by Taira Sadafumi, *Kokinshū* 965:

> Life will end, I shall not stay forever.
> Waiting, I would be free of these myriad sorrows.

I am not likely to escape his cruelty; and so, precisely because my hopes for the next world are dim, I must turn to him again, unchastened, in this one.'*

Thus she fought to hold back the tears, but today she was not up to the effort. She had done everything these last days to keep her thoughts to herself. She had not wanted him to know that he had hurt her. But too many sad thoughts came pouring in at once, and after the first tears the flow was not easy to stop. Embarrassed, angry at herself, she turned away.

He pulled her to him. 'The wonderful way you have of answering exactly to what a man wants — it has always been your principal virtue. Am I to believe that you have let something come between us? Have your feelings changed in one short night?' He brushed her tears away with his own sleeve.

' "Have your feelings changed in one short night?" ' She managed a trace of a smile. 'I can think of someone who might be asked the question.'

'Come, my dear. You are being very childish. I have nothing to hide from you, nothing on my conscience; and if I tried to hide anything, do you think it would do me any good? You are very innocent, and that is one of my reasons for loving you, but innocence is not always the easiest thing in the world to live with. Put yourself in my place, if you can, for a moment. Give the matter a little thought. I am in no position to let my person "go where my heart would lead it."† I have certain hopes, and if anything comes of them I shall soon have ways of demonstrating how deep, how very deep indeed, my affection for you is. I would not argue that it is going to be easy for you, but "let us see, while life permits." '‡

*Anonymous, *Kokinshū* 631:

> Unchastened, I stir again these empty rumors,
> For I go through the world with one whom I cannot hate.

The thought with which the soliloquy concludes is very obscure. It could mean that, with his promises for the next life to give her strength, she must put up with his unkindness in this.

†See note*, page 896.

‡Anonymous, *Kokinshū* 377:

> We cannot be sure. Let us see, while life permits,
> Whether I will forget, or you will cease to visit.

Just then the messenger whom he had sent to Rokujō returned, hopelessly drunk. Forgetting that the situation called for a certain restraint, he came staggering up to the front veranda of this west wing, quite buried in the wondrous silks and satins* with which the Rokujō house had rewarded him. The stupidest of serving women would have had no trouble guessing his mission – though she might have had to give a thought or two to the question of when Niou had found time for his letter. He had nothing which he really wished to conceal from Nakanokimi. The abruptness of the confrontation had been unfortunate, but it would do no good now to reprove the messenger for his tactlessness.

A woman brought in the letter. For better or worse, thought Niou, no secret must henceforth stand between them. It was a small relief to see that the letter seemed to be not in the hand of Rokunokimi herself but that of her stepmother.† He put it aside, for these things were embarrassing, even when a scrivener intervened.

The hand was strong and practiced. 'I urged her to write her own letter, since I did not wish to seem forward; but she is not entirely herself.

> 'It droops, the maiden flower, as never before.
> The dew this morning has left it all too swiftly.

'Did you have to go so soon?'
'Complaining, always complaining. Why won't they just let me be alone with you? I do find myself in the oddest situations.'

Most people, accustomed to thinking that one wife is enough for a man, would have found it difficult to sympathize. But his affairs were complicated, and what had happened had to happen sooner or later. The world had chosen to single him out, even among princes of the blood, and no one could have reproved him for taking as many wives as he wished; and so no one need think Nakanokimi's situation a notably cruel one. Quite the reverse: it was the general view that she was lucky, swept into an embrace so ardent and at the same time so estimable. To Nakanokimi herself, this sudden event was the more shocking for the fact that she had

---

*Literally: 'He had dived deep into the wondrous seaweed which the fishermen gather.'
†The widow of Kashiwagi.

begun to take his affection for granted. She had wondered, reading old romances, why women were always fretting at such length over these little problems. They had seemed very remote. Now she saw that the pain could be real.

'And this refusal to eat – it is not at all good for you, you know,' he said gently, with every indication of real concern. He ordered her favorite fruits immediately, and put his most famous cook to work on other dishes he thought might tempt her; but her thoughts were elsewhere. It was all very disturbing.

Toward evening he withdrew to the main hall. The breeze was cool, and it was a time of the year when the skies had a particular fascination. Very much the man of fashion, he today presented an even more elegant figure than usual; but for Nakanokimi the very care that he gave to his dress deepened gloom that was already next to unbearable. The song of the evening locust made her yearn for 'the mountain shadows.'*

'My sorrows would have their limits, were I yet there.
The locust's call this autumn eve – I hate it!'

He was on his way while the evening was still young. She heard his outrunners withdrawing into the distance, and an angler might have wanted to have a try at the waters by her pillow.† Even as she wept, she rebuked herself for having surrendered so weakly to jealousy. Why should she be wounded afresh, when he had been inconsiderate from the start? Matters were of course complicated by her pregnancy. What did the future have in store for her? She came from short-lived stock, and might herself be marked for an early death. Though she had no great wish to live on, the thought of death saddened her, and the sin would be great if she left behind a motherless child. She passed a sleepless night.

The empress being indisposed, Niou went to the palace the next day. He found the whole court assembled. She proved to be suffering from no more than a slight cold, however, and Yūgiri, as he left, invited Kaoru to share a carriage with him. He wanted the

---

*Anonymous, Kokinshū 204:

> I hear the locust, think that eve has come.
> But no – it is only the dark of the mountain shadows.

†Probably a poetic allusion.

evening's ceremonies to be of unprecedented brilliance, though of course there is a limit beyond which not even the wealthiest of commoners is expected to go. He felt somewhat uncomfortable with Kaoru. Yet among his near relatives there was no one whom he thought it so necessary to have at these last nuptial ceremonies. No one could more gracefully do honor to the occasion. But at the same time Yūgiri was annoyed. Kaoru had left court with unwonted alacrity, and he showed not the smallest sign of regret that Rokunokimi had gone to another; and now he threw himself into the preparations as if he were one of her brothers.

It was after dark when Niou made his appearance. A room had been prepared for him at the southeast corner of the main hall. The prescribed silver dishes were laid out most grandly on eight stands, and there were two smaller stands as well, and the ceremonial rice cakes were brought on trays with the festoon-shaped legs so much in style. But enough: why should I describe arrangements with which everyone is perfectly familiar?

Arriving at the banquet, Yūgiri pointed out to Niou, who had not yet emerged from the bridal chambers, that it was growing very late and his company was much missed. But Niou still loitered among the ladies, whose company he was enjoying enormously. In attendance upon him were Yūgiri's brothers-in-law, a guards commander and a councillor. Finally the bridegroom emerged, a very spruce figure indeed. Yūgiri's son the captain was acting as master of ceremonies and pressed wine upon Niou. The cups were emptied a second time and a third, and Niou smiled at Kaoru's diligence in seeing that they were refilled. No doubt he was remembering his own complaints about this excessively proper household. But Kaoru was all solemnity, and pretended not to notice. Niou's retinue, which included numbers of ranking and honored courtiers, was meanwhile being entertained in the east wing. For six men of the Fourth Rank there were ladies' robes and cloaks, and for ten men of the Fifth Rank double-lined Chinese robes and trains in several colors for the several stations. Four men of the Sixth Rank received trousers and brocade cloaks. Chafing at the limits imposed upon even the most illustrious statesman, Yūgiri had exhausted his ingenuity in seeing that the dyeing and cutting were of the finest, and some might have thought the gifts for the handymen and grooms rather excessive. Why is it – because the pleasures the eye takes in are the best, perhaps – that old romances seem to give these lively events first priority? But we are always being told that not even they manage to get in all the details.

Some of Kaoru's outrunners, victims of the darkness, seem not to have been noticed when the wine was passed out. 'Now why couldn't he have married her himself, like a good boy?' they grumbled as they saw his carriage in through the garden gate. 'He may enjoy his bachelor's life, but we don't.'

Kaoru smiled. It was late and they were sleepy. Niou's men would be sprawled about here and there happily sleeping off the wine. But what a strained affair it had been, he thought as he went in and lay down. The father of the bride, a close enough relative of the groom too,* had come in with such portentous ceremony. The lights turned up high, this person and that had pressed drinks upon the groom, who had responded with unexceptionable poise and dignity. It had been a performance the very memory of which brought pleasure. If he had had a well-endowed daughter of his own, thought Kaoru, he would have found it hard to pass over Niou even in favor of an emperor. Yet he knew that in all the court not one father of an eligible daughter failed to think of Kaoru himself even as he thought of Niou. No, his was not a name they scoffed at. A touch of self-congratulation creeping into his soliloquy, he thought what a pity it was that he should be a crabbed old recluse. Supposing the emperor, and there certainly were hints enough, was having thoughts about the Second Princess and Kaoru. It would not do to give too withdrawn and self-contained an impression. Prestige the match would certainly bring, and yet he wondered. And all that aside, what sort of lady would she be? Might she just possibly resemble Oigimi? It would seem that he was not, after all, wholly uninterested in the Second Princess.

Troubled once more with insomnia, he went to the room of a certain Azechi, a woman of his mother's who was his favorite, in some measure, over the others, and there passed the night. No one could have reproved him for sleeping late, but he jumped from bed as if duty were calling.

Azechi was evidently annoyed:

---

*Yūgiri is Niou's maternal uncle.

'Clandestine my rendezvous at Barrier River.
No good this sudden departure will do for my name.'

He had to admit that he was not being kind:

'Viewed from above, its waters may seem shallow.
But deep is Barrier River, its flow unceasing.'

Even 'deep' had a doubtful ring to it; and 'shallow,' one can imagine, did little to dispel Azechi's bitterness.

'Do come for a look at this sky.' He opened the side door. 'How can you lie there as if it didn't exist? I would not wish to seem affected, but the dawn after one of these long nights does fill a person with thoughts about this world and the next.' Spreading confusion behind him, he made his departure.

Although he did not have a large repertory of pretty speeches, he was a man of taste, thought by most people to be not entirely without warmth. Women with whom he had exchanged little pleasantries hoped for more. And this household of a princess no longer a part of the world was a target for properly introduced serving women, and each, after her rank and fashion, could no doubt have told stories to which one might listen with interest and sympathy.

Seeing his bride for the first time in daylight, Niou was pleased. She was of moderate height and attractive proportions, her face was well molded, and her hair flowed in a heavy cascade over her shoulders. It was a proud, noble face, the skin almost too delicate, the eyes such as to make a rival feel somehow defective. Not a flaw detracted from her beauty, he could say quite without reservation. He might have feared a certain immaturity, but, in her early twenties, she was no longer a child. A flower at its best, product of the most careful nurturing, so adequate an object of attention as to make a father forget that he had other duties. But of course there was a different kind of beauty, a more winsome kind, and here the honors had to go to Niou's lady at Nijō. Rokunokimi was not forward, but she did not fail to make herself understood. And so, in sum, the new wife had much to recommend her, and her more apparent charms seemed to have intelligence and cultivation behind them. In her retinue were thirty carefully chosen young women and six little girls, all of more than ordinary comeliness. Each could indeed have been described as a real beauty, and not one showed less than the best taste in dress and grooming. Yūgiri knew that he had a demanding son-in-law to please, and his ingenuity in seeing that every detail was the best of its kind was astonishing (appalling, some might have said). Not even when his oldest daughter, by Kumoinokari herself, had become the bride of the crown prince had he taken such pains – evidence, no doubt, of his hopes for this other prince.

Niou was not able to spend as much of his time at Nijō as he would have wished. Princes of the blood did not set forth casually in the middle of the day. He had taken up residence again in the southeast quarter at Rokujō, where he had lived as a child, and he could not, when night came, slip calmly past his new wife and set out for Nijō.

And so Nakanokimi was kept waiting. She had tried to prepare herself for this turn of events, but of course one is never prepared. Now that it had come she was left asking herself how love could fade so quickly. She had acted precipitately. Sensible people did not forget their own insignificance and seek to enter the grand world. She must have been quite bereft of her senses when she let herself be brought down the mountain path from Uji. She longed to go back, not in grand defiance, but simply to rest, to regain her composure. He should not mind, if she made it clear that she was not trying to teach him a lesson.

Shyly, her thoughts at length too much for her, she sent off a letter to Kaoru. 'The abbot has told me in detail of your attentions the other day. I cannot tell you how great a consolation your kindness in remembering has been. I am deeply grateful, and would like if possible to offer my thanks in person.'

It was written quietly on plain Michinoku paper, most touching in its directness. The sincerity of her gratitude for the memorial services, which had been conducted with unpretentious solemnity, was apparent, though stated without exaggeration or rhetorical flourish. There had always been something stiff, reserved, hesitant, in what should have been the most casual of notes from her. And now she wanted to see him! Niou, so quick to jump from this fad and that infatuation to the next, was clearly neglecting her. Almost in tears, Kaoru read the simple note over and over again.

His answer, on matter-of-fact white paper, was, he hoped, equally direct. 'Thank you for your letter. I set off by myself the other day, as silently as a monk, because there seemed to be reasons for not informing you. I resent very slightly your choice of the word 'remembering,' because it implies that forgetfulness might have been possible. But we must talk of all this when I see you. In the meantime, please be assured of my very great esteem.'

The next evening he made his visit. His heart a tangle of secret emotions, he gave more than usual attention to his dress. The perfume burnt into his soft robe blended with his own and that of his cloves-dyed fan to be if anything too subtle. And so he set forth, a figure of incomparable dignity.

Nakanokimi had not of course forgotten their strange evening together. Witness once more to his kindness, so at odds with what she now judged to be the ordinary, she might even have had regrets, one may imagine, for not having become his wife. She was mature enough by now to compare him with the man who had wronged her, and could think of no scale on which he was not to be marked the higher. It would be a pity to keep him at a distance. She invited him inside her anteroom and addressed him from her parlor, through a blind and a curtain.

'You did not mean to honor me with a special invitation, I know, but I was delighted at this indication – the very first, I believe – that you would not object to my presence, and wanted to come immediately. Then I was told that the prince would be with you, and so I waited until now. Here I am inside the first barrier – dare I congratulate myself that after all these years I am being rewarded?'

She still had great trouble finding words; but at length, faint and hesitant from deep in the room, he caught her reply: 'I am so mute and frozen always, I was wondering how I might let you know even a little of my gratitude for the other day, and the happiness it gave me.'

She was really *too* shy. 'How very far away you seem. There are so many things I would like to tell you.'

She granted his point and came closer. He held himself under tight control as he moved from subject to subject, offering a few words of consolation, avoiding direct criticism of Niou and his rather astonishing volatility.

As reluctant as he to complain, she had little to say, and that little she said by indirection, implying that she did not blame the world so much as her own destiny for what had befallen her.

Behind her words were sad hints that she wanted to go back to Uji for a time and wanted him to take her.

'Alas, I am in no position to promise anything of the sort. You must ask him, as clearly and directly as you can, and do as he wishes. And I must beg of you not to give him the slightest excuse for thinking you frivolous or undependable. Once you have made everything clear to him I shall have no misgivings at all about going with you and bringing you back again. He knows me well enough not to suspect anything improper.'

The knowledge that his path was strewn with lost opportunities was always with him. 'Might I have it back again?'* But he only hinted at his feelings.

It was growing dark.

'I am afraid that this sort of talk rather tires me.' He was making her nervous, and the time had come to withdraw. 'Perhaps when I am feeling a little better.'

'No, please tell me – if you are serious.' He groped for words with which to detain her. 'When would you like to go? The road will be overgrown, and I must have it cleared.'

She turned back. 'Let us say the first of next month. This month is almost over. I think we should go very quietly. Do you really think I need his permission?'

The soft voice was so like Oigimi's, more than he had ever known it to be. Abruptly, he leaned towards the pillar by which he was sitting and reached for her sleeve.

She should have known! She slipped deeper into the room. He pushed his way after her as if he were one of the family and again took her sleeve.

'You misunderstand completely. I thought I heard you say you wanted to go quietly off to Uji, and was delighted, and hoped to make sure I had heard you correctly. That is all. You have no reason to run away.'

She would have preferred not to answer. He was becoming a nuisance. But at length she composed herself for a soft reprimand: 'Your behavior is so very strange at times. Try to imagine what all these people will be thinking.'

She seemed on the edge of tears. She was right, in a way, and he was sorry for her. Yet he went on: 'Have I done anything that I

*Probably a poetic allusion.

need feel guilty about? Remember, please, that we had one rather intimate conversation. I do not entirely relish being treated like a criminal when, after all, you were once offered to me. But please do not fret. I will do nothing that might shock you and the world.'

Though he did not seem prepared to release her, he spoke calmly enough of the regrets that had been building up over the months and were by now almost too much for him. She felt helpless, cornered – but the words that come most easily do little to describe her anguish. She was in tears, more shamed and outraged than if it had been possible to dismiss him as merely a boor.

'You are behaving like a child, my dear,' he said at length, aroused once more to pity by her fragile charms. Beneath the distraught exterior he sensed a deep, calm strength, telling him how she had matured since the Uji days. Why had he so heedlessly given her up? He had done it, and deprived himself of all repose since, and he would have liked to cry out his regrets to the world.

Two women were in close attendance upon her. Had he been a stranger, they would have drawn closer against the possibility of something unseemly. But he was an old friend, and the conversation was evidently of a confidential nature. Tactfully, with a show of nonchalance, they withdrew, and unwittingly made things worse for Nakanokimi. Though he had not succeeded in keeping his regrets to himself, today as on other days he was behaving with admirable restraint. She could not think of curtly dismissing him.

One must presently draw a curtain upon such a scene. It had been a useless sort of visit, and, everything considered, he thought it best to take his leave.

Already it was dawn, and he would have said, if asked, that the sun had only just set. His fear of gossip had much less to do with his own good name than with concern for hers. The cause of her indisposition was by now clear enough. She had tried to hide the belt that was the mark of pregnancy. He had respected her shyness, and said nothing. A stupid sort of reticence – and on the other hand any show of forwardness would have gone against his deeper wishes. To surrender to the impulse of a moment would have been to make future meetings more difficult; to demand secret meetings, whatever her wishes, would have been to complicate his own life infinitely and to leave her in the cruelest uncertainty. Would it be better not to see her at all? But the briefest interval away from

her was torment. He had to see her. And so, in the end, the workings of his wayward heart prevailed.

Though her face was somewhat thinner, her delicate beauty
was as always. It was with him after his departure, driving everything else from his thoughts. He debated the possibility of taking
her to Uji, but it was not likely that Niou would agree, and it
would be most unwise to go in secret. How could he follow her
wishes and the mandates of decorum at the same time? He lay
sunk in thought.

Very early in the morning he got off a note, folded into a formal envelope:

'An autumn sky, to remind me of days of old:
I made my way in vain down a dew-drenched path.

Your cruelty is, I should say, both intolerable and senseless.'

She did not want to answer, but knew that her women noticed
any departure from routine. 'I have received your letter,' she said
briefly, 'and, not at all well, am not up to a reply.'

It offered little consolation to its recipient, still haunted by the
events of the evening before. She had been dismayed by his behavior, for she had little way of guessing what another man might
have done; and yet she had sent him off with composure and dignity and no suggestion of rudeness. The memory was not comforting. He could tell himself that he had been exposed to all the
varieties and stages of loneliness.

She had improved enormously since the Uji days. If Niou were
to reject her, then he himself would be her support. They could
not meet openly, perhaps, but she would be his heart's refuge. A
reprehensible heart, that it should have room for only this – but
such are the shortcomings one finds in men of apparent depth and
discernment. He had grieved for Oigimi, and his present sufferings
seemed far worse.

Thus the thoughts came and went. Upon hearing that Niou
had put in an appearance at the Nijō house, he quite forgot, in his
jealousy, that he had set himself up as her guardian.

Feeling guilty about his long absence, Niou had paid an unannounced visit. Nakanokimi was determined to show no resentment. She had wanted to go off to Uji, and now she saw that the
man who was to take her could not be depended upon. The world
seemed to close in more tightly by the day. She must accept

her fate, and greet whatever came, so long as she lived, with an appearance of cheerfulness. So successful was she in carrying through her resolve, so open and charming, that Niou's affection and delight rose to new heights. He apologized endlessly for his neglect. Her pregnancy was beginning to show, and the belt that was its mark and had been such a source of embarrassment the night before both moved and fascinated him, for he had never before been near a woman in her condition. Coming from the strained formality of Rokujō, he felt pleasantly relaxed here at Nijō, and his promises and apologies flowed on and on. What a very clever talker, thought Nakanokimi. The memory of Kaoru's alarming behavior came back. She was grateful to him, as she long had been, but he had gone too far. Though little inclined to put faith in Niou's vows, she found herself yielding before the flood. What a wretched position Kaoru had put her in, lulling her into a sense of security and then plunging into her room. He had said that his relations with her sister had been pure to the end, and she had believed and admired him; but it would not do to be too friendly. Apprehension turned to terror at the thought of what a really prolonged separation from Niou might bring. She said nothing of her fears, and her manner, more girlishly endearing than ever, quite ravished him. And then he caught a telltale scent. It was not one of the scents that people purposely burn into their garments. Something of a connoisseur in such matters, Niou had no doubt about its origins.

'And what is this unusual perfume?'

She was speechless. It was true, then; something was going on between the two of them. His heart was pounding. He had long been convinced that Kaoru's feelings went beyond friendliness. She had changed clothes and still that scent clung to her.

'Really, my dear, you cannot go on pretending that you have kept him at a distance.' His carefully measured speech left her feeling utterly helpless. 'I have given you no cause, not the slightest, to doubt the intensity of my affection. *You* are "the first to forget."* I must accuse you, indeed, of bad taste − of forgetting what is expected of people like us. Perhaps you think I have stayed away

*Ise, *Kokin Rokujō, Zoku Kokka Taikan* 32974:

> Had I known I was facing one so cruel
> I should have wished to be the first to forget.

long enough to justify what you have done. I have not, and I am deeply disappointed to find this strain of insensitivity.' His reproaches seemed endless, and were quite beyond transcribing. Her silence adding fuel to his rancor, he presently capped them with an accusing poem:

> 'Most friendly it was of him to give to your sleeve
> The scent that maddens, sinks into the bones.'

It was too much. She had to reply.

> 'The familiar robe has been a source of comfort.
> And now, for cause so paltry, must I lose it?'

The fragile, weeping figure could not fail to move him – and at the same time could not be permitted to escape responsibility for what had happened. His agitation increased until he too was in tears (for he had few defenses against tears). However terrible the mistake, it was not possible to cast her off. Such touching gentleness did not permit resentment to last, and soon he was seeking to comfort her.

He left Nijō the next morning after ablutions and a leisurely breakfast. Used to a blaze of Chinese and Korean hangings, to layer upon layer of damasks and brocades, he found the furnishings here intimate and reposeful, and her women, some of them in soft, unstarched robes, lent the place a quiet dignity. Nakanokimi herself was wearing a soft robe of lavender and over it a cloak of deep pink lined with blue. It was a quiet dress, and yet he thought her entirely capable of competing with the rather florid lady who, at Rokujō, seemed almost vain in her attention to clothes. He was as susceptible to retiring beauty as to bold, and did not think that Nakanokimi had cause to feel inferior to her rival. She had had a charmingly round face, but emaciation and a new pallor had not spoiled its beauty. Even before he had caught that alarming scent, he had been aware of an unsettling possibility: given the quiet charms that so raised her above the ordinary, any man not a close relative would have had trouble staying away once he had come to know her. Niou knew all too well what his own inclinations would have been, and he was always ready to judge others by himself. And so he had for some time made it a practice to go nonchalantly through this cabinet and that chest in search of evidence. He had found nothing suspicious. There were, to be sure, brief,

matter-of-fact notes mixed in among other papers, though not in
such a manner as to suggest a particular wish to preserve them.
There had to be more somewhere. The absence of letters and the
presence of that perfume made a particularly alarming combination. When Kaoru was drawn to someone he was drawn irresistibly. Would Nakanokimi be capable of repulsing him? They were
a good match, and no doubt they had much in common. Niou
was sad, angry, jealous, too much a prey to these various emotions
to leave her. He sent off two and three apologetic letters to
Rokujō. It did not take him long to think of new things to say,
grumbled some of the old women.

Kaoru continued to fret over Niou's presence at Nijō. How
stupid, how undisciplined he was, he told himself again. He had
undertaken to see that she was looked after, and what right had he
now to be jealous? Forcing his thoughts in a new direction, he
managed a certain semblance of happiness at this evidence that
Rokujō had not overwhelmed her. He thought of the somewhat
dowdy women in attendance upon her and decided to consult
with his mother.

'I wonder if you might have a few clothes you don't need just
at the moment? I know a house that could use something decent.'

'I believe that some things will be coming for the services next
month,* but the dyers have been so busy. Suppose we send off an
order.'

'Please don't bother. Whatever you have ready will do.'

He sent off to see what the seamstresses had on hand and was
offered a wide selection of women's robes, some fine cloaks, and
several bolts of undyed silk and damask. For the princess herself he
found a red singlet in his own stores, the gloss from the fulling
mallets uncommonly fine, and numerous garments of white
damask and the like. Though he had no women's trousers, he did
come upon an ingenious cord, which he knotted, and, with this
poem, added to the collection:

'I shall not go on always and always resenting
     The cord that now has bound you to another.'

He sent them all to Tayū, an elderly serving woman with
whom he was on good terms.

*She regularly has the Lotus Sutra read.

'Here are some bits and scraps I happened to find lying about. Hand them out quietly, please, as seems appropriate.'

Though not so as to make a great show of the matter, he had the gifts for Nakanokimi wrapped with special care. Tayū was used to these attentions, and she neither gave the princess a full report nor thought it necessary to stand on formality and return the gifts. Taxing herself no further with these refinements, she distributed the cloth to the women, and they set about making new clothes for themselves. It was only right that the better materials should go to the young women in immediate attendance upon the princess. The menials, who were beginning to have trouble hiding their tatters, caught the eye the more pleasingly for the modesty of the unlined white robes in which they now were dressed. Who but Kaoru, they asked, would have thought of all this? Niou was warmhearted enough, and would of course not let them starve; but he had no eye for the fine details that made all the difference in running a household. The pampered darling of the whole world, he was not very keenly aware of its sorrows and frustrations, of its persistent refusal to go in every respect as one would wish. For him 'cold' signified nothing more piercing than the touch of dew, and life was a gay parade of style and elegance. Yet, given the circumstances, he *was* considerate, seeing to fairly routine matters with the passing of the seasons, provided they concerned someone of whom he was fond. A few of his women, including his nurse, thought indeed that he occasionally went too far. Nakanokimi was, all the same, embarrassed at the shabbiness of her retinue, and she sometimes feared that a mansion so fine only set her off to incongruous effect. And there were Rokunokimi and *her* household to be considered, the luxury and extravagance that were the talk of the day. To Niou's men the Nijō house must seem scarcely fit for human habitation. Kaoru observed and understood, and, though he would have hated to be thought discourteous or unfeeling in sending off garments so unremarkable that he would not have dreamed of letting a stranger have them, he had to keep certain notions of propriety in mind. What would people have said if he had sent the products of the greatest cutters and weavers in the land? And so, with his usual care and sobriety, he had had a collection neither extravagant nor mean put together, including a robe woven especially for Nakanokimi, and damasks and other fineries. He too was the spoiled pet of the great, his manner so proud that some might have called it aloof and arrogant, his tastes such as might, at times, have seemed overrefined. The Eighth Prince's mountain dwelling, its solitude and melancholy, had wrought a great change in him and led him to an awareness of the tears of ordinary life. In rather sad ways the prince had been of service!

Kaoru had been determined to behave so as to add nothing to her worries, but she was more than ever on his mind. His letters were more detailed, and suggested that his feelings were no longer very securely under control. And so, thought Nakanokimi, her agitation rising with each letter, the complications in her life refused to leave, and indeed increased. If he were a complete stranger, she could easily dismiss him as a lunatic and send him on his way; but he had been a great source of strength over the years, and a sudden breach would only make people ask questions. He had been kind and gentle, and she was grateful; but she must avoid giving the impression that she condoned his behaviour. All the women who might be young enough to understand seemed too new and too unfamiliar with events at Uji, and those who were adequately informed were all very old. Quite alone, with no one whom she could really talk to, she longed more than ever for her sister. Kaoru would surely be able to control these improper tendencies if Oigimi were still alive. Nakanokimi almost thought them more distressing than the possibility that Niou might weary of her.

One quiet evening, the yearning at length too much for him, Kaoru paid a visit. Nakanokimi had a cushion set out for him on the veranda and sent word through one of her women that she was not feeling well and would be unable to receive him. Though almost in tears, he was determined to control himself before her women.

'When you are not well, you invite strange priests to sit beside you. Can you not at least treat me like your physician? Can you not let me inside your room? If we have to have people running back and forth with messages, then I might as well not have come at all.'

Very improper, said the women who had been present at the scene that earlier evening. They lowered a blind between the veranda and the main hall and showed him to the seat usually occupied by the priest in night attendance. Nakanokimi was extremely uncomfortable, but had to agree that open hostility would be misguided. Shyly and without enthusiasm, she edged a little closer, and the few words that came to him in a faint little voice so reminded him of Oigimi in the days after she fell ill that forebodings were added to his sorrow. The lights seemed to dim before his eyes. He could only blurt out short and disconnected phrases. Her refusal to answer seemed intolerable. Reaching through the blind in the manner he had as of being one of the family, he pulled the curtain slightly aside and leaned towards her.

In a panic, she called out to a woman named Shōshō. 'I seem to be rather short of breath. I wonder if I might ask you to massage me for just a moment or two.'

'That sort of thing only makes matters worse.' With a sigh, he drew back again – but not because any great measure of calm had returned to him. 'Why do you go on feeling so unwell? I have asked about people in your condition and been told that there may be great discomfort at first but that it goes away in time. Might you perhaps be making a little too much of it all?'

'I do feel unwell sometimes,' she replied, much embarrassed to have to talk of her condition. 'It was so with my sister too. I have heard people describe it as a sign that neither of us was meant to live long.'

Yes, he thought, in an access of pity. One had to realize that life was far shorter than 'the thousand years of the pine.'* Shōshō's presence no longer enough to restrain him, he began to speak of his feelings over the years. He did, it was true, choose his words with care and circumspection, avoiding matters that might be compromising or inconveniently clear to an outsider. A gentleman of remarkable sensitivity, thought Shōshō.

Everything reminded him of Oigimi, who seldom left his thoughts. 'From very early in my life I turned my back on the world, and I hoped to end my days a bachelor. But fate seems to have intervened. One would have to say that your sister was a rather chilly lady, and yet something about her struck up a most extraordinary response, and my saintly resolutions, for what they were worth, began to waver. I admit that I went out looking for comfort after she died. I glanced at this and that woman and even

---

*Anonymous, *Kokin Rokujō, Zoku Kokka Taikan* 32948:

> How sad that love should be thwarted in this brief span,
> As if we had the thousand years of the pine.

kept company with one or two for a time. It was only that I wanted to stop thinking of her.' He was in tears and his voice had taken on a pleading note. 'And to no purpose at all. I have been drawn to no one else. Sometimes – I am only human – I have not been able to keep myself under very tight control. But it would hurt me very much indeed to think that you have ever had cause to doubt my motives. You would have every right to be shocked and revolted if you were to detect even a hint of anything improper in my behaviour toward you. Do please let me go on seeing you from time to time. Who could possibly object if we were to talk of the little trifles that interest us? I have no tendencies, I assure you, that need make you feel in danger. I am not like other people, I swear I am not.'

'But I do trust you. You do not know me very well if you think I would allow such extraordinary intimacy otherwise. You have been kindness itself over the years, and it is because I know so well what you will do for me that I have asked favors of you.'

'Favors? I am not aware of any worth mentioning – or dare I hope that in your plans for your mountain village you will finally decide you have found a use for me? If that is so, then we have evidence that you have read a part of my feelings. I am delighted.' He had not finished complaining, but he thought that her women had heard enough.

It was growing dark and the humming of insects was loud. The hillock in the garden was falling back into night. He sat quietly on, leaning against an armrest. She wished very much that he would leave.

'An end to sorrow,'* he whispered. 'No, it is too much. Let me have a Silencetown† somewhere, a place for quiet tears. Somewhere near that monastery of yours. No, I don't need a whole monastery. If I could just have a statue or a picture of her, and set out offerings before it.'

---

*See note†, page 706.

†Anonymous, *Kokin Rokujō*, *Zoku Kokka Taikan* 32156:

> As one who cannot reduce his tears to silence,
>
> I long to be shown, somehow, to Silencetown.

Though no village by this name is known, there is an apparent association with Otonashi no Taki, 'the Waterfall of Silence,' in Yamashiro.

'A very kind thought. But just a moment – you speak of having an image made, and that somehow suggests the river Mitarashi.* And so perhaps you are not being so kind to my sister after all. Or a picture: much depends, you know, on what you are willing to pay. An artist can do very badly by a person.'†

'That is true, of course. And in any case, no sculptor or painter could really give me what I want. Short of a miracle, which I would not reject. I know of a sculptor who one day not long ago brought flowers raining down from the skies.'‡

She at length took pity on him, convinced that he had indeed been unable to forget, and came a little nearer.

'This image you speak of reminds me of something. Something very strange.'

'Yes?' Delighted at this new amiability, he reached under the curtain for her hand.

So here they were again! But her indignation did not keep her from wanting to quiet him somehow and make reasonable discussion possible; and there was the problem of Shōshō, sitting right beside her.

She managed to go on. 'I heard recently of a lady whose existence I had not dreamed of. Someone whom I could not keep at a distance, and at the same time whom I had no great wish to be friendly with. The other day she came calling, and the resemblance to my sister astonished me and moved me deeply. You insist on seeing my sister in me, on thinking of me as a sort of legacy, and yet these women tell me that no two people could have been more unlike. Strange that in both cases it should be the opposite of what one would expect – that a lady with no cause to look like her should be her very image.'

Might he be dreaming? 'Some very strong bond has brought you together, of that we can be sure. But why had you told me nothing of this before?'

*Kaoru has used the word *hitokata*, which suggests the images floated down rivers during lustration ceremonies. *Mitarashi* can have general reference to any stream so used, or specific reference to the stream flowing through the precincts of the Lower Kamo Shrine in Kyoto.

†See note†, page 251.

‡Unclear, though it may be imagined that the reference is to a sculptor so skillful that he caught the attention of the powers above.

'Bond? I have no notion what that might be. Father's great fear was that we would become drifters and beggars, and now that I am alone I have reason to think I am finally beginning to understand what he meant. And now this unfortunate affair comes along, and I shudder to think of the harm it will do to his memory if we let the world get wind of it.'

Her manner suggested that she was referring to 'this keepsake, this child,'* left by some lady with whom her father had kept secret company. He wanted to hear more about the resemblance to Oigimi.

'Having said this much, you ought to go on, I think. Surely you do not mean to leave me dangling.'

But she was reluctant to give him the details. 'You might want to visit her. There is much that I do not know myself, but I can tell you in a general way of her whereabouts. And revealing too much sometimes takes away from the interest.'

He pressed her for more. 'If it were in pursuit of your sister, I would give myself up to wandering the wide, gloomy world, I would search to the depths of the sea.† I would of course be less single-minded in pursuit of this new lady. But since I had thought that even an image of your sister would be some slight comfort, why should we not enshrine the other in that mountain village? Please tell me everything, and as clearly as you can.'

'No. He did not recognize her as one of his children, and I should not have told you as much as I have. It was just that I felt sorry for you and doubtful about this request for a miraculous sculptor.

'She grew up in the far provinces. Her mother thought it a pity that she should be hidden from the world and mustered up courage to write to me. I could not bring myself to ignore the letter, and so the girl herself came to see me. It may be of course that there was not time for a really good look at her, but she seemed less countrified in every way than I would have expected. It would be great good fortune for her poor mother – she really seemed quite desperate – if you were to enshrine the girl. But I hardly think that matters will go so far.'

*See note†, page 181.

†Po Chü-i has the emperor Hsüan-tsung going to such extremes in his search for Yang Kuei-fei.

He was resentful, sensing behind the apparent innocence with which she told him of this new discovery a wish to turn away unwelcome attentions. Still he was interested. She evidently found his presence next to intolerable; and yet his heart beat faster at the thought that she was not able to send him on his way, evidence, surely, that she understood and sympathized. It was very late. She wondered what her women would be thinking. Taking advantage of his bemusement, she slipped away to the rear of the house. She was right to do so, of course, but he was unable to keep back tears of chagrin and resentment. His agitation was increased by the presence of her women. But rash action would make her unhappy and do him no good. He fought to maintain at least a semblance of composure. Sighing deeper sighs than usual, he made his way out.

A helpless captive of yearning, he could hope for no lessening of the pain. How, without calling down upon himself the reproaches of the whole world, was he to find solace? Not having known a great deal of love, he let it lure him into fantasies that could be of no use to either of them; and so he passed the night. She had said that this new girl resembled her dead sister. How might he learn whether or not she was right? The girl was of a low enough station in life that he could doubtless approach her with no difficulty; but he was less than enthusiastic. Having approached her, he might be embarrassed to find her not entirely to his taste.

Nostalgia for Uji was mounting again. The long intervals between his visits somehow made the past withdraw more rapidly into the distance. Toward the end of the Ninth Month he paid a visit. In the wail of the winds, the Uji house had only the rushing waters for company. The human presence was scarcely to be detected. His eyes clouded over at the infinite sadness of the place. Asking for Bennokimi, he was received at a dark-blue curtain drawn before her rooms.

'I am much honored by this visit. I am even older and uglier than when last you saw me and would be ashamed to face you.' She remained behind her curtains.

'I can guess how sad life is for you. I have come because only you understand certain things I long to talk about.' There were tears in his eyes. 'How quickly time does go by!'

The old woman was weeping quite openly. 'Here we are again at the time of the year when my older lady was suffering so. There is no particular season for weeping, of course, but it is the autumn wind that hurts most. And I have had dim rumors that things have turned out for my younger lady as my older lady feared they would – that her relations with the prince are not good. One must go on worrying, it seems.'

'I suppose that everything arranges itself in the end, if only you live long enough, but I cannot help blaming myself that her last days were so unsettled. But you speak of the prince's recent behavior. There is nothing in the least unusual about it, you know. It is exactly what one would have expected. He has taken another wife, but that is no cause for your lady to be upset. No, I fear that my own sorrow is the greater. I know that the day will come when I too will vanish into the skies. "The dew falls soon and late"* – but that knowledge does not make the wait any easier.'

Sending for the abbot, he gave instructions for memorial services. 'My visits here do me no good,' he said. 'What good is it to grieve? I think we should move this house to your monastery and do it over as a memorial hall. Something of the sort will be necessary someday, I am quite sure, and the sooner the better.'

He drew sketches and they discussed the arrangement of chapels, galleries, and cells.

'A most admirable undertaking,' said the abbot.

'Some will think it cruel, I know, to change a house that has so much of its owner in it. But we have pious motives that would have accorded completely with his own. His great trouble seems to have been an inability to pursue them, out of concern for the daughters he would leave behind. This land will have passed through his second daughter to Prince Niou, and we are hardly in a position to make it a holy precinct, whatever our personal wishes in the matter may be. And of course it is too near the river and too open, and so I think we should move the house and have something else put up in its place.'

'In every respect a most excellent plan. There once was a man who lost his children and in his grief went for long years carrying their remains in a kerchief around his neck. Then through the benign powers of the Blessed One he cast them away and entered the realm of enlightenment.† For you this house is similarly

See note, page 772.

†The source of this edifying tale is not known. Probably it was part of an oral tradition.

disquieting, a barrier along the holy way. A temple will be a source of grace in lives to come. Let us get to work immediately. We will have the soothsayers choose a good day and find two or three carpenters who know what they are about, and in matters of detail we need only follow the specifications laid down by the Blessed One himself.'

Kaoru gave all the necessary instructions. Summoning men from his manor, he told them to obey the abbot's orders while the work was in progress. It was by then evening. He decided to stay the night. He wandered here and there, knowing that this might be his last visit. The images had already been taken to the monastery, with only a few ritual implements left behind for Bennokimi's convenience. It was a lonely life she led, thought Kaoru. And what was to become of her now?

'There are rather urgent reasons for rebuilding the house,' he explained, 'and while we are about it perhaps we could ask you to make do with this gallery. If there are things you want sent to your lady, I can ask one of my men to deliver them.'

So he busied himself with domestic details. It is not the usual thing for young men to be interested in aged women, but he called her to his side and questioned her about old times. Since there was no danger of being overheard, she spoke at great length of his father.

'I can see him now as he lay dying. He did so want to see the child. And now, coming upon you at the far end of my outrageously long life, I feel as if I were having my reward for having been with him then. I am happy, and I am sad. And ashamed, too, for having lived all these wretched years and seen and known all these things. My lady writes telling me to visit her occasionally. She asks if I intend to shut myself off from her and forget about her completely. But I cannot be seen as I am. I want to be in attendance only upon Lord Amitābha.'

She also talked at great length of Oigimi: of her nature and conduct over the years, of remarks she had made on this and that occasion, of the fugitive poems she had composed when the cherries were in bloom or the autumn leaves at their best. The old woman expressed herself well, though her voice wavered from time to time. Kaoru was deeply moved. There had been something mutely childlike about Oigimi, but she had been a lady of sensibility all the same. He compared her in his mind with her sister. Nakanokimi was the more cheerful and modern of the two, even though she could be very cold to attentions she found unwelcome. With him, however, she was evidently reluctant to seem *too* withdrawn. He presently found his chance to mention the girl Nakanokimi had said resembled her dead sister.

'I cannot be sure whether she is in the city or not,' replied Bennokimi. 'I have only heard rumors. It was before the prince came to these mountains to live, and shortly after he lost his wife. Among his attendants was a woman named Chūjō, of good family and an amiable enough disposition. For a very short time he favored her with his attentions. No one knew of the affair, and presently she had a daughter. He was embarrassed, yes, even disgusted, knowing that it might well be his. He did not want to be troubled further and refused to see her again. It was self-loathing, I should imagine, that turned him into the saint he became in his last years. The woman was of course in a difficult position and soon left his service. Some time later she married the governor of Michinoku and went off with him to his province. Back in the capital after some years, she let it be known that the girl was in good health. The prince told her very brusquely that the news had nothing to do with him or this house; and so the poor woman could only lament her inability to do anything for the girl. I heard nothing of her for some years – I should imagine it was because she was off in Hitachi, where her husband had been posted as governor.* Then this spring there was a report that she had called upon my lady. The daughter will be about twenty,† I should imagine. I did once have a long letter from the mother saying that she was far too pretty to be wasted in the provinces.'

Fascinated by these remarks, Kaoru concluded that there must be a great deal of truth in what Nakanokimi had said. 'I have been telling myself that I would go to the far corners of the earth for a glimpse of someone who resembled your dead lady even a little. The prince may not have counted this other girl among his

---

*The husband is consistently called the governor of Hitachi, but, since the governor of that province was always a prince of the blood, he must in fact be the vice-governor.

†Which would make her five years younger than Nakanokimi. The Eighth Prince's wife died almost immediately after Nakanokimi was born, and so the old woman's story does not quite hang together.

children, but that she is can hardly be denied. I suppose she will visit you here someday. When she does, please tell her what I have said, though without seeming to make a great point of it.'

'Chūjō is a niece of my ladies' mother, and so the two of us are related;* but because we worked for different families, we were never very close. I have had a letter from Tayū – she is in the city with my lady, you will remember – saying that the girl would like to pay her respects at her father's grave, and that I should be prepared for a visit; but so far she does not seem to have thought of writing us directly. When she does come, I shall pass your message on to her.'

As he prepared to leave in the morning, he gave the abbot silks and cottons that had been brought after him. He gave similar gifts to Bennokimi and even to her women and the ordinary priests. It was a lonely mountain dwelling, but with this steady flow of gifts she was able to pursue the religious vocation in quiet security and in a manner befitting her station.

The trees had been stripped bare by the cruel winds. There were no tracks through the leaves. Hating to depart for what he feared would be the last time, he gazed on at the melancholy scene. The ivy climbing the twisted mountain trees still had traces of autumn color. He broke off a sprig, thinking that even so small a gift would please Nakanokimi.

> 'Memories of nights beneath the ivy
> Bring comfort to the traveler's lonely sleep.'

This was Bennokimi's answer:

> 'Sad must be the memory of lodging
> Beneath this rotting, ivy-covered tree.'†

Though he would not have called it a modish, up-to-date poem, it was not without charm, and it brought consolation of a sort.

---

*Bennokimi is a first cousin of the prince's wife.

†'Lodging' and 'ivy' are contained in the single word *yadoriki*. *Yadoriki* or *yadorigi* means specifically 'mistletoe.' The context makes clear that it can apply to climbing as well as parasitic plants, however, and seems to demand 'ivy', certain varieties of which are much admired for their autumn colors.

Niou chanced to be with the princess when the ivy was delivered.

'From the Sanjō house,' said the woman nonchalantly.

So she would have to go through it all over again! Nakanokimi wished that she could somehow hide the gift.

'Most remarkable,' said Niou, his manner richly insinuating.

He took up the ivy and a letter that said in part: 'Have you been better these last few days? I paid a visit to your mountain village, and lost my way among the clinging mountain mists. I shall tell you all about it when I see you. The abbot and I went over plans for rebuilding the house as a memorial hall. When I have your approval I shall see to arrangements for moving it. Perhaps I may ask you to give Bennokimi the necessary instructions.'

'Very cool and distant,' said Niou. 'He must have known I would be here.'

There was possibly a grain of truth in it; but Nakanokimi, delighted that the letter was so innocuous, now found herself damned by the very innocuousness. Her irritation was visible, and so charming that he had to forgive her everything.

'Send off an answer, now. I won't watch.' He turned away.

Since a show of reluctance would only make matters worse, she took up her brush.

'I am very envious of you, running off to the mountains. I have been thinking that very much the disposition you suggest should be made of the house; and I think too that, rather than seek some other "cave among the rocks"* when the time comes for me to leave the world, I would like to keep it in repair. I shall be very pleased indeed if you remodel it as you find appropriate.'

It seemed an easy, relaxed friendship, thought Niou, that offered no ground for jealousy; but he was suspicious all the same, knowing that he himself would not dream of allowing everything to meet the eye. It was not an easy situation for Nakanokimi.

Below the veranda autumn grasses beckoned, their plumes bending and swaying over beds of withered flowers. Some, not yet headed, fragile in the evening breeze, were flecked with dew. It was an ordinary enough breeze, and yet it was strangely moving.

See note, page 234.

'The autumn grass is keeping something back.
Beneath the dew, it beckons and it beckons.'*

He had on an informal robe over a pleasantly rumpled singlet.
Taking up a lute, he tuned it to the *ōjiki* mode. It was so charming
a performance that Nakanokimi, who knew a great deal about
music, could not go on being annoyed. She was a charming figure
herself. Leaning against an armrest, she peeped shyly out from
behind a low curtain.

'Weakly, weakly the wind glides over the grasses.
One knows that the moor is at the end of autumn.'

To her poem she added only the words: 'Left alone.'†
Embarrassed at her inability to hold back tears, she hid her face
behind a fan. She was a delight, and he pitied her; and at the same
time he could see that precisely this appeal would make it difficult
for other men to stay away. His doubts came back, and his resentment.

The chrysanthemums had not yet taken on their last color, for
the more carefully cultivated the chrysanthemum, the slower it is
to change. Yet a single blossom, for whatever reason, had changed
to that most beautiful of colors. The prince had it brought to him.

' "I do not love, among flowers, the chrysanthemum only," '‡
he whispered. 'One evening long ago, a certain prince was admiring chrysanthemums, and a spirit came down from the heavens to
help him at his lute.** We must resign ourselves to doing without
such services in this inferior age of ours.'

'We may not be as imaginative as they were,' said Nakanokimi,
not wanting him to put the instrument down, and always eager to
add to her own repertoire, 'but that hardly means that we are not
up to playing what has been given to us.'

---

*The meaning is that Kaoru is in surreptitious correspondence with her.
†See note*, page 949.
‡Yüan Chên, *Wakan Rōeishū* 267:

> I do not love, among flowers, the chrysanthemum only;
> But when it blooms and falls, there are no more.

**Tradition has it that the prince was Minamoto Takaakira (914-82), a son of the
emperor Daigo, and that the heavenly being was Yüan Chên.

'I get lonesome, all by myself. You must join me.' He had a koto brought out for her.

But she quite refused to touch it. 'I did once have a few lessons, but I'm afraid I wasn't as diligent as I might have been.'

'How difficult you are, my dear, even with these little trifles. The lady at Rokujō is still almost a stranger, but she does not try to hide her weaknesses from me. Our good friend Kaoru gives it as his view that women should be docile and straightforward. No doubt you are more open with him.'

And so, finally, he had said it. She sighed and played a brief melody. The strings being somewhat slack, she tuned her koto to the *banjiki* mode.* Even the few notes she plucked by way of tuning made it clear that her touch was excellent. Niou sang 'The Sea of Ise'† in very good voice, and Nakanokimi's women, wreathed in smiles, came up close behind the curtains.

'Yes, it would be nice if he could make do with only our lady, but fine gentlemen are what they are. We have to live with it, and I say she's been lucky. Can she really think of running back to those awful mountains? Why, years could go by without anything half as interesting as this.'

The younger women would have preferred just to listen.

With music and other diversions to break the monotony, he stayed at Nijō for some days. He sent word to Rokujō that a defilement had made a period of abstinence necessary. The lady there thought the excuse altogether too transparent.

One day Yūgiri himself stopped by, on his way home from court.

'He always makes such a parade of it,' grumbled Niou, going to the main hall.

'What fond memories this place does call up. I ought to come more often, I suppose, but, not having much by way of excuse –' Yūgiri talked of the old days for a time, and when he left he took Niou with him.

It was indeed a parade, row upon row of sons and courtiers. Nakanokimi's women looked out and sighed, having before them evidence that their mistress faced impossible competition. 'But what a really handsome gentleman he is,' said one of them. 'What

*A note higher than his *ōjiki*. Said to be a mode suited for winter.

†See note†, page 267.

a *really* handsome gentleman. He has that platoon of sons, each as good as the rest, and all of them so young and healthy; but he outshines them all.'

Others were less pleased. 'I don't think it's in very good taste, really, making such a show of things. Our poor lady has troubles enough already.'

Nakanokimi had her own thoughts. What she had seen over the years had been sufficient to convince her that she was not meant to mingle with these grand people. She was an insignificant little thing, as the world could plainly see. It would be better to return quietly to her mountains.

And so, like other years, this one came to an end.

She was in great discomfort from late in the First Month. Niou, for whom this was a new experience, was beside himself. He had services performed at this temple and that, and went on commissioning new ones. When Nakanokimi's distress was greatest, there came an inquiry from the empress. The marriage was now in its second year. Though aware of the fact that such steadfastness on Niou's part was worth noting, the world had not paid a great deal of attention to Nakanokimi. Now courtiers high and low began sending expressions of concern.

Kaoru was no less apprehensive than Niou. He made discreet inquiries and commissioned services of his own, but his visits could not be as frequent as he would have wished.

The court was astir during these same weeks with preparations for the Second Princess's initiation. The emperor gave them his personal attention and found it rather a relief that she had no maternal relatives. The princess of course had her mother's treasures, to which were added rich stores from the palace and from appropriate provincial offices as well. Kaoru was to become her bridegroom immediately after the ceremonies. He too should have been busy with preparations, but he could think only of Nakanokimi.

At an extraordinary levee toward the end of the Second Month, he was appointed General of the Right and given a supernumerary seat on the council. (A vacancy had been created when the Minister of the Right,* who had also been General of the Left,

---

*Because of difficulties created by Chapter 44, 'Bamboo River,' there is doubt as to whether this is Yūgiri or Kōbai.

resigned the latter position.) He went about making the courtesy calls which this happy event demanded, and in the course of them visited the Nijō mansion. Knowing that Nakanokimi would have Niou with her in this difficult time, he went directly to her apartments. In some confusion, Niou informed him that the place was swarming with priests and that the main hall might be more appropriate. Changing to court dress slightly less formal than Kaoru's, he received his caller at the foot of the stairs, and the scene the two presented was dignity itself. Kaoru was giving a banquet that evening for officers of the guard, he said, and would be most honored if Niou might be present. Because of Nakanokimi's condition, Niou did not commit himself.

The banquet took place at Rokujō, where everything had been done to insure an affair no less grand than a similar one on the occasion of Yūgiri's becoming a minister.* Princes of the blood and high courtiers were present in numbers no fewer than at the earlier banquet. Some, indeed, might have argued for less display. Niou did put in an appearance, but hurried back to Nijō before the festivities were over. Yūgiri and his family were not pleased. The princess at Nijō was of as high a rank as Yūgiri's Rokunokimi, but nearness to the sources of power sometimes has a heady effect on people.

At dawn a prince was born. Niou was delighted – they had endured great uncertainty, and been rewarded. For Kaoru, preferment was joined by a second cause for rejoicing. He paid a brief call of congratulation and of thanks for Niou's presence at the banquet the evening before. No one of rank would have dreamed of missing a visit to Nijō, the prince being in residence there.

As is the custom, the celebration on the third night was private. On the fifth night Kaoru sent fifty servings of ceremonial rice, prizes for the Go matches, and other stores of food,† as custom demanded. To Nakanokimi he sent thirty trays on stands, five sets of swaddling clothes, and diapers and the like. There was nothing grand or obtrusive about these various gifts, but close inspection revealed uncommonly fine taste. To Niou went twelve trays of aloeswood, and, on stands, steamed cakes of the five-colored

*Here and elsewhere, Yūgiri's promotion from Minister of the Right to Minister of the Left in 'Bamboo River' seems to be forgotten.

†Literally, 'rice in bowls,' but probably to be interpreted more generally.

cereals. The women in attendance upon Nakanokimi received trays on stands, of course, and thirty cypress boxes. Everything was in the best taste, in nothing was there even a hint of wanton display. On the seventh day the festivities were sponsored by the empress. The crowds were even larger. Courtiers of medium and high rank were numberless, and at their head was Her Majesty's own chamberlain. The emperor sent a sword – was he not to show his delight, he said, at Niou's having become a father? On the ninth day it was Yūgiri's turn. The occasion was for him a somewhat distasteful one, but he did not want to risk offending Niou. All of his sons were in attendance, and the greatest care was taken that there be no suggestion of hostility. No doubt Nakanokimi, whose physical discomfort had not been helped by worries about her rival, found all these attentions cheering.

Kaoru's feelings were mixed. She would be even more aloof and inaccessible now that she had become a mother, and she would be showered with affection; and on the other hand he could scarcely object to the fact that his original plans had worked out so well.

Toward the end of the month, following the initiation ceremonies, Kaoru took the Second Princess for his bride. There were private evening rites at the palace.

Some complained. 'Everyone has been talking about what a fuss he makes over her – and now he gives her to a commoner! She must have expected something better. It would have been all right, perhaps, to give his august permission *eventually* – but why did he have to rush things so?'

But the emperor, once he had made a decision, was a man to carry it out with alacrity. Provision would eventually have to be made for the princess, and he was prepared to go against precedent in making it now. Yet it must be said that though princesses are always marrying, few daughters of emperors so young and vigorous can have been rushed so precipitously into marriage with commoners.

'What a singular esteem for him our sovereign shows, and how singularly lucky he is,' said Yūgiri to his own Second Princess. 'Your late father bestowed your sister upon my father only when he was in his last years and about to retire from the world. And just look at me, if you will, picking up a princess without a by-your-leave.'

It was true, she thought, flushing. She did not answer.*

On the third night after the wedding, the emperor had gifts presented to all those who had been of service to his daughter, her maternal uncles and the rest. Quietly and without display, he took notice too of Kaoru's guards, outrunners, grooms, and footmen. The stiffness of court etiquette was avoided in all these attentions. Kaoru regularly and dutifully waited on his bride, but his heart was still in the past. The daytime hours he spent at home in brooding despondency. He would set out to visit her early in the evening, all the while telling himself that he must move her to Sanjō.

Delighted, his mother offered to let him have the main hall. Altogether too much, he replied. He had a gallery extended to the chapel, with the apparent intention of moving his mother to the west side of the main hall.† The east wing had been beautifully rebuilt after the fire, and still greater care was now taken to see that it was perfect in every detail. The emperor heard of these plans, and was uneasy. Was it wise for his daughter to give herself up so soon after marriage to life in her husband's house? In their concern for their children monarchs are no different from ordinary men. He wrote to his sister, Kaoru's mother, of his worries. She had been committed to his special care by their father, the late Suzaku emperor, and his concern had not diminished when she became a nun. Whatever she asked was granted, with great care that no detail be overlooked.

Kaoru was thus favored by the fondest attentions that two people of the very highest station had to offer; and still he was not happy. One could come upon him sunk in thought, intent only upon hurrying his plans for the Uji monastery.

Counting off the days, he was also immersed in preparations for the infant prince's fiftieth-day ceremonies. He saw to the details of baskets and cypress boxes for rice cakes and the like. Determined that the celebration be no ordinary one, he brought together troops of aloeswood and sandalwood carvers and workers of gold and silver, and each sought to outdo all the others.

He visited the Nijō mansion, choosing as usual a time when Niou would not be at home. Perhaps it was her imagination, but

---

*Yūgiri's remark is very unkind. See Chapters 37 and 39.

†Not at all clear. It seems that he means to share the main hall with his mother. The chapel is perhaps behind or to the west of the west 'side' (*hisashi*).

to Nakanokimi he seemed to have taken on a maturer dignity. She received him confidently – he would surely have left behind those troublesome ways of his.

But no. He choked with tears, and pity for himself was undisguised. 'The world seems a darker place than ever. I have gone against the demands of my own heart.'

'Please, you must not say so. What if someone were to catch even a whisper of it?' But in fact she was deeply moved, the tenacity of his affection for her sister being quite evident. He was unable to forget, and not even the enviable match he had made for himself seemed to help. If only her sister had lived! But then of course she would be in the same predicament as Nakanokimi herself; neither would have cause to envy the other. Their origins simply were not such as to command the respect of the world. Her sister's decision not to give herself to Kaoru seemed more than ever the wise one.

Kaoru begged to see the child. She had reservations, but told herself that it would be cruel to refuse him. There was the one unpleasant matter in which his resentment was a fact she must be resigned to living with, but in everything else she would follow his wishes. Not giving a direct answer, she sent the child out with its nurse. One would have expected a child of such parents to be beautiful, but in fact it had a skin so fair as almost to arouse forebodings, and it babbled and laughed in high, sweet tones. If only it were his, thought Kaoru – not, it would seem, having entirely given up thoughts of this world. If the one for whom he longed had followed the way of the world and left behind a child, he might find consolation. And such were the workings of his intractable heart that he had had no thought over the days of the possibility that his wellborn wife might have a child. Still, one would not wish to describe him as merely perverse. Had he been a man of reprehensible tendencies, the emperor would surely not have insisted upon having him for a son-in-law. In high matters of state, one would imagine, he showed uncommon talents.

Touched and pleased that the princess had consented to let him see the child, he talked on at greater length than usual, and presently it was dark. The pity was that he could not stay on into the night, making himself quite at home. Sighing and sighing again, he departed.

'What a remarkable perfume,' said the women. Indeed some of

the younger ones found it rather a trial. ' "So noisy the warbler"*
– I imagine we will be pestered by warblers looking for our blossoms.'

The approach to the Sanjō mansion from the palace was in a
direction which would be interdicted by the stars once summer
had come. He therefore moved his wife to Sanjō late in the Third
Month – before what is called, I believe, 'the parting of the seasons.' On the day before her removal, the emperor was host at a
wisteria viewing in her mother's apartments. (It being a state
assembly, the princess did not herself act as hostess.) The blinds
were rolled up and the royal seat put out on the south veranda.
The keepers of the palace larder saw that the courtiers of various
ranks were suitably entertained. Yūgiri and Kōbai were in attendance, as were two of Higekuro's sons, a councillor and a guards
captain. Two princes of the blood, Niou and Prince Hitachi, were
also present. Courtiers of medium rank were seated beneath the
wisteria arbors in the south garden, with court musicians disposed
along the east side of the Kōrōden Gallery, immediately beyond.
As dusk came on they played a strain in the *sōjō* mode.† Musical
instruments were brought out from the princess's rooms for the
emperor's delectation. Yūgiri and certain lesser officials delivered
them to the imperial presence. Yūgiri also presented two koto
scores in the late Genji's own hand. Genji had given them to
Kaoru's mother, and now, for presentation to the emperor, they
were attached to felicitous pine branches. Lutes as well as kotos of
the several varieties were brought out, all of them once the
property of the Suzaku emperor. Then there was the flute that had
been the source of a revelation in a dream, memento of a man
long dead,‡ which the emperor had on an earlier occasion pronounced to be of unexcelled tone: thinking there would not be
another affair so brilliant, it would seem, its owner had it brought
out. The emperor gave a Japanese koto to Yūgiri and a lute to
Niou. Kaoru quite outdid himself on the flute. Numbers of
medium-ranking courtiers famous for their voices serenaded the
emperor most admirably. The princess sent out cakes of the five-
colored cereals. As for the table settings, there were four trays of

*See note‡, page 588.
†Tonic G, thought to be appropriate for spring.
‡See Chapter 37.

aloeswood and stands of sandalwood, and cloths of varied lavender embroidered with wisteria branches. There were glass cups* and silver saucers,† and indigo decanters.‡ The guards captain busied himself seeing that the cups were kept full. Since it would not do to press too many drinks upon Yūgiri, and since no princes of the blood were present who could appropriately receive the royal cup, His Majesty turned to Kaoru. The young man protested that he was unworthy of the honor, but presently, whatever he may have read into the august invitation, he accepted and raised the cup high.

'To Your Majesty's health.'** Even so ordinary a toast he managed to utter with a difference – or perhaps his very special position made it seem so to the assembly. He transferred the wine to another cup, and with incomparable dignity descended to the garden to offer ritual thanks. Men of the highest rank, ministers and princes of the blood and the like, find such attentions flattering; and for Kaoru there was the singular honor of having been received as a royal son-in-law. His rank did carry its limitations, however, and in the end he had to return to his low seat.

Kōbai was annoyed. He had hoped to be so honored. He had had intentions upon the girl's mother, and had continued to write to her even after her presentation at court; and his thoughts had then turned to the daughter. He had let it be known that he would not be averse to being looked upon as her protector. The mother had chosen not to inform the emperor, however, and Kōbai had not emerged from the affair with grounds for satisfaction.

'No doubt,' he said, 'our friend was born under better stars than the rest of us, but I do think His Majesty is making a bit of a fool of himself. All this fuss over getting a daughter married! And I don't think it sets a very good precedent when a commoner no different from you and me takes over rooms practically next door to the celestial chamber itself, and is treated today as if he were the guest of honor.'

He had not wanted to be left out of what promised to be a brilliant assembly, but he was not happy.

*Ruri, perhaps lapis lazuli.

†Yōki, formal utensils of some description.

‡Again, perhaps of lapis lazuli.

**Oshi. The precise meaning is doubtful.

Torches were lighted. Each guest, as he placed his poem upon the lectern, seemed more pleased with himself than the one before. Sure that the poems would be of the usual trite and fusty sort, I did not think I would trouble myself to write them down; but I do seem to have made note of a few after all, by way of remembering the occasion. (I must warn that rank bears little relation to performance as a poet.)

This would seem to be Kaoru's, presented with a sprig of wisteria for the royal cap:

> 'Wisteria, thought I, to grace the august bonnet;
> And my sleeve has caught upon a high, high branch.'*

Such are the airs one assumes when one marries a princess. And this His Majesty's reply:

> 'Its fragrance shall last through all the centuries.
> We shall not then be weary of it today.'

Someone else† presented this:

> 'The wisteria spray that graces the august bonnet
> Competes with the purple clouds of paradise.'

And yet another:

> 'It sends its cascade of flowers to the loftiest heights.
> Of a most uncommon hue is this wisteria.'

The last would seem to be by the unhappy Kōbai.

I may have made mistakes in transcribing certain of these attempts at poetry, but can give assurance that none was conspicuous for its originality.

The hours passed, the concert was more and more interesting. Kaoru was in splendid voice as he sang 'How Grand the Day.'‡ Kōbai joined in, and one still recognized the voice for which he had been famous as a youth. Yūgiri's seventh son, a mere child, played the *shō* pipes so charmingly that he was given a robe by the emperor. Yūgiri himself descended to the garden to offer the ritual thanks. It was almost dawn when the emperor withdrew to his

---

*'I have married far above my station.'

†Probably Yūgiri. His poem is in praise of Kaoru's bride.

‡See note*, page 402.

rooms, having made certain that appropriate gifts were at hand for ranking courtiers and princes of the blood. The princess had gifts, each appropriate to his rank, for lesser courtiers and for the musicians.

The next night she was escorted to Kaoru's Sanjō mansion. The ceremonies accompanying the move were of unusual grandeur, with all the royal ladies in attendance. The princess rode in a brocaded carriage with a wide, flaring roof. In the procession were three carriages similarly brocaded but with plain roofs, six carriages whose facings of plaited palmetto were embossed with gold, twenty such carriages without the gold, and two carriages with wickerwork facings. There were thirty ladies-in-waiting, each attended by eight little maids of honor and eight serving women, and they were joined by women who had been sent from Kaoru's house in twelve carriages. The ranks of courtiers down to the Sixth Rank quite exhausted the possibilities of gorgeous display.

And so Kaoru had her with him, and could observe her at his leisure; and he was not unhappy with what he saw. She was small, pretty, and quiet, with no defects that immediately caught the eye. He had been lucky – and when would he have a better chance to forget Oigimi? Yet he continued to grieve. He could not hope for comfort on this earth, he feared. If only he might find enlightenment, and an understanding of what their strange, unhappy relationship had been a punishment for, he might be able to send it on its way. He lost himself in plans for the Uji villa.

Toward the end of the Fourth Month, when the excitement of the Kamo festival had passed, he set out once again for Uji. He inspected the building and gave appropriate orders, and, thinking it would be unkind not to visit the 'rotting, ivy-covered tree' while he was on the precincts, he made his way to the nun's quarters. A procession of some dignity was just then coming across the bridge: a modest woman's carriage guarded by a band of rough East Country soldiers with quivers at their hips, and attended by a considerable number of servants. Some provincial lady or other, he said to himself as he started inside. His men were noisily making their way through the gate when it became apparent that the other procession was coming to the villa. Quieting his men, Kaoru sent to ask who they might be.

The answer came in rustic accents: 'Our lady's the daughter of the old governor of Hitachi. She's been to the temple at Hatsuse. We put up here on the way out too.'

Well, now: this was someone of whom he had had news! He ordered his men to take cover.

'Please bring her carriage in,' he sent by messenger. 'There is someone else staying here, but he is over in the north wing.'

His men were in travel dress not notable for its finery. The newcomers seemed ill at ease all the same, apparently sensing that the guest was of high rank. Leading their horses aside, they stood at rigid attention. The carriage was pulled up at the west end of a gallery joining the main hall to an outbuilding. The house was without blinds, quite exposed to the public gaze. Kaoru took up his position in a room with lowered shutters, and a search revealed a convenient aperture in one of the doors to the east.* To guard against tell-tale rustling, he stripped down to a singlet and trousers.

The lady was reluctant to leave her carriage. She sent to inquire of the nun who this apparently well-placed guest might be. But Kaoru had said that his identity was under no circumstances to be revealed.

'Please do come in,' said a servant who knew what was expected of him. 'We do have a guest, but he is in another part of the house.'

A young woman climbed out and turned to raise the carriage blinds. She was far less countrified than the guards. Then came an older woman.

'Be quick about it, please, if you will,' she said to her mistress.

'But I have a feeling I'm being watched.' The low voice suggested considerable refinement.

'There you go again. Always imagining things.' The woman seemed very confident of herself. 'You remember perfectly well that the shutters were down the last time too. And where would anyone be watching from?'

Hesitantly, the lady came out. The hair and the shape of the head, the bearing of the slight little figure, added to the impression of good breeding – and reminded him astonishingly of Oigimi. His heart raced with longing to see her face, which was hidden behind a fan. The carriage, a high one, had been stopped at a

*It seems that Kaoru is in the second room – the *futama* – from the eastern veranda of the main hall, and that the girl's carriage has been pulled up at the point where the gallery joins that veranda. *Futama* can also be taken to signify a room two beam spans or some four yards wide.

hollow in the ground. The other two women had jumped down with agility, but their mistress seemed afraid. Hesitantly, she at length climbed down and made her way inside. She had on a robe of deep red, and over it a cloak that seemed to be of pink lined in lavender, with another cloak, of pale green, showing beneath. A screen four feet or so high had been spread against the door through which Kaoru was watching, but he had a clear view, the aperture being yet higher. The lady seated herself beside an armrest. She was evidently suspicious of these doors, for her face was turned carefully away.

'You've had a hard day. Wasn't the Kizu awful?'

'It was so much lower when we crossed last spring. But this is nothing compared to the roads in the east.'

The two women showed no sign of fatigue. Their mistress had lain down, in silence. The arm upon which she rested her head was plump and pretty. Such a charming girl, one knew, could not have been sired by a boor like the governor of Hitachi. Kaoru's back was beginning to ache, but he stood motionless, lest they sense his presence.

'What a fine smell,' said the younger woman. 'Some high-class incense, I imagine. Something the nun will be burning, maybe?'

'A really fine smell. These ladies from the capital go on being all elegant and stylish even when they run off to the mountains. The governor's lady was pretty pleased with herself when it came to perfumes and such, but way off there in the east what chance did she have of putting together a smell like this one? You can say it's a nunnery if you want, but I say she does pretty well for herself. Quality shows through even when you have to stick to blues and grays.'

A girl came in from the veranda beyond. 'Something that might make your lady feel better,' she said. Boxes were brought in one after another.

'Do have some of this,' said the women, pressing sweets upon their mistress.

She did not open her eyes, however, and so the two of them, with loud crunches, commenced devouring chestnuts or something of the sort. It was a noise he was not used to, and it bothered him. He drew away from the door. But again and again he came back. How strange that he should be so drawn to her when he was able to keep company quite as he wished with the grandest of

ladies, even the empress, women of great beauty and elegance –
and so cold to ordinary femininity that people thought the matter
worth commenting upon – how strange that he should be unable
to pull himself away from this less than remarkable young lady.

The nun sent over greetings; but his men, knowing that there
were matters to conceal, said that he was not feeling well, and was
resting. He had suggested that he wished to meet the girl, thought
the nun; and now, seeing his opportunity, he would be waiting for
nightfall. How could she know that he was even now indulging
himself? As always, provisions came from his manor in numerous
hampers and boxes. He had several sent to the nun, who passed a
good portion on to the new arrivals and otherwise saw to their
needs. Putting her dress in order, she presently came to offer formal greetings. Her dress did indeed suggest 'quality,' and in her
features there remained traces of her youthful beauty.

'I was expecting you yesterday. What delayed you?'

'Our lady was so tired you couldn't believe it,' said the older
woman, 'and we stopped last night by the Kizu ferry. And this
morning she took her time about feeling better.'

They awakened her. Shyly, she turned away from the nun, and
Kaoru had a clear view of her face. It was true: he had not been
able to examine Oigimi's features with any great care, but the lines
about the eyes, the flowing hair, were so like hers that he was in
tears. The voice was gentle and well bred, and this time he was
reminded astonishingly of Nakanokimi.

What a sad life the girl had led! The tragedy was that he had
not met her before. And she was so like her sisters! He would have
been drawn to a girl of low status, a girl from some minor cadet
branch of the family, had he been able to detect such a resemblance; and the girl before him, though unrecognized, was without doubt the Eighth Prince's own daughter. He wanted to go in
immediately and say to her: 'So you were deceiving us. You are
still alive.' There had been an emperor across the seas who sent an
emissary to the land of the dead for spangles and bodkins, mementos of his love;* and they had offered little consolation. This lady
was, to be sure, not Oigimi, but it seemed that there might be
some lessening of the pain. A bond from another life had brought
them together.

*Hsüan-tsung and Yang Kuei-fei.

The nun withdrew after a very short interview. The perfume that had been detected by the women, it would seem, had led her to suspect what was happening, and rendered conversation difficult.

It was growing dark. Kaoru slipped out and, making himself presentable, called the nun to her door, slightly open, as always. 'How lucky that I should be here now. You will remember what I asked of you?'

'I had been waiting for an opportunity to tell her of your wishes. And so last year went by, and then this spring I saw them, mother and daughter, when they passed through on their way to Hatsuse. I did let drop a hint to the mother. A very inadequate substitute her daughter would be for our dead lady, she said. I knew you would be busy, and thought I would wait for another time, and that is why I did not tell you. Then I heard that she would be going to Hatsuse again this month. I'm sure she makes a point of stopping here because of her father. This time something, I don't know what, kept the mother in the city, and the girl came alone; and so it did not seem right to tell her about you.'

'I didn't want these country people to see me dressed as I am and so I swore my men to silence. But I know them, and doubt very much if they will have kept the secret. So what shall we do now? I disagree with you. I think the very fact that she is alone makes things easier. Tell her, if you will, please, that there must be a bond between us. How else are we to account for this meeting?'

'A most convenient bond, appearing for us straight from the blue.' She smiled. 'I will tell her.' And she went inside.

'I had heard the call of that strange and lovely bird,*
And parted the grasses, hoping to find its kin.'

It was a poem that he whispered as if to himself; but she took it in to the lady.

---

*The *kaodori* of the *Manyōshū* seems to have been a specific bird, but by the period of the *Genji* its identity was no longer known.

CHAPTER 50

The Eastern Cottage

Mount Tsukuba beckoned, there in Hitachi, but Kaoru hesitated to approach even the verdant foothills.* He had his good name to think of. It would be indiscreet even to write to the girl. Though from time to time the nun Bennokimi gave the girl's mother a hint of what he had said, the mother found it hard to believe that his intentions were serious. She was glad that he had noticed the girl, but she was aware of his exalted rank; and she could only lament that their own was not high enough to make a match possible.

The governor had numerous children by a former wife, now dead. By his present wife he had a daughter who was known as Himegimi,† much pampered, and five or six other children, all of them very young. His affections monopolized by the others, he tended to treat the Eighth Prince's daughter, Ukifune,‡ like an outsider. The mother greatly resented this partiality, and the thought never left her mind of shaming them all by finding a splendid husband for the girl. She would not have fretted so had Ukifune been no prettier than the others – she was, after all, legally the governor's daughter. But her beauty and grace were more pronounced as she grew older. How deplorable, thought the mother, that they should go unnoticed.

Aware that the family was well supplied with daughters, several men from the ranks of the petty nobility had indicated an interest in one or another of them. Even now, with two or three of the

---

*Minamoto Shigeyuki, *Shinkokinshū* 1013:

> Dense are the woods of the hills of Tsukuba;
> But he who has the will can find a way.

Tsukuba, a famous mountain in Hitachi, is introduced because the Eighth Prince's unacknowledged daughter is the adopted daughter of the governor (or vice-governor) of that province.

†Which means something like 'princess.' There is a note of sarcasm in so designating the girl.

‡'Boat upon the waters,' from a poem in the next chapter.

older girls already married, the governor's wife refused to abandon her high hopes for Ukifune, who was the center of her life.

The governor could not have been called a man of low estate. He numbered among his relatives several high courtiers. Being a man of considerable private wealth, he indulged himself as his status allowed, and presided over an orderly and not at all vulgar household. A strangely coarse and rustic manner, however, belied these tasteful surroundings. Probably because he had long been buried in the remote East Country, he was incapable of uttering a syllable that struck the cultivated ear as correct. Aware of this defect, he kept his distance from higher circles at court, and in general maintained a watchful aloofness. He cared little for flute and koto, but he was an expert archer. Numbers of well-favored women, indeed women rather too good for such a household, had been pulled into its service by the power of money. In dress they were excessively modish, and they wrote bad poetry and fiction and otherwise sought to cultivate the skills that see one through the Kōshin vigil.*

This noisy way of life came to be noticed, and Ukifune acquired a certain vogue among the young gallants. They assumed her to be an accomplished young lady, and very pretty as well. Among those who had thrown themselves into the competition for her hand was a certain guards lieutenant. In his early twenties, he was a quiet man who was reputed to have a scholarly bent. He was unable to hold his own in the world of high fashion, and perhaps for this reason had given up his pursuit of other women and commenced paying ardent court to Ukifune. Her mother had decided that he was the most promising of her suitors. He was an honorable man, she said, and a man of discrimination. Though not inexperienced in amorous matters, he was no philanderer. And beautiful though the girl was, she was not likely to attract anyone better.

The mother accepted his letters, and on suitable occasions had the girl send friendly replies. As far as *she* was concerned, everything was settled. The governor might favor the other girls, but she herself was prepared to sacrifice everything for Ukifune. There

---

*As if in imitation of the bad poetry, the sentence is somewhat incoherent. It was thought dangerous to fall asleep on the night of the Kōshin, which occurred once in every cycle of sixty days.

was not the slightest chance, once the lieutenant had laid eyes on her, that he would spurn her because of her low rank. It was presently agreed that the marriage would take place in the Eighth Month. The mother began putting a trousseau together. When some trifle, some little piece of lacquer or inlay, would catch her eye for its high quality and good design, she would put it aside for Ukifune, commending to the governor's attention, for the use of his other daughters, something altogether inferior. He was no judge in these matters, but he collected indefatigably, until they were barely able to see out over the mountains of gimcrackery. A teacher was summoned from the palace to give them lute and koto lessons, and when he had seen them safely through a piece the governor would kowtow with gratitude and bury the man in gifts. On a pleasant evening he would have them at a lively strain, and the effusions with which the governor greeted the performance were quite deafening. Knowing what was good and what was not, his wife would look on contemptuously and refuse to join in the paeans. She might make note now and then, he was constantly saying, that his girls had their good points too.

The lieutenant was becoming impatient. Must they wait until the Eighth Month? But the governor's wife was beginning to have second thoughts. Perhaps she should have consulted her husband – and was she quite sure she could trust the man?

The intermediary stopped by one day.

'I have so many things to worry about,' said the mother, calling him aside. 'It's a long time to wait, I know, and I wouldn't want to seem rude, putting off such an important gentleman. And of course everything *is* decided. But she has no father to look after her, and I have had to do everything myself. I would hate to have him think I have mismanaged things. All the others have someone to look after them, and I don't worry a great deal about them. But this one – what will happen to her when I am gone? I have not set any conditions, because everyone says he is a gentleman of understanding. But sometimes a person *will* wonder, you know. Might he have a change of heart and leave the poor girl for people to laugh at?'

The intermediary passed all of this on to the lieutenant. A look of consternation came over his face.

'You mean she's not the governor's daughter? The first I'd heard of it. You may say she's his stepdaughter and that's just as good, but I'd be lowering myself before the whole world. It won't do. Thank you for not looking into things before you came to me. Thank you very much indeed.'

'I swear I didn't know,' said the intermediary, guiltily. 'Someone at my place told me what you had said. Seeing that she was the favorite, I naturally assumed she was his daughter. I didn't think to ask whether he had a stepdaughter. I hadn't heard anything even suggesting it. I *had* heard that she was beautiful and well behaved, and that her mother couldn't do enough for her and was set on getting her a really good husband. You said you wanted a go-between. Well, I was your man, and I told you so — and how was I to guess that you didn't know all about her? I don't think you have any right to call me careless.'

He was a crafty man, and a good talker.

The lieutenant's reply was not very elegant. 'It's not a family a man would want to marry into for what it is. I'm just doing what all the others do, and no one can blame me for it. I thought that if I could get the governor of Hitachi behind me I might overlook a few other details. He may think of her as no different from his own daughters, but people will say that it doesn't seem to matter to me what I get. The Minamoto councillor and the governor of Sanuki strut in and out of the house, and how would I feel, the last and smallest in the whole long line?'*

The intermediary was an unprincipled man. He was sorry for what had happened, because he had expected favors from both sides.

'You want one of the governor's own daughters, then? They're still very young, but maybe I could tell him. The next-oldest they call Himegimi. I hear she's his favorite.'

'Well — it might not seem very nice just to drop the poor girl and ask for another, now that I've gone this far. But let me tell you how I really feel. I got into this because the governor is a man of substance who handles himself well, and I wanted his backing. That's all. I don't ask for beauty or superior morals. It wouldn't be any trouble at all to find that sort of thing, and good manners and

---

*The lieutenant's speech is difficult, but he seems to be saying that he is willing to overlook a great deal for a share in the governor's wealth. The Minamoto councillor and the governor of Sanuki would seem to be the husbands of the oldest daughters.

a good family to boot. But a poor man who marries a girl with tastes beyond his means is asking for trouble, and can't expect much praise from the world. No, I've seen enough examples of that sort of thing, and I think I'd be willing to put up with a little roughness for a safe, dependable marriage. If you tell the governor how I feel and if he feels the same, I don't see how anyone could object.'

The intermediary had undertaken the assignment because he had a sister in the west wing of the governor's mansion. He was not personally acquainted with the governor. He marched directly into the governor's quarters all the same.

'There is something we ought to discuss.'

'I'd heard about you and your visits.' The governor's manner was not friendly. 'But I don't recall ever inviting you.'

'I am here at the request of the guards lieutenant.'

The governor consented to an interview. The man edged closer, as if finding the matter hard to broach.

'For quite a while now he has been in touch with your lady. They had arranged for him to marry her daughter. They had even picked a lucky day. He is an impatient man. But then someone, I don't know just exactly who, seems to have told him that the girl is your wife's daughter but not yours. It wouldn't look good, you know, for him to marry a governor's step-daughter. Everyone would say it didn't seem to matter to him what he got. When fine gentlemen marry governors' daughters, it's to have the backing of their father-in-law, to be treated like their own prized sons. When there seems like a good chance of it, then that sort of marriage can sometimes be arranged. But what would be the point otherwise? What would be the point if the man found that his father-in-law, the governor, hardly recognized him, treated him like the last and smallest of them all? People have been saying things, and he is upset. He tells me he hit on you immediately, sir, because His Majesty himself had spoken of the brilliance and solidity of your house, and so he asked me to approach you. He had not known, he tells me, that one of the young ladies was not your daughter. And now, seeing that you have so many daughters – yes, we know they are very young – but seeing you have so many, he would like to go back to his very first hope, and would be pleased if he might have your cooperation. He asked me to sound you out.'

'I hadn't heard in any detail what he had in mind. The girl is treated exactly like any daughter of my own. But it's true that I have several other silly girls, and I'm not very good at these things, and it's more than I can do to look after them all. So her mother has the notion that I treat the girl like an outsider, and she's always complaining, and I have no say in the girl's affairs. I heard that something was going on – but that the young gentleman should be looking to me for support – well, I am delighted. I have a daughter I'm fond of. More than fond of – I'd give my life for her. She's had proposals, but I haven't been able to make up my mind. The reports I get about the younger generation aren't good, and I've been thinking my best might not be enough to make her happy. Day and night I ask myself how I'm to go about finding a good, safe man for her. I know the lieutenant. When I was young I worked for his father, the general, now deceased. I could see from close up what a fine, talented boy he was. I hoped I might work for him too someday.* But then I was away in the provinces all those years, and since I've been back I've been shy about making friends again. I'm very glad to hear how he feels about me. Why, I could let him have my girl tomorrow. The only trouble is I wouldn't want her mother to think I'm trying to snatch a husband away from the other girl.'

The intermediary was delighted. Things were going nicely.

'Why hold back? If you agree, everything is as good as settled. What he really wants is a bride with a father who loves her, it doesn't matter how young she is. He knows he made a mistake when he let himself get involved with the other one. He's a fine young fellow, and everyone expects great things from him. And he's a good deal quieter and steadier than you'd expect such an important young fellow to be. He knows his way around, and he has land scattered all over the country. Of course he doesn't have much money yet, but to the manner born, as they say. You'd do a good deal better to have him than some flashy upstart, I don't care how rich he might be. Next year he'll make the Fourth Rank, not a doubt about it. His Majesty himself has promised to make him a privy secretary, so you see there's absolutely not a doubt about it. His Majesty goes on to say it's a crying shame that such a fine young fellow, why you couldn't find a flaw in him, should still be

*There is a chronological difficulty, for the lieutenant would have been a mere infant. Or perhaps the governor is intentionally exaggerating.

single. Go get yourself a wife, His Majesty keeps saying, and useful in-laws. One of these days he'll be right in there with the best of them – His Majesty says he'll be there himself to promise it. His Majesty doesn't have a more devoted servant, and knows it. Two people couldn't be closer. Talented, serious, dedicated – all this and more. Why not make up your mind right here on the spot? A man might almost say if you asked him that this is more than you bargained for. Hundreds of people would jump at the chance to have him for a son-in-law. If you hesitate you're lost. What I say I say because I have your interests at heart.'

It had been a long and persuasive speech. The countrified governor had listened smiling.

'I don't care whether he has money or not. I can smother him in money. Do you think I'd leave him short? It's true I might die on him, but I've decided to leave everything, land and warehouses and everything, to my Himegimi. No one can say anything about her right to them. I have all sorts of children, but she's far and away my favorite. Just let him be good to her, and I'll see him all the way, I'll make a minister of him. He won't have to ask for a thing, even if I have to borrow money while I'm getting things done. Why, anyone that close to His Majesty doesn't have to worry about whether he can depend on *me* or not. What a match for the both of them, him and my girl, maybe, if you know what I mean.'*

He spoke as if arrangements were complete. Overjoyed, the intermediary did not bother to tell his sister what had happened, or to call on the governor's wife. He went directly to the lieutenant. Everything was in order, he said, describing the interview. The lieutenant was not at all unhappy, though he thought it somewhat provincial to talk of buying a ministry.

'And have you spoken to his wife? She's been dead set on marrying me to the other girl. People will say I have bad manners. They may even say I'm not honest.' He was having brief doubts.

'Come, now. This Himegimi is her *real* favorite. It's only that she thought the oldest daughter should marry first, and so she aimed her in your direction. You were a good solution to her problem.'

---

*The governor's last statement is made to indicate sudden doubt, probably to comical effect.

It seemed a little odd to the lieutenant that the younger daughter should suddenly have replaced Ukifune as the favorite. But it was better to take the long view, even at a risk of having to endure the displeasure of the mother and the reproaches of the world for a time. He was a practical young man, and he quickly made up his mind. On the evening of the very day that had been selected for his marriage to Ukifune he went to the second daughter.

In ignorance of all this, the governor's wife was pushing ahead with the arrangements. Her women were all decked out in nuptial finery and their rooms were properly appointed, and she had seen to the needs of the bride herself, washed her hair, helped her to dress. She was too good for the lieutenant. Her father was dead, of course, but if he had recognized her and she had grown up with her sisters, then it would not have been wholly out of the question, though perhaps just a little presumptuous, to think of marrying her to Kaoru. But the sad truth was that she would always be looked down upon as an adopted daughter and a girl whose father had not recognized her.

Enough of these thoughts. She was passing her prime, and here was this man, from a not inconsiderable family, of not despicable rank, with his solemn proposals. Keeping her own counsel, the mother had made her decision. The intermediary was a skillful persuader, able to get around even the governor; and it was not at all surprising that he should have succeeded with a woman.

The hour was approaching. Mother and daughter were very busy.

In came the governor with a headlong account of what had happened.

'In that sneaky way of yours, you tried to take away my girl's husband. What you need is a good long look at your place in the world. Don't go thinking fine young gentlemen might be interested in that girl of yours. My own may be ugly little things, but for some reason, I don't just know what it is, men seem to like them better. You had your plans, and pretty good ones too. He had different ones. If it was all the same, he said, he'd like to have one of my girls, and I said yes.'

It was a graceless description of the case and it took no account of his wife's feelings.

She was stunned. She sat for a time on the verge of tears, recalling one after another the cold, hard ways of the world. Abruptly, she got up and left.

She went to Ukifune's room. The girl was charming, beautiful – a superior girl, without question, despite what had happened. In tears, the governor's wife told the nurse her story.

'Men are utterly cruel. I have always said to myself that I must have no favorites among my sons-in-law, but I have known that I would give up everything for the husband of this one. And look at him, throwing her over because she has no father, taking a mere child in her place. He's impossible. I do not want to be where I have to see him or hear his voice. Just listen to them if you will – as if it were the greatest honor in the world. They're a match for each other, that man and my good husband. I want no part of it. I only wish that I could get out of this house.'

The nurse was incensed. It was good of him to look down upon her lady. 'But there's nothing to carry on about. I say she's lucky this has happened. If that's the sort of person he is, well, let's just say that he has no taste. We'll wait for someone with good taste to come along. I had just the quickest glimpse of the gentleman at Uji the other day, and it added years to my life. If he says he's interested, well, all we have to do is let things run their course.'

'You're mad. Everyone says it takes the most extraordinary kind of woman to interest him. Lord Yūgiri and Lord Kōbai and Prince Hotaru all went down on their knees, they say, and he sent them away and finally got one of His Majesty's own daughters. I imagine he just thinks of putting the child in his mother's service and seeing her now and then. It would be a fine house to be in, of course, but I would worry even so. Everyone says how lucky her sister is, and certainly she has her worries. The only man you can trust is the man who is willing to make do with one wife. I know that well enough from my own experience. The prince at Uji was a fine, sensitive gentleman, but he treated me as if I were less than human. I can't tell you how much I suffered. The governor is a complete boor and not at all good-looking, but the years have gone quietly by because he has been faithful to me. The sort of thing he did tonight isn't easy to live with, but he has never given me reason to be jealous. When we have had our quarrels they have been out in the open. All those grand houses, ministers and princes and that sort of people – they may be so stylish they make you dizzy. But a woman has to remember her place in the world. That's what makes all the difference, and that's why I'm so sad for the poor child. I only wish I could make her a match that people wouldn't laugh at.'

The governor, busy with his own preparations, looked in upon them once more. 'You have all these pretty young things. Send them over to be with my Himegimi. And I understand you have new bed curtains. We haven't had much time, so we'll just make do with them.'

Jumping up and sitting down and jumping up again, he directed the operations. The rooms had been appointed in quiet good taste, but he had screens brought in until they made solid walls, and vanities and cupboards until they seemed to be fighting for space. He was very pleased with himself. His wife had better taste, but she kept her peace, resolved not to interfere. Ukifune had withdrawn to an inner room.

'I know you,' he said. 'Well, my girl is your girl too, and maybe you could help just a little. But it doesn't matter. Plenty of girls get by without mothers.'

Himegimi's nurse had been at work since noonday, and the results were not at all displeasing. Himegimi was fifteen or sixteen, small and plump, with hair that trailed to the hems of her skirts and was thick and luxuriant to the farthest edges. The governor was very proud of it.

'Maybe I should feel guilty about taking a man my wife had other ideas about. But he's too good to let get away. The whole town's after him, and someone might get him, and I wouldn't want that to happen.' The go-between had been very successful.

As for the lieutenant, his future seemed bright. The governor was known to be very rich. Not even bothering to change the date, he made his nuptial visit.

The mother and the nurse were outraged. Poor Ukifune was as good as homeless.

And so the mother wrote to Nakanokimi, Prince Niou's wife:* 'I have thought that it would be impertinent of me to approach you without good reason, and so I have not written. Certain developments now make life rather difficult for my daughter, and

---

*She is here called Niou's *kitanokata*, 'main wife' or 'principal wife,' for the first time in an expository passage.

it seems advisable that she be away from here for a time. If there were a place in your house where she could hide, attracting the attention of no one, I should be very happy indeed. It is not possible for an insignificant person like myself to see adequately to her needs, and sad events do have a way in this world of piling one upon another. I have no one to turn to except you.'

She was in tears as she wrote. Nakanokimi was deeply moved, but in a quandary. Would it be right for her, the guardian of his memory, to take in the daughter to whom her father had to the end denied recognition? And on the other hand it would not be easy to look away while her sister suffered and perhaps went to ruin. Nor would it do honor to the memory of her father if, for no good reason, the two were to become strangers. What was she to do?

In an agony of indecision, she appealed to the woman Tayū.

'She must have her reasons,' said Tayū. 'Please do not answer in a way that might strike her as even slightly unfriendly. Daughters of low-ranking mistresses are always keeping company with daughters of proper wives. Your good father was altogether too inflexible.'*

The princess sent off her answer: 'We have a place in the west wing where she may hide. It will be uncomfortable, I am sure, but if she can bear with it she is most welcome.'

The mother was delighted, and the two of them, mother and daughter, slipped out of the house. Ukifune was by now rather happy at her misfortune, because it offered a chance for new intimacy with her sister.

The governor had been determined that his new son-in-law be received with the utmost splendor; but the restraint that makes for true brilliance was foreign to him. He scattered East Country silks in all directions, and at the banquet, a clamorous affair, the dishes threatened to crowd one another off the tables. The underlings were delighted at all this largesse, and even the lieutenant was pleased. It had been clever of him to woo the governor. The governor's wife suffered in silence, acquiescing in her husband's demands, for she could hardly be absent from the festivities. This room was to be for the lieutenant, those over there for his

---

*The last sentence, which is missing from numbers of texts, is unclear. It could be construed as a repetition of the plea that Nakanokimi be kind to the girl.

attendants, and in the end scarcely a room was left in the whole vast house. The Minamoto councillor occupied the east wing, and the governor had many sons. Himegimi having taken over Ukifune's west wing, Ukifune herself would have to make do with a corner of a gallery somewhere.

It was in these desperate circumstances that the governor's wife thought of Nakanokimi. With no powerful relatives, poor Ukifune would suffer increasing scorn and abuse. The governor's wife did not find it easy to seek the help of a lady whose father had refused to accept his responsibilities.

The girl's nurse and two or three young attendants went with them. A room had been prepared at the northwest corner of the west wing, remote from the main activities of the house. They had lived far apart over the years, the princess and the governor's wife, but they were not, after all, complete strangers.* The princess received her guests warmly. Used to a different sort of company, the governor's wife thought her charming. Yet envy at the young mother and child before her was mixed in with the pleasure. Was she herself so utterly inferior to the wife of the Eighth Prince? No, he had refused to accept her only because she had been in domestic service. There could be no other reason for such scorn. Forcing her daughter upon the princess had not been easy for her. Word having been sent out that the girl was in retreat, no one came to her room. The mother stayed for several days, quietly studying the household.

Niou appeared one day. Overcome with curiosity, the governor's wife looked out through a crack between two doors, and thought him radiant as a cherry in full bloom. Numerous courtiers of the Fourth and Fifth ranks waited upon him, far superior in manner and appearance to the husband upon whom she depended, and whom, maddening though he might be, she did not mean to reject. Nakanokimi's stewards came in to discuss this and that problem in their several domains. Among the young courtiers of the Fifth Rank were many whom she did not recognize. Her own stepson, a secretary in the ministry of rites, came with a message from court, but he was of too inferior a rank to address the prince. What glory, she thought; and what happiness to be near him! Why should an outsider like herself have thought that, grand though he

---

*The governor's wife is a niece of Nakanokimi's mother.

might be, he meant unhappiness for his princess? She should have known better. So remarkable were his face and his bearing as he took the child in his arms that any woman should be delighted at the meager prospect of an annual interview, like the stars at their midsummer meeting.* The princess was behind a low curtain, which he pushed aside as he spoke to her. They were a perfect match. The governor's wife thought of the Eighth Prince and the lonely life he had led, and knew that there were princes and there were princes.

Niou withdrew to the bedchamber. Nurses and young serving women were left in charge of the child. Visitors† came in swarms, but he said that he was not feeling well and stayed in bed until nightfall. The elegance of each small detail quite dazzled the governor's wife. She had thought herself dedicated to the pursuit of good taste, and she saw now that there was a certain point beyond which ordinary people could not go. But she had one daughter, at least, who could mix with the best of them. They too were her daughters, the girls the governor talked of buying ministries and thrones for; yet how different! She must not give up, she must persist with her high ambitions. She lay awake all night, thinking of the future.

The sun was high when Niou arose. The empress was again indisposed, he said, changing to court dress, and he must inquire after her. Still consumed with curiosity, the governor's wife looked out through the same aperture. In formal dress he was incomparable. He sat dandling the child, clearly reluctant to leave; but finally, after a light breakfast, he made his way out. His escort had emerged from the barracks. Among them was one who, though dressed well enough (he had on a lined robe and wore a sword), had not one mark of real distinction. Indeed, he was rather homely. Before the prince he shrank to a cipher.

The women were talking.

'That's the lieutenant, the governor of Hitachi's son-in-law. He was supposed to marry our new guest, but he thought he'd do better for himself if he married one of the governor's daughters. So he got himself a little dwarf of a thing.'

'The lady hasn't said a word.'

---

*Tanabata, the seventh day of the Seventh Month, when Altair and Vega meet.
†Or possibly ladies-in-waiting.

'But we have our ways. We have our spies over there.'

Only half listening, the governor's wife was suddenly attentive, and startled. So that was who the man was! What a fool she had been to think him even remotely acceptable! She had only contempt for him now.

On hands and knees, the little prince was peering from under a blind. Niou came back and gave him another bouncing.

'If the empress is feeling better, I'll come straight home. Otherwise I suppose I'll have to stay until morning. I do hate to be away for even a single night.'

The governor's wife gazed on and on until finally he made his departure, and when he was gone she was somehow lonely.

She could not find strong enough words of praise. Nakanokimi smiled, thinking the lack of restraint a bit countrified.

'You were a mere infant when your mother died. All of us, and your father too, wondered what would become of you. You were born under lucky stars. That's why you could grow up way off in the mountains and still be the fine young lady you are. What a tragedy that your sister had to leave us.'

She was in tears, and Nakanokimi's eyes were moist. 'A person lives on, and there are times when anger and resentment seem very far away. I have become resigned to a great many things – that I was fated to live longer than those who were most important to me, that I was not meant to know my own mother. But I do go on weeping for my sister. Why did she have to die, when a man like the general, a man of real feeling, could not take his mind from her?'

'But isn't he just a little *too* pleased with himself, now that the emperor has singled him out for special attention? If your sister were still alive, there would be the other princess standing between them.'

'I wonder. We would have been alike, you mean, with the whole world laughing at us? You may be right. It may be better that she died. He goes on grieving, I suppose, because she never let him come near. But it is more than that. He seems completely unable to forget – it is very odd, really. And he has taken care of all the memorial services for Father.' She did not mention the more troublesome aspects of their relationship.

'He seems to have told the nun at Uji that he would like to have my daughter, useless little thing, in place of your poor dead sister. It is not for me to say it, I know, but there are "those laven-der grasses." '*

In tears, she went on to tell of Ukifune's troubles. Thinking that Nakanokimi might have heard of the affair, though not per-haps in detail, she spoke obliquely of how the girl had been wronged by her stepfather and the lieutenant.

'While I am alive we can somehow get by, I suppose. I can take care of her after a fashion, and we can be a comfort to each other. But what awful things will happen to her when I die and leave her behind? I worry, and have almost decided that it would be best to give up the idea of finding a husband for her, and put her in a nunnery somewhere off in the mountains.'

'Yes, it is very sad. But we who have been left behind must learn to live with insults. It was not possible for my sister and me to go into a nunnery, and so Father chose the next-best thing, and taught us to live alone, away from the world. And here I am, living this strange life, right in the middle of the city. No, you mustn't think of it. I couldn't bear to see her in those awful blacks and grays.'

It had been spoken with care and gravity, and the governor's wife was much comforted. Though no longer young, she dressed with modest good taste. She had not, however, been able to con-trol a tendency toward fleshiness, and her generous proportions made her an admirable match for His Eminence of Hitachi.

'Your esteemed father was not kind to her, I have always thought, and that is why the world chooses to treat her as if she were less than human; but what you have said does a great deal to help me forget the old sorrow.' She talked of her life over the years and of places she had seen, wild, remote places like Ukishima.† 'I was "left alone to think these dismal thoughts," ‡ and now I find such pleasure in your company that I would like to stay on and on, and possibly give you some idea of what it is like to live at the foot of Tsukuba, where there is no one, literally no one, to talk to. But all those other tiresome children will be raising a great stir, I know, and I am, after all, a little restless. I know better than most what it means to lose your proper place in the world, and so I shall leave her with you, and say no more.'

See note, page 116.

†Near Shiogama, in the present Miyagi Prefecture.

‡See note*, page 949.

The list of her grievances stretched on. Nakanokimi did indeed hope that something could be done for the girl, who was certainly attractive and seemed to have a pleasant disposition. She was quiet and composed and yet not excessively shy, and her way of avoiding the scrutiny of even Nakanokimi's women suggested that she was not wanting in intelligence. Her speech was astonishingly reminiscent of Oigimi's. Yes, thought Nakanokimi, remembering that there had been talk of a statue of her sister. She would like to have him see *this* image.

And just then there came a shouting. 'The general is here, the general is here!'

The usual care went into arranging the curtains.

'I must have a look at him,' said the governor's wife. 'Everyone says he's wonderfully handsome, but of course he can't possibly be as handsome as the prince.'

'We don't know about *that*,' replied the women. 'We'd be hard put to choose between them.'

'When they are side by side,' said Nakanokimi, 'my husband seems rather short on good looks; but when they are apart it really is impossible to decide which one is the better-looking. The way good looks have of blotting out everyone else can be rather annoying.'

'This is just talk,' laughed one of her women. 'It would take a very extraordinary man to blot out Prince Niou.'

Now he was getting out of his carriage, came the report; but he was concealed by his retinue, shouting to clear the way. Then they saw him approaching. Yes, thought the governor's wife: these were not the showy kind of good looks, but the impression was of a gentle elegance such as to make one feel rather common. She smoothed her hair at the forehead.

He had a large retinue, for he was on his way home from court.

'I was told last night that Her Majesty was ill. She seemed lonely without her children, and so I stayed on in place of the prince. He was late this morning too. You must be charged with responsibility for these delinquencies, I fear.'

'Very kind of you,' she answered simply, 'I am sure.'

He of course had something on his mind, for he had come at a time when he knew that Niou would be at court. His manner was, as always, affectionately nostalgic. He spoke with circumspection of his inability to forget the past and his unhappiness with his marriage. How, she wondered, could he go on forever thinking of her sister? Or was there an element of pretense in his tenacity? Having been so ardent at the outset, he would not have it thought that he had forgotten? But he seemed so open with her that, not being a log or a stone, she had presently to recognize the genuineness of his sorrow. She sighed. Then, perhaps hoping to wash away* part of the pain, she mentioned the 'image' of which they had spoken. An image had come in secret to this very house, she let it be known.

This was exciting news. He longed to be shown to the girl's presence, but feared that he might seem capricious.

'It would indeed be a comfort if an idol were to come at my command. But a bad conscience would only muddy the waters.'

'It is not easy to be a saint.' She laughed a soft laugh which the governor's wife found charming.

'But you might at least describe my feelings to them. I am reminded of an earlier case of evasion and it does not bode well for the future.' There were tears in his voice, which he sought to cover with a playful poem.

> 'The permanent loan, if you please, of a useful image,
> A handy memento, to take away the gloom.'†

> 'To float downstream afresh at each atonement,
> And yet to have forever at your side?

No, there are too many hands tugging at you.‡ I would fear for the poor girl.'

'You know very well which shoal I shall come upon in the end. Please do not pretend that you do not. I am like the foam that

---

*The imagery of the lustration ceremony is resumed, and pursued in the following conversation.

†The image is of *nademono*, dolls to which, during lustration ceremonies, impurities and afflictions were transferred by bodily contact. They were then cast away down a stream.

‡Anonymous, *Tales of Ise* 47 and *Kokinshū* 706:

> Too many hands are tugging at the *nusa*.
> My love it may command, but not my faith.

Nusa (here *ōnusa*, 'large *nusa*'), sacred branches hung with strips of paper, were used in lustration ceremonies much as were *nademono*.

sinks and rises again,* and I find your talk of being floated downstream very much to the point. Where will the foam come to rest?'

It was growing dark, and she had her guests to think about. 'I do seem to have some people with me at the moment, and must have a thought or two for appearances. Suppose you go home early, this one time.'

'You might tell her, if it would not be too much trouble, that these feelings have been with me for some years, and that it would be wrong of her to think herself the victim of a sudden whim. But I tend to be wrapped up in myself, and handle these matters clumsily.'

And he went out.

The governor's wife thought him splendid, indeed quite flawless. Bennokimi had on more than one occasion spoken of a possibility which she had dismissed as altogether too remote; but now she thought that one could easily wait a whole year to bathe in the light of such a star. She was determined that her daughter go to no ordinary man; and she was aghast at her want of discrimination (for she had long kept company with rough East Country people) in thinking the lieutenant acceptable. As for the perfume left at the cypress pillar and upon the cushion, she despaired of finding words to describe it.

And those who knew him well had to praise him afresh. 'The good books tell us that a strong perfume is one of the real signs of grace. It must be true. There's that sandalwood from Oxhead Mountain (awful name) that the Lotus Sutra makes so much of.† The first whiff of him and you know what it means. He's been at his books and beads ever since he was a little boy.'

And another: 'What I'd like to know is what he was up to in other lives to deserve it all.'

---

*Ki no Tomonori, Kokinshū 792:

> As the foam, which sinks to rise again,
> I drift along, and know my time will come.

†In the Medicine King (Yakuō) section of the Lotus Sutra, we are informed that they who follow well the precepts of the Medicine King exude a fragrance as of the sandalwood of Oxhead Mountain, in southern India. Oxhead is an 'awful name' because of the association with the oxheaded demons of hell.

The governor's wife listened smiling.

Nakanokimi relayed certain of his remarks. 'And once he has made up his mind to something, it becomes an obsession with him. Nothing can budge him. Yes, I know that his life is complicated; but if you really have thought of sending her off to a nunnery, you have nothing to lose by giving him a try.'

'Yes, it is true that I've thought of sending her where "no birds fly singing overhead."* I've thought of it as the only way to protect her. But now I see that just being near him, just being one of his servants, would give new meaning to life; and if that is the effect he has upon me, think what he must do to a young girl. But I don't know – she is such an unattractive little thing – we might just be asking for trouble. Life is not good to us women. All of us, high and low, have to live with unhappiness, in this life and all the others. I want to weep, just thinking about it. But I leave everything to you. I know you will do the right thing.'

'As I have said, he has been honesty itself through the years.' Nakanokimi sighed. This new responsibility was not entirely welcome. 'But we can never be sure of the future.' She said no more.

The next morning a carriage came for the governor's wife, and with it a strongly worded letter. The governor was angry.

'I shouldn't, I know, but I do leave everything to you. Keep her hidden for a while. She is useless, but keep her with you, and teach her what she needs to know. I'll be thinking what to do with her, whether to send her off to some cave among the rocks,† or what.' She was in tears as she got into her carriage.

This was Ukifune's first separation from her mother, and she was of course sad; and yet the prospect of living with her sister for a time in a bright, fashionable house was not unpleasing.

The carriage left at dawn. Niou and his retinue, on their way from court, were just then coming in the gate. Having slipped away for a quiet visit with his son, he had few attendants and his carriage was plainer than his rank called for. The governor's wife had her carriage pulled aside while his was brought up to a gallery. He glared at the other party suspiciously. And who would they be, sneaking away in the night? So it was, he said to himself, that an

See note, page 611.
†See note*, page 234.

adventurer made his escape. He had a not very lovable way of judging others by himself.

One of her attendants identified her as 'a noble person from Hitachi.'

'A noble person from Hitachi!' His young men roared with laughter. 'Suppose we give them a bit of the real thing for their troubles.'

Yes, sighed the governor's wife, it had been a poor choice of words; in such company she was scarcely to be called noble. And she so longed to make a decent match for her daughter, who certainly deserved a better than ordinary husband.

Niou made his way inside. 'And so you have had a noble person from Hitachi with you? A carriage and guard disappearing in the night – I think most people would find it suspicious.'

He was impossible. She turned away in a show of annoyance which he thought charming.

'It was an old friend of Tayū's – no one interesting enough for *you* to concern yourself with. Why must you always put the wrong meaning on things? You seem absolutely intent on turning people against me.'

He slept on as if the sun had not risen. Presently a party of courtiers arrived, and he went to receive them in the main hall. The empress was better, it seemed, her indisposition not having been serious. Thus relieved of court duties, he passed several pleasant hours with Yūgiri's sons and others, in such pursuits as Go and rhyme guessing.

In the evening he returned to the princess's rooms. She was having her hair washed. Most of her women had withdrawn. He sent a little girl in with a message: 'A very nice time you have chosen for laundering your hair. I don't suppose you expect me to watch? And so I am to sit with my boredom?'

'Yes, it is unfortunate,' agreed Tayū. 'She usually washes her hair while you are away, but she has been putting it off and putting it off. This is the last good day before the end of the month, and of course she can't do it next month or the month after.* And so I have been at work on it.'

Several women were putting the baby prince to bed. Wander-

*Hair washing during the Ninth and Tenth months seems to have been thought sacrilegious.

ing restlessly here and there, Niou came upon a girl whom he had not seen before, out towards the west veranda. A new maid-servant, perhaps? Midway along the partition* a door was slightly open. About a foot beyond he saw a screen, and beside it a curtain backed by a blind. One section had been folded over the frame. From beneath protruded the sleeves of a bright lavender robe and a cloak of greenish yellow. He could see without being seen, for one panel of the screen was folded back. He softly opened the door a few inches more and edged closer to the mysterious lady. The garden, enclosed by a gallery, was in the best of taste, a profusion of flowers with high rocks along a brook. The girl was at the edge of the veranda, leaning on an armrest and gazing out. He opened the door yet a little more and peered from behind the screen. She was very pretty indeed as she looked up, thinking that one of the women had come in. Never one to hold back on such occasions, he clutched at her skirt. He pushed the door shut with his other hand and seated himself beside the screen. Aware now that there was something unusual about the visitor, she brought a fan to her face, and, very engaging in her shyness, turned to see who he might be. He took the hand that held the fan.

What was she to do? And who might he be? He had caught her quite unawares. His face averted, he was sitting in the shadow of the screen. The gentleman who had expressed such an improbable interest in her, perhaps? The fragrance suggested as much.

Her nurse, sensing the presence of the invader, pushed aside the screen. 'What is going on in here? Something very odd is going on in here.'

But he was not to be put off by so minor a reproof. Though the encounter had been quite unplanned, he was at no loss for words. He talked of this and that, and soon it was evening.

'What is your name? I won't let you go till you tell me.'

He stretched out familiarly beside her. The nurse was horrified, for she had at length guessed who he was.

Lamps were being lighted at the eaves. The maids announced that Nakanokimi's toilet was finished and that she had returned to the main room. From other parts of the hall came the sound of

---

*This sentence and the next are not at all clear. Probably the partition runs along the west side of the central chamber (*moya*), and the screens and the curtain are at right angles beyond, the latter parallel to the blind.

shutters being closed. Ukifune's quarters, in a remote corner, were furnished with but a pair of highboys. Crated screens lay about in much disorder. A door had been left open for routine comings and goings. Ukon, a daughter of Tayū also in Nakanokimi's service, was closing the shutters, gradually nearer.

'My, but it's dark in here. No one has brought you a light? Well just look at this, will you. I've been in such a rush getting these things shut that I don't even know where I am.' She opened a shutter she had just closed. Niou was mildly disconcerted.

'Come here and listen to what *I* have to tell you.' The nurse was an emphatic woman. 'The most dreadful thing has been going on in here. I've worn myself out keeping watch. I haven't been able to budge from this spot.'

Ukon groped her way through the darkness, and came upon a fragrantly reclining figure in a man's singlet. So he was at it again! She knew immediately that he did not have Ukifune's permission.

'It most certainly *is* dreadful. What shall I do? Go this minute and tell our lady?'

She started off. No, said the other, that would hardly be the proper thing to do. Niou was not in the least worried. But he was puzzled. Here was this wonderfully attractive girl, and he could tell from Ukon's manner that she was more than a new maid-servant. At great length, he tried to coax her from her silence. There was nothing ill-natured or disagreeable about it, but he could see that she was near distraction. He was genuinely sorry and put much feeling into his efforts to comfort her.

Ukon hurried off to tell Nakanokimi. 'Very sad, very sad,' she said. 'I can imagine how the poor girl feels.'

'That awful habit of his. Her mother will think it very careless of us. I don't know how many times she told me to take care of the child.'

But what was she to do? He had a remarkable way of spying out everyone in the household who was even moderately young and attractive. How had he learned that the girl was here? She fell into an outraged silence.

Ukon had gone on to take a woman named Shōshō into her confidence.

'Usually when he's at games with those fine gentlemen they play on into the night. And so he caught us off guard. There we were, sprawled all over the house. But the question is what to do now.'

'That nurse of hers is quite a woman. Nothing could make her budge an inch. I almost thought she was going to separate them by main force.'

Just then a messenger arrived from court with the news that the empress had suffered a relapse. She had been in great pain since earlier in the evening.

'How very inconsiderate of her, when he was having such a good time.' Ukon started in with the message.

'What's done is done,' said Shōshō. 'Don't go scolding him and making yourself look silly.'

'But I doubt if it *is* quite done.'

They were whispering busily to each other. And what would all the rest be thinking? sighed Nakanokimi. People with an ordinary sense of propriety would be reproving her as well as Niou.

Ukon relayed the message, embroidering upon it somewhat.

'And who was the august messenger?' he asked, showing no disposition to move. 'I'm sure he overdid it.'

'A chamberlain to Her Majesty who announced himself as Taira no Shigetsune.'

He was in no hurry to go, whatever all the others might be thinking. Ukon went for the messenger, who came to the west veranda. With him was the man who had earlier brought in his message.

'Prince Nakatsukasa is already at court, and I saw Her Majesty's chamberlain leaving his house.'

She did from time to time have these seizures. He started out, leaving behind many complaints and promises. It would not do to be thought unfilial.

Soaked in perspiration, Ukifune sat with bowed head. It was as if she had awakened from a nightmare. Her nurse was beside her, wielding a fan as she offered her views in the matter.

'This place is not for us. We have no defenses, none at all, and it will be even worse now that he knows you are here. I'm terrified. He may be a royal highness and all that sort of thing, but his conduct is inexcusable. No – you must find someone outside the family. Your own brother-in-law – why the shame of it had me glowering at him like a proper devil.* I can't have been a pretty

---

Gama no sō, scowl like that with which Acala (Fudō) wards off devils.

sight, and I think I possibly had him a little frightened. He gave my hand a playful little tweak. I almost had to laugh at that.

'There was a battle at the other house today. His Honor the governor said your mother only cared about you and had as good as abandoned all the others. It was a complete disgrace for her to be out of the house, he said, just when they had this new bridegroom coming in. For a minute or so they thought he might hit her. They heard it all, and they were all on her side. It was that lieutenant's fault, they said. If it hadn't been for him and his grand ideas, they said, well, there might have been a little fighting in the family from time to time, but things would have gone on pretty much the same.'

But the girl was beyond worrying about her mother. Added to terror such as she had not known before was concern for Nakanokimi's feelings. She sat weeping, her head bowed.

The nurse now commenced painting a brighter picture. 'Oh, come now – there's no need for all these tears. It's all *so* much sadder for a girl who has no mother. People may have a way of looking down on a girl with no father, but there's nothing worse, let me tell you, than a nasty stepmother. You have your mother to look after you, and she'll do it too, somehow. So stop this carrying on. You've been to Hatsuse time after time and you're not used to traveling, and the Blessed One is sure to have noticed. People may be mean to you now, but I'm praying for the day when you'll make a marriage that will startle them all. You'll have the last laugh, I know you will.'

Niou hurried out. As he went through this west gate, which seemed to be nearer the place, he was singing some of his favorites from the anthologies. He had an uncommonly good voice, but it did not please her. His retinue was simple, some ten guardsmen on plainly fitted horses.*

Nakanokimi guessed what Ukifune would be going through and sent for her as if nothing had happened. 'The prince has gone to inquire after Her Majesty and will probably not be back tonight. Washing my hair somehow depresses me and I am still up. Do come over and keep me company. You must be bored.'

Ukifune sent her nurse with a reply. 'I am not feeling well myself. I think I should rest for a while.'

*Utsushiuma, the meaning of which is doubtful.

Another message came immediately. 'And what will the trouble be?'

'Nothing in particular, really. It is just that I am not quite myself.'

Ukon and Shōshō exchanged glances. *They* knew what was the matter, and the fact that all the others knew too did not help.

It was really too sad for the poor girl, Nakanokimi was thinking. Kaoru had indicated an interest in her, and he would have little admiration for her failure to defend herself. As for Niou, he was outrageous, always sniffing out scandals in her life when his own was riddled with them, always making baseless charges while conveniently overlooking his own vulnerability. And Kaoru, keeping his bitter counsels, of such gravity and restraint as to make one despair of ever reaching a similar level – he now had Ukifune to worry about. She and Ukifune had lived apart over the years, but now that they had met nothing must separate them. Yes, it was all very sad. The world was full of the most remarkable complications. She had her own troubles, but she must count herself among the lucky ones. She had seemed destined for just such misfortunes, but something had kept her from falling the whole distance. If she could but see that infatuation of Kaoru's smoothly transferred elsewhere, her troubles would be over. Her hair, thick and long, was very slow to dry. She had lain down, a winsome, delicate figure in a white singlet.

Ukifune was still in a daze. Her nurse, though sympathetic, urged her to action. 'This will not do at all. She will think that something really happened. Pull yourself together, do, and go in to her. I will tell Ukon everything.' She went to the door. 'I would like to speak to Ukon, please.'

'This horrible affair has left her running a fever,' she continued when Ukon had come out, 'and she is in a bad state. Have your lady comfort her, please, if you will. She has not done a thing to apologize for, and here she is all guilt and regrets. That's how she is – a little more experience and she would think nothing of it.' She went on fussing over the girl and presently saw her to the princess's rooms.

Ukifune was in an agony of embarrassment. What would they all be thinking? Almost too docile and yielding, she allowed herself to be led off.

She sat turned away from the light, lest they see that her hair was wet from tears. The women had thought their mistress unique, but here was her match. She could not very well hide herself from her own sister, and the two women, Ukon and Shōshō, were able to have a good look at her. They shuddered to think what would happen if Niou were to give her his full attention. He was always being attracted to new women who had far less to recommend them.

'You are to think of this as your own house, and you are not to be forever on your guard,' said Nakanokimi in intimate, affectionate tones. 'I have not for one moment stopped mourning for my sister, and I have been angry at myself for living on without her. You are a great joy and comfort – you do so look like her. There is no one who really cares for me. It would please me enormously if you could learn to think of me as she did.'

Ukifune was shy and still somewhat countrified, and had trouble finding an answer. Finally she said in an almost childlike voice: 'All those years I thought of you, miles and miles away. It is a great comfort for me too, seeing you after so long.'

The princess took out illustrations to old romances, which they examined while Ukon read from the texts. Absorbed now in the pictures and facing her sister in the lamplight, Ukifune had a delicate, girlish beauty that was perfection of its kind. The quiet elegance of the face, with a slight glow about the eyes and at the forehead, was so like Oigimi that Nakanokimi herself was paying little attention to the pictures. A longing for the past flooded over her. She compared the two in her mind. How could they be so alike? No doubt the girl took after their father. Old women long in the Eighth Prince's service had said that Oigimi looked like her father, Nakanokimi herself like her mother. What affection and yearning she did call up, this girl so like the two now gone! Nakanokimi felt tears coming to her eyes. Oigimi had been a lady of cold, proud nobility, but she had had an affectionate strain and could be docile and accommodating to excess. Ukifune still had not outgrown a certain childish awkwardness, and perhaps because of it and because of her shyness one would have had to put her down as rather inferior to Oigimi in the sort of undeniable beauty that immediately catches the eye. Given a certain mellowing and deepening, however, she would not seem in any degree a mismatch for Kaoru. Nakanokimi was begining to behave like an elder sister.

They talked until dawn, when they lay down side by side to sleep. Nakanokimi spoke of her father, though at no great length, and of the life they had lived at Uji. Ukifune sighed that she had not been allowed to share it.

Meanwhile others who knew something of what had happened were also talking.

'How far do you suppose it went? She really is very pretty – and what horrid luck! Our lady may be fond of her, but small good that will do her now.'

'Oh, I don't think it went far at all,' replied Ukon. They were conversing in whispers. 'That nurse of hers pulled me in and had a few things to say, but she didn't make it sound as if she had allowed much to happen. And then the prince was reciting the poem about "meeting and not meeting"* when he went out. But I don't know – maybe he did it to put me off the track. You never can tell. But remember how calm and cool she was when she was sitting with our lady? She certainly didn't look like someone with a great deal to hide.'

The nurse borrowed a carriage and went to the governor's house. The governor's wife was stunned. The whole Nijō house would be scandalized – and what of Nakanokimi herself? Jealousy favored no particular rank, she knew from her own experience. She rushed off to Nijō that night. It was a great relief to find Niou away.

'She is still a child. I thought she would be safe here. But with the cat away, as they say.† All those silly people at home are at me day and night.'

'Oh, she's not all that much of a child,' laughed Nakanokimi. 'The trouble is having you off there watching us, like the cat you say is away.'‡

This calm beauty only stirred new doubts. What would she really be thinking? The governor's wife could not of course ask.

'I thought I had finally found what I had been hunting for all these years, and told myself that no one would ever look down on

---

*It has not been satisfactorily identified.

†Literally: 'I feel as if I had a mink beside me.' There are numerous theories as to the meaning.

‡Literally: 'It bothers me to have you shading your eyes and looking suspiciously at me.' The mink was believed to shade its eyes while scanning a stranger from afar.

us again.' She was weeping. 'I see now that I should not have come to you. I was right the first time. She must go into a nunnery.'

'What is it that worries you so?' Nakanokimi was deeply moved. 'You would have cause to object if I seemed not to want her here. Yes, I know there is a man who is not as much in control of himself as he might be and who occasionally misbehaves; but everyone knows about him and keeps watch. I will see to it myself that nothing happens to her. What can have turned you against me?'

'I certainly do not accuse you of behaving as if you did not want her. Why should I hold you responsible for the way your father treated us? No, I turned to you not because of him but because of that other bond between us.'* There was deep urgency in her voice. 'In any case, she must be in retreat tomorrow and the next day. She must see no one. I have a very quiet place in mind for her. I will bring her again one day soon.'

And she took the girl off with her.

All most unfortunate, thought Nakanokimi, seeking to detain her no further. The governor's wife was so badly shaken that she rushed out with scarcely a word of farewell.

She had a cottage for use when the stars demanded a change of direction. It was a tasteful place, modestly furnished and still in process of construction.

'What a time I do have trying to find you a home. It is better for a woman to die young, when the whole world seems against her. I would not mind the worst sort of loneliness and humiliation and degradation if I had only myself to think of; but here we are friends again after all the years of bitterness. The world would roar with laughter if anything were to go wrong. It's all very sad, but anyway –' She was picking herself up to depart. 'This isn't a very elegant place, I know, but bear with it for a while, and don't let anyone see you. I'll think of something else one of these days, I promise you.'

The girl was a sad little figure, weeping tears of utter dejection, sorry even to be alive. Matters were no better with the governor's wife. It would be a shame to waste such beauty, she had told herself. She had hoped that the girl, seen safely to womanhood, might

*The relationship through Nakanokimi's mother.

make a good marriage for herself. And now they had the scorn of the world to look forward to, and must face charges of rashness and frivolity. She was not an insensitive woman, but she tended to be headstrong and somewhat erratic. Though it would not have been impossible to hide Ukifune in a corner of the governor's mansion, she had dismissed the thought as too unfeeling. They had always been together and the separation was cruel for both of them.

'This place won't be really safe either until it is finished. Do be careful. I've sent some women to look after you and given orders to the guards. But I know I'll go on worrying – and everyone at the other house is furious.'

The governor had gained in the lieutenant what was for him a priceless jewel. He was still out of sorts. His wife might be a little more helpful, he complained.

But it was because of the man's callousness that all the trouble had arisen, that the daughter she so doted upon had fallen into disgrace. She would have nothing to do with him. The poor figure he had cut in Niou's presence had so filled her with contempt that she had no wish to wait upon him as a mother-in-law might be expected to. Still she was curious. She had not yet had a good look at him. It was high noon of a day when she knew he would be at his ease in the west wing. She hurried over and took up a position behind a screen. He was near the edge of the veranda, looking out at the garden. He had on a singlet of soft white brocade and a robe of deep pink beaten to a rich glow on the fulling blocks. He did not seem so inferior after all. Indeed, he was rather handsome. Her daughter, leaning on an armrest beside him, was a mere child. They could hardly have competed with Niou and his Uji princess, and yet as he exchanged quips with the women he was not at all the colorless figure she had seen at Nijō. Might it have been another lieutenant?

'The *hagi* at Prince Niou's is especially good,' he was saying. 'I wonder where he found the seeds. It comes in the usual shapes, but somehow it seems more graceful. I happened to be there just as he was going out the other day, and I didn't have a chance to break off a branch. He recited the poem about the fading *hagi*.* I

---

*Ise, *Shūishū* 183:

> The weight of dew all but breaks the *hagi* twigs,
> When even its fading color saddens one.

just wish you could have seen him. You know the one.' And he recited it himself.

'The beast, the craven beast,' she muttered. 'And what a cheap article he did look beside the prince. I wonder how he is as a poet.'

He did not seem to be wholly without accomplishments. She thought she would put him to the test.

This was the poem she sent out:

'Of the plighted *hagi*, the upper leaves seem quiet.
What will have caused a change in the underleaves?'

It seemed to make him feel a little guilty.

'Had I known it to be of the meadow of Miyagi,
With the fragile *hagi* I would have kept my faith.*

'Perhaps we can discuss the matter sometime.'

So he had learned who the girl's father was. All the old yearning to make a decent life for her, to give her the security that was Nakanokimi's, came back. The governor's wife wished she were not always thinking of Kaoru. Though both of them, Niou and Kaoru, were magnificent men, she was not so foolish as to think that Niou took her daughter seriously. And she was incensed at what he had done. Kaoru had indicated an interest in the girl and even made inquiries, and yet, curiously, he remained silent. If he was so much on her mind, how much more must he be on her daughter's. Yes, she had been stupid to let her thoughts dwell upon the lieutenant. They were now upon Ukifune as she examined this and that pleasant prospect for the future. None seemed quite within reach. The princess who was already married to this uniquely eminent and well-favored young man must herself be superior; and truly superior another girl would have to be to catch his fancy. It had been her experience that one's station in life made all the difference in matters of comportment and sensibility. Not one of her other daughters could stand comparison with Ukifune. She herself had seen how the lieutenant, who cut such a swath in this house, shriveled to nothing in the presence of Niou. What

*'The meadow of Miyagi,' near Sendai, was famous for its *hagi*. The first two syllables of Miyagi suggest a prince or princess of the blood. Hence: 'I would not have let her go had I known her to be a prince's daughter.'

then of Ukifune in the presence of a gentleman who had taken for his bride a treasured daughter of the emperor? Her thoughts were beginning to blur and waver.

Meanwhile the girl passed monotonous days in her temporary and unfinished lodgings. Even the grasses seemed oppressive. She heard only coarse East Country voices and there were no flowers to comfort her. As the days went by in a dreary procession, her thoughts turned with intense nostalgia to Nakanokimi. She thought too of Niou. His behaviour had been deplorable and the memory of it still filled her with terror; and yet, whatever he may have meant by them, he had said many charming things. It seemed to her that, faintly, his fragrance was still with her.

An affectionate letter came from the governor's wife, alive to her maternal duties as never before. The girl was sad for her mother too. She had tried so hard, and in vain. The letter said in part: 'I can imagine how unhappy you must be in a strange house, but you must try to bear it for a time.'

'No, I am not at all unhappy,' the girl sent back. 'Indeed I am having a very pleasant time.

> 'If I could think it a place apart from the world,
>   In happy procession then might pass the days.'*

The childlike innocence brought tears to the mother's eyes. How cruel it was that the girl should be driven from home, robbed of all security!

> 'Though it be in a house apart from this gloomy world,
>   I pray that the best may yet be mine to see.'

And so they exchanged simple, straightforward poems.

It was Kaoru's practice to visit Uji in late autumn. Every morning he awoke to sad thoughts of Oigimi. He set out one day to inspect the new hall, having been informed that it was finished. Many weeks had passed since his last visit. The autumn leaves were at their best. There the new hall was, all bright and shining, where the villa had stood. It had been a simple place, a veritable hermitage. The thought of it brought poignant memories. Almost

*Anonymous, *Shūishū* 506:

> Would I might have a place apart from the world,
> There to hide what time has done to me.

regretful that he had had it moved, he was plunged into deeper melancholy than usual. The prince's rooms had been appointed with stern solemnity, while his daughters' had shown remarkable grace and delicacy. Now the plaited screens and all the other austere furnishings had been sent off to fit out cells at the monastery. No expense had been spared to see that the new house was appointed as a mountain villa should be, and the results were most satisfying.

He went into the garden and sat on a rock by the brook. The scene was not an easy one to pull himself away from.

'They still flow on, these waters clear and clean.
Can they not reflect the image of those now gone?'

Brushing away a tear, he went to look in upon the nun. His sorrow was so apparent that she too was moved to tears. He sat in the doorway and raised the blind a few inches. She was seated behind a curtain.

'I heard the other day that the young lady was staying in Nijō.' The conversation had taken a turn that accommodated the interesting subject. 'But it had seemed rather awkward to think of visiting. Perhaps you would tell her of my feelings.'

'I had a letter from the governor's wife not long ago. It seems that she has the girl moving from house to house, trying to avoid unlucky directions. At the moment she is hidden in a shabby little cottage somewhere. The best thing would be to leave her here with me – but the mountain roads seem to frighten her.'

'And here I am. All these years I have been coming over the roads that frighten them so. Why should it be? What have we inherited from other lives to account for it?' As was so often the case, there were tears in his voice. 'Send off a message, if you will, to wherever it is that she seems to think so safe. Or might I ask you to go yourself?'

'It would be very easy to pass on a message, but I am afraid I am no longer up to going into the city. I do not even think of visiting my lady.'

'You must be bolder. If we see that no one knows, then no one will talk. After all, even the hermits on Atago* went to the city

---

*Tradition holds them to be Shinzei, a disciple of Kōbō Daishi, and Kūya. Atago is a mountain to the west of Kyoto.

occasionally. And you know it is a good thing to break the most solemn vow if it means making someone else happy.'

'I am not all that holy – no bridge to see the others across.'* She was genuinely perplexed. 'But there is sure to be unpleasant talk.'

'This is the best chance you will ever have.' It was not like him to be so insistent. 'I will send a carriage day after tomorrow. In the meantime please find out where she is staying. You know very well,' he concluded with a smile, 'that I would not dream of making complications.'

She was not so sure. What would be on his mind? He was not a reckless or thoughtless man, however, and he had his own name to think of.

'Very well,' she finally answered. 'I will do as you say. The house is very near your own, and possibly it would be a good idea if you were to get off a note. I wouldn't want to seem like a busybody. I am too old to be playing the wise fox.'†

'I could very easily do that. But people do talk, and it will be noised around that I have my eye on the daughter of His Eminence the governor of Hitachi. I understand he is a very rough fellow.'

She was both touched and amused.

It was dark when he left. He broke off some flowers from under the trees and some autumn branches, which he took to his wife, the Second Princess. She could not have been described as unhappy with her marriage, but Kaoru seemed remote and somehow ill at ease. Out of the concern any father would feel, the emperor had written to his sister, the nun at Sanjō, of what he sensed to be the situation. For his part, Kaoru paid his wife the respect her place demanded; but life was complicated. To see to the needs of a lady so doted upon by his mother and the emperor himself was no easy task, and now had come a new affair.

---

*The empress Onshi, *Gosenshū* 1118:

> No bridge am I, to see others safely across.
> And why have I passed a life like a long, long bridge?

†Literally: 'the fox of Iga.' The precise meaning is unclear, but something in the nature of an officious meddler seems called for. Iga was a small province east of Nara.

Early on the morning of the appointed day he sent off a carriage, escorted by a rather obscure courtier in whom he had great confidence and another minor functionary. He instructed them to fill out the guard with men from his Uji estate.

He had said that she must come, and so, bracing herself, the nun finished her toilet and got into the carriage. The mountain scenery brought memories. She was sunk in thought the whole of the journey. The cottage, when she arrived, was quiet and next to deserted, and her carriage attracted no notice. She sent in to explain why she had come. Young women whom she recognized from Ukifune's pilgrimages came to help her in. Ukifune, for whom the days had been an uninterrupted passage of gloom and boredom — and it was a wretched little house — was delighted that she now had someone with whom she could exchange reminiscences. She felt especially close to this woman who had served her father.

'You have been on my mind constantly. I have cut myself off from the world and do not even visit my lady, but he was more stubborn than I have ever seen him, and I knew that I would have to come.'

The girl and her nurse had been pleased that Kaoru, such a fine gentleman, should not have forgotten them; but they had not dreamed that he would so quickly contrive to be in communication with them.

Late in the night there came a soft knocking at the gate. 'Someone from Uji,' it was announced. One of Kaoru's men, thought the nun, ordering the gate opened. She was startled to see a carriage being pulled in.

'Show us to the nun,' said a man who announced himself as the superintendent of Kaoru's Uji manor. She went to the door. A gentle rain was falling and a remarkable fragrance came in on the cool breeze to tell them who in fact their visitor was, so stately a visitor that he both delighted and upset them. The cottage was a poor one and he had caught them unprepared. What could it possibly mean? they asked one another, bustling about to receive him.

'May I perhaps speak to the lady in private?' he sent in. 'I should like to tell her of certain feelings I have scarcely been able to keep to myself these last months.'

The girl was perplexed for an answer.

'He's here, and there's nothing you can do about it,' said her nurse impatiently. 'You can at least ask him to sit down. We can have someone slip out and tell your mother. She's so near.'

'Don't be silly – there's no need to tell her,' said the nun. 'A couple of young people want to speak to each other, and you assume they're going to fall in love on the spot? He is a quiet, thoughtful young man, not at all the sort to force himself on a lady.'

It was raining harder. The watchmen on their rounds called out in strange East Country accents. 'That spot over by the southeast corner, you have to keep an eye on it. Get that wagon inside and close the gate. They don't have common sense, these people.'

It was all very strange and rather forbidding. Seated at the edge of a veranda as of a rustic cottage, he whispered to himself:

'And there is no shelter at Sano.*

> 'Are there tangles of grass to hold me back, that I wait
> So long in the rain at the eaves of your eastern cottage?'†

No doubt the perfume that came in on the breeze was a source of great wonderment to the eastern rustics.

Concluding at length that it would be impossible to turn him away, the girl had a cushion set out in the south room. Urged on by her women she slid the door‡ open a crack.

'I am not used to looking at doors and I resent even the carpenter** who makes them.' And he pushed his way inside.

He did not mean, it would seem, to describe his thoughts about having her as a substitute for her sister. 'You will not have been aware of it, I am sure, but I once had a glimpse of you through a

---

*Naganoimiki Okimaro, *Manyōshū* 265:

> How cruel that rain should fall when there is no shelter
> At the ferry of Sano of Miwagasaki.

Miwagasakisano was in the province of Kii.

†See note*, page 154.

An 'eastern cottage' was a compact rectangular building with lean-to chambers at each of the four sides.

‡*Yarido*, a sliding door of wood, seems to suggest a modest and even rustic dwelling.

**Literally: 'the carpenter of Hida.' The province of Hida, in the mountains of central Japan, was noted for its master carpenters.

crack in a door. You have been very much on my mind ever since. I suppose it was meant to be, but you have been so much on my mind that I find it a little odd.'

Small and pretty, very much in control of herself, she quite lived up to his expectations. Indeed, he was delighted with her.

Though it would soon be morning, no cocks were crowing. From the main street, very near at hand, came the sleepy voices of peddlers offering wares with which he was quite unfamiliar. The women among them, he had heard, could look like veritable demons as they strode about in the dawn with their wares balanced on their heads. It was a new experience, passing the night in a tangle of wormwood, and he was not at all bored. At length he heard the guards going off duty.

Ordering his carriage brought to a hinged door at a corner of the house, he took the girl up in his arms and carried her out.

The women were in a panic. And here it was the inauspicious Ninth Month. What *could* he be thinking of?

Bennokimi was as startled as the rest, and as concerned for the girl; but she also saw the need to be calm. 'Don't worry. He knows what he is doing. You say it is a bad month – but if I'm not mistaken tomorrow will be the first day of winter.'

It was the thirteenth of the month.*

'This time I cannot go with you,' she continued. 'It will not do if my lady hears that I have slipped into town and gone back without seeing her.'

But Kaoru wanted to keep word of the escapade from Nakanokimi as long as he could. 'You can apologize later. You must be my guide. And we will need another one too.'

Bennokimi got into the carriage with Jijū. The nurse and the girl who had been Bennokimi's companion were left behind in a daze.

They would not be going far, thought Bennokimi; but in fact they were taken to Uji. Kaoru had arranged for a change of oxen. It was daybreak when they crossed the Kamo River and passed the

---

*Both the transition from spring to summer and that from autumn to winter seem to have been thought bad times to marry. It would not be impossible for the first day of winter by solar reckoning to fall in the middle of the Ninth Month by lunar reckoning.

Hōshōji Temple.* Jijū could now see his face, albeit dimly, and it so excited her that she was gaping openly. Ukifune sat with bowed head, too stunned to look about her. The rocky stretches might be difficult, he said, and took her in his arms. A thin curtain hung between the two of them and the women behind. Bennokimi wished that he had had the consideration not to drag her out in broad daylight. And how it would have pleased her, she sighed, to have seen her lady going off with him thus. One was witness to strange, sad happenings when one lived too long. Try though she might to control herself, her face was presently contorted with grief. What a silly old woman, thought Jijū. A nun was not in any case the sort of chaperone a person wanted on such a happy excursion, and why did she have to add nasty tears to her own nasty presence? Well, old people cried a great deal, and that was that.

Kaoru had not been disappointed in the girl, but something about the sky and the day brought back all of his longing for Oigimi. As they entered the mountains he too found his eyes clouding over. He sat leaning against an armrest, deep in memories. He noticed, as a wheel of the carriage pulled out of a rut, that his sleeves were hanging far beneath the blind, and, in the river mist, the red of a singlet and the blue of the robe over it had come together.† A poem formed in his mind:

> 'I think to find her equal, and my sleeves
>   Are deep in tears as the land in morning mist.'

The nun heard him, and would have liked to wring her own sleeves dry. All very odd, and not very pretty, thought Jijū. Such a jolly outing – and these people seemed determined to spoil the fun. The nun's sobs were coaxing sniffles from Kaoru.

But he had to think of the girl beside him. 'It is just that memories come back of all the times I have been over this road. Do look at the colors in the hills. You have not said a word to me.'

He forced her to look up. Her face shyly hidden by a fan, she was remarkably like Oigimi. But there was something too docile and passive about her. It made him uneasy. Oigimi had been

---

*To the southeast of the old city, within the environs of the present city. It does not survive.

†To produce an ashen color, as of mourning.

similarly fragile and childlike, but she had also been of a solemn, meditative turn. His longing seemed to fill the very skies.*

They had arrived at Uji. And would Oigimi even now call it home? Here he was, lost in aimless wandering – and because of whom? He left Ukifune for a time, that he might be with the other.

Ukifune was as upset for her mother as for herself, but she had the memory of his soft words to console her. Bennokimi had insisted on being let out near her own rooms, though such reticence hardly seemed called for.† Farmers came from his manor, as usual, in noisy troops. Bennokimi brought lunch. The road had been heavily overgrown, and here the prospect was bright and open. The house had been planned to take advantage of the river and the colors in the hills. Ukifune felt the gloom of the recent days leave her. Yet great uncertainty remained. What plans would he have for her?

He sent off notes to his mother and his wife in the city. 'I had had decorations commissioned for the chapel. Today being a lucky day, I rushed off to inspect them. I am not feeling well and have just remembered that I should be in retreat. So I shall stay on through today and tomorrow.'

Ukifune found him even handsomer in casual dress. She still felt shy before him, but no longer thought it necessary to hide her face. Though great attention had gone into her clothes, they still had a certain rustic plainness about them. He remembered how elegant Oigimi had managed to look even in old clothes, and had to conclude that Ukifune was not quite her equal. She did have beautiful hair, however, thick and smooth to the very ends. The Second Princess had unusually fine hair, but this was perhaps even lovelier.

And what now? There would be talk if they received her openly at Sanjō. Yet something more than ordinary treatment was surely called for. He would leave her at Uji for a time. Knowing how lonely she would be, he talked affectionately with her until

---

*Anonymous, *Kokinshū* 488:

> My longing so has grown that it fills the skies.
> I wish that it would leave me – but where can it go?

†Apparently she is treating Ukifune as the mistress of the house.

evening. He spoke in fascinating detail of her father and of events long ago, and he essayed an occasional pleasantry. Her shyness seemed excessive, but it offered possibilities of its own. There was hope for such a girl, even if an occasional mistake was made in her training. He would be her teacher. Had she been the loud, garrulous sort of provincial, he would have had to give up all thought of making her a substitute for Oigimi.

He had kotos brought out. She would be less adept at music, he feared, than at the other polite accomplishments. Sadness for the past flooded over him as he began to play. He had not touched a koto in the Uji house since the prince's death, he did not himself know why. He played on, sunk in thought, and the moon came out. There had been nothing insistent about the prince's koto, but it had, in its quiet way, had a strange power to move.

'If you had grown up here I think you might have had a rather different feeling for things. We were no kin to each other, but the prince had a strong hold on my affections. It is a pity that you spent so many years so far away.'

She was toying shyly with a fan. Her profile was an unblemished white, and her forehead, between the rich strands of hair, brought memories of her sister. He must give her music lessons and otherwise make her a lady for whom he need not apologize.

'Have you had a try at the koto? Perhaps you have had lessons on the East Country koto?'*

'I do not even speak the language of the capital. Should you expect me to play a capital koto?'†

She was clever. He was already sad at the thought of having her at Uji and seeing her only rarely. It was not often that he felt such regrets.

---

*Literally: 'the koto known as my dear wife.' Azuma as a general designation of the eastern regions is traditionally derived from the homophonous 'my wife.' The dual reference to a wife and the east seems to be an oblique allusion to the Saibara 'The Eastern Cottage.'

†The six-stringed Japanese koto is also called the *yamatokoto*. Ukifune adds a syllable to make *yamatokotoba*, 'the speech of Yamato.' It refers to the speech of the court, and to the composition of the thirty-one syllable *waka* or *yamatouta* as well.

'The voice of "the koto in the night, on the terrace of the king of Ch'u," '* he whispered to himself.

Daughter of a region where one heard only the twang of the bow, Jijū was entranced. It was the mark of her want of culture that her delight should be so unconditional, and take no account of such matters as the proper color of a fan, and what it told of a noble lady's boudoir. But why, he was asking himself, had he chosen that particular poem from all the poems he knew?

Refreshments were brought from the nun's rooms. Sprigs of ivy and maple had been laid out tastefully on the lid of the box, and on the paper beneath (one may imagine that he was hungry) he caught a glimpse, in the bright moonlight, of a poem in a shaky old hand:

'Autumn has come, the leaves of the ivy change;
And bright as of old, the moon of memories.'

The hand was an old-fashioned one, but it made him feel somehow inadequate. He softly intoned a poem of his own, though not as if by way of answer:

'The village still calls itself Uji, and here in my rooms
The moon streams in upon another face.'†

It would seem that Jijū took the poem to the nun.

---

*Minamoto Shitagō, *Wakan Rōeishū* 380:

> The hue of the fan in autumn, in the boudoir of Lady Pan.
> The koto in the night, on the terrace of the king of Ch'u.

Lady Pan, deposed as the favorite of the emperor Han Ch'êng-ti, wrote a poem likening her situation to that of the summer fan put away in the autumn. The koto and Ukifune's fan bring the poem to Kaoru's mind; and then, remembering the significance of the fan, he realizes that he has chosen an unfortunate poem to quote from. Jijū, the robust East Country girl, is not alive to such refinements.

†'The village bears the same gloomy name,' with the usual pun on Uji and *ushi*, 'sad' or 'gloomy.'

CHAPTER 51

A Boat upon the Waters

Niou had not for a moment forgotten the dim evening light in which he had seen the girl. She would not appear to have been of the highest rank, and yet her clean grace left him deeply dissatisfied (for he was very susceptible) that he had not had his way. He managed to work up considerable resentment at Nakanokimi.

'I would not have expected it of you,' he said, so frequently that she began to wonder whether she ought not to tell him the whole story.

But no. The girl had attracted the notice of someone who – though he did not, it seemed, mean to make her his principal wife – was so taken with her that he had hidden her away. It was not for Nakanokimi to reveal secrets. Besides, Niou could not be expected to sit idly by once he had learned the truth. Let him embark upon some fleeting dalliance with one of the women around him, and temptation would promptly lead him off to places where a prince ought not to go. The case of the girl who had been so on his mind over the days and weeks was almost certain to be troublesome. Nakanokimi could do nothing, of course, if he were to learn the facts from someone else. It would be sad for both Kaoru and Ukifune, but he would not be held back by the most persuasive arguments. And the effect upon Nakanokimi herself would be far more painful than the effect of all his other intrigues combined. Well, she would in any case make sure that she herself was guilty of no carelessness. This sulking was not easy to live with, but she would say nothing. Incapable of clever fabrication, she kept her peace and let him think her just another jealous woman.

Kaoru's self-control, meanwhile, approached the unbelievable. The girl would be expecting him, he knew, but a man in his position had to have good excuses for such a journey. The road was more forbidding than if it had been proscribed by the gods.* He would in the end do his duty by her. She would be his companion

*Tales of Ise 71:

> Come to me, if longing so afflicts you.
>
> The gods, you know, have not proscribed the way.

in that mountain village. He would invent some pretext for spending a few quiet days with her, but for the time being she must remain out of sight. When she was somewhat more settled and composed, he would arrange an acceptable sort of liaison, one that would not damage his good name. He did not want people to be asking what this sudden development meant, and who the girl might be, and when it had all begun; his aim in visiting Uji was certainly not to attract attention. And on the other hand he would not wish Nakanokimi to think that he had turned his back on a place so rich in memories and left the past behind. With his usual care and deliberation, he turned the arguments over in his mind.

Not that he was wholly inactive: he had commenced work on the house to which he would presently bring the girl. He was a busy man, but he continued to visit Nakanokimi regularly. Though some of her women thought it all rather odd, Nakanokimi herself, more familiar now with the ways of the world, was much moved. Here was a man who did not forget, whose affections did not wear thin with the passage of time. The years seemed to improve him, even as the hopes the world had for him rose. Seeing, by contrast, how deplorably capricious and unreliable her husband was, she could only sigh at the strange, sad fate that seemed to be hers. Oigimi's plans for her had come to nothing, and she had found herself married to a man whose chief contribution to her life was gloomy foreboding.

Yet it was difficult to receive Kaoru with the warmth she really felt. The Uji years were receding into the distance. People of the lower classes might presume upon such a relationship, muttered some of her women, unfamiliar with happenings at Uji, but it certainly was most irregular for grandchildren of emperors. In the natural course of events, then, she began to seem more distant, even though her feelings for him were as they had always been. Niou might upset her from time to time with his erratic ways, but the little prince was growing up, more of a delight each day. Thinking it unlikely that another lady would favor him with so pretty a child, he lavished great affection upon her, affection, indeed, such as the lady at Rokujō did not enjoy. In spite of everything, Nakanokimi was feeling more sure of herself.

At about noon one day early in the New Year, when Niou was playing with the child, now in its second year, a little girl came bounding in and handed the princess a rather fat letter in a fine,

cream-colored envelope. With it were a small 'whiskered basket'*
attached to an artificial seedling pine, and a second letter, more
formally folded.

'And where might they be from?' asked Niou.

'The man said from Uji, for Madame Tayū. I didn't know what
to do with them, and I thought my lady might like to see them.
She always does.' The girl was confused. 'Just look at this basket,
will you. Metal, and it's colored all over. And look at this pine.
Look at the branches. You might think it was real.'

She smiled, and Niou smiled back. 'Yes, do let me have a look
at it.'

'Take them to Tayū immediately.' Nakanokimi flushed. She
did not want him to read the letters.

Would they be from Kaoru? They did look like women's letters, but he could easily have disguised them, and Uji would have
been an apt choice for their source. He took one of them up. But
he too was confused. He hoped that his suspicions would not
prove correct.

'I'm going to open it. Will you be angry with me?'

'It's not good manners to look at private notes between
women.' Nakanokimi managed to seem unconcerned.

'You really must let me see them. What might it be like, I
wonder, a letter from one woman to another?'

'I have been very remiss about writing, and here we are, going
into the New Year. Our gloomy mountains offer no break in the
winter mists.' The hand was that of a very young woman. 'These
are cheap trinkets, but give them to the little prince, if you will.'

There was nothing remarkable about the letter. But he was
curious to know who the writer might be. He took up the other.
It too was, as she had said, in a woman's hand.

'And how will our lady be, now that the New Year has come?
I have no doubt that you yourself have a long list of blessings to
count over. This is a beautiful house and we are well taken care of,
and yet it seems a pity that the young lady should be shut away in
the mountains. I have been telling her that she must stop brooding, that she must pick herself up and visit you from time to time;
but she refuses because of that awful thing and goes on brooding.

---

*Higeko, a basket with the plaits left uncut at the rim.

She is sending streamers to decorate the little prince's room. Please show them to him when his father is away.'

It was not a very pleasing letter. It was wordy and complaining and not at all in keeping with the happy season. Puzzled, he read it again.

'You must tell me everything. Who is it from?'

'I am told that the daughter of a woman who was in service with us at Uji has been obliged to go back there.'

But it did not seem the hand of an ordinary maidservant, and the mention of 'that awful thing' was a valuable hint. The streamers were charming, obviously the work of someone with a great deal of spare time, perhaps, indeed, too much. A branch at a fork in the pine had been strung with artificial red berries, and a poem attached to it:

'Our seedling pine has not known many years.
I see for it, withal, a pine's long life.'

It was not a particularly distinguished poem. Yet he continued to read it over, sensing that it would be from a lady who had been much on his mind.

'Send off an answer. You must not be rude, and I see no need for secrecy.' He turned to go. 'I have no choice but to leave you when you are in one of your moods.'

The princess summoned her women. 'A great pity,' she said softly. 'You had to let them fall into the hands of an infant, did you?'

'You surely don't think we wanted it that way! No, that child is cheeky and forward and not as bright as she might be. It doesn't take long to sort out the ones with possibilities. The quiet ones are the ones to watch.'

'Oh, don't be angry with her,' said Nakanokimi. 'She's so young.'

The child had been put into Nakanokimi's service the winter before. She was a pretty little thing and Niou was fond of her.

All very strange, thought Niou, back in his own rooms. Having had reports that Kaoru continued to visit Uji, and a further report that he occasionally spent the night there, he had smiled and said to himself that his friend had strange ways, even granting the associations that Uji had for him. So a lady was hidden there!

Niou remembered a certain official, a privy secretary, who had been of service to him in scholarly matters and who had close friends among Niou's retainers. He asked the man to bring anthologies for a game of rhyme guessing.

'Just leave them in the cabinet over there, if you will. By the way: they tell me that the general is still making trips to Uji. His monastery must be very splendid – I only wish I could go have a look at it.'

'Very splendid indeed, I understand, very dignified. Especially the Chapel of the Holy Name, people tell me. I understand that he has been going more often since last fall, and his men have been spreading rumors about a lady there, someone he does not find at all unattractive, I'm sure. He's told the people at his manor to do everything they can for her, and they post guards every night, and then he keeps sending out secret supply wagons from town. A very lucky lady – but she must be lonely and bored off there in the mountains. That's what they say, or were saying along towards the end of last year.'

What a delightful piece of intelligence! 'They haven't said who she might be? I've heard that he visits a nun who's lived there for a very long time.'

'The nun lives in a gallery. The lady herself is in the main hall, the new one. She gets by comfortably, I believe, with acceptable enough women to wait on her.'

'Very, very interesting. What plans might he have for her? And what sort of woman is she? He has his ways, you know, not at all like yours and mine. I hear that his good brother is always after him for overdoing the religious thing and spending his nights off in mountain temples. And people say that he could find plenty of other places to be religious in if he had to, and needn't go sneaking off to Uji. It has to be because of the late princess, people say. So here we are. Interesting, do you not think? The saint who is so much better than the rest of us does have his little secrets.'

It was *very* interesting. The secretary was the son-in-law of Kaoru's steward and so was apprised of very intimate matters. Niou wondered how to go about learning for certain whether it was the girl he had seen at Nijō. She must in any case be unusual if she had caught Kaoru's eye. And why should she be close to Nakanokimi? It so irritated him that he could think of nothing else, the quite evident fact that Kaoru and Nakanokimi had spirited the girl away.

The archery meet and the literary banquet were over and there were no great demands on his time. The provincial appointments that created such a stir on certain levels were no concern of his. He could think only of slipping off to Uji. The secretary from whom he had learned Kaoru's secret had certain ambitions, and was adept at currying favor. Niou did nothing to discourage him.

'Suppose I were to ask something really difficult of you,' he said one day. 'Would you do it for me?'

The man bowed deeply.

'Well, here we are then, and I hope I won't shock you. I've learned that the lady at Uji might be someone I knew for a very little while a long time ago. She disappeared, and I've had reports that the general may have taken her away. I can't be really sure. I'd like to do a bit of sleuthing. Do you think something might be arranged without attracting notice?'

This would be difficult, thought the man. Still he could not refuse. 'The road leads through wild mountains, but not so very far, really. If you leave in the evening you should be there by a little after ten. And it might be best to be home by dawn. No one needs to know except the men who go with you, and not even they need to know everything.'

'My feelings exactly. I've made the trip before – but do try to keep it secret. There are always gossips who seem to think that people like me should stay at home.'

Though he knew that he was being reckless, it was now too late to withdraw. He took along two or three men who had been with him on other trips to Uji, this secretary, and the son of his old nurse, a young man who had just been promoted to the Fifth Rank for his work as a privy secretary. They were all among his closer confidants. The secretary had orders to inquire carefully into comings and goings at Sanjō, and was certain that Kaoru would not be visiting Uji in the next day or two.

Memories came flooding back. Niou found himself pulled in several directions at once. In the old days he had felt remarkably close to Kaoru, who had taken him by the hand and led him off to Uji. It bothered him a little to think what he was now doing to his good friend, and he was a little frightened too, for he was a prince, and even in the city his adventures were never secrets. Such were his thoughts as, in drab incognito, he mounted his horse; but he was of an impressionable, eagerly responsive nature. His heart rose as they pushed deeper into the mountains. Would it be much longer? Would she let him see her? A tragedy indeed if he were denied even a glimpse of her!

He had come by carriage as far as the Hōshōji Temple and from there on horseback. Making very good time, he was in Uji by perhaps eight in the evening. The secretary having questioned an attendant of Kaoru's who was familiar with the arrangements at Uji, they were able to pull up at an unguarded spot to the west of the house. Breaking through the reed fence, they slipped inside. The secretary himself was somewhat uncertain, not really knowing his way about, but the grounds did not seem to be heavily guarded. He saw a dim light and heard a rustling of garments at the south front of the house.

'There still seem to be people up. Come this way, please, if you will.'

Niou made his way softly up the stairs and leaned forward to take advantage of a crack he had found in a shutter. The rustling of an Iyo blind* gave him brief pause. The house was new and clean, and but roughly furnished. As if in confidence that no one would be looking in on them, the women inside had not bothered to cover the openings. The curtain beyond the shutter had been lifted back across its frame. In the bright light, three or four women were sewing. A pretty little maidservant was spinning thread. It was a face he had had a glimpse of in the torchlight at Nijō. Or was he perhaps mistaken? Then he saw the young woman who had announced herself as Ukon.† Ukifune herself lay gazing into the light, her head pillowed on her arm. Her eyes, charmingly girlish and not without a certain dignity, and her forehead, thick hair spilling down over it, reminded him astonishingly of his princess at Nijō.

'But if you do go, I don't imagine you'll be coming back very soon.' It was Ukon, busy creasing a robe. 'We had that messenger from the general yesterday, you know. The general will be coming on about the first of the month, we can be sure of it, once the

---

*A rough sort of blind, likely to make more noise than a finer blind. Iyo was a province on Shikoku.

†The name is casually dropped as if this were the Ukon in the service of Nakanokimi, but it presently becomes apparent that the two cannot be the same.

business of the provincial appointments is out of the way. What has he said in his letters?'

Evidently sunk in thoughts of her own, the girl did not answer.

'It won't look at all good, running off when you know he'll be coming.'

'I think you ought to let him know about your plans,' said the woman facing Ukon. 'It won't seem very nice to go dashing off without a word to him. And I think you ought to come back as soon as you've had time for a prayer or two. I know this is a lonely place, but it's a safe, quiet place too. Once you're used to it you'll feel more at home than you ever did in the city.'

'Don't you think the polite thing,' said another woman, whom he could not see, 'would be to wait a little while? After you're in the city you can have a good visit with your mother. The old woman here is much too quick with her good ideas. Careful plans turn out best in the end. It is true now and it has always been true.'

'Why didn't you stop her? Old people are such a nuisance.' These reproaches seemed to be directed at Ukifune's nurse.

Yes, to be sure, thought Niou: there had been a troublesome old woman with the girl. The memory of that evening had a misty, spectral quality about it.

The talk went on, so open that he was almost embarrassed. 'I say the lucky one is our lady in the city. The minister throws his weight about and makes a big thing of having royalty for a son-in-law, but since our little master was born our side has had the better of it. And there aren't any nasty, pushy old women at Nijō, and our lady can do very much as she pleases.'

'Oh, but our own lady will be doing just as well if the general keeps his promises. She'll be there with the best of them.'

'There with the best of them!' Ukifune raised herself on an elbow. 'Did you have to say that? You know I don't want you comparing me with the lady at Nijō. What if she were to hear?'

How might the two of them be related, this girl and his own lady? There was an unmistakable resemblance. The girl was no match for the other in proud, cool elegance. She was winsome and pretty, no more, and her features were delicately formed. A suggestion of less than the rarest refinement, however, was not enough to make him withdraw when he had before his eyes a girl who had been so long and persistently on his mind.

This first good look at her left him in an agony of impatience to make her his own. It would appear that she was going on a journey. And she seemed to have parents. When would he have another such chance? What might he hope to accomplish in the course of the night?

He gazed on and on, in growing agitation.

'I'm very sleepy,' said Ukon, gathering up half-sewn garments and hanging them over the curtain rack. 'I don't know why, but I hardly slept at all last night. I can finish tomorrow morning. Even if your mother gets an early start it will be noon by the time she gets here.' Leaning on an armrest, she seemed about to doze off. The girl retired somewhat farther into the room and lay down. After disappearing into a back room for a time, Ukon reappeared and lay down at her feet. Soon she was fast asleep.

At a loss for other devices, Niou tapped on the shutter.

'Who is it?' asked Ukon.

He cleared his throat. A most genteel sound, thought Ukon. It would be Kaoru. She came to the shutter.

'Raise it, if you will, please.'

'You've chosen a strange hour. It must be very late.'

'I heard from Nakanobu* that your lady would be going away, and I came running. It was a terrible trip, terrible. Do raise the shutter, please.' She obeyed, not guessing who it would be. He spoke in undertones and skillfully imitated his friend's mannerisms. 'I'm all in tatters. Something really frightful happened along the way.'

'It must have been, I'm sure.' Uncertain what to do, she put the light at a distance.

'I don't want anyone to see me. Please don't wake them.'

He was a clever mimic. Since their voices were similar, he was able to give a convincing enough imitation of Kaoru that he was shown to the rear of the hall. How trying for the poor man, thought Ukon, withdrawing behind a curtain. Under rough travel guise he wore robes of a fine, soft weave. His fragrance scarcely if at all inferior to Kaoru's, he undressed as if he were in his own private rooms and lay down beside Ukifune.

'Why not where you usually sleep?'

He did not answer. Ukon spread a coverlet over her mistress, and, arousing the women nearby, asked them to lie down some

---

*Kaoru's steward, it later becomes evident, and the father-in-law of the secretary who is being so helpful to Niou.

slight distance away. Since it was the practice for Kaoru's men to be accommodated elsewhere, no one sensed what was happening.

'How very sweet of him, so late at night. Doesn't she understand?'

'Oh, do be quiet.' Some people understand too well, thought Ukon. 'A whisper in the middle of the night can be worse than a scream.'

Ukifune was stunned. She knew that it was not Kaoru; but whoever it was had put his hand over her mouth. (If he was capable of such excesses at home, with everyone watching, what would he not be capable of here?) Had she known immediately that it was not Kaoru, she might have resisted, even a little; but now she was paralyzed. She had hurt him on an earlier occasion, he said, and she had been on his mind ever since; and so she quickly guessed who he was. Hideously embarrassed, horrified at the thought of what was being done to her sister, she could only weep. Niou too was in tears. It would not be easy to see her again. Might it have been better not to come at all?

And so the night sped past. Outside, an attendant coughed to warn of the approach of dawn. Ukon came out. Niou did not want to leave, for he had had far from enough of the girl's company – and it *would* be difficult to come again. Very well: let them raise any sort of commotion they wished. He would not go back today. One loved while one lived. Why go back and die of longing?

He summoned Ukon. 'You will think it unwise, I am sure, but I propose to spend the day here. Have my men hide somewhere not too far away, and send Tokikata to the city with good excuses – maybe he can say I'm busy praying at a mountain temple.'

Ukon was aghast. Why had she not been more careful? But she was soon in control of herself once more. What was done was done, and there was no point in antagonizing him. Call it fate, that he should have gone on thinking about Ukifune after that strange, fleeting encounter. No one was to blame.

'Her mother is sending for her today. What do you intend to do? I know that some things have to be, and there is nothing anyone can do about them; but you've really picked a very bad day. Suppose you come again, if you still feel in the mood.'

An able woman, thought he. 'No, I've been wandering around in a daze all these weeks. I haven't cared what they might be saying about me. A man in my position doesn't go sneaking off into the night, you know, if he's still worried about appearances. Just tell her mother there's been a very unfortunate defilement, and send them back again. Don't give them a hint that I'm here. For her sake and for mine. I don't think that's asking a great deal, and I won't settle for less.'

He did seem so infatuated with the girl that he no longer worried about the reproaches he might call down upon himself.

Ukon went out to a man who had been nervously seeking to get Niou on his way, and informed him of these new intentions. 'Go tell him, please, that this will not do. He is behaving outrageously. I don't care what *he* may be thinking, what your men are thinking is more important. Are you children, bringing him out into these wilds? Country people can be unruly, you know, and they don't always respect rank.'

The secretary had to agree that things might be difficult.

'And which of you is Tokikata?' She passed on Niou's orders.

'Oh, but of course,' laughed Tokikata. 'Any excuse to get away from that tongue of yours. But seriously: he seems very fond of her, and I intend to do what I can, even if it means, as you say, taking childish risks. Well, I'm off. They'll soon be changing the guard.'

Ukon was in a quandary. How was she to keep Niou's presence a secret?

'The general seems to have had reasons for coming incognito,' she said when the others were up. 'Something rather awful happened to him along the way. He's having fresh clothes sent out tonight.'

'Mount Kohata *is* a dreadful place. That's what happens when you go around without a decent guard. How really dreadful.'

'Don't shout about it, if you please. Give the servants a hint and they'll guess everything.'

Ukon did not like it at all. She was not a natural liar. And what would she find to say if a messenger were to come from Kaoru? 'Please,' she prayed, bowing in the direction of Hatsuse. 'Please let this day pass like all the others.'

Ukifune and her mother were to go on a pilgrimage to Ishiyama. The women had been through all the necessary fasting and purification. For nothing, it now became apparent. How very unfortunate!

The sun had risen, the shutters were open. Ukon stayed near her mistress. Blinds were lowered to darken the main hall and bills posted announcing a retreat. Should Ukifune's mother ask to come in, Ukon would have to say that there had been forbidding dreams in the night. She brought water to Niou and her mistress. The morning ablutions were in no way out of the ordinary, but it seemed infinitely strange to him that this new girl should be waiting on him. He invited her to wash first. Used to Kaoru's quiet ways, she now found herself with a gentleman who proclaimed himself incapable of tolerating a moment's separation. This must be the sort of thing people meant when they spoke of love. But what if word of this new shift in her destinies – strangest of destinies – were to get abroad? What, before anything, of Nakanokimi?

He still did not know who she was. 'You are being very unkind, and I can tell you that I am not at all happy. Tell me everything, everything. There's no need to be shy. I'll only like you better, I vow it, whatever you tell me. Tell me your family doesn't amount to a thing, and I'll still like you better.'

She remained silent despite his importunings, but on other subjects she answered with a pleasing openness. He was delighted to see that she was not ill disposed toward him.

The sun was high when a retinue from the city – two carriages, seven or eight mounted warriors, rough East Country people, as always, and numbers of foot soldiers as well – arrived to escort her back. Embarrassed at their uncouth speech and manners, the women of the house shooed them out of earshot. What could she possibly say to them? Ukon was asking herself. That Kaoru was on the premises? But the lie would be transparent. Everyone knew the whereabouts of someone so prominent.

Confiding in none of the other women, she got off a letter to the girl's mother: 'Night before last her monthly defilement came on, and, to compound her unhappiness at having to cancel the pilgrimage, she had a bad dream last night. Complete retirement has seemed necessary. We are very sorry indeed – no doubt some evil spirit has been at work.'

She fed the guards and sent them on their way, and, again offering the monthly defilement as her excuse, informed the nun that they would not after all be going to Ishiyama.

Ukifune had been living in unrelieved gloom and boredom,

such as to make her wonder, looking moodily out into the mist that clung to the mountains, how she could go on; but today she had interesting company, and begrudged the passage of each moment. The day sped by, a calm spring day. There was nothing to distract Niou from present delights. Her face, at which he gazed and did not tire,* was pretty and gentle, and free of anything that could be counted a blemish. She was not, to be sure, the equal of his princess at Nijō, nor was she to be compared to his lady at Rokujō, now in the finest glow of youth. But there did come these occasions when the moment seemed sufficient unto itself, and he thought her the most charming creature he had ever seen. She, for her part, had thought Kaoru the handsomest of men, but here was a luster, a glow, with which he could not compete.

Niou sent for an inkstone. He wrote beautifully, even though for his own amusement, and he drew interesting pictures. What young person could have resisted him?

'You must look at this and think of me when I am not able to visit you.' He sketched a most handsome couple leaning towards each other. 'If only we could be together always.' And he shed a tear.

> 'The promise is made for all the ages to come,
> But in these our lives we cannot be sure of the morrow.

'No. I am inviting bad luck. I must control myself. It will not be easy to visit you, my dear, and the thought of not seeing you makes me want to die. Why do you suppose I have gone to all this trouble when you were not at all kind to me the last time we met?'

She took up the brush, still inked, and jotted down a poem of her own:

> 'Were life alone uncertain of the morrow,
> Then might we count upon the heart of a man.'

It amused him that she should be reproving him for future infidelities. 'And whose heart is it that you have found so undependable?' He smiled, and pressed her to tell of her arrival at Uji and of the days that had followed.

*Ki no Tomonori, *Kokinshū* 684:

> At the cherries in the mists along the hills
> One gazes, and at you, and never tires.

'Why must you keep asking questions that I cannot answer?' There was an open, childlike quality about the reproach that he found enchanting. He knew that the whole story would presently come out. Why then must he have it from her lips?

Tokikata returned in the evening. 'There was a message from Her Majesty,' he said to Ukon. 'She is very angry, and so is the minister. These secret expeditions of his suggest very bad judgment, she said, and could have embarrassing consequences. And she said – it was quite a scolding – that her own position would be impossible if His Majesty were to hear of them. I said he had gone off to visit a learned, learned man in the eastern hills.' And he added: 'Women are the root of it all. Here we are, the merest bystanders, and we get pulled in, and end up telling lies.'

'How kind of you to make my lady a learned, learned man. A good deed, surely, that wipes out whatever may have been marked against you for lying. But where *did* he pick up his bad habits? If he had let us know in advance, well, he is a very well-placed young gentleman, and we could have arranged something. But she is right. He shows bad judgment.'

She went to transmit Tokikata's report. True, thought Niou: they would be worried. 'It is no fun,' he said to Ukifune, 'living in shackles. I wish I could run about like all the others, just for a little while. But what do you think? People will find out, whatever we do. And how will my friend Kaoru take it? We have been close friends. That is only natural. But actually we have been closer than close, and I hate to think what the discovery will do to him. As they say,* he may forget that he has kept you waiting and blame you for everything. I wish I could hide you somewhere from the whole world.'

He could not possibly stay another day. 'My soul,' he whispered as he made ready to go, 'does it linger on in your sleeve?'†

Wishing to be back in the city before daylight, his men were coughing nervously. She saw him to the door, and still he could not leave her.

---

*A reference to a proverb?

†Michinoku, *Kokinshū* 992:

> I feel that my soul has quite abandoned me.
> Unsatisfied, does it linger on in your sleeve?

'What shall I do? These tears run on ahead
And plunge the road I must go into utter darkness.'

She was touched.

'So narrow my sleeves, they cannot take my tears.
How then shall I make bold to keep you with me?'*

A high wind roared through the trees and the dawn was heavy
with frost. Even the touch of their robes, in the moment of parting, seemed cold.† He was smitten afresh as he mounted his horse,
and turned back to her; but his men were not prepared to wait
longer. In a daze of longing, he at length set out. The two courtiers of the Fifth Rank‡ who had come with him led his horse
through the mountains and mounted their own only when they
had come to open country. Everything, even the clattering of
hoofs on the icy riverbank, brought melancholy thoughts. The
pull of Uji and love, and that alone, now and in the old days, had
the power to bring him through wild mountains. What strange ties
he did seem to have with that remote mountain village!

Back at Nijō, he went to his own rooms, hoping to rest for a
time. He had another reason for wanting to be away from Nakanokimi: he was still annoyed at her for having concealed the other
girl's whereabouts. But he could not sleep. He was lonely, and his
thoughts were too much for him. Presently he gave up and went
to her wing of the house. Innocent of what had happened, she was
at her most beautiful. She was more beautiful than the one who
had made the night before such an unmixed delight. The closeness
of the resemblance brought back the full flood of his longing.
Pensively, he went into her boudoir and lay down. She followed.

'I am not feeling well. I wonder if it might be something serious. I have been fond of you, and I am sure that if I were to
disappear you would find a replacement in no time. He will win
out in the end, I am sure.'

What a terrible thing to say – and he was not joking. 'How do

*Narrow sleeves indicate a low rank.

†Anonymous, *Kokinshū* 637:

> A trace of dawn comes over the eastern sky.
> Our very robes seem cold in this moment of parting.

‡Tokikata and the secretary, the commentators agree.

you suppose he will feel if he hears of these snide insinuations?' She turned away. 'I have worries enough without having to defend myself against completely groundless charges.'

He looked at her solemnly. 'And how will you feel if you find that I am really angry with you? I have done rather a great deal for you, I think. There are those who say I have done too much. You obviously rank me several grades below him. Well, that I can accept as fate. But it hurts me that you should seem so bent on keeping secrets from me.'

All the while he was marveling upon the forces of destiny that had made him seek the girl out. Tears came to his eyes. Moved to pity, Nakanokimi wondered what sort of rumors he could have picked up. She fell silent. His first visit to her had been the merest prank, and he could not have come away with any high regard for her determination to guard her honor. The mistake had been in admitting and indeed in feeling grateful for the services of a gentleman who, though without close ties to the Uji family, had chosen to act as intermediary. It was because of the initial mistake that she must put up with these insults. She presented a charming and pathetic figure as she lay sunk in her worries. Not wanting her to know for a time that he had found Ukifune, he sought to make her think he had good reasons for berating her. She concluded that her apparent flirtation with Kaoru lay at the heart of the matter. Someone had been talking. Unable to guess what exactly he might be charging her with, she wanted to run and hide.

An unexpected letter came from the empress. Careful to go on looking displeased, Niou withdrew to his own rooms. It said in part: 'His Majesty was much upset at your absence yesterday. Unless you are indisposed, please do come today. It has been rather a long time since I last saw you myself.'

He was sorry to discommode his parents, but he really was not feeling well. He did not go to court. Large numbers of high-ranking courtiers came by but he stayed behind blinds the whole day. In the evening Kaoru called. Asking that he be shown in, Niou received him in dishabille.

'Her Majesty was terribly alarmed when she heard that you had not been well. What might the trouble be?'

The sight of him made Niou's breath come more rapidly. Here I am in the presence of our resident saint, he was thinking; but he smells a little of the vagrant saint,* I fear. Such a sweet girl, and he keeps her off in the mountains all for himself, and leaves her waiting week after week. Niou thought his friend sanctimonious, giving assurances of his sincerity when nothing in the conversation seemed to call for them. Always assiduous in his search for openings, was he not to take delicious advantage of this new secret? But sarcasm did not fit his mood. He wished that Kaoru would go away.

'This will not do,' said Kaoru most solicitously as he got up to leave. 'You may think it is nothing at all, but when these little complaints refuse to clear up after a few days they can be dangerous. You must take care of yourself.'

The man had a remarkable way of making one feel defeated, thought Niou. And how would the girl at Uji be rating them against each other, Kaoru and himself? So each passing incident brought her back – not that she was ever far away.

At Uji the days went by in dull procession, now that the trip to Ishiyama no longer offered relief. Niou wrote at almost tedious length of his impatience and frustration. Knowing that he could not be too careful, he chose for his messenger a man of Tokikata's who knew little of the situation at Uji. The man always went to Ukon.

'We were very fond of each other, once upon a time,' said Ukon to her fellows. 'He discovered me here when he came with the general, and now he wants to be friends again.' She had become adept at lying.

The First Month passed. A trip to Uji was for Niou almost an impossibility, however restless he might be. He was sure that this new obsession was taking years from his life; and so there came thoughts of death to intensify the gloom.

Kaoru, meanwhile, having a brief respite from his duties, set off in his usual quiet way for Uji. He went first to pay his respects and offer a prayer at the monastery. In the evening, after distributing gifts to the monks whom he had put to invoking the holy name, he went on to the Uji villa. Though incognito might have been appropriate, he had made no attempt to hide his rank. In informal but careful court dress, he was the embodiment of calm nobility. How could she possibly receive him? thought Ukifune, in near

*Yamabushi, itinerant, mendicant monks.

panic. The very skies seemed to reproach her. The dashing figure of his rival came back to her. Could she see him* again? Niou had said that she had every chance of driving all his other ladies away and capturing his affections for herself alone. She had heard that he was ill and had sharply curtailed his affairs, and that his house echoed with services for his recovery. How hurt he would be when he learned of this visit! Kaoru was very different. He had an air as of unsounded depths and a quiet, meditative dignity. He used few words as he apologized for his remissness and he said almost nothing that suggested loneliness and deprivation. Yet he did say, choosing his words most carefully, that he had wanted to see her, and his controlled earnestness moved her more than any number of passionate avowals could have. He was very handsome; but that aside, she was sure that he would be a more reliable support, over long years, than Niou. It would be a great loss if he were to catch word of the strange turn her affections had taken. Niou's improbable behavior had left its mark, and she had to thank him for it; but he was altogether too impetuous. She could expect nothing of an enduring nature from him. She would be very sad indeed if Kaoru were to fling her away in anger.

She was a sad little figure, lost in the turmoil of her thoughts. She had matured, acquired new composure, over the months. No doubt, in the boredom of country life, she had had time for meditation.

'The house I am building is almost finished.' His tone was more intimate and affectionate than usual. 'I went to see it the other day. The waters are gentle, as different as they can be from this wild river, and the garden has all the flowers of the city. It is very near my Sanjō place. Nothing need keep us from seeing each other every day. I'd like to move you there in the spring, I think, if you don't mind.'

Niou could scarcely have known of his friend's plans when, in a letter the day before, he had spoken of finding a quiet place for her. She was very sorry, but she should not yield further, she knew, to his advances. And yet his image did keep floating before her eyes. What a wretched predicament to be in!

'Life was much easier and much pleasanter,' said Kaoru, 'back in the days when you were not quite so given to tears. Has

---

*The antecedent could be either Kaoru or Niou.

someone been talking about me? Would a person in my position come over such a long and difficult road if he had less than the best intentions?'

He went to the veranda railing and sat gazing at the new moon. They were both lost in thoughts, he of the past, of days and people now gone, she of the future and her growing troubles. The scene was perfection: the hills were veiled in a mist, and crested herons had gathered at a point along the frozen strand. Far down the river, where the Uji bridge cut its dim arc, faggot-laden boats were weaving in and out. All the details peculiar to the place were brought together. When he looked out upon the scene it was always as if events of old were fresh before his eyes. Even had he been with someone for whom he cared nothing, the air of Uji would have brought on strange feelings of intimacy. How much more so in the company of a not unworthy substitute for Oigimi. Ukifune was gaining all the while in assurance and discernment, in her awareness of how city people behaved, and she was more beautiful each time he saw her. At a loss to console her, for it seemed that her tears were about to spill over, he offered a poem:

'No need to grieve. The Uji bridge stands firm.
They too stand firm, the promises I have made you.

'I am sure that you know what I mean.'
She replied:

'The bridge has gaps, one crosses gingerly.
Can one be sure it will not rot away?'

He found it more difficult than ever to leave her. But people talked, and he would have his fill of her company once he had moved her to the city. He left at dawn. These evidences of improvement added to the sorrow of parting.

Toward the middle of the Second Month the court assembled to compose Chinese poetry. Both Niou and Kaoru were present. The music was appropriate to the season, and Niou was in fine voice as he sang 'A Branch of Plum.'* Yes, he was the most accomplished of them all, everyone said. His one failing, not an easy one to forgive, was a tendency to lose himself in amorous dalliance of an unworthy sort.

*See note**, page 542.

It began to snow and a wind had come up. The festivities were quickly halted and everyone withdrew to Niou's rooms, where a light repast was served. Kaoru was called out to receive a message. The snow, now deeper, was dimly lit by the stars. The fragrance which he sent back into the room made one think how uselessly 'the spring night's darkness' was laboring to blot it out.*

'Does she await me?'† he said to himself, able somehow to infuse even such tiny, disjointed fragments of poetry with sudden life.

Of all the poems he could have picked, thought Niou. His heart racing, he pretended to be asleep. Clearly his friend's feelings for Ukifune passed the ordinary. He had hoped that the lady at the bridge had spread her cloak for him alone, and it was sad and annoying that Kaoru should have similar hopes. Drawn to such a man, could the girl possibly shift her affections to a trifler like himself?

The next day, with snow drifted high outside, the courtiers appeared in the imperial presence to read their poems. Niou was very handsome, indeed at his youthful best. Kaoru, perhaps because he was two or three years older,‡ seemed the calmer and more mature of the two, the model of the personable, cultivated young aristocrat. Everyone agreed that the emperor could not have found a better son-in-law. He had unusual literary abilities and a good head for practical matters as well. Their poems read, the courtiers withdrew. The assembly was loud in proclaiming the superiority of Niou's, but he was not pleased. How easygoing they were, he said to himself, how fortunate to have room in their heads for such trivia.

Some days later, unsettled still at Kaoru's behavior that snowy evening, Niou made elaborate excuses and set out for Uji. In the capital only traces of snow remained, as if awaiting a companion,** but in the mountains the drifts were gradually deeper. The road was even more difficult than he had remembered it. His men were near tears from apprehension and fatigue. The secretary who had

---

See note, page 587.

†See note†, page 848.

‡This is inconsistent with what we have been told before. Niou was born in Chapter 35, Kaoru in Chapter 36.

**See note†, page 588.

been his guide to Uji was also vice-minister of rites. Both positions carried heavy responsibilities, and it was ridiculous to see him hitching up his trousers like any ordinary foot soldier.

The people at Uji had been warned, but were sure that he would not brave the snow. Then, late in the night, word was brought in to Ukon of his arrival. So he really was fond of her, thought Ukifune. Ukon's worries – how would it all end? she had been asking herself – dropped away, at least for the night. There was no way of turning him back, and she concluded that someone else must now be made a partner in the conspiracy. She chose the woman Jijū, who was another of Ukifune's special favorites, and who could be trusted not to talk.

'It is most improper, I know,' said Ukon, 'but we must stand together and keep it from the others.'

They led him inside. The perfume from his wet robes, flooding into the deepest corners of the hall, could have been troublesome; but they told everyone, convincingly enough, that their visitor was Kaoru. To go back before dawn would be worse than not to have come at all; yet someone was certain to spy him out in the morning light. He had therefore asked Tokikata to have a certain house beyond the river made ready. Tokikata, who had gone on ahead to see to the arrangements, returned late in the night and reported that everything was in the best of order. Ukon too was wondering how he meant to keep the escapade a secret. She had been awakened from deep slumber and she was trembling like a child lost in the snow.

Without a word, he took Ukifune up in his arms and carried her off. Jijū followed after and Ukon was left to watch the house. Soon they were aboard one of the boats that had seemed so fragile out on the river. As they rowed into the stream, she clung to Niou, frightened as an exile to some hopelessly distant shore. He was delighted. The moon in the early-morning sky shone cloudless upon the waters. They were at the Islet of the Oranges* said the boatman, pulling up at a large rock over which evergreens trailed long branches.

'See,' said Niou, 'they are fragile pines, no more, but their green is so rich and deep that it lasts a thousand years.

*Tachibana no Kojima.

'A thousand years may pass, it will not waver,
     This vow I make in the lee of the Islet of Oranges.'

What a very strange place to be, thought the girl.

'The colors remain, here on the Islet of Oranges.
     But where go I, a boat upon the waters?'

The time was right, and so was the girl, and so was her poem: for him, at least, things could not have been more pleasingly arranged.

They reached the far bank of the river. An attendant helped him ashore, the girl still in his arms. No one else was to touch her, he insisted.

The custodian of the house was wondering what sort of woman could have produced such an uncourtly uproar. It was a temporary house, rough and unfinished, which Tokikata's uncle, the governor of Inaba, had put up on one of his manors. Crude plaited screens such as Niou had not seen before offered almost no resistance to the wind. There were patches of snow at the fence, clouds had come up, bringing new flurries of snow, and icicles glistened at the eaves. In the daylight the girl seemed even prettier than by candlelight. Niou was dressed simply, against the rigors of the journey. A fragile little figure sat huddled before him, for he had slipped off her outer robe. And so here she was, she said to herself, not even properly dressed, before a royal prince. There was nothing, nothing at all, to protect her from his gaze. She was wearing five or six white singlets, somewhat rumpled, soft and lustrous to the hems of the sleeves and skirts, more pleasing, he thought, than any number of colors piled one upon another. He seldom saw women with whom he kept constant company in quite such informal dress. He was enchanted.

And so Jijū too (a pretty young woman) was witness to the scene. Who might she be? Niou had asked when he saw her climbing uninvited into the boat. She must not be told his name. Jijū, for her part, was dazzled. She had not been in the company of such a fine gentleman before.

The custodian made a great fuss over Tokikata, thinking him to be the leader of the party. Tokikata, who had appropriated the next room for himself, was in good form. He made an amusing game of evading the questions the custodian kept putting in reverent tones.

'There have been bad omens, very bad, and I must stay away from the city for a while. No one is to see me.'

And so Niou and Ukifune passed pleasant hours with no fear of being observed. No doubt, thought Niou, once more in the clutches of jealousy, she was equally amiable when she received Kaoru. He let it be known that Kaoru had taken the emperor's own daughter for his bride and seemed devoted to her. He declined (let us say out of charity) to mention the snatch of poetry he had overheard that snowy evening.

'You seem to be cock of the walk,' he said when Tokikata came with towels and refreshments. 'But keep out of sight while you're about it. Someone might want to imitate you.'

Jijū, a susceptible young lady, was having *such* a good time. She spent the whole day with Tokikata.

Looking towards the city over the drifting snow, Niou saw forests emerging from and sinking back into the clouds. The mountain above caught the evening glow as in a mirror. He described, with some embroidering, the horror of last night's journey. A crude rustic inkstone having been brought to him, he set down a poem as if in practice:

> 'I pushed through snowy peaks, past icy shores,
>   Dauntless all the way – O daunting one!'

'It is true, of course, that I had a horse at Kohata.'*
In her answering poem she ventured an objection:†

> 'The snow that blows to the shore remains there, frozen.
>   Yet worse my fate: I am caught, dissolve in midair.'

This image of fading in midair rather annoyed him. Yes, she was being difficult, she had to agree, tearing the paper to bits. He was always charming, and he was quite irresistible when he was trying to please.

He had said that he would be in retreat for two days. Each unhurried hour seemed to bring new intimacy. The clever Ukon contrived pretexts for sending over fresh clothes. Jijū smoothed her mistress's hair and helped her into a robe of deep purple and a

See note, page 911.

†Unclear. Perhaps she inks out his poem, or immediately after having written it, her own.

cloak of figured magenta lined also with magenta – an unexceptionable combination. Taking up Jijū's apron,* he had Ukifune try it on as she ladled water for him. Yes, his sister the First Princess would be very pleased to take such a girl into her service. Her ladies-in-waiting were numerous and wellborn, but he could think of none among them capable of putting the girl to shame.

But let us not look in too closely upon their dalliance.

He told her again and again how he wanted to hide her away, and he tried to extract unreasonable promises from her. 'You are not to see him, understand, until everything is arranged.'

That was too much to ask of her. She shed a few silent tears. He, for his part, was almost strangled with jealousy. Even now she was unable to forget Kaoru! He talked on and on, now weeping, now reproaching her.

Late in the night, again in a warm embrace, they started back across the river.

'I doubt if the man to whom you seem to give the top ranking can be expected to treat you as well. You will know what I mean, I trust.'

It was true, she thought, nodding. He was delighted.

Ukon opened the side door and the girl went in, and he was left feeling utterly desolate.

As usual after such expeditions, he returned to Nijō. His appetite quite left him and he grew paler and thinner by the day, to the consternation of the whole court. In the stir that ensued he was unable to get a decent letter off to Uji.

That officious nurse of Ukifune's had been with her daughter, who was in confinement; but now that she was back Ukifune was scarcely able to glance at such letters as did come. Her mother hated having her off in the wilderness, but consoled herself with the thought that Kaoru would make a dependable patron and guardian. The indications were that he would soon, albeit in secret, move her to a place near his Sanjō mansion. *Then* they would be able to look the world square in the face! The mother began seeking out accomplished serving women and pretty little girls and sending them off to her daughter. All this was as it should be, Ukifune knew; yet the image of the dashing, impetuous Niou, now reproaching her, now

---

Shibira, an overgarment of some description. He is treating her like an underling, to see how she might perform in the service of his sister.

wheedling and cajoling, insisted upon coming back. When she dozed off for a moment, there he would be in her dreams. How much easier for everyone if he would go away!

The rains continued, day after day. Chafing at his inability to travel that mountain road, Niou thought how constricting was 'the cocoon one's parents weave about one'* – and that was scarcely a kind way to characterize the concern his royal parents felt for him. He sent off a long letter in which he set down his thoughts as they came to him.

> 'I gaze your way in search of the clouds above you.
> I see but darkness, so dreary these days of rain.'

His hand was if anything more interesting the less care he took with it. She was still young and rather flighty, and these avowals of love set up increasingly strong tremors in response. Yet she could not forget the other gentleman, a gentleman of undoubted depth and nobility, perhaps because it was he who had first made her feel wanted. Where would she turn if he were to hear of this sordid affair and abandon her? And her mother, who lived for the day when he would give her a home, would certainly be upset, and very angry too. Prince Niou, judging from his letters, burned with impatience; but she had heard a great deal about his volatility and feared that his fondness for her was a matter of the passing moment. Supposing he were indeed to hide her away and number her among his enduring loves – how could she then face Nakano-kimi, her own sister? The world kept no secrets, as his success in searching her out after that strange, fleeting encounter in the dusk had demonstrated. Kaoru might bring her into the city, but was it possible that his rival would fail to seek her out there too? And if Kaoru were to turn against her, she knew that she would have herself to blame.

Her thoughts had reached this impasse when a second letter came, this one from Kaoru. Ranged side by side, the two letters seemed to reproach her. She went off and lay down with Niou's, the longer of the two. Ukon and Jijū exchanged glances: so the game was over, and Niou had won.

---

*Hitomaro, *Shūishū* 895:

> How tight the cocoon one's parents weave about one.
> Its prisoner, I may not see my love.

'Perfectly natural,' said Jijū. 'I really thought I had never seen a finer man than the general, but the prince is *so* handsome, especially when he's just being himself. If he ever paid that much attention to me, I can tell you, I'd be making my plans right now. I'd be looking for a place with Her Majesty, and then I could see him every day of the week.'

'I can see that you bear watching. But I don't agree. The general is the finest of them all. I don't care about looks. Manners and disposition, those are the things that count. But she has worked herself into a fine predicament, on that I think we can agree. Whatever will become of her?'

Life was easier for Ukon, however. It was easier to tell lies and invent excuses now that there were two of them.

'I have been very remiss,' said Kaoru's letter in part, 'though you may be sure that you have been constantly on my mind. I would be very pleased indeed if I might have a note from you now and then. Can you have led yourself to believe that I do not care for you?

> 'The long, dark rains go on, one's heart is dark.
>   Will it be so in yon village of rising waters?*

'My longing to see you is greater with each passing day.'

It was on prim white paper in a formal envelope. The writing lacked subtlety, perhaps, but suggested breeding and sensitivity.

Niou's letter was interesting too. Long and detailed and intricately folded, it was as different from Kaoru's as a letter could possibly be. She must answer it first, while no one else was with her, said one of the two women. She took up her brush – but no, she could not possibly. As if by way of practice, she set down a poem:

> ' "Gloom" is the name of Uji in Yamashiro.
>   It speaks of the lives of us who dwell in its compass.'

Sometimes she would take out the sketch Niou had made for her, and weep. His love would not last, it could not, she told herself, wishing that quiet resignation would come to her. But she wept more bitterly at the thought that she might one day be torn from him.

Ochi no sato, here translated 'yon village,' may be a place name.

At length she sent an answer. He wept quite unapologetically as he read it:

> 'I wish to be as the cloud that darkens the peak.
> Better so than aimlessly drifting through life.*

'Were I to join them . . .'†
She did, after all, seem fond of him. He thought again of that pathetic little figure, huddled up as if in defense against its own thoughts.

And the more proper of the two suitors was meanwhile reading *his* note over and over. He deeply sympathized, and wanted very much to see her. This was her poem:

> 'The tedious days of rain, incessant rain,
> They speak to me of me. Yet wetter my sleeves.'

'I have hesitated to mention it, not for the world wanting to offend you,' he said to his wife; 'but the truth is that I have left an old friend out in the country, and she is so unhappy there that I am thinking of bringing her into town. I have always been an odd sort of man, reconciled to living an odd life; but you have made me see that I am not capable of running away from the world. And so it makes me feel sad and guilty to have these little secrets.'

'I see no reason at all to be jealous,' she replied.

'But what will people say to your father? They will talk, you know, and gossip can be a nuisance. Not that she is important enough to produce a really good scandal.'

He had a house for the girl, but he squirmed at the thought of having it said that he was readying himself a pleasant trysting place. In the greatest secrecy he commissioned paintings for the doors. And the man whom he chose to make his special confidant was the father-in-law of the secretary who had taken Niou to Uji. The news, nothing omitted, was promptly relayed to Niou.

'He has the services of artists whom he trusts completely. It is an out-of-the-way little place, but he doesn't seem to care a thing about the expense.'

---

*Possibly she is saying that she wants to die, and possibly, since the 'cloud' is literally 'rain cloud,' *amagumo,* and *ama* is also 'nun,' she is saying that she wants to enter a nunnery.

†A poetic allusion?

Niou saw that he must act quickly. He remembered that his old nurse had a house in the lower reaches of the city and that she would shortly be going to a remote province with her husband, who was to be governor.

'I have someone whom it seems important to keep out of sight,' he said to her.

The nurse and her family had misgivings. What sort of woman would he be after this time? But it was not theirs to refuse what seemed important to him. Something would be arranged, they sent back, and his spirits revived. The governor was to leave towards the end of the month. Niou decided to move the girl into the house on the very day of his departure. Word was sent to Uji, with emphasis on the need for secrecy. It would of course be out of the question for Niou to go there himself, and word came back that there might be complications because of that overzealous nurse.

Kaoru was meanwhile making his own plans: he would send for Ukifune on the tenth day of the Fourth Month. Though Ukifune was not disposed to follow 'whatever waters beckon,'* she could not imagine what else she was to do with herself. Utterly distraught, she wanted only to go home, there to spend a few days in quiet thought. But the governor's house would be overrun with priests and noisy with prayers and incantations, for the sister, the lieutenant's wife, was in confinement. Nor would it be possible, in the circumstances, to think of a trip to Ishiyama.

One day her mother came calling.

The nurse bustled about playing the good hostess. 'The general has been so nice about clothes and all. I would have been very glad, I'm sure, to do it all myself, but of course I'm just a woman. We women do make the worst bungle of things.'

Faced with all this joy, the girl could only think of impending disaster. The whole world would be laughing at them.

There had come yet another letter from the importunate Niou. He would seek her out, he declared, even if she hid behind the eightfold mountain mists.† The two of them would then have no recourse but to die. Far better to slip off somewhere together.

*Ono no Komachi, *Kokinshū* 938:

> Alone, adrift, like a rootless water weed,
> I shall give myself to whatever waters beckon.

†Probably a poetic allusion.

What was she to do? In hopeless indecision, she lay down again.

'My, but you do look pale.' Her mother was openly surprised. 'And I think you've lost weight.'

'She hasn't been herself for days and days. She won't eat a bite, and she seems so tired and mopish all the time.'

'Something has gotten at her. Oh, my! Could it be *that*, I wonder. But of course we did have to cancel the trip to Ishiyama.'*

The girl looked away.

In the evening the moon was bright. She was on the edge of tears as she thought of the moon in the dawn that other night. But she must drive it from her mind.

The governor's wife invited Bennokimi over to exchange memories of days long past. The nun spoke of Oigimi, of what a sober, deliberate lady she had been and of how, in her worries, she had faded away before their eyes.

'And if she had lived, she too would have had your daughter to share her thoughts with. What a consolation that would have been for them.'

What right had they to look down upon her daughter? the governor's wife was muttering to herself. Was she not one of them? Well, if fate proved as kind as they now had reason to expect, she *would* be one of them.

'Over the years she has been my great worry, and now things seem to be going a little better. Once she's moved into town I don't suppose I'll have much reason to come all these miles out into the country. But don't think I haven't enjoyed it. So nice to have a good, quiet talk now and then about old times.'

'I seem to bring people bad luck, and so I've kept my distance. I haven't really had a decent talk with her yet. I'll be lonely all the same when she leaves me. But this is no place for a young girl. It's best that she go. I've said that the general isn't one for quick, easy flirtations, and that only a very unusual attraction could bring him all this way; and I haven't lied to you.'

'A person can never tell, of course, what will happen over the years; but at the moment he does seem pleased with her. I'm sure I have you to thank for it. Her sister at Nijō was far kinder to her

---

*Menstruation was given as the reason for canceling the pilgrimage to Ishiyama, late in the First Month. It is now the Third Month.

than she had any right to expect, but there was that unfortunate incident, you know, and where was I to leave her?'

The nun smiled. 'Yes, he is a troublemaker, a young gentleman of affairs, altogether too many of them. Sensible women think several times before they go to work in that house. Tayū's daughter Ukon* says he's a very attractive young man, but he has his ways, and they are always holding their breath, wondering what might happen next to upset their lady.'

Ukifune listened in silence. Serving women, thought she, mere serving women; and what of her, Nakanokimi's own sister?

'Disgusting. But the general now. He's married a royal princess but I say – it may not be my place, but I say – it doesn't matter a bit who he takes in now and whether it works or not. You may tell me it's not my place to say so, but that's what I think. But if something were to happen, something to set tongues to wagging, well, I would be very sorry, of course, but that would be that. She wouldn't be my daughter any more.'

The girl felt as if she were being cut to shreds. She wanted to die. It could only be a matter of time before word reached her mother.

And outside the river roared. 'There are gentler rivers,' said her mother, somewhat absentmindedly. 'I'm sure the general feels guilty about leaving her all this time in this godforsaken place.'

Yes, it was a terrible river, swift and treacherous, said one of the women. 'Why, just the other day the ferryman's little grandson slipped on his oar and fell in. Any number of people have drowned in it.'

If she herself were to disappear, thought Ukifune, people would grieve for a while, but only for a time; and if she were to live on, an object of ridicule, there would be no end to her woes. Death would cancel out the accounts, nothing seemed to stand in the way. But no – that would be too cruel to her mother. Her thoughts in a turmoil, she pretended to be asleep, and before her was a vision of her bereaved mother, wailing and lamenting.

They must arrange for invocations to the Blessed One, said the governor's wife, remarking again upon these alarming evidences of decline, and there must be lustrations and propitiatory rites to the native gods as well.

*It is becoming clear that the Ukon at Uji and the Ukon whom we saw at the Nijō mansion are not the same person.

She rambled on, quite unaware of what these 'lustrations' of hers might mean to her daughter, of the stain the girl would want to wash away in the river Mitarashi.*

'You don't have enough people here,' continued the mother, overlooking nothing. 'Hunt up people you can trust and leave these new ones out. She may think it's easy enough to rub elbows with the great ones, but if things go a little wrong there's bound to be fighting. Be careful, and don't let anyone know what you're up to. Well, I must be off. I *am* a little worried about the other girl, you know.'

Utterly helpless in the face of disaster, half convinced that they would not meet again, the girl clung to her mother. 'I am not at all well, and I hate being alone. Let me come with you, just for a few days.'

'I wish it were possible, really I do. But the house is so small, and you can't imagine what it's like now. And you do have to get ready, you know. Your girls couldn't get the tiniest thing done there.' She was weeping. 'I'd find ways to see you, believe me I would, even if you were to go off to Takefu.† But you know how it is. There's very little I can do for you.'

Kaoru wrote asking after her health, for she had told him that she was not well. 'I wish I could see you, but I am quite buried in trivial paperwork. We do not have much longer to wait – and the result is that waiting becomes more difficult each day.'

And another letter came from Niou. 'What are you worried about this time? I wonder. I too am worried, indeed beside myself with worry. Might something have led the smoke "in a rather

---

See note, page 367.

†'Gateway,' a Saibara:

> Tell my parents I am here,
> O wind that blows between us,
> At the governor's seat in Takefu,
> The gateway to the north,
> O wind that blows between us,
> O noble gentlemen.

It is generally agreed that the young Murasaki Shikibu lived for a time at Takefu, seat of the governor of Echizen.

surprising direction"?'* This was far from all. His letters tended to be much longer than Kaoru's.

The two messengers had crossed paths that rainy day and today they met again. Kaoru's messenger, a guardsman, had occasionally seen the other, a groom, in the house of that accommodating secretary.

'And what brings your honorable self out into the country so often?' he asked.

'Well, you see, there's someone here I write little notes to.'

'Come, now. You deliver your own notes? I suspect you're not telling me everything.'

'Well, as a matter of fact, the governor,† you see, is in touch with someone here.'

It all seemed very odd, very improbable. This was not, however, the time to press the matter, and they went their separate ways. Kaoru's man, who had a good head, turned to the boy with him.

'Trail him and see if he goes to the governor's house.'

'He went to Prince Niou's,' reported the lad, 'and gave the letter to the vice-minister of rites.'

Niou's man, less intelligent, had not guessed that they would take the trouble to follow him, and in any case (sad but true) he did not really know what he had been up to.

The guardsman arrived back at Sanjō just as Kaoru, in casual court dress, was setting out for Rokujō, where the empress was in residence. His retinue was modest.

'I'm a little late,' said the man, handing his note to someone in the retinue, 'because I've been looking into something very odd.'

Kaoru overhead. 'And what was it?' he asked, coming out.

But the man only bowed, not wanting the other to hear. Kaoru understood and started on his way.

The empress again being indisposed, though lightly, all her sons were with her, and the Rokujō house swarmed with high-ranking courtiers. The secretary, a very busy man (he was also vice-minister of rites, as we have seen), was late in making his appearance. Niou took Ukifune's note, along with several others, at the doorway to one of the withdrawing rooms. On his way from an

See note, page 534.
†Tokikata.

interview with the empress, Kaoru sensed something furtive in the meeting and stopped to watch. Niou opened the most important letter first. It seemed to be in a delicate hand on fine red paper. Engrossed, Niou did not look Kaoru's way. Just then Yūgiri passed on his way from the royal bedchamber. Stepping from behind a door, Kaoru coughed to warn his friend. Niou shoved the letter out of sight as Yūgiri moved on, and, in confusion, redid his blouse strings.

'I think I will go too,' said Kaoru, bowing deeply* and hurrying after Yūgiri. 'It makes you wonder, when she hasn't had one of these spells in such a long time. Maybe we should send off to Hiei for the abbot.'

It was late in the night when the last of the courtiers left the empress. Yūgiri, with Niou leading the way and his sons of various ranks trooped around him, went off to his own quarter. Kaoru started for home a few minutes later. Curious about the man who had been to Uji, he took advantage of a moment when his attendants were down in the garden readying torches.

'What were you talking about?'

'At Uji this morning there was a man who works for Lord Tokikata, the governor of Izumo. He had a very interesting letter, on purple tissue paper, tied to a cherry branch, and he gave it to a woman at the west door. When I asked him about it afterwards, his answers didn't make much sense. I was sure he was lying. I couldn't imagine why he would want to lie to me and so I had the boy trail him. He went to Prince Niou's and gave the answer from Uji to Lord Michisada.'

Very odd indeed. 'What was the answer like, and who gave it to him?'

'It was handed out from another door and I didn't see it myself. But the boy said it was a very elegant note on red paper.'

Without doubt the note that had so enthralled Niou. Kaoru was much impressed with the man's perspicacity, but he was not as lavish with his praise as he would have wished to be. People might be listening.

His thoughts on the way home were far from pleasant. What a very clever fellow his friend was! How had he learned that the girl was at Uji? How had he arranged to be in communication with

---

*It is actually a more profound gesture of respect: he kneels.

her? Kaoru had thought that so far from the city she would be in no danger. He had been naïve. Niou could have as many ladies as he wished if they were his alone; but how could he be so unfeeling towards the friend who had been so close to him, who had acted as guide and intermediary, indeed almost as procurer, in the Uji days? Kaoru had kept his longing for Nakanokimi under tight control, and now his forbearance seemed merely stupid. His feelings for her went far beyond a passing attachment of yesterday and today. There was that bond between them over so many years. He had controlled himself, wanting to spare her pain, and wanting to have nothing on his own conscience; and he had been very stupid indeed. With all those hordes of people around the empress, how had Niou managed to get a letter off to distant Uji? Had he already seen the girl? Love did have a way of keeping one on the road. And Niou's whereabouts *had* given cause for speculation and inquiry these last days, and he had been vaguely unwell, and his ailments could frequently be traced to amatory sources. Kaoru thought of Niou's distress – everyone had been so sorry for him – at being unable to see Nakanokimi. Ukifune's moodiness on their last meeting no longer puzzled him.

Such was the human heart. So charming and quiet on the surface, she was a good match for Niou. They were meant for each other. Perhaps he should withdraw in Niou's favor. But he had never, not in his most sentimental moments, thought her the only one for him. He would leave her to other affairs as she chose to have them, and take her for what she was. He knew that a decision to send her away would not come easily.

His men could see all too clearly that he was lost in a black reverie.

If in his anger he were to abandon her, Niou would no doubt take her in; but Niou was not one to dwell carefully and compassionately upon the distant future. There were already two or three women of whom he had wearied and whom he had put in the service of the First Princess. Kaoru did not want to hear that Ukifune had joined the company. He would not, he concluded once again, find it easy to dismiss her.

He wrote inquiring after her health. Choosing a moment when there was no danger of being overheard, he summoned that astute guardsman.

'Is Lord Michisada still with Nakanobu's* daughter?'

'Yes, my lord, it seems that he is.'

'And does he make it a practice to send that man to Uji? There is a lonely lady there and he may have his eye on her.' He sighed. 'Well, see that no one goes trailing *you*. We'd look very silly.'

The man bowed. He remembered that Michisada was always prying into Kaoru's affairs and had asked about the situation at Uji, but it seemed wise not to tell unsolicited tales. Kaoru questioned him no further. Too much had been spied out already, he feared.

At Uji, the increasing frequency of his messages was a new worry. The latest said only:

> 'It yet stands firm, the pine-clad mount of Sué,
> Thought I. And even then the waves engulfed it!†

Do not, I pray, make us an object of unkind laughter.'

An odd thing to say – what could he mean? She did not wish to make it seem that he had scored a hit, and it was always possible that there had been a mistake.

She refolded the note and added a note of her own: 'This seems to have been missent. I am not at all well, and am sure that you will forgive me for not writing a decent letter.'

He smiled as he read it. This talent for evasion had not been apparent earlier. He could not really be angry with her.

She was in despair. He had not exactly said so, but he had hinted rather broadly that he knew. The strangest, unhappiest of fates was pressing down upon her.

'Why are you sending the general's letter back?' Ukon had come in. 'That's as good as inviting bad luck.'

'It doesn't seem to be for me. The address must be wrong.'

Ukon thought her mistress's behavior very odd, and (knowing perfectly well that good servants should be more reticent) unfolded the note as she took it back to the messenger.

'Very sad,' she said to Ukifune, not letting it be known that she had seen the letter. 'For you, for me, for all of us. The general seems to have guessed.'

Ukifune flushed and did not answer. She concluded that some-one had been talking. She did not ask who it might be. How

---

*Nakanobu is Kaoru's steward, described earlier as Michisada's father-in-law.

†See note*, page 275.

would she seem to her women, what would be on their minds? She had not asked for these complications. Her hapless destiny was working itself out.

'Let me tell you about my sister,' Ukon was saying to Jijū. 'It was when we were off in Hitachi. This sort of thing can happen to the likes of us too, you know. She had two men after her, and she just couldn't make up her mind, they both seemed so fond of her. Then she began edging toward the new one and the other up and killed him. And never spoke to her again. So we lost a good soldier, and the other one, the one who did the murdering, he was a good man too, but naturally he couldn't be kept on. So he was ordered to leave Hitachi, and my sister was let go from the governor's house, because, after all, nothing would have happened if it hadn't been for her and her bad habits. She stayed on in the east and (more's the sin) Nurse* goes on weeping for her to this very day. You may think I'm asking for trouble when I say so, but it's just not the sort of thing people do. I don't care what sort of families they come from, a muddle is a muddle. It doesn't always end up in bloodshed, of course, but things every bit as bad can happen, I don't care whether you're a princess or a laundress. I don't know, maybe it's even worse for a princess. Maybe she'd be better off dead than in a predicament like my sister's. Well, my lady. Make up your mind. If the prince seems so fond of you, just panting after you, then go to him, and stop moping. There's no point at all in letting yourself waste away. Your mother is so worried, and Nurse is all in a dither about the general and his plans for you. Myself, I wish the prince would just go away and stop trying to snatch you from under the general's nose.'

'You're dreadful.' Jijū preferred Niou and did not hesitate to say so. 'No one can fight his destiny, my lady, and yours is to go to the one you're even a little fonder of. And really, the prince is so warm about it all, so sincere, why, my lady, you couldn't think of throwing it all away. I can see that you're not happy about these people trying to rush you off into the general's arms. You may have to hide yourself for a little while, but I say you should go to the one you like best.'

'I don't care which one she goes to. I just want her to go safely, and I've said my prayers at Hatsuse and at Ishiyama too. The

---

*Mama. Ukifune's officious nurse is apparently the mother of both Ukon and the sister left behind in Hitachi.

people on the general's land are thugs, there's no other way to describe them, and this town is swarming with them, all related to each other. Everyone here in Yamashiro and over in Yamato is related to Udoneri and that Ukonnodaibu,* you know, his son-in-law, the ones the general left to look after us. I'm not saying, mind you, that a fine gentleman like the general himself would order any rough business, but you can't tell about country people, and they're the ones who take turns guarding the house. Every last one of them is determined that nothing will go wrong while he is on duty – it's a point of honor – and, why, anything could happen. It was very foolish and very careless of the prince to do what he did the other night. He's so bent on secrecy that he comes incognito with no guard to speak of at all. Anything could happen, I tell you, if one of those men were to catch him.'

Ukifune listened in an agony of embarrassment. It was clear that they had guessed everything, even her feelings toward Niou. She had not decided upon either of the two. Niou's ardor quite dizzied her, and left her incredulous that she should be its cause and object; and on the other hand she could not bring herself to say her final farewells to the man who had so long† been her chief source of strength. Hence her agony and the paralyzing indecision. And how awful if Niou's heedlessness really were to invite 'rough business.'

'Leave me alone, please. Please – just let me die.' She lay with her face pressed against a cushion. 'Has anyone, the lowest beggar, ever had more to worry about than I have?'

'You are not to say so. I was only trying to make things a little easier for you. You used to throw off worries as if they weren't there, and now you fret and fret. I really don't understand you.'

For the two women who knew the truth, the tension mounted. Nurse, meanwhile, hummed a happy song as she went on with her preparations, dyeing this piece of cloth, cutting that. 'Now here's someone who might amuse you,' she said, calling to Ukifune's side a pretty little girl who had just come into their service. 'Do you have to lie around the house all day long when there's nothing in

---

*These are not properly names, but functional designations, telling us that both men belong to the warrior class.

†'Over the years,' the text says literally; but Kaoru and Ukifune have known each other for only about six months.

the world the matter with you? I wonder if someone might be trying to get at you and spoil everything.'

The days went by and there was no answer from Kaoru. One afternoon that Udoneri whom Ukon had described as so menacing came to the house. He was an old man with a rough growl, not at all refined; yet something in his manner commanded respect.

'I want to speak to one of the ladies.' Ukon came out. 'The general sent for me and I went to town this morning. I've just come back. He gave me a long list of orders. He'd trusted us to keep guard all night and hadn't sent guards from town. Now he's heard that men with no business here have been seen around the place. Our fault, nobody else's, he said. We might try keeping our eyes open. If we weren't up to it, well, he'd have to think of something else, and it might not be good for us. He sent out a man with his orders and that's what he told the man to tell me. I told the man to tell him I'd been sick myself and off duty, and wouldn't know what might be going on. They had been told to keep their eyes and ears open, I said, and they'd have told me if they'd seen any prowlers. The general said he'd know what to do with us if it happened again. What was he talking about? It didn't make me feel very good, you can guess.'

An owl hooting beside her pillow could not have given Ukon a more unpleasant start. Silently, she went back into the house. 'I was right. The general knows everything. That's why he's stopped writing.'

Nurse had overheard only a part of Udoneri's remarks. 'Good. He needed a dressing down. They've been careless and there are robbers all over the place. He sends plowboys to keep watch. Nobody really keeps watch at all.'

Ukifune saw doom approaching. Niou wrote asking over and over again to be kept abreast of the preparations, and pleading the unhappiness of 'waiting, as the moss beneath the pines.'* Doom seemed to come yet a few steps closer. One or the other of the two men was certain to be made desperately unhappy, and the obvious solution was for her to disappear. Long ago there had been a maiden who drowned herself for no greater cause than that

*Anonymous, *Shinchokusenshū* 734:

> Waiting, as the moss beneath the pines,
> I find my passions growing more unruly.

two men seemed equally fond of her.* Why should she have regrets for a world that promised only torment? Her mother would grieve for a time; but she had all those other children and would presently gather grasses of forgetfulness. Death would bring less lingering sorrow than disgrace. Ukifune was on the surface a gentle, docile, obedient girl, but perhaps because she had been reared on the outer edges of society, she was capable of sudden, impulsive action. Unobtrusively, she began tearing up suggestive papers, burning them in her lamp and sending the ashes down the river. Women not in her confidence assumed that she was destroying fugitive notes written to beguile the tedium and not worth taking to the city.

But Jijū too saw what was happening. 'My lady! Whatever are you doing? I can understand not wanting people to see your little love notes, but the day will come when you will regret burning them. The thing to do – they all do it, princesses and servants too – is put them away in a corner of some box and take them out from time to time. He does express himself so beautifully, and his letters even *look* beautiful. How can you be so heartless?'

'Heartless? I do not have long to live, I'm afraid, and I wouldn't want to leave them behind. For his sake, really. Think what people would say. She wanted us to know all about it – that's what they would say.'

She remembered having heard, back before she knew much of the world, that to die in advance of one's parents is a grave sin – but she had reached something like a decision, and, so paralyzing were the thoughts that trailed one another through her mind, she feared she would not have the strength to reach another.

The end of the month approached. The house to which Niou proposed moving her was to be vacated on the twenty-eighth.

'I will send for you that night, I promise you,' wrote Niou. 'Do not let your women know what is happening. I will not breathe a word of it myself.'

If he were to come in the usual incognito, she would have to turn him away, and be resigned to not seeing him again. She could not invite him into the house, even to rest a moment for the

---

*There are two possible precedents: the maiden of Unai, *Tales of Yamato* 147, and Tekona of Mama, *Manyōshū* 1807 and 1808. The latter was pursued by numerous suitors.

return journey. His image (so tenacious, that image), defeated and going off angry, came before her again and would not leave. She pressed his letter to her forehead, trying to control herself; but soon she was weeping bitterly.

'Please, my lady, please,' said Ukon. 'These people will guess what has happened. I'm afraid that some of them are suspicious already. You must make up your mind. Tell him you will go to him, if that is what you want. I will not leave you. I am ready for anything, even if he carries you off through the skies, tiny little thing that you are.'

The girl managed to control her sobs for a time. 'I'm sure you want to help, but you don't understand. It would be so easy if that seemed the right thing to do. He makes it seem that I am begging him to come for me. What will he do next? It is all too awful.'

She did not answer the letter.

Niou had his own worries. She gave no sign of surrender, and he seldom even heard from her any more. Kaoru's reasonable arguments had no doubt led her in the safer direction. He could not deny their justice. Yet he boiled with resentment and jealousy. She had been fond of him and he had been defeated by the women around her. His gloom and longing seemed to spread until the heavens offered them no further refuge.*

Impulsively, as always, he rushed off to Uji.

He tried the reed fence that had admitted him before, but the guards were more alert.

'Who's there?' came voices.

He withdrew and this time sent a man who knew the precincts well. Again came the challenge. Matters were not as simple as they had been.

'An emergency message from the city,' said the man, asking for one of Ukon's maids.

Ukon was in consternation. 'It will be quite impossible for him to disturb her tonight. I am very sorry indeed that he should have come all this way for nothing.'

Niou was wringing his hands. How could they be so unfeeling? He called Tokikata. 'Go and arrange something with Jijū.'

A devious fellow, Tokikata contrived an interview.

See note, page 1050.

'It will be difficult.' Jijū could only second Ukon. 'The guards have had some special order from the general, I don't know what or why. It touched their pride and they are being careful. My lady has been very upset to think that the prince might come all this way for nothing, but if they catch you things will only be worse. Suppose you tell him that we are making our plans and not letting anyone know, and we will be ready when the night he has spoken of comes.' And she added that Nurse was even jumpier than usual.

'You know of course that he can't run off on these trips every day. If you make me go slinking back to tell him she just won't see him, he'll think I'm not worth my keep. Come with me, and the two of us can try to explain.'

Out of the question, completely out of the question. And as they argued the night wore on.

Still on his horse, Niou waited some distance away. Numbers of dogs had come bounding up and were barking most inelegantly. His men were in the cruelest apprehension. There were very few of them and they were far from help. What would they do if someone were to leap out from the underbrush?

'Enough of this.' Tokikata dragged the protesting Jijū after him. Her long hair under her arm, she was very pretty even in this extremity. Since she quite refused to get on his horse, he walked beside her, helping with her skirts. He appropriated the rough clogs of a guardsman for himself and let her have his shoes.

It did not seem prudent to confer in an exposed position. Tokikata spread a saddle blanket* at a spot backed by a woodcutter's fence and protected by brambles and matted grasses. Niou dismounted.

What a queer fix to be in, he was thinking, told of what had happened. Suppose he really were to take a bad fall on this road he had chosen and lame himself for life? He was in tears, and to the susceptible Jijū his plight seemed even sadder. Had he been a veritable fiend of an enemy, his powers of persuasion would still have had their way.

'Can't I have a single word with her?' He struggled to control his tears. 'Why have things come to this, after all that has happened? You people have turned her against me.'

*Aori, a sort of mudguard.

She explained recent events as carefully as she could. 'Don't let anyone know what day you have decided on. You have been very good to come all this way, and I will do everything I can, even if it means ruining myself.'

Terrified of being found out, he could not reprove her for this caution. His men chased the dogs away repeatedly but still they barked. From the villa came the twang of bowstrings and the rough voices of the guard alerting the house to the danger of fire.

We need not seek words to describe Niou's feelings as Jijū hurried him on his way.

'I weep, I go — to lose myself! — where soar
　　No mountains but know the white of clinging clouds.

'Hurry home yourself.'

Jijū wept the whole of the way back. There was nothing in the world to compare with his gentle persuasions and the perfume from his robes, drenched in the late-night dew.

Hopelessly, Ukifune listened to Ukon's story. Then Jijū came in with hers. Ukifune made no comment. She wished they would go away and let her weep unobserved.

Ashamed of her swollen eyes, she was late in arising the next morning. She put her dress in a semblance of order and took up a sutra. Let my sin be light, she prayed, for going ahead of my mother. She took out the sketch Niou had made for her, and there he was beside her again, handsome, confident, courtly. The sorrow was more intense, she was sure, than if she had seen him the night before. And she was sad too for the other gentleman, the one who had vowed unshakable fidelity, who had said that they would go off to some place of quiet retirement. To be laughed at, called a shallow, frivolous little wench, would be worse than to die and bring sorrow to such an estimable gentleman.

'If in torment I cast myself away,
　　My sullied name will drift on after me.'

She longed to see her mother again, and even her ill-favored brothers and sisters, who were seldom on her mind. And she thought of Nakanokimi. Suddenly, indeed, the people she would like to see once more seemed to form in troops and battalions. Her women, caught up in preparations for the move, dyeing new robes and the like, would pass by with this and that remark, but she paid no attention. She sat up through the night, ill and half distraught, wondering how she might steal into the darkness unobserved. Looking out over the river in the morning, she felt nearer death than a lamb on its way to the slaughter.

A note came from Niou, telling once more of his unhappiness. Not wishing to compromise herself at this very late date, she sent back only a poem:

'Should I leave no trace behind in this gloomy world,
    What target then would you have for your complaints?'

She wanted also to tell Kaoru of her last hours; but the two men were very close friends and the thought of their comparing notes revolted her. It would be better to speak openly of her decision to neither.

A letter came from her mother: 'I had a most ominous dream of you last night, and am having scriptures read in several temples. Perhaps because I had trouble getting back to sleep, I have been napping today, and I have had another dream, equally frightening. I waste no time, therefore, in getting off this letter. Do be careful. You are so far away from all of us, the wife of the gentleman who visits you is a disturbingly strong-minded lady, and it worries me terribly that I should have had such a dream at a time when you are not well. I really am very worried. I would like to visit you, but your sister goes on having a difficult time of it. We wonder if she might be in the clutches of some evil spirit, and I have the strictest orders from the governor not to leave the house for a moment. Have scriptures read in your monastery there, please, if you will.'

With the letter were offerings of cloth and a request to the abbot that sutras be read. How sad, thought the girl, that her mother should go to such trouble when it was already too late. She composed her answer while the messenger was off at the monastery. Though there was a great deal that she would have liked to say, she set down only this poem:

'We shall think of meeting in another world
    And not confuse ourselves with dreams of this.'

She lay listening to the monastery bells as they rang an accompaniment to the sutras, and wrote down another poem, this one at the end of the list that had come back from the monastery of the sutras to be read:

'Join my sobs to the fading toll of the bell,
To let her know that the end of my life has come.'

The messenger had decided not to return that night. She tied her last poem to a tree in the garden.

'Here I am having palpitations,' said Nurse, 'and she says she's been having bad dreams. Tell the guards to be extra careful. Why *will* you not have something to eat? Come, a cup of this nice gruel.'

Do please be quiet, Ukifune was thinking. The woman was still alert and perceptive enough, but she was old and hideously wrinkled. Yet another one who should have been allowed to die first – and where would she go now? Ukifune wanted to offer at least a hint of what was about to happen, but she knew that the old woman would shoot bolt upright and begin shrieking to the heavens.

'When you let your worries get the best of you,' sighed Ukon, asking to lie down near her mistress, 'they say your soul sometimes leaves your body and goes wandering. I imagine that's why she has these dreams. Please, my lady, I ask you again: make up your mind one way or the other, and call it fate, whatever happens.'

The girl lay in silence, her soft sleeve pressed to her face.

CHAPTER 52

The Drake Fly

The Uji house was in chaos. Ukifune had disappeared, and frantic searching had revealed no trace of her. I need not seek to describe the confusion, for my readers will remember old romances that tell of maidens abducted in the night, and of how it was the next morning.

Her first messenger having failed to return, Ukifune's mother sent a second. 'I left the city while the cocks were still crowing,' he said.

Nurse and the other women made no sense. They had no notion what might have happened, and they moved in utter confusion from one possibility to the next. Ukon and Jijū, the only two among them who had known of the crisis, remembered their lady's growing moodiness and feared she might have thrown herself into the river. In tears, they opened the mother's letter.

'My worries have left me quite unable to sleep, and so I suppose I shall not see you tonight even in my dreams. Nightmares, rather; nightmares dominate my life and have driven me to distraction. I am very, very worried and am going to send for you, even though you are so shortly to move to the city. Today, of course, we are likely to have rain.'

Ukon opened the girl's note to her mother and soon was sobbing helplessly. It had happened. There could be no other explanation for so sad a little poem. And why had she not given Ukon even a hint of it all? They had been such friends since they were little girls. Ukon had not been separated from her for a moment, had not kept the tiniest mote of a secret from her. Why, at the most important time of all, had she given no indication of what was coming? It was too much. Ukon wept like a thwarted child.

They had known that the girl was despondent, but they had not thought her capable of such extraordinary, such frightening resolve. But how, exactly, had she committed the dreadful act?

Nurse was less help than any of them. 'What shall we do, what *shall* we do?' she asked over and over again.

Sensing something out of the ordinary in her last note, Niou immediately dispatched a messenger. She had not found his company distasteful, he was sure. Worried about his well-known fickleness, then, had she hidden herself away? His messenger arrived at a house given over to wailing and lamenting and could find no one to take his letter.

What had happened? he asked a maidservant.

'Our lady died last night. We are stunned, completely stunned. We don't know where to turn. The gentleman who has been such a help isn't here to help now.'

Not knowing a great deal about the Uji household, the man did not press the matter. Back in the city he reported to Niou, for whom the news was like a sudden, horrible visitation. She had been indisposed, it was true, but not seriously ill; and that last note had shown a certain flair rather wanting in most of her notes. What could have happened?

He summoned Tokikata. 'Go and see what you can find out, please.'

'I don't know what rumors the general has picked up, but he has reprimanded the guard, and now not even the servants can get in and out of the house without being stopped. If I were suddenly to appear and he were to hear of it, I'm afraid he would guess everything. And of course the place will be in a frightful stir, swarms of people rushing in all directions.'

'Perhaps; but I have to know the truth. You're a clever fellow. Find a way to see that Jijū. She'll know everything. I want the truth. We can't believe what we hear from servants.'

Unable to resist feelings on such open display, Tokikata set out for Uji that evening. He was not of a rank to require a retinue and he wasted no time. Though the rain had stopped, he had dressed as if for a difficult and dangerous journey and he looked more like a foot soldier than an intimate of royalty. The Uji house was, as he had expected, a bedlam.

'We must have the services immediately, tonight,' someone was saying. Startled, he asked for Ukon. She refused to see him.

'I cannot get myself to my feet,' she sent back. 'It seems a pity that I cannot even say hello. I don't suppose that you will be coming this way again.'

'But how can I go back with nothing to report? Let me talk to your friend, then, please.'

He was so insistent that Jijū presently came forward. She was sobbing uncontrollably. 'Please tell the prince that it is all too terrible. He cannot possibly have foreseen that she would be capable of such a thing. We are stunned, dazed – no, I can't think of the right word. When I am a little more myself, I may be able to tell you about her last days, and how sad she was, and how she hated sending him away that night. Come again, please, when I can really talk to you. I would not want to pass the defilement on to you.'*

Wails echoed from the inner rooms. He recognized Nurse: 'Where are you, my lady? Please come back. You haven't even let us see you, and why should we want to go on living? I was with you from the start and I still have not seen enough of you. My one thought through all the years was to make you happy. And now you have left me, disappeared, not even told me where you might be going. I can't believe that you have let a devil take you away. I can't believe it. And so we must pray. We must pray to Lord Taishakuten.† Give her back to us, whoever you are, man or devil or whoever. Let us look at her, even if she is dead.'

There were numerous obscure points in all this. 'Tell me the truth. Has someone taken her away? I am here because he wants the facts. There is nothing to be done now, I suppose, whatever has happened, and if he should learn the truth and find it at variance with what I have told him, then he is sure to think me incompetent and irresponsible. You can imagine, can you not, the intensity of feeling that prompted him to send me, hoping against hope that what he had heard would not be true? In other countries even kings have fallen too deeply in love and lost their senses, but I think there can be no other example anywhere of such absolute devotion.'

Yes, thought Jijū, Niou was showing a most laudable concern. And the details of this unusual event would not be kept secret forever. 'If there were even the slightest chance that someone had run off with her, do you think we would be carrying on as you see us? She had been in bad spirits for some time, and then there were those unpleasant hints that the general had found out, and her mother and Nurse here – it's she who is making all the noise – they were all caught up in the excitement of sending her off to the

---

*The defilement of having been in the presence of death. Jijū is making it seem that Ukifune's body is on the premises.

†The *Sambōekotoba* of the late tenth century tells how Taishakuten (Śakrodevānām Indraḥ) brought Śākyamuni himself back to life.

man who seemed to have first claim; and so I would imagine that longing for the prince just drove her out of her mind. It was too much for her. And now she had done away with herself, body and soul, and that is the reason for the sentiments you are getting such an earful of.'

She still had not precisely come out with it. Ambiguities remained. 'Well, I'll come again. Too much is left out when you can't sit down* for a good talk. I rather imagine that the prince will be visiting you.'

'That would be a very great honor. If the world were to learn that he was fond of her, then it would seem that her stars were good to her. But she did keep it a secret, and perhaps she would rest more easily if he were to do the same. We do not mean to tell anyone that she died an unnatural death.' She did not want him to know that the body had not been found. He was clever and would soon guess the truth, and so she hurried him on his way.

Ukifune's mother, quite beside herself, arrived in a pouring rain. 'It is sad enough to have someone die before your eyes. But that is the way of the world. What *can* have become of her?'

Unaware of the dilemma that had so filled these last days, she had no reason to suspect that the girl had thrown herself into the river. Might some fiend have devoured her? Might a fox spirit, or some equally sinister force, have led her off? There were strange incidents in old romances, and there was one lady in particular whom the girl had cause to fear.† Had some malicious nurse, perhaps, resenting the proposed move to the city, been conspiring against her?

The mother's first thought was of the serving women. 'Is there anything suspicious about the new ones?'

'None of them are here, my lady. We are so far away from things that the ones who hadn't really settled down kept complaining about not being able to get anything done. So they went home, all of them, and took along the things they were getting ready for the move to the city, and said they'd be back.'

The house did seem rather inadequately attended. Even women who had been in service at Uji since the Eighth Prince's time had gone home. Jijū and the others spoke of the girl's unhap-

*He avoids pollution by declining to take a seat.
†Probably Kaoru's wife, the Second Princess.

piness over the days. She had said more than once, weeping, that she wanted to die.

Under an inkstone Jijū found the poem about the 'sullied name.' She looked out at the river, and shuddered at the roar of the waters.

She conferred with Ukon. 'It is sad to have them go on wondering. The affair with Prince Niou was not her responsibility and there is no reason at all for her mother to feel guilty or ashamed – he *is* a prince, after all. Suppose we tell her. The suspense must be killing her. We can't produce a body, and it's only a matter of time till rumors get out. Yes, we must tell her, and see what we can do then to make things look somewhat respectable.'

In quiet tones, they told what they knew, and sank back into silent grief. So the child had fallen victim to this awful river, thought the governor's wife, only half conscious of what she had heard. She had hated it so herself, and now she wanted to jump in after the girl.

'Let's send people out to look for her, then. Let's at least find the body and have a decent funeral.'

'There would be no point in it. She will be drifting out to sea by now, and there would be talk.'

The mother had no further suggestions.

Ukon and Jijū ordered a carriage and loaded it with the girl's cushions and quilts (she had slipped from them the night before) and personal belongings. The monks were summoned who might be expected to preside over services. The nurse's son was among them, and his uncle the abbot,* and various disciples, and other old gentlemen with whom the girl had been on more or less friendly terms. The procession was made to look as if there were a body to escort to a pyre. Mother and nurse were near collapse from grief and (the omens were not good) foreboding.

Udoneri, who had so intimidated them all, stopped by with his son-in-law. 'We ought to let the general know of the funeral, and allow time to do it right.'

'We want it to be very quiet, before the night is over.'

The funeral carriage proceeded to the moor at the foot of the mountain. No one was allowed near save the few monks who

---

*Ukifune's nurse and the abbot are brother and sister? There has been no earlier indication that 'Nurse' has such close ties with Uji.

knew what had happened. In a moment or two the coffin was smoke. Country people tend to be stricter in these matters than city people, and superstitious as well. They had unfriendly comments to make upon what they had seen.

'Pretty strange, I say. Call that a proper funeral? Why, they might as well be taking care of a scrubwoman that died on them.'

'I don't know. I hear city folk do it without a fuss when brothers are left.'*

Even these rustic comments had Ukon and the others on their guard; and they had Niou and Kaoru to worry about. The world kept no secrets. If Kaoru were to learn that there had been no body to cremate, he would draw certain conclusions. He and Niou were close friends. He might suspect for a time that Niou had spirited the girl off, but he would not go on forever in ignorance. He would proceed to suspect other people, to look for other abductors. She had seemed much the pet of fortune while she lived, and now it did indeed seem that a sullied name must live after her.

Given the confusion of the morning, some of the menials might even now be guessing the truth. Strict precautions seemed necessary.

'We will have to let it out someday, bit by bit, I suppose, if we live long enough. But just now I'm afraid I don't have the strength. He may hear things that will turn him against her, and that will be sad, of course.' Uneasy consciences had given them reason to keep the secret.

His mother having been ill, Kaoru had gone on a pilgrimage to Ishiyama. Uji was much on his mind, but no one informed him of the disaster. At Uji his silence was embarrassing. Then a message came from his manor. He was stunned. Early the next morning he sent off a letter.

'I know I should have gone running to you the moment I got this terrible news, but my mother is not well, and I must stay in retreat for some days. About the funeral last night: why did you have to hurry through it in what I am told was such a casual

---

*Unclear. Perhaps the country people are justifying the simplicity of the services on the grounds that Ukifune has brothers; or perhaps they believe that she has none and that she should therefore be sent off more elaborately. It is not even certain that *katae* should be rendered 'brothers.'

fashion? You should have let me know, and postponed it long enough to make decent arrangements. Nothing is to be done now; but it is sad to learn that even the hill people are talking.'

His messenger was that Nakanobu who had been such a close adviser. At Uji, Nakanobu's arrival brought new outbursts of grief. The women could think of nothing to say, and made these floods of tears their excuse for not essaying a proper answer.

Kaoru was in despair. He had chosen the wrong place, an abode of devils, perhaps. Why had he left her there all alone? The disaster had occurred because he had in effect made things easy for Niou. He was angry at his own carelessness and his inability to behave like other men. Quite unable to give himself up to his prayers, he went back to the city.

'Though not of great importance,' he sent to his wife, 'something distasteful has happened to a person rather close to me; and I shall be in retreat until the shock has passed.'

What a fleeting affair it had been! The pretty face, those winning ways, were gone forever. Why had he been so slow to act while she was alive, why had he not pressed his cause more aggressively? Numberless regrets burned within him, so intense that there was no quenching them. For him, at least, love seemed to be unrelieved torment. Perhaps the powers above were angry that, against his own better impulses, he had remained in the vulgar world. They had a way of hiding their mercy, of subjecting a man to the sorest trials and imposing enlightenment upon him. So the black thoughts ran on. He lost himself in prayer.

Niou's grief was more open. His household was in great confusion. What sort of malign spirit could have taken possession of him? Presently the tears dried and the anguish subsided; but for him too the memory of her face and her manner brought unquenchable longing. Though he thought of devising clever ways to make it seem that he was genuinely ill, and so to hide these stupidly tear-swollen eyes, everyone guessed the truth. Who, people asked, could have sent him into a despondency so profound that it seemed to threaten his life?

Kaoru of course had full reports. His suspicions were true. Niou and Ukifune had been more than acquaintances who exchanged little notes. She was the sort Niou liked, a girl he would have had to make his own once he had caught a glimpse of her. If she had lived on, she and her friend might have made Kaoru himself look very clownish (for he and the friend were not strangers). He found the thought somehow comforting.

Everyone was talking about Niou's indisposition. A stream of well-wishers flowed in and out of his rooms. People would think it odd, thought Kaoru, if, in mourning for a woman of no consequence, he failed to call. His uncle Prince Shikibu* had recently died, rather opportunely, and Kaoru had put on somber robes. In his own mind he could call them weeds for Ukifune. Loss of weight had if anything improved him.

He made his visit on a melancholy evening after other callers had withdrawn. The illness was not so severe as to keep Niou in bed. He did not, it was true, receive people with whom he was on less than familiar terms, but he turned away no one whom he would in ordinary circumstances have admitted to his inner chambers. But he wished Kaoru had not come. The encounter was sure to bring tears.

'Nothing serious, really,' he said controlling himself for a time, 'but I'm told I must be careful. I hate to upset Their Majesties so. I've been sitting here thinking how little there really is for us to depend upon.'

He pressed a sleeve to his eyes, able to hold back the tears no longer. All very embarrassing; but of course his friend, unaware of the cause, could tax him with no more than unmanliness.

It was as he had suspected, Kaoru was in fact thinking. And when had they managed to strike up a liaison? How the two of them must have been laughing at him all these months! His grief seemed to vanish quite away.

A very cool sort his friend was, thought Niou; indeed a rather chilly sort. He himself, when his thoughts were too much for him, needed no such disaster – the call of a bird flying over was enough – to bring on waves of sorrow. Kaoru would hardly be repelled by these weak tears, even if he had guessed their source. But perhaps this was the usual way with people who understood the transience of things? Niou was envious, and he was fascinated. Kaoru had known the girl too, had been the cypress pillar† on which she had leaned. Niou looked at his friend again, this time more affectionately, as at a memento.

*One of Genji's brothers. He is mentioned only once before, in Chapter 50.

†*Makibashira*. Perhaps a poetic allusion.

The desultory talk went on. Kaoru began to feel uncomfortable about the significant spot that was being reserved for silence. 'When I have something on my mind – it has always been so – I find myself nervous and restless if I go for even a little while without telling you of it. But I have risen now to a modest place in the world, and you of course have far more important matters to occupy you, and so we seldom find a chance for a quiet talk. The days go by and I do not ask for an audience with you unless I have a good reason. But let me come to the point. I recently learned about a relative of the lady who died in that mountain village, you will know the one I am speaking of – I recently learned that she was living in a rather odd place. I thought of helping her, but unfortunately I found myself in circumstances that made me afraid of gossip. So I left her there, and a wretched place it was, too, and scarcely visited her at all. As time went by I came to suspect that I was not the only one she was looking to for support. But I would not want you to think that I was dreadfully upset. I had certainly not thought of her as the love of my life. No one seemed seriously at fault. She was amiable, and she was attractive, and that was all. And then, very suddenly, she died. It is a sad world we live in. But perhaps I am speaking of something you have already been informed of.' He had been dry-eyed until now. He would have preferred not to join his friend in this tasteless weeping, but once they had started the tears were not to be held back.

Niou found this break in the calm touching and at the same time threatening. He chose to feign ignorance. 'Very sad, very sad. I did hear something about it, just yesterday. I wanted to offer condolences, but I heard that you were avoiding publicity.' He stopped short. Under the cool surface were complex and powerful emotions.

'That is the story. I hoped there might sometime be a chance to introduce you. Or perhaps you happened to run into her somewhere? Perhaps she visited Nijō? She was of course related to your princess.' The innuendos were becoming broader. 'But I forget myself. I should not be bothering you with these trivia when you are not feeling well. Do please be careful.' And he went out.

So Niou had been genuinely in love with her, he was thinking. Her life had been a short one, but her destinies had borne her to high places. Here was Niou: the pet of Their Majesties, the handsomest and stateliest of men, with two noble beauties for wives. And he had pushed them aside to make room for her! Was not this illness, on which so many scriptures and ceremonies were being concentrated, the result of an uncontrollable love? And Kaoru could point to himself too, not immodestly: high position, a royal bride, everything; and the girl had bewitched him even as she had bewitched Niou. And in death she seemed to have a stronger hold on him than in life.

What utter folly! He would think of it no more. But he was dizzy with memory and longing. 'We are not sticks and stones, we all have hearts,'* he whispered to himself as he lay down.

And how, he wondered, sadness giving way to irritation, had Nakanokimi responded to news of that hasty funeral? He was not at all happy with it himself. Possibly the mother, a common sort of woman, had dispensed with ceremony on the theory that the grand ones do so out of deference to surviving brothers and sisters.

Faced with so many obscure points, he would have liked to run off to Uji and ask about Ukifune's last days; but were he to make serious inquiries he would have a long purification to look forward to, and on the other hand he would not wish to go such a distance and turn back immediately.

The Fourth Month came. The evening of the day appointed for her move to the city was especially difficult. The scent of the orange blossoms near the veranda brought memories. A cuckoo called and called a second time as it flew overhead. 'Should you stop by her dwelling, O cuckoo.'† His heart heavy with memory and yearning, he broke off a sprig of orange blossom and sent it with a poem to Nijō, where Niou was spending the night.

'It sings in the fields its muted song of the dead.
      Your muted sobs may have joined it – to no avail.'‡

The poem found Niou and his princess sunk in thoughts of the dead girl. How very much the sisters had resembled each other, he

---

*Po Chü-i, Collected Works, IV, 'Madame Li.'

†Anonymous, Kokinshū 855:

> Should you stop by the dwelling of the one now gone, O cuckoo,
> Tell her that even now she may hear my sobs.

‡The cuckoo, which comes at planting time, was believed to be a messenger from the land of the dead.

was thinking – and did his friend have to hint so broadly at what had happened?

This was his answer:

> 'Where orange blossoms summon memories
> The cuckoo now should sing most cautiously.*

'A very great trial, I am sure.'

Nakanokimi was by now familiar with the whole story. Her sisters had died so young, no doubt because they had both of them been of a too introspective nature. She, the one without worries, had lived on. And how long would it be until she joined them?

Since she obviously knew everything, the pretense at conceal-ment was becoming awkward. Arranging matters somewhat to his own advantage, now laughing and now weeping, he made his confession. 'I was very annoyed at you for hiding her,' he con-cluded. How very affecting it was to have the girl's own sister for his audience!

He was more comfortable here at Nijō. At Rokujō everything was so grand and ceremonious. When he was indisposed they all fussed over him so. He had no defenses against well-wishers, and Yūgiri and his sons made genuine nuisances of themselves.

But everything still seemed so vague and dreamlike. Her sud-den death had not been properly explained. He sent for Ukon.

At Uji, the roar of the waters stirred the governor's wife to thoughts of suicide. There could be no rest from her grief. Sadly, she returned to the city. The Uji house settled into near silence, the monks its chief source of strength and cheer. This time the troublesome guards made no attempt to challenge Niou's emis-saries. How sad, the latter were thinking, that what had proved to be their lord's last chance for a meeting had come to nothing. It had not been pleasant to watch the effects of his clandestine love, and now the memory of those nocturnal visits, and of the girl too, so fragile and so beautiful on the night of the river crossing, was enough to dissolve the least sensitive of them in tears.

They told Ukon why they had come.

'It would not do to stir up gossip at this late date,' she said, 'and I doubt that any explanations I might make would satisfy him. I shall think up a good excuse to visit him once we are out of

*See note‡, page 228.

mourning. I can tell people that I have business to discuss with him. It is true that I do not want to outlive my own grief, but if someday I manage to pull myself together, I shall call on him, you may be sure, whether he sends for me or not, and describe this nightmare to him.' They could not persuade her to go with them.

'I did not have all the details and was not in a good position to judge,' said Tokikata, 'but I did sense something very unusual in his feelings for her. I looked forward to the day when I might myself be of service to you, and saw no need to rush things; and this sudden disaster has only strengthened my good intentions. We seem to have this carriage, and I would hate to take it back empty. What about the other lady?'

'Yes, by all means.' Ukon summoned Jijū. 'You go.'

'But I would have even less to tell him than you. And we are in mourning, you know. I wouldn't want to pass the defilement on.'

'He is being careful of his health, but I doubt if that would worry him. He has been so upset by it all that I rather imagine he would welcome a few days' retreat. And you won't be in mourning much longer in any case. Come along, now, one or the other of you.'

Jijū agreed to go. She did want to see Niou again, and when could she hope for another chance? She was a handsome figure herself when she had put her somber robes in order. Because formal dress could be dispensed with in the absence of one's lady, she had not been wearing formal trains, and she had none dyed in the proper hues of mourning. A lavender one was the best she could find. Thinking of her lady's secret but triumphal progress along this same road had she but lived, she wept the whole of the way into the city.

She had always been partial towards Niou, and he was pleased and touched that she had come. Wishing to avoid a scene, he did not tell Nakanokimi of the visit. He went to the main hall and asked Jijū to alight at a gallery adjoining it.

She told him in great detail of Ukifune's last days. 'My lady had been in low spirits for some time and she was weeping when she went to bed that night. She seemed so wrapped up in herself, she had even less to say than usual. She was not a lady to complain about her troubles, you will remember, and that may be why she didn't leave a proper letter behind. It hadn't occurred to us in our wildest dreams that she would be capable of such a thing.'

All the sadness of those days came back. One somehow manages to accept a natural death – but to throw herself into those savage waters! What could account for such resolve? If only he had been there himself. He pictured himself on the spot, pulling her from the river, and regret attacked him more fiercely, to no purpose, of course.

'What fools we were not to guess when she burned her letters.'

They talked the night through. She told him too of the poem they had found in the tree. He had not paid much attention to her until now, and she interested him.

'Would you think of joining us here at Nijō? You and the lady in the other wing are not strangers, after all.'

'No, it would be too sad. Let me at least wait until we are out of mourning.'

'Do come again.' He was sorry to see her go.

As she left in the dawn, he gave her a comb box and a clothespress he had had made for Ukifune. Though he had in fact put together a considerable collection of boxes and chests, he gave her only what she could take with her. She had not expected such largesse, and was a little embarrassed at the thought of displaying it to her fellows. There being little relief these days from the tedium, however, she did show Ukon her new treasures when no one else was near. The designs were most elegant, the workmanship was superb – and this and much more their lady had thrown away! The contents of the clothespress quite dazzled them, but of course women in mourning had no use for such finery.

Numerous questions still on his mind, Kaoru paid a visit. His thoughts on the road were of long ago. What strange legacy had brought him and the Eighth Prince together? A bond from an earlier life, surely, had tied him to this family and its sad affairs, and made him see to the needs of this last sad foundling, even. He had first sought an audience with the prince in hopes of divine revelation. His mind had been on the next world; and in the end he had wandered back to this. Perhaps it was the Buddha's way of making him see his own inadequacies.

'I still do not know what happened,' he said to Ukon. 'I am in such a state of shock that I can't somehow make myself believe it all. You will soon be out of mourning, I have told myself, and it would be better to wait; but I found that I could wait no longer. What exactly was it that took her so suddenly?'

The nun Bennokimi would have guessed the truth, thought Ukon, and if she herself sought to dissemble, the combined result would be impossible confusion. Though she had grown used to lying, this solemn honesty made her forget the several stories she had put together. She told him a good part of the truth.

For a time he said nothing. It could not be. A girl so quiet, so sparing even of commonplaces – how could she have done it? No – these women had conspired to deceive him. For a moment he was furious. But Niou's grief seemed genuine, and here they all were, down to the lowest maid-servant, wailing and lamenting.

'Did anyone else disappear? Tell me more precisely, if you can, what happened. I cannot believe that anything I myself did can have turned her against the world. Was there a crisis, something that left her with nowhere to go? I do find it hard to believe.'

Ukon was sad for him, and at the same time troubled. She was afraid that he had guessed more of the truth than she had told him.

'You will have heard all about it, I am sure. She was unlucky from the beginning, and after she came here to live, so far away from everyone, she seemed to slip deeper and deeper into herself. But she did look forward to your visits. They were a consolation, you may be sure. She did not actually say so, but she also looked forward, I know she did, to the time when you could be together. We were delighted when we began to find reason for hoping that it might actually come. I can't tell you how relieved and how pleased her mother was. Those were happy days for us all, her mother too, when we were busy getting her ready. And then that odd note came from you, and those awful guards – how they did frighten us – started saying you had given them a dressing down, and after that they were so strict that we could only think there had been a misunderstanding. And there was no word from you for so long. Over the years she had come to think that she was just unlucky, and she was sad for her poor mother too, who only wanted her to live a decent, respectable life. It would be too awful, she thought, after all your kindness, if some scandal were to ruin everything and make a laughingstock of them. I can think of nothing else that can have had her in such a state. Some say that this house is cursed. I've always thought myself that if it is then the devils ought to make themselves more evident.'

He understood everything. He too was in tears.

'I am not able to do exactly as I would wish, and so I lived with my worries, sure that I would soon have her near me, where I could protect her and see to her needs. She thought me cold and distant, it seems, and I can't help suspecting that she preferred someone else. Well, let me say it. I would far rather not, but while no one is listening – the affair with Prince Niou. When did it begin? He is very good at ruining women's lives. Wasn't he responsible, wasn't it that she wanted to see more of him? Tell me everything, please. I do not want you to leave anything out.'

So he knew. How sad for her poor lady! 'You ask very difficult questions. I never once left her side.' She fell silent for a time. 'You will have heard of it. One day when my lady was in hiding at her sister's, the prince stole in upon her in a way that seemed to us shockingly improper. We would have none of it, and he left. My lady was terrified and moved into the queer little house where you found her. We tried to keep our move here a secret, but – I can't think where he might have found out – letters started coming late last spring, a considerable number of them. She refused to look at them. We told her that she should feel honored, and that he would think her rude, and so she did answer once or twice. And that is all I know.'

Just what he might have expected. It seemed pointless and even cruel to inquire further. He lapsed into his own thoughts. The girl had fallen victim to Niou's charms, but she had not found Kaoru's own advances distasteful. And so she had been caught in an impossible dilemma, and here was the river, beckoning, and she had given in to it. If he had not left her in this wilderness, she might have found life difficult, but she would hardly have sought a 'bottomless chasm.'* How sinister his ties had been with this river, how deep its hostility flowed! Drawn by the Eighth Prince's daughters, he had come the steep mountain road all these years, and now he could scarcely endure the sound of those two syllables 'Uji.'† There had been bad omens, he now saw, from the start: in that 'image,' for instance, of which Nakanokimi had first spoken, an image to float down a river. At fault himself all along, he had

---

*Anonymous, *Kokinshū* 1061:

> Suppose at each sad thought we throw ourselves in,
> We shortly will see the bottomless chasm made shallow.

†The common pun on *ushi*, 'gloomy.'

been unhappy with the girl's mother for the almost casual simplicity of the funeral services. He had attributed it to bad breeding.
Now that he knew the facts he wondered what the unfortunate
woman would be thinking of him. The girl had been well favored
for one of her station in life. Unaware of the liaison with Niou,
the mother would no doubt have thought the tragedy somehow
related to Kaoru himself. Suddenly he was very sad for her.

There had been no remains and so there could be no pollution.
Wishing to maintain appearances before his men, he stayed on a
side veranda all the same, not far from his carriage. After a time it
came to seem a not very dignified position, and so he went to sit
in the garden, deep-shaded moss for his cushion. He did not think
that he would again be visiting this ill-starred house.

'Should even I, sad house, abandon you,
    Who then will remember the ivy that offered shelter?'

The abbot had recently become an archdeacon.* Kaoru summoned him, gave instructions for memorial services, asked that
several more priests be set to invoking the holy name, and specified the images and scriptures to be dedicated each week. Suicide
was a grave sin. He wished to leave out nothing that might lessen
the burden of guilt. It was dark when he set out for the city. If
Ukifune were still alive, he thought, sending for the nun, he
would not be leaving at such an hour.

She refused to see him and he did not press the matter. 'Alone
with my own ugliness,' she sent back, 'I have thoughts of nothing
else. You would see me sunk in abysmal dotage.'

All the way back he cursed himself for his neglect. Why had he
not called Ukifune to the city earlier? The sound of the river,
while he was still within earshot, seemed to pound and flail at him.
There could have been no sadder an ending to it all. Even the
earthly remains had disappeared. Among what empty shells, under
what waters?

Ukifune's mother had not been allowed to go home. The governor made a serious issue of the defilement, the younger daughter
still not having had her child. The mother spent comfortless days
in unfriendly wayside lodgings. The other girl was a worry of

---

*Risshi. This matter-of-fact statement seems to inform us that we are to hear no
more of the old gentleman.

sorts; but presently the child was delivered. Still kept at a distance, the governor's wife had no further room in her thoughts for her surviving daughters.

A courteous and friendly note came from Kaoru. It aroused her from the lethargy and brought new twinges of sorrow.

'My first thought was to send condolences in this horrible affair; but I have been very upset, and my eyes have been dark with tears. How much more impenetrable the darkness must be for you. After that first thought it came to me that I should allow you time to recover somewhat, and so the days have slipped aimlessly by. How is one to describe the evanescence of it all? If I should survive this most difficult of times, and I sometimes think I shall not, please look upon me as a memento of sorts, and come to me when you think I might be of assistance.'

Nakanobu, his emissary, had another message, which had not been committed to writing. 'I had thought that there was no hurry, and so the months went by. You may have had doubts about my intentions. I hereby make solemn vow that in everything I am at your service. Always remember, if you will, that I have said so. I have heard that you have several other youngsters, and I shall consider it my duty to watch over them when the time comes for them to seek positions.'

The governor's wife insisted that Nakanobu come inside. It had not been the sort of pollution, she said, that was likely to rub off on others. She wept as she composed her answer.

'I wanted nothing more than to die, and perhaps I have lived on that I might have these kind words from you. I blamed her loneliness over the years upon my own insignificance. Then came the great honor of your acquaintance and your undertakings, and I looked forward to seeing her finally in honorable circumstances. And nothing came of my hopes. Yes, Uji is a gloomy village, and our bonds with it were as gloomy. If a few more years are granted me, I shall remember your good offer of support. I am blind with tears at the moment, and can say no more.'

It was hardly a time for gifts. Yet she was uncomfortable at sending Nakanobu away empty-handed. She took out a sword and a belt, both beautifully wrought, the latter inlaid with mottled sections of rhinoceros horn. She had meant them to go one day to Kaoru. She ordered that they be put in a pouch, which she sent out to Nakanobu as he was getting into his carriage.

'In memory of my daughter.'

Kaoru too thought it an odd time to be giving gifts.

'She made me come in,' said Nakanobu, 'and between her sobs she told me among other things how grateful she was for what you had said about the other children. She was so unimportant herself, she said, that she could not do very much, but she would ask you to find something for them when the time came. Though of course they were such poor things, she said, that she couldn't expect too much. And she said she wouldn't breathe a word about your reasons for being interested in them.'

It was true, thought Kaoru, that the bond between them was not cause for pride; but had not emperors, even, taken women of low status? Such matches seemed dictated by fate and no one called them in question. Among commoners the precedents were legion for taking lowborn women and women who had been married before. Let people say that he had become son-in-law to His Eminence of Hitachi – well, never from the outset had his intentions for the girl been such as to demean him. The governor's wife had lost one child, and he only meant to let her know that the loss would bring profit to the others.

The governor came briefly to see his wife. He was very angry. Why had she left home at such a time? She had not informed him of Ukifune's whereabouts, and he had assumed that the girl had fallen upon hard times, and asked no questions. The mother had been saving her news for the girl's removal to the city, but there was no longer any point in secrecy. Weeping, she told him everything. She showed him Kaoru's letter. In growing wonderment, he read and reread it, for he was well provided with a certain rustic snobbishness.

'So she died on us just when she was having all this good luck? I was with his family for a while, but he was way up there on top, and I didn't really know him. So he's thinking of the others, is he?'

The mother lay sobbing. Such cause for joy, and Ukifune was not here to partake of it.

The governor managed a tear or two of his own. He thought it unlikely, however, that Kaoru would have paid much attention to them if the girl had lived. He had been wrong and he wanted to make amends, that was all, and, within these limits, he was prepared to put up with a little gossip.

The time came, on the forty-ninth day after her disappearance, for the most elaborate of the memorial rites. Kaoru was not entirely sure that she was dead, but rites could do her no harm, living or dead. He made arrangements in secret with the Uji monastery, sending rich offerings to the sixty priests who were to read the sutras. The governor's wife visited Uji and made arrangements of her own. Niou sent Ukon a silver bowl filled with pieces of gold. Since he naturally wanted to stay in the background, Ukon made the offering as if it were her own. Those of her comrades who were not privy to the secret wondered how she could have come by so much. Kaoru asked all his particular intimates to be in attendance.

All rather astonishing, said the general public. 'Why, we never even heard of her, and now such a stir. Whoever can she have been?'

The astonishment mounted when His Eminence put in an appearance at Uji and grandly took over the house. He had meant to outdo himself in honor of his new grandchild, and his own house was jammed with ritual utensils and trappings, Chinese and Korean hangings and the like; but there was a limit to what a provincial governor could do. And here were *these* ceremonies – secret, if you please, and just look at them! The girl would have done all right for herself if she had lived. His Eminence would have had a hard time getting an audience with her.

Nakanokimi also sent offerings, as well as food for the seven monks whose services she herself had commissioned. The emperor, learning for the first time of the girl's existence, was sad that Kaoru should have been so fond of her and yet should have felt constrained, out of deference to the Second Princess, to keep her in hiding.

Niou and Kaoru continued to grieve, but Niou was recovering. The loss had been particularly affecting because it had come just at the climax of a love that should not have been. Soon he was looking here and there for consolation. The heavier duties were passed on to Kaoru, who meant to leave nothing undone. The sorrow still lay too deep for words.

The empress was in provisional mourning at Rokujō. Her second son had become minister of rites and seldom found time to visit. Niou came often, seeking to beguile his sorrows in the apartments of his sister, the First Princess. It annoyed him that so many of the beauties surrounding her should be so skillful at concealing

themselves. Among them was one Kosaishō, famous for her elegance and grace, of whom Kaoru had with some difficulty made the
secret acquaintance. He admired her for her artistic accomplishments. When she struck up a melody on koto or lute the sound
was somehow different, and she had her own style too when she
jotted down a poem or granted an interview. Niou had not failed
to make note of the name she was acquiring for herself, and once
again he considered devices for thwarting his friend. Kosaishō had
turned him coldly away. She was not among those who came running, she let it be known. Yes, thought Kaoru, she was unusual.

Unable to remain silent in the face of such grief, she wrote to
him on paper that only a lady of great refinement could have
selected.

> 'Pray think me not less feeling than the others.
> But I am no one. Silent pass my days.

'And were I she, would sorrow then . . . ?'*

She had somehow known that it would be for him an evening
of unusual melancholy.

> 'Yes, I know the sadness that all is fleeting.
> But I did not mean that you should hear my sighs.'

And immediately he went to see her, to tell her how much her
delicate sense of timing had meant to him. He was so solemn and
withdrawn, and her rooms were not meant for receiving men of
rank; and indeed he did seem ridiculously confined, over in a corner by the door. There was no suggestion of obsequiousness, however, in her answers. She *did* have something, a certain depth and
gravity, that one seldom found in serving women. He wondered
why she had gone into the service of even a princess. He did not
know, but he wished that something more appropriate might be
arranged. No hint of these thoughts was allowed to slip into the
conversation.

---

*The emperor Uda, *Gosenshū* 1365:

> Change for autumn leaves your pillow of grass.
> Would sorrow then be eating out your heart?

The lady is saying that she herself would be incapable of inspiring such grief.
The 'pillow of grass' suggests travel. Hence, Ukifune.

When the lotuses were at their best, the empress ordered a solemn reading of the Lotus Sutra. Images and scriptures were consecrated to the memory of her father and of Murasaki, who had reared her. The services were extraordinarily beautiful and dignified, reaching a climax with the fifth of the eight books, and concluding on the morning of the fifth day. The assembly was large and varied, for everyone who knew a lady in the household managed an invitation. The partition between the main hall and the north rooms had been taken down, and as serving women swarmed in and out removing the votive decorations and otherwise restoring the hall to its normal state, the First Princess withdrew with her retinue to the west gallery. In the evening most of her women, fatigued after the long services,* went off to their own rooms.

Having changed to an informal court robe, Kaoru strolled down to the angling pavilion. There were certain monks with whom he had matters to discuss, but unfortunately they had all left. He went on to take the evening cool by the lake. That gallery, it came to him, would provide withdrawing rooms for the First Princess and her few attendants, Kosaishō among them, and there would be only curtains to conceal them. He caught a rustling of silk. A sliding door above a board walk happened to be open a crack. Looking in, he saw that, for such secluded precincts, it offered a remarkably bright and unobstructed view. The curtains were somewhat disordered, permitting him to see far inside. Three women and a little girl who had removed their cloaks were chipping busily at a large block of ice on a tray of some description. They could scarcely be in the royal presence – but there the princess was, marvelously beautiful in a robe of white gossamer (she had evidently changed since the services), ice in hand, half smiling at the labors in progress before her. He had seen beautiful ladies, but none, he thought, as beautiful as she. The day being a warm one, her hair, indescribably rich and lustrous, had been pushed to one side, revealing her full profile. By comparison her women seemed rather plain. But then, collecting himself for a better look, he saw that there was another worth making note of: in a yellow singlet of raw silk and a lavender train, she sat quietly fanning herself. Yes, she had a certain manner.

*The Lotus Sutra is about as long as the New Testament.

'You'll only wear yourselves out. Just take it as it is.' The smile was charming, and he recognized the voice of the lady he had called upon.

The others were at length having some success with the ice. They would probably not have put chunks of it quite so indiscriminately to foreheads and bosoms had they known that they were being observed. Kosaishō wrapped ice in paper for herself and for the princess. The hands the princess held out were white and delicately modeled.

'I think not, thank you. See how I'm dripping already.'

So low that he almost failed to catch it, her voice excited him enormously. He had seen her once before, when they were both children, and been delighted with her. Since then he had not been admitted to her presence. What supernatural powers, he wondered, would have arranged this secret audience? Or might it be only for purposes of adding to his torments?

Just then a servant who had been cooling herself on the north veranda came scampering back. She evidently remembered that, having slid the door open for some momentarily urgent reason, she had forgotten to close it again. She would be taken to task if someone were to notice and make use of it. And, dear me, there was a man in casual court dress! She ran down the veranda, oblivious to the fact that she was quite exposed herself. Somewhat guiltily Kaoru slipped out of sight. How embarrassing, thought the woman. He had been able to look past the curtains, almost any distance! Who might he have been? One of Yūgiri's sons, probably. Strangers would hardly have penetrated to these forbidden corners. She must not let her dereliction be found out, for there would be reprisals. The man's robe and trousers had been of raw silk, it seemed, and she could be fairly certain that no one had heard.*

Kaoru fled the scene in great disquiet. Headed resolutely down the road to enlightenment, he had gone astray, and now woman after woman made demands upon his attention. If he had renounced the world when the thought had first come to him, he would now be off in some deep mountain retreat, away from all this torment. Why had he so longed over the years for another glimpse of the First Princess? Well, now he had seen her, and found for himself further pain and frustration.

---

*Raw silk evidently does not rustle as glossed silk does.

The Second Princess was looking unusually fresh and radiant when she arose the next morning. She would have been by no means out of place in a contest with her sister, and yet despite a certain family resemblance they did not really look alike. For clean beauty and elegance, no one, he was sure, could quite match the princess he had seen so briefly at Rokujō; but perhaps he had so idealized her over the years that his eyes had played him false, and perhaps the moment had been right.

'It is very warm,' he said to the Second Princess. 'Suppose you put on something lighter. Something you don't ordinarily wear. It can make things more interesting, you know.' And to one of the women: 'Go have Daini do up something in gossamer.'

Her women were pleased. She was at her best, and gossamer would surely become her.

It was his usual practice to retire late in the morning for prayers. When he appeared again at noon, the gossamer robe was hanging over a curtain rack.

'Do try it on. You will feel half undressed, I know, with all these ladies around, but don't let them worry you.'

He held the new robe for her to slip into. Her trousers were scarlet, as her sister's had been, and, like her sister's, her hair fell in long, thick cascades. But not one of us is like any other. The effect was very different. Still not ready to admit defeat, he sent for ice. Some men find comfort in pictures, and his princess should have afforded far more comfort than any picture. He permitted himself a sigh. How he would have liked to join that party yesterday, and gaze on and on, quite openly, at the First Princess.

'Are you in correspondence with your sister?'

'I wrote occasionally when I was in the palace. His Majesty said I should. But I haven't now in a very long time.'

'Do you suppose she has stopped writing because you married a commoner? That would make me unhappy. I shall tell Her Majesty you resent it very much.'

'Resent it? What is there to resent? No, please don't.'

'I shall tell her that your sister is arrogant. I shall say that she treats you like an underling.'

He stayed at home that day and the next morning went again to be in attendance upon the empress. Niou was also at Rokujō. He had on a thin saffron singlet and over it an informal blue robe, in the very best of taste. No less well favored than his sister, he was handsomer for the pallor and loss of weight. Yes, the resemblance was extraordinary, sighed Kaoru. Remembering himself, he sought to control these wayward thoughts, and found the effort very considerable. Niou had brought along a number of pictures, most of which he sent off to his sister's quarters. He followed shortly himself. Kaoru congratulated the empress upon the faultless handling of the ceremonies, and they exchanged reminiscences of old times.

'My princess at Sanjō,' he said, taking up the pictures that had been left behind, 'is rather despondent at having, as they say, descended from the clouds. I feel very sorry for her. She thinks her sister has dropped her now that things have been arranged so unsatisfactorily for her. It would be nice if she had pictures to look at from time to time, but of course it would not be the same if I were to take them to her myself.'

'Why should her sister do any such thing? They had rooms very near each other in the palace, and I believe they exchanged notes. No, it is just that they live farther apart now. I shall see that she writes. And there is no need for your own princess to hold back.'

'No, I suppose not. You have not been very friendly yourself, you know, but after all she is now your own sister-in-law, and it would please me enormously if you might find it possible to favor her with a little of your attention. The two of them were once so close. It would be a pity if they were to drift apart.'

The empress did not guess his motives.

He passed in front of the main hall and went on to the west wing, thinking to call on Kosaishō. Hidden behind blinds, the women looked out upon a most stately and graceful figure. Even the gallery walls, he was thinking, might somehow bring comfort.

Yūgiri's sons seemed to be in possession of the gallery. Kaoru came up to a side door.

'I am of course often in attendance upon Her Majesty,' he said to the women, looking off towards the assembly of nephews. 'But it seems that I do not see you as often as I would like. And so time has gone by, and here I am feeling like an old man. I thought this might be a good chance for a talk, though I'm sure you are wishing the old man would go away.'

'Oh, we'll take years off your age, just give us a chance.' Even when they were far from serious, they did not take leave of the peculiar refinement that was their lady's. Talking of this and that (he had no real business), he began to feel rather close to them, and stayed longer than he had planned.

The First Princess had gone to her mother.

'But the general seems to be over in your wing,' said Her Majesty.

'I think Kosaishō will keep him entertained,' said one Dainagon, a lady-in-waiting to the princess.

'A woman has to know what she is doing,' replied the empress, 'when a solemn and resolute young man takes up the pursuit. He will see through all her pertness if she isn't careful. But I think that Kosaishō can take care of herself.'

Though they were brother and sister, she did not feel at ease with Kaoru, and evidently she was warning her women against any appearance of impropriety.

'It's always Kosaishō's room that he goes to. They talk on and on, all by themselves, and sometimes he is there till very late. But it doesn't seem to be what one might expect. She has a low opinion of Prince Niou, and won't even answer his letters.' Dainagon laughed. 'Believe me, *I* wouldn't be wasting such an opportunity.'

The empress too was amused. 'Yes, she can be relied upon to take care of herself if she sees what is wrong with my good son. Is there no way to reform him? You must know, I am sure, how uncomfortable it makes me to have him come into the conversation.'

'I heard something interesting the other day. The lady who died at Uji seems to have been the younger sister of his princess at Nijō. A half sister, actually. Some say that the wife of a governor of Hitachi is her mother, some say that she's an aunt. I don't know which to believe. Prince Niou visited the girl secretly, very secretly, they say. The general seems to have had thoughts of his own, and he learned of the prince's visits. He had plans for bringing her to the city. So he posted guards and gave them very strict orders. The prince went off on another of his secret visits, and they kept him outside on his horse (I can't imagine that it was very dignified) and then trundled him back to the city. And very suddenly she disappeared. It may be that she died of longing. Her nurse and the others think she may have thrown herself into the river. I am told that they are quite out of their minds, the poor dears.'

The empress was scandalized. 'Wherever did you hear such a thing? It is sad and it is horrible. But perhaps it isn't true. Word of anything so unusual is bound to get out, and I would have expected my brother to say something. But he just goes on mooning about how things change, and says what a pity it is that people seem to live such short lives at Uji.'

'You can't really believe servants. But a little girl who was in service at Uji has been with Kosaishō's family, and she spoke of it as solid fact. The Uji lady picked such a strange way to disappear that I gather they don't want people to know. It all sounded like a curse, really, and I can believe that they would want it kept secret. It may be that they did not even tell the general.'

'That girl is not to say another word about it.' The empress was openly perturbed. 'A foolish boy who ruined himself over women – that's what the talk will be, you can be sure.'

The Second Princess had a note from her sister. The hand, delicate but sure, delighted Kaoru. He should have thought of this device sooner. The empress sent interesting paintings to the Second Princess and Kaoru gathered even finer ones for the First Princess. One of the finest called to mind his own situation: consumed with desire for the First Princess, the son of the Serikawa general* is out walking of an autumn evening. If only the real princess might be as generous as the princess in the story.

'The autumn wind that brings the dew to the rushes,
    It chills, it saddens most when evening comes.'

He would have liked to jot down his poem beside the painting, but it would not do to give the smallest hint of his feelings. Always he came to the same useless conclusion: Oigimi would have had the whole of his affection. He would not have taken a royal princess for his bride. Indeed, if the emperor had heard of the events at Uji he would probably not have wanted Kaoru for a son-in-law. She was the source of all his sorrow, the lady at the bridge!

His thoughts jumped to Nakanokimi, and presently the jumble of longing and resentment and frustration began to seem ridiculous even to him; and so he moved on to the third Uji sister, who had died such a terrible death. She was to be taxed with a kind of childishness, with rashness and indiscretion, but she had suffered. Sensing a change in Kaoru's own feelings, she had had a very bad conscience to live with. He thought of her last days. A lovable sort

*The title of or a major figure in a romance that has been lost.

of companion she might have been, someone not to be taken very seriously or offered too exalted a place. He no longer felt angry with Niou, and he could no longer reprove the girl. He had only his own erratic ways to blame.

Such thoughts occupied much of his time.

If they could prey upon a man so carefully in control of himself, they found a far easier victim in Niou, who had no one to share his memories with, no one to tell of his quest for solace. Nakanokimi did speak now and then of Ukifune's sad lot; but the sisters had not grown up together, and their acquaintance had been short. There was a limit to the grief one might expect from her. Besides, the affair that was the source of his loneliness rested uncomfortably between them.

He sent again for Jijū.

The Uji house was by now almost deserted. Nurse and Ukon and Jijū, who had been especially close to the dead girl, were reluctant to leave her last dwelling behind. Though the outsider,* Jijū remained a part of the company even when most of the others had left. But that savage river, which she had somehow lived with while there had been a prospect of happier shoals, had at last become unendurable. She had recently moved to a shabby little place in the city. Niou searched her out and once again offered her a position at Nijō, but again she declined. She was grateful for the invitation, but there would be gossip if she took service in the house that had been at the beginning of the whole sad story. She said that she would prefer a position with Her Majesty.

'Splendid. We needn't tell anyone our little secret.'

And so, in her loneliness and the insecurity of her life, Jijū went through an intermediary, as custom demanded, and obtained a place with Her Majesty. Of inconspicuous rank and good appearance, she had no enemies. She frequently saw Kaoru, who was in and out of the empress's apartments and the sight of whom stirred powerful and conflicting emotions. She found no one in the empress's retinue who seemed a match for her dead mistress, and this despite the fact that the empress took in only ladies of unexceptionable breeding.

The daughter of that Prince Shikibu who had died in the spring was meanwhile having difficulties with her stepmother. The

---

*Nurse and Ukon are mother and daughter.

stepmother's brother, an undistinguished cavalry captain, had for some time had his eye on her, and it had been decided (for the stepmother wasted no affection upon the girl) that he should be her husband.

The empress had heard of it all. 'What a pity, and what a waste. Her father was so fond of her.'

The girl's brother, a chamberlain, had taken the empress at her kind word, and so the princess, known as Miyanokimi,* had recently come into the royal service. She was singled out for special favors, since she was, after all, the granddaughter of an emperor. She remained a lady-in-waiting all the same, and one was touched and saddened to see her wearing the train which the royal presence required, although she was granted a dispensation in certain other matters of ceremony.

Niou was greatly excited. Might she resemble Ukifune? Quite possibly, since their fathers were brothers. It will be seen that volatility continued to be among his more striking traits: one moment he would be lost in thoughts of his dead love, and the next he would be desperately impatient to meet her cousin.

Kaoru thought it all very sad. Until yesterday Miyanokimi's father had considered marrying her to the crown prince, and he had hinted that Kaoru himself might be an acceptable son-in-law. How very uncertain were the destinies of even a princess. One could understand why Ukifune had thrown herself into the river. Kaoru more than anyone sensed what Miyanokimi would be going through.

The empress had more spacious and comfortable apartments at Rokujō than in the palace, and the people who tended to be somewhat lazy about waiting upon her were with her now. Indeed, the wings and galleries that wandered over the wide grounds were packed with them. Yūgiri was as lavish in seeing to their needs and whims as his father would have been – more so, it might almost have been said, for the house was if anything more prosperous. The fun Niou might have had if he had been more his usual self rather defies the imagination. He was so subdued and withdrawn that people began to suspect an unlikely regeneration. But he was returning to form, and had dedicated himself to the pursuit of Miyanokimi.

*Which means 'princess.'

The weather being somewhat cooler, the empress thought of removing to the palace.

But her younger women objected. 'This is the place for autumn colors. Do let us stay and see them.'

They were all of them gathered at Rokujō. They went boating on the lake and they enjoyed the moonlight. Day and night, song to koto and lute floated over the grounds. Niou was not one to overlook such excitement. To the ladies, even those who saw him morning and night, he was like a fresh flower upon each appearance. Kaoru visited less frequently and they found him forbidding and unapproachable. One day Jijū chanced to look out from behind a screen and saw the two of them side by side. If only her lady had lived, become the bride of the one or the other, and reaped blessings (people would have said) from former lives! How utterly forlorn was the reality of her passing compared with the possibilities she had thrown away. But no one must be vouchsafed the smallest hint of the truth. Jijū must evince no more than any girl's interest in the two men.

Niou was transmitting all the court gossip to his mother. Kaoru got up to leave and Jijū slipped out of sight. She did not want him to know that she had taken service again before even the year of mourning was over. He would think her lacking in steadfastness and dedication.

He went to the east galleries, where numbers of women were whispering to one another just inside an open door.

'How pleasant if we could all be friends. You can trust me, you know, just as you trust one another, and it is possible that I might have a thing or two to teach you. Do you know what I mean? Yes, I rather think you do, and I am pleased.'

The poor girls were at a loss for an answer. Presently an older and very experienced woman named Ben spoke up. 'I fear that the ones who have no good cause to answer are the ones with all the answers. Isn't that the unfortunate way of the world? You are not to understand, of course, that good cause makes a girl speak up in response to just any passing query; and on the other hand it would be odd for us brazen ones to sit here like lumps.'*

'So those who have good cause to be friendly tend to be shy, and you are not such a one? How very sad for both of us.'

*Ben's speech is very obscure. Perhaps there is an element of deliberate obfuscation.

She seemed to have slipped off her cloak and pushed it away, and, in dishabille, to be at practice on her calligraphy. It seemed too that she had been toying with flowers, for several delicate sprays lay on the lid of her writing box. He was treated to an elegant array of ladies, though some had slipped behind curtains and the others had turned so that their faces could not be seen through the open door.

He pulled the inkstone nearer.

'Now through a field of riotous maiden flowers
    I go, untouched by any drop of dew.

'Do you still not trust me?'

He handed it to a lady who sat turned away from him, very near the door. Calmly, quickly, with scarcely a motion, she set down an answering poem.

'A flower whose name may suggest a want of judgment,
    It does not bend for every passing dew.'

It was a tiny sample to go by, but he found the hand pleasing and distinguished. Perhaps en route to the royal audience chamber she had found him blocking the way.

'Well,' resumed Ben, 'I must say that you make yourself very clear, and you do, as you have indicated, show signs of senility.

'Suppose you too have a nap among the flowers.
    Then may we see how well you resist their hues.

'And then we will be in a position to make up our minds about you.'

Kaoru was ready with another poem:

'I shall stay the night, if I have your invitation,
    Though common hues, I warn you, tempt me not.'

'That was not kind. I spoke in generalities.'

He had said little, but it had interested them.

'Well, I see that I am in the way. I shall leave it unobstructed. And I seem to have come at a time that calls for unusual reticence.'*

---

*Kaoru's last remark is cryptic. It seems to hark back to Ben's implied view that women with cause to speak lapse into silence, and may hint at a suspicion that Niou has been at work in the vicinity.

They only hoped, thought some of the women as he turned to leave, that he had not taken Ben for their spokesman.

He leaned against the east railing and as the color of evening came over the sky gazed at the flower beds before the empress's apartments. Lost again in sad thoughts, he whispered to himself: 'The autumn skies are the cruelest of all.'*

There was a rustling of silk as the woman who had answered his poem slipped inside the main hall.

Niou had come up beside him. 'Who was that?'

'Chūjō,' replied a second woman. 'She is with your royal sister.'

She should not have said it, thought Kaoru. Ladies were not supposed to offer up the names of other ladies in response to any chance question. And along with distaste at this impropriety he felt a twinge of jealousy. Niou's presence seemed to offer no cause for shyness. Niou was so impetuous, so direct – no doubt he swept them all before him. Kaoru's own friendship with the prince had brought mainly sorrow. He played with the possibility of reprisal. If Niou was after one of these beauties, then there might be ways to make him sip of his own medicine. Women of true discernment should prefer Kaoru to Niou – but where were they? His thoughts moved to Nakanokimi and the unhappiness Niou's various activities had brought. Yet she kept up the appearances demanded of her as Niou's wife. Kaoru thought it all very touching, and very admirable too. Would there be such women here? No frequenter of the women's quarters, he did not know. He might have enjoyed a try at nocturnal wandering himself, to beguile the long, sleepless hours; but such adventures were alien to his nature.

He had, however – and it seemed odd – acquired a liking for that west gallery, where he had espied the First Princess. Though she spent her nights with her mother, her women were assembled there, enjoying music and gossip. He interrupted a gentle strain upon a koto.

'Such music makes me impatient to see the musician.'†

*Po Chü-i, Collected Works, XIV, 'Evening.'

†This remark and the two following refer to the *Yu Hsien K'u* ('Cavern of Disporting Fairies,' Sir George Sansom has called it), a T'ang story preserved in Japan. The hero is attracted to the beautiful 'fairy' by the sound of a koto. We are informed that in mien she resembles her maternal uncle and in manner her elder brother. Chūjō's remark is obscure. It may be that she is telling Kaoru to go gaze upon Niou if he

He had caught them by surprise, but they left the blinds slightly raised. One of them came forward.

'And is there an elder brother for one to resemble?' It was Chūjō's voice.

'That I do not know,' he answered brightly, 'but there *is* a maternal uncle loitering about. Your lady is with her mother, I suppose? And how does she spend these days of freedom from palace restraints?' He was disappointed to find her away.

'Oh, she's not so very busy whether she is here or whether she is there. You have caught us at the sort of thing we do.'

For them life seemed to be very interesting. He sighed. Then, fearing that the sigh might have been detected, he pulled a Japanese koto towards him, and, making use of the scale on which one of the women had been at practice, played the opening bars of a song. It was not unsuccessful, since minor scales are thought especially suited to the moods of autumn; but he broke off before he had finished. The women had been listening with great interest and half wished he had not begun at all.

His mother was a princess too, and was she so inferior to Niou's eldest sister? The First Princess's mother had been named empress, and his own grandmother had not been so honored, and that was the whole of the difference. Both of them, his mother and the princess, were the much-loved daughters of emperors. Yet there was something ineffably different about the princess. A remarkable place, that Akashi coast, where her mother had been born. He must go someday for a look at it. He could hardly say that fate had slighted him, for the Second Princess was his. Yet how much kinder if it had given him the First Princess too! He was of course asking the impossible.

Miyanokimi had rooms in the west wing. Numerous other young women had gathered to enjoy the moonlight. She too was a princess, he thought, and sighed again, this time at the uncertainty of human destinies. He started toward her rooms, remembering that he had been among the tentative candidates for her hand. Two or three little girls, very pretty in formal livery, had been strolling up and down the veranda. They retreated at his

wishes to know what the First Princess is like; but the absence of honorifics seems to call for a more general interpretation. Kaoru is of course, so far as the world knows, maternal uncle to the princess.

approach. There was nothing to be shy about, thought he, but such was the way with little girls. He stopped before the south door and coughed to attract attention. An elderly woman came out.

'I might say that I have had secret thoughts about your lady, but I fear I would sound altogether too gauche and unimaginative. So here I am, seeking as best I can to describe "what lies beyond mere thoughts." '*

A forward sort, the woman chose to make reply in her mistress's stead. 'In the rather unexpected pass we have arrived at, the views of my lady's royal father come frequently to mind. I have more than once heard her speak of them. I feel sure that these indirections of yours would give her much pleasure.'

He was being put off like any wayward young man. He had failed to make his point.

'I have never been one to abandon people near me, and now more than ever, in this "unexpected pass," it would please me if she might find cause to look to me for support. But one is not always delighted to be confronted with an intermediary, you may perhaps have guessed, when one wishes to address a lady.'

Somewhat discommoded, she seems to have stirred her lady to action.

'I have "not even the aged pines of Takasago"† for comrades.' This time it was Miyanokimi's own voice, gentle and youthful. 'Your assurance that you have not forgotten gives me comfort.'

Though the remark was acceptable enough in itself, he was of two minds about it. Here was a princess of the blood reduced to addressing a man, albeit briefly, as if she were an ordinary lady-in-waiting. He longed for a glimpse of her, since there could be no doubt about her grace and distinction; and then a flicker of wry amusement crossed his mind. Niou would be ill again!

*Anonymous, *Kokin Rokujō, Zoku Kokka Taikan* 33486:

> I think of you. So much I may easily say.
> But how to add what lies beyond mere thoughts?

†Fujiwara Okikaze, *Kokinshū* 909:

> Whom shall I call my friend? No comrades they,
> Not even the aged pines of Takasago.

One could go searching a very long while for a perfect woman. He had been idealizing this royal princess. No rule of nature dictated that princesses be without equals.

The truly remarkable thing was that a hermit who had reared his two daughters like mountain rustics should have produced two such paragons. And the other girl, whom he had taxed with flightiness and poor judgment, of whom he had really seen so little: she too had delighted him.

So his thoughts returned always to the same family. As he sank deeper in memories of Uji, of his strange, cruel ties with the Uji family, drake flies, than which no creatures are more fragile and insubstantial, were flitting back and forth in the evening light.

> 'I see the drake fly, take it up in my hand.
> Ah, here it is, I say – and it is gone.'

And he added softly, as always: 'Here, and perhaps not here at all.'

CHAPTER 53

At Writing Practice

The bishop of Yokawa, on Mount Hiei, a holy and learned man, had a mother some eighty years old and a sister in her fifties. In fulfillment of a vow made long ago, they had been on a pilgrimage to Hatsuse. The bishop's favorite disciple had been with them. Having finished their prayers and offered up images and scriptures, they were climbing the Nara Slope on the return journey when the old woman was taken ill. She was in such discomfort that they could not ask her to go on. What were they to do? An acquaintance had a house at Uji, and it was decided to stop there for a day or two. When the old woman failed to improve, word was sent to the bishop. He had determined to remain in his mountain retreat until the end of the year, not even venturing down to the city, but there seemed a danger that his mother, of such an age that she could go at any time, might die on the journey. He hurried to her side. He himself and certain of his disciples whose ministrations had on other occasions been successful set about prayers and incantations – though one might have told them, and they would not have denied it, that she had lived a long enough life already.

The Uji acquaintance was troubled. 'I have plans for a pilgrimage to Mitake, and for a week now I have been fasting and otherwise getting ready. Can I risk having a very old and ailing lady in the house?'

The bishop understood, and the house was in any case small and shabby. They would proceed back towards Hiei by easy stages. Then it was discovered that the stars were against them, and that plan too had to be abandoned. The bishop remembered the Uji villa of the late Suzaku emperor. It would be in the vicinity, and he knew the steward. He sent to ask whether they might use it for a day or two.

The messenger came back to report that the steward and his family had left for Hatsuse the day before.

The caretaker, a most unkempt old man, came with him. 'Yes, if it suits your convenience, do please come immediately. The main hall is vacant. Pilgrims are always using it.'

'Splendid.' The bishop sent someone to make an inspection. 'It is a public building, you might say, but it should be quiet enough.'

The caretaker, used to guests, had simple accommodations ready.

The bishop went first. The house was badly run-down and even a little frightening. He ordered sutras read. The disciple who had been to Hatsuse and another of comparable rank had lesser clerics, to whom such tasks came naturally, prepare torches. For no very good reason, they wandered around to the unfrequented rear of the main hall. Under a grove of some description, a bleak, forbidding place, they saw an expanse of white. What could it possibly be? They brought their torches nearer and made out a seated human figure.

'A fox? They do sometimes take human shapes, filthy creatures. If we don't make it come out I don't know who else will.' One of the lesser monks stepped forward.

'Careful, careful,' said another. 'We can be sure it's up to no good.' Not letting his eyes wander for an instant from the thing, he made motions with his hands towards exorcising it.

The bishop's favored disciple was sure that his hair would have been standing on end if he had had any. The bold torchbearer, however, advanced resolutely upon the figure. It was a girl with long, lustrous hair. Leaning against the thick and very gnarled root of a tree, she was weeping bitterly.

'Why, this is strange. Maybe we should tell the bishop.'

'Very strange indeed,' said another, running off to report the discovery.

'People are always talking about foxes in human form,' said the bishop, 'but do you know I have never seen one?' He came out for a look.

All the available domestics were at work in the kitchen and elsewhere, seeing to the needs of the unexpected guests. These postern regions were deserted save for the half-dozen men watching the thing. No change was to be detected in it. The hours passed, the night seemed endless. Daylight would tell them whether or not it was human, thought the bishop, silently going over appropriate spells, and seeking to quell whatever force it might be with mystic hand motions.

Presently he reached a conclusion. 'It is human. It is no monstrous apparition. Go ask her who she is and why she is here. Don't be afraid. She is no ghost – though possibly a corpse thrown away hereabouts has come back to life.'

'A corpse thrown away at the Suzaku emperor's own villa? No, Your Reverence. At the very least it is someone a fox spirit or a wood spirit or something of the sort has coaxed away from home and then abandoned. The place will be contaminated, and for our purposes the timing could hardly be worse.'

Someone called for the caretaker, and the summons echoed menacingly across the empty grounds. He came running out, a somewhat ludicrous figure with his cap perched high on his head.

'Do you have any young women living here? Look at this, if you will.'

'Ah, yes. The foxes are at it again. Strange things are always turning up under this tree. Two years or so ago, in the fall it would have been, a little boy, maybe two years old, he lived up the road. They dragged him off and left him right here at the foot of this tree. It happens all the time.' He did not seem in the least upset.

'Had the child been killed?'

'Oh, no. He's still alive, I'd imagine. Foxes are always after people, but they never do anything really bad.' His manner suggested that such occurrences were indeed commonplace. The emergency domestic arrangements seemed to weigh more heavily on his mind.

'Suppose we watch for a while,' said the bishop, 'and see whether or not we observe foxes at work.'

He ordered the brave torchbearer to approach and challenge the strange figure.

'Who are you? Tell us who you are. Devil, fox, god, wood spirit? Don't think you can hold out against His Reverence. He won't be cheated. Who are you? Come on, now, tell us who you are.'

He tugged at a sleeve. The girl pressed it to her face and wept all the more bitterly.

'Come on, now. The sensible thing would be to tell us.' He tugged more assertively, though he rather hoped he would not be permitted a view of the face. It might prove to be the hideous mask of the eyeless, noseless she-devil* he had heard about. But he

---

Meoni has been taken by some commentators to mean not 'she-devil' but the homophonous 'eye devil.' An eyeless and noseless monster was held in medieval commentaries to inhabit Mount Hiei, whence the brave torchbearer has come.

must give no one reason to doubt his mettle. The figure lay face in arms, sobbing audibly now.

'Whatever it is, it's not the sort of thing you see just every day.' He peered down at the figure. 'But we're in for a storm.* She'll die if we leave her out in it, that's for sure. Let's move her in under the fence.'

'She has all the proper limbs,' said the bishop, 'and every detail suggests that she is human. We cannot leave her to die before our eyes. It is sad when the fish that swim in the lake or the stag that bays in the hills must die for want of help. Life is fleeting. We must cherish what we have of it, even so little as a day or two. She may have fallen into the clutches of some minor god or devil, or been driven from home, a victim of foul conspiracy. It may be her fate to die an unkind death. But such, even such, are they whom the Blessed One will save. Let us have a try at medicines and seek to revive her. If we fail, we shall still have done our best.'

He had the torchbearer carry her inside.

'Consider what you are doing, sir,' objected one of the disciples. 'Your honored mother is dangerously ill and this will do her no good.'

'We do not know what it is,' replied another, 'but we cannot leave it here for the rain to pound to death.'

It would be best not to let the servants know. The girl was put to bed in a remote and untenanted part of the hall.

The old nun's carriage was brought up, amid chatter about the stubbornness of her affliction.

'And how is the other?' asked the bishop when the excitement had somewhat subsided.

'She seems to have lost her very last ounce of strength – sometimes we wonder if she is still breathing – and she has not said a word. Something has robbed her of her faculties.'

'What is this?' asked the younger nun, the bishop's sister.

'Not in my upwards of six decades have I seen anything so odd.' And the bishop described it.

'I had a dream at Hatsuse.' The nun was in tears. 'What is she like? Do let me see her.'

---

*There is mention in the preceding chapter of a heavy rain on the day after Ukifune's disappearance.

'Yes, by all means. You will find her over beyond the east door.'

The nun hurried off. No one was with the girl, who was young and pretty and indefinably elegant. The white damask over her scarlet trousers gave off a subtle perfume.

'My child, my child. I wept for you, and you have come back to me.'

She had some women carry the girl to an inner room. Not having witnessed the earlier events, they performed the task equably.

The girl looked up through half-closed eyes.

She did not seem to understand. The nun forced medicine upon her, but she seemed on the point of fading away.

They must not let her die after she had been through so much. The nun called for the monk who had shown himself to be the most capable in such matters. 'I am afraid that she is not far from death. Let her have all your best spells and prayers.'

'I was right in the first place,' he grumbled. 'He should have let well enough alone.' But he commenced reading the sutra for propitiating the local gods.

'How is she?' The bishop looked in. 'Find out what it is that has been at her. Drive it away, drive it away.'

'She will not live, sir, I am sure of it. And when she dies we'll be in for a retreat we could perfectly well have avoided. She seems to be of good rank, and we can't just run away from the corpse. A bother, that is what I call it.'

'You do talk a great deal,' said the nun. 'But you are not to tell anyone. If you do you can expect an even worse bother.' She had almost forgotten her mother in the struggle to save the girl. Yes, she was a stranger, nothing to them, if they would have it so; but she was a very pretty stranger. Everyone who saw her joined in prayers that she be spared. Occasionally she would open her eyes, and there would be tears in them.

'What am I to do? The Blessed One has brought you in place of the child I have wept for, I am sure of it, and if you go too, I shall have to weep again. Something from another life has brought us together. I know that too. Speak to me. Please. Say something, anything.'

'I have been thrown out. I have nowhere to go.' The girl barely managed a whisper. 'Don't let anyone see me. Take me out when it gets dark and throw me back in the river.'

'She has spoken to me! But what a terrible thing to say. Why must you say such things? And why were you out there all by yourself?'

The girl did not answer. The nun examined her for wounds, but found none. Such a pretty little thing – but there was a certain apprehension mingled with the pity and sorrow. Might a strange apparition have been dispatched to tempt her, to challenge her calm?

The party remained in seclusion for two days, during which prayers and incantations went on without pause. Everyone was asking who this unusual person might be.

Certain farmers in the neighborhood who had once been in the service of the bishop came to pay their respects.

'There has been a big commotion over at the prince's place,' one of them remarked by way of apology. 'The General of the Right was seeing the prince's daughter, and then all of a sudden she died, of no sickness at all that anyone could see. We couldn't come yesterday evening when we heard Your Reverence was here. We had to help with the funeral.'

So that was it. Some demon had abducted the Eighth Prince's daughter. It scarcely seemed to the bishop that he had been look- ing at a live human being. There was something sinister about the girl, as if she might at any moment dissolve into thin air.

'The fire last night hardly seemed big enough for a funeral.'

'No, it wasn't much to look at. They made it as small as they could.' The visitors had been asked to remain outside lest they communicate the defilement.

'But who might it be? The prince's daughter, you say – but the princess the general was fond of has been dead for some years. He has another princess now, and he is not the sort to go out looking for new wives.'

The old nun was better and the stars no longer blocked the way. Everything that had happened made them want to leave these inhospitable precincts as soon as possible.

'But the young lady is still very weak,' someone objected. 'Do you really think she can travel?'

They had two carriages. The old nun and two others were in the first and the girl was in the second, with an attendant.* They

---

*The commentators are agreed that the bishop's sister is in the second carriage.

moved at an easy pace with frequent stops. The nuns were from Ono, at the west foot of Mount Hiei. It was very late when they arrived, so exhausted that they regretted not having spent another night along the way. The bishop helped his mother out. With many pauses, the younger nun led the girl into the nunnery. It was a sore trial to have lived so long, the old nun, near collapse, was no doubt saying to herself. The bishop waited until she had recovered somewhat and made his way back up the mountain. Because it had not been proper company for a cleric to find himself in, he kept the story to himself. The younger nun, his sister, also enjoined silence, and was very uneasy lest someone come inquiring after the girl. Why should they have found her all alone in such an unlikely place? Had a malicious stepmother taken advantage of an illness in the course of a pilgrimage, perhaps, and left her by the wayside? 'Throw me back in the river,' she had said, and there had been not a word from her since. The nun was deeply troubled. She did so want to see the girl restored to health, but the girl did not seem up to the smallest effort in her own behalf. Perhaps it was, after all, a hopeless case – but the very thought of giving up brought a new access of sorrow. Secretly requesting the presence of the disciple who had offered up the first prayers, the nun told of her dream at Hatsuse and asked that ritual fires be lighted.

And so the Fourth and Fifth months passed. Concluding sadly that her labors had been useless, the nun sent off a pleading letter to her brother: 'May I ask that you come down and see what you can do for her? I tell myself that if she had been fated to die she would not have lived this long; and yet whatever has taken possession of her refuses to be dislodged. I would not dream, my sainted brother, of asking that you set foot in the city; but surely it will do you no harm to come this far.'

All very curious, thought the bishop. The girl seemed destined to live – in that matter he had to agree with his sister. And what then would have happened if they had left her at Uji? All that could be affirmed was that a legacy from former lives had dictated a certain course of events. He must do what he could, and if then she died, he could only conclude that her destiny had worked itself out.

Overjoyed to see him, the nun told of all that happened over the months. 'A long illness generally shows itself on a person's face; but she is as fresh and pretty as ever she was.' She was weeping copiously. 'So very many times she has seemed on the point of death, and still she has lived on.'

'You are right.' He looked down at the girl. 'She is very pretty indeed. I did think all along that there was something unusual about her. Well, let's see what we can do. She brought a store of grace with her from other lives, we can be sure of that. I wonder what miscalculation might have reduced her to this. Has anything come to you that might offer a clue?'

'She has not said a word. Our Lady of Hatsuse brought her to me.'

'Everything has its cause. Something in another life brought her to you.'

Still deeply perplexed, he began his prayers. He had imposed upon himself so strict a regimen that he refused to emerge from the mountains even on royal command, and it would not do to be found in ministrations for which there was no very compelling reason.

He told his disciples of his doubts. 'You must say nothing to anyone. I am a dissolute monk who has broken his vows over and over again, but not once have I sullied myself with woman. Ah, well. Some people reveal their predilections when they are past sixty, and if I prove to be one of them, I shall call it fate.'

'Oh, consider for a moment, Your Reverence.' His disciples were more upset than he was. 'Think what harm you would be doing the Good Law if you were to let ignorant oafs spread rumors.'

Steeling himself for the trials ahead, the bishop committed himself silently to vows extreme even for him. He must not fail. All through the night he was lost in spells and incantations, and at dawn the malign spirit in possession of the girl transferred itself to a medium.

Assisted now by his favorite disciple, the bishop tried all manner of spells toward identifying the source of the trouble; and finally the spirit, hidden for so long, was forced to announce itself.

'You think it is this I have come for?' it shouted. 'No, no. I was once a monk myself, and I obeyed all the rules; but I took away a grudge that kept me tied to the world, and I wandered here and wandered there, and found a house full of beautiful girls. One of them died, and this one wanted to die too. She said so, every day and every night. I saw my chance and took hold of her one dark night when she was alone. But Our Lady of Hatsuse was on her side through it all, and now I have lost out to His Reverence. I shall leave you.'*

'Who is that addresses us?'

But the medium was tiring rapidly and no more information was forthcoming.

The girl was now resting comfortably. Though not yet fully conscious, she looked up and saw ugly, twisted old people, none of whom she recognized. She was assailed by intense loneliness, like a castaway on a foreign shore. Vague, ill-formed images floated up from the past, but she could not remember where she had lived or who she was. She had reached the end of the way, and she had flung herself in – but where was she now? She thought and thought, and was aware of terrible sorrows. Everyone had been asleep, she had opened the corner doors and gone out. The wind was high and the waters were roaring savagely. She sat trembling on the veranda. What should she do? Where was she to go now? To go back inside would be to rob everything of meaning. She must destroy herself. 'Come, evil spirits, devour me. Do not leave me to be discovered alive.' As she sat hunched against the veranda, her mind in a turmoil, a very handsome man came up and announced that she was to go with him, and (she seemed to remember) took her in his arms. It would be Prince Niou, she said to herself.

And what had happened then? He carried her to a very strange place and disappeared. She remembered weeping bitterly at her failure to keep her resolve, and she could remember nothing more. Judging from what these people were saying, many days had passed. What a sodden heap she must have been when they found her! Why had she been forced against her wishes to live on?

She had eaten little through the long trance, and now she would not take even a drop of medicine.

'You do seem bent on destroying all my hopes,' said the younger nun, the bishop's sister, not for a moment leaving her side. 'Just when I was beginning to think the worst might be over. Your temperature has gone down – you were running a fever all those weeks – and you seemed a little more yourself.'

---

*One is to understand not that the possession caused Ukifune's unhappiness but that the unhappiness gave the possessing spirit its opportunity.

Everyone in the house was delighted with her and quite unconditionally at her service. What happiness for them all that they had rescued her! The girl wanted to die; but the indications were that life had a stubborn hold on her. She began to take a little nourishment. Strangely, she continued to lose weight.

'Please let me be one of you,' she said to the nun, who was ecstatic at the prospect of a full recovery. 'Then I can go on living. But not otherwise.'

'But you are so young and so pretty. How could you possibly want to become a nun?'

The bishop administered token orders, cutting a lock of hair and enjoining obedience to the five commandments.* Though she was not satisfied with these half measures, she was an unassertive girl and she could not bring herself to ask more.

'We shall go no further at the moment,' said the bishop, leaving for his mountain cell. 'Do take care of yourself. Get your strength back.'

For his sister, these events were like a dream. She urged the girl to her feet and dressed her hair, surprisingly untangled after months of neglect, and fresh and lustrous once it had been combed out its full length. In this companionship of ladies 'but one year short of a hundred,'† she was like an angel that had wandered down from the heavens and might choose at any moment to return.

'You do seem so cool and distant,' said the nun. 'Have you no idea what you mean to me? Who are you, where are you from, why were you there?'

'I don't remember,' the girl answered softly. 'Everything seems to have left me. It was all so strange. I just don't remember. I sat out near the veranda every evening, that I do half remember. I kept looking out, and wishing I could go away. A man came from a huge tree just in front of me, and I rather think he took me off. And that is all I remember. I don't even know my name.' There were tears in her eyes. 'Don't let anyone know I am still alive. Please. That would only make things worse.'

---

*Against killing, stealing, wantonness, deceit, and drunkenness.

†In episode 63 of Tales of Ise, the hero is pursued by a lady 'but one year short of a hundred.'

Since it appeared that she found these attempts at conversation tiring, the nun did not press further. The whole sequence of events was as singular as the story of the old bamboo cutter and the moon princess,* and the nun was uneasy lest a moment of inattention give the girl her chance to slip away.

The bishop's mother was a lady of good rank. The younger nun was the widow of a high-ranking courtier. Her only daughter, who had been her whole life, had married another well-placed courtier and died shortly afterwards; and so the woman had lost interest in the world, taken the nun's habit, and withdrawn to these hills. Yet feelings of loneliness and deprivation lingered on. She yearned for a companion to remind her of the one now gone. And she had come upon a hidden treasure, a girl if anything superior to her daughter. Yes, it was all very strange – unbelievably, joyously strange. The nun was aging but still handsome and elegant. The waters here were far gentler than at that other mountain village. The house was pleasingly furnished, the trees and shrubs had been set out to agreeable effect, and great care had obviously gone into the flower beds. As autumn wore on, the skies somehow brought a deepened awareness of the passing days. The young maidservants, making as if to join the rice harvesters at the gate, raised their voices in harvest songs, and the clacking of the scare-crows† brought memories of a girlhood in the remote East Country.

The house was set in against the eastern hills, some distance above the retreat of Kashiwagi's late mother-in-law, consort of the Suzaku emperor. The pines were thick and the winds were lonely. Life in the nunnery was quiet, with only religious observances to break the monotony. On moonlit nights the bishop's sister would sometimes take out a koto and a nun called Shōshō would join in with a lute.

'Do you play?' they would ask the girl. 'You must be bored.'

As she watched these elderly people beguiling the tedium with music, she thought of her own lot. Never from the outset had she been among those privileged to seek consolation in quiet, tasteful pleasures; and so she had grown to womanhood with not a single

---

*Kaguyahime, in the tenth-century 'Tale of the Bamboo Cutter' (*Taketori monogatari*). She returns to the moon at the end of the story.

†*Hita*, clappers of wood and bamboo manipulated from a distance by a string.

accomplishment to boast of. Her stars had not been kind to her. She took up a brush and, by way of writing practice, set down a poem:

'Into a torrent of tears I flung myself,
    And who put up the sluice that held me back?'

It had been cruel of them to save her. The future filled her with dread. On these moonlit nights the old women would recite courtly poems and talk of this and that ancient happening, and she would be left alone with her thoughts.

'Who in the city, now bathed in the light of the moon,
    Will know that I yet drift on through the gloomy world?'

Many people had been in her last thoughts – or what she had meant to be her last thoughts – but they were nothing to her now. There was only her mother, who must have been shattered by the news. And Nurse, so desperate to find a decent life for her – how desolate she must be, poor thing! Where would she be now? She could not know, of course, that the girl was still alive. Then there was Ukon, who had shared all her secrets through the terrible days when no one else had understood.

It is not easy for young people to tell the world goodbye and withdraw to a mountain village, and the only women permanently in attendance were seven or eight aged nuns. Their daughters and granddaughters, married or in domestic service, would sometimes come visiting. The girl avoided these callers, for among them might be one or two who frequented the houses of the gentlemen she had known. It seemed absolutely essential that her existence remain a secret, and no doubt strange theories about her origins were going the rounds. The younger nun assigned two of her own maidservants, Jijū and Komoki, to wait upon the girl. They were a far cry from the 'birds of the capital'* she had known in her other life. Had she found for herself the 'place apart from the world' the poet speaks of?† The bishop's sister knew that such extreme reserve must have profound causes, and told no one of the Uji events.

---

*In the ninth episode of *Tales of Ise*, the exiled hero is reminded of home by the *miyakodori*, 'bird of the capital,' the black-headed gull.
†See note*, page 1043.

Her son-in-law was now a guards captain. His younger brother, a court chaplain and a disciple of the bishop, was in seclusion at Yokawa. Members of the family often went to visit him. Once on his way up the mountain the captain stopped by Ono. Outrunners cleared the road, and the elegant young gentleman who now approached brought back to the girl, so vividly that it might have been he, the image of her clandestine visitor. Ono was little nearer the center of things than Uji, but the nunnery and its grounds showed that the occupants were ladies of taste. Wild carnations coyly dotted the hedge, and maiden flowers and bell-flowers were coming into bloom; and among them stood numbers of young men in bright and varied travel dress. The captain, also in travel dress, was received at the south veranda. He stood for a time admiring the garden. Perhaps twenty-seven or twenty-eight, he seemed mature for his age. The nun, his mother-in-law, addressed him through a curtained doorway.

'The years go by and those days seem far away. It is good of you to remember that the darkness of our mountains awaits your radiant presence. And yet –' There were tears in her voice. 'And yet I am surprised, I must admit, that you so favor us.'

'I have not for a moment forgotten the old days; but I fear I have rather neglected you now that you are no longer among us. I envy my brother his mountain life and would like to visit him every day. But crowds of people are always wanting to come with me. Today I managed to shake them off.'

'I am not at all sure that I believe you. You are saying what young people say. But of course you have not forgotten us, and that is evidence that you are not like the rest of them. I thank you for it, you may be sure, every day of the year.'

She had a light lunch brought for the men and offered the captain lotus seeds and other delicacies. Since this was of course not the first time she had been his hostess, he saw no cause for reticence. The talk of old times might have gone on longer had a sudden shower not come up. For the nun, regret was added to sorrow, regret that so fine a young man had been allowed to become a stranger. Why had her daughter not left behind a child, a keepsake? Quite lost in the nostalgia these occasional visits induced, she sometimes said things she might better have kept to herself.

Looking out into the garden, alone once again with her thoughts, the girl was pathetic and yet beautiful in the white singlet, a plain, coarse garment, and drab, lusterless trousers in harmony with the subdued tones of the nunnery. What an unhappy contrast she must be with what she had once been! In fact, even these stiff, shapeless garments became her.

'Here we have our dead lady back, you might almost think,' said one of the women; 'and here we have the captain too. It makes you want to weep, it really does. People will marry, one way and another, and it would be so nice if we could have him back for good. Wouldn't they make a handsome couple, though.'

No, never, the girl replied silently. She had no wish to return to the past, and the attentions of a man, any man, would inevitably pull her towards it. She had been there, and she would have no more of it.

The nun having withdrawn, the captain sat looking apprehensively up at the sky. He recognized the voice of the nun Shōshō and called her to him.

'I am sure that all the ladies I knew are here, but you can probably imagine how hard it is for me to visit you. You must have concluded that I am completely undependable.'

They talked of the past, on and on, for Shōshō had been in the dead lady's service.

'Just as I was coming in from the gallery,' he said, 'a gust of wind caught the blind, and I was treated to a glimpse of some really beautiful hair. What sort of damsel do you have hidden away in your nunnery?'

He had seen the retreating figure of the girl and found her interesting. How much more dramatic the effect would certainly be if he were to have a good look at her. He still grieved for a lady who was much the girl's inferior.

'Our lady was quite unable to forget her daughter, your own lady, and nothing seemed to console her. Then quite by accident she came on another girl, and she seems to have recovered somewhat from her grief. But it is not at all like the girl to have let you see her.'

Now this was interesting, thought the captain. Who might she be? That single glimpse, a most tantalizing one, had assured him that she was well favored. He questioned Shōshō further, but her answers were evasive.

'Oh, everything will come out in the end. Just be patient.'

It would not have been good manners to press for more.

'The rain has stopped and we do not have much more day-light,' said one of his men.

Breaking off a maiden flower below the veranda, he was heard to murmur as he went out: 'Why should our nunnery be bright with maiden flowers?'*

The older women recognized the allusion and thought it grati-fying. Even a dashing young gentleman could worry about appearances.

'He always was pleasant to look at,' said the bishop's sister, 'and the years have been good to him. Yes, how nice if things could be as they were. I am told that he has not actually been neglecting the Fujiwara councillor's daughter,† but that he's not too awfully fond of her. He spends most of his time at home, I am told. But come: you are not being very kind, my dear, letting your own thoughts occupy you so. Do cheer up a bit, please do. Tell yourself that what had to be had to be. For five and six years I grieved and I yearned, and now I have you to fill my life, and I must confess that she has quite gone out of it. Someone, somewhere, may have grieved and yearned for you too, but whoever it is must by now have given you up, of that I am sure. Nothing lasts, everything changes. That is the way of the world.'

'I don't want to keep secrets from you,' said the girl, choking with tears. 'But it is all so strange, that I am alive, that you found me where you did, everything. It is all like clinging to something in a dream. Like being born into a different world, I should think. If there are people who worry about me, I cannot remember who they are. I have only you.'

A smile on her face, the nun listened quietly. How beautiful the girl was, and how unaffected!

The captain reached Yokawa. The bishop too enjoyed his visits. The talk went on and on and presently monks of good voice were called in to read sutras. With this and that diversion, the night went pleasantly by.

The captain remarked in the course of it: 'I stopped by Ono on

---

*Henjō, *Shūishū* 1098, upon seeing maidens in the monastery garden:

> Must our gardens be bright with maiden flowers?
> For cause far less the world is wont to gossip.

†The captain's new father-in-law has not otherwise been identified.

my way here. It was a pleasure to see your sister again. She may
have left the world, but there aren't many who have her taste and
discrimination.' He paused and continued: 'The wind caught one
of the blinds and I was treated to a glimpse of a long-haired
beauty. I gather that she did not want to be seen. She was running
off to another part of the house. But what I did see struck me as
most uncommon. A nunnery is an odd place for young beauty, I
must say. She sees nuns and more nuns, morning and noon and
night, and one of these days she will be looking like a nun herself.
We would not wish that to happen.'

'I have heard,' said his brother, 'that they went to Hatsuse this
spring and found her somewhere along the way.' Not himself a
witness to these events, he offered no details.

'That is very interesting, and very sad. Who might she be?
Someone in the most trying circumstances, I should think, that she
should want to hide from the world. But how very interesting.
There is something a little storybookish about it, you might almost
say.'

He found Ono hard to pass by on his descent to the city.

The nun was prepared this time, and so lavish with her hospitality that he was reminded of other years. Though Shōshō no
longer wore the bright robes of old, she was still a woman of taste.
The bishop's sister was in tears as she received him.

'And who,' he asked nonchalantly, 'is the young lady you have
hidden away?'

She was startled. But a moment's consideration told her that he
had seen the girl and that evasion would do her no good. 'My sins
went on accumulating because I was unable to forget my daughter,
and for several months now I have had another girl to look after,
and she has brought a certain comfort. I do not know the details
myself, but she seems to have rather dreadful problems, and does
not even want it known that she is alive. I thought surely these
mountain fastnesses would be safe from prying eyes. How do you
happen to know about her?'

She had not completely satisfied his curiosity. 'Even if my
motives were less than honorable, I might, I think, claim a certain
measure of credit for having braved these mountain roads. I had
expected a better reward. You are being somewhat ungenerous if
you insist on hiding the facts and treating me as if they were no
concern of mine. If she serves as a substitute for my lamented wife,

then I think I may say that they are. Why is she so set against the world? It is just possible that I might offer comfort.' And he indited a poem on a piece of notepaper he had with him:

'O maiden flower, bend not to Adashino's gales.
I came the long road to make for you a windbreak.'*

The bishop's sister saw the note, which he sent in through Shōshō. 'You must answer, you really must. He is an honest and serious young man, and you have nothing to worry about.'

But the girl would not be moved. 'I write so dreadfully,' she said.

Not wanting him to go off annoyed, the nun herself sent an answer. 'I have warned you that she is eccentric, and we may not reasonably expect conventional behavior of her.

'We have brought the maiden flower to a hut of grass
Away from the world, and yet the world torments it.'

Concluding that nothing more was to be expected, he started for the city. Further attempts at correspondence would seem inappropriate and even childish. Yet he could not forget the figure of which he had had a glimpse that afternoon. He pitied the girl, though of course he still did not know what reasons there were for pity.

Toward the middle of the Eighth Month, on a falconing expedition, he again visited Ono.

He called Shōshō and gave her a note for the girl. 'The sight of you has left me restless and utterly at loose ends.'

Since it seemed unlikely that the girl would answer, the nun sent back: 'She awaits "I know not whom on Matsuchi Hill." '†

'You have told me that she has troubles,' he said when the nun

---

*The sound of the name Adashino, 'the moor of Adashi,' in the western reaches of the modern city, suggests fickleness and promiscuity; here, an enterprising young man.

†Ono no Komachi, *Shinkokinshū* 336:

Awaiting I know not whom on Matsuchi Hill,
The maiden flower has a bond with autumn, it seems.

Matsuchiyama, on the border between the provinces of Kii and Yamato, suggests waiting.

came out to receive him. 'I would like more details, if you don't mind. Few things go as I would wish them. I often think of withdrawing to the mountains myself; but people hold me back, and time goes by. I am of a rather morose turn, I fear, and sunny dispositions do not particularly suit me. Perhaps if I might talk of my troubles with someone who has troubles too?'

He seemed very interested indeed, thought the nun. 'If you are looking for someone who is not very talkative, I suspect that you have come to the right place. But her distrust of the world is almost frightening, and she seems determined not to do as other women do. It was not easy for me, even, to say goodbye to the world, and I have so little time ahead of me. I do not know how a girl with everything ahead of her can even think of it.' As she bustled back and forth between girl and caller, it was as if she had become a mother once more. 'You are not being kind,' she said to the girl. 'You must let him have an answer, even if it is only a word or two. People like us should be more understanding than most.'

But the girl was cold to her persuasions. 'I know nothing at all, not the way they answer these things, nothing.'

'I beg your pardon?' said the captain. 'No answer? That is too unkind. It is a lie, then, about Matsuchi Hill?

' "I wait," said the voice from the pines; and I have come
   And find myself wandering lost through dew-drenched reeds.'*

'Do try to feel a little sorry for him,' said the nun. 'You must answer at least this one time.'

But the thought of even a delicate show of interest horrified the girl, and a response was sure to invite further challenges. She remained silent.

This evidence of apathy was not to the nun's liking. She sent an answer herself, and her manner as she set about it suggested that she had not always been of an ascetic bent.

'Though the dew on the autumn moors may have wet your sleeves,
   You do wrong, O hunter, to blame our weed-grown lodgings.

---

*The voice is that of the *matsumushi*, 'pine cricket.' The common pun on *matsu* suggests waiting.

'I but forward her reply to your message. As you see, it is not encouraging.'

The nuns had warm feelings towards the captain, and of course they could not know how deeply it distressed the girl to have word get out, despite her own wishes, that she was still alive. They seemed intent upon pushing her into his arms. 'Just have a try at letting him talk to you when these little chances come up. You will be surprised, I am sure you will, at how silly you have been to hold back. No, it needn't be the usual sort of thing. Just let him know that you don't dislike him.'

They were far from as withdrawn and unworldly as she would have wished, and the youthful zest with which they turned out bad poetry did nothing to restore her composure. What further humiliations must she expect? – for she still had life, unbearable burden which she had sought to be rid of. If only they would turn her out, rejected by the whole world.

The captain heaved a sigh, perhaps because other worries had crossed his mind. Taking out a flute, he played a muted tune upon it, and when he had finished he intoned softly, as if to himself: ' "The call of the hart disturbs the autumn night." '* He did appear to be a man of taste. 'I seem to have come all this way just to be tormented by memories,' he said, getting up to leave, 'and I fear that my new friend will not be much comfort. No, your retreat does not seem to lie along my "mountain path away from the world." '†

'Such a beautiful night, and it is just beginning.' The nun came out towards the veranda. 'Must you go?'

'What possible reason have I to stay? I sense very great distances between us.'

He had no wish at this point to seem eager. The one fleeting glimpse had been interesting, and had offered possible relief from

---

*Mibu Tadamine, *Kokinshū* 214:

> Lonely the mountain village, lonelier yet
> When the call of the hart disturbs the autumn night.

†Mononobe Yoshina, *Kokinshū* 955:

> I would start down a mountain path away from the world,
> Did thoughts of one still there not pull me back.

loneliness and boredom. That was all. Her haughtiness was rather out of keeping with her circumstances, and cooled his ardor.

The nun was reluctant to see even the flute go. She sought to detain him with a verse, though not a very clever one:

> 'A stranger to the late-night moon in its glory
>   That he now disdains our house at the mountain ridge?'

She had been clever in one respect: she had made it seem that the girl's own sentiments were in the poem. His interest revived, he sent an answering poem:

> 'I shall watch till the moon goes behind the mountain ridge,
>   To see how it slips through the boards that roof your chamber.'

The old nun, the bishop's mother, had caught a dim echo of a flute. She tottered eagerly forward, coughing and sputtering, her voice tremulous as she made her wishes known. Though she should have been overwhelmed by memories, she said nothing of the old days. Perhaps she did not recognize their guest.

'Play, play! Play on flute and koto. Oh, but a person does want a flute on a moonlit night. Come on, you over there. Bring out a koto.'

The captain had guessed who was addressing him. So she still lived on in these mountains! How was it possible? Life dealt itself out capriciously, giving some people more than their share of it. He offered the old lady a deft melody in the *banjiki* mode.

'Now for the koto.'

'I think you have improved,' said the younger nun, rather a connoisseur, 'but then you always were good. It may be that I have listened too long to the wind in the pines. I am sure to disgrace myself in such competition.' And she played a melody on the koto.

Not much in vogue these days, the seven-stringed koto had its own charm. The wind blew a counterpoint through the pines, and the flute seemed to be urging the moon to new splendors. Delighted, the old nun was prepared to stay up until dawn.

'I used to do tolerably well on the Japanese koto myself; but my son tells me it is in bad taste. I suppose the fashions have changed. He says he can't bear the thing, and besides I am wasting my time. I ought to be spending my time with my beads, every last minute of it, he says, and so I am out of practice. If I could just give you something on that koto of mine, such a fine, clear tone it does have.'

She would like nothing better than to perform for them, the captain could see. 'Your reverend son has strange ideas of what you should and should not be doing. Does he not know, and like all the rest of us think it admirable, that the powers above play on instruments like these and the angels dance to them? What sin can there be in music, what harm can it do to your prayers? I for one cannot think of any. Come, let's have a tune or two.'

The old lady was in ecstasy. 'Tonomori,' she coughed. 'Bring me that koto, the Japanese one.'

The others looked forward to the performance with a certain dread, but since even her son had aroused her ire, it hardly seemed politic to discourage her. Not bothering to ask what mode the captain had been using, she smartly plucked out a gamut that suited her fancy. The flutist had fallen silent, doubtless, she thought, lost in admiration.

'*Takefu chichiri chichiri taritana.*'* It was a brave, sturdy effort, though not a very modish one.

'How interesting,' said the captain. 'Not the sort of thing one hears very often these days.'

She did not quite catch his words, which had to be relayed to her by someone a little nearer.

'Young people seem to have given up this sort of thing,' she cackled. 'Take the girl who has been with us these last few weeks. She's very pretty, I'm sure, but she lives in a world all her own. None of our little frivolities for *that* one, I can tell you.'

To her daughter and the others she was beginning to seem a bit too pleased with her own world; and a beautiful night was being spoiled.

The captain set out for the city, his flute coming in rich and full on the wind from the mountain. There was no sleep at the nunnery that night.

Early in the morning a note was delivered: 'It was because of all my troubles that I took my leave so early.

> 'Ancient things came back, I wept aloud
> At koto and flute and a lady's haughty ways.

---

*A solfeggio, apparently. Some have argued that the old nun is filling in for the now silent flute; and some that the first syllables are a reference to the Saibara 'Gateway' (see note†, page 1083).

'Do teach her a little, if you will, of the art of sympathy. If I were able to endure in silence, would I thus be serenading you?'

Sadder and sadder, thought the nun, on the edge of tears as she composed her reply:

> 'With the voice of your flute came thoughts of long ago,
> And tears wet my sleeve, and sped you on your way.

'You will have guessed, from the remarks my mother was so generous with, that the girl is so withdrawn as to suggest insensitivity.'

It was not a letter that interested him a great deal.

As insistent as the wind through the rushes, the girl was thinking. How very insistent men were! Memories of the Uji days, and especially of Niou, were coming back. Well, she knew a way to be free of them all. She quite gave herself up to her preparations, to study and prayer and invocation of the holy name. The bishop's sister was forced to conclude that the girl had never been young, that she had somehow been withdrawn and gloomy from the start. But pretty she certainly was, so pretty that dissatisfaction with her could not last. Indeed, the nun's life had come to center upon her, and a rare little chuckle from her was a delight among delights.

In the Ninth Month the nun made a pilgrimage to Hatsuse. All those months had done little to ease her grief, and now she had found a girl whom she could only think of as a daughter; and the pilgrimage was by way of showing her gratitude to Our Lady of Hatsuse.

'Suppose you come along, my dear. No one need hear of it. You may say that one holy image is very much like another, but Hatsuse does seem to produce very special results. Do come with me.'

Her mother and nurse had said exactly that, she remembered, and had more than once taken her to Hatsuse; and what good had their efforts done? In those last desperate days, she had not even been allowed to dispose of her own life. And the thought of going on a long journey with a near stranger somehow frightened her.

But she made no effort to argue the matter. 'I am not myself,' she said quietly, 'and I am not at all sure what the trip would do to me.'

Yes, poor child, she had every right to be apprehensive, thought the nun. She said no more.

She came upon a scrap of paper on which, by way of writing practice, the girl had jotted down a verse:

'On shoals unsought, I ask no further view
Of cedars twain beside that ancient river.'*

'Two cedars, is it?' said the nun banteringly. 'So there actually are two persons you might want to see again?'

The girl started and flushed crimson. The nun had said more than she intended to. She thought this confusion charming, and rattled off a not very distinguished poem:

'I know not the roots of the tree by the ancient river,
But it takes the place, for me, of one now gone.'

She had hoped to steal off almost by herself, but everyone clamored to go along. Fearing that the girl would be lonely, she left three attendants behind: the sensitive and cultivated Shōshō, an elderly woman called Saemon, and a little girl. Gazing moodily after the pilgrims, Ukifune felt the loneliness close in upon her even more threateningly. Indeed, she felt quite defenseless, her one ally now off for Hatsuse. In upon the tedium and loneliness, as her thoughts wandered now to the past and now to the perilous future, came a letter from the captain. Shōshō asked her at least to glance at it, but she refused.

'Come, now. This gloom is getting to be contagious. Let's see if I can best you at Go.'

'Of course you can. I always lose.' The girl seemed not unhappy at the suggestion, however, and the board was brought out. Expecting an easy victory, Shōshō let her have the first play. But the girl was no weakling, and in the next match Shōshō was easily persuaded to play first.

'What a charming surprise. Something to tell my lady about, if she will just hurry back. She is rather good at it herself. Her honored brother has always been fond of the game, and there was a time when he was taking on airs like the gentleman they called the High Priest of Go.† It was just about then that he challenged my lady to a match. He promised that he would be a generous and

*See note†, page 197.
†Tachibana Yoshitoshi, a minor courtier of the late ninth and early tenth centuries, acquired the sobriquet.

forbearing conqueror, and he lost two in a row. I am sure you would have no trouble besting His Reverence the High Priest of Go. You are very, very good, I do not hesitate to tell you.'

Shōshō was warming to her subject. But the girl was beginning to fear that this unlovely, bald-pated person might be too insistent a companion. She was a little tired, she said, and went to lie down.

'A game now and then would do you a world of good. It seems such a pity that a girl as attractive as you should be forever moping. The flaw in the gem, as they say.'

The night wind moaning outside brought memories.

Just as the moon came flooding over the hills the captain appeared. (There had been that note from him earlier in the day.) The girl fled aghast to the rear of the house.

'You are being a perfect fool,' said Shōshō.* 'It is the sort of night when a girl should treasure these little attentions. Do, I beg of you, at least hear what he has to say – or even a part of it. Are you so clean that his very words will soil you?'

But the girl was terrified. Though someone ventured to tell him that she was away, he probably knew the truth. Probably his messenger had reported that she was alone.

His recriminations were lengthy. 'I don't care whether or not I hear her voice. I just want to have her beside me, prepared to decide for herself whether I am such an ugly threat. She is being quite heartless, and in these hills too, where it might be imagined that there would be time to cultivate the virtue of patient charity. It is more than a man should be asked to bear.

'In a mountain village, deep in the autumn night,
    A lady who understands should understand.

'And I do think she should.'

'There is no one here to make your explanations for you,' said Shōshō to the girl. 'You may if you are not careful seem rude and eccentric.'

'The gloom of the world has been no part of my life,
    And how shall you call me one who understands?'

The girl recited the poem more as if to herself than by way of reply, but Shōshō passed it on to him.

*Probably it is she, though no subject is given.

He was deeply touched. 'Do ask her again to come out, for a moment, even.'

'I seem to make no impression upon her at all,' said Shōshō, who was beginning to find his persistence, and with it a certain querulousness, a little tiresome. She went back inside – and found that the girl had fled to the old nun's room, which she had not before so much as looked in upon.

Shōshō reported this astonishing development.

'With all this time on her hands,' said the captain, 'she should be more than usually alive to the pity of things, and all the indications are that she is a gentle and sensitive enough person. And that very fact, you know, makes her unfriendliness cut more cruelly. Do you suppose there is something in her past, something that has made her afraid of men? What might it be, will you tell me, please, that has turned her against the whole world? And how long do you expect to have her with you?'

Openly curious now, he pressed for details; but how was Shōshō to give them?

'A lady whom my lady should by rights have been looking after was lost for a number of years. And then, on a pilgrimage to Hatsuse, we found her again.'

The girl lay face down, sleepless, beside the old nun, whom she had heard to be a very difficult person. The nun had dozed off from early evening, and now she was snoring thunderously. With her were two nuns as old as she, snoring with equal vigor. Terrified, the girl half wondered whether she would survive the night. Might not these monsters devour her? Though she had no great wish to live on, she was timid by nature, rather like the one we have all heard of who has set out across a log bridge and then changed her mind.* She had brought the girl Komoki with her. Of an impressionable age, however, Komoki had soon returned to a spot whence she could observe this rare and most attractive caller. Would she not please come back, would she not *please* come back? Ukifune was asking; but Komoki was little help in a crisis.

The captain presently gave up the struggle and departed.

'She is so hopelessly wrapped up in herself,' said the women, 'and the worst of it is that she is so pretty.'

At what the girl judged would be about midnight the old nun

*A reference, apparently, to a story or proverb, not identified.

awoke in a fit of coughing and sat up. In the lamplight her hair was white against her shawl.

Startled to find the girl beside her, she shaded her eyes with her hand as the mink (or some such creature) is said to do* and peered over.

'Now this is strange,' she said in a deep, menacing voice. 'What sort of thing might you be?'

The moment had come, thought the girl. She was going to be devoured. When that malign being had led her off she had not resisted, for she had not had her senses about her. But what was she to do now? They had dragged her ignominiously back into the world, and black memories were a constant torment; and now came a new crisis, one which she seemed incapable of surmounting or even facing. Yet perhaps if she had had her way, if she had died, she would this moment be facing a crisis still more terrible. Sleepless, she thought back over her life, which seemed utterly bleak. She had not known her father and she had divided all those years between the capital and the remote provinces. And then she had come upon her sister. For a time she had been happy and secure; but that untoward incident had separated them. Some relief from her misfortunes had seemed in prospect when a gentleman declared himself ready to offer her a respectable position, and she had responded to his attentions with that hideous blunder. It had been wrong to permit even the smallest flutter of affection for Niou. The memory of her ultimate disgrace, brought on by his attentions, revolted her. What idiocy, to have been moved by his pledge and that Islet of Oranges and the pretty poem it had inspired!† Her mind moved from incident to incident, and longing flowed over her for the other gentleman. He had not exactly burned with ardor, but he had seemed calm and dependable. From him above all she wanted to keep news of her whereabouts and circumstances. Would she be allowed another glimpse of him, even from a distance? But she sternly dismissed the thought. It was wrong. She must not harbor it for a moment.

After what had seemed an endless night, she heard a cock crowing. It was an immense relief – but how much greater a

*There is a similar reference in Chapter 50.
†See Chapter 51.

delight had it been her mother's voice awakening her! Komoki was still absent from her post. The girl lay in bed, exhausted. The early snorers were also early risers, it seemed. They were noisily at work on gruel and other unappetizing dishes. Someone offered her a helping, but the donor was ugly and the food strange and unappetizing. She was not feeling well, she said, not venturing an open refusal. The old women did not sense that their hospitality was unwelcome.

Several monks of low rank came up to the nunnery. 'The bishop will be calling on you today.'

'What brings him so suddenly?'

'An evil spirit of some sort has been after the First Princess. The archbishop* has been doing what he can, but two messengers came yesterday to say that only His Reverence offers real hope.' They delivered these tidings in proud voices. 'Then late last night the lieutenant came, the son of the Minister of the Left, you know.† He had a message from Her Majesty herself. And so His Reverence will be coming down the mountain.'

She must summon up her courage, thought the girl, and have the bishop administer final vows. Today there were no meddling women to gainsay them. 'I fear I am very ill,' she said, rousing herself, 'and when he comes I hope I may ask him to let me take my vows. Would you tell him so, please?'

The old nun nodded vaguely.

The girl went back to her room. She did not like the thought of having anyone except the bishop's sister touch her hair, and she could not dress it without help. She loosened the cords that had bound it up for the night. Though of course she had no one but herself to blame for what was about to happen, she was sad that her mother would not see her again in lay dress. She had feared that her hair might be thinner because of her illness, but could detect no evidence that it was. Remarkably thick, indeed, it was a good six feet long, soft and smooth and beautifully even at the edges.

Zasu, the chief abbot of Mount Hiei.

†One of Yūgiri's sons, and so a first cousin of the princess.

'I cannot think,' she whispered to herself, 'that she would have wished it thus.'*

The bishop arrived in the evening. The south room had been readied for him. Suddenly full of shaven heads, it was an even less inviting room than usual. The bishop went to look in on his mother.

'And how have you been these last months? I am told that my good sister is off on a pilgrimage. And is the girl still with you?'

'Oh, yes. She didn't go along. She says, let me see, she's not feeling well. She'd like to take her vows, she says, and she'd like you to give them to her.'

'I see.' He went to the girl's room and addressed her through curtains. Shyly, she came forward.

'I have felt that only a bond from a previous life could explain the curious way we met, and I have been praying my hardest for you. But I am afraid that as a correspondent I have not been very satisfactory. You will understand, I am sure, that we clerics are supposed to deny ourselves such pleasures unless we have very good reasons. And how have you been? It is not an easy life women lead when they turn their backs on the world.'

'You will remember that I had no wish to live on, and my strange survival has only brought me grief. But of course I am grateful, in my poor way, for all you have done. Do, please, let me take my vows. I do not think I am capable of the sort of life other women lead. Even if I were to stay among them, I do not think I could follow their example.'

'What can have brought you to such a conclusion, when you have your whole life ahead of you? No, it would be a grave sin. The decision may at the time seem a firm one, but women are irresolute creatures, and time goes by.'

'I have never been happy, not since I was very young, and my mother often thought of putting me in a nunnery. And when I began to understand things a little better I could see that I was different from other people, and must seek my happiness in another world.' She was weeping. 'Perhaps it is because I am so

---

*Henjō, *Gosenshū* 1241, upon taking holy orders:

> I cannot think that she would have wished it thus,
> My aged mother, stroking my raven hair.

near the end of it all – I feel as if everything were slipping away. Please, reverend sir, let me take my vows.'

The bishop was puzzled. Why should so gentle a surface conceal such a strange, bitter resolve? But he remembered that malign spirit and knew that she would not be talking nonsense. It was remarkable that she was still alive. A terrible thing, a truly hideous thing, to be accosted by forces so evil.

'Your wish can only have gained for you the smiling approval of the powers above. It is not for me to deter you. Nothing could be simpler than administering vows. But I have come down on most pressing business, and must tonight be at the princess's side. The services begin tomorrow. In a week they will be over, and I shall see that your petition is granted.'

But by then the younger nun would have come back, and she would surely object. It must be made to appear that the crisis was immediate.

'Perhaps I have not explained how unwell I am. I fear that vows will do me little good if I am beyond accepting them wholeheartedly. Please. I see my chance today, the only one I shall be blessed with.'

Her weeping had touched his saintly heart. 'It is very late. I used to have no trouble at all climbing up and down the mountain, but I am old, and matters are no longer so simple. I had thought to rest here awhile and then go on to the city. If you are in such a hurry, I shall see to your wishes immediately.'

Delighted, the girl pushed scissors and a comb box towards him.

'Have the others come here, please.' The two monks who had been with him that strange night at Uji were with him again tonight. 'Cut the young lady's hair, if you will.'

It was a most proper thing they were doing, they agreed. Given the perilous situation in which they had found her, they knew that she could have been meant for no ordinary life. But the bishop's favored disciple hesitated even as he raised the scissors. The hair pushed forward between the curtains was altogether too beautiful.

The nun Shōshō was off in another wing with her brother, a prefect who had come with the bishop. Saemon too was having a chat with a friend in the party; and such modest entertainment as they were capable of providing for these rare and most welcome visitors occupied most of the household.

Only Komoki was present. She scampered off to tell Shōshō what was in progress. A dismayed Shōshō rushed in just as the bishop was going through the form of bestowing his own robe and surplice upon the girl.

'You must now make obeisance, if you will, in the direction of your father and mother.'

The girl was in tears, for she did not know in which direction that would be.

'And what, may I ask, are you doing? You are being utterly irresponsible. I cannot think what our lady will have to say when she gets back.'

But the proceedings were at a point beyond which expressions of doubt could only disturb the girl. Shōshō said no more.

'. . . as we wander the three worlds,'* intoned the bishop.

So, at length, came release. Yet the girl felt a twinge of sorrow: there had in fact been no bonds to break.

The bishop's assistant was having trouble with her hair. 'Oh, well. The others will have time to trim it for you.'

'You must admit no regrets for the step you have taken,' said the bishop, himself cutting the hair at her forehead. He added other noble admonitions.

She was happy now. They had all advised deliberation, and she had had her way. She could claim this one sign of the Buddha's favor, her single reward for having lived on in this dark world.

The visitors left, all was quiet. 'We had thought that for you at least,' said her companions, to the moaning of the night wind, 'this lonely life need not go on. We had looked forward to seeing you happy again. And this has happened. Have you thought of all the years that lie ahead of you? It is not easy for even an old woman to tell herself that life as most people know it has ended.'

But the girl was serene. 'Life as most people know it' – she need no longer think about that. Waves of peace flowed over her.

But the next morning she avoided their eyes, for she had acted selfishly and taken no account of their wishes. Her hair seemed to scatter wildly at the ends, and no one was prepared to dress it for her in charitable silence. She kept her curtains drawn.

She had never been an articulate girl, and she had no confidante with whom to discuss the rights and wrongs of what had hap-

*Although the text from which the bishop is reciting has been lost, the reference would seem to be to the cycle of birth and rebirth.

pened. She seated herself at her inkstone and turned to the one pursuit in which she could lose herself when her thoughts were more than she could bear, her writing practice.

> 'A world I once renounced, for they and I
>   Had come to nothing, I now renounce again.

'Finally, this time, I have done it.'
The poem moved her to set down another:

> 'I thought that I should see the world no more,
>   And now, once more, 'no more' is my resolve.'

As she sat jotting down poem after poem, all very much alike, a letter came from the captain. In the midst of the uproar, someone had sent word of what Ukifune had done. He was of course much distressed. There was a consistency in it all, her determination accounting for her coldness and her reluctance to embark upon even the beginning of a correspondence. Still it was very disheartening. He had begged the other night to be granted a closer look at the rich hair that had so interested him, and the nuns had told him that his time would come. He sent off a bitter reply by return messenger:

'What would you have me say?

> 'Make haste, make haste, lest I be left behind.
>   The fisher boat even now rows far from the shore.'*

The girl surprised them by showing an interest in the letter. It was a time for sadness, and she was touched by this sign that he had finally lost hope. Whatever she may have had in mind, she took up a rough scrap of paper and wrote this poem on a corner of it:

> 'My soul may have left the shores of this gloomy world,
>   But on driftwood it floats, who knows to what far shore?'

In her usual fashion, she jotted it down as if in writing practice. Someone folded it in a cover and sent it off to the captain.
'You could at least have recopied it.'
'I did not want to risk miscopying.'
The girl's answer came as a surprise, and added to the regrets.

Amabune, 'fisherman's boat,' also means 'nun's boat.'

The younger nun returned from her pilgrimage. She was aghast at the news that awaited her.

'I have taken vows myself, and I had thought that I should encourage you in your wishes. But what do you propose to do with the years you have ahead of you? I may tell you now why I went on that pilgrimage. I cannot be sure whether I shall be alive tomorrow, and I wanted to pray to Our Lady of Hatsuse to watch over you.'

So great was her agitation that she took to her bed. The girl was sorry for her, of course, but even sorrier for her own mother, who must have carried on even thus over a daughter who had disappeared and left no earthly remains to mourn over. Silent as always, the girl was extraordinarily young and pretty as she sat turned away from the company.

'What a useless little person I do seem to have taken in.' The bishop's sister soon recovered sufficiently to order a nun's habit for the girl. It was a garb they were very familiar with, and soon the girl was wearing a dull gray robe and surplice. The other nuns, helping her into them, could not find strong enough words with which to condemn the bishop's recklessness and irresponsibility. She had been a comfort to them over the days, an unexpected light in the mountain gloom; and now the light had gone out.

It was as his fellows had said: the bishop's powers were extraordinary. The First Princess having recovered, his name inspired yet greater reverence. Since complications can follow an apparent recovery, however, the services were continued. The bishop remained at court for a time. One still, rainy night when he was among the clerics on duty, he was summoned for nocturnal rites. The ladies-in-waiting, exhausted from the strain of these last few days, were resting. Only a few were in the royal presence. The empress herself was among them.

'I have thought so all along,' she said, 'and now I feel more than ever that we may look to you for assistance in this life and the next.'

'I have been informed by the Blessed One that I have not long to live and that this year and next are particularly dangerous ones for me; and so I had thought to stay in solemn retreat, concentrating upon the holy name. Your Majesty's own summons has brought me here.'

The empress spoke of how stubborn the malign spirit in

possession of her daughter had been, and how frightening it is when these spirits insist upon announcing themselves under a variety of names.

'Your Majesty has chosen to speak of malign spirits. I am reminded of a most unusual happening. Late this spring my mother, a very old lady, went on a pilgrimage to Hatsuse by way of fulfilling a vow. Taken ill on the return journey, she stopped over at the late Suzaku emperor's Uji villa. Evil spirits have a way of occupying large houses that have been neglected over the years, and I feared that she had chosen an unfortunate spot for her convalescence. I was right.' And he described how they had found Ukifune.

'What an extraordinary thing!' Quite unnerved, the empress aroused the women nearby. That Kosaishō in whom Kaoru had shown a certain interest had heard the bishop's story. The others had been asleep. The bishop, noting the royal perturbation, saw that his narrative had perhaps been too vivid, and did not go into further details.

'But let me just tell you a little about the young lady. On my way down from the mountain I looked in on the nuns at Ono. She wept as she told me how desperately she wanted to leave the world, and I administered vows. My sister, the widow of the guards captain, seems to adore the girl, and even to look upon her as a substitute for her own daughter. No doubt she is berating me for what I have done. The girl is a very pretty, I must say, a most elegant young lady, and it does seem a pity that she should be wasted in a nunnery. I have no notion who she might be.'

'But why should such a pretty girl have been left in such a place?' asked Kosaishō. 'Surely you have found out who she is?'

'No, I fear I have not – though she may have told my sister. If she is what she appears to be, a girl of good family, then the secret cannot be kept forever. Not of course that I would wish to be understood as saying that there are no beauties among girls of the lower classes. Ours is a world in which even the ogre maiden finds salvation.* But if she should prove to be a person of no background, then the fact that she is so lovely would mean that she

---

*The bishop makes reference to the Lotus Sutra and the doctrine of universal Buddhahood.

came into this life with a remarkably light burden of sin from other lives.'

The empress remembered having heard of a girl who disappeared in Uji or thereabouts, in the spring it must have been. Kosaishō had had the sad story from the girl's sister. But of course they could not be sure that this was the same girl. And the bishop had said that the girl wanted her very existence to be kept secret, and had hidden herself away like a fugitive from some terrible enemy. He found it all very strange, the bishop said again, as if he did not want to elaborate further; he had brought the matter up only because it had occurred to him that Her Majesty might be interested. Kosaishō thought it best to keep the story to herself.

'It may well be the same girl,' said the empress when the bishop had withdrawn. 'Suppose we tell my brother.'

But secrecy was important to both of them, it seemed, and no one was entirely sure of the facts; and Kaoru was such a difficult man to talk to in any case.

The princess having recovered, the bishop returned to his mountain retreat. He looked in on the nuns once more. His sister assaulted him with great vehemence.

'You must be charged with a grave sin, sir, in condemning a mere child to a nunnery. How can you have done it without asking me first? I can think of no reasonable explanation for your conduct.'

But of course these recriminations came too late.

'Be diligent with your prayers,' said the bishop to Ukifune. 'Life is uncertain for old and young alike. It is most proper that you should have awakened to the facts of this fleeting world.'

The girl disliked even such oblique reference to her past.

'Have a new habit made for yourself,' he said, taking out gossamers and damasks and unfigured silks. 'I shall see to your needs, I promise you, while I am here to do it. You need not feel uncertain on that score. It would seem that, for me, for you, for most of us, bonds with this transient world are not easy to break so long as we remain preoccupied with its illusory triumphs and glories. Lose yourself in your devotions, here in the forest depths, and shame and regret need not be a part of your life. This wordly existence "is but a thin blade of grass."' And he added after a moment:

' "Now comes dawn to the gate among the pines,
        And lingers yet the moon in the sky above." '*

His knowledge ranged far beyond the scriptures, and such allusions gave his homilies a certain grandeur. To the girl it seemed (though she may not have understood everything) that he was saying exactly what she wanted to hear.

The wind moaned the whole day through. 'The wandering monk off in the mountains wants to sob aloud on such a day,' said the bishop.

She had become one of the wanderers herself, thought the girl, and it was perhaps for that reason that she was so given to weeping.

Gazing out from the veranda, she saw in the distance a troop of men in variegated travel robes. Even people on their way up the mountain tended to pass the nunnery by, though occasionally the nuns would catch a glimpse of a monk, from perhaps Black Valley.† Men in lay dress were a very rare sight indeed. These proved to be in attendance upon the captain whom she had so disappointed. He had come with further complaints, now useless, of course, but the autumn leaves, just at their best, more richly tinted here at Ono than elsewhere along the range, made him forget them for a time. What a start it would give a man, he thought, to come upon a bright, lively girl in such a place.

'I had a bit of spare time, and it seemed meant for your autumn colors.' He gazed admiringly about him. 'Yes, your trees do invite one to spend a night among them – to borrow a night from the past, so to speak.'

The bishop's sister, generous as ever with her tears, offered a poem:

'Harsh the winds that come down these mountain slopes.
    Our trees are bare. They give not shade or shelter.'

He replied:

'Mountain trees, I know, where none awaits me;
    And yet I cannot easily pass them by.'

*Both quotations are from Po Chü-i's 'The Women at the Tomb,' Collected Works, IV. The mention immediately below of the moaning wind alludes to the same poem.

†Kurotani, at the west base of Mount Hiei.

'Let me at least see her in her new robes,' he said to Shōshō, in the course of lengthy observations about the girl now beyond retrieving. 'Allow me a single sign that you remember your promises.'

Shōshō went inside. Yes, she did indeed want to show the girl off, slight, delicate, graceful, in a cloak of light gray and a singlet of a quiet burnt yellow, her rich hair spread about her like a five-plaited fan. The fine skin was as if it had been freshly and tenderly powdered. More than show her off: Shōshō would have liked to paint a picture of the little figure engrossed in prayer, a rosary hung over a curtain rack nearby, a sutra unrolled before her. Shōshō wanted to weep. How much more extreme was the effect likely to be upon a man who had come as a suitor! The moment seemed propitious. She pointed to a small aperture below the latch and pushed aside curtains and the like that might obstruct his view. He had not been prepared for such beauty. A flawless creature – and she had become a nun! The regrets and the sorrow were as if some dreadful mistake of his own had brought matters to this pass. He withdrew, unable to hold back his tears and afraid that he might break into open sobbing. Was it conceivable that no one would be searching for this lost paragon? He would have heard if a daughter of one of the great families had disappeared or turned in bitterness from the world.

An enigma, certainly; but one did not look with aversion upon nuns when they were great beauties. Indeed, their condition added to the excitement. Concluding that the girl was worth a secret visit from time to time, he appealed to the bishop's sister.

'I can see that there were reasons for shyness before she had these new defenses, but I should think that we might now have a quiet talk. Suggest as much to her, if you will. I have called on you from time to time because I have not been able to forget the past, and now I have another reason.'

'Yes,' said the nun, in tears, 'I have worried about her a great deal, and I would be much happier if I could think that she had a friend, someone who would promise in all honesty to see her from time to time. I shall not be here forever, you know.'

But who might the girl be? The nun's words suggested that she was a relative.

'I may not live long myself, and I am not of much consequence in any case; but I keep a promise when I have made one. Tell me:

does no one come to see her? You must not think that I am holding back because I do not know who she is – and yet it does somehow stand between us.'

'If she had any notion that the world ought to be paying its respects, then she would have no lack of callers, I am sure. But as you see, she has quite given up such things. She seems interested in her prayers and nothing more.'

He sent a note in to the girl:

'You have chosen to turn your back upon the world.
It pains me to think that I have been the occasion.'

He could not have been warmer or more courteous, said the woman who brought the note.

'Think of me as a brother,' he persisted. 'The most trivial sort of conversation would be such a comfort.'

'I fear that your remarks are above me,' she sent back, not attempting a real answer.

Those disastrous events had so turned her against men, it seemed, that she meant to end her days as little a part of the world as a decaying stump. The gloom of the last months lifted a little, now that she had had her way. She would joke with the bishop's sister and they would play Go together. She turned to her studies of the Good Law with a new dedication, perusing the Lotus Sutra and numbers of other holy texts. It was winter, the snows were deep, and there were no visitors; and now if ever was the tedious time.

The New Year came, but spring seemed far away. The silence of the frozen waters seemed to speak with its own sad voice. Though she had turned away in disgust from the prince who had found her so 'daunting,'* she thought all the same of the days when she had known him.

At the writing practice that was her chief pleasure in recesses from her devotions, she set down a poem:

'I gaze at snow that swirls over mountain and moor,
And things long gone have still the power to sadden.'

Memories of the past were much with her. It was a year now since her disappearance. Would there still be those to whom memories of her were important?

*In Chapter 51.

Someone brought the first spring shoots in a coarse rustic basket. The nun sent them in with a poem:

'Their prize these shoots that break through the mountain snows.
My joy the abundant years you have before you.'

And the girl replied:

'On drifted moors I shall gather early shoots.
May years of your life add to years, as snow upon snow.'

How very dear of her to say so – and how much greater the joy if, over those years, she might live the life she deserved.

A rose plum was blooming near the eaves of the girl's room, its color and its perfume as they had always been. It was her favorite among all the flowering trees. It told her that the spring was 'the spring of old,'* perhaps because she remembered the perfume of which she 'knew no surfeit.'†

Early one morning as she was setting out votive water in preparation for the matins, she had a nun rather younger and of lower rank than the others break off a sprig. Petals fell as if in protest, and seemed to send out a suddenly more compelling fragrance. A poem formed itself in the girl's mind:

'He whose sleeve brushed mine is here no more,
And yet is here in the scent of the dawning of spring.'

A grandson of the old nun who had recently returned from his duties as governor of Kii came to pay his respects. He was a handsome man, perhaps thirty, and he seemed very sure of himself.

'And how have you been?' he asked the old lady. 'I have not seen you in two whole years, you will remember.'

But she did not seem to understand.

He went to his aunt's rooms. 'She has aged terribly, poor thing. She has been on my mind a great deal, even though I have been too far away to call on her. I have known of course that she has not many more years to live. Yes, she has been like a mother to me since my own mother died. Does Hitachi ever come to see you?'

See note, page 948.

†Prince Tomohira, *Shūishū* 1005:

> Recalling your fragrance, of which I knew no surfeit,
> I break this morn a flowering branch of plum.

It would seem that he was referring to his sister.

'Not a great deal breaks in on our loneliness and boredom. It has been a very long time since we last heard from Hitachi. Indeed I sometimes wonder if Mother will see her again.'

Though not especially interested in the conversation, the girl caught the name Hitachi.*

The governor went on: 'I have been back in the city for several days now, but one quickly gets caught up in court business. I meant to come yesterday and then at the last minute I found that I had to go off to Uji with Lord Kaoru. We spent the day at the Eighth Prince's villa. One of the prince's daughters, with whom, I believe, His Lordship was keeping company, died some years ago, and then a younger daughter — I am told that he took her there in secret — died last spring. It was the anniversary of her death, and he had asked the archdeacon there to see to memorial services. I suppose I'll have to contribute something myself, a lady's robe or two would be the thing. I wonder — might I ask you to have them made up if I give orders to the weavers as soon as I get back to town?'

Here was a story that did interest the girl. She turned away from the doors lest her agitation be noticed.

'I have heard, I believe, that the saintly prince had *two* daughters. One of them is married to Prince Niou. Now which would it be? I wonder.'

'The second of Lord Kaoru's ladies would seem to have been the daughter of a concubine of not very high rank. He was not as good to her as he might have been, and so now of course he is all the sorrier. They say he was terribly upset when the first princess died. He even thought of becoming a monk.'

The girl was in terror. The man seemed to be among Kaoru's intimates.

'It seems strange,' the governor continued, 'that they should both have died at Uji. He was in very low spirits yesterday, very low indeed. There were tears in his eyes when he went down to the river. He came back to the house and wrote a poem on one of the pillars:

*The governor's brother-in-law, husband of the sister in question, is or has been governor (more probably vice-governor) of Hitachi. So of course was Ukifune's stepfather.

' "I cannot halt the tears that join the flow
    Of waters that gave her image, and do so no more."

'He said very little, but you could see that he was in very low spirits. I should imagine that the two ladies adored him. I have known him for a very long time myself and have been aware all along of his extraordinary kindness and sensitivity. Yes, if I can count on his support, then I have no wish to be on the chancellor's own personal staff.'

It did not take a very discerning person, thought the girl, to observe Kaoru's superiority.

'Although I should suppose,' said the nun, 'that no one we have with us these days compares with the gentleman they used to call "the shining Genji" or something of the sort. I hear that his house collects more honor for itself as the years go by. What sort of man might his older son be?'

'Very handsome, very cultivated, respected by everyone. Certainly one of the most powerful men in the country. But the *really* handsome one is Prince Niou. Sometimes I almost wish I were a woman, and could have my turn at waiting on him.'

It was as if he had come with a prepared speech. Ukifune listened in sorrow and fascination to a story as from another life. The talk went on for a time, and the governor left. It touched her to know that she had not been forgotten. Again the thought of her mother's sorrow came first. But she did not want to be seen in this unbecoming dress. She watched the women at work preparing clothes – in memory of herself! She said not a word about the strangeness of it all.

A nun came to her with a singlet. 'Suppose you do this for us. We've seen how good you are at turning a hem.'

But the thought was somehow repellent. 'I'm afraid I'm not feeling well.' She lay with her back turned upon all the activity.

'What is the matter?' The bishop's sister anxiously put aside her work.

Another nun held up a red singlet and a damask robe with a cherry-blossom pattern in the weave. 'If only we could ask you to try this on for us. It seems such a waste that you should always be in grays and blacks.'

'Shall I, having taken the habit of the nun,
    Now change to robes of remembrance, think of the past?'

The girl sighed as she jotted down her poem. This world kept no secrets, and if she were to die and the bishop's sister to learn the truth, her secretive ways would no doubt seem cold and unfeeling.

'I have forgotten everything,' she said, 'but when I see you at this sort of work something does seem to come back, and make me very sad.'

'I have no doubt that you remember something, indeed a great many things, and it does you no good to go on hiding them. I have forgotten a great many things myself. The bright colors they wear down in the city, for example; and so I have lost my touch for this kind of work. If my daughter had only lived! Surely there is someone who is to you as I was to her? I saw her remains right there before my eyes, and I went on believing that she had to be alive, somewhere, and wanted to run off and look for her. And you just vanished – surely there is someone out looking for you?'

'Yes, I did have a mother, back when I was a part of it all. But I rather think she died not long ago.' She sought to hide her tears. 'It hurts to try to remember, and I really have nothing at all to tell you. Do please believe that I am not trying to keep things from you.' Always a girl of deep reserve, she fell silent.

The memorial services were over. What a fragile bond it had been, thought Kaoru. He found posts for such of the Hitachi sons as had come of age, one with the privy council, another in his own offices. He considered taking one of the more presentable boys into his personal retinue.

On an evening of quiet rain he went to see the empress. She had little to occupy her time.

'I have for some years been visiting an out-of-the-way mountain village,' he remarked in the course of the conversation. 'People used to criticize me for calling on a certain lady there, but I told myself that there was no point in trying to fight destiny, and went on seeing her all the same. I think almost anyone would have done as I did – and what else is a man to do when his affections have become involved? There was an unfortunate incident. It made me feel that the very name of the place must carry a curse, and the road began to seem longer and more difficult than I could negotiate. So I stayed away for a very long time. The other day I had to go there on business, and it made me think all over again how uncertain things are. The house I used to visit, I thought, the house of that saintly prince, must have been put up on purpose to urge the votary along on his way.'

Very sad, thought the empress, remembering what she had heard from the bishop. 'Has some evil spirit taken up residence there, do you suppose? How did she die?'

She would be referring to the deaths of two sisters in such quick succession. 'Evil spirits do have a way of choosing lonely, remote places. But her death was unusual even so.' He did not go into the details.

It would be bad manners, she thought, to hint that she had considerable information about the realm he was so carefully skirting, and she remembered how depressed Niou had been, how he had even fallen ill. She remained silent out of deference both to her brother and to her son.

'My brother the general still seems to mourn the girl at Uji,' she said in confidence to Kosaishō. 'I was so sorry for him that I was on the point of telling him everything, but in the end I held myself back. It might not be the same girl, after all. You heard what the bishop said. Sometime when you are having one of your talks with the general, just give him the substance of it. But do be careful not to say anything that might hurt him.'

'Please, Your Majesty. If you think it improper to tell him yourself, do consider how much more improper it would be for one of us others.'

'These things depend entirely on the circumstances. I have my reasons.'

Kosaishō understood and was interested. One day she found her chance to tell him the bishop's story.

He was astounded. The empress had probably known at least a part of it when he visited her; and why had she not told him? But then he had been somewhat furtive himself – and even now that he had learned the truth he was no more open. He feared that anything he said would make him look more eccentric. Perhaps the gossips were already at work. Even when a man and woman were alive and present and alert, their secrets had a way of getting out.

'It sounds very much like someone I had been wondering about,' he replied guardedly. 'And is she still at Ono?'

'The bishop administered vows the day he came down from the mountain. She insisted on it, even though everyone wanted her to wait until she had regained a little of her strength.'

The place was right, and not one of the circumstances was at variance with what he knew. Half hoping he would be spared the knowledge that it was indeed she, he cast about for a way to learn the truth. He would present an awkward figure if he were to lead the hunt himself. And if he were to treat Niou to the sight of his restlessness, his friend would no doubt seek ways to block the path the girl had chosen. Had Niou extracted a vow of silence from his mother? That would explain her curious reluctance to talk about a matter so extraordinary. And if Niou was already part of the conspiracy, then however strong the yearning, Kaoru must once again consign Ukifune to the realm of the dead. If indeed she still lived, then some chance turn of the wind might one day bring them together, to talk, perhaps, of the shores of the Yellow Spring.* He would not again think of making her his own.

Though the empress was evidently determined not to discuss these events, he found another occasion to seek her out.

'The girl I told you about, the one who I thought had died such a terrible death – I have heard that she is still alive. She has come on unhappy circumstances, I am told. It all seems very unlikely – but then the way she disappeared was unlikely too. I find it hard to believe that she hated the world enough to think of such desperate measures. And so the rumors I have picked up may not be so unlikely after all.' And he described them in more detail. He chose his words carefully when they touched upon Niou, and he did not speak at all of his own bitterness. 'If he hears that I would like to find her he is sure to credit me with all the wrong motives. I do not propose to do anything even if I discover that she is still alive.'

'I was rather frightened when I had the story from the bishop, and did not listen as carefully as I should have. But how could my son possibly have learned of it? I know all about his deplorable habits, and have no doubt that news of this sort would send him into a fever. The talk I pick up about his little escapades worries me terribly.'

He knew that she would never, in what seemed to be the frankest of conversations, let slip something she had learned in confidence.

---

*Yomi, the land of the dead.

The mystery haunted him, day and night. In what mountain village would the girl be? How might he with dignity seek her out? He must have the facts directly from the bishop of Yokawa. He made solemn offerings on the eighth of every month, sometimes at the main hall on Mount Hiei, sacred to Lord Yakushi.* This time he would go on to Yokawa. He took the girl's brother with him. He did not mean to tell her family for the moment, not until he had more precise information. Perhaps he hoped that the boy's presence would bring an immediacy to an encounter that might otherwise seem unreal. If the girl in the bishop's story should indeed prove to be Ukifune, and if, further, she had already been the victim of improper advances, even in strange new dress, off among strange new women – the truth would not be pleasing.

Such are the thoughts that troubled him along the way.

---

*Bhaiṣajyaguru, the Buddha of medicine. The eighth of the month was among his feast days.

CHAPTER 54

The Floating Bridge of Dreams

Kaoru made the usual offerings of images and scriptures at the main Hiei monastery and the next day went to Yokawa. The bishop received his unexpected visitor with much ceremony. Although Kaoru had occasionally consulted him on liturgical matters, they had not been close. Kaoru had been much impressed at the effectiveness of the bishop's recent ministrations to the First Princess, however. The new bond between them, thought the bishop, fluttering with excitement over the visit, had brought this eminent gentleman so far out of his way. They talked on and on, like the oldest and most intimate of friends. A light repast was brought.

'I believe you have a house in Ono?' remarked Kaoru when the excitement had subsided.

'Yes, a shabby little place. As a matter of fact, my mother is living there – she is a nun, and a very old woman. I had no place in the city that seemed right, and I decided that if I was to live up here away from the world I wanted her to be where I could look in on her at any odd hour.'

'I have heard that Ono used to be lively enough, but that of recent years it has been neglected. Indeed, they say it is rather lonely.' He lowered his voice. 'But tell me. I have hesitated to mention it because I have not been sure of the facts and I have been afraid you might think me forward and a little eccentric. I have heard that a person I once knew well is hiding there. I thought that when I had learned a few of the facts I might ask you exactly what had happened, and now I hear that you have taken her under your protection and made a nun of her. Might I ask whether it is true? She is very young and her parents are living, and I feel somewhat responsible for her disappearance.'

The bishop was at a loss for an answer. He had guessed from her appearance that she was a girl of some standing, and Kaoru's manner suggested very strongly that she was important to him. The bishop must conclude that, although he had been faithful to his pious duties, he had acted recklessly. It seemed likely that Kaoru knew the essential facts. Attempts at evasion, now that so much had been found out, could only complicate matters.

'Ah, yes,' he said after a time. 'The young lady who has so puzzled us all these months. The nuns at Ono went to Hatsuse with some request or other, and on the way back my mother was suddenly taken ill. It was at the Uji villa. Her condition seemed critical and someone came for me. I arrived to find a very strange situation indeed.' He lowered his voice as he told how they had come upon Ukifune. 'My sister seemed completely devoted to the girl. She as good as left our mother to take care of herself. The girl was still breathing, but that was the only sign of life. It was all very strange indeed. I was reminded of stories I had heard of people who had come back to life at their own funerals. I called my disciples, the ones who had made names for themselves, and had them take turns at prayers and spells. I was with our mother myself. She is so old that I shouldn't have had any regrets for her, I know, but there she was away from home, and I wanted her at least to give herself up unconditionally to the holy name. So I was not able to observe the girl in any detail. I would imagine from what the others told me that some goblin or wood spirit had led her astray. We brought her back to Ono with us, but for three months or so she might as well have been dead. My sister is a nun too. You may possibly have heard of her, the widow of a guards captain. She lost her only daughter and she went on grieving, and now she had found a pretty girl, a most elegant girl, indeed, of about the same age. She saw it all as an answer to her prayers at Hatsuse. I could not help being moved by her pleas, poor woman. She seemed desperate to save the girl. And so I came down from the mountain and conducted services. The girl began to emerge from her trance and after a few days seemed to make a complete recovery; but she was afraid that the evil spirit, whatever it might have been, was still after her, and she wept and begged me to let her take vows. She had to escape, she said, and look to the next world for happiness. I have taken vows myself and it was natural for me to encourage her, and I did as she asked. How could I have dreamed, sir, that she was somehow of importance to you? It was all so strange, I suppose, that we should have made inquiries, but my mother and sister feared complications if word got out, and we kept our own counsel over the months.'

Kaoru had come a great distance to confirm his suspicions, and now the knowledge that the dead girl was alive made him feel like a sleep-walker. Since it would not do to have the sage see him in disarray, he struggled to control the tears that surged forward.

The bishop was feeling guilty. He should not have taken it upon himself to help so important a lady leave the secular world. 'It must have been something she brought from an earlier life,' he said, 'that she should have been so vulnerable to the assaults of evil spirits. I should imagine that she is from a good house. What could possibly have reduced her to such unhappy circumstances?'

'We shall say that she is an obscure cousin of the emperor himself. I happen to know her, though not at all intimately. I would not have dreamed that anything so terrible could happen to her. But her disappearance was very strange indeed, and all sorts of theories were propounded. Some even hinted that she had thrown herself into the river. Now I know the truth. I am content with it, and must thank you. It is all for the good, I am sure, that she has taken vows and should be trying to lighten the burden of sin. But it would seem that her mother still grieves for her. I ought to inform her of what I know, I suppose; but the shock might be too much for her, and then your good sister has seen fit to keep the secret all this time. It is not easy for a mother to give up a child. I am sure the unfortunate woman would be quite unable to deny herself the comfort of a visit.

'You will think me excessively demanding, I am sure,' he continued after a moment, 'but might I ask you to go down to Ono with me? I cannot ignore the girl, now that I know the truth. It all seems very unreal, but I would still like to have a talk with her.'

The bishop was in a difficult position. He understood Kaoru's wishes, and the girl could be said to have taken a step that was irreversible. But the most ascetic of clean-shaven monks had strange urges occasionally, and nuns were still more susceptible. He would be putting the girl to a cruel and unnecessary test, as much as inviting transgression.

'I fear that circumstances compel me to be here on the mountain for a few days more. I will get off a note early next month.'

Kaoru was unhappy, but it would have been unseemly to press further. He had no choice but to wait, he concluded, making ready to start back for the city. He called the girl's brother, the handsomest of the governor's sons.

'This lad is a very close relative of the young lady's. Perhaps I might ask you to give him a message for her, please, if you don't mind. Even a short note will do. You might not want to mention me by name, but perhaps you could warn her that someone may shortly be inquiring after her.'

'It would, I fear, be wrong of me to do as you suggest. I have told you the facts, and in some detail. I doubt that anyone would reproach you for going in person and doing what seems necessary.'

Kaoru smiled. 'Wrong, good sir? You quite fill me with shame. Here I am looking as if I still belonged in the world, and even to me it all seems very strange. I have longed to take vows since I was a mere boy. But there is my mother, and the bond, as you say, is not an easy one to break. She is lonely, and I am really all that she has, little though it may be. I have been caught up in affairs at court and I have moved ahead bit by bit, without doing much to deserve it. I have worried a great deal, you may be sure, about leaving undone the one thing I have really wanted to do, and so the years have gone by. Duties pile up, there is no avoiding them; but I have tried not to let my affairs, which I keep to a minimum, bring me in conflict with the holy injunctions, or such small fragments of them as I am not in complete ignorance of. I try to think of my life as little different from that of a recluse like yourself. Can you imagine that I would even dream of risking so grievous a sin for so small a cause? It is quite out of the question. On that score you need have not the smallest doubt. I am sad for her mother, that is all, and now that I have learned the truth I want her to know it too. Then and only then will I be at peace with myself.'

The bishop nodded approvingly. 'Most praiseworthy,' he said.

It was growing dark. Ono would be a convenient place to spend the night. But Kaoru might be embarrassed to learn that he had after all been mistaken. After some hesitation he set out directly for the city.

The bishop's eye had meanwhile fallen on the boy, in whom he was finding much to praise.

'Suppose you let him take a letter, then,' suggested Kaoru once more, 'and give her a hint of what to expect.'

The bishop dashed off a note. 'Let us have an occasional visit from you too,' he said to the boy. 'Don't for a moment think it would be to no purpose.'

Though puzzled by this attention, the boy took the note and started off with Kaoru.

Kaoru deployed his guard as they reached the foot of the mountain. 'So as not to attract too much attention,' he said.

With little to relieve the monotony, Ukifune sat gazing into the heavily wooded hills. Only the fireflies along the garden brook served to remind her of the Uji days. From far beyond the eaves that looked out over the valley came voices of outrunners cautiously clearing the way, and soon torches, large numbers of them, were tossing among the trees. What might this commotion mean? the other nuns were asking as they came to the veranda.

'Whoever it is, he certainly does have himself a big escort. When we sent that seaweed to the bishop this morning, he said in his note that we couldn't have picked a better time. He all of a sudden had a general to entertain, he said. Which general do you suppose it could have been?' It was the sort of talk one hears in remote, unfrequented places. 'The general that is married to the Second Princess?'

The girl knew who it would be; and there among the voices of the outrunners, unmistakably, were some she had heard clearing the mountain path to Uji. What could be the profit, after all that had happened, in remembering? She tried to lose herself in meditation upon the holy name, and had even less to say than usual.

Travelers to Yokawa gave secluded Ono what precarious ties it had with the larger world.

Kaoru would have liked to send the bishop's letter in immediately, but he had attracted too large an audience. He dispatched the boy the next day, escorted by two or three trusted courtiers of low rank and a guardsman who had often taken messages to Uji.

He was careful to let no one overhear his instructions to the boy. 'You remember your dead sister well enough to recognize her, I suppose? Well, I had resigned myself to the fact that she was no longer among us, but now it seems quite clear that I was wrong. But it would not do to have people know, and especially the people closest to her. See what you can find out. You are not to tell your mother, not for the moment, at least. The news might unsettle her, and we must prepare her gradually; and there is always the possibility that people who shouldn't be in on the secret might hear. My main reason for wanting to find your sister is that I feel so sorry for your mother.'

Very young and impressionable, the boy had continued to

grieve for his sister, much superior to his many other siblings. Delight at this news brought him close to tears.

'Yes, my lord,' he answered gruffly, trying not to weep.

A letter from the bishop had been delivered at the nunnery early in the morning. 'Did a young page come yesterday with a message from the general? Please tell the lady that, having been given a description of the actual circumstances surrounding her case, I am overcome by a rather surprising sense of remorse and guilt for what should have been an act of piety. There are numbers of things we must talk about. I shall visit you in the next few days.'

The bishop's sister, astounded, took the letter in to Ukifune. The girl flushed crimson. The rumor was abroad, finally, it seemed. The nun would be furious at her secretiveness. She could find no answer.

The nun was indeed reproachful. 'You must tell me the truth. Your silence is cruel, that is the only word for it.' Still apprised of only a part of the truth, she was in great agitation.

'A message from the mountain,' came a voice at the gate. 'A message from the bishop.'

Confused, the nun ordered that the new messenger be shown in. He would shed light on the mystery. A very handsome and well-groomed boy came forward. Offered a cushion, he knelt deferentially beside the blind.

'I was ordered to deliver it personally.'

The bishop's sister took the note. 'To the young lady who has recently become a nun,' and, with the bishop's signature, 'From the mountain.' This time the girl was not permitted the excuse that the message was for someone else. She slipped deeper into the room and sat with her face averted.

'You are a quiet girl, and always have been,' said the nun; 'but there is a limit.'

She looked at the bishop's letter. 'The general came this morning and asked about you, and I told him everything. You have turned your back upon human affections and have chosen to live among mountain people. This I know. Yet I was disturbed to learn the facts, and have come to fear that, contrary to our intentions, what we have done might call down the wrath of the holy powers. We must be resigned to it; and now you must go back, surely and without hesitation, to the general, and dispel the clouds of sin brought on by tenacious affections. Draw comfort from the thought that a single day's retreat brings untold blessings. I shall myself go over the problem carefully with you. The lad who brings this can no doubt give you a general description of what has occurred.'

There was no trace of ambiguity in the letter, and yet it was worded so discreetly that an outsider would not immediately have guessed the meaning.

'Who is the boy?' asked the nun. 'Must you go on keeping secrets from me even now?'

The girl looked out through the blind. It was the brother who had been especially on her mind that last terrible night at Uji. She had always thought him an impudent, arrogant, and generally unpleasant little urchin, but he had been a favorite of their mother's whom she had occasionally brought with her to Uji. Yes, they had been fond of each other in their childish way; but the memory was like a dream. She longed for news of her mother. She had in the course of events had word of others, but none at all of her mother. At the sight of the boy all the old sadness came back. Tears were streaming from her eyes.

He was a very attractive boy indeed. The nun thought she detected a family resemblance. 'Your brother, I am sure of it. Suppose we ask him in. He will want to talk to you.'

But he would long ago have sent her off in his thoughts to another world, and she was ashamed to have him catch even a glimpse of her nun's habit. 'I am sorry that you think me furtive,' she answered after some hesitation. 'I am very sorry indeed. But I have nothing to say. You must have had any number of questions when you found me. I was out of my mind then, of course, and even now I cannot remember a thing. Possibly I have given away my own soul, if that is what you wish to call it, and borrowed someone else's. The other day when I heard what your nephew the governor had to say, I had a vague feeling that it was about a place I once knew. I have thought and thought, but nothing really comes back. There was a lady who worried about me and wanted to make me happy, and that is all I know. I keep wondering how she is, but somehow it makes me very sad to think of her. I may have known this boy when we were small – but please, I can't make myself try to remember. If you don't mind, I would rather let him go on thinking I am dead. I do not know whether my mother is still alive. If she is I might want to see her – but no one else. The gentleman the bishop speaks of: I would rather he too went on thinking I am dead. Please tell the boy that there has been a mistake.'

'That will not be easy. Even as people of saintly honesty go, my brother is not a man to hold things back. He will have revealed every last detail. The truth will not consent, I fear, to go back into hiding again, and the fact that the general is a man who must be reckoned with does not make matters less complicated.'

She was not prepared to accept evasions this time, and she had the support of the other nuns. 'The most obstinate little creature,' they said, 'the world ever saw.'

A curtain was hung near the veranda of the main hall and the boy invited inside the blinds. Though he knew that he was in his sister's presence, he was still a child, and shy about speaking without adequate preliminaries.

Eyes on the floor, he presently essayed: 'There is another letter I'd like to give her. What the bishop said is true, I'm sure. But she seems so unfriendly.'

'She is indeed. What a handsome lad you are. Yes, here she is, the person the letter is for. We outsiders are somewhat puzzled by it all. Have a talk with her yourself. You do seem terribly young, but he must have had good reasons for choosing you.'

'What can I say when she won't answer? She is treating me like a stranger. No, I have nothing more to say. But he told me I had to put the letter in her hands and no one else's, and so I have to.'

'You do indeed.' The nun pushed the girl towards the curtain. 'Be civil to him, please do. You really are very stubborn.'

The boy was certain, from the dumbness as of one in a trance, that the object of these remarks would be his sister. He edged closer and pushed the letter towards her.

'As soon as you can let me have your answer I will be off.' Hurt by her aloofness, he had no wish to dawdle.

The nun opened the letter and handed it to the girl.

It was in the familiar hand. Sending forth the extraordinary fragrance, it quite dizzied the more forward of the nuns, who made sure that they had a glimpse of it.

'Out of deference to the bishop, I shall excuse the rash step you have taken. Of that I shall speak no further. For my own part, I am seized with so intense a longing to speak to you of those nightmarish events that I can scarcely myself accept it as real. I cannot imagine how it might seem to others.'

As if unable to find adequate words, he continued with a poem:

'I lost my way in the hills, having taken a road
　　That would lead, I hope, to a teacher of the Law.

'Have you forgotten this boy? I keep him here beside me in memory of one who disappeared.'

It was friendly, even ardent. She could not pretend, such was the clarity of the detail, that it was meant for someone else. She dreaded a visit, perhaps unannounced. She did not want him to see her drab robes and her cropped hair. The uncertainty too much for her, she collapsed in tears. The nun gazed at her helplessly. What a silly child she was!

'And may I have your answer?'

'Let me collect myself just a little, please, if you don't mind. I try to remember but I cannot. It is all like a strange, frightening dream. I think possibly I may be able to understand when I have calmed myself a little. Send it back, please, today at least. There may have been a mistake.' Not even refolding the letter, she pushed it towards the nun.

'You are being rude, my dear, nothing else, and if you persist in your rudeness we too will be held responsible.'

The girl was trembling violently and wished to hear no more. She lay with her face buried in her sleeves.

The nun came forward to converse briefly with the boy. 'Some evil powers may be at her again. She is seldom herself and she goes on feeling unwell, and so she has taken vows. I have feared all along that if someone were to come looking for her we would be in trouble, and here we are. It is all very sad and very disturbing. I must apologize for what has happened and admit that it is a great waste. She has never been strong. Today she is less in control of herself than usual, and I fear we cannot expect even the sort of inadequate response we usually get.'

A most elegant lunch of mountain delicacies was brought in; but the boy's young thoughts were elsewhere. 'My lord sent me all this way,' he said, 'and what am I to take back? Let me have a word from her, please, just a word.'

'What you say is entirely reasonable.' The nun relayed the appeal, but Ukifune was silent.

'All I can suggest,' said the nun, coming forward again, 'is that you remind him of our vulnerability. The mountain winds may blow, but we are not separated from the city by so fearfully many banks of clouds, and I am sure that you will find occasion to visit again.'

Nothing more was to be done, clearly, and the boy feared that he was beginning to look ridiculous. Saddened and chagrined at his failure to exchange even a word with his so grievously lamented sister, he started for the city.

Kaoru waited with much anticipation, which the boy's report was quick to dispel. He might better have done nothing at all.

It would seem that, as he examined the several possibilities, a suspicion crossed his mind: the memory of how he himself had behaved in earlier days made him ask whether someone might be hiding her from the world.